THE
CRONIN
OMNIBUS

THE CRONIN OMNIBUS

HATTER'S CASTLE
THE CITADEL
THE KEYS OF THE KINGDOM

A. J. CRONIN

VICTOR GOLLANCZ

LONDON

Hatter's Castle first published in Great Britain 1931
by Victor Gollancz Ltd, copyright A. J. Cronin 1931
The Citadel first published in Great Britain 1937
by Victor Gollancz Ltd, copyright A. J. Cronin 1937
The Keys of the Kingdom first published in Great Britain 1942
by Victor Gollancz Ltd, copyright A. J. Cronin 1942

The Cronin Omnibus first published in Great Britain 1958

This edition published in Great Britain 1994
by Victor Gollancz
A Division of the Cassell group
Villiers House, 41/47 Strand, London WC2N 5JE

A catalogue record for this book is
available from the British Library

ISBN 0 575 05836 6

Printed in Finland by Werner Söderström Oy

THE
CRONIN
OMNIBUS

CONTENTS

HATTER'S
CASTLE

CONTENTS

BOOK I

I

THE spring of 1879 was unusually forward and open. Over the Lowlands the green of early corn spread smoothly, the chestnut spears burst in April, and the hawthorn hedges flanking the white roads which laced the countryside, blossomed a month before time. In the inland villages farmers exulted cautiously and children ran bare-footed after watering-carts; in the towns which flanked the wide river the clangour of the ship-yards lost its insistence and, droning through the mild air, mounted to the foothills behind, where the hum of a precocious bee mingled with it and the exuberant bleating of lambs overcame it; in the city clerks shed their coats for coolness and lolled in offices execrating the sultry weather, the policy of Lord Beaconsfield, the news of the Zulu War, and the high cost of beer. Thus over the whole estuary of the Clyde, from Glasgow to Portdoran, upon Overton, Darroch, Ardfillan—those towns which, lying between the Winton and Doran hills, formed the three cardinal points of the fertile triangle upon the right bank of the firth—over the ancient Borough of Levenford, which stood bisecting exactly the base line of this triangle at the point where Leven entered Clyde, over all lay the radiance of a dazzling sun and, lapped in this strange benignant heat, the people worked, idled, gossiped, grumbled, cheated, prayed, loved, and lived.

Over Levenford, on this early day of May, thin wisps of cloud had hung languidly in the tired air, but now in the late afternoon these gossamer filaments moved slowly on to activity. A warm breeze sprang up and puffed them across the sky, when, having propelled them out of sight, it descended upon the town, touching first the high historic rock which marked the confluence of the tributary Leven with its parent stream, and which stood, a land-mark, outlined clearly against the opal sky like the inert body of a gigantic elephant. The mild wind circled the rock, then passed quickly through the hot, mean streets of the adjoining Newtown and wandered amongst the tall stocks, swinging cranes, and the ribbed framework of half-formed ships in the busy yards of Latta and Co. along the river's mouth. Next it wafted slowly along Church Street, as befitted the passage of a thoroughfare dignified by the Borough Hall, the Borough Academy, and the Parish Church, until, free of the sober street, it swirled jauntily in the advantageously open space of the Cross, moved speculatively between the rows of shops in the High Street, and entered the more elevated residential district of Knoxhill. But here it tired quickly of sporting along the weathered, red sandstone terraces and rustling the ivy on the old stone houses, and seeking the countryside beyond, passed inland once more, straying amongst the prim villas of the select quarter of Wellhall, and fanning the little round plots of crimson-faced geraniums in each front garden. Then, as it drifted carelessly along the decorous thoroughfare which led from this genteel region to the adjacent open country suddenly it chilled as it struck the last house in the road.

It was a singular dwelling. In size it was small, of such dimensions that it could not have contained more than seven rooms, in its construction solid, with the hard stability of new grey stone, in its architecture unique.

The base of the house had the shape of a narrow rectangle with the wider aspect directed towards the street, with walls which arose, not directly from the earth, but from a stone foundation a foot longer and wider than themselves, and upon which the whole structure seemed to sustain itself like an animal upon its deep-dug paws. The frontage arising from this supporting pedestal, reared itself with a cold severity to terminate in one half of its extent in a steeply pitched gable and in the other in a low parapet which ran horizontally to join another gable, similarly shaped to that in front, which formed the coping of the side wall of the house. These gables were peculiar, each converging in a series of steep right-angled steps to a chamfered apex which bore with pompous dignity a large round ball of polished grey granite and, each in turn, merging into and become continuous with the parapet which, ridged and serrated regularly and deeply after the fashion of a battlement, fettered them together, forming thus a heavy stone-linked chain which embraced the body of the house like a manacle.

At the angle of the side gable and the front wall, and shackled likewise by this encircling fillet of battlement, was a short round tower, ornamented in its middle by a deep-cut diamond-shaped recess, carved beneath into rounded, diminishing courses which fixed it to the angle of the wall, and rising upwards to crown itself in a turret which carried a thin, reedy flagstaff. The heaviness of its upper dimensions made the tower squat, deformed, gave to it the appearance of a broad frowning forehead, disfigured by a deep grooved stigma, while the two small embrasured windows which pierced it brooded from beneath the brow like secret, close-set eyes.

Immediately below this tower stood the narrow doorway of the house, the lesser proportion of its width giving it a meagre, inhospitable look, like a thin repellent mouth, its sides ascending above the horizontal lintel in a steep ogee curve encompassing a shaped and gloomy filling of darkly stained glass and ending in a sharp lancet point. The windows of the dwelling, like the doorway, were narrow and unbevelled, having the significance merely of apertures stabbed through the thickness of the walls, grudgingly admitting light, yet sealing the interior from observation.

The whole aspect of the house was veiled, forbidding, sinister, its purpose, likewise hidden and obscure. From its very size it failed pitifully to achieve the boldness and magnificence of a baronial dwelling, if this, indeed, were the object of its pinnacle, its ramparts and the repetition of its sharp-pitched angles. And yet, in its coldness, hardness, and strength, it could not be dismissed as seeking merely the smug attainment of pompous ostentation. Its battlements were formal but not ridiculous, its design extravagant but never ludicrous, its grandiose architecture containing some quality which restrained merriment, some deeper, lurking, more perverse motive, sensed upon intensive scrutiny, which lay about the house like a deformity, and stood within its very structure like a violation of truth in stone.

The people of Levenford never laughed at this house, at least never openly. Something, some intangible potency pervading the atmosphere around it, forbade them even to smile.

No garden fronted the habitation but instead a gravelled courtyard, bare, parched, but immaculate, and containing in its centre the singular decoration of a small brass cannon, which, originally part of a frigate's broadside, had long since joined in its last salvo, and after years in the junk yard, now stood prim and polished between two attendant symmetrical heaps of balls, adding the last touch of incongruity to this fantastic domicile.

At the back of the house was a square grassy patch furnished at its corners with four iron clothes poles and surrounded by a high stone wall, against which grew a few straggling currant bushes, sole vegetation of this travesty of a garden, except for a melancholy tree which never blossomed and which drooped against a window of the kitchen.

Through this kitchen window, screened though it was by the lilac tree, it was possible to discern something of the interior. The room was plainly visible as commodious, comfortably, though not agreeably furnished, with horse-hair chairs and sofa, an ample table, with a bow-fronted chest of drawers against one wall and a large mahogany dresser flanking another. Polished wax-cloth covered the floor, yellow varnished paper the walls, and a heavy marble timepiece adorned the mantel-piece, indicating by a subtle air of superiority that this was not merely a place for cooking, which was, indeed, chiefly carried on in the adjacent scullery, but the common room, the living room of the house where its inhabitants partook of meals, spent their leisure, and congregated in their family life.

At present the hands of the ornate clock showed twenty minutes past five, and old Grandma Brodie sat in her corner chair by the range making toast for tea. She was a large-boned, angular woman, shrunken but not withered by her seventy-two years, shrivelled and knotted like the bole of a sapless tree, dried but still hard and resilient, toughened by age and the seasons she had seen. Her hands, especially, were gnarled, the joints nodular with arthritis. Her face had the colour of a withered leaf and was seamed and cracked with wrinkles; the features were large, masculine, and firm; her hair, still black, was parted evenly in the middle, showing a straight white furrow of scalp, and drawn tight into a hard knob behind; some coarse short straggling hairs sprouted erratically like weeds from her chin and upper lip. She wore a black bodice and shawl, a small black mutch, a long trailing skirt of the same colour, and elastic-sided boots which, although large, plainly showed the protuberance of her bunions and the flatness of her well-trodden feet.

As she crouched over the fire, the mutch slightly askew from her exertions, supporting the toasting fork with both tremulous hands, she toasted two slices of bread with infinite care, thick pieces which she browned over gently, tenderly, leaving the inside soft, and when she had completed these to her satisfaction and placed them on that side of the plate where she might reach out quickly and remove them adroitly at once whenever the family sat down to tea, she consummated the rest of her toasting negligently, without interest. While she toasted she brooded. The sign of her brooding was the clicking of her false teeth as she sucked her cheeks in and out. It was simply an iniquity, she reflected, that Mary had forgotten to bring home the cheese. That girl was getting more careless than ever, and as undependable in such important matters as a half-witted ninny. What was tea to a woman without cheese? Fresh Dunlop cheese! The thought of it made her long upper lip twitch, sent a little river of saliva drooling from the corner of her mouth.

As she ruminated, she kept darting quick recriminative glances from under her bent brows at her grand-daughter, Mary, who sat in the opposite corner in the horse-hair armchair, hallowed to her father's use, and by that token a forbidden seat.

Mary, however, was not thinking of cheese, nor of the chair, nor of the crimes she committed by forgetting the one and reclining in the other. Her soft brown eyes gazed out of the window and were focused upon the far-off distance as if they saw something there, some scene which shaped itself enchantingly under her shining glance.

Occasionally her sensitive mouth would shape itself to smile, then she would shake her head faintly, unconsciously, activating thus her pendant ringlets and setting little lustrous waves of light rippling across her hair. Her small hands, of which the skin wore the smooth soft texture of petals of magnolia, lay palm upwards in her lap, passive symbols of her contemplation. She sat as straight as a wand, and she was beautiful with the dark serene beauty of a deep tranquil pool where waving wands might grow. Upon her was the unbroken bloom of youth, yet although she was only seventeen years of age there rested about her pale face and slender unformed figure a quality of repose and quiet fortitude.

At last the old woman's growing resentment jarred her into speech. Dignity forbade a direct attack, and instead she said, with an added bitterness from repression:

"You're sitting in your father's chair, Mary."

There was no answer.

"That chair you're sitting in is your father's chair, do you hear?"

Still no answer came; and, trembling now with suppressed rage, the crone shouted:

"Are you deaf and dumb as well as stupid, you careless hussy? What made you forget your messages this afternoon? Every day this week you've done something foolish. Has the heat turned your head?"

Like a sleeper suddenly aroused Mary looked up, recollected herself and smiled, so that the sun fell upon the sad still pool of her beauty.

"Were you speaking, Grandma?" she said.

"No!" cried the old woman coarsely, "I wasna speakin'. I was just openin' my mouth to catch flies. It's a graund way o' passin' the time if ye've nothing to do. I think ye must have been tryin' it when ye walked doun the toun this afternoon, but if ye shut your mouth and opened your een ye might mind things better."

At that moment Margaret Brodie entered from the scullery, carrying a large Britannia metal teapot, and walking quickly with a kind of shuffling gait, taking short flurried steps with her body inclined forward, so that, as this was indeed her habitual carriage, she appeared always to be in a hurry and fearful of being late. She had discarded the wrapper in which she did the house-work of the day for a black satin blouse and skirt, but there were stains on the skirt, and a loose tape hung untidily from her waist, whilst her hair, too, straggled untidily about her face. Her head she carried perpetually to one side. Years before, this inclination had been affected to exhibit resignation and true Christian submission in periods of trial or tribulation, but time and the continual need for the expression of abnegation had rendered it permanent. Her nose seemed to follow this deviation from the vertical, sympathetically perhaps, but more probably as the result of a nervous tic she had developed in recent years of stroking the nose from right to left with a movement of the back of her hand. Her face was worn, tired, and pathetic; her aspect bowed and drooping, yet with an air as if she continually flogged her jaded energies onwards. She looked ten years older than her forty-two years. This was Mary's mother, but now they seemed as alien and unrelated as an old sheep and a young fawn.

A mistress from necessity of every variety of domestic situations, Mamma, for so Mrs. Brodie was named by every member of the house, envisaged the old woman's rage and Mary's embarrassment at a glance.

"Get up at once, Mary," she cried. "It's nearly half-past five and the tea not infused yet. Go and call your sister. Have you finished the toast yet, Grandma? Gracious! you have burned a piece. Give it here to me. I'll eat it. We can't have waste in this house." She took the burned toast and laid it ostentatiously on her plate, then she began needlessly to move everything on the tea-table as if nothing had been done right and would, indeed, not be right until she had expiated the sin of the careless layer of the table by the resigned toil of her own exertions.

"Whatna way to set the table!" she murmured disparagingly, as her daughter rose and went into the hall.

"Nessie—Nessie," Mary called. "Tea—time—tea-time!"

A small treble voice answered from upstairs, singing the words:

"Coming down! Wait on me!"

A moment later the two sisters entered the room, providing instantly and independent of their disparity in years—for Nessie was twelve years old—a striking contrast in character and features. Nessie differed diametrically from Mary in type. Her hair was flaxen, almost colourless, braided into two neat pigtails, and she had inherited from her mother those light, inoffensive eyes, misty with the delicate white flecked blueness of speedwells and wearing always that soft placating expression which gave her the appearance of endeavouring continually to please. Her face was narrow with a high delicate white forehead, pink waxen doll's cheeks, a thin pointed chin and a small mouth, parted perpetually by the drooping of her lower lip, all expressive, as was her present soft, void smile, of the same immature and ingenuous, but none the less innate weakness.

"Are we not a bit early to-night, Mamma?" she asked idly as she presented herself before her mother for inspection.

Mrs. Brodie, busy with the last details of her adjustments, waved away the question.

"Have ye washed your hands?" she answered without looking at her. Then with a glance at the clock and without waiting for a reply she commanded with an appropriate gesture: "Sit in!"

The four people in the room seated themselves at table, Grandma Brodie being, as usual, first. They sat waiting, while Mrs. Brodie's hand poised itself nervously upon the tea-cosy; then into the silence of their expectation came the deep note of the grandfather's clock in the hall as it struck the half-hour and at the same moment the front door clicked open and was firmly shut. A stick rattled into the stand; heavy footfalls measured themselves along the passage; the kitchen door opened and James Brodie came into the room. He strode to his waiting chair, sat down, stretched forward his hand to receive his own special large cup, brimming with hot tea, received from the oven a large plateful of ham and eggs, accepted the white bread especially cut and buttered for him, had hardly seated himself before he had begun to eat. This, then, was the reason of their punctual attendance, the explanation of their bated expectancy, for the ritual of immediate service for the master of the house, at meal-times as in everything, was amongst the unwritten laws governing the conduct of this household.

Brodie ate hungrily and with obvious enjoyment. He was an enormous man, over six feet in height and with the shoulders and neck of a bull. His head was massive, his grey eyes small and deep set, his jaw hard and so resolutely muscular that as he chewed, large firm knobs rose up and subsided rhythmically under the smooth brown jowl. The face itself was broad and strong and would have been noble but for the insufficient depth of the forehead and the narrow spacing of the eyes. A heavy brown moustache covered his upper lip, partly hiding the mouth; but beneath this glossy mask his lower lip protruded with a full and sullen arrogance.

His hands were huge, and upon the backs of these and also of the thick spatulate fingers dark hairs grew profusely. The knife and fork gripped in that stupendous grasp seemed, in comparison, foolishly toyish and inept.

Now that Brodie had commenced to eat it was permissible for the others to begin, although for them, of course, there was only a plain tea; and Grandma Brodie led the way by fastening avidly upon her soft toast. Sometimes when her son was in a particularly amiable humour he would boisterously help her to small titbits from his plate, but to-night she knew from his demeanour that this rare treat would not come her way, and she resignedly abandoned herself to such limited savour as the food at her disposal provided. The others began to partake of the meal in their own fashion. Nessie ate the simple food heartily, Mary absent-mindedly, while Mrs. Brodie, who had privately consumed a small collation an hour before, trifled with the burnt bread upon her plate with the air of one who is too frail, too obsessed by the consideration of others, to eat.

An absolute silence maintained, broken only by the sucking sound which accompanied the application of the moustache cup to the paternal lips, the clanking of Grandma's antiquated dentures as she sought to extract the fullest enjoyment and nutriment from the meal, and an occasional sniff from Mamma's refractory nose. The members of this strange family tea-party manifested neither surprise, amusement, embarrassment, nor regret at the absence of conversation, but masticated, drank, swallowed without speech, whilst the minatory eye of Brodie dominated the board. When he chose to be silent then no word might be spoken, and to-night he was in a particularly sullen mood, lowering around the table and between mouthfuls casting a black glower upon his mother who, her eagerness rendering her unconscious of his displeasure, was sopping her crusts in her tea-cup.

At last he spoke, addressing her.

"Are ye a sow to eat like that, woman?"

Startled, she looked up, blinking at him. "Eh, wha' James? What for, what way?"

"What way a sow would eat, slushing and soaking its meat in the trough. Have ye not got the sense to know when you're eatin' like a greedy pig? Put your big feet in the trough as well, and then you'll be happy and comfortable. Go on! get down to it and make a beast o' yersel'. Have ye no pride or decency left in the dried-up marrow of your bones?"

"I forgot. I clean forgot. I'll no' do it again. Ay, ay, I'll remember." In her agitation she belched wind loudly.

"That's right," sneered Brodie. "Remember your pretty manners, you old faggot." His face darkened. "It's a fine thing that a man like me should have to put up with this in his own house." He thumped his chest with his huge fist, making it sound like a drum.

"Me," he shouted, "me!" Suddenly he stopped short, glared around from under his lowered bushy eyebrows and resumed his meal.

Although his words had been angry, nevertheless he had spoken, and by the code of unwritten laws the ban of silence was now lifted.

"Pass your father's cup, Nessie, and I'll give him some fresh tea. I think it's nearly out," inserted Mrs. Brodie propitiatingly.

"Very well, Mamma."

"Mary dear, sit up straight and don't worry your father. I'm sure he's had a hard day."

"Yes, Mamma," said Mary, who was sitting up straight and worrying nobody.

"Pass the preserves to your father then."

The smoothing down of the ruffled lion had commenced, and was to be continued, for after waiting a minute Mamma began again on what was usually a safe lead.

"Well, Nessie dear, and how did you get on at the school to-day?" Nessie started timidly.

"Quite well, Mamma."

Brodie arrested the cup he was raising to his lips.

"Quite well? You're still top of the class, aren't ye?"

Nessie's eyes fell. "Not to-day, father! only second!"

"What! you let somebody beat you! Who was it? Who went above ye?"

"John Grierson."

"Grierson! That sneakin' corn hawker's brat! That low-down bran masher! He'll crow about it for days. What in God's name came over you? Don't you realise what your education is going to mean to you?"

The small child burst into tears.

16

"She's been top for nearly six weeks, father," put in Mary bravely "and the others are a bit older than her."

Brodie withered her with a look.

"You hold your tongue and speak when you're spoken to," he thundered. "I'll have something to say to you presently; then you'll have plenty of chance to wag your long tongue, my bonnie woman."

"It's that French," sobbed Nessie. "I can't get those genders into my head. I'm all right with my sums and history and geography but I can't do that other. I feel as if I'll never get it right."

"Not get it right! I should think you will get it right—you're going to be educated, my girl. Although you're young, they tell me you've got the brains—my brains that have come down to you, for your mother's but a half-witted kind of creature at the best o' times—and I'll see that you use them. You'll do double home-work to-night."

"Oh! yes, father, anything you like," sighed Nessie, choking convulsively over a final sob.

"That's right." A transient unexpected gleam of feeling, which was partly affection, but to a far greater extent pride, lit up Brodie's harsh features like a sudden quiver of light upon a bleak rock.

"We'll show Levenford what my clever lass can do. I'm looking ahead and I can see it. When we've made ye the head scholar of the Academy, then you'll see what your father means to do wi' you. But ye must stick in to your lessons, stick in hard." He raised his eyes from her to the distance, as though contemplating the future, and murmured, "We'll show them." Then he lowered his eyes, patted Nessie's bowed, straw-coloured head, and added: "You're my own lass, right enough! Ye'll be a credit to the name of Brodie."

Then as he turned his head, his gaze lit upon his other daughter, and immediately his face altered, his eye darkened.

"Mary!"

"Yes, father."

"A word with you that's so ready with your jabbering tongue!"

In his sardonic irony he became smooth, leaning back in his chair and weighing his words with a cold, judicial calm.

"It's a pleasant thing for a man to get news o' his family from outsiders. Ay, it's a roundabout way no doubt, and doesna reflect much credit on the head o' the house—but that's more or less a detail, and it was fair stimulatin' for me to get news o' ye the day that nearly made me spew." As he continued his tone chilled progressively. "But in conversation with a member of the Borough Council to-day I was informed that you had been seen in Church Street in conversation with a young gentleman, a very pretty young gentleman." He showed his teeth at her and continued cuttingly: "Who I believe is a low, suspicious character, a worthless scamp."

In a voice that was almost a wail, Mrs. Brodie feebly interposed:

17

"No! no! Mary! It wasn't you, a respectable girl like you. Tell your father it wasn't you."

Nessie, relieved to be removed from the centre of attention, exclaimed unthinkingly:

"Oh! Mary, was it Denis Foyle?"

Mary sat motionless, her glance fixed upon her plate, a curious pallor around her lips; then, as a lump rose in her throat, she swallowed hard, and an unconscious force drove her to say in a low, firm voice:

"He's not a worthless scamp."

"What!" roared Brodie. "You're speaking back to your own father next and for a low-down Irish blackguard! A blackthorn boy! No! let these paddies come over from their bogs to dig our potatoes for us but let it end at that. Don't let them get uppish. Old Foyle may be the smartest publican in Darroch, but that doesn't make his son a gentleman."

Mary felt her limbs shake even as she sat. Her lips were stiff and dry, nevertheless she felt compelled to say, although she had never before dared argue with her father:

"Denis has got his own business, father. He won't have anything to do with the spirit trade. He's with Findlay & Co. of Glasgow. They're big tea importers and have nothing at all to do with—with the other business."

"Indeed now," he sneered at her, leading her on. "That's grand news. Have ye anything more ye would like to say to testify to the noble character of the gentleman. He doesna sell whisky now. It's tea apparently. Whatna godly occupation for the son of a publican! Well, what next?"

She knew that he was taunting her, yet was constrained to say, appeasingly,

"He's not just an ordinary clerk, father. He's well thought of by the firm. He goes round the country on business for them every now and then. He—he hoped he might get on—might even buy a partnership later."

"Ye don't say," he snarled at her. "Is that the sort of nonsense he's been filling up your silly head wi'—not an ordinary clerk—just a common commercial traveller—is that it? Has he not told ye he'll be Lord Mayor o' London next? It's just about as likely? The young pup!"

With tears streaming down her cheeks Mary again interposed, despite a wail of protest from Mamma.

"He's well liked, father! Indeed he is! Mr. Findlay takes an interest in him. I know that."

"Pah! ye don't expect me to believe what he tells ye. It's a pack of lies, a pack of lies," he shouted again, raising his voice at her. "He's a low-down scum. What can ye expect from that kind of stock? Just rottenness. It's an outrage on me that ye ever spoke to him. But ye've spoken to him for the last time." He glared at her compellingly, as he repeated fiercely: "No! Ye'll never speak to him again. I forbid it."

"But, father," she sobbed, "oh! father, I—I——"

"Mary, Mary, don't dare answer your father back! It's dreadful to hear you speak up to him like that," came Mamma's voice from the other end of the table. But although its purpose was to propitiate, her interjection was on this occasion a tactical errc r, and served only to direct momentarily the tyranny of Brodie's wrath upon her own bowed head, and with a jerk of his eyes he flared at her:

"What are you yammerin' about? Are you talkin' or am I? If ye've something to say then we'll all stop and listen to the wonder o' it, but if ye've nothing to say then keep your mouth shut and don't interrupt. You're as bad as she is. It's your place to watch the company she keeps." He snorted and, after his habit, paused forcibly, making the stillness oppressive, until the old grandmother, who had not followed the trend of the talk or grasped the significance of the intermission, but who sensed that Mary was in disgrace, allowed the culmination of her own feelings to overcome her, and punctuated the silence by suddenly calling out, in a rancorous senile tone:

"She forgot her messages the day, James. Mary forgot my cheese, the heedless thing she is"; then, her ridiculous spleen vented, she immediately subsided, muttering, her head shaking as with a palsy.

He disregarded the interruption entirely and returning his eyes to Mary, slowly repeated:

"I have spoken. If you dare to disobey me, God help you! And one more point. This is the first night of Levenford Fair. I saw the start o' the stinking geggies on my way home. Remember! No child of mine goes within a hundred yards of that show ground. Let the rest of the town go; let the riff-raff of the countryside go; let all the Foyles and their friends go; but not one of James Brodie's family will so demean themselves. I forbid it."

His last words were heavy with menace as he pushed back his chair, heaved up his huge bulk and stood for an instant upright, dominating the small feeble group beneath him. Then he strode to his armchair in the corner and sat down, swept his adjacent pipe-rack with the automatic action of established habit, selected a pipe by sense of touch alone, withdrew it and, taking a square leather tobacco pouch from his deep side pocket, opened the clasp and slowly filled the charred bowl; then he lifted a paper spill from the heap below the rack, bent heavily forward, ignited the spill at the fire and lit his pipe. Having accomplished the sequence of actions without once having removed his threatening eyes from the silent group at table, he smoked slowly, with a wet, protruding underlip, still watching the others, but now more contemplatively, more with that air of calm, judicial supremacy. Although they were accustomed to it his family inevitably became depressed under the tyranny of this cold stare, and now they conversed in low tones; Mamma's colour was still high; Mary's lips still trembled as she spoke; Nessie fiddled with her teaspoon, dropped it, then blushed shamefully as though discovered in a wicked act; the old woman alone sat impassive, pervaded by the comfortable sense of her repletion.

At this moment there were sounds of someone entering the house, and presently a young man came into the room. He was a slender youth of twenty-four, pale-faced and with a regrettable tendency towards acne, his look slightly hangdog and indirect, his dress as foppish as his purse and his fear of his father would allow, his hands, particularly noticeable, being large, soft, dead white in colour, with the nails cut short to the quick, leaving smooth round pads of flesh at the finger ends. He sidled into a chair without appearing to regard anyone in the room, accepted silently a cup of tea which Mamma handed him, and began to eat. This, the last member of the household, was Matthew, sole son and, therefore, heir to James Brodie. He was permissibly late for this meal because, being employed as a clerk in the ship stores department in Latta's Shipyard, his hours of work did not cease until six o'clock.

"Is your tea right, Matt?" asked his mother solicitously, in a low voice.

Matthew permitted himself to nod silently.

"Have some of that apple-jelly, dear. It's real nice," begged Mamma in an undertone. "You're lookin' a bit tired the night. Have ye had a lot to do in the office to-day?"

He jerked his head non-committally whilst his pale, bloodless hands moved continuously, cutting his bread into small accurate squares, stirring the tea, drumming upon the table-cloth; he never allowed them to be still, moving them amongst the equipage of the table like an acolyte performing some hasty sacramental rite upon an altar. The downcast look, the bolted mouthfuls, this uneasy inquietude of his hands were the reactions upon his unstable nerves of that morose paternal eye brooding behind his back.

"More tea, son?" whispered his mother, stretching out her hand for his cup. "Try these water-biscuits too, they're new in to-day"; then adding, as a sudden thought struck her: "Has your indigestion bothered you to-day?"

"Not too bad," at last he murmured in reply, without looking up.

"Eat your tea slowly then, Matt," cautioned Mamma confidentially. "I sometimes think ye don't chew your food enough. Don't hurry!"

"Got to see Agnes to-night, though, Mamma," he whispered reprovingly, as though justifying his haste.

She moved her head in a slow, acquiescent comprehension.

Presently the old grandmother arose, sucking her teeth and brushing the crumbs from her lap, wondering, as she took her chair, if her son would talk to her to-night. When in the humour he would regale her with the choicer gossip of the town, shouting to her of how he had got the better of Waddel and taken him down a peg, how Provost Gordon had slapped him heartily upon the back at the Cross, how Paxton's business was going down the hill. No one was ever praised in these conversations, but they were delicious to her in their disparaging piquancy, toothsome in their sarcastic aspersion, and she enjoyed them immensely, fastening upon each morsel of personal information and devouring it greedily, savouring always the superiority of her son over the victim of the discussion.

But to-night Brodie kept silent, occupied by his reflections which, mellowed by the solace of his pipe, flowed into a less rancorous channel than that which they had followed at table. He would, he considered, have to tame Mary, who, somehow, did not seem like his child; who had never bowed down to him as lowly as he desired, from whom he had never received the full homage accorded him by the others. She was getting a handsome lassie though, despite her unsubdued nature— took the looks from him—but he felt he must, for his own satisfaction and her good, subdue that independent spirit. As for her acquaintance with that Denis Foyle, he was glad that the noise of it had reached his ears, that he had crushed the affair at the outset.

He had been astounded at her temerity in answering him as she had done to-night and could find no reason for it, but now that he had marked that tendency towards insubordination he would watch her more carefully in the future and eradicate it utterly should it again occur.

His gaze then rested upon his wife, but only for an instant; considering it her only worth that she saved him the expense of a servant in the house, he quickly looked away from her, with an involuntary, distasteful curl of his lips, and turned his mind to pleasanter things.

Yes, there was Matthew, his son! Not a bad lad; a bit sly and soft and sleek perhaps; wanted watching; and spoiled utterly by his mother. But going to India would, he hoped, make a man of him. It was getting near the time now and in only two or three weeks he would be off to that fine job Sir John Latta had got for him. Ah! folks would talk about that! His features relaxed, as he considered how everyone would recognise in this appointment a special mark of Sir John's favour to him, and a further tribute to his prominence in the town, how, through it, his son's character would benefit and his own importance increase.

His eye then fell upon his mother, less harshly, and with a more indulgent regard than that he had directed towards her at table. She was fond of her food, and even as she sat nodding over the fire he read her mind shrewdly, knew that she was already anticipating, thinking of her next meal, her supper of pease brose and buttermilk. She loved it, repeated like a wise saw: "There's naethin' like brose to sleep on! It's like a poultice to the stomach." Ay! her god was her belly, but losh! she was a tough old witch. The older she got, the tougher she grew, she must have good stuff in her to make her last like that, and even now she looked, to his mind, good for another ten years. If he wore as well as that, and he might wear better, he would be satisfied.

Finally he looked at Nessie and immediately his bearing became tinged, almost imperceptibly, with a faint indication of feeling, not manifest by any marked change of feature, but by his eye which became flecked with a softer and more considerate light. Yes! Let Mamma keep her Matt, ay, and Mary too—Nessie was his. He would make something of her, his ewe lamb. Although she was so young she had the look of a real smart wee thing about her and the Rector had said to him only the other night that she had the makings of a scholar if she stuck in hard to her work. That was the way to do it. Pick them out young and keep them at it. He was looking ahead, too, with something up his sleeve for the future. The Latta Bursary! The crowning success of a brilliant scholastic career. She had it in her to take it, if she was nursed the right way. Gad! what a triumph! A girl to win the Latta—the first girl to win it, ay, and a Brodie at that! He would see that she did it. Mamma had better keep her soft spoiling hands off his daughter. He would see to that.

He did not quite know what he would make of her, but education was education; there were degrees that could be taken later on at College, and triumphs to be won. They all knew in the Borough that he was a man of progress, of broad and liberal ideas, and he would bring this more emphatically before them, yes, ram it into their silly mouths. "Did ye hear the latest!" he could hear them chatter. "That clever lass o' Brodie's is awa' up to the College—ay, she's taken the Latta—fair scooped the pool at the Academy, and he's lettin' her travel up and down to the University. He's a liberal-minded man for sure. It's a feather in *his* bonnet right enough."

Yes! he would show them in the town. His chest expanded, his nostrils quivered, his eye became fixed and distant, as he gave rein to his fancy, while his unnoticed pipe went out and grew cold. He would make them recognise him, make them look up to him, would force them somehow, some day, to see him as he really was.

The thought of Nessie faded gradually from his mind, and he ceased to contemplate her future but, making himself the central figure of all his mental pictures, steeped himself delightfully in the glory she would bring to his name.

At length he bestirred himself. He knocked out the ashes of his pipe, replaced it in the rack and, with a last silent survey of his family, as though to say: "I am going, but remember what I've said, I'll still have my eye on ye!" he went into the hall, put on his square felt hat with the smooth well-brushed nap, took up his heavy ash stick, and was out of the house without a word. This was his usual method of departure. He never said good-bye. Let them guess where he was going in his spare time—to a meeting, to the council, or to the club; let them remain uncertain as to his return, as to its time and the nature of his mood; he liked to make them jump at his sudden step in the hall. That was the way to keep them in order, and it would do them a deal of good to wonder where he went, he thought, as the front door closed behind him with a slam.

Nevertheless, the removal of his actual presence seemed to bring some measure of relief to his family, and with his departure a cloud of constraint lifted from the room. Mrs. Brodie relaxed the muscles which for the last hour had been unconsciously rigid and, while her shoulders sagged more limply, the tension of her mind was released and her spirit revived feebly.

"You'll clear up, won't you, Mary?" she said mildly. "I feel kind of tired and far through to-night. It'll do me no harm to have a look at my book."

"Yes, Mamma," replied Mary, adding dutifully as was expected of her every evening. "You've earned a rest. I'll wash up the dishes myself."

Mrs. Brodie nodded her inclined head deprecatingly, but none the less in agreement, as she arose and, going to her own drawer in the dresser, took from its place of concealment a book, *Devenham's Vow*, by one Amelia B. Edwards, which, like every book she read, was on loan from the Levenford Borough Library. Holding the volume tenderly against her heart she sat down, and soon Margaret Brodie had sunk her own tragic, broken individuality in that of the heroine, comforting herself with the one of few solaces which life now held for her.

Mary quickly cleared the dishes from the table and spread upon it a drugget cover, then, retiring to the scullery, she rolled up her sleeves from her thin arms and began her task of washing up.

Nessie, confronted by the unencumbered table, which mutely reminded her of her father's incitement to work, glanced first at the engrossed figure of her mother, at her grandmother's unheeding back, at Matt now tilted back in his chair and picking his teeth with an air, then with a sigh began wearily to withdraw her books from her school satchel, laying them reluctantly one by one in front of her.

"Come and play draughts first, Mary," she called out.

"No, dear, father said home work. Perhaps we'll have a game after," came the reply from without.

"Will I not dry the dishes for you to-night?" she suggested, insidiously trying to procrastinate the commencement of her toil.

"I'll manage all right, dear," replied Mary.

Nessie sighed again and remarked to herself sympathetically, in a voice like her mother's:

"Oh! dear me!"

She thought of the other children she knew who would be fraternising to play skipping ropes, rounders, cat and bat, and other magical frolics of the evening, and her small spirit was heavy within her as she began to work.

Matthew, disturbed in his transitory reverie, by the reiterated murmurs close to his ear: je suis, tu es, il est, now restored his quill to his vest pocket and got up from his chair. Since his father had gone his manner had changed, and he now adopted the air of being slightly superior to his surroundings, as he shot his cuffs, looked at the clock significantly and went out of the room, with a slight but pronounced swagger.

The room was now silent but for the rustle of a turning page, the slight clink of china invading it from without, and the harrowing murmur: nous sommes, vous êtes, ils sont; but in a few moments the audible evidence of activity in the scullery ceased and shortly afterwards Mary slipped quietly through the room into the hall, mounted the stairs and tapped at her brother's room. This was a nightly pilgrimage, but had she now been suddenly bereft of every sense but that of smell, she could still have found this room by the rich, unctuous odour of cigar smoke which emanated from it.

"Can I come in, Matt?" she murmured.

"Enter," came a studied voice from within.

She entered. As she came in he who had spoken so dispassionately did not look up, but seated in his shirt-sleeves upon the bed in the exact position where, with the looking-glass upon his chest of drawers tilted to the correct angle, he could best see himself, continued placidly to admire himself and to puff great clouds of smoke appreciatively towards his image.

"What a lovely smell your cigar has, Matt," she remarked, with ingenuous approval.

Matthew removed the weed from his lips in a dashing manner, still regarding himself approvingly.

"Yes," he agreed, "and it should have at the money. This is a Supremo, meaning the best. Five for sixpence, but this single one cost me three halfpence. It was a sample, and if I like it I'll go in for a few. The smell is good, Mary, but the bouquet is what we smokers appreciate. No cigar is really first class unless it has bouquet. This has what is called a nutty bouquet." He removed his eyes unwillingly from the mirror and contemplating his cigar more closely, added: "Now I'll stop, I think I've smoked enough."

"Oh! go on," she encouraged. "It's lovely! Far nicer than a pipe!"

"No! I must keep the other half for this evening," he replied firmly, carefully extinguishing the glowing end against the cold china of his wash-basin and preserving the stub in his waistcoat pocket.

"Does Aggie Moir like you to smoke?" she murmured, drawing her conclusions from his actions.

"Agnes, if you please—not Aggie," he replied in a pained voice. "How often have I told you not to be familiar like that. It's vulga It's—it's a liberty on your part."

She lowered her eyes. "I'm sorry, Matt."

"I should hope so! Remember, Mary, that Miss Moir is a young lady, a very worthy young lady, and my intended as well. Yes! if you must know she does like me to smoke. She was against it at first but now she thinks it manly and romantic. But she objects to the odour of the breath afterwards and therefore gives me cachous. She prefers the variety called 'Sweet Lips.' They're very agreeable."

"Do you love Agnes very much, Matt?" she demanded earnestly.

"Yes! and she loves me a great deal," he asserted. "You shouldn't talk about things you know nothing about, but you've surely the sense to know that when people are walking out they must be fond of one another. Agnes worships me. You should see the things she gives me. It's a great thing for a young man to have an affinity like that. She's a most estimable girl."

Mary was silent for a moment, her eyes fixed upon him intently, then suddenly pressing her hand to her side, she asked involuntarily, wistfully:

"Does it hurt you when you think of Agnes—when you're away from her?"

"Certainly not," replied Matthew primly. "That's not a nice thing to ask. If I had that pain I should think I had indigestion. What a girl you are for asking questions, and what questions you do ask! We'll have no more of it, if you please. I'm going to practise now, so don't interrupt."

He rose up and stooping carefully to avoid creasing his best trousers, took a mandolin case from under the bed and extracted a mandolin decorated with a large bow of pink satin ribbon. Next he unrolled a thin yellow-covered music book entitled in large letters: *First Steps in the Mandolin,* and in smaller print below: *Aunt Nellie's Guide for Young Mandolin Players, after the method of the famous Señor Rosas,* opened it at page two, laid it flat upon the bed before him, and sitting down beside it, in an attitude of picturesque ease, drew the romantic instrument to him and began to play. He did not, alas, fulfil the expectation which his experienced posture aroused, or dash ravishingly into an enchanting serenade, but with a slow and laborious touch picked out two or three bars of "Nelly Bly," until his execution grew more and more halting and he finally broke down.

"Begin again," remarked Mary helpfully.

He rewarded her with an aggrieved look.

"I think I asked you to remain silent, Miss Chatterbox. Remember this is a most difficult and complicated instrument. I must perfect myself in it before I leave for India. Then I can play to the ladies on board during the tropical evenings. A man must practise! You know I'm getting on splendidly, but perhaps you would like to try as you're so clever."

He did, however, begin again and eventually tweaked his way through the piece. The succession of tuneless discords was excruciating to the ear, and, in common with the art of smoking, could only be indulged in during the absence of his father; but Mary, nevertheless, with her chin cupped in her hands, watched, rather than listened, admiringly.

At the conclusion Matthew ran his fingers through his hair with a careless, yet romantic gesture.

"I am perhaps not in my best form, to-night; I think I am a little 'triste,' pensive, Mary you know. Perhaps a little upset at the office to-day—these confounded figures—it disturbs an artistic temperament like mine. I'm not really understood down at the Yard." He sighed with a dreamy sadness befitting his unappreciated art, but soon looked up, anxious for encouragement, asking:

"But how did it really go? How did it seem?"

"Very like it," replied Mary reassuringly.

"Like what?" he demanded doubtfully.

"The Saucy Kate Galop, of course!"

"You little ninny," shouted Matthew. "It was 'Nelly Bly.' " He was completely upset, looked at her crushingly, then jumped off the bed and put the mandolin away in a huff, remarking, as he bent down: "I believe you only said it to spite me," and asserting disdainfully as he got up: "You've no ear for music, anyway." He did not seem to hear her profuse apologies, but turning his back took a very stiff high collar and a bright blue spotted tie from a drawer, and still occupied by his pique, continued:

"Miss Moir has! She says I'm very musical, that I've got the best voice in the choir. She sings delightfully herself. I wish you were more worthy to be her sister-in-law."

She was quite upset at her clumsy tongue and well aware of her unworthiness, but she pleaded:

"Let me tie your neck-tie anyway, Matt."

He turned sulkily and condescendingly permitted Mary to knot the cravat, a task she always undertook for him, and which she now performed neatly and dexterously, so that presenting himself again before the mirror, he regarded the result with satisfaction.

"Brilliantine," he demanded next, forgiving her by his command. She handed him the bottle from which he sprinkled copious libations of mellifluous liquid upon his hair and with a concentrated mien he then combed his locks into a picturesque wave.

"My hair is very thick, Mary," he remarked as he carefully worked the comb behind his ears. "I shall never go bald. That ass Couper said it was getting thin on the top the last time he cut it. The very idea! I'll stop going to him in future for his impertinence."

When he had achieved the requisite undulation amongst his curls, he extended his arms and allowed her to help him to assume his coat, then took a clean linen handkerchief, scented it freshly with Sweet Pea Perfume, draped it artistically from his pocket, and surveyed the finished result in the glass steadily.

"Smart cut," he murmured, "neat waist. Miller does wonderfully for a local tailor, don't you think?" he queried. "Of course I keep him up to it, and he's got a figure to work on! Well, if Agnes is not pleased with me to-night, she ought to be." Then, as he moved away, he added inconsequently, "And don't forget, Mary, half-past ten to-night, or perhaps a little shade later."

"I'll be awake, Matt," she murmured reassuringly.

"Sure now?"

"Sure!"

This last remark exposed the heel of Achilles, for this admirable, elegant young man, smoker, mandolinist, lover, the future intrepid voyager to India, had one amazing weakness—he was afraid of the dark. He admitted Mary to his confidence and companionship incontestably for the reason that she would meet him by arrangement on these nights when he was late and escort him up the obscure and gloomy stairs to his bedroom, without fail and with a loyalty which never betrayed him. She never considered the manner of her service to him, but accepted his patronising favour gratefully, with humility, and now as he went out, leaving behind him a mingled perfume of cigars, brilliantine, and sweet pea blossom and the memory of his bold and dashing presence, she followed his figure with fond and admiring eyes.

Presently, bereft of the tinsel of his personality, Mary's spirits drooped, and unoccupied, with time to think of herself, she became disturbed, restless, excited. Everyone in the house was busy: Nessie frowning over her lessons, Mamma deeply engaged in her novel, Grandma sunk in the torpor of digestion. She wandered about the kitchen, thinking of her father's command, uneasy, agitated, until Mamma looked up in annoyance.

"What's wrong with you—wanderin' about like a knotless thread? Take up your sewing, or if you've nothing to do, away to your bed and leave folks to read in peace!"

Should she go to bed? she considered perplexedly. No! it was too ridiculously early. She had been confined in the house all day and ought perhaps to get into the open for a little, where the freshness of air would restore her, ease her mind after the closeness of the warm day. Everyone would think she had gone to her room, she would never be missed. Somehow, without being aware of her movements, she was in the hall, had put on her old coarse straw bonnet with the weather-beaten little bunch of cherries and the faded pink ribbon, had slipped on her worn cashmere coat, quietly opened the front door and moved down the steps.

She was startled, almost, to find herself outside, but thought reassuringly that with such clothes it was impossible for her to go anywhere, and as she reflected that she had no really nice things to wear, she shook her head sadly so that the woebegone cherries which had hung from her hat through two long seasons, rattled in faint protest and almost dropped to the ground. Now that she was in the open her mind moved more freely and she wondered what Denis was doing. Getting ready to go to the fair, of course. Why was everyone else allowed to go and not she? It was unjust, for there was no harm in it. It was an institution recognised, and patronised tolerantly, by even the very best of the townspeople. She leant over the front gate swinging to and fro gently, drinking in the cool beauty of the dusk, fascinated by the seductive evening, so full of dew-drenched odours, so animate with the awakening life that had been still during the day. Swallows darted and circled around the three straight silver birches in the field opposite, whilst a little further off a yellow-hammer called to her, entreatingly: "Come out! Come out! Jingle, jingle, jingle the keys, jingle, jingle, jingle the keys!" It was a shame to be indoors on a night like this! She stepped into the roadway, telling herself that she would take a little walk, just to the end of the road before coming back for that game of draughts with Nessie. She sauntered on unobserved, noting unconsciously that in the whole extent of the quiet road no person was in sight. Denis was expecting her to-night at the fair. He had asked her to meet him, and she, like a mad woman, had promised to be there. The pity of it that she could not go! She was terrified of her father and he had absolutely forbidden it.

How quickly she reached the end of the road, and although she seemed to have been out only for a moment she knew that she had come far enough, that it was now time for her to go back; but as her will commanded her to turn, some stronger force forbade it, and she kept on, her heart thumping furiously, her steps quickening in pace with her heartbeats. Then, through the magic of the night, the sound of music met her ears, faint, enticing, compelling. She hastened her gait almost to a run, thought: "I must, oh! I must see him," and rushed onwards. Trembling, she entered the fair ground.

II

LEVENFORD FAIR was an annual festival, the nucleus of which was the congregation of a number of travelling troupes and side-shows, a small menagerie, which featured actually an elephant and a cage of two lions, an authentic shooting gallery where real bullets were used, and two fortune-tellers with unimpeachable and freely displayed credentials, which, together with a variety of other minor attractions, assembled at an agreed date upon that piece of public land known locally as the Common.

The ground was triangular in shape. On one side, at the town end, stood the solidly important components of the fair, the larger tents and marquees, on another the moving vehicles of pleasure, swings, round-abouts and merry-go-rounds, and on the third, bordering the meadows of the river Leven, were the galleries, coco-nut shies, lab-in-the-tub and molly-dolly stalls, the fruit, lemonade, hokey-pokey, and nougat vendors, and a multitude of small booths which engaged and fascinated the eye. The gathering was by far the largest of its kind in the district and, its popularity set by precedent and appreciation, it drew like a magnet upon the town and countryside during the evenings for the period of one scintillating week, embracing within its confines a jovial mass of humanity, which even now slowly surged around the trigon on a per-petually advancing wave of pleasure.

Mary plunged into the tide and was immediately engulfed. She ceased to become an entity and was absorbed by the sweep of pushing, laugh-ing, shouting, gesticulating beings, which bore her forward independent of her own volition, and as she was pushed this way and that, yet always borne onwards by this encompassing force, she became at once amazed at her own temerity. The press of the rough crowd was not what her idyllic fancy had pictured, the blatant shouts and flaring lights not the impressions of her imagination, and she had not been five minutes on the ground before she began to wish she had not come and to perceive that, after all, her father might be right in his assertion, wise to have forbidden her to come. Now she felt that, though the sole purpose of her coming was to see Denis, it would be impossible for him to discover her in such a throng, and as a sharp, jostling elbow knocked against her ribs, and a fat ploughboy trod upon her foot and grinned uncouthly in apology, she grew wretched and frightened. What manner of feeling had drawn her amongst these vulgar clowns! Why had she so impru-dently, rashly, dangerously disobeyed her father and come with such light and ardent unrestraint at the beck of a youth whom she had known for only one month?

As she swayed around she viewed that month in retrospect, recollect-ing with a melancholy simplicity that the swing doors of the Borough Public Library had been, in part, responsible. These doors bore on the inside the authoritative word "Pull," and, in obedience to that terse mandate, when coming out of the Library, one was supposed to pull strenuously upon them; but they were so stiff and heavy that, when one was cumbered with a book and unobserved by the compelling eye of the janitor of the Borough Buildings, it was much easier to disregard the law and push. Upon one memorable occasion she had, undoubtedly, pushed, and thrusting forward with no uncertain hand, had launched herself straight into the waist-coat of a young man in brown. The impetus of her exit allowed her to observe fully the colour of his neat suit. His hair, too, was brown, and his eyes, and his face which had tiny freckles of a deeper brown dusted upon it; and as she raised her startled eyes she had noticed immediately, despite her discomposure, that his teeth, when he smiled, as he did instantly, were white and perfect. Whilst she stared at him with wide eyes and parted lips, he had composed his features, had politely collected her fallen book, calmly opened it, and looked at her name on the borrower's ticket.

"I am sorry to have upset you, Miss Mary Brodie," he had said gravely, but smiling at her the while out of his hazel eyes. "These doors are exceedingly treacherous. They ought, of course, to have glass windows to them. It is entirely my fault, for hot having brought the matter before the Borough Council."

She had giggled insanely, immodestly, but alas, irrepressibly at his delicious raillery and had only ceased when he added, tentatively, as though it were of no importance: "My name is Foyle—I live in Darroch." They looked at each other for a long moment, while she, of course, had flushed like a fool (since then he had told her that it was an adorable blush) and had said timidly: "I'm afraid I must be going." What a weak remark, she now reflected! He had not attempted to detain her, and with perfect courtesy had stepped aside, lifted his hat and bowed; but all the way down the street she had felt those lively brown eyes upon her, respectful, attentive, admiring. That had been the beginning!

Presently she, who had never before seen him in Levenford, for the good reason that he had seldom come there, began to see him frequently in the streets. They were, in fact, always encountering each other, and although he had never had the opportunity to speak, he always smiled and saluted her, cheerfully yet deferentially. She began to love that gay spontaneous smile, to look for the jaunty set of his shoulders, to desire the eager radiance of his glance. Sometimes she discerned him with a group of the hardier and more intrepid spirits of Levenfold standing at the newly opened ice-cream saloon of Bertorelli's, and perceived with awe that these bold striplings accepted him as an equal, even as a superior, and this, together with the knowledge that he should frequent a place so wild and reckless as an Italian ice-cream shop, made her tremble. His slight acquaintance with her had, too, given her distinction, and, even in his absence, when she passed this group of the youthful elect a polite silence immediately ensued, and as one man the members of the band swept off their hats to honour her—thrilling, but disconcerting her.

A week later she had again visited the Library, and despite the fact that this time she carefully pulled the doors as a public gesture of self-reproach and censure, openly avowing her penitence, she again found Denis Foyle outside.

"What a coincidence, Miss Brodie!" he had said. "Imagine us meeting here again. Strange that I should be passing just at this moment." How could she know, poor thing, that he had been waiting for two hours on the opposite side of the street.

"May I see what book you are reading this week?"

"*Pomeroy Abbey*, by Mrs. Henry Wood," she had stammered.

"Ah! yes, volume two. I saw you had volume one last time you were here."

He had, she mused, given himself away there, and as she observed a slight, shy eagerness in his glance, realised that he was altogether less composed, less assured than upon their previous encounter, and a melting tenderness filled her as she heard him say fervidly:

"Will you permit me to carry your book for you please, Miss Brodie?" She blushed darkly now at her unladylike and unpardonable conduct, but the unalterable fact remained that she had given him the book, had surrendered the volume without a word, as though in effect she had meekly proffered him the modest volume in return for the sweet acceptance of his attentions. She sighed as she thought of that small, and apparently trivial beginning, for since that occurrence they had met on several, no, on many occasions, and she had become so enwrapped by a strange and incomprehensible regard for him that it left her hurt and lonely to be away from him.

With a start she came out of the past. By this time she had been once round the fair without seeing anything but a blur of gaudy colours, she became once more aware of her unpleasant predicament, of the hopelessness of ever distinguishing amongst this nightmare sea of faces that seethed around her the one she sought, and as she was now opposite an opening in the crowd which permitted access to the street she began with difficulty to squeeze her way out.

Suddenly a warm hand clasped her small, cold fingers. Hurriedly she looked up, and saw that it was Denis. A wave of security enveloped her and invaded her veins in a delicious sense of comfort, filling her with such relief that she pressed his hand in hers and in the open simplicity of her nature said hurriedly, ardently, before he could speak:

"Oh! Denis, I've been so miserable here without you! I felt as if I had lost you for ever."

He looked at her tenderly, as he replied:

"I was a fool to ask you to meet me here in all this crowd, Mary. I knew I would find you, but I quite forgot that you might get into the crush before then. My train was late, too. Have you been here long?"

"I don't know how long," she murmured. "It seemed like years, but I don't care now that you're here."

"I hope you didn't get pushed about in the crowd," he protested. "I blame myself for letting you come on by yourself. Indeed I do! I should have met you outside, but I hadn't an idea there would be so many here to-night. You're not annoyed?"

She shook her head negatively; and without concealing her delight in him, without upbraiding him for his tardiness or permitting him to see the risk she had taken in coming to meet him here, replied guilelessly, happily:

"It's all right, Denis. I don't mind the crowd—nothing matters now that you've found me."

"What a girl you are, Mary," he cried. "It's an angel you are to forgive me. But I'll not rest till I've made it up to you. Let's make up for lost time. I'll not be happy till I've given you the time of your life. What shall we do first? Say the word and it's as good as done."

Mary looked round. How changed everything was! how glad she was to have come! She saw that the people around were not rough but merely boisterous and happy, and had she now been confronted with the heavy-footed ploughboy she would have returned his rustic grin with an understanding smile. She saw everywhere colour, excitement, and movement; the shouts of the showmen animated her, the cracking of shots in the shooting-gallery thrilled without daunting her; the blare of music around intoxicated her, and as her sparkling eye was drawn by a ring of hobby horses leaping gaily round, circling, prancing, gambolling to the tune of the Kandahar Waltz, she laughed excitedly and pointed to them.

"These," she gasped.

"Sure!" cried Denis. "Your word is law, Mary! We'll kick off on the leppers. All aboard for the Donegal Hunt," He grasped her arm, leading her forward while magically the crowd, which had so oppressed her, seemed to melt before them.

"Here we are," he exclaimed gaily. "Two together, with tails like lions and teeth like dromedaries. Up you go, Mary! Yours will jump the side of a house by the wicked look in his eye."

They were seated on the horses, grasping the reins, waiting, circling at first slowly, then quickly, then whirling to the mad music, thrilled with the joy of movement, tearing round above the gaping, unmounted commoners who seemed far below the flying hoofs of their prancing chargers, chasing together through wide celestial spaces, soaring upwards in a spirited nobility of movement. When, at last, they slowly came to rest, he refused to allow her to dismount, but compelled her willing presence beside him for another, and another and still another turn, until, as her experience grew, and her confidence in the saddle increased, she relaxed the tenseness of her grip upon the reins and directing her mount by the light touch of one hand, relaxed her body to its curvetting movement and exhibited proudly to him the address and dexterity of her horsemanship. He praised her, encouraged her, revelling in her enjoyment, until at length Mary's conscience pricked her and, feeling that he would be ruined through her prodigal rashness, she implored him to come off. He laughed till his sides shook.

"We could stay on all night if you wanted to! It's nothing at all if you're happy."

"Oh! yes it is, Denis! It's an awful expense. Do let us get down," she begged. "I'm just as happy watching!"

"All right, then! We'll get off to please you, Mary; but we're only beginning. To-night it's a millionaire you're with. We're goin' through the whole bag of tricks."

"If you're sure you can afford it, Denis," replied Mary doubtfully. "It's simply wonderful here! But I don't want you to spend too much on me."

"Sure I couldn't spend enough on you, Mary!" he replied warmly, "if I spent every farthing I've got!"

That was the raising of the curtain; and now they plunged into the throng, feasting their eyes upon the panorama of gaiety and absorbing the merriment around them eagerly, joyously, and together.

An hour later, having experienced every variety of movement offered for their delectation, thrown balls at all conceivable objects from coconuts to sallies, seen the flea-bitten lions and the apathetic elephant, prodded the fat boy at the earnest request of the showman to ensure there being no deception, admired the smallest woman in the world, shuddered appreciatively at the living skeleton, and purchased every edible commodity from honey pears to cough candy, they stood, the most joyously animated couple in the whole show ground, before the biggest tent in the fair. It was the famous McInally's, which provided, as its posters indicated, a feast of refined and elegant entertainment. In front of the tent was a wooden platform now illuminated by four naphtha flares, and upon the centre of this stage stood the famous McInally himself, easily distinguishable by his glossy top hat and flowing frock coat, by his largely checked trousers and the enormous brass albert that stretched, yellow as gold and thick as a mayoral chain, across his whitish velvet waistcoat. On either side of him stood, to quote again from the red and blue lettered advance notices that plastered the walls and gateposts of the countryside, a coruscating galaxy of talent. On his right a tall, soulful gentleman in full but musty evening dress leant with a melancholy grace against a pole of the marquee, directing his romantic gaze upwards from the mob as though he sought upon an ethereal balcony some Juliet who might be worthy of him, and concealing as best he might the soiled condition of his linen by elongating his coat sleeves and folding his arms manfully across his shirt front. But this sombre Romeo did not constitute the sole attraction of the show, for at the other end of the stage on McInally's left, was poised a bewitching creature clad in pink tights and white ballet skirt, with a peaked yachting cap set at a rakish angle upon her head, executing from time to time a few mincing steps hinting at the promise of more ravishing movements to come and throwing kisses to the multitude below with an airy, graceful action of her arms that suggested she was drawing yards of streamers from her lips.

"Isn't she lovely?" whispered Mary, who by this time had drawn so close to her companion that she had taken his arm.

"If you saw her in daylight you would be surprised," replied the more sophisticated Denis. "I've been told something about her. As a matter of report," he continued slowly, as though liberating a baleful secret, "they say she squints."

"Oh! Denis, how can you say such a thing!" cried Mary indignantly. But she gazed doubtfully at the suggestive angle of the yachting cap. Was it merely saucy, or was its purpose more profoundly significant?

"Walk up, ladies and gentlemen, walk up!" shouted McInally, removing his hat with a flourish and holding it extended in a courtly gesture of invitation. "The Performance is going to begin. We are just about to commence. Positively the last Performance of the evening. An entertainment of the highest class, admission twopence and twopence only. Artistic, refined, and elegant—Gentlemen, you may bring your wives and sweethearts, an entertainment without a blush. The one and only McInally, positively of the highest class and one class only. Just about to begin! Gentlemen! on my left Madame Bolita in the most wonderful and artistic Terpsichorean exhibition of the century." At the mention of her name Madame pirouetted lightly, smiled coyly, extended her wrists coquettishly and drew out fresh streamers, which were, if anything, more tenacious than before.

"Ladies! on my right Signor Magini, the most renowned, accomplished vocalist, direct from the Opera Houses of Paris and Milan, in the illuminated song-scena of the age." Signor Magini, whose real name was Maginty, looked more romantically melancholy than ever and bowed dreamily as though ladies had mobbed him with bouquets in Paris and fought for his favour in Milan. "We are about to commence to begin. We are about to begin to commence! Walk up! Walk up! The last show to-night. We are closing down for the evening. Thanking you one and all for your kind attention. Walk up, walk up."

"It must be going to begin, said Denis. "He's told us so often. Shall we chance it?"

"Yes," thrilled Mary.

They went inside.

In the tent it smelt of paraffin, hot sawdust, and orange-peel and, feeling their way through the dim, redolent interior they found a vacant place, seated themselves, and after a moment of expectant waiting, were rewarded by the opening of the programme. This was divided into two

34

parts, the first given over to Madame Bolita, the second to the Signor from Paris and Milan; but whether the great McInally was drawn by the compelling odour of his supper of steak and onions issuing from his caravan at the rear, or whether he felt that there was time for yet another performance which should be positively the last, is impossible to say; certainly the entertainment was the essence of brevity.

Madame pirouetted, postured, and leaped heavily, accentuating the thuds of her descent upon the thin sounding board of the stage by short involuntary expirations which might in a less accomplished artiste have been mistaken for grunts, and accompanying her lighter movements by much snapping of her fingers and shrill cries of: "La! la! oh! la, la!" She would pirouette tremulously at the back of the platform, trip forward skittishly to the row of footlights, thrust back one substantial leg into the air with a disdainful kick, advance her chin languishingly upon one extended forefinger, and, swaying slightly upon her remaining support, survey the audience with an air of profound achievement. Then, mingling the faint, intermediate rattle of applause with a self-congratulatory "oh! la, la!" she would toss her head enticingly and bound off into a circular gambol which took her conveniently back to her original position. The climax of the first part of her act came with a noble effort when, her arms outstretched, her face contorted by endeavour, she subsided slowly and painfully into the splits, a position from which, however, she did not attempt to arise, but was rescued by the timely fall of the curtain.

"Not bad, considering her age," remarked Denis, confidentially, "but she'll go right through that stage one day, and never be heard of again."

"Oh! Denis," whispered Mary reproachfully. "You don't really mean that. Surely you liked her?"

"If you liked her, I liked her! But don't ask me to fall in love with her," he replied teasingly. "We'll see what she does next," he added, as, after an adequate pause, the curtain again rose to reveal a darker stage into which the adipose figure of the incomparable Bolita swung slowly. Shrouded in a long white gown, bereft of the yachting cap, but still discreetly veiled by long yellow tresses which hung luxuriantly about her, and wearing a large and incontestably angelic pair of wings, she floated through the obscure air and remained poised seraphically before their astonished gaze. Gone now were the fripperies of the dance, the tinsel of the ballet, as though, reformed and purged, she now disdained the creature who had cried: "Oh! la, la!" and performed the atrocity of the splits; thus she swam piously about the stage to the accompaniment of an audible creaking of the wire and pulley which supported her and the tinkling out of "The Rock of Ages," upon the piano in the wings. There was much applause chiefly in the shape of shrill whistles from the back benches and loud cries of "'core, 'core";

35

but encores were unheard of in the McInally régime and Madame, having taken her bow with fluttering wings, retired gracefully and turned into her caravan to see if little Katie Maginty, her grandchild, had gone to sleep.

Mary clapped her hands enthusiastically and turned to Denis.

"What's your opinion now?" she enquired earnestly, as though daring him to belittle such a heavenly creature. They sat very close together on the thin wooden form, their hands clasped, their fingers interlocked, and Denis, looking at her entranced upturned face, pressed her fingers as he replied, meaningly:

"I think you're wonderful!" It was the height of repartee! Mary laughed outright, but at the sound of her own laughter, so unusually gay and unrestrained, inversely there arose in her mind, as if by contrast, the picture of her home, and suddenly chilled, as though she had been plunged into icy water, she shivered and lowered her head. But with an effort she thrust away her despondency; comforted by Denis' nearness she looked up again to see that Magini was holding the stage. A white screen had been lowered and now the magic lantern at the back of the tent flashed upon it the title: "Tender and True" or "The Mariner's Maid." The jingling piano struck up the opening bars of the ballad and Magini began to sing, while as he sang the honeyed words, richly coloured slides were shown upon the screen, demonstrating the touching vicissitudes attending the progress of true love. The meeting of the sailor and the miller's daughter by the mill-stream, the parting, the lonely mariner in his hammock, the trials of the noble-hearted seaman on the deep, and the no less lachrymal tribulations of his beloved at home, the still horrors of the shipwreck, the stark heroism of the rescue, flashed in turn before the breathless gaze until the final reunion of the well-deserving lovers, with clasped hands by that same mill-stream—the first slide repeated—gave relief and satisfaction to the entire audience.

He next sang, by special request, "Juanita," dealing with the seductive charms of a lady, darker and more passionate than the sailor's dove-like affinity, and holding a wilder and more dangerous appeal. When he concluded, the cheering from the back benches was vociferous and prolonged and it was some time before he could be heard to announce his last number as "The Land of Love," a favourite song, he informed his audience, of Ciro Pinsuti's. In contrast to the others it was simple, melodious, and touching, and although the vocalist had never been further south than the limits of McInally's circuit at Dumfries, he sang with a pure and natural voice. As the soft waves of sound floated through the dark tent Mary felt herself swept towards Denis in a rush of throbbing tenderness and sympathy. The sublime elevation of her emotion filled her eyes with tears. No one had ever treated her like Denis. She loved him. Raised far above the level of her confined and monotonous existence by the glitter of the evening and the glamour of the music, she would, if he had demanded it, have died willingly for this young god-like creature whose side was pressed against her side in a bitter-sweet union: sweet because she adored him, and bitter because she must leave him.

The song was ended. With a start she realised that the performance was over, and linked by an understanding silence she passed with Denis out of the tent into the fresh night air. Now it was dark, the ground illuminated by flares, the crowd diminished but still gaily surging, yet for these two, filled by a deeper enchantment, the attraction of the rair had waned. They looked around undecidedly.

"Shall we do any more of this?" asked Denis slowly. Mary shook her head. The evening had been so wonderful she felt it should have lasted for ever; but it was over, finished, and the hardest task of all was to say good-bye to him. She would have to walk back, a weary way out of that land of love, and now, alas! it was time for the journey to begin.

"Come for a little stroll then," he urged. "It's not late yet, Mary. We'll not go far."

She could not leave him! With a premonitory sadness rising in her throat at the very thought of her departure, she felt blindly that she must be with him a little longer. She wished to delay the sad reaction from this excitement and enchantment; she wanted his presence always, to soothe her and comfort her. The poignancy of her present feeling for him hurt her like a wound in her side, and its potency drove from her mind the thought of her home, her father, every deterring thought that might have prevented her accompanying him.

"Come, Mary dear," he pleaded. "It's still early."

"For a little way then," she consented in a whispered tone.

The path they took followed the winding bank of the Leven with the rippling river on one side and on the other meadows of dewy pasture land. A full moon that shone like a burnished plate of beaten silver, hung high in the sky, amongst a silver dust of stars, and was bosomed in the mysterious depths of the dark water beneath. At times thin pencils of misty cloud streaked this white nimbus that lay so far above and yet so deeply within the river, like ghostly fingers shielding from the eyes a luminance too brilliant to endure. As they walked, silent in the beauty of the silvery radiance, the air, cool with the dew-drenched freshness of night and sweet with the scents of lush grass and wild mint, encompassed them softly and settled upon them like a caress.

Before them two large grey moths pursued each other along the path-way, fluttering fantastically among the tall sedges and rushes of the bank, silently circling and crossing, flitting, but always following each other, always together. Their wings shone in the white light like large sailing motes within a moonbeam and the whisper of their flight fell upon the quietude like the downward flutter of a falling lea..

The river, too, was almost silent, gurgling and sucking softly at its banks, and the low purling song of the stream became part of the stillness of the night.

They had walked some distance and now the fair ground was marked only by a faint glare in the sky extinguished by the moon, and the brassy music by a weak whisper on the breeze obliterated by the stillness; yet Mary and Denis knew nothing of the music or the moon, and though unconsciously they absorbed the beauty around them they were aware only of each other. That she should be for the first time alone with Denis and isolated from the world, filled Mary with a tremulous happiness, set her heart beating in a wild and joyous sweetness.

Denis, too, the sophisticated young man of the town, was overwhelmed by an emotion that was strange and new. The easy currents of conversational small-talk which made him always the life and soul of a party, the blandishments that flowed naturally from his lips, were dried up at the source. He was silent as a mute at a funeral, and, he told himself, as dismal. He felt that his reputation was at stake, that he must make some remark, no matter how trivial. Yet while he cursed himself inwardly for a dolt, a blunderer, a simpleton, imagining that he was estranging Mary by his dumb stupidity, his tongue still remained dry and his quick brain so flooded by his emotions that he could not speak.

Outwardly they both walked placidly and sedately, but inwardly there surged in each a tide of pent-up feelings, and because they did not speak this feeling grew more intense.

In Mary's side there came an actual pain. They were so close together that the sense of intimacy filled her with inexpressible yearning, an unfathomable longing which found its only ease in the firm clasp upon her arm that linked her pulsating body to his and soothed her like a divine balm.

At length they stopped suddenly, involuntarily, turned, and faced each other. Mary lifted her face to Denis. The small oval of her features bore the pallor of the moonlight with a spiritual translucency. He bent and kissed her. Her lips were soft and warm and dry, and they offered themselves to his like an oblation. It was the first time she had kissed any man, and although she was perfectly innocent and entirely ignorant, yet the instincts of nature throbbed within her, and she pressed her lips close against his.

Denis was overwhelmed. His mild experience as a gallant had encompassed nothing like this, and, feeling as if he had received a rare and wonderful gift, without knowing what he did, he dropped spontaneously upon his knees beside Mary and, clasping his arms around her, pressed his face in homage against her dress. The smell of the rough worn serge of her skirt was fragrant to him; he felt her legs, so pathetically slender and immature, tremble slightly under his touch. Clasping her hand he drew her down beside him. Now he could see the little hollow in her neck and from it a tiny blue vein running down. As he took off her hat a ringlet of hair fell over her smoothly pale brow, and first he kissed that awkwardly, humbly, with a clumsiness which did him credit, before he laid his lips upon her eyes and closed them with his kisses.

Now they were in each other's arms, sheltered by rushes and bushes of broom, the soft grass plastic beneath them. The contact of their bodies gave them a delicious warmth so that there was no need of speech, and in silence they left the world, knowing and caring nothing but for each other. Her head lay back on his arm, and between her parted lips her teeth shone in the moonlight like small white seeds. Her breath was like new milk. Again he saw in the arch of her neck the small vein threaded under the smooth skin, like a tiny rivulet through virgin snow, and caressingly, he stroked it, gently tracing with his finger tips its lovely downward passage. How firm and round her breasts were, each like a smooth and perfect unplucked fruit enclosed within his palm for him to fondle! The pressure of his hand sent the hot colour into her face, and though her breath came faster, yet she suffered him. She felt these small virgin breasts, the consideration of which had never before invaded the realm of her consciousness, grow turgid, as if an ichor from her blood had filled them, and all her puny strength surged into them as though from her nipples drops might well forth to an invisible suckling. Then her mind was dazzled, and, as she lay with closed eyes in his embrace, she forgot everything, knew nothing, ceased to be herself, and was his. Her spirit rushed to meet his swifter than a swallow's flight and together uniting, leaving their bodies upon the earth, they soared into the rarer air. Together they floated upwards as lightly as the two moths and as soundlessly as the river. No dimension contained them, no tie of earth restrained the ecstasy of their flight.

The lights in the fair-ground went out one by one; an old frog, its large, sad eyes jewelled in the moonlight, broke through the grasses beside them, then noiselessly departed; a dim white mist sheathed the radiance of the river like breath upon a mirror; then, as the lace veils of vapour loomed over the land, crepuscular shadows filled the hollows of the meadows, and the earth grew faintly colder as though its heat had been chilled by the rimed air. With the falling mist all sound was blotted out and the stillness became absolute until after a long time a trout jumped upstream and splashed heavily in its pool.

At the sound, Mary stirred slowly, and consciousness of the world half returning, she whispered softly:

"Denis I love you. Dear, dear Denis! But it's late, very late! We must go."

She lifted her head heavily, moved her drugged limbs slowly, then, like a flash the recollection of her father, her home, her position here, invaded her mind. She started up, terrified, horrified with herself.

"Oh! what have I done? My father! What will become of us?" she cried. "I'm mad to be here like this."

Denis stood up.

"No harm will come to you, Mary," he said as he essayed to soothe her. "I love you! I will take care of you."

"Let me go then," she replied while tears ran down her pale cheeks. "Oh! I must be back before he gets in or I'll be shut out all night. I'd have no home!"

"Don't cry, dear Mary," he entreated, "it hurts me to see you cry. It's not so very late—not eleven o'clock yet! Besides I am responsible for everything, all the blame is mine."

"No! No!" she cried, "it's all my fault, Denis. I should never have come. I disobeyed my father. I'll be the one to suffer."

Denis placed his arm around her trembling form and, looking again into her eyes, said firmly:

"You will not suffer, Mary! Before we go I want you to understand one thing. I love you. I love you above everything. I am going to marry you."

"Yes, yes," she sobbed. "Only let me get home. I must. My father will kill me! If he's not late to-night something terrible will happen to me—to us both." She started off at a run up the path, slipping and stumbling in her anxiety to make haste, whilst he followed, trying to console and comfort her, uttering words of the most endearing tenderness. But, although at his words she ceased to weep, she still ran and did not speak again until they reached the edge of the town. There she stopped abruptly.

"Don't come any further, Denis," she panted. "This is enough! We might meet him—my father."

"But it's so dark on the road," he protested. "I'm afraid to leave you."

"You must go, Denis! He might come on us together."

"But the darkness?"

"I can't help that. I'll run all the way."

"It'll hurt you if you race home like that, Mary, and it's so black, the road seems so lonely now."

"Leave me! you must!" she cried. "I'll go myself! Good-bye!"

With a last touch of his hand she fled from him; her figure dissolved into the blackness, and was gone.

As he gazed into the impenetrable gloom, vainly trying to follow her rapid flight, wondering if he should call to her or follow her, he raised his arms in perplexity, as though beseeching her to return to him, then slowly he lowered them and, after a long passivity, turned heavily upon his heel, and took his dejected way towards his own home.

Meanwhile in a panic of urgency; Mary forced her tired body along the road, the same road that she had so lightly traversed earlier on this same evening, having lived, it seemed to her, a whole century in time and experience during the space of these few intervening hours. It was unthinkable that she, Mary Brodie, should be at this time of night alone in the open streets; the sound of her solitary footsteps frightened her, echoing aloud like a reiterated accusation for her father, for everyone to hear, shouting out the madness, the iniquity of her present situation. Denis wanted to marry her! He must be mad too— madly unaware of her father and of the circumstances of her life. The echoes of her steps mocked her, whispering that she had been bereft of her senses to plunge herself in this predicament, making the very contemplation of her love for Denis a painful and grotesque absurdity.

As she neared her home, suddenly she became aware of another figure in front of her, and the dread that it might be her father filled her with numb apprehension. Although he frequently did not return from the club until after eleven o'clock, sometimes he was earlier, and as she drew nearer, silently gaining upon the figure, she felt that it must be he. But, all at once, a gasp of relief escaped her, as she perceived that it was her brother, and, abandoning her caution, she ran up to him, panting:

"Matt! Oh! Matt! Wait!" and stumbling against him, she clutched his arm like a drowning woman.

"Mary!" he exclaimed, starting violently, hardly able to believe his eyes.

"Yes! It's me, Matt, and thank God it's you! I thought it was father at first."

"But—— But what on earth are you out for at this time of night?" he cried, in shocked amazement. "Where have you been?"

"Never mind just now, Matt," she gasped. "Let us get in quick before father. Please, Matt, dear! Don't ask me anything!"

"But what have you been up to? Where have you been?" he repeated. "What will Mamma think?"

"Mamma will think I've gone to bed, or that I'm reading in my room. She knows I often do that when I'm sitting up for you."

"Mary! This is a terrible escapade. I don't know what to do about it. It's shameful to find you out in the street at this time of night." He moved on a few steps then, as a thought struck him, stopped abruptly. "I wouldn't like Miss Moir to know about this. It's disgraceful! Such a going-on by my sister might prejudice me in her eyes."

"Don't tell her, Matt! Don't tell anybody! Only let us get in. Where is your key?" Mary urged.

Muttering under his breath, Matthew advanced to the front steps, and while Mary gasped with relief to see that the outer door was unbolted, which meant that her father had not returned, he opened the door.

The house was still, no one awaited her, no recriminations or accusations were hurled at her, and realising that she was miraculously undiscovered, in a transport of thanksgiving Mary took her brother's hand, and in the darkness they crept noiselessly up the stairs.

Inside her own room she drew a deep breath, and as she felt her way securely about its known confines, the very touch of familiar objects reassured her. Thank God she was safe! Nobody would know! She tore off her clothes in the dark and crept into bed, when instantly the cool sheets soothed her warm weariness and the soft pillow caressed her aching head. Her hot, tired body relaxed in an exquisite abandon, her trembling eyelids closed, her fingers uncurled from her palms, her head drooped towards her shoulder, and with her last waking thought of Denis, her breathing grew regular and tranquil. She slept.

III

JAMES BRODIE awoke next morning with the sun streaming in through his window. He had especially designated this room at the back of the house as his bedroom because, with an animal appreciation of sunshine, he loved the bright morning rays to strike in and waken him, to soak through the blankets into his receptive body, and saturate his being with a sense of power and radiance. "There's no sun like the morning sun," was one of his favourite sayings, one of his stock of apparently profound axioms which he drew upon largely in his conversation and repeated with a knowing and astute air. "The mornin' sun's the thing! We don't get enough o' it, but in MY room I've made sure o' all that's goin'."

He yawned largely and stretched his massive frame luxuriously, observed with half-opened yet appreciative eyes the golden swarm of motes that swam around him, then, after a moment, blinked questioningly towards the clock on the mantelpiece, the hands of which marked only eight o'clock; becoming aware that he had another quarter of an hour in bed, he put his head down, rolled over on his side, and dived beneath the blankets like a gigantic porpoise. But soon he came up again. Despite the beauty of the morning, despite the brosy odour of the boiling porridge which his wife was preparing downstairs and which, arising, gently titillated his nostrils, his present humour lacked the full complacency which he felt it should have held.

Moodily, as though seeking the cause of his discontent, he turned and surveyed the hollow on the other side of the big bed, which his wife had left a full hour ago when, according to custom, she had arisen in good time to have everything in order and his breakfast ready upon the table the moment he came down. What good, he reflected resentfully, was a woman like that to a man like him? She might cook, wash, scrub, darn his socks, brush his boots, aye, and lick his boots too; but what kind of armful was she now? Besides, since her last confinement, when she had borne him Nessie, she had been always ailing, in a weak, whining way, offending his robust vigour by her flaccid impotence, and provoking his distaste by her sickly habits. Out of the corner of his eye when she thought herself unobserved, as in the early hours of the morning when she left the bed before him, he would contemplate her almost stealthy dressing with disgust. Only last Sunday he had detected her in the act of concealing some soiled garment, and had roared at her like an angry ram: "Don't make a midden of my bedroom! It's bad enough for me to put up with you without havin' your dirty clothes flung in my face!" She had, he considered bitterly, long since been repugnant to him; the very smell of her was obnoxious to him, and had he not been a decent man, he might well have looked elsewhere. What had he dreamed last night? He thrust out his lower lip longingly and stretched his legs powerfully as he played with the vision of his sleep, thinking of the tantalising young jade he had chased through the woods who, though he had run like a stag, had been saved by the fleetness of her foot. She had run, faster than a deer, her long hair flying behind her, and with not a stitch on her back to cumber her, but still, despite her speed, had turned to smile at him enticingly, provokingly. If he had only gotten a grip of her, he thought, allowing his erotic fancy to riot delightfully as he lay back, basking his ponderous body in the sun, his parted lips twitching with a half lewd, half sardonic amusement, he would have made her pipe to a different tune.

Suddenly he observed that it was quarter past eight and, without warning, he jumped out of bed, put on his socks, trousers, and slippers, and pulled off his long nightgown. His naked torso gleamed sleekly and the muscles of his shoulders and back undulated like pliant knotted ropes under the white skin which shone like smooth satin, except where the thick brown hair was felted on the chest, dense and adherent as lichen upon a rock. For a moment he stood thus, placed before the small mirror above the washstand, admiring his clear eye, his strong white teeth, and running his fingers with a bristling sound over the stubble on his heavy jaw. Then, still stripped to the waist, he turned, took up a mahogany box of razors wherein lay seven special hollow-ground Sheffield blades with their ivory handles marked each with a day of the week, carefully picked out the one inlaid with the word Friday, tried the temper appreciatively against his thumb nail and began to strop it slowly upon the leather thong which hung near from its appointed hook. The strap was thick, and, as Matthew and Mary had testified in their younger days, of an enduring toughness, and as Brodie worked the razor slowly up and down upon its tan surface it set the true blade to an infinite keenness. When he had adjusted the edge to his satisfaction, he went to the door, picked up his hot shaving water which was there, steaming, to the minute, returned to the mirror, lathered his face copiously, and began to shave with long, precise movements. He shaved meticulously, leaving his chin and cheeks as smooth as silk, cautiously avoiding the glossy curl of his moustache and sweeping the razor against his tense skin with such firm, measured strokes that it filled the silence of the room with a regularly intermittent rhythm of crisp, rustling sound. Shaved, he cleaned the razor upon a slip of paper taken from a specially cut pile, which it was Nessie's duty to prepare and replenish, re-stropped it and replaced it in its case; then, decanting the large ewer into its basin, he washed extravagantly in cold water, splashing it upon his face and sluicing lavish handfuls about his chest, head, and arms. This prodigal use of cold water even on the iciest mornings of winter was his inflexible habit, maintaining, he claimed, his perfect health, and saving him from the catarrhal colds which so frequently affected his spouse. "I slunge myself in cold water," he would often boast, "as cold as I can get it. Ay! I wad break the ice to dook myself, and the more frozen it is the warmer it makes me after. It doesna make me chatter or snivel wi' a red nose, like some folks I could mention. No! No! It makes me glow. Give me plenty cold, cold water—there's health in it"; and now, as he vigorously applied a coarse rough towel to his body, whilst he hissed between his teeth like an ostler, he felt a ruddy glow sweep through him and dispel in part the rankness of his early mood.

He finished his dressing by assuming, with scrupulous care, a shirt of fine, expensive linen, starched Gladstone collar and bird's-eye cravat fixed with a gold horseshoe pin, embroidered grey waistcoat, and long coat of superfine broadcloth. Then he went downstairs.

Breakfast he invariably ate alone. Matthew left the house at six, Nessie at half-past eight, his mother was never up before ten o'clock, Mrs. Brodie and Mary took their morning meal privately and when they chose in the dim regions where cooking was performed, and it fell therefore that Brodie sat down to his large bowl of porridge in solitary dignity. He enjoyed all his meals, but to breakfast in particular he brought, in the freshness of morning, a more lively appetite, and he now addressed himself eagerly to his porridge, and after, to the two fresh eggs lightly boiled to the requisite second and shelled into a large cup, to the large soit rolls and thick fresh butter, and to his coffee, a beverage of which he was inordinately fond and one permitted to no one else in the household.

As Mary passed soundlessly in and out of the room during the meal to serve him he noticed from beneath his lowered lids how pale she looked, but he made no remark, for it was his policy not to encourage his womenfolk to consider themselves ill; it gave him, nevertheless, an inward satisfaction as he attributed the subdued look and dark circles under her eyes to the shrewd attack he had launched on her on the previous night.

According to custom, when he had breakfasted, and that in silence, he left the house at nine-thirty precisely, and stood for a moment at his front gate looking back appreciatively at his property. His proud glance swept the small domain, observing that not a weed sprouted in the gravelled yard, not a spot disgraced the paintwork, not a blemish marked the grim grey stone, and approving with intense complacency the work of his own creation. It was his! Five years ago he had bought the land and approaching Urie the builder, had spoken to him at length, drawn rough diagrams, and described fully the nature of the house he desired. Urie, a blunt man and a man of substance, had looked at him in astonishment, saying:

"Man alive! you're not a stone-mason or you wouldna let your ideas run awa' wi' you like that. Your head must be in the clouds. Do ye realise what that sketch would look like in stone and mortar?"

"I'm going to live in it, Urie—not you," Brodie had replied steadily.

"But there's so much unnecessary work on it. Just take the expense o' piercin' this wee piece o' parapet! What good is it?" and Urie flicked the pencilled outline before him.

"I'm payin' for it, Urie—not you," again replied Brodie.

The builder had pushed his hat over his ears, scratched his head uncomprehendingly with his pencil, and expostulated: "You're not serious, Brodie! It would be all right if it were ten times as big, but you're only wantin' a six room and kitchen house. It's preposterous. You'll make yoursel' the laughin' stock o' the town."

"I'll attend to that," cried Brodie grimly. "God help the man that laughs at James Brodie to his face!"

"Come, come now, Brodie," the other had conciliated, "let me put you up a solid respectable bit villa, not this wee kind o' sham castle that you're haverin' about."

Brodie's eyes took on a strange expression, as though a dark fire flickered there, and he shouted out:

"Damn ye, Urie! Keep your tongue civil when ye speak to me. I want none o' your smug bandboxes. I want a house that befits me"; then in a flash he had recovered himself and in a normal, quiet tone added: "If you don't like it ye needna touch it. I'm givin' ye the chance, but if ye don't wish to take it there are other builders in Levenford."

Urie stared at him and whistled.

"Sits the wind in that quarter. Well! Well! If you're set on it I'll get a plan and an estimate out for you. A wilful man maun have his way. But don't forget I warned ye. Don't come and ask me to take the house down again once it's up."

"No! No! Urie," Brodie had sneered. "I'll only come back to ye if ye don't give me what I'm askin' for, and then it'll not be pleasant hearin' for ye. Get ahead wi' it now and don't blabber so much."

The plans had been prepared, passed by Brodie, and the building begun. From day to day he had seen it grow, going along in the cool evenings to the slowly mantling building, observing the exact adherence to his design, gloating over the smooth, white stone, testing the mortar between his fingers, caressing the shining lead pipes, weighing and fingering approvingly the heavy square slates. Everything had been of the best materials, and though this had taken heavy toll upon his purse, had in fact drained it—for he had always spent money freely upon himself, would indeed never have saved but for this one object— he was proud to have achieved it, proud to have left the rented house in Levengrove Place, proud in the possession of the inmost desire of his heart. He was right too. Nobody laughed openly. One night, shortly after the house had been completed, a loafer at the Cross stepped out from the toping gang that loitered there, and accosted Brodie.

"Good evening, Mr. Brodie," he hiccoughed, looking round at his fellows for approbation, then back at Brodie. "And how is the castle to-night?"

Brodie looked at him calmly. "Better than you," he replied, and smashed his fist with terrific violence into the rowdy's face, then, taking the clean linen handkerchief from his pocket, and wiping the blood from his knuckles, he threw it contemptuously on the ground beside the fallen man and walked quietly away.

Certainly Brodie's position in the town had altered sensibly in these last five years, and since the building of his house he was regarded with more significance, detachment, and misgiving; his social value increased at the price of singularity, and he became gradually a more notable figure with many acquaintances and no friends.

Now he took a final look at his property, squared his shoulders, and set off down the road. He had not proceeded far before he caught a glimpse of a peering face from behind the front-room curtains of one of the semi-detached houses further down, and he jeered inwardly to see that it was little Pettigrew, the grocer, who had recently moved into the select neighbourhood, and had at first sought to establish himself by walking ingratiatingly to the town with Brodie. The big man had tolerated this liberty for the first day, but when on the second morning he found the diminutive, unimportant grocer again waiting for him, he had stopped short. "Pettigrew," he had said calmly, "I'm afraid I'm not seein' so weel this mornin'. You're kind o' wee and shilpet to me the day and to-morrow I mightna see you ava'. Besides I'm a fast walker. Gang your own gait, man, but don't strain your bandy wee legs keepin' pace with me. Good morning to you." Now he smiled sardonically as he passed the house, reflecting that since then the nervous Pettigrew had avoided him like a plague and had formed the habit of watching him well out of sight before venturing into the street.

Soon he had traversed the quieter residential district and entered the town where, at the south end of Church Street, an artisan carrying his bag of tools touched his cap to him in passing. Brodie's chest expanded at this act of deference, accorded only to the most important figures in the town. "Good morning to you," he cried affably, setting his head further back in a proud geniality, marching round the corner into the High Street with his stick over his shoulder, and tramping up the incline like a soldier until he reached the crest of this main thoroughfare. There he stopped opposite an inconspicuous shop. The shop was old and quiet with a narrow, unostentatious front marked by a small single window that displayed no merchandise, but masked its face discreetly behind an interior screen of fine-meshed wire, which, though it veiled the window, revealed the hidden secret of the shop by bearing upon its drawn grey filigree, in faded gilt lettering, the one word—Hatter. It was, then, apparently a hat shop, but although it held the most commanding situation in the town, it not only disguised its character but seemed to remove itself from public observation, receding slightly from the common frontage of the street, and permitting the adjacent buildings to project beyond and above it, as though it wished to remain, despite the fixed solidity of its position, as unobserved and unobtrusive as it might, reserving its contents, and striving to conceal itself and all that lay within from vulgar, prying eyes. Above its doorway the sign, too, was bleached by age and weather, its paint finely cracked by sun, and smoothly washed by rain; but, still distinguishable upon it in thin sloped letters across its surface, was the name—James Brodie. This was Brodie's shop. Each morning, as he regarded it, the fact that he should possess it never failed to amuse him, and for twenty years he had inwardly regarded his business with a tolerant derision. It was of course the sole means of his livelihood, the unimpressive source of his stately and inspiring habitation, its solid, steady business the origin of his fine clothes and the money he rattled so easily in his pockets; yet his attitude towards it was that of a man who views with an indulgent yet contemptuous air some trifling and unbecoming foible within his own nature. He—Brodie—was a hatter! He was not ashamed of the fact, but gloried in its ridiculous incongruity, revelled in the contrast between himself and the profession of his adoption which he knew must continually present itself to the world at large. He turned and surveyed the street from his elevated position like a monarch offering himself freely to the public gaze. He was only a hatter! The richness of the absurdity of his position was always before him, inevitably appealed to him, and now an internal diversion shook him as he moved into his shop to start another day's work.

Inside, the shop was dark, neglected, and almost dingy, its dim interior bisected by a long counter which ran the length of the room, acting as a barrier between the public and the private divisions of the establishment and bearing upon its worn, indented surface at one end a graduated series of tarnished brass stands each supporting a hat or cap of different style and colour. At the other distant end, the counter joined the wall as a ledge capable of elevation, thus permitting ingress to a short row of steps leading to a door with a ground glass window on which was inscribed the word Office. Running backwards, beside and underneath this elevated compartment, was a small L-shaped cupboard of a back shop that, deprived of its original dimensions by the more recent imposition of the Office, contained with some difficulty in its limited extent an ironing-board and an iron stove which, with its perpetual blast, dried more thoroughly the already sapless and vitiated air. In the shop itself the walls were covered in a drab crimson paper upon which hung several old prints; although few hats were to be seen, and upon these no prices were displayed, behind the counter stood a series of wide mahogany drawers for caps, and a long line of shelves upon which stacks of cardboard boxes ranged from floor to ceiling.

Behind the counter, and in front of this abundant but hidden stock, stood a young man whose appearance suggested that his stock of virtues must also be concealed. He was thin, with an etiolated countenance which palely protested against the lack of sunlight in the shop, and which was faintly pitted with honourable scars gained in his perpetual struggle against an addiction to boils, a disorder to which he was unhappily subject, attributed by his devoted mother to thin blood and against which she continually fortified him with Pepper's Quinine and Iron Tonic.

The general engaging aspect of his features was not, however, marred to any extent by these minor blemishes, nor by a small but obtrusive wart which had most inconsiderately chosen its location upon the extremity of his nose, and was well set off by a shock of dark hair, feathered, despite its careful oiling, and so frosted with dandruff that it shed its surplus flakes and formed a perpetual rime upon his coat collar.

The remainder of his person was pleasing, and his dress suited soberly to his position; but about him clung a peculiar, sour odour occasioned by a tendency towards free perspiration, particularly from his feet, a regrettable but unavoidable misfortune that occasionally induced Brodie to fling him out of the back door, which abutted upon the Leven, together with a cake of soap and a profane injunction to wash the offending members. This was Peter Perry, messenger, assistant, salesman, disciple of the stove and ironing-board, lackey of the master, and general factotum enrolled in one.

As Brodie entered he inclined his body forward, his hands pressed deeply on to the counter, fingers extended, elbows flexed, showing more of the top of his head than his face and, in a passion of obsequiousness, awaited his master's greeting.

"Mornin', Perry."

48

"Good morning, Mr. Brodie, sir," replied Perry with nervous haste showing a little less of his hair and a little more of his face. "A very beautiful morning again, sir! Wonderful for the time of year. Delightful!" He paused appreciatively before continuing: "Mr. Dron has been in to see you this morning, on business he said, sir."

"Dron! what the devil does he want?"

"I'm sure I couldn't say, sir. He said he'd come back later."

"Humph!" grunted Brodie. He strode into his office, flung himself into a chair and, disregarding the several business letters that lay on the desk, lit his pipe. Then he tilted his hat well back on his head—it was a sign of personal superiority that he never removed it at his business —and took up the *Glasgow Herald*, that had been placed carefully to his hand.

He read the leading article slowly, moving his lips over the words; although occasionally he was obliged to go over an involved sentence twice in order to grasp its meaning, he persisted tenaciously. At times he would lower the paper and look blankly at the wall in front, using the full power of his sluggish mentality, striving to comprehend fully the sense of the context. It was a stern, matutinal task which Brodie set himself to assimilate the *Herald's* political editorial, but he considered it his duty as a man of standing to do so. Besides, it was thus that he provided himself with weighty argument for his more serious conversation, and to this purpose he never failed to accomplish the task, although by next morning he had completely forgotten the gist of what he had read.

Half a column had been battled with in this dogged fashion when a diffident tap upon the glass panel disturbed him.

"What is it?" shouted Brodie.

Perry, for only Perry could have knocked like that, replied through the closed door:

"Mr. Dron to see you, sir."

"What the devil does he want? Does he not know I'm at the *Herald's* leader and can't be disturbed?"

Dron, a dejected, insignificant individual, was standing close behind Perry and could hear every word, a fact of which Brodie was maliciously aware, and which induced him, with a satirical humour, to couch his replies in the most disagreeable terms and in the loudest tones he could. Now, with a faint grin upon his face, he listened over his lowered paper to the muffled consultation outside the door.

"He says, Mr. Brodie, he won't keep you a minute," insinuated Perry.

"A minute, does he say! Dearie me, now. He'll be lucky if he gets a second. I havena the least desire to see him," bawled Brodie. "Ask him what he wants, and if it's not important the little runt can save his breath to cool his porridge." Again there was a whispered colloquy, during which Perry, with vigorous pantomime more expressive than his words, indicated that he had done everything to further the other's interests compatible with his own safety and security.

"Speak to him yourself, then," he mumbled finally, in self-acquittal, seceding from the cause and backing away to his counter. Dron opened the door an inch and peered in with one eye.

"You're there, are you?" remarked Brodie, without removing his eyes from the paper, which he had again raised in a grand pretence of reading. Dron cleared his throat and opened the door a little further.

"Mr. Brodie, could I have a word wi' you just for a wee minute? I'll not keep ye more nor that," he exclaimed, working himself gradually into the office through the slight opening he had cautiously made for himself.

"What is it, then?" growled Brodie, looking up in annoyance. "I've no dealings wi' you that I'm aware of. You and me are birds that don't fly together."

"I ken that well, Mr. Brodie," replied the other humbly, "and that's the very reason I've come to see ye. I came more or less to ask your advice, and to put a small suggestion before ye."

"What is't, then? Don't stand there like a hen on a hot griddle."

Dron fumbled nervously with his cap. "Mr. Brodie, I havena been doin' too well lately at my trade, and I really came in regarding that little property o' mine next door."

Brodie looked up. "You mean the tumble-down shop that's been empty these three months past. Who could help seeing it? Man, it's an eyesore in the street."

"I ken it's been empty a long time," replied Dron meekly, "but it's an asset in a way—in fact it's about the only asset I've got now—and what wi' gettin' a bit desperate one way and another an idea struck me that I thocht might interest you."

"Indeed, now," sneered Brodie, "is not that interestin'! Ye have the lang head on ye, sure enough, to get all these inspirations—it'll be the Borough Council for ye next. Well! what is the great idea?"

"I was thinking," returned the other diffidently, "that with your grand business and perhaps a shop that was a little too small for ye, ye might consider extendin' by taking in my place and making one big premises with perhaps a plate-glass window or two."

Brodie looked at him cuttingly, for a long moment.

"Dear, dear! And it was to extend my business you worked out all this and came in twice in the one mornin'," he said at last.

"Indeed no, Mr. Brodie. I've just told ye things have been goin' rather ill with me lately, and what with one thing and another, and the wife expecting again soon, I must get a bend on to let my property."

"Now that's too bad," purred Brodie. "It's you small, snuffy men that will have the large families. I hope ye're not makin' me responsible for your latest addition though. Ay, ye're fond o' the big family, I know.

I've heard tell ye've that many weans ye can't count them. But," he continued in a changed voice, "don't make me responsible for them. My business is my own and I manage it my own way. I would as soon th'nk of a cheap-lookin' plate-glass window as I would of giving away pokes o' sweeties with my hats. Demn you, man, don't you know I've the most distinguished people in the borough as my clients and my friends? Your empty shop's been a fester on my respectable office for months. Let it for God's sake. Let it by all means. Let it to auld Nick if ye like, but you'll never let it to me. Now get out and don't ever bother me like this again. I'm a busy man and I've no time for your stupid yammerin'!"

"Very well, Mr. Brodie," replied the other quietly, twisting his hat in his hands. "I'm sorry if I've offended ye, but I thought there was no harm in asking—but you're a hard man to speak to." He turned disconsolately to depart, but at that moment an agitated Perry shot himself into the room.

"Sir John's gig is at the door, Mr. Brodie," he stammered. "I saw it drive up this very minute!"

The assistant might deal with the less important, with, indeed, the bulk of the customers, to whom it was his duty to attend without disturbing Brodie, but when a personage came into the shop he knew his orders, and raced for his master like a startled greyhound.

Brodie lifted his eyebrows with a look at Dron which said: "You see!"; then, taking him firmly by the elbow, as he had no wish to be confronted by Sir John in the other's undistinguished company, he hurried him out of the office and through the shop, expediting his passage through the outer door with a final push. The indignity of this last, powerful, unexpected shove completely upset Dron, and, with a stagger, he slipped, his legs shot from under him, and he landed full upon his backside at the very moment that Sir John Latta stepped out of his gig.

Latta laughed vociferously, as he entered the shop and came close up to Brodie.

"It's the most amusing thing I've seen for ages, Brodie. The look on the poor man's face would have brought the house down at Drury's," he cried, slapping his thigh with his driving gloves. "But it's a blessing he wasn't hurt. Was he dunning you?" he asked slyly.

"Not at all, Sir John! He's just a bit blether of a man that's always making a public nuisance of himself."

"A little fellow like that?" He looked at the other appraisingly. "You know you can't realise your own strength, man! You're an uncommon powerful barbarian."

"I just flicked him with my pinkie," declared Brodie complacently, delighted to have so opportunely attracted the other's notice, and feeling it sweet incense for his pride to receive attention from the distinguished principal of the famous Latta Shipyard. "I could whip up a dozen like him with one hand," he added carelessly—"not that I would soil my fingers that way. It's beneath my consideration."

Sir John Latta was gazing at him quizzically along his finely chiselled nose. "You're a character, Brodie, you know! I suppose that's why we cherish you," he said. "The body of a Hercules and the mind of— well——" He smiled. "Shall we put a glove on it for you? You know the tag, 'odi profanum vulgus et arceo'?"

"Quite so! Quite so!" replied Brodie agreeably. "You've a neat way o' puttin' things, Sir John. There was something like that in the *Herald* this mornin'. I'm with you there!" He had not the least idea what the other was talking about.

"Don't let things run away with you though, Brodie," said Sir John, with a warning shake of his head. "A little of some things goes a long way. You're not to start knocking the borough about. And don't offer us too much baronial caviare. I hope you get my meaning. Well," he added, abruptly changing the subject and his manner, allowing the latter to become formal, more distant, "I mustn't dally, for I'm in really a hurry—I have a meeting—but I want a panama hat—the real thing, you know. I haven't felt sun like this since I was in Barbados. Get some down from Glasgow if needs be. You have my size."

"You shall have a selection to choose from at Levenford House this very afternoon," replied Brodie complacently. "I'll not leave it to my staff. I'll see to it myself."

"Good! And by the by, Brodie," he continued, arresting himself on his way to the door. "I almost forgot that my agents write me from Calcutta that they're ready for your boy. He can leave on the *Irrawaddy* on June the fourteenth. She's a Denny-built packet, nineteen hundred tons, you know. Fine boat! Our people will look after his berth for him."

"That is more than kind of you, Sir John," purred Brodie. "I'm deeply grateful. I'm most indebted for the way you've put yourself about for me over that matter."

"Nothing! Nothing!" replied the other absently. "We've got plenty young fellows at this end, but we want them at our docks out there— the right kind that's to say! The climate's really nothing to speak of, but he'll need to watch the life out there. It sometimes knocks a young fellow off his feet. I'll have a word with him if I've time. I hope he does well for your sake. By the way, how is that remarkably pretty daughter of yours?"

"Quite fair."

"And the clever little sprat?"

"Splendid, Sir John."

"And Mrs. Brodie?"

"Middling well, thank ye."

"Good! Well, I'm off now! Don't forget that hat of mine."

He was into his gig, a fine, spare, patrician figure of a man, had taken the reins from his groom and was off, spanking down the High Street, with the smooth, glossy flanks of the cob gleaming, and the high lights flashing on whirling spokes, gleaming metal, shining liveried cockade, and upon the rich lustre of varnished coachwork,.

Rubbing his hands together, his eye dilating with a suppressed exultation, Brodie returned from the doorway, and, to Perry, who had remained, a drooping, nebulous shadow in the background, he cried, with unwonted volubility:

"Did ye hear that conversation we had? Was it not grand? Was it not enough to make these long lugs o' yours stand out from your head? But I suppose the half of it was above ye. You'll not understand the Latin. No! but you heard what Sir John said to me—gettin' that post for my son and speirin' all about my family. Answer me, ye puir fool," he called out. "Did you hear what Sir John Latta said to James Brodie?"

"Yes, sir," stammered Perry, "I heard!"

"Did you see how he treated me?" whispered Brodie.

"Certainly I did, Mr. Brodie!" replied the other, with returning confidence, perceiving that he was not to be rebuked for eavesdropping. "I wasn't meaning to—to overhear or to spy on you, but I did observe you both, sir, and I agree with you. Sir John is a fine man. He was more than good to my mother when my father died so sudden. Oh! yes, indeed, Mr. Brodie, Sir John has a kind word and a kind action for everybody."

Brodie eyed him scornfully. "Faugh!" he said contemptuously. "What are you ravin' about, you witless creature! You don't know what I mean, you poor worm! You don't understand." Disregarding the other's crushed appearance as beneath his notice, he stepped upwards into his office once more, arrogantly, imperiously, and resumed his big chair, then, as he gathered together the sheets of his morning paper before his unseeing eyes, he muttered softly to himself, like one who dallies wantonly, yet seriously, with a profound and cherished secret: "They don't understand. They don't understand!"

For a full minute he remained staring blankly in front of him, while a dull glow lurked deeply in his eye, then, with a sudden toss of his head and a powerful effort of will, he seemed to thrust something violently from him as though he feared it might master him; shaking his body like a huge dog, he recollected himself, observed the paper in front of him, and, with a visage once more composed and tranquil, began again to read.

IV

"MARY, put the kettle on the fire. We'll be back in time for me to give Matt some tea before he goes off to see Agnes," said Mrs. Brodie, drawing on her black kid gloves with prim lips and a correct air, adding: "Mind and have it boiling, now, we'll not be that long." She was dressed for one of her rare sorties into the public street, strangely unlike herself in black, flowing paletot and a plumed helmet of a hat, and beside her stood Matthew, looking stiff and sheepish in a brand new suit, so new indeed that when he was not in motion his trouser legs stood to attention with edges sharp as parallel presenting swords. It was an unwonted sight on the afternoon of a day in midweek, but the occasion was sufficiently memorable to warrant the most unusual event, being the eve of Matthew's departure for Calcutta. Two days ago he had, for the last time, laid down his pen and picked up his hat in the office at the shipyard, and since then had lived in a state of perpetual movement and strange unreality, where life passed before him like a mazy dream, where, in his conscious moments, he became aware of himself in situations both unusual and alarming. Upstairs his case stood packed, his clothing protected by camphor balls, so numerous that they had invaded even the inside of the mandolin, and so powerful that the entire house smelled like the new Levenford Cottage Hospital, greeting him whenever he entered the house with an odious reminder of his departure. Everything that the most experienced globe trotter could desire lay in that trunk, from the finest obtainable solar topee given by his father and a morocco-bound Bible by his mother to the patent automatic opening water-bottle from Mary and the small pocket compass that Nessie had bought with the accumulation of her Saturday pennies.

Now that his leave-taking was at hand Matthew had experienced during the last few days a well-defined sinking feeling in the vicinity of his navel, and though of his own volition he would willingly and self-sacrificingly have abandoned the thrill of such a disturbing emotion, like a nervous recruit before an action, the pressure of circumstances forbade his retirement. The lions which had arisen in his imagination and leapt glibly from his tongue a short week ago to engage the fascinated attention of Mary and Mamma, now returned growling, to torment him in his dreams. Renewed assurances from people connected with the yard that Calcutta was at the least a larger community than Levenford failed to comfort him, and before retiring each night he cultivated the habit of searching for snakes which might be perfidiously concealed beneath his pillow.

For Mrs. Brodie the emotional influence of the occasion had provided a strong stimulus, as though she felt at last able to identify herself in a situation worthy of a leading character in one of her beloved novels.

Like a Roman matron renouncing her son to the State with spartan fortitude, or, more sensibly, a Christian mother sending out a second Livingstone on a mission of hope and glory, she forsook her meek despondency and, bearing up nobly, packed, repacked, devised, succoured, comforted, encouraged, and exhorted, and sprinkled her conversation with text and prayer.

Brodie had not missed the change in her, gauging with a sardonic eye the explanation of the transient phase. "You're makin' a bonny exhibition o' yourself, my woman," he had sneered at her, "wi' your posing and posturin', and your runnin' after that big gowk o' yours, and your cups o' tea and snashters at a' hours. Ye would think ye were Queen Victoria to look at ye. Is it a general ye're sendin' out to the war or what? that you're blowin' yerself out like a pig's bladder. I know well what will happen. Whenever he's away ye'll collapse, and we'll have ye back on our hands more o' a dreich empty bag than ever. Faugh! Let some sense in that silly skull o' yours, for God's sake."

She had felt him cold, unfeeling, even callous, as she feebly expostulated: "But, father, we maun give the boy his start. There's a great future in front o' him"; and though, thereafter, concealing her endeavours from her husband, she had redoubled, with an outraged, conscious rectitude, these spirited efforts on behalf of her young, potentially illustrious pioneer.

Now, having adjusted her gloves to a smooth, though nodose, perfection, she remarked: "Are you ready, Matt dear?" in a tone of such forced cheerfulness that it chilled Matthew's very blood. "We are going down, Mary, to the chemist's," she continued in a chatty manner. "The Rev. Mr. Scott told Agnes the other day that the best remedy for malaria was quinine—a wonderful cure he said, so we're off to get a few powders made up." Matthew said nothing, but visions of himself lying, fever-racked, in a crocodile-infested swamp rushed through his mind, and considering glumly that a few scanty powders seemed a paltry protection against such an evil, in his mind he sullenly repudiated the reverend gentleman's suggestion. "What does he know about it, anyway? He's never been there. It's all very fine for him to talk," he thought indignantly, as Mrs. Brodie took his arm and led him, an unwilling victim, from the room.

When they had gone Mary filled the kettle and put it on the hob. She seemed listless and melancholy, due, no doubt, to the thought of losing her brother, and for a week had moved in a spirit of extreme dejection which might reasonably have been entirely attributed to sisterly solicitude. Curiously, though, it was just one week since she had been with Denis at the fair, and though she longed for him, she had not seen him since. That had been an impossibility, as she knew him to be in the North travelling on business, from a letter posted in Perth which, startlingly, she had received from him. It was an event for her at any time to receive a letter (which, on such rare occasions, was inevitably perused by the entire household), but fortunately she had been first down that morning and so no other had seen it, or the sudden throbbing gladness of her face, and she had thus avoided detection, interrogation, and certain discovery.

What felicity it had been to hear from Denis! She realised with an inward thrill that he must have held this paper in his own hands, the hands which had touched her so caressingly, brushed the envelope with those lips which had sealed themselves upon hers, and, as she read the letter behind the locked door of her room, she flushed even in this privacy, at the impetuous, endearing words he wrote. It became evident to her that he desired to marry her and, without considering the obstacles which might be between them, took for granted apparently that she had accepted him.

Now, seated alone in the kitchen, she took the letter from her bodice and re-read it for the hundredth time. Yes! He wrote fervently that he was pining for her, that he could not exist without her, that life to him was now an endless waiting until he should see her, be near to her, be with her always. She sighed, ardently, yet sadly. She, too, was pining for him. Only ten days since that night by the river's brink, and each day more piteous, more dolorous than the one before!

On the first of the seven she had felt ill physically, while the realisation of her boldness, her disobedience of her father, the defiance of every canon of her upbringing struck her in one concentrated blow; but as time passed and the second day merged into the third and she still did not see Denis, the sense of iniquity was swamped by the sense of deprivation, and she forgot the enormity of her conduct in a straining feeling of his necessity to her. On the fourth day, in her sad bewilderment, when she had essayed so constantly to penetrate the unknown and unrealised depths of her experience that it began to appear to her like a strange, painful unreality, his letter had come, raising her at once to a pinnacle of ecstatic relief. He did, then, love her after all, and everything became obliterated in the joy of that one dazzling fact; but on the succeeding days she had gradually slipped from the heights, and now she sat realising the hopelessness of ever obtaining sanction to see Denis, asking herself how she could live without him, wondering what would become of her.

As she pondered, carelessly holding the letter in her hand, old Grandma Brodie entered unobserved.

"What's that you're reading?" she demanded suddenly, peering at Mary.

"Nothing, Grandma, nothing at all," Mary blurted out with a start, stuffing the crushed paper into her pocket.

"It looked to me gey like a letter, and ye seemed in a big hurry to hide it. You're always mopin' and moonin' over something now. I wish

I had my specs. I would soon get to the bottom o' it." She paused, marking the result of her observation malevolently on the tables of her memory. "Tell me," she resumed, "where's that glaikit brother o' yours?"

"Gone to get quinine at the chemist's with Mamma."

"Pah! what he needs is gumption—not quinine. He would need a bucket o' that to stiffen him up. Forbye, some strained castor oil and a drop of good spirits would be more useful to him outbye there. I've no time for sich a palaver that has been goin' on. Everything's upset in the house with the fiddle faddle of it a'. Tell me, is tea earlier to-night?" She clicked her teeth hopefully, scenting like a harpy the nearness of sustenance.

"I don't know, Grandma," replied Mary. Usually the old woman's unbashful eagerness for food left her indifferent, but to-night, in her own troubled perplexity, it nauseated her; without further speech she got up and, feeling that she must be alone and in a less congested atmosphere, went out into the back garden. As she paced back and forwards across the small green she felt it strangely cruel that life should continue to move heedlessly around her in the face of all her sadness and confusion, that Grandma Brodie should still crave greedily for her tea, and the progress of Matt's departure march indifferently along. The current of her thoughts had never flowed so despondently as, with restless movements, she seemed dimly to perceive that the circumstances of her life were conspiring to entrap her. Through the back window she saw Matthew and her mother return, saw Mamma bustle to prepare the table, observed Matthew sit down and begin to eat. What did they care that her brain throbbed with perplexity behind a burning forehead, that she wished one word of compassionate advice but knew not where to seek it? The barren drabness of this back garden, the ridiculous rear view of the outlines of her home, enraged her, and she desired with bitter vehemence to have been born into a family less isolated, less exacting, less inhuman, or, better, not to have been born at all. She envisaged the figure of her father, bestriding, like a formidable colossus, the destiny of the Brodies, and directing her life tyrannically—with an ever watchful, relentless eye. His word it was which had withdrawn her at the age of twelve from school, which she loved, to assist in the duties of the household; he had terminated her budding friendships with other girls because this one was beneath her, or that one lived in a mean house, or another's father had incensed him; his mandate had forbidden her to attend the delightful winter concerts in the Mechanics' Hall on the grounds that she demeaned herself by going; and now he would destroy the sole happiness that life now held for her.

A torrent of rebellion swirled through her; as she felt the injustice of such unnatural restraint, such unconditional limitation of her freedom, she stared defiantly at the meek currant shoots which grew half-heartedly in the hard soil around the garden walls. It was easier, alas, to put them out of countenance than Brodie, as though they, too, infected by the tyranny of their environment, had lost the courage to hold their slender tendrils erect.

A touch on her shoulder startled her, she who had just dared to show fight. It was, however, merely Matthew, who had come to speak to her for a moment before leaving to visit Miss Moir.

"I'll be home early to-night, Mary," he said, "so don't worry about —you know, staying up. And," he added hastily, "now that I'm going abroad I know you'll never mention it to a soul—I would never like it to be known—and thank you a lot for what you've done for me."

This unexpected gratitude from her brother, although its origin lay in a premature wave of nostalgia, and was fostered by the cautious instinct to safeguard his memory against his absence, touched Mary.

"That was nothing to do for you," she replied. "I was only too pleased, Matt. You'll forget all about that worry out there."

"I'll have other things to bother about, I suppose." She had never seen him so subdued, or less self-complacent, and a glow of affection for him warmed her, as she said, "You'll be off to see Agnes now. I'll walk to the gate with you."

As she accompanied him round the side of the house, taking his arm in hers, she sensed the change from the modish young man about town of a fortnight ago to this uncertain timorous youth now by her side. "You'll need to cheer up a bit, Matt," she remarked kindly.

"I don't feel like going now it's come to the bit," he ventured casually.

"You should be glad to get out of here," she replied. "I know I would gladly go. This house seems like a trap to me. I feel I'll never get away from it, as if I might wish to but could not." She paused a moment, then added, "But then you're leaving Agnes behind! That's bound to make all the difference. That's what's making you sad and upsetting you."

"Of course," agreed Matthew. The idea had not occurred to him before in this particular light, but as he turned it over in his mind it was distinctly comforting, and, to his vacillating self-esteem, profoundly reassuring.

"What does father think of Agnes and you?" Mary asked suddenly.

He gazed at her with astonished eyes before he replied, indignantly:

"What do you mean, Mary? Miss Moir is a most estimable girl. No one could think a word against her. She's a remarkably fine girl! What made you ask that?"

"Oh! nothing in particular, Matt," she replied vaguely, refusing to liberate the absurd conception which had arisen in her mind. Agnes Moir, worthy and admirable in every other way, was simply the daughter of a small and completely undistinguished confectioner in the town, and as Brodie himself, in theory at least, kept a shop, he could not repudiate Agnes on that score. But it was he who had obtained this position for Matthew, had insisted upon his going; and Matthew would be absent five years in India. She remembered like a flash the grim, sardonic humour in her father's eyes when he had first announced to his shrinking wife and his startled son, his intention of sending the latter abroad, and for the first time a faint glimmering dawned upon her of her father's mentality. She had always feared and respected him, but now, at the sudden turn of her thoughts, she began almost to hate him.

"I'm off, then, Mary," Matthew was saying. "Ta-ta just now."

Her lips opened to speak, but even as her mind grappled dimly with her suspicions, her eyes fell upon his weak, daunted countenance, striving ineffectually against discouragement, and she let him go without a word.

When he left Mary, Matthew tramped along more confidently, warming his enervated self-assurance at the glow she had unconsciously kindled within him. To be sure he was afraid of leaving Agnes! He felt that at last he had the reason fo his dejection, that stronger men than he would have wavered for a slighter cause, that his despondency did him credit as a noble-hearted lover. He began to teel more like Livingstone again and less like the raw recruit, whistled aloud a few bars of "Juanita," recollected his mandolin, thought, rather inconsistently, of the ladies on the *Irrawaddy*, or possibly in Calcutta, and felt altogether better. He had regained a faint shadow of his normal dash by the time he reached the Moir domicile and he positively leaped up the stairs to the door, for, as, unhappily, the Moirs were compelled to live above their shop, there were many stairs, and, worse, an entry by a close. He had, indeed, so far recovered that he used the knocker with considerable decision, and his manner had the appearance of repudiating the slightly inferior aspect of his surroundings as unworthy of a man whose name might one day shine in the annals of the Empire. He gazed, too, with a superior air, at the small girl who helped in the shop and who, now lightly disguised as a maid, admitted him and ushered him into the parlour where Agnes, released from the bondage of the counter—although business hours were not yet over—sat awaiting her Matt; to-morrow she could not be spared from her post of duty, and would be unable to accompany him to Glasgow, but to-night she had him for her own.

The parlour was cold, damp, unused, and formal, with large mahogany furniture whose intricate design lost itself in a voluptuous mystery of curves, with antimacassars veiling the sheen of horsehair, and waxcloth on the floor that glittered like a wet street. From the walls Highland cattle, ominous in oils, looked down dispiritedly upon the piano, that hall-mark of gentility, which bore upon its narrow, crowded surface three stuffed birds of an unknown species, perched mutely under a glass case amidst a forest of photographs. Agnes as an infant, as a baby, as a child, as a girl, as a young woman, Agnes in a group at the bakers' and confectioners' annual trip, at the Band of Hope social, at the church workers' outing—all were there!

Here, too, was Agnes in the flesh: literally, for although short in stature she was already inclined, like the furnishings of the room, to a redundancy of curves, which swelled particularly around her hips and bosom, that were full, with the promise of greater amplitude to come. She was dark, with sloe eyes under sable eyebrows, with olive cheeks and red almost thick lips, and upon her upper lip was a smooth umber shadow that lay softly, but with a dark, threatening menace of the future.

She kissed him with great warmth. She was five years older than Matthew, and she treasured him accordingly, and now, taking his hand, she led him forward and sat down with him upon the unsympathetic sofa which, like the parlour, was sanctified to their courtship.

"And this is the very last night," she mourned.

"Oh! don't say that, Agnes," he replied. "We can always think of each other! We'll be with each other in spirit."

Ardent church worker though she was, Agnes, from her appearance, had potentialities for a closer communion than this. She was, of course, unaware of it and would have repudiated it hotly, but her sigh was heavy as she said: "I wish you were nearer than India!" and came closer to him now.

"The time will fly, Agnes. In no time I'll be back with plenty of rupees." He was proud of his knowledge of the foreign currency and added: "A rupee is about one shilling and fourpence."

"Never mind the rupees just now, Matt; tell me you love me."

"I do love you, that's why I'm so upset at going away. I haven't been myself at all these last few days—quite off colour!" He felt truly noble to have laid the burden of his suffering at her feet.

"You won't even speak to any of these foreign ladies, will you, Matt? I wouldn't trust them as far as I could see them—a pretty face may cover a wicked heart. You'll remember that, won't you, dear?"

"Certainly, Agnes."

"You see, dear, there must be great temptations for a handsome young man out in these hot countries. Women will go to such lengths to get hold of a man once they get their eye on him, especially if he's a good young man—that excites them all the more, and your little Agnes won't be there to watch over you, Matt. I want you to promise to be careful for my sake."

It was delightful for him to feel that he was so ardently desired, that already she was jealous of him to desperation, and, with one eye fixed already upon his future conquests abroad, he murmured solemnly: "Yes, Agnes, I see the truth of what you say. The way may be hard for me, but I'll let no one spoil me for you. It'll not be my fault if anything comes between us."

"Oh! Matt, dear," she whispered, "don't even speak of that. I'll hardly be able to sleep for thinking of all the hussies that might be after you. Of course I am not unreasonable, dear. I would like you to meet good, earnest women, perhaps lady missionaries or workers in the Christian field out there. A few motherly women out there would be nice for you to know. They would take good care of you, perhaps darn your socks for you. If you were to let me know I could write to them."

"Of course, Agnes," he replied, unattracted by her suggestion and with a strong conviction that such elderly ladies as she had just described would not constitute the society of his election. "Of course, I can't say I'll meet anyone like that. I'll have to see how things are first."

"You'll fall on your feet all right, Matt," she assured him fondly. "You couldn't help it the way you get round people. Then your music will be a great help to you socially. Have you got all your songs packed?" He nodded his head complacently, saying: "And the mandolin. I put a new pink ribbon on it yesterday!"

Her sable brows contracted at the thought of those who might receive the benefit of this decoration, knotted on such a romantic instrument, but she did not wish to press him too far so, with an effort, she controlled her apprehensions and, forcing a smile, deflected the conversation into a nobler channel.

"The church choir will miss you, too, Matt. The choir practice won't be the same place without you." He protested modestly, but she would not permit his humility. "No!" she cried, "don't deny it, dear. Your voice will be missed in that church. Do you remember that night after the practice when you first walked home with me, dear? I'll never forget the way you spoke to me. Don't you remember what you said?"

"I can't think the now, Aggie," he answered inattentively. "Did you not speak to me first?"

"Oh! Matt," she gasped, widening her eyes at him reproachfully, "how can you? You know you smiled at me over your hymn book all that night, and you did speak first. I only asked if you were going my way." He nodded his head apologetically, as he replied: "I remember now, Agnes! We ate all that big bag of liquorice all sorts you had with you. They were real nice, too."

"I'm going to send you out a big tin box of sweets every month," she promised eagerly. "I wasn't going to mention it, but as you speak of it I might as well tell you, dear. I know you're fond of a good sweet and you'll never get good confectionery out in those parts. They'll carry perfectly well if I send them in a tin." He thanked her with a satisfied smile, but, before he could speak, she hurried on, striking on the heat of his gratitude.

"There's nothing your Agnes will not do for you, Matt, if you just

61

don't forget her," she continued fervently. "You've never to forget me for a minute. You've got all my photographs with you! Put one in your cabin straight away, won't you, dear?" She laid her head more heavily on his shoulder and gazed up at him entrancingly. "Kiss me, Matt! That was nice. It's so delightful to feel that we are engaged. It's almost as binding as matrimony. No good girl could feel like I do without being affianced to her young man."

The couch being apparently without springs, Matt began to feel uncomfortable under the considerable weight he was supporting. His calf-love for Miss Moir, developed under the insidious flattery of her attentions, was not strong enough to stand the strain of this powerful amatory embrace.

"Would you permit me to smoke?" he suggested tactfully. Agnes looked up, her liquid eyes swimming beneath the inky tangle of her hair.

"On the last night?" she asked reproachfully.

"I thought it might pull me together," he murmured. "The last few days have been very heavy for me—all that packing has been such a strain on a man."

She sighed and raised herself reluctantly, saying:

"All right then, dear! I can refuse you nothing. Have just a few puffs if you feel it will so you good. But you're not to over-smoke yourself in India, Matt. Remember your chest is not strong." Then, graciously, she added: "Let me light this one for you as it's the last time." She timidly ignited the slightly bent weed he withdrew from his waist-coat pocket and watched him fearfully as he blew out thick clouds in manful taciturnity. Now she could only love and admire him from a distance, but at arm's length she still fondled his watch chain.

"You'll miss your little Aggie, won't you, Matt?" she asked soulfully, but coughing slightly as she inhaled the noxious odour from his cigar.

"Most dreadfully," he replied solemnly. This was what he really enjoyed, himself smoking heroically, she at his feet in fond womanly admiration. "It will be—unbearable." He would have liked to say, dashingly: "Hell," but out of respect he used the less manly expression, and he shook his head as if he doubted his ability to stand the strain of it all.

"We must suffer for each other's sake," said Agnes, with a sigh. "I feel it will make you do great and good work out there, Matt. You'll write and tell me all your doings."

"I'll write to you and Mamma every mail," promised Matthew.

"I'll be in close touch with Mamma, of course," responded Agnes, as if she were already a daughter of the house.

He felt that the prayers of two loyal adoring women would ascend in unison for him as he faced his stern task abroad, but the cigar, despite his efforts to prolong it, was burning his lips, and at length he regretfully discarded it. Immediately Agnes nestled her head upon his chest: "Kiss me again, dear!" she said. Then after a pause she whispered, suggesting alluringly, "You'll come back to me a big, strong, fierce man, won't you, Matt? I like to be crushed hard in your arms, as hard as ever you like." As he placed a limp arm around her shoulders he felt somehow that too much was being demanded of a man who had to face the perils of an arduous and unknown journey in the morning.

"I'm really ashamed to show my feelings like this," she continued bashfully, "but there's no harm in it, Matt, is there? We'll be married whenever you come back. Indeed it breaks my heart to think we couldn't have got married before ye left. I would willingly have gone out with you!"

"But, Agnes," he protested, "it's not the country for a white woman, at all."

"There's plenty go out there, Matt, plenty! Officers' wives, and what not! I'll go back with you if you've got to go out again when your time's up," she said firmly. "It's just the fact that you've got to make your way that has hindered us, dear."

He was silent, startled at the decision in her words, never having viewed himself as being so near the altar, nor having quite suspected the extent of her ascendancy over him, thinking too, that the embrace, was being protracted indefinitely. At length he said:

"I'm afraid I must be going now, Aggie."

"But it's so early yet, Matt," she asserted petulantly. "You never leave before ten o'clock as a rule."

"I know, Agnes, but I've got a big day ahead of me to-morrow," he replied importantly. "Got to get on the packet by noon."

"This separation is going to kill me," said Agnes dramatically, unwillingly releasing him.

As he stood up, straightening his tie, shaking down his trousers, and inspecting the damage to his creases, he felt that it was worth while, that it was good to know that women would die for him.

"Good-bye, then, Agnes," he exclaimed gallantly, straddling his legs and throwing out both hands towards her. "We shall meet again." She flung herself again into his proffered arms and buried her head against him, whilst the force of her sobs rocked them both.

"I feel I should never let you go," she cried, brokenly, as he separated from her, "I should never give you up like this. You're going too far away. I'll pray for you, though, Matt! May God take care of you for me," she wept as she saw him down the stairs.

Out again in the street he felt consoled, uplifted, strengthened by her grief, as though the devastation he had wrought within her virgin heart ennobled him, added inches to his stature. But as he retired early to bed in preparation for the fatigues of the next day he reflected in his

more mature and worldly vein that perhaps Miss Moir had been lately
a little pressing in her attentions upon him, and as he fell asleep he
realised that a man might as well think twice before tying himself up
in a hurry, especially if that man were such a knowing blade as Matthew
Brodie.

Next morning, although he awoke early, it was nine o'clock before
Mamma let him get up.

"Don't rush! we'll take it easy. Conserve your strength, my boy,"
she said, as she brought him his morning tea. "We've plenty of time,
and you've a long journey ahead of you."

She apparently visualised him journeying to Calcutta without repose,
and in consequence of his deterred rising he was only half-dressed when
his father called to him from the foot of the stairs. Brodie would not
depart an inch from his habit; he would, indeed, have considered it a
weakness to wait to see his son away, and at half-past nine he was off
to business in the usual fashion. As Matthew came scuttering down the
stairs in his braces, a towel in his hand, his wet hair over his pallid
brow, and came up to his father in the hall, Brodie fixed a magnetic
eye upon his son and held for a moment the other's wavering glance.
"Well, Matthew Brodie," he said, looking down at his son, "you're
off to-day, and that means good-bye to your home for five years. I hope
to God you are goin' to prove yourself in these years. You're a sleekit,
namby-pamby fellow and your mother has a' but spoiled ye, but there
must be good in ye. There must be good," he cried, "because you're
my son! I want that brought out in ye. Look a man between the eyes
and don't hang your head like a dog. I'm sending you out there to make
a man of ye. Don't forget that you're the son, ay, and the heir of James
Brodie.

"I've got you everything you want," he continued. "A position of
trust and of great possibilities. I've given you the best outfit money can
buy and best of all I've given you a name. Be a man, sir, but above all
be a Brodie. Behave like a Brodie wherever you are, or God help you."
He shook hands firmly, turned, and was gone.

Matthew finished dressing in a maze, aided by Mamma—who
continually darted in and out of his room—ate his breakfast without
tasting it, and was startled by the cab at the door before he could
collect himself. Other farewells were showered upon him. Old Grandma
Brodie, cross at being disturbed so early, called out from the head of
the stairs as she clutched her long nightgown above her bare, bony feet:
"Good-bye to ye, then, and watch you don't get drouned on the way
over." Nessie, in tears long before the time, from the very solemnity of
the occasion, could only sob incoherently: "I'll write to you, Matt!
I hope the compass will be useful to you." Mary was deeply affected.
She clasped her arms round Matthew's neck and kissed him fondly.
"Keep a stiff upper lip, Matt dear. Be brave, and nothing can hurt

you, and don't forget your own loving sister."

He was in the cab with Mamma, sitting in hunched apathy, being bumped unmercifully, on the way to the station, while Mrs. Brodie looked proudly out of the window. In her mind's eye she saw people nudging each other as they watched the sweep of her spanking equipage, and saying: "That's Mrs. Brodie seein' her laddie off to Calcutta. She's been a good mother to that boy, ay and a fine fellow he is, too, an' all, an' all." Indeed it was not every day that a mother in Levenford took her son to the boat for India, she reflected complacently, drawing her paletot more becomingly around her, and sitting up grandly in the decrepit vehicle as though it were her private carriage.

At the station she paid the cabman with a conscious air, glancing sideways from under her hat at the few chance loungers under the archway, and to the man who carried the luggage she could not forbear to remark, casually: "This young gentleman is for India." The porter, staggering under the heavy case and stupefied by the reek of camphor which emanated from it, twisted his red neck round the angle of the box and gaped at her obtusely, too overcome to speak.

Although they were now on the platform the train of destiny was late, for the schedule of the Darroch and Levenford joint railway, never the object of public approbation, did not to-day belie its reputation and was apparently not working to any degree of accuracy. Mamma tapped her foot restlessly, pursed her lips impatiently, looked repeatedly at the silver watch that hung around her neck by its chain of plaited hair; Matthew, filled with a despairing hope that there might have been a breakdown on the line, looked vaguely, disconsolately, at the porter who, in turn, gazed with open mouth at Mrs. Brodie. He had never seen her before and, as his oafish look engulfed her brisk, nonchalant demeanour, so outwith the compass of his local experience, he took her for a prodigy—a traveller at least of European experience.

At last a clanking noise was heard in the distance, sounding the knell of Matt's last hope. The train smoked its way into the station, and in a few minutes puffed out again with Mrs. Brodie and Matthew inside, facing each other on the hard wooden seats, and leaving the porter looking incredulously at the penny piece which the lady had magnificently pressed into his palm. He scratched his head, spat disgustedly, dismissed the whole episode as a mystery beyond the powers of his comprehension.

In the train Mrs. Brodie utilised every lull in the din, when her voice might be audible, to utter some lively remark to Matthew, and between these parentheses she contemplated him vivaciously. Matthew squirmed in his seat; he knew he was the object of a cheering-up process and he loathed it. It's all right for her, he thought moodily, she hasn't got to go.

At length they reached Glasgow, after a journey that was, for Matthew, mournfully short. They made their way out of the station down Jamaica

Street and along the Broomielaw to where the S.S. *Irrawaddy* was lying at Stobcross dock with steam up, and two tugs in attendance. She seemed to them an enormous ship with paddles wide as the spread of a bat's wings, and a funnel which dwarfed the masts of all the other shipping, and Mamma remarked, admiringly: "My word! that's a great big boat, Matt! I'll not be so feared for ye when I think on ye aboard o' that. That lum is as high as the Town steeple. Look at a' these folks on deck too. I suppose we maun go on board." Together they advanced up the gangway and gained the deck, where the flurry of embarkation had begun and an exaggerated bustle and confusion prevailed. Sailors leaped about the deck performing miracles with ropes; officers in gold braid shouted importantly and blew whistles loudly; stewards pursued passengers and passengers ran after stewards; Anglo-Indians returning to the country of their selection glared passionately at all who got in their way; relatives on the verge of bereavement stubbed their toes over iron stanchions and piles of luggage.

In the face of this hustling activity Mrs. Brodie's spirit quailed. The superior look of the purser as he directed them below intimidated her, and though she had intended at least to approach the captain of the vessel and turn over Matthew, in the appropriate manner, to his especial care, now she wilted; as she sat in the stuffy confines of the den which was to serve Matt as cabin for the next eight weeks, and felt the gentle lift and fall of the boat against the fenders of the quay, she realised that the sooner she went ashore the better.

Now that the actual farewell was at hand the spurious exaltation derived from her romantic imagination collapsed, as her husband had sardonically foreseen, like a pricked bladder. She was herself again, the weak woman who had given birth to this child, suckled him at her breast, seen him grow to manhood, and now was about to see him leave her. A tear crept slowly down her cheek.

"Oh! Matt," she cried, "I've tried to bear up well for ye, son—for your own dear sake, but I'm sorry to lose you. I doubt if you're the man for these foreign parts. I would rather you stayed at home."

"I don't want to go either, Mamma," he implored ea gerly, as though at the last moment she might stretch out her hand and plluck him from his awful predicament.

"You'll need to go now, my son. It's gane too far to be altered now," she replied sadly, shaking her head. "Your father has it wished all along. And what he says must be done. There's just no other way about it. But you'll do your best to be a good boy, won't you, Matt?"

"Yes, Mamma."

"You'll send home something of your pay for me to put in the Building Society for you?"

"Yes, Mamma."

"You'll read a chapter of your Bible every day?"

"Yes, I will, Mamma."

"And don't forget me, Matt."

Matthew burst into broken, uncouth sobs.

"I don't want to go," he blubbered, catching at her dress. "You're all sending me away and I'll never come back. It's my death I'm goin' out to. Don't let me go, Mamma."

"Ye maun go, Matt," she whispered. "He would kill us if we came back thegither."

"I'll be sick on the boat," he whined. "I feel it comin' on already. I'll get the fever out there. You know I'm not strong. I tell ye, Mamma, it'll finish me."

"Wheesht, son!" she murmured, "ye maun calm yoursel'. I'll pray to the Lord to protect ye."

"Oh! well, Mamma, if I'm to go, leave me now," he wailed. "I can't stand any more. Don't sit there and mock me. Leave me and be finished with it!" His mother stood up and drew him into her arms; at last she was a woman. "Good-bye, son, and God bless you," she said quietly. As she left the cabin with streaming eyes and shaking head, he flung himself impotently upon his bunk.

Mrs. Brodie stepped off the gangway and set out for Queen Street station. As she retraced her steps through the docks her feet dragged along the very pavements over which she had advanced so airily; gradually her body drooped forward, her dress trailed behind heedlessly; her head inclined itself pathetically; a mantle of resignation descended upon her; she had emerged completely from her dreams, and was again the hapless and handless wife of James Brodie.

In the train homewards she felt tired, exhausted by the rapid flight of emotions that had traversed her being. A drowsiness crept over her and she slept. In the shadows of her sleeping brain spectres sprang from their lurking places and tormented her. Someone was thrusting her downwards, crushing her with stones; square grey stones were all around, compressing her. Upon the earth beside her lay her children, their cadaverous limbs relaxed in the inanition of extreme debility, and, as the walls slowly drew in nearer upon them, she awoke with a loud shriek which mingled the blast of the engine's whistle. The train was entering the outskirts of Levenford. She was home.

V

On the following morning about ten o'clock, Mrs. Brodie and Mary were together in the kitchen, according to their custom of consulting together to discuss the household plans for the day when the master of the house had departed after breakfast. This morning, however, they sat without reviewing the possibilities of their cleaning or mending, without debating whether it should be stew or mince for the day's dinner, or considering whether father's grey suit required pressing, and instead remained silent, somewhat subdued, with Mrs. Brodie mournfully sipping a cup of strong tea and Mary gazing quietly out of the window.

"I feel good for nothing, to-day," said Mamma at length.

"No wonder, Mamma, after yesterday," Mary sighed. "I wonder how he's getting on? Not homesick already, I hope."

Mrs. Brodie shook her head. "The seasickness will be the worst, I'm gey afeared, for Matt was never a sailor, poor boy! I remember only too well when he was just twelve, on the steamer to Port Doran, he was very ill—and it wasna that rough either. He would eat greengages after his dinner, and I didna like to stop him and spoil the day's pleasure for the wee man, but he brought them up and the good dinner too, that had cost his father a salt half crown. Oh! but your father was angry with him, and with me too, as if it was my fault that the boat turned the boy's stomach."

She paused reminiscently, and added: "I'm glad *I* never gave Matt a hard word, anyway, now that he's away far, far. No! I never gave him a word in anger, let alone lifted my hand to him in punishment."

"You always liked Matt best," Mary agreed, mildly. "I'm afraid you'll miss him sorely, Mamma!"

"Miss him?" Mrs. Brodie replied. "I should just think I would. I feel as weak as if—as if something inside of me had gane away on that boat and would never come back. But he'll miss me too, I hope." Her eye glistened, as she continued: "Ay, grown man though he is, he broke down in his cabin like a bairn when he had to say good-bye to his mother. It's a comfort to me, that, Mary, and will be, until I get the consolation of his own dear letters. My! but I'm lookin' forward to these. The only letter he's ever written me was when he was nine years old and was away for a holiday at Cousin Jim's farm, after he had been poorly with his chest. It was that interestin' too—all about the horse he had sat on, and the wee trout he had caught in the river. I've got it in my drawer to this very day. I maun redd it out for mysel'. Ay!" she concluded, with a melancholy pleasure, "I'll go through all my drawers and sort out a' the things of Matt's, that I've got. It'll be a wee crumb o' comfort till I hear from him."

"Will we do out his room to-day, then, Mamma?" asked Mary.

"No, Mary—that's not to be touched. It's Matt's room, and we'll keep it as it is until he wants it again—if ever he does." She drank a mouthful of tea appreciatively. "It was good of you to make me this, Mary, it's drawing me together. He ought to get good tea in India, anyway, that's the place for tea and spices. Cold tea should be refreshin'

68

to him in the heat," she added. Then, after a pause, "Why didn't you take a cup yourself?"

"I feel upset a bit myself this morning, Mamma."

"You've been looking real poorly these last few days. You're as pale as paper, too."

Mary was the least beloved by Mrs. Brodie of all her children, but in the deprivation of the favourite, Matthew, she drew closer to her.

"We'll not do a bit of cleaning in the house to-day, either of us; we both deserve a rest after all the rush we've had lately," she continued. "I might try and ease my mind in a book for a wee, and you'll go out this morning for your messages to get a breath of air. It'll do ye good to get a walk while it's dry and sunny. What do we need now?"

They conned the deficiencies of the larder, whilst Mary wrote them down on a slip of paper against that treacherous memory of hers. Purchases at various shops were involved, for the housekeeping allowance was not lavish, and it was necessary to buy every article in the cheapest possible market.

"We maun stop our order o' the wee Abernethies at the baker's, now that Matt's away. Your father never looks at them. Tell them we'll not be requirin' any more," said Mamma. "My! but it's an awfu' emptiness in the house to think on the boy bein' away; it was such a pleasure for me to give him a nice, tasty dish."

"We'll not need so much butter either, Mamma! He was fond of that too," suggested Mary, with her pencil reflectively tapping her white front teeth.

"We don't need that anyway this morning," retorted Mamma, a trifle coldly, "but I want you to get this week's *Good Thoughts* when you're out. It's the very thing for Matt, and I'm going to send it to him every week. It'll cheer him up to get it regularly, and do his mind a world o' good."

When they had examined and weighed up all the requirements of the household, and carefully estimated the total cost, Mary took the money counted out from her mother's thin purse, slipped on her bonnet, picked up her fine net reticule, and set out upon her errands. She was happy to be in the open, feeling, when she was out of doors, freer in her body and in her mind, less confined, less circumscribed by the rooted conformity of her environment. Additionally, each visit to the town now held for her a high and pulsating adventure, and at every turn and corner she drew a deep, expectant breath, could scarcely raise her eyes for the hope and fear that she might see Denis. Although she had not had another letter, mercifully, perhaps, for she would then surely have been detected, an inward impression told her that he was now home from his business circuit; if he in reality loved her he must surely come to Levenford to seek her. An instinctive longing quickened her steps and made her heart quicken in sympathy. She passed the

Common with a sense of embarrassment, observing, with one quick, diffident glance, that nothing remained of the merry-making of last week but the beaten track of the passage of many feet, blanched squares and circles where the booths and tents had stood, and heaps of debris and smoking ashes upon the worn, burned-out grass; but the littered desolation of the scene gave her no pang, the departure of its flashing cohorts no regret, for in her heart a memory remained which was not blanched, or trampled, or burned out, but which flamed each day more brightly than before.

Her desire to see Denis intensified, filled her slender figure with a rare æther, setting a mist upon her eyes and a freshness upon her cheeks like the new bloom upon a wild rose; her aspiration rose into her throat, and stifled her with a feeling like bitter grief.

Once in the town she lingered over her shopping, delaying a little by the windows, hopeful that a light touch upon her arm might suddenly arouse her, taking the longest possible routes and traversing as many streets as she dared, in the hope of encountering Denis. But still she did not see him, and now, instead of veiling her glance, she began to gaze anxiously about her, as though she entreated him to come to her to end the unhappiness of her suspense. Slowly the list of her commissions dwindled and, by the time she had made her last purchase, a small furrow of anxiety perplexed her smooth brow, while her mouth drooped plaintively at its corners as the latent antithesis of her longing now took possession of her. Denis did not love her, and for that reason he would not come to her! She had been mad to consider that he could continue to care for her, a creature so little befitted to his charm and graceful beauty; and, with the bitter certainty of despair, she became aware that he would never see her again, and she would be left like a wounded bird, fluttering feebly and alone.

Now it was impossible to procrastinate her return, for, with a sudden pathetic dignity, she felt she could not be seen loitering about the streets, as though she lowered herself commonly to look for a man who had disdained her; and she turned quickly, with the reticule of parcels dragging upon her arm like a heavy weight as she moved off towards home. She now chose the quiet streets, to hide herself as much as possible, feeling miserably that if Denis did not wish her, she would not thrust herself upon him; and in a paroxysm of sad renunciation, she kept her head lowered and occupied the most inconsiderable space possible upon the pavement which she traversed.

She had so utterly resigned herself to not seeing Denis that, when he suddenly appeared before her from the passage leading out of the new station, it was as if a phantom had issued from the unsubstantial air. She raised her downcast eyes as though, startled and unbelieving, they refused to allow the sudden transport of the vision to pass beyond into her being, to flood it with a joy which might be unreal, merely the delusive mirage of her hopes. But no phantom could hurry forward so eagerly, or smile so captivatingly, or take her hand so warmly, so closely, that she felt the pulse of the hot blood in the ardent, animate hand. It was Denis. Yet he had no right to be so gay and elated, so carefree and dashing, his rapture untouched by any memory of their separation. Did he not understand that she had been forced to wait through weary days of melancholy, had only a moment ago been plunged in sad despondency, even to the consideration of her abandonment?

"Mary, it's like heaven to see you again, and you've the look of one of the angels up above! I only got back home late last night and I came the first moment I could get away. How lucky to catch you like this!" he exclaimed, fervently fixing his eye upon hers.

Immediately she forgave him. Her despondency melted under the warmth of his flow of high spirits; her sadness perished in the gay infection of his smile; instead, a sudden, disturbing realisation of the sweetly intimate circumstances of their last meeting seized her, and a mood of profound shyness overtook her.

She blushed to see in the open day this young gallant who, cloaked by the benign darkness, had pressed her so closely in his arms who had been the first to kiss her, to touch caressingly her virgin body. Did he know all that she had thought of him since then? all the throbbing recollections of the past and the mad, dancing visions of the future that had obsessed her? She dared not look at him.

"I'm so delighted to see you again, Mary, I could jump for joy! Are you glad to see me again?" he continued.

"Yes," she said, in a low, embarrassed voice.

"I've so much to tell you that I couldn't put in my letter. I didn't want to say too much for fear it would be intercepted. Did you get it?"

"I got it safely, but you mustn't write again," she whispered. "I would be afraid for you to do that."

What he had said was so indiscreet that the thought of what he had left unsaid made a still higher colour mantle in her cheeks.

"I won't need to write for a long time, again," he laughed meaningly. "Sure, I'll be seeing you ever so often now. I'll be at the office for a month or two until my autumn trip; and speaking of business, Mary dear, you've brought me the luck of a charm—I've twice as many orders this time. If ye keep inspirin' me like that you'll make a fortune for me in no time Bedad! you'll have to meet me if only to share the profits!"

Mary looked around uneasily, feeling already in the quiet street a horde of betraying eyes upon her, sensing in his impetuosity how little he understood her position.

"Denis, I'm afraid I can't wait any longer. We might be seen here."

"Is it a crime to talk to a young man, then—in the morning anyway?" he replied softly, meaningly. "Sure there's no disgrace in that. And if ye'd rather walk I could tramp to John o' Groats with you! Let me carry your parcels for a bit of the way, ma'am."

Mary shook her head. "People would notice us more than ever," she replied timidly, already conscious of the eyes of the town upon her, during that reckless promenade.

He looked at her tenderly, protectingly, then allowed his resourceful glance to travel up and down the street with what, to her devoted eyes, seemed like the intrepid gaze of an adventurer in a hostile land.

"Mary, my dear," he said presently, in a jocular tone, "you don't know the man you're with yet. 'Foyle never knows defeat,' that's my motto. Come along in here!" He took her arm firmly and led her a few doors down the street, then, before she realised it and could think even to resist, he had drawn her inside the cream-coloured doors of Bertorelli's café. She paled with apprehension, feeling that she had finally passed the limits of respectability, that the depth of her dissipation had now been reached, and looking reproachfully into Denis' smiling face, in a shocked tone she gasped:

"Oh, Denis, how could you?"

Yet, as she looked round the clean, empty shop, with its rows of marble-topped tables, its small scintillating mirrors, and brightly papered walls, while she allowed herself to be guided to one of the plush stalls that appeared exactly like her pew in church, she felt curiously surprised, as if she had expected to find a sordid den suited appropriately to the debauched revels that must, if tradition were to be believed, inevitably be connected with a place like this.

Her bewilderment was increased by the appearance of a fat, fatherly man with a succession of chins, each more amiable than the preceding honest one, who came up to them, smilingly, bowed with a quick bend of the region which had once been his waist, and said:

"Good-day, Meester Doyle. Glad to see you back."

"Morning, Louis!"

This, then, was the monster himself.

"Had a nice treep, Meester Doyle? Plenty business, I hope."

"Plenty! you old lump of blubber! Don't you know by this time I can sell anything. I could sell a ton of macaroni in the streets of Aberdeen."

Bertorelli laughed and extended his hands expressively, while his chuckle wreathed more chins around his full, beaming face.

"That woulda be easy, Meester Doyle. Macaroni is good, just the same as porreedge; makes a man beeg like me."

"That's right, Louis! You're a living example against the use of macaroni. Never mind your figure, though. How's all the family?"

"Oh! just asplendeed! The bambino weel soon be as beeg as me. Already he has two chins."

As he rolled with laughter, Mary again gazed aghast at the tragic spectacle of a villain, who concealed his rascality under the guise of a

72

fictitious mirth and a false assumption of humanity. But her conflicting thoughts were interrupted by Denis, as he tactfully enquired:

"What would you like, Mary—a macallum?"

She had sufficient hardihood to nod her head; for although she would not have known a macallum from a macaroon, to have confessed her ignorance before this archangel of iniquity was beyond her.

"Very good, very nice," agreed Bertorelli, as he ambled away.

"Nice chap, that," said Denis, "straight as a die; and as kind as you make them!"

"But," quavered Mary, "they say such things about him."

"Bah! He eats babies, I suppose! Pure, unlovely bigotry, Mary dear. We'll have to progress beyond that some day, if we're not to stick in the dark ages. Although he's Italian he's a human being. Comes from a place near Pisa, where the famous tower is, the one that leans but never falls. We'll go and see it some day—we'll do Paris and Rome too," he added casually.

Mary looked reverently at this young man who called foreigners by their Christian names and who toyed with the capitals of Europe, not boastingly like poor Matt, but with a cool, calm confidence, and she reflected how pulsating life might be with a man like this, so loving, and yet so strong, so gentle, and yet so undaunted. She felt she was on the way to worshipping him.

Now she was eating her macallum, a delicious concoction of ice-cream and raspberry juice, which, cunningly blending the subtly acid essence of the fruit with the cold mellow sweetness of the ice-cream, melted upon her tongue in an exquisite and unexpected delight. Under the table Denis pressed her foot gently with his, whilst his eyes followed her naïve enjoyment with a lively satisfaction.

Why, she asked herself, did she enjoy herself always so exquisitely with him? Why did he seem, in his kindness, generosity, and tolerance, so different from anyone she had known? Why should the upward curl of his mouth and the lights in his hair, the poise of his head, make her heart turn with happiness in her breast?

"Are you enjoying this?" he asked.

"It really is nice here," she conceded, with a submissive murmur.

"It's all right," he agreed. "I wouldn't have taken you, otherwise. But anywhere is nice so long as we are together. That's the secret, Mary!"

Her eyes sparkled back at him, her being drew in the exudation of his courageous vitality, and, for the first time since their meeting, she laughed spontaneously, happily, outright.

"That's better," encouraged Denis. "I was beginning to worry about you." He leant impulsively across the table, and took her thin, small fingers in his.

"You know, Mary dear, I want you so much to be happy. When I first saw you I loved you for your loveliness—but it was a sad loveliness.

You looked to me as if you were afraid to smile, as if someone had crushed all the laughter out of you. Ever since our wonderful time together, dear, I've been thinking of you. I love you and I hope that you love me, for I feel we are just made for each other. I couldn't live without you now, and I want to be with you, to watch you unfold out of your sadness and see you laugh at any silly, stupid joke I make to you. Let me pay my court to you openly."

She was silent, moved immeasurably by his words, then at last she spoke:

"How I wish we could be together," she said sadly. "I—I've missed you so much, Denis. But you don't know my father. He is terrible. There is something about him you don't understand. I'm afraid of him and he—he had forbidden me to speak to you."

Denis' eyes narrowed.

"Am I not good enough for him?"

Mary gripped her fingers, tightly, involuntarily, as though he had wounded her.

"Oh! don't say that, dear Denis. You're wonderful and I love you, I'd die for you; but my father is the most domineering man you could ever imagine, oh!—and the proudest man too."

"Why is he like that?—He has nothing against me? I've nothing to be ashamed of, Mary. Why do you say he is proud?"

Mary did not reply for a moment. Then she said slowly: "I don't know! When I was little I never thought about it, my father was like a god to me, so big, so strong, every word that he uttered was like a command. As I grew older I seemed to feel there was some mystery, something which makes him different from ordinary people, which makes him try to mould us into his own fashion, and now I almost fear that he thinks——" She paused and looked up at Denis nervously.

"What?" he urged.

"I'm not sure, oh! I can hardly say it." She blushed uncomfortably as she haltingly continued: "He seems to think we are related in some way to the Winton family."

"To the Wintons," he exclaimed incredulously. "To the Earl himself! How on earth does he make that out?"

She shook her head sadly, miserably. "I don't know. He never lets himself speak of it, but I know it's in the back of his mind all the time. The Winton family name is Brodie, you see—oh! but it's all so ridiculous."

"Ridiculous!" he echoed. "It does seem ridiculous! What does he expect to get out of it?"

"Nothing," she exclaimed bitterly. "Only the satisfaction to his pride. He makes life miserable for us at times. He compels us, makes us live differently from other people. We're apart in that house of ours that he built himself, and like him it oppresses us all." Carried away by the expression of her fears, she cried out finally: "Oh! Denis, I know it's not right for me to talk like this about my own father, but I'm afraid of him. He would never—never allow our engagement."

Denis set his teeth. "I'll go and see him myself. I'll convince him in spite of himself, and I'll make him let me see you. I'm not afraid of him. I'm not afraid of any man living."

She jumped up in a panic. "No! No, Denis! Don't do that. He would punish us both dreadfully." The vision of her father, with his fearful, brute strength, mauling the beauty of this young gladiator, terrified her. "Promise me you won't," she cried.

"But we must see each other, Mary. I can't give you up."

"We could meet sometimes," said Mary.

"That leads nowhere, dear; we must have some definite understanding. You know I want to marry you." He looked at her closely; he knew her ignorance to be such, he was afraid to say any more. Instead, he took up her hand, kissed the palm softly, and laid his cheek against it.

"Will you meet me soon?" he asked inconsequently. "I would like to be in the moonlight with you again to see it shining in your eyes, to see the moonbeams dancing in your hair." He lifted his head and looked lovingly at her hand, which he still held in his. "Your hands are like snow-drops, Mary, so soft and white and drooping. They are cool like snow itself against my hot face. I love them, and I love you."

A passionate longing seized him to have her always with him. If necessary he would fight; he would be stronger than the circumstances that separated them, stronger than fate itself; in a different voice he said firmly:

"Surely you will marry me even if we've got to wait, won't you, Mary?"

While he sat silent, against the garish background of the empty shop, his hand lightly touching hers, awaiting her answer, she saw in his eyes the leaping of his kindred soul towards her, in his question only the request that she be happy with him always, and, forgetting instantly the difficulty, danger, and total impossibility of the achievement, knowing nothing of marriage but only loving him, losing her fear in his strength and sinking herself utterly in him, her eyes looked deeply into his, as she answered:

"Yes."

He did not move, did not cast himself upon his knee in a passion of protesting gratitude, but in his stillness a current of unutterable love and fervour flowed from his body into hers through the medium of their touching hands and into his eyes there welled up such a look of tenderness and devotion that, meeting hers, it fused about them like an arch of radiance.

"You'll not regret it, dear," he whispered, as he leaned across the table and softly kissed her lips. "I'll do my utmost to make you happy,

Mary! I've been selfish, but now you will always come first. I'll work hard for you. I'm making my way fast and I'm going to make it faster. I've got something in the bank now, and in a short time, if you'll wait, Mary, we'll just walk off and get married."

The dazzling simplicity of the solution blinded her, as, thinking how easy it would be for them to run away suddenly, secretly, without her father knowing, to loose themselves utterly from him, she clasped her hands together and whispered:

"Oh! Denis, could we? I never thought of that!"

"We can and we will, dear Mary. I'll work hard so that we can manage soon. Remember my motto! we'll make that our family crest. Never mind the Wintons! Now, not another word or another worry for that little head of yours. Leave everything to me, and remember only that I'm thinking of you and striving for you all the time. We may have to be careful how we meet, but surely I can see you occasionally— even if it's only to admire the elegant little figure of you from a distance."

"I'll have to see you sometimes; it would be too hard to do without that," she murmured, and added ingenuously: "Every Tuesday I go to the Library to change Mamma's book, and sometimes my own."

"Didn't I find that out for myself, you spalpeen!" smiled Denis. "Sure enough I'll know all about your mother's taste in literature before I'm finished. And don't I know the Library! I'll be there, you may be sure. But can you not give me a photo of your own dear self to keep me going, in between times?"

She hung her head a little, conscious of her own deficiencies and the oddity of her up-bringing, as she replied: "I haven't got one. Father didn't approve of it."

"What! Your parents are behind the times, my girl. We'll have to waken them up. To think that you've never been taken is a shame; but never mind, I'll have your sweet face before the camera the moment we're married. How do you like this?" he enquired, as he produced a misty brown photograph of a jaunty young man standing with cheerful fortitude, mingled with an inappropriate air of hilarity, amongst what appeared to be an accumulation of miniature tombstones.

"Denis Foyle at the Giants' Causeway last year," he explained. "That old woman that sells shells there, you know the big curly ones that sing in your ear, told my fortune that day. She said I was going to be the lucky, lucky gossoon, and indeed she must have known I was going to meet you."

"Can I have this, Denis?" she asked shyly. "I think it's lovely."

"It's for you, and no other, provided you wear it next your heart."

"I must wear it where nobody sees it," she answered innocently.

"That'll suit me," he replied, and smiled teasingly at the sudden rush of colour and understanding which flooded her modest brow. But immediately he amended, honourably:

76

"Don't mind me, Mary. As the Irishman said, 'I'm always puttin' me foot in it with me clumsy tongue.' "

They both laughed, but as she dissolved in gaiety, feeling that she could have listened to his banter for ever, she saw the purpose behind it, and loved him for the attempt to hearten her against their separation. His courage made her valiant, his frank but audacious attitude towards life stimulated her as a clear cold wind might arouse a prisoner after a long incarceration in stagnant air. All this rushed upon her as she said involuntarily, simply:

"You make me glad and free, Denis. I can breathe when I'm with you. I did not know the meaning of love until I met you. I had never thought of it—did not understand—but now I know that, always, for me, love is to be with you, to breathe with the same breath as you——"

She broke off abruptly, covered with confusion at her boldness in speaking to him like this. A faint recollection of her previous existence, of her life apart from him, dawned upon her, and, as her eye fell upon the heap of parcels beside her, she remembered Mamma, who would be wondering what had become of her; she thought of her already appalling lateness, of the necessity for prudence and caution, and starting up abruptly, she said, with a short sigh:

"I'll really need to go now, Denis." .

Her words burdened him suddenly with the imminence of her departure, but he did not plead with her to stay, and he stood up, like a man, at once, saying:

"I don't want you to go, dear, and I know you don't want to go either, but we've got the future straightened out better now. We've only got to love each other and wait."

They were still alone. Bertorelli, in vanishing irrevocably, had, monster though he might be, betrayed none the less a human understanding and a tactful appreciation of their situation which might weigh in the balance—however lightly—against the atrocities that had been imputed to him. They kissed quickly, when her lips swept his like the brush of a butterfly's wing. At the door they shared one last look, a silent communion of all their secret understanding, confidence, and love, which passed between them like a sacred talisman before she turned and left him.

Her reticule now a featherweight, her steps rapid, fluent to her dancing heart, her head in the air, her curls straying and sailing buoyantly behind her, she was home before the rapture of her thoughts had abated. As she swept into the kitchen Mrs. Brodie looked at her questioningly from around the inclination of her nose.

"What kept you, girl? You took a long time to get that pickle of messages. Did you meet anyone you knew? Was anybody speirin' about Matt?"

Mary almost giggled in Mamma's face. For a ridiculous instant she considered the effect upon her mother were she to tell her she had just eaten an ambrosial sweetmeat, served by an outrageous ruffian, who tortured bambinos with macaroni, in a forbidden haunt of iniquity, and in company with a young man who had virtually proposed a honeymoon in Paris. It was well that she refrained, for had she yielded to this absurdity in the exhilaration of her spirits Mrs. Brodie, if she had not doubted her daughter's sanity, would certainly have swooned immediately.

"The air must have done you good, anyway," continued Mamma, somewhat suspiciously. "You've got quite a colour."

Credulous as she was, the maternal instinct that was in her doubted such immediate efficacy in the usually impotent Levenford air.

"Yes! I feel much better now," replied Mary truthfully, with twitching lips and sparkling eyes.

"Grandma was saying something when you were out about a letter she had seen you reading," persisted Mrs. Brodie, trailing after her nebulous idea. "I hope you're not up to any mischief your father would disapprove of. Don't set yourself up against him, Mary. Them that has tried it have aye regretted it. There's only one finish to that!" She sighed reminiscently, and added: "He finds out eventually, and he'll be at you in the end, ay, and make it a bitter, bitter end."

Mary shook off her mantle with a shrug of her shoulders. In the space of the last hour her slim figure had regained its youthful and imperious vitality. She stood erect, filled with a fierce and confident joy.

"Mamma," she said gaily, "don't worry about me. My motto is now, 'Mary never knows defeat!'"

Mrs. Brodie shook her pathetically inclined head sadly, and, filled with a vague, uncomprehending foreboding, gathered up the messages; with a more melancholy inclination of her head, like an incarnate presage of misfortune and ill-omen, she passed slowly out of the room.

VI

"Nessie! Mary!" shrilled Mrs. Brodie, in a fine frenzy of service, as she skittled about helping Brodie to dress, "come and put on your father's gaiters."

It was the morning of Saturday the twenty-first of August, and one of the red-letter days in James Brodie's calendar. In a large-patterned, black and white check knickerbocker suit he sat, his face like a full red sun, trying to struggle into his gaiters, which had not been used since a year that day, when, though he now chose to forget the fact, he had experienced the same difficulty in assuming them.

"What kind of witless trick was it to put a man's gaiters away damp?" he girned at his wife. "They'll not meet on me now. Desh it all, can't a man keep a thing decent in this house? These have shrunk."

Inevitably, when anything went wrong, the onus was thrust upon his wife's narrow shoulders.

"A man can't leave a thing about, but some senseless creature wastes it for him. How am I to go to the Show without gaiters? Ye'll be askin' me to go without my collar and tie next."

"But, father," meekly replied Mrs. Brodie, "I think you must be wearing a shade larger boot this year. This new pair I ordered for you myself were something broader than the others."

"Nonsense!" he grunted. "You'll be saying that my feet have got bigger next."

Here Nessie burst into the room like a young foal, followed more slowly by Mary.

"Quick, girls," urged Mamma, "do up your father's gaiters for him. Look sharp now, he's behind time!" The young handmaidens launched themselves upon their knees, applying their nimble fingers with dexterity and strength to the task before them, whilst Brodie lay back, simmering, darting black glances at the apologetic figure of his wife. The catastrophe was the more unfortunate for Mrs. Brodie as, upon this day in particular, he might reasonably be relied upon to be in a good temper, and the thought of spoiling for herself the rare chance of a day without a rage, of having activated the passive volcano, was more humiliating to her than the actual insults of the moment.

It was the day of the Levenford Cattle Show, an outstanding agricultural event, which drew the pedigree of the county as regards both its stock and its human inhabitants. Brodie loved the show and made his attendance of it an unfailing annual institution. He loved the sleek cattle with their swollen udders, the full-muscled Clydesdale stallions, the high-stepping cobs in the ring, the fat-flanked porkers and thick, close-knit sheep, and he prided himself on his judgment of a beast.

"I, a hatter!" he seemed to say, as he stood close to the judges, one hand gripping his famous ash plant, the other deep in his front pocket, "I'm more fitted for the job than them."

He was in his element, in the forefront of the judging, prominent amongst the best of them. Then, sauntering round the marquees with his hat well back on his head, he would slice with his penknife a sliver from this cheese and a sliver from that, tasting them critically; savour the different butters, the cream, the buttermilk; rakishly chaff the sonsiest of the dairymaids, who stood behind their exhibits.

That part of him which lay close to the soil flourished on days like these. From his mother's family, the Lumsdens, who had for generations farmed in the Barony of Winton, he drew that deeply rooted inheritance of the love of the land, its produce and beasts. His body craved the hardy exercise of the farm, for in his youth he had driven his team through the loam of Winton, and had known also the thrill of the feel of the gun butt against his cheek. From his father, James Brodie, that bitter, morose, implacable man, of whom he was the sole child, he had derived a pride which nourished itself upon a desire to possess the land. Only the vicissitudes following his impoverished father's death, when the latter had killed himself by falling from his horse, had driven him, as a young man, into the abomination of trade.

But another, and a stronger reason, existed which impelled him to the Show, namely, the craving to associate on equal terms with the gentry of the county and the borough. Conducting himself there not obsequiously, but rather with a trace of arrogance, nevertheless a nod of recognition, a word of greeting, or a few moments conversation with a notability of rank or distinction gratified him inwardly, and intoxicated him with an aberrant delight.

"I've done it, father. I've finished first!" cried Nessie triumphantly. With her small fingers she had succeeded in buttoning up one of the refractory spats.

"Come along, Mary," implored Mrs. Brodie. "You're such a slow-coach. Your father hasn't got all day to wait."

"Let her take her time," said Brodie sardonically. "I might as well be late now I'm about it. In fact, you might like to keep me here all day between you."

"She is never as quick at a thing as Nessie," sighed Mamma.

"That's it," at last said Mary, standing up with benumbed fingers. Her father eyed her critically.

"You know you're getting lazy, that's what's wrong with you, my girl. Good sakes, now I look at you you're getting as big as the side of a house. You should eat less and work more."

He stood up, contemplating himself in the mirror, whilst Mamma led the girls from the room, and, as his reflection gazed back at him from the glass with gradually increasing approval, his self-complacency was eventually restored. His thick muscular legs were set off to perfection by the rough knickerbockers, and under the fleecy homespun stockings his calves swelled nobly; his shoulders were as broad and straight as a wrestler's; not an ounce of fat marred his body; his skin was as unblemished as a child's. He was the perfect figure of a country gentleman, and, as the fact which he already knew was borne in upon him more forcibly by the glamour of his image, he twirled his moustache and smoothed his chin with satisfied vanity.

At this point the door of his room slowly opened and Grandma Brodie put her head round the door jamb, insinuatingly, espying how his mood lay before she spoke.

"Can I have a look at you before you go, James?" she wheedled, after a cautious pause. This day produced upon her decaying sensibility an emotion akin to excitement, sponsored by the forgotten memories of her youth which rushed incoherently in upon her. "You look real grand. Ye're the fine figure o' a man," she told her son. "Losh! but I wish I was going with ye."

"You're too old in the tooth for me to show you, mother," jibed Brodie, "although ye might get a ribbon for toughness."

Her dull ears prevented her from hearing properly, her distant thoughts from understanding the full import of his remark. "Ay, I'm gettin' a trifle old to go," she lamented, "but I've seen the day I would have been among the foremost there at the milkin', and the showin', and the jiggin' after, and then the tig-taggin' on the lang drive hame in the cool o' the night air. It a' comes back to me." Her dull eyes glistened. "What grand scones and bannocks we used to have there, though I paid but little heed to them in they days." She sighed regretfully, at her lost opportunities.

"Tuts, woman, can ye not keep your mind off your meat? You would think you were starved to hear you," Brodie chided her.

"No! No! James. I'm very grateful for all that you give me, and that's plenty. But maybe to-day if you were to see a nice, wee bit Cheddar cheese, no' too dear—there's a wheen o' bargains to be had at the end o' the day—perhaps you might pick it up for me." She leered at him ingratiatingly.

Brodie burst into loud laughter. "Gad! you'll be the death of me, woman. Your god's in your belly. I expect to be seeing Sir John Latta to-day. Do you want me to be carrying pokes and parcels when I meet him," he shouted at.her as he strode uproariously out of the room.

His mother hastened to the window of her room to see him swagger out of the house. She would sit there most of the day, straining her vision upon any passing stock, feasting her eyes upon the coloured cards—the red firsts, the blue seconds, the green thirds, and the indifferent yellows, which meant only highly commended—revelling in the press and bustle of the country throng, trying, but always unsuccessfully, to catch a glimpse of some old, familiar face amongst the passing crowd. There was always the chance too, ever present in her mind—its very improbability whetting her fancy provokingly—that her son might bring her back some small gift. She had asked for this, at any rate, and could do no more, she reflected complacently, as she settled herself eagerly in her chair to begin her pleasant vigil.

Downstairs on his way out, Brodie turned to Mary: "You better go down to the business and remind that ass Perry I'll not be in all day." The shop was known in the Brodie household only under the term of "the business"; the former term would have been considered paltry, even degrading. "He mightna remember that there's no holiday for him to-day. He's quite capable of forgetting his head, that one is. And run all the way, my lassie, it'll take some of the beef off you."

To Mamma he said, "I'll be back when you see me!" This was his valediction on such rare occasions as he chose to bid his wife farewell, but it was, in reality, a mark of unusual magnanimity, and Mamma accepted it with an appropriate gratitude.

"I hope you'll enjoy yourself, James," she said timidly, suiting her reply to his mood and the memorable nature of the event. Only on such infrequent and remarkable occasions did she dare use his baptismal name, but when they arose she ventured it in her reply, feeling that it consolidated what small and unsubstantial position she held in his esteem.

She did not dare to consider the attraction which the Show might offer to her; it was deemed sufficient gratification for her to admire the retreating, well set-up figure of her husband, as he went off by himself upon any excursion of pleasure, and the preposterous idea that she might accompany him never entered her head. She had no clothes, she was required at home, her strength was insufficient to support the hardships of a day in the fresh air—any one of these, or of a dozen further reasons, was, by her timid logic, sufficient to debar her from going. "I hope it'll keep fine for him," she murmured as, well pleased, she went back to wash the breakfast dishes, whilst Nessie waved good-bye to her father's back from the parlour window.

When the door had closed behind the master of the house Mary went slowly upstairs to her room, sat down on the edge of her bed and looked out of the window. She did not, in the clear brightness of the morning, see the three tall birch trees, their smooth boles shining with a lustrous sheen, standing upright like silver masts; she did not hear the whispered rustle of the leaves, flickering dark and light as they turned in the faint breeze. Engrossed within herself, she sat thinking of that remark which her father had made, turning it over in her mind uneasily, unhappily. "Mary, you're getting as big as a house," he had sneered, meaning, she fully realised, that she was developing, filling out, as befitted her age and rapid growth. Nevertheless, that single utterance, like a sudden shaft of light darting in, then out, of the darkness of her ignorance, had suddenly originated in her mind a profound disquiet.

Her mother, like a human ostrich, burying her head nervously at the slightest suggestion of the subject when it appeared on the domestic horizon, had not enlightened her on even the most elementary aspects of sex, and to any direct, ingenuous question which her daughter might address to her in this connection, Mamma would reply, in horror: "Hush at once, Mary! It's not a nice thing to talk about. Good girls don't think of such things. That was a shameful thing to ask." Her acquaintance with other girls had been always so slight that she had never achieved information on this matter through the light, tittering remarks in which even the most simpering, pink and white maidens of the town occasionally indulged. Stray fragments of such conversations which she might have overheard fell upon uncomprehending ears, or were repudiated by the natural delicacy of her feeling, and she had lived in an unconscious simplicity, discrediting perhaps, if she ever considered this, the fable that babies were achieved through the assistance of the stork, but being sublimely unaware of the most rudimentary realities of procreation.

Even now the fact that for three months the normal functions of her body had been disturbed had not ruffled the limpid pool of her virgin mind, but this morning her father's coarse remark, twisted by some hidden convolution of her mind into a different sense, distorted into a different interpretation, had struck her with a crushing violence.

Was she different now? Agitatedly she ran her hands over her limbs and body. It was her body, her own, belonging entirely to herself; how could it have altered? In a panic she jumped up, locked her bedroom door, and tore off her cashmere bodice and skirt, her petticoat, her clinging slip, undressed completely until she stood, bewildered, in a chaste nudity, touching her body with confused hands. Never before had she studied her figure with anything but a passing interest. She gazed stupidly at her creamy white skin, raised her arms above her head, lengthened her lithe, lovely figure into a taut, flawless beauty. The small mirror upon her table revealed in its inadequate depths no blemish or imperfection to confirm or allay her unformed fears, and, though she twisted her head this way and that, her frightened eyes could detect no branding disfigurement crying aloud of an inward ugliness. She could not tell whether she was different, whether her bosom was fuller, the shell pink of her nipples less delicate, the soft curve of her lips more profound.

A fearful indecision took possession of her. Three months ago, when she had lain in Denis' arms in a state of unconscious surrender, her instincts had blindly guided her, and with closed eyes she had abandoned herself utterly to the powerful currents which permeated her being. Neither reason, had she wished it, nor knowledge, had she possessed it, intervened; in effect, while experiencing the rending emotions of a pain intolerably sweet, and a pleasure unbearably intoxicating, she had been so moved out of her own being that she had known nothing of what was actually taking place. Her feelings then had lifted her above consideration, but now she dimly wondered what mysterious chemistry had been inaugurated by the power of their embrace, if, perhaps, her lips against his, in some strange combination, had altered her irrevocably in some profound, incomprehensible manner.

She felt powerless, lost in a perplexity of indecision, feeling that she must act to dispel immediately this sudden ferment in her mind, but unaware of how she should accomplish this. As she sombrely resumed the garments that lay scattered around her feet, she abandoned immediately the idea of approaching her mother, knowing well that Mamma's timid soul would leap in terror at the very mention of the topic. Involuntarily she turned towards the thought of Denis, her perpetual consolation, but instantly, and adding to her dismay, she was aware that she would not see him for at least a week, reflected, further, that she might see him on this next occasion for a moment only. Since that wonderful talk with him in Bertorelli's their meetings had been short—although so sweet—and by agreement carefully guarded, and while such fleeting glimpses of Denis as she thus obtained constituted the only felicity of her life, she felt now conclusively that, in these hasty exchanges of encouragement and love, she would never muster courage to invoke, even indirectly, his advice; at the mere idea a shameful blush pervaded her.

She was again dressed, and, unlocking the door, went downstairs, where Mamma, having finished what she called putting a face on things, had settled down luxuriously to an uninterrupted hour with her book. There were no problems like hers in such books, sadly reflected Mary, no indication in the vows, kissed finger tips, sweet speeches, and happy endings, of the elucidation of her difficulty.

"I'll go down to the business with father's message. He asked me to go in the forenoon," she said, after a moment's indecision, addressing her mother's bowed, rapt figure.

Mrs. Brodie, sitting in the drawing-room of a Sussex manor, surrounded by the society of her election, and in earnest conversation with the evangelical vicar of the parish, did not reply, did not even hear her daughter's voice. When immersed in a book she was, as her husband had put it, its slave.

"You're a perfect slave to that trash," he had once sneered at her when she had failed to respond to his question. "To see ye slaverin' ower it is like a drunkard wi' a bottle. Ye wad sit readin' there if the house was burnin' about our ears."

Observing, therefore, with a clouded eye that it was useless to disturb her mother, that under the present circumstances she could not obtain from her a coherent, still less a comforting word, Mary departed silently, and unnoticed, to execute her errand.

On the way to the town she remained immersed in her sad, questioning thoughts, walking limply, her head drooping, with slow steps; but although her journey was thus protracted, she reached her destination before she had even glimpsed the solution of her enigma.

In the shop Peter Perry was alone, lively, expanded, important, in the magnificence of sole responsibility, and he welcomed her with nervous effusion, his face lighting up with delight and his white cheeks becoming even more pale from the joyous shock of seeing her.

"This is an unexpected pleasure indeed, Miss Mary. Not often we have the pleasure of seeing you down at the business! Dear me! A great pleasure! A great pleasure!" he repeated agitatedly, rubbing his thin,

84

transparent, tapering fingers together with quick, rustling movements; then he paused, completely at a loss. He was actually unnerved by the stroke of circumstances which had delivered Mary at the shop on the very day when, her father being absent, he might be permitted to talk to her, and, in his confusion, the scintillating conversations he had so frequently conducted in his imagination between himself and a bevy of queenly young ladies of the highest society, and which he regarded as a form of rehearsal for an occasion such as that which now presented itself, fled from him on the four winds. He was silent, he who had longed for this opportune moment, saying: "If a fellow could get the chance he might cut a pretty good dash with Miss Mary," and tongue-tied, he who addressed his ironing-board, through the steam in the back shop, with fluent, contemptuous ease. A paralysing dumbness lay upon the man who, in his romantic leisure moments in bed on Sunday mornings, his eye fixed on his brass bed-knob as on a coronet, had charmed a duchess with his courtly speech. He felt his flesh wilt, his skin tingle damply, the perspiration exude clammily from his pores; he lost his head completely and, his professional manner taking the bit between its teeth, he blurted out: "Pray be seated, madam, what can I do for you to-day?"

He was horrified, and what blood lay in his veins rushed painfully to his head, making her image swim before him through a haze of embarrassment. He did not colour—that was an impossibility for him—but his head swam with giddiness; yet to his amazement and relief, Mary manifested neither indignation nor surprise. In plain truth her thoughts were still sadly distant, she had not quite recollected herself from the march of her dreary reverie, had not heard him, and instead of showing astonishment, she took quite gratefully the chair he had automatically proffered, and sank down upon it with a tired sigh.

Then in a moment she looked up, as though seeing him for the first time.

"Oh! Mr. Perry," she exclaimed, "I—I must have been thinking. I had no idea you were there."

He was slightly dismayed. Looking at his emasculate figure, it seemed the last possibility in the world that he should cherish, in the traditional manner, a secret passion for his employer's daughter, but such was indeed the case, and, in his highest, wildest, and most furtive flights, he visualised even a partnership for an exceedingly worthy young man, to be achieved through an alliance to the house of Brodie more binding than that of sordid trade. Mary, completely unaware of such optimistic visions, but vaguely pitying in her heart the timorous youth who lived in such manifest apprehension of her father, gazed at him mildly.

"I have a message for you, Mr. Perry," she said. "Mr. Brodie will not be in to-day and asks that you will attend to the business in his absence."

"Oh! quite, Miss Brodie! I quite understood that your father would be at the Show to-day. In fact I have made all arrangements to be here all day! I shall lunch here. I know well that the chief is extremely fond of such functions." Had Brodie heard himself referred to in such terms he would have annihilated his assistant with a single glance, but Perry had now recovered himself, was prepared to do himself justice, and privately considered his last florid remark rather good. "But even in the chief's absence the work will go on, Miss Brodie—and I hope—go on well," he continued euphoniously. "You, personally, may rest assured I shall do my best, my very utmost to make things go smoothly." He was so earnest in his manner, his moist eye glistened so eloquently that, despite her apathy, Mary found herself thanking him, though for what reason she scarcely knew.

Just then a customer came in, a shipwright who demanded a new cap and, though Mary would have gone at his entry, a languor of mind held her passive and relaxed, a lassitude of body bound her to the soothing comfort of the chair. She felt disinclined to begin her return home, and under her eye, although it followed his movements indifferently, Perry, seizing a delightful chance to exhibit his ability, served his client magniloquently, accomplishing feats of extreme nimbleness and dexterity with boxes and the short step ladder, and eventually with paper and string. When the purchaser had gone he returned with a conscious air and, leaning across the counter, remarked confidentially: "Your father has a wonderful business here, Miss Brodie—practically a monopoly." He was proud of that too, and although it came out of a book on Economics he was wrestling with at nights, he gave the term the flavour of his own deep and original deduction. "Not that—if I might venture to suggest it—it might not be increased by a few new ideas, a little novelty, perhaps, some new developments, even an extension of the business—it could be done," he added insinuatingly.

She did not reply, which oppressed him with the feeling that somehow he did not seem to be holding her attention; the conversation appeared to him rather one-sided.

"I hope you are well?" he enquired, after a considerable pause.

"Quite well," she echoed mechanically.

"You look to me, if I may say so, somewhat thinner in the face."

She raised her eyes.

"You think I'm thinner."

"Decidedly!" He seized the opportunity to regard her impassive, shadowed face with an expression of respectful solicitude and, as he leaned upon the counter, supported his small chin in his long fingers and posed his figure generally with an air of studied admiration.

"In fact," he continued boldly, "although as beautiful as ever, if you will permit me to say so, you look slightly indisposed. I am afraid the heat of the day is trying you. Could I get you a glass of water?"

86

Before she could refuse he had raised himself in a passion of service, was off like a shot, returned instantly with a brimming tumbler of sparkling water and had pressed the cold, clouded glass into her unresistant hand. "Drink it, Miss Mary," he insisted, "it will do you good." As she took a few sips so as not to hurt his feelings, a sudden anxious thought filled him with concern.

"I trust you have not been ill. You are so pale. Have you seen your physician?" he enquired in his best manner.

At his affected words Mary stopped with the glass half raised to her lips as though a light had broken upon her with a sudden effulgence, showing her a pathway she must follow. She looked at Perry with the full force of her attention, then turned her gaze through the open doorway and beyond, whilst her mind filled with a sudden resolution that made her lips firm and straight.

For a moment she remained still, then, with a quick impulse, she got up and murmured: "I must go now, Mr. Perry. Thank you for your kindness"; and before he could collect himself, she moved quietly away and went out of the shop, leaving him gazing blankly at the tumbler, the vacant chair, the empty air. What a strange girl, he thought, to go like that when he was behaving so admirably to her; but then, to be sure, women were strange creatures, and on the whole he had, he considered, acquitted himself very creditably. Mr. Perry began to whistle.

When Mary walked into the street she turned, not to the right, which was the direction for home, but to the left which would take her, if she pursued the road to its termination, to the far, Knoxhill end of the Borough. Peter Perry's chance remark had given her the solution she had been blindly seeking, and it was that which now impelled her in this contrary direction. She would go and see a doctor. Doctors were wise, trustworthy, kind; they healed, advised, comforted, yet respected one's confidence. Immediately she thought of the only practitioner she knew, Dr. Lawrie who, although he had not been in her home once in ten years, was nominally the family doctor, and she now remembered vividly the last time he had spoken to her, when he had placed his hand upon her small head and remarked with a pompous benignity: "Penny for a curl, young lady! Come along! Is it a bargain? You'll never miss it." She had been ten then, and while he had not secured the ringlet she had received the penny. Although she had not met him since, she saw him frequently, driving in his dogcart, everywhere and at every hour, always in a hurry and, in her eyes, maintaining always the look her childish mind had memorised, of one learned, august, and apart. He lived at Knoxhill, in a large residence, old, mottled by lichen, but still imposing, breasting the ascent half-way up the hill, and as she made her way resolutely along the street she recollected having heard that his hour of consultation began at noon.

It was a considerable distance to the doctor's house, and soon she was forced to ease the impulsive rapidity of her pace, she who a few months ago could have run the whole way without once losing breath. As her steps flagged her resolution faltered slightly, and she began to wonder how she would approach him. The thought of seeking his advice had dawned upon her so happily that the difficulties of achieving this object had not occurred to her; but now they obtruded themselves upon her notice painfully, obviously, and with every step became more insurmountable. Should she begin by consulting him about her health? He would, she realised, instantly marvel that she should have come alone, without the escort and protection of her mother. Such a thing was unheard of and she conceived that he might even refuse to see her in her unaccompanied state; if he consented to see her and she advanced, in her inexperience, some insufficient reason for her visit, she felt certain that with a few searching questions he would riddle any flimsy tissue which she might fabricate, and leave her helpless and ashamed. At this she reflected sadly that the only way would be to tell the truth absolutely, and to throw herself upon his mercy. Suppose, then, he were to disclose the visit to her parents, did the purpose she sought to achieve justify such a frightful hazard? Her thoughts wandered in on a maze of unreasoning perplexity as she began to ascend the incline of Knoxhill.

At length she reached the gate of the doctor's residence, where his big, brass plate, dented in its early, uneasy days by an occasional stone from some mischievous urchin, and now polished into a smooth, undecipherable, respected serenity, shone like the eye of an oracle, compelling thither the weary and the sick.

Outside the gate, as she stood for a moment quelling her misgivings and mustering her courage, she saw approaching in the distance an elderly man whom she recognised as an acquaintance of her father's, and realising with a sudden start that she could not risk going in whilst he was in sight, she turned her back upon him and walked slowly past the house. From out of the corner of her eye she observed the big, solid house with its severe Georgian porch, its windows swathed in mysterious saffron curtains, felt it, with a growing uneasiness, looming more largely upon her, felt her doubts rush back upon her with a greater and more disquieting force. It was a mistake to visit a doctor who knew her so well. Denis might not like her taking a step like this without first consulting him; another time would be more propitious for her visit; she was not ill, but well and as normal as ever; she was making herself the victim of her own imagination, obviously, unnecessarily, dangerously.

Now the street was clear and she perceived that she must enter at once or not at all; telling herself that she would go in first and face her difficulties afterwards, she had placed her hand upon the gate-handle when she recollected that she had no money with her to pay the fee which, even if he did not demand it, she must at once discharge to avoid a complication leading to discovery. She withdrew her hand, and was again beginning to resume her indecisive pacing upon the pavement, when, abruptly, she saw a maid looking from behind the curtains of a front window. Actually the maid observed nothing, but to Mary's excited fancy the servant's eye appeared to be regarding her suspiciously, and in the accusation of this apparent scrutiny the last shreds of her resolution dissolved. She felt she could endure the suspense of her indecision no longer, and with a guilty countenance she moved off hastily down the street, as though detected in some atrocious action.

As she fled down the street, retracing the whole of the weary way she had come, the repression of her unrelieved desire almost stifled her. She felt herself a blunderer and a coward; her face burned with shame and confusion; she felt she must at all costs avoid the public gaze. To keep away from anyone who might know her, and to return home as quickly as possible, she did not follow the High Street but took instead the alternative route—a narrow, shabby alley named College Street, but referred to always as the Vennel—which branched off the circuitous sweep of the main thoroughfare and drove, under the railway, directly towards the Common. With lowered head she plunged into the murk of the Vennel as if to hide herself there, and hurried along the mean, disreputable street with its ill-paved causeway and gutters filled with broken bottles, empty tins, and the foul litter of a low quarter. Only the desire to rush from recognition drove her through this lane which, tacitly forbidden to her, she never entered; but even in her precipitate flight its misery laid a sordid hand upon her.

Women stared at her from open courts as they stood idle, slatternly, bare armed, talking in groups; a mongrel dog chased her, barking, snapping at her heels; a cripple, dirty and deformed, taking his ease upon the pavement, shouted after her for alms, pursuing her with his voice whiningly, importunately, insultingly.

She hurried with a greater speed to escape from the depressing confines of the lane, and had almost made her way through, when she discerned a large crowd of people bearing down upon her. For one tragic, transient instant she stood still, conceiving this to be a mob rushing to assault her. Immediately, however, the sound of a band fell upon her ears, and she observed that the host, surrounded by an attendant rabble of dirty children and racing, mangy curs, descending upon her like a regiment marching to battle, was the local branch of the Salvation Army, newly formed in Levenford. In the rush of its youthful enthusiasm its devoted members were utilising the holiday by parading the low quarters of the town—even at this early hour of the day—to combat and offset any vice or debauchery that might be liberated on the occasion of the Cattle Show.

Onwards they came, banners flying, dogs barking, cymbals crashing, the band blaring out the hymn: "Throw out the Life-line," whilst the soldiers of both sexes joined their voices loudly with harmonious fervour.

As they advanced she pressed herself against the wall, wishing the pavement to open beneath her feet and engulf her, and while they swept past, she shrank into herself as she felt the buffet and sway of the surging bodies coarsely against her own. Suddenly, as they rolled past, a female private of the army, flushed with righteousness and the joy of her new uniform, seeing Mary there so frightened and humiliated, dropped for a moment her piercing soprano and, thrusting her face close to Mary's, whispered in one hot, penetrating breath:

"Sister, are you a sinner? Then come and be saved; come and be washed in the Blood of the Lamb!"

Then, merging her whisper into the burden of the hymn, she sang loudly: "Someone is sinking to-day," swung again into the fervent strains and was gone, tramping victoriously down the street.

A sense of unutterable degradation possessed Mary as she supported herself against the wall, feeling with her sensitive nature that this last disgrace represented the crowning manifestation of an angry Providence. In the course of a few hours the sudden, chance direction of her thoughts into an obscure and foreign channel had altered the whole complexion of her life. She could not define the feeling which possessed her, she could not coherently express or even understand the dread which filled her, but as she stumbled off upon her way home she felt, in a nausea of self-reproach, that she was unworthy to live.

VII

On the Monday after the Cattle Show a considerable commotion occurred in the Brodie household. The ra-ta-tat of the postman on that morning was louder than usual and his mien fraught with a more important significance, as he handed to Mrs. Brodie a letter embellished by a row of strange stamps, a thin, flimsy oblong which crackled mysteriously between her agitated fingers. Mamma, with a palpitating heart, looked at this letter which she had been anticipating for days. There was no need for her to consider who had sent it, for she recognised immediately the thin, "foreign" envelopes which she had herself solicitously chosen and carefully packed for Matt. She was alone, and, in a transport of gratitude and expectation, she pressed the envelope to her lips, then close against her bosom, until, after a moment, as though she had by contact absorbed its hidden message directly into her heart, she withdrew it and turned it over in her red, work-wrinkled hands.

Although she felt that the letter was exclusively hers she saw that it was addressed to Mr. and Mrs. James Brodie, and she dared not open it; she dared not run upstairs and cry joyfully to her husband: "A letter from Matt!"; instead she took this first, precious, unsubstantial bulletin from abroad and placed it carefully upon her husband's plate. She waited. She waited submissively, yet with an eager, throbbing impatience, for the news from her son, returning from time to time into the kitchen from the scullery to reassure herself that the letter was still there, that this phenomenal missive, which had miraculously traversed three thousand leagues of strange seas and exotic lands to reach her sarely, had not now suddenly vanished into the empty air.

At last, after what seemed to her an eternity, Brodie came down, still showing in his disposition, she observed thankfully, remnants of the previous day's pleasure. Immediately she brought him his porridge and, having placed this gently before him, stood expectantly a short distance off. Brodie took up the letter, weighed it silently on the palm of his huge hand, seemed to consider it dispassionately, weighed it ostentatiously again, then put it down unopened before him and commenced to eat his porridge. As he supped one spoonful after another, bent forward in a crouching attitude with both elbows upon the table, he kept his eyes fixed upon the envelope and maliciously affected not to see her.

Under the refinement of his malice she remained in the background, her hands pressed tightly together, her body tense with a fever of anticipation, until she could no longer endure the suspense.

"Open it, father," she whispered.

He affected a violent, exaggerated start.

"Bless my soul, woman, you near scared the life out me. What are ye hangin' about there for? Oh! I see! I see! It's this bit o' a thing that's drawin' ye." He jerked his spoon towards the letter and lay back negligently in his chair, contemplating her. He was, he told himself in the full flush of his amiability, having a rare game with her. "Ye've the look o' a wasp ower the jam pot," he drawled. "The same kind o' sickly hunger about ye. I was thinkin' mysel' it looked pretty thin; pretty poor stuff, I've no doubt."

"It's the thin note-paper I bought for him to save postage," Mamma pleaded. "Ye can get a dozen sheets o' it into the one envelope."

"There's not a dozen sheets here. No, I question if there's more nor two or three at the outside. I hope that doesna mean bad news," he said sadly, cocking one small, spiteful eye at her.

"Oh! will ye not open it and put my mind at rest, father?" she implored. "I'm fair eaten up with anxiety, ye must surely see."

He lifted his head arrestingly.

"There's plenty time—plenty o' time," he drawled, spinning out the words. "If ye've waited ten weeks another ten minutes 'll not burst ye. Away and bring me the rest o' my breakfast."

Sighing with uncertainty, she was obliged to drag herself away from the letter, and go back to the scullery to dish up his bacon and eggs whilst she trembled continually in the fear that he might read the epistle and suddenly destroy it in her absence.

"That's the spirit," he cried broadly, as she hastily returned. "I havena seen ye run like that since the day ye ate the green grosets. I know how to make ye souple. I'll have ye dancin' in a minute."

But she did not reply; he had baited her into dumbness. Accordingly when he had finished breakfast he again picked up the letter.

"Well, I suppose we better see what is inside it," he drawled casually, taking as long as he could to slit the envelope and extract the largely written sheets. Silence reigned whilst he protracted his reading of the epistle intolerably, but all the time Mamma's anxious eyes never left his face, seeking there some expression which might transmit to her a verification of her hopes and a negation of her fears. At length he threw it down, declaring:

"Nothing in it! A pack o' nonsense!"

The moment he relinquished them, Mrs. Brodie threw herself upon the sheets and, seizing them with longing, brought them close to her myopic eyes and drank the closely written lines thirstily. She observed at once from the superscription that the letter had been written on board the *Irrawaddy*, and that it had been posted almost immediately the ship berthed.

"Dear Parents," she read on, "I take up my pen to write you after a most fearful and unending attack of mal de mer, or more plainly, sea-sickness. This dreadful affliction settled upon me first in the Irish Sea, but in the Bay of Biscay I was so ill I wished to die, and would have prayed to be thrown to the fishes but for the thought of you at home. My cabin being close and unendurable, and my berth companion turning out to be a vulgar fellow—addicted to a heavy indulgence in drink —I at first attempted to remain on deck, but the waves were so gigantic and the sailors so uncharitable that I was forced to descend again to my hot, disagreeable quarters. In this confined space, as I lay in my bunk I was rattled about in a most awful and distressing manner, sometimes being lifted up to the ceiling and sticking there for a minute before falling heavily. When I had fallen back on my berth my stomach seemed to have remained above, for so much did I experience a feeling of emptiness and exhaustion that it seemed as if my middle was devoid of its contents. To make matters worse I could in addition eat nothing, but vomited all the time, night as well as day. My cabin-mate, as the term goes here, who occupied the lower bunk, used the most frightful language on the first night when I was sick and made me get up in my nightshirt in the cold, heaving cabin to change places with him. The only thing which kept down and indeed which kept my poor body and soul together was a nourishing drink which one of the stewards kindly brought me. He called it stingo, and I must confess that I found it agreeable and that it was truly the means of saving my life for you Altogether it was a frightful time I can well assure you.

"Well, to continue, by the time we had passed Gibraltar, which is nothing but a bare one-sided rock, much bigger than our own Levenford Rock but not so pretty, and were well into the Mediterranean, I managed to get my sea legs. The sea here was more blue than anything I have seen—tell Nessie it was more blue even than her eyes—and I was the more able to enjoy this and also the lovely colours of the sunsets as it was so mercifully calm. I could still hardly swallow a bite, but at Port Said we took in supplies of fruit and I was able to eat some fresh dates and some very delicious oranges, which were very sweet, and skinned easily like tangerines, but much larger. I had also a fruit called a papaia which is juicy like a small melon but with a green skin and a pinkish colour of flesh. Very refreshing! I think they did me good, in fact I am sure they did me great good.

"I did not go ashore here as I had been warned that Port Said was a very wicked place and dangerous for Europeans unless armed. A gentleman on board here told me a long story about an adventure he had in a heathen temple and in other places there, but I will not repeat it from motives of modesty and also as I am not sure that he was speaking the truth. But it seems that there are astonishing things out here. In this connection tell Agnes I am true to her memory. I forgot to say that they come off to the ship in boats at Port Said and sell very good rahat-lakoum which is an excellent sweet although you would never judge so from the name.

"We passed very slowly through the Suez Canal, a narrow ditch bounded on either side by miles of sandy desert with purple mountains in the distance. This canal is not much to look at and passes through some dull-looking sheets of water called the Bitter Lakes, but it is, they say, very important. Sometimes we saw men with white cloaks, mounted —not on camels as you at home might have expected—but on fast horses on which they galloped away whenever they caught sight of the ship. I must tell you that I also saw palm trees for the first time—just like the one in the church hall, only very much larger and thicker. In the Red Sea the heat was very great but after we had well passed Aden and some curious islands called the Twelve Apostles, when I was just hoping to have a nice time by joining the ladies in deck games, conversation, and music, the heat again suddenly became frightful. Mamma, those drill suits you got me are no use they are so thick and heavy. The correct thing to do is to have them made in India by a native. They say they are very clever at it and have the right material which is tussore silk and certainly not that drill you got me. Also while on this subject please tell Mary that the glass piece of the flask she gave me smashed in the first storm, and Nessie's compass is points different from the one on the ship.

"Anyway I went down with the heat, and although eating better—I like the curries very much—I lost pounds. I am sure I got very thin and this caused me much embarrassment which, together with my lack of energy, debarred me from joining in social life and I could only sit alone, thinking of my unused mandolin, and looking unhappily at the ladies and at the sharks which followed the ship in great numbers.

"After the heat came the rain, what is referred to here as a monsoon—a chota (small) monsoon, but it was wet enough for me—just like a never-ending Scotch mist which drenched everything all day long. We went through the mist until we reached Ceylon, putting in at Colombo. This has a wonderful harbour. I could see miles and miles of calm water. Very comforting! We had had it rough in the Indian Ocean. Some people went ashore to buy precious stones, moonstones, opals, and turquoises, but I did not go as they say you are simply robbed and that the moonstones are full of flaws, that is cracks. Instead my friend the steward gave me a choice Colombo pineapple. Although it was large I was surprised to find that I could finish the whole of it. Very palatable! My bowels were a trifle loose on the following day and I thought I had dysentery but mercifully have been spared this, also malaria, so far. It must have been the pineapple.

"However, the worst thing of all was yet to come. In the Indian Ocean we had a typhoon, which is the worst kind of horrible storm you could ever imagine. It all began by the sky going quite purple, then dark yellow like brass. I thought it very pretty at first but suddenly all we passengers were ordered below and I took this rightly as a bad omen, for all at once the wind hit the ship like a blow. A man who was standing at his cabin had his hand caught by the sudden slam of the door and his thumb was torn right off. A seaman had his leg broken also. It was terrible.

"I was not sick, but must now confess I was almost apprehensive. The sea came up, not like the waves in the Bay of Biscay, but with a fearful high swell—like round hills. I was obliged soon to give over looking through the porthole. The ship groaned so much in her timbers I thought she would surely burst asunder. The rolling was most awful; and on two occasions we went over so far and remained there so long I feared we should never come back. But Providence was kind and finally we reached the delta of the Ganges, great banks of sand and very muddy water. We had a pilot to take us up from the mouth of the Hooghly—and we went up the river so slowly that we took days. On the banks are a multitude of little patches of cultivation all irrigated by ditches. I have seen coco-nut palms, also bananas growing on the trees. The natives here are, of course, black and seem to work in nothing but loin cloths, although some have turbans. They squat on their haunches as they work on their patches, but some also cast nets in the yellow river water and catch fish which are said to be good. The whites have sun helmets—father, your topee is the very thing.

"Now I must close. I have written this letter at intervals, and now we have docked. I am much impressed with the size of the place and the docks. The sky here seems full of house tops and minarets.

"I read a bit of my Bible every day. I am not indisposed. I think I shall do well here.

"With love to all at home, I remain,
"Your dutiful son,
"MATT."

Mamma drew in her breath ecstatically, as she wiped away the tears which seemed to have escaped from her overflowing heart. The frail instrument of her being swelled in a pæan of joy and gratitude, singing within her: "What a letter! What a son!" The news seemed too potent for her, alone, to contain, and a wild impulse seized her to run into the open street, to traverse the town waving aloft the letter, crying out the brave chronicle of this epoch-making voyage.

Brodie read her mood distinctly, with a derisive penetrating eye. "Call out the bellman," he said, "and shout the news through the Borough. Go on. Have it blurted out to everybody. Pah! wait till ye get, no' his first, but his twenty-first, letter. He's done nothing yet but eat fruit and be namby-pamby."

Mamma's bosom heaved indignantly.

"The poor boy's had a dreadful time," she quivered. "Such sickness! Ye mustna begrudge him the fruit. He was aye fond o' it." Only this aspersion upon her son made her answer him back. He looked at her sardonically: "It seems ye made a fine mess of the outfit! My topee was the only fit article he had," he said, as he rose from the table.

"I'll take it up with that manager at Lennie's this very day," cried Mamma in a choking voice. "He told me with his own lips that drill was being worn out there. The idea of such deceit! It might have sent my son to his death o' sunstroke."

"Trust you to make a mess o' anything, auld wife," he launched at her pleasantly, as a parting shot. But now his arrows did not penetrate or wound; they did not reach her as she stood in that far-off land, where tall palms waved majestic fronds against an opal sky, and soft bells pealed from temples in the scented dusk.

At last she started from her reverie.

"Mary!" she called out to the scullery. "Here's Matt's letter! Read it and take it to Grandma when you've finished with it"—adding presently in an absent voice, "then bring it back to me." Immediately she returned to her sweet meditation, considering that in the afternoon she would send the precious missive to Agnes Moir. Mary should take it down, together with a jar of home-made jam and a cake. Agnes might have had a letter herself, although that, Mrs. Brodie complacently reflected, was doubtful; but at any rate she would be overjoyed to hear, in any manner, of the heroic tidings of his journey and the splendid news of his arrival. To send down the letter at once was also, Mamma was well aware, the correct thing to do, and the added libations of cake and jam would embellish the tit-bit delightfully for Agnes, a good, worthy girl of whom she consistently approved.

When Mary returned, Mamma demanded: "What did Matt's grandma say about his letter?"

"Something about wishing she could have tasted that pineapple," remarked Mary indifferently.

Mamma bridled as she carefully took the sacred letter from her daughter. "The like of that," she said, "and the poor boy nearly drowned and consumed by sharks. You might show a little more interest yourself with your brother in such danger. Ye've been trailing about like a dead thing all morning. Now, are ye listening to me? I want you to run over to Agnes with it this afternoon. And you're to take a parcel over to her as well."

"Very well," said Mary. "When am I to be back?"

"Stay and have a chat with Agnes if you like. And if she asks you to wait for tea, I'll allow you to do so. You can come to no harm in the company of a Christian girl like that."

Mary said nothing, but her lifeless manner quickened. A frantic plan, which had hung indefinitely in her mind during the previous sleepless night, began already to take substantial form under this unexpected offering of chance.

She had resolved to go to Darroch. To venture there alone would be for her, at any time, a difficult and hazardous proceeding, fraught with grave possibilities of discovery and disaster. But if she were to undertake such an unheard of excursion at all, the timely message of Mamma's was clearly her opportunity. She knew that a train left Levenford for Darroch at two o'clock, covering the four miles between the two towns in fifteen minutes, and that the same train made the return journey, leaving Darroch at four o'clock. If, incredibly, she ventured upon the expedition, she saw that she would have more than one hour and a half to accomplish her purpose, and this she deemed to be adequate. The sole question which concerned her was her ability to deliver her message successfully before two o'clock, and, more vitally, whether she could disentangle herself from the embarrassing and effusive hospitality of Agnes in time for her train.

With the object of speed in her mind she worked hard all morning, and had finished her household duties before one o'clock when, snatching a few mouthfuls of food, she hurried upstairs to change. But, as she reached her room at the head of the stairs, a remarkable sensation overtook her. She felt suddenly light, ethereal, and giddy; before her startled eyes the floor of her bedroom moved gently upwards and down-

96

wards, with a slow see-sawing instability; the walls, too, tottered in upon her like the falling sides of a house of cards; across her vision a parabola of lights danced, followed instantly by darkness. Her legs doubled under her and she sank silently down upon the floor in a faint. For a long time she lay recumbent upon her back, unconscious. Then gradually her prone position restored her feeble circulation, tiny currents of blood seemed to course again under the dead pallor of her skin, and with a sigh she opened her eyes, which fell immediately upon the hands of the clock that indicated the time to be half-past one. Agitatedly she raised herself upon her elbow, and, after several fruitless attempts, at last forced herself to stand upright again. She felt unsteady and languid, but her head was light and clear, and with soft, limp fingers, that felt to her useless for the purpose, she compelled herself to dress hastily. Then hurriedly she went downstairs.

Mamma met her with the letter and the package and a host of messages, greeting, and injunctions for Agnes. So engrossed was she in her benevolent generosity that she failed to notice her daughter's distress.

"And don't forget to tell her it's the new season's jam," she called out, as Mary went out of the gate, "and that the cake has two eggs in it," she added. "And don't leave the letter. Say I want it back!" she shouted, finally.

Mary had twenty minutes to get to the station, which was enough time and no more. The heavy parcel, containing two pounds of cake and two pounds of jam, dragged upon her arm; in her weak state the thought of the rich cake sickened her, and the sweet jam smeared itself cloyingly over her imagination. She had no time to deliver it to Agnes, and manifestly it was impossible for her to carry it about all afternoon. Already in her purpose she stood committed to a desperate act, and now an incitement to further rashness goaded her. Something urged her to dispose of Mamma's sumptuous present, to drop it silently in the gutter or cast it from her into an adjacent garden. Its weight oppressed her, and her recoil from the contemplation of its contents thrust her into sudden recklessness. Beside the pathway stood a small boy, ragged, barefooted, and dirty, who chalked lines disconsolately upon a brick wall. As she passed, with one sudden, unregenerate impulse, Mary thrust the bundle upon the astounded urchin. She felt her lips move, heard herself saying: "Take it! Quick! Something to eat!"

The small boy looked up at her with astonished, distrustful eyes which indicated, more clearly than articulate speech, his profound suspicion of all strangers who might present him with heavy packages under the pretext of philanthropy. With one eye still mistrustfully upon her, he tore open the paper cover to ensure he was not being deceived, when, the richness of the contents having been thus revealed to his startled eyes, he tucked the parcel under his arm, exploded into activity before this peculiar lady might regain her sanity, and vanished like a puff of śmoke down the street.

Mary felt shocked at her own temerity. A sudden pang struck her as to how she would conceal from Mamma her inexcusable action, or failing this, how she might ever explain away the dissipation into thin air of the fruits of her mother's honest labour. Vainly she tried to obtain comfort by telling herself she would deliver the letter to Agnes when she returned after four, but her face was perturbed as she hastened onwards to the station.

In the train for Darroch she made a powerful effort to concentrate her fatigued attention upon the conduct of her scheme, tracing mentally in advance the steps she would take; she was determined that there should be no repetition of the weakness and indecision of the day before. Darroch she knew sufficiently well, having visited it several times before it had become vested for her with a halo of glamour and romance as the place in which Denis lived. Since she had known that he resided there, the drab town, consisting in the main of chemical and dye works, the effluent of which frequently polluted the clear Leven in its lower reaches, had undergone a manifest and magical metamorphosis. The ill-cobbled, narrow streets assumed a wider aspect because Denis moved along them, and the smoke-splashed buildings became more splendid because amongst them he had his being.

As she drew slowly nearer to this enchanted place Mary, in spite of her crushing anxiety, felt actually a breathless anticipation. Although it was not her intention to see Denis, she could not suppress a throb of excitement at drawing near to him in his own environment.

When the train steamed into Darroch station she quickly left her compartment, surrendered her ticket, and was amongst the first of the small handful of passengers to leave the platform. Walking without hesitation, and as rapidly as her strength permitted, she passed along the main street, inclined sharply to the left, and entered a quieter residential locality. None of the persons she encountered knew her; her appearance caused neither stir nor interest. Darroch, though lacking the county atmosphere, was as large a township as Levenford, was, indeed, the only other large town within a radius of twelve miles, and it was easy for Mary to slip unnoticed through the busy streets, and to submerge her identity beneath that of the crowd which thronged them. It was for these very reasons that she had chosen Darroch for her present purpose.

When she had proceeded half-way along the secondary street she observed, to her relief, that her memory had served her correctly, and, confronted by a crescent of terrace-houses she advanced resolutely to the end house, and at once rang the bell loudly. A diminutive maid in a blue cotton overall opened the door.

"Is the doctor at home?" asked Mary.

"Will you please to come in," replied the small domestic, with the indifferent air of one who is tired of repeating the formula endlessly.

Mary was shown into the waiting-room. It was a poor room with dull walls and a thin, worn carpet upon the floor, furnished by an array of chairs, in varying degrees of decrepitude, and a large oak table bearing several tattered, dog-eared, out-of-date periodicals and a pink china pot containing a languishing aspidistra.

"What is the name?" apathetically enquired the slave of the door.

"Miss Winifred Brown," replied Mary distinctly.

Clearly she was, she now saw, a liar! Whilst she should have been in Levenford, sitting in amiable conference with her brother's legitimately engaged fiancée, here she was, having cast her mother's parcel from her, four miles away, giving a false name, and waiting in the house of a strange doctor, whose name and domicile she had recollected only by fortunate chance. The faint colour, which had entered her face as she enunciated the fictitious name, now violently flushed it at these thoughts, and it was with difficulty that she essayed to thrust the feeling of guilt from her as she was ushered into the consulting-room.

The doctor was a middle-aged man, bald, untidy, disillusioned, and the possessor of an indifferent, cheap practice. It was not his usual consulting hour, which caused him a justifiable annoyance, but his economic position was such as to compel him to see patients at any hour. He was a bachelor and his housekeeper had just served him up a midday meal of fat boiled beef with suet puddings, which he had eaten hurriedly, and, as a result, the chronic indigestion, due to badly cooked food, irregular hours, and septic teeth, to which he was a martyr, was beginning to gnaw at him painfully. He looked surprisedly at Mary.

"Is it a call?" he enquired.

"No! I have come to consult you," she replied, in a voice which seemed far away and unrecognisable as her own.

"Be seated, then," he said abruptly. Immediately he sensed the unusual and his irritation deepened. He had long ceased to derive interest from the clinical aspect of his cases, and any deviation from the humdrum routine of ordinary practice associated with the rapid issuing of bottles, containing dilute solutions of cheap drugs and colouring agents, always dismayed him; he was, in addition, anxious to get back to his couch and lie down; a spasm of pain gripped his middle as he remembered that his evening surgery would be heavy this night.

"What is it?" he continued, shortly.

Haltingly she began to tell him, blushed, faltered, went on again, speaking in a daze. How she expressed herself she did not know, but apparently his aroused suspicions were confirmed.

"We must examine you," he told her coldly. "Will it be now, or shall you return with—your mother?" Hardly understanding what he meant, she did not know how to reply. His impersonal manner discouraged her, his callous air chilled her, and his general slovenly appearance, with ragged, untrimmed moustache, uncared for finger nails, and grease spots on his waistcoat, affected her equally with a sense of strong antipathy. She told herself, however, that she must go through with her ordeal, and in a low voice she said: "I cannot come back again, doctor."

"Take your things off, then, and prepare yourself," he told her bluntly, indicating the couch as he went out of the room.

In her awkward timidity she had barely time to loosen her clothing and lie down upon the shabby, torn settee before he returned. Then with eyes shut and clenched teeth she submitted herself to his laboured and inexpert examination. It was agony for her, mentally and physically. She shrank in her fastidious mind from his coarse and uncouth presence, and the touch of his unskilful fingers made her wince with pain. At last it was over and, with a few short words, he again left the room.

Inside the space of five minutes she was back again in her chair, dressed, and gazing dumbly at him as he lumbered back to his desk.

The doctor was for once slightly at a loss. He had met this calamity frequently in women of a different class, but he was, despite his obtuse, case-hardened intellect, aware that this girl, who was nothing more than a frightened child, was uninstructed and innocent. He felt that her unconscious defloration had undoubtedly coincided with her conception. He realised why she had so self-consciously given him an assumed name, and in his dry, empty heart a vague pity stirred. At first, with all the anxiety of the unsuccessful practitioner jealous of his meagre reputation, he had suspected that she desired him to apply some means of terminating her condition, but now he realised fully the extent of her sublime ignorance. He moved uncomfortably in his chair, not knowing how to begin.

"You are not married?" he said at length, in a flat voice.

She shook her head with swimming, terrified eyes.

"Then I advise you to get married. You are going to have a baby."

At first she hardly understood. Then her lips contorted with a quivering spasm, her eyes overflowed and tears ran soundlessly down her face. She felt paralysed, as though his words had bludgeoned her. He was talking to her, trying to tell her what she must do, what she must expect, but she scarcely heard him. He receded from her; her surroundings vanished; she was plunged into a grey mist of utter and incomparable dejection, alone with the obsessing horror of certain and inevitable calamity. From time to time fragments of his meaning came to her, like haggard shafts of daylight glancing suddenly through the swirling wreaths of fog which encircled her.

"Try not to worry," she heard him say; then again through the enveloping pall came the words, "You are young, your life is not wasted."

What did he know or care? His well-meant platitudes left her untouched and cold. Instinctively she realised that to him she represented merely a transient and unwelcome incident in his monotonous day, and, as she rose and asked to know his charge, she detected instantly in his eye a half-veiled flicker of relief. Her intuition had not deceived her, for, having taken his fee and shown her to the door, he fled immediately to his bismuth bottle, took a large dose, settled himself down, with a sigh of relief, to rest and straight away completely forgot her.

As she passed out of the house into the street it was just three o'clock. She had an hour to wait for her train—if ever she would take it. In a torture of mind she walked down the street whispering to herself: "God! O God! why have You done this to me? I've never done You any harm. Stop this from happening. Stop it!" A blind unreason possessed her as to why, and how, her body had been singled out by the Almighty for this obscene experiment. It struck her as a supremely unjust manifestation of the Divine omnipotence. Strangely, she did not blame Denis; she felt herself simply the victim of some tremendous, incomprehensible fraud.

No! she did not blame Denis; she felt, instead, that she must fly to him. Caution was now abandoned to the winds in the extremity of her anguish and, with a strained face, she walked along Main Street, at the far end of which stood the Lomond Wine and Spirit Vaults—Owen Foyle, proprietor. Around the corner was a wide, double gate leading into a yard, from which an open, winding stair ascended to the Foyle house.

She crept up this stairway and knocked faintly at the door. From inside came the tinkle of a piano. The tinkle continued, but no one came in answer; then she heard a voice cry, "Rosie, me chick, is that somebody at the door? See if anybody's there." Someone replied, in childish tones: "I'm at my scales, mother; you go, or wait and let them knock again." And the sound of the piano was resumed with redoubled energy and a loudness expressive of intense application.

After a moment's irresolute pause Mary was about to knock upon the door more loudly, when suddenly, as she advanced her hand, a sharp whistle shrilled from outside the yard, and drew gradually nearer to her.

She turned and, at the same moment, Denis appeared at the foot of the stairs, his head tilted back enquiringly, his eyes widening with surprise as he perceived her. Observing immediately that Mary was in acute distress, he ran up the steps.

"Mary!" he exclaimed hurriedly, "what is it?"

She could not reply, could not utter his name.

"What is the matter, dearest Mary?" murmured Denis, coming close to her, taking her cold hand and smoothing it gently in his. "Is it your father?"

She shook her head without gazing at him, knowing that if she did so, she must break down abjectly.

"Come away," she whispered. "Come away before anyone comes."

Oppressed, he followed her slowly down the steps.

In the street, he asked fiercely: "Have they been bad to you at home? Tell me quickly what the trouble is, dear? If anybody has touched you I'll kill him."

There was a pause, then she said slowly, indistinctly, painfully, dropping each word from her lips like a leaden weight:

"I am going to have a baby."

His face whitened as if he had received a frightful wound and became gradually more pale, as though his strength and vigour flowed out from him. He dropped her hand and looked at her with dilated, starting eyes.

"Are you sure?" he jerked out at last.

"I'm sure."

"How do you know?"

"Something seemed wrong with me. I went to a doctor. He told me."

"A—a doctor? It's certain, then?"

"Certain," she echoed, dully.

It was irrevocable, then. With one sentence she had thrust upon his shoulders a load of misery and responsibility, which turned him from a gay, whistling boy into a mature and harassed man. Their love-making had been a trap, the playful dalliance and the secret meetings of the past merely snares to lure and entangle him in this draggled predicament. The pleasant, sanguine expectations of marrying her, all the alluring preparations which he had contemplated, now felt like chains binding and drawing him towards an obligation he must inevitably fulfil. A heavy sigh burst from him. In the masculine society in which he moved nothing was considered more derogatory to the male, or more ridiculous, than to be victimised into a marriage of necessity. His prestige would be lost, he would be lampooned at the street corners, his name would become an obloquy. He felt the position so intolerably for himself that he was moved by a desire to escape and in a flash he thought of Canada, Australia, America. He had often thought of emigrating, and the prospects that existed in these new countries for an unattached young man never appealed to him more entrancingly than at this moment. Another thought struck him.

"When did the doctor say that you would——" He paused, unable to complete the sentence. Nevertheless she was now able to understand his meaning.

"He said February," she replied, with an averted face.

Only five more months and he would be the father of her child! That exquisite night they had spent together by the Leven was to produce a child, a child that would be nameless unless he married her immediately. The pressing necessity for marriage again obtruded itself distastefully upon him. He did not know how long she might remain undiscovered before the condition of her pregnancy became obvious.

102

Although he had at times heard stories bandied amongst his companions, of how peasant girls working on the land had remained in this state of pregnancy, undetected until the actual birth occurred, he doubted if Mary had the strength or fortitude to continue the concealment for any length of time. And yet she must do so. He was not in a position to provide a home for her immediately. She must wait. There was, of course, nothing visible yet. He looked at her closely, and as he observed her pendent figure, weighted with an infinitely heavier despondency than his, for the first time he began to think of her rather than himself.

Now that she had told him she waited helplessly, as if, attending in submission for him to direct her movements, her attitude invoked him dumbly as to what she should do. With a powerful effort he pulled himself together, yet, as he spoke, his words sounded harsh and unconvincing in his ears.

"This is a bit of a mess we're in, Mary, but we'll straighten it out all right. We must go and talk it over."

"Have I got to go back home to Levenford?" she asked in a low tone.

He pondered a minute before replying: "I'm afraid it's best for you to do that. Did you come in by train?"

"Yes, and if I'm going back I must leave here at four." He took out his watch, which indicated half-past three. Although they had exchanged only a few sentences they had been standing there, in the street, for half an hour.

"You can't wait till the next," he agreed. "It's too late."

An idea struck him. The waiting-room at the station was usually empty at this time; they could go there until her train departed. He took her arm and drew it into his. At this, the first sign of tenderness he had manifested towards her since she had told him the dreadful news, she looked at him piteously and her drawn features were transcended by a pale smile.

"I've only got you, Denis," she whispered, as they moved off together. At the station, however, the waiting-room was unfortunately full; an old woman, some farm servants, and two dye-workers from the print works sat staring at each other and at the plain board walls. It was impossible to talk there, so Denis took Mary to the far end of the platform, where, as the short walk had given him time to collect himself and the soft feel of her arm reminded him of her charm and beauty, of the delightful attractions of her fresh body, he mustered a smile.

"It's not so bad, Mary, after all, so long as we stick together."

"If you left me now, Denis, I should drown myself in the Leven. I'd kill myself somehow."

As her eyes met his, he could see that she meant absolutely every grim word she uttered, and he pressed her arm again, tenderly. How could he, even for an instant, have considered leaving this lovely, defenceless creature who, but for him, would still have been a virgin and who now, because of him, was soon to be a mother. And how passionately attached to him she was! It thrilled him with a fierce joy to see her complete dependence upon him and her submission to his will. His spirit was recovering from the cutting injury which it had received, and he began to think coherently, as his normal self.

"You'll leave everything to me!" he said.

"Everything," she echoed.

"Then you must go home, dear, and try to behave as if nothing had happened. I know how difficult it will be, but you must give me as long as possible to make our arrangements."

"When can we be married?" It cost her a powerful effort to utter the words, but in her new-found knowledge she felt dimly that her body would remain unchaste until she knew when he would marry her.

He reflected.

"I have a big business trip towards the end of the year—it means a lot. Could you wait until after then?" he asked doubtfully. "I could fix up everything by then—and we could be married and go straight into a little cottage somewhere—not in Darroch or Levenford—but perhaps in Garshake."

His idea of a cottage in Garshake cheered them both, and each immediately visioned the quiet, old village that clustered so snugly around an arm of the estuary.

"I could wait for that," Mary replied wistfully, viewing in her mind's eye one of the small, whitewashed cottages of which the village was composed—one smothered in red rambler roses, with a doorway festooned by creeping nasturtiums—in which her baby would mysteriously come into her arms. She looked at Denis and almost smiled.

"I'll not fail you, dear," he was saying. "If you will be brave—and hold out as long as ever you can."

The train was now in the station, and the old woman, the farm servants, and the two workmen were scrambling to their places. She had time only to take a hurried farewell of him as he helped her into a seat, but, as the train began to move, he ran along beside her until the last moment, holding her hand, and before he was forced to let go, she called to him, courageously:

"I'm remembering your motto, Denis, dear!" He smiled and waved his cap bravely, encouragingly, in reply, until the train circled the bend and they were torn from each other's sight.

She was certainly valiant, and now that she knew the worst she was prepared to exercise all her hardihood to achieve her only hope of happiness. Seeing Denis had saved her. He was, and would be, her salvation, and strengthened by the thought that he shared her secret, she now felt fortified to endure anything until he would take her away with him for good. She shuddered at the recollection of her visit to the doctor, but firmly she blotted out from her mind the odious experiences of the last two hours. She would be brave for Denis!

Back again in Levenford she hastened to deliver the letter to Agnes Moir, and discovered to her relief that Agnes had gone upstairs for tea. She therefore left the letter for her at the shop with all Mrs. Brodie's messages of attachment and affection, and escaped, mercifully, without questioning.

As she took the way home she reflected that her mother was sure to discover at a later date her defection in the matter of the parcel, but, involved in a deeper and more serious trouble, she did not care. Let Mamma scold, weep, or bewail, she felt that she had only a few months more until she would be out of a house which she now detested. Every sense within her turned towards the suggestion Denis had tentatively advanced, and in her imagination she consolidated it into actuality; thrusting the thought of her present condition from her, she concentrated her sanguine hopes eagerly upon the cottage she would share with him in Garshake.

VIII

BRODIE sat in his office reading the *Levenford Advertiser*, with the door slightly open so that he could, at infrequent intervals, raise a vigilant eye towards the shop without interfering with the comfortable perusal of his paper. Perry was ill, confined to bed, as his agitated mother had announced to Brodie that morning, from a severe boil which partially prevented his walking and debarred him entirely from sitting down. Brodie had muttered disagreeably that he required his assistant to stand up, not to sit down, but on being assured that the sufferer would certainly be relieved through constant poulticing and be fit for duty in the morning, he had consented with a bad grace to allow him the day off. Now, enthroned on his chair at the top of the row of steps leading to his sanctum, Brodie devoted an almost exclusive attention to the report of the Cattle Show. He was glad that business was quiet this morning and that he was not constrained to lower himself to the menial work of the shop, which he detested, and which was now entirely Perry's obligation. A few moments ago he had been obliged to leave his seat to serve a labouring man who had rolled uncouthly in, and, in his indignation, he had hustled the man out with the first hat he could lay hands on. What did he care, he asked himself, whether or not the thing suited? He couldn't be bothered over these infernal trifles; a thing like that was Perry's job; he wanted to read his paper in peace, like any other gentleman.

With an outraged air he had come back and began again at the opening lines of the report.

"The Levenford and District Annual Cattle Show," he read, "took place on Saturday the 21st inst. and was attended by a large and distinguished gathering." He perused the whole report slowly, carefully, sedulously, until at the finish of the article he came upon the paragraph beginning: "Amongst those present." His eye glimmered anxiously then flared into triumph, as he saw that his name was there! Amongst the distinguished names of the borough and county, towards the end of the list no doubt, but not absolutely at the end, stood the name of James Brodie. He banged his fist triumphantly upon his desk. By Gad! that would show them! Everyone read the *Levenford Advertiser*—which was published once a week, on Friday—and everyone would see his name flourishing there, near to no less a personage than the Lord Lieutenant of the County. Brodie glowed with vanity. He liked the look of himself in print. The capital "J" of the James had a peculiar, arresting curl, and as for his surname—nay his family name—spelt in the correct manner, not with a "y," but with the terminal "ie," he was prouder of this than of all his other possessions together. He cocked his head to one side, never removing his eyes from this arresting name of his. Actually he had read through the wordy report, tantalising himself in its verbosity, simply to find himself living in the public eye through the medium of these two printed words. He gloated over them.

James Brodie! His lips unconsciously formed the words as he rolled them silently over upon his tongue. "You're a proud man, Brodie," he whispered to himself. "Eh! you're proud; and by God! you have reason to be." His eyes blurred with the intensity of his feeling, and the entire list of dazzling personages, with their titles, honours, and distinctions, fell out of focus into one solitary name which seemed indelibly to have stamped its image upon his retina. James Brodie! Nothing seemed to surpass these simple yet suggestive words.

A slight deviation of the current of his ideas caused his nostrils to dilate with resentment at the thought of having been called upon to lower himself in his own eyes, by serving a common workman this very morning. That had been well enough twenty years ago when he was a struggling man forced into business by necessities over which he had no control. But now he had his hired servant to do this work for him. He felt the encounter of this morning a slur upon his name, and a choleric indignation swelled within him at the unfortunate Perry for having failed him.

"I'll boil him," he cried, "the pimply little snipe." He had never been meant for business, that he had always known, but, as he had been compelled to adopt it, he had transmuted its substance into something more appropriate to his name and bearing. He had never considered himself a man of commerce but had, from the first, adopted the part of the impoverished gentleman obliged to live by an unfitting and unbecoming occupation. Yet his very personality had, he felt, strangely dignified that occupation into something worthy of him. It had ceased to be paltry and had become unique. From the outset he had never run after people; they had, indeed, been obliged to whistle to his tune and to meet him in all his foibles and vagaries.

In his early days he had once thrown a man out of his shop for an impolite word; he had startled the town into recognising him; he did not curry favour, but stood bluntly as if to say: "Take me as I am or leave me"; and his anomalous policy had been singularly successful. He had achieved a reputation for rude honesty and downright dealing; the more arbitrary of his maxims were repeated like epigrams in the gossip of the town; amongst the gentry he had been recognised—in the local term—as a "character," and his original individuality had acquired for him their patronage. Yet, the more his personality had unfolded, the more he had disdained the vehicle of its expansion.

He felt himself now a personage, superior to the claims of trade. A vast satisfaction possessed him that he should have attained eminence despite the unworthy nature of his profession. His vast pride could not differentiate between the notoriety he had achieved and the more notable distinction which he desired. He was spurred onward by his success. He wished to make his name resound. "I'll show them," he muttered arrogantly. "I'll show them what I can do."

At that moment someone came into the shop. Brodie looked up in irritation, his lordly glance daring the intruder to demand attention from the compeer of the county's nobility; but curiously, he was not asked to descend. A young man leapt lightly over the counter, mounted the steps, and came into the office, shutting the door behind him. It was Denis Foyle.

Three days ago, when Denis had seen the train take Mary away from him, an avalanche of remorse had fallen upon him and had immediately swept over and engulfed him. He considered that he had acted towards Mary with a cold and cowardly selfishness. The sudden blow to his self-esteem had taken him so completely unawares, that he had, for the moment, forgotten how much he really cared for her. But he did love her; indeed, he realised more maturely, and in her absence, that he craved for her. The burden of her condition lent her, in his more complete consideration, a pathetic appeal which he had previously resisted. If his situation was unpleasant, hers was unbearable, and he had offered nothing in alleviation but a few weak and mawkish condolences. He had writhed inwardly to contemplate what she must now think of his abject and unresourceful timidity, and the realisation that he had no certain access to her to tell her all that he now experienced, to express his contrition and adoration with the utmost fervency, filled him with despair.

For two days he endured these steadily growing feelings, when, suddenly, a definite and extraordinary line of action presented itself to him.

He thought it bold, strong, and daring. In reality it was the reflex of the battery of self-reproaches upon his taut nerves, and although it was merely rash, presumptuous, and foolish, it represented an outlet for his constrained feelings, and he saw in it the opportunity to vindicate himself in his own and in Mary's eyes.

Essentially, it was this urge to justify himself which now moved him, as he stood before Brodie, saying:

"I came in like this, Mr. Brodie, because I thought you mightn't agree to see me otherwise—I'm Denis Foyle of Darroch."

Brodie was astounded at the unexpectedness of this entry and at the audacity it betokened, but he made no sign. Instead he settled himself more deeply in his chair; his head seemed to sink right into the magnitude of his shoulders, like a rock sunk on the summit of a hill.

"Son of the pub keeper?" he sneered.

"Exactly," replied Denis politely.

"Well, Mister Denis Foyle"—he emphasised the mister ironically—"what do you want here?" He began to hope to goad Foyle into an assault, so that he might have the pleasure of thrashing him.

Denis looked straight at Brodie and, disregarding the other's manner, proceeded according to his plan.

"You may be surprised at my visit, but I felt I must come to you, Mr. Brodie. I have not seen your daughter, Miss Mary Brodie, for over three months. She has consistently avoided me. I wish to tell you frankly that I have an attachment for your daughter, and have come to ask your permission to allow me to see her."

Brodie gazed upwards at the young man with a heavy mask-like face which permitted nothing to penetrate of the tide of rising amazed anger he felt at the other's demand. After a moment's lowering stare at Foyle, he said, slowly: "I am glad to hear from your own lips I have been obeyed! My daughter has refused to see you because I forbade her to look at ye! Do ye hear me. I forbade her, and now that I've seen what ye are I still forbid her."

"Why, Mr. Brodie, may I ask?"

"Must I explain my actions to you? The fact that I order it is enough for my daughter. I do not explain to her, I command."

"Mr. Brodie, I should be glad to know your objection to me. I should do my best to meet you in any way you desired." With all his power Foyle tried to propitiate the other. "I'm very anxious to please you! Let me know what to do and I'll do it."

Brodie fleered at him:

"I want ye to take your smooth face out o' my office and never show it in Levenford again; and the quicker ye do't the better ye'll please me."

With a deprecating smile Foyle replied:

"Then it's only my face you object to, Mr. Brodie." He felt he must win the other round somehow!

Brodie was beginning to become enraged; the fact that he could not beat down this young sprig's eyes, nor yet provoke him to temper, annoyed him. With an effort he controlled himself and said, sneeringly:

"I'm not in the habit of exchanging confidences with your kind, but as I have a moment to spare, I will tell you what I object to. Mary Brodie is a lady, she has blood in her veins of which a duchess might be proud, and she is my daughter. You are a low-down Irish scum, a nothing out of nothing. Your father sells cheap drink, and I've no doubt your forebears ate potato peelings out o' the pot."

Denis still met his eyes unflinchingly, although the insults quivered inside him. Desperately he forced himself to be calm. "The fact that I am Irish surely does not condemn me," he replied in a level voice. "I don't drink—not a drop. In fact I'm in a totally different line of business, one which I feel will one day bring a great return."

"I've heard about your business, my pretty tatie-picker. Long trips over the countryside, then back to loaf about for days. I know your kind. If ye think that you can make money by hawkin' tea round Scotland then you're stupid, and if ye think ye can make up for your rotten family by takin' up a trashy job like that, then you're mad."

"I wish you would let me explain to you, Mr. Brodie."

Brodie contemplated him savagely.

"Explain to me! You talk like that to me, you damned commercial traveller. Do you know who you're speakin' to? Look!" he roared, flourishing the paper and thrusting it in front of the other. "See this, if you can read! These are the people I associate with——" He inflated his chest and shouted: "I would as soon think of letting my daughter consort with you as I would let her mix with swine."

With a considerable effort Foyle controlled his temper.

"Mr. Brodie," he pleaded. "I wish you would listen to me. Surely you must admit that a man is what he makes himself—that he himself controls his own destiny irrespective of what his parents may be. I am not ashamed of my ancestry, but if that is what you object to, surely it does not damn me."

Brodie looked at the other frowningly.

"Ye dare to talk that damned new-fangled socialism to me!" he roared angrily. "One man is as good as another, I suppose! What are we comin' to next. You fool! I'll have none of ye. Get out!"

Denis did not move. He saw clearly that this man was not amenable to reason; that he might batter his head against a stone wall with more avail; he saw that, with such a father, Mary's life must be a procession of terrifying catastrophes. But, because of her, he determined to maintain his control, and, quite quietly, he said: "I am sorry for you, Mr. Brodie. You belong to an age that is passing; you do not understand progress. And you don't understand what it is to make friends; you must only make enemies. It is not I who am mad!"

Brodie got up, lowering, his rage like that of an angry bull. "Will you get out, you young swine?" he said thickly, "or will I smash you?" He advanced towards the other, heavily. In a second Denis could have been out of the office, but a hidden antagonism had been roused in him by Brodie's insults and, although he knew he ought to go for Mary's sake, nevertheless he remained. Confident that he could take care of himself, he was not afraid of the other's lumbering strength and he realised, too, that if he went now, Brodie would think he had driven him out like a beaten dog. In a voice suffused by resentment he exclaimed:

"Don't touch me! I've suffered your insults, but don't go any further!"

At these words Brodie's anger swelled within him until it almost choked him.

"Will I not, though," he cried, his breath coming in quick noisy gusts. "I've got ye like a rat in a trap, and I'll smash ye like a rat."

With a heavy ferocious stealth he advanced slowly towards the other, carefully manœuvred his towering bulk near to him; then, when he was within a yard of Denis, so near that he knew it was impossible for him to escape, his lips drew back balefully upon his gums, and suddenly he raised his mammoth fist and hurled it with crushing force full at young Foyle's head. A sharp, hard, brittle crack split the air. There had been no head for him to hit; quicker than a lightning flash, Foyle had slipped to one side, and Brodie's hand struck the stone wall with all the power of a sledge-hammer. His right arm dropped inertly to his side; his wrist was broken. Denis, looking at him with his hand on the door knob, said quietly:

"I'm sorry, Mr. Brodie. You see that after all there are some things you do not understand. I warned you not to try anything like that." Then he was gone, and not a moment too soon. The heavy, mahogany, revolving chair, thrown across the room by Brodie's left arm, like a shot from a catapult, crashed against the light door and shivered the glass and framework to atoms.

Brodie stood, with heaving nostrils and dangling arm, staring stupidly at the wreckage. He felt conscious of no pain in his injured arm, only an inability to move it, but his swelling breast was like to burst with defeated fury. The fact that this young pup above everyone had bearded him, and gotten away with it, made him writhe with wounded pride; the physical hurt was nothing, but the damage to his pride was deadly.

The fingers of his left hand clenched convulsively. Another minute, he was certain, he would have cornered him and broken him. But to have been outdone without so much as a blow having been struck against him! Only a faint remnant of self-control and a glimmering of sense prevented him from running blindly into the street after Foyle, in an effort to overtake and crush him. It was the first time in his life that anyone had dared to take the upper hand of him, and he ground his teeth to think that he had been outfaced and outwitted by the effrontery of such a low-born upstart.

"By God!" he shouted to the empty room, "I'll make him pay for it."

Then he looked down at his useless hand and forearm which had already become blue, swollen, and œdematous. He realised that he must have the condition seen to and also that he must invent some story to explain it—some balderdash about having slipped on the stairs, he thought. Sullenly he went out of the shop, banged shut the front door, locked it, and went off.

Meanwhile it had dawned upon Denis, since his departure, that by his rash action he had done incalculable harm to Mary and himself. Before the interview he had imagined that he might ingratiate himself with her father, and so obtain his consent to see her. This, he had assumed, would make it easy for them to arrange the events towards a definite plan of escape. Indeed, he had fondly estimated that Brodie might view him with less disapproval, might even conceive some slight regard for him. To have succeeded in this project would undoubtedly have expedited the course of such sudden steps as they might later be obliged to take, would also have tempered the shock of the subsequent and inevitable disclosure.

He had not then known Brodie. He had frequently considered Mary's delineation of him, but had imagined that her account was perhaps tinged with filial awe, or that her sensitive nature magnified the stature of his odious propensities. Now he fully understood her terror of Brodie, felt her remarks to have erred on the side of leniency towards him. He had a few moments ago seen him in a condition of such unbalanced animosity that he began to fear for Mary's safety; he cursed himself repeatedly for his recent imprudent action.

He was completely at a loss as to what step to take next, when, suddenly, as he passed a stationer's shop in the High Street, it occurred to him that he might write her a letter, asking her to meet him on the following day. He entered the shop and bought a sheet of notepaper and an envelope. Despite his anxiety his power of blandishment remained, and he wheedled the old lady behind the counter to sell him a stamp, and to lend him pen and ink. This she did willingly, with a maternal smile, and whilst he wrote a short note to Mary, she watched him solicitously, out of the corner of her eye. When he had finished he thanked her gracefully and, outside, was about to drop the letter in the pillar-box when a thought struck him, and he withdrew his hand, as if it had been stung. He turned slowly round to the kerb and then, after a moment, at the confirmation of his thought, he tore the letter into small pieces and scattered them in the gutter. He had suddenly realised that if, by chance, this communication were intercepted, Brodie would immediately apprehend that he had wilfully deceived him, that Mary had been meeting him continually and clandestinely. He had made one serious mistake that day and he was determined not to commit another. Buttoning up his jacket tightly, he plunged his hands in his pockets and, with his chin thrust pugnaciously forwards, he walked quickly away. He had decided to reconnoitre the neighbourhood of the Brodie's house.

Unfamiliar with the locality, he became slightly out of his reckoning in the outskirts of the town, but, by means of his general sense of direction, he made a series of detours and at length arrived within sight of Mary's home. Actually he had never seen this house before, and now, as he surveyed it, a feeling of consternation invaded him. It seemed to him more fitted for a prison than a home, and as inappropriate for the housing of Mary's soft gentleness as a dark, confined vault might be for a dove. The squat, grey walls seemed to enclose her with an irrevocable clasp, the steep-angled ramparts implied her subjection, the deep, embrasured windows proclaimed her detention under a constrained duress.

As he surveyed the house, he murmured to himself: "I'll be glad to take her away from there, and she'll be glad to come. That man's not right! His mind is twisted somewhere. That house is like him, somehow!"

With his mind still clouded by apprehension, he wormed himself into a hollow in the hedgerow behind him, sat down on the bank, lit a cigarette, and began to turn over certain projects in his mind. Faced with the imperative necessity of seeing Mary, he began to review mentally a series of impossible plans and incautious designs of achieving the object. He was afraid of making another imprudent blunder, and yet he felt that he must see her at once, or the opportunity would be for ever lost. His cigarette was almost burned out when, suddenly, the stern look vanished from his face, and he smiled audaciously at the obvious simplicity of the excellent expedient which had struck him. Nothing was to prevent him, now, in open daylight, from advancing boldly, and knocking upon the front door. Mary would almost assuredly open the door herself, whereupon he would signify immediately for silence and, after delivering a note into her own hands, leave as urbanely and openly as he had come. He knew enough of the household to understand that, with Brodie at business and little Nessie at school, the only other person who might answer the door would be Mrs. Brodie. If this latter contingency occurred, she did not know him, Brodie would not yet have warned her against him, and he would merely enquire for some fictitious name, and make a speedy and apologetic departure.

Rapidly he tore a leaf out of his pocket-book and scribbled on it, in pencil, a short message, telling her that he loved her and asking her to meet him outside the Public Library on the following evening. He would, for preference, have selected a more secluded meeting-place, but he feared that the only pretext she might advance for leaving the house would be to visit the Library. When he had finished he rolled the paper into a small, neat square, pressed it tight in his palm, and, flicking the dust from his clothing, sprang up. He turned his head briskly towards his objective and had assumed all the ingenuous artlessness of a simple visitor, when all at once his face fell, his brow darkened, and he flung himself violently back into his hiding-place. Coming along the pavement, and approaching the house from the lower end of the road, was Brodie himself, his wrist bandaged, his arm supported by a sling.

Denis bit his lip. Nothing, apparently, went right with him! It was impossible for him to approach the house now, and he realised bitterly that Brodie, in his resentment, would almost certainly caution the household against him, and so jeopardise the chances of utilising his scheme successfully upon another occasion. With a heavy heart he considered, also, that Brodie's anger might react upon Mary, although he had so carefully protected her during his unhappy interview at the shop. He watched Brodie draw nearer, detected with concern that the injured wrist was encased in plaster, observed the thunder blackness of his face. saw him crash open the gate and finally let himself into the house. Denis experienced a strong sense of misgiving. So long as Mary lived beside that monstrous man, and in that monstrous house, he realised that he would never be at rest. Straining his ears for some sound, some cry, some call for help, he waited outside interminably. But there was only silence—silence from behind the cold, grey walls of that eccentric dwelling. Then, finally, he got up and walked dejectedly away.

IX

MARY BRODIE sat knitting a sock for her father. She leaned slightly forward, her face pale and shadowed, her eyes directed towards the long steel needles which flashed automatically under her moving fingers. Click-click went the needles! Nowadays she seemed to hear nothing but that sound, for in every moment of her leisure she knitted. Mamma had decreed sententiously that, as the devil found work more readily for idle hands, Mary must keep hers employed, even in her spare moments, and she had been set the task of completing one pair of socks each week. She was now finishing her sixth pair!

Old Grandma Brodie sat watching, with her lips pursed up as if they had been stitched together. She sat with her withered legs crossed, the pendent foot beating time to the clinking music, saying nothing, but keeping her eyes perpetually fixed upon Mary, inscrutable, seeming to think all manner of things that no one, least of all Mary, could know of. Sometimes, Mary imagined that those bleared, opaque eyes were penetrating her with a knowing, vindictive suspicion, and when her own eyes met them, a spark of antagonism was struck from the stony pupils. She had, of late, felt as if the eyes of the old sibyl were binding some spell upon her which would compel her to move her tired fingers ceaselessly, unwillingly, in the effort to utilise an unending skein of wool.

It was an agreeable diversion for the crone to watch the young girl, but, in addition, it was her duty, the task assigned to her six weeks ago. Her head shook slightly as she recollected that incredible afternoon when her son had come in, with his arm bandaged and his face black as night, remembered the solemn conclave between Brodie and his wife behind the locked door of the parlour. There had been none of the usual bluster, no roaring through the house, only a dour grinding silence! What it had been about she had been unable to guess, but certainly some grave disaster had been in the air. Her daughter-in-law's face had been drawn with fright for days afterwards; her lips had twitched while she had enrolled her as an auxiliary in the watching of Mary, saying only: "Mary's not allowed out of the house. Not a step beyond the front gate. It's an order." Mary was a prisoner, that was all, and she, in effect, the gaoler. Behind the mask of her face she revelled in the thought of it, of this disgrace for Mary. She had never liked the girl, and her occupation now afforded her the deepest gratification and delight.

Her present meditations were interrupted by the entry of Mrs. Brodie. Mamma's eyes sought out Mary.

"Have you turned the heel yet?" she enquired, with a forced assumption of interest.

"Nearly," replied Mary, her pale face unchanging from its set, indifferent apathy.

"You're getting on finely! You'll set your father up in socks for the winter before you've finished."

"May I go out in the garden a minute?"

Mamma looked out of the window ostentatiously. "It's smirring of rain, Mary. I think you better not go just now. When Nessie comes in maybe it'll be off, and you can take her out for a stroll round the back."

Mamma's feeble diplomacy! The will of Brodie, wrapped up in too plausible suggestions, or delivered obviously in the guise of uplifting quotations from Scripture, had pressed round Mary like a net for six weeks, each week of which had seemed like a year—a year with long, long days. So oppressed and weakened in her resistance was she now, that she felt obliged to ask permission for her every action.

"May I go up to my room for a little, then?" she said dully.

"Certainly, Mary! If you would like to read, dear, take this"; and, as her daughter went slowly out of the room, Mrs. Brodie thrust upon her a bound copy of Spurgeon's sermons that lay conveniently ready upon the dresser. But immediately Mary had gone, a glance passed between the two women left in the room, and Mamma nodded her head slightly. Grandma at once got up, willingly forsaking her warm corner by the fire, and hobbled into the parlour, where she sat down at the front window, commanding from this vantage a complete view of anyone who might attempt to leave the house. The constant observation ordained by Brodie was in operation. Yet Mamma had hardly been alone a moment before another thought crossed her mind. She pondered, then nodded to herself, realising this to be a favourable opportunity to execute her husband's mandate, and, holding her skirts, she mounted the stairs, and entered her daughter's room, determined to say a "good word" to Mary.

"I thought I would come up for a little chat," she said brightly. "I havena had a word with you for a day or two."

"Yes, Mamma!"

Mrs. Brodie considered her daughter critically. "Have you seen the light yet, Mary?" she asked slowly.

Mary knew instinctively what was coming, knew that she was to receive one of Mamma's recently instituted pious talks which had made her at first either tearful or rebellious, which had never at any time made her feel better spiritually, and which now merely fell senselessly upon her stoic ears. These elevating discourses had become intolerable during her incarceration and, together with every other form of high-minded exhortation, had been thrust upon her, heaped upon her head like reproaches, at all available opportunities. The reason was not far to seek. At the conclusion of that awful session in the parlour Brodie had snarled at his wife: "She's your daughter! It's your job to get some sense of obedience into her. If you don't, by God! I'll take the strap across her back again—and over yours too."

"Do you feel yourself firm on the rock yet, Mary?" continued Mamma earnestly.

"I don't know," replied Mary, in a stricken voice.

"I can see you haven't reached it yet," Mamma sighed gently. "What a comfort it would be to your father and me if we saw you more abounding in faith, and goodness, and obedience to your parents." She took Mary's passive hand. "You know, my dear, life is short. Suppose we were called suddenly before the Throne in a state of unworthiness—what then? Eternity is long. There is no chance to repent then. Oh! I wish you would see the error of your ways. It makes it so hard for me, for your own mother that has done everything for you. It's hard that your father should blame me for that stiff, stubborn look that's still about ye—just as if ye were frozen up. Why, I would do anything. I would even get the Rev. Mr. Scott himself to speak to you, some afternoon when your father wasna in! I read such a comforting book the other day of how a wayward woman was made to see the light by one of God's own ministers." Mamma sighed mournfully, and after a long impressive pause, enquired:

"Tell me, Mary, what is in your heart now?"

"I wish, Mamma, you'd leave me a little," said Mary, in a low tone. "I don't feel well."

"Then you've no need of your mother, or the Almighty either," said Mamma with a sniff. Mary looked at her mother tragically. She realised to the full the other's feebleness, ineptitude, and impotence. From the very beginning she had longed for a mother to whom she could unbosom her inmost soul, on whom she might have leaned clingingly, to whom she might have cried passionately: "Mother, you are the refuge of my torn and afflicted heart! Comfort me and take my suffering from me! Wrap me in the mantle of your protection and shield me from the arrows of misfortune!"

But Mamma was, alas, not like that. Unstable as water, and as shallow, she reflected merely the omnipresent shadow of another stronger than herself. Upon her lay the heavy shade of a mountain whose ominous presence overcast her limpid nature with a perpetual and compelling gloom. The very tone of this godly conversation was merely the echo of Brodie's irresistible demand. How could she speak of the fear of Eternity when her fear of Brodie dwarfed this into insignificance, into nothingness? For her there was only one rock, and that the adamantine hardness of her husband's furious will. Woe! Woe! to her if she did not cling submissively to that! She was, of course, a Christian woman, with all the respectable convictions which this implied. To attend church regularly on Sundays, even to frequent, when she could escape from her duties, an occasional fervent, week-night meeting, to condemn the use of the grosser words of the vocabulary, such as "Hell" or "Damn," fully justified her claim to godliness; and when, for her relaxation, she read a work of fiction, she perused only such good books as afforded the virtuous and saintly heroine a charming and godly husband in the last chapter, and as afforded herself a feeling of pure and elevated refinement. But she could no more have supported her daughter in this crisis of her life than she could have confronted Brodie in his wrath.

All this Mary comprehended fully.

"Will you not tell me, Mary?" Mamma persisted. "I wish I knew what was goin' on inside that stubborn head of yours!" She was continually in fear that her daughter might be secretly contemplating some discreditable step, which would again arouse Brodie's ungovernable fury. Often in her shuddering anticipation she felt, not only the lash of his tongue, but the actual chastisement with which he had threatened her.

"There's nothing to tell you, Mamma," replied Mary sadly. "Nothing to say to you."

She was aware that, if she had attempted to unburden herself, her mother would have stopped her with one shrill, protesting cry and, with deaf ears, have fled from the room. "No! No! I don't tell me! Not a word more. I won't hear it. It's not decent," Mary could almost hear her crying as she ran. Bitterly she repeated:

"No! I've nothing at all to tell you!"

"But you must think of something. I know you're thinking by the look of you," persisted Mrs. Brodie. Mary looked full at her mother.

"Sometimes I think I would be happy if I could get out of this house and never come back," she said bitterly. Mrs. Brodie held up her hands, aghast.

"Mary!" she cried, "what a thing to say! Ye should be thankful to have such a good home. It's a good thing your father doesna hear ye— he would never forgive such black ingratitude!"

"How can you talk like that," cried Mary wildly. "You must feel as I do about it. This has never been a home to us. Can't you feel it crushing us? It's like part of father's terrible will. Remember I haven't been out of it for six weeks and I feel—oh! I feel broken to pieces," she sobbed.

Mrs. Brodie eyed these tears gratefully, as a sign of submission. "Don't cry, Mary," she admonished; "although ye should be sorry for talking such improper nonsense about the grand place you're privileged to live in. When your father built it 'twas the talk o' Levenford."

"Yes," sobbed Mary, "and so are we. Father makes that so, too. We don't seem like other people. We're not looked on like ordinary people."

"I should think not!" bridled Mrs. Brodie. "We're far and above them."

"Oh, mother," cried Mary, "you would never understand what I mean. Father has frightened you into his own notions. He's driving us, driving us all into some disaster. He keeps us apart from people. We've got no friends. I never had a chance like anybody else; I've been so shut off from everything."

"And a good job, too," interposed Mamma. "It's the way a decent girl should be brought up. You should have been shut off a bit more, by the way you've been goin' on."

Mary did not seem to hear her, but, gazing blindly in front of her, pursued that last thought to its bitter end. "I was shut up in a prison— in darkness," she whispered; "and when I did escape I was dazzled and lost my way." An expression of utter hopelessness spread slowly over her face.

"Don't mumble like that," cried Mamma sharply. "If ye can't speak up honestly to your mother, don't speak at all. The idea! Ye should be thankful to have folks to take care of ye, and keep ye in here out of harm."

"Harm! I haven't done much harm in the last few weeks," echoed Mary, in a flat voice.

"Mary! Mary!" cried Mamma reprovingly, "you should be showing a better spirit. Don't answer so sulkily. Be bright and active, and show more respect and deference to your parents. To think of the low young men of the district running after you should bring the blush of shame to your face. You ought to be glad to stay in to escape from them, and not be always hanging about looking so gloomy. Why! when I think what you're being protected from——" Mamma stopped for very modesty, and shuddered virtuously as she pushed Spurgeon's sermons nearer Mary. Concluding on the highest and most elevated note, she arose and, as she retreated to the door, said significantly: "Have a look at that, my girl. It'll do ye more good than any light talk ye might hear outside." Then she went out, closing the door behind her with a soft restraint which harmonised with the godly thoughts which filled her mind. But Mary did not touch the book that had been so persistently thrust upon her; instead, she looked hopelessly out of the window. Heavy masses of cloud shut out the sky, turning the short October afternoon more quickly towards the night. A soft, insistent rain blurred the window panes; no wind stirred; her three silver birches, bereft of leaves, were silent in a misty, melancholy reverie. She had of late gazed at them so often, that she knew them in every mood, and thought of them as her own. She had seen them shed their leaves. Each leaf had come fluttering down sadly, slowly, like a lost hope, and with each fall Mary had cast away a fragment of her faith. They had been like symbols to her, these three trees, and so long as they had breathed through their living foliage, she had not despaired. But the last leaflet had gone and this evening, like her, they were denuded, enwrapped in cold mist, lost in profound despondency.

Her child was living in her womb. She had felt it throb with an ever increasing surge of life; this throbbing, living child that no one knew of but Denis and herself. She was undiscovered. Concealment, which had at first so much worried her, had not been easy, but now it did not trouble her at all; for, at this moment, her mind was occupied by a deeper and more awful contemplation.

Yet, as she sat so passive by her window, she recollected how the first movement within her had caused her a pang, not of fear, but of sublime yearning. She had been transcended by a swift illumination which lit up the dark spaces of her mind, and a fierce desire for her child had seized her. This desire had, through many dark hours, sustained her fortitude, had filled her with a brave endurance of her present misery. She had felt that she now suffered for the child, that, the more she endured, the more she would be recompensed by its love.

But that seemed a long time ago, before hope had finally left her. She had then still believed in Denis.

Since that afternoon when she had gone to Darroch she had not seen him. Imprisoned in the house by the will of her father, she had lived through these six, unendurable weeks without a glimpse of Denis.

Sometimes she had imagined she had seen his figure lurking outside the house; often, at night, she had felt that he was near; once she had wakened with a shriek to a faint tapping on her window; but now she realised that these had merely been illusions of her disordered fancy, and she was finally convinced that he had deserted her. He had abandoned her. She would never see him again.

She longed for night to come to bring sleep to her. In the beginning of her sorrow she had been unable to rest, then, strangely, she had slept profoundly, with a slumber often pervaded by exquisite dreams, dreams that were filled with an extraordinary felicity. Then she was always with Denis amongst enchanting surroundings, exploring with him a sunlit land of gay, old cities, and mingling with laughing people, living upon strange and exotic foods. These pleasant phantasies, by their happy augury for the future, had at one time cheered and comforted her; but that was past; she sought now no visions of unreality. The sleep which she desired was a dreamless one. She had resolved to kill herself. Vividly she remembered her words to him on Darroch Station, when she had, with an unconscious, dreadful foreboding, told what she would do if he deserted her. Her only refuge lay in death. Unknown to anyone she had concealed in her room a packet of salts of lemon which she had removed from the high shelf above the wash-tubs in the scullery. To-night she would go to bed in the usual way and, in the morning, they would find her dead. The living child that had never breathed would be dead too, she realised, but that was the best thing that could happen. Then they would bury her with her unborn child in the wet earth and she would be finished and at peace. She got up and opened a drawer. Yes! it was there safely. With calm fingers she opened slightly one end of the white packet and gazed at the harmless appearance of the contents within. Unconsciously, she reflected how strange it was that these inert, innocent crystals should be so full of deadly potentiality; yet she was aware that they held no menace for her, but only a benign succour. They would enable her with a single, quick motion to escape from the hopeless, cumulative bondage of her existence and, when she swallowed them, she would drain in one final, convulsive gulp the last bitter dregs of life itself. Tranquilly, she reflected that at bed-time she must bring up water in a cup to dissolve the crystals.

She replaced the packet, closed the drawer, and, returning to the window, sat down and began again to knit. She would finish the sock to-night for her father. As she thought of him she had no active emotion towards him—everything within her was passive, as though her feelings had already died. He never spoke to her. His arm was healed. His life went on unchanged and, even after she was dead, would go on unchanged, with the same unfailing regularity, in the same proud indifference, smoothed by the same adulation and cringing subservience from Mamma.

She stopped knitting for a moment and glanced out of the window. Nessie was coming in from school. Compassion invaded her for her small, susceptible sister who had been at first infected with her misery. She would be sorry to leave Nessie. Poor Nessie! She would be all alone! Strangely, however, the diminutive figure did not enter the gate, but instead, stood in the gathering dusk making a peculiar, determinate sign. It was not Nessie, but another small girl who, posted indomitably in the rain, waved her arm upwards with a significant, yet hidden intention. Mary looked at her fixedly, but as she did so the movements ceased, and the little puppet moved away. Two people then came into view and passed out of sight down the road, leaving it void and black as before. A sigh burst from Mary, expressive of the dispersion of a dim, unborn hope; she rubbed her eyes vaguely and covered them dumbly with her hands.

She removed her hands, and immediately again viewed the child waving more emphatically, more appealingly than before. She stared uncomprehendingly, then, feeling that she must be the victim of some strange hallucination of her disordered senses, expecting the phenomenon to vanish as instantaneously and magically as it had appeared, slowly, unbelievingly, she opened her window and looked out. Immediately, out of the dim obscurity, a round object, thrown with unerring accuracy, struck her upon the shoulder and dropped with a soft thud at her feet, whilst at the same instant the street became vacant and empty. Mechanically, Mary closed the window and sat down again. She would have dismissed the whole episode as a delusion of her tired brain but for the fact that upon the floor lay the missile which had impinged upon her out of the gathering darkness, like a small innocuous meteor falling from the invisible sky. She looked at the round object more closely. It was an apple.

She stooped and retrieved the apple, which felt smooth and polished and warm, as if for a long time it had been harboured in hot, human hands, and as she held it in her small palm, she scarcely knew why she should have abandoned her knitting for the contemplation of so absurd an object. It was, she recognised—of the pippin variety—a King Pippin—and immediately there flashed across her memory a remark once made to her by Denis: "We're fond of apples at home," he had said; "we always have a barrel of King Pippins standing in the pantry." At this sudden thought, from merely looking perplexedly at the apple, she began to inspect it closely, and discovered, to her surprise and growing agitation, a faint circular cut made necessarily by a fine blade, encircling the entire core. Her wan cheeks flooded with a high, nervous colour as she plucked at the short dried stem which was still adherent to the apple, but they paled instantly, and the blood drained from her face, as a neat round plug of the firm, white fruit came away easily in her grasp, revealing a hollowed-out centre which was packed tightly with a roll of thin paper. With frantic haste and a pitiful agitation her nervous fingers fumblingly extracted and unrolled the cylinder, then, suddenly, the action of her fluttering heart almost ceased. It was a letter from Denis! He had written to her. He had not abandoned her. Her wild, incredulous eyes fastened themselves avidly upon this letter which had reached her with all the timely mercy of a reprieve. Feverishly she read on, saw that it had been written almost a fortnight previously, that it addressed her in most fervent terms. A great joy came upon her like a full, dazzling light suddenly turned upon her, blinding her by its unexpectedness, warming her with its radiance. The words of the letter shone before her eyes, their meaning flooded her like a glow of heat penetrating a chilled and icy body. She had been mad to doubt him. He was Denis—her Denis—and he loved her!

He loved her, had tried with all his power to reach her, had attempted, even, to place a message through her window by night. She saw now that she had been right in feeling that he was near to her, but her foolish cry of fear had driven him away. Still, nothing mattered in the face of his wonderful news. Her heart beat as she read that he had taken their house—the cottage in Garshake. They could move into it upon the first of January. It was called Rosebank—in summer a bower of roses, in winter a warm, safe haven to enclose them both. He was doing all that lay within his power, and he was not afraid! She was touched beyond measure at his endeavours, at what he had done for her. How he had worked for her! He would have come to her openly, but for the fact that their plans were not mature. They must have a roof to cover them, a house to shelter them, before they could take any drastic step; until then, he must be wary for her sake. Yes! she must wait—wait a little longer; wait until his last summer trip of the year was over, until he could devote himself to her. Then he would take her away with him for ever, care for her, and look to her safety and comfort. Her eyes grew dim with tears of happiness as she read his promises to cherish her. Could she wait? She must wait. She could endure anything, so long as he took her to him in the end.

When she had finished the letter, for a moment she remained quite still, as though the shock of unexpected happiness had petrified her into stone and she sat like a marble effigy, rigid and motionless. Then, slowly, a pulsating essence flowed through her veins; mysterious currents, set in motion by the moving words of his letter, circulated in her being; after what had been an eternity of death-like inanition she lived and, as in an awakening Galatea, a tinge of life pervaded her, colour rushed into her face, her body, her limbs. Her eyes sparkled eagerly with the joy of living, her constrained lips parted softly, fervidly, and the sad immobility of her face was transfigured by a rush of sanguine joy. Like a watcher forgotten upon some solitary isle, who, worn with an endless, fruitless vigil, has long abandoned hope, the sudden sight of the means of her rescue filled her with an unbelievable, almost unbelieving ecstasy. The loud beating of her reawakened heart sang in her ears with a rapturous refrain; the pale hands holding the letter became animate, vitalised, and active; eagerly the fingers seized a pencil that lay near and wrote urgently on the reverse side of the paper.

It was a short note, saying that she was well and, now that she had heard from him, happy. She said nothing of the tortures of mind she had suffered, or of the abyss into which she had been sinking. She told him she would abide gladly in her present home if only he came for her in December, and she blessed him repeatedly for his letter. She had not time to write more, for, outside the house, in the rapidly fading light, she discerned that the patient, tenacious figure of the child had again reappeared, and was gazing expectantly towards the window. It was Rose—it must be Rose—that small devoted sister he had spoken of. She blessed Rose! And now, replacing the message in the hollow apple, she raised the window sash and, throwing with all her strength, watched the sphere go sailing through the air and bound twice upon the road before coming to rest. Dimly she glimpsed Rose running to recover it, saw her extract the letter and place it in her coat pocket, observed her wave her hand significantly, triumphantly, and, as if to symbolise the sweetness of her triumph, go off down the road, exultantly munching the bruised and battered pippin. A quiver of grateful admiration ran through Mary as the small figure passed out of sight, marching indomitably with the same invincible air, the same jaunty courage as Denis. A slight smile of recollection moved her as she remembered Rose's careless touch upon the piano. The folly of judging the intrepid messenger by the execution of those scales!

And now Mary arose and stretched her limbs luxuriously. She raised her arms above her head in an attitude of unconscious aspiration and whilst her figure seemed to draw itself upwards, her head fell back, her throat grew taut. As she gazed towards heaven, her face filled with a supreme thanksgiving, which seemed insensibly to pass into an invocation for the future. She was alive again, brave, filled with new hope, new courage. Little pricking streams ran through her skin. Suddenly, as she lowered her arms and again relaxed her body, she felt hungry. For weeks she had eaten nothing but the insipid, choking mouthfuls thrust down at meal times under the eye of her father, and the delicious return of the zest to live now made her voracious.

Within her body the unformed child leapt and throbbed, as if in sympathy and gratitude for the reprieve which had been granted to it.

And Mary, feeling the weak impotence of that thankful impulse, was moved with a sudden pity. In the revulsion of her feeling she turned quickly, in a passion of self-reproach, to the drawer where she had concealed the salts of lemon, and lifting the packet in a frenzy of disgust, concealed it in her hand and hastened downstairs. As she hurried past the half-open door of the parlour, she saw old Grandma Brodie nodding drowsily, and she realised happily that Rose had not been observed, that for once the sentinel slept at her post. Quickly she went through the kitchen and entered the scullery where, with a feeling of aversion, she thrust the contents of the packet, not back upon its shelf, but into the sink, where a rapid stream from the tap washed it away from her for ever. Then, with a new freedom, she went to a cupboard, poured out a glass of milk and cut herself a thick wedge of cold steamed pudding left over from dinner. The pudding was luscious and full of soft, sweet currants; her teeth bit into it with a sapid relish. The milk tasted like a draught of some rich nectar, cool as the froth from melting snow-flakes. She was prolonging her meal as long as possible, by sipping slowly and nibbling the last crust of pudding, when her mother entered the scullery. Mamma looked at Mary curiously.

"You're hungry?" she remarked. "I wish I could eat like that. The sermons have improved your appetite."

"Let me cut you a piece of this, Mamma."

"No! we're to have it heated up to-morrow. It doesn't matter about me."

By her attitude Mrs. Brodie conveyed that Mary was selfish to consume the pudding, that she herself would have desired it, but that she was deliberately sacrificing her personal gratification in the interests of the common good. Mary looked apologetic. With the first mouthful she had enjoyed for weeks she had been made to feel greedy.

"I'm glad to see you in a better frame of mind, anyway," said Mamma, noting the look. "Keep it up for your father to-night. I want him to see I've been speaking to you."

Here a light step sounded in the hall. This time it was, in reality, Nessie, who came in gaily, glistening like a young seal from the rain.

"It's awfully wet now," she cried; "and I want a piece and jelly."

Her mother looked at her fondly. "Ye've a braw colour on your cheeks, dear. That's the way I like my bairns to look; not white and miserable." This was a veiled hint to Mary, and as a further reproof to her elder daughter, Mamma gave Nessie, as a treat, not bread and jelly, but white bread with butter and carraway seeds spread upon it.

"Carvie! Lovely!" cried Nessie; "and I deserve it. Oh! Mary, you do look better to-night yourself. I'm glad! You'll soon be bonny like me," she added with a giggle, inconsequently twirling about.

"Why do you deserve it, pettie?" queried Mamma.

"Well!" replied Nessie importantly, "we had the school inspector this afternoon, and the whole junior school had what he called a memory test, and who do you think was first?"

"Who?" demanded Mamma, with bated breath.

"Me!" shrieked Nessie, waving her bread and carvie.

"My word!" said Mamma, "your father will be pleased." She looked at Mary, as if to say: "That's the kind of daughter I prefer." Actually she was not in the least exultant at the scholastic success. What delighted her was that she had, in this achievement, a tangible asset to put the lord and master of the house in a complacent frame of mind.

Mary looked at Nessie tenderly, feeling how near she had been to leaving her for ever.

"That was just splendid!" she said, and placed her cheek lovingly against her sister's cold, wet face.

X

A STILLNESS lay over Levenford. Sunday afternoon was always quiet; the morning bells had then rung themselves out; the bustle of the shops and the noise of shipyards were hushed; no step echoed in the empty street; the people, sunk in the lethargy produced by a heavy dinner following a long sermon, sat indoors, stiffly trying to read, or slept uncomfortably in their chairs.

But this afternoon was unusually still. A dull, yellow sky pressed down upon the town and imprisoned it in a vault of heavy silence. Within this vault the stagnant air was difficult to breathe and filled the lungs with a sense of vitiation. The streets seemed narrowed, the houses nearer to each other, and the Winton and Doran Hills, usually so majestic and remote, were low and close at hand as if, cowering from the encroaching sky, they crept in upon the town for protection. The trees stood petrified in the sultry air, their stripped branches dropping like stalactites in a cave. No birds were to be seen. Desolate and depopulated, the landscape lay in such an oppressive silence as might precede a battle, and the deserted town, empty of life and movement, stood like a beleaguered city fearfully awaiting the onset of an attack.

Mary sat upstairs at her bedroom window. Now, at every opportunity, she stole away to her room, finding in that retreat alone, a sanctuary in which she obtained solitude and refuge. She felt ill. In church that morning an intolerable sickness had seized her, and during dinner she had been compelled to remain quiescent and uncomplaining while her head and body ached incessantly. Now, as she sat with her chin cupped in both hands, looking out upon the strange immobility of the land, she wondered if it lay within her power to last out the next two days.

With a faint shudder, she reviewed in her mind her struggles of the past eight weeks. In his first note Denis had asked her to wait only until the middle of December, but it was now the twenty-eighth day of that month, and she had still to endure the torture of her life at home for another two days. It was, she realised, not his fault. He had been obliged to extend the scope of his business activities in the North and was now acting for his firm in Edinburgh and Dundee. They were pleased with his work; the delay was in actuality advantageous; but at present she found it hard to bear.

Only two more days! Then with Denis beside her in their snug, strong cottage by the Garshake shore—a fastness to enclose them both—she could face anything. She had visioned their cottage so continuously that it stood always firm, white, and steadfast in her mind, like a beacon, a shining emblem of protection, drawing her towards its safety. But she was losing faith in her ability to continue the struggle against the growing lassitude of her body and the ever-present dread of discovery.

She was, in effect, seven and a half months pregnant, but her fine, firm body had, until lately, retained its shape adequately. She had grown more mature, and paler in her face, but no gross distortion in her form had taken place, and any alteration in her appearance had been attributed to the effects of the more rigid discipline to which she had been subjected. But recently, she had been obliged to lace herself more tightly, and to strain to hold her back and shoulders erect in order to maintain, in the face of greater difficulty, and with unceasing effort, the semblance of her natural figure. The cramping grip of her corset almost stifled her, but she was now compelled to suffer this continually, to sit passively under the cold eye of Brodie whilst she felt her child turn protestingly under the unnatural restraint, and to preserve in the face of everything an aspect of unconcern and tranquillity.

She imagined, too, that of late, in spite of her every precaution, Mamma had entertained a vague uneasiness regarding her. Frequently she had looked up to intercept a doubting, questioning glance levelled acidly at her. Faint unformed suspicions, she realised, moved like latent shadows in her mother's mind, and only the preposterous nature of their purport had hitherto prevented them from assuming a more definite shape.

The last three months had dragged past more slowly and more fearfully than all the years of her life which had preceded them, and now, with the climax imminent and relief at hand, her strength seemed to be leaving her. To-day, a numb pain in her back added to her distress, and at intervals small, sweeping waves of suffering traversed her. As the memory of all that she had endured rose poignantly before her, a tear splashed down her cheek.

This quiet movement, the coursing of a tear-drop upon her face which disturbed her sad, statuesque passivity, had its counterpart in nature. Whilst she gazed, the front gate, which had all day hung half-open upon its listless hinges, was impelled into sluggish motion, and swung slowly shut with a loud clang, as though an invisible hand had negligently pushed it. A moment later, a heap of dead leaves which lay in the far corner of the courtyard, stirred, and a handful eddied, raised themselves spirally upwards on the air with a sighing susurrus, then subsided and were still.

Mary viewed both of these movements with a sensation of disturbance; perhaps her state induced such disquiet, for they had been in themselves insignificant, but the contrast of the sudden, unwarranted movements against the close, imperturbable quiet of the day was starkly arresting. The hush outside deepened, whilst the brassy sky grew more sombre and crept lower to the earth. As she sat, quiescent, awaiting another surge of pain, the front gate again swung gently open, hesitated, and recoiled with a more resounding concussion than before; the long, drawn-out noisy creak of the opening gate came to her like an interrogation and the quick-following clang like an abrupt and decisive reply. A faint ripple undulated across the field which lay opposite and the long grasses ruffled like smoke; under her staring eyes, a wisp of straw lying in the roadway was suddenly whisked high into the air and flung far out of sight by an unseen and inexplicable force. Then the silent air was filled with a soft, quick pattering, and a mongrel dog came racing down the street, its sides panting, its ears laid back flat, its eyes cowering. With a startled curiosity Mary marked its stricken aspect, and asked herself the reason for its haste and terror.

The answer to her unspoken question came like a sigh from a long way off, a low-pitched hum which swept in from beyond the Winton Hills, and echoed around the house. It encircled the grey walls, twisted sinuously through the embrasures of the parapet, whirled amongst the chimneys, spun around the solemn, granite balls, dwelt an instant at Mary's window, then receded in a gradual diminuendo, like the roar of a defeated wave upon a shingle shore. A long silence ensued, then the sound returned, swelling in from the distant hills more loudly, remaining longer than before, and retreating more slowly to a vantage point less remote.

At the end of this last, shivering drone the door of the bedroom opened, and Nessie came precipitately in. "Mary, I'm frightened," she cried. "What's t!.at noise? It's like a great, big, humming-top."

"It's nothing but the wind."

"But there's no wind at all. Everything's as quiet as the grave—and what a colour the sky is! Oh! I'm feared of it, Mary."

"There's going to be a storm, I think, but don't worry, you'll be all right, Nessie."

"Oh! dearie me," cried Nessie, with a shiver, "I hope there'll be no lightning. I'm that scared of it. If it hits you they say it burns you up, and if you sit near steel that attracts it more than anything."

"There's not a steel thing in the room," Mary reassured her.

Nessie came closer.

"Let me stay with you a little," she entreated; "you seem to have been far away from me lately. If ye let me bide with you that sound will not seem so fearsome." She sat down and placed her thin arm around her sister; but instinctively Mary drew away.

"There you are again! You won't even let me touch you. You don't love me like you used to," Nessie grieved, and, for a moment, it looked as though she would rise and go out in childish pique. Mary sat silent; she could not justify her action, but she took Nessie's hand and pressed it gently. Partly reassured by this gesture, Nessie's hurt expression faded and she pressed Mary's hand in return. Thus, hand in hand the two sisters looked out silently upon the panting earth.

The atmosphere had now become dry and rare, and infused with an acrid, saline character which irritated the nostrils like brine. The dun sky had darkened to a blackish purple, meeting the near horizon like smoke, blotting out distant objects and throwing into strange relief those that were near. The sense of increasing isolation from the outer world thus produced was terrifying to Nessie. She gripped Mary's hand more tightly as she cried: "These clouds are coming on top of us. It's like a big black wall. Oh! I'm feared of it. Will it fall on us?"

"No, dear," whispered Mary, "it can't hurt us." But the dark, enclosing barrier still advanced, and upon its summit streaks of lighter saffron lay, like spume upon the crest of a breaking comber. Against this background the three birch trees had lost their soft, silvery mobility; stiff and livid, they gripped the soil more tenaciously with their sinewy roots, their stems standing straight, with closely furled branches, like masts awaiting oppressively the batter of a hurricane.

From amongst the now hidden hills came a secret mutter like the tattoo of muffled drums. It seemed as if it rolled along the crests of the hill-tops, bounding down the ravines, across the streams and up the gulleys, the close following notes chasing each other with a frantic revelry.

"That's thunder," shivered Nessie. "It's like guns firing."

"It's a long way off," Mary comforted her. "It may pass over us without breaking here."

"I feel it's going to be a terrible storm. Will we both go to Mamma, Mary?"

"You go if you like," replied Mary, "but you're just as safe here, dear."

The thunder drew nearer. It ceased to rattle continuously, and instead pealed brokenly; but now each peal was loud as an explosion, and each succeeding explosion more violent than the one before. This ominous quality of approach conveyed to Nessie the impression that she was the focus of some blind, celestial fury, which was surely converging upon her, and would ultimately destroy her.

"I'm sure it'll get us," she gasped. "Oh! there's the lightning."

An ear-splitting crash accompanied the first flash of lightning, a thin, blue streak which darted raggedly across the dead sky, as if the detonation of the thunder had suddenly cracked the bowl of the firmament, allowing, for one quivering instant, a dazzling and unearthly light to penetrate.

"It's forked!" cried Nessie. "That's more dangerous than sheet. Come away from the window!"; she tugged at Mary's arm.

"You're as safe here as anywhere," Mary repeated.

"Oh! it's no good saying that. This room of yours gets the worst of it! I'm going away to Mamma. I'll put my head below the blankets in her room till that awful lightning stops. Come away or you'll be struck"; and she rushed out of the room in a panic.

Mary did not follow her but continued to watch the growing storm alone. She felt like a lonely watcher in a tower, obsessed by pain and danger, for whose diversion a gigantic tourney was waged by nature's forces. The discord which raged outside was a drastic anodyne, which served to distract her from her increasing pain, the pangs of which seemed to her to be slowly intensifying. She was glad to be alone once more, glad that Nessie had left her. It was easier for her to suffer in solitude. The thunder fulminated wildly, and the lightning cascaded like fluid across the sky with a blinding intensity. Often, the onset of her pain would synchronise with a flash, and then she felt that she, a speck within the universe, was linked by the chain of light to this titanic upheaval of the heavens.

As the distracting influence of the storm upon her failed, the disturbance ceased to be palliative; she began, involuntarily, to interpret it in terms of her bodily suffering, and became herself involved in the tumult around her. The rolling waves of thunder lifted her in their upward sweep, and carried her off upon their undulating echoes, until, suddenly, a violet lightning flash would stab her with pain, and cast her down again upon the ground. When the thunder failed, the wind, which had been rapidly increasing in volume, swept her back again into the midst of the chaos. This wind especially frightened Mary, began, indeed, to terrify her. The first soughing onset and retreat which had whirled the leaves then left them motionless, had been but the prelude to a series of deeper and more powerful attacks. Now there was no retreat, and with crushing vigour the full force of the blast struck the land. Mary felt the strong, stout house tremble to its foundations, as though an infinity of tearing fingers were rending each stone from its bed of mortar. She saw her own trees whipped downwards, like drawn bows bent double under some prodigious strain; with each gust they bent, then, liberated, again sprang upwards with a twanging sound. The arrows they released were invisible, but they penetrated Mary's room as shafts of pain. The long grasses in the field were no longer gently ruffled, but were flattened as though a gigantic scythe had decimated them. Each fierce blast of the gale battered at the windows, rattling them in their frames, then rushed howling around the house, with all the uncouth demons of sound loosed and rampant upon its wings.

'Then the rain began. It fell at first in heavy, solitary gouts whicn stained the wind-swept pavements with spots each as large as a crown piece. Faster and faster came the drops, until a solid sheet of water deluged the earth. Water splashed upon the open roadways, hissed and dripped from the roofs and gutters of houses, spattered against trees, flattened shrubs and bushes by its very density and weight. Water flooded everything. The gutters were at once filled to overflowing and ran like torrents; the streets became watercourses, and running streams, filled with floating debris, sluiced along the main thoroughfares.

With the commencement of the rain the lightning gradually ceased, the thunder passed over, and the air chilled perceptibly; but the storm, instead of abating, grew more violent with every moment. The wind gained velocity. Mary heard it drive the rain in waves, like sea surf, upon the roof of the house, then she faintly heard a snap and saw the flag-staff, riven from the turret, fall clattering to the ground.

At this she got up, and began to pace up and down the room, hardly able to endure the racking ache which now seemed continually an element of her being. She had felt nothing of the kind before, nothing to equal this in all her life. She wondered, uncertainly, if she should ask her mother for some remedy, thinking that a hot application might perhaps do good, but, reluctantly, she abandoned the idea as dangerous. She did not know that such an antidote would have been ineffectual, for, although she had no apprehension of her condition, she was already advanced in the throes of a premature labour. Like the untimely dark-ness of the premature night which now began to fall upon the outraged earth, this precipitate travail had already, and too soon, begun to lay its mantle of suffering upon her. The mental hardships she had undergone were demanding an undreamed of toll, which she could not escape, and she had now, in all her unpreparedness, unconsciously begun to solve the dreadful mystery of the nativity of her child.

By this time she felt that it was impossible for her to go downstairs for tea, and, in despair, she loosened her corset, and began again to pace up and down the narrow confines of her room. Between these pacings she stopped, supporting her body between her open palms. She dis-covered that it was easier for her to meet the paroxysms in a stooping posture and, from time to time, she stood crouching against the end of her bed, her forehead pressed downwards against the cold metal of the rails.

As she remained heedlessly like this, in one of these spasms, suddenly the door opened, and her mother entered the room. Mrs. Brodie had come to satisfy herself that Mary had suffered no ill effects from the storm, and to reprimand her for not taking greater precautions, for Nessie had run to her with the story that lightning was striking into the room. She was herself terrified by the tempest, and her overstrung nerves were quiveringly set for an outburst of recrimination. But now, as she stood, unobserved, regarding her daughter, the rebuke that lay half-formed upon her lips remained unuttered. Her jaw dropped slowly, she gasped, whilst the room, rocked by the fury of the wind, seemed to oscillate about her. Mary's abandonment, her relaxed attitude, the profile of her unrestrained figure, plucked at the instrument of the mother's memory and touched a hidden chord in her mind, bringing back suddenly the unforgettable remembrance of her own travail. An illuminating flash, more terrible than any lightning stroke, pierced her understanding. All the latent, the unthought of and unthinkable misgivings, which had been dormant within her, bounded before her in one devastating conviction. The pupils of her eyes dilated into pools of horror and, clutching her shrunken bosom with her left hand, she raised her right drunkenly, and pointed her finger at Mary.

"Look—look at me!" she stammered.

With a start Mary turned and, her brow dewed with perspiration, looked at her mother dumbly. Immediately the mother knew, knew inexorably, and Mary saw that she was discovered. Instantly a shriek burst from Mrs. Brodie like the cry of an outraged animal. Higher and more piercing than the wind it shrilled inside the room, and echoed screechingly through the house. Again, and again, she shrieked, lost in the grasp of hysteria. Blindly, Mary clutched at her mother's dress.

"I didn't know, Mamma," she sobbed. "Forgive me. I didn't know what I was doing."

With short, stabbing blows Mrs. Brodie thrust Mary from her. She could not speak; her breath came stertorously from her in panting spasms.

"Mamma! dear Mamma! I understood nothing! I didn't know I was wicked. Something's hurting me now. Help me!" she begged her.

The mother found her tongue with difficulty.

"The disgrace! Your father!" she moaned. "Oh! it's a nightmare. I'm not awake."

She screeched again, madly. Mary was terrified; this outcry imprisoned her in a cell o iniquity; she heard in each scream the wide broadcast of her disgrace.

"Oh! please, Mamma, don't call out like that," implored Mary, her head hanging abjectly; "only stop, and I'll tell you everything."

"No! No!" shrieked Mamma. "I'll hear nothing! Ye'll have to face your father. I'll be party to nothing. I'm not responsible. It's only yourself to blame."

Mary's limbs trembled violently. "Dear Mamma! is there no excuse for me?" she whispered. "I was so ignorant."

"Your father will kill ye for this," screamed Mrs. Brodie. "It's your fault."

"I implore you, Mamma," pleaded Mary feverishly, "not to tell father. Help me for two days more—only two days"—she cried desperately, trying to bury her head on her mother's breast—"dear, kind Mamma. Keep it between us till then. Only two days more! Please— Oh! please!"

But again her mother, terrified beyond reason, thrust her off and cried out wildly:

"You must tell him at once. I'm no' to blame. Oh! the wickedness of ye to get us into such trouble. Oh! the wickedness, the wickedness!"

Then, with a bitter finality, Mary realised that it was hopeless to entreat her mother further. A great fear descended on her and, with it, the rushing desire to escape. She felt that if she left her, Mamma might recover her control. She desired urgently to get out of the room, and pushing past her mother, she began hastily to descend the stairs. But when she was half-way down, suddenly she raised her head and saw at the foot of the staircase, standing in the hall, the heavy figure of her father.

Brodie had the custom, every Sunday afternoon after dinner, of resting. He went with the regularity of clockwork into the parlour, closed the door, drew the curtains, removed his frock coat, and laid his ponderous bulk down upon the sofa, where he slept heavily for two or three hours. But to-day he had been disturbed by the storm, and he had slept only in snatches, which was worse than not sleeping at all. The loss of his sleep had aggravated him, rendering his temper sour, and, in addition, he took it as a matter of great annoyance to his sense of order that his time-honoured ritual should have been deranged in such an outrageous fashion. The culmination of his vexation had been achieved when he had been aroused from a snatch of sleep by the fall of the flagstaff from his house. He was in a flaming rage and, as he stood in his shirt-sleeves, looking at Mary, his upturned face reflected the bitter resentment of his mood.

"Have we not enough noise outside that you must start that infernal din upstairs?" he shouted. "How can a man sleep with such a fiendish blattering in his ears? Who was making that noise? Was it you?" He glared at her.

Mamma had followed Mary, and now stood swaying upon the top landing, rocking herself to and fro, with her arms clasped upon her breast. Brodie turned his inflamed eye upon her.

"This is a braw house for a man to rest in," he flared. "Do I not work hard enough for ye through the week? What is this day made for, will ye tell me? What's the use of all that godly snivellin' talk of yours if ye must go and ring our ears like this. Can I not lay down for a minute without this damned wind howlin', and you howlin' like a hyena too?"

Mrs. Brodie did not reply but still swayed hysterically at the top of the stairs.

"What are you going on about? Are you gone silly?" bawled Brodie. "Has the thunder turned your reason to make ye stand like a drunken fish wife?"

Still she was silent, and it then dawned upon him, from her manner, that some disaster had occurred.

"What is it?" he shouted roughly. "Is it Nessie? Has the lightning hit her? Is she hurt?"

Mamma shook her whole body in a frantic negation—the catastrophe was worse than that!

"No! No!" she gasped. "It's her—her!" She raised her hand accusingly against Mary. Not even the most shadowy instinct of protection was in her. Her terror of Brodie in this awful calamity was so unbounded that her only impulse was to disclaim all responsibility, all knowledge of the crime. She must at all costs defend herself from any charge of liability in the matter.

"For the last time," raged Brodie, "I ask ye what it is. Tell me, or by God I'll come up to ye both."

"It wasn't my fault," cringed Mrs. Brodie, still shielding herself from the undelivered charge, "I've brought her up always like a Christian girl. It's her own natural badness." Then, realising that she must tell or be beaten, she strained her body to the utmost, threw her head back and, as if each word cost her an unbearable effort of ejaculation, sobbed: "If you must know. She's going—she's going to have a child."

Mary stiffened, whilst the blood drained from her face. Her mother, like Judas, had betrayed her. She was lost—trapped—her father below, her mother above.

Brodie's great frame seemed to shrink imperceptibly; his bellicose eyes became faintly bemused, and, in a muddled fashion, he looked at Mary.

"What wha'——" he muttered. He raised his eyes uncomprehendingly to Mamma, saw her frantic plight, and again lowered his gaze upon Mary. He paused, whilst his mind grappled with the inconceivable, unfathomable news. Suddenly he shouted: "Come here!"

Mary obeyed. Each step she took seemed to lower her into her own tomb. Brodie seized her roughly by the arm and looked her up and down. A sickening feeling went through him. "My God!" he repeated to himself, in a low tone. "My God! I believe it's true. Is it?" he cried thickly. Her tongue lay mutely in her mouth from shame. Still holding her arm he shook her unmercifully, then, releasing her suddenly, allowed her to recoil heavily upon the floor.

"Are you with child? Tell me quickly or I'll brain you," he shouted.

As she told him, she thought he would surely kill her. He stood there looking at her as if she were a viper that had stung him. He raised his arm as if to strike her, to crush her skull with one blow of his hammer fist, to wipe out with one blow her obliquity and his dishonour. He wanted to strike her, to trample on her, grind her under the heels of his boots into a mangled, bloody pulp. A vast brutal passion seethed in him. She had dragged his name into the mire. The name of Brodie! She had lowered his heritage into the slime of ill-fame. The whole place would reek of it. He would see the smirks, the sneers, the significant nods as he strode down the High Street; at the Cross he would hear the stray word of mockery and the half-muffled laugh of derision. The niche he had cut and was still carving for himself would be shattered, the name, the reputation he had made for himself would be ruined, and he himself cast downwards in contumely through this thing that lay weeping at his feet. But he did not strike her. The intensity of his feeling burned suddenly into a heat which turned his gross rage into a subtle and more dangerous channel. In a different manner he would show her! He saw sharply a means of vindicating his honour. Yes! by God, he would show them in the Borough how he dealt with this sort of thing .They would see the stand that he was taking. She was now no daughter of his. He would cast her from him as unclean.

Then, suddenly, a second, loathsome suspicion came into his mind, a suspicion which gathered in aversion, becoming more certain the longer he contemplated it. He roused Mary with his huge, heavy boot.

"Who was the man?" he hissed at her. "Was it Foyle?" He saw from her look that he was right. For the second time that hateful young upstart had dealt him a crushing blow, this time more deadly than before. He would rather it had been anyone, the basest and most beggarly scoundrel in the town, anyone but Foyle! But it was he, the smooth-faced, blarneying, young corner boy who had possessed the body of Mary Brodie; and she, his child, had suffered him to do so. A lucid mental picture, revolting in its libidinous detail, rose up and tortured him. His face worked, the skin around his nostrils twitched, a thick, throbbing vessel corded itself intumescently upon his temple. His features, which had at first been suffused with a high angry flush, now became white and hard as chiselled granite. His jaw set ruthlessly like a trap, his narrow forehead lowered with an inhuman barbarity. A cold ferocity, more terrifying than the loud-mouthed abuse which he usually displayed, tempered his rage like an axe blade. He kicked Mary viciously. The hard sole of his boot sank into her soft side.

"Get up, you bitch!" he hissed, as he again spurned her brutally with his foot. "Do you hear me? Get up."

From the staircase the broken voice of Mamma senselessly repeated: "I'm not to blame! I'm not to blame!" Over and over came the words: "I'm not to blame. Don't blame me." She stood there abjectly, cringingly, protesting ceaselessly in a muttering voice her inculpability, whilst behind her the terrified figures of Nessie and the old woman were dimly outlined. Brodie gave no heed to the interruption. He had not heard it.

"Get up," he repeated, "or I'll help ye up"; and, as she rose, he lifted her to her feet with a final jerk of his foot.

Mary staggered up. Why, she thought, did he not kill her and be done with it? Her side, where he had kicked her, stabbed with a lancinating hurt. She was too terrified to look at him. She felt that he was torturing her only to destroy her in the end.

"Now," he ground out slowly from between his clenched teeth, with words that bit into her like vitriol, "you'll listen to me."

As she stood there, bent and drooping, he moved his head slightly and thrust forward his hard, relentless face into hers. His eyes gleamed closely, with a concentrated, icy glitter that seared her with its chill.

"You'll listen to me, I say. You'll listen to me for the last time. You are not my daughter any longer. I am going to cast you out like a leper! Like a leper—you filthy slut! That's what I'm going to do to you and your unborn bastard. I'm going to settle with your fancy man in my own time, but you—you're going out to-night."

He repeated the last words slowly, whilst he pierced her with his cold eyes. Then, as though reluctant to abandon the satisfaction of her abasement under his glare, he turned slowly, walked heavily to the door and flung it open. Immediately a terrific inrush of wind and rain filled the hall, clattering the pictures on the walls, billowing the hanging coats on the stand, and rushing upwards with the force of a battering-ram towards the clinging group upon the stairs.

"It's a beautiful night for a stroll," snarled Brodie, with drawn lips. "It's dark enough for you to-night! You can walk the streets to your heart's content to-night, you strumpet!"

With a sudden thrust of his arm he caught her by the neck and compressed it within his huge, prehensile grasp. No sound but the howling of the wind filled the hall. Of the three terrorised onlookers, the uncomprehending child, the mother, and the half-fearful, half-gloating old woman, not one spoke. They stood paralysed to silence. The feel of her soft yet resistant throat fascinated him; he wanted to squeeze it like a pipe-stem until it snapped, and, for an instant, he stood thus, fighting the impulse; but he started violently and, with a sudden tug, dragged her to the door. "Now," he shouted, "you're going out and you'll never come back—not until you crawl back and grovel down to lick these boots that have kicked you."

At that, something within Mary spoke. "I will never do that," she whispered from her pale lips.

"No!" yelled Brodie. "You will never come back, you harlot!"

He pushed her, with a violent, final thrust, from him. She disappeared into the raging blackness beyond. As she vanished completely to sight and sound, as though she had stepped over a precipice, he stood there in an ecstasy of passion, his fists clenched, filling his lungs with the wet, saline air, shouting at the pitch of his voice: "Don't come back, you whore! you whore!" He shouted the last word again, and again, as if its repetition afforded him, in its coarse vituperation, a satisfaction, an alleviation of his fury. Then he turned upon his heel and shut her out into the night.

XI

MARY rested where she had fallen. She felt stunned, for Brodie's final, brutal thrust had thrown her, heavily, flat upon her face, into the rough, gravel courtyard. The rain, driven in straight, parallel spears, impinged painfully upon her lightly covered body and spattered the surface of the puddle in which she lay. Already she was soaked to the skin, but the wetness of her rain-saturated clothing brought, at that moment, only a refreshing coolness to the fever that burned within her. She had felt under her father's terrible eyes that he would surely murder her and now, although her bruised and aching body still burned, a sense of escape filled her mind and transfigured its terror to lightness and relief. She had been cast out shamefully, but she was alive, she had left for ever a home which had become lately a hated prison; and now she plucked together her shattered forces and bravely fixed her mind upon the future.

Denis, she became aware amongst the fearful confusion of her thoughts, was perhaps sixty miles away; she was enveloped in a storm of unprecedented magnitude; she had no coat, no hat, insufficient clothing and no money; but now she had courage. Firmly, she compressed her wet lips as she desperately endeavoured to examine her position. Two courses lay open to her: the one to attempt to reach the cottage at Garshake, the other to go to Denis' mother at Darroch.

It was twelve miles to Garshake and, beyond the fact that she knew that it was named Rosebank, she had no knowledge of where the cottage stood; besides, even if she succeeded in getting inside, she would be alone, penniless, and without food; and now she realised that she needed succour of some kind. She therefore abandoned all thought of reaching Rosebank and turned, inevitably, to the alternative idea. She must go to Denis' mother! At least she would receive shelter from her, shelter until Denis returned. His mother would not refuse her that; and she hearteningly recollected that once Denis had said to her: "If the worst happened, you could come to my mother." She would do that! She must do that.

To get to Darroch she would be obliged to walk. She was not aware of any train which left Levenford for Darroch on Sunday night; and if one did, indeed, run she did not know its time of departure, nor had she the cost of her ticket. Two routes therefore offered themselves for her choice. The first was the main artery of communication between the two places, a broad main thoroughfare nearly five miles long, the other, a narrow, unfrequented road running directly across the open countryside, narrowing here to a lane and there to a mere track, but avoiding the circuitous windings of the outskirts of both towns, and shorter than the former by almost two miles. Her strength was now so insufficient, and her sufferings so great, that she decided to take the latter route because it was the lesser distance. She thought she could walk three miles.

Prostrate upon the ground and protected by the high wall of the courtyard she had not appreciated the full power of the storm, which was, indeed, the worst which had ravaged the Scottish Lowlands for over a century. The wind, springing from the south-west, tore past at the unprecedented velocity of sixty miles an hour. In the town only those driven by necessity were abroad, and, of these, only the hardiest remained for more than a few moments in the open. Slates torn from the roofs of houses sailed downwards through the air, each with the force and cutting violence of a falling guillotine; whole chimney-pots were wrenched off, flung through the air entire, and dashed upon the cobblestones below; the large, thick, plate-glass window of the Building Society's office was blown into pieces, like dry parchment, by the force of the wind alone. Amongst the roar of the hurricane the reports of falling objects as they struck upon the streets came continuously, like a bombardment. In the Newtown the gable of a newly erected house was caved in by the blast and the wind, entering the aperture like a wedge, prised off the roof and seized it. Off flew the entire roof, its sides extended like the planing wings of a bird, soaring through the air, until finally the wind ceased to support it and it dived like a plummet into the black water of the estuary a full three hundred yards away.

In the low-lying parts of the town the ceaseless rain caused such flooding that entire areas lay under water; houses stood apart like isolated dwellings rising from a strange lagoon, and the deluge, rushing around them, percolated the walls, entered through doors and windows, and completely inundated the lower floors.

The lightning which ran riot over the surrounding countryside produced a less diffuse but more deadly havoc. A shepherd, herding on the Doran hills, was struck instantly dead by a fulgent stroke; two farm servants sheltering under a tree were struck down and their charred bodies crushed by the fall of the riven tree; livestock suffered severely; countless sheep and cattle were killed as they lay in the open or sought a more precarious shelter under trees, and a full score of cattle crouching against a wire fence were electrocuted by the conduit of the fluid current.

A thunderbolt fell, and, crashing into a sailing barque at anchor in Port Doran Bay, sank it instantly. Other ships, in the river mouth and in the Firth, dragged their anchors and broke their moorings and were battered by the waves as they ran aground on the Doran shore.

Unaware of all this, Mary slowly raised herself to her feet. The wind took hold of her and almost cast her down again, but she bore against it, and, inclining her body sharply into the teeth of the gale, set out through the pitch of the night. Her sodden garments flapped about her like drenched sails and hampered her movements, clinging bindingly to her legs at each step she took. As she left the front of her home a leaden gutter, stripped from the coping by a single gust, came hurtling viciously towards her, like a last malevolent gesture from the house; but, though it passed dangerously near her head, it missed her and buried itself deeply into the wet ground.

She had not proceeded a hundred yards before she was compelled to rest. Though this point marked the situation of the last lamp-post of the road, now the darkness was unrelieved and, for a moment, she imagined the light had been blown out, but as she resumed her way, she tripped upon the prone column of the disrupted lamp. With head downwards she stumbled on, feeling her way like a blind woman and keeping the road only through her sense of direction and by her familiarity with it. The noise about her was frightful, so deafening that if she had shouted aloud she would not have heard her own voice. The wind, like some gigantic orchestra, traversed madly the gamut of its compass. The deep diapason of the pipe-organ mingled with the reedy treble of clarionets; bugles shrilled against the bass of oboes; the wailing of violins, the clash of cymbals, the booming of drums were blended together into an unearthly cacophony of dissonance.

Every now and then, out of the blackness, unseen objects struck her. Flying twigs of trees stung her face, torn-up branches and shrubs flung themselves against her. Once a soft, sessile tentacle entwined itself about her neck and arms. She shrieked with terror, lifting her soundless voice against the hurricane, thinking that living arms had corded themselves about her, but, as she raised her hands in panic, she discovered that she was enveloped by a sheaf of hay blown from some obliterated stack.

With the utmost difficulty she had now traversed about a mile of her journey, and, though she was not yet half-way towards her objective, the most fearful part lay immediately ahead. Here the road closed in almost to a pathway and wandered, unflanked by any guiding fence or boundary, without line of demarcation from the adjacent woodland, through a thick grove of firs. This wood was always tenebrous, with gloomy trees that whispered elegies, but now, in this fearsome night, which itself lay around her like a dense forest, the wood became frightful and repulsive, like the central darkness, the very heart of the forest of the night. She shuddered to think of entering it. Once, when a child, upon an expedition with some others, she had lost herself amongst these stern, austere trees, had run amongst them, forlornly seeking her companions, and she now recalled with painful vividness her youthful terror, a terror which returned upon darker wings as, mustering all her courage and her strength, she plunged into the coppice.

It was almost impossible to trace the pathway. Gropingly she crept along, keeping both arms extended, with flat palms outstretched in front of her. This extension of her arms gave her an excruciating hurt in that side of her chest where her father had kicked her, but she was obliged to hold them so in order to protect her head and face from the contact of the trees, and to ascertain more exactly the direction of her laborious progress.

The wind which, in the open land, had maintained a constant direction, now whirled around the tree trunks with a hundred currents and eddies, in a manner which rendered direct forward movement impossible. Mary was tossed this way and that way, like a ship beating its course amongst a swirl of treacherous tides, without moon or stars to guide her in the perilous pitch of the night. She had begun to wander from the path when, suddenly, an erratic vortex caught her, swept away her balance, and flung her violently to the left. She fell with all her weight, and the palm of her left hand impaled itself upon the dagger-sharp point of a low, broken fir branch which projected horizontally from the main trunk. For one agonising moment her hand remained nailed to the wood, then she plucked it free, and staggered to her feet.

Onwards she went. She was now utterly lost. She wanted to get out of the wood but she could not. Dizzily she felt her way from tree to tree, the blood streaming from her wounded hand, permeated by terror, by the throbbing of her injured side and the recurrent pains within her body. Chilled to the bone, her wet hair streaming dankly, her skin infiltrated with rain water, she mazed about the wood in the darkness. She stumbled, and got up, swayed backwards and staggered onwards, to the insane music of the tornado as it bellowed through the trees. The pandemonium of sound dinning upon her ears seemed of itself to swing her about, controlling her movements by its stupendous rhythm. Light-headedly she gyrated, amongst the rending avulsion of uprooting trees, lost to everything but pain and her desire to escape from the horror of this besetting forest.

Her head became light and giddy, and now it seemed to her that the blackness was peopled with wild, living creatures that dashed about her, touching her, plucking at her with their fingers, pressing against and hurrying past her in an orgy of stampeding movement. She felt the cold, gusty breathing of the wet things as they slid their way and buffeted through the forest. They whispered into her ears strange, sad tidings of Denis and of her child; they bellowed loudly in her father's tones, and wailed like her mother. Every sound about her she construed into the weird and incoherent speech of these visionary beings. At intervals she knew she was going mad, that no forms surrounded her, that she was alone, deserted, forgotten in the wood, but, as she staggered on, her mind again became obscured, clouded by the visions of her terror.

Suddenly, when it seemed as though she must completely lose her reason, she paused in a kind of numb wonder. She raised her tortured eyes upwards to the sky and beheld the moon, a thin crescent, pale and without radiance, which lay flat upon its back amongst the banked clouds, as though the gale had blown it over. She saw it only for a moment, then it was obscured by the racing clouds, but she observed that the wind now came upon her in one direct, tearing line of motion that she no longer felt the hard trunks of the firs. She was out of the wood! She sobbed with relief, and immediately ran blindly to escape from it, and from the gibbering creatures it contained. She had lost the road, together with all sense of her bearings, and the instinct of flight alone impelled her as, with a crouching, stumbling motion, she hastened anywhere. The wind was now assisting her, lifting her from her feet and lengthening her shambling steps. She was in some kind of field, and long, dank grasses whipped her legs as she slid forward upon the soft turf. It was not cultivated land, for she passed amongst clumps of bracken, slipped and stumbled against half-buried, moss-grown boulders, and ripped through clusters of bramble bush; but she was now beyond logical thought and did not pause to deduce her whereabouts from the nature of the country she traversed.

Then, all at once, amongst the tumult, she became aware of a deep, sonorous cadence, which, as she went on, grew louder, and swelled to the roar of rushing water. It was the sound of a broad river, swollen to overflowing, and so engorged by turbid waters that its rushing turbulence sounded in her ears like the resonance of a cataract. With every step she took this sound grew louder till it seemed as though the river, glutted with the debris of the uplands, advanced menacingly upon her, bearing, unseen amongst the seething waters, palings and fencing, the debris of a dozen bridges, whole tree trunks, and the bodies of dead sheep and cattle.

She was now upon its brink before she understood that it was the Leven; the same Leven which had sung to her so softly with its lilting purl, which had added to the rapture of Denis and herself as, meandering past, it had serenaded them to love. Now, like herself, it was altered beyond recognition. The moon was still obscured, and nothing was visible to her, but as she stood terrified, listening upon the high, exposed bank, for an instant, in her fearful extremity, she was tempted to let herself slide into these invisible, booming waters below, to forget and be forgotten. A shudder ran through her bruised body as she repulsed the thought. Like a command to live came the thought that, no matter what happened, she still had Denis. She must live for Denis, and now she felt him beckoning to her. She turned abruptly from the sound as though to cut off its appeal but, as she moved, in the careless hurry of her recoil, her wet shoe slipped, she stumbled, her foot again slithered on the surface of a greasy clod and she shot feet first down the steep slope. Her hands clutched desperately at the short grass and rushes of the bank, but the weeds that she grasped broke immediately in her clasp, or uprooted easily from the wet soil. Her feet tore two furrows in the yielding clay as she dug them fiercely into it in a fruitless effort to save herself. With her arms she clung to the wet bank, but she found nothing to retard her descent.

The smooth surface of the declivity was as steep and treacherous as that of a glacier and, instead of arresting her fall, these frantic movements only served to increase her speed. She was precipitated with irresistible momentum into the unseen river below. She entered the water with a soundless splash and immediately sank down amongst the long water weeds which grew from the bottom, whilst water rushed into her lungs as she gasped from shock and terror. The force of the current drove her body rapidly along the river bed, amongst the entangling grasses, and swept her down stream for thirty yards before she came at last to the surface.

She could not swim but, instinctively, with the effort of preservation, she made a few, feeble, despairing strokes, trying to keep her head above the surface of the water. It was impossible. The intense spate of the torrent had raised a series of high, undulating waves which swept repeatedly over her, and finally, a swirling undertow caught her legs and sucked her down. This time she remained under so long that her senses almost left her. Bells rang in her ears, her lungs were ballooned, her eyeballs bursting; red stabs of light danced before her; she was suffocating. But she came once more to the surface and, as she emerged, inert and half insensible, the end of a floating log of wood was flung by a wave into her right armpit. Unconsciously, she seized it and feebly clasped it against her. She floated. Her body was submerged, her hair streaming behind her in the current, but her face lay above water and, with great, gasping breaths, she filled and refilled her chest with air. With all feeling suspended but the necessity of respiration she clung to the log, amidst the strange flotsam that dashed every now and then against her, and was borne rapidly down the river. Her rate of movement was so great that, as consciousness returned to her more fully, she realised that, if she did not quickly reach the bank, she would soon be swept amongst the sharp rocks which spiked the rapids that lay immediately above Levenford. With the remains of her strength, and still clinging to the log, she kicked out with her legs. The cold of the river water was infinitely more cutting than of the rain, cutting from the frigidity of an ice-crusted, snow-capped mountain source, and from the added chill of tributary hill streams fed by melted snow. This cold pierced to the marrow of Mary's bones; her limbs lost all sensation and, although her legs moved feebly at the command of her will, she did not feel them stir. The air, too, had become so frigid that hailstones began to fall. They were large pellets, hard as stone, sharp as icicles, that churned the water like shot and bounced off the log like bullets. They rained mercilessly upon Mary's face and head, bruising her eyes, whipping her cheeks, and cutting her lower lip. Because she must hold the log so grimly with both her hands she could not shield herself and she was compelled to suffer this pitiless, pelting shower, unprotected. Her teeth chattered; her wounded hand was seared and freezing; dreadful cramps seized her middle; she felt she was perishing from the cold. The immersion in the glacial water was killing her. At that moment, as she struggled towards the bank, a single thought obsessed her—not of herself or of Denis, but of the child within her. A compelling instinct suddenly flowered within her as though a message, passing by some strange communication between the child and her own being, had suddenly told her that, if she did not quickly get out of the water, it must die.

Never before had she thought so lovingly of the child. At times she had hated it as part of her own despicable body, but now an overpowering desire for it overtook her. If she died it must die. She thought of the living infant, entombed in her drowned body, floating out to sea, moving more and more feebly in the prison of her lifeless flesh. Without speech she prayed that she might live, live to give it birth.

She had now reached a point where the engorged river had burst its banks and overflowed into the neighbouring fields. She could feel this quieter water to the left of her and, with her puny force, she essayed to direct herself to it. Again and again, she tried to draw away from the main stream only to be sucked back again. She had almost abandoned hope when, at a sharp bend of the river, her log was suddenly deflected from its course by a powerful eddy, and she floated into an area where she could feel no waves, no swirl, no wild onrush. She let the log drift on until it came to rest, then, trembling, she lowered her legs. They touched bottom and she stood up, thigh deep in the water. The weight of the water and her frozen state almost prevented her moving, but, though gaining only inches at a time, she moved slowly away from the sound of the river. At length she was clear of the flood. She looked round. To her intense joy she saw, amidst the impenetrable darkness around her, a light. The sight of this light was like a divine balm laid suddenly upon each of her wounds. For what seemed to her like years she had been moving in a world of tenebrous shadows, where each step was fraught with obscure suspense and an unseen danger that might annihilate her. The faint, unflickering ray gleamed serenely, and in the dim illumination she saw comfort and serenity. Hereabouts she recollected was situated a small and isolated croft, but whosoever dwelt here could never refuse to shelter her in her terrible condition on so terrible a night. Cowering, she advanced towards the light.

Now she could hardly walk. Low in her body a heavy weight seemed to bear her down and lancinating pains tore her with every movement. Bent almost double, she persisted on her way. The light had been so near and yet, the further she advanced, the more it seemed to recede from her! Her feet squelched deep into the inundated ground so that it was an effort to withdraw them, and with each step she seemed to sink deeper into the marshland which she was now obliged to cross. Still, she progressed, going deeper and deeper into the swamp, sinking to her knees as she plodded through a foul admixture of mud and water. One of her shoes was plucked from her foot by the adhesion of the quagmire and she was unable to retrieve it; her skin, blenched white by her prolonged immersion, now became smeared and splashed with mire; the remnants of her clothing trailed behind in draggled tatters.

At length, it appeared to her that she was slowly gaining ground and approaching nearer to the light of the croft, when abruptly, following a forward step, she failed to find bottom with her feet. She began to sink into the bog. She shrieked. The warm, quaggy mud sucked at her legs with a soft insistence, drawing her downwards into its embrace. She was unable to withdraw either foot and, at her struggles, gaseous bubbles erupted from the slough and stifled her with their miasma. Downwards she sank. It seemed to her that she had been saved from the clean, cold death of the river in order to be destroyed more fittingly here. This sludge was a more suitable winding sheet than the pure water of the mountain streams. In such corruption as this her violated body had been destined to disintegrate and, dissolving, become finally part of its substance. To have surmounted such peril as she had that night endured, and to be robbed of succour when within sight of it, infuriated her. In a passion of endeavour she struggled to support herself; with a shriek she flung herself forward, clawing wildly at the wet moss which covered the surface of the morass. The glutinous stuff offered little hold, but with such frenzy did she tear at it with her extended fingers that she succeeded, with a last superhuman effort, in drawing herself clear by the power of her arms alone. Then, pantingly, she dragged her body to a firmer part of the marsh, where she lay completely exhausted. She could now no longer walk, and therefore, after a few moments rest, she began to crawl slowly forward on all fours like a stricken animal. But in escaping from the bog she had utilised the last dregs of her strength; although she was on solid ground and no more than fifty yards from the house, she realised that she would never attain it. She gave up, and, sobbing weakly, lay on the ground, hopeless, with powerless limbs relaxed, whilst a fresh downpour of rain deluged her. Yet, as she lay there, the faint lowing of cattle came to her through the storm. After a moment she again heard the sound and, looking to the right, she perceived, dimly outlined in the obscurity, the darker outlines of a low building. She became aware through the drifting vapours in her brain that here was shelter of some kind. Raising herself, she staggered with a last, delirious effort, into the shed, and collapsed unconscious upon the floor.

The sanctuary she had attained was a poor outbuilding, the mean byre of the small farm. Being built of thick stones with the crevices closely stuffed with moss, it was warm inside, and, having so insignificant a height, the chilling blast rushed over it, so that it had, in addition, escaped the fury of the wind. The air was filled with the blended odours of straw, dung, and the sweet smell of the animals themselves. The three milch cows standing in their stalls moved with gentle, resigned movements, their bodies almost invisible, but their pale udders faintly luminous amongst the shadows. The cows, their large, sad eyes inured to the darkness, looked with a docile timidity at the strange human creature which rested, scarcely breathing, upon the floor of the byre. Then, having identified it as passive and harmless, they turned their heads disinterestedly, and again began calmly ruminating with silent moving jaws.

For only a few moments Mary remained in happy insensibility. She was restored to consciousness by the powerful spur of pain. Waves of pain swept over her. The pain began in her back, travelled round her body and down the inside of her thighs with a slow, fulminating grip which gradually crept to an intolerable crisis. Then suddenly it left her, limp, drained, and helpless.

During the whole of her tragic journey she had endured these pangs. Now they became insupportable, and, lying amongst the ordure of the shed, she suffered with closed eyes. Her arms and legs were extended flaccidly; her body, which Denis had named his shrine, was pressed into the steaming dung and plastered with drying mud. Moans of pain broke from between her clenched teeth; a damp sweat beaded her forehead and trickled slowly over her shut eyelids; her features, disfigured by filth and distorted by her insupportable experiences, were rigidly set, but around her head the emanation of her sufferings seemed to have condensed in a faint, translucent radiance which encircled her dying face like a nimbus.

The inactive intervals of her pains grew shorter whilst the paroxysms lengthened. When a pain abated the passive anticipation of the next was torture. Then it would begin, graspingly envelop her, permeate her with agony, and squander itself through her every nerve. Her cries were combined with the shriek of the ever-present wind. Everything she had undergone was as nothing compared to her present torture. Her body writhed about the stone floor feebly; blood mingled with the sweat and dirt about her. She prayed for death. Dementedly she called upon God, on Denis, on her mother. She besought the clemency of her Savour in gasps, which broke in anguish from between her clenched teeth. In answer to her cries only the wind responded. Rising up, it shrieked and mocked at her as it rushed about the shed. She lay abandoned until, at last, when she could not have lived through one further exacerbation, the gale rose to its loudest, highest pitch and, amidst the culmination of the storm, she was delivered of a son. Till the last torture abated she was conscious. Then, when there was no more pain for her to endure, she relapsed into the deep well of forgetfulness.

The child was small, puny, premature. Bound still to its insensible mother it clawed feebly at her, and at the empty air, with its diminutive fingers. Its head sagged upon its frail neck. It rested there, scarcely breathing, while the mother lay slowly blanching from a slow, seeping

F

hæmorrhage. Then it cried with a weak and fitful cry.

As if in answer to that call the door of the shed opened slowly, and the rays of a lantern dimly penetrated the darkness. An old woman came into the byre. A thick, plaid shawl was wrapped round her head and shoulders; her wooden, solid clogs clattered as she walked. She had come to reassure herself as to the safety and comfort of her beasts and now she went to them, smoothing their necks, patting their sides, talking encouragingly to them. "Eh, Pansy lady," she muttered. "Come up, Daisy! Come awa', Belle; come up, leddy, leddy! Come, leddy, leddy! But what a night! What a storm! But dinna steer, dinna fash, ye're a' richt, my hinnies! You've a good, stout roof abin ye, ye maunna be frichted! I'm near enough tae ye. You'll be——" Abruptly she broke off, and raised her head into a listening attitude. She imagined she had heard within the byre a faint, puling cry. But she was old and deaf and her ears rang with the echo of the hurricane, and, mistrusting her own perception of the sound, she was about to turn away and resume her task when she distinctly heard the slight, plaintive call repeated.

"Guidsakes! what—is't—at a', at a'," she murmured. "I'm shair I heard something—— Something. unco' like a wean greetin'." With an unsteady hand she lowered her lantern, peering about in the darkness; then suddenly she paused, with incredulous, awestruck eyes. "The Lord save us!" she cried, "it's a bairn and—and its mother. God in Heaven, she's deid! Oh! the nicht that this has been! What a thing for ma auld een to see!" In a second she had placed her lantern on the stone floor and was down upon her aged knees. She had no fastidious delicacy as she plied her coarse hands with the adept, experienced movements of a woman of the soil to whom nature was an open book. Quickly, but without flurry, she disengaged the child and wrapped it warmly in a corner of her plaid. Then she turned to the mother and, with an expert pressure, at once evacuated the womb, and controlled the bleeding. All the time she spoke to herself, while she worked: "Did ye see the like! She's nearly gane! the puir thing! and her so young and so bonnie. I maun dae ma best for her. That's better though. What in God's name did she no' come to the house, though. I would have letten her in. Ah, well, 'twas the will o' the Almighty I cam' out to the beasts." She slapped Mary's hands, rubbed her cheeks, covered her with the remainder of the plaid, and hastened off.

Back in her comfortable kitchen she shouted to her son, who sat before the huge crackling log fire: "Quick man! I want ye to run like fury to Levenford for a doctor. Ye maun get yin at a' costs. There's an ill woman in the byre. Go, in God's name, and no' a word frae ye. It's life or death."

He stared at her dully. "What," he cried stupidly, "in our byre?"

"Ay," she shouted, "she's been driven in by the storm. If ye dinna hurry she'll be gane. Haste ye! Haste ye awa' for help."

He got up mazedly and began to struggle into his coat.

"It's the maist unheard o' thing," he muttered; "in our byre. What's wrang wi' her, ava', ava'?"

"Never mind," she flared; "gang awa' this meenute. Never mind the horse. Ye maun rin like fury."

She hustled him out of the door, and when she had assured herself that he had gone, took a pan, poured into it some milk from a jug on the dresser, and hurriedly heated it upon the fire. Then she took a blanket from the kitchen bed, her own bed, and rushed again to the cowshed, with the blanket on her arm and the hot milk in her hand. She wrapped Mary tightly in the blanket and, raising her head gently, poured with difficulty a few drops of hot milk between her blue lips. She shook her head doubtfully. "I'm afraid to move her," she whispered, "she's gae far through."

Taking the infant in the crook of her arm, she removed it to the warm kitchen, and returned with a clean, damp cloth and another blanket for Mary.

"There, ma bonnie, that'll hap ye up warm," she whispered, as she encompassed the limp form in this second covering. Then, tenderly, with the cloth, she wiped the inspissated mud from the white cold face. She had done all that was possible, and now she waited patiently, crouching down, without once removing her eyes from Mary, from time to time chafing the lifeless hands, stroking the cold brow beside her. For almost an hour she remained thus.

At last the door was flung open, and a man entered the byre in a bluster of wind and rain.

"Thank God ye've come, doctor," cried the old woman. "I was feared ye wouldna."

"What is the trouble?" he demanded abruptly, as he advanced towards her.

In a few words she told him. He shook his head dispassionately and bent his tall, spare form down beside the figure on the floor. He was a young man, this Dr. Renwick, skilful in his work, but new to Levenford and anxious to build up a practice, and this had drawn him out on foot on such a night when two other doctors approached before him had refused to go. He looked at Mary's pale, sunken face, then felt her soft, fluttering pulse; whilst he contemplated the second hand of his watch with a serene tranquillity the old woman gazed at him anxiously.

"Will she die, think ye, doctor?"

"Who is she?" he said.

The old wife shook her head negatively.

"I dinna ken, ava', ava'. But what a bonnie, wee thing to suffer so much, doctor." She seemed to entreat him to do all he could.

"The baby?" he enquired.

"In the kitchen! 'Tis alive the now, but 'tis a puir, feeble bit bairn."

The physician in him looked coldly, critically at the inert figure before him, but the man in him was touched. He seemed to trace, with his experienced eye, the record of all her sufferings, as though the history of these was indelibly delineated upon her features. He saw the pinched nostrils of the thin straight nose, the sunken rings of her dark eyes, and the piteous droop of the pale, soft lips. A feeling of compassion awoke in him, tinctured by a strange, flowing tenderness.

He took up again the frail, relaxed hand and held it in his as though to transfuse a current of life from his vital body into hers, then, as he turned the hand, and saw the gash which transfixed the palm, he cried, in spite of himself: "Poor child! She's so young and helpless." Then, ashamed of his weakness, he continued roughly: "She's in a bad way. Hæmorrhage, bad hæmorrhage, and shock. Shock from God knows what misery. It's a case for the Cottage Hospital," he added finally.

At these words the young farmer, who had been silent in the background, spoke from the door:

"I'll have the horse in the shafts of the cart in a minute if ye like, doctor."

Renwick looked at the old woman for confirmation. She nodded eagerly, her hands supplicating him.

"Very well, then!" He braced his shoulders. In this case he saw no chance of fee, only its difficulties and danger, and a hazard to his unformed reputation. But he was moved to take it. He felt he must take it. His dark eyes lit with a flashing desire to save her. "It's not only the shock," he said aloud; "I don't like her breathing. Might be pneumonia there, and if so——" He shook his head significantly, turned and bent over his bag, and, extracting from it some temporary restoratives, applied these as best the circumstances permitted. When he had finished, the cart, a rough farm waggon as deep and heavy as a tumbrel, stood ready at the door. The infant was swaddled in blankets and placed carefully in one corner, then they lifted Mary up and placed her beside her child. Finally, Renwick clambered in and, while he supported Mary in his arms, the crofter jumped into his seat and whipped up the horse. Thus they set out into the night for the Cottage Hospital, the strange ambulance bumping and jolting slowly along, the doctor protecting the limp figure in his arms, as best he could, from the shocks of the rough road.

The old woman saw them disappear, then she sighed, turned, shut the byre door, and with bowed back went slowly into her house. As she entered the kitchen the grandfather's clock in the corner chimed eight, solemn strokes. She went quietly to the chest of drawers, picked up her Bible and, slowly assuming her old, steel spectacles, opened the book at random and began soberly to read.

XII

THE wind, which blew fiercely in the west, blew still more furiously in the east. On the Sunday afternoon, when havoc ranged in Levenford and amongst the surrounding townships, still greater devastation roamed amongst the counties of the Eastern sea-board.

In Edinburgh, as Denis buffeted his way along Princes Street, the wind, tearing along the grey, weather-beaten thoroughfare, ballooned his coat about his ears and lifted him off his feet. He loved that wind; it made him feel strong to fight a passage against it. Hat in hand, his hair disordered, his lips parted, he cleaved his way along. The wind sang against his teeth like the song of a gigantic humming-top, and he sang too, or uttered spontaneous, inarticulate sounds, expressive of the virile exuberance that seethed within him. Of the few people in the street, most turned involuntarily to look at him, and muttered enviously, from blue, shivering lips: "My certies, he's a hardy chiel, that one!"

It was quarter to four. Denis had made an early tea at McKinleys' "Family and Commercial Temperance Hotel." They did things well there, no show, indeed, but a lavish abundance of good food, and he had eaten his way through a large trencher of sausages and white-pudding, cleared a plateful of oatcakes, and emptied the tea-pot in Ma McKinley's own, private parlour. Old Mother McKinley would do anything for Denis—just the way he had with her, and with most people —and he always went there when in Edinburgh. She had, in parting, given him a thick packet of sandwiches to sustain his body until his late arrival in Dundee, and a large, smacking embrace to support his spirit until she saw him again. It was good to have friends like that, he thought warmly, as he felt the comforting wad of sandwiches buttoned against his side, whilst he strode out on his way to Granton, to take the ferry-boat across the Firth of Forth for Burntisland. His only grievance against the weather was his fear that it might prevent them running the ferry, but if there was no boat, he was, he told himself facetiously, feeling vigorous enough to swim across the firth.

Although it blew so hard, there was as yet no rain and, as it was only three miles to Granton, he disdained the usual conveyance to the ferry and decided to walk. It was fine to be alive! This wind intoxicated him; the feel of it upon his cheek made him want to live for ever. As he drove his feet hard upon the pavement he knew he would cover the distance easily under the hour at his disposal.

His reflections, as he strode along, were pleasant. Business was opening out beyond his expectations and to-morrow, in Dundee, he hoped to consolidate his position with Blain & Co. Young Mr. Blain was the force in the firm; he liked him immensely, and he felt that if he could convince him, persuade him to deal with Findlay's, the day would be won. He began to think out a smart, little speech to open his conversation on the morrow. He declaimed the address magnificently to the wind and to the empty streets as he walked along, enjoying himself immensely, emphasising his points by telling gesticulations, so that by the time Granton was reached he had riddled young Mr. Blain with epigrams, bombarded him with technicalities, and reduced him to impotence by solid argument. Now, to his relief, he observed that the ferry bumped at her small pier with every indication of departure, and hastening his steps, he went on board the vessel. From the low deck of the boat the firth looked darker and more threatening than from the jetty, with white spume slapping over the crests of the slate-grey waves. The small boat rocked heavily, and the rope hawsers attached from the vessel to the squat bollards on the quay creaked and thumped, as the combined strain of wind and tide pulled upon them. Denis, however, was an excellent sailor and, unperturbed, he joined three other passengers who were gathered in the bow of the boat, looking gloomily across the firth, a disconsolate sense of danger binding them closer together.

"I don't like the look o' it," said one.

"Ay, it's gey and threatenin' like," said another.

"I'm beginning to wish I had taken the wife's advice and stayed at home," said the third, with a feeble attempt at jocularity.

Denis rallied them.

"Do you think the captain would put out the boat if he wasn't sure of getting over?" he cried, heartily. "It's only five miles across—a mere nothing. Why, in twenty years we'll be jumping across a ditch like this, or walking over on stilts."

They looked at him doubtfully, but he laughed, joked, bantered them until they surrendered, and, in the space of five minutes, he had them enrolled under his banner. They accepted him as a leader; their fearful anticipation vanished; indeed, one of the group produced a small, flat bottle.

"Will we have a wee drappie before we start?" he asked, with a wink. It was the height of conviviality! The host partook first, then the two others sipped with the moderation of guests, but Denis refused.

"I'm so full of sausage, I'm afraid to chance it," he replied, with a gesture of broad pantomime towards the unruly water, indicating that his sole desire in life was to retain the excellent meal he had just paid for. They laughed delightedly; the fact that this reckless, intrepid youth might be as ridiculously ill as he suggested, filled them with a returning sense of their own worth. And Denis encouraged them, adapting himself to the level of their society with verve, and telling stories with such spirit that they did not fully observe the departure, or the tossing in the firth. One grew greenish, and another swallowed queasily, but they would have died rather than disgrace themselves in the eyes of this young Hector now relating to them, in the climax of his fifth story, the brilliant repartee which the Irishman had made to the Englishman and the

Scotsman, under circumstances of a particularly ludicrous and embarrassing character.

The few other passengers were less assured, and remained huddled together as the boat pitched about like a cockleshell in the stormy water. They clung to the stanchions, lay upon the deck, or were openly sick, whilst the spray-laden wind howled through the rigging, and the fierce, snapping waves burst over the low bulwarks, covering the deck with a sheet of water which flooded from side to side with each roll of the ship.

But at length they drew near Burntisland, passed out of the stormy water and, after considerable manœuvring, made fast. The skipper of the little vessel came off the bridge, dripping in his oilskins.

"I'm not sorry to be in," Denis heard him say. "I didna like it. It's the worst crossing we've ever made."

The passengers disembarked hastily, although some had suffered so acutely that they were obliged to be carried off the ship on to the jetty, and here the small band of heroes bade Denis farewell.

"You're not going any further, then?" said Denis.

"Na! Na!" said the spokesman, looking up at the clouds, "we're all Burntisland lads, praise be, and it'll be a long time before we have another jaunt o' this nature to Edinburgh. Hame looks guid enough to me after that blatter o' sea."

They shook hands with him solemnly, feeling that they would never forget him. "Man, he was a cure, yon fellow that cam' ower the Forth i' the storm," they would repeat to each other long afterwards. "He didna give a hang about anything."

When they had left him, Denis made his way to the station. The train for Dundee, being run in conjunction with the Granton ferry, and due to depart at 5.27 p.m., was already waiting, and as it was now twenty minutes past five, he walked along the platform looking through the windows to secure an empty third-class compartment. A larger number of people than might have been expected from the nature of the weather, were travelling, and he traversed the length of the train up to the engine without seeing a vacant carriage. At the engine, the guard stood talking to the driver and Denis, recognising in the former an acquaintance that he had made—with his usual facility—upon a previous journey, went up and accosted him.

"And how's Davie McBeath?" he cried. The guard turned his head, and, after a moment's hesitating scrutiny, his eye cleared.

"It's yourself, then, Mr. Foyle," he replied cordially. "I couldna place ye for a minute.

"Sure there's not another like me out of Donegal," grinned Denis.

"Do you get weather like this over there?" asked McBeath. "Mitchell," he indicated the driver, "and me are just discussing the gale; we're no' so sure of the wind. It's in a bad quarter."

"Will it push the old, puffing billy backwards?" laughed Denis. Mitchell shook his head doubtfully.

"It's no' just exactly that," he exclaimed, and his look spoke more than his words; then, turning to his mate in the cab he asked:

"How is the gauge, John?"

The black face of the stoker looked up, his teeth showing whitely as he smiled.

"You've enough steam to take ye to Aberdeen!" he said. "Ay, and further than that if ye like."

"Dundee'll be good enough for me, and for you, too, Johnnie Marshall," replied the other, dryly.

"Will she stand it, think ye?" enquired McBeath seriously, for the moment ignoring Denis.

"I canna say," replied Mitchell cryptically, "but we're shair tae find out, ay, and soon enough."

"What's all the mystery?" asked Denis, looking from one to the other.

The grinning face of the stoker looked up from the open door of the furnace, whilst the reflection of the flames played across his dusky, shining face.

"They're a' feared o' a wee bittie o' a brig," he guffawed, as he shovelled; "they dinna ken what steel and cement mean yet."

"Get awa' wi' ye, man," growled Mitchell angrily. "Ye've twa mile o' it and that wind is blowin' richt at it—ay and hammerin' like the picks o' ten thousand devils." At his words a hush seemed to fall on the group, then with a start McBeath looked at his watch. "Well," he said, "whatever we think, the schedule says go, and go we must. Come away, Mr. Foyle."

"What exactly is the trouble?" asked Denis, as he walked up the platform with the guard. Davie McBeath glanced at him out of the corner of his eye, but he did not reply; instead, he changed the subject significantly, saying:

"That's a grand new ulster you've got."

"You like it."

"Ah! I do that! It's a real cosy thing for a night like this, and real smart too."

"Is it smart enough for a wedding, Davie?" asked Denis, nudging the other confidentially.

"It is that!" replied the guard unthinkingly; then he looked up, interestedly.

"What! what! ye're not thinkin' o'——" Denis nodded his head.

"I'm not thinking, man. I'm certain. Tuesday's the day, and like enough I'll wear this coat. Sure, it's part of my trousseau!"

McBeath gazed at the other quizzically, then his dry features relaxed, and they both laughed heartily.

"Weel! weel! you don't say!" cried Davie. "Man! you're a caution! Ye're moving ahead fast. I'm sure I wish ye the best o' everything
—to you and the wee lass, whoever she may be. She'll be braw, if I ken
ye richtly. Come along, now. We canna put a bridegroom in with all
these people in the thirds." He looked along his nose at Denis as he
opened an empty first-class compartment. "It wouldn't be safe."

"Thanks, Davie," said Foyle, appreciatively. "You're a good sort.
I'll send you a bit of the cake to sleep on." Then he added, more
seriously: "See you later, at Dundee." The guard gave him a smile
and a nod as he walked off, and a moment later the whistle blew, the
flag waved, and the train moved out of the station.

Alone in his magnificence, Denis looked about him with satisfaction,
and, reclining back upon the cushions, he raised his feet upon the
opposite seat and fixed his eyes meditatively upon the ceiling. But
slowly his gaze grew distant, and, piercing the low roof, reached far
away. He was thinking of Mary.

He would, he reflected soberly, be married on Tuesday, not exactly
in the manner he had hoped, nor in the fashion he had sometimes
planned, but married none the less. The manner of the marriage did not
matter, the fact remained that he would be no longer a bachelor, and
already he began to feel older and more responsible. A comforting glow
pervaded him as he considered the nobility of his action in accepting,
so willingly, this responsibility. He repulsed the thought that he had
ever wished to repudiate the consequences of his love. "No," he cried
aloud, "I'm not the sort of skunk to let down a girl like Mary." He
became aware vividly of her trust, her loveliness, her faith in him,
thought of her at first tenderly, then with a faint anxiety; thinking of the
storm, he hoped, for her sake, that it had not touched Levenford. Here,
despite the happy tenor of his mind, he began to feel unaccountably
depressed; the subdued happiness, which had succeeded his exuberance
at the commencement of his journey, now turned slowly to an unaccountable melancholy. He tried to shake this off, fixing his mind on the
roseate future that awaited Mary and himself in their cottage at
Garshake, envisaging the wonderful career he would carve for himself,
thinking of the holidays, the trips abroad they would later enjoy—but
he could not dispel the shadow that had clouded his bright optimism.
He began to be afraid for her, and to ask himself if he had been wise
to postpone taking her from her home until so late.

It began now to rain, and the windows of his compartment became
blurred with a dismal covering of wet and slush. The pounding wind
flung great gobs of sleet against the sides of the train with a sound like
the slash of a wet cloth, whilst the rain hissed upon the roof of the
carriage like fierce streams from the nozzle of a gigantic hose. His
depression deepened, and his mind filled with a more mournful misgiving, as, with a sad regret, he visioned the sweet, mysterious beauty of

her body and thought how he had deflowered that beauty. At his violating touch a child had become a woman, who must have suffered bitterly by his act; her slender virginity had become bloated through him, and, in the effort of concealment alone, she must have endured misery; the intimate symmetry of her form appeared to him as something which he had destroyed, which she would never again regain. A sigh broke from him as, slowly, the train drew to a standstill at a wayside station. The train, which was not express, had already made several halts at intermediate stations without his having particularly observed them, but here, to his annoyance, the door of his compartment opened and an old countryman entered. He seated himself blandly in the opposite corner, steaming from the rain, whilst puddles of water ran off him on to the cushions and floor; emanating from him, and mingling with the steam, came the spirituous odour of a liquid more potent than rain-water. Denis stared at him, then remarked coldly: "This is a first-class compartment."

The old fellow took a large red and white spotted handkerchief from his pocket and blew his nose like a trumpet.

"'Deed it is," he said solemnly, affecting to look round the carriage. "I'm glad you told me. It's a rale pleasure for me to travel in style; but the first-class that ye speak o' doesna make muckle difference to me, for I havena got a ticket at all"; and he laughed uproariously, in a tipsy fashion.

Denis was so far below his normal humour that he failed to appreciate the situation. In the ordinary way he would have amused himself intensely with this unexpected travelling-companion, but now he could only gaze at him glumly.

"Are you going far?" he finally asked.

"To Dundee—bonnie Dundee. The town ye ken—not the man. Na! Na! I'm not thinkin' o' the bonnets o' bonnie Dundee—I mean the bonnie town o' Dundee," the other replied, and having thus explained himself with a grave and scrupulous exactitude, he added, meaningly: "I hadna time to get my ticket, though."

Denis sat up. He would, he realised, have to endure this for the rest of the journey, and he resigned himself to it.

"What's the weather like now?" he asked. "You look wet!"

"Wet! I'm wet outside and inside. But the one counteracts the other ye ken, and to a hardy shepherd like me wet clothes just means lettin' them dry on ye. But mind ye, it is a most awful, soughin' night all the same, I'm glad I'm not out on the hills."

He nodded his head several times, took a small, foul stump of clay pipe from his pocket, lit it, covered it with its metal cap, and, inverting it from the corner of his mouth, sucked noisily; when he had filled the carriage with smoke, he spat copiously upon the floor without removing the pipe from his mouth.

Denis looked at the other with compassionate disgust, and as he tried to picture this gross, bibulous old yokel as a young man, then wondered moodily if he himself might ever degenerate to such a crapulous old age, his melancholy grew more profound. Unconscious of the effect he had produced, the old shepherd continued: "Ah! It's good-bye to the hills for me. That sounds kind o' well, think ye no'? Ay! Good-bye to the hills. Man!"—he laughed, slapping his thigh—"It's like the name o' a sang. Good-bye to the Hills. Weel, onyway, I'm going back to my native town, and you'll never guess what for." He tittered vehemently, choking himself with smoke.

"You've come into some money, perhaps?" hazarded Denis.

"'Deed, no! The bit of money I've got is what I've saved by hard and honest work. Try again." As Denis remained silent he went on, garrulously.

"Ay! you'd never think it, but the plain truth is that I'm going——" He paused to wink prodigiously, then blurted out, "I'm goin' to Dundee to get married." Observing with manifest enjoyment the effect he had produced, he meandered on——

"I'm a hardy blade, although I'm not so souple as I was, and there's a fine, sonsie woman waiting for me. She was a great friend of my first wife. Ay! I'm to wed early the morn's mornin'. That's the way I'm takin' this train and breakin' the Sabbath. I maun be in time, ye ken."

As the other wandered on, Denis gazed at him with a curious repulsion, due, in the main, to the strange coincidence of his own circumstances. Here, then, was another bridegroom, linked to him in this narrow compartment by a bond of corresponding position. Did this disreputable veteran mirror the image of his contumely, or reflect to him a dolorous premonition of his future?

In dismay Denis asked himself if he were not as contemptible in the eyes of his own kind as this grey-beard was in his. A tide of self-depreciation and condemnation rushed over him as he began to review the manner of his life. An unusual humility startled him by the rapidity and force of its onset, and in this despair he remained, subdued and silent, until the train clattered into the station of St. Fort. Here his companion rose and got out of the compartment, remarking, as he did so: "We've a good way to go yet. I'll just get out and see if I canna get haud o' something to keep out the cauld. Just a wee dram to warm the inside o' the stammack." In a moment, however, he came back, to say reassuringly: "I'll be back! I'm not away, mind ye. I wouldna leave ye like that. I'll be back to keep ye company till we get to Dundee." Then he tramped off.

Denis looked at his watch and saw that it was five minutes past seven. The train was up to time, yet, as he put his head out of the window, he found that the strength of the wind had increased beyond endurance.

Passengers getting out of the open doors were bowled along the platform, and the heavy train, as it stood stationary, seemed to rock upon its wheels. Surrounding McBeath he saw a wind-beaten group clamouring:

"Is it safe for us to gang on, guard?"

"What a wind it is! Will the train stand it?"

"Will it keep on the line?"

"Lord, save us, what a night this is! What about the bridge? Oh! I wish we were a' hame!"

He thought his friend the guard looked perturbed and irritable, but although McBeath did indeed feel anxious, with the charge of a hundred people upon his mind, he maintained in his replies the even and imperturbable calm of officialdom.

"Safe as the Bank of Scotland, Ma'am."

"Wind forsooth! Tuts, it's only a bit breezie, man. Think shame o' yourself."

"Ay, it'll haud the line and ye'll be hame wi' your lassock in an hour, ma fine wumman!" Denis heard him repeat placidly, composedly, impenetrably. His calmness seemed to reassure them completely, and at his comforting words the people broke up and entered their compartments.

At length the all clear was given and the train again began to move. As it did so Denis observed the figure of his travelling companion staggering against the wind in an effort to attain the rearmost carriage, but in his anxiety and haste, the old shepherd slipped and fell prostrate upon the platform. The train drew away from him, he was irrevocably left behind and, as they moved out of the station Denis caught a last glimpse, under the gusty flicker of the station lamp, of the perplexed, discomfited face, filled with almost ludicrous desolation. As he sat in his corner, while the train approached the southern edge of the Tay Bridge, Denis reflected with a sombre humour that the other would assuredly be late for his nuptials in the morning. Perhaps it was a lesson meant for him. Yes, he must profit by this strange, unpleasant coincidence. He would not fail Mary on Tuesday!

The train moved on and, at thirteen minutes past seven, it reached the beginning of the bridge. At this point, before entering upon the single line of rails over the bridge, it slowed down opposite the signal cabin, to allow the baton to be passed. Without this exchange it was not permitted to proceed, and, still filled by a sense of misgiving, Denis again lowered his window and looked out, to observe that everything was correct. The force of the gale almost decapitated him but, in the red glare cast by the engine, he discerned, stretching dimly into the distance, the massive girders of the bridge, like the colossal skeleton of an enormous reptile, but of steel, strong and adamantine. Then, all at once, he saw the signalman descend the steps from his box with consummate care, clutching the rail tightly with one hand. He surrendered the baton to the stoker, and, when he had accomplished this, he climbed back into his cabin with the utmost difficulty, fighting the wind and being assisted up the last few steps by the hand of a friend held out to him from within.

And now the train moved off again, and entered the bridge. Denis raised his window and sank back in his seat composedly, but, as he was carried past the signal-box, he received the fleeting impression of two pale, terrified faces looking at him from out of it, like ghostly countenances brushing past him in the blackness.

The violence of the gale was now unbounded. The wind hurled the rain against the sides of the train with the noise of a thousand anvils, and the wet snow again came slobbering upon the window panes, blotting out all vision. The train rocked upon the rails with a drunken, swaying oscillation, and although it proceeded slowly, cautiously, it seemed, from the fury and rush of the storm, to dash headlong upon its course. Thus, as it advanced, with the blackness, the noise of the wheels, the tearing rush of the wind, and the crashing of the waves upon the pier of the bridge below, there was developed the sensation of reckless, headlong acceleration.

As Denis sat alone, in the silent, cabined space of his compartment, tossed this way and that by the jactation, he felt suddenly that the grinding wheels of the train spoke to him. As they raced upon the line he heard them rasp out, with a heavy, despairing refrain: "God help us! God help us! God help us!"

Amidst the blare of the storm this slow, melancholy dirge beat itself into Denis' brain. The certain sense of some terrible disaster began to oppress him. Strangely, he feared not for himself, but for Mary. Frightful visions flashed through the dark field of his imagination. He saw her, in a white shroud, with sad, imploring eyes, with dank, streaming hair, with bleeding feet and hands. Fantastic shapes oppressed her which made her shrink into the obliterating darkness. Again he saw her grimacing, simpering palely like a sorry statue of the Madonna and holding by the hand the weazened figure of a child. He shouted in horror. In a panic of distress he jumped to his feet. He desired to get to her. He wanted to open the door, to jump out of this confining box which enclosed him like a sepulchre. He would have given, instantly, everything he possessed to get out of the train. But he could not.

He was imprisoned in the train, which advanced inexorably, winding in its own glare like a dark, red serpent twisting sinuously forward. It had traversed one mile of the bridge and had now reached the middle span, where a mesh of steel girders formed a hollow tube through which it must pass. The train entered this tunnel. It entered slowly, fearfully, reluctantly, juddering in every bolt and rivet of its frame as the hurricane assaulted, and sought to destroy, the greater resistance now offered to it. The wheels clanked with the ceaseless insistence of the tolling of a

155

passing-bell, still protesting, endlessly: "God help us! God help us! God help us!"

Then, abruptly, when the whole train lay enwrapped within the iron lamellæ of the middle link of the bridge, the wind elevated itself with a culminating, exultant roar to the orgasm of its power and passion.

The bridge broke. Steel girders snapped like twigs, cement crumbled like sand, iron pillars bent like willow wands. The middle span melted like wax. Its wreckage clung around the tortured train, which gyrated madly for an instant in space. Immediately, a shattering rush of broken glass and wood descended upon Denis, cutting and bruising him with mangling violence. He felt the wrenching torsion of metal, and the grating of falling masonry. The inexpressible desolation of a hundred human voices, united in a sudden, short anguished cry of mingled agony and terror, fell upon his ears hideously, with the deathly fatality of a coronach. The walls of his compartment whirled about him and upon him, like a winding-sheet, the floor rushed over his head. As he spun round, with a loud cry he, too, shouted: "God help us!" then, faintly, the name: "Mary!"

Then the train with incredible speed, curving like a rocket, arched the darkness in a glittering parabola of light, and plunged soundlessly into the black hell of water below, where, like a rocket, it was instantly extinguished—for ever obliterated! For the infinity of a second, as he hurtled through the air, Denis knew what had happened. He knew everything, then instantly he ceased to know. At the same instant as the first, faint cry of his child ascended feebly in the byre at Levenford, his mutilated body hit the dark, raging water and lay dead, deep down upon the bed of the firth.

BOOK II

I

THE cutting cold of a March morning lay upon the High Street of Levenford. Large, dry snowflakes, floating as gently and softly as butterflies, insistently filled the air and lay deeply upon the frosted ground. The hard, delayed winter had been late of coming and was now tardy of passing, thought Brodie, as he stood in the doorway of his shop, looking up and down the quiet, empty street. Strangely, the quietness of the street consoled him, its emptiness gave him freer space to breathe. During the last three months it had been hard for him to face his fellow townsmen, and the lack of stir about him came as a respite to his suffering but unbroken pride. He could, for a moment, relax his inflexible front and admire his own indomitable will. Yes, his task had been difficult for the last three months but, by God, he had done it! The arrows they had launched at him had been many and had sunk deeply, but never by a word, never by a gesture, had he betrayed the quivering of his wounded and outraged pride. He had conquered. He pushed the square hat further back upon his head, thrust his thumbs into the armholes of his waistcoat, and, with his blunt nostrils doggedly sniffing the keen air, gazed aggressively down the silent thoroughfare. In spite of the biting cold he wore no overcoat or scarf; his intense satisfaction in the hardihood of his physique was such that he disdained this sign of weakness. What would I do with a coat, with MY constitution? was his contemptuous attitude, despite the fact that this morning he had been obliged to break a thin skin of ice upon the cold water in his ewer before he could sluice himself. The algid weather suited his disposition. He revelled in the iron frost, filled his chest invigoratingly with the chilled air, whilst the suction of his breath drew the white, sailing snowflakes on to his tongue, where they lay like melting hosts, filling him with a new refreshing force.

Suddenly, he saw a man approaching. Only Brodie's stimulated pride kept him at his door, for he recognised the figure as that of the glibbest, smoothest gossip in the Borough. "Damn his sleekit tongue," he muttered, as he heard the slow, muffled steps approach and saw the other deliberately cross the roadway. "I would like to rive it from his mouth. Ay! he's comin' over. I thought he would."

Up came Grierson, wrapped to his blue ears. As Brodie had anticipated, he stopped.

"Good morning to you, Mr. Brodie," he began, stressing the "you" with a nicety of accent that might have been interpreted as deferential, or merely as ironic.

"Morning," said Brodie shortly. He had suffered acutely from the hidden venom of that tongue in the past, and he distrusted it profoundly.

"The frost still holds firm, I fear," continued the other. "It's been a hard, hard winter, but, man, it doesna seem to affect you a bit. I believe you're made o' steel, you can thole anything."

"The weather suits me weel enough," growled Brodie, eyeing the other's blue nose contemptuously.

"The trouble is, though," replied Grierson smoothly, "that a' these hard frosts maun break some time. The ice has got to crack one day. There maun be a thaw, and the harder the frost the softer the thaw. There'll be a big change in the conditions here some day." He raised a guileless glance towards the other.

Brodie fully understood the double significance of the words, but he was not clever enough to reply in kind. "Is that so?" he said heavily, with a sneer. "Man, you're clever, clever."

"Na, na, Mr. Brodie. It's juist fair intuition! What the Romans ca'ed takin' the omens frae the weather."

"Indeed! ye're the scholar as weel, I see."

"Man!" went on Grierson, unperturbed, "this morning a wee robin-redbreast flew into my house—it was so perished like." He shook his head. "It must be awfu' weather for the birds—and onybody that hasna got a home to go to." Then, before Brodie could speak he added: "How are all the family?"

Brodie forced himself to reply calmly: "Quite well, thank ye. Nessie's gettin' on grandly at school, as no doubt ye've heard. She'll be runnin' awa' with all the prizes again this year." That's one for you, thought Brodie, with your big, stupid son that's always done out of first place by my clever lass.

"I hadna heard! But it's fine all the same." Grierson paused, then in a soft voice, remarked: "Have ye had ony word from the other daughter lately—Mary, I mean?"

Brodie gritted his teeth, but he controlled himself and said slowly: "I'll thank you not to mention that name again in my hearing."

Grierson manifested a great show of concern.

"'Deed, I'm sorry if I've upset you, Mr. Brodie, but I had aye a bit regard for that lass o' yours. I was gey upset at her lang illness, but I had heard tell the other day that she had gotten a post away in London, and I was wonderin' if it was through these folks in Darroch—the Foyles, I mean. Still I've nae doubt ye ken as little as me." He screwed up his eyes and glanced sideways at the other, as he continued: "Ay, I took great notice o' the affair. In a human sort o' way, ye ken. I was real touched when the wee, bit bairn died in the hospital."

Brodie eyed him stonily, but the torture continued.

"They say it was a real bonny wean, and the doctor was much upset when it slipped through his fingers. He took a great interest in the mother's case. I'm no' surprised either, it was so unusual, with the complications o' pneumonia and all." He shook his head, mournfully. "Man! what a calamity though, that the father wasna' spared to make an honest woman o'—ahem, ahem! Forgive me, Mr. Brodie! I clean forgot! I was just lettin' my silly tongue run away wi' me." Grierson was abjectly apologetic. He had rubbed Brodie on the raw, made him wince, and was clever enough to know when to withdraw.

Brodie looked right through the other. Inwardly he writhed, but in a low, strained voice he said: "Let your mealy-mouthed tongue run on like the Wellhall burn, it makes no odds to me."

It was a mistaken attitude, for it immediately offered an opportunity to renew the baiting which Grierson was not slow to seize. He laughed, with a soft, unctuous titter.

"That's richt, that's richt! That's the spirit that never flinches! I can't but admire ye, Mr. Brodie," he went on, "at the firm stand ye've taken amongst the disgrace o' it all. A man that had such an important standin' in the Borough might easily have been broken richt to bits by such a come-down, for there's no doubt that for months the whole town has been ringin' wi' it."

"The gabble of the Cross is of no moment to me," retorted Brodie, with a heaving breast. He could have killed the other with his glance, but he could, with dignity, use no other weapons, and his pride forbade him to retreat.

"Ay, ay," replied Grierson speculatively, "but it might shake up *another* man to be the butt o' a' these dirty divots, and the laughin' stock o' the place. Man!" he added, in a low tone, almost as an afterthought, "it would be enough to drive an ordinary man to the drink for consolation."

Brodie lowered at him from beneath his bushy eyebrows. Had they been calumniating him on that score, too? "Nothing like a wee droppie to cheer up a man, especially in this weather," drawled Grierson, in an insinuating tone.

"Well, I maun be off. It's cold work standin' bletherin'. Good day to you, Mr. Brodie." Grierson passed quickly out of range with meek, bowed head, without giving the other time to reply. Although he shivered from his stand in the freezing air, inwardly he warmed himself at a fire of delicious self-appreciation. He glowed at the thought of the quiver in Brodie's fierce eye as his delicately pointed barbs had sunk home, and feasted his recollection on the great, heaving sigh that the cumulation of their poison had finally produced. He chuckled at the richness of the jest to relate at the club this evening; they would laugh till they burst at the story, as he would tell it. He tee-heed to himself in anticipation. And why shouldn't he have lowered the stuck-up runt? What did he think he was, with his insolent, haughty airs? Besides, what man would have turned his own child out, like a dog, on such a night? It had been the death of the bairn. Ay, he had nearly killed Mary by it too, if reports were to be believed! Pneumonia, and child-birth fever, and God only knows what she had suffered. It was scandalous, yes, even if she was a precious ———. He went on, and out of sight, still hugging his reflection closely.

Brodie watched him down the road, his lips drawn into a thin, crooked line. That was the way of them, he thought. They would try to stone him, to kick him, to batter him to bits now that he was down. But, at the very idea, he drew himself up proudly. He was not down! Let them that suggested it wait and see. The whole, damnable business would have blown over, would be only dimly remembered, in another month or two. His real friends, the gentry, the big people of the district, must feel for him only sympathy and regret. But, at the memory of what he had endured, his tense lips quivered slightly. All those weeks, whilst Mary had lain between life and death at the Cottage Hospital, he had stood with the hard, craggy indifference of a rock, immovable in his determination to outcast his daughter. By her own act she had outlawed herself, and he had proclaimed openly that he would let her rot beyond the bounds of decent society. Under the wordless wilting of his wife, under the loud-tongued gossip and hotly fluctuating opinion of the town, under the pressure of a biting, private interview with Dr. Renwick, under the contumely of public affronts and reproaches, he had remained immutable and unyielding. He had not looked near her, and the consideration of his inflexible resolution now soothed his ruffled spirit. But they did not know what he had suffered; the blow to his pride had been almost mortal. With a grim relief he diverted his thoughts to the solace which had comforted him through these bitter months, and he allowed his mind to dwell gloatingly upon the Tay Bridge disaster! He did not consider with any satisfaction the death of the bastard infant—he had from the first disowned it—but the thought of Foyle's broken body— the pitiful remains of which had been recovered, and now lay putrefying in Darroch soil—had rarely been out of his thoughts. It was the salve for his wounded arrogance. His imagination had riotously indulged itself amongst a host of vivid, morbid details. He did not care that a hundred others had perished; the loss of the entire train was but the instrument of a just vengeace. This one man had wronged him, had dared to oppose him, and now he was dead. It was a sweet consolation!

He was turning to go into his shop when he was again accosted. A little man, with all the restless timidity of a rabbit, had bolted out from next door to speak with him. It was Dron. Contempt marked Brodie's drawn features as he gazed at the jerky agitation of the other, and his self-assurance, restored always by an appreciation of the terror he could inspire in others, returned, whilst he surmised disdainfully the object of the little man's visit. Would he be going to tell him about the arrival of his brat? he wondered, as he noted the peculiar, suppressed look that marked him.

Dron's aspect was certainly remarkable, as, trembling with a repressed excitement, rubbing his hands rapidly together with a rustling sound, his pale eyelashes blinking ceaselessly, his legs shaking as though with tetanus, he essayed, stammeringly, to speak.

"Out with it, then," sneered Brodie. "and don't keep me on my own door-step any longer. What species o' animal is it ye've been blessed wi' this time?"

"It's no exactly that," said Dron hurriedly, with a fresh spasm of fidgets. Then he added slowly, like one who has rehearsed it carefully: "I was just wonderin' if you were quite sure you didna want these premises o' mine I offered you last back end." He jerked his head in the direction of the empty shop. "You may have forgotten that you threw me out on the pavement that day, but I havena! I havena forgotten that ye flung me out on the broad o' my back." His voice rose in a shrill crescendo at the last words.

"Ye fell down, my little mannie, that was all. If ye chose to sit on your backside outside my place o' business I canna blame ye; but if it's no' as pleasant a position as ye might find, then talk to your wife about it. It's no affair o' mine," said Brodie, calmly. Yet the other's eye fascinated him, pervaded as it was by two antagonistic emotions warring for supremacy, filled by such a look as might occupy the half-terrified, half-exultant eye of a rabbit .hat views an enemy caught in its own snare.

"I was askin' ye if ye were sure," Dron palpitated, without heeding the interruption; then he hurried on:

"I say are ye quite sure ye dinna want these premises o' mine? Because if ye did want the shop, ye canna have it. I havena let it! I havena let it! I've sold it! I've sold it to the Mungo Hat & Hosiery Company." He shouted out the last words in triumph, then he rushed on. "I've gotten more than my price—for they have unlimited capital. They're going to fit up a grand, big emporium with everything, and a special window and a special department for hats and caps. I knew ye would like to hear the news, so I couldna wait. The minute I had signed the contract I came round." His voice rose gloatingly, almost to hysteria. "Put that in your pipe and smoke it, you gurly, big bully!" he yelled. "Smoke it till it sickens ye. That'll learn ye to mishandle folks weaker than yoursel'." Then, as if in fear that Brodie would attack him, he whirled round and scuttled off to his burrow.

Brodie stood perfectly still. Dron's pusillanimous ebullition disturbed him not at all, but his news was catastrophic. Would misfortune never desert him? The Mungo company, originating in, and at first confined solely to, Glasgow, had for some time past been reaching out tentacles

161

into the adjacent countryside; like pioneers, realising the advantage of the principle of multiple shops, they had invaded most of the townships in Lanarkshire and now they were stretching slowly down the Clyde. This incursion, Brodie knew, had meant disaster for many a local shopkeeper; for, not only did the Company indulge in such flashing pyrotechnics as bargain sales and glittering window displays, wherein their articles were marked, not in plain honest shillings, but in deceptive figures ending cunningly in 11¾d., and were actually adorned by trumpery cards which tempted the fancy seductively under such terms as: "The Thing for the Bairns," or "Real Value," or even "Exquisite," but they cut prices ruthlessly in the face of competition. They were in Darroch and Ardfillan, that he knew, but, although they were not exclusively hatters, he had often flattered himself into thinking that they would leave Levenford alone because of his old-established, deeply rooted business. He had told himself disdainfully that they wouldn't sell a hat in a year. And now they were coming! He was aware that it would be a fight, and he would make it a bitter fight, in which he would let them try what they could do to James Brodie, then take the consequences. A sudden realisation took him of the proximity they would occupy to him, and bitter a surge of black resentment made him shake a menacing fist at the empty shop as he turned and went into his own.

To Perry, meekly ubiquitous as always, he threw out: "What are ye glumping at there, you dough-faced sheep? Do some work for a change. That empty look of yours fair scunners me."

"What would you like me to do, sir? I'm not serving."

"I can see you're not serving. Do you mean to infer that I have no customers, me that's got the best and most solid business in the town. It's the snow that's keeping folks away, you fool. Clear up the place a bit, or take a bar of soap and go out and wash your feet," shouted Brodie as he banged into his office.

He sat down. Now that he was alone, and his bold front to the world slightly lowered, the almost imperceptible change in him became faintly discernible in the tincture of hollowness which touched the smooth, firm line of his cheek, in the tenuous line of bitterness that ran downwards from the angle of his mouth. On his desk the *Herald* lay unopened—he had not looked at a paper for months, an omission supremely significant —and now, with a gesture of negligent distaste, he slashed it off his desk and on to the floor with a fierce swap of his open palm. Immediately his hand sought his pocket, and he drew out, with familiar unconsciousness, his pipe and tobacco pouch, looked at them suddenly as if he wondered how they had come into his hands, then laid them on the desk before him, with a grimace of aversion. He did not wish to smoke on this morning which had been so consistently miserable for him. Although there was a bright coal fire in the room and, despite his vaunted indifference to the inclemency of the weather, he suddenly felt chilly: whilst a shiver ran through him he reflected on what Grierson had said. "There's nothing to keep out the cold, or cheer a man up, like a wee droppie." A wee droppie! what an expression for a grown man to use, thought Brodie; but it was like Grierson to talk like that, with his soft, pussy voice and his creeping, sneaking ways. The obvious construction of the remark which rose to his mind was that, at the Cross, they had him a drunkard already, he who hadn't touched drink for months.

He jerked out of his seat impatiently, and looked through the frosted window at the snow which was everywhere, on the ground, on the frozen Leven, on the house tops, in the air, falling relentlessly, as though it would never cease to fall. The drifting flakes appeared to Brodie each like an oppression in itself supportable, but becoming insufferable by weight of numbers. As he cogitated, a dormant molecule of thought began to swell within his mind. He felt in his dull brain the blind injustice of the veiled accusation that he had been consoling himself with drink. "That's it," he muttered. "I'm gettin' the blame, and none of the comfort." The desolation of the scene again struck frigidly upon him. He shivered once more and continued to talk to himself. This propensity of articulate self-communion was entirely new, but now, as he spoke thus, the process of his ideas became more lucid and less entangled. "They say I'm takin' a dram do they; it's the sort of thing the measly swine would say, without rhyme nor reason; but by God! I will take them at their word. It's what I'm needin' anyway, to take the taste o' that braxy out o' my mouth—the poor, knock-kneed cratur' that he is, wi' his 'wee droppies.' Him and his sleekit 'beg your pardons' and 'by your leaves,' and his scrapin' and bowin' down in the dirt. Some day I'll kick him and keep him down in it. Ay. I maun have something to clean my mouth after this mornin's wark." His face grimaced dourly as he added ironically, still addressing the empty room: "but thank you all the same, Mister Grierson—thank you for your verra acceptable suggestion."

Then his features changed; suddenly he experienced a wild and reckless desire to drink. His body felt strong, so brutally powerful that he wanted to crush iron bars; so eagerly alive, with such vast potentiality for enjoyment, that he felt he could empty huge reservoirs of liquor. "What good does it do me to live like a blasted stickit minister—they talk about me just the same. I'll give them something to babble about, blast them!" he cried, as he pulled his hat down over his eyes and strode darkly out of the shop.

A few doors off stood a small, quiet inn, "The Winton Arms," owned by an elderly, respectable matron named Phemie Douglas, famed for her liquor, her virtue, and her snug sitting-room—known as "Phemie's wee back parlour" to the choicer spirits amongst the better class of the townspeople, for whom it was a favourite howff. Brodie, however, on entering the tavern, avoided this social centre, as he now had no time for words; he wanted to drink, and the longer he waited the more he desired it. He entered the public bar, which was empty, and demanded from the barmaid a large whisky toddy. "Hurry up and bring it," he said, in a voice dry from the violence of his craving. Now that he had ordained that he would drink, nothing could stop him, nothing arrest the swelling urge which made his throat dry, caused his hands to clench and unclench restlessly, made his feet stamp chafingly upon the sawdust floor of the bar whilst he awaited the hot whisky. When she brought it he drank the scalding liquid in one, long breath.

"Another," he said impatiently.

Altogether he had four, large whiskies, hot and potent as flame, which he consumed as rapidly as he obtained them, and which now worked within him like the activation of some fiery ferment. As he glowed, he began to feel lighter; the shadows of the last three months were lifting; they still swirled like smoke clouds about his brain, but nevertheless they lifted. A sardonic leer played about his mouth as a sense of his superiority, and of his invulnerable personality, impressed him, but this was the sole expression of the thoughts which rushed within him. His body remained quiet, his actions grew cautious, more restrained; he remained absolutely within himself, whilst his bruised pride healed itself in the roseate thoughts which coursed swiftly through his mind. The barmaid was young, attractive, and quite desirous of being talked to by this strange, huge man, but Brodie ignored her, did not even observe her, as, wrapped in the splendid emancipation from his hateful despondency, and engrossed in the incoherent but dazzling consideration of his future plans and triumphs, he remained silent, staring blankly in front of him. Finally he asked for a bottle of whisky, paid for it, and went out.

Back in his office he continued to drink. His brain clarified with each glass, grew more dominant, more compelling; his body responded more quickly and more perfectly to his movements; he now sanctioned with an intense approval all his recent actions.

The empty bottle stood on the table before him, bearing on the label the words: "Mountain Dew," which struck his bemused fancy as notably appropriate; for now he felt as powerful as a mountain and as sparkling as dew.

"Yes," he muttered, addressing himself to the bottle, "you mark my words; they can't down me. I'm more than a match for them. I can master them. Everything I did was right. I wouldna draw back a step o' the road I took wi' her. Just you wait and see how I'll go ahead now. Everything will be orgotten and nothing will stop me! I'll get the whip hand o' them."

Actually he did not know whom he was indicting, but he included largely and indeterminately in that category, all who he imagined had opposed him, slighted him, or failed to recognise him as the man he was.

He did not now think of the threatened opposition to his business, which became, in the swollen magnitude of his disdainful pride, too petty, too ridiculously ineffectual to affect him adversely. The opposition which he recognised was universal, intangible, yet crystallised in the feeling that any man's hand might be raised against his sacrosanct dignity: and now this obsession, always latent within him, strengthened and became more corrosive in his mind. And yet conversely, whilst the danger to his position loomed the more largely before him, his faith in his ability to conquer such a menace was augmented and exalted in such a manner as to render him almost omnipotent.

At last he started, took out his watch and looked at it. The hands, which appeared larger and blacker than usual, showed ten minutes to one.

"Time for dinner," he told himself agreeably. "Time to see that braw, tidy wife o' mine. It's a grand thing for a man to have such a bonnie wife to draw him hame." He got up impressively, but with a slight, almost imperceptible sway, and walked solidly out of his office, disregarding the awestruck, cringing Perry absolutely. He stalked through the shop and into the street, gained the middle of the street, and held it like a lord. Along the crown of the causeway he swaggered, head erect, shoulders thrown back, planting his feet in front of him with a magnificent sense of his own importance. The few people who were abroad gazed at him in amazement, and as, from the corner of his eye, he saw them glance, their astonishment fed his vanity, his intoxicated assurance battened on their wonder. "Take a good look," his attitude seemed to say. "It's Brodie you're lookin' at—James Brodie, and, by God, he's a man!" He walked through the snow the whole way home as though he headed a triumphal procession, keeping so exactly in the centre of the road, and holding so undeviatingly to his course, that such traffic as traversed the streets had perforce to go round him, leaving him the undisputed king of the causeway.

Outside his house he paused. The white envelope of snow vested it with an unreal and delusive dignity, softening the harsh lines, relieving the squat and rigid contours, blending the incongruous elements with its clinging touch so that, before his fuddled eyes, it reared itself in massive grandeur, looming against the opaque, slate-coloured sky with an illusion of infinite dimensions. He had never liked it so well or admired it so much, and a sense of elation that he should possess it held him as he marched to the front door and entered his home.

In the hall he removed his hat and, with wide extravagant gestures, scattered in all directions the thick snow that had caked upon it, amusedly watching the mushy gobbets go slushing against the roof, the walls, the pictures, the chandelier; then, wildly, he stamped his heavy boots upon the floor, dislodging hard, pressed lumps of ice and snow. It would give that handless slut of his something to do to clean up his mess, he thought, as he walked into the kitchen with the air of a conqueror.

Immediately, he sat down and delved into the huge, steaming bowl of broth, sweet with the essence of beef and bones, and stiff with the agglutination of barley, that stood on the table anticipating his arrival, the ignored reminder of his wife's devotion and forethought. Just the thing for a cold day, he thought, as he supped greedily with the zest of a ravenous animal, lifting huge, heaped spoonfuls rapidly to his mouth and working his jaws incessantly. The meat and small fragments of bone that floated through the pottage he rent and crushed between his hard teeth, revelling in the fact that for weeks his appetite had not been so keen or the taste of food so satisfying upon his tongue.

"That was grand," he admitted to Mrs. Brodie, smacked his lips coarsely at her, "and a good thing for you. If ye had singed my broth on a day like this I would have flung it about your lugs." Then, as she paused at the unusual praise, he bellowed at her: "What are ye gawkin' at; is this all I've to get for my dinner?"

At once she retreated, but, as she hastily brought in the boiled beef and an ashet of potatoes and cabbage, she wondered fearfully what had drawn him from out his perpetual, grim taciturnity to this roaring, devilish humour. He hacked off a lump of the fat beef and thrust it upon his plate, which he then loaded with potatoes and cabbage, began to eat, and with his mouth full, regarded her derisively.

"My, but you are the fine figure of a woman, my dear," he sneered, between champing mouthfuls. "You're about as straight as that lovely nose o' yours. No, don't run away." He raised his knife, with a broad, minatory gesture, to arrest her movement, whilst he finished masticating a chunk of beef. Then he went on, with a fine show of concern: "I must admit ye havena got bonnier lately; all this worry has raddled ye; in fact, you're more like an old cab-horse than ever now. I see you are still wearin' that dish clout of a wrapper." He picked his teeth reflectively with a prong of his fork. "It suits you right well."

Mamma stood there like a wilted reed, unable to sustain his derisive stare, keeping her eyes directed out of the window, as though this abstracted gaze enabled her better to endure his taunts. Her face was grey with an ill, vitreous translucency, her eyelids retracted with a dull, fixed despondency; her thin, work-ugly hands played nervously with a loose tape at her waist.

Suddenly a thought struck Brodie. He looked at the clock. "Where's Nessie?" he shouted.

"I gave her some lunch to school, to save her coming back in the snow."

He grunted. "And my mother," he demanded.

"She wouldna get up to-day for fear of the cold," she whispered.

A guffaw shook him. "That's the spirit you should have had, you fushionless creature. If ye'd had that kind o' gumption ye would have stood up better, and no' run done so quick." Then, after a pause, he continued: "So it's just you and me together. That's very touchin', is't not? Well! I've grand news for ye! A rich surprise!"

Immediately her look left the window; she gazed at him with a numb expectation.

"Don't excite yourself, though," he scoffed. "it's not about your fine, bawdy daughter. You'll never know where she is! It's business this time. You're always such a help and encouragement to a man that I must tell ye this." He paused importantly. "The Mungo Clothing Company have taken the shop next door to your husband—ay—next door to Brodie—the Hatter." He laughed uproariously, "So maybe ye'll find yourself in the poor-house soon!" He howled at his own humour.

Mrs. Brodie restored her gaze into space. She suddenly felt weak and sat down; but as she did so his mocking eye darkened, his face, already flushed with hot food, flamed sullenly.

"Did I tell ye to sit down, ye limmer! Stand up till I've done with ye."

Like an obedient child, she rose.

"Maybe the fact that these blasted swine are goin' to have the audacity to settle on my door-step doesna mean much to you. You get your meat and drink too easy perhaps, while I've got to work for it. Does your weak mind not see it's going to be a fight to a finish—to their finish?" He banged his fist on the table. His ranting gaiety was wearing off and giving place, instead, to a morose reactionary temper. "If ye canna think—ye can serve. Go and get my pudding."

She brought him some steamed apple dumpling, and he began to attack it wolfishly, whilst she stood like some bedraggled flunkey at the other end of the table. The news he had given her caused her little concern. In the shadow of Brodie's dominant personality she did not fear pecuniary disaster; although he kept her household allowance parsimoniously tight, she understood, always, that money was free with him, and often she had seen him draw out from his pocket a shining handful of golden sovereigns. Her dejected spirit was grappling with another care. She had not received a letter from Matthew for six weeks, and, before that, his communications to her had been growing increasingly brief, and so irregular as to cause her the deepest vexation and misgiving. Mary she had now abandoned as irrevocably lost to her; she did not even know her whereabouts, except that it had been rumoured that the Foyles had found her a situation of some sort in London, but of what nature she did not know; now it was Matthew upon whom she built her entire hopes and affection. Nessie was so absolutely Brodie's exclusive favourite that only Matt was now left to Mamma. But, apart from this, she had, indeed, always loved him best and, now that he was neglecting to write to her, she imagined that ill-health or misfortune had surely befallen him. Suddenly she started.

"Give me some sugar. What are you moping and 'moonin' about?" Brodie was shouting at her. "This dumplin' tastes like sourocks. You've got as much hand for a dumplin' as my foot." The more the effect of the liquor left him the more surly he became. He snatched the sugar basin from her, sweetened the pudding to his liking, then consumed it with every indication of dissatisfaction.

Finally, he rose, shaking himself in an effort to dispel the heavy lethargy which was beginning to affect him. Going to the door he turned to his wife and said cuttingly: "Ye'll get sitting down now! I've no doubt the moment my back's turned you'll be crouching at the fire wi' your trashy books, while I'm away working for you. Don't tell me you're not lazy; don't tell me you're not a slut. If I say so, then ye are—and that's the end o't. I know ye for what you are—you lazy besom." In his own increasing ill-temper he sought sullenly for some new means of wounding her, and, as an idea of a parting shot of extreme subtlety struck him, his eyes gleamed, maliciously, with the humour of using Dron's news of this morning, speciously, as a pretext for her discomfiture.

"Now that we've got opposition in the business," he continued slowly, pausing at the door, "we must economise. There'll have to be less wastin' and throwin' out in this house, and for a start I've made up my mind to cut down your allowance for the house. Ye'll get ten shillings a week less from now on, and don't forget I want no savin' on my food. Ye maun just cut out what ye waste and give me the same as usual. Do ye hear me. Ten shillings a week less for ye! Think over that when ye're at your novelettes." Then he turned, and left the room.

II

WHEN her husband had gone Mrs. Brodie did, indeed, sit down, feeling that if, by his departure, she had not been permitted to rest her tired body, she would have fallen at his feet upon the floor from sheer weariness and from a gnawing pain within her side. This pain was peculiar, like a slow, harassing stitch which, though she was so inured to it as almost to ignore it, continually dragged upon her strength and rendered her, when she remained standing for any length of time, unduly and incomprehensibly fatigued. But, as she sat there, it was apparent from her features, which had aged considerably in the last three months, and which now bore the look of remote concentration, that she was not selfishly occupied by the consideration of her own physical disabilities, but was influenced by a deeper and more moving cause for sorrow.

Brodie's last threat had not yet greatly affected her, she was, at the moment, too crushed to realise its portent, and, although she vaguely understood that his conduct had been unusual and his manner exceptional, she had no suspicion of the cause. Nor was she greatly perturbed at his abuse. On this especial side of her nature she was so calloused to the lash of his tongue that she now hardly noticed a variation in the mode of her chastisement, and against any of his sneering charges it never occurred to her to attempt to defend herself; she could not have uttered the mildest or most logical assertion in her favour contrary to his will. Long ago she had realised, with a crushing finality, that she was chained to a man of domineering injustice, that her sole defence would be to develop a supine indifference to every irrational imputation with which he vilified her. She had not entirely succeeded, and he had broken her, but she had at least evolved the faculty of inhibiting him from her meditation in his absence from the home. Therefore, the moment he went out, she directed her thoughts away from him, and automatically they returned to the object of her recent solicitude—her son.

At first, Matt's letters had reached her with a satisfying and affectionate regularity, and with these initial letters he had every month sent her the sum of five pounds to invest for him in the Levenford Building Society. She had loved the tone of these early letters; they had been to her so engrossingly interesting, of such an elevated sentiment, and so filled with strongly expressed moral rectitude. Then, gradually, a slow transition had occurred, and his letters, though still appearing regularly with each mail, had dwindled in volume, and altered in principle, so that, though she had devoured the few husks of scanty and frequently disturbing news within them, her maternal craving had not been satisfied; nor had the half-hearted, stereotyped expression of regard, with which they had invariably concluded, stifled her vague misgivings. When he had thus cut down his epistles to the shortest and most meagre limits, she had begun to write to him reprovingly, but alas, ineffectually, and his acknowledgment of her first letter in this spirit had been to ignore it completely, and to miss the mail for the first time since he had left her. His omissions subsequently had grown more frequent, more disturbing, and now she had not heard from him for nearly six weeks.

Agnes Moir had suffered in the same respect, and his later letters to her had been indifferent in sentiment to the point of actual coldness, filled with veiled, then direct allusions, to the unsuitability of the Indian climate for a wife, and interpolated by intimations as to his unworthiness, or unwillingness, to accept her chastely proffered matrimonial relationship. Miss Moir's soft, amorous nature had received a rude and painful check, by these chilling and infrequent effusions. Now, as she thought of Agnes, Mamma, with the irrational yet inherent notion of seeking consolation in a despondency equal to her own, decided despite her own lassitude and the inclemency of the weather, to visit her future daughter-in-law. A glance at the clock told her that she had two free hours which she could utilise for this purpose without being missed by any of the household—an important point as, since Mary's banishment, Brodie expected her to account to him for her every absence from the house.

Accordingly, she got up and, ascending to her room, discarded her wrapper by allowing it to slide from her to the floor; without once regarding herself in the glass she made her toilet by giving her face a quick wipe with the wetted end of a towel. She next withdrew from the wardrobe what was revealed to be, after removing several pinned, protecting sheets of paper, an old sealskin jacket. The jacket, a relic of the days before her marriage, was now worn, frayed, shiny, and in places of a drab, brownish tinge. It had been kept and worn intermittently for a period of over twenty years, and this decayed and dilapidated coat, which had once enclosed her young, virgin figure, held as much tragedy as Margaret Brodie herself. She did not, however, view it in this sombre light, regarding it as sealskin, real sealskin, no longer perhaps elegant in cut, but still genuine sealskin, and treasuring it accordingly as the most splendid garment she possessed. For a moment she forgot her sorrow as, holding up the jacket, denuded of its wrappings, to the satisfaction of her appraising eyes, she shook it gently, touched the faded fur with caressing fingers, then, with a sigh, as though she had shaken out from its musty texture faded recollections of her forgotten youth, slowly she assumed it, when at least it had the merit of covering her rusty gown and sheathing warmly her decrepit figure. Her next action was to cram upon her untidy hair, and to stab carelessly into position, a black hat plumed with a withered pinion which trailed, with a frightful travesty of coquetry, behind her left ear; having thus accomplished completely her vesture for the outer air, she hastened downstairs and left the house with a mien which was almost stealthy.

In the street, unlike her husband, she did not swagger her way down the middle of the road, but instead, crept along the inside of the pavement with short, shuffling steps, her head inclined, her face blue with cold, her figure shirking observation, her entire aspect a graphic exposition of resigned martyrdom. The snow turned her dull sealskin to glittering ermine, blew into her eyes and mouth and made her cough, penetrated her thin, inadequate boots and soaked her feet so profusely that, long before she reached the Moirs' shop, they squelched at every step.

Despite the unexpectedness of this visitation, Agnes was delighted to see her, and welcomed her warmly, whilst a quick look passed between the two women, each searching the other's eyes for some recorded sign of better tidings. Immediately they knew their eager hope to be unfulfilled, deferred, and their eyes fell dejectedly; but they still voiced the question which each had, silently, already answered.

"Have you had anything this week, Aggie?"

"Not yet, Mamma." She fondly addressed Mrs. Brodie by that term in the sanguine anticipation of her future relationship. "Have you?"

"No, dear, not yet, but maybe the mail is delayed by the bad weather," said Mrs. Brodie, in a despondent tone.

"I shouldn't be surprised," replied Agnes, forlornly.

Actually each attempted to delude the other, for they knew by heart the incidence of the posts from India, and the mystery of the passage of mail ships was now to them an open book; but to-day, under the intolerable burden of their growing uncertainty, this feeble effort of deception was useless and they now gazed at each other blankly, for a moment, as if they had already exhausted their entire range of conversation. Agnes, by virtue of her position as hostess, recovered first, and collecting her forces said, considerately:

"You'll have a cup of tea with me, Mamma. You're all wet and cold from the snow."

Mrs. Brodie assented dumbly and followed her into the little back shop where, amidst a profusion of empty biscuit tins, sweet bottles, and wooden chocolate boxes, a small iron stove threw out a meagre heat.

"Sit down there, Mamma," continued Agnes, opening the metal window of the stove and placing a chair before this small glowing mouth. "The weather's keeping us as quiet as can be, so I'll have time for a crack with you."

By mutual consent an armistice was tacitly proclaimed for the cessation of their unhappy exchanges, and, whilst Agnes boiled the kettle, Mamma steamed her damp boots at the fire and agreed, meditatively:

"Ay! 'Twas snowin' heavy again as I came along. It's good to see a blink of heat on a day like this."

At these words Agnes threw a small shovelful of coke on to the red embers, and enquired:

"Will you have tea or cocoa, Mamma? I've got some fresh Epps' in this week."

"I think I would prefer the cocoa. It's more sustaining, and nourishing like, than tea on a cold day. That's one thing about you, Agnes, you always offer a body something tasty."

"I can surely do that for you, Mamma," replied Miss Moir, pursing her lips significantly. "It would be a pity if I couldn't put myself about a bit for you. Will ye not take your coat off?" and she made an advance to assist in the removal of the sealskin.

"No! No! thanks," cried Mamma hastily, with a drearful consciousness of her deficiencies underneath. "I'll not be biding that long." But her eyes watered gratefully as she took the cup of hot cocoa and sipped it appreciatively; she even accepted and nibbled a sweet biscuit; then, as comfort stole through her, she sighed:

"It's been a hard winter for me. I don't know how I've come through it."

"I well know that, Mamma! You have suffered."

"Ay, I've suffered! I never thought I could have endured such disgrace, Agnes, I didn't merit it. And I think her father blames me for not having watched Mary better." She could hardly bring herself to articulate her daughter's name, it had been so firmly proscribed from her lips.

"Nobody could be blamed for her fall but herself, Mamma. Your influence could only have been for good—wickedness is in the person that sins. You'll just need to let me take her place."

"That's good o' ye, Agnes, but there's times at night I can't get her out of my head. I never thought I should miss her so much—she was always that quiet and douce about the house—and I don't even know where she is."

"You must forget her now," insisted Agnes gently.

"Her father wouldna let me speir a word about her. Not even when she was near dyin' in the hospital. Not even when the puir bairn died."

Agnes drew her mouth together.

"I'm not sure if I should tell you, Mamma," she began, slowly, "and it's not a pleasant subject for me—it's not the thing for a nice girl to be connected with even indirectly—but I heard the other day that she was in London." She gave to the name of the city an accent of imputation and opprobrium which seemed to summarise her opinion of its manifold potentialities for wickedness.

"Do ye know what she's doing?" cried Mamma.

Agnes veiled her eyes and shook her head.

"I can't be sure," she replied, lowering her voice, "but I've been told—only been told mind you—that it's service."

"A servant!" gasped Mamma. "Oh dearie me! what a thing to come to! It's terrible! What would her father say if he knew! A Brodie a servant!"

"What else is she fitted for," replied Agnes, with a faint toss of her head. "We should be thankful it's an honest occupation, if indeed it is so."

Despite the bond between Mrs. Brodie and herself it gave her a pleasurable sense of moral and social superiority to impart this news, which she had avidly sought amongst the tittle-tattle of the town.

"A servant in London!" repeated Mamma, faintly, "It's awfu'. Could these folks in Darroch no' have done something for her?"

"Indeed that's the very point," cried Agnes. "These Foyles wanted the child for the sake of the son's memory, so as to take it back to Ireland with them—they've gone back there ye know. Ye can't believe all ye hear; of course there's all sorts of stories about, but I believe the truth is that, when it died, they took a spite at her and got rid of her the quickest they could!"

Mrs. Brodie shook her head negatively.

"That wouldna be difficult," she retorted. "Mary was always an independent girl; she would take charity from nobody—no, she would work for her living first."

"Well, anyway, Mamma, I didn't like telling you, but I thought it best you should know. Anyway, your responsibility for her is ended. Mind you, although she has lowered the name of my intended, I bear no grudge against her. I hope she may in time repent; but you have got others to think of."

"Ay, that's true, Agnes! I maun swallow the bitter pill; but I will say this—I never thought much of Mary, never valued her until I lost her. Still I maun forget if I can, and think of them that's left to us." She sighed heavily. "What's come over our poor Matt at all, at all? It fair breaks my heart not to have news o' him. Can he be ill, think ye?" They were now embarked upon the consideration of the subject vital to them both, and, after a moment's thought, Miss Moir shook her head, dubiously.

"He's said nothing about his health," she replied. "He's been off his work once or twice I know, but I don't think it was from sickness."

"Maybe he wouldn't like to frighten us," said Mrs. Brodie, diffidently. "There's agues and fevers and jaundice and all kinds of awfu' troubles out in these foreign parts. He might even have got sunstroke, although it's strange to think of such a thing with all this snow about us here. Matt was never a strong boy." Then she added, inconsequently: "He aye had a weak chest in the winter, and bronchitis, that needed thick garments."

"But, Mamma," cried Agnes impatiently, "he would never get bronchitis in a hot country. They would never get snow like this in Calcutta."

"I ken that, Agnes," replied Mrs. Brodie firmly, "but a weakness like that might work inwardly in a hot country, and forbye if he opened his pores he might sit doun and get a chill, as easy as look at ye."

Agnes did not seem to take kindly to this train of thought and she arrested it by a pause, after which she said, slowly:

"I've been wondering, Mamma, if some of these black persons have not been exerting an evil influence over Matt. There's people called Rajahs—rich heathen princes—that I've read awful things about, and Matt might be led away. He might be easily led," she added solemnly—recollecting, perhaps, her own enticement of the receptive youth.

Mrs. Brodie instantly had visions of all the potentates of India luring her son from grace with jewels, but indignantly she repudiated the sudden, baleful thought.

"How can ye say that, Agnes?" she cried. "He kept the best of company in Levenford. You should know that! He was never the one for bad companions or low company."

But Agnes who, for a Christian woman, had an intensive knowledge of her subject, which must necessarily have come to her through the marvellous intuition of love, continued relentlessly:

"Then, Mamma, I hardly like to let the words cross my lips, but they have wicked, wicked attractions out there—like dancing girls that—that charm snakes and dance without——" Miss Moir, with downcast eyes, broke off significantly and blushed, whilst the down on her upper lip quivered modestly.

Mrs. Brodie gazed at her with eyes as horrified as if they beheld a nest of those snakes which Agnes so glibly described; demoralised by the appalling suddenness of a suggestion which had never before entered her mind, she wildly visualised one of these shameless houris abandoning the charming of reptiles to charm away the virtue of her son.

"Mat's no' a boy like that!" she gasped.

Miss Moir compressed her lips delicately and bridled, then raised her heavy eyebrows with an air of one who could have revealed to Mrs. Brodie secrets regarding the profundities of Matthew's passionate nature which had hitherto been undreamed of. As she sipped her cocoa her attitude seemed to say: "You ought to know by now the propensities of your children. Only my inviolate and virtuous maidenhood has kept your son pure."

"Ye've no proof, have ye, Agnes?" wailed Mrs. Brodie, her apprehension strengthened by the other's strange air.

"I have no definite proof, of course, but I can put two and two together," replied Miss Moir coldly. "If you can read between the lines of these last letters of his he's always at that club of his, and playing billiard matches, and out at night with other men, and smoking like a furnace." Then, after a moment's silence she added, petulantly: "He should never been allowed to smoke. It was a step in the wrong direction. I never liked the idea of these cigars; it was downright fast!"

Mrs. Brodie wilted visibly at the obvious insinuation that she had countenanced her son's first step on the road to ruin.

"But, Aggie," she blurted out, "you let him smoke an' all, for I mind well he persuaded me by saying ye thought it manly."

"You're his mother. I only said to please the boy. You know I would do anything for him," retorted Agnes with a sniff which verged almost into a sob.

"And I would do everything for him, too," replied Mrs. Brodie hopelessly; "but I don't know what's going to come of it at all."

"I've been seriously wondering," pursued Agnes, "if you ought not to get Mr. Brodie to write a strong letter to Matt, sort of, well, reminding him of his duties and obligations to those at home. I think it's high time something was done about it."

"Oh! that wouldna do at all," cried Mamma hastily. "It would never do. I could never approach him. It's not in me, and besides it's not the kind of thing his father would do." She trembled at an idea so antagonistic to her invariable line of conduct towards Brodie, so contrary to her usual concealment of everything that might provoke that imperial wrath, and she shook her head sadly, as she added: "We maun do what we can ourselves, for his father wouldna stir his finger to help him. It may be unnatural, but it's his style. He thinks he's done a' he should do."

Agnes looked grieved. "I know Matt was always afraid—always respected his father's word," she said, "and I'm sure you don't want any more discredit on the family."

"No, Agnes, I don't like to contradict you to your face, but I'm certain you're not on the right track. I would never believe wrong of my boy. You're anxious, like me, and it's put you on the wrong idea. Wait a bit and you'll have a grand, big budget of good news next week."

"It can't come quick enough for me," replied Miss Moir, in a frigid tone which coldly indicated her grievance against Mrs. Brodie in particular, and her growing resentment, fed by the recollection of Mary's recent disgrace, against the name of Brodie in general. Her breast heaved and she was about to utter a bitter, contumacious reproach when suddenly the shop door bell went "ping," and she was obliged, with heightening colour, to rise servilely to answer the call, and to serve a small boy with an inconsiderable quantity of confectionery. This supremely undignified interruption did nothing towards restoring her equanimity but, instead, activated her to a lively irritation and, as the penetrating voice of her client demanding a halfpennyworth of black-striped balls clearly penetrated the air, the obstinate perversity of her temper deepened.

Unconscious of the working of this angry ferment in Miss Moir's exuberant bosom Mrs. Brodie, in her absence, sat huddled in her chair before the stove, her thin chin sunk in the scraggy wetness of the sealskin coat. Surrounded externally by struggling currents of steamy vapour, there struggled also, within her mind, a dreadful uncertainty as to whether she might not be responsible for some vague and undetermined weakness in Matt, through a fault in his upbringing. A frequent expression of Brodie's a decade ago flashed into her mind, and she now saw vividly, in her anguish, her husband's contemptuous face as, discovering her in some fresh indulgence towards Matthew, he snapped at her: "You're spoiling that namby-pamby brat of yours. You'll make a braw man o' him!" She had, indeed, always attempted to shield Matt from his father, to protect him from the harshness of life, to give him extra luxuries and privileges not accorded to her other children. He had never had the courage to play truant from the Academy, but when he had desired, as he frequently did, a day off or had been for some reason afraid to attend school, it was to her that he had come, limping and whining: "Mamma, I'm sick. I've got a pain in ma belly." Whenever he had feigned illness, of whatever kind, he had affected always that limping, hobbling, lame-dog gait, as though the agony arising in any

G

organ of his body flew immediately to one leg, paralysing it and rendering him incapable of locomotion. She had seen through him, of course, but though undeceived by his pretences, a wave of her foolish maternal love would rush over her and she would compliantly answer: "Away up to your room then, son, and I'll fetch ye up something nice. Ye've got a friend in yer mother, anyway, Matt." Her stultified affections were obliged to find an outlet, and she had lavished them upon her son, feeling the imperative need, in that harsh household, of binding him to her by bonds of love. Had she spoiled his manhood by her indulgence? softened her son into a weakling by lax, tolerant fondness? Immediately her mind formulated the idea, her heart indignantly repudiated it, telling her that she had shown him nothing but kindness, gentleness, and lenience, had wished for him nothing but what was good; she had slaved for him, too, washed, darned, knitted for him, brushed his boots, made his bed, cooked the most appetising meals for him.

"Ay," she muttered to herself, "I've served that laddie hand and foot. Surely he can never forget me? I've taken the very bite out my mouth for him."

All the toil she had expended upon her son, from the washing of his first napkins to the final packing of his trunk for India, rose up before her, and she was confronted with a sense of the bewildering futility of all her love and service in the face of his present treatment of her. She blindly asked herself if it were her incompetence alone which had rendered her enormous and unremitting efforts useless, so that he now used her so indifferently and left her in such harassing suspense.

Here, a sudden sound startled her, and she looked up wanly, to observe that Agnes had returned and was addressing her in an uneven tone of ill-repressed vindictiveness.

"Mamma," she cried, "I'm going to marry Matt. I'm going to be his wife and I want to know what's going to be done about this. You've got to do something at once."

Mamma regarded her humbly, with the mild, moist blue eyes that shone meekly from under the grotesque, bedraggled black hat.

"Don't start on me, Agnes, dear," she said submissively. "I've had enough to stand in my time without having a hard word from you. I'm not fit to answer ye back, ye can surely see," and she added feebly, "I'm just a done woman."

"That's all very well," cried Agnes in a huff, "but I'm not going to have Matt taken away like this. He belongs to me as much as anyone. I'm not going to give him up."

"Aggie," replied Mamma, in a dead voice, "we don't know anything; we can't tell what's happening; but we can pray. Yes! that's what we can do. I think I would like us to put up a prayer in this very room. Maybe the Almighty, the same Lord God that looks down on Matt in

India, will look down on us two anxious women here and show us a light to comfort us."

Agnes, touched on her weakest side, was mollified, and the stiffness of her figure relaxed, the glitter faded from her eye as she said: "Maybe you're right, Mamma. It would be a comfort." Then, more as a polite formality than anything else, she asked: "Will you speak, then, or will I?"

"You do it better than me," said Mrs. Brodie, unassumingly. "You put up a word for us both."

"Very well, Mamma," replied Agnes complacently.

They knelt down in the small, stuffy room, amongst the jumbled clutter on the floor of bottles, boxes, tins, surrounded by the untidy litter of straw packing and sawdust, their altar a packing-case, their ikon a framed advertisement upon the wall. Still, they prayed.

Agnes, kneeling straight and upright, her thick, short body tense with an almost masculine vitality, and potent with the pressure of her restraint, began to pray in a loud, firm voice. Amongst the godly people in the church movements with which she was identified Miss Moir was noted for the power and richness of her spontaneous prayer, and now the words flowed from her lips in an eloquent stream, like the outpourings of a young and fervent priest supplicating for the sins of mankind. Yet she did not petition, she seemed indeed to demand, and her dark eyes glowed, her full bosom heaved with the intensity of her appeal. All the fire of her nature entered that passionate prayer. Her words were proper, modest, stereotyped, but in essence it was as though she throbbingly implored the Almighty not to cheat her of the man she had captivated and subdued by the meagre charms with which He had endowed her. No one had ever looked at her but Matt, she knew her attractions to be limited, and, if he failed her, she might never marry. All the suppressed feeling dammed within her had been restrained within bounds only by visions of the joyous promise of the future, and she now tacitly implored the Almighty not to defraud her of the fulsome fruition of these desires in the state of holy matrimony.

Mamma, on the contrary, seemed to sink down in a supine mass, like a heap of discarded, draggled clothing; her head sagged with a pleading humility; the faint, speedwell blue of her pathetic eyes was washed with tears; her nose flowed with lacrymation. As the loud, fervent words fell upon her ears, the image of her son rose before her and, while at first she applied her handkerchief furtively, soon she used it profusely, and at length she wept openly. All the time, her heart seemed to beat out the words: "O God! If I did wrong over Mary, don't punish me too much. Don't take Matt away from me. Leave me, still, my son to love me." When the prayer was ended there was a long pause, then Agnes rose, extended her hand to Mamma and helped her to her feet; facing each other closely, amicably, the two women now regarded each other with a glow of understanding and sympathy. Mamma nodded her head gently, as if to say: "That'll do it, Agnes. It was wonderful." New life seemed to have possessed them both. This outpoured confession of all their hopes, fears, and desires to the unknown heavens towards a Supreme, Omniscient, and Omnipotent Being left them assured, comforted, and fortified. Now they were positive that all would be well with Matthew and, as Mamma at length turned to go, invigorated and refreshed, a look passed between them expressive of their sweet, secret co-operation and they kissed each other a sanguine, affectionate good-bye.

III

Towards the middle of March, the empty shop next door to Brodie's became the nucleus of a seething activity. Previously, when, in its unoccupied wretchedness, it had been to him a perpetual eyesore against the refinement of his establishment, he had viewed it with contemptuous disgust; but, immediately after Dron's communication that it had been sold, he began to see it with a different, a peculiar, and more intense disfavour. Every time he passed in or out of his own business he darted a furtive, antagonistic glance at the vacant, dilapidated premises, quickly, as if he feared to have that glance intercepted, yet vindictively, as though he vented his spleen upon the inanimate building. Its two empty windows were no longer vacuous, but became to him hateful, and each morning as he came along, fearing, yet hoping, that signs of the incoming of the new company would be evident, and still the same shabby, void aspect met his gaze, he experienced a compelling desire to hurl a heavy stone with all his force, to shiver the blank and glass panes. As day followed day for an entire week, and still nothing happened, this deferred action angered him—he had been so strung up for battle and he began to ponder, obtusely, if the whole idea was simply a spiteful invention of Dron's, concocted in order to irritate him. For the space of one full day he felt convinced that the shop had not been sold and, during that time, he scoffed openly, with a flaunting triumph, but immediately, a short announcement in the *Levenford Advertiser*, stating briefly that the Mungo Company would open a new branch at 62 High Street at the beginning of the month of April, and that the fullest details would be given in the following week's issue, destroyed this transitory illusion; the conflict, occurring solely in Brodie's own perverted mind, between himself and the inert building, reopened more bitterly than before.

Shortly after this pretentious announcement in the *Advertiser*, a dapper, urbane visitor had come into Brodie's shop and, with an agreeable, yet deprecatory, smile, presented his card in introduction.

"Mr. Brodie, I am, as you see, the district manager of the Mungo Hat & Hosiery Company. I want us to be friends," he said, holding out his hand affably.

Brodie was dumbfounded, but beyond ignoring the proffered hand, he gave no indication of his feelings and made no departure from his usual manner. "Is that all ye want?" he asked abruptly.

"I understand your very natural feelings," the other began again. "You already consider us your enemies. That is really not strictly so. Although we are, in a sense, business opponents, we have found by experience that it is often mutually advantageous for two establishments of the same nature—such as yours and ours—to be together."

"Do ye tell me, now," said Brodie ironically, as the other paused impressively, and, not knowing his man or the symptoms of his gathering wrath, expansively continued.

"Yes, that *is* so, Mr. Brodie. We find that such a combination attracts more people to that particular centre, more shopping is done there, and this, of course, is advantageous to both shops. We multiply the trade and divide the profits! That's our arithmetic," he concluded, as he imagined, rather neatly.

Brodie looked at him icily.

"You're talkin' a lot of damned lies," he said roughly. "Don't think ye can pull the wool over my eyes like that, and don't refer to my business in the same breath as your own gimcrack huckster's trade. You've come here to try and poach on my preserves and I'm goin' to treat you like a low poacher."

The other smiled. "You surely can't mean that! I represent a reputable firm; we have branches everywhere, we are not poachers. I am going to open the new branch myself, and I want to be with you. And you," he added flatteringly, "well—you certainly don't look like a man who could fail to understand the value of co-operation."

"Don't talk to me about your blasted co-operation," cried Brodie, "if that's the name ye give to stealing other folks' custom."

"I hope you don't mean us to infer that you have the exclusive rights to monopolise the hat trade here," said the other, with some indignation.

"I don't care about the right, I have the might, and I tell ye I'll smash you!" He flexed up his great biceps with a significant gesture. "I'll smash you to bits."

"That surely is a childish attitude, Mr. Brodie! Co-operation is better than competition every time. Of course, if you choose to fight," he waved his hand deprecatingly, "we have large resources. We have had to cut our prices before, in similar circumstances, and we can easily do it again."

Brodie threw a glance contemptuously at the pasteboard of the visiting-card which lay crushed in his hand. "Man! Mr.—whatever your name is—you talk like a penny novelette. I don't intend to reduce my prices one farthing," he drawled, pityingly. "I have the connection here, that's all, and I'm just man enough to keep it."

"I see," the other had replied succinctly; "you are definitely going out of your way to demand open hostility."

"By God!" Brodie thundered at him, "that's the only true word you've spoken yet, an' I hope it's the last thing ye will say."

At these final and unmistakable words the other had turned and walked quietly out of the shop, then, upon the following day—the fifteenth of March—a small corps of workmen had descended upon the place next door.

They were working now, irritating him intensely by the sound of their labour, by each tap of their hammers which beat with exasperating monotony into his brain. Even in the intervals of silence he was harassed by their presence, kept anticipating the onset of the staccato tattoo, and, when it recommenced, a pulse within him throbbed dangerously in the same tapping rhythm. When the rending of saws on wood came through the dividing wall he winced, as if the saw had rasped his own bones, and at the cold steely sound of the chisels upon stone he frowned, as if they carved upon his brow, above and between his eyes, a deep, vertical furrow of hatred.

They were gutting the shop. The men worked quickly and in the rush to complete their operations as rapidly as possible, worked also overtime; double wages apparently meant nothing to the Mungo Company! At the end of a week they had cleared out the old window frames, the doorway, the dilapidated shelves and counter, the whole worn wreckage of a bygone age, and now the denuded frontage leered at Brodie like a mask, its window spaces the sightless sockets of eyes and its empty doorway the gaping, toothless mouth. Then the plasterers and decorators added their efforts to those of the joiners and masons, altering visibly, from day to day, by their combined exertions and skill, the entire aspect of the structure. Brodie hated every phase of its change, and he encompassed within his growing aversion for the transformed building these workmen who, through their labours, were reconstructing it so admirably, and making it the finest and most modern shop in the Borough. On an occasion when one of these had entered Brodie's establishment and, touching his cap, asked civilly if he might be obliged with a bucket of water to make tea for himself and his mates next door, as their own supply had been temporarily suspended at the main, Brodie had shot the astonished man out of his shop. "Water!" he had snarled. "Ye want water, and ye have the impertinence to come here for your favours. Ye'll get none of it. If the whole gang o' ye were fryin' in hell I wouldna so much as put a drop on one o' your tongues. Get out!"

But his animadversion had no effect upon their activities, serving only, or so it seemed to him, to stimulate these, and moodily he observed thick, scintillating plate-glass windows of a green actinic translucency come into place, rich show-cases appear like mushrooms in the space of a night, an ornately lettered sign-board emerge—glittering! Finally, under his eyes, in broad daylight—the crowning anathema—a model of a huge top-hat, sumptuously and opulently gilt, was erected above the doorway, where it swung jauntily from its supporting pole with every breath of air.

Brodie's demeanour to the town during this period gave, in general, no marked indication of the emotions which he repressed. He manifested outwardly only calm indifference, for his very pride forbade him to speak; and to his acquaintances who rallied him on the matter of the encroachment he exhibited an air of profound contempt towards the new company, met Grierson's gall-dipped witticisms at the Philosophical Club with the assumption of a careless and superior unconcern.

The general opinion was that Brodie would undoubtedly carry the day against the invaders.

"I give them six months," remarked Provost Gordon judiciously, to the select junto of the club one evening, in Brodie's absence, "before Brodie drives them out. He's an unco' deevelish man that, for an enemy. Dod, he's quite capable o' layin' a charge o' gunpowder under their braw new shop."

" 'Twould be a risky job wi' that sparky temper o' his," inserted Grierson.

"He'll spark them out," replied the Provost. "He fair beats me, does James Brodie. I know of no man alive who would have come through a' that awfu' pother and disgrace about his daughter without turnin' a hair, or once hangin' his heid. He's a black deevil when his purpose is set."

"I'm not so sure, Provost; na, na, I'm not just so sure," drawled the other, "that the very deliberateness o' him michtna thwart its aim purpose, for he's that obstinate he would try to outface a mule. Forbye, Provost, he's gotten so big for his shoes now that folks—aye, even the county folks who liket it at first—are beginnin' to get a wheen sick o' it. That grand style o' his is juist like the lordly salmon; a wee bittie is all right, but if ye get it served up a' the time, man, ye get awfu' scunnered by it."

Seeing himself thus the object of their speculation, and sensing its slightly favourable tone, Brodie began to feel that the public eye was turned encouragingly towards him as a defender of the old, solid order of the Borough against the invasion of the trumpery new, and he became, in his appearance, even more of the dandy, ordered two new suits of the finest and most expensive cloth, bought himself in the jeweller's at the Cross a smart, opal tiepin which he now wore in place of his plain gold horseshoe. This pin was immediately the object of criticism amongst the cronies, and was passed from hand to hand in admiration.

" 'Tis a bonnie stone—although I'm no judge," tittered Grierson. "I hope it hasna ruined you to buy it."

"Don't judge my savings by yours. I know weel enough what I can afford," retorted Brodie roughly.

"Na! Na! I wouldna dream o' doin' that. Ye're so lavish wi' your money ye maun be worth a mint o' it. I'll warrant ye'll have a wheen o' siller stowed away for a rainy day," lisped Grierson ambiguously, as his eye flicked Brodie's with ironic insight.

"They say an opal's gey unlucky. The wife's sister had an opal ring that brought her a heap o' misfortune. She had an unco' bad slip the very month she got it," demurred Paxton.

"That'll no' happen to me," replied Brodie coarsely.

"But are ye not feared to wear it?" persisted Paxton.

Brodie looked at him fixedly.

"Man," he said slowly, "you ought to know I'm feared of nothing on this God's earth."

Curiously, although he directed the most scrupulous attention towards his own attire and personal appearance, he would not for an instant entertain the idea of sprucing up his business premises by renewing the drab aspect of his shop, but seemed actually to glory in its unalterable, but recently accentuated, dinginess. When Perry, who had cast a persistently envious eye upon the growth of the dazzling magnificence next door, remarked upon the contrast and timidly suggested that perhaps a touch of paint might benefit the exterior, he said, impressively: "Not a finger do we lay on it. Them that wants to buy their hats in a painted panopticon can do so, but this is a gentlemen's business and I'm going to keep it so." In this attitude he waited the first attack of the enemy.

With the final steps of restoration and reconstruction completed, at last the opening day of the rival establishment arrived. Astonishing progress had been made during the last week of March and a full blaring column in the *Advertiser* had announced that the first of April would mark the inauguration of the new establishment. Behind the thick green blinds and shuttered entrance, a feeling of occult mysticism had prevailed during the whole of the previous day, and through this veil the district manager of the company, who had been deputed to take charge of the local branch for the initial months, had been observed flitting restlessly, like a shadow, symbolic of secrecy. Obviously the policy of the Mungo Company was to dazzle Levenford by their display in one sudden, blinding revelation; they would rend the cover from the windows and the Borough as a whole would be staggered by the vision of what it saw. Such, at least, were Brodie's ironic thoughts as, on the first of April, he left his house at 9.30 to the second, no sooner no later, and began the usual walk to his business in exactly his usual manner. As he came down the High Street in perfect composure he looked, although his manner was perhaps a trifle over-emphasised, the least perturbed man in Levenford. The satirical nature of his reflections fed his vanity and consolidated his rooted belief in himself, stifling the vague misgiving that had for days fluttered at the back of his brain. Now that the moody period of waiting was at an end and the fight actually begun, he became once more the master of his fate and his bearing now seemed to say: "Let me get at it. I've been waitin' on this. And now you're ready for me, by God, I'm ready for you." He loved a fight. Furthermore, he felt spurred in this incentive to contest, by his additional anticipation that the heat of the battle would remove his mind from the dull depression into which the blow to his intimate family pride had recently plunged him. Already his heart lifted to the joy of the fight as he told himself that he would show them the stuff that James Brodie was made of, would demonstrate again to the town the spirit that was in him, would, by a crushing defeat to these Mungo upstarts, restore his prestige in the eyes of the Borough to even a higher level than before. With a stiff back and expanded chest, with his stick cocked over his shoulder—an exultant mannerism he had not indulged in for months—he strode confidently along the street.

He reached the new shop, saw instantly that, at last, it was open. Whilst a lesser man might have, more circumspectly, completed his inspection by peering from the corner of his eye as he walked past, this prying was not in Brodie's nature, and he arrested himself openly, ostentatiously, in the middle of the pavement, and with his stick still upon his shoulder, his feet planted firmly apart, his massive head thrown back, he gazed sardonically at the double-fronted spectacle before him. A deliberate smile spread over his features. A ponderous guffaw shook him. His whole attitude became expressive of his delightful realisation that the display before him was more trashy and new-fangled than he had dared to hope, more ludicrous than he had preconceived even in his wildest expectations. One window was crammed from floor to ceiling with hats, hats of every conceivable form, variety, and style, mounting upwards in graduated tiers amongst festoons of ties and sprouting bouquets of coloured handkerchiefs, ornamented at tasteful intervals by garlands of socks and stockings, and embellished by an array of gloves arranged like fern fronds, with limp yet politely extended fingers. The indication that the purpose of this strikingly artistic exhibition was not purely decorative was clearly, yet tactfully, conveyed by the fact that each article bore a small ticket stamped M.H.H., with the price in plain red figures below. But although he perceived this composite tableau, it was, however, the other window which riveted Brodie's quizzical attention, where his contemptuous eyes observed the unthought-of novelty of two wax figures. Wax figures—incredible! Still, there they were, a gentleman of perfect complexion and address gazing with fixed, ambiguous fondness upon the form of a small boy who, from his clear skin, wide blue eyes, and bland innocuous simper was undoubtedly the model son of this model father. They stood, the right hand of the father and the left hand of the son extended with the same delicate gesture, as if to say: "Here we are. Gaze upon us. We are here for your admiration."

Their clothing was immaculate, and Brodie's eye travelled from the creases of their trousers to the brilliance of their ties, over the glaze of their collars, the snowy whiteness of their prominent handkerchiefs, the sheen of sock and stocking, to the curly brimmed Derby on the parental brow and the natty pill-box upon the juvenile head, until finally it rested upon the neat card on which was printed: "Dressed by the M.H.H. Co. Let us do the same for you."

"Dummies," muttered Brodie. "Demned dummies. It's not a hat shop; it's a demned waxworks." They represented to him the joke of a lifetime, for these figures had never been seen in Levenford—although it had been recently rumoured that such innovations were appearing in the larger Glasgow warehouses—and he considered that they would soon be the laughing-stock of the Borough.

As he remained in arrogant contemplation, suddenly a man came out of the shop, carrying a brown paper parcel. Instantly Brodie's sneer was transfixed by a sudden mortifying apprehension, and a pang shot through him like a knife stab. Had they, then, begun to do business already? He had never seen the man before, and he tried to reassure himself that, in all probability, this was merely a belated workman performing some omitted task or collecting his forgotten gear; nevertheless, a neat parcel aroused his suspicion, disturbed him deeply, and in a less arrogant manner, he moved his firmly rooted limbs and went slowly through his own doorway.

Perry, inevitably, was there to greet him, moved this morning, by the progress of current events, to a more obsequious deference, and bearing in his mind perhaps the faint aspiration that he might, in the face of this new opposition, have the opportunity to show to his patron something of his real value, to achieve in some measure a realisation of his blighted hopes.

"Good morning to you, Mr. Brodie, sir." For this especial occasion Perry had concocted a mild witticism which he considered in his own mind both clever and amusing, and, plucking up all his courage, he now had the temerity to liberate it upon Brodie. "This is the first of April, sir," he said nervously. "Do you observe the inference, since they"—he always referred to his new neighbours in this ambiguous manner—"since they have opened on All Fools' Day."

"No," growled Brodie, looking from under his brows, "but tell me, you that's so clever."

"Well, it's all through the town, Mr. Brodie, that you'll make April gowks of them," gushed Perry, and, as he saw the effect of his remark, he tittered sympathetically, then writhed in the exuberance of his satisfaction, for Brodie had laughed shortly, pleased by the notion of the general adulation of the town implied in Perry's flattering, but, though he knew it not, fabricated remark. His huge fingers flexed in slowly on his palm.

"Ay, I'll mak' a gowk o' them, right enough! I'll take some o' the conceit out o' them, take some o' the gilt off their gingerbread. They don't know who they're up against yet, but, by gad, I'll learn them." How, exactly, he did not quite know, but at this moment, although he had no vestige of a settled policy in his brain, his confidence in his own ability to crush the opposition was supreme.

"Did ye notice the stookies in the window?" he queried, absently.

"Yes! oh yes! Mr. Brodie. A new idea from the larger houses. Rather original, of course, and up to date." In the first flush of his conversational success he had almost the optimism to hope that "the guv'nor" might perhaps order a brace of these intriguing models on the spot. His eyes glowed enthusiastically, but he had perforce to lower them under Brodie's glower, realising that he had this time said, apparently, the wrong thing.

"Up to date, ye say. It's a deshed museum! They'll have a crowd round that bluter of a window o' theirs."

"But, sir," ventured Perry timidly, "is that not desirable. If you would attract people and draw their attention outside, they're more likely to come inside. It's a sort of advertisement."

Brodie looked at him obtusely for a moment, then growled, angrily: "Has the same bug been bitin' you, that you're itchin' for the common herd to batter at our doors. If it has, get the poison out your system quick, or it'll be as much as your job is worth."

Perry looked at him humbly, and observed, meekly: "It's all grist to your mill though, sir." Then, removing himself to safer ground, he hastened to observe: "I see they're going in for a sort of general outfitting as well, Mr. Brodie, sir."

Brodie nodded sullenly.

"You wouldn't care to branch out with a few extra lines yourself, sir, a novelty or two perhaps. Say a brace or a smart glove! Very refined indeed, a nice glove, sir." Perry almost pleaded at the bubbling urge of all the ideas repressed within him.

But his bright, insinuating suggestions fell on deaf ears. Brodie paid no heed to him, but stood, moved by an unusual impulse of self-analysis, absorbed in the contemplation of his strange departure from his invariable routine. Why, he asked himself, was he hanging about the shop instead of entering his office with his usual imperial negligence? He was going to smash them next door, of course, but would he do it by sitting calmly at his desk, attempting to read the *Glasgow Herald*? He felt he must do something, take some definite line of conduct, but as he moved about, chafing at his desuetude, his sluggish mentality offered him no tangible suggestions towards the powerful action which he craved. If only he could have used the terrific strength of his body in this present cause, then he would have toiled till the sweat poured from him, till his joints cracked with the strain of his effort; he would willingly have embraced the supporting pillars of the opposing shop and, uprooting them, have dragged down the entire edifice about him; but some dim perception of the uselessness of his brute force dawned upon him and stung him bitterly.

At this point a woman, holding by the hand a small child of about six years of age, entered the shop. She was obviously of a poor class, and advanced to Perry who greeted her deferentially.

"I wanted a bonnet for ma wee boy. He's goin' to the school next week!" she said, confidentially.

Perry beamed upon her.

"Certainly, madam! What can I show you for the little man?"

Suddenly a strange impulse, a fierce inclination against his hated opposition, seized Brodie, and, although these customers were obviously of an inferior class, and clearly of that type whom he invariably left to his assistant, he was impelled to go forward.

"Let me do it," he said, in a harsh, unreal tone.

The woman gazed at him timidly and, instinctively in awe of him, her lightly worn assurance fell from her; she became, not a lady who was selecting, yes and paying for, a hat to set her son bravely out upon the adventure of school, that first step upon the mysterious highway of life, but merely a mean, shabby, workman's wife.

"This young gentleman served me the last time," she whispered irresolutely, indicating Perry. "I was in last year and he suited me nicely."

The little boy instantly sensed his mother's discomfiture, felt also the lowering oppression of the huge, dark figure above him, and, burying his face in his mother's dress, he began to whine plaintively.

"Mammie! Mammie, I want to go hame," he sobbed. "I don't want to stay here. I want hame."

"Stop greetin' now. Stop your greetin' at once, will ye." The poor woman, utterly humiliated, stood discomposed and faltering whilst the wailing child burrowed his head dourly into the sanctuary of her person; she shook him, and the more fiercely she shook him the louder he howled; her face coloured with shame and annoyance; she herself was near enough to tears. "Can that black-browed Brodie not keep out o' the place? it's the bairn's hat I wanted—not him," she thought, angrily, as she lifted the yelling child in her arms and said with great embarrassment: "I better come back another time. He's a bad boy. I'll come again when he can behave himself." While she cast, for appearance sake, this specious aspersion against her own child, her outraged maternal instinct assured her that she would never return. She had turned to go, and would have vanished irrevocably, when Perry in a low, tactful voice suggested tentatively from the background:

"Perhaps a sweetie——?" and from an unsuspected recess in a drawer he adroitly produced a large peppermint drop and poised it prominently, alluringly, between his finger and thumb. Instantly the child stopped crying and, exposing one large, brimming, doubtful eye from out the folds of its mother's bodice, lifted it calculatingly towards the sweet. The mother, at this indication of trust, halted, questioningly regarding the child.

"Would you?" she queried.

With a final, convulsive sob the boy nodded his head trustingly towards Perry, and stretched forward a small, avid claw. They returned. The sweet quickly bulged the wet, shining, young cheek, and, peace now being restored, Perry continued to soothe the child, to propitiate the mother, to minister to them both until finally, the notable purchase, for such he now made them feel it to be, was satisfactorily effected. As they departed, he showed them to the door with the same ubiquitous courtesy, receiving the mother's last grateful glance upon the top of his lowered unassuming head, whilst Brodie, who had moved sullenly, ponderously to the background, looked on gloomily.

Perry returned, rubbing his hands with satisfaction. Strange young man that he was, he built his conceit only upon his imaginary powers and took no credit for the undoubted attributes of quickness and intuition which were actually his; though he had just achieved a triumph of diplomacy and tact, yet his sole feeling was a humble satisfaction that he had saved the customer for Brodie before the eyes of the august master himself. He glanced up deferentially as the other spoke.

"I didna know we gave away sweeties wi' our hats," was all that Brodie said, as he turned sombrely into his office.

The day had begun; and it wore steadily on, with Brodie remaining still shut up in his room, immersed in his own, intimate thoughts. Across his stern face shadows drifted like clouds across the face of a dark mountain. He suffered. Despite the iron hardness of his will he could not prevent his responsive ears from quickening to every sound, from anticipating the gradual halting of footsteps as they drew near his shop, from analysing the lightest noise without his office, as if to differentiate the entry of a customer from Perry's restless pacings; yet, to-day, he felt that, though he had never before consciously noted them, the sounds were few and unsuggestive. The sun poured through the window upon him, the slush of the thaw which had succeeded the long frost was now completely gone, and the day was crisply dry, yet warm, so that in this dawning hint of spring the streets would, he knew, fill with people, happy, eager, thronging the shops; yet no chatter of enquiring voices broke the outer silence.

The blank, dividing wall which stood before him seemed to dissolve, under his piercing gaze and reveal, in the premises next door, a bustling and successful activity. A reaction from his sneering confidence of the morning took him, and he now morbidly visioned crowds of people jostling each other there in a passionate eagerness to buy. Savagely, he bit his lip and again picked up his discarded paper in an effort to read; but in a few moments, to his annoyance, he returned to himself to find that he gazed stupidly at the wall in front: as though it hypnotised him.

Moodily, he reflected how delightful it had been in the past to lie back in his chair—for what else had he done—with an eye through the half-open door, lording it over Perry and those who entered his domain. The menial duties of the business were entirely Perry's, who fetched and carried to his royal word, and he himself had not mounted the steps or lifted his hand to the shelves, or bound up a parcel for longer than he could remember. Most customers he ignored; with some he would stroll in whilst they were being served, nod casually, pick up the hat under review, pass his hand over its nap or bend the brim in haughty approval of his own merchandise, saying with his air: "Take it or leave it, but ye'll not get a better hat anywhere." Towards only a few, a handful from the best families of the county, did he actually direct his personal service and attention.

It had then been so delightful to feel assured that people must come to him, for, in his blind autocratic way, he had scarcely realised, had not paused to consider, that the absence of competition and lack of choice might drive many people to him, that necessity might be the mainstay of his business; but now, as he sat alone, he became unhappily aware that, for the time being at least, his monopoly was at an end. Nevertheless he would not, he firmly determined, alter his conduct; if he had not been obliged to run after people to solicit their paltry custom, he would not now be coerced into so doing; he had run after no man in his life and he now swore a solemn oath that he would never do so.

The dim, early days of his beginning in Levenford, so long since that he had almost forgotten, returned mistily to him; but through these mists he saw himself as a man who had never curried favour, nor fawned, nor acted the subservient toady. Though there had been no Perry then, he had been upright and honest and determined, had worked hard and asked no favour. And he had succeeded. He glowed as he thought of his slow rise in importance and consequence, of his recognition by the Council, his election to the Philosophical Club, of the gradual conception of his house, of its building, and, since that date, of the growing and subtle change in his situation to that unique, isolated, notable position which he now held in the town. It was, he told himself, the good blood that ran in his veins which had done that for him, which had brought him to the top, where he belonged, despite the handicaps which had beset him in his youth, that blood of his ancestors which—as in a noble horse—would always tell, and which would not fail him now.

Waves of anger at the injustice of his present position swept in on him, and he jumped to his feet. "Let them try to take it from me," he cried aloud, raising up his fist; "let them all come! I'll wipe them out like I destroy all who offend me. There was a rotten branch on the tree of my name," he shouted loudly, "and I cut it off. I'll smash everybody that interferes with me. I am James Brodie, and be damned to everybody and everything. Let them try to hinder me, to thieve my trade from me, try to take all I've got; let them do it! Whatever comes, I am still *myself*."

He subsided in his chair, unconscious of the act that he had arisen, unaware that he had shouted to the empty room but hugging only, with a gloating satisfaction, that last precious thought. He was himself —James Brodie—no one but he understood, could ever comprehend, the full comfort, the delicious pride which that possession gave him. His thoughts rioted away from his present vicissitudes into a land of exalted dreams and longings, and, with his head sunk in his chest, he lost himself in the sublime contemplation of some future day when, unchecked, he would unleash the uncontrolled desires of his pride, when he would appease to satiation his craving for eminence and homage.

At last he sighed and, like a man awakening from the dreams of a drugged sleep, he blinked and shook himself. He looked at his watch, realised with a start that the end of this day, and of his self-ordained seclusion, was approaching. He arose slowly, yawned prodigiously, stretched himself, and, banishing from his features all traces of his recent, indulgent reverie, hardened his face again into a mask of hard indifference and went into the shop to review, as was his custom, the business of the day. This was invariably a pleasant duty, into which he infused a lordly dignity, giving himself the air of a feudal ruler receiving tribute from his vassal. Always Perry had a heap of gleaming silver, often a few gleaming sovereigns, and sometimes a rustling bank note to be transferred to the master's deep, hip pocket; and, when this had been effected, Brodie would run a casual eye over the lists of sales —casual, inasmuch as he recognised that Perry would never cheat him —it would, in his own words, "have been a pity for the little runt had he tried"—would slap his bulging pocket, assume his hat and, with a last curt command, be off, leaving Perry to close up and shutter the shop.

But, to-night, an unusual air seemed to cling to Perry, giving him an aspect at once blurred and disconsolate. Usually he opened the cash drawer with a proud and subservient flourish, as though to say: "We may not be much, but this is what we've done for you to-day, Mr.

Brodie, sir"; now, however, he pulled the drawer timidly open, with a faint deprecating twitch.

"A very quiet day, sir," he said meekly.

"The weather's been good," remonstrated Brodie testily. "What have you been playin' at? There's been plenty folks about."

"Oh! there's been a stir on the streets," replied Perry, "but quite a number—that's to say, a few have gone in——" He faltered. "They had an attractive window," he concluded lamely.

Brodie looked down at the drawer. Only six, miserable, silver shillings lay in the till.

IV

THE Levenford Philosophical Club was in convocation. Although to-night the session was by no means a plenary one, the room was comfortably filled by smoke and by a gathering of six members who, now ranged in comfortable chairs around the cordial fire which blazed upon the hearth, philosophised in this congenial atmosphere at their ease. Of those present two were engaged upon a silent game of draughts, easy, harmonious, relaxed, whilst the others lay back, smoked, talked, and wooed the inspiration of worthy thoughts by frequent, comforting sips of their grog.

The conversation was sporadic, the pauses, despite the choice richness of the language employed, sometimes more pregnant than the actual spoken words, the wave of a pipe more pungent than a pithy adjective, the glances of the members abstract, cogitative, and intellectually remote. Wearing modestly the distinction of their higher cerebration, they sat within the hallowed precincts of the club—the rallying-point of all these honest burghers in Levenford who might claim to be more notable than their fellow men—and, in the consciousness of their distinction, were at least content. To have achieved this club was, in itself, a feat which immediately conferred a cachet upon these happy individuals and rendered each the envy of less fortunate beings. To these the member would remark, of an evening, with, perchance, a nonchalant yawn: "Well! I think I'll away down to the club. There's a bit discussion on the night," and saunter off, whilst jealous eyes followed him down the street. To outsiders, those not of the elect, the social prestige of the club loomed largely, but so, also, did the suggestion of its profound intellectual significance, for the sonorous name—Philosophical—breathed of the rarer and more refined realms of pure reason. True, a classical master who had come to the Levenford Academy, bearing the letters of a degree of Oxford University after his name, had remarked to a colleague: "I was keen to join when I heard the name but, to my disgust, I discovered it was nothing more than a smoking and drinking clique." What did he know, the ignorant English clown? Was he unaware of the six lectures, followed by lengthy debates, which took place at regular intervals during the winter? Had he not seen the neatly printed syllabus, which, like an amulet, reposed invariably in each member's top, right-hand, waistcoat pocket, containing the titles of this year's subjects of information and discussion? Had he but chosen he might have cast his grudging eyes upon such profound themes as:

"Our Immortal Bard—with Readings,"
"The Homing Pigeon in Health and Sickness,"
"The Growth of Shipbuilding in the Royal Borough on the Clyde,"
"Scottish Wit and Humour—with Local Anecdotes," or even,
"From Rivet-boy to Provost—the Life Story of the Late Respected Mathias Gloag of Levenford."

Such, indeed, were the weighty lectures to be delivered, but if, on these evenings when the associates' brains were not taxed by these deep matters, and their minds disengaged from solving the problems of race and nation, some trifling relaxation occurred—what disgrace lay in a gossip or a smoke, a game of the dambrod or even whist? And, as Phemie's tidy house was convenient to the back door, what harm was it to send round occasionally for a bit glass or even to adjourn at times to the "wee back parlour"?

Such arguments were, of course, unanswerable! It was, in addition, the function and practice of this unofficial town council to discuss in detail, and sit in deliberation upon, the people of the Borough, and their affairs. The ramifications of this subsidiary branch of their philosophising ranged from such diverse matters as the shrewish temper of Gibson's wife to the appropriate remonstration to be made to Blair of the Main's Farm, regarding the insanitary propensities of his cows upon the public highway; and a singularly reassuring feature, speaking volumes for Levenford equity, was the fact that the very members themselves had no prerogative or privilege immunising them from discussion by their fellow commentators. To-night, James Brodie was the subject of the discussion initiated by a chance glance at the empty chair in the corner, a contemplative pause, and the remark:

"Brodie's late to-night. I wonder will he be comin'."

"He'll be here, right enough," remarked Provost Gordon. "I've never known him so regular. He maun keep up his morale, ye ken." He looked round for approval at the use of this appropriate and noble-sounding word. "What I mean to infer," he explained, "is that he's got to put a face on things now, or else go under a' thegether."

The others sucked at their pipes and nodded silently. One of the draughts players moved a man, then looked up reflectively into the warm aromatic air, and said:

"Dod! time passes like a flash! It must be nearly a year now since he flung out that daughter o' his, on the night o' the big storm."

Paxton, who had the reputation of a head for figures, remarked:

"It'll be a year exactly in a fortnight's time; but it might be a single day for all that Levenford's seen o' Mary Brodie since then. I aye maintained, and I still maintain, that it was a bitter cruel thing that James Brodie did that night."

"Where is the lassock now?" queried someone.

"Weel," responded Paxton, "the story was that the Foyles of Darroch got her a position; but that's a' nonsense. She went off all by herself. The doctor wished to help her but she just up and away. It's said now that she's got a post in a big house in London—nothin' more nor less than a servant she would be—puir thing. The Foyles didn't do a thing for her afore they went back to Ireland."

"That's right," said the second draughts player; "old Foyle was fair broken up by the loss o' that boy o' his. 'Twas an awfu' thing, and no mistake, that Tay Bridge disaster. I'll never forget that night. I had been out at the guid sister's and had to get back hame in the teeth o' the wind, when a flyin' slate skiffed my ear by an inch. It nearly took ma heid off."

"That wad have been a worse calamity to the town than the loss o' the Bridge, John," sniggered Grierson from his corner. "We would need to ha' put ye up a braw monument at the Cross, like the braw new Livingstone statue in George Square up in the city. Think what ye've missed. If it had struck ye, man, ye would have been another o' Scotland's heroes."

"Weel, the new bridge maun be a bit stronger before they get me to gang across it. 'Twas a perfect scandal that a' they good lives were flung awa'. I contend there should have been a punishment for them that was to blame," said the first draughts player, covering the discomfiture of his companion.

"Man! Ye canna punish the Almighty," drawled Grierson; "'twas an act of God, and ye canna claim damages off Him—at least not successfully."

"Wheesht, man, Grierson," admonished the Provost—by virtue of his position. "Watch that tongue o' yours; that's downright blasphemy ye're talkin'."

"Na! Na! Provost," soothed Grierson. "It's just the law—a wee bit o' the law ye ken. No offence to the company, or the Almighty, or yourself," he added, with a leer.

There was an uncomfortable pause, when it looked as if the harmony of the discussion might be destroyed, but eventually the Provost continued:

"Brodie maun be losing trade hand over fist these days. I never see a soul in his shop."

"The prices the Mungo Company's sellin' at wad emptv anybody's shop that tried to compete wi' them," said Paxton, with some show of sympathy. "They've made up their minds to feenish him first and make their profits after. He's got on the wrang side o' the fence a' thegether. It looks to me gey like ruin."

"Ruin is the richt word," drawled Grierson, who from his corner looked knowingly as if he could, if he chose, disclose a large, ripe plum of information on the subject.

"But he maun be a warm man though, Brodie. He's aye free o' his money—splashin' it about like water, spendin' it on anything that might take his fancy. He has the best o' everything, and then ye wad think that wasna good enough for him. Look at his dress, look at his braw new tiepin and signet ring, and besides," the speaker looked round cautiously before he uttered the next words, "look at his graund country-castle." A slight smirk seemed to traverse the entire party, and covert glances of well-subdued amusement were exchanged.

"Look at his auld wife's boots, her elegant clothes, and braw appearance," replied Grierson. "Look at his bank balance—his wee Nessie was a fortnight late wi' her fees at the Academy this quarter. Look at the flicker in his proud eye when he thinks ye're not watchin' him. I tell you that the big, big man—that he thinks he is—is beginnin' to feel a wee bittie vexed about things." An intense undercurrent of innuendo lay behind the words as he continued: "I may be wrong but, in my humble opinion, I consider that James Brodie is goin' through the worst time o' his life. And if he's not careful he'll be down where he's flung many another man—right down in the gutter!"

"Ay, he's an awfu' man to make enemies. Speakin' o' the gutter, though, I maun tell you this one." Paxton took a few reflective draws at his pipe. "I was passin' Brodie's shop the other Saturday night when a kind o' commotion stopped me." He puffed again twice. "There was a big, drucken street-worker in the shop, fu' as a whelk, and fu' o' his week's wages—in the mood to fling out the pound notes like a harrier's trail—I saw the roll o' notes in his hand—and he stood there swayin' afore Brodie, ordering a couple o' hats and a couple o' bonnets, and this and that and goodness knows a' what. He was in the mood to buy up the whole shop, ay and pay for't too. Brodie, and God knows he must have needed the money sorely, stood glarin' at him out o' his starin' red eye." Reaching the climax of his story he sucked interminably at this pipe, before removing it, pointing it emphatically, and proceeding: " 'If ye can't say "please" when ye address me,' Brodie was snarlin', 'then ye'll get nothing here. Other places,' he sneered, 'might stand that style o' thing. Go there if ye choose, but if ye come to me ye'll behave yourself or get out.' I didna hear what the other said in reply, but it must have outraged Brodie frightful, for he louped the counter and gripped the other's neck, and before ye could say knife had flung him out o' the shop right into the dirty gutter, where he lay, knocked stupid, at my feet."

A pregnant pause succeeded the anecdote.

"Ay," sighed the first draughts player at last, "he has an unco' temper. His pride is fair terrifyin' now. It's his worst enemy. He used no' to be so conspicuous in that respect, but of late years it's fair run awa' wi' him. He's as proud as Lucifer."

"And 'tis my belief he'll have the same fall," inserted Grierson. "He's bloated with his own vanity! It's worked on him till it's like a very mania."

"And the rideeclous cause o't too!" said Paxton, in a low cautious tone; "that claimin' kinship wi' the Wintons! I'll swear he thinks he should be the Earl himself. 'Tis strange, too, the way he hides it, yet feasts on it."

"They wouldna own him. Brodie may have the name. He may look like the Wintons. But what's in a name and what's in a likeness?" said the first draughts player. "He hasna a shadow o' proof."

"I'm afeared what proof there was had a big, black bar through it," remarked Grierson judicially; "for I'm gey and certain that ony-thing that might have happened lang back took place the wrang side o' the blanket. That's why our friend willna blatter it out. That's maybe the bonnie kinship."

" 'Tis not only kinship that he claims," said Provost Gordon slowly. "Na! Na! the disease has swelled beyond that. I hardly like to come over it to ye and deed I'm hardly sure myself, but I'll mention no names and ye mustna repeat it. I had it from a man who saw James Brodie when he was the worse o' liquor, mad ravin' drunk. There's no' many has seen that," he continued, "for he's a close man in they things. But this night his dour tongue was loosed and he talked and——"

"Another time, Provost," cried Paxton suddenly.

"Wheesht, man, wheesht."

"Talk o' the deevil."

"About that new trap o' yours now, Provost, will ye——"

Brodie had entered the room. He came in heavily, blinking at the sudden transition from the darkness to the lighted room, and frowning from the bitter suspicion that he had been at the moment of his entry the object of their backbiting tongues. His dour, hard face had to-night a pale grimness, as he looked round the company, nodding his head silently several times in salutation, more in the manner of a challenge than a greeting.

"Come away in, come away in," remarked Grierson smoothly, "we were just wonderin' if the rain that was threatenin' had come on yet."

"It's still dry," said Brodie gruffly. His voice was flat, had lost its old resonant timbre, was, like the brooding mask of his face, inexpressive of anything but stoic endurance. He took out his pipe and began to fill it. An old man, the messenger and factotum of the club, dignified as such by a green baize apron, put his head round the door in speechless enquiry, and to him Brodie shortly remarked: "The usual."

A momentary silence descended upon the group whilst the old man retreated, was absent, returned shamblingly with a large whisky for Brodie, then finally departed. The Provost felt it his duty to break the awkward stillness which had descended upon the group and, looking at Brodie, he said, in a kindly tone, moved in spite of himself by the other's ghastly look:

"Well, Brodie man, how are things with ye? How's the world waggin' now?"

"Oh! fair, Provost! very fair," replied Brodie slowly. "Nothing to complain about." The grim assumption of indifference in his tone was almost tragic, and deceived none of the assembly, but Gordon, with an assumption of heartiness, retorted:

"That's fine! That's the ticket! We're expectin' every day to see the Mungo Company wi' the shutters up."

Brodie accepted this polite fiction and the spurious murmur of assent from the group which followed it, not with the blatant satisfaction which it would have provoked six months ago but, in the face of his present position, with a blank indifference which the others did not fail to observe. They might discuss him freely in his absence, criticise, condemn, or even vilify him, but when he was in their midst their strongly expressed feelings weakened sensibly under the shadow of his actual presence, and they were impelled, often against their wish, to make some flattering remark which they did not mean, and which they had not intended to utter.

He was a man whom they thought wiser to humour, better to keep on the right side of, safer to propitiate than to enrage, but now, as they noted his moody humour, and slyly watched his oppressed demeanour, they wondered if his iron control might be at last beginning to fail him.

A gentle, insinuating voice from the corner, addressing the company at large, broke into their general air of meditation.

"If you're thinkin' o' the Company's shutters goin' up you'll have a' to bide a wee—na, na, they'll not be shuttin' up shop—for a bit any way—not for a bittie," drawled Grierson.

"How's that?" queried someone.

"Oh! just a little private information," answered Grierson complacently, pursing his lips, placing his finger tips together and beaming on the company, especially upon Brodie, with an aspect of secret yet benevolent comprehension. Brodie looked up quickly from beneath his tufted eyebrows, not fearing the man but dreading, from his past experience, the sly, meek attitude which betokened in the other a deep and calculating venom.

"What is it then, man?" asked Paxton. "Out with it!"

But now that he had thoroughly aroused their curiosity, Grierson was in no haste to divulge his secret information and still smiled sleekly, keeping them on tenterhooks, tantalising them with the plum which would not drop from his lips until it was juicy with ripeness.

"Odd! you wouldna be interested," he purred. "'Tis just a leetle piece o' local news I happened to get wind o' privately."

"Do you know yourself, Brodie?" asked Paxton, in an effort to terminate the irritating procrastination.

Brodie shook his head mutely, thinking bitterly how Grierson got his finger first into every pie, how he was always the last to remove it.

"It's just a wee, insignificant bit of information," Grierson said, with increased satisfaction.

"Then out with it, ye sly deevil!"

"Well, if you must know, the district manager o' Mungo's is goin' away, now that they're so firmly established. I'm told they're doin' uncommone wel." He smiled blandly at Brodie and continued: "Ay! they've made a clever move, too, in offering the vacant post—and a real fine post it is an' all—to a Levenford man. He's been offered it and he's accepted it."

"Who is't then?" cried several voices.

"Oh, he's a real deservin' chap, is the new local manager o' the Mungo Company."

"What's his name then?"

"It's our friend's assistant, none other than young Peter Perry," drawled Grierson, with a triumphant wave of his hand towards Brodie.

Immediately a babble of comment broke out.

"Man, ye don't say so!"

"The auld, weedowed mother will be unco' pleased about that."

"What a step up for the young fellow!"

"He would jump at it like a cock at a groset."

Then, as the first flush of excitement at the unexpected tit-bit of local gossip subsided, and the real realisation of its meaning to Brodie dawned upon them, a silence fell, and all eyes were turned upon him. He sat perfectly still, stunned at the news, every muscle in his huge body rigid, his jaw set, his teeth gripping the stem of his pipe with the increasing pressure of a slowly closing vice. So Perry was leaving him, Perry upon whom of late he had come to depend utterly, realising at last that he had himself got out of the way of serving, that he was above it now, and was unable to lower himself to such lackey's work had he even desired it. A sharp crack split the attentive silence, as, with the onset of a pang of sudden bitterness, his teeth compressed themselves with such a vicious, final force upon his pipe that the stem snapped through.

As though in a trance, he looked at the riven pipe in his hand for a long second, then spat out the broken end coarsely upon the floor, looked again stupidly at the ruined meerschaum, and muttered to himself, unconscious that they heard him:

"I liked that pipe—liked it weel. It was my favourite."

Then he became aware of the ring of faces regarding him as though he sat in an arena for their contemplation, became aware that he must show them how he met the bitter shock of the blow, or better, show them that it held no bitterness for him. He stretched out towards his glass, raised it to his lips with a hand as steady as a rock, looked steadily back at Grierson, whose gaze immediately slipped off that unwavering stare. He would at that moment have given his right hand for the power to utter some cutting, withering retort which would shrivel the other by its very potency, but, despite a fury of endeavour, his brain was not sufficiently agile, his slow, ponderous wit refused to function, and all that he could do was to say, with an attempt at his habitual, sneering grimace:

"It's of no concern, not the slightest! Not the slightest concern to me!"

"I hope he'll not take any o' your trade with him," said Paxton solicitously.

"Now I come to think on't 'tis a downright dirty trick, Mr. Brodie," came in a toadying tone from one of the draughts players. "He kens a' your customers."

"Trust these Mungo bodies to move smartly. They're a deevelish clever lot in my opeenion," said another voice.

"Myself, I think it's raither a poor spirit," drawled Grierson consideringly. "Somehow it gives me the impression that he's just like a rat leavin' the sinkin' ship."

There was a sudden hush whilst everyone sat aghast at the audacity of this remark, the most direct affront that had ever been offered to Brodie in that club room. They expected him to arise and rend the puny form of Grierson, tear him apart by the sudden exertion of his brute strength, but instead he remained inert, unheeding, as if he had not heard or understood the other's remark. With his thoughts sunk in a gloomy abyss, he reflected that this was the most deadly blow he had suffered of any, although already they had smote him hip and thigh.

They had lavished their abundant capital in the struggle against him. In a dozen ways had exercised their ingenious cunning, but now in taking Perry they had snapped his last mainstay. Appropriately, he recollected his assistant's strange suppressed manner that night, his half-intimated, half-exultant look, as if he had been glad yet regretful, as if he had wished to speak and yet could not summon courage to do so. Strangely, he did not blame Perry, realising in justice that the other had merely accepted a better offer than he could have made, and

197

instead any animosity that stirred within him turned against the Mungo Company itself. His feeling, however, was at this moment, not truly one of hatred, but rather of curious compassion for himself, a sad consideration that he, so noble, so worthy, should suffer at such treacherous hands, should in consequence be compelled continually to assume this false front of indifference, when hitherto his careless arrogance had, unwittingly, protected him like armour. Then, amongst his meditations, he became again aware of the circle of watching eyes and the imperative need for speech, and hardly knowing what he said, yet whipping himself to anger, he began:

"I've always fought fair! I've always fought wi' clean hands. I wouldna lower myself to the level o' bribery and corruption, and if they've bribed that pimply, little snipe to leave me then they're gey and welcome to him. It'll save me the bother o' sackin' him—ay, they can keep him while they last. I don't give a tinker's curse about the whole affair." Reassured by his own speech, carried away by the expression of a sentiment he had not felt, his words grew louder, more confident, his glance more defiant and assured. "No! not a tinker's damn do I give," he cried. "But I'll not have him back again. Oh, dear, no! Let him draw his bribes while he can—and when he's able—for when they're burst and a' to hell, and he comes whinin' back for his auld job, then I'll see him in hell as weel, before I lift a hand to help him. He's unco' quick to run away. I've no doubt he thinks his fortune's made—the poor fool—but when he's back in the sheuch I took him out o', he'll regret the day he ever left the house o' James Brodie."

He was transfigured, exalted by his speech, now believing utterly in this declamation which contrasted so absolutely with his sombre, sensible perception of a moment before, and, his spirit asserting itself more powerfully in the very recognition of its power he glared back at them with wide, excited pupils. He hugged within himself the reflection that he could still control, dominate, overawe them, and as at last an idea, delightful and appropriate, struck him he drew himself up and cried:

"No! it'll take more than that to upset James Brodie in spite o' what our wee friend in the corner has had the nerve to suggest. When ye hear me complainin' it'll be enough to get out your crape, and it'll be a lang, lang time before ye need mournin' on that account. It's a joke though"—his eye flickered round them with a rampant facetiousness—"by gad! it's a joke that's worth a dram to us a'. Gentlemen," he cried, in a lordly voice, "shall we adjourn so that you may join me in a glass?"

They at once applauded him, delighted with his generous spirit, delighted at the thought of free refreshment, scenting ahead the chance of a carousal.

"Good for you, Brodie!"

"Scotland for ever! A man's a man for a' that."

"I'm wi' ye, juist a wee deoch-an-dorris to keep out the cauld."

"There's life in the auld horse yet!"

The Provost himself slapped him on the back. "Man, Brodie! you're a caution. Ye've the pluck o' a lion, the strength o' a bull, ay and the pride o' the deevil—there's no beatin' of ye. I believe ye wad dee before ye took a lickin'." At these words they stood up, concurring, and all but Grierson swarmed round him so that he stood amongst them, his fierce glance encompassing them, encouraging yet rebuking, sanctioning yet subduing, approving yet admonishing, like an emperor surrounded by his court. His blood, the blood that was noble like an emperor's, coursed more imperially in his veins than did the thin, serous fluid that was in theirs. In his heavy brain he felt he had achieved a great and noble action, that his gesture, in the teeth of disaster, had been sublime.

"Lay on, MacDuff," they cried, stirred by the unwonted laxity and magnanimity of his usually unapproachable nature, impatient to savour the rich, golden liquor he would provide for them. As he led them through the back door of the club into the outer air and they filed, eventually, into Phemie's wee back parlour, he felt the danger was over, that he was again the master of them.

Soon the drinks were flowing as they toasted him jubilantly, in McDonald's finest Chieftain whisky, for his generosity, his discrimination, his strength. As he flung out a golden sovereign, birling it grandly on to the round, mahogany table, a faint glimmering of sense at the back of his mind whispered to him how little he could afford it now, but he thrust the thought back again, stamped it out fiercely with a loud: "Here's to us—wha's like us?"

"It's a be-autiful dram, this," purred Grierson, smacking his lips appreciatively as he held his glass up to the light. "A beautiful dram, mild as mother's milk and smooth as—weel smooth as the nap on one o' our friend's braw hats. The only pity is that it's so dreshed more expensive than orner stuff." He tittered spitefully, knowingly towards Brodie.

"Drink it up then, man!" replied Brodie loudly. "Lap it up when ye get the chance. You're no' payin' for't. By God, if we were a' as mean as you, the world would stop goin' round."

"That's one to put in your pipe, Grierson," laughed Paxton, hoarsely.

"Speakin' o' stinginess—did ye hear the latest one about our wee friend here?" cried the Provost, with a nod towards Grierson, and a wink at Brodie.

"No! what was it?" they chorused. "Tell us, Provost."

"Weel," replied Gordon, with a knowing look, "it's short and sweet. The other day a wheen bairns were playin' about outside our friend's grain store, beside a big sack o' beans at the door, when up comes the son o' the house. 'Get away, boys,' young Grierson cries, 'and don't touch these beans or my feyther'll find out. He's got every one o' them counted!' "

A roar of appreciation arose from the assembly, through which Grierson murmured easily, blinking through the smoke:

"I'll no deny I ken how many beans make five, Provost, but it's a handy thing these days wi' so much hardship and poverty about."

But Brodie, upon his throne, the already warmed pith of him flaming under the potent whisky, neither heard nor heeded the innuendo as, filled with a wild elation, the desire to act, to liberate his strength, to smash something, seized him, and, raising his empty glass high above his head, he suddenly shouted, without point in the conversation: "To hell with them! To hell with these measly Mungo swine!" and shattered the heavy tumbler violently against the wall.

The others, now mellow for his mood, responded gleefully.

"That's the spirit!"

"Another round, gentlemen."

"No heeltaps."

"Gie us a song, Wullie."

"Speech! Speech!" came their shouts.

At this point a discreet knock upon the door, followed by the noiseless entry, felt-slippered yet formidable, of the landlady interrupted the fluid current of their hilarity.

"Ye're merry the night, gentlemen," she said with a thin, tight-lipped smile which inferred that their gaiety was not entirely becoming to them or wholly pleasing to her. "I hope ye'll no' forget the good name o' the house." Much as she valued their connection she was too remote, too virtuous, altogether too much of an institution to be imposed upon by them. "I dinna like to hear the smash o' glass," she added, acidly.

"Tits, Phemie, woman, it'll be payed for," cried Brodie. She nodded slightly, as though to convey to him that she had already taken that for granted, but in a slightly mollified tone she remarked:

"What's the occasion?"

"Just a little celebration given by our esteemed member at the head o' the table," murmured Grierson. "I dinna ken what it's to celebrate exactly, but ye micht ca' it a beanfeast without any beans."

"Never mind him, Phemie, send us in another hauf mutchkin," cried a voice.

"Will ye have a wee hauf yersel', Phemie?" remarked the Provost, breezily.

"Come awa' and sit on my knee, Phemie," cried one of the erstwhile draughts players—now, alas, incapable of differentiating a crowned man from a peppermint oddfellow.

"Send in the whisky, Phemie," demanded Brodie. "I'll make them a' behave themselves."

200

She reproved them individually and collectively with her glance, raised a warning forefinger, and padded out as silently as she had come murmuring as she went:

"Dinna forget the name o' the house. I'll send ye in the speerits, but ye maun keep quiet, ye maun mind the good name o' the house."

When she had gone the ball of their gaiety rolled off again, quickly gathered speed, and bounded more exuberantly than before.

"Never mind Phemie," cried a voice, "her bark is waur than her bite, but her face is waur than the two o' them thegither."

"Ye wad think this public o' hers was a tabernacle o' righteousness," cried another, "she's that uncommon godly about it. She wad have ye drink like ye were in the kirk."

"There's a braw, wee tittie in the front pews, onyway," replied the more bibulous draughts player. "They say Nancy, the barmaid, is as obleegin' as she's bonnie." He winked round the assembly knowingly.

"Tits, man, tits!" cried the Provost reprovingly. "Don't file the nest that you're sittin' in."

"That's the cuckoo ye wad be meanin'," replied the other agreeably; "but I'm no' that."

"Would ye like me to give ye a verse o' Burns?" called out Paxton. "I'm just ripe to let ye have 'The Devil amang the Tailors.'"

"Our chairman promised us a bit speech, did he not?" remarked Grierson, insinuatingly.

"Ay! Come awa' wi' that speech ye were goin' to give us," cried the Provost.

"Speech!" they insisted again. "Speech from the chairman."

Brodie's soaring pride, wafted higher by their tipsy cries, reached upward to a sublimated region where his limitations ceased, in the refined air of which his tongue seemed fluent, his incapacity for the articulate utterance of his inner thoughts forgotten.

"Very well," he called out, "I'll give ye a speech." He rose, inflating his chest, widening his eyes at them, swinging slightly from side to side on the fulcrum of his feet, wondering, now that he had risen, what he should say.

"Gentlemen," he began at length, slowly, but amidst ready applause, "ye all know who I am. I'm Brodie, James Brodie, and what that name means, maybe ye can guess." He paused, surveying each member of the group in turn. "Ay, I'm James Brodie, and in the Royal Borough of Levenford, and beyond it, too, it is a name that is respected and esteemed. Show me the man that says a word against it and I'll show you what these two hands will do to him." He shot out his huge hands wildly and let them throttle the vacant air before him, missing in his emotion the general apathy, the gloating relish in Grierson's satirical eyes, and seeing only reverence. "If I but chose I could tell you something that would startle ye to the very core." Then, as his eyes swept round the table, he lowered his voice to a hoarse, confidential whisper, shook his head cunningly. "But no! I'm not goin' to do it! Guess if ye like, but I'm not goin' to tell ye now—ye may never know. Never!" He shouted the word. "But it's there; and so long as I breathe breath into this body o' mine I will uphold my name. I've had an unco' trouble lately that would have bent a strong man and broken a weaker one, but what has it done to me? I'm still here, still the same James Brodie, but stronger, more determined than before. 'If your hand offend ye cut it off' says the Scriptures—I've had to cut my own flesh and blood, ay but it was without flinchin' that I used the axe. I've had trouble within and trouble without, sneakin' rogues and thievin' swine at my very ain' door, false friends and dirty enemies round about me, ay and sly, sleekit backbiters as weel." He looked grimly at Grierson. "But through it all and above it all James Brodie will stand hard and fast like the Castle Rock, ay and wi' his head as high above the air," he shouted, thumping his chest with his big fist and concluding in a loud full voice: "I tell ye I'll show ye all! I'll show every one o' ye." Then, having reached the climax of his feelings, for the spontaneous words had rushed from him unknowingly at the urge of his emotions, he sat down heavily, saying in a natural undertone: "And now we'll have another dram all round."

The last part of his speech was appreciated, loudly cheered, applauded by a rattle of glasses upon the hard table, echoed by Grierson's suave drawl:

"Good! I havena enjoyed a speech like that since Drunken Tam harangued the Baillies through the windae o' the jail."

They drank to him, to his oration, to his future; someone sang in a broken falsetto; Paxton protested, unheeded, that he, too, wanted to make a speech; the second draughts player attempted to tell a long, involved, and unseemly story; there were several songs with shouted choruses. Then, abruptly, Brodie, who had, with altered mood, remained cold, impassive, and disdainful amongst their mirth, jerked back his chair and got up to go. He knew the value of these sudden departures, felt the restrained dignity of his leaving the sodden dogs to sing and rant in the fashion that fitted them, whilst he departed at the moment when he could so retire with majesty and honour.

"What's the matter, man? Ye're not awa' hame yet," cried the Provost. "It's not near struck the twal' yet!"

"Bide a wee and we'll punish another haulf mutchkin atween us a'."

"Is the wee wifie waitin' on ye, then?" whispered Grierson blandly.

"I'm away," he cried roughly, buttoning up his jacket and stamping his feet, and, ignoring their profuse protests, he looked at them solemnly, saying:

"Gentlemen! Good night."

Their shouts followed him out of the room into the cool night wind, and filled him with a thrilling elation which increased inversely as the sounds of their homage weakened; the cries were like hosannahs, diminishing, yet pursuing, on the cold, sweet air that rose like frosted incense from the rimed streets. It had been a night, he told himself, as he made his way homewards amongst the white-limned houses that stood like silent temples in a deserted city, and, as he swelled with self-esteem, he felt he had justified himself in his own and in their eyes. The whisky in him made his step elastic, springy, and youthful; he wanted to walk over mountains in this crisping exaltation that sparked equally within him and in the delicious atmosphere around him; his body tingled and he thought in terms of wild, erotic, incoherent desires, peopling the dark rooms of every house he passed with concealed yet intimate activity, feeling, with a galling sense of injustice, that he must in future find some outlet for the surge of his suppressed and unattracted flesh. The short distance which he traversed to his home whetted his appetite for some fitting termination to the glorious evening and, almost in expectation, he let himself into his house and shot home the lock of the outer door with a flourish of the heavy key.

A light, he observed, still burned in the kitchen, a manifestation at once unusual and disturbing, as, when he came in late, all lights had been extinguished save that which burned faithfully in the hall, waiting to illuminate his return. He looked at his watch, saw the time to be half-past eleven, then viewed again the light which winked at him in the dim hall as it shone from beneath the closed door. With a frown he replaced his watch, stalked along the lobby, and seizing the door-handle firmly, with one push burst into the kitchen; there he stood erect, surveying the room and the figure of his wife as she sat crouching over the dull embers of the fire. At his entry she started, oppressed, although she awaited him, by the sudden intrusion into her dejected reverie of his frowning, unspoken disapproval. As she looked round in trepidation, showing red, inflamed eyes, he glared at her more angrily. "What's the matter with you?" he said, emphasising the last word like a gibe. "What are ye doin' up at this hour wi' your bleary, baggy een like saucers?"

"Father," she whispered, "ye'll not be angry, will ye?"

"What in God's name are ye snivelling for?" Was this the kind of homecoming that he merited, and on such a night as this had been? "Can ye not be in bed before I come in," he gnashed at her. "I don't have to look at ye there, ye auld trollop. You're a beautiful specimen o' a thing to come hame to, right enough. Did ye expect me to tak' ye out courtin' on this braw, moonlight night? You that's got as much draw in ye as an auld, cracked pipe."

As she looked upwards into his dark, disgusted face she seemed to shrink more into herself, her substance became less than a shadow, coherent speech failed her, but tremblingly, indistinctly, she articulated one word: "Matt!"

"Matt! Your dear, wee Matt! What's wrong wi' him next?" he fleered at her. "Has he swallowed another plum stane?"

"This letter," she faltered. "It—it came for me this mornin'. I've been feared to show you it all day," and, with a shaking hand, she handed him the crushed sheet of paper which she had all day hidden against her terrified, palpitating breast. With a derisive growl he rudely snatched the letter from her fingers and slowly read it, whilst she rocked herself to and fro distractedly, wailing with a tongue which was now loosed in the defence of her son: "I couldna keep it to mysel' a minute longer. I had to sit up for ye. Don't be angry wi' him, father. He doesna mean to vex you, I'm sure. We don't know the facts and it must be a terrible country out there. I knew something must be wrong wi' the boy when he stopped writin' regular. He'll be better at hame."

He had finished reading the few scrawled lines.

"So your big, braw, successful son is comin' hame to ye," he snarled. "Hame to his loving mother, and all her loving care."

"Maybe it's for the best," she whispered. "I'll be glad to have him back and to nurse him back to strength if he needs it."

"I ken you'll be glad to have him back, ye auld fool—but I don't give a damn for that." He again considered the crushed sheet with aversion before compressing it into a ball within his shut fist and jerking it furiously into the fireplace.

"What's the reason o' him throwin' up his good job like this?"

"I know no more nor yourself, father, but I think he must be poorly in himself. His constitution was aye delicate. He wasna really fitted for the tropics."

He showed his teeth at her.

"Fitted, your silly, empty head. 'Twas you made him a milk and water softie with all your sapsy treatment o' him. 'Matt dear,' he mimicked, 'come to your mother and she'll gie ye a penny. Never mind your father, lambie dear, come and Mamma will pet ye, dearie.' Is't that what brings him fleein' back to your dirty apron strings? If it is I'll string them round his neck. 'P.S. Please tell father,' " he sneered, quoting the burnt letter. "He hasna even the gumption to write to me himself, the washy, pithless pup. He's got to get his sweet, gentle mother to break the guid news. Oh! he's a right manly whelp."

"Oh! James, would ye no' comfort me a little?" she implored. "I'm that downright wretched. I dinna ken what has happened and the uncertainty is fair killin' me. I'm feared for my bairn."

"Comfort ye, auld wife!" he sang at her. "I would look well, would I not, puttin' my arm round a bag like you?" Then, in a harsh tone of repugnance, he continued: "I canna thole ye! Ye know that! Ye're as much good to me as an empty jeely jar. Ye're just about as much a success o' a wife as ye are o' a mother. One o' your litter has made a bonnie disgrace o' ye, and this one seems to be on his way. Ay, he seems well on his way. He's a credit to your upbringing o' him." Then his eyes darkened suddenly. "Take care though ye don't interfere wi' my Nessie. She belongs to me. Don't lay a finger on her. Keep your soft fiddle faddle away from her or I'll brain ye."

"Ye'll give him a home, father," she moaned. "Ye'll not show him the door?"

He laughed hatefully at her.

"It would kill me if ye turned him out like—like——" She broke down completely.

"I'll have to think about it," he replied, in an odious tone, revelling in the thought of keeping her in suspense, diverting against her all his indignant displeasure at Matthew's sudden defection and thrusting the entire blame upon her of this failure of her son. Hating her already in his defeated desire for the pleasure she could not give him, he loathed her the more inordinately because of this failure of her son, and he would, he told himself, let her pay for it dearly, make her the chopping block for the keen blade of his wrath. The fact that Matthew should have given notice and be sailing for home was entirely her offence; invariably the faults of the children made them hers, their virtues his.

"You're too just a man not to hear what he's to say, or what he wants, father," she persisted, in a ridiculous, wheedling voice. "A fine, big man like you wouldna do onything like that. Ye would give him a hearin', let him explain—there's bound to be a reason."

"There'll be a reason right enough," he sneered at her. "He'll want to come and live off his father, I've no doubt, as if we hadna enough to do without feedin' his big, blabby mouth. That'll be the reason o' the grand home comin'. I've no doubt he thinks he's in for a grand soft time here, wi' me to work for him and you to lick the mud off his boots. Damn it all—— It's too much for a man to put up wi'." A gust of passion mixed with a cold sleet of antipathy caught him. "It's too much," he yelled at her again. "Too blasted much." Raising up his hand as though to menace her with its power, he held it there for one tense moment, then with a sudden gesture he directed it towards the gas, turned out the light and, throwing the effacing darkness around her, went heavily out of the room.

Mrs. Brodie, left in the obliterating blackness, the last dying spark of the cinders of the fire barely silhouetting the amorphous outlines of her contracted figure, sat cowed and still. For a long time she waited, silent and reflective, while her sad thoughts flowed from her like dark waves, oppressing and filling the room with a deeper and more melancholy obscurity. She waited whilst the embers grew cold, until he would be undressed, in bed, and perhaps asleep, then she moved her set, unwilling frame, crept out of the kitchen, like a hunted animal from its cave, and crawled warily upstairs. The boards which had groaned and creaked when Brodie ascended were noiseless under her frail weight but, though her movements were soundless, a faint sigh of relief emanated from her into the darkness as, at the door of the bedroom, the heavy sound of her husband's breathing met her. He slept, and, eeling her way into and about the room she shed her shabby, spotted garments; laying them in a heap on her chair ready for the morning, she crept cautiously into bed, fearfully keeping her wilted body away from his, like a poor weak sheep couching itself beside a sleeping lion.

V

"MAMMA," said Nessie, on the following Saturday, "what is Matt coming back for?"

She was playing about the house and dragging after her mother in the desultory, querulous manner of a child to whom a wet Saturday morning is the worst evil of the week.

"The climate wasna suitable to him," replied Mrs. Brodie shortly. It was deeply rooted in the mind of Mamma as an essential tenet of the Brodie doctrine that from the young must be kept all knowledge of the inner workings of the affairs, relationships, and actions of the house, the more so if they were disagreeable. To questions concerning the deeper and more abstract aspects of Brodie conduct and, indeed, of life in general the consoling answer was: "You'll know some day, dear. All in good time!" and, to divert interrogations, the issue of which could not be avoided, Mamma considered it no sin to lie whitely and speciously to maintain inviolate the pride and dignity of the family.

"There's dreadful fevers out there," she continued; and a vague idea of improving Nessie's natural history made her add, "and lions, tigers, elephants, and giraffes, and all manner o' curious beasts and insects."

"But, Mamma!" persisted Nessie, "Jenny Paxton said it was all through the Yard that our Matt had got the sack for not attendin' to his work."

"She told a wicked untruth then. Your brother resigned his position like a gentleman."

"When will he be back, Mamma? Will he bring me anything, do you think? Will he bring me a monkey and a parrot? I would like a parrot better than a monkey. A monkey would scratch me but a parrot would talk to me and say, 'Pretty Polly,' and that's more than a canary can do, isn't it?" She paused meditatively, then resumed, "No; I'll not have that, I would have to clean its cage. I think I would like a pair of honky-tonky, morocco slippers or—or a bonnie, wee string o' coral beads. Will ye tell him, Mamma?"

"Be quiet, girl! How can I write to him when he's on his way home? Besides, Matt has more to think of than beads for you. You'll see him soon enough."

"Will he be here soon, then?"

"You'll know all in good time, Nessie." Then, voicing her own hopes, she added: "It might be in about ten days, if he left soon after his letter."

"Ten days! that's fine," Nessie chanted, and began to skip about with a more lively air. "I'll maybe have some fun when Matt comes back, forbye the wee string o' beads. It's been terrible since——" She stopped abruptly against the blank, forbidding wall of a subject absolutely interdicted, looked timidly at her mother, paused for a moment in confusion, then, as she saw that she was not to be reprimanded, began again, by a childish association of ideas: "What does it mean to be in deep water, Mamma?"

"What are ye talkin' about now, Nessie. Ye run on like a spoutin' waterfall. Can ye not let me get my work done."

"One of the girls in the class asked if my father could swim, because she heard her father sayin' that James Brodie was gettin' into deep water."

"Will you stop tormentin' me with your silly nonsense, Nessie," cried Mamma. "Your father can look after himself without your help. It's an impertinence for his name to be lifted like that." Nevertheless, the childish question touched her with a sharp, sudden misgiving, and, as she picked up a duster and went out of the kitchen, she wondered vaguely if there was any intrinsic reason for the exacerbation of Brodie's meanness with her, for the whittling and paring of her housekeeping allowance which had for months past made it impossible for her to make ends meet.

"Oh! it's not me, Mamma," replied Nessie, narrowing her small mouth virtuously, and following her mother into the parlour. "It's what the other girls in the class say. You would think there was something funny about us the way they go on. I'm better than them amn't I, Mamma? My father could beat all theirs tied together."

"Your father's a man in a million." It cost Mrs. Brodie an effort to say these words, but she uttered them heroically, unconscious of the ambiguous nature of her phrase, striving only to maintain the best traditions of the house. "Ye must never listen to a thing against him. Folks say bitter things when they're jealous o' a man."

"They're just a lot of cheeky, big things. I'm going to tell the teacher if they say another word about us," concluded Nessie, pressing her nose against the window like a small blob of putty. "It's still raining, coming down heavy as heavy—hang it!"

"Nessie! Don't say hang it. It's not right. You're not to use bad words," reprimanded Mamma, interrupting her polishing of the brass candlesticks on the burr walnut front of the piano. She would take no chances with Nessie! The first sign of error must be corrected! "Remember, now, or I'll tell your father," she threatened, addressing her heated face again towards the piano which, open for the nonce, smiled at her in fatuous agreement, its exposed keys grinning towards her like an enormous set of false teeth.

"I wanted to go and play—that was all," came the plaint from the window, "but there's puddles everywhere, even if it does go off. I've got to work so hard at these old lessons through the week, it's a shame if a girl can't get a little bit of playtime on a Saturday." Disconsolately, she continued to view the dismal prospect of the wet December landscape, the wet roadway, the rain-drenched fields, the still, dripping branches of the birches opposite, the melancholy lack of movement save for the steady downward fall of water. But her facile prattle did not cease for long and, despite the depressing scene, in a moment she had recommenced: "There's a sparrow sittin' on our cannon. Oh! there's another—there's two wee sparrows cowriein' down in the rain on our brass cannon. What do we keep a cannon like that for? It doesn't shoot and it always needs cleanin'. I've never noticed how funny it looked till the now, Mamma!" she pestered, insistently, "what is it there for? Tell me."

"A kind of ornament to set off the house, I suppose that was your father's idea," came the harassed voice from the back of the piano.

"It would have been better to have had a plot of pansies, or a wee monkey-puzzle tree like Jenny Paxton has in front o' her house," replied Nessie; then, continuing slowly, voicing her facile thoughts aloud, she chattered on: "There's not a breath in these trees across the fields. They're standin' like statues in the rain. 'Rain rain go to Spain! Never more come back again!' That'll not put it away though. That's only a story like Santa Claus. He's got a white beard. What is a Spaniard like I wonder. Has he a black face? The capital of Spain is Madrid. Correct. Up to the top of the class, Nessie Brodie. Good for you! That'll please father. What a day for a Saturday holiday. Here am I doin' geography on it. Not a body on the street. No! I'm wrong, I believe there's a man. He's comin' up the road. It's not a man, it's a telegraph boy!" It was a rich and unusual discovery in the dull, uninteresting prospect, and she fastened upon it delightedly. "Mamma! Mamma! somebody's going to get a telegram. I see the boy in the road. He's comin' right up here. Oh! look, look," she called out in a rapturous effervescence of expectation and excitement, "he's comin' into our house!"

Mrs. Brodie dropped her duster and flew to the window, through which she saw the boy coming up the steps, and immediately she heard the door-bell peal with such violence that it sounded in her startled ears like a sound of alarm. She stood quite still. She feared telegrams with a dreadful intensity as the harbingers of swift, unexpected calamity; they spoke not to her of happy births or joyous weddings but of the sudden, unconceived disaster of death. As she stood motionless a second, ominous ring of the bell fell upon her ears, and, as though the powerful pull tugged at the cords of her memory, reminded her of that previous solitary occasion in her life when she had received a telegram, the message which had announced the death of her mother. Without looking at Nessie she said, hoarsely: "Go to the door and see what it is."

Yet when Nessie, bubbling with anticipation, had run out of the room, she sought to calm herself; she reflected that perhaps the messenger had come only to collect information regarding an unknown name or an undecipherable address, as, living in the last house in the road, such inquiries were not infrequently addressed to them. She strained her hearing to the utmost, essaying to catch some hopeful sounds that might indicate a colloquy at the door, but vainly, for immediately Nessie was back, waving an orange slip with all the triumph of her own personal discovery.

"It's for you, Mamma," she announced breathlessly; "and is there an answer?"

Mamma took the telegram into her hand as though she touched a poisonous viper and, turning it over fearfully, inspected it with the profound horror with which she might have viewed this dangerous reptile. "I can't see without my glasses," she murmured, afraid to open the telegram, and trying feebly to gain time.

In a flash Nessie had gone and in a flash returned, bearing the steel-rimmed spectacles. "Here you are, Mamma! Now you'll manage to read it. Open it."

Mrs. Brodie slowly put on her glasses, again looked timorously at the dreadful thing in her hand and, turning to Nessie in a panic of indecision and fear, faltered:

"Perhaps I better leave it to your father. It mightna be my place to open a thing like this. It's a job for your father, is't not, dear?"

"Oh, come on, Mamma, open it," urged Nessie impatiently. "It's addressed to you and the boy's waiting for the answer."

Mrs. Brodie opened the envelope with stiff, ungainly fingers, tremblingly extracted the inner slip, unfolded it, and looked at it. For a long time she looked at it, as though it had contained, not nine words, but a message so lengthy and complicated that it passed her comprehension. As she gazed, gradually her face became dead, like grey ashes, and seemed to shrink into a smaller and more scanty compass; her features became pinched and drawn, as though some sudden icy blast had extinguished the feeble glow which animated them and frozen them into a strange, unnatural immobility.

"What is it, Mamma?" asked Nessie, on her tiptoes with curiosity.

"Nothing," repeated Mrs. Brodie in a dull, mechanical voice. She sat down limply upon the sofa with the rustling slip of paper fluttering between her shaking fingers.

Outside in the porch, the waiting boy, who had for some moments been moving impatiently, now began to whistle restlessly and to kick his toes noisily against the step, thus informing them in his own fashion, that it was no part of his duty to wait upon this doorstep for the duration of an entire day.

"Do you want the boy to wait for an answer?" continued Nessie curiously, observing, but not fully comprehending, her mother's strained immobility.

"No answer," automatically replied Mamma.

At Nessie's injunction the telegraph boy departed, still whistling loudly and unconcernedly, recognising his importance as the instrument of destiny, yet totally unmoved by the ravages of his missive of destruction.

Nessie came back to the parlour and, regarding her mother, thought her appearance ever moré strange, seemed with a more prolonged scrutiny hardly to recognise her.

"What's the matter with you, Mamma? You look so white." She touched her mother's cheek lightly, felt it, under her warm fingers, to be be cold and stiff as clay; then, with an uncanny intuition, she continued:

"Was it something about Matt in the telegram?"

At the name of her son Mrs. Brodie returned from her frigid rigidity into the conscious world. Had she been alone she would have melted into an abandoned flood of tears, but in Nessie's presence her weak spirit made a powerful effort to check the sobs rising in her throat and, struggling for control, she endeavoured to think with all the forces of her benumbed intellect. Urged by the strongest motive in nature to an effort of mind and will which would nominally have been far beyond her, she turned with a sudden movement to the child.

"Nessie," she breathed, "go up and see what Grandma's doing. Don't mention this wire, but try and find out if she heard the bell. You'll do that for Mamma, won't you, dear?"

With the quick perception that was the basis of her smartness Nessie understood exactly what her mother required of her, and embracing gleefully the task, which was that kind of confidential mission she adored to perform, she nodded her head twice, slowly, understandingly, and strolled casually out of the room.

When her daughter had gone, Mrs. Brodie unrolled the ball into which the telegram had been crumpled within her contracted fingers, and although the message had seared itself upon her memory, unconsciously she gazed at it again, whilst her quivering lips slowly framed each individual word—"Wire my forty pounds Post Restante Marseilles immediately. Matt."

He wanted his money! He wanted the savings that he had sent home to her, the forty pounds that she had invested for him in the Building Society! She saw immediately that he was exiled in Marseilles, in trouble, in some desperate strait, and that the money was a vital and immediate necessity to remove him from the meshes of a dreadful and dangerous entanglement. Someone had stolen his purse, he had been sandbagged and robbed, the vessel had sailed and left him stranded, without any of his belongings, in Marseilles. Marseilles—the very name—unknown, foreign, sinister, chilled her blood and suggested to her every possible evil that might befall her beloved son, for, on the sole evidence of this cryptic and appalling demand, she conceived him to be, definitely, the innocent victim of deplorable and harrowing circumstances. Sifting the available facts to the uttermost she observed that the wire had been handed in at Marseilles that morning—how soon had travelled the unhappy tidings!—which indicated to her that he had been in a fit state to dispatch the message, that he should be, at least, in no immediate physical danger. He had recovered, perhaps, from the effects of the vicious assault upon him, and now merely awaited patiently and anxiously the arrival of his own money. As her thoughts ran through these innumerable winding channels of her supposition they converged inevitably, despite a dozen deviations in their courses, to the one, common, relentless termination, to the conclusion that she must send this money. A pitiful shudder shook her at the very thought. She could not send it; she could send nothing. She had spent every penny of his forty pounds.

During the past nine months her financial struggles had been desperate. Brodie had progressively cut her allowance until he had at length reduced it by half, yet he expected the same excellent food supplied, where he was concerned, in the same excessive quantities; and did she manifest the slightest indication of economy upon the table she became the object of a fierce sarcastic tirade, in which he vituperated her as an incompetent bungler who lacked the ability even to manage adequately the petty exchequer of the home. He taunted her with the superior ability of his old mother, producing specious evidence of the old woman's housewifely efficiency, relating in detail the delicious, inexpensive meals she had prepared for him before his marriage, threatening, despite his mother's age, to transfer the management of the house into her more competent hands. It had been useless for Mamma to protest weakly that he gave her insufficient money, that food prices were rising, that the growing Nessie required more clothes, new boots, more expensive school books, that Grandma Brodie would not relinquish one single item of the comforts and luxuries to which custom had habituated her. It would have been equally ineffective, had she attempted it, to convince him that she spent not one farthing upon her own personal expenses, that she had not bought herself a new garment for three years, that in consequence she was the epitome of bedraggled inelegance, exposing herself, by the very unselfishness of this economy, to his gibes and sneers. Seeing her thus, despite a few feeble, ineffective initial protests, accept the reduced amount and apparently manage with it, he concluded that he had been too lavish in the past and, as money was so tight with him that he exulted in the opportunity to economise at her expense, he had tightened his purse strings to the limit and ground her further under the pressure of his heel.

Although she struggled to make one shilling do the work of two by buying in the cheapest markets, by bargaining and wheedling until she had achieved a reputation for mean shrewishness, it could not continue. Bills had become overdue, tradesmen had become impatient and finally, in despair, she had chosen the path of least resistance and drawn upon Matthew's money. Immediately, matters became easier. Brodie's growls about the food became less frequent, the old woman's whining, senile recriminations abated, Nessie had a new coat, the school fees were paid, and the long-suffering butcher and grocer were appeased. She herself obtained nothing, no clothing, no trivial trinket, no indulgence of her fancy, nothing but a transient immunity from the reproaches of her husband and the worries of her debts. She had consoled herself for her action by telling herself that Matt had really meant the money for her, that he loved her so that he would desire her to take it; again, she had reasoned that she had not spent it upon herself, that she would undoubtedly save and collect it for him in better times and fairer financial weather.

Forty pounds! It was a ruinous sum! Although she had expended it so easily the thought of obtaining it again was incredible. Under her former circumstances, and by the most penurious thrift, she might achieve this amount in, perhaps, the long term of a year; but the sum was required immediately. Her lips quivered as her heart quailed within her, but immediately she rallied herself, bracing herself to be brave for Matt's sake. She set her mouth firmly and looked up as Nessie returned to the room.

"Grandma was tidying up her drawer," whispered Nessie to her mother, with the air of a conspirator. "She didn't hear the bell and she doesn't know a thing about it. I found out ever so carefully!"

"That's a good, clever girl," said Mamma. "Nobody's to know about that telegram, Nessie. You're not to open your mouth yourself, about it. That was for me and nobody else. I trust you now! And I'll give ye something nice if ye don't tell." Then she concluded vaguely, feeling that some form of explanation was expected of her: "It was just from an old friend in the country—an old friend of Mamma's who is in some slight distress."

Nessie placed her left forefinger on her closed lips, delighted to share in a confidence of her mother's, implying by this precocious gesture that she was worthy to be trusted with the most private and mysterious secrets of the universe.

"That's right, now. Don't forget that you've given your word. Your father need know nothing about it," said Mrs. Brodie, as she got up. She desired to remain passively considering the situation, but it was nearly noon, and she had the dinner to prepare. No matter what anxiety affected her, the work of the house must go on, meals must appear upon the table with an inexorable punctuality, the master must be propitiated, fed adequately and succulently. As she began to peel a large potful of potatoes she tried to reach some decision as to what she should do.

At the outset she realised that she would obtain no help from her husband. She would have steeled herself to anything for Matt's sake, but it was an impossibility for her to face her husband and demand a sum of the absurd magnitude of forty pounds, realising with certainty, as she did, beforehand, that he would infallibly refuse to send the money. To bring the matter uselessly, in this manner, to his knowledge would be to reveal to him her own culpability, arouse his prodigious wrath, and yet obtain no tangible result. Even as she reasoned thus she could visualise him sneering: "He's in Marseilles, is he? Well! let him walk or swim back. It'll do the poor dear a heap o' good."

She next considered the possibilities associated with Agnes Moir. There was no doubt but that Agnes, who, like Mamma, could refuse him nothing, would be instantly willing to send money to Matthew, despite the shameful coldness and neglect she had suffered from him during the last few months, but it was, unhappily, an equal certainty that she did not possess forty pounds. The Moirs, although respectable, were poor, privation lay very near to their door, and it was unthinkable, even if they wished Agnes to have the money, that they could suddenly produce a large sum like this. Additionally, there had been a strong hint of reproach in Miss Moir's attitude to her lately which contained a justifiable suggestion of suffering and injured innocence. How could she then, in the face of such wounded purity of conscience, confess herself the thief of her own idolised son's money. The impeccable Miss Moir would condemn her immediately, would perhaps repudiate her before the eyes of the entire town.

She therefore abandoned Agnes, but, whilst she mechanically performed the actions of cooking the dinner, her mind continued to work furiously, racing against time. When Brodie came in she served the meal without once removing her fierce concentration from the problem that obsessed her, and with such unusual abstraction that she placed before Brodie, in mistake, Nessie's small plate.

"Are ye drunk, woman?" he roared at her, gazing at the diminutive portion, "or am I expected to repeat the miracle o' the loaves and fishes?"

As she hastily changed the plates Mamma blushed guiltily at this outward manifestation of her secret cogitations; but how could she have said, in extenuation: "I was thinking of how I could raise forty pounds for Matt?"

"She'll have been takin' a wee sook at the bottle to keep her strength up," tittered Grandma Brodie maliciously. "That's how she'll have been passin' the time this mornin'."

"So that's where the money for the house goes," sneered Brodie, taking up his mother's lead; "in tipple! well, we maun see what's to be done about that."

"Maybe that's what's gie'n her that red neb and watery een, I'm thinkin'," replied the old woman.

Nessie said nothing, but her too obvious side-glances of fealty and co-operation towards Mamma were so pregnant with meaning that they almost defeated their object. Still, the crisis was not precipitated and, after dinner, when Brodie had departed and the old woman retreated upstairs, Mamma breathed more freely, and turning to Nessie, said:

"Will you clear up, dear? I've got to go out for a few messages. You're a great help to Mamma to-day, and if you've got the dishes washed when I come back, I'll bring you a pennyworth of sweeties." In her awful dilemma she was capable even of subtle strategy in a small matter like this and, although the rain had ceased, Nessie consented willingly, lured by the bait of sweetmeats, charmed to be recognised by her mother as so supremely grown up.

Mrs. Brodie put on a hat and coat, the latter the very paletot she had worn when she escorted Matt to Glasgow on his departure, and hurried out of the house. She quickly crossed the Common and took the road which ran behind the station, then, at the junction of Railway Road and College Street, she paused outside a small, low-browed shop which bore above the crooked lintel of its doorway the disreputable insignia of three brass balls. Upon the window was a notice which stated in dirty white letters, and, through the defection of certain letters and the broken condition of others, with some uncertainty: Gold, Silver, Old False Teeth Bought, Money Lent; whilst behind this, chalked on a small un-prosperous looking slate, was the terser and less prepossessing phrase: Rags Bought. With a fearful misgiving Mrs. Brodie contemplated this, the only pawnshop in the respectable Borough of Levenford. To enter these precincts was, she knew, the most abysmal humiliation to which a respectable person could descend; and the greater crime of being de-tected entering therein meant disgrace, dishonour, and social annihila-tion. She realised all this, realised further her inability to cope with the hidden horrors within, yet she compressed her lips and glided bravely into the shop as quickly and unsubstantially as a shadow. Only the loud revealing tinkle of the bell attached to the door marked her entry, and, surrounded by its mellifluous reiterations, she found herself facing a counter in a small box-like compartment which appeared to be one of three. Here the number three had apparently a cabalistic significance both without and within, yet in the compartment she was more private than she could have hoped. Even in this debased society there were apparently instincts of delicacy! When the tinkle of the bell had ceased, her nostrils became gradually and oppressively aware of an odour, emerging permeatingly from some unseen point, of boiling fat tinctured with the aroma of onions. With a sudden faintness at the greasy, nauseating odour, she closed her eyes, and when she opened them a moment later, a short, squat man magically confronted her, having issued unseen, like a genie, from behind the heavy opaque cloud of vapour that infiltrated the inner shop. He had a long, square beard, iron grey and slightly curling, bushy eyebrows of the same colour and texture beneath which bright, beady eyes twinkled like a bird's; his hands and shoulders moved deferentially, but these black pellets of eyes never left Mrs. Brodie's face. He was a Polish Jew whose settlement in Levenford could be adduced only to his racial proclivity for courting adversity and who, failing to eke out an existence by usury in the hard soil of the Borough, was reduced to merely subsisting—or so it seemed—by the buying and selling of rags. Being mild and inoffensive he did not resent the abusive epithets which greeted him as, shouting: "Anyrag anybone! anybottle to-day!", he drove his donkey-cart upon his rounds, and he made no complaints except to bewail, to such as would hear him, the absence of a synagogue in the town.

"Yeth?" he now lisped to Mrs. Brodie.

"You lend money," she gasped.

"Vot you vont to pawn?" he thrust at her. Although his voice was gentle, she was startled at such crudity of expression.

"I've nothing here now. I wanted to borrow forty pounds."

He glanced sideways at her, regarding her rusty, unfashionable clothing, her rough hands and broken nails, the tarnish on the thin, worn, gold band of her solitary ring, her ludicrous battered hat—missing, with his glittering eyes, no item of her sad and worthless attire. He thought she must be mad. Caressing his fleshy, curved nose between his finger and thumb he said, thoughtfully:

"Zat es a lot of monesh. Ve must ave security. You must bring gold or jewels if you vish to raise zat amount."

She should, of course, have had jewels! In her novels these were the touchstone of a lady's security, but, apart from her wedding ring, she had only her mother's silver watch—which she might, with good fortune, have pledged for fifteen shillings—and, realising something of the insufficiency of her position she faltered:

"You would not lend it on my furniture or—or on note of hand. I saw—in the papers—some people do that, do they not?"

He continued to rub his nose, considering, beneath his benignly tallowed brow, that these Gentile women were all alike—scraggy and worn and stupid. Did she not realise that his business was conducted on the basis of shillings, not of pounds? and that, though he could produce the sum she required, he would require security and interest which he had realised at his initial survey to be utterly beyond her? He shook his head, gently but finally, and said, without ceasing to be conciliatory, using indeed, to that end his deprecating hands:

"Ve don't do zat beesness. Try a bigger firm—say en ze ceety. Oh yes! Zey might do et. Zey have more monesh zan a poor man like me."

She regarded him with a palpitating heart in stunned, humiliated silence, having braved the danger and suffered the indignity of entering his wretched hovel without achieving her purpose. Yet she was obliged to accept his decision—she had no appeal—and she was out once more in the dirty street amongst the puddles, the littered tin cans and the garbage in the gutter, without having procured even one of the forty pounds she required. She was utterly abased and humiliated yet, as she walked quickly away, she appreciated with a growing anxiety that, though she had achieved nothing, Matt would at this very moment be waiting in immediate anticipation of the arrival of the money. Lowering her umbrella over her face to avoid detection she hastened her steps feverishly towards home.

Nessie awaited her in a small imitation apron, triumphantly playing the housewife over her neat pile of clean crockery, preparing herself for her just reward of sweetmeats, but Mamma thrust her roughly aside.

"Another time, Nessie," she cried. "Don't bother me! I'll get you them another time." She entered the scullery and plunged her hand into the box where old copies of newspapers and periodicals, brought home by Brodie, were kept for household purposes, chiefly the kindling of fires. Removing a pile of these she spread them out upon the stone floor and flung herself before them, on her knees, as though she grovelled before some false god. She hurriedly ran her eye over several of these sheets until, with an inarticulate cry of relief, she found what she sought. What had that wretched Jew said? "Try a bigger firm," he had told her, in his indecently garbled English, and, accordingly, she chose the largest advertisement in the column, which informed her with many glowing embellishments that Adam McSevitch—a genuine Scotsman—lent £5 to £500, without security, on note of hand alone, that country clients would be attended promptly at their own homes, and, memorable feature, that the strictest and most inviolable secrecy would be preserved —nay, insisted upon—between the principal and his client.

Mrs. Brodie breathed more calmly as, without removing her hat or coat, she rose to her feet, hurried to the kitchen and sat down and composed a short, but carefully worded letter, asking Adam McSevitch to attend her at her home on Monday forenoon at eleven o'clock. She sealed the letter with the utmost precaution, then dragged her tired limbs out of the house and into the town once more. In her haste the constant pain in her side throbbed more intensely, but she did not allow it to interfere with her rate of motion and, by half-past three, she succeeded in reaching the general post office where she bought a stamp and carefully posted her letter. She then composed and dispatched a wire to "Brodie: Poste Restante: Marseilles," saying, "Money arrives Monday sure. Love. Mamma." The cost of the message left her stricken, but though she might have reduced the cost by omitting the last two words, she could not force herself to do so. Matt must be made to understand, above everything, that it was she who, with her own hands, had sent the wire, and that she, his mother, loved him.

A sense of comfort assuaged her on her way home; the feeling that she had accomplished something, and that on Monday she would assuredly obtain the money, reassured her, yet nevertheless, as the day dragged slowly to its end, she began to grow restless and impatient. The consolation obtained from her definite action gradually wore off and left her sad, inert, and helpless, obsessed by distressing doubts. She fluctuated between extremes of indecision and terror; felt that she would not obtain the money, then that she would be surely discovered; questioned her ability to carry through the undertaking; fled in her mind from the fact, as from an unreal and horrid nightmare, that she of all people should be attempting to deal with money-lenders.

Sunday dragged past her in an endless succession of interminable minutes, during the passage of which she glanced at the clock a hundred times, as if she might thus hasten the laboured transit of time and so terminate her own anxiety and the painful expectancy of her son. During the slow hours of the tardily passing day, she formed and re-formed the simple plan she had made, trembled to think how she would address Mr. McSevitch, was convinced that he would treat her as a lady, then felt certain that he would not, re-read his advertisement secretly, was cheered by his comforting offer to lend £500, then shocked by the amazing effrontery of it. When she retired eventually to rest, her head whirled with confusion, and she dreamed she was overwhelmed by an avalanche of golden pieces.

On Monday morning she could hardly maintain her normal demeanour, she shook so palpably with apprehension, but, mercifully, her anxiety was not detected and she sighed with relief when first Nessie, and then Brodie, disappeared through the front door. She now had only Grandma Brodie to dispose of, for, from the moment she had written her letter she had fully appreciated the obvious danger of having the inquisitive, garrulous, and hostile old woman about the house at the time fixed for the interview. The danger that she might stumble upon the entire situation was too great to be risked, and Mamma, with unthought of cunning, prepared to attack her upon her weakest point. At half-past nine therefore, when she took up to the old woman, upon a tray, her usual breakfast of porridge and milk, she did not, as was her usual custom, immediately leave the room, but instead sat down upon the bed, and regarded its aged occupant with an assumed and exaggerated expression of concern.

"Grandma," she began, "you never seem to get out of the house these days at all. You look real peaky to me the now. Why don't you take a bit stroll this morning?" The old dame poised the porridge spoon in her yellow claw, and cast a suspicious eye upon Mamma from under her white, frilled nightcap.

"And where would I stroll to on a winter's day?" she asked, distrustfully. "Do ye want me to get inflammation of the lungs so as you can get rid o' me?"

Mamma forced a bright laugh, an exhibition of gaiety which it tortured her heart to perform.

"It's a lovely day!" she cried, "and do ye know what I'm going to do with ye? I'm just going to give you a florin, to go and get yourself some Deesides and some oddfellows."

Grandma looked at the other with a dubious misgiving, sensing immediately a hidden motive, but tempted by the extreme richness of the enticement. In her senile greediness she loved particularly the crisp biscuits known as "Deeside," she doted upon those large, flat, round sweets so inappropriately named oddfellows; in her own room she endeavoured, always, to maintain a stock of each of these delicacies in two separate tins inside her top drawer; but now, as Mamma was well aware, her supplies were exhausted. It was a tempting offer!

"Where's the money?" she demanded, craftily. Without speaking, Mamma revealed the shining florin in the middle of her palm.

The crone blinked her bleared eyes at it, thinking with rapid, calculating glances, that there would be enough for the Deesides, the oddfellows, and maybe a wee dram over and above.

"I micht as weel take a dauner, then," she muttered slowly, with the semblance of a yawn·to indicate indifference.

"That's right, Grandma—I'll help ye," encouraged Mamma as, trembling with an exultation she feared to display, realising that so far victory was hers, she assisted the other out of bed. Before the old woman could have time to change her mind, she happed her in her voluminous clothing, tied a multitude of tapes, drew on the elastic-sided boots, brought her the jet-spangled bonnet, held out and enveloped her in the black, beaded cape. Then she presented her with her false teeth upon the charger of a cracked saucer, handed her the two-shilling piece and, having thus finally supplied her with the weapons and the sinews of the war about to be waged on the Deesides, she led the old woman down the stairs, and saw her go tottering out along the road, before the clock showed half-past ten. Exercising the utmost dispatch, she now made all the beds, washed the dishes, tidied the house, made herself, in her own phrase, decent, and sat down breathlessly at the parlour window to await her visitor.

As the hands of the marble timepiece on the parlour mantelpiece drew near to eleven, Mamma shook with trepidation, as though she expected a cab to dash up to the house and the front bell to ring, simultaneously with the first stroke of the hour. As the clock eventually struck eleven strokes, and was silent, she wondered if Mr. McSevitch would bring the money in golden sovereigns in a bag, or present it to her in immaculate notes; then, as the hands indicated five minutes, ten minutes, then fifteen minutes past the appointed time and still no one came, she grew restless. If her visitor did not come at the hour she had specially indicated, all her carefully thought out arrangements would go for nothing, and she shuddered to think what would happen if he arrived during the dinner hour, when her husband would be in the house.

At twenty minutes to twelve she had almost abandoned hope when, suddenly, she observed two strange gentlemen appear opposite the house. They arrived on foot and carried no bag, but were dressed exactly alike, in a manner which Mrs. Brodie felt might represent the peak of elegance, the most dashing summit of contemporary male fashion. Their Derby hats, that curled till brim met crown, were tilted rakishly above glossy side whiskers; their very short jackets were tight to the waist, with long rolling lapels, so that the chest of each had the appearance of swelling forward like that of a pouter pigeon, whilst the curve of the lower part of the back swept protrudingly, but equally enticingly, in an obverse direction; their check trousers, maintaining an agreeable looseness in the upper portions, clung more sympathetically to the figure as they descended, and terminated finally with the tightness of spats around small, inconspicuous, but none the less shining, shoes. Each wore a large, heavy watch chain high up across his spotted, fancy waistcoat whilst, even at such a distance as that from which she viewed them, she noted upon their fingers a coruscation of jewelled rings which sparkled and flashed with every fluent movement. No strangers of such composed address or brilliant plumage had, in the memory of Mrs. Brodie, ever flitted down upon the town of Levenford and, with a beating heart and a fascinated eye, she realised instinctively—although her anticipation had visualised a patriarchal gentleman in an Inverness cloak with a bluff manner and a benevolent shaggy beard—that these men of the world were the emissaries of McSevitch—genuine Scotsman.

From the middle of the roadway they looked knowingly at the house, as though their eyes, having embraced and criticised every architectural feature of its outer aspect, bored like gimlets through the hard stone walls, examining the inadequacies of its inner structure, and contemptuously discovering a host of deficiencies hitherto concealed even from its occupants.

At length, after a prolonged, impassive stare, one of the two turned his head slowly and, out of the corner of his mouth, said something to his companion, who on his part pushed his hat further back upon his head, veiled his protuberant eyeballs, and laughed with an experienced air.

Like a sudden, startled victim of diplopia, Mrs. Brodie now saw them advance simultaneously, proceed through the gateway abreast, saw them glance in unison at every stone on the courtyard, and, as they paused before the cannon in front the porch, she shrank back behind the concealment of her curtain.

"Bit o' junk that, but solid stuff—brass by the look on it," she heard one say as he fingered his large, pearly tiepin. The other flicked the gun barrel with his finger nail, as though he wished to see if it might ring true, but immediately he withdrew the finger and thrust it hastily into his mouth. "Ow! it's bloody hard, anyway," floated in through the half-open window towards Mamma's astounded ears. The bell rang. Mechanically she went to answer it and, as she threw open the door, she was confronted by two identically competent smiles which met and returned her shrinking gaze with a dazzling exhibition of gold and ivory.

"Mrs. Brodie?" said one, extinguishing his smile.

"You wrote?" said the other, doing likewise.

"Are you from Mr. McSevitch?" she stammered.

"Sons," said the first, easily.

"Partners," said the second, gracefully.

Overcome by the ease of their manners, but none the less shaken by a faint misgiving, she hesitatingly took them into the parlour. Immediately their sharp eyes, which had been glued upon her, detached themselves, and darted round every object in the room, in abstracted yet eager estimation until, finally, as the orbits of their inspection intersected, their glances met significantly and one addressed the other in a tongue unknown to Mrs. Brodie. The language was strange, but the tone familiar, and, even as she winced at its disparaging note, her cheeks coloured with a faint indignation as she thought that such words as these were, at least, not genuine Scottish. Then, alternately, they began to bombard her.

"You want forty pounds, lady?"

"On the quiet—without anyone knowin'—not even the old man, lady."

"Been havin' a little flutter, perhaps?"

"What do you want it for, lady?"

Their well-informed glances devastated her as they moved their fingers, sparkling their rings affluently, demonstrating agreeably that they had the money, that she it was who desired it. She was at their mercy.

When they had drawn everything from her regarding the house, her husband, herself, and her family, they exchanged a nod and, as one man, arose. They toured the parlour, then tramped loudly and indifferently through the house, fingering, handling, stroking, twiddling, and weighing everything in it, peering, poking, and prying into every room with Mamma at their heels like a debased and submissive dog. When they had reviewed the most intimate details of the life of the household as manifested to them in the interior of cupboards, the inside of wardrobes, the contents of drawers, and made her blush painfully as, penetrating even to her bedroom, they regarded with a knowing air the space beneath her bed, they at last descended the stairs, looking everywhere but at her. She could see refusal in their faces.

"I'm afraid it's no good, lady. Your furniture's poor stuff, heavy, old-fashioned, won't sell!" said one, at last, with an odious show of candour. "We might lend you two tens on it—or say even twenty-four pounds. Yes, say twenty-five at the outside limit and on our own terms of interest," he continued, as he produced a quill toothpick from his waistcoat pocket and assisted his calculations by its assiduous application. "What say?"

"Yes, lady," said the other, "times is bad these days, and you're not what you might call a good loan. We're always polite to a lady—funny the number of ladies we does business with—but you haven't got the security."

"But my things are all good," quavered Mamma in a faint voice; "they've been handed down in the family."

"You couldn't given them away now, ma'am," the gentleman with the toothpick assured her, shaking his head sadly. "No, not even in a downright gift. We've reached the limit, the fair limit. How about that twenty-five pounds of good money?"

"I must have forty pounds," said Mamma, weakly, "anything else is no good." She had set the fixed sum in her mind and nothing short of its complete achievement would satisfy her.

"You've nothing else to show, lady?" said one insinuatingly. "Funny what you ladies will shake out when you're put to it. You've nothing up your sleeve for the last?"

"Only the kitchen," replied Mrs. Brodie humbly, as she threw open the door, loath to allow them to depart, desiring despairingly to entice them into the plain apartment for a last consideration of her appeal. They went in, following her reluctantly, disdainfully, but immediately their attention was riveted by a picture which hung conspicuously upon the wall, framed in a wood of mottled, light yellow walnut. It was an engraving entitled "The Harvesters," was marked First Proof, and signed J. Bell.

"Is that yours, lady?" said one, after a significant pause.

"Yes," said Mrs. Brodie, "it's mine. It was my mother's before me. That small pencil sketch in the corner of the margin has been much admired."

They talked in low tones before the picture, peered at it through a glass, rubbed it, pawed it possessively.

"Would you like to sell this, lady? Of course it's nothing to make a noise on—oh dear, no!—but we would offer you—yes—five pounds for it," said the second eventually, in an altered, ingratiating tone.

"I can sell nothing," whispered Mamma. "Mr. Brodie would notice it at once."

"Say ten pounds then, lady," exclaimed the first, with a great show of magnanimity.

"No! No!" returned Mamma, "but if it's worth something will ye not lend me the rest of the money on it? If it's worth something to buy it's surely worth something to lend on." She waited in a fever of anxiety, hanging upon the inflections of their voices, upon their quick, expressive gestures, upon the very lift of their eyebrows while they held colloquy together upon her picture. At last, after prolonged argument, they agreed.

"You win, then, lady," said one. "We'll lend you the forty pounds, but you'll have to give us your bond on the picture and the rest of the furniture as well."

"We're giving the money away, lady," said the other, "but we'll do it for your sake. We see you need the money bad; but you must understand that if you don't pay up, that picture and your furniture belongs to us."

She nodded dumbly, feverishly, filled with a choking, unendurable sense of a hard-bought victory. They went back into the parlour and sat down at the table, where she signed the endless papers that they produced for her, appending her signature where they indicated with a blind, reckless indifference. She understood that she would have to repay three pounds a month for two years, but she cared nothing for that and, as they counted out the money in crisp pound notes, she took it like a woman in a dream, and, like a sleepwalker, she showed them to the door. In spite of everything she had got the money for Matt.

Early that afternoon she wired off the money. In the overwrought state of her imagination she seemed to see the clean bank notes actually rushing through the blue to the salvation of her son and, when they had gone, for the first time in three days she breathed peacefully, and a mantle of tranquillity descended upon her.

VI

ON the following morning Brodie sat at breakfast, cold, moody, detached, the two, sharp, vertical furrows—lately become more intensely grooved

—marking the centre of his forehead between his sunk eyes like cicatriced wounds, and giving to his gloomy visage a perpetual air of brooding perplexity. Caught in the unrelieved severity of the pale morning light his unwary countenance, relieved of observation, seemed to justify the idle remark uttered in the Paxton home that now he was beyond his depth, and, from behind that low wall of his harassed forehead, the confusion of his mind seemed to obtrude itself so forcibly that, even as he sat still and quiet at table, he appeared to flounder helplessly with all the impotent brute strength of a harpooned whale. His diminutive intellect, so disproportionate to his gigantic body, could not direct him towards safety and, while he lashed out in the most mistaken directions in his efforts to avoid a final catastrophe, he still saw that disaster steadily closing in upon him.

He, of course, knew nothing of the wire or of Mamma's action on the previous day. Mercifully, he was not aware of the unauthorised feet that had so boorishly tramped through his domain, yet his own worries and misfortunes were more than sufficient to render his temper like tinder, ready to ignite and flame furiously at the first spark of provocation, and now, having finished his porridge, he awaited with ill-concealed impatience his special cup of coffee which Mrs. Brodie was pouring out for him at the scullery stove.

This morning cup of coffee was one of the minor tribulations of Mamma's harassed existence, for, although she made tea admirably, she rarely succeeded in making coffee to Brodie's exacting taste, which demanded that it must be freshly brewed, freshly poured, and steaming hot. This innocent beverage had become a convenient peg upon which to hang any matutinal grievance, and most mornings he complained bitterly about it, on any or every pretext. It was too sweet, not strong enough, had too many grounds in it; it burned his tongue or was full of the straggling skin of boiled milk. No matter how she made it the result was declared unsatisfactory. The very action of carrying his cup to the table became to her a penance as, knowing the tremor of her hand, he insisted further that the cup must be brimming full and that not a single drop must be spilled upon the saucer. This last transgression was the most deadly that she could commit, and when it occurred he would wilfully allow the drop from the bottom of the cup to fall upon his coat, and would then roar:

"Ye careless besom, look what you've done! I can't keep a suit of clothes for your feckless, dirty ways."

Now, as she entered with the cup, he flung at her an irascible look for having kept him waiting exactly nine seconds, a look which developed into a sneering stare as, maintaining the brimming cup erect and the saucer inviolate by a tense effort of her slightly trembling hand, she walked slowly from the scullery door to the table. She had almost achieved her objective when suddenly with a frantic cry she dropped everything upon the floor and clutched her left side with both hands. Brodie gazed with stupefied rage at the broken crockery, the spilled coffee, and, last of all, at her distorted figure writhing before him amongst the wreckage on the floor. He shouted. She did not hear his bellow, she was so pierced by the sudden spasm of pain which transfixed her side like a white-hot skewer from which burning ripples of agony emanated and thrilled through her flesh. For a moment she suffered intensely, then gradually as though this awful cautery cooled, the waves of pain grew less and with a bloodless face she rose to her feet and stood before her husband, heedless at that instant of her enormity in upsetting his coffee. Relief at her emancipation from pain gave her tongue an unusual liberty.

"Oh! James," she gasped, "that was far the worst I've ever had. It nearly finished me. I really think I should see the doctor about it. I get the pain so much now and I sometimes feel a wee, hard lump in my list." Then she broke off, becoming aware suddenly of his high, affronted dignity.

"Is that a fact now?" he sneered; "we're goin' to run to the doctor for every touch o' the belly ache that grips us, we can so well afford it! And we can afford to scale the good drink on the floor and smash the china! Never mind the waste! Never mind my breakfast; just smash, smash a' the time." His voice rose with each word, then changed suddenly to a sneering tone—"Maybe ye would like a consultation of a' the doctors in the town? They might be able to find something wrang wi' ye if they brought round a' their learned books and put their empty heads together about ye! Who was it ye would be speirin' to see now?"

"They say that Renwick is clever," she muttered, unthinkingly.

"What!" he shouted, "ye talk o' goin' to that snipe that fell foul o' me last year. Let me see you try it!"

"I don't want to see anybody, father," cringed Mamma; "it was just the awfu' pain that's been grippin' me off and on for so long; but it's away now and I'll just not bother."

He was thoroughly infuriated.

"Not bother! I've seen you botherin'! Don't think I havena seen you with a' your dirty messin'. It's been enough to scunner a man and I'll put up wi' it no longer. Ye can take yersel' off to another room. From to-night onwards ye'll get out of my bed. Ye can move out o' my road, ye fusty old faggot!"

She understood that he was casting her out of their marriage bed, the bed in which she had at first lain beside him in love, where she had borne for him her children. For nearly thirty years of her life it had been her resting place; in sorrow and in sickness her weary limbs had stretched themselves upon that bed. She did not think of the relief it would afford her to have her own, quiet seclusion at nights away from his sulky oppression, to retire to Mary's old room and be alone in peace; she felt only the cutting disgrace of being thrown aside like a used and worn-out vessel. Her face burned with shame as though he had made some gross, obscene remark to her, but, as she looked deeply into his eyes, all that she said was:

"It's as you say, James! Will I make ye some more coffee?"

"No! keep your demned coffee. I'll do without any breakfast," he bawled. Although he had already eaten a large bowl of porridge and milk, he felt that she had wilfully defrauded him out of his breakfast, that he was again suffering because of her incompetence, her malingering assumption of illness. "I wouldna be surprised if ye tried to starve us next, with your blasted scrimpin'," he shouted finally, as he pranced out of the house.

His black resentment continued all the way to the shop, and although his mind left the incident, the sense of injustice still rankled while the thought of the day before him did nothing to restore his serenity. Perry had now left him, amidst a storm of contumely and reproaches no doubt, but he had nevertheless gone, and Brodie had been able to substitute for his rare and willing assistant only a small message boy who merely opened the shop and ran the errands. Apart from the loss of trade through the defection of the competent Perry, the onus of supporting the entire work of the shop now lay upon his broad but unaccustomed shoulders, and, even to his dull comprehension, it became painfully evident that he had entirely lost the knack of attending to such people as now drifted into his shop. He hated and despised the work, he never knew where to find things, he was too irritable, too impatient, altogether too big for this occupation.

He had, also, begun to find that his better-class customers, upon whose social value he had so prided himself, were insufficient to keep his business going; he realised with growing dismay that they patronised him only upon odd occasions and were invariably neglectful, in quite a gentlemanly fashion of course, of the settlement of their indebtedness to him. In the old days he had allowed these accounts to run on for two, three, or even four years, secure in the knowledge that he would eventually be paid; they would see, he had told himself in a lordly fashion, that James Brodie was not a petty tradesman grasping for his money, but a gentleman like themselves who could afford to wait another gentleman's convenience. Now, however, with the acute drop in the cash income of the business, he was in such need of ready money that these large, outstanding amounts by the various county families became a source of great anxiety, and although he had sent out, with much laborious auditing and unaccustomed reckoning, a complete issue of them, apart from a few, including the Latta account, which were paid to him immediately, the entire bundle might have been posted into the middle of the Leven for all the result that immediately accrued to him. He fully realised that it was useless to send them out again, that these people would pay in their time and not in his; the mere fact that he had already requested settlement with an unusual urgency might possibly estrange them from him altogether.

His own debts to the few, conservative, wholesale houses whom he favoured had grown far beyond their usual limits. Never a good business man, his usual method had been to order goods when, and as, he pleased, and to pay no heed to amounts, invoices, or accounts until the dignified representative of each house visited him at recognised intervals, in the accepted and friendly manner consonant between two firms of standing and reputation. Then, after a polite and cordial conversation upon the topics of the moment, Brodie would go to the small, green safe sunk in the wall of his office, unlock it grandly, and produce a certain canvas bag.

"Well," he would remark, imposingly, "what is our obligation to-day?"

The other would murmur deprecatingly, and, as if urged against his will to present the bill, would produce his handsome pocket book, rustle importantly amongst its papers, and reply suavely:

"Well, Mr. Brodie, since you wish it, here is your esteemed account"; whereupon Brodie, with one glance at the total, would count out a heap of sovereigns and silver from the bag in settlement. While he might more easily have paid by cheque, he disdained this as a mean, pettifogging instrument and preferred the magnanimous action of disbursing the clean, bright coins as the worthier manner of the settlement of a gentleman's debts. "That's money," he had once said in answer to a question, "and value for value. What's the point o' writin' on a small slip of printed paper. Let them use it that likes it—but the braw, bright siller was good enough for my forebears, and it'll be good enough for me." Then, when it was stamped and signed, he would negligently stuff the other's receipt in his waistcoat pocket and the two gentlemen would shake hands warmly, and part with mutual expressions of regard. That, considered Brodie, was how a man of breeding conducted such affairs.

To-day, however, although he expected a visit of this nature, he took no proud satisfaction from the thought but, instead, dreaded it. Mr. Soper, himself, of Bilsland & Soper Ltd., the largest and most conservative firm with whom he dealt, was coming to see him and, contrary to the usual procedure, he had actually been advised of this call by letter, an unexpected and unwonted injury to his pride. He well knew the reason of such a step, but nevertheless he felt the full bitterness of the blow to his self-esteem, anticipated, too, with sombre dismay the interview which was in prospect.

When he reached the shop he sought to lose his unhappy forebodings in the work of the day, but there was little to occupy him; business was at a standstill. Yet, attempting some show of activity, he walked cumbersomely about the shop with the ponderous movements of a restless

226

leviathan. This spurious display did not deceive even the small errand boy who, peering fearfully through the door of the back shop, saw Brodie stop every few moments whilst in the midst of some unnecessary operation and gaze blankly in front of him, heard him mutter to himself in a vague yet intense abstraction. With the street urchin's cunning he guessed that his employer was on the verge of disaster and he felt, with a strong measure of relief, that it would not be long before he was obliged to set about finding for himself another, and a more congenial, situation.

After an interminable, dragging hiatus, during which it seemed as if the entire hours of the forenoon would pass without a customer appearing, a man entered whom Brodie recognised as an old customer. Thinking that here was someone who, if not important, was at least loyal, he advanced with a great show of heartiness and greeted him.

"Well, my man," he said, "what can we do for you?" The other, somewhat taken aback by such cordiality, asserted laconically that he only required a cloth cap, a plain ordinary cap like the one he had purchased some time before, a grey check, size six and seven eighths.

"Like the one you're wearing?" asked Brodie, encouragingly.

The other looked uncomfortable.

"Naw," he replied, "this is a different yin; this is ma Sunday bonnet."

"Let me see," said Brodie, and struck by a dim idea he put out his hand, suddenly removed the cap from the other's head, and looked at it. Inside, on the shiny sateen lining, was stamped M. H. & H., the hated symbol of his rival next door. Immediately his face flooded with angry resentment and he flung the cap back at its owner. "So!" he cried, "ye've been goin' next door for your braw and fancy stuff, have ye? To wear on Sundays forsooth! And then ye've the impertinence to come in to me for a plain, ordinary bonnet after ye've given them the best o' your trade. Do ye think I'm goin' to take their leavin's? Go back and buy a' the trashy rubbish in their waxworks museum. I'll not serve ye for a pound note."

The other looked exceedingly discomfited. "Aw! Mr. Brodie. I didna mean it like that. I juist gie'n them a trial for a kind o' novelty. It was really the wife's doin'. She egged me on to see what the new place was like. That's like the women ye ken—but I've come back to ye."

"And I'm not goin' to have ye," roared Brodie. "Do ye think ye can treat me like that? I'll not stand it. It's a man that's before ye, not a demned monkey on a stick like they've got next door," and he banged his fist on the counter.

It was a ridiculous position. It was as though he expected the man to fawn at his feet and implore to be reinstated as a customer; as though, in his absurd rage, he expected the other to beg to be allowed the honour of buying from him. Something of this amazement dawned in the workman's face; he shook his head, uncomprehendingly.

"I can get what I want elsewhere. I've nae doubt you're a grand gentleman, but you're cuttin' off your nose to spite your face."

When he had gone, Brodie's passion suddenly subsided, and his face took on a mortified expression as he realised that he had done a foolish thing which would react injuriously upon his business. This man that he had refused to serve would talk, talk exaggeratedly in his resentment, and probably a garbled version of his action would be circulating freely in Levenford in the course of a few hours' time. People would make unfavourable comments about him and his high-handed ways, and although in the past he would have revelled in their adverse gossip, exulted uncompromisingly in their cackle, now he felt, in the light of his past experience, that people who heard the story would determine that they would not be subject to a similar indignity, that they would give his business a wide berth in the future. He wrinkled up his eyes at these disturbing thoughts and he damned the man, the people, and the town.

When one o'clock arrived he threw out to the boy that he would be gone for half an hour. Since Perry's departure had deprived him of a responsible person to leave in charge, it was only on rare occasions that he went home for his mid-day meal and, on such occasions, although his business had diminished so considerably, he was impatient to the point of irritability when he undertook the longer journey home for dinner; he felt, with a strange and unwarranted optimism, that he might be missing something which might vitally affect the business for the better. To-day, therefore, he took only a few paces down the street and went into the Winton Arms. Previous to the last twelve months it was unthought of for him to enter these doors except in the late evening, and by the special, private door allotted to himself and his fellow Philosophers; but now these visits had become usual and to-day, Nancy, the pretty barmaid, had a cold pie and some pickled red cabbage for his lunch.

"What will ye drink to-day, Mr. Brodie—a glass of beer?" she asked him, from under her dark curling lashes.

He looked at her heavily, noticing, despite his despondency, how a few, tiny, yellow freckles set off her creamy white skin like the delicate, golden specks upon a robin's egg.

"You ought to know I never drink beer, Nancy. I can't abide it. Bring me some whisky and cold water."

Nancy opened her lips to speak, but, although she wished to say that she thought it a pity to see a fine man like himself taking so much drink through the day, she was afraid, and she uttered no words. She thought Mr. Brodie a grand upstanding gentleman with, if her information was accurate, a perfect scarecrow of a wife, and, mingled with her interest, was compassion, an especial sorrow for him now that he bore this air of deep yet melancholy abstraction. He was, for her, invested with the essential elements of romance.

When she brought him his whisky he thanked her with an upward look of his dark, moody face, which seemed not to dismiss but to encourage her, and as she hovered about the table whilst he ate his lunch, waiting for an opportunity to anticipate his needs, he observed her carefully out of the corner of his eyes. She was a fine little jade, he thought, his gaze travelling upwards from her small foot in its neat shoe, over her well-turned ankle under the close black stocking, sweeping her tight firm hips and breasts, neat yet full, rising to her lips, which were red like the outer petals of fuchsia flowers against the whiteness of her skin. And, as he surveyed her, he was suddenly moved. A sudden, terrific desire for all the lustful pleasures that he had been denied rushed over him; he wished to rise immediately from the table and crush Nancy in his huge embrace, to feel a young, hard, resistant body in his arms instead of the torpid, slavish lump that he had for so long been obliged to accept. For the moment he would scarcely swallow, and his throat went dry with the urge of another appetite. He had heard stray, little whispers and veiled allusions about Nancy that whetted his hunger fiercely, told him it was a hunger which would be easy to appease; but with a tremendous effort of will he controlled himself and went on eating mechanically, his glowing eyes fixed upon his plate.

"Some other time," he kept telling himself, realising that this important engagement of the afternoon must be faced, that he must restrain himself, curb himself against the time of the interview with Soper, which might be filled with a critical significance for the future of his business. He did not look at her again during his short meal, although now her presence fascinated him, and the brush of her body against his arm as she removed his plate made him clench his teeth. "Some other time! Some other time!"

Silently he accepted the biscuits and cheese she brought him and quickly consumed them, but when he had finished he got up and, standing close to her, significantly pressed a coin into her warm hand.

"You've looked after me real well these last weeks," he said, looking at her strangely. "I'll not forget ye."

"Oh! Mr. Brodie, I hope this doesna mean you'll not be back," she cried in concern. "I would miss ye if ye didna come in again."

"Would ye miss me, then?" he replied slowly. "That's good! You and me would suit not bad thegither I'm thinkin'. So don't worry. I'll be back all right." He paused and added in a low voice: "Yes! and maybe ye ken what for."

She mustered a blush and affected to hang her head, feeling, despite her fear to the contrary, that he had noticed her and was disposed to favour her with his regard. She was interested in him, obsessed by his strength; because she was not a virgin her nature responded more ardently to the suggestion of vital force which emanated from him. He was such a free man with his money, too, was Mr. Brodie!

"A big man like you couldna see much in such a wee thing as me," she murmured, provokingly; "ye wouldna want to try!"

"I'll be back," he repeated and looked at her intently, penetratingly, then turned on his heel and was gone.

For an instant she stood quite still, her eyes sparkling with satisfaction, her affectation of meekness abandoned, then she ran to the window and stood on tiptoes to watch him go down the street.

Back again in his shop Brodie made a powerful effort to dismiss the warm images which so pleasantly permeated his mind and tried to prepare his ideas for the forthcoming visit of Mr. Soper. But his thoughts lacked continuity or coherence, he was unable, now as always, to formulate any definite, original plan of campaign; the instant he started to consider the possibilities of an idea his mind wandered off at a tangent and he began to think again of Nancy, of the warm look in her eyes, of the chances of arranging a meeting with her. In disgust he gave up the struggle, and feeling that he must blindly await the developments of the interview before he could attempt to cope with them, he got up and went into his shop to await the arrival of his visitor.

As he had said so exactly in his letter, at three o'clock precisely Mr. Soper arrived at the shop, and Brodie, who stood ready, immediately came forward and greeted him; but as they shook hands, Brodie seemed to sense more firmness and less effusiveness in the other's grasp, though he ignored this suspicion and said, with a great assumption of cordiality:

"Come away into my office, Mr. Soper. Moderate weather for the time of year. Yes! very mild indeed."

Somehow his visitor was not inclined to discuss the weather. As they sat down on opposite sides of the desk he looked at Brodie with a politely formal mien, then looked away. He was well aware of Brodie's position and for the sake of old association had intended to be kind; but now, the rank odour of spirits which clung to the other and the loose, easy manner of his greeting prejudiced him intensely. Soper himself was a man of well-defined ideas on moral grounds, being a strong adherent of the sect of Plymouth Brethren, and, in addition, a handsome contributor to the Scottish Temperance Association; as he sat there in his rich, well-fitting clothes, contemplating his admirably kept finger nails, he drew in his lips in a manner totally adverse to Brodie's interest.

"If this open weather continues they'll be gettin' on well with the ploughin'. I saw they had made a bend at the Main's Farm the other day I was out," Brodie persevered, his sluggish wit failing to attune itself to the other's inimical attitude, his obtuse mind compelling him to continue to force remarks in the usual strain set by the precedent of such interviews in the past. "I often take a bit run into the country when I have the opportunity—ay! I'm real fond o' seein' a good pair o' horses turnin' up the fine, rich land up by there."

Soper let him run on, then suddenly, in a cold, incisive voice he cut in.

"Mr. Brodie, your total indebtedness to my firm is exactly one hundred and twenty-four pounds ten shillings and sixpence. I am here at the request of my co-partners to request payment."

Brodie stopped as if he had been shot.

"Wha'—what?" he stammered, "what's come on ye?"

"I appreciate that it is a large sum, but you have postponed payment of our bills on the last three visits of our representative, and in consequence of the large amount involved and the fact that you are an old client I have, as you may have surmised, made this personal visit to request settlement."

In Brodie's mind two opposing forces, rage at the other's manner and consternation at the amount of his debt, dragged against each other violently. Although he had no records for verification, he knew at once that Soper's figure must, although it appalled him, be correct; these people never made mistakes. But the other's chilling attitude left him aghast, and the fact that he was powerless to deal with it as he would have wished infuriated him. If he had possessed the money he would have paid Soper instantly and closed his account with the firm on the spot; but he was well aware of his inability to do this and, with an effort, stifled his fury.

"You'll surely give an old client like myself time to settle?" he managed to articulate, as a negative confession of his inability to find the money.

"You have paid us nothing for over twelve months, Mr. Brodie, and we are naturally becoming anxious. I'm afraid I must ask you to meet this bill now."

Brodie looked at him, then at his safe set in the wall which contained, he knew, less than five pounds, thought futilely of his banking account which had dwindled to an inconsiderable trifle.

"If you don't," Soper was continuing, "I'm afraid we must press. We don't like it, but we shall have to press."

Brodie's eye grew sullen like that of a baited bull.

"I cannot pay," he said. "I cannot pay to-day. But there will be no need for ye to press, as ye call it; ye should well know that James Brodie is an honest man. I'll pay ye—but you must give me time to raise the money."

"How do you propose to do that, might I ask, Mr. Brodie?"

"Ye can ask till you're blue in the face, man, but it's no duty of mine to enlighten you. All that ye need to know is that you'll have your precious money by the end o' the week. I have said it and my word is my bond."

Looking at him, Soper's face softened slightly.

"Yes," he said after a pause, "I know that. I know you've had your difficulties, Mr. Brodie. These undercutting companies with their modern shops," he shrugged his shoulders expressively. "But we have our troubles as well, and we have our own obligations to meet. There's little room for sentiment in business, nowadays. But still—how exactly are things with you?"

As Brodie tried to think of a devastating reply, suddenly it seemed to him with a grim humour what nothing would shock the other more than the plain truth.

"Less than three pounds has come into the business in two weeks," he shot out abruptly. "How do ye like that?"

The other raised his well-kept hands in horror.

"Mr. Brodie, you shock me! I had been told, but I did not know it was as bad as that." He looked at Brodie's harsh face for a moment then said, in a more kindly tone: "There's a saying on 'change, man, which you might well consider. It's sometimes better to cut your losses. Cut your losses rather than go under. Don't batter your head against a brick wall. You'll forgive me—but you understand what I mean." He rose to go.

"I don't understand! What the devil do you mean?" asked Brodie. "I'm here, I've always been here, and, by God, I'll stay here."

Soper paused on his way to the door.

"I mean this kindly to you, Mr. Brodie," he exclaimed, "and what I say is offered to you in a helpful spirit of advice. You can take it or leave it, but experience tells me that you are in an impossible position here. You've had a grand thing here in your day but now, these folks next door have got you beat a hundred ways. Man alive, remember this is the year 1881. We're all moving with new ideas and up-to-date methods but you, and the wheels of progress have run ye down. It's a wise man who knows when he's beat, and if I were you I would shut up my shop and get out with what I could. Why don't you get out of here and try something else? A big man like you could stock a farm and work it with the best." He held out his hand frankly, and said in parting: "You'll not forget us at the end of the week!"

Brodie gazed after him with a flat expressionless face, gripping the edge of the desk until the sinews on the back of his hands showed white under the dark, hairy skin, and the veins rose up like twisted cords.

"Stock a farm!" he muttered. "He surely doesna know what little I have left"; and, as his thoughts rushed outwards into open spaces in a wild regret, he whispered to himself: "He's right though! That would have been the life for me if I could have managed it. I could have settled down close to the land I love so weel, the land that should be mine. But I canna do't now. I maun battle on here."

He was now aware that he would have to bond his house, his sole remaining asset, in order to find the money to settle his account with Soper and to discharge the remainder of these obligations which had gradually accumulated upon him. No one would know, he would go secretly to a lawyer in Glasgow, who would arrange everything, but already, he felt dully as if his own house did not belong to him. It was as if, with his own hand, he was compelled to begin the destruction and disintegration of the solid structure he had seen arise stone by stone, like the gradual erection of an edifice of his own hopes. He loved his house, yet he would have to pledge it to maintain the honour of his name. Above everything he must keep untarnished his reputation for equity and honesty, must demonstrate at once that he—James Brodie—could owe no man a penny. There were some things that he could not do! Then, with a sudden turn of his mind, he seemed by contrast to remember something; his eye glistened, his lower lip protruded slowly, and his mouth twisted into a warped smile. Amongst the desert of his troubles he suddenly espied a green oasis of pleasure. There were some things that he could do! Darkly, a hidden purpose concealed within him like the secret of a crime, he went out of the shop, heedlessly leaving it untenanted, and slowly directed his course towards the Winton Arms.

VII

Mrs. Brodie was resting on the parlour sofa, an unwonted indolence on her part, more especially at this early hour of the afternoon when she should have been industriously occupied in washing the dinner dishes. To-day, however, her forces had spent themselves sooner than usual and she had felt that she must rest before nightfall.

"I'm so knocked up," she mentioned to Grandma Brodie, "I feel ready to drop. I think I'll lie down a wee."

The old woman had eyed her reprovingly and, moving hastily out of the room for fear she herself might be asked to wash up, had replied:

"It surely doesna take much to upset you, you're always moanin' and groanin' about your health they days. When I was your age I did twice your work and never blinked an eye ower it."

Nevertheless, on her departure, Mamma had gone quietly into the parlour and lain down, and now, feeling better, refreshed and restored, she reflected idly that if only she had made a habit of this short afternoon repose earlier in her life she might have worn better; still, she felt thankful that, for the past ten days she had suffered no recurrence of her excruciating pain but merely that dragging ache which, through long familiarity, she now almost ignored.

Nearly three weeks had elapsed since the dispatch of the money to Matt, and for all the acknowledgment which she had received, the forty pounds might still have rested securely in the coffers of McSevitch.

To think, even of that ridiculous, hateful name made her shiver slightly, it was costing her so dear to scrape together the first instalment of her debt, to stint and save parsimoniously so that, from time to time, she might thankfully place some coins in the tin box specially put aside, hidden in her own drawer for this not to be forgotten purpose. It seemed to her, from the painful difficulty of her accumulation, as if this debt would hang threatening above her head for the next two years, like a perpetually suspended sword.

Here, of course, she made no allowance for Matt, and now, amidst the harassing thoughts of her present position, the mere consideration of his return caused a pallid smile to enliven her features. She was firmly assured in her inmost heart that the moment he came back he would stretch out his hand lovingly, compassionately, and with one word relieve her of this racking responsibility. The corners of her drawn lips relaxed as she reflected that it would not be long before her son was once more in her arms, comforting her, rewarding her a hundredfold for the superhuman effort she had made on his behalf. She pictured the last stages of his journey, saw him, an impatient manly figure, pacing the deck of the ship, disembarking impetuously, now driving hurriedly through crowded, thronging streets, sitting restlessly in the corner of his railway compartment, and finally flinging himself eagerly into the cab which would restore him to her.

The vision of his return hung before her, dazzled her with its imminence, yet as she looked idly out of the window and gradually observed that a cab, loaded with luggage, had driven up at the gate, her brow became furrowed incredulously, as if she failed to believe what she saw. It could not be Matt—her boy—her own son—and yet, miraculously, it was he, home to her at last, stepping out of the cab nonchalantly, as though he had not traversed three thousand miles of sea and land to come to her. With an incoherent cry she raised herself, stumbled to her feet, ran precipitately out of the house, and had enveloped him in her arms almost before he was out of the cab.

"Matt!" she panted, overcome by the excess of her feelings. "Oh! Matt!"

He started back a little, protesting,

"Half a chance, Mamma. Take it easy. You'll smother me if you go on like that."

"Oh! Matt! my dear boy!" she whispered, "you're back to me at last."

"Whoa up, Mamma!" he cried. "Don't weep all over me. I'm used to a dry climate. There now! Don't make a handkerchief of my new tie."

At his protests she at last relinquished her embrace, but would not altogether let him go, and clutching his sleeve fondly, as though fearful that she might again lose him, exclaimed fervently:

"I can hardly believe I've got you back again, son. It's a sight for

234

my tired eyes to see you, for I was thinking about you the minute you drove up. I've missed you wearily, wearily!"

"Well, we're certainly here again, old girl," he quizzed her; "back to the same old Levenford, same old ancestral home, and same old Mamma!"

Mrs Brodie looked at him dotingly. Everything here might be the same, but he had altered, was profoundly different from the raw youth who had left her only two years ago.

"My! Matt!" she cried, "you've got a real smart look about you. There's an air about you that fair takes my breath away. You're a man now, my son!"

"That's right," he agreed, surveying his surroundings rather than her. "I've learned a thing or two since I saw you last. I'll show them some style in this old Borough before very long. Gad! but everything here seems poky compared with what I've been used to." Then, turning commandingly to the cabby he shouted:

"Bring in my luggage you! *jilde!*"

She observed proudly that he, who had departed with one small, brass-bound chest, now returned with a galaxy of bags and trunks; and could he, on that memorable day when she had let him go fluttering from under her wings, have addressed a cabman in terms of such auto-cratic disdain? She could not forbear from expressing her fond admira-tion at the change as she followed his swaggering figure into the hall.

"Oh! that's nothing," he exclaimed carelessly; "I've been used to a retinue of servants out there—blacks you know—and a man gets so accustomed to ordering them about, 'tis no trouble to make this old *gharry wallah* jump to it. Pay him, though, will you, Mamma! I happen to have run out of change at the moment." His look conveyed a sense of superiority to the task of paying a mere cabman, and with a final condescending survey, he moved off and entered the house. Mamma ran for her purse and at once settled with the man, and as she returned, closing the front door securely lest her son might suddenly be taken from her again, the pile of boxes in the hall gladdened her, her heart sang joyously the words: "He's back! Matt's back for good!"

She rejoined him in the kitchen where he was reclining in the arm-chair, his legs extended, his arms drooping over the sides of the chair, his whole pose indicative of fashionable ennui.

"Rather fatiguing journey!" he murmured, without moving his head. "I find the trains in this country very noisy. Give a man a con-founded headache."

"Rest ye—rest ye then, my boy," she exclaimed. "You're home now, that's the main thing." She paused, having so many things to say that she did not know where to begin, yet realising that, before she could permit herself to indulge her selfish curiosity, she must restore his strength with some honest food prepared by her own loving hands.

"I'm dying to hear all about it, Matt," she said, "but let me get you a bite of something first."

He waved the suggestion of food aside.

"Yes! dear—a little cold ham or a cup of lentil soup. You could surely take that. You mind that nice nourishing soup I used to make for you. You were always fond of it."

Matt shook his head definitely, saying: "I don't want to eat just now. I'm used to a late dinner at night now—besides I had a snack in Glasgow."

She was slightly disheartened, but still insisted: "You'll be thirsty after your journey, son. Have a cup of tea. There's nobody can make it like me."

"All right, then," he assented. "Go ahead if that's the best you can do!"

She did not quite grasp his meaning, but rushed in a passion of love to get him the tea and, when she brought him the large steaming cup, she seated herself upon a low stool before him, watching with hungry eyes his every gesture. He was not discomposed by her eager stare but, as he sipped his tea, he casually drew a bright leather case from his pocket and, extracting a thick cheroot, withdrew the straw from it and lit up, demonstrating more plainly than words could tell that he was master of himself, a finished man of the world.

Whilst she studied his easy gestures and admired the fashionable negligence of his suit of smooth, light cloth, she became aware with some concern that his face had altered, grown older than she had expected. His eyes, particularly, had aged and seemed darker than before, with a fine network of wrinkles besetting the corners of the lids; his features had sharpened, his complexion turned to a more sallow, even yellowish tinge, whilst his cheeks seemed to be tightly stretched upon the framework of his jaws. She felt convinced now that some harsh and bitter experience had marred his separation from her and, deeming him to have recovered somewhat, her tone was gentle as she said:

"Tell me, Matt, all about it."

He regarded her from beneath his half-closed eyes, and replied abruptly:

"About what?"

"Oh! just everything, son! Ye can't deceive your mother's eyes. Somebody's been hard on you—unjust too. But I know so little. Tell me how you left India and what—what happened on the way back?"

His eyes opened more fully and, waving his cigar, he immediately grew voluble.

"Oh! that!" he said, "that's soon explained. There's nothing to tell there. I simply threw up my job because it got on my nerves! To be quite honest, Mamma. I couldn't stand the damned dock *wallah* who

236

ran the office. Everything was a fault with him. If a man were a bit late in the morning, after an evening at the club, or if there happened to be a day taken off work—just for a little social engagement you know— he was simply unbearable." He contemplated her with an injured air as he drew at his cigar, and added indignantly: "You know how I could never abide being put upon. I was never the one to endure being bossed about by anyone. It's not my nature. So I told him in plain language what I thought and walked out on him."

"Did ye not speak to Mr. Waldie about it, Matt?" she queried sharing his resentment. "He's a Levenford man and a good man. He has a great name for fairness."

"It's him I mean, the *soor*!" retorted Matthew bitterly. "He's the very one that tried to drive me like a coolie. Not a gentleman!" he added. "Nothing but a damned, psalm-singing slave driver."

Mamma's expression grew vaguely troubled and confused.

"Was that the reason of it, son? It wasna right if he did that to you." She paused, then ventured timidly: "We thought it might be your health?"

"Health's as sound as a bell," said Matthew sulkily. "It was the blasted job. I liked everything else out there. It was a fine life if I had been left alone. But he won't cook me, the old swine. I'll go abroad again—Burma! or Malay this time. I'll never stay in this rotten place after what I've seen."

Mrs. Brodie's heart sank. Here was her son barely home, restored only this moment to her arms, and in the next breath he talked of leaving her, of returning, like Alexander, to attempt fresh conquests in these wild foreign lands which terrified her.

"Ye'll not be thinkin' of that for a bit, dear," she quavered. "Maybe you'll get a post at home that would suit you better. Then you wouldna need to leave me again."

He laughed shortly.

"Do you believe I could live in a hole like this after the kind of life I've had out there. What can you offer me here to make up for it? Think of it," he cried. "I had the club, dinners at the mess, dances, the races, polo matches, servants to wait on me hand and foot—every single thing I could want."

He dazzled her with his romantic mendacity so that she saw him mixing in exclusive Society, at regimental dinners, rubbing shoulders with officers in their red mess jackets, with ladies in gleaming satin, and, overcome by the inadequacy of anything that she could offer in return, she could only say weakly:

"I know there's not much of that at home, son. But I'll—I'll do my best to attend to you, to make you comfortable here." He made no reply and, at his eloquent silence, she hesitated, dismayed that the conversation should languish in this fashion, as though after two years he had nothing to tell her, no eagerness to discover how she had fared in his absence. "Did ye have a good voyage home?" she ventured at last.

"Tolerable! Quite tolerable," he admitted. "Weather was good but I got bored towards the end. I left the ship at Marseilles."

"That was where I sent ye the—your money," she remarked haltingly. "Ye got it safe?"

"Yes, I got it all right," he replied, negligently. "Took a devilish age to come through though. Long to come and quick to go."

"I suppose ye had some grave need of a' that siller, Matt?"

"That's right," he replied. "*I* needed it—that was enough, wasn't it?"

"True enough, Matt," she answered. "I knew from your wire you had sore need of it. But it was such a sum of money!"

"Sum of fiddlesticks," he retorted angrily. "You would think it wasn't my own the way you talk. I worked for it, didn't I? I didn't rob ye for it. It was mine to spend as I liked."

"Spend," she echoed; "ye needed it for something more than just the spendin' of it."

He burst into a high laugh.

"Mamma! you'll be the death of me! You know I came back overland. How could a man get along without a little pocket money?" He broke off and regarded her with mock solemnity. "I tell you what I did, Mamma. I went around all the blind beggars in Paris and shared out the cash amongst them. That was the last little fling I had in gay Paree before getting home to this excitin' spot."

She was totally submerged, and the vision of Paris rose before her, indicating clearly that she had demeaned herself, thrust herself into the clutches of unchristian moneylenders for the sole purpose of sending him with a full purse into the unchaste delights of a wicked city. For what wild and reckless extravagances on his part would she be compelled to pay tribute over the next two years? Despite her burning love she said reproachfully, and at the grave risk of offending him:

"Oh! Matt, I would rather ye hadna visited such a like place. I'm not saying you did wrong with the money, dear, but that—that city must be full of temptations for a young man. I'm afraid it was a mistaken thing to do, and I'm sure Agnes would think the same."

Again he laughed rudely.

"What Agnes thinks or says means as much to me now as the squeak of an old boot. I know what she would think all right, and as for her talk there's too much hymn book about that for my taste. I'll never sit on her sofa again. No! She's not the woman for me, Mamma! I'm finished with her."

"Matt! Matt!" burst out Mamma. "Don't talk like that. Ye can't mean what you say. Agnes is devoted to you."

"Devoted!" he retorted. "Let her keep that for them that wants it. What else has she got? Nothing! Why," he continued expansively, I've met women with more in their little finger than she has in her whole body. Charm! Vivacity! Life!"

Mrs. Brodie was horrified and, as she gazed at her son appealingly, a sudden thought struck her.

"Ye havena broken the pledge, have ye, son," she quavered anxiously.

He looked at her queerly, asking himself if the old girl thought he was still at her apron strings. Perhaps he had been too unguarded with her.

"Just a spot of Hollands occasionally," he replied smoothly. "We have to take it out there, you know, for the good of the liver."

She immediately visioned his liver as a dry, absorbent sponge driving him to imbibe spirits to saturate it, and feeling the mercy of his return to what was, in a double sense, a more temperate climate, she returned bravely to the charge.

"Agnes is a good girl, Matt! She would be the salvation of any man. She's waited on you faithfully. It would break her heart if ye gave her up now."

"All right, Mamma," he replied sauvely. "Don't worry! Don't get excited! I'll see her if you like." It suddenly occurred to him that, imbued with his more potent worldly experience, it might be amusing to see Miss Moir again.

"That's good of you, son. You go and see her. I knew you would do that for me." She was at once relieved, feeling the power of her love over him, knowing that when the young people came together everything would be right again. If he had strayed, Agnes would bring him back to the narrow pathway, and now, hastily, for fear he might suddenly take back his promise, she passed on, reclaiming him further.

"I'm afraid you have had a very gay life out there, Matt! I don't blame ye, my boy, but it would be difficult to keep your mind fixed on the more godly matters of life." His vague allusions had shocked her; she must know more, be at all costs reassured. And she continued interrogatively: "Still you did read your chapter every day, didn't you, son?"

He moved restlessly in his chair, glanced at her resentfully.

"That sounds just like old Waldie, Mamma," he replied impatiently. "You'll be asking me if I walked down Chowringee Road with a text slung round my neck, or thumped a bible out on the maidan in the evenings "

"Don't, Matt! Don't! I don't like to hear you talk so lightly," trembled Mamma. Far from allaying her suspicions he was increasing them. "Maybe you'll go to the meeting again with Agnes now you're back. You mean so much to me now. I want ye to be happy, and there's never any happiness apart from goodness in this life, dear."

"What do you know about happiness?" he retorted. "You always looked miserable enough before."

"You'll go to the meeting with Agnes, won't ye, Matt?" she persisted. "Try just the once to please me."

"I'll see," he replied evasively. "I'll go if I want to go, but don't sermonise me any more. I don't like it, I'm not used to it and I won't have it."

"I know that you'll go for my sake," she whispered, placing her worn hand on his knee. "Ye ken that Mary's away now and that I've nobody but you. You were aye my own boy!"

"I knew Mary was away all right," he snickered. "Where is she since her little accident?"

"Hush! Hush! Don't speak like that," she returned hastily. "That's shameful talk!" She paused, shocked, then added: "She's in London we think, but her name's forbidden in the house. For goodness' sake don't talk that way before your father."

He threw off her caressing hand.

"What do I care for father," he blustered. "I'm a man now. I can do what I like. I'm not afraid of him any longer."

"I know that, Matt! You're a fine big man," she wheedled, "but your father's had an awfu' time since ye left. I'll rely on ye not to try his temper too much. I'll just get the brunt of it if ye do. Don't tell him any of these things you've told me. He's that touchy nowadays he mightna like it. He's worried—business is not what it used to be."

"It serves him right," he said, sulkily, as he rose, feeling that she had, as usual, rubbed him the wrong way. "You would think I cared an anna piece what happened to him. Let him try any tricks on me and it'll be the worse for him." He made his way to the door, adding: "I'm going up for a wash now."

"That's right, Matt! Your own room's prepared. I've kept it ready for you since the day ye left. Not a soul has been in it, and not a hand has touched it but my own. The bed has been well aired for you, too. You go and freshen yourself up and I'll lay the tea while you're upstairs." She watched him eagerly, awaiting some expression of appreciation for her forethought, but he was still offended at her and went into the hall without a word. She heard him pick up a bag and march upstairs and, straining her ears, listening to every movement he made above; she heard him go into Grandma's room, heard this new, swaggering laugh of his as he greeted the old woman with a boisterous flourish. Despite her confused disquiet the sounds which he made above comforted her and she became filled with a glowing sense of gratitude at the feeling of his proximity; she had her own son actually in the house beside her after all these weary months of separation. She breathed a prayer of gratitude as she quickly began to make preparations for the evening meal.

Soon Nessie came bounding in. She had seen the trunks in the hall and rushed up to Mamma in a flutter, crying:

"Is he home, Mamma? What great big boxes! Where is he? I wonder if he's brought me a present from India. Oh! I want to see Matt! Where is he?" At Mrs. Brodie's word she dashed upstairs, calling out expectantly to Matt, all eagerness to see him. In a few moments, however, she came down slowly, stood again before Mamma, this time dejectedly, frowning her little petulant frown, her swelling excitement entirely collapsed. "I hardly knew him," she remarked, in her old-fashioned way. "He's not like our Matt a bit. He didn't seem in the least glad to see me."

"Tuts, Nessie!" exclaimed Mamma. "You're haverin'. He's had a long journey. Give him time to settle down."

"When I went in he was drinkin' something out a wee leather bottle. He said not to bother him."

"He would be doing his unpackin', child. Don't be so impatient. He's got other things to think of just now, forbye you."

"When I asked him about my compass he said he had thrown it away—he said something I didna understand—something about it bein' like your nose."

Mrs. Brodie coloured deeply, but made no reply. She felt sure that Nessie must be making some mistake, must have misconstrued the remark, yet her heart was heavy at the thought of what might have been implied.

"I thought he might have brought me a wee string o' coral beads or something like that," persisted Nessie. "Grandma's real upset too, she thought he might have minded her with a keepsake. He seems to have brought nothing for anybody."

"Don't be selfish, Nessie!" cried Mamma sharply, venting all her pent-up feeling in this rebuke. "Your brother has enough to do with his money without squandering it on you. Not another word out of your head! Away and call Grandma down to make the toast," and, pursing her lips closely together, Mrs. Brodie inclined her head more rigidly to its angle of endurance, set herself resignedly to arrange the tea things upon the table.

When tea time drew near Matthew came down to the kitchen. A faint flush tinged the yellow of the skin around his prominent cheek bones, his speech was more profuse than when he had arrived, and, detecting a faint but suggestive odour upon his breath, instantly Mamma knew that he had been fortifying himself for the meeting with his father. Observing him covertly she perceived that, despite his vaunting talk, he dreaded this coming encounter; at once her recent humiliation was forgotten and all her instincts rose again to his protection.

"Sit down by the table, on your chair, son! Don't tire yourself out any more."

" 'S all right, Mamma," he replied. "I'll keep on my pins. Been cramped up travelling these last few days. I like to stretch myself a bit." He moved restlessly about the room, nervously fingering everything within reach, looking repeatedly at the clock, and getting in her way as she passed to and from the table.

Grandma Brodie, who had entered behind him and now sat by the fireside, called out:

"Man! you're like a knotless thread. Is that a habit you've picked up off these black men to wander about like that? It fair makes my head giddy to look at ye." She was still bitter about not having received a present from him.

Eventually he sat down, joining the others at the table. In spite of all his resistance the approach of half-past five was cowing him; all the firm resolutions which he had formed for days past to stand up to his father and assert himself as a man of the world began to ooze from him, and his especial determination to maintain a nonchalant assurance at this first interview gradually wilted. Coming home, it had been easy for him to tell himself that he cared nothing for his father—now, as he sat in his old chair at the same table and within the same unaltered room, waiting, his ears anxiously alert for that firm heavy footstep, the overwhelming sweep of old associations deluged him, and, losing all his acquired dash and hardihood, he became the nervously expectant youth once more. Instinctively he turned to his mother, and to his annoyance found her limpid eye regarding him with a sympathetic understanding. He saw that she appreciated his emotions, that his apprehension was apparent to her, and a furious resentment against her stirred him as he exclaimed:

"What are you looking at now? It's enough to make a man jump when you look at him like that." He stared at her angrily until she lowered her eyes.

At half-past five the well-remembered click of the door startled him; the sound was exactly to the second, for Brodie, after a prolonged period of irregularity in his meals, had now resumed, with an utter disregard for business, his habits of scrupulous punctuality. Now, as his father came into the room, Matthew gathered himself together, controlled the movements of his hands, prepared himself for a bitter onslaught of words. But Brodie did not speak, did not once look at his son. He sat down and began to partake comfortably of his tea, which he seemed to enjoy immensely. Matthew was abashed. In all his visualisations of the meeting nothing like this had ever occurred, and now he had an almost irresistible impulse to cry out, like a schoolboy in disgrace: "Look, father, I'm here! Take notice of me!"

Brodie, however, took no notice of him, but went quietly on with his meal, staring straight ahead of him, and saying no word until it seemed as though he had no intention of recognising his son. But at last, after a long time, when the tension in the room had grown almost unbearable, he turned and looked at Matthew. It was a penetrating gaze which saw everything and expressed everything, pierced the outside shell of hard bravado into the soft, shrinking flesh beneath, permeated and illuminated the deep recesses of Matthew's mind, and which said:

"You've returned at last, then. I know you! Still a weakling and now a failure!"

Under that glance Matthew seemed to diminish visibly in stature and, although he fought with all the strength in him to meet his father's eyes, he could not. His own gaze wavered, quailed, and, to the intense humiliation of his swaggering vanity, fell downwards to the ground.

Brodie smiled grimly, then having, without uttering one word, brow-beaten the other to subjection, he spoke, saying only, with a cutting inflection:

"You've arrived!" Yet, expressed within the short compass of these simple words were a dozen sarcastic, objectionable meanings. Mamma trembled. The baiting of her son had begun and, though she saw that it was going to be worse than she had feared, she dared not say a word for fear of aggravating her husband's mood. Her eyes fell upon her Matt with a terrified, compassionate sympathy as Brodie continued: "It's a real pleasure to see your braw, handsome face again, although it has turned as yellow as a guinea. Ye were aye a bit pasty faced now I think o't, but all the gold ye've been savin' out by there has fair jaundiced ye." He surveyed Matthew critically, warming to his work, finding an outlet in this sardonic onslaught for all his bitter sufferings of the past months.

"It's worth it, though, no doubt it's worth it," he continued. "You'll have brought us a hantle o' gold from these foreign parts ye've been slavin' in. Ye'll be a rich man now? Are ye rich?" he shot out again.

Matthew shook his head dismally, and at this silent negation, Brodie's eyebrows lifted in a stupendous sneer.

"What!" he cried, "ye havena brought back a fortune? That beats a'! I thought from the way you've been jauntin' about Europe and from those grand big boxes in the hall that ye must be worth a mint o' money at least. Then, if ye're not as rich as all that, why did ye get yoursel' thrown out o' your position?"

"I didn't like it," muttered Matthew.

"Dear! dear!" remarked Brodie, appearing to address the company at large. "He didna like his position. He maun be a big man to be so hard to please as all that; and the downright honesty of the man to admit that he didna like it." Then, turning to Matthew, and hardening his tone, he exclaimed: "Do ye not mean that it didna like you? I've been told here in Levenford that you were soundly kicked out o' it— that they got as sick of the sight o' ye out there as I am already." He paused, then continued suavely: "Still, I may be wronging you. I've no doubt ye've got something splendid in view—some marvellous new position. Have ye not?"

His tone demanded a reply and Matthew muttered: "No," sulkily hating his father now with a violence which shook him, feeling it an unbearable humiliation that he, the travelled, the experienced, the sophisticated buck, should be spoken to like this; he swore inwardly that, though at present he made no resistance, when he was stronger, more recovered from his journey, he would be revenged for every insult.

"No new post to go to!" Brodie continued, with assumed affability. "No post and no money! You've just come back to live off your father. Come back like a beaten dog. Ye think it's easier to sponge on me than to work, I suppose."

A tremor ran through Matthew's frame.

"What!" cried Brodie, "are ye cold? It's the sudden change from the great heat ye've been called upon to endure when you were workin' yourself into the jaundice outbye. Your dear mother will have to get ye some warm clothes out o' these grand, big cases o' yours. I mind weel she was aye plaisterin' ye with flannels when ye were a boy. And now that you're a braw, full-grown man she mustna let ye get a chill. Na! Na! you're too precious and valuable for that." He passed up his cup for more tea, remarking: "I havena made such a good tea for a long time! It fair gives me an appetite to see your pokey face back again."

Matthew could endure these taunts no longer, and giving up the pretence of eating, he got up, mumbling to Mamma in a broken voice: "I can't stand this any longer. I don't want any tea. I'll away out!"

"Sit down!" thundered Brodie, pushing the other back with his closed fist. "Sit down, sir. Ye can go when I tell ye to and not before. I'm not done with ye yet." Then, as Matthew subsided into his seat, he continued, cuttingly: "Are we not to have the privilege of your society next? Ye've been away two years and yet you canna bide in the house two minutes. Can ye not see that we're all waiting to hear about these wonderful adventures you've had out there? We're just hanging on the words that are ready to drop from your lips. Come on! tell us all about them."

"Tell you about what?" answered Matthew sullenly.

"About the grand, excitin' time ye've had outbye. About the rajahs and princes you've been hob-nobbin' with—about the elephants and the tigers ye've shot—tell us quick before ye've time to mak' it up. Ye'll be a perfect daredevil now, I suppose? There'll be no end to what ye can do?"

"I can maybe do more than you think," muttered Matthew under his breath.

"Indeed, now!" sneered Brodie, catching at the other's words. "You're going to surprise us, are ye? It's the same story as before, always what you're goin' to do. Never what ye've done, mind ye, but always what's comin' off next! Gad! when I look at ye there with that cringin' look about ye, and all these fine, flashy clothes on ye, it makes me wonder what ye will do." His anger rose until it almost choked him, but with an effort he controlled it and continued in his smooth, ironic voice: "Never mind though! It's such a treat to have ye back that we mustna be too hard on ye. The main thing is that you've come back safe and sound from all the terrible dangers that ye're too modest to speak about. We must have the notice o' your return put in the *Advertiser*. Then all your braw friends—especially your lady friends —will ken that you're home. They'll be swarmin' round ye like flies round a honey pot. That's what ye like, isn't it—to have the women pettin' ye and runnin' after ye?"

Matthew made no reply and after a moment's pause Brodie continued, drawing back his lips sardonically:

"I suppose next Sunday that mother o' yours will have ye all toshed up and have ye out at the kirk for the general admiration o' her braw congregation. Ye might even squeeze your way into the choir again if ye were sleekit enough, to let them all hear your bonnie voice lifted up in praise o' the Lord. It would be a real manly thing to sing in the choir again—would it not? Answer me, ye dummy. Do ye hear what I'm sayin' to ye?"

"I'll not sing in any choir," retorted Matthew, thinking sullenly that it was like his father to bring up this memory of the past and use it, derisively, to force him into a ridiculous position.

"The prodigal son refuses to sing," sneered Brodie. "Did ye ever hear the like o't—and him that had the lovely, lovely voice. Well my fine man," he continued with a snarl, "if ye'll not sing for your mother you'll sing for me. You'll sing to the tune I pipe. Don't think that I can't see through ye. I do! ye've disgraced yourself and me. Ye hadna the grace to stick to your job like a man—ye must come running back home to your soft mother like a beaten cur. But don't think ye can try that with me. Keep yourself in order when I'm about or, by God! it'll be the waur o' ye. Do ye understand what I mean?" He rose from the table abruptly, and stood glaring down at his son. "I'm not finished with ye yet. I'll knock the fancy notions out o' your head before I'm done with ye. I warn ye—keep out of my path, sir, or I'll smash ye down as ye stand. Do ye hear me?"

Matthew, emboldened by seeing that his father was about to go and goaded by the very humiliation of his position, raised his head and looked sideways at the other, muttering:

"I'll keep out of your way, all right."

Brodie's eye flamed fiercely in return. He grasped Matthew's shoulder.

"You dog!" he shouted, "don't look at me like that. Don't dare to do it or I'll break you. You thing that calls yourself by the name o'

Brodie. You're a disgrace to me, sir, yes! a bigger disgrace than your bitch of a sister." Then as Matthew's eye again fell, he continued, disgust mingling with his anger: "It scunners me to think a man of noble blood could beget a whelp like you. You're the first Brodie to be called a coward, but by God you are one none the less. You're a hangdog coward and I'm ashamed o' ye!" He shook his son like a sack of bones, then suddenly released his hold and allowed him to collapse inertly back into the chair.

"Watch what you're about, my man. I'll have my eye on ye," he cried, forbiddingly, as he walked out of the room.

When he had gone Nessie and Grandma continued silently to look at Matthew, but Mamma dropped on her knees beside him and placed her arm around his shoulder.

"Never mind, Matt! never mind, my own son! I love ye, onyway!" she wept.

He thrust down her arm whilst the muscles of his face twitched under the pale skin.

"I'll pay him out yet," he whispered, as he rose up. "I'll get even with him. If he's not done with me I'm not done with him."

"You're not going out now, son," cried Mrs. Brodie fearfully. "Ye'll bide in with me to-night, won't you? I want ye to be beside me."

He shook his head.

"No!" he said, controlling his voice with an effort, "I must go out." He licked his dry lips. "I've got some—some old friends to look up. I'm goin' out now. Give me a key."

"Don't go, son," she implored. "Don't let what your father said upset ye. He doesna mean it. He's worried himself. Stay in with your mother now, there's a good lad. Ye've had no tea at all. Stay in and I'll make ye something nice. I love ye, Matt. I love ye so much I would do anything for ye!"

"Give me the key, then," he replied. "That's what I want."

Silently she gave him her own key. He thrust it into his pocket, saying: "I'll be late! Don't sit up for me."

She followed him, wavering in fear, to the door. "Ye'll be careful, Matt, won't ye. Keep out o' mischief for my sake, son. Don't let him drive ye to anything rash. I couldna bear it now that you're safely back to me."

He made no reply but was gone, disappearing rapidly into the darkness beyond. Her ears followed his steps until they died into the quiet of the night, then, with a short, dry sob she turned and went back to the kitchen. She did not know what was going to happen, but she feared exceedingly.

VIII

NEXT morning Mrs. Brodie woke early, while it was still almost dark, but, as she stirred, she heard in the distance the first, faint, challenging cock crow, betokening, despite the obscurity, the imminent dawn of another day. Although she had waited up late on the night before, she had not seen Matthew come in, and now, after a troubled sleep, her first thought was to assure herself that he was well. As she dressed there was no need for her to be timorously silent for fear of disturbing her husband, since she was now alone in the small room that had been Mary's, yet, from long habit, her actions were as stealthy and inaudible as the movements of a shadow. The dim light entered the window of the bedroom and vaguely revealed her ghostly, drooping figure as she shivered into her clothes. Her underclothing was so patched, darned, and repaired as to become at any time a puzzle to assume and now, in the cold obscurity of the chill February air, her insensitive, roughened fingers fumbled confusedly with the coarse, worn garments. As she dressed thus, by sense of touch, her teeth chattered slightly, giving the sole audible indication of her presence and activity.

When she had covered her body by solving the intricate riddle of her enigmatical vestments, she rubbed her hands soundlessly together to induce some sign of circulation and slid out of the room in her stockinged feet.

Matthew's bedroom, being at the back of the house and facing east, was better illuminated; as she silently entered it she saw amongst the disordered confusion of bedclothes, the outlines of his regularly breathing form, and she too again breathed regularly with relief. His face looked leaden in the bluish pallor of the morning light, as the corners of his mouth dry sordes had formed, and sleaves of dark hair lay tangled upon his brow. Between his lips his tongue seemed to pro trude slightly as though it had become too swollen and bulky for its normal confines, and with each respiration it acted as a dull sounding-board for the hoarse passage of his breath.

Mamma gently restored the blankets and coverlet to a more orderly comfort, ventured even to stroke the tumbled locks of hair from his eyes, but as, at her touch, he stirred uneasily and muttered, she drew back, quickly removing her hand, yet leaving it poised in mid air above his head as though unconsciously she blessed him in his sleep. Her gaze, too, was like a benediction, maintained for a many moments. At length, reluctantly, she slowly withdrew her eyes from his face and turned to go. On her way out of the room she observed that his coat, vest, and trousers were strewn in disarray on the floor, that his shirt had been flung into one corner, his collar and tie into another and, as though glad to render him service, she stooped, picked up the scattered garments, folded them neatly upon a chair, looked again at his sleeping face, and went quietly away.

Downstairs, everything lay exposed in the stale, repugnant ebb of the low tide of early daybreak; the night, receding like an ocean, had left the furniture disordered, the dead fire dirty with grey, powdered ashes, the pile of unwashed dishes cluttering the scullery sink obscenely, like wreckage upon a desolate shore.

In the usual way, before she stirred herself into jerky activity to lay and light the fire, blacklead the grate, wash the dishes, sweep the floor, boil the porridge, and perform the endless necessities of the morning, she would first indulge herself with a cup of strong tea, feeling, in her own words, that it drew her together. The hot, fragrant liquid was like a healing draught, comforting her, warming her, clearing away the mists in her brain, and resigning her to the hardships of another day.

This morning, however, although she hurriedly infused and poured out a cup of tea, she did not herself drink it but, having carefully cut and delicately buttered two thin slices of bread, she placed these, together with the tea, appetisingly upon a tray, which she then carried up to Matthew's room.

"Matt," she whispered, touching him lightly upon the shoulder, "here's some tea for ye, son. It'll freshen ye up." Although she bent over him he still snored on, exuding with each breath the reeking halitus of stale liquor, which disturbed her deeply, made her, in her agitation, speak more loudly. "Matt! Here's something nice for ye!" That was what she used to say to him, coaxingly, when he was a boy, and at her words he stirred, half awake, twisted impatiently, and with eyes still closed, muttered:

"Let me sleep, boy. Go to hell. Don't want any chota hazri."

Unhappily, she shook him.

"Matt, dear, this tea will do you good. It's nice for ye in the morning."

At this he opened his eyes and surveyed her from under listless, stuporous lids; within his dark pupils she could see the dull, unhappy comprehension of his position slowly reawaken.

"It's you, is it," he slurred; "what you want wakenin' me like this. Let me sleep."

"But the nice tea, dear! so refreshing. I went straight down and made it myself."

"You're always flinging tea at me! Let me sleep, damn it all!" He hunched round his back at her and was at once asleep again.

Mamma looked miserably from his prone figure to the tray still in her hands, as though unable to comprehend his refusal or the full force of his abuse, then, moved by the thought that he might later reconsider his decision, she laid the tray down on a chair by the bedside, covered the cup warmly with the saucer, inverted the plate protectingly over the fresh bread, and turned disconsolately away.

He was on her mind all morning. The fire kindled, the dishes became clean, the boots were brushed, the porridge bubbled, she took up her husband's shaving water, then began to lay the table whilst she thought of him, lamenting the words he had used to her, mourning the revealing odour of his breath, yet all the time excusing him in her mind. The shock of coming home, of his father's treatment, had upset him; as for his language, he had, poor boy, been in a rough land, and had not been fully awakened when he spoke to her. Whilst she forgave him, the still house began to stir, light and heavy sounds vibrated through the ceiling, doors were opened and shut upstairs, and now, confronted by the fear that some further disturbance might arise between Brodie and her son, she listened anxiously for the noise of some sudden outburst, the clash of angry voices, even for the sound of a blow. To her intense relief none came, and after Nessie had come downstairs and been hurriedly fed, and packed off with her satchel of books, Brodie descended and began to breakfast in sombre, solitary silence. She had taken the utmost care that everything should be perfect for him this morning in order to lull him into a more amiable mood, was prepared, even, to lie blatantly about Matt's coming in late; but although his mood seemed to her unpropitious, her fear proved to be unfounded and he departed without a single reference to his son.

When he had gone she breathed more easily and, her tranquillity further restored by a belated cup of tea, she prepared Grandma's breakfast and took it upstairs shortly before ten o'clock. When she had visited the old woman she tiptoed across the landing and listened with her ear to the door of Matt's room; hearing only the rise and fall of his breathing she softly opened the door. She saw at once that nothing had been touched and, to her wounded feelings, it seemed as though the undisturbed tray mutely rebuked her, that the plate still investing the untouched bread and butter, and the saucer still uselessly covering the long since cold tea, were like tokens of her folly and presumption. He still slept. Confusedly she wondered if his removal from what she considered to be an antipodean hemisphere might not have inverted the hours of his repose, and, in rendering him active at night and drowsy by day, have thus made it a necessity for him to sleep through certain hours of the forenoon. Unconvinced in mind but none the less eased a little in heart, feeling that if not this, perhaps some kindred reason existed for his behaviour, she did not disturb him, and again passed quietly out of the room.

Hesitatingly she addressed herself to her household duties in an effort to divert her attention, but as the forenoon drew on, uneasiness gradually possessed her; she comprehended that if their son was still in bed when Brodie returned for dinner a disastrous scene might take place. Anxiously she pricked her ears for the first evidence of his retarded activity and, towards noon, was rewarded by hearing the faint creak of his bed as it surrendered his body, the sound of his step upon the boards above. Hastily decanting water into a jug from the kettle which stood ready boiling, she rushed upstairs to leave it outside his door.

He was a long time dressing, but about quarter to one he came slowly downstairs and entered the kitchen. She greeted him fondly.

"I'm glad that you've had a nice long sleep, dear, but you've had no breakfast. Will you have a bite before your dinner? Just say the word, it'll not be the least bother for me to get ye a——" It had been on her tongue to offer him the universal panacea—a cup of tea—but mercifully she recollected his remark of the morning in time and added: "anything that's in the house."

"I never eat much in the morning." He was smartly dressed in a different suit from the day before, in a smooth, fawn hopsack with a puce shirt and natty brown tie to match; as he fingered the bow of his tie with white plastic fingers that trembled slightly, he eyed her doubtfully, judging erroneously from her adulatory manner that she could not fully have realised his discomfiture of the night before. "I miss the fresh fruit my servants used to bring me," he asserted, feeling that some further explanatory remark might be required of him.

"You'll have some nice apples to-morrow, Matt," she replied eagerly. "I'll put in the order sure. If ye just tell me what you'd like, or the kind of food you've been used to outbye, I'll do my best to get it for ye."

His attitude repudiated the idea of such sour wizened apples as she might obtain for him in this unproductive land; he waved his hand eloquently, and retorted shortly:

"I meant mangoes, fairy bananas, pineapple. Nothing but the best is any use to me."

"Well, son, we'll do our utmost, anyway," she replied bravely, although somewhat out of countenance at the grandiloquence of his remark. "I've got a nice dinner for ye anyway. Then, if ye feel like it afterwards, I was thinking maybe we might have a bit stroll together."

"I'm going out for *tiffin* " he inserted coldly, as though her suggestion was ridiculous and to be seen walking with her decrepit, outlandis figure the last thought his superior mind would entertain.

Her face fell, and she stammered:

"I—I had such nice nourishin' broth for ye, boy, as sweet as anything."

"Give it to the old man," he retorted bitterly. "Give him a bucketful. He can stand it." He paused for a moment, then continued in a more ingratiating tone: "I wonder though, Mamma, if you would lend me a pound or two for to-day. It's such a confounded nuisance, but my bank drafts have not come through from Calcutta yet." He frowned at the annoyance of it all. "It's causing me no end of inconvenience. Here am I stuck up for a little ready cash all through their beastly delay. Lend me a fiver and you shall have it next week."

A fiver! She almost burst into hysterical tears at the word, at the painful absurdity of his request that she should lend him at a moment's notice five pounds—she who was bleeding herself white to scrape together the monthly toll that would soon be levied on her, who had, apart from the three pounds she had laboriously collected for the purpose, only a few paltry copper and silver coins in her purse!

"Oh! Matt," she cried. "Ye don't know what you're askin'. There isna such a sum in the house!"

"Come on now," he replied rudely, "you can do it fine. Toll out. Where's your bag?"

"Don't speak to me like that, dear," she whispered. "I canna bear it. I would do anything for ye, but what you're askin' is impossible."

"Lend me one pound then, seeing you're so stingy," he said, with a hard look at her. "Come on! give me a miserable pound."

"Ye can't understand, son," she pleaded. "I'm so poor now I can hardly make ends meet. Your father doesna give me enough for us to live on." A yearning desire took hold of her to tell him of the manner in which she had been obliged to raise the money to send to him at Marseilles, but she stifled it, realising with a sudden pause that this moment, above all, was not propitious.

"What does he think he's doing? He's got his business and this precious wonderful house of his," Matthew sneered. "What is it he's spending the money on now?"

"Oh! Matt, I hardly like to tell ye," she sobbed, "but things seem to be in a bad way with your father in the business. I'm—I'm feared the house is bonded. He hasna said a word to me but I saw some papers lyin' in his room. It's terrible. It's the opposition that's started against him in the town. I've no doubt he'll win through, but in the meantime I've got to make one shillin' do the work of two."

He looked at her in sullen amazement, but refused, none the less, to be diverted from the issue.

"That's all very well, Mamma!" he grumbled. "I know you. You always had something tucked away for a rainy day. I want a pound. I tell you I've got to have it. I need it."

"Oh, my dear, have I not told ye how ill-off we are," she wept.

"For the last time, will ye lend me it?" he threatened.

As she again sobbingly refused him she thought, in her agitation, for the space of a horrified instant, that he was about to strike her, but abruptly he turned upon his heel and left the room. As she stood there, her hand clutching her side, she heard him banging about through the rooms upstairs and finally come down, pass through the hall without speaking, and slam out of the house.

When the reverberating echoes of the bang of the door had died upon the air they still resounded in her brain like an ominous portent of the

251

future, and involuntarily she raised her hands to her ears to blot them out as she sat down at the kitchen table, an abject, disillusioned figure. She felt, as she rested there, her head supported in her hands, that the story of the bank draft must be a specious lie, that he, having spent the forty pounds, was now penniless. Had he almost threatened her? She did not know, but he had wanted the money badly, and she, alas, had been unable to give it to him. Before she could analyse her emotions further, and realising now that she should have been in a position to accede to his later demand, that in a fashion the fault had been hers, on top of her misery came a great rush of tenderness. Poor boy, he had been used to mixing with gentlemen who spent money freely, and it was only fair that he should have money in his pocket like the rest. It was, in fact, a necessity after the high society life he had been leading. It was not just to expect a young man as well put on as Matt to go out without the means of backing up his smart appearance. He had really not been to blame and, in some degree, she regretted not having given him at least a few shillings, if he would have accepted them from her. As the affair became thus presented to her in a more satisfactory light and she was filled by a sense of her own inadequacy she rose and, drawn by an irresistible attraction she went up to his room and with loving care began to tidy the litter of wearing apparel which encumbered it. She now discovered that his clothing was not so plentiful as might have been expected from first appearances, finding one trunk to be completely empty, two of his cases to be filled with thin drill suits and another stuffed untidily with soiled linen. Eagerly, she seized upon socks to darn, shirts to mend, collars to starch, feeling it a joy to serve him by attending to these needs, beatitude even to touch his garments.

Eventually, having restored order amongst his things and arranged, for her attention, a large bundle which she bore away in triumph, she entered her own room, made her bed, and began in a more cheerful spirit to dust the furniture. As she came to the shallow china toilet tray that rested on the small table by the window an undetermined sense of perplexity affected her; a familiar impression to which she had long been accustomed in her subconscious mind was now lacking. She pondered absently for a moment, then suddenly realised that she did not hear the intimate, friendly tick of her watch which, except on those state occasions when she wore it, lay always upon this small tray of hers which now confronted her, denuded of all but a few stray hairpins. When she had been compelled to change her room she had of course brought this tray with her and the watch had still remained upon it; indeed, for twenty years the touch of this tray had been consonant with her audition of the watch, and at once she appreciated the variation.

Although she knew that she was not wearing the watch she clutched at her bodice, but it was not there, and immediately she began to look for it in a flurry, searching everywhere in her own room, in Brodie's room, downstairs in the parlour and in the kitchen. As her unsuccessful search was prolonged, a worried look appeared on her face. It was her mother's watch, a fine scrolled silver shell with a gilt face, delicate spidery hands, and a Swiss mechanism which never failed to register the exact minute, and although it was not valuable she had for it, and for the small faded daguerreotype of her mother clipped inside the case, a rare and sentimental affection. It was her only trinket and for this fact alone she treasured it deeply. As she stooped to survey the floor she knew that she had not mislaid it and she asked herself if someone had not accidentally interfered with it. Suddenly she straightened up. Her face lost its annoyance, and instead became stricken. She realised in an illuminating flash that Matt had taken her watch. She had heard him in her room, after she had refused to give him the money, and he had rushed out without speaking to her. She knew irrevocably that he had stolen her watch for any paltry sum he might obtain for it. She would gladly have given him it as she had given him everything in life that was hers to give, but he had thieved it from her with a sly, sneaking baseness. With a hopeless gesture she pushed back a wisp of grey hair that had been disarranged in her futile search. "Matt! my son," she cried out aloud, "you know I would have given you it! What way did ye steal it?"

On this, the day following her son's return, when she had glowingly anticipated content and the mitigation of her worries, she found herself sunk more deeply into the well of her dejection. Dinner passed and the afternoon proceeded eventlessly towards evening. Amidst the trouble of her thoughts the fall of dusk and the fading of the short grey twilight made her wish poignantly to see him. Only let them be alone together, the mother and the son, and she felt she would soften any hardness in his heart. He could not, she was convinced, withstand the entreaty of her affection; he would be at her feet in penitence and remorse if only she could express to him in words the love that was in her heart. But still he did not appear and, when the clock struck the half hour after five and he did not come in for tea, she was immeasurably distressed.

"I suppose that braw mannie o' yours is ower feared to come in," Brodie sneered at her as she handed him his tea. "He's deliberately avoidin' me—skulkin' outside there until I've gane out again. Then he'll come sneakin' in for your sympathy and consolation. Don't think I don't see through it all, although it's behind my back."

"No, indeed father," she quavered, "I assure ye there's nothing to keep from ye. Matt has just gone out to look up some o' his friends."

"Is that so, now?" he answered. "I didna ken he had any friends, but from what you make out he must be the popular hero right enough! Well, tell your model son, when ye see him, that I'm savin' up a' that I've got to say until I meet him next. I'll keep it hot for him."

She made no reply, but served him with his meal, and when he went out set herself again to wait.

At seven o'clock, about an hour after Brodie had left the house, Matthew did, indeed, return·He came in quietly with a slight indication upon his face of the old downcast expression of his youth, sidled into the room and, looking at Mamma ingratiatingly, said in a soft voice:

"I'm sorry I'm late, Mamma dear. I hope I haven't put you about?"

She looked at him eagerly.

"I *have* worried about you, Matt! I didn't know where you had gone!"

"I know," he replied in a subdued voice. "It was downright thoughtless of me. I don't think I have quite got used to being here. I may have got a little careless since I've been away, Mamma, but I'll make up for it to you."

"It's not like you to be careless," she cried, "except to yourself, going without your food like this. Have you had your tea?"

"No," he replied, "I haven't, but I'm real hungry now, though. Have you something for me to eat?"

She· was touched, convinced, despite her day of despondency, that this was her own son again who had sloughed off the skin of his wicked Indian experiences.

"Matt!" she said earnestly, "you ought to know better than ask. Your supper is in the oven this very minute." She ran to the oven and produced, impressively, for his inspection a thick cut of findon haddock cooked in milk, a dish of which he had been particularly fond in the past. "Wait just half a minute," she cried, "and I'll be ready for you."

Grandma Brodie had gone up to her room but Nessie was occupying the table with her homework. Nevertheless, in a few moments, Mamma had spread a white cloth upon half of the table and had covered it with every requisite of an appetising meal.

"There, now," she said, "I told ye I wouldn't be long. There's no one can do a thing for ye like your own mother. Sit in, Matt, and let us see what *you* can do."

He rolled his eyes up at her gratefully and bowed his head.

"Oh! Mamma, you're too kind to me! I don't deserve it. It's like heaping coals of fire on my head after the way I've gone on. It does look good though, doesn't it?"

She nodded her head happily, watching him eagerly as he drew in his chair, sat down, and began to eat with large, quick mouthfuls. "Poor boy, he must have been starving," she thought, as the succulent white flakes of the fish melted magically under the soft, relentless attack of his knife and fork. Nessie, sucking the stump of a pencil at the other end of the table, watched him over the edge of her book with a different emotion.

"Some folks are luckier than others," she remarked enviously. "We didn't get finnan haddie to-night."

Matt looked at her with a wounded expression, then placed the last large piece of fish carefully in his mouth.

"If I had known, Nessie," he expostulated, "I would have offered yousome. Why did you not speak before?"

"Don't be so selfish, girl," cried Mamma sharply. "You've had enough and plenty, and you know it. Your brother needs some decent food now. He's had a hard time lately. You get on with your lessons. Here, Matt—try some of these oatcakes."

Matt thanked her with a warm, upward look and continued to eat. At his attitude Mamma was overjoyed and, the loss of her watch now completely forgotten, she regarded him benevolently, happily, every mouthful he took causing her an intense enjoyment, as if the food which he consumed was savoured by her own palate with infinite relish. She observed with sympathy that his face was marked by smuts; amazed at her own shrewdness, she surmised that he had brushed into a dusty hedge, that he had been hiding outside from his father. She was concerned, so that benevolence gave way to protection; he was her own boy once more and she would shelter and defend him against the world.

"Did ye enjoy that, son?" she asked finally, hungering for his praise. "I took special pains with it. I knew ye always liked it."

He smacked his lips.

"It was lovely, Mamma! Better than all the curries I had to put up with out in India. I tell you I've missed your cooking. I've never had a decent dish like that since I left."

"Is that the case, son," she exclaimed. "It gladdens me to hear it. Now! is there anything else you would like?"

Out of the corner of his eye he saw on the dresser a dish of small apples which he imagined she must have procured for him. He looked at her for a moment reflectively.

"I think, Mamma, I would like an apple," he said with the simplicity of one who has pure desires. She was overjoyed to have anticipated his wish and at once brought over the dish.

"Just what I thought. I gave the boy the order this morning," she said delightedly, proving her thoughtfulness of his every wish. "You said you wanted fruit and I said that you should have it."

"Thank you, Mamma! I don't wish to smoke," he explained, as he bit with difficulty into the hard fruit, "and I'm told an apple destroys the craving. What need have I to smoke, anyway? It doesn't do me any good."

Mrs. Brodie laid her hand caressingly on his shoulder as she murmured:

"Matt, it does my heart good to hear you say that. It's worth more to me than anything on this earth. I'm happy. I feel we're going to understand each other better. now. It must have been the long separation that upset us both, but these misunderstandings are sent from above to try us. I prayed for understanding to come to the both of us, and the prayer of an unworthy woman has been answered."

He lowered his eyes, for a moment, in remorse while he persisted in his efforts with the apple, then, looking up and choosing his words with extreme care, he said slowly, unveiling another rapturous surprise for her:

"You know, Mamma, I saw Agnes this afternoon."

She started with surprise and pleasure.

"Of course," he hurried on, before she could speak, "I can't say much just now. You mustn't ask me anything. My lips must be sealed on what passed between us, but it was very satisfactory." He smiled at her deprecatingly. "I thought you would be pleased to hear, though."

She clasped her hands in ecstasy, her bliss only tempered by the thought that it was not she herself, but another woman in the person of Miss Moir, who had, perchance, turned her son's steps back to righteousness. Still, she was overjoyed and, stifling the unworthy thought, she ejaculated:

"That's good! that's grand! Agnes will be as happy as I am about it." Her bowed back straightened slightly as she raised her moist eyes to heaven in a pæan of unspoken gratitude; when she looked down again to earth Matthew was addressing Nessie.

"Nessie, dear! I was selfish a minute ago but I'll make up for it now. I'm going to give you this half of my apple if you leave Mamma and me together a little. I want to talk to her privately."

"Nonsense, Nessie!" exclaimed Mamma, as Nessie stretched out her hand agreeably. "If you're to have a bit apple don't take the bite out your brother's mouth."

"Yes, Mamma. I'm going to give this to Nessie!" insisted Matt, in a kindly voice, "but she must let you and me have a little chat now. I've got something to say that's for your ears alone!"

"Well, Nessie," said Mrs. Brodie, "take it, and thank Matt for it, and don't let us have any more of your ungrateful remarks in the future. You can leave your homework in the meantime and go into the parlour and do your practising for half an hour. Away with you, now, Take the matches, and be careful how you light the gas."

Glad to be relieved from her hated books, Nessie skipped out of the room and soon the halting tinkle of the piano came faintly into the kitchen, interpolated at first by pauses barren of melody, co-related to the lifting of the apple from the bass end of the keyboard.

"Now, Matt," said Mrs. Brodie warmly, drawing her chair close to his, feeling that her improbable dream of the morning was about to be fullfiled, and hugging herself with a trembling satisfaction.

"Mamma," began Matthew smoothly, inspecting his hands carefully, "I want you to forgive me for being so—well—so off hand since I came back; but you know I've been worried. I've had a lot on my mind."

"I could see that, son!" she agreed, compassionately. "My heart has gone out to you to see how you've been upset. It's not everybody that understands your sensitive nature the way I do."

"Thank you, Mamma," he exclaimed; "you're kind as ever you were, and if you forget any hard words I've said I'll be grateful. I'll try and be a better man."

"Don't belittle yourself in that fashion, Matt," she cried. "I don't like to hear it. You were aye a good boy. Ye were always my own son—I never knew ye do a really wrong action."

He lifted his eyes for an instant and shot a quick furtive glance at her, then immediately veiled them, murmuring:

"It's nice to be in with you again, Mamma."

She smiled devotedly at his words, recollecting that as a boy it had been a manifestation of his childish pique to be "out with her," and, when she was eventually restored to favour to be "in with her."

"We'll never be out with each other again, will we, dear?" she countered, fondly.

"That's so, Mamma," he agreed, and allowed an impressive pause to elapse before remarking casually: "Agnes and I are going to the prayer meeting to-night."

"That's splendid, Matt," she whispered. He was definitely reclaimed! "I'm that pleased about it. Oh, but I would like to come with you both!" She halted timidly. "Still—I—I suppose ye would rather be your two selves. It's not for me to interfere."

"It might be as well, perhaps, Mamma," he admitted deprecatingly. "You know how it is!"

She looked at the clock, observing that it was quarter to eight. She regretted exceedingly having to break up this heart to heart talk, but with true unselfishness, she said, with a not unhappy sigh:

"It's nearly eight as it is, I'm afraid. You'll have to be stirring now or you'll be late," and she made as though to move.

"Just a minute, though, Mamma!"

"Yes, dear!"

"I wanted to ask you another thing!" He hesitated and looked at her soulfully, having, from his point of view, reached the critical point of the interview. "Mamma," he murmured irresolutely.

"What is it, Matt, my dear?"

"It's just like this, Mamma! I may as well be honest with you! I've been an awful spendthrift," he confessed. "People have taken advantage of my generosity. I have no money just now. How can I go about with Agnes with nothing in my pocket?" He had the air of one, the victim of his own open-handedness, from whom the words fell shamefully. "I'm used to having some cash always with me. It makes me feel so small to be without it, specially when I'm with a lady, back in my own town. Could you not help me, Mamma, until I get started again?"

She saw at once that it was a supremely reasonable request. She had been right in assuming that her boy, accustomed to high and lavish society, could not confront Levenford penniless; still less could he encounter Miss Moir in such a penurious predicament. In the flush of her reunion to him she threw caution to the winds and, with a magnificent sacrifice, she arose silently, unlocked her drawer and withdrew from it the square box which contained her accumulated savings for the initial repayment of her heavy debt. She looked adoringly at Matthew, heedless of the future, remembering only that she was the mother of this loving and devoted son.

"This is my all, Matt," she said soberly, "and I've saved it dearly for a most important and necessary cause. But I am going to give ye some of it."

His eyes gleamed as she opened the box and took out a pound.

"Take this for your pocket, son," she said simply, holding out the note to him in her outstretched hand, her worn face softened by love, her bent figure drooping a little towards him. "I give it to you gladly. It's yours!" It was a sacrifice of supreme and touching beauty.

"How much have ye altogether?" asked Matthew ingenuously, rising up and going close to her. "You've got a lot in there, right enough."

"There's nearly three pounds here," she replied, "and it's been a weary job for me to save it. Times are hard with us now, Matt—harder than ye might think. I'll need every penny of this by the end of the month."

"Mamma! Let me keep it for you," he said wheedlingly. "I'll keep it till the end of the month. I'll not spend it. I might as well keep it in my pocket as let you lock it in that old tin box. What a funny place to keep your money!" He made the idea of her little box as a receptacle for money appear almost ludicrous. "I'll be your banker, Mamma! It's nice for me to feel I have something to fall back on, even if I never have the need for it. Just the feel of it beside me would make me comfortable. Come on, Mamma! a pound is nothing, really, to a fellow like me." He held out his hand coaxingly.

She looked at him with a vague, frightened doubt in her eyes.

"It's most important for me to have this money by the end o' the month," she stammered. "I don't know what'll happen if I haven't got it."

"You shall have it then," he assured her. "What a worrier you are! Leave it to me. I'm as safe as the Bank of England!" He took the money out of the open box as he continued talking volubly, reassuringly. "You're not going to let your Matt go about like a pauper, are you, Mamma?" He laughed at the very idea. "A gentleman needs a little ready brass to give him assurance. You'll be right as rain, Mamma," he continued, edging into the hall. "I'll see to that! Don't sit up for me now, I'll like as not be late."

He was out and away with a last, gay wave, and she was left with the open, empty box in her hands, staring at the panels of the front door that had closed behind him. She sighed convulsively whilst the piano chattered in her ears with a false sprightliness. Blindly she suppressed the recurrent thought of her missing watch and an inchoate doubt as to the wisdom of so weakly allowing him to take the money. Matt was a good boy! He was hers again and their mutual love would surmount any obstacle and conquer all difficulties. He was on his way to worship God with a good Christian girl. Happiness flowed into her heart once more, and she returned to the kitchen, well content with what she had done.

She sat down, gazing into the fire, a faint reminiscent smile upon her face at the memory of his tenderness to her. "He did relish that fish, the boy," she murmured to herself. "I maun make him some more nice dishes." Then, suddenly, as she was about to recall Nessie to her lessons the door bell rang with a short, trenchant peal. Mamma felt startled as she got up, it was so far beyond the time of an ordinary visitor. Matthew had his key, he could not have returned like this; the least thing upset her nowadays, she reflected, as she cautiously opened the door. Miss Moir, palely outlined in the glimmer of the lobby lamp, stood before her.

"Oh! Aggie dear, it's you," she exclaimed in some relief, pressing her hand to her side. "I got quite a fright. You've just missed Matthew by a few minutes."

"Can I come in, Mrs. Brodie?" Again Mamma was startled. Not once in the space of three years had Agnes addressed her in such terms, and never in such a strange, unnatural voice.

"Come in—of course ye can come in, but—but I'm telling you Matthew has gone out to meet ye."

"I would like to speak to you, please."

In amazement Mamma admitted a frozen-faced Agnes. They went into the kitchen.

"What's it a' about, dear?" she faltered. "I don't understand this in the least. Matt's away to meet you. Are ye not well?"

"Quite well, thank you," came from Miss Moir's stiff lips. "Did you know that—that Matthew came to see me this afternoon?" She had the utmost difficulty in uttering his name.

"Yes! he's just told me. He's gone to take you to the meeting; Matt has gone to get you," repeated Mrs. Brodie stupidly, mechanically, as a fearful spasm gripped her heart.

"It's a lie!" exclaimed Agnes. "He's not gone to see me or to look near any meeting."

"What!" faltered Mamma.

"Did he tell you what happened to-day?" said Agnes, sitting up straight and gazing in front of her with hard eyes.

"No! No!" halted Mamma. "He said he couldna speak about it yet."

"I can well believe that," cried Agnes bitterly.

"What was it, then?" whimpered Mrs. Brodie; "tell us for God's sake."

Agnes paused for a moment, then, with a quick indrawing of her breath, she steeled herself to her humiliation. "He came in smelling of drink, in fact he was nearly the worse of it. In spite of that I was glad to see him. We went into the back shop. He talked a lot of nonsense—and then he tried to borrow—to borrow money off me." She sobbed dryly. "I would have given him it, but I saw he would just spend it on spirits. When I refused he called me awful names. He swore at me. He said I was a ——" She broke down completely. Her big eyes gushed tears. Her full bosom panted with hard sobs; her large mouth drew into bibbering grimaces. In a frenzy of lamentation she flung herself at Mrs. Brodie's feet. "But that wasna everything," she cried. "I had to go into the shop a minute. When I came back he tried to—he tried to insult me, Mamma. I had to struggle with him. Oh! if only he had been kind to me I would have given him what he wanted. I don't care whether I'm wicked or not. I would! I would!" she shrieked. Her sobs strangled her. "I love him, but he doesn't love me. He called me an ugly bitch. He tried to take—to take advantage of me. Oh! Oh! Mamma, it's killing me. I wanted him to do it, if only he had loved me. I wanted it!" she repeated in a high hysteria. "I had to tell ye. I'm worse than Mary was. I wish I was dead and finished."

She flung back her head and gazed wildly at Mrs. Brodie. The eyes of the two women met and fused in a dull horror of despair, then Mamma's lips twisted grotesquely, her mouth drew to one side, she made as though to speak but could not, and with an incoherent cry she fell back helplessly in her chair. As Agnes gazed at the limp figure her eyes slowly grew startled, her thoughts withdrew gradually from her own sorrow.

"Are ye ill?" she gasped. "Oh! I didn't think it would take you like that. I'm so upset myself I never thought it might make you feel as bad as that. Can I not get you anything?"

Mamma's eyes sought the other's face, but still she did not speak.

"What canI do for you?" cried Agnes again. "You look so bad I'm frightened. Will I get you some water—will I get the doctor? Speak to me."

At last Mamma spoke.

"I thought my boy was going out with ye to worship the Lord," she whispered in a strange voice. "I prayed that it should be so."

"Oh! don't talk like that," exclaimed Agnes. "You'll need to come and lie down a wee. Come and lie down till you're better!"

"My side hurts me," said Mamma dully. "It must be that my heart is broken. Let me go to my bed. I want to be quiet and by my lone in the darkness."

"Let me help you, then," cried Agnes, and taking the other's passive arm she drew her to her feet, supported her, and led her unresistingly up the stairs to her bedroom. There she undressed her, and assisted her to bed. "What else can I do for you?" she said, finally. "Would you like the hot bottle?"

"Just leave me," replied Mamma, lying on her back and looking directly upwards. "Ye've been kind to help me, but I want to be by myself now."

"Let me sit with you for a bit! I don't like to go away yet awhile."

"No! Agnes. I want ye to go!" said Mrs. Brodie, in a dull flat voice. "I want to shut myself in the darkness. Turn out the gas and leave me. just leave me be."

"Will I not leave the gas in a peep?" persisted Agnes. "No matter what's happened I can't think to go away like this."

"I wish the darkness," commanded Mrs. Brodie, "and I wish to be alone."

Agnes made as though to speak but, feeling the futility of further protest, she took a last look at the inert figure upon the bed, then, as she had been bidden, turned out the gas. Leaving the room in blackness she passed silently from the house.

IX

As Matthew shut the front door upon Mamma, and ran lightly down the steps, he was filled with a lively humour and as he smiled knowingly, the sham meekness fell from his face like a mask. "That's the way to work the old woman. Smart! Done like an artist too," he chuckled to himself, "and not bad for a first touch." He was proud of his achievement, and felt in agreeable anticipation that he would do even better next time, that Mamma must have a tidy sum tucked away in a safe place. It would be his for the asking! The few shillings which he had received by pawning her watch had disgusted him, for he had expected it to be worth considerably more, but now that he had a few pounds in his pocket, his prestige and cheerfulness were restored. Just let him have the cash, he told himself gleefully, and he was all right. He knew how to disport himself with it!

The lights of the town twinkled invitingly. After Calcutta, Paris, London, he would find Levenford contemptibly small, yet this very disdain filled him with a delightful self-esteem. He, the man of the world, would show them a few things in the town to-night; yes, by gad! he would paint it a bright, vermilion red! At his thoughts a throaty laugh broke from him exultantly and he looked about him eagerly. As he swung along he saw dimly on the other side of the street the moving figure of a woman and, looking after the indistinct figure, he leered to himself: "That one's not much good to a man, she's in too much of a hurry. What does she want to run like that for?" He did not know that it was Agnes Moir on her way to see his mother.

He quickened his steps through the darkness that wrapped him like a cloak, revelling in this obscurity which made him feel now more dashing, more alive than the broad light of day. What manner of youth had he once been, to be afraid of this stimulating opacity? It was the time when a man woke up, when he could have some fun! Memories of lotus-eating nights he had spent in India recurred vivaciously to him and, as they rose before him, whetting his anticipation, he muttered: "These were the nights. These were the splurges. I'll go back all right. Trust me!" Gaily he plunged into the first public-house in the street.

"Gin and angostura," he cried in an experienced tone, banging a pound note down on the bar. When the drink came he drained it in a gulp and nodded his head affirmatively, sophisticatedly. With the second glass in his hand he gathered up his change, slipped it into his pocket, tilted his hat to a rakish angle, and looked round the saloon.

It was a poor sort of place he noted indifferently, with drab red walls, poor lights, dirty spittoons and sawdust on the floor. Heavens! sawdust on the floor, after the rich, thick piled carpet into which his feet had sunk so seductively in that little place in Paris. Despite his demand there had been no bitters in his gin. Still, he did not care, this was only the opener! His first and invariable proceeding on these jovial excursions was to get a few drinks into himself quickly. "When I've got a bead in me," he would say, "I'm as right as the mail. Man! I'm a spunky devil then." Until he felt the airy spinning of wheels within his brain he lacked drive, daring, and nerve; for, despite his bluster, he was at heart the same soft, irresolute weakling as before and he required this blurring of his impressionable senses before he could enjoy himself in perfect self-confidence. His susceptible nature reacted quickly to the suggestive urge of alcohol and his bold dreams and pretentious longings were solidified thereby into actualities, so that he assumed with every glass a more superior aspect, a more mettled air of defiance.

"Anything happening in this hole to-night?" he enquired largely of the barman—it was the class of tavern which, of necessity, had a large, powerful male behind the bar. The barman shook his close-cropped bullet head, looking curiously at the other, wondering who the young swell might be.

"No!" he replied cautiously, "I don't think so. There was a mechanics' concert in the Borough Hall on Thursday!"

"Gad!" replied Matthew, with a guffaw. "You don't call that sort of thing amusement. You're not civilised here. Don't you know anything about a neat little place to dance in, with a smart wench or two about. Something in the high-stepping line."

"You'll no' get that here," replied the tapman shortly, wiping the bar dry with a cloth, and adding sourly: "this is a decent town you're in."

"Don't I know it," cried Matt expansively, embracing with his glance the only other occupant of the room—a labouring man who sat on a settle against the wall watching him with a fascinated eye from behind a pint pot of beer. "Don't I know it. It's the deadest, most sanctimonious blot on the map of Europe. Aha! but you should see what I've seen. I could tell you stories that would make your hair stand on end. But what's the odds. You don't know the difference here between a bottle of Pommeroy and a pair of French corsets." He laughed loudly at his own humour, viewing their incredulous faces with an increasing merriment, then suddenly, although gratified at the impression he had created, he perceived that no further amusement, no further adventure was to be had there, and, moving to the door with a nod of his head and a tilt of his hat, he lounged out through the swing doors into the night.

He sauntered slowly along Church Street. That delicious woolly numbness was already beginning to creep round the back of his ears and infiltrate his brain. An easy sensation of well-being affected him; he wanted lights, company, music. Disgustedly he looked at the blank, shuttered shop windows and the few, quickly moving pedestrians, and parodying contemptuously the last remark of the barman, he muttered to himself: "This is a decent graveyard you're in." He was seized by a vast and contemptuous loathing for Levenford. What good was a town of this kind to a seasoned man like him whose worldly knowledge stretched from the flash houses in Barrackpore to the Odeon bar in Paris?

Moodily, at the corner of Church Street and High Street, he turned into another saloon. Here, however, his glance immediately brightened. This place was warm, well lit, and filled with the animated chatter of voices; a glitter of mirrors and cut glass threw back myriads of coruscating lights; stacks of bottles with vivid labels were banked behind the bar, and through half-drawn curtains he saw, in another room, the smooth, green cloth of a billiard table.

"Give me a Mackay's special," he ordered impressively. "John Mackay's and no other for me."

A plump, pink woman with jet drop ear-rings served him delicately. He admired the crook of her little finger as she decanted the spirits, considering it the essence of refinement, and although she was matronly he smiled at her blandly. He was such a lion with the ladies! A reputation like his must be sustained at all costs!

"Nice snug little place you've got here," he remarked loudly. "Reminds me of Spinosa's bar in Calcutta. Not so large but pretty well as comfortable!" There was a hush in the conversation, and feeling with satisfaction that he was being stared at, he sipped his whisky appreciatively, with the air of a connoisseur and went on: "They don't give you the right stuff out there, though! Not unless you watch them! Too much blue vitriol in it. Like the knock-out gin at Port Said. Nothing like the real John Mackay." To his satisfaction a few people began to collect round him; an English sailor in the crowd nudged him familiarly and said, thickly:

"You been out there too, cocky?"

"Just back!" said Matt affably, draining his glass. "Back across the briny from India."

"And so have I," replied the other, staring at Matthew with a fixed solemnity, then gravely shaking hands with him, as though the fact that they had both returned from India made them brothers now and for all time. "Bloody awful heat out there, isn't it, cocky? Gives me a thirst that lasts till I get back."

"Have a wet, then?"

"Naow! You have one along o' me!"

Agreeably they argued the point until they finally decided by tossing.

"Lovely lady," cried Matthew with a killing glance at the fat barmaid. He won, and the sailor ordered drinks for everyone in the small coterie. "Right with the ladies every time," sniggered Matthew. He was glad that he had won and the sailor, in the exuberance of his drunken hospitality, glad to have lost. Whilst they drank they compared their amazing experiences and the mob gaped whilst they discussed mosquitoes, monsoons, bars, bazaars, ship biscuits, pagodas, sacred and profane cows, and the contours and anatomical intimacies of Armenian women. Stories circulated as freely as the drinks until the sailor, far ahead in the matter of inebriation, began to grow incoherent, maudlin, and Matt, at the outset of his night's enjoyment and swollen with an exuberant dignity, set himself to look for an excuse to shake him off.

"What can a man do in this half-dead town?" he cried. "Can't you squeeze out some excitement here." This was not the society he had moved in before leaving for India and no one recognised him; as, indeed, they did not know him to be a son of the ancient Borough he preferred them to regard him as a stranger, a dashing cosmopolitan.

They could think of nothing worthy of him and were silent until finally someone suggested:

"What about billiards?"

"Ah! a game of pills," said Matt thoughtfully, "that's something in my line."

"Billiards!" roared the seaman. "I'm true blue I am! I'll play anybody alive for—for anything you like to—what—I——" his voice deteriorated into a drunken dribble of sound. Matthew considered him dispassionately.

"You're the champion are you? Good enough. I'll play you fifty up for a pound a side," he challenged.

"Right," shouted the other. He surveyed Matthew with lowered lids and an oscillating head, indicating, in incoherent yet unmistakable picturesque language, that he would be soused for a son of a sea cook if he would go back on his word. "Where's your money?" he asked solemnly, in conclusion.

Each produced his stake, which the onlooker who had first suggested the game had the honour of holding, and, as no one had ever played in the place for such an unheard of sum, the crowd, simmering with excitement, surged into the billiard-room behind them amidst considerable commotion, and the game commenced.

Matthew, looking dashingly proficient in his shirt sleeves, began. He was, he fully understood, a good player, having practised assiduously in Calcutta, often indeed during the daytime when he should have been perched upon his office stool, and he realised with an inward complacency that the other, in his present condition, could be no match for him. Professionally, he ran his eye along his cue, chalked it and, feeling that he was the focus of the combined admiration of the gathering, broke the balls, but failed to leave the red in baulk. His opponent, swaying slightly upon his feet, slapped his ball on the table, took a rapid sight at it and slammed hard with his cue. His ball struck the red with terrific violence and, pursuing it eagerly all round the table through a baffling intricacy of acute and obtuse angles, finally bolted after it into the bottom right-hand pocket. The crowd voiced its appreciation of the prodigious fluke. He turned and, supporting himself against the table, bowed gravely, then exclaimed triumphantly to Matthew:

"Whadeye think of that, cocky? Who's topsy-boozy, now? Didn't I say I was true blue? Wasn't that a shot? I'll play you with cannon balls next time." He wanted to stop the game for a profound dissertation upon the merits of his marvellous stroke and a lengthy explanation of how he had performed it, but, after some persuasion, he was prevailed upon to continue. Though he readdressed himself to the game with the air of a conqueror his next shot was hardly so successful, for his ball, struck hard on the bottom, bounced skittishly across the cloth, hurdled the edge of the table in its stride, and landed with a thud on the wooden floor amidst even louder and more prolonged applause than had greeted his previous effort.

"Wha' do I get for that?" he enquired, owlishly, of the assembly at large.

"A kick on the arse!" shouted somebody at the back. The seaman shook his head sadly, but they all laughed, even the fat barmaid who was craning her neck to see the fun and who tittered involuntarily, but recovering herself with a start, quickly merged her merriment into a more modest cough.

It was now Matthew's turn to play, and though the balls were favourably placed, he began with great caution, making three easy cannons and then going in off the red. Next, he began to play a series of red losing hazards into the right middle pocket, so accurately that at every stroke the object ball returned with slow, unerring exactitude to the required position below the middle of the table. The crowd held its breath with profound and respectful attention whilst he continued his break. Under the bright lights his white, fleshy hands swam over the smooth baize like pale amœbæ in a green pool; his touch upon the cue was as delicate and as gentle as a woman's; the spirits in him steadied him like a rock. This was the greatest joy that life could offer him, not merely to show off his perfect poise and masterly ability before this throng, but to draw upon himself this combined admiration and envy. His empty vanity fed itself upon their adulation greedily.

When he had made thirty-nine he paused significantly, rechalked his cue, and neglecting, obviously, an easy ball which lay over the pocket, he addressed himself ostentatiously to a long and difficult cushion cannon. He achieved it, and with three, further, quick shots ran out with his unfinished break of fifty. A storm of cheering filled the room.

"Go on sir! Don't stop! Show us what you can do!"

"Who is he? The man's a marvel!"

"Stand us a pint, mister. It's worth that, anyway!"

But with a lordly assumption of indolence he refused to continue, pocketed his winnings, and flung his cue into the rack; now that he had made his reputation he was afraid to mar it. They surrounded him, clapping him on the back, pushing and shoving each other, trying to shake hands with him, whilst he gloried in his popularity, laughing, talking, gesticulating with the rest. His opponent, having been with difficulty convinced that the game was over, manifested no regrets, but flung his arm tipsily round Matthew's shoulder.

"Did you see that shot of mine, cocky?" he kept repeating, "it was worth a pound—worth five pounds. It was a—a regular nor'easter— a pickled ripsnorter. I'm true blue I am," and he glared defiantly round, seeking for anyone who might dispute it.

They all went back to the bar where the whole assembly had beer at Matthew's expense. He was their hero; they toasted him, then dispersed into small groups throughout the room discussing, stroke by stroke, the memorable achievement of the victor.

Matt swaggered about the room, lording it over them. He had no false reticence, no mock modesty, but visited each group, saying to this one: "Did you see that cannon of mine off the cushion? Pretty neat, wasn't it? Judged to a hair's breadth!" to another: "Dash it all, I've made a break of two hundred on my day—more than two hundred!"

and to a third: "The poor barnacle, what chance had he against the likes of me? I could have beat him with my walking-stick." He lauded himself to the skies and the more he drank the more his silly vanity ballooned itself, until the room seemed to him to become filled with a babble of voices all lifted up to him in honeyed, fulsome flattery. His own tongue joined in the pæan, the light gleamed about him like a thousand candles lighted in his honour, his heart swelled with gratification and delight. He had never had a triumph like this before; he considered himself the finest billiards player in Levenford, in Scotland, in the Kingdom; it was something to be able to make a break of fifty like that; why did they want to degrade him by shoving him into an office when he could play billiards in such a marvellous fashion?

Suddenly, at the height of his jubilation, the fickle favour of the crowd waned; a heated argument had developed between two new-comers— an Irish navvy and a bricklayer—and the general attention left him and fixed itself upon the protagonists, whilst the mob goaded on each in turn in the hopes of provoking a fight. After all, he had only bought them beer—the price of popularity was higher than that—and almost at once he found himself alone, in a corner, friendless and forgotten. He almost blubbered with dismay at the sudden change in his condition, reflecting that it was always the same, that he could never maintain the centre of the stage for a sufficient length of time but was shoved, before he wished it, into the background. He wanted to run after them and recapture their errant favour, to shout: "Look! I'm the man that made the break of fifty! Don't forget about me. I'm the great billiards player. Gather round me again! You'll not see a player like me every day!" His vexation deepened, merged insensibly into resentment, and in his disgust he swallowed two large whiskies, then, with a last indignant look which swept scowlingly over them all, he went out of the bar. No one noticed him go.

Outside, the pavements tilted slightly as he walked, moving like the deck of a liner in a mild swell; yet, cunningly, he adapted his balance to this gentle regular roll so that his body swayed slightly from side to side—but nevertheless maintained its upright poise. The exhilaration of the movement charmed him and soothed his wounded conceit. As he traversed the High Street he became aware that, in manœuvring so skilfully amongst the intricate difficulties of this perpetually alternating plane, he was accomplishing a noted feat, one ranking equally, perhaps, with his remarkable achievement at billiards.

He felt that it was not late, and with great difficulty he attempted to make out the time from the lighted dial of the Town clock; with his legs wide apart and his head thrown back he struggled with the abstruse dimensions of time and space. The steeple oscillated gently and wavered in harmony with the earth, the hands were indistinct, but he thought that it was just ten o'clock and his satisfaction at his cleverness was unbounded when, a moment later, the clock struck ten. He counted the chiming notes with sage, explanatory beats of his arm as though he himself were tolling the bell.

Even for a dead and alive town like Levenford it was too early for him to go home. A man like Matthew Brodie to return home at the childish hour of ten o'clock? Impossible! He rammed his hand into his trousers pocket and feeling the reassuring crackle of a pound note and the clinking touch of silver coins, he thrust his hat more firmly on his head and once more set off down the street. Disappointingly few people were about. In a real city he would have known what to do; it was the easiest thing in the world to fling himself into a cab and, with a knowing wink, tell the driver to take him to the *bona robas*; he had only to lie back, luxuriously, and smoke his cigar whilst the spavined horseflesh dragged him happily to his destination. But here there were no cabs, no excitement, no women. The one girl whom he discovered and addressed gallantly ran from him panic-stricken, as though he had struck her, and he damned the town for its blatant, bourgeois piety, cursed the female population in its entirety for the reputable habit of retiring early, for the unhappy integrity of its virtue. He was like a hunter after game who, the more it evaded him, became the more desperate in his pursuit and he swayed up the High Street and down again, fruitlessly essaying to find some means of combating the melancholy of drunken despondency which began slowly to settle upon him. At last, when he felt that he must enter another tavern to drown the sorrow of his failure all at once he remembered! He paused abruptly, slapped his thigh extravagantly at his unaccountable lapse of memory, and allowed a slow smile to expand his features as he recollected that house in College Street which, in his youth, he had always hurried past with averted eyes and bated breath. Rumours regarding this tall, dark, narrow house, sandwiched between the Clyde Dress Agency and the mean pawnshop at the foot of the Vennel, had spread from time to time like tiny ripples on the flat, impeccable surface of Levenford's respectability, giving the house a mysterious but tacitly acknowledged reputation amongst the knowing youth of the town. Its curtains were always drawn and no one entered by day, but at night lights discreetly appeared, footsteps came and went, sometimes music was heard. Such an iniquity, however veiled, must long ago have been expunged from so ancient and reputable a Borough, but a controlling hand of protection seemed to lie over the house, not perhaps sanctioning but rather concealing its inoffensively, immoral existence; it was even hinted by malicious individuals that certain baillies and prominent citizens found a not infrequent occasion upon which to make use of this rendezvous, in, of course, an eminently sedate and genteel manner.

"That's the hidey-hole for you, Matt. You'll see if ye were right or wrong. You've often wondered what's inside and now you're going to find out," he muttered to himself, delightedly, as he lurched towards College Street, bent upon investigating the horrors at which his immature experience had shuddered. It struck him suddenly as the most ludicrous jest imaginable that he should be on his way to a bawdy house in Levenford, and he burst into peals of laughter so that he was obliged to stop, and roll helplessly against the side of a wall, whilst inane guffaws shook him and tears of mirth coursed down his face. When he was able to proceed, his despondency of a few short moments ago was gone, and he felt with a delicious, inward appreciation that he was enjoying himself infinitely more than he had expected. The alcohol he had absorbed had not yet reached the zenith of its stimulation and, with every floundering step he took, he became more stupidly heedless and more sublimely hilarious.

He entered the Vennel. The narrow street seemed more full of life than all the wide main streets of the town together; it teemed with an unseen activity. From the pens and closes and from behind even the thin walls of the houses came an endless variety of sounds—voices, laughter, the howl of a dog, the music of a melodeon, singing. He perceived that they did not retire early here, felt that he was in his element, and outside a lighted window, from which emerged a roistering chorus, he stood rooted, then suddenly, like a provoked dog, he threw back his head and lifted his loud, inebriate voice in unison with the harmony within. The music ceased immediately and, after a pause, the window was thrown up and a stream of slops descended in a curving arch towards him. It missed him, however, by a foot, merely splashing slightly about his legs, and he retired down the street gaily, with the full honours of the encounter.

Half-way down, his nostrils dilated to the succulent odour of frying ham arising from the cooking of some belated supper in a house which he was passing, and reaching him through the night in a spicy, savoury vapour. Immediately he felt hungry and, looking around, discerned over the way a small shop still open, a nondescript eating house devoted to the sale of such delicacies as pies, puddings, potted head, and tripe and onions. Moved by a sudden impulse, he strode across the street and muttering to himself drunkenly: "Ladies can wait. Matt needs little nourishment. Must keep strength up, m'boy " he entered the place magnificently. Inside, however, his whisky-hunger overcame his style and he shouted: "Throw us a meat pie quick, and swill in plenty of gravy."

"Penny or twopenny?" queried the greasy youth behind the counter.

"Sixpenny! you *soor*," replied Matthew, amiably. "Do you think I want any of your small trash? you *bobachee*. Pick me the biggest in the bunch and push it over here, *jilde*!" He slapped the coin down, took up the newspaper-wrapped package offered in return and, disdaining to consume the pie upon the premises, walked out. Down the street he went, tearing off the paper wrapping and stuffing handfuls of the delicacy into his mouth, eating voraciously, leaving behind him a track which became at once the joy and contention of all the starveling cats of the alley.

When he had finished, he breathed a sigh of content and, recollecting his manners, sucked his fingers and wiped them fastidiously upon his handkerchief. Then he hurried more urgently forward, full of meat and drink, ready now for the subtler and more piquant enchantments of the dessert. He came eventually to the house, found it, indeed, without difficulty, for it was not easy to forget one's way in Levenford, and for a moment he stood outside, contemplating the narrow veiled illumination of the windows. As he remained there, momentarily a faint return of his adolescent awe touched him strangely, made him hesitate, but urged by the wild thought of the pleasure that lay therein for him, he seized the knocker and hammered loudly at the door. The clangour thundered up and down the street with a rude insistence, and, when he desisted, echoed to and fro across the narrow canyon of the lane, leaving, after the final reverberation had ceased, a startled silence which seemed to fall upon the outside, to grip even the inside of the house. There was a long pause during which he stood swaying upon the doorstep and, when he had almost made up his mind to knock again, the door was opened slowly, and for a small way only. Still, he was not dismayed by the inhospitable meagreness of this narrow aperture but, wise in his experience, immediately thrust his foot into the opening.

"Good evening, dear lady," he simpered. "Are you at home?"

"What do you want?" said a hard, low-toned, female voice from the interior darkness.

"The sight of your pretty face, my deah," he replied, in his best manner. "Come along now. Don't be so cruel and heartless. Give me a look at your bright eyes or your neat ankles."

"Who are you?" repeated the other harshly. "Who told you to come here?"

"I'm an old inhabitant, sweet creature, lately returned from abroad and not without the wherewithal." He jingled the money in his pocket enticingly, and laughed with a short, empty laugh.

There was a pause, then the voice said firmly:

"Go away! You've made a mistake. This is a respectable house. We'll have nothing to do with you whatever," and she made as though to close the door in his face. In the ordinary way he would have been deterred by this rebuff and would undoubtedly have slunk off, but now his foot prevented the door from closing and he replied, with some show of bluster:

"Not so fast, ma'am. Don't be so high and mighty! You're dealing with a tough customer here. Let me in or I'll make such a hullabaloo you'll have the whole street at your door. Yes, I'll bring the town down about your ears."

"Go away at once or I'll get the police on you," said the other in a less firm tone, after a momentary silence that seemed fraught with indecision.

He winked triumphantly at the darkness, feeling that he was winning, realising proudly that he could always bluff the women.

"No you won't," he replied craftily, "you don't want any police down here. I know that better than you do. I'm the gentleman you want to-night—just wait till you see."

She made no answer and, her silence encouraging him, her reticence serving to excite his lust, he muttered:

"I'll come and take a peep at you, Dolly," and, pressing his shoulder into the slight open space of the doorway, he forcibly insinuated himself into the hall. There he blinked for a moment in the light of the lamp which she held in her hand and which was now thrust forward into his face, then his jaw dropped and he stared boorishly, incredulously at her. Across the thrawn, forbidding face of the woman a gross purple nævus lay like a livid weal, stretching like a living pappy fungus which had eaten into and destroyed her cheek and neck. It fascinated him morbidly with the attraction of a repulsive curiosity.

"What do you want?" she repeated in a rasping voice. He was disconcerted; with an effort, he removed his eyes from her face, but as he gazed round the wide, high-vaulted hall his confidence returned at the thought that there were other rooms in the house, rooms sealed with an alluring mystery. She herself was only the bawd; there must be plenty of fun waiting for him behind one of these doors in the house. He looked at her again and immediately her disfigurement obtruded itself upon him, so forcibly that he could not release his attention from it and, despite himself, muttered stupidly:

"Woman, that's an awful mark on your face. How did ye come to get it?"

"Who are you?" she repeated, harshly. "For the last time I ask you, before I have you thrown out."

He was off his guard.

"My name's Brodie—Matthew Brodie," he mumbled in an absent, sottish voice. "Where are the young wenches? It's them I want to see! You'll not do!"

As he spoke she, in her turn, stared at him and, in the flickering light of the lamp, it seemed as if amazement and agitation in turn swept across her grim features. At length, she said, slowly:

"I told you that you had mistaken the kind of house that this is! You'll not find much to amuse you here. Nobody lives in this house but me. That's the plain truth. I advise you to leave at once."

"I don't believe you," he cried sullenly, and, his anger growing, he set up a great hubbub, shouting: "You're a liar, I tell you. Do you think I'm a fool to be put off with a yarn like that? I'll see you further before I go away. Do you think I'll let myself be put off by a thing like you?—me that's travelled to the other end of the world. No! I'll break into every room in this damned house sooner than be beat."

At the uproar which he created a voice called out from upstairs and immediately she thrust her hand over his face.

"Shut your mouth, will you," she cried fiercely. "You'll have the whole place about my ears. What the devil are you to come in and disturb an honest woman like this? Here! wait in this room till you're sober. Then I'll have it out with you. Wait until I come back or it'll be the worse for you." She seized him by the arm and, opening a door in the lobby, pushed him roughly into a small sitting-room. "Wait here, I tell you, or you'll regret it all your born days," she shot at him, with a forbidding look, as she shut the door and enclosed him within the cold, uninviting chamber. She was gone before his fuddled brain had realised it and now he looked round the small cold parlour into which he had been thrust with a mixture of disgust and annoyance. Luscious memories recurred to him of other houses where he had moved in a whirl of mad music and wild, gay laughter, where bright lights had danced above the rich warmth of red plush and eager, undressed women had vied with each other for the richness of his favours. He had not been three minutes in the room before his drunken senses collected themselves and, as his mind realised the absurdity of having permitted himself—a man of such experience—to be shut up out of the way in this small cupboard, his will shaped itself towards a fiery resolution. They would not close him up in this box of a place with fine sport going on under his very nose! He moved forward and, with a crass affection of caution, opened the door and tiptoed once more into the wide lobby, where a faint murmur of voices came to him from upstairs. Surreptitiously he looked round. There were three other doors opening out of the hall and he surveyed them with a mixture of expectation and indecision, until, choosing the one immediately opposite, and advancing carefully, he turned the handle and looked in. He was rewarded only by the cold darkness of a musty, unoccupied room. Closing this door, he turned to the one which adjoined it, but again he was disappointed for he discovered here only the empty kitchen of the house; and swinging round with a snort of disgust, he plunged heedlessly into the last room.

Immediately he stood stock still, whilst the thrill of a delicious discovery ran through him. Before his eyes, seated reading a newspaper beside the comfortable fire, was a girl. Like a frantic searcher who has at last discovered treasure he uttered deep in his throat a low exultant cry and remained motionless, filling himself with her beauty, fascinated by the warm reflection of the firelight upon the soft curve of her pale cheek, noting her slender body, the shapely curve of her ankles, as, still unconscious of him, she held her feet to the fire. She was attractive and, seen through the haze of his distorted, craving senses, she became to him at once supremely beautiful and desirable. Slowly he advanced towards her. At the sound of his step she looked up, her face at once became disturbed, and she dropped her paper, saying quickly: "This room is private, reserved."

He nodded his head wisely, as he replied:

"That's right. It's reserved for me and you. Don't be afraid; nobody will disturb us." He sat down heavily on a chair close to her, and tried to take her hand in his.

"But you can't come in here!" she protested in a panic. "You've no right to do such a thing. I'll—I'll call the landlady."

She was as timid as a partridge, and, he told himself greedily, as smooth and plump. He longed to bite the round contour of her shoulder.

"No! my dear," he said thickly, "I've seen her already. We had a nice long talk outside. She's not bonny, but she's honest. Yes! she's got my money, and I've got you."

"It's impossible! You're insulting me," she cried out. "There's been a mistake. I never set eyes on you before. I'm expecting someone here any minute."

"He can wait till I've gone, dearie," he replied coarsely. "I like the look of you so well I would never let you go now!"

She jumped to her feet indignantly.

"I'll scream," she cried. "You don't know what you're about. He'll kill you if he comes in."

"He can go to hell, whoever he is. I've got you now," shouted Matt, gripping her suddenly before she could shriek.

At that moment, when he hugged her close to his rampant body, whilst he bent down to her face, the door opened and, as he raised his head furiously to vituperate the intruder, he gazed straight into the eyes of his father. For what seemed an eternity of time the three figures remained motionless as though the three emotions of surprise, anger, and fear had petrified them into stone; then gradually, as Matt's arm relaxed, the limp figure of the girl slipped silently out of his embrace. Then as if this movement induced him to speak, yet without for an instant removing his eyes from his son's face, and in words as cold and penetrating as steel, Brodie said:

"Has he hurt ye, Nancy?"

The pretty barmaid of the Winton Arms came slowly up to him and tremblingly sobbed:

"Not much. It was nothing at all. He didna hurt me. Ye just came in time."

His lips compressed themselves firmly, and his gaze became more fixed as he replied:

"Don't weep then, lassie! Run awa' out."

"Am I to wait in the house for ye, dear?" she whispered. "I will, if ye wish it."

"No!" he exclaimed, without an instant's hesitation.

"Ye've had enough to thole. Run awa' hame." His eyes dilated and his hands opened and shut as he continued slowly: "I want to have this —this gentleman to myself—entirely to myself."

As she brushed past him he stroked her cheek, without looking at her, without relaxing a muscle of his face.

"Dinna hurt him," she whispered fearfully. "He didna mean anything. Ye can see he's not himself."

He did not reply, but when she had gone he shut the door quietly and came close up to his son. The two men looked at each other. This time Matt's eyes were not beaten down for he immediately lowered them and gazed deliberately at the floor. Through his inebriated mind a wild succession of thoughts whirled. The immediate sinking fear he had experienced was replaced by a contrary emotion which rushed upwards in a fierce and bitter resentment. Was his father inevitably doomed to thwart him? The memory of each humiliation, every taunt, all the beatings he had endured from the other throughout his life seethed through his pot-valiant brain like white fire. Was he to submit patiently to another thrashing because he had unwittingly obtruded upon his father's low woman? Mad with drink and frustrated lust, inflamed by the hot tide of his hate, he stood still, feeling blindly that now, at least he was beyond fear.

Brodie gazed at the lowered head of his son with a burning passion which at last burst the bonds of his iron control.

"You dog!" he hissed from between his clenched teeth. "You dared to do that! You dared to interfere with me and with what is mine. I warned ye to keep out of my way and now I'll—I'll strangle you." He put out his great hands to clutch the other's neck but with a jerk Matt broke away from him, staggering to the other side of the table, from where he glared insanely at his father. His pale face was bedewed with sweat, his mouth worked convulsively, his whole body shook.

"You're as bad as me, you swine!" he yelled. "Don't think you can come it over me any longer. You wanted that bitch for yourself. That was all. But if I can't get her I'll see that you don't. I've suffered enough from you. I'm going to suffer no more. Don't look at me like that!"

"Look at ye!" roared Brodie. "I'll do more than look at ye! I'll choke ye till I squeeze the breath out of your worthless body."

"Let me see you try," shouted the other, with a heaving breast. "You'll choke me none—you'll grind me down no longer. You think I'm feared of you, but by God! I'm not. I'll show you something you don't expect."

A more brutal rage surged in Brodie at this unexpected defiance and his eye glared but, without speaking, he began slowly to advance round

274

the table towards his son. Yet, strangely, Matthew did not move. Instead, with a wild shout of delirious exultation he plunged his hand into his hip pocket and withdrew a small derringer which he clutched fiercely in his grasp and pointed directly at his father.

"You didn't know I had this, you swine," he shrieked. "You didn't know I had brought this from India. There's a bullet in it that's a keepsake for you. Take it now, damn ye. Take it now, you sneering bully!" And shutting his teeth behind his pale lips, he jerked back his forefinger and pulled the trigger. There was a bright yellow flash and a sharp explosion which sounded loudly within the confines of the room. The bullet, fired at close range, furrowed Brodie's temple and buried itself in the mirror of the overmantel, amidst a crashing of glass which tinkled upon the floor amongst the dying echoes of the shot.

For a second, Brodie stood aghast, then, with a loud cry, he rushed forward and struck his son a fearful blow with his mallet fist full between the eyes. Matthew dropped like a pole-axed animal, striking his head against the table leg as he fell. He lay senseless upon the floor, bleeding from his nose and ears.

"You murderer!" panted Brodie, staring with glittering eyes at the insensate form beneath him. "You tried to murder your own father." Then, as he stood thus, a furious knocking came upon the door, and the woman of the house burst into the room, trembling, her gruesome face becoming more ghastly as she gazed at the pistol and the inanimate figure on the floor.

"My God!" she gasped. "Ye havena—ye havena shot your own son?"

Brodie pressed his handkerchief to his raw, scorched temple, his face rigid, his chest still heaving painfully.

"Leave us," he commanded, still keeping his gaze upon Matthew. "It was him tried to kill me."

" 'Twas him fired at you, then," she cried, wringing her hands. "I knew no good would come o' him bustin' in like he did. Whatna noise that pistol made, too!"

"Get out o' here then," he ordered roughly. "Get out or there'll be more noise—if that's all that concerns you."

"Dinna do anything rash," she implored him. "Remember the name o' the house."

"Damn you and your house! The only name it has is a bad one," he shouted, forcing his fierce gaze on her. "Don't ye know I was nearly deid," and seizing her by the shoulder, he thrust her out of the room. When he had closed the door behind her he turned and again grimly contemplated the prone figure, then advancing, he stood over it and stirred it with his foot.

"You would have murdered your father," he muttered. "By God I'll pay you for it." Then he moved slowly to the table, sat down and, folding his arms across his chest, patiently awaited the other's recovery.

For five minutes there was absolute silence in the room, except for the slow tick-tock of a clock that hung against the wall and the occasional fall of a cinder in the grate; then, suddenly, Matt groaned and moved. Holding his head in both hands, whilst blood still streamed from his nose, he tried to sit up but failed, and subsided again upon the floor with a low moan of pain. The blow which he had received had almost fractured his skull and now he felt sick with concussion. He had yet no consciousness of his father's presence as the room swam around him and a violent nausea affected him. He felt deathly sick, hiccoughed and then vomited. The disgusting accumulation of his stomach contents gushed from his mouth and mixed revoltingly with the pool of blood upon the floor. It appeared as if he would never stop retching, as though the reflex straining of his body would kill him, but at last he ceased, and after lying weakly upon his side, he rose, and staggered dizzily to a chair by the table. His face was pale and streaked with blood, his eyes puffed and swollen, but with such vision as was left to him he now saw, and gazed dumbly at, his father.

"You're still here you see," whispered Brodie softly, "and so am I." He uttered the last words with a slow intensity as he drew his chair nearer to that of his son. "Just the two of us alone in this room. Isna' that grand? It's a rare delight for me to be with ye like this, and to see ye so close to me." He paused for a moment, then snarled: "Your dear mother would love ye if she could only see you now. The sight o' your face would fair fill her heart with joy! The look o' these smart clothes that you've spewed such a braw new pattern ower would fair chairm her! Her big braw son!" Matthew was incapable of speaking, but speech was not required of him; Brodie picked up the pistol and, turning it over ostentatiously before his son's shrinking gaze, continued, in a more restrained and contemplative tone: "Man, when I see you there, I'm surprised that a thing like you had the courage to try to murder me. Ye're such a poor bit o' dirt. But although I'm not anxious to have a bullet in my brain it's a pity, in a way, that ye didna succeed. Ye would have danced so brawly at the end of a halter, swingin' from side to side with the rope round your yellow neck."

Matthew, now quite sober, turned a dead, piteous face towards his father, and, impelled by the instinct of flight, weakly tried to get up, in an endeavour to escape from the room.

"Stay where you are, you dog!" flared Brodie. "Do you think I'm done with ye yet? Ye'll leave here at my pleasure, and there's just the chance ye might never leave at all."

"I was out of my head, father," Matt whispered. "I didn't know what I was doin'—I was drunk."

"So ye take a dram, do ye?" sneered his father. "The very idea, now! That's another gentlemanly habit ye brought back from abroad.

No wonder ye have such a bonny aim wi' a gun."

"I didna mean to fire," whispered the other. "I only bought the pistol for show. Oh! I'll never, never do it again."

"Tuts! man," jibed Brodie, "dinna make such rash promises. Ye might want to murder somebody in real earnest to-morrow—to blow their brains out so that they lay scattered on the floor."

"Father, father, let me go," whined Matthew. "Ye can see fine I didn't mean it."

"Come! come!" jeered Brodie, "this'll never do. That's no' like the big man you are—that's not like your mother's dashin' son. Ye must have spewed a' the courage out o' ye by the look o' things. We maun gie you another drink to pull ye together." He seized the bell that lay on the table and rang it loudly. "Just consider," he continued with a dreadful laugh, "a dead man couldna have rung that bell. Na! I couldna have given ye a dram if ye had murdered me."

"Don't say that word again, father," Matt sobbed. "It makes me feared. I tell ye I didn't know what I was doing."

Here the landlady of the house came in and, with tight lips, silently regarded them.

"We're still a' alive, ye see," Brodie sang out to her gaily, "in spite of all the pistols and gunpowder and keepsakes from India; and since we're alive we're goin' to drink. Bring us a bottle o' whisky and two glasses."

"I don't want to drink," Matt quailed. "I'm too sick." His head was splitting in agony and the very thought of liquor nauseated him.

"What?" drawled Brodie. "Ye don't say! and you the seasoned vessel that carries revolvers about wi' ye. Man, ye better tak' what's offered, for ye'll need a good stiffener before I hand ye over to the police!"

"The police!" gasped Matt, in terror. "No! No! you wouldna do that, father." His fear was abject. He was now, through the blow, the reaction of his feelings, and the close proximity of his father, reduced to the level of an invertebrate creature who would have willingly crawled at the other's feet if he could thereby have propitiated him.

Brodie eyed his son repugnantly; he read his mind and saw the arrant cowardice staring from his bloodshot eyes. He was silent whilst the woman entered with the bottle and glasses, then, when she had withdrawn, he muttered slowly to himself:

"God help me! Whatna' thing is this to bear my name?" Then bitterly he took up the bottle and poured out two glasses of neat spirit.

"Here" he shouted, "we'll drink to my big, braw son. The fine man from India! The lady's man! The man that tried to kill his father!" Fiercely he thrust the glass at his son. "Drink it, you dog, or I'll throw it in your teeth." He drained his glass at a gulp, then fixed a minatory eye upon the other whilst Matthew painfully forced himself to swallow his portion of the spirit.

"Now," he sneered, "we'll make a fine comfortable night o' it, just you and me. Fill up your glass! Fill it up, I say!"

"Oh! father, let me go home," cried Matt—the sight and taste of the whisky now loathsome to him—"I want to go home. My head is bursting."

"Dear! dear!" replied Brodie, in a broad mimicry of his wife's voice. "Our Matt has a wee bit headache. That must have been where I struck you, son. That's terrible! What shall we do about it?" He affected to think deeply whilst he again emptied his glass. "Man, I can't think of anything better than a leetle speerits. That's the remedy for an honest man like you—some good honest whisky." He filled out another full glass of the raw liquor and bending forward, seized his son's jaw with vice-like fingers, prised open the weak mouth, then quickly tilted the contents of the glass down Matt's gullet; whilst Matthew gasped and choked he continued, with a frightful assumption of conviviality: "That's better! That's much better! And now tell me—don't hesitate, mind ye, but be quite frank about it—tell me what ye thought of Nancy. She's maybe no so weel born as your mother, ye ken, but she doesna stink in her person. Na! she's a clean wee body in some respects. A man canna have it both ways, apparently." Then dropping his assumed smoothness he suddenly snarled, in a devilish voice: "Was she to your taste, I'm askin' you?"

"I don't know. I can't tell," whined Matthew, realising that whatever answer he gave would be the wrong one.

Brodie nodded his big head reflectively.

"Man, that's true enough! I didn't give ye enough time to sample her. What a pity I came in so soon. I might have given ye another ten minutes thegither." Deliberately he whipped his own imagination on the raw with a dark unconscious sadism, knowing only that the more he tortured himself the more torment he gave his son. The more he saw his son's painful thoughts revolt from the consideration of his recent excesses, the more thickly he thrust these repugnant ideas upon him.

"Man," he continued, "I couldna help but admire the bold, strong way you handled her, although she couldna have refused anything to a braw callant like you. Ye would have thocht ye were fetchtin' wi' a man the way ye gripped her."

Matthew could endure it no longer. He had reached the limit of his endurance and laying his head, which throbbed with the beat of a hundred hammers, upon the table, and bursting outright into weak, blubbering tears, he cried:

"Father, kill me if ye like. I don't care. Kill me and be done with it but, for God's sake, let me be."

278

Brodie looked at him with baffled, embittered fury; the hope he had entertained of taunting his son into another wild assault so that he might experience the delight of again battering him senseless to the floor, died within him. He saw that the other was too weak, too broken, too pitifully distressed to be provoked into another outburst and a sudden, rankling resentment made him bend over and catch him a tremendous buffet on the head, with his open hand.

"Take that, then, you slabbering lump," he shouted loudly; "you haven't even got the guts of a sheep." All the refinement of his anger, the sneering, the sarcasm, the irony, vanished, and instead, his rage foamed over like a raging sea whilst his face grew black with rabid fury like the dark clouding of an angry sky. "You would lay your fingers on my woman! You would lift your hand against me! Against me!" he roared.

Matt raised his eyes weakly, imploringly. "Don't look at me," bellowed Brodie, as though a sacrilege had been committed by the other. "Ye're not fit to lift your eyes above the level o' my boots. I canna look at ye but what I want to spit on ye. Take that, and that, and that." With every word he cuffed the other's head like an empty cask, sending it juddering against the table. "God!" he cried in disgust, "what are ye! Your head sounds like an empty drum. Have ye got to be drunk before ye can stand up for yourself? Have ye no sense of pride in the blood that's in ye? Have ye no pride to be heir to the name I gave ye?" Then, in the height of his fury, he suddenly seized Matt by the arm and, lifting him like a huddled marionette, dragged him to his feet. "For what am I wasting my time on ye here? We'll go home!" he cried. "I'll take ye home. Now we must deliver ye safely to your mother, out o' this wicked house. It's not the place at all for the son of such a godly woman." He linked his arm through Matt's and propped the staggering, half insensible figure against his own, then, flinging some money on the table, he rammed his hat on his head. "Can ye sing?" he shouted, as he trailed Matt out into the drab, empty street. "We maun have a bit chorus on the way home. Just you and me—to show folks what good friends we are. Sing, you dog!" he threatened, twisting the other's arm agonisingly. "Sing, or I'll kill ye!"

"What will—what will I sing?" came the panting, tormented voice of his son.

"Sing anything. Sing a hymn. Ay!" he gloated over the idea, "that's verra appropriate. Ye've juist missed murdering yer faither—ye maun sing a hymn o' praise and thanksgiving. Give us the Old Hundred, my big, braw man. Begin!" he ordered.

"All people that on earth do dwell," quavered Matt.

"Louder! Quicker!" shouted Brodie. "Give it pith! Put your heart into it. Pretend ye're just out o' the prayer meetin'." He marched the other off, supporting him, dragging him, bolstering him up when he

279

staggered on the uneven street, beating time to the tune, and from time to time joining his voice in the refrain with a blasphemous satire.

Down the narrow Vennel they went, towards their home, the words ringing sonorously through the stillness of the imprisoned air. Fainter grew their steps and more faintly came the sound until, finally, the last fading whisper was lost in the peaceful darkness of the night.

X

MRS. BRODIE lay on the thin, straw mattress of her narrow bed, encompassed by the darkness of her room and the silence of the house. Nessie and Grandma were sleeping, but since Agnes had left her, she had remained strainingly awake for the sounds of Matt's return. Her mind, since the shock she had received earlier in the evening, was blank and dully incapable of thought, but, whilst she waited, she suffered physically. Her acute pain had returned to her! Restlessly she twisted from side to side, trying one position and then another in an effort to alleviate the boring volleys of pain which enfiladed the entire length of her body. Her feet were cold and her hot hands moved constantly on the fretted surface of the patchwork quilt that covered the bed. Automatically, in the darkness, her fingers moved over each pattern as though she unconsciously retraced the labour of her needle. Dimly, she longed for a hot bottle to draw the blood from her congested head into the icy numbness of her legs and feet, but she was too languid to stir and she feared, too, in a vague way, to move from the safe harbour of her room, dreading that some new misfortune might beset her, that she might perhaps encounter some fresh and terrifying experience on the stairs.

Slowly the seconds ticked into minutes, sluggishly the minutes dragged into hours and, through the peace of the night, she heard actually the faint distant note of the Town clock as it struck twelve whispering notes. In effect, another day had begun when she must soon face the melancholy round of the daylight hours and all that the new dawn would bring to her. But her introspection did not follow this course. As the significance of the hour broke upon her she murmured only: "He's late! They're both awfu' late!" With the characteristic pessimism of a defeated spirit, she now sounded the abyss of melancholy possibility to its deepest extent, and wondered, miserably, if Matt had encountered his father in the town. Intangible contingencies following upon the chance of this meeting made her tremble, even as she lay passive upon the bed.

At length, when her anxiety had reached an intolerable pitch, she heard steps outside in the road. Desperately she wished to rush to the window to try to penetrate the gloom outside, but she could not make the effort, and was compelled to lie still, waiting with anxious fears for the click of the front door latch. Soon, indeed, she heard this sound but with the opening of the door her perturbation increased, for, immediately, she distinguished the loud bawling voice of her husband, derisive, compelling, dominant, and in reply the cowed, submissive tones of her son. She heard the ponderous movement of a heavy body noisily ascending the stairs and the slurred footsteps of a lighter, less vital, and more exhausted frame following behind. On the landing outside her room her husband said, in a loud, hectoring voice:

"Go to your kennel now, you dog! I'll be ready for you again in the morning." There was no answer but the quick scuffle of feet and the loud bang of a door. Comparative quiet again descended upon the house, penetrated only by an occasional sound from Brodie's bedroom, the creaking of a board, the scrape of a chair, the clatter of his boots as he discarded them upon the floor, the creak of the springs as he flung his huge bulk upon the bed. With this final sound, unbroken silence did, again, completely envelop the house.

The helplessness of her position seemed to intensify her perception and give her intuition an added force. She realised that the possibility she had dreaded had actually taken place and, in addition, that some crushing misadventure had befallen her son. She had at once sensed this latter fact from the shambling irregularity of his step and the hopeless impotence of his voice, but now her imagination ran riot, and she began to fill the torpid hush of the night with distressing sounds. She thought she heard someone weeping. Was it, she asked herself, a faint movement of air around the house or, in truth, the subdued sobbing of her son? If it were he, what rash act might not such misery induce? She pictured him, the errant but still beloved child, contemplating some desperate means of self-destruction. Immediately the sobbing turned to soft sad music which swelled with the funereal insistence of a dirge. She tried, with all her power, to compose herself to sleep but could not. In the suspended state of her mind, swinging between reality and dreams, the lament broke over her like grey waves upon a forgotten shore, mingling with the lost, desolate cries of sea-birds. She saw, amidst pouring rain and the raw, wet clods of fresh-turned clay, a rough, plank bier upon which lay a yellow coffin, saw this lowered, and the heavy clotted lumps of earth begin to fall upon it. With a low cry she twisted upon her back. Her half-conscious visions suddenly became dissipated by a fierce onset of bodily suffering. The excruciating pang, that had stricken her occasionally before, now flung itself upon her with a fierce and prolonged activity. It was unbearable. Hitherto this particular spasm had been, though of deadly intensity, only of short duration, but now her agony was continual. It was, to her, worse by far than the pangs of childbirth, and it flashed upon her that she suffered so fearfully because she had betrayed her daughter and allowed her to be cast headlong in her labour into the storm. She felt her enfeebled heart fibrillate with the stunning violence of the pain. "O God!" she whispered, "take it from me. I canna thole it longer." Yet it did not leave her but increased in strength until it was impossible for her to endure it; wildly, she struggled up, clutching her long night-gown about her. She swayed as she walked, but her anguish forced her on; she tottered in her bare feet into her son's room, and almost fell across his bed.

"Matt," she panted, "my pain is on me. It willna leave me—run—run for the doctor. Run quick, son!"

He had been hardly asleep and now he sat up, startled to be confronted by this new, terrifying apparition; she frightened him horribly, for he could discern only a long white shape that lay supinely across his bed.

"What is it?" he cried. "What do you want with me?" Then, as he perceived dimly that she was ill, he exclaimed: "What's wrong with you, Mamma?"

She could hardly breathe. "I'm dyin'. For the Lord's sake, Matt—a doctor! I canna live wi' this pain. It'll finish me if ye dinna hurry."

He leapt out of bed, his head swimming with the residue of his own recent experience, and, as a passion of remorse gripped his already prostrate spirit, he became again a frightened, remorseful boy.

"Is it my fault, Mamma?" he whined; "is it because I took your money? I'll not do it again. I'll get the watch for you too. I'll be a good boy!"

She scarcely heard him, was far beyond understanding his words.

"Run quick!" she moaned. "I canna thole this longer."

"I'll go! I'll go!" he ejaculated, in a passion of abasement. Frantically, he struggled into his trousers, flung on his jacket, and pulled on his shoes, then ran downstairs and out of the house. With long, lurching steps he raced down the middle of the road whilst the wind of his passage lifted the matted hair from off his bruised and swollen forehead. "O God!" he whispered as he ran, "am I going to kill my mother next? It's all my fault. It's me that's to blame. I haven't done right with her." In the dejection following his debauch he felt himself responsible, in every way, for his mother's sudden illness and a gross, lachrymal contortion shook him as he shouted out to the Deity wild, incoherent promises of reformation and amendment if only Mamma might be spared to him. As he careered along, with head thrown back, bent elbows pressed against his sides, his shirt widely open over his panting chest, his loose garments fluttering about him, he ran like a criminal escaping from justice, with no apparent motive but that of flight. Though his broad purpose was to reach the town, he had at first, in the misery and conflict of his thoughts, no definite objective, but now, when his breath came in short, flagging puffs and a stitch penetrated his side, making him feel that he could run no further, he bethought himself more urgently of finding a doctor. In the distress of his exhausted condition he perceived that he could not continue the whole way to Knoxhill for Dr. Lawrie.—It was too far! Suddenly he remembered that Mamma, in one of her voluminous letters, had mentioned a Dr. Renwick of Wellhall Road in a sense which he imagined to be favourable. With this in mind he swerved to the left at the railway bridge, and, after spurring on his jaded body to a further effort, he saw, to his relief, a red light outside one of the shadowy houses in the road.

Panting, he drew up at the door, searched in a flurry for the night-bell, found it, and tugged at the handle with all his pent-up fear. So violent had been his pull that, as he stood there, he heard a long-continued pealing inside the silent house; then, after a few moments, a window above him was thrown up and the head and shoulders of a man protruded.

"What is it?" called out an incisive voice from overhead.

"You're wanted at once, doctor!" cried Matthew, his anxious upturned face gleaming palely towards the other. "My mother's ill. She's been taken very bad."

"What's the nature of her trouble?" returned Renwick.

"I couldn't tell you, doctor," exclaimed Matthew brokenly. "I knew nothing about it till she just collapsed. Oh! But she's in awful pain. Come quickly."

"Where is it, then?" said Renwick, resignedly. He did not view the matter from the same unique and profoundly disturbing aspect as Matthew; it was, to him, merely a night call which might or might not be serious, the repetition of a frequent and vexatious experience—the loss of a good night's rest.

"Brodie's the name, doctor. You surely know the house at the end of Darroch Road."

"Brodie!" exclaimed the doctor; then, after a short pause, he said in an altered, interrogative tone: "Why do you come to me? Your mother is not a patient of mine."

"Oh! I don't know anything about that," cried Matthew feverishly. "She must have a doctor. Ye must come—she's suffering so much. I beg of ye to come. It's a matter of life or death."

It was a different Renwick from two years ago, one to whom success had given the power of differentiating, of refusing work he did not wish, but now he could not resist this appeal.

"I'll come, then," he said shortly. "Go on ahead of me. I'll be after you in a few moments."

Matthew sighed with relief, poured forth a babble of effusive gratitude towards the now closed window, then turning, hurriedly made his way home. Yet, when he arrived at the house, he was afraid to go in alone and stood shivering outside, in his insufficient garments, feeling that he must wait for the doctor's support before he could enter. Although he buttoned his jacket to the neck and held it close about him, the chilly night air pierced him like a knife, yet the fear that he might make some terrible discovery, that he might perhaps find Mamma lying lifeless upon his bed, kept him standing indecisively at the gate, trembling with cold and fear. He had not long to wait, however, for soon the yellow blurs of two gig lamps came into sight round the bend of the road and approached towards him with a more diffuse brilliancy. Finally they drew into the side of the road and stopped with their full glare upon him and, from the darkness behind, Renwick's voice came crisply:

"Why haven't you gone in? It's folly to stand like that after running. You'll catch your death of cold hanging about there with every pore of you open." He jumped out of his gig and, from the contrasting obscurity beyond, advanced towards the other into the circle of light. "Man alive!" he said suddenly, "what's happened to your head? Have you had a blow?"

"No!" stammered Matthew awkwardly, "I—I fell down."

"It's an ugly bruise," returned Renwick slowly, looking at the other questioningly; yet he said no more but swung his bag forward in his hand and with it motioned the other towards the house.

They went in. Stillness and blackness immediately surrounded them.

"Get a light, man, for heaven's sake," said Renwick irritably. The longer he was with Matthew the more his quick judgment estimated and condemned the other's weakness and indecision. "Couldn't you have seen to all this before I arrived? You'll need to pull yourself together if you want to help your mother."

"It's all right," whispered Matthew, "I have a box in my pocket." With a shaking hand he struck a match and lit the small gas jet in the hall, and, in this dim, wavering gleam together they moved forward, following their own flickering shadows as they mounted the stairs. The door of Mrs. Brodie's room stood half open and, from within, came the sound of quick breathing, at which Matthew broke down and sobbed: "Thank God, she's alive!"

By a miracle of heroic endeavour she had made her way back to her own room and now lay helpless, like a wounded animal that, by a last supreme effort, has reached its lair. The doctor took the matches from Matthew's useless fingers and, having lit the gas in the bedroom, guided him quietly out of the room, then closing the door, he turned and seated himself beside the figure upon the bed. His dark, sombre eyes fixed themselves upon the outlines of her ravaged figure, and as he gently felt the quick, compressible pulse and noted the sunken hollows where emaciation had already touched her, his face shadowed slightly at the suspicion already forming in his mind. Then he laid his palm upon her body softly, with a sensitive touch which registered immediately the abnormal resistance of her rigid muscles, and simultaneously the concern of his face deepened. At this moment she opened her eyes and fastened them appealingly upon his, then whispered, slowly:

"You've come!" Her words and her regard recognised him as her deliverer. He altered his expression, adapting his features, the instant she looked at him, to an air of kind and reassuring confidence.

"It hurts you here," he indicated gently, by a pressure of his hand, "This is the place."

She nodded her head. It was wonderful to her that he should immediately divine the seat of her pain; it invested him with a miraculous and awe-inspiring power; his touch at once seemed healing and his gently moving hand became a talisman which would discover and infallibly reveal the morbid secret of her distress. Willingly she submitted her racked body to his examination, feeling that here was one in whom lay an almost divine power to make her well.

"That's better," he encouraged, as he felt her relax. "Can you let me go a little deeper—just once?" he queried. Again she nodded her head and, following his whispered injunction, tried to breathe quietly, whilst his long, firm fingers sent shivers of pain pulsating through her. "That was splendid!" He thanked her with a calm consideration. "You are very brave." Not by so much as the flicker of his eyelids could she have discerned that, deep in the tissues of her body, he had discovered nodules of a wide-rooted growth which he knew to have progressed far beyond the aid of any human skill. "How long have you had trouble?" he asked casually. "Surely this is not the first attack you've had?"

With difficulty she spoke.

"No! I've had it for a long time, off and on, doctor, but never for such a spell as this. The pain used to go away at once, but this one is a long time in easin'. It's better, mind you, but it hasna gone."

"You've had other symptoms—surely, Mrs. Brodie," he exclaimed, his speaking eye conveying a meaning beyond his simple words. "You must have known you were not right. Why did you not see about it sooner?"

"I knew well enough," she answered, "but I seemed never to have the time to bother about myself." She made no mention of her husband's intolerance as she added: "I just let it gang on. I thought that in time it would go away "

He shook his head slowly in a faint reproof, saying:

"You've neglected yourself sadly I'm afraid, Mrs. Brodie. It may mean that you'll be laid up in bed for a little. You must make up your mind for a rest—that's what you've needed for a long time. Rest and no worry!"

285

"What's wrong with me, then," she whispered. "It's—it's nothing serious?"

He raised himself from the bed and surveyed her kindly.

"What did I say about worrying," he replied. "I'm coming again to-morrow for a fuller examination, when you have no pain. Just now you are going to have a good sleep. I've something here to give you relief."

"Can you ease me?" she murmured weakly. "I couldna bear yon again."

"You'll have no more of that," he comforted her. "I'll see to it." She watched him silently as he picked up his bag, opened it and produced a small phial from which he measured some drops carefully into a glass; then, as he added some water and turned to her again, she placed her worn hand on his and said, movingly: "You're so kind to me. It's no wonder your name's on a' bodies' tongues. I canna but thank you for your goodness in coming to me to-night, and thank you I do with all my heart."

"You drink this, then," he murmured, gently pressing her dry, calloused fingers. "It's the very thing for you."

She took the glass with all the sublime trust of a young child and drained it to the dark dregs, forced even a faint, tragic smile to her pale lips as she whispered:

"That was bitter, doctor. It maun be good medicine."

He smiled back at her reassuringly.

"Now rest," he ordained. "You need a good long sleep"; and, with her hand still in his, he sat down again beside her, waiting whilst the opiate took effect. His presence reassured her by its benign, magnetic power; the talisman that she clasped as though she feared to relinquish it, comforted her; occasionally her eyes would open to regard him gratefully. Then her pupils contracted slowly, the drawn lines of her features became erased, drowsily she murmured:

"God bless you, doctor. 'Twas you saved my Mary's life, and ye'll make me better too. Come to me again—please." Then she slept.

Slowly he disengaged his hand from her now flaccid grasp, repacked his bag, and stood gazing at her dormant form. His face, wiped clean of its protecting film of sanguine assurance, was heavy with a sad knowledge, mingled with a pensive, human sympathy. He remained motionless for a moment, then he covered her more warmly with the bedclothes, lowered the gas, and went out of the room.

At the foot of the stairs Matt was awaiting him, his pale, apprehensive countenance shiny with the blanched pallor of a sickly moon.

"How is she?" he asked in a low tone. "Is she better?"

"She is out of pain now, and sleeping," answered Renwick. "That was the immediate necessity for your mother." He looked directly at the other, wondering how much he could tell him.

"Where is your father?" he asked, finally. "I feel I ought to see him."

Matthew's glance wilted, his bruised eyes fell downwards, his body moved uneasily as he whispered:

"He's asleep in bed. I don't want to disturb him. No! we better not wake him. It wouldn't do any good."

Renwick's face became stern at the other's abject look. What manner of house was this? he asked himself, and what manner of people? The mother, the son, yes, even that poor child Mary, all were terrified of the one omnipotent being, the master of the house, this outrageous Brodie.

"I do not know," he said at length, enunciating his words with cold distinctness, "whether it will be desirable for me to continue the conduct of this case, but you may tell your father that I shall call to see him to-morrow."

"Is she going to be bad for long, then?" mumbled Matthew.

"For about six months at the outside."

"What a long time!" said Matt, slowly. "She does all the work. How will we manage in the house without her?"

"You will have to manage," said the doctor, severely. "And high time it is that you started to learn."

"What way?" asked Matthew stupidly.

"Your mother is dying of an incurable, internal cancer. She will never get out of that bed again. In six months she will be in her grave."

Matt collapsed as if the other had struck him; weakly, he sat down upon the stairs, Mamma dying! Only five hours ago she had been running after him, had served him with a delicate meal cooked by her own hands, but now she lay stricken upon a bed from which she would never arise. With his head bowed upon his hands he did not see the doctor go out or hear the sound of the closing door. Prostrated by grief and remorse he looked, not forward, but backward; his mind, swayed by memory, roamed through the whole period of his life; his vivid recollection strayed through all the pathways of the past. He felt the tender petting of her hands, the caress of her cheek, the touch of her lips upon his brow. He saw her coming to his room as he lay petulantly on his bed, heard her say soothingly: "Here's something nice for you, son." Her features appeared before him in every expression, coaxing, pleading, wheedling, but all bearing the same indefinable stamp of love for him. Then he saw her face finally composed in the calm, complacent rigidity of death, and in its serenity he still observed upon the pale lips the smiling tenderness which she had always shown to him.

Alone on the stairs he broke down, and whispered to himself, again and again:

"Mamma! Mamma! ye were aye so good to me!"

XI

"WHERE's my hot water?" shouted Brodie. "Hot water! My shaving water!" He stood upon the landing outside his room, dressed in his shirt and trousers, bawling to the regions below. For the first time since he could remember, his shaving water was not ready for him at his door at the precise second when he required it; he had, with the established action of habit, bent down to lift the jug and there had been no jug for him to lift. At this unprecedented and atrocious evidence of neglect, amazement had immediately given way to a sense of personal affront which had added to the bitter temper in which he had arisen from bed. This morning he had awakened to a different perception of the incidents of the previous night, and on turning over the matter in his mind, had slowly become infuriated to think that his son had stumbled on his intrigue with Nancy, had discovered the meeting-place at the house in College Street. Resentment that such a weakling as Matt should have dared to interfere with the manner of his life made him forget the danger which he had survived; the unusual incident of the shooting faded into the realm of the unreal and it was the interference with his pleasure which now aroused his bitter anger. His head felt stuffed from the heaviness of his sleep; the ever-present worry of his failing business, lying perpetually in the background to greet him when he awoke, added to his bitter moody vexation; and now, when he wanted especially to get shaved and freshened up in order to adjust his tangled thoughts, he could not obtain his hot water. It was always the same, he told himself; a man could never get what he wanted in this infernal house, and, with the full force of a legitimate grievance, he bellowed out once more: "Water! Bring it up at once! Damn it all, am I to stand here all day cooling my heels on your pleasure! Water, confound you!"

Nothing happened! To his bewilderment, Mamma did not come panting up the stairs in a paroxysm of abasement and haste, with the familiar steaming jug in her hand and a quivering apology upon her lips. An unusual quiet prevailed below. He sniffed with dilated nostrils like an angry bull scenting the wind, but could discern no appetising smell of cooking ascending from the kitchen. With a snort, he was about to plunge downstairs to make his wants known more forcibly, when suddenly the door of Matt's room opened and, in response to the muffled sound of a parting injunction, Nessie came out and timidly advanced towards her father.

His anger moderated at the sight of her, the frown faded from his forehead, the bitter twist of his lips softened slightly. The inevitable effect of her presence was to soften the harshness of his nature, and it was, indeed, for this reason she had been selected to break the news to him.

"Father," she said diffidently, "Mamma's not up this morning."

"What!" he cried, as though hardly able to believe his ears, "not up yet? Still in her bed at this hour?"

Nessie nodded.

"It's not her fault though, father," she murmured placatingly. "Don't blame her—she's not well. She tried to get up but she couldn't move."

Brodie growled. He knew she was lazy, malingering, that the whole affair was a subterfuge to prevent him from getting his shaving water. Then he thought of his breakfast. Who was to get him that? Abruptly he took a step towards Mamma's room to see if his presence would not make her forget her indisposition, liven her up to a more useful activity.

"Mamma was awful bad through the night," Nessie interposed. "Matt had to run out in the middle of the night and get a doctor."

He stopped dead at this new and startling information, and exclaimed, in amazed displeasure:

"The doctor! What way was I not told? Why was I not consulted about this? Is everything to be done in this house over my head, without telling me about it? Where is Matt?"

Matthew, who had been listening to the conversation through the half-open door, emerged slowly upon the landing. From his streaked, haggard face he looked as if he had not slept and now he regarded his father uncomfortably in the broad light of day. Still, Nessie had done her part in imparting the petrifying news; it would be easier for him to explain.

"Why did ye not tell me about this—this affair, sir?" repeated Brodie fiercely. He refused to refer to it directly as an illness; in his opinion the whole thing was a fabrication against his comfort, a conspiracy to annoy him. "Why did you not come to me first?"

"I didn't want to disturb you, father," mumbled Matt. "I thought you would be asleep."

"You're gey considerate o' me all of a sudden," Brodie sneered "You're not always so solicitous about my health, are ye?" He paused significantly and added:

"Ye brought Lawrie into the house—well? what did he say about her?"

"It wasn't him," replied Matthew humbly, "I couldn't get him father. It was Renwick that came."

A thrill of anger ran through Brodie's frame.

"What!" he roared, "Ye brought that snipe to my house. What were ye thinking about, you fool! Do ye not know him and me are sworn enemies. Of course he would put Mamma to her bed. Certainly!" he jeered, "I suppose he wants to keep her there for a week. I suppose we've a' been killin' her here. I've no doubt it'll be chicken and champagne ordered for her now, whilst we've got to scrint to pay his bills."

"Oh! father," entreated Matthew, "I don't think so. He said it was —it was really serious."

"Bah!" snarled Brodie, "there's nothing I wouldna put past a thing like him—and you're as bad for lettin' him in here behind my back. I'll pay ye for that as well. That's something else I owe ye."

"Anyway," faltered Matt, "he said—he said he would come to examine her more thoroughly this morning—that he would be seein' you."

"So!" said Brodie. He stood silent, his lips drawn back in an ugly sneer. Renwick was coming to his house this morning, was he? To start, maybe, a course of daily visits, thinking, no doubt, that with a soft, spineless creature like Mamma, he would have a grand, imaginary invalid to play about with. Brodie's fist clenched involuntarily, as it did always when a powerful resolution moved him, and he gritted his teeth together. "I'll wait on him myself," he said aloud, in a tone of concentrated animosity. "I'll see what he has to say for himself. I'll surprise him. It'll not be her that he'll see, but me."

Then, after a moment during which he gazed ahead of him into space, he turned.

"Nessie," he said, "you go and get your father some hot water. Take care not to scald yourself, pettie! Then get that old mother o' mine up. She maun get some kind o' breakfast made for us. If Mamma can lounge in her bed there's others that have work to do. Off you go now," and, patting her thin shoulders, he went back again into his bedroom.

The hot water arrived quickly and he began to perform the usual routine of his morning toilet. But his thoughts were not upon what he did. Every now and then he would stop short, his eye, glooming into space, would kindle with an angry fire and he would toss his head fiercely, contemptuously.

"He would keep my wife in bed," he muttered angrily, taking it now as a deliberate hit at him by Renwick that his wife should be in bed. "The infernal impudence of him. I'll learn him, though! I'll teach him to interfere with me again!"

Ever since the terrible illness of his daughter, he had borne Renwick a bitter grudge for the aspersions made during that memorable interview when he had refused to visit and assist his daughter in the crisis of her pneumonia. A fulminating antagonism now flared inside him as he considered, in advance, all the cutting insults he would fling at the other. Not for a moment did it occur to him that he should visit his wife; she was an insignificant pawn amongst the movements of this affair, and when he had dealt successfully with Renwick she would unques tionably get up and cook his dinner—an extra good dinner, too, it had better be, to compensate for her defection of the morning.

"Yes! I'll settle him," he muttered, repeatedly, to himself. "I'll chuck his fee in his face and tell him to shift out o' my house."

He could scarcely swallow his breakfast for the surge of his resentment; not that the meal was tempting, in any case. The porridge was singed and watery and, gloomily, he looked at his old mother, with her skirt kirtled round her waist above her striped petticoat, as she made a great commotion of her preparations.

"These porridge are wasted," he flung at her moodily. "They're not fit for pigs to eat."

Everything was wrong. The toast was soft and limp; his tea—he was obliged to accept this instead of his favourite coffee—was weak and made with water which had not reached the boiling point; his egg was like leather and his bacon like cinders.

"She'll need to get up!" he exclaimed aloud. "I can't stand this kind of thing. This meat is enough to poison a man."

The dirty fireplace stared at him, his boots were unbrushed, he had cut himself whilst shaving; flaming, he heaved himself up from the table and sat down in his chair to wait for Renwick. His eye followed with disgust the senile, inept movements of his mother, his ears were jarred by the clatter of a breaking dish which came to him from the scullery. Then, perceiving that Nessie hung about the room, he sent her sharply off to school. She was at least an hour late, and had hoped in the rarity of the occasion to be overlooked, or perhaps excused, but he ordered her to go and, without attempt at protest, she departed. Matthew did not appear but remained invisible upstairs. No sound was heard from Mamma.

Brodie could not settle. He looked at the clock, saw that it was half-past ten, became aware that he was at least an hour late for business, that his shop would be standing open, empty, untended, with only his stupid, careless boy to gape uselessly at any person who might come in; then he reflected bitterly that his absence was of little consequence, that actually it did not matter, so few people did come into his business now.

He got up and restlessly moved about. The kitchen seemed somehow unfamiliar to him in this light; disturbed in his routine, he felt everything strange and unusual about him. The infringement of his daily custom, following so closely upon the unnatural events of the preceding night, gave to him a sensation of monstrous unreality which baffled his mediocre comprehension, and the irritation produced by this puzzled perplexity served like fuel to feed his flaming anger further. Restless as a caged tiger he paced up and down the lobby. The longer he was obliged to wait the more his resentment swelled until, as if in an endeavour to hasten Renwick's arrival, he went into the parlour and gazed fretfully out of the window. Then the thought struck him that the doctor might see his peering face and take it as a sign of weakness upon his part, and at the hateful idea he drew away violently from the window and returned to the kitchen where he forced himself again into his chair, forced himself to a semblance of control. Outwardly impassive, but inwardly seething, he waited, the only sign of his hot impatience the quick action of his foot as it made a ceaseless, tapping movement through the empty air.

At eleven o'clock the door-bell rang. Like a runner who has long awaited the sound of the start, to unleash his restrained store of energy, Brodie leaped out of his chair, strode, himself, to the front door and with a defiant, sweeping gesture threw it wide to the wall. His huge bulk filled the opening, blocking the passage into the house.

"Well! what is it?" he growled. "What do ye want?"

Dr. Renwick stood upon the door-step, dispassionately immaculate in his well-fitting morning coat, and dignified by the background of his man, his well-groomed cob, and smart gig. Secure now in the possession of his large and lucrative practice, he made not the slightest motion towards coming in, but paused appreciably before replying pleasantly:

"Ah! Mr. Brodie, himself, this morning I see!"

"Never mind me," said Brodie loweringly. "What do ye want here?"

"Really," said Renwick tranquilly, "you are the epitome of courtesy. You have not altered since our last meeting—at least not for the better."

"Your purpose, sir?" breathed Brodie heavily. "Don't flash your glib tongue at me. Answer me straight."

"Well! Since you are so blunt I will be equally so. I came last night at the urgent request of your son, and rather against my inclination, to see your wife, and despite your pretence of ignorance I am convinced that you know I was here." He paused and negligently flicked his sleeve with his glove before continuing. "This morning I had proposed to pay a final visit"—he emphasised deeply the word final—"in order to confirm, by a further examination, the melancholy diagnosis which I made last night."

Brodie glowered at him. Renwick's aloof imperturbability infuriated him infinitely more than any display of furious rage would have done. That, he could meet with equal violence. But his clumsy wit was as useless against this quick coolness of mind as a bludgeon against a flashing rapier; he was pricked in a dozen places before he could swing the heavy weapon of his reply.

The other had, indeed, almost disarmed him by the assertion that he proposed to make no further calls, and he had aroused Brodie's attention by the veiled implication of his reference to Mamma's condition.

"What are ye makin' out to be wrong wi' her, then?" he sneered, unconsciously changing his attitude. "She's a graund subject for the bed."

Renwick raised his eyebrows delicately, without speaking, a slight gesture which had, nevertheless, the immediate effect of making the other feel the exceeding bad taste of his remark. Raging at this unspoken contempt Brodie rushed on to his inevitable resort when all else failed him—the descent to personalities.

"Don't mock at me like that with your creashy smirk," he cried. "It doesna improve the look of your ugly face, anyway."

Renwick continued to look at him dispassionately. Most men, from their physical stature, were compelled to look upwards to James Brodie and Brodie revelled in this fact; it gave him a sense of superiority and power to stand over a man. Renwick, however, was fully as tall as he, and from the slight eminence of the outer porch, he reversed the usual order of things, and he, instead, looked down upon Brodie.

"I shall not waste my time here further," he said at last, coldly. "If you are not a busy man I am. In your state of mind you are not amenable to reason. You have a delusion of grandeur which makes you wish everyone to be in awe of you. The unfortunate members of your family are, no doubt, afraid of you, but I, happily, am not! Understand that clearly if you can. And now, good morning to you!" He turned on his heel and was about to descend the steps when the other caught hold of his arm. "Wait! Wait!" shouted Brodie. The interview was not proceeding as he had anticipated, for he had visioned himself grudgingly permitting Renwick to have access to the house after he had been scraped and bowed to, after his offended dignity had been suitably appeased. In his heart he felt he must know what the doctor thought of his wife, and though he had desired, first of all, to make Renwick feel like a paid servant who could be discharged contemptuously with his fee, he did not wish to be left completely ignorant of Mamma's condition.

"Don't go like that," he cried. "Ye havena told me what's wrong wi' my wife. What are ye paid for if ye can't tell me what you came here for last night? You'll have to justify yourself in some way."

The other showed him a coldly contemptuous profile.

"The question of fee has not arisen, so far as I am aware. As to the other matter, I have already informed you that I shall give you my definite diagnosis only after a further and internal examination"; and he shook off Brodie's detaining hand and made to resume his exit.

"Damn it all, then," cried Brodie suddenly. "Come in and do what ye want. Since ye are here we may as well make use of ye."

Renwick came back slowly, and with a maddening suavity he said:

"Since you beg of me to come back I shall do so, but understand this, it is only for your wife's sake"; then he pushed past the bulky form before him and quickly mounted the stairs.

Brodie, fuming and nonplussed, was left standing in the hall. He bent his brows angrily, rubbed his chin indecisively, stretched out his hand to shut the front door, then refrained from shutting it, as the thought crossed his insulted mind that it would amount almost to subservience for him to close the door for Renwick.

"Let him shut the door for himself," he muttered. "Anyway he'll not be long. He'll soon be out again, and then it'll be for good." He gazed moodily out of the open door at the doctor's spanking turn-out at his gate, his dark envious eye noting the fine legs of the cob, its muscled shoulders, its supple arched neck. He estimated clearly the money which lay in the splendid animal, in the sound coach-built gig, in the man's smart livery, even in the cockaded hat which sat jauntily upon his head, and this tangible vision of the other's prosperity was like gall to him. With a jerk he withdrew his gaze, began to pace up and down the hall. "Will he never come down?" he asked himself. "What does he think he's doin' up there a' this time?"

He reflected impatiently on what must be taking place upstairs, writhed at the thought of what the nature of the examination might be. Although he had finished with his wife in every aspect of his sexual life, and had indeed cast her from him in contumely, the thought of another man interfering, as he mentally worded it, with her made him furious. Although his wife was old, jaded, and worn out, yet she was still his property, his chattel, his possession. He would never need the possession nor use the chattel, yet she must remain wholly and subserviently his. That was his mentality and, had he lived in another age, he would surely have destroyed each mistress when he had tired of her in the perverted fear that she would fall into another's hands. Ridiculous and abominable thoughts now began to torment him.

"By God!" he cried out, "if he doesna come down I'll go up myself."

But he did not go up! Something in Renwick's cold disdain had chilled his animal mind and although, of course, he feared no one, yet the temper of the other's spirit so far surpassed his that it surmounted and even subdued him. Always, a superior, fearless mind aroused in him a faint, lowering distrust, the prelude to hatred, to an unbridled antipathy that weakened, to his undoing such reason as usually controlled his motives. And so he chafed and stamped about in the hall until, when he had been made to wait a full half-hour, he did at last hear Renwick come down. Watching the doctor descend the stairs slowly, he felt, uncontrollably, that he must voice his severe displeasure.

"Did you say you were busy?" he girned. "What a time you were."

"Not too long, surely, for a last visit," said Renwick impassively.

"What's wrong with her then?" shot out Brodie. "I've no doubt you've been puttin' some grand, fancy ideas in her head all this time."

"Which reminds me," continued the doctor tranquilly, ignoring the interjection, "that you must arrange for your own medical man to be called in without fail to-morrow. If you wish, I will communicate

294

with him. Your wife must have constant and unremitting attention."

Brodie stared at him incredulously, then laughed sneeringly.

"Does she need a nurse next?" he exclaimed.

"Your good wife most assuredly does. That is," Renwick added quietly, "if you can afford it."

Brodie drew from the other's words a humiliating imputation.

"Be careful," he breathed. "I asked you what was wrong with her."

"Advanced, incurable cancer of the womb," said Renwick slowly.

Brodie's jaw dropped at the dreadful word. "Cancer," he echoed. "Cancer!" Despite his iron control his cheek blenched slightly; but he fought to recover himself.

"It's a lie!" he exclaimed loudly. "You're trying to get even with me. You're tryin' to frighten me with a demned lie."

"I wish it were a lie, but I have satisfied myself, beyond all shadow of a doubt, that my diagnosis is correct," said Renwick sadly. "There is nothing to be done for the poor soul but to alleviate her pain—and she will never leave the bed she now lies on."

"I don't believe you," snarled Brodie. "I don't give that for your opinion." He snapped his fingers in the other's face like the crack of a whip, caring, not so much for the dreadful affliction which might lie upon his wife, as for the humiliating position into which he imagined the doctor was trying to force him. "I'll have better advice than yours," he cried. "I'll have my own physician. He's head and shoulders above you in skill. If she's ill he'll cure her!"

Renwick inclined his head.

"I hope sincerely that he does, and I must tell you," he added severely, "that in medicine the basis of any treatment is rest and freedom from anxiety."

"Thank ye for nothing," cried Brodie roughly. "Here! what is your fee for a' this tarradiddle?—what do we pay you for tellin' her to lie in bed?" and he plunged his hand into his trousers pocket.

The doctor, on his way to the door, turned and said, with a penetrating look which revealed the fullness of his knowledge of Brodie's unhappy financial position:

"Really, no! not from you, in your present circumstances. I couldn't think of it." He paused and added: "Remember, I shall not call again unless I'm sent for"—then he was gone.

Brodie, his fists clenched, stared impotently at the retreating figure. Only when the gig was out of sight did a suitable retort occur to him.

"Send for him again," he cried. "He'll never come into this house again! The infernal snipe! I don't believe a word of his damned lies. A pack of lies," he repeated, as if to convince himself.

As he stood in the lobby he did not know what to do, but through his indecision, despite his assumed contempt of Renwick's opinion, the word cancer kept beating into his brain with a dire significance. Cancer of the womb! It seemed to him the most horrid manifestation of the dread disease. Although he had violently professed unbelief, now a seeping tide of conviction swept over him; bit by bit he began to piece evidence together which was in itself conclusive. Her ailing look had not, then, been assumed—those secretive ways not an indecency, a reproach to him, but only a piteous necessity.

Suddenly a devastating thought struck him! Had the scourge been passed to him? Knowing nothing of the laws of contagion or infection, still he wondered if he himself might be contaminated, and immediately the recollection of her previous nearness to him, of past contacts, rushed over him, making him feel unclean. Involuntarily he glanced over his muscular body as if it might reveal already some sinister index of the malady. His glance reassured him, but, following the thought, came, inevitably, a small wave of resentment against his wife. "Could she no' have watched herself better?" he muttered, as if she were in measure responsible for her own calamity.

He shook himself and braced out his barrel chest to rid himself of all the oppressive, conflicting ideas within him. Without realising it, he wandered into the cold, unused parlour and sat down in the inhospitable room where he again set himself to decide what he must do. Although he must, of course, justify his threat to Renwick and call in Dr. Lawrie, already he knew it to be useless. This had been merely the spiteful taunt of his inferior mind and, in his inmost heart, he knew Lawrie's skill to be far below the other's. He realised, too, that he must go up to his wife, but he had no heart for this duty, for under the stigma of this awful distemper she had become to him even more unwelcome and repugnant than before. He shrank equally from her and from his onerous duty to visit her. Shifting his mind quickly from her he began to consider the domestic situation. What a mess, he thought; and not unlike the state of his business! A look that was almost piteous in its perplexity slowly invaded the hard, massive face, softening its harshness, driving out the bitterness, lifting the frown from the brow. But that compassionate expression was for himself! He was thinking, not of his wife but of himself, sympathising with himself, pitying James Brodie for the troubles that beset him.

"Ay," he muttered, gently, "it's a good job you're a man amongst a' this injustice. Ye have a wee thing or two to thole." With these words he rose and ascended the stairs as slowly and heavily as if clambering up a ladder; outside Mamma's room he paused, drew himself up, and went in. She had heard him coming up and already was turning to greet him with a pleading, ingratiating smile.

"I'm sorry, father," she immediately murmured. "I tried hard to get up but it was just beyond me. I'm real sorry ye've been so upset. Did ye get a decent breakfast?"

He seemed to be seeing her with new eyes, observing now that her face looked ghastly, with hollowed temples and jaws, that her form appeared to have become suddenly wasted. He did not know what to say. It was so long since he had addressed a kind word to her that his tongue refused to utter one, and in his hesitation he felt uncomfortable, incongruous, absurd. His motive in life was to drive, to demand, to chastise, to flagellate; he could not sympathise. He stared at her desperately.

"You're not angry, I hope, father," she said timidly, misconstruing his look. "I'll be up in a day or two. He says a bit rest is what I need. I'll see that you're not put about more than need be."

"I'm not angry, woman," he said hoarsely. Then after a pause, with an effort, he added: "Ye maun lie still till we see what Dr. Lawrie can do for ye."

Immediately she flinched.

"Oh! no! no! father," she cried, "it's not him I want. I like Dr. Renwick so much I feel he'll make me well. He's so kind and so clever. His medicine made me feel better at once."

He gritted his teeth impotently as her protests rang on endlessly. Previously he would have rammed his intention in her teeth and left her to swallow it as best she liked, but now, in the novelty of her condition, and indeed, of his, he knew not what to say. He resolved that she would have Lawrie, that he would send him in, but modifying his retort with an effort, he exclaimed:

"We'll see then! We'll see how ye get on."

Mrs. Brodie gazed at him doubtfully, feeling that if he took Renwick from her she would surely die. She had loved this doctor's serene assurance, had expanded under his unusual gentleness. Unconsciously she was drawn to him as the one who had attended her daughter, and he had already spoken to her of Mary, in terms that paid tribute to the patience and fortitude of her child under the trials of an almost mortal illness. Now she sensed at once that her husband was antagonistic to her desire, but she knew better than to argue; hastily, she sought to propitiate him.

"What are we goin' to do about you, James?" she ventured. "Ye must be looked after properly. You must have your comforts."

"I'll be all right," he managed to say. "The old lady will do her best."

"No! No!" she urged, "I've been thinkin' out plans all morning. I must get up as soon as I'm able, but in the meantime, could we not get a girl in, someone who would get your meals as ye like them. I could tell her—tell her just what to do—how to make the broth as ye like it, and how to season your porridge, and the airin' o' your flannels and——"

He interrupted her by a definite, intolerant shake of his head. Could she not realise that it cost money to keep a servant? Did she think he was rolling in wealth? He wanted to say something crushing that would shut off her silly twaddle. "Does she think I'm a helpless wean, the way she's going on?" he asked himself. "Does she think the house couldna go on without her?" Yet he knew that if he opened his mouth to speak he would blunder into some blunt rejoinder—the niceties of expression were beyond him—so he closed his lips and maintained a chafing silence.

She looked at him closely, encouraged by his silence, wondering fearfully if she dared to venture the subject nearest her heart. His unaccustomed placidity made her brave and, with a sudden gasp, she exclaimed:

"James! To mind the house now—could we not—could we not have Mary back?"

He recoiled from her. His assumed serenity was not proof against this, and losing control of himself, he shouted:

"No! we will not. I warned ye not even to lift her name. She'll not come back here till she crawls on her bended knees. Me *ask* her to come back! Never! Not even if ye lay on your death-bed."

The last word rang through the room like a trumpet call and, slowly, a frightened look came into Mamma's eyes.

"As you say, James," she trembled. "But please dinna mention that awfu' word. I'm not wantin' to die yet. I'm goin' to get better ye ken. I'll be up soon."

Her optimism exasperated him. He did not realise that the habits of half a lifetime had ingrained in her the feeling that she must always exhibit in his presence this spurious cheerfulness, nor did he understand that the desire to get up arose from an ever-pricking urge to fulfil the innumerable demands that harassed her.

"The doctor didna say much," she continued propitiatingly, "beyond that it was a kind of inflammation. When that goes down I'm sure I'll get my strength up in no time. I canna bear this lyin' in bed. I've got so many things to think of." She was worrying about the payment of her debt. "Just a wee bits o' things that nobody would bother about but me," she added hastily, as if she feared he might read her mind.

He looked at her gloomily. The more she glossed over her illness the more he became convinced that she would not survive it; the more she spoke of the future the more futile she became in his eyes. Would she be as inept when confronted by death as she had been in the face of life? He tried desperately to find something to say; what could he say to this doomed but unconscious woman?

And now his manner began to puzzle her. At first she had assumed gratefully that his quiet had betokened a forbearance in the face of her sickness, a modification of the same feeling which made her move throughout the house on tiptoes when she had nursed him, on such rare occasions as he had been ill. But a curious quality in his regard now perturbed her, and suddenly she queried:

"The doctor didna say anything about me to you, did he? He didna tell you something that he keepit from me? He seemed a long time downstairs before I heard him drive away."

He looked at her stupidly. His mind seemed, from a long distance off, to consider her question slowly, detachedly, without succeeding in arriving at an appropriate answer.

"Tell me if he did, James," she cried apprehensively. "I would far rather know. Tell me." The whole of her appearance had altered, her demeanour, from being calm and sanguine, had become agitated, disturbed.

He had come into the room with no fixed motive as to how he should deal with her. He had no sympathy, no tact, and now no ingenuity to lie to her. He felt confused, trapped, like a blundering animal before the frail, raddled creature on the bed. His temper flared suddenly.

"What do I care what he thinks!" he found himself saying, harshly. "A man like him would say ye were dyin' if ye had a toothache. He knows nothing—less than nothing. Haven't I told ye I'm goin' to get Lawrie to ye." His angry, ill-chosen words struck her like a thunderbolt. Instantly she knew, knew with a fearful conviction that her illness was mortal. She shivered, and a film of fear clouded her eyes like a faint, shadowy harbinger of the last, opaque pellicle of dissolution.

"Did he say I was dying then?" she quavered.

He glared at her, furious at the position into which he had been forced. Angry words now poured from his mouth.

"Can ye not shut up about that runt," he cried. "Ye wad think he was the Almighty to hear you. He doesna ken everything. If he canna cure ye there's other doctors in Levenford! What's the use o' makin' such a fuss about it a'?"

"I see. I see now," she whispered. "I'll no' make any more fuss about it now." Quiescent upon the bed she gazed at him and behind him; her gaze seemed to transcend the limits of the narrow room and focus itself fearfully upon a remoteness beyond. After a long pause she said, as though to herself: "I'll not be muckle loss to you, James! I'm gey and worn out for you." Then she whispered, faintly: "But oh! Matt, my own son, how am I to leave you?"

Silently she turned to the wall and to the mystery of her thoughts, leaving him standing with a sullen, glouting brow, behind her. For a moment he looked lumpishly at her flaccid figure, then, without a word, he went heavily out of the room.

XII

A SUDDEN burst of vivid August sunshine, penetrating the diaphanous
veil hung by the last drops of a passing shower, sprayed the High
Street with a misty radiance, whilst the brisk breeze which had thrown
the fleecy, wool-pack clouds from off the pathway of the sun, now
moved the rain slowly onwards in a glow of golden haze.

"Sunny-shower! Sunny-shower!" chanted a group of boys, as they
raced along the drying street on their way to bathe in the Leven.

"Look," cried one of them, importantly, "a rainbow!" and he
pointed upwards to a perfect arc which, like the thin beribboned handle
of a lady's basket, spanned glitteringly the entire length of the street.
Everyone paused to look at the rainbow. They lifted their eyes above
the drab level of the earth and gazed upwards towards the sky, nodded
their heads, smiled cheerfully, exclaimed with delight, shouted to each
other across the street.

"It's a braw sight!"

"Look at the bonnie colours!"

"It puts auld Couper's pole in the shade, richt enough." The sudden,
unexpected delight of the phenomenon cheered them, elevating their
minds unconsciously to a plane that lay above the plodding commonplace of their existence, and, when they looked downwards again, the
vision of that splendid, sparkling arch remained, inspiring them for the
day before them.

Out of the Winton Arms into this bright sunshine came James Brodie.
He saw no rainbow, but walked dourly, with his hat pulled forward, his
head down, his hands deeply in his outside pockets, seeing nothing, and,
though a dozen glances followed his progress, saluting no one. As he
plodded massively, like a stallion, over the crest of the street he felt
that "they"—the peering inquisitive swine—were looking at him with
prying eyes, knew, though he ignored it, that he was the focus of their
attention. For weeks past it had appeared to him that he, and the
moribund shop that he tenanted, had been the nidus of a strange and
unnatural attention in the Borough, that townspeople, some that he
knew and some whom he had never seen before, strolled deliberately
outside his business to stare openly, curiously, purposely, into the depths
within. From the inner obscurity he imagined that these empty, prying
glances mocked him; he had cried out to himself: "Let them look then,
the glaikit swine! Let them gape at me for all they're worth. I'll give
them something to glower about." Did they guess, he now asked himself bitterly, as he strode along, that he had been celebrating—celebrating the last day in his business? Did they know that, with a ferocious
humour, he had just now swallowed a liberal toast to the wreck of his
affairs? He smiled grimly to think that to-day he ceased to be a hatter,

that shortly he would walk out of his office for the last time, and bang the door behind him finally and irrevocably.

Paxton, from across the road, whispered to his neighbour:

"Look, man, quick, there's Brodie," and together they stared at the strong figure on the opposite pavement. "Man! I'm sorry for him somehow," continued Paxton; "his come down doesna fit him weel."

"Na!" agreed the other, "he's the wrang man to be ruined."

"For a' his strength and power," resumed Paxton, "there's something blunderin' and helpless about him. It's been a fearfu' blow to him. Do ye mark how his shoulders have bowed, as if he had a load on his back."

His neighbour shook his head.

"I canna see it like that! He's been workin' for this for a lang, lang time. What I canna stand about the man in his black, veecious pride that grows in spite o' a' things. It's like a disease that gets waur and waur, and the source o't is so downright senseless. If he could but see himself now, as others see him, it micht humble him a wee."

Paxton looked at the other peculiarly.

"I wouldna talk like that about him," he said slowly, "it's a chancy thing even to whisper like that about James Brodie, and at this time more than ordinar'. If he heard ye he would turn on ye and rend ye."

"He's not listenin' to us," replied the other, a trifle uncomfortably; then he added, "He has drink in him again, by the look o' him. Adversity micht bring some men to their senses, but it's drivin' him the other way round."

They both turned again and glanced at the slowly retreating figure. After a pause Paxton said:

"Have ye heard, lately, how his wife goes on?"

"Not a word! From what I can make out not a body sees her. Some leddies from the kirk took up a wheen jellies and the like for her, but Brodie met them at the gate and sent them a' richt about turn. Ay, and waur nor that, he clashed the guid stuff they had brought about their ears."

"Do ye say so! Nobody maun tamper wi' him or his," exclaimed Paxton; then he paused and queried: " 'Tis cancer, is't not, John?"

"Ay! so they say!"

"What a waesome affliction!"

"Man!" replied the other, as he moved away: "it is bad but to my mind 'tis no waur than for that puir woman to be bound body and soul to a man like James Brodie."

By this time Brodie had entered his shop, his footsteps echoing loudly through the almost denuded premises where only a tithe of his stock remained, the rest having been disposed of through the interest and consideration of Soper. The evanescent boy had finally vanished and he was alone in the barren, unhappy, defeated place, where the faint gossamer of a spider's web, spun across the remaining boxes on the shelves, mutely indicated the ebb to which his business had fallen. Now, as he stood in the midst of this dereliction, unconsciously he peopled it with the figures of the past, the past of those lordly days when he had walked with a flourish about the place, disdaining the humbler of his clients but meeting equally and agreeably all persons of importance or consequence. It seemed incomprehensible to him that they should now be merely shadows, entering only in his imagination, that he would no longer laugh and jest and talk with them in these precincts which had enclosed his daily life for twenty years. It was the same shop, he was the same man, yet slowly, mysteriously, these living beings had withdrawn from him, leaving only unhappy, unsubstantial memories. The few old customers, chiefly the country gentlepeople, who had still clung to him had seemed only to prolong the misery of his failure, and now that it was finished a vast surge of anger and sorrow invaded him. With his low forehead contracted he tried, abortively, to realise how it had been accomplished, to analyse how all this strange, unthinkable change had come about. Somehow he had permitted it! A convulsive, involuntary sigh shook his thick chest, then, as if in rage and disgust at such a weakness, he bared his lips over his pale gums, ground his teeth, and went slowly into his office. No letters, no daily paper now cumbered his desk, awaiting his disdainful attention; dust alone lay there, lay thickly upon everything. Yet, as he stood within the neglected office, like the leader of a hopeless cause when he has finally abandoned it, a faint measure of sad relief tinctured his regret, and he became aware that he now faced the worst, that the suspense of this unfair fight was at an end.

The money he had raised by mortgaging his house was finished; though he had eked this out to the last driblet his resources were now entirely exhausted. But, he reflected, he had discharged his obligations to the utmost; he owed no man a penny, and if he were ruined, he had scorned the ignominious refuge of bankruptcy. He sat down upon his chair regardless of dust, scarcely noticing, indeed, the cloud that rose about him, unheeding of the powdery layer that settled on his clothing—he had grown so careless of his person and his dress. He was unshaven, and against the dark, unkempt stubble on his face the white of his eyes glared savagely; his finger nails were ragged and bitten to the quick, his boots were unbrushed, his cravat, lacking the usual pin, was partially undone as though, desiring suddenly more liberty to breathe, he had unloosed it with a single wrench. His clothes, too, were flung untidily upon him as he had dressed that morning regardless of anything but despatch. Now, indeed, his main concern was to leave as quickly as possible a house pervaded with sudden and disturbing cries of pain, filled with disorder and confusion, with unwashed dishes and the fœtor of drugs, a house wherein he was nauseated by ill-cooked and ill-served food, and irritated by a snivelling son and an incompetent old woman. Sitting there, he plunged his hand suddenly into his inside pocket and drew out carefully a flat, black bottle, then, still staring in front of him, without viewing the bottle, he sunk his strong teeth in the cork and with a quick jerk of his thick neck withdrew the cork. The sharp, plucking report filled the silence of the room. Placing the neck of the bottle between his cupped lips he raised his elbow gradually and took a long gurgling drink, then with a sharp intake of breath over his parted teeth, he placed the bottle in front of him on the table and fixed his glance on it. Nancy had filled it for him! His eye lit up, momentarily, as though the bottle mirrored her face. She was a good one, was Nancy, an alleviation of his melancholy, the mitigation of his depression; despite his misfortunes he would never let her go; he would stick to her whatever happened. He tried to penetrate the future, to make plans, to decide what he must do; but it was impossible. The moment he set himself to think deeply his mind wandered off into the remotest and most incongruous digressions. Fleeting visions of his youth revolved before him—the smile of a boy who had been his playmate, the hot sunny wall in the crevices of which, with other boys, he had hunted for bumble bees, the smoke about his gun-barrel when he had shot his first rabbit; he heard the swish of a scythe, the purling of cushat-doves, the sharp skirling laughter of an old woman in the village.

With a shake of his head he banished the visions, took another pull at the bottle, considering deliberately the immense solace that spirits brought to him. His depression lightened, his lip curled sneeringly, and "they," the unheard critics, the antagonists ever present in his mind became more contemptible, more pitiful than ever. Then suddenly, through this new mood, a sparkling idea struck him, which as he considered it more fully, forced from him a short, derisive laugh. With the eyes of the town upon him, peering sneakingly upon his misfortunes, expecting him to slink abjectly from the scene of his ruin, he would nevertheless show them how James Brodie could face disaster. He would provide a fitting climax for his exit with a spectacle that would make their spying eyes blink. Fiercely he drained the last of the whisky, pleased that his brain had at last given him an inspiration to spur him to motion, delighted to loose the confined brooding of his mind in a definite physical activity, no matter how inordinate it might be. He arose and, sending his chair sprawling on the floor, passed into the shop where, surveying with a hostile eye the remaining boxes stacked behind the counter, he advanced upon them and began rapidly to spill their contents upon the floor. Eagerly he tumbled out hats of all descriptions. Disdaining to open the boxes calmly, his huge hands gripped them fiercely and rent the cardboard like tissue paper, furiously ripping and tearing at the boxes as though in frantic avulsion they dismembered the bodies of his dead enemies. He flung the tattered debris from him in every direction with loose, whirling movements, till the fragmentary litter filled the room and lay about his feet like fallen snow. Then, when he had thus roughly shelled each box of its contents, he gathered the pile of hats from the floor into his wide arms and, massing them together in his colossal embrace, marched triumphantly to the door of his shop. A wild exultation seized him. As the hats were useless to him, he would give them away, distribute them freely, spite his enemies next door and spoil their custom, make this noble offering of largess his last remembered action in the street.

"Here," he bawled, "who wants a hat?" The whisky had broken down the restraining barriers of his reserve and the foolish extravagance of his act seemed to him only splendid and magnificent. "It's the chance of a lifetime," he shouted, with a curl of his lip. "Come up, all you braw honest bodies, and see what I've got for ye."

It was nearly noon and the street was at its busiest. Immediately a crowd of urchins surrounded him expectantly, and outside this ring an increasing number of passing townsfolk commenced to gather, silent, the incredulous, yet nudging and glancing at each other significantly.

"Hats are cheap to-day," shouted Brodie at the pitch of his lungs. "Cheaper than you can buy them at the waxworks," he cried, with a ghastly facetiousness, hoping that they would hear the jibe next door. "I'm givin' them away! I'll make ye have them whether ye want them or no' "; and immediately he began to thrust hats upon the onlookers. It was as he had said, something for nothing, and dumbly, amazedly, they accepted the gifts that they did not desire and might never use. They were afraid to refuse, and, seeing his dominance over them he gloated, glaring at them the more, beating their eyes to the ground as they met his. A deep-buried, primitive desire in his nature was at last being fed and appeased. He was in his element, the centre of a crowd who hung upon every word, every action, who looked up to him gapingly and, he imagined, admiringly. The fearful quality in his eccentric wildness made them forbear to laugh, but gazing in awed silence, ready to fall back should he run berserk suddenly amongst them, they stood like fascinated sheep before a huge wolf.

But now the mere handing out of the hats began to pall on him and he craved for less restrained, more ungoverned action. He began, therefore, to toss the contents of his arms to the people on the outskirts of the crowd; then, from merely throwing the hats, he commenced to hurl them violently at the onlookers in the ring, hating suddenly every one of the white, vacuous faces; they became his enemies, and the more he despised them the more mercilessly he pelted them, in a growing, turbulent desire to hurt and disperse them.

"Here," he bellowed, "take them a'. I'm finished with them for good. I don't want the blasted things although they're better and cheaper than you'll get next door. Better and cheaper!" he howled over and over again. "If ye didna want them before, I'll make ye take them now."

The mob retreated under the force and accuracy of his fusillade, and as they dispersed, with back-turned, protesting faces, he followed them with long, skimming shots.

"Stop it?" he shouted sneeringly. "I'll be damned if I do. Do you not want them, that you're runnin' awa'? You're missing the chance of a lifetime."

He gloated in the commotion he was causing, and, when they were out of range, he seized a hard hat by its brim and sent it bowling down the hill where, with the full force of the following breeze, it rolled gaily like a ball in a bowling alley and finally skittled against the legs of a man walking far down the street.

"That was a good one!" cried Brodie, laughing with boisterous delight. "I aye had a grand aim. Here's another, and another." As he sent a further volley whizzing after the first shot, hats of all descriptions went madly leaping, whirling, dancing, swerving, bounding, as they pursued each other down the declivity. It was as though a hurricane had suddenly unbared the heads of a multitude; such an unparalleled and monstrous sight had never before been seen in Levenford. But at last his stock was almost exhausted, and with his final missile in his great paw, he paused selectively, weighing the last shot in his locker—a stiff, board-like strawbasher which, by reason of its shape and hardness, he felt dimly to be worthy of a definite and appropriate billet. Suddenly, out of the corner of his eye, he observed the pale, aghast face of Perry, his old assistant, peering from the adjacent doorway. He was there, was he, thought Brodie—the rat that had saved his own skin by leaving the sinking ship; the beautiful manager of the Mungo Panopticon!—In a flash he skimmed the flat projectile like a whirling quoit full at the sallow, horrified face. The hard serrated brim caught Perry full in the mouth, splintering a tooth and, as he saw the blood flow, and the terrified young man bolt back indoors, Brodie yelled with a roar of triumph at the success of his aim.

"That'll fit you to superintend the waxworks, you poor trash. That's something I've been owin' you a long time." It seemed to him the fitting and culminating achievement of a rare and remarkable display. Throwing up his arms into the air he waved them exultantly, then with an elated grin he turned again into the shop. Inside, as he gazed at the emptiness, complete but for the wreckage of the boxes, the smile on his lips stiffened slowly to a fixed, sardonic spasm; but he did not stop to allow himself to think. He walked through the scattered rubbish into his office where, in the continuance of his wild mood of destruction, be dragged out all the drawers in the desk, smashed the empty whisky bottle against the wall, and overturned the heavy desk with a single, powerful heave. Surveying the scene with a moody, wanton satisfaction, he picked up the door key from its hook beside the window, lifted his stick and, with his head in the air, went again through and out of the shop, closing the outer door behind him. This last, single action affected him, suddenly, with a sense of such absolute finality that the key in his grasp became a foolish redundancy; when he withdrew it from the lock he looked at it senselessly as it lay in his palm, then suddenly drew back, and hurled it far over the top of the building—listening intently until he heard the faint splash as it dropped into the river behind. They could get into the place how they liked, he thought bitterly; he, at any rate, was finished with it.

On his way home he still could not, or at least refused to think, remaining without even a remote idea as to the conduct of his future. He had a fine stone house, heavily mortgaged, to maintain, an old decrepit mother, an invalid wife, and a useless son to support, and a young daughter who must be educated, but beyond the fact that he was strong, with a physique powerful enough to uproot a fair-sized tree, his assets towards these responsibilities were negligible. He did not actively consider in this fashion but, the abandon of his recent mood subsided, he felt dimly the uncertainty of his position and it weighed upon him heavily. He was affected chiefly by the lack of money in his pocket, and as he neared his house and saw standing outside a familiar, high gig and bay gelding, his brow darkened. "Damn it all," he muttered, "is he in, again? How does he expect me to pay the blasted long bill he's runnin' up?" It pricked him with an irritating reminder of his circumstances to see Dr. Lawrie's equipage at his gate and, thinking to spare himself the necessity of a tedious encounter by entering the house unobserved, he was more deeply annoyed to meet Lawrie face to face at the front door.

"Just been having a peep at the good wife, Mr. Brodie," said the doctor, with an affectation of heartiness. He was a pompous, portly man with blown-out cheeks, a small, red mouth, and an insufficient chin inadequately strengthened by a grey, imperial beard. "Trying to keep her spirits up, you know; we must do all we can."

Brodie looked at the other silently, his saturnine eyes saying, more cuttingly than words: "And much good ye have done her, ye empty wind bag."

"Not much change for the better, I'm afraid," continued Lawrie hurriedly, becoming a trifle more florid under Brodie's rude stare. "Not much improvement. We're nearing the end of the chapter I fear." This was his usual stereotyped banality to indicate the nearness of death, and now he shook his head profoundly, sighed, and smoothed the small tuft on his chin with an air of melancholy resignation.

Brodie gazed with aversion at the finicking gestures of this pompous wiseacre, and though he did not regret having brought him into his house to spite Renwick, he was not deceived by his bluff manner, or by his great display of sympathy.

"Ye've been tellin' me that for a long time," he growled. "You and your chapters! I believe ye know less than onybody what's goin' to happen. I'm gettin' tired of it."

"I know! I know! Mr. Brodie," said Lawrie, making little soothing gestures with his hands, "your distress is very natural—very natural! We cannot say definitely when the unhappy event will occur. It depends so much on the reaction of the blood—that is the crux of the question—the reaction of the blood with regard to the behaviour of the corpuscles! The corpuscles are sometimes stronger than we expect. Yes! the corpuscles are sometimes marvellous in their activities," and, satisfied with his show of erudition he again stroked his moustache and looked learnedly at Brodie.

"You can take your corpuscles to hell," replied Brodie contemptuously. "You've done her as much good as my foot."

"Come now, Mr. Brodie," said Lawrie in a half-expostulating, half-placating tone, "don't be unreasonable. I'm here every day. I'm doing my best."

"Do better then! Finish her and be done wi't," retorted Brodie bitterly, and turning abruptly, he walked away and entered the house, leaving the other standing aghast, his eyes wide, his small mouth pursed into an indignant orb.

Inside his home, a further wave of disgust swept over Brodie as, making no allowance for the fact that he was earlier than usual, he observed that his dinner was not ready, and he cursed the bent figure of his mother amongst the disarray of dishes, dirty water, pots, and potato peelings in the scullery.

"I'm gettin' ower auld for this game, James," she quavered in reply. "I'm not as nimble as I used to be—and forbye the doctor keepit me back."

"Move your auld bones then," he snarled. "I'm hungry." He could not sit down amongst such chaos, and, with a sudden turn of his black mood, he decided that he would fill in the time before his meal by visiting his wife—the good wife, as Lawrie had called her—and give her the grand news of the business.

"She maun hear some time," he muttered, "and the sooner the better. It's news that'll not stand the keepin'." He had lately fallen into the habit of avoiding her room, and as he had not seen her during the last two days, she would no doubt find the unexpectedness of his visit the more delightful.

"Well!" he remarked softly, as he went into the bedroom, "you're still here I see. I met the doctor on my way in and he was gi'en us a great account o' your corpuscles o' the blood—they're uncommon strong by his report."

She did not move at his entry, but lay passive, only the flicker of her eyes showing that she lived. In the six months that had elapsed since she had been forced to take to her bed she had altered terrifyingly, and one who had not marked the imperceptible, day by day decline, the gradual shrinking of her flesh, would not have found her unrecognisable even as the ailing woman she had then appeared. Her form, beneath the light covering of the sheet, was that of a skeleton with hip bones which stuck out in a high, ridiculous protuberance; only a flaccid envelope of sagging skin covered the thin, long bones of her legs and arms, while over the framework of her face a tight, dry parchment was drawn, with cavities for eyes, nose, and mouth. Her lips were pale, dry, cracked, with little brown desiccated flakes clinging to them like scales, and above the sunken features her bony forehead seemed to bulge into unnatural, disproportioned relief. A few strands of grey hair, withered, lifeless as the face itself, straggled over the pillow to frame this ghastly visage. Her weakness was so apparent that it seemed an impossible effort for her to breathe, and from this very weakness she made no reply to his remark, but looked at him with an expression he could not read. It seemed to her that there was nothing more for him to say to wound her.

"Have ye everything ye want?" he continued, in a low tone of assumed solicitude. "Everything that might be necessary for these corpuscles o' yours? Ye've plenty of medicine anyway—plenty of choice, I see. One, two, three, four," he counted, "four different bottles o' pheesic. There's merit in variety apparently. But woman, if ye go on drinkin' it at this rate, we'll have to raise another loan frae your braw friends in Glasgow to pay for it a'."

Deep in her living eyes, which alone of her wasted features indicated her emotions, a faint wound reopened, and they filled with a look of dull pleading. Five months ago she had, in desperation, been forced to confess to him her obligation to the money-lenders and though he had paid the money in full, since then he had not for a moment let her forget the wretched matter, and in a hundred different ways, on the most absurd pretexts, he would introduce it into the conversation. Not even her present look moved him, for he was now entirely without sympathy for her, feeling that she would linger on for ever, a useless encumbrance to him.

"Ay," he continued pleasantly, "ye've proved yoursel' a great hand at drinkin' the medicine. You're as gleg at that as ye are at spendin' other folks' money." Then abruptly he changed the subject, and queried gravely: "Have ye seen your big, braw son the day? Oh! ye have, indeed," he continued, after reading her unspoken reply. "I'm real glad to hear it. I thocht he michtna have been up yet, but I see I'm wrong. He's not downstairs though. I never seem to be fortunate enough to see him these days."

At his words she spoke at last, moulding her stark lips to utter, in a weak whisper:

"Matt's been a good son to me lately."

"Well, that's only a fair return," he exclaimed judiciously. "You've been a graund mother to him. The result o' your upbringing o' him is a positive credit to you both." He paused, recognising her weakness, hardly knowing why he spoke to her thus, yet, unable to discard the habit of years, impelled somehow by his own bitterness, by his own misfortunes, he continued in a low voice: "Ye've brocht up a' your children bonnie, bonnie. There's Mary now—what more could ye wish for than the way she's turned out? I don't know where she is exactly, but I'm sure she'll be doin' ye credit nobly." Then, observing that his wife was attempting to speak, he waited on her words.

"I know where she is," she whispered slowly.

He gazed at her.

"Ay!" he answered, "ye know she's in London, and that's as much as we a' ken—as much as ye'll ever know."

Almost incredibly she moved her withered hand, that looked incapable of movement, and lifting it from the counterpane stopped him with a gesture; then, as her shrunken arm again collapsed, she said weakly, and with many tremors:

"Ye mustna be angry with me, ye mustna be angry with her. I've had a letter from Mary. She's a good girl—she still is. I see more clearly, now, than ever I did that 'twas I that didna do right by her. She wants to see me now, James, and I—I must see her quickly before I die." As she uttered the last words she tried to smile to him pleadingly, placatingly, but her features remained stiff and frigid, only her lips parted slightly in a cracked, pitiful grimace.

The colour mounted slowly to his forehead.

"She dared to write to you," he muttered, "and you dared to read it."

" 'Twas Dr. Renwick, when you stoppit him comin', that wrote to London and told her I was not—not likely to last long. He's aye had a great interest in Mary. He said to me that morning that Mary—my daughter Mary—was brave, ay, and innocent as well."

"He was a brave man himself to raise that name in my house," returned Brodie in a low, concentrated tone. He could not shout and rave at her in her present state, prevented only by some shred of compunction from turning violently upon her, but he added, bitterly: "If I had known he was interferin' like that I would have brained him before he went out the door."

"Don't say that, James," she murmured. "It's beyond me to bear bitterness now. I've had a gey and useless life I think. There's many a thing left undone that should have been done, but I must—oh! I must see Mary, to put things right between her and me."

He gritted his teeth till the muscles of his stubbled jowl stuck out in hard, knotted lumps.

"Ye must see her, must ye," he replied—"that's verra, verra touchin'.

We should a' fall down and greet at the thought o' this wonderful reconciliation." He shook his head slowly from side to side. "Na! Na! my
woman ye'll not see her this side o' the grave, and I have strong misgivings if ye'll see her on the other. You're never to see her. Never!"

She did not answer, but, withdrawing into herself, became more
impassive, more aloof from him. For a long time her eyes remained
fixed on the ceiling. There was silence in the room but for the drowsy
drone of an insect as it circled around the few sprays of sweet-scented
honeysuckle that had been gathered by Nessie and placed by her in a
vase that stood beside the bed. At length a faint tremor ran through
Mamma's wasted body.

"Weel, James," she sighed, "if you say it, then it maun be so—
that's always been the way; but I wanted, oh! I did want to see her
again. There's times though," she went on, slowly, and with great
difficulty, "when the pain o' this trouble has been to me like the carryin'
of a child—so heavy and draggin' like—and it's turned my mind to that
bairn o' hers that never lived for her to see it. If it had been spared I
would have liket to have held Mary's bairn in these arms"—she looked
downwards, hopelessly, at the withered arms that could scarcely raise
a cup to her lips—"but it was the will of God that such things couldna
be, and that's all there is about it."

"Woman, you're not squeamish to take such a notion into your head
at this time o' day," scowled Brodie. "Have ye not had enough to do
with your own children without draggin' out the memory of—of that."

"It was just a fancy," she whispered, "and I've had many o' them
since I lay here these six, long months—so long they've been like weary
years." She closed her eyes in a tired fashion, forgetting him as the
visions that she spoke of rushed over her again. The sweet perfume of
the honeysuckle flowers beside her wafted her thoughts backwards, and
she was out of the close, sickly room, home again on her father's farm.
She saw the stout, whitewashed buildings, the homestead, the dairy, and
the long, clean byre forming the three snug sides of the clean yard, saw
her father come in from the shooting with a hare and a brace of pheasants
in his hand. The smooth, coloured plumage delighted her as she stroked
the plump breasts.

"They're as fat as you are," her father cried, with his broad, warm
smile, "but not near as bonnie."

She had not been a slut then, nor had her form been the object of
derision!

Now she was helping her mother with the churning, watching the
rich yellow of the butter as it clotted in the white milk like a clump of
early primroses springing from a bank of snow:

"Not so hard, Margaret, my dear," her mother had chided her, for
the quickness of her turning. "You'll turn the arm off yourself."

She had not been lazy then, nor had they called her handless!

Her thoughts played happily about the farm and in her imagination she rolled amidst the sweet mown hay, heard the creak of the horses moving in their stalls, laid her cheek against the sleek side of her favourite calf. She even remembered its name—"Rosabelle," she had christened it. "Whatna name for a cow!" Bella, the dairymaid, had teased her. "What way not call it after me and be done wi' it?" An overpowering wave of nostalgia came over her as she remembered long, hot afternoons when she had lain with her head against the bole of the bent apple tree, watching the swallows flirt like winged, blue shadows around the eaves of the white, sun-drenched steadings. When an apple dropped beside her she picked it up and bit deeply into it; even now, she felt the sweetly acid tang refreshing upon her tongue, cooling its parched fever. Then she saw herself in a sprigged muslin frock, beside the mountain ash that grew above the Pownie Burn and, approaching her, a youth to whose dark, dour strength her gentleness drew near. She opened her eyes slowly.

"James," she whispered as her eyes sought his with faint, wistful eagerness; "do ye mind that day by the Pownie Burn when ye braided the bonnie, red, rowan berries through my hair? Do ye mind what ye said then?"

He stared at her, startled at the transition of her speech, wondering if she raved; here was he on the brink of ruin, and she drivelled about a wheen rowans thirty years ago. His lips twitched as he replied, slowly:

"No! I dinna mind what I said, but tell me, tell me what I said."

She closed her eyes as though to shut out everything but the distant past, then she murmured, slowly:

"Ye only said that the rowan berries were not so braw as my bonnie curly hair."

As, unconsciously, he looked at the scanty, brittle strands of hair that lay about her face, a sudden, fearful rush of emotion swept over him. He did remember that day. He recollected the quiet of the little glen, the ripple of the stream, the sunshine that lay about them, the upward switch of the bough after he had plucked the bunch of berries from it; now he saw the lustre of her curls against the vivid scarlet of the rowans. Dumbly, he tried to reject the idea that this—this wasted creature that lay upon the bed had on that day rested in his arms and answered his words of love with her soft, fresh lips. It could not be—yet it must be so! His face worked strangely, his mouth twisted as he battled with the surging feeling that drove against the barrier of his resistance like a torrent of water battering against the granite wall of a dam. Some vast, compelling impulse drove at him with an urge which made him want to say blindly, irrationally, in a fashion he had not used for twenty years:

"I do mind that day, Margaret, and ye were bonnie—bonnie and sweet to me as a flower." But he could not say it! Such words as these

311

could never pass his lips. Had he come to this room to whine some stupid phrases of endearment? No, he had come to tell her of their ruin, and tell her he would, despite this unnatural weakness that had come upon him.

"Auld wife," he muttered with drawn lips, "ye'll be the death o' me if ye talk like that. When ye're on the parish ye maun give me a crack like this to cheer me up."

At once her eyes opened enquiringly, anxiously, with a look which again stabbed him; but he forced himself to continue, nodded at her with a false assumption of his old, fleering jocosity.

"Ay!" he cried, "that's what it amounts to now. I'll have no more fifty pounds to fling away on ye. I've shut my door of the business for the last time. We'll all be in the poorhouse soon." As he uttered the last words he saw her face change, but some devilish impulse, aroused by his own present weakness, and moving him more fiercely because he knew that in his heart he did not wish to speak like this, made him thrust his head close to her, goaded him to continue: "Do ye hear! The business is gone. I warned ye a year ago—don't you remember that wi' your demned rowan berry rot? I tell ye we're ruined! You that's been such a help to me, that's what ye've brought me to. We're finished, finished, finished!"

The effect of his words upon her was immediate, and terrible. When his meaning burst in upon her a frightful twitching affected the yellow, weazened skin of her features as though a sudden, intense grief attempted painfully to animate the moribund tissues, as though tears essayed with futile effort to well out from the dried-up springs of her body. Her eyes became suddenly full, intense, and glowing and, with a tremendous, shivering effort, she raised herself up in the bed. A stream of words trembled upon her tongue but she could not utter them, and as a dew of perspiration broke upon her brow in cold, pricking droplets she stammered incoherently, stretched her hand dumbly before her. Then, as her face grew grey with endeavour, suddenly she spoke:

"Matt," she cried in a full, high tone. "Matt! come to me!" She now stretched out both her quivering arms as though sight failed her, calling out in a weaker, fading tone: "Nessie! Mary! Where are ye?"

He wished to go to her, to start forward instantly, but he remained rooted to the floor; yet from his lips broke involuntarily these words, strange as a spray of blossoms upon a barren tree:

"Margaret, woman—Margaret—dinna mind what I said. I didna mean the hauf o't!"

But she did not hear him, and with a last, faint breath she whispered slowly:

"Why tarry the wheels of thy chariot, O Lord? I'm ready to go to ye!"

Then she sank gently backwards upon the pillow. A moment later a last, powerful expiration shook the thin, withered body with a convulsive spasm, and she lay still. Limp and flat upon her back, with arms outstretched upon the bed, the fingers slightly flexed upon the upturned palms, she lay, in shape and stillness, as if she had been crucified. She was dead.

XIII

BRODIE looked round the company assembled uncomfortably in the parlour with a brooding eye which passed over Nessie, Matthew, and his mother, lit impatiently upon his wife's cousins—Janet and William Lumsden—and settled with a scowling finality upon Mrs. William Lumsden. They had just buried all that remained of Margaret Brodie, and the guests, clinging even in the face of Brodie's inhospitable frowns, to the privileges endowed to them by old-established precedent, had returned to the house after the funeral to partake of refreshment.

"We'll give them nothing!" Brodie had exclaimed to his mother that morning. His momentary, belated tenderness towards his wife was now forgotten and he resented bitterly the threatened intrusion of her relations. "I don't want them about my house. They can go hame whenever she's ditched." The old woman had herself hoped for a savoury high tea, but in the face of his remark she had modified her demands.

"James," she had pleaded, "ye maun gie them a sip o' wine and a bite o' cake for the honour o' the house."

"None o' our ain folks are left to come," he growled. "What does it matter about hers? I wish I had choked them off when they wrote."

"They're ower scattered for mony o' them to come," she had placated, "but ye canna get ower offerin' them something. It wouldna be decent to do otherwise."

"Give them it, then," he cried, and as a sudden thought struck him, he added: "Ay, give them it, then. Feed the swine. There'll be somebody here to lend ye a hand."

Now it gave him a saturnine pleasure to see Nancy enter briskly with cake, biscuits, and wine and hand them round. He was his own man again, and it appeared a delicious stroke of satire for him to have her enter his house the moment his wife's body had been carried out; the two women—the dead and the quick—had, so to speak, passed each other at the gate; his eyes met hers in a glow of hidden buffoonery.

"Go ahead, Matt," he jeered significantly at his son, as Nancy handed the latter wine, with a pertly conscious air. "Take up a glass. It'll do ye good after all your greetin'. You'll be quite safe. I'm here to see it doesna fly to your head." He watched his son's trembling hand with disgust. Matt had again disgraced him by breaking down abjectly at the graveside, snivelling and whimpering before these relations of Mamma's, and grovelling hysterically on his knees as the first spadeful of earth clumped heavily upon the coffin.

"Nae wonder he's upset," said Janet Lumsden, in a kindly voice. She was a fat, comfortable woman with a high, amiable bosom protruding above the upper edge of her ill-fitting corsets. Now she looked round the assembly and added, agreeably: " 'Twas a merciful release, though, I'm led to believe. She'll be happier where she is now, I'll warrant."

" 'Tis a pity the puir thing wasna allowed a wreath or two," said Mrs. William Lumsden, with a sniff and a toss of her head. Her lips were tight and her mouth downturned beneath her long, sharp, penetrating nose; as she helped herself from the tray she looked intently at Nancy, then looked away again with a slow and upward twist of her head. "A funeral is never the same without flowers," she added, firmly.

"Ay, they're sort o' comfortin' like," said Janet Lumsden placatingly. "They big lilies are bonnie."

"I had never been to a burial before, without flowers," replied Mrs. Lumsden acrimoniously. "The last interment I attended there was a full, open carriage of flowers, forbye what covered the coffin."

Brodie looked at her steadily.

"Weel, ma'am," he said politely, "I hope ye'll have a' the blossoms ye require when ye go to yer ain last repose."

The other looked along her nose at him doubtfully, not knowing exactly whether to accept the remark as a compliment or an insult, then, in her uncertainty, she turned commandingly to her husband for support. He, a small wiry man, uncomfortable in his stiff, shiny black suit, his starched dickey, and tight "made" tie, magnificent, yet none the less still smelling of the stable, interpreted the familiar look, and dutifully began:

"Flowers gang well at a funeral—it's a matter of opinion no doubt, but I would say they were a consolation to the bereaved. But the strangest thing to my mind is that they should gang well with a weddin' too. It's a fair mystery to me how they should suit such opposite ceremonies." He cleared his throat and looked sociably at Brodie. "Ye ken I've been to many a funeral—ay, and to many a weddin' too. Ance I went as far as forty miles away from hame, but would ye believe me, man," he concluded triumphantly, "for thirty-two years I havena slept a nicht out o' ma ain bed."

"Indeed," said Brodie curtly, "I'm not interested."

At this rudeness there was an uncomfortable pause, a silence punctuated only by a small residual sob from the red-eyed Nessie. The two groups looked at each other distrustfully, like strangers on opposite sides of a railway compartment.

314

"It's a gey appropriate day for a funeral, anyway," said Lumsden at last, defiantly, looking out at the drizzling rain; and at his remark a low conversation amongst the three visitors, and confined exclusively to them, again recommenced and slowly gained impetus.

"Ay! it's miserable enough for onything here."

"Did ye mark how heavy the rain cam' on at the graveside whenever the cords were lowered?"

" 'Tis remarkable to me that the meenister wouldna come back to the house to gie us a few words."

"He'll have his reasons, I have nae doubt."

"What he did say at the grave's heid he said unco' weel, onyway. It's a pity she couldna have heard it hersel', puir body."

"What was't he said, 'a loyal wife and a devoted mother,' wasn't no'?"

They looked out of the corners of their eyes at Brodie as though expecting him to confirm decently this last tribute, but he seemed not to have heard them and now gazed broodingly away from them out of the window. And now, seeing Brodie's apparent inattention, they grew bolder.

"I wad like to have seen the puir thing again, but I had the surprise o' my life when I heard she had been screwed down before we arrived."

"She must have altered sadly wi' sicca trouble, ay and a' the worry she cam' through."

"She was a bricht, lively kimmer in her young days. She had a laugh like the song o' a mavis."

"She was a' that," said Janet at last, with a reproachful look at the figure by the window, implying by her words, "She was too good for you."

There was a moment's pause, then, with a guarded look at Nessie that encompassed her blue serge dress, Mrs. Lumsden murmured:

"It fair affronts me to see that puir child without the decent mournin's to her back. It's nothing short of shameful."

" 'Twas the sma' sma' funeral that surprised me," returned Janet. "Only the twa carriages, and not a single body frae the town."

He heard them, actually he had listened to every word—only the heedlessness of his embittered humour had allowed them to proceed—but now he turned to them coarsely:

" 'Twas my express wish that the funeral should be private, and as quiet as might be. Did ye wish the town band out for her, and free whisky and a bonfire?"

They were frankly shocked at such brutality, drew more closely together in their resentment, began to think of leaving.

"Weelum! do ye know onywhere in Levenford we're likely to be able to get our tea before the train goes?" said Mrs. Lumsden, as an indication of departure, in a trembling but rancorous tone. She had expected, instead of this thin, sour wine and bought seed cake a lavish display of hot and cold cooked meats, baked pastries, scones, tea bread, and other appropriate delicacies; coming from a distant village in Ayrshire they knew nothing of Brodie's failure, and thought him well able to provide a more worthy and substantial repast than that of which they were now partaking.

"Will ye no' have another biscuit then, if ye're hungry?" said old Grandma Brodie, with a slight titter—"they're Deesides—I can recommend them." The wine was like nectar to her unaccustomed palate, and she had partaken freely of it, so that a faint flush marked the yellow, wrinkled skin over her high cheek-bones; she was enjoying the occasion immensely, making high festival of the return to earth of the poor remains of Margaret Brodie. "Have a wee drap mair wine, will ye not?"

"Thank ye! No!" said Mrs. Lumsden, compressing her mouth superciliously into the smallest possible compass, and issuing her words disdainfully from the diminutive aperture. "I'll not indulge if ye don't mind. I'm not addicted, and besides I couldna fancy that what you're drinkin'. Do ye know," she continued, drawing on her black kid glove, "that's a bold-looking quean ye have about the house at a time like this. Have ye had her long?"

As Grandma Brodie made to answer, a polite hiccough disturbed her.

"I dinna ken her," she replied confusedly, "she's juist come in now. 'Twas James sent her in to gie me a haund."

Mrs. Lumsden exchanged a significant glance with her cousin by marriage. Each nodded her head with a slight downward gesture of disparagement, as though to say: "Just what we thought," and both turned ostentatiously compassionate eyes upon Nessie.

"What in the world will ye do without your mother, dearie?" remarked one.

"Ye maun come doun to us, child, for a spell," said the other. "Ye would like to play about the farm, would ye not?"

"I can look after Nessie," inserted Brodie icily; "she needs neither your help nor your pity. When ye do hear o' her she'll be shapin' for something that you and yours could never attain."

As Nancy entered the room to collect the glasses, he continued:

"Here, Nancy! these two ladies have just remarked that you're a brazen—was it quean ye said, leddies—ay, a brazen quean. In return for this good opinion would mind ye showin' them out o' the house— and I suppose this bit gentleman they've brocht wi' them better go too."

Nancy tossed her head pertly.

"If it was my house," she said, with a bold look at Brodie, "they would never have been in it."

The two women, scandalised, stood up.

"The language—and the behaviour! In front of the child too," gasped Janet, on her way to the door, "and at such a time as this."

Mrs. Lumsden, equally shocked, but less intimidated, drew herself up to her tall, angular height and threw her head back defiantly.

"I've been insulted," she shrilled from between thin, compressed lips, "in a house where I came a long and expensive journey to bring comfort. I'm goin', oh! indeed yes, I'm goin', nothing would stop me, but," she added emphatically, "before I leave I want to know what has been left to our side o' the family by my puir cousin."

Brodie laughed shortly in her face.

"Indeed now! and what had she to leave, pray?"

"I happen to know from Weelum that forbye the china, pictures, and the ornaments on the best bedroom mantelpiece, and her mother's watch and locket, Margaret Lumsden took a pickle siller wi' her into the house," she cried angrily.

"Ay, and she took a pickle out o' it," answered Brodie harshly. "Get away wi' ye! the sight o' your sour, graspin', avaricious face fair scunners me!" With whirling movements of his arms he herded them to the door. "Get away with ye a', there's nothing for ye here. I'm sorry I let ye break bread in my house."

Mrs. Lumsden, almost in tears from rage and vexation, turned on the doorstep.

"We'll have the law on ye about it," she cried. "I'm not surprised that puir Margaret Lumsden withered out here. She was ower guid for ye, wi' your bold besoms. Ye've made a cryin' scandal out of the burial of the puir soul. Come awa' home, Weelum."

"That's right," shouted Brodie tauntingly, "take Weelum away hame to his bed. I'm not surprised he's so fond o' it wi' such a tricksy ornament as yersel' below the blankets." He leered at her, insultingly. "Ye're richt not to let him out it for a nicht, for if ye did ye might never get him back."

As she disappeared with the others, her head high, her colour flaming, he cried out after her:

"I'll not forget to send ye your flowers whenever ye require them."

But when he returned to the parlour his hard assumption of indifference had dropped from him and, wishing to be alone, in a different, quiet voice he bade them leave him. As they filed out he turned to Matthew and said to him meaningly:

"Away out and find work. I want no more of your useless, watery tear-bag nonsense. Get something to do. Ye'll not live off me much longer"; but as Nessie passed he patted her head and said, gently:

"Don't greet any more, pettie, your father will take care of ye. Dry your eyes, now, and run and take up a book or something. You needna worry. I'm goin' to look after you in future."

That, he considered, as he sat down again in the empty room, was the course towards which his life must immediately shape itself—the

317

vindication of himself through Nessie. She was his asset, clever, yes, he told himself, brilliant! He would nurse her, encourage her, thrust her forward to triumph after triumph until her name and his own should resound in the town. He saw in his colossal failure and in the recent misfortunes which had beset him only a temporary eclipse from which in time he must necessarily emerge. "Ye cannot keep a good man down," one of his frequently repeated maxims, occurred again to him now comfortingly. He would be up again presently, more dominant than before, and in his own mind he considered it an almost masterly strategy to plan a return to his old, favoured position through Nessie. He heard in anticipation the name of Nessie Brodie upon everyone's lips, became aware of himself sharing largely in the universal adulation. "There's been no holdin' him since his wife died," he heard them say; "she must have been a muckle hindrance to the man." How true that was! His main feeling, as he helped to lower the light coffin into its shallow trench, had been one of relief, that he was at last free of a useless encumbrance, a drag upon both his patience and his purse. He remembered nothing in her favour, treasured nothing of her virtues, but dwelt only upon the weakness, the lack of physical attraction that she had manifested in her later years. No gentle sentiment, such as had faintly throbbed within him at her death-bed, no remembrance of the earlier days of their life together now stirred him; his memory was clouded like an overhung sky that refused to allow one single, relieving gleam to penetrate from the clearer air behind. He imagined that she had failed him in everything, in her companionship, in the oblation of her physical being, in the very geniture of her children. No credit was due to her for Nessie, whom he felt to be entirely of his substance, and such obituary as his consideration gave her was epitomised in the single word—incompetent. As the irrevocable finality of her departure struck him with a sudden and forceful reality, a feeling of a strange emancipation came over him. The lightness of her restraint had been—from its very feebleness—galling to him. He was a young man yet, and virile, for whom many pleasures lay in store which might be tasted freely now that she was gone. His lower lip hung thickly forward as his thoughts dallied appreciatively upon Nancy, then roamed forward in anticipation amongst the lush, erotic pastures of his mind. Nancy must be always about him—now she could remain in the house ror good. There was nothing to prevent her being beside him, no possible objection to her serving him, cheering him, and—yes, a man must, after all, have a housekeeper!

Satisfied at this comforting decision, insensibly his meditations turned again upon his younger daughter. His mind, incapable of embracing any but one purpose at a time, pursued that purpose, when it had been adopted, with a relentless obstinacy; and now, he realised that in order to continue living in his house, to maintain Nessie and to educate her

318

as he wished, he must quickly find some means of income. His lips tightened, and he nodded his head profoundly, as he resolved to carry into effect, immediately, a plan which had for the last two days been maturing in his brain. He got up and entered the hall where he put on his hat, took his silk umbrella from the stand, and went slowly out of the house.

Outside it was cool and fresh, with a fine, impalpable rain—soft and subtile as dew—which misted his garments and touched his warm brow like a caress. As he filled his lungs with great draughts of the balmy, misty vapour it felt good to him that he did not lie in a narrow, wooden box beneath four feet of dank earth, but walked in the air, invigorated, alive, and free. Characteristically, in the constrained capacity of his intellect, the memory of his humiliation in business, even the final scene in the High Street when he had given that madly unrestrained exhibition, was now completely obliterated; his failure appeared to him in a different light; he was not crushed and beaten, but a gentlemanly victim of malicious circumstances. The ebullition of temper provoked by the Lumsdens had subsided and, his present mission filling him once more with a conscious dignity, he walked gravely through the streets, addressing no one, but saluting seriously such of those he encountered as he felt to merit his recognition. He responded strongly to his own suggestion that, disencumbered of his wife, and with Nessie as the medium of his expression, a new and more important book of his life was beginning.

At the head of Church Street he turned at right angles and proceeded directly away from the High Street, towards the Newtown. Shops became infrequent; on his left lay a row of workmen's dwellings, mean houses which abutted, without gardens, directly upon the street, and upon his right a high, stone wall ran continuously. Above this wall small, bristling forests of tall, branchless, spars erected themselves, and from over its summit, carried on the salty breeze, a hundred gradations of noise reached his ears. Some few hundred yards along, he drew up opposite a block of buildings which, intersecting the smooth continuity of the lofty wall, fronted the street imposingly; there, opposite the main door, he paused. His appearance was that of one who studied carefully the inconspicuous, brass plate before him—the sign which said neatly, above: Levenford Shipbuilding Yard and, below: Latta & Co.—but actually he was mustering all his forces to enter that doorway which confronted him. Now that he had arrived, an unusual vacillation possessed and weakened his purposeful determination; the sight, even, of the outer confines of the immense yard, the dim realisation of the immense wealth which it represented, impressed him, in his reduced financial situation, with a sensation of inferiority. Angrily he thrust this from him, assuring himself, in his own axiom, that it was the man, not the money that mattered, and, with a quick gesture, he swaggered his way through the imposing portals.

His precipitate entry carried him past the small, sliding window marked "Enquiries" without his observing it, and immediately he became lost in a labyrinth of corridors. For some moments he moved about the corridors, blundering angrily like a trapped minotaur in a maze, until by chance he encountered a young man whom, from the short wooden pen that projected like a spit behind one ear, he correctly adjudged to be a clerk.

"I want to see Sir John Latta," he announced fiercely. He felt a fool in these corridors. "I want to see him at once."

The youth blenched at the august name. For him an impassable regiment of chief clerks, managers, heads of departments, and superintendents intervened upon his road of access to that supreme head.

"Have you an appointment?" he asked, vaguely.

"No!" said Brodie, "I haven't."

"It's nothing to do with me of course," replied the youth, disclaiming immediately all responsibility, "but you would have more chance if you had an appointment." He spoke the last word as though it were an emblem of high solemnity, like a key that was necessary to open a sacred door.

"Never mind your appointments. I must see him," cried Brodie, so fiercely that the young man felt compelled to offer another suggestion.

"I could see Mr. Sharp for you," he observed, mentioning his own particular demi-god.

"Take me to him then," said Brodie impatiently, "and hurry up about it."

With surprising ease the youth threaded the corridors and, presenting him before Mr. Sharp with a few explanatory words, fled spontaneously as though repudiating all consequences of his act.

Mr. Sharp was not sure, was, in fact, extremely doubtful of Sir John's ability to see anyone to-day. The head of the firm was deeply engaged, had asked not to be disturbed, was shortly going out, and, in fact, unless the business was of the most important nature, Mr. Sharp was exceedingly distrustful of himself intruding upon Sir John with Mr. Brodie's name.

Brodie gazed at the other out of his small, angry eyes.

"Tell Sir John that James Brodie asks to see him," he exclaimed hotly. "He knows me well. He'll see me at once."

Mr. Sharp departed in a huff but came back, after some time, to ask Mr. Brodie in a frigid tone to be seated, and to say that Sir John would see him presently.

With a triumphant look at the other which said: "I told ye so, ye fool," Brodie sat down and waited, watching idly, as the moments passed, the hive of busy clerks that hummed around him, their activities controlled, apparently, by the waspish eye of Sharp. As the minutes dragged slowly on, whilst he cooled his heels he reflected, in his suspense, that "presently" must mean a very considerable period, and the longer he waited the more his exultation faded, the more Mr. Sharp's obvious satisfaction increased; it was borne in on him that he could not enter Sir John's office in the easy fashion that Sir John entered his, that it was appreciably more difficult to interview the other here than it had been to accost him casually at the Cattle Show. A heavy depression settled upon him which was scarcely dispelled by the sudden, eventual summons to the office of the head of the firm.

Sir John Latta looked up quickly from his desk as Brodie was shown into the room and, silently indicating a chair, resumed his intent consideration of a plan that lay before him. Brodie lowered his ponderous bulk into the chair and glanced round the sumptuous room, observing the rich, teak panelling and softly tinted colours, the flowing marine paintings on the walls, the exquisite models of ships upon their graceful pedestals; as his feet sank deeply into the many piles of the carpet and he viewed the buhl inlay of the desk and the gold cigar box upon it, his nostrils dilated slightly and his eye glistened with a deep sense of appreciation. "I like these things," his attitude seemed to say; "these are the manner of possessions that should be mine."

"Well, Brodie," said Sir John at last, but without looking up, "what is it?"

The other could scarcely have failed to observe the lack of warmth in the tone, but nevertheless he began, eagerly:

"Sir John! I've come to ask ye for your advice. Ye're the one man in Levenford that I would approach like this. Ye understand me, and all that's to me, Sir John. I've felt that in the past over and over again, and now I've come to ask your help."

Latta looked at him curiously.

"You are talking in riddles, Brodie," he retorted coldly, "and it is a form of speech that does not suit you. You are more suited to direct action than indirect speech"; then he added, slowly: "and action does not apparently always become you."

"What do ye mean, Sir John?" blurted out Brodie. "Who has been speakin' of me behind my back?"

The other picked up a fine ivory ruler and, as he lightly tapped his desk with it, answered slowly:

"You are out of favour with me, Brodie. We cannot help but hear the news and bruit of the town at Levenford House—and you have been making a fool of yourself, or worse."

"Ye don't mean that nonsense about—about skiting away the hats?"
Latta shook his head.

"That certainly was folly, but in you a comprehensible folly. There are other things you must know of. You have lost your wife and I believe you have lost your business. You have had disappointments, so I shall not say too much. Yet I hear bad reports of you. You know I never hit a man when he's down, but," he continued quietly, "I take interest in all our townspeople, and I am sorry to hear ill things spoken even of the meanest labourer in my shipyards."

Brodie hung his head like a whipped schoolboy, wondering vaguely if it were Matthew's failure or the Winton Arms that lay in the background of Sir John's mind.

"You may have observed," continued Latta quietly, "that I have not patronised your establishment since the beginning of last year. That is because I heard then of an action of yours which I consider was both unjust and unmerciful. You behaved like a blackguard and a bully to your unfortunate daughter, Brodie, and though some might condone your act on grounds of outraged propriety, we can have nothing to do with you whilst you are under a stigma of this sort."

Brodie's hands clenched tightly and the frown deepened upon his pendent forehead. Latta, he thought bitterly, was the only person in Levenford who would have dared to address him like this, the only man, indeed, who could have uttered such words with impunity.

"I can do nothing," he said sulkily, restrained in his action only through a glimmering sense of his dependence upon the other's good will. "It's all past and done with now."

"You can forgive her," replied Latta sternly. "You can promise me that she shall have refuge in your house if ever she might require it."

Brodie sat sullenly silent, his mind filled, not by Mary but, strangely, by the picture of Nessie. He must do something for her! It was, after all, easy for him to make an acquiescence of some description, and with his head still lowered and his eyes upon the carpet he blurted out: "Very well, Sir John! It'll be as ye say."

Latta looked for a long time at the huge, lowering figure. He had at one time viewed Brodie, in the limited sphere of their mutual encounter, with the connoisseur's eye for the unusual; regarded him with appreciation as a magnificent mountain of manhood; smiled at his obvious conceit and tolerated, with a puzzled curiosity, his strange, bombastic, and unfathomable allusions. He had observed him with the man of breeding's appreciation of a unique and eccentric specimen, but now he felt the other's presence strangely distasteful to him, thought him altered and debased, considered that some deeper explanation might exist of that bluff, yet pretentious assumption of dignity. Quickly he rejected the thought—after all, the man had conceded his point.

"How can I help you then, Brodie?" he said seriously. "Tell me how you stand."

Brodie at last raised his head, becoming aware that the interview had turned, though he knew not how, into the channel which he desired it to take.

"I've closed my business, Sir John!" he began. "Ye know as well as I do how I've been used by these"—he swallowed and restrained himself—"by that company that sneaked into the town and settled beside me like a thief in the night. They've used every low trick they could, stolen my manager from me; they've undercut me, sold rotten trash instead of honest goods, they've—they've sucked the very blood out o' me."

As memory stirred under his own words, his eye filled with self-sympathy and his chest heaved; he stretched out his arm demonstratively.

But Latta was somehow not impressed and raising his hand, deprecatingly, to stop the other he remarked:

"And what did you do, Brodie, to combat these tactics? Did you branch out into new directions or—or exert yourself more agreeably towards your customers?"

Brodie stared at him with a stupid, mulish obstinacy. "I went my own way," he exclaimed stubbornly, "the way I've always gone."

"I see," said Latta slowly.

"I fought them!" exclaimed Brodie. "I fought them like a gentleman and I fought fair. Ay, I would have riven them to bits with these two hands if they had shown the courage to meet me. But they skulked beneath me—and how could I lower myself down to their level, the dogs?"

"And are you involved now, in your affairs?" asked Sir John. "Are you in debt?"

"No!" replied Brodie proudly, "I'm not. I'm finished—but I owe no man a farthing. I've bonded my house but, if I have nothing, I owe nothing. I can start fair, Sir John, if you've a mind to help me. That wee Nessie of mine must have her chance. She's the cleverest lass in Levenford. She's cut out for the bursary your own father founded if she only gets the opportunity."

"Why don't you sell that ridiculous house of yours?" considered Latta, impressed more favourably by the other's words. "It's too large for you now, anyway. Then you can clear your bond, and start afresh in a smaller house with the balance."

Brodie shook his head slowly.

"It's my house," he said heavily. "I built it, and in it I'll bide. I would drag it down about my head sooner than give it up." Then after a pause he added, sombrely: "If that's all ye have to suggest I'll not take any more o' your time."

"Sit down, man," cried Latta. "You're as touchy as tinder." He toyed absently with his ruler, deep in thought, whilst doubtfully, uncomprehendingly, Brodie watched the quick passage of emotions over the other's face. At last Latta spoke. "You're a strange man, Brodie!" he said, "and your mind puzzles me. I was of opinion, a minute ago, to let you whistle for assistance, but somehow I feel a drag upon me which I can't resist. I will make you an offer. Business is not for you now,

Brodie. You are too big, too slow, too cumbersome. You would never succeed by opening up again in your own line, even if this were possible for you. You ought to be working with these great muscles of yours, and yet I suppose you would consider that beneath you. But you can use a pen, keep books, reckon up figures. We might find a place for you here. As I say, I am making you an offer—it is the most I can do—you may refuse it if you choose."

Brodie's eye gleamed. He had known all along that Sir John would help him, that the strong tie of friendship between them must draw the other to help him, and help him royally; he felt that something large and important was looming near for him.

"Ay, Sir John," he said eagerly, "what do ye suggest? I'm at your disposal if I can assist ye."

"I could offer you," Latta continued, evenly, "a position in the office as a clerk. It so happens that there is a vacancy in the wood department at this moment. You would have something to learn, yet, out of consideration for you, I would increase the salary slightly. You would have two pounds ten shillings a week."

Brodie's jaw dropped, and his face crinkled into striped furrows of bewilderment. Hardly able to believe his ears, his eyes clouded with surprise and chagrin whilst the rosy visions which he had suddenly entertained of sitting in a luxurious room—one such as this perhaps—and of directing a bevy of rushing subordinates, faded slowly from his eyes.

"Think it over a moment," said Latta quietly, as he got up and moved towards an inner room. "You must excuse me just now."

Brodie strove to think. Whilst the other was out of the room he sat crushed, overcome by his humiliation. He—James Brodie—to be a clerk! And yet what other avenue than this could he possibly pursue. For Nessie's sake he must accept; he would take the wretched post—but only—only for the meantime. Later, he would show them all—and this Latta more than any.

"Well," said Latta, coming into the office again, "what is it to be?"

Brodie raised his head dully.

"I accept," he said in a flat voice, and added, in a tone into which he strove to insert an inflection of satire, but which succeeded merely in becoming pathetic, "and thank ye."

Dazedly, he saw Latta pull the bell beside his desk, heard him exclaim to the boy who instantly appeared:

"Send Mr. Blair to me."

Blair came, apparently as quickly and mysteriously as the boy, though Brodie hardly looked at the small, precise figure, or gazed into the eye which outdid Sharp's in formal coldness. He did not hear the conversation between the two others yet, after a period of time which he knew not to be long or short, he felt himself being dismissed by Latta.

He stood up, followed Blair slowly out of the rich room, along the passage, down flights of steps across a courtyard, and finally through the door of a small, detached office.

"Though it is apart from the main department I trust you will take no advantage of this fact. This will be your desk," said Blair coldly. It was clear that he regarded Brodie as an interloper and, as he proceeded to explain the simple nature of the duties to him, he infused as much icy contempt into his tone as he might. The two other clerks in the room, both of them young men, peered curiously from over the edge of their ledgers at the strange sight before them, incredulous that this could be their new colleague.

"You have followed me, I trust?" exclaimed Blair finally. "I've made it clear?"

"When do I begin?" asked Brodie dully, feeling that some acknowledgment was expected of him.

"To-morrow, I suppose," answered the other. "Sir John did not exactly specify. If you wish to get a grasp of the books you can begin now if you choose"; and he added witheringly, as he passed out of the room: "But it's only half an hour till the horn goes. I should imagine it would take you longer than that to master the work."

Mutely, as if he knew not what he did, Brodie sat down upon the high stool before the desk, the open ledger a white blur in front of him. He did not see the figures with which, in the future, he must occupy himself, nor did he feel the staring eyes of the two silent youths bent upon him in a strange constraint. He was a clerk! a clerk working for fifty shillings a week. His mind writhed from the unalterable fact yet could not escape it. But no! he would never stand this—this degradation. The moment he was out of this place he would plunge away somewhere and drink, drink till he forgot his humiliation, steep himself in forgetfulness till the memory of it became a ridiculous nightmare. How long had that other said? Half an hour till the horn went! Yes, he could wait until then! He would remain for that short space of time in this ignoble bondage, then he would be free. A tremor seemed to run through him as, blindly, he reached out for a pen and dipped it into the inkwell.

BOOK III

I

"THEY couldna wear such a thing out there, even if they do have black skins," said Nancy, with a slight titter. "You're just tryin' to take a rise out of me." She cocked her head knowingly at Matt, as she surveyed him from her seat upon the kitchen table, and swung her well-exposed ankles towards him to point her remark more emphatically.

"Sure as anything," he replied in an animated tone, whilst from his reclining position against the dresser he ogled her with his eye, his posture, his air of elegance. "That's what the native ladies—as ye're pleased to call them—wear."

"Get away, you," she cried roguishly, "you know too much. You'll be tellin' me the monkeys in India wear trousers next." They roared together at her joke, feeling that they were having a precious fine time, she, that it was good to break the monotony of her empty forenoon, to have a change from that dour black father of his, he, that the conversation was exhibiting his social graces to the best advantage—almost as if he dazzled her as she sat behind a glittering saloon bar.

"You're a great blether," she resumed, in an admonishing yet encouraging tone. "After tellin' me that they niggers chew red nuts like blood and clean their teeth with a bit of stick you'll be askin' me to believe that they comb their hair wi' the leg o' a chair—like Dan, Dan the funny, wee man." Again they laughed in unison until, drawing herself up with mock modesty she resumed: "But I don't mind these kinds of fairy tales. It's when ye start a' these sly jokes o' yours that ye fair make me blush. You've got a regular advantage over a poor, inno-cent girl like me that's never been abroad—you that's visited such grand, interestin' countries. Now tell me some more!"

"But I thought ye didn't want to hear," he teased her. She pouted her richly red lips at him.

"Ye know fine what I mean, Matt. I love hearin' about a' these strange things out there. Never mind the ladies. If I had been out there I wouldna have let ye even have a glink at them. Tell me about the flowers, and the braw coloured birds and beasts, the parrots, the leopards, the tigers. I want to know about the bazaars, the temples, the gold and ivory images—I just can't get enough about them."

"You're the lass to egg me on to it," he replied. "There's no satisfyin' you. What was I speakin' about before ye asked me about the—about what I'm no allowed to mention?" He grinned. "Oh! I remember now, 'twas about the sacred cows. Ay! Ye mightn't believe it, Nancy, but the cow is a sacred animal to millions of folks out in India. They'll have images of the animal stuck up in all places and in the streets of the native quarters you'll see great big cows slushing about, with flowers on their horns and garlands of marigolds round their necks, poking their noses everywhere like they owned the place, into the houses and into the stalls—that's like the shops you know—and not a body says 'no' to them. I once saw one of the beasts stop at a stall of fruit and vegetables and before you could say 'knife' it had cleared the place from end to end, and the man what owned the shop was obliged to sit helpless and watch it eat up all his stuff, and when it had finished he could do nowt but put up a bit prayer to it or string the remains of his flowers around its big neck."

"Ye don't say, Matt," she gasped, her eyes wide with interest; "that's a strange thing you're tellin' me. To think they would worship the likes of a cow!"

"There's all kinds of cows though, Nancy," replied Matt with a wink; but immediately he resumed, more seriously: "Yes! but what I'm telling you is nothing. I couldn't describe all that I've seen to you, ye've got to travel to appreciate such marvellous sights that you would otherwise never dream of. And there's other places finer than India, mind you, where the climate's better, with less mosquitoes and just as much freedom."

She considered him deliberately as, carried away by his own enthusiasm, he talked; and, viewing the slender figure in the natty brown suit, the engaging neatness of his appearance, the inherent yet not unpleasing weakness of his pale face, she was amazed that she could ever have fled from him as she had done at their first encounter. During the six weeks that had elapsed since Mrs. Brodie's funeral—when she had been formally installed as housekeeper to the Brodie mènage—she had gradually come to regard Matthew with favour, to protect him against his father, to look forward to his lighter conversation after the heavy taciturnity and laboured monosyllables of the elder man.

"You're not listening to me, you little randy," he exclaimed, suddenly. "What's the good of a man using his breath and all his best adjectives if the bonnie lassie pays no heed to him?—and you that asked for it and all."

"Do you think I'm bonnie, then, Matt," she replied, continuing to regard him in a dreamy manner, yet making her eyes more seductive, her whole saucy pose more provocative.

"I do that, Nancy," he cried eagerly, his glance lighting. "You're as bonnie as a picture. It's a treat to have you about the house. I've always thought that since ever I saw you."

"Ay," she continued musingly, "ye were a richt bad boy the first time ye met me, but your manners have improved extraordinar' since then. In fact, when I came here I began to think ye were something feared to talk to me, but I see that's all gone now, and indeed I'm not sorry, though I wonder what your father would say to the change if he but knew."

He had raised himself slightly as though about to move towards her, but, at her last words the kindling gleam in his eye was suddenly quenched, and relaxing his body again upon the dresser, he replied, moodily:

"I don't know what a young thing like you can see in an old man like him, with his sour, crabbed ways. He doesn't seem to fit you like a younger man would."

"There's strength in him though, Matt," she replied reflectively, but still drawing him with her eyes, "and it pleases me to see that strength break down before me. The way things have turned out now I could have him like water in my hands. But don't forget," she added, with a change of manner and a sudden toss of her head, "I'm only the housekeeper here."

"Yes," he exclaimed bitterly, "you've got a grand post! You've settled down pretty well here, Nancy."

"And what about you?" she retorted pertly. "You've settled down no' so badly yoursel', for all your fine talk of finding these grand positions abroad."

He laughed at her admiringly.

"Woman! I can't but admire that gleg tongue o' yours. You could strip a man with it if ye chose."

"I could do all that," she answered meaningly; "quick enough."

How she seemed to fire his blood, this coquettish baggage who belonged entirely to his father, who was so absolutely forbidden to him by the taboo of his father's possessions.

"Ye know as well as I do, Nancy, that it's only a matter of time until I fix it up," he replied earnestly. "I've got my name down with half a dozen firms. The first vacancy is mine. I couldn't stay in this rotten hole of a town for the rest of my life. There's nothing to keep me here now since—since my mother died. But I'm telling you to your face it'll be hard to leave you."

"I'll believe ye better when you've gotten the job, Matt," she remarked tartly. "But ye shouldna let the old fellow down ye so much. Stick up for yourself. Have more faith in your own powers. What I think ye need is a woman, with a good level head on her, that would stiffen ye up and give ye a notion of how to face things out."

"I'll get even with him all right," he asserted sulkily. "My chance will come. I'll make him pay for all that he's done to me——" he paused, and added virtuously, "ay and for all that he made my poor mother suffer. He's drinking himself to death anyway."

She did not reply, but throwing back her head, gazed upwards meditatively at the ceiling, exposing the fine, white arch of her throat and drawing her skirt almost to her knees by the graceful backward inclination of her body.

"You're wastin' yourself on him, I'm tellin' you," he continued eagerly. "He's nothing but a great, surly, big bully. Look what he's doing to Nessie—driving her on at these lessons. Look what he did to Mamma! He's not worth it. Do you not see that yourself?"

A secret merriment shook her as she replied:

"I'm not feared, Matt. I can take care of myself. I'm only thinkin' one or two things all to my wee self. Just a secret between Nancy and me," she whispered captivatingly.

"What is it?" he cried ardently, aroused by her manner.

"I'll tell ye some day, if you're good."

"Tell me now," he urged. But she refused to enlighten him and, with a flirt of her head, looked at the clock, then replied: "Tuts! I was just thinkin' it was time to throw a bit dinner on the stove. I maun remember my official responsibilities and not forget what I'm here for or I'll be gettin' the sack. You'll be out for lunch as usual, I suppose."

He, too, regarded the clock to estimate his margin of safety before he must clear out of the house to avert an encounter with his father; the policy he had followed since Mamma's death was to avoid his father as much as possible.

"Ay, I'll be out! You know it chokes me to eat at the same table as him—not that I'm feared of him, for he's so changed he hasn't got a word in him—but the more we keep out of each other's way the better for everybody concerned. It's just a matter of good sense on my part."

As he moved his position with a great show of indifference and independence, she raised her hands behind her head as though to support its backward tilt and continued to smile at him faintly, enigmatically.

"Come here a minute, Matt," she murmured, at length.

He looked at her doubtingly as he came towards the table on which she sat, advancing so slowly that she urged:

"Closer, man, closer. I'll not bite ye."

He would, he thought, have willingly submitted to such desirable punishment as he caught the glint of her white, even teeth shining under the red, smiling lips, lips that grew more vivid against the pallor of her skin the nearer he approached to her.

"That's more like it," she said at length; "that shows more spunk. Ye know, Matt, your father's an awfu' stupid, senseless man to leave two young folks like us hangin' about this dreich house with time so heavy on our hands. If he had but a grain o' sense to sit down and reflect over the matter he would never have allowed it. I havena been

330

out of the house for days now, except for messages, and he would never think of takin' a lassie out for a bit entertainment. Now listen to me. There's a concert on in the Borough Hall to-morrow, Matt," she whispered, lifting her dark lashes enticingly; "what do you say if you and me take a turn down there? He'll never know a thing about it, and forbye, I'll get the money for our seats out of him somehow."

He gazed at her with a fascinated stare, thinking not of her words, which he hardly heard, but noting how from her posture her firm breasts protruded eloquently towards him, and—as not only he had seen—how the faint, golden freckles dusted her small, straight nose and finally touched the softly rounded curve of her short upper lip. He knew now that he wanted her, although he was afraid to take her, and as he gazed deeply into her dark eyes some half-hidden flicker incited him to a rash, tempestuous action, made him blurt out unconsciously:

"Nancy! Nancy! you're a devil to draw a man!"

For a second her expression lost its enticing look and changed to one of pleased complacency.

"I'm beginning to see that now," she murmured, "and the next man that gets me is not goin' to get me cheap." Then, immediately, her voice altered, and she resumed wheedlingly: "But what about the concert, Matt—it's the McKelvie family—they're grand. I'm just dyin' for a little amusement. You and I could hit it off fine at a concert like that. We've always had such good fun together and this'll brighten us both up. Come on, Matt, will you take me to it?"

He felt her breath fan his cheek with a warm intimacy as he blurted out awkwardly, oddly:

"All right, Nancy! I'll take ye! Anything you like—you've just to say the word."

Her smile rewarded him; she leapt lightly from the table and touched his cheek airily with her finger tips.

"That's settled, then," she cried, gaily. "We'll have a rare time and no mistake. You leave it all to me, tickets and everything. We can arrange to meet at the Hall, but you maun come back that long dark road wi' me," she added slyly. "I would be feared to come home myself. I might need your protection." Then, with a sudden upward glance, she cried: "Sakes alive, will ye look at that clock! I've hardly time to fry up the sausages. Away out with ye, Matt, unless ye want to run slap into that big father o' yours. Away the now, but come back when the coast's clear and we'll have a tasty bite together—just you and me."

She warmed him with a last glance and without a word he went out of the room, the inward struggle of his emotions binding his tongue, making his passage clumsy and his step ungainly.

When he had gone, she commenced her belated preparations for the midday meal, not with any degree of urgency but with an undisturbed and almost deliberate carelessness, flinging a pound of sausages into the frying-pan and leaving them to cook themselves upon the stove whilst she spread a soiled cover upon the table, rattled some plates into their appointed places, and flanked each carelessly by a knife and fork.

The slovenly nature of her housewifery was markedly in contrast to her own trig, fastidious person but was further strongly evidenced by the general appearance of the kitchen. The dust which lay thickly upon the mantelpiece and shelves, the spotted, rusty grate, the unswept floor and hearth, the lax indefinite air of untidiness and neglect that hung upon the room, all became explained in the light of her present actions. The aspect of the interior had changed sadly since the days when Mamma had been unjustly maligned for her sluttishness, when her unappreciated efforts had at least maintained a spotless cleanliness inside the house; now, as the protesting sausages spluttered their grease over the adjacent walls, they seemed to smirch the room with a melancholy degradation.

Suddenly, above the crackle of this cooking, into the fat-drenched vapour that filled the scullery, came the sound of the front door opening and shutting, followed by a heavy but sluggish tread along the hall. This, however, although she recognised it as Brodie's step, did not in the least perturb the unprepared Nancy who still maintained her unconcerned and wary survey of the frying-pan. For her no frantic running with savoury broths, brimming coffee cups, or Britannia metal teapots! As she heard him come ponderously into the kitchen and silently sit down at the table she waited a moment, then called out brightly:

"You're too early the day, Brodie. I'm not nearly ready for ye," then, as he did not reply, she continued to shout out, addressing him— who had never deviated a second from his routine—"You're that uncertain these days I never know when to expect you, or else the clocks in this house o' yours are all wrong. Anyway, hold on and I'll be in the now."

He "held on," waiting without a word. In the short space of time which had elapsed since his entry into the offices of Latta & Co. a change, more striking and profound than that of the room in which he sat, but shaped in a similar direction, had affected him. Now, as he sat, his eyes fixed downwards upon the plate before him, he seemed to have shrunken slightly so that his clothes appeared not to fit him, but to have been made for some larger frame than his, while his upright, firm-chested, and always belligerent bearing had been replaced by a faint yet clearly perceptible stoop. His features, from being rugged, had become morose, his eye, no longer piercing, was fixed, brooding, and shot with faint threads of blood, while his cheeks, too, were veined by a fine, reticulated network of reddish vessels. His lips were dry, compressed; his temples, and indeed his cheeks, gaunt, slightly hollowed, and upon his brow the furrow of his frown had seared itself like a deep-grooved stigma. It was as though the firm outlines of the man had become blurred, his craggy features corroded, the whole solidity of his being eaten and undermined by some strange, dissolving acid in his blood.

When Nancy entered, bearing the platter of sausages, he glanced up quickly, drawn by the magnet of her eyes, but as she placed the plate before him he looked at it and said, in a harsh voice that came like the note of a faintly warped instrument:

"Have ye no soup to-day for me, Nancy?"

"No," she replied shortly, "I have not."

"I would have liked a drop broth to-day," he replied with a shadow of displeasure. "There's a nip in the air already; still, if ye haven't got any that's all about it. Where's the potatoes, then?"

"I hadna time to make any potatoes for ye to-day. I've been fair rushed off my feet. Ye canna expect me to do everything for ye a' days, and dippin' my hands in cold dirty water to peel potatoes is what I've never been used to. Ye were glad enough to get a simpler dinner than that when ye used to come in to see me at the Winton Arms, and things are no better off with ye now. Eat it up and be content, man!"

The pupils of his eyes dilated as he looked at her, his lips shaped themselves to an angry reply, but with an effort he restrained himself, helped himself from the plate before him, and, taking a slice of bread, began his meal. She stood beside him for a moment, her hands upon her hips, flaunting her figure near to him, filled by the conscious sense of her power over him until, as Grandma Brodie entered the room, she flounced back into the scullery.

The old woman came forward to the table with a half-bemused expression upon her sallow, wrinkled visage and as she sat down murmured to herself: "Tch! these things again"; but at her scarcely perceptible words Brodie turned and, showing his teeth at her in his old manner, snarled:

"What harm have the sausages done? If ye don't like plain, honest meat ye can go to the poorhouse, and if ye do like it then shut your auld girnin' mouth!"

At his words, and more especially at the accompanying glance, she at once subsided into herself, and with her tremulous hands began, but without much eagerness, to assist herself to the food she had so indiscreetly condemned. Her ageing, muddled brain, incapable of fully comprehending the significance of the changes around her, accepted only the fact that she was now uncomfortable, presented with scanty, unpalatable meals, and as her weak jaws champed with a dry disrelish she vented her displeasure in quick, darting glances towards the hidden presence in the scullery.

After a few moments during which the two ate in silence, Brodie paused suddenly in his indifferent mastication, raised his head slightly at the light sound of someone entering the house and, fixing his eyes upon the door leading to the hall, waited expectantly for the entry of Nessie. She came in immediately and, although Brodie resumed his eating mechanically, he followed her everywhere about the room with his eyes. She slipped the thin elastic from under her chin and released her plain straw hat, threw this upon the sofa, discarded her blue serge jacket and laid it beside the hat, fluffed out her light flaxen hair and finally subsided in her chair beside him. She sat back in her chair, languidly, surveying the table with a faint childish air of petulance, saying nothing, but feeling in her own mind that the sight of the solidifying grease before her had removed what little appetite she had possessed, that though she might have eaten, and enjoyed, perhaps a little stewed mince or even a small lamb chop, now she turned from the very thought of food. At her present age of fifteen years she had reached that period of her life when her budding and developing body required an additional attention, a more selective dietary, and though she realised nothing of this she felt instinctively, with her slightly throbbing head and the onset of her significant though unmentionable malaise, that it was an injustice to present her with the food she now surveyed. As she rested thus, her father, who had observed her continuously since her entry, spoke; with an unchanged face but in a voice which he tried to render light, persuasive, he said:

"Come on now, Nessie dear, and get your dinner begun. Don't sit and let it get cold. A big lassie like you should be hungry as a hunter and dashin' in for her meals as though she could eat the house up!"

At his words she came out of her meditation and at once began to obey, murmuring in explanation, almost apologetically:

"I've got a headache, father, just right on the front of my brow, like a strap goin' round it," and she pointed listlessly to her forehead.

"Come, come now, Nessie," he replied in a low tone which could not carry to the scullery, "you're aye talkin' about that headache. If you're always crying 'wolf, wolf' we'll not be believing you when it does come to the bit. So long as ye don't have the strap on the palm o' your hand ye shouldna mind it on the front o' your head."

"But it ties my brow so tight sometimes," she murmured mildly; "like a tight band."

"Tut! tut! it's the brain behind that matters, no' the brow, my girl. Ye should be thankful that ye're so well equipped in that respect." Then, as she began negligently to eat, he continued with extravagant approval: "That's better. Ye canna work without food. Take your fill o' whatever is goin'. Hard work should give a young lass like you an appetite, and hunger's guid kitchen." He suddenly shot a rancorous glance at his mother as he added harshly: "I'm pleased ye're not so particular and fasteedious as some folks."

Nessie, gratified that she was pleasing him and unfolding to some extent at his praise, redoubled her flagging efforts to eat but regarded him from time to time with a strained look in her eye as he continued reminiscently:

"When I was your age, Nessie, I could have eaten an ox when I came rushin' in from the fields for my dinner. I was a hardy chiel—ay—ready for what I could get. I could never get enough though. No! No! Things were different for me than they are for you, Nessie! I didna have your chance. Tell me," he murmured confidentially, "how are things goin' to-day?"

"Quite well," she replied automatically.

"You're still top of the class," he insisted.

"Oh! father," she expostulated, "I'm tired of explaining to you that we don't have that sort of thing now. I've told you half a dozen times in the last three months that it all goes by quarterly examinations." With a faint note of vanity in her voice she added: "Surely you understand that I'm past that stage now."

"Ay! ay!" he hastily replied, "I was forgettin' that a big girl and a fine scholar like you wouldna have to be fashed wi' such childish notions. True enough, it's examinations that you and me are concerned with." He paused, then in a sly tone remarked: "How long have we now till the big one?"

"About six months, I suppose," she answered half-heartedly, as she pallidly continued her meal.

"That's just fine," he retorted. "No' that long to wait and yet plenty of time for ye to prepare. Ye can't say ye havena had warnin' o't." He whispered almost inaudibly: "Ay! I'll keep ye to it, lass—you and me'll win the Latta between us."

At this point old Grandma Brodie, who had been sitting expectantly for a second course to follow and who, regardless of the conversation had been itching, but afraid, to say: "Is there nothin' else comin' " or "Is this a' we're to get," at last abandoned hope; with a resigned but muffled sigh she scraped back her chair from the table, raised her stiff form, and dragged disconsolately from the kitchen. As she passed through the door she was unhappily aware that little comfort was in her, that in the sanctuary of her room two empty tins awaited her like rifled and unreplenished tabernacles mutely proclaiming the prolonged absence of her favourite Deesides and her beloved oddfellows.

Wrapped in the contemplation of his daughter Brodie did not observe his mother's departure, but remarked in a tone that was almost coaxing:

"Have ye no news at all then, Nessie? Surely someone said something to ye. Did nobody tell ye again that ye were a clever lass? I'll warrant that ye got extra good marks for your home work." It was as though he besought her to inform him of some commendation, some pleasing attribute bestowed upon the daughter of James Brodie; then, as she shook her head negatively, his eye darkened to a sudden thought and he burst out savagely: "They havena been talkin' about your father, have they, any o' these young whelps? I daresay they listen to what the backbitin' scum o' their elders might be sayin', but if they come over a thing to ye, just let me know. And dinna believe it. Keep your head up, high up. Remember who ye are—that you're a Brodie—and demand your due. Show them what that means. Ay and ye will show them, my girl, when ye snap awa' wi' the Latta from under their snivellin' nebs." He paused, then, with a twitching cheek, bit out at her: "Has that young brat o' Grierson's been makin' any of his sneakin' remarks to ye?"

She shrank back timidly from him, exclaiming: "No! no, father! Nobody has said anything, father. Everybody is as kind as can be. Mrs. Paxton gave me some chocolate when she met me going down the road."

"Oh! she did, did she?" He hesitated, digesting the information; apparently it disagreed with him, for he sneered: "Well, tell her to keep her braw presents the next time. Say we have all we want here. If ye're wantin' sweeties, like a big saftie, could ye not have asked me for them? Do ye not know that every scandalmonger in the town is just gaspin' for the chance to run us down? 'He canna afford to give his own daughter a bit sweetie next,' that's what we'll be hearin' to-morrow, and by the time it gets to the Cross they'll be makin' out that I'm starvin' ye." His annoyance was progressive and he worked himself up to a climax, crying: "Bah! ye should have had more sense. They're all against us. That's the way o't now. But never mind! Let them fling all the mud they like. Let the hand of every man be turned against me—I'll win through in spite o' them." As he concluded he raised his eye wildly upwards when, suddenly, he observed that Nancy had come into the room, and was watching him from under her raised brows with a critical and faintly amused detachment. At once his inflated bearing subsided and, as though caught in some unwarrantable act, he lowered his head while she spoke.

"What's all the noise about! I thought that somebody had taken a fit when I heard ye skirlin' like that," and as he did not reply she turned to Nessie.

"What was the haverin' about? I hope he wasna flightin' at you, henny?"

With Nancy's advent into the kitchen a vague discomfort had possessed Nessie and now the skin of her face and neck, which had at first paled, flushed vividly. She answered confusedly, in a low voice:

"Oh! no. It was nothing—nothing like that."

"I'm glad to hear it," replied Nancy. "All that loud rantin' was enough to deafen a body. My ears are ringin' with it yet." She glanced round disapprovingly and was about to retire when Brodie spoke, looking sideways at Nessie, and with an effort making his voice unconcerned.

"If you've finished your dinner, Nessie run out to the front and wait for me. I'll not be a minute before I'm ready to go down the road with you." Then, as his daughter arose, picked up her things from the sofa and went silently, uneasily, out of the room he turned his still lowered head; looking upwards from under his brows, he regarded Nancy with a strong, absorbed intensity, and remarked:

"Sit down a minute, woman. I havena seen ye all the dinner hour. Ye're not to be angry at that tantrum. You should know my style by this time. I just forgot myself for a minute."

As she sat down carelessly in the chair Nessie had vacated his look drew her in with a possessive gratification which told more clearly than his words how she had grown upon him. So long without a fresh and vital woman in his house, so painfully encumbered by the old and useless body of his wife, this firm, white, young creature had entered into his blood like an increasing fever, and, by satisfying his fierce and thwarted instincts, had made him almost her slave.

"Ye didna give us any pudding, Nancy," he continued, clumsily taking her hand in his huge grasp; "will ye not give a man something to make up for't—just a kiss, now. That'll not hurt ye, woman, and it's sweeter to me than any dish ye could make."

"Tuts, Brodie! You're always on at the same thing," she answered, with a toss of her head. "Can ye not think o' something else for a change? Ye forget that you're a burly man and I'm but a wee bit lass that canna stand a deal of handlin'." Although the words were admonitory she threw an inflection of seductiveness into them which made him tighten his clasp on her fingers, saying:

"I'm sorry if I've been rough with ye, lass. I didna mean it. Come and sit closer by me, Come on now!"

"What!" she skirled, "in broad daylight. Ye maun be mad, Brodie, an' after last night too, you great lump. Ye'll have me away to shadow —no! no! ye'll not wear me out like ye did the other." She looked little like a shadow with her plump cheeks and solid form that had filled out more maturely from her six months of easy, indolent existence, and, as she regarded him with a substantial appreciation of his dependence upon her, she became aware that he was already losing his hold upon her, that the strange strength which had drawn her was being sapped by drink and her embraces, that he had now insufficient money to gratify her fancies, that he looked old, morose, and unsuited to her. She had almost an inward contempt for him as she resumed slowly, calculatingly: "I might gie ye a kiss, though. Just might, mind ye. If I did, what would ye give me for it?"

"Have I not given ye enough, woman?" he answered gloomily. "Ye're housed and fed like myself and I've sold many a thing out this house to meet your humour. Don't ask for the impossible, Nancy."

"Tuts, ye wad think ye had given me a fortune to hear ye," she cried airily. "As if I wasna worth it, either! I'm not askin' ye to sell any more tiepins or chains or pictures. I'm only wantin' a few shillin's for my purse to go out and see my Aunt Annie in Overtoun to-morrow. Give us five shillin's, and I'll give ye a kiss."

His lower lip hung out sulkily.

"Are ye goin' out again, to-morrow? Ye're aye goin' out and leavin' me. When will ye be back?"

"Man! I believe ye would like to tie me to the leg o' this table. I'm not your slave; I'm only your housekeeper." That was one for him, she thought, as she delivered the pert allusion to the fact that he had never offered to marry her. "I'll not be away all night. I'll be back about ten o'clock or so. Give us the two half-crowns and if ye behave I'll maybe be kinder to ye than ye deserve."

Under her compelling eyes he plunged his hand into his pocket, feeling, not the handful of sovereigns that had once reposed there, but some scanty coins, amongst which he searched for the sum she asked.

"Here ye are, then," he said eventually, handing her the money. "I can ill afford it but ye well know I can deny ye nothing."

She jumped up, holding the money triumphantly, and was about to slip away with it when he, too, got up, and catching her by the arm, cried:

"What about your bargain! You're not forgettin' about that! Do ye not care for me at all?"

Immediately she composed her features, lifted up her face, opened her eyes wide at him with an ingenious simplicity, and murmured:

"I should think I do care for ye. Do ye think I would be here if I didna? Ye shouldna get such strange ideas in your head. That's the way mad folk talk. You'll be sayin' I'm goin' away to leave ye next."

"No, I wouldna let ye do that," he replied, crushing her fiercely against him. As he strained her small unresisting form against his own bulk he felt that here was the anodyne to his wounded pride, forgetfulness of his humiliation, while she, turning her face sideways against his chest, looked away, thinking how ridiculous to her, now, was his infatuated credulity, how she wanted someone younger, less uncouth, less insatiable, someone who would marry her.

"Woman! what is it about ye that makes my heart like to burst when I have ye like this?" he said thickly, as he held her. "I seem to lose count of everything but you. I would wish this to go on for ever."

A faint smile creased her hidden features as she replied:

"And why should it not? Are ye beginnin' to get tired of me?"

"By God! you're fresher to me than ever ye were." Then after a pause he suddenly exclaimed: "It wasna just the money ye wanted, Nancy?"

She turned an indignant face to him, taking the opportunity to release herself.

"How can ye say such a thing? The very idea? I'll fling it back at ye in a minute if ye don't be quiet."

"No! No!" he interposed hurriedly, "I didna mean anything. You're welcome to it, and I'll bring ye something nice on Saturday." This was the day upon which he drew his weekly wage and with the sudden realisation of his subordinate position, of the change in his life, his face darkened again, became older, and looking down he said: "Well, I better go, then. Nessie's waitin' for me." Suddenly a thought struck him. "Where's that Matt, to-day?" he demanded.

"I couldn't say." She stifled a yawn, as though her lack of interest made her positively languid. "He went out straight away after breakfast. He'll not be back now till supper I expect."

He gazed at her for a moment then said, slowly:

"Well I'll away myself, then. I'm off!"

"That's right," she cried gaily. "Off with ye, and mind ye come straight back from the office. If ye have a single drink in ye when ye come in I'll let ye have the teapot at your head."

From under his heavy eyebrows he looked at her with an upward, shamefaced glance that sat ill upon his lined and sombre countenance; nodding his head to reassure her, he gave her arm a final squeeze and went out.

In the front courtyard, now thickly covered by sprouting weeds and denuded of the ridiculous ornament of the brass cannon—which three months ago had been sold for its value as old metal—he found Nessie patiently awaiting him, supporting her unformed drooping figure against the iron post of the front gate. At the sight of him she raised herself and, without a word, they set out together upon their walk to the point where their paths diverged at the end of Railway Road, where he would proceed to his work in the shipyard and she to hers at school. This daily pilgrimage had now become an established custom between Brodie and his daughter, and during its course he had the practice of encouraging and admonishing her, of spurring her onward to achieve the brilliant success he desired; but to-day he did not speak, tapping along with his thick ash stick, his coat sagging upon him, his square hat, faded and unbrushed, thrust back in a painful caricature of his old-time arrogance, marching silently and apart, with an air of inward absorption which made it impossible for her to speak to him. Always, now, in the public gaze he retired into himself, holding his head erect, looking directly in front of him and seeing no one, creating thus, for himself, wide depopulated streets filled, not with curious, staring, sneering faces, but by the solitude of his single presence.

When they reached their place of separation, he stopped—an odd arresting figure—and said to her:

"Away and work hard now, Nessie. Stick into it. Remember what I'm always tellin' you—'what's worth doin' is worth doin' well.' Ye've

339

got to win that Latta—that's a' there is about it. Here!"—he put his hand in his pocket—"Here's a penny for chocolate." He almost smiled. "Ye can pay me back when you've won the Bursary."

She took the coin from him, timidly yet gratefully, and went on her way to face her three hours of work in a stuffy classroom. If she had taken no breakfast and little lunch, she would at least be sustained and fortified against her study by the ample nourishment of a sticky bar of raspberry cream chocolate!

When she had gone the faint show of animation in his face died out completely and, bracing himself up, he turned and continued his progress to the office which he hated. As he drew near to the shipyard he hesitated slightly in his course, wavered, then faded into the doorway of the "Fitter's Bar" where, in the public bar, filled by workmen in moleskins and dungarees, yet to him tenanted by no one but himself, he swallowed a neat whisky, then quickly emerged and, retaining the fumes of the spirit by a compression of his lips, morosely entered the portals of Latta & Co.

II

ON the evening of the following day, when Nancy had departed to visit her aunt at Overton, and with Matt, as he always was at this hour, out of the house, a sublime and tranquil domesticity lay upon the kitchen of the Brodie home. So, at least, it seemed to the master of the house as, reclining back in his own chair, head tilted, legs crossed, pipe in mouth, and in his hand a full glass of his favourite beverage, hot whisky toddy, he contemplated Nessie, seated at the table, bent over her lessons, her pale brows knitted in concentration, then surveyed his mother who, in the temporary absence of the hated intruder, had not retired to her room, but sat crouched in her old corner beside the blazing fire. A faint flush marked Brodie's cheeks, his lips, as he sucked at his pipe, were wet and full, the eye, now turned meditatively upon the contents of the steaming tumbler, humid, eloquent; by some strange transformation his troubles were forgotten, his mind filled contentedly by the thought that it was a delightful experience for a man to spend an evening happily in his own home. True, he did not now go out in the evenings, or indeed, at any hours but those of his work, shunning the streets and the club, banned, too, from the small back parlour of the virtuous Phemie, and it should logically have been an event of less moment for him to hug the fire, and one less productive of such unusual gratification. But to-night, recognising that he would not be called upon to account to his housekeeper for his lateness at the tea-table, he had dallied by the wayside on his return from work, and now, mellowed further by a few additional drinks and the thought of more to come, the sadness of his separation from Nancy tempered by the exhilaration of his unwonted liberty and by the consideration of their reunion later in the evening, his induced felicity had enveloped him earlier and more powerfully than on most nights. Viewed from his armchair, through the clear amber of the toddy, his position in the office became a sinecure, his subordinate routine merely an amusing recreation; it was his whim to work like that and he might terminate it at his will; he was glad to be finished with his business, an ignoble trade which had clearly never suited his temper or his breeding; he would, however, shortly abandon the hobby of his present post for a more prominent, more lucrative occupation, startling the town, satisfying himself and delighting Nancy. His Nancy—ah! that was a woman for a man! As her image rose before him he toasted her, hoping enthusiastically that she might now be having a pleasant time with her aunt at Overton. Rosy mists floated through the dirty ill-kept room, tinting the soiled curtains, veiling the darker coloured square which marked the disappearance from the wall of Bell's engraving, sending a glow into Nessie's pale cheeks and softening even the withered, envious face of his mother. He watched the old woman's starting eyes over the edge of his glass as he took a long satisfying drink and, when he had drawn his breath, cried jeeringly:

"Ye're wishin' you were me, ye auld faggot. Ay, I can see from the greedy look about you that you wish this was goin' into your belly and not mine. Well, take it from me, in case ye don't know, it's a great blend o' whisky, the sugar is just to taste and the water is right because there's not too much o't." He laughed uproariously at his own wit, causing Nessie to look up with a scared expression, but catching his glance, she immediately lowered hers as he exclaimed:

"On with the work, ye young limmer! What are ye wastin' your time for? Am I payin' for your education for you to sit gogglin' at folks when you should be at your books." Turning to his mother again, he shook his head solemnly, continuing volubly: "I must keep her at it! That's the only way to correct the touch o' her mother's laziness that's in her. But trust me! I'll make her a scholar in spite of it. The brains are there." He took another pull at his glass and sucked noisily at his pipe.

The old woman returned his glance sourly, dividing her gaze between his flushed face and the whisky in his hand as she remarked:

"Where is that—where is she gane to-night?"

He stared at her for a moment then guffawed loudly. "Ye mean Nancy, ye auld witch. Has she put a spell on you, too, that you're feared even to lift her name?" Then after a pause during which he assumed a leering gravity, he continued: "Well, I hardly like to tell

341

ye, but if ye must know she's awa' to the Band of Hope meetin'."

She followed the vehemence of his mirth, as he shook with laughter, with an unsympathetic eye, and replied as tartly as she dared:

"I don't see much to laugh about. If she had gone to the Band o' Hope when she was younger she might have——" she stopped, feeling his eye upon her, thinking that she had gone too far.

"Go ahead," he gibed; "finish what ye were sayin'. Let us all have our characters when you're about it. There's no pleasin' some folk. Ye werena satisfied with Mamma, and now ye're startin' to pick holes in my Nancy. I suppose ye think you could keep the house yoursel'— that maybe ye might get an odd pingle at the bottle that way. Faugh! the last time ye cooked my dinner for me ye nearly poisoned me." He considered her amusedly from his elevated position, thinking of how he might best take her down a peg. Suddenly a wildly humorous idea struck him, which, in its sardonic richness, made him slap his thigh delightedly. She was grudging him his drink was she, eyeing it like a cat would a saucer of cream, gasping for it, ready to lap it up at the first opportunity. She should have it then, she who was so quick to run down other people! By Gad! she should have it. He would make her fou, yes, fou as a whelk. He realised that he had plenty of whisky in the house, that in any case it would take very little to go to the old woman's head, and as some foretaste of the drollery of his diversion invaded him, he rocked with suppressed hilarity and smote his leg again exuberantly. Losh! but he was a card!

Then all at once he cut off his laughter, composed his features and, narrowing his small eyes slyly, remarked cunningly:

"Ah! it seems hardly fair o' me to have spoken to ye like that, woman, I can see it's put ye right down. You're lookin' quite daunted. Here! would ye like a drop speerits to pull ye together?" Then, as she looked up quickly, suspiciously, he nodded his head largely and continued "Ay, I mean it. I'm quite serious. What way should I have it an' no' you? Away and get yoursel' a glass."

Her dull eye lighted with eagerness, but knowing his ironic tongue too well, she still doubted him, was afraid to move for fear a burst of his derisive laughter should disillusion her, and moistening her lips with her tongue she exclaimed, in a tremulous voice:

"You're not just makin' fun o' me, are ye?"

Again he shook his head, this time negatively, vigorously, and reaching down to the bottle conveniently beside his chair he held it out enticingly before her.

"Look! Teacher's Highland Dew. Quick! Away and get yoursel' a tumbler!"

She started to her feet, eagerly, as though she were beginning a race, and made her way to the scullery, trembling at the thought of her luck, she who had not lipped a drop since the day of the funeral and then only wine, not the real, comforting liquor. She was back, holding out the glass, almost before he had controlled the fresh exacerbation of amusement which her avid, tottering progress had afforded him; but, as he poured her out a generous allowance, he remarked, in a steady, solicitous voice:

"An old body like yersel' needs a drop now and then. See, I'm givin' you plenty, and don't take much water with it."

"Oh no, James," she protested. "Don't give me ower much. You know I'm not fond o' much o't—just a wee drappie to keep out the cold."

At her last words a sudden memory cut across his jocularity like a whip lash, and he snarled at her:

"Don't use these words to me! It minds me too much of somebody I'm not exactly fond of. Why do ye speak like a soft and mealy-mouthed hypocrite?" He glowered at her while she drank her whisky, quickly, for fear he should take it from her, then, urged by a more vindictive spirit he cried out: "Come on. Here's some more. Glass about."

"Na! Na!" she exclaimed mildly. "I've had enough. It's warmed me nicely and gie'n my mouth a bit flavour. Thenk ye all the same, but I'll no' hae any more."

"Ye'll not say no to me," he shouted roughly. "What are ye to refuse good spirits? Ye asked for it and you'll have it, even if I've to pour it down your auld thrapple. Hold out your glass; we'll drink fair."

Wonderingly she submitted, and when he had given her another liberal helping, she drank it more slowly, appreciatively, smacking her lips and rolling it over her tongue, murmuring between her sips: "It's the real stuff richt enough. It's unco' kind o' ye, James, to spare me this. I've never had so much afore. Troth I'm not used to it." She was silent whilst the liquid in her glass dwindled, then all at once she burst out: "It's got a graund tang on your tongue—has it no? 'Deed it almost makes me feel young again." She tittered slightly. "I was just thinkin' ——" she tittered more loudly.

At the sound of her levity he smiled darkly.

"Yes," he drawled, "and what were ye thinkin', auld woman? Tell us so that we can enjoy the joke."

She snickered the more at his words, and covering her wrinkled face with her knotted hands, abandoned herself to a delicious, inward humour until at last she coyly unveiled one senile, maudlin eye and whispered brokenly:

"Soap! I was just thinkin' about soap."

"Indeed now, ye were thinkin' about soap!" he mimicked. "That's very appropriate. Was it a wash that ye were wantin'? For if that's the case I can assure ye that it's high time ye had one."

"Na, na," she giggled, "it's no' that. It just flashed into my heid what the wives used to do in my young days, when they wanted a drop

343

o' speerits without the guid-man knowin' about it. They—they wad go to the village grocer's for their gill and get it marked to the book as soap—Soap!" She was quite overcome by her enjoyment of this delicious subtlety, and again buried her face in her hands; but she looked up after a moment to add: "Not that I ever did a thing like that! No! I was aye respectable and could scrub the house without that kind of cleanser!"

"That's right! Blow your own trumpet," he sneered. "Let us know what a paragon o' virtue you were. I'm listenin'."

"Ay! I did weel in these days," she continued reminiscently, losing, in the present fatuity of her mind, all awe of her son, "and I had muckle to put up wi'. Your father was as like you are now as twa peas in a pod. The same grand way wi' him, and as touchy as gunpowder. Many the night he would come in and let fly at me if things werna to his taste. But I stood up to him in a' his rages! I'm pleased to think on that." She paused, her look becoming distant. "I can see it like it was yesterday. Man, he was proud, proud as Lucifer."

"And had he not reason to be proud?" he exclaimed harshly, becoming aware that the drink was not taking her the way he had expected, that she was ceasing to amuse him. "Do ye not know the stock he came from?"

"Oh, ay, I kenned a' about that lang syne," she tittered spitefully, filled by a heady, rancorous imprudence. "He had the airs o' a duke, wi' his hand me this and reach me that, and his fine clothes, and his talk o' his forebears and what his rights were if he but had them. Oh! he was aye splorin' about his far-back connection wi' the Wintons— But I often wonder if he believed it hissel'. There's a' kinds o' connections," she sniggered, "and 'tis my belief that the lang syne connection was on the wrang side o' the blanket."

He glared at her, unable to believe his ears, then finding his tongue, he shouted:

"Silence! Silence, ye auld bitch! Who are you to talk like that about the Brodies? Ye bear the name yersel' now. How dare ye run it down before me," and he grasped the neck of the bottle as though to hurl it at her.

"Now, now, Jims," she drivelled, quite unperturbed, raising one uncertain, protesting hand, "ye mustna be unreasonable. I'm not the kind o' bird that files its ain nest—this is a' atween the family so to speak —and ye surely know it was a' gone intill and found out that the whole trouble began lang, lang syne wi' an under the sky affair atween Janet Dreghorn, that was the heid gardener's daughter, and young Robert Brodie that cam' to the title mony years after. Na! na, they were never bound by ony tie o' wedlock."

"Shut your blatterin' mouth," he roared at her. "If ye don't I'll tear the dirty tongue out o' it. You would sit there and miscall my name

344

like that. What do you think ye are? Ye were lucky my father married you. You—you——" He stammered, his rage choking him, his face twitching as he looked at her senseless, shrunken features. She was now completely intoxicated, and unconscious equally of his rage and of Nessie's frightened stare, continued:

"Lucky!" she babbled, with a drunken smirk, "maybe I was and maybe I wasna, but if ye kenned the ins and outs o' it all ye might think that ye were lucky yoursel'!" She broke into peals of shrill laughter, when suddenly, her false teeth, never at any time secure and how dislodged from her palate by her moist exuberance, protruded from between her lips like the teeth of a neighing horse, and impelled by a last uncontrollable spasm of mirth, shot out of her mouth and shattered themselves upon the floor. It was, in a fashion, a fortunate diversion, for otherwise he must certainly have struck her, but now they both gazed at the detached and scattered dentures that lay between them like blanched and scattered almonds, she staring with collapsed, grotesque cheeks and shrunken, unrecognisable visage, he with a muddled amazement.

"They're lyin' before ye like pearls before swine," he exclaimed at last. "It serves ye right for your blasted impudence."

"My guid false teeth!" she moaned, sobered by her loss yet articulating with difficulty, "that I've had for forty years! They were that strong, too, with the spring atween them. What will I do now? I canna eat. I can hardly speak."

"That'll be a good job, then," he snarled at her, "if it keeps you from gabblin' with your lyin' gongue. It serves you right."

"They'll not mend," she whined. "Ye maun get me a new set." Her forlorn eyes were still fixed upon the floor. "I canna just suck at my meat. Ye don't get the good out o' it that way. Say you'll get me another double set, James."

"Ye can whistle for that," he retorted. "What good would new teeth be to an auld deein' thing like you? You're not goin' to last that much longer. Just look on it as a judgment on ye."

At his words she began to whimper, wringing her bony hands together, and mumbling incoherently: "What a to do! I'll never get ower it. What's to become o' me that's had them so lang. It was a' the fault o' the speerits. I could aye manage them fine. It'll mean the end o' me."

He regarded her ludicrous, whining figure with a scowl, then, moving his glance, he suddenly observed the drawn face of Nessie watching the scene with a frightened yet fixed attention.

"What are you playin' at next?" he growled at her, his mood changed by his mother's recent remarks. "Can ye not get on with your own work? You'll get a braw lot done with that glaikit look about you. What's the matter with ye?"

"I can't get on very well with the noise, father," she replied timidly, lowering her eyes; "it distracts my attention. It's not easy for me to work when there's talking."

"So that's it!" he replied. "Well! there's plenty of room in the house now. If the kitchen isn't good enough for you, we'll put ye in the parlour. You'll not hear a sound there. Then ye'll have no excuse for idlin'." He got up and, before she could reply, advanced with a slight lurch to the table where he swept her books into one disordered heap; clutching this between his two enormous hands, he turned and stalked off, crying: "Come on. Into the parlour with ye. The best room in the house for my Nessie. You'll work in peace there, and work hard too. If ye can't study in the kitchen you'll gang into the parlour every night."

Obediently she arose and followed him into the cold, musty room where, after stumbling about in the darkness, he flung her books upon the table and at length succeeded in lighting the gas. The pale light gleamed from its frosted globe upon the chilly, uncovered mahogany table, the empty, unused fireplace, upon all the cold discomfort of the neglected, dust-shrouded chamber and lit up finally the overbearing figure of Brodie and the shrinking form of the child.

"There you are now," he cried largely, his good humour partially restored. "Everything's ready and to your hand. Draw up your chair and begin. Don't say that I havena helped ye." He put two fingers upon the pile of books and spread them widely over the surface of the table, disarranging them still more and losing all her places. "See! there's plenty o' room for a' your orders. Can ye not say thank ye!"

"Thank you, father," she murmured submissively.

He watched her with a complacent eye whilst she sat down and bent her thin shoulders in a presence of study, then he tiptoed with heavy, exaggerated caution from the room, protruding his head round the door as he went out to say:

"I'll be back in a minute to see how you're gettin' on." As he returned to the kitchen he told himself that he had done the right thing by Nessie, that he was the one to make her get on, and in a mood of self-congratulation he sat down again in his chair and in reward poured himself out another glass of whisky. Only then did he become aware of his mother, still sitting motionless, stupid, like a bereaved woman, with a hollow look, as if some power had sucked her empty.

"Are ye still here?" he shot at her. "You're far too quiet for one that had such a glib tongue in her head a minute ago. When I didna hear ye I thought ye would be away to sleep off your exertions. Go on—get away now, then. Away ye go, I'm sick of the look o' ye." And as she was slow in moving, he shouted: "Quick! out of my sight."

While he had been in the parlour she had collected the wreckage of her dentures from the floor, and now, clutching these fragments tightly in her hand she faded soberly from the room, her bowed, dejected carriage contrasting sadly with the gay eagerness with which she had rushed for the tumbler towards her own undoing.

Alone and untrammelled in the kitchen, Brodie addressed himself more assiduously to the bottle, washing away the unpleasant memory of her presence and the bitter recollections occasioned by her remarks. He knew, well, that unhappy truth lay in the foundation of her senile yet disconcerting reminiscences, but now, as always he chose to blind himself to their accuracy—a process never difficult to his obtuse and lumbering mind and one now rendered easier than ever by the liberality of his potations. Soon he had ¡orgotten the entire incident except for the ludicrous remembrance of her sudden and embarrassing edentation, and reclining at ease in his chair, and toping steadily, he mounted into the higher altitudes of intoxication. With the gradual elevation of his spirits he began to regret his solitary condition and with an impatient, swinging foot and eager glances at the clock he sought to anticipate the return of Nancy. But it was only nine o'clock, he knew that she would not arrive before ten, and, as the hands moved with a regular and monotonous slowness despite his efforts to expedite their progress, he got up and began to walk about the room. A wild idea of promenading the streets of the town, of bursting in upon the assembly at the club and disconcerting them with a few lurid and well-chosen words presented itself to him, but although he played with the appealing notion, he finally rejected it on the grounds that his Nancy would not approve. He had now lost his morose and gloomy oppression and, striding clumsily within the confines of the kitchen, his hair ruffled, his wrinkled clothes hanging more awkwardly upon him, his hands dangling like inactive flails, he felt he wanted to express the exultation of his mood in some definite and appropriate action. His past was for the moment forgotten and his outlook bounded only by the compass of the next few hours; he was himself again, yet from time to time, when the sound of his steps rang too loudly in his ears, he would pause with a profound concern for his student next door and, admonishing himself with a shake of his head, resume his pacing more silently, with a greater and more exaggerated caution.

At length the limits of the room became inadequate, failed to contain him. Insensibly he passed out of the doorway and began to wander about the house. He ascended the stairs, moved across the top landing, opened the door of his mother's room and flung an objectionable remark at her, chuckled to himself, entered Matt's bedroom, where he viewed with disgust the array of toilet lotions and hair pomades, and, having lit every gas so that the house blazed with light, finally he stood within his own apartment. Here, drawn by a hidden force, he went slowly forward to the chest of drawers where Nancy kept her clothing and, a sly leer mingling with his shamed consciousness, he commenced to pull out and examine the fine embroidered garments which she had bought with the money he had given her. He handled the smooth lace-edged vestments, touched soft lawn, fingered thin cambric, held the long empty stockings in his ponderous grasp, and his mouth curved with an upward slant while he invested the fragrant garments with the person of their owner. His shot eye, fixed upon the whiteness before him, saw actually the alabaster of her body, always to him a source of wonder and delight, and to his mind the texture of the stuff he handled seemed to have absorbed its colour from contact with that milky skin. As he remained there, displaying with stretched arms and for his sole enjoyment these flimsy articles of finery, he looked like some old and uncouth satyr who, stumbling upon the shed raiment of a nymph, had seized upon it and now, by contemplation, whetted his worn fancy capriciously.

At length he closed the drawers by a pressure of his knee and glancing sideways as he walked, moved stealthily from the room, shutting the door silently behind him. Outside, it was as though he had accomplished successfully and without detection some secret enterprise, for his shamed slyness dropped from him, he rubbed his hands noisily together, puffed out his cheeks, and heavily descended the stairs. In the hall he opened the parlour door, and cried, with a facetious assumption of gravity.

"Can I come in, ma'm? or are ye not at home?" Then without waiting for the reply, which indeed she did not utter, he entered the parlour, saying in the same manner: "I've been round my house to see that everything's in order, so there'll be no burglars to trouble ye to-night. Lights in all the windows! A fine splore o' illumination to show a' the rotten swine that we're gay and bricht in the Brodie house." She did not in the least understand what he meant but watched him with her blue, placating eyes that now seemed to be enlarged, to stand out from her cold, stiff face. With arms crossed and shivering, her thin-stockinged legs curled under her for warmth, having lost all sensation but that of numbness in her feet and hands, and her impressionable mind stamped by the scene she had witnessed in the kitchen, having failed completely to make headway with her study, she now regarded him fearfully.

"How are ye gettin' on?" he continued, looking at her closely. "Have ye enough quietness here to suit you? What have ye done since ye came in?"

She started guiltily, knowing that she had done nothing, unable to conceal anything from him.

"I haven't got on very well, father," she replied humbly. "It's so terribly cold in here."

"What! Ye havena got on well—and me that's been keepin' as quiet, as quiet for ye. What are ye thinkin' of?"

"It's the cold room," she repeated again. "I think it must be freezing outside."

348

"The room!" he cried, raising his brows with a tipsy gravity. "Did ye not beg and beseech me to bring ye in here? Did I not carry in your books in my own hands, and light the gas for ye, and set you down to it? Ye wanted in here and now you turn on me and complain!" Here his flushed face indicated an aggrieved and exaggerated disapproval. "Not got on well, forsooth! Ye·better get a bend on and look sharp about it."

"If there had been a fire!" she ventured diffidently, observing now that he was not in his severe vein towards her. "I'm all goose flesh and shivering."

Her words penetrated, struck some responsive chord in his soaked brain, for he started and, with a complete change of manner, cried with profuse pathos:

"My Nessie shiverin'! Here am I as warm as toast and my own, wee lassie freezin' and wantin' a fire! And what for no? It's reasonable. It's more than reasonable. Ye shall have a fire this minute if I've got to get it with my own hands. Sit still now, and wait and see what your father'll do for ye." He held up an admonishing finger to bind her to her seat and, moving unwieldily out of the room and into the cellar that adjoined the scullery, he fumbled in the dark amidst the coal and finally secured what he sought—a long, iron shovel. Then, brandishing this like a trophy, he advanced to the kitchen fire, and knocked down the front bars of the grate; thrusting the shovel under the glowing coals, he secured a flaming heap of red-hot cinders which he bore triumphantly back to the parlour, leaving a smoky trail behind him. Flinging the burning embers into the cold fireplace he cried, in a knowing voice: "Wait a minute! Just wait a minute! Ye havena seen it a' yet," and again disappeared, to return immediately with a huge bundle of sticks in one hand and the shovel, replenished this time with coal, in the other. Kneeling down clumsily he laid the sticks upon the cinders, and lying flat on his stomach, blew them stertorously until they blazed to his satisfaction. With a grunt he now raised himself and sitting within the confines of the hearth like a playful bull within its stall, he fed the flames sedulously with coal so that he achieved, eventually, a high crackling pyramid of fire. With both hands and one full glowing cheek grimed by smoke and coal dust, and his knees somewhat soiled by soot, he nevertheless surveyed his masterpiece with supreme approval, and cried: "Look at that, now! What did I tell ye! There's a fire for ye—fit to roast an ox. Ye couldna be cold at a blaze like that. On wi' the work now that ye've got your fire. There's not many a man would take such a trouble for his daughter, so don't let a' my bother be wasted. On ye go. Stick into the lessons."

Following this exhortation he seemed loath to get up and remained gazing at the leaping flames appreciatively, murmuring from time to time: "A beautiful fire! It's a bonnie blaze!"; but eventually he heaved himself up, and kicking the shovel to one side, muttered: "I'll away and bring my dram in beside ye," and went out of the room. As he departed Nessie—who fully realised from the unnatural manner of his conduct that her father was once again drunk—threw a quick glance, deeply charged with apprehension, at his retreating back. She had not done a stroke of work all evening and was now becoming thoroughly alarmed at her father's extraordinary behaviour. Although his treatment of her had lately been more peculiar—acts of sudden and unaccountable indulgence interpolating his perpetual coercion of her to study—she had never seen him so odd as he appeared to-night. At the sound of his step, when he returned with the remainder of the bottle of whisky, she sat rigid, pretending, with pale moving lips, to be engrossed in her work although she could not see the page which she held so closely before her.

"That's right," he muttered. "I see you're at it. I've done my bit for ye—now you do yours for me. That's another thing doun on my account for ye to settle when ye win the Latta." He subsided in a chair by the fireside and began again to drink. It seemed to him now that the evening had been long, as long even as a year, during which he had experienced a variety of profound and moving sensations, a period which had been a delightful prolongation of accomplishment and anticipation to be capped shortly by his reunion with Nancy. He became more joyful than ever. He wanted to sing! Fragments of tunes ran deliciously through his head, making him nod extravagantly and beat time with his foot and hand to this internal harmony. His small eyes seemed to protrude from his head as they roamed the room seeking some outlet for his culminating beatitude. Suddenly they lit upon the piano. Laud's sake! he told himself, what was the good of that if it wasn't to be used, that fine burr walnut instrument that had come from Murdoch's— bought and paid for these twenty years! It was a scandal to see it lying idle there, when a man had spent money on music lessons for his daughter.

"Nessie," he shouted, making her jump with fright. "You've got a' that book off by heart now. Put it away. You're goin' to have your music lesson now and I'm the teacher." He guffawed, then corrected himself: "No! I'm not the teacher—I'm the vocalist." He threw out his arm with a sweeping gesture. "We'll have some guid Scotch songs. Away— away over and give us 'O' a' the airts the wind can blaw' for a start."

Nessie slipped off her chair and looked at him doubtfully, knowing that he had forbidden the piano to be opened for months, feeling that she must obey, yet fearful of doing so; but as she stood indecisively he cried vehemently:

"Come on! Come on! What are ye waitin' for? 'O' a' the airts the wind can blaw,' I tell ye! I havena felt like this for months. I'm ripe for a sang!"

It was after ten o'clock and, as it was past her bedtime and she was worn by the strain of the long evening, she felt exhausted, but she was too terrified, too much in awe of him, to protest; and going, therefore, to the piano, she opened it, found the Scottish Song Book that had been Mary's, sat down, and began to play. Her small trembling fingers brought out as best they could the air that he demanded whilst from the seat by the fire, waving his pipe in undulating curves, Brodie sang the words boisterously.

> "*O' a' the airts the wind can blow,*
> *I dearly lo'e the west.*
> *It's there the bonnie lassie lives,*
> *The lassie I lo'e best.*"

"Louder! Louder!" he shouted. "Hit it harder! I'm singin' about my Nancy. We maun give it pith! 'By day and nicht my fancy's flight is ever with my Jean'!" he roared at the pitch of his voice. "By God! that was good. If we call her Jean—ye're none the wiser. Come on. Give us the second verse again, and sing yoursel'. Sing! Sing! Are ye ready! One, two, three!—

> "*I see her in the dewy flower.*"

She had never seen him like this before and in a panic of shame and fear she joined her quavering voice to his bellow so that together they sang the song.

"That was graund!" he cried, when they had finished. "I hope they heard us at the Cross! Now we'll have 'My Love is like a red, red Rose,' although mind ye she's more like a bonnie white rose. Have ye not found it yet? You're awfu' slow and clumsy the nicht. I'm as light as a feather though. I could sing till dawn."

She struck painfully into the song which he made her play and sing twice, and after that she was forced through "The Banks and Braes," "O Rowan Tree," and "Annie Laurie," until with her hands so, cramped and her head so giddy that she felt she must fall from the stool, she turned imploringly, and with tears in her eyes, cried:

"Let me go, father. Let me go to my bed. I'm tired." He frowned upon her heavily, her interruption cutting in rudely upon his blissful state. "So ye can't even play for your father," he exclaimed, "and after he's taken all the trouble to go and put on a fire for ye, too. The minute it's on ye want away to your bed. That's gratitude for you. Well, if ye'll not do it for right you'll do it for might. Play! Play till I tell ye to stop, or I'll take the strap to ye. Play my first song over again!"

She turned again to the piano and wearily, with eyes blinded by tears, began again, "O' a' the airts the wind can blaw," whilst he sang, emphasising every discord which her agitation led her to produce by a black look directed towards her bowed and inoffensive back.

They had proceeded half-way through the song when suddenly the parlour door opened and Nancy—her eyes sparkling, the cream of her cheek tinted by a faint colour from the cold, her hair crisping under her attractive toque, the neat fur tippet setting off her firm bust to perfection—Nancy—his Nancy, stood before him. With mouth wide open and pipe poised in mid air he stopped singing, regarding her stupidly, realising that he had failed to hear the opening of the front door, and he continued to stare thus while the unconscious Nessie, as though accompanying his silent astonishment and admiration, played through the song to its end, when silence descended upon the room.

At length Brodie laughed, a trifle uncomfortably. "We were just singin' a wee song to ye, Nancy, and troth ye deserve it for you're lookin' as bonnie as a picture."

Her eyes sparkled more frostily and her lips tightened as she replied:
"The noise comin' up the road was enough to draw a crowd round the house—and lights blazin' out o' every window. And ye've been at your soakin' again and then ye've the impertinence to make me the grounds for it a'! You're a disgrace! Look at your hands and your face. You're like an auld coal-heaver. What a thing for me to come home to, after an elevatin' evenin' like I've had."

He looked at her humbly, yet drinking in, even at its coldness, the freshness of her young beauty, and in an attempt to change the subject, he murmured heavily:

"Did ye have a nice time at your aunt's? I've missed you, Nancy. It's like a year since I saw ye last. Ye were a long time comin' to me."

"And I wish I had made it longer," she exclaimed, with a hard glance at him. "When I want music I know where to get it. Don't bawl at me and don't drink to me—ye blackfaced drunkard."

At these terrible words Nessie, sitting petrified upon the piano stool, shrank back, expecting her father to rise and fling himself upon the mad woman who had uttered them: but to her amazement he remained passive, drooping his lip at Nancy and muttering:

"I tell ye I've been missin' you, Nancy. Don't turn on a man that's so fond o' ye."

Disregarding his daughter's presence entirely, he continued blatantly, with an almost maudlin' sentiment: "You're my white, white rose, Nancy. You're the breath in my body. I had to pass the time somehow! Away up and take off your things and dinna be cross wi' me. I'll—I'll be up mysel' in a minute."

"Oh! you will!" she cried, with a toss of her head. "You're drinkin' like a fish, you rough, big bully. Go up any time ye like for all I care. It makes no odds to me—as you'll soon see," and she flounced up the stairs out of his sight.

With lowered head he sat quite still, filled by the melancholy thought that she was angry with him, that when he went upstairs he would have to appease her, pacify her, before she manifested her kindness towards him. In the midst of his dejected meditations he suddenly realised his daughter's presence and, considering moodily that he had betrayed himself to her, he muttered thickly, without looking up:

"Away up to your bed, you! What are ye sittin' there for?" And when she had slipped like a shadow from the room he continued to sit by the rapidly dying embers of the fire until he adjudged that Nancy might be in bed, and more amenable to his advances. Then, blind to the complete reversal of his position in the house since the days when he had left his wife to brood by the dismal remnants of a dead fire, anxious only to be beside his Nancy, he got up and, having turned out the gas, passed slowly and as lightly as he could, up the stairs. He was consumed by eagerness, eaten by desire, as he entered his lighted bedroom.

It was empty!

With unbelieving eyes he gazed round until it slowly dawned upon him that this night she had kept her word and forsaken him; then, after a moment, he turned and, moving silently across the dark landing, tried the handle of the door of that small room to which his wife had retired —the room, indeed, where she had died. This, as he expected, was locked. For one instant a torrent of resentment surged within him and he gathered himself together to hurl himself against and through the door, to batter it down by the strength of his powerful and desirous body. But immediately came the realisation that such a course would not benefit him, that inside the room he would still find her bitter, more bitter and unyielding than before, more icy, more determined to oppose his wish. She had enslaved him, insidiously yet completely, and for that reason was now stronger than he. His sudden fury died, his hand dropped from the door and slowly he re-entered his own room and shut himself within it. For a long time he remained in sullen silence, then impelled by an irresistible impulse he went to the drawer he had opened earlier in the evening, slowly pulled it out once more, and with a heavy brow stood staring inscrutably at the contents within.

III

MATTHEW BRODIE came out of Levenford Station, leaving the platform, splashed with its pale yellow lamplight, behind him and entered the cold, exhilarating darkness of the frosty February night with a lively feeling of elation. His steps upon the hard ground rang out quick and clear; his face, blurred in the surrounding obscurity, radiated nevertheless a faint excited gleam; the fingers of his inquiet hands twitched continually from the suppression of his pervading exultation. He walked rapidly along Railway Road, through the tenuous low-lying haze above which the tops of trees and houses loomed like darkly smudged shadows against the lighter background of the sky. Towards his expanded nostrils came, from across the open space of the Common, the faint aromatic odour of a distant wood fire and, as he sniffed it, filling his lungs deliciously with the tingling savour of the air, he was permeated by a vivid sense of the zest of living. Despite the forward thrust of his mood, memories rushed across him at that acrid, yet spicy breath, and he became enveloped in a balmy dusk that was filled with strange quiescent sounds, fragrant subtle scents, and the white and liquid shimmer of a tropic moon. His drab and evasive existence of the last six months fell away from his recollection while he considered the glamour of his life abroad, and as if to answer the appeal of such a free and enchanting land, he further accelerated his pace and swung along the road with impetuous eagerness in the direction of his home. This haste, in one who, when approaching the house in the evenings, displayed usually a flagging step, indicative of his disinclination to encounter his father, seemed to betoken an important change in the current of Matt's life. He was indeed, at this moment, bursting with the news of that change, and as he rushed up the steps, opened the front door of the house, and entered the kitchen he trembled, actually, with his excitement.

The room was empty except for Nancy, who, slowly and tardily clearing the tea-table of its dishes, looked up at his sudden appearance with an expression of surprise, mingled also with an unguarded and engaging familiarity which at once indicated to him that his father was not at hand.

"Where is he, Nancy?" he exclaimed, immediately. She rattled a dish contemptuously upon the tray as she replied:

"Out for the usual, I suppose. There's only one thing takes him out at this hour, and that's to get the black bottle filled up again." Then she added slyly: "But if you're wantin' to see him he'll be back soon."

"I'm wantin' to see him, all right," he blustered, looking at her significantly. "I'm not feared to meet him. I've got news for him that'll make him sit up and take notice."

She glanced at him quickly, noting now his slightly hurried breathing, the glitter in his eye, the general concealed importance of his bearing.

"Have ye news, then, Matt?" she said slowly.

"I should think I have!" he declared. "The best that I've had for nine months. I'm just this minute off the train. I've only had word o' the thing an hour ago, and I couldna get back quick enough to tell it— to fling it in that auld devil's face."

She left the dishes entirely and advanced deliberately towards him, saying ingratiatingly:

"Was it only your father ye wanted to tell, Matt? Am I not to know first? I'm gey interested to hear."

A broad smile spread over his features.

"Of course you're to know! Ye ought to understand that by this time."

"What is it then, Matt?" she whispered.

As he saw her eagerness, he swelled the more, and, determining to edge her curiosity, he suppressed his own excitement, moved to his favourite spot by the dresser, and reclining in his particular manner, surveyed her with a boasting eye.

"Come, come now. Can ye not guess? Surely a clever wee body like yourself can guess? You haven't got that trig head on your shoulders for nothing."

She knew positively now what the purport of his tidings must be, but, seeing that he was pleased to exhibit his air of consequence, it suited her to pretend ignorance, and with a charming assumption of simplicity, she shook her head and replied:

"No, Matt! I can hardly think. I'm almost afraid to say. Would it be about your father?"

He wagged his head from side to side portentously.

"No! Not this time, Nancy, dear. Leave him out of the question. It's about another man altogether. Somebody younger, that can take a glass without soakin' in it, that can take a lass out to a concert and let her enjoy herself. Think on somebody that's fond of you."

"It's yourself, Matt! Oh!" she gasped, widening her eyes, "ye don't mean to say ye've got that post."

"Did I say I hadn't got it?" he leered at her.

"Have ye, though? Tell us quick, Matt. I'm that excited about I can hardly stand still!"

"Yes!" he cried, unable to restrain himself longer. "I have got it. The job's signed, sealed, and delivered into my hands. It's me for South America—passage paid—free livin'—and plenty of money in my pocket. To hell with this rotten town, and this blasted house and the drunken, auld bully that owns it. It'll be something for him to smoke in his pipe when he hears."

"He'll be pleased enough, Matt," she replied, again advancing to him as he leaned against the dresser.

"Ay, glad to be rid of me, I suppose," he answered sulkily. "But I'm glad enough to go. And I'll be even with him yet. He'll maybe get something he doesn't like before long."

"Never mind about him. He's just an auld ɪool. I'm as sick o' him as you are. I canna think what I ever saw in him." She paused, then added ingenuously, pathetically; "I'm real pleased too, that ye've got the job, Matt, although—although——"

"Although what," he replied largely, looking down at her soft, appealing eyes. "Surely I've waited long enough for it."

"Ay—it was just nothing," she answered with a sigh, stroking his hand absently, almost unconsciously, with her soft finger tip. "It's a wonderful opportunity for ye. It must be grand for you to gang abroad like that. I can see the big boat drivin' through the blue sea, wi' the sun on it. I can just fancy the lovely place that you're goin' to—Rio—what was it ye called it again?"

"Rio de Janeiro," he replied grandly. "I'll only be a couple of miles out of it. It's a wonderful city and a beautiful climate. There's a chance for a man out there, a hundred times better than in India."

"I'm sure ye'll do well," she murmured, now holding his hand entirely in her soft clasp. "But I'll be that lonely without ye. I don't know whatever I'll do. It's hard for a young lass like me to be tied up here!"

He gazed at her as though his suppressed feeling had not entirely left him, as though, escaping only in part, it had left still an effervescence behind.

"You're not wantin' me to go," he remarked slyly. "I can see that!"

"Of course I am, you wicked man! I wouldn't for the world stop you. It's a grand chance." She gave his hand an admonitory squeeze, and added: "And you said it was such good money too?"

"Yes! it's a handsome salary," he assented impressively, "and they've flung in a bungalow with it as well. I couldn't wish for more. My experience out East has done me a good turn after all."

She was silent, gazing with an appealing candour at his face, but seeing instead, a strange mysterious city, shadowed by exotic trees, with cafés in its streets, a band in the square, with herself there smiling, dashing along gaily in a carriage, veiled in a lace mantilla, drinking red wine, happy, free. Her thoughts were so poignant, so touching, that without difficulty she pressed a tear from her swimming eyes and allowed it to steal slowly, entrancingly down the smooth curve of her cheek as, with a gentle movement, she leant against him and whispered:

"Oh! Matt, dear, it'll be hard to do without ye! You're goin' to leave me just when I'm beginnin' to——"

A strange exultation possessed him as she pressed against him and, seizing her downcast face between his palms, he made her look at him.

"Don't say you're beginning—say you do love me."

She did not speak but, more potently than any words, veiled her soft eyes as though she feared to let him see the intensity of her passion for him.

"Ye do!" he cried. "I can see that ye do!" His lips twitched, his nostrils dilated as a fierce delight filled him, not from the touch of her form alone, but from the understanding that he had ousted his father, that fate had delivered into his hands a powerful weapon of revenge.

"I know I'm a bad girl, Matt," she whispered, "but I mean to do well. I'm goin' to leave him. I went to the front room myself all last night. That—that's finished. I would never look at another man unless

356

I married him, and then I would stick to my man through thick and thin."

He continued to look at her fixedly, whilst she continued, with great feeling:

"I think I could make a man happy if I tried. There's wee things about me that he might like one way and another. I would do my best to give him a' that he wanted!" She sighed and drooped her head against his shoulder.

His thoughts twisted incoherently amongst the conflict of his emotions, but through the warm mists in his brain he saw that this was doubly desirous to him—not only to strike his father but, additionally for his own gratification. Nancy was a woman in a thousand, lovely, entrancing, ardent, not with the strong and clumsy vehemence of Agnes Moir but with a subtler, a more delicate and alluring flame which pervaded her pale white body like an essence and drew him towards its clear heat. Her beauty, too, surpassed by far the merely tolerable comeliness of the unfortunate Agnes; her figure was, not sturdy, but elegant; no umber shadow menaced the exquisite curve of her soft upper lip; not only was she beautiful, but she was, he was convinced, enamoured of him to the point of passionately abandoning his father because of her feeling for him. Filled by these thoughts he was confirmed in his resolution and, in a choked voice, he exclaimed:

"Nancy! There's something I've got to tell you—something else that you don't know. Something that might interest you. Would you like to hear it?"

She looked at him languishingly, throwing her head back so that the inclination of her poise invited his embrace, and was about to murmur "Yes," when suddenly the front door of the house clicked open and was heavily shut, and the sound of footsteps was heard along the hall. Like a flash Nancy recovered herself from the apparent profundity of her feeling and, pushing Matt to the fireplace she cried, in a sharp whisper:

"Bide there, and don't let on. He'll never know," then in the same instant her hands had flown to her hair and, moving as lightly as quick fluttering birds, had adjusted, patted smooth such small disorder as might have existed. She was back at the table immediately, clattering the dishes, when Brodie entered the room.

For a moment Brodie paused in the doorway, an unwrapped bottle swinging in his hand, surveying first his son, whom he so rarely saw, with a black lowering disgust, allowing his glance to travel questioningly to Nancy, then returning it restlessly to the uneasy figure by the fireplace. His dull understanding appreciated nothing of the undercurrent of the events he had disturbed, but his moody eye perceived the faint flush upon Matt's sallow cheek, the downcast look, the nervous agitation of his attitude, and instinctively his memory rushed back to that scene in the house in the Vennel, when he had surprised his son with Nancy struggling in his arms. He knew nothing, suspected nothing, but he was none the less tormented by this vision of his memory, felt instinctively that some secret activity had been in process at his entry; his glance became black and darting, impaling Matt, who moved more uneasily, and hung his head with greater embarrassment, the longer that silent stare continued.

Nancy, at the table, her inveterate hardihood rendering her composed, perfect mistress of her features, inwardly furious at the flustered ineptitude of the hero to whom she had so passionately avowed her devotion, attempted to rescue him by remarking, tartly, to the elder man:

"What are ye standin' there for, Brodie—like a big bear? Come in and sit down, and don't swing that bottle as though ye wanted to brain us. Ye look downright uncanny. Come awa' in." But Brodie did not seem to hear her, and, allowing her remark to pass unheeded, still continued to view his son from the vantage point of the door, still swinging the bottle like a club, until at length he spoke, saying with a snarl:

"What's the honour o' this visit due to? We're not usually so fortunate when we come in at this time—no! your home's not good enough for you in the evenings now. You're one o' these late birds we never seem to see at all."

Matt opened his dry lips to speak, but before he could reply Brodie continued, fiercely:

"Have ye been sayin' anything to Nancy here that ye might like to repeat to me?—If ye have I'm listenin' and waitin'."

Here Nancy broke in, flinging her hands upon her hips, squaring her neat shoulders, and tossing her head indignantly.

"Are ye mad, Brodie, that ye go on like that? What are ye talkin' about at all, at all? If you're goin' to rave in that fashion I'll be muckle obliged if ye'll kindly keep my name out o' it."

He turned slowly and surveyed her. His drawn brows relaxed.

"I know, woman! I know it's all right! I would never doubt ye and I know he's too feared of me to dare it, but somehow the sight o' the glaikit, fushionless loon aye embitters me. He looks as if butter wouldna melt in his mouth and yet I can never forget that he tried to shoot me." He swung round again to Matt who had paled at these last words and exclaimed, bitterly: "I should have given ye over to the police for that —you that tried to shoot your father. Ye got off too easy that night. But I'm no' so good humoured as I used to be, so don't try any more tricks on me or by God! I'll lay your skull open wi' this very bottle. Now will ye tell me what you're doin' here."

"He was tellin' me about some job or other," cried Nancy shrilly, "but I didna ken what it was a' about." Would he never speak? she thought, the stupid fool that was standing there as white and flabby as a soft lump of putty, giving the whole affair away by his lack of gumption.

"What job?" said Brodie. "Speak for yourself, sir!"

At last Matthew found his tongue, he who on the homeward journey had visualised his superior attitude during the interview and traced the manner in which he would gradually lead up to it, who had just told Nancy how he would throw his new position in this old devil's teeth.

"I've got a position in America, father," he stammered, Brodie's face did not change but after a pause he sneered:

"So you're goin' to do some work at last. Weel! weel! Wonders will never cease. The heir to the house o' Brodie is goin' to work? It's a good thing too, for though ye've kept out of my way right well, now that I've seen ye again I feel I would soon have flung ye out." He paused. "What is this grand position? Tell us all about the marvels of it."

"It's just my own work," stammered Matt, "storekeeping. I've had my name down for months with two or three firms, but it's not often a chance like this crops up."

"And how did a thing like you get hold o' the chance? Was it a blind man that engaged ye?"

"It was an emergency," replied Matt apologetically. "The man that had the job died suddenly. He was flung off his horse and they wanted somebody in a hurry. I'll have to leave at once—within a week—to fill the place as soon as ever I can. Maybe ye've heard o' the firm. They're ——" Here a cup fell clattering from the tray, and smashed with a sudden, ringing cadence upon the floor.

"Guidsakes," cried Nancy in a great commotion, "that's what comes o' standin' haverin' like auld wives. It's always the way if ye take your mind off what you're doin'—you're sure to go and break something or other." She bent down to pick up the fragments and as she stooped she flashed a glance at Matthew, quick, covert, but full of suppressed and significant warning. "I'm sorry if I interrupted you," she murmured to Brodie as she got up.

Matthew had observed the glance, interpreted its meaning and though his embarrassment grew, swollen from another source, with a feeble attempt at strategy he lowered his eyes and murmured:

"They're—they're in the wool business. It's to do with sheep."

"By God! they've got the right man," cried his father, "for a bigger sheep than yoursel' never went bleatin' about this earth. Take care they don't crop ye, by mistake, at the shearin' time. Look up, ye saft sheep! Can ye not hold your head up like a man and look at me? A' this flash and dash that's come on ye since ye went to India doesna deceive me. I thought it might make a man o' ye to go out there, but I see through the rotten gloss that it's gie'n ye, and you're but the same great, blubberin' sapsy that used to greet and run to your mother whenever I put my een on ye."

He stood looking at his son, filled by a profound and final repugnance which sickened him even of the thought of baiting Matt, who, he considered disgustedly, was not worth even the lash of his tongue. Thank God he was going away, to quit his home, to abandon this sneaking, sponging existence, to be irrevocably out of his sight, out of the country, forgotten.

Suddenly he felt tired, realised dimly that he was not the man he had been and, with a quick rushing desire for the nepenthe of forgetfulness, he wanted to be alone with Nancy, wanted to drink. To his son he said, slowly:

"You and me are finished, Matt. When ye've gone ye'll never come back into this house. I never want to see ye again," then, turning to Nancy, and regarding her with a fond and altered glance he added:

"Bring me a glass, Nancy. He doesna deserve it, but I'm goin' to give him a toast." As she silently departed to obey he followed her with the same glance, feeling that she was warming to him again, that with his son out of the house, they would be more private, more unrestrainedly together than before. "Thank ye, Nancy," he said mildly, as she returned and handed him the glass. "Ye're an obleegin' lass. I don't know how I ever got on without ye." Then he continued, reassuringly: "I'm not goin' to take ower much to-night. No! no! This bottle will do me for a week. I know fine ye don't like me to take too much and I'm not goin' to do it. But we must pledge this big maunderin' sheep before he goes out to join the flock. Will ye have just a wee taste yer'sel', Nancy? It'll do ye no harm. Come along now," he added with a clumsy ingratiating manner, waving his arm at her, "away and get yourself a glass—and I'll give ye just enough to warm ye."

She shook her head, still without speaking, her eyes half-veiled, her lips smoothly parted, her expression neither hostile nor friendly but shaded by a vague reticence which gave to her an air of enigmatic subtlety that encouraged him, drew him towards her by its very mystery. Actually, behind the mask of her face lay a bitter contempt of him, activated the more fiercely as she saw that in choosing thus to humiliate Matt before her he was intimidating his son, making it more difficult for her to achieve the purpose she had set herself.

"No?" he said affably, "well! I winna drive ye, woman. You're a mare that needs gentle guidin'—as I've proved to my cost. Ye maun be humoured—not driven." A short laugh broke from him as he uncorked the bottle, and holding the glass to the level of his eye, which glittered at the first sight of the trickling liquor, slowly poured out a large measure, raised the bottle, paused, moistened his lips with his tongue, then quickly added a further quantity of the spirit. "I may as well take a decent glass to begin with. It saves goin' back and back. And I can stand it onyway," he muttered, keeping his head down and away from her, as he placed the bottle upon the dresser and transferred the glass of whisky to his right hand. Then, stretching out his arm he cried:

"Here's a toast to the heir to the house o' Brodie—the last I'll ever drink to him. May he go to his grand job and may he stay there! Let him get out o' my sight and keep out o' it. Let him go how he likes and where he likes, but let him never come back, and if ever he tries to get on to that horse he was speakin' about, may he fall off and break his useless neck like the man that had the place before him!" He threw back his head and, with a tilt of his wrist, drained the glass at a gulp, then, surveying Matthew with a sardonic grin, he added: "That's my last good-bye to ye. I don't know where ye're goin'—I don't even want to know. Whatever happens to ye makes no odds now, for it'll never reach my ears!" And with these words he ceased to regard his son, ignored him utterly. Now that he had swallowed the whisky he felt more vigorous. Lifting his eye again to the bottle on the dresser, he considered it speculatively for a moment, cleared his throat, straightened himself up and, his head averted from Nancy, remarked solemnly: "But I canna drink a toast to a thing like him and pass over a braw lass like my Nancy." He shook his head at the injustice of the thought as, with the empty tumbler still in his hand, he approached the table. "No! that would not be fair!" he continued, pouring himself out another portion. "I couldna do that in all conscience—we must give the girl her due. There's nothing I wouldna do for her, she means so much to me. Here, Nancy!" he cried, wheedlingly, turning to her: "This is a wee salute to the bonniest lass in Levenford."

She had controlled her temper so long that now it seemed impossible for her to contain herself further, and her veiled eyes sparkled and a faint colour ran into her cheeks as though she might immediately stamp her foot and assail him furiously with her tongue. But instead, she stifled the words she wished to utter behind her tight lips, and, turning on her heel, marched into the scullery where she began noisily to wash the dishes. With a chastened expression Brodie stood, his head slightly on one side, listening to the clatter of china; he heard in it some suggestion of her exasperation, but soon, returning his eyes again to the glass in his hand, he slowly raised it to his lips and slowly drained it; then, advancing to his chair he lowered himself heavily into it.

Matt, who had remained at the place by the fireplace where he had been thrust by Nancy, a silent and dismayed spectator of his father's recent actions, now moved uneasily upon his feet, subdued more abjectly by the closer proximity of the other as he sat brooding in his chair. He moved his eyes restlessly round the room, bit his pale lips, rubbed his soft, damp hands together, wishing fervently to leave the room but, thinking his father's eye to be upon him, was afraid to stir. At length, emboldened by the continued silence in the room, he widened the scope of the sweeping circles of his eye and allowed his flickering glance to touch for a swift second upon the face of the other beside him. Immediately he saw that Brodie was not, as he had feared, contemplating him but instead gazing earnestly towards the open doorway of the scullery and, reassured by the other's abstraction, he ventured one tentative foot in front of him, was not observed, and, continuing his stealthy progress—slid quietly out of the kitchen.

His intention had been to escape from the house as quickly as possible, resigning himself to an interminable wait in the streets outside until his father had gone to bed, but he was arrested, in the dimness of the hall, by a segment of light striking out from the parlour. As he paused, suddenly it occurred to him that since Nessie was within, he might spend a few moments more comfortably with her before departing into the frosty night outside. He felt, too, unconsciously, the pressing need for the opportunity to declaim upon the merit of the attainment of his new post, and the desire for some approving tribute to restore the damage inflicted upon his self-esteem. Consequently he opened the door and looked into the room.

Nessie, seated at the table, surrounded by the inevitable accompaniment of her books, did not look up at his entry but remained with folded arms, hunched shoulders, and bent head. But when he spoke, with a sudden quick start she flinched as though the unexpected waves of speech had struck her across the stillness of the room.

"I'm coming in a minute," was all that he had said.

"Oh! Matt," she cried, pressing her small closed hand into her left side, "what a start you gave me! I didn't hear you come in. I seem to jump at anything these days."

As he observed her present attitude, the inclination of her head, the mild and limpid eyes, filled with a mute apology for her weakness, a striking memory presented itself to him, making him for the moment forget his own concerns.

"My goodness, Nessie," he exclaimed, staring at her. "You're getting as like Mamma as life. I can almost see her looking out of your face the now!"

"Do you think so, Matt," she replied, flattered in some degree to be the object of his interest. "What makes you say that?"

He seemed to consider.

"I think it's your eyes; there's the same look about them as though you thought something was going to happen to you and were looking ahead for it."

At his words she was hurt and immediately lowered these betraying eyes, keeping them fixed upon the table as he continued:

"What's come over you lately?—you don't seem the same to me at all. Is there anything wrong with you that's making you like that?"

"Everything's wrong," she answered slowly. "Since Mamma died I've been at miserable as could be and I haven't had a soul to speak to about it. I can't suffer to be near to—to Nancy. She doesn't like me. She's always at me for something. Everything is different. The house has been so different that it's not like the same place—father's different, too."

362

"You've nothing to be feared of from him. You were always his pet," he retorted. "He's always sucking round you in some way."

"I wish he would leave me alone," she replied dully. "He's just driving me on all the time with this work. I can't stand it. I don't feel well in myself."

"Tuts! Nessie," he exclaimed reprovingly, "that's Mamma all over again. Ye should pull yourself together. What's the matter with you?"

"I've always got a headache! I wake up with it in the morning and it never leaves me all day. It makes me so stupid that I don't know what I'm doing. Besides, I can't eat the food we get now and I'm always tired. I'm tired at this very minute."

"You'll be all right when you've got this exam. over. You'll win the Latta all right."

"I'll win it all right," she exclaimed wildly. "But what's going to become of me then! What is he going to do with me after? Tell me that! Am I to be shoved on like this all the time and never know what's going to come of it? He'll never say when I ask him. He doesn't know himself."

"You'll be a teacher—that's the thing for you."

She shook her head.

"No! that wouldn't be good enough for him. I wanted to do that myself—to put down my name to go on to the Normal, but he wouldn't allow it. Oh! Matt," she cried, "I wish I had somebody to put in a word for me. I'm so downright wretched about it and about everything else—I wish sometimes I had never been born!"

He shifted his gaze uncomfortably from her appealing face which, stamped by a forlorn wistfulness, seemed to implore him to help her.

"You should get out the house and play with the other girls," he advanced, somewhat uncertainly. "That would take your mind off things a bit."

"How can I?" she exclaimed frantically. "Ever since I was a wee thing I've been kept in at these lessons, and now I'm flung in here every night, and will be, too, for the whole of the next six months. And if I dared to go out he would leather me. You would'nt believe it, Matt, but I sometimes think I'll go out of my mind the way I'm kept grindin' at it."

"I go out," he exclaimed valiantly. "He didn't stop me goin' out."

"You're different," she replied sadly, her puny outburst subsiding and leaving her more dejected than before. "And even if I did go out what good would it do? None of the other girls would play with me. They'll hardly speak to me as it is. One of them said the other day that her father said she was to have nothing to do with anyone that came out of this house. Oh! I do wish you could help me, Matt!"

"How can I help you?" he replied roughly, irritated at her entreaties. "Don't you know I'm goin' away next week?"

She gazed at him with a slight wrinkling of her brow and repeated, without apparently comprehending:

"Going away next week?"

"To South America," he replied grandly; "to a splendid new position I've got out there. Miles and miles away from this sink of a town."

Then she understood, and in the sudden perception that he was leaving immediately for a far-distant land, that she, of all the Brodie children, would be left in a solitary, unprotected state to face the dreadful unhappiness of her present existence in the home, she paled. Matt had never helped her much, and during these latter months had, indeed, comforted her still less, but he was her brother, a companion in her distress, and she had only a moment ago appealed to him for assistance. Her lips quivered, her eyes became blurred, she burst into tears.

"Don't go, Matt," she sobbed. "I'll be left all alone if ye go. I'll have nobody at all in this terrible house."

"What are ye talking about," he retorted savagely. "You can't know what you're saying. Am I going to give up the chance of a lifetime —money and freedom and—and everything for the likes of you? You're mad!"

"I'll be mad if you go," she cried. "What chance will I have here all by myself?—Mary away, and you away, and only me left! What'll become of me?"

"Stop your howling," he shot at her, with a quick glance towards the door. "Do you want everybody to hear you with that bawling? He'll be in at us in a minute if you're not careful. I've got to go and that's all about it."

"Could ye not take me with you then, Matt," she gulped, stifling her sobs with difficulty. "I know I'm young but I could keep the house for ye. That's always the sort of thing I've wanted to do—and not these miserable lessons. I would do everything for you, Matt." Her attitude apprised him that she would serve him like a slave, her eyes implored him not to leave her desolate and forsaken.

"They would never hear of ye going out. The sooner you get it out of your head the better. Can you not look pleased at your brother getting a fine job like this instead of moaning and groaning about it."

"I am pleased for your sake, Matt," she sniffed, wiping her eyes with her saturated handkerchief. "I—I was just thinking about myself."

"That's it," he shot out. "You can't think of anybody else. Try to have some consideration for other people. Don't be so selfish!"

"All right, Matt," she said, with a last convulsive sigh. "I'll try. Anyway, I'm sorry."

"That's better," he replied largely, in a more affable tone; but even as he spoke he shivered, and, changing his tone to one of complaint, he cried: "Gosh! it's cold in here! How do you expect a man to stand talking to you if you haven't got a fire? If your circulation can stand this, mine can't. I'll need to put my coat on and away out to walk up my circulation." He stamped his feet then turned abruptly, calling to her: "I'm away out then, Nessie."

When he had gone she remained rigid, the small, wet ball of the handkerchief clutched tightly in her hand, her red-lidded eyes fixed upon the door, which had closed upon her like the door of a prison. The avenue of the future down which she gazed was gloomy, and amidst the dark, forbidding shadows she saw the figure of Nessie Brodie pass fearfully and alone. No one could now come between her and her father, no one interpose between her frailty and the strength of his unknown purpose. Matthew would go as Mary had gone. Mary! She had thought so much of her lately that she longed now for the comfort of her sister's arm around her, for the solace of her quiet smile, the sustaining courage that lay within her steady eyes. She needed someone to whom she might unburden her weary mind, in whom she could confide her sorrows and the thought of her sister's tranquil fortitude drew her. "Mary!" she whispered, like an entreaty, "Mary, dear! I didn't love you as you deserved when you were here, but oh! I wish I had you near me now!"

As the almost incredible words left her lips the expression on her pinched, tear-stained face grew suddenly transfigured, illuminated as from a sudden light within. Hope again shone in the sorrowful eyes mingled by a purpose so rash that only her present despair could have induced her to consider it. Why, she thought, should she not write to her sister?—A terrible consideration, but her only chance of succour! Upstairs, hidden in a secret corner of her bedroom, lay the letter which Mamma had given her some days before she died and which bore the address in London where Mary lived. If she acted carefully her father would never know; she knew, too, that Mary would never betray her, and with the renewed consciousness of her sister's love she got up from her chair, and, as though walking in a dream, went out of the room and tiptoed silently upstairs. After a moment she returned and shutting the door, listened attentively, trembling violently in all her limbs. She had the letter, but she was terrified at what she had done, at what she proposed to do. Nevertheless she persisted in her purpose. At the table she tore out a leaf from one of her copy-books and hurriedly composed a short note of pathetic entreaty, telling Mary in a few words how she was situated and imploring her assistance, entreating her to come to her if she could. As she wrote, she looked up from time to time with agitated glances, as though expecting her father to enter, but soon the few scribbled lines, blotted by haste and the fall of an irrepressible tear, were completed. She folded the ragged-edged sheet and thrust it in the envelope she had brought from upstairs. Then she addressed the envelope, copying each word carefully, and thrust it into the bosom of her dress; finally, with a pale face and palpitating heart she resumed her bent

position over her books and made pretence to study. But her precaution
was unnecessary. No one entered the room during the whole evening.
She was undiscovered and, early next morning, on her way to school,
she posted the letter.

IV

JAMES BRODIE was awakening. No sun streamed through his window to
stimulate gently his recumbent figure, or set the golden motes swimming
through straight rivers of light across his sleep-filled gaze. Instead, a
cold fine rain smirred the dripping panes, dulling the interior of the
room to one drab monotone and meeting his half-opened, glutinous
eye like a melancholy reminder of his altered condition. He marked
the unhappy aspect of the weather moodily, then from the window, his
visible eye, now more fully opened to reveal the sticky, white coagulum
at its corner, turned to the clock, and, observing that the dim hands
pointed to ten minutes past eight, ten minutes beyond his appointed
but unkept hour of rising, grew more gloomy. To-day he would, he
realised, be late at the office once again, would suffer another sharp
rebuke from the upstart chief clerk who now attempted to control his
working hours, who had threatened even to report him to the under
manager should he fail to observe a more constant punctuality.

At this reflection his face, against the lighter background of the pillow,
seemed to darken, the lines that marked it deepened like sharp incisions,
and the eyes, losing their innate melancholy, were filled instead by a
dull, morose obstinacy. Be damned to them all, he thought, they would
not order him about; he would have another five minutes in bed in
spite of the whole board of directors of the Latta Shipyard! He would,
of course, make up the time by omitting to shave which struck him
now, as it frequently did, as a cunning way of defeating the powers which
sought to move him to their rule and pattern of life. Such a ruse as this
suited him, too, in his own inclination, for he was now averse to shaving
in the mornings when his unsteady hand so often behaved erratically,
trying his temper to control it, and on occasions making him gash his
cheek. The early hours of the day never found him at his best, for not
only did his hand refuse to obey him, but his head ached, or his tongue
felt like dry wood, or his stomach turned within him at the mere consideration of his breakfast. It was, he was well aware, the whisky which
was responsible for these unwelcome visitations, and in this grey morning's light he felt, with a gloomy insight, that he must cut down his
allowance. When he had made such resolutions in the past he had
never, he told himself, been really serious, but now he must definitely

366

make up his mind to take himself in hand, to drink nothing before dinner and thereafter to abstain until the evening, when he would be moderate, when indeed, he must be moderate if he were to please Nancy, whose favour was now of such vital necessity to him. Certainly she had been better disposed towards him during the last two days and he reflected, with a more equable turn of mind that, although she had not come back to his room since their quarrel on the night of her visit to the aunt at Overton, the obvious reason which she had advanced in excuse must surely be correct in view of her recent kindness and more tolerant treatment of him. He could not do without Nancy! She had become as necessary to him and as indispensable as breath to his body, and for this reason alone he must be careful how he addressed himself to the bottle in future. Impossible that he should ever live without her! She would come to him again to-night, the fresher for his enforced abstinence, or he would know the reason why!

Some semblance of his old complacency seemed to flow into him at this last thought and, flinging off the bedclothes, he got out of bed; but as the cold air of the room struck his body he shivered, frowned, and losing his satisfied look, reached hurriedly for his clothes, which lay in a disordered heap upon a near-by chair. He struggled into these garments with the utmost dispatch, giving his face alone some transient attention with water and soap before assuming his soiled linen collar, knotting his stringy tie and throwing on his baggy coat and waistcoat. The economy in time was considerable, for the whole process of dressing had not taken five minutes, and now he was ready, albeit after a fashion, to descend the stairs and consume his morning meal.

"Good mornin' to you, Brodie," cried Nancy agreeably, as he entered the kitchen. "You're on time all right to-day! How did ye sleep?"

"Not so weel as I would have liked," he replied heavily. "I was cold! Still, I've a feeling I'll be cosier to-night."

"You're not blate so early in the mornin'," she answered, with a toss of her head. "Sup up your porridge and be quiet."

He considered the porridge with pursed lips and some show of repugnance as he exclaimed:

"I don't feel like them somehow, Nancy. They're heavy on a man's stomach at breakfast time. They might do for supper but I can't think of them the now. Have ye anything else?"

"I've got a nice, sweet kipper in the pan just done to a turn," she cried complacently. "Don't eat the porridge if ye're not in the mood. I'll get ye the other this very minute."

He followed her active figure, observing the swirl of her skirts, the fluent movements of her neat feet and ankles as she rushed to carry out her words, and he was filled by a sudden appreciation of the marked improvement in her attitude towards him. She was coming near to him again, no longer looked at him with that sparkle of animosity in her eyes, was even now running after him in a fashion strangely reminiscent of his wife's eagerness to serve him. He felt the comfort of being once more looked after with this devotion, especially as it came from his beloved but independent Nancy, and when she returned with the dish, he looked at her from the corner of his eyes and remarked:

"You're drawin' round to me again, I see. I can mind of mornings when some burnt porridge was good enough to fling at a poor man for his breakfast, but this juicy kipper is more to my taste, and your way o' lookin' at me is more to my likin' still. You're fond of me, Nancy, aren't ye?"

She gazed down at his tired face, lined, hollowed, disfigured by a two days' stubble of beard and split by a forced and unbefitting smile, envisaged his bowed and slovenly figure, his tremulous hands and uncared for finger-nails, and with a shrill little laugh she cried:

"True enough, man! I've such a feelin' for ye now that I hardly like to own it. It fair makes my heart loup when I look at ye sometimes."

His smile was extinguished, his eyes puckered intently, and he answered:

"It's a treat for me to hear ye say that, Nancy! I know it's downright wrong o' me to tell ye, but I can't help it, I've got to depend on ye now something extraordinar'." Then, still disregarding his breakfast, he continued, almost apologetically, as though he defended his conduct: "I never would have believed I could draw to anybody so much. I didna think I was that kind o' man, but ye see, I had to do without for so lang, that when—when we came thegither—weel—ye've fair taken hold of me. That's plain truth. Ye're not angry at me for tellin' ye a' this, are ye now?"

"No! No!" she exclaimed hurriedly. "Not a bit, Brodie. I should understand ye by this time. But come on now, don't waste the good kipper I've taken the trouble to cook ye. I'm wantin' to hear how ye like it. And I'm anxious for ye to make a good breakfast, for you'll have to take your dinner out to-day."

"Take my dinner out! What for?" he exclaimed, in some surprise. "Ye were away at Overton only last week—ye're surely not goin' to see that aunt o' yours again?"

"No, I'm not!" she cried, with a pert toss of her head, "but she's comin' to see me! And I'm not wantin' you runnin' round after me, with her, that's a decent unsuspectin' body—ay and one that's fond o' me—starin' the eyes out of her heid at your palavers. Ye can come home in the evenin'. Then I'll be ready for ye."

He glared at her for a moment with a dark countenance, then, suddenly relaxing, he shook his head slowly: "Damnation, woman! but ye have the cheek on ye. To think that you've got the length o' entertainin' your friends in my house! Gad! it makes me see how far ye can go with me. I should have warmed the backside o' ye for doin' a thing like that without first askin' me—but ye know I canna be angry with ye. It seems there's no end to the liberties you'll take with me."

"What's the harm," she demanded primly. "Can an honest house-keeper body not see her relations if she wants to? It'll do ye good to have a snack outside, then I'll have a surprise all ready for ye when ye come."

He looked at her doubtfully.

"Surprise is the right word, after the way you've been treatin' me." He paused and added, grimly: "I'm damned if I know what makes me so soft wi' ye."

"Don't talk like that, Brodie," she reprimanded mildly. "Your language is like a heathen Chinaman's sometimes."

"What do you know about Chinamen?" he retorted moodily, at last turning his attention towards the kipper, and beginning to consume it in slow, large mouthfuls. After a moment he remarked, in an altered tone: "This has a relish in it, Nancy—it's the sort of thing I can fancy in the mornin's now."

She continued to look at him in an oddly restrained fashion as he conveyed the food to his lowered mouth, then suddenly a thought seemed to strike her, and she cried:

"Guidsakes, what am I dreamin' about! There's a letter came for ye this mornin' that I forgot a' about."

"What!" he retorted, arresting his movements and glancing up in surprise from under his thick, greying eyebrows. "A letter for me!"

"Ay! I clean forgot in the hurry to get your breakfast. Here it is." And she took a letter from the corner of the dresser and handed it to him. He held the letter for a moment in his outstretched hand, drew it near to him with a puzzled look in his eyes, observed that it was stamped by the postmark of London, then, carelessly inserting his thick thumb, ripped the envelope open and drew out the sheet within. Watching him with some slight interest as he read the written words Nancy observed the expressions of bewilderment, amazement, enlightenment, and triumph sweep across his face with the rapidity of clouds traversing a dark and windy sky. Finally his expression assumed a strange satisfaction as he turned the letter, again read it slowly through, and, lifting his eyes, fixed them upon the distance.

"Would ye believe it," he muttered, "and after all this time!"

"What?" she cried. "What is it about?"

"She has climbed down and wants to come crawlin' back!" He paused, absorbed in his own considerations, as though his words had been sufficient to enlighten her fully.

"I don't know what you mean," she exclaimed sharply. "Who are ye talkin' about?"

"My daughter—Mary," he replied slowly; "the one that I kicked out of my house. I swore she would never get back until she had licked my boots, ay, and she said she never would come back, and here she is, in this very letter, cadging to win home and keep house for me. God! it's a rich recompense for me after a' these years!" He held up the letter between his tense fingers as though his eyes would never cease to gloat upon it, sneering as he read: " 'Let the past be forgotten! I want you to forgive me.' If that doesna justify me my name's not Brodie. 'Since Mamma has gone I would like to come home. I am not unhappy here but sometimes lonely,' " he continued with a snarl. "—Lonely! By God, it's what she deserves. Lonely! Long may it continue. If she thinks she'll get back here as easy as that she's far mistaken. I'll not have her. No! Never!" He returned his eyes to Nancy as though to demand her approval and, with twisted lips, resumed, "Don't ye see how this puts me in the right, woman! She was proud, proud as ye make them, but I can see she's broken now. Why else should she want home? God! what a come down for her to have to whine to get taken back like this and—what a triumph for me to refuse her. She wants to be my housekeeper!" He laughed harshly. "That's a good one, is it no', Nancy? She doesna know that I've got you—she's wantin' your job!"

She had picked the letter from his hand and was reading it.

"I don't see much of a whine here," she replied slowly. "It's a decent enough written letter."

"Bah!" he cried, "it's not the way it's written I'm thinkin' of! It's the meanin' of it all that concerns me. There's no other explanation possible, and the very thought of it lifts me like a dram o' rare spirits."

"You're not goin' to let her come back, then?" she queried, tentatively.

"No!" he shouted, "I'm not! I've got you to look after me now. Does she think I want the likes o' her. She can stop in this place in London that she's in, and rot there, for all I care."

"Ye mustna decide in a hurry," she admonished him; "after all she's your own daughter. Think it over well before ye do anything rash."

He looked at her sulkily.

"Rash or not rash, I'll never forgive her," he growled, "and that's all there is to it." Then his eye suddenly lighted as he exclaimed: "I tell ye what might be a bawr though, Nancy—and something that would cut her to the quick. Supposin' ye were to write back and tell her that the post she applied for was filled. That would make her feel pretty small, would it not? Will ye do't, woman?"

"No, I will not," she cried immediately; "the very idea. Ye maun do it yoursel' when you're about it."

"Well, at least ye'll help me to write my answer," he protested. "Suppose you and me do it thegether to-night when I come home. That smart head o' yours is sure to think on something clever for me to put in."

"Wait till to-night, then," she replied after some consideration, "and I'll think about it in the meantime."

"That's grand," he cried, playing in his mind with the idea of collaborating with her in the evening over this delightful task of composing a cutting reply to his daughter. "We'll lay our heads together. I know what you can do when you try."

As he spoke a faint horn sounded in the distance, swelling and falling at times, but always audible, entering the room with gentle though relentless persistency.

"Gracious," cried Nancy quickly, "there's the nine o'clock horn and you not out of the house yet. Ye'll be late as can be if ye don't hurry. Come on now, away with ye!"

"I'm not carin' for their blasted horns," he replied sullenly. "I'll be late if I like. You would think I was the slave of that damned whistle the way it draws me away from ye just when I'm not wantin' to go."

"I don't want ye to get the sack though, man! What would ye do if ye lost your job?"

"I would get a better one. I've just been thinkin' about that lately myself. What I've got is not near good enough for me."

"Wheesht! now, Brodie," she conciliated him, "you're well enough as ye are. Ye might look further and fare worse. Come on and I'll see ye to the door!"

His expression softened as he looked at her and rose obediently, exclaiming:

"Don't you worry anyway, Nancy. I'll always have enough to keep you." At the front door he turned to her and said, in a voice which sounded almost pathetic: "It'll be a' day until I see you again."

She drew back a little and half shut the door as she replied, irrelevantly:

"What a mornin', too. Ye should take an umbrella instead o' that auld stick. Are you minding about gettin' your dinner out, to-day?"

"I'm mindin' about it," he answered submissively. "You know I heed what you tell me. Come on now—give us a kiss before I go."

She was about to shut the door in his face when, at his attitude, something seemed to melt within her and, raising herself on her toes, inclining her head upwards, she touched with her lips the deep furrow that marked the centre of his forehead.

"There," she whispered under her breath, "that's for the man that ye were."

He stared at her uncomprehendingly with eyes that gazed at hers appealingly, inquiringly, like the eyes of a devoted dog.

"What were ye sayin'?" he muttered, stupidly.

"Nothing," she cried lightly, withdrawing herself again. "I was just biddin' ye good-bye."

He hesitated, stammered uncomfortably:

"If it was—if ye were thinkin' about—about the drink, I want to tell ye that I'm going to cut it down to something reasonable. I know ye don't like me to take so much and I want to please ye, woman."

She shook her head slowly, looking at him curiously, intently.

" 'Twasna that at all. If ye feel ye need a dram, I suppose ye maun have it. It's the only—it's a comfort to ye, I suppose. Now away with ye, man."

"Nancy, dear, ye understand a man weel," he murmured in a moved voice. "There's nothing I couldna do for ye when you're like this." He shifted his feet heavily, in some embarrassment at his own outburst, then in a gruff voice full of his suppressed feeling exclaimed: "I'll—I'll away, then, woman. Good-bye just now."

"Good-bye," she replied evenly.

With a last look at her eyes he turned, faced the grey and melancholy morning, and moved off into the rain, a strange figure, coatless, crowned extravagantly by the large, square hat, from under which thick tufts of uncut hair protruded fantastically, his arms behind his back, his heavy ash plant trailing grotesquely behind him in the mud.

He walked down the road, his brain confused by conflicting thoughts amongst which mingled a sense of abashment at the unexpected exhibition of his own emotion; but, as he progressed, there emerged from this confusion a single perception—the worth to him of Nancy. She was human clay like himself, and she understood him, knew the needs of a man, appreciated, as she had just remarked, that he required sometimes the comfort of a glass. He did not feel the rain as it soaked into his clothing, so enwrapped was he in the contemplation of her, and into the dullness of his set face small gleams of light from time to time appeared. As he approached the shipyard, however, his reflections grew less agreeable, evidenced by the unrelieved harshness of his countenance, and he was concerned by his lateness, by the possibility of a reprimand, and affected by a depressing realisation, which time had not eradicated, of the very humiliating nature of his employment. He thought, too, in a different light of the letter that he had just received, which appeared to him as an intolerable presumption on the part of her who had once been his daughter, and which now reminded him bitterly of the past. An acrid taste came into his mouth at his own recollection whilst the salt, smoked fish which he had eaten for breakfast made him feel parched and thirsty; outside the "Fitter's Bar" he deliberately paused and, fortified by Nancy's parting remark, muttered: "Gad, but I'm dry, and I'm half an hour late as it is. I may as weel make a job o' it while I'm about it."

He went in with a half-defiant glance over his shoulder at the block of offices that lay opposite and, when he emerged, a quarter of an hour later, his bearing had regained something of its old challenging assertion. In this manner he entered the main swing doors of the offices and, threading the corridors, now with the facility of habit, entered his own room with his head well in the air, surveying in turn the two young clerks who looked up from their work to greet him.

"Has that auld, nosey pig been round yet?" he demanded; "because if he has I don't give a tinker's curse about it."

"Mr. Blair?" replied one of the pair. "No! he hasn't been round yet!"

"Humph!" cried Brodie, fiercely annoyed at the sudden feeling of relief which had swept involuntarily over him. "I suppose ye think I'm lucky. Well! let me tell ye both that I don't give a damn whether he knows I've been late or not. Tell him if ye like! It's all one to me," and, flinging his hat upon a peg and his stick into a corner, he sat heavily down upon his stool. The other clerks exchanged a glance, and after a slight pause, the spokesman of the two remarked diffidently:

"We wouldn't say a word, Mr. Brodie. You surely know that. But look here, you're wringing wet—will you not take your jacket off and dry it?"

"No! I'll not take it off!" he replied roughly, opening his ledger, lifting his pen, and beginning to work; but after a moment he raised his head and said in a different tone: "But thank ye all the same. You're good lads both, and I know you've lent me a hand in the past. The truth is I've had some news that upset me, so I'm just not quite my usual this mornin'."

They knew something of his affairs from certain bouts of rambling dissertations during the past months, and the one who had not yet spoken remarked:

"Not Nessie I hope, Mr. Brodie?"

"No!" he answered, "not my Nessie! She's as right as the mail, thank God, workin' like a trooper and headin' straight for the Latta! She's never given me a moment's trouble. It was just something else, but I know what to do. I can win through it like I've done with all the rest."

They forbore to question him further, and the three resumed work in a silence broken only by the scratching of pens on paper, the rustle of a turning page, the restless scrape of a stool, and the mutter from Brodie's lips as he strove to concentrate his fogged brain in the effort to contend with the figures before him.

The forenoon had advanced well upon its course when a precise step sounded in the corridor outside, and the door of the room opened to admit the correct figure of Mr. Blair. With a sheaf of papers in his hand he stood for a moment, adjusting his gold-rimmed pince-nez upon his elevated nose, and scrutinising at some length the three clerks now working under his severe eyes. His gaze eventually settled upon the sprawling form of Brodie from whose damp clothing the steam now rose in a warm, vaporous mist, and as he looked his glance became more disapproving; he cleared his throat warningly and strode forward, fluttering the papers

373

in his grasp like feathers of his ruffled plumage. "Brodie," he began sharply, "a moment of your attention, please!"

Without changing his posture Brodie lifted his head from the desk and regarded the other mordantly:

"Well," he replied, "what is it this time?"

"You might get up when you address me," expostulated Blair. "Every other clerk does so but you. It's most irregular and unusual."

"I'm a kind o' unusual man, ye see; that's maybe the reason o' it," retorted Brodie slowly. "I'm just as well where I am! What is't you're wantin'?"

"These accounts," shot out the other angrily. "Do you recognise them? If you don't I may inform you that they represent your work—or so-called work! Every one of them is in error. Your figures are wrong the whole way through and your total is outrageously incorrect. I'm sick of your blundering incompetence, Brodie! Unless you can explain this I shall have to report the whole matter to my superior."

Brodie glowered from the papers to the other's starched and offended face, and, filled by a sense of the insupportable indignity of his position he replied sullenly, in a low voice:

"I did the best I could. I can do no more."

"Your best is not good enough, then," retorted Blair in a high, almost a shrill tone. "Lately your work has become atrociously bad and your behaviour is, if anything, worse. Your very appearance is lowering to the dignity of this office. I'm sure if Sir John knew he would never permit it. Why," he stuttered, choked by indignation, "already your breath is reeking with the smell of drink. It's abominable!"

Brodie sat quite still, his eyes lowered, his mind blurred, wondering if it were he, James Brodie, who remained passive under the insults of this primly insignificant creature. He saw himself leap up, seize the other by the throat, shake him within an inch of his life then hurl him, as he had hurled a man twice his size, ignominiously out of the door. But no, he was still sitting motionless upon his stool, muttering in a dull voice:

"My time is my own outside this place. I can use it how I like."

"You must come to this office in a fit condition to work," insisted Blair coldly. "You're a bad example to these young men here—the look of you is a slur on the whole place!"

"Leave my appearance alone, damn you," ground out Brodie with a sudden fierceness. "I'd rather be as I am than have your smug face on me."

"None of your impertinence, please," cried Blair, a flush rising to his pale countenance. "I'll report you for insolence."

"Well, leave me alone," cried Brodie, looking up from his crouched position on the desk like a wild animal, broken by captivity, but still ferocious. "Don't push me too far or it'll be the worse for ye."

A sense of the latent danger to himself in the other's wild eye restrained Blair from further disparaging comment but, thrusting the file of papers disdainfully upon Brodie's desk, he remarked icily:

"Let me have these corrected at once—faultless if you please—or I'll know the reason of it!" then, turning, he stepped formally out of the office.

With the closing of the door no outburst occurred, but the stillness of the room became more oppressive than any storm. Brodie sat like an effigy in stone turning over within his mind the insults he had just endured, feeling in his humiliation, that the combined glances of the other two were fixed upon him derisively. Out of the corner of his eye he observed a hand appear over the edge of his desk and silently remove the offending accounts and, although he knew that he was again being aided through the good-nature of his colleagues, the hard-hewn moroseness of his features did not relax. He sat thus for an interminable time without lifting his pen, observed, without speaking, the corrected documents slide back again in front of him, maintained his attitude of rigid indifference until the dinner-whistle blew at one o'clock; then he rose immediately from his stool, seized his hat, and walked quickly from the room. Some insults might be washed out in blood, but he now sought urgently, in a different manner, to eradicate the memory of his indignity.

When he returned, punctual to the hour, at two o'clock he was altered, as though some mysterious, benign influence had been at work upon him, potently dispersing his melancholy, smoothing the harsh outlines of his face, injecting into his veins a fluid gaiety which now coursed through him joyously, and emanated radiantly from his being.

"I'm here first, lads, ye see," he cried with a heavy facetiousness, as the two other clerks appeared together shortly after he had arrived, "and on the stroke of the clock too! But what do you mean by comin' in late. It's abominable. If you don't improve your blunderin' irregularity I'll report you to your superior—that pasty pie-face that was in here this mornin'." He laughed boisterously and continued: "Can you not take your example from me that's held up to you as such a paragon o' virtue?"

"You're in fettle now, Mr. Brodie," doubtfully replied one of the youngsters.

"And what for no'," he exclaimed. "I wouldna let a thing like what happened this forenoon put me down. Not on your life, my mannie. It was just the thought of other considerations that forbade me to wring the puir creature's stiff neck for him. You know," he continued confidentially, "he's aye been jealous o' the way I got into this office under his very nose, but I had the influence and he couldna prevent it." He drew his pipe from his pocket, rapped it noisily against the desk, and began to fill it.

"You're not goin' to smoke, Mr. Brodie," cried the first clerk, looking up from his ledger in some concern. "You know it's strictly forbidden."

Brodie glowered at him, swinging a little on his stool, as he answered: "And who would stop me? I'll do as I like in here. A man like me shouldna have to beg and pray for permission to light his pipe." He effected this action now, defiantly, sucking noisily and flinging the spent match disdainfully upon the floor. Then, with a profound movement of his head, between puffs he resumed: "No! and I'm not agoin' to do it. Gad! if I had my rights I wouldna be sittin' in this rotten office. I'm far above this kind o' work, far above any kind o' work. That's true as death, but it just canna be proved, and I've got to thole things as best I can. But it doesna alter me. No! by God. No! There's many a man in this Borough would be glad to have the blood that runs in my veins." He looked round for approval but, observing that his listeners, tired of the stale recitation of his pretensions, had bowed their heads in a feigned indifference, he was displeased; none the less he turned their defection to account by producing a small, flat bottle from his hip, quickly applying it to his lips, and stealthily returning it to his pocket. Thus refreshed he continued, as though unconscious of their lack of attention: "Blood will tell! There's nothing truer than that. I'll come up again. It's nothing but a lot of rotten jealousy that's put me here; but it'll not be for long. Ye can't keep a good man down. I'll soon be back again where folks'll recognise me again for what I am, back at the Cattle Show rubbin' shoulders with the Lord Lieutenant o' the County and on the best o' terms—equal terms mind ye"—he emphasised this to the air by a jerk of his pipe—"ay, on equal terms with the finest blood in the county, and with my name standin' out brawly in the paper amongst them all." As he viewed the future by regarding the glory of the past his eye moistened, his lower lip drooped childishly, his breast heaved, and he muttered: "God! that's a grand thing to happen to a man."

"Come on now, Mr. Brodie," entreated the other clerk, breaking in upon his meditation, "put away your pipe now you've had a smoke. I don't want to see you getting into trouble."

Brodie glowered at him for an instant then suddenly guffawed:

"Man, you're awfu' feared. True enough, it's as you say. I've had a smoke, but I'm goin' to have another—and more than that—I'm goin' to have a dram as well!" He slyly produced the bottle again and, whilst they watched him with startled eyes, partook of a long pull. Instead of returning the flask to his pocket he stood it before him on top of his desk, remarking: "Ye'll be handier for me there, hinny, and I can look at ye as well, and watch ye goin' down inch by inch." Then, flattered to find himself the focus of their anxious stares, he continued: "Speakin' of trouble—there's one thing that little runt said to me this mornin' that was so ridiculous it's stuck in my head." He frowned prodigiously at the very memory. "I think I mind of him sayin' 'the look o' ye is a slur on the whole place'—ay, that was it—these were his very words. Now tell me, lads—what the devil was he talkin' about? Is there anything wrong with my appearance?" He glared at them with a bellicose mien whilst they shook their heads from side to side, doubtfully. "I'm a fine-lookin' man, am I not!" he shot at them, watching their silent assent with a large and exaggerated approval. "I knew it," he cried. "It was just his measly spite. Ay! I was always a grand upstandin' figure of a man, well set up, with a skin on me as clear as a bairn's. Besides," he continued, looking at them sideways, craftily, as he stroked the coarse stubble on his sallow chin with a rustling sound, "there's another reason why I know he's wrong. Ye're maybe ower young to hear but it's no harm to tell ye that a certain lass—ay, the bonniest in Levenford, puts me first abune everybody else. Odd, I maun have a drink at the very thought of her." He drank a toast with decorous solemnity in honour of the loveliest lady in Levenford, and was for some time silent whilst he considered her happily. He wanted to talk about her, to boast proudly of her attractions, but a shadow of restraint held him back and, searching with contracted brows amongst the recesses of his mind for the reason of his reserve, a sudden illumination shone upon him. He became aware that he could not speak more freely about her because she was not his wife. At this startling realisation of his mused brain he silently reviled himself for his negligence. "Losh," he muttered to himself, "ye havena acted fair, man. Ye should have thought on this before." He shook his head deprecatingly, took another swig of spirits to assist his meditations, and a profound pathos for the plight of Nancy seized him as he whispered in a maudlin tone: "I believe I'll do it. By God! I will do it for her." He almost shook hands with himself at the nobility of the sudden resolution he had formed to make an honest woman of her. True, she was not of much consequence in the social scale, but what of it, his name would cover her, cover them both, and if he married her he would, in one magnificent gesture, keep her more securely in the house, put himself right in the eyes of the town, and still for ever these sad, questioning glances which he had observed from time to time on Nessie's face. He banged his fist on the desk, crying out: "I'll do it! I'll mention it this very night," then, grinning at the strained faces before him he remarked, with an assumption of lofty rectitude: "Don't be alarmed, lads. I've just been planning out things and I've just decided to do something for my wee Nessie. She's well worth it." Then, lowering his elevated tone, he leered at them cunningly and added: "A little matter of domestic policy that you're sure to hear of sooner or later." He was about to enlighten them more lucidly when one of the clerks, perceiving perhaps in advance the drift of the revelations that might follow, hurriedly sought to deflect his attention by exclaiming:

"And how is Nessie getting on, Mr. Brodie?"

He blinked for a moment at the questioner before replying:

"Fine! Ye know she's gettin' on fine. Dinna ask stupid questions, man. She's got the Latta in her pocket already." Then, launching out on this fresh subject that now presented itself to his muddled mind he continued: "She's a great comfort to me is that lass. To see her puttin' a spoke in that young Grierson's wheel time after time is a rich treat to me. She always beats him ye know, and every time she does it, it must be gall and wormwood to that smooth sneakin' father o' his. Ay! Gall and wormwood it must be!" He sniggered at the very reflection of it and, with a more acute tilt of the bottle to his mouth, was emptying it completely of its contents when, failing in the attempt to laugh and drink simultaneously, he choked and burst into a prolonged fit of hoarse coughing. "Pat my back, damn ye," he gasped with congested face and running eyes as he bent forward, heaving like a sick and emaciated elephant. "Harder! Harder!" he cried as one of the others, leaping from his stool, began to thump his bowed back.

"That's a nasty cough," said the young fellow when the paroxysm had finally abated. "That's what comes of sitting in damp clothes."

"Bah! it wasna a hoast at all—that," replied Brodie, wiping his face with his sleeve. "I've never wore a coat yet and I never will. I've lost my umbrella somewhere, but it doesna matter, the rain aye seems to do me good. I'm strong as a Clydesdale stallion," and he extended his gaunt structure to show them the manner of man he was.

"Nessie doesn't take after you, Mr. Brodie," remarked the first speaker. "She doesna look too strong!"

Brodie glowered at him, exclaiming angrily:

"She's as sound as a bell. Are you another o' these safties that are aye trying to make out folks to be ill. She's as right as the mail I tell you. She had a wee bit turn last month, but it was nothing. I had her at Lawrie and he said she had a heid on her in a thousand—ay, in a million, I would say!" He glanced round triumphantly, looked to the bottle to express his elation, but, observing that it was empty, seized it and with a fortunate aim hurled it into the waste-paper basket in the corner—whence it was later retrieved and cast into the Leven through the charity of one of his long-suffering colleagues. "That's an aim for ye," he cried gaily. "I've got an eye in my head! I could bring down a running rabbit at fifty paces without a blink. A rabbit! Damnation! If I was where I should be I would be at the butts bringing down the grouse and the pheasants like droppin' hailstones." He was about to embark once more on the nobility of his estate when suddenly his eyes fell upon the clock. "Gad! would ye believe it. It's nearly five o'clock. I'm the man to pass the hours away." He cocked his eye facetiously, snickered, and resumed: "Time passes quick when you're workin' hard, as that stickit whelp Blair would say. But I'm afraid I must leave ye, lads. Ye're fine fellows and I'm gey an' fond o' ye, but I've something

378

more important to attend to now." He rubbed his hands together in a delightful anticipation and added, with a leer: "If the fancy man comes in before five just tell him his accounts are in order and say I've gone to buy him a rattle." He got off his stool ponderously, slowly assumed his hat, adjusting it twice before the tilt of its dusty brim pleased him, picked up his heavy stick and stood with a gravity now definitely drunken, framing the doorway with his swaying bulk. "Lads!" he cried, apostrophising them with his stick, "if ye knew where I was goin' now, the eyes would drop out your heads for pure jealousy. You couldna come, though. No! No! There's only one man in this Borough could gang this bonnie bonnie gait." Surveying them impressively he added, with great dramatic gusto: "And that's me!"—swept their forbearing but disconcerted faces with a final glare and swung slowly out of the room.

His star was in the ascendant, for as he strode noisily along the passages, bumping from side to side in his erratic career, he met no one and, at five minutes to five, shot through the main swing doors into the open and set his course for home.

The rain had now ceased and the air came fresh and cool in the darkness through which the newly lighted lamps shimmered upon the wet streets, like an endless succession of topaz moons upon the surface of black, still water. The regular repetition of these reflections, each one of which seemed to float insidiously towards him as he walked, amused Brodie monstrously, and he grinned as he told himself he would assuredly inform Nancy of his experience with this strangely inverted celestial phenomenon. Nancy! He chuckled alond at the consideration of all they had to talk of to-night, from the composition of a real stinger of a letter for that one in London to the delicious proposition which he had determined to put before her. She would of course be perturbed to see him return with perhaps—and he admitted this magnanimously to the darkness—a heavier dram in him than usual, but the sudden delight at his offer of matrimony would dispel all her annoyance. He knew she had always wanted an established position, the randy, such as a fine man like him could give her, and now he heard her over-whelmed voice exclaiming: "Do ye mean it, Brodie! Losh! man, ye've fair sweepit me away. Marry ye? Ye know I would jump at the chance like a cock at a groset. Come till I give ye a grand, big hug." Yes! she would be kinder to him than ever after this sublime concession on his part, and his eyes flickered at the thought of the especial manifestations of her favour which this should elicit from her to-night. As he advanced, warmly conscious that each staggering step took him nearer to her, he could find no comparison strong enough to adequately describe her charm, her possessing hold upon him. "She's—she's bonnie!" he muttered inarticulately; "the flesh o' her is as white and firm as the breist of a fine chicken. I could almost make a meal o' her." His thoughts

379

grew more compelling, served to intensify his longing, to add to his excitement, and with a final rapid struggle he launched himself up the steps of his house, fumbled impatiently at the lock with his key, opened the door, and burst into the obscurity of the hall. "Nancy," he cried loudly, "Nancy! Here I am back for ye!" He stood for a moment in the darkness awaiting her answering cry, but, as she did not reply, he smiled fatuously to think that she should be hiding, waiting for him to go to her, and taking a box of matches from his pocket, he lit the lobby gas, planted his stick firmly in the stand, hung up his hat, and went eagerly into the kitchen. This, too, was in darkness.

"Nancy," he shouted, in astonishment not unmixed with annoyance, "what are ye playin' at? I don't want a game o' blind man's buff. I want none o' these fancy tricks, woman! I want you. Come out from wherever ye be." Still there was no response, and, advancing awkwardly to the gas-bracket above the mantelpiece he lit this gas, turned to survey the room, and to his amazement observed that the table was not laid, that no preparation for tea had been begun. For a moment he remained quite still, fixing the bare table with an astounded gaze, compressing his lips angrily, until suddenly a light seemed to break in upon him and he muttered slowly, with a loosening of his frown: "She's awa' to the station with that aunt of hers. Has not she the nerve though? She's the only body that would dare to do it. Sends me out for my dinner and then keeps me waitin' for my tea." A faint thrill of amusement ran through him, deepening to a roar of laughter as he contemplated, almost proudly, her hardihood. Gad, but she was a fit mate for him! Yet when his mirth had subsided he did not quite know what to do, presumed eventually that he must await the pleasure of her return and, standing with his back to the fireplace, he allowed his gaze to wander idly round the room. To him, the very atmosphere breathed of her presence; he saw her flitting airily about, sitting nonchalantly in his armchair, smiling, talking, even flighting him. Yes! the very hat-pin sticking into the dresser was an indication of her own saucy, impudent, inimitable indifference. But something else lay upon the dresser, held in place by that pin, a letter—that presumptuous communication which he had received at breakfast-time from his daughter—and moving forward he took it up disdainfully in his hands. Suddenly his expression changed, as he observed that it was not the same envelope but another, addressed to him in his son's sloping clerkly hand, a penmanship so like Matt's own smooth plausibility that it had always irritated him. Another letter! and from Matthew! Was the sly, sneaking coward so afraid of him now that he must write his messages instead of delivering them face to face like a man? Filled by a profound contempt he gazed at the neat writing on the envelope which, however, became modified as, tilting his head to one side he considered inconsequently how well his own name looked —almost as well as in print—in these precise characters now before him. James Brodie, Esquire! It was a name to be proud of, that one! Smiling a little, a large and lordly appreciation swept over him, restoring him again to complacency and, in the excess of his own satisfaction, he carelessly tore open the letter and pulled out the single sheet within.

"Dear Father," he read, "You were too high and mighty to hear about my new post or you would have learned that it was a position for a married man. Don't expect Nancy back. She's come to see that I don't fall off my horse! Your loving and obedient son, Matt."

Seized by a vast stupefaction he read over the scanty words twice, looked up, unseeingly, as he muttered incredulously: "What does he mean? What has Nancy got to do with the fool's horse? Your loving and obedient son—the man must be mad!" Then suddenly, blindingly, he felt that he too was mad, as the purport of the note penetrated his dull, fuddled brain, as he observed upon the back of the paper, scrawled in Nancy's childish, illiterate hand these words: "Matt and me are off to be married and have a high old time. You were too fond of your bottle to marry me so you can take it to bed with you the night. You auld fool!"

A great cry burst from his lips. At last he understood that she had left him. The letter faded from his sight, the room swung round and away from him, he was alone in a vast immensity of blackness. Out of his distorted face his wounded eyes gazed dumbly from below his brow, now corroded by the full knowledge of his loss. Matt, his own son, had taken Nancy from him! In the shock of his despair he felt it would have been better far had he been killed outright by that pistol bullet in the house in the Vennel, that this blow his son had delivered was more frightful, more agonising than death! His weakling and despised son had triumphed over him. Complete understanding of the deception to which he had been subjected in the past week flashed upon him—Nancy's indifference, followed by her assumed yet restrained affection, the locking of her door, the fictitious relation at Overton, the complete obliteration of Matthew from the house—he understood all, remembered, too, the scene where he had surprised them in the kitchen, when she had broken the cup at the very moment that he questioned his son about the post. God! what a fool he had been. "An auld fool!"—that was what she called him, and how she must have laughed at him, how they must both be mocking him now. He knew nothing, neither how they had gone nor where they had gone. He was powerless, knowing only that they were together, powerless except to stand and think of them in an inconceivable intimacy which made him writhe with anguish.

He was recalled from his dark oblivion, like an insensible man to whom consciousness momentarily returns, by the voice of Nessie who, entering the kitchen, gazed fearfully at him and murmured, timidly:

"Will I make some tea for you, father? I've not had any tea or any dinner either."

He lifted his tortured face, looked at her stupidly, then cried, thickly:

"Go away! Go to the parlour. Go to your lessons. Go anywhere, but let me alone!"

She fled from him and he sank again into the torment of his thoughts, filled by a profound self-pity as he realised that there was now no one to look after him or Nessie but his dotard and incapable mother. She would have to come back—Mary, his daughter! He would have to allow her to return and keep the house, if only for Nessie's sake. Mary must now come back! The full significance of his discussion of this matter with Nancy struck him like a fresh blow as he recollected how he had coaxed her to write the letter of refusal. And she had known all the time that she was leaving him. He had been too late with his offer of marriage; and now, how would he ever do without her? A piercing anguish took him as he thought of her, even now, in his son's arms, opening her lips to his kisses, offering her firm, white body gladly to his embrace. As though vainly to obliterate the torture of the vision, he raised his hand and pressed it upon his throbbing eyes, whilst his lips twisted painfully and a hard, convulsive sob burst from his swelling breast and echoed through the quiet of the room.

V

THE three-twenty train from Glasgow to Ardfillan, the first half of the journey accomplished successfully, had left Overton behind, and traversing the low, dripping, smoke-filled arches of Kilmaheu Tunnel, emerged into the breezy March afternoon with a short, triumphant whistle, that sent a streamer of steam swirling behind the engine like a pennant, and presently began to coast gently down the slight incline of the track, which marked the approach to Levenford Station. The train was lightly laden, having many of its carriages empty and several with but one passenger in each and, as though conscious of having achieved the sharp ascent of Poindfauld and traversed the dark, grimed caverns of Kilmaheu, it now proceeded at an easier and more leisured pace through the soft, dun countryside across which the railway track advanced like a long, narrowing furrow.

Within the train, alone in a compartment, in a corner facing the engine, and with the small portmanteau that constituted her entire luggage beside her, sat a girl. Dressed in a plain, grey costume of serviceable, inexpensive serge, shaped to a neat yet unfashionable cut, and wearing upon her dark, close-coiled hair a grey velvet hat relieved only by a thin, pink ribbon gathered at one side into a simple bow, she remained upright yet relaxed, directing her gaze out of the window, viewing eagerly, yet wistfully, each feature of the fleeting landscape. Her face was thin, the nose straight and fine, the nostrils delicate, the lips sensitive and mobile, the smooth, pale sweep of the brow accentuated by the dark, appealing beauty of her eyes; and upon the entire countenance lay a melancholy sweetness, a pure and clarified sadness, as though some potent, sorrowful experience had stamped upon every lineament the subtle yet ineradicable mark of suffering. This faint, sombre shadow which lightly touched, accentuating even, the dark beauty of the face, made her seem more mature than her actual age of twenty-two years and gave to her an appearance of arresting delicacy, of refined sincerity which was intensified by the severe simplicity of her apparel. Like the face, but in a different sense, her hands, too, immediately engaged attention, as, denuded of gloves, which lay upon her knee, they rested lightly, palm upwards, passive upon her lap. The face was that of a madonna but the hands, red, conspicuous, coarse-grained, and slightly swollen, were the hands of a servant; and if it was suffering which had sublimated the face to a more exquisite beauty, the hands spoke eloquently of bitter toil that had blemished them into this pathetic, contrasting ugliness.

As she gazed intently out of the window she remained quiescent, passive as her own work-worn hands, yet across her sensitive features a faint excitement quivered which betokened the inner agitation of her turbulently beating heart. There, she thought, was the Mains Farm, its brown, furrowed fields lapped by the wind-beaten, crested waters of the Estuary, its stack-yard a square, yellow patch against the low, white-washed huddle of the homestead; there, too, was the weathered pile of the Linten Lighthouse, and, equally unchanged, the blue, massive outlines of the Rock itself; there, against the sky, the long, skeleton tracery of the Latta Shipyards, and now, swinging into view, the sharp, stippled steeple of the Borough Hall. Affected by the touching familiarity of all that she saw, she considered how unaltered everything was, how permanent, secure, and solid. It was she, Mary Brodie, who had changed, and she now longed wistfully to be as she had been when she had lived in these surroundings, before the branding iron of circumstance had set its seal upon her. As she meditated thus, with a sudden, wrenching pang like the tearing open of a wound, she observed the Levenford Cottage Hospital where for two months she had lain facing death, where, too, her infant child had died; and, at the sudden poignant reminder, the serenity of her countenance broke and though no tears flowed— they had all been shed before—her lips quivered painfully. She marked the window through which her fixed eyes had ceaselessly sought the sky, the gravel walk flanked by laurel bushes along which she had directed the first, flagging steps of her convalescence, the very gatepost to which she had then clung, fluttering and exhausted from the feebleness of her state. She willed the train to stop that she might linger with her memories, but it bore her quickly away from this sad reminder of the past and, circling the last bend, gave to her spasmodic, transient glimpses of Church Street, a line of shops, the Public Library, the Cross, then swept her into the Station itself.

How small the platform seemed, with its diminutive waiting-rooms and insignificant wooden ticket office, yet when she had once stood in this same station to take the train for Darroch she had, in the agitation of her adventure, trembled at its very magnitude; and, indeed, she trembled now as she realised that she must leave the solitary seclusion of her compartment and venture forth into the public gaze. She stood up firmly, gripping her portmanteau, and although a faint colour tinged her cheeks, she set her soft lips into the mould of fortitude and stepped bravely out upon the platform. She was back again in Levenford after four years!

To the porter who approached, she surrendered her bag with instructions that it should be delivered to her at the next round of the station van and, having given up her ticket, she descended the short flight of steps to the street and set out with a throbbing bosom for her home. If she had been beset by memories in the train, now they rushed in upon her with an overpowering force, and it seemed to her as if each step she took brought before her some fresh remembrance to further strain her already bursting heart. There was the Common, fringed in the distance by the Leven; here was the school she had attended as a child; and, as she passed the portals of the Public Library, still guarded by the same swing doors, she became aware that it was here, on this very spot, that she had first met Denis. The thought of Denis brought no pang, no bitterness, but now merely a sad regret, as though she felt herself no longer his beloved nor yet the victim of his love, but only the helpless puppet of an irresistible destiny.

While she proceeded along Railway Road she observed coming towards her a woman whom she had known in the days before her banishment, and she settled herself for the wound of a sharp, contemptuous glance; but no glance came, no sharp wound, for the other drew near and passed her with the placid countenance of complete unrecognition. How much I must have changed, thought Mary sadly, as she entered Wellhall Road, and, coming upon Dr. Renwick's house, she wondered with a curious detachment if he, too, might find her changed, should she ever encounter him. He had been so good to her, that even to pass this dwelling moved her strangely. While she did not consider the fact that he had saved her life, as though this were of slight importance, she remembered vividly the letters he had written her—first when she had gone to London and later to inform her of her mother's illness, and subsequently of her death—all filled with a kind and unmistakable sympathy. She might never have returned to Levenford but for these letters, for, had she not received the second, she would not have written home and Nessie would never have known her address to send her that frantic appeal. Poor, frightened Nessie! Thoughts of her sister and of her father now invaded her, and as she drew near to her home, with the memory of the night on which she had left it stamped like an indelible background upon her mind, she became outwardly agitated; the calm, long-set tranquillity of her appearance was at last melted by the warm, surging currents set racing by the unwonted action of her fast-beating heart.

Again she felt herself tremble at the prospect of meeting her father; she shuddered slightly as, of her own volition, she moved towards the oppressive influence of the dwelling which had once contained her like a prisoner.

When, finally, she reached her home, it was with a shock that she observed the outer aspect of the house, wondering, in her first bewilderment, if it were she who viewed it with different eyes, but in a moment, noting more intently the subtle, individual alterations which gave it an appearance at once slovenly and sordid. The windows were dirty, with such curtains as veiled them soiled and draggled, with blinds hanging unevenly; in the turret one small window was open and uncovered, the other completely shuttered, like a closed eye, so that the face of the tower winked at her with a fixed, perpetual leer. The clean, grey stone of the frontage was stained by a long, irregular, rusty smear, drawn by the rush of water from a broken gutter, and straggling across the house face like a defilement; the gutter sagged, a slate drooped drunkenly from the straight line of the eaves, whilst the courtyard in front was empty, unraked, and green with weeds.

Startled by these slight but revealing variations which so transfigured the exterior of the house, and stirred with a sudden fear of what she might discover within, Mary moved quickly up the steps and rang the bell. Her trepidation increased as she stood for a long time waiting, but at last the door opened slowly and she beheld, against the dimness beyond, the thin, unformed figure of Nessie. The sisters looked at each other, exclaimed together "Nessie!" "Mary!" then, with a mingling cry, rushed into each other's arms.

"Mary! Oh, Mary!" Nessie cried brokenly, unable in her emotion to do more than repeat the name, and clinging to her sister in utter abandon. "My own, dear Mary!"

"Nessie! dear Nessie!" whispered Mary, herself overcome by an excess feeling, "I'm so happy to see you again. I've often longed for this when I've been away."

'You'll never leave me any more, will you, Mary?" sobbed Nessie. "I've wanted you so much! Hold me tight and never let me go."

"I'll never leave you, dearie! I've come back just to be with you!"

"I know! I know!" wept Nessie. "It's good of you to do it, but oh! I've needed you sorely since Mamma died. I've had nobody! I've been frightened!"

"Don't cry, dearest," whispered Mary, drawing her sister's head against her breast and gently stroking her brow. "You're all right, now. Don't be frightened any more."

"You don't know what I've come through," cried Nessie frantically. "It's like heaven to see you back; but it's a wonder I'm here at all."

"Hush! dearie, hush! I don't want you to upset yourself and be ending up with a sore, wee head."

"It's my heart that's been sore," said the younger sister, turning up her red-lidded, burning eyes. "I didn't love you enough when I had you, Mary, but I'll make up for it. Everything's so different now. I need you so much I'll do anything, if you'll just bide with me."

"I'll do that, dear," replied Mary consolingly. "Just dry your eyes and you can tell me all about it. Here's my handkerchief for you!"

"It's just like old times for you to give me this," sniffed Nessie, releasing her sister's arm, taking the proffered handkerchief, and applying it to her wet face. "I was aye losing mine." Then as her sobs subsided and she regarded her sister from a slight distance she exclaimed, suddenly: "How bonnie you've got, Mary! There's a look about your face that makes me want never to take my eyes off you."

"It's just the same old face, Nessie."

"No! you were always bonnie, but now there's something seems to shine out of it like a light."

"Never mind about me," replied Mary tenderly. "It's you I'm thinking of, dear. We'll need to see about putting some flesh on these thin arms of yours. You've been needing someone to look after you."

"I have, indeed," answered Nessie pathetically, looking down at her own unsubstantial form. "I can't eat anything. We've had such bad food lately. It was all because of that—that——" She threatened to break down again.

"Hush, pettie, hush—don't cry again," whispered Mary. "Tell me some other time."

"I can't wait to tell you," cried Nessie hysterically, her words coming in a rush. "My letter told you nothing. We've had a terrible woman in the house and she's run away with Matt to America. Father was nearly out of his head and he does nothing but drink from mornin' till night and oh! Mary! he's driving me on to study so much that it's just killing me. Don't let him do it, Mary—will you? You'll save me, won't

386

you, Mary?" and she held her hands out beseechingly towards her sister.

Mary stood quite still; the torrent of the other's speech had overwhelmed her. Then she said, slowly: "Is father changed, Nessie? Is he not good to you now?"

"Changed!" whimpered Nessie. "He's so changed you wouldn't know him. It frightens me to see him sometimes. When he's not had whisky he's like a man walkin' in a dream. You wouldn't believe the change in everything"—she continued with a rising voice, and, seizing her sister's arm, she began to draw her towards the kitchen—"you wouldn't believe it unless you saw it. Look here! Come and see the sight of this room," and she flung open the door widely as though to demonstrate visibly the extent of the alteration in the circumstances of her life.

Mary stood dumbly envisaging the frowsy room, then she looked at Nessie and said, wonderingly:

"Does father put up with this?"

"Put up with it!" cried the other; "he doesn't even notice it, and he looks worse even than this room, with his clothes hanging off him, and his eyes sunk away, down in his head. If I try to lay a finger on the place to clear it up he roars my head off and keeps shouting at me to get on with my work and threatens me in all manner of ways, simply scares me out of my wits."

"Is it as bad as that, then?" murmured Mary, almost to herself.

"It's worse," cried Nessie, mournfully, looking up at her sister with wide eyes. "Grandma does the best she can, but she's near helpless now. Nobody can manage him. You and me better go away somewhere quick before anything happens to us." Her attitude seemed to entreat her sister to fly instantly with her from the ruins of their home. But Mary shook her head, and speaking firmly, cheerfully, said:

"We can't run away, dear. We'll do the best we can together. I'll soon have the place different for you," and, advancing to the window she threw it up and let a gust of the cool, sharp wind come rushing in the room. "There, now; we'll let the breeze in for a little, while we have a walk in the back, then I'll come in and straighten things out." She took off her hat and coat and, laying them on the sofa, turned again to Nessie, put her arm round the other's thin waist, and drew her out of the back door into the outer air.

"Oh, Mary!" cried Nessie ecstatically, pressing her side close against her sister as the two began to walk slowly up and down, "it's wonderful to have you back. You're so strong, I've an awful faith in you. Surely things will go right now." Then she added inconsequently: "What's been happening to you? What have you been doing all this time?"

Mary held out her free hand for a moment.

"Just using these," she said lightly; "and hard work never killed anybody, so here I am."

The younger girl looked with a shocked gaze at the rough calloused palm, seared by a deep white scar; and turning her eyes upwards remarked, wonderingly:

"What gave you that big mark? Was it a cut ye got?"

A quick expression of pain flitted across Mary's face as she replied:

"That was it, Nessie; but it's all better now. I told you never to mind about your stupid old sister. It's wee you we're to think about."

Nessie laughed happily, then stopped short in amazement.

"Would ye believe it!" she exclaimed, in an awestruck tone; "that was me laughin'—a thing I haven't done for months. Goodness! I could be downright happy if it wasn't for the thought of all the work for that old Bursary exam." She shivered exaggeratedly. "That's the worse thing of any."

"Will you not get it?" asked Mary solicitously.

"Of course I will!" exclaimed the other with a toss of her head. "I mean to get it all right, just to show them all—the way some of them have behaved to me at school is a disgrace. But it's father. He goes on about it and worries me to death. I wish he would only leave me alone." She shook her head and added, in an old-fashioned tone that might have been her mother's voice: "My head's like to split the way he raves at me sometimes. He's got me away to a shadow."

Mary looked commiseratingly at the fragile form and thin precocious face beside her and, squeezing her sister's puny arm reassuringly, she said:

"I'll soon get you all right, my girl. I know exactly what to do, and I've a few tricks up my sleeve that might surprise you."

Nessie turned, and using a favourite catchword of their childhood, remarked, with an assumption of great simplicity:

"Is it honky-tonky tricks you've got up there, Mary?"

The sisters gazed at each other, while the years fell away from them, then suddenly they smiled into each other's eyes, and laughed aloud together, with a sound which echoed strangely in that desolate back garden.

"Oh! Mary," sighed Nessie rapturously "this is better than I expected. I could hug you, and hug you. You're lovely. I've got my bonnie, big sister back. Was it not brave of me to write and ask you to come back? If he had found me out he would have taken my head off. You'll not let on it was me though, will you?"

"No, indeed," cried Mary fondly, "I'll not say a word."

"He'll be in soon," said Nessie slowly, her face falling again at the thought of her father's imminent return. "You know all about—about his comin' to work in the Yard I suppose."

A faint colour suffused Mary's cheeks as she answered:

"Yes! I heard about it, just after Mamma's death."

"Such a come down!" said Nessie in a precocious tone. "Poor Mamma was well out of it. It would have finished her if the other hadn't." She paused, and sighed, adding with a sort of sorrowful comfort: "I would like us to go up and put some flowers on her grave some day soon. There's not a thing on it—not even an artificial wreath."

A silence now came between the sisters whilst each followed her own thoughts, then Mary started, and said: "I must go in and see to things, dear. I want to get everything ready. You wait here in the air, for I think it'll do you good. Wait and see how nice I'll have everything for you."

Nessie gazed at her sister doubtfully.

"You're not going to run away and leave me?" she demanded, as though she feared to allow Mary out of her sight. "I'll come in and help you."

"Nonsense! I'm used to this work," replied Mary. "Your business is to stay here and get an appetite for tea."

Nessie loosed her sister's hand, and as she watched her go through the back door cried, warningly:

"I'll keep my eye on you through the window to see you don't go away."

Inside the house, Mary set to work to restore cleanliness and some degree of order to the kitchen and, having assumed an apron which she discovered in the scullery, and directing her activities with the precision of experience, she quickly burnished and blackened the grate, lit the fire and swept the hearth, scrubbed the floor, dusted the furniture, and rubbed the window panes to some degree of brightness. Then, searching for the whitest table cover she could find, she spread this upon the table and commenced to prepare as appetising a tea as the scanty contents of the larder would permit. Standing there by the stove, flushed and a little breathless from the rapidity of her exertions, she seemed to have sloughed off the intervening years and—as though she had never suffered the bitter experiences of her life—to be again a girl engaged in getting ready the evening meal of the household. While she remained thus, she heard a slow shuffling tread in the lobby followed by the creak of the kitchen door as it swung open, and turning, she observed the bowed and decrepit figure of old Grandma Brodie come hobbling into the room, diffidently, uncertainly, like a spectre moving among the ruins of its past glory. Mary left the stove, advanced, and called: "Grandma!"

The old woman looked slowly up, presenting her yellow, cracked visage with its sunken cheeks and puckered lips, and, staring incredulously, as though she too observed a phantom, she muttered at length: "Mary! it canna surely be Mary." Then she shook her head, dismissing the evidence of her aged eyes as unthinkable, removed her gaze from Mary, and with an indeterminate step moved towards the scullery, whispering to herself:

"I maun get some tea thegither for him. James' tea maun be got ready."

"I'm getting the tea, Grandma," exclaimed Mary; "there's no need for you to worry about it. Come and sit in your chair," and taking the other's arm she led her, tottering but unresisting, to her old seat by the fire, into which the crone subsided with a vacant and unheeding stare. As Mary began, however, to journey to and fro from the scullery to the kitchen and the table assumed gradually an appearance such as it had not borne for months, the old woman's eye became more lucid and looking from a plate of hot pancakes, steaming and real, to Mary's face, she passed her blue-lined, transparent hand tremulously over her brows and muttered: "Does he know you're back?"

"Yes, Grandma! I wrote and said I was coming," replied Mary.

"Is he goin' to let you bide here?" croaked the other. "Maybe he'll put ye out again. When was that? Was it before Marg'et deed? I canna think. Your hair looks unco' bonnie that way." Her gaze then faded and she seemed to lose interest, murmuring disconsolately as she turned towards the fire: "I canna eat so weel without my teeth."

"Would you like a hot pancake and butter?" asked Mary in a coaxing tone.

"Would I no'!" replied the other instantly. "Where is't?" Mary gave the old woman her pancake, saw her seize it avidly and, crouching over the fire, begin eagerly to suck it to its destruction. Suddenly she was aroused from her contemplation by a whisper in her ear:

"Please, I would like one too, Mary dear!" Nessie had come in and was now presenting a flatly suppliant palm, waiting to have it covered by the warm solace of a new-made pancake.

"You'll not have one, you'll have two," cried Mary recklessly. "Yes! as many as you like. I've made plenty."

"They're good," exclaimed Nessie appreciatively. "Good as good! You've made them so quick too, and my word what a change you've made in the room! It's like old times again! as light as a feather! That's the way my mother used to make them, and these are just as good, ay, better than we used to get. Yum—yum—they're lovely!"

As Mary listened whilst Nessie talked on in this fashion and watched her quick, nervous gestures as she ate, she began to study her more intently than she had hitherto done, and slowly an impression of vague but deep uneasiness stole in upon her. The facile, running speech of her sister, the jerky and slightly uncontrolled movements perceptible now on her closer observation, seemed to betoken a state of unconscious nervous tension which alarmed her, and as she traced the thin contours

390

of the other's growing body and noted her faintly hollowed cheeks and temples she said, involuntarily:

"Nessie, dear, are you sure you're feeling all right?"

Nessie stuffed the last of the pancake into her mouth before she replied, expressively:

"I'm getting better and better—especially since I've had that. Mary's pancakes are good but Mary herself is better." She chewed for a moment then solemnly added: "I've felt real bad once or twice, but I'm right as the mail now."

Her sudden idea was, of course, mere nonsense, thought Mary, but nevertheless she determined to use every effort in her power to obtain for Nessie some respite from the studies which seemed, at least, to be overtaxing the inadequate strength of her immature frame. A strong feeling, partly from love of her sister, but chiefly from a strong maternal impulse towards the other's weakness, gripped her, and she laid her arm protectingly round Nessie's narrow shoulders, drew her close and murmured, warmly: "I'll do my best for you, dear. I really will. There's nothing I wouldn't do to see you look happy and well."

Whilst the sisters stood together thus the old woman raised her head from the fire and, as she considered them, a sudden, penetrating insight seemed to flash through the obscurity of her senile mind, for she remarked sharply:

"Don't let him see ye like that. Don't hing thegither and show you're so fond o' one another in front of him. Na! Na! he'll have no interference wi' Nessie. Let her be, let her be." The edge in her voice was blunted as she uttered these last words, her gaze again became opaque and, with a slow, unconcealed yawn she turned away, muttering: "I'm wantin' my tea. Is it not tea time yet? Is't not time for James to be in?"

Mary looked interrogatively at her sister and the shadow fell again on Nessie's brow as she remarked, moodily:

"You can infuse the tea. He'll be in any minute now. Then you'll see for yourself—the minute I've finished a cup it'll be the signal for me to be shoved off into the parlour. I'm tired to death of it."

Mary did not reply but went into the scullery to infuse the tea, and filled now by a sudden, private fear at the immediate prospect of meeting her father, the unselfish consideration of her sister slipped for the moment from her mind and she began to anticipate, tremblingly, the manner of his greeting. Her eyes, that were fixed unseeingly upon the steamy clouds issuing from the boiling kettle, flinched as she recollected how he had kicked her brutally as she lay in the hall, how that blow had been in part responsible for the pneumonia which had nearly killed her, and she wondered vaguely if he had ever regretted that single action, if he had, indeed, even thought of it during the four years of her absence. As for herself, the memory of that blow had lived with her for months the pain of it had lasted during the long delirium of her illness, when she had suffered a thousand savage kicks from him with each stabbing respiration; the indignity had remained until long afterwards, when she would lie awake at night, turning in her mind the outrage upon her body of the inhuman impact of his heavy boot.

She thought again of these thick-soled boots which she had so often brushed for him, which she would, in her voluntary servitude, brush for him again, and as she remembered, too, the heavy tread which had habitually announced his entry, she started, listened, and once again heard his foot in the hall, slower, even sluggish, less firm, almost dragging, but still her father's step. The moment which she had foreseen, had visualised a thousand times, which, though she dreaded it, was of her own seeking, was upon her and, though she shook in all her limbs, she turned and advanced bravely, but with a fluttering heart, to meet him.

They came face to face in the kitchen, where the man who had come in looked at her silently, swept the room, the table, the brightly burning hearth with his dark eye, then returned his glance to her. Only when he spoke did she know actually that it was her father, when his old bitter sneer distorted his furrowed visage and he said:

"You've come back then, have ye?" and walked without further speech to his chair. The devastating change in him, such a change that she had failed almost to recognise him, shocked her so profoundly that she was unable to speak. Could this be her father, this old, shrunken man with his unkempt hair, his stained, untidy clothing, his morose unshaven face, his wild, wretched, malignant eye. Nessie had been right! She could not have believed the magnitude of this change until she had seen it, and even now she could scarcely credit the evidence of her eyes. In a dazed manner she moved herself forward and began to pour out and hand round the tea and, when she had accomplished this, she did not sit down with the others, but remained standing, waiting to serve them, still filled with an incredulous dismay at her father's dreadful appearance. He, on his part, continued to ignore her and to partake of his meal silently, with a careless, almost slovenly manner of eating, apparently regardless of what he consumed or the fashion in which he consumed it. His glance was distrait, oblique, and when it assumed a cognisance of his surroundings, it fell not upon her, but always upon Nessie, as though some rooted conception of his brain was centred upon her, making her the focus of his conscious attention. The others, too, ate without speaking and, although she had not yet had the opportunity to address her father, to break that period of silence now four years long, she passed quietly out of the kitchen into the scullery where she remained intent, listening, and perturbed. When she had determined to sacrifice herself for Nessie's sake and return home she had envisaged herself in combat with an oppression of a different nature, loud, hectoring, even savage, but never with such a strange, inhuman preoccupation as this which she now felt to have possessed her father. His strong and virile character seemed, like his flesh, to have crumbled from him, leaving a warped structure of a man engrossed with something, she knew not what, which had mastered him and now controlled each thought, each action of his body.

She had been in the scullery only a few minutes, considering him thus, when to her straining ears came the harsh, different sound of his voice, saying:

"You've finished, Nessie! You can get into the parlour and begin your work now!" Immediately she steeled herself and re-entered the kitchen, and, observing Nessie rising in a sad, dejected manner with a cowed look in her eyes to obey his command, at the submission of the child she felt a sudden rush of courage within her and in a quiet voice she addressed her father.

"Father, could Nessie not come for a walk with me before she begins her work?"

But he might have been deaf to her words, and utterly oblivious of her presence, for any evidence which he manifested of having heard or seen her, and continuing to look at Nessie, he resumed, in a harder tone:

"Off with you, now. And see you stick into it. I'll be in to see how you're getting on."

As Nessie went humbly out of the door Mary bit her lip and flushed deeply, finding in his silent contempt of her first words to him, the realisation of how he proposed to treat her.—She could be there, but for him she would not exist! She made no comment, but when he had arisen from the table, and the old woman, too, had finished and gone out of the room, she began to clear away the dishes into the scullery, observing as she passed in and out of the kitchen, that he had taken a bottle and glass from the dresser and had settled himself to drink steadily, with an appearance of habitual exactitude as though he proposed to continue imbibing regularly for the course of the entire evening.

She washed and dried the dishes, cleaned and tidied the scullery, then, with the intention of joining Nessie in the parlour, she entered the kitchen and was about to pass through it, when suddenly, and without looking at her. Brodie shouted from his corner in a fierce, arresting tone:

"Where are you going?"

She halted, looking at him appealingly as she replied:

"I was only going in to see Nessie for a moment, father—not to speak —only to watch her."

"Don't go, then," he shot at her, still fixing his eye upon the ceiling and away from her. "I'll do all the watching of Nessie that's required. You'll kindly keep away from her."

"But, rather," she faltered, "I'm not going to disturb her. I haven't seen her for so long, I like to be near her."

"And I like that you shouldn't be near her," he replied bitterly.

"You're not the company I want for my daughter. You can cook and work for her and for me too, but keep your hands off her. I'll brook no interference with her or with the work she's set on." This indeed was what she expected, and asking herself why she had come back if it were not to succour Nessie, she stood firmly contemplating him with her quiet gaze, then, mustering all her courage, she said:

"I'm going to Nessie, father," and moved towards the door.

Only then he looked at her, turning the full force of his malignant eyes upon her, and, seizing the bottle by his side he drew himself to his feet and advanced slowly towards her.

"Move another step towards that door," he snarled, "and I'll smash your skull open"; then as though he hoped that she might disobey him he stood confronting her, ready to swing fiercely at her head. She retreated, and as she slipped back from him he watched her sneeringly, crying: "That's better. That's much better! We'll have to teach ye manners again, I can see. But by God! keep away from Nessie and don't think *you* can fool me. No woman living can do that now. Another step and I would have finished ye for good." Then, suddenly his ferocious manner dropped from him and he returned to his chair, sat down and, sinking back into his original air of morose and brooding apathy, he resumed his drinking, not apparently for the achievement of gaiety, but as though in a vain, despairing endeavour to obtain oblivion from some secret and unforgettable misery.

Mary sat down at the table. She was afraid to leave the room. Her fear was not physical, not for herself, but for Nessie, and had she not been concerned solely for her sister, she would a moment ago have advanced straight into the threatening sweep of the weapon with which her father had menaced her. Life was of little value to her now, but nevertheless she realised that if she were to help Nessie from the frightful danger which threatened her in this house, she must be not only brave, but wise. She saw that her presence and, indeed, her purpose in the house would mean a bitter perpetual struggle with her father for the possession of Nessie, and she felt that her own resources were insufficient to cope with this situation to which she had returned. As she sat there watching Brodie soak himself steadily, yet ineffectually, in liquor, she determined to seek assistance without delay, and planned carefully what she would do on the following day. When her conception of what she must do lay clearly defined in her mind, she looked around for something to occupy her, but could find nothing—no book to read—no sewing which she might do, and she was constrained to remain still in the silence of the room, gazing at her father, yet never finding his gaze upon her.

The evening dragged slowly on with lagging hours until she felt that it would never end, that her father would never move, but at last he got up and saying, coldly: "You have your own room. Go to it, but

leave Nessie alone in hers," went out and into the parlour, where she
heard his voice, questioning, admonishing Nessie. She put out the light
and went slowly upstairs to her own, old room where she undressed
and sat down to wait, hearing first Nessie come up, then her father,
hearing the sounds of their undressing, finally hearing nothing. Silence
filled the house. She waited a long time in this small room where she
had already known so much waiting and so much bitter anguish. Fleeting visions of the past rushed before her, of her vigils at the window when
she gazed so ceaselessly at the silver trees, of Rose—where was she now?
—and the throwing of the apple, of the storm, of her discovery, and in
the light of her own sad experience she resolved that she would save
Nessie from unhappiness, even at the sacrifice of herself, if it lay within
her human power. At this thought she arose noiselessly, opened her
door, crept across the landing without a sound, passed into Nessie's
room, and slipped into bed beside her sister. She folded her arms around
the cold, fragile figure of the child, chafing her frigid feet, warming her
against her own body, stilling her sobs, comforting her in endearing
whispers and at last soothing her into sleep. There, holding in her
embrace the sleeping form of her sister, she remained awake long into
the night, thinking.

VI

Mary looked at the picture, which hung in solitary distinction against
the rich, deep red background of the wall of the room, with a rapt contemplation which removed her momentarily from the anxiety and confusion which beset her. She stood, her clear profile etched against
the window beyond, head thrown back, lips faintly parted, her luminous
eyes fixed absorbedly upon the painting out of which breathed a cool,
grey mist that lay upon still, grey water, shrouding softly the tall, quiet
trees—as silvery as her own trees—and sheathing itself around the thin,
immobile wands of the rushes which fringed the pool; she was elevated
from the confusion of mind in which she had entered this house, by the
rare and melancholy beauty of the picture which, exhibiting with such
restraint this passive mood of nature, seemed to move from out its frame
and touch her like a reverie, like a sad yet serene meditation upon the
sorrow of her own life.

So engrossed was she by her consideration of the picture, which had
caught her eye as she sat embarrassed, amongst the tasteful furnishings
of the room, so moved from her conflicting feelings by the strange,
appealing beauty of the painting which had compelled her to rise involuntarily to stand before it, that she failed to observe the smooth

movement of the polished mahogany door as it swung open upon its quiet hinges; nor did she observe the man who had entered the room, and who now gazed at her pale, transfigured profile with a sudden intentness, as silent and as entranced as her own contemplation of the picture. He stood as motionless as she did, as though afraid to break the spell which her appearance had laid upon him, but regarding her with pleasure, waiting, too, until she should have filled her eyes enough with the loveliness of the placid pool.

At last she withdrew her glance, sighed, turned unconsciously and, again raising her dark eyes, suddenly perceived him. Immediately all her dispelled confusion rushed back upon her, heightened now to the point of shame, and she flushed, hung her head as he advanced towards her and warmly took her hand.

"It is Mary," he said, "Mary Brodie come back again to see me."

With a great effort she forced her disconcerted gaze upwards, looked at him, and replied, in a low tone:

"You remember me, then. I thought you would have forgotten all about me. I've—I've changed so much."

"Changed!" he cried. "You haven't changed, unless it's that you're bonnier than ever! Tut! Don't look so ashamed of it, Mary. It's not a crime to look as lovely as you do."

She smiled faintly at him as he continued, cheerfully: "As for forgetting you, how could I forget one of my first patients, the one who did me most credit, when I was struggling along with nothing in this very room but the empty packing case that my books had come in."

She looked round the present rich comfort of the room and, still slightly discomposed, she replied, at a tangent to her main thoughts:

"There's more than that here now, Dr. Renwick!"

"You see! That's what you've done for me," he exclaimed. "Made my name by your pluck in pulling through. You did the work and I got the credit!"

"It was only the credit you got," she replied slowly. "Why did you return the fee I sent you?"

"I got your address from the letter—you that ran away without saying good-bye," he cried; "that was all the fee I wanted." He seemed strangely pleased to see her and strangely near to her, as though four years had not elapsed since he had last spoken to her, and he still sat by her bedside compelling her back to life by his vital animation. "Tell me all that you've been doing," he ran on, endeavouring to put her at her ease. "Wag your tongue! Let me see you haven't forgotten your old friends."

"I haven't forgotten you, doctor, or I wouldn't be here now. I'll never forget all that you've done for me."

"Tuts! I don't want you to wag the tongue that way! I want to hear about yourself. I'm sure you've got all London on its knees before you by this time."

She shook her head at his words and, with a faint humour lurking in her eyes, replied:

"No! I've done the kneeling myself—scrubbing floors and washing steps!"

"What!" he cried, in amazed concern. "You haven't been working like that?"

"I don't mind hard work," she said lightly. "It did me good; took my thoughts away from my own wretched troubles."

"You were never made for that sort of thing," he exclaimed reproachfully. "It's scandalous! It was downright wicked of you to run away as you did. We would have found something more suitable for you to do."

"I wanted to escape from everything, then," she answered sadly. "I wished help from no one."

"Well, don't do it again," he retorted with some asperity. "Will you rush away like that again, without saying good-bye to a man?"

"No!" she replied mildly.

He could not forbear to smile at her air of submission as he motioned her to sit down and, drawing a small chair close up beside her, said:

"I have been forgetting such manners as I have to keep you standing like this, but really, Miss Mary, it is such a sudden and unexpected pleasure to see you again! You must be lenient with me." Then after a pause he asked, "You would get my letters? They were dismal reminders of this place were they not?"

She shook her head.

"I want to thank you for them. I would never have known of Mamma's death if you hadn't written. These letters brought me back."

He looked at her steadily and replied:

"I knew you would come back some day. I felt it." Then he added, "But tell me what has actually brought you back?"

"Nessie! my sister Nessie!" she said slowly. "Things have been dreadful at home and she has suffered. She needed me—so I came home. It's because of her I've come to see you. It's a great liberty on my part after you've done so much for me already. Forgive me for coming! I need help!"

"Tell me how you wish me to help you and I'll do it," he exclaimed. "Is Nessie ill?"

"Not exactly ill," said Mary, "although somehow she alarms me; she is so nervous, so easily excited. She laughs and cries by turns and she has got so thin, seems to eat so little. But although it worries me I really did not come about that." She paused for a moment gathering courage to tell him, then continued, bravely: "It is about my father. He treats her so peculiarly, not unkindly, but forcing her so unreasonably to work at her lessons, to study all the time, not only at school, but the whole long evening—and every evening. She is shut up by herself and made to 'stick in' as he calls it, so that she will win the Latta Bursary. He has set his mind on that. She tells me that he throws it at her head every time she sees him, threatening her with all manner of penalties if she fails. If he would leave her alone she would do it in her own way, but he drives and drives at her and she is so fragile I am afraid of what is going to happen. Last night she cried for an hour in my arms before she went to sleep. I am very anxious!"

He looked at her small, sad, earnest face, was filled with a quick vision of her comforting and consoling her sister, thought suddenly of the child which, despite his every effort, had been lost to her, and with a grave face answered:

"I can see you are anxious, but it is a difficult matter to interfere in. We must consider it. Your father is not actually cruel to her?"

"No! but he terrifies her. He used to be fond of her, but he is so changed now, that even his fondness is changed to something strange and terrible."

He had heard, of course, the stories concerning Brodie's altered habits, but forbore to question her more deeply on this particular point and, instead, he exclaimed:

"Why is he so eager for her to win the Latta? It's usually a boy that wins that—is it not—never a girl?"

"That may be the reason," replied Mary sadly; "he's always been mad for some unusual kind of success to bring credit on himself, always wanted Nessie to do well because of his own pride. But now I'm certain he doesn't know what he'll do with her when she's won it. He's shoving her on to no purpose."

"Is young Grierson in the running for the Bursary?" queried Renwick, after a moment's consideration. "Your father and Grierson are not exactly on good terms I believe."

Mary shook her head.

"It's deeper than that I'm sure," she answered. "You would think the winning of it was going to make father the envy of the whole town the way he talks."

He looked at her comprehendingly.

"I know your father, Mary, and I know what you mean. I'm afraid all is not right with him. There was always something—— Well—I've come across him in the past too——" he did not say that it had been chiefly on her behalf, "and we have never agreed. There would be little use in my going to see him if, indeed, it were permissible for me to do so. Any direct action of mine would serve only to aggravate him and make his conduct worse."

As she sat observing him while, with an abstracted gaze, he pondered the question, she thought how wise, how kind and considerate he was towards her, not rushing blindly, but reasoning coherently on her behalf; her eyes moved slowly across his strong dark face, vital yet austere, over his spare, active, and slightly stooping form until they fell at length upon his hands, showing sensitive, strong, and brown against the immaculate, white bands of his starched linen cuffs. These firm, delicate hands had probed the mysteries of her inanimate body, had saved her life, such as it was, and as she contrasted them in her mind with her own blotched and swollen fingers she felt the gulf which separated her from this man whose help she had been bold enough to seek. What exquisite hands! A sudden sense of her own inferiority, of her incongruity amongst the luxury and taste of her present surroundings afflicted her, and she diverted her eyes quickly from him to the ground, as though afraid that he might intercept and interpret her glance.

"Would you care for me to see the Rector of the Academy about Nessie?" he asked at length. "I know Gibson well and might in confidence ask his assistance in the matter. I had thought at first of speaking to Sir John Latta, but your father is engaged at the office of the shipyard now and it might prejudice him there. We doctors have got to be careful of what we are about. It's a precarious existence——" He smiled. "Would you like me to see Gibson, or would you rather send Nessie to me to let me have a look at her?"

"I think if you saw the Rector it would be splendid. He had a great influence with father once," she replied gratefully. "Nessie is so frightened of father she would be afraid to come here."

"And were you not afraid to come?" he asked, with a look which seemed to comfort her with its knowledge of her past fortitude.

"Yes," she answered truthfully. "I was afraid you would refuse to see me. I have no one to ask for help for Nessie but you. She is so young. Nothing must happen to her!" She paused, then added in a low tone: "You might not have wished to see me. You know all about me, what I have been!"

"Don't! Don't say that, Mary! All that I know of you is good. I have remembered you for these years because of your goodness, your gentleness, and your courage." As he looked at her now he would have added: "and your loveliness," but he refrained and said, instead: "In all my life I never met such a sweet, unselfish spirit as yours. It graved itself unforgettably upon my mind. I hate to hear you belittle yourself like that."

She flushed at the warm comfort of his words and replied:

"It's like you to say that, but I don't deserve it. Still, if I can do something for Nessie to make up for my own mistakes I'll be happy."

"Are you an old woman to talk like that! What age are you?" he cried impetuously. "You're not twenty-two yet. Good Lord! you're only a child, with a whole lifetime in front of you. All the pain you've suffered can be wiped out—you've had no real happiness yet worth the name. Begin to think of yourself again, Mary. I saw you looking at that picture of mine when I came in. I saw how it took you out of yourself. Make your life a whole gallery of these pictures—you must amuse yourself—read all the books you can get—take up some interest. I might get you a post as companion where you could travel abroad."

She was, in spite of herself, strangely fascinated by his words and, casting her thoughts back, she recollected how she had been thrilled in like fashion by Denis, when he had opened out entrancing avenues for her with his talk of Paris, Rome, and of travel through wide, mysterious lands. That had been a long time ago, when he had moved horizons for her with a sweep of his gay, audacious hand and whirled her abroad on the carpet of his graphic, laughing speech. He read her thoughts with a faculty of intuition which confounded her and said, slowly:

"You still think of him, I see."

She looked up in some slight dismay, divining that he misjudged the full tendency of her emotion, which was merely a retrospective sadness, but, feeling that she could not be disloyal to the memory of Denis, she did not speak.

"I would like to do something for you, Mary," he resumed quietly, "something which would make you happy. I have some influence. Will you allow me to find some post which is suited to you, and to your worth, before I go away from here."

She started at his words, bereft suddenly of her warm feeling of comfort, and stammered:

"Are you going away, then?"

"Yes," he replied, "I'm off within six months. I'm taking up a special branch of work in Edinburgh. I have the chance to get on the staff there—something bigger than the Cottage Hospital. It's a great opportunity for me."

She saw herself alone, without his strong resolute support, vainly endeavouring to protect Nessie from her father, interposing her own insignificant resolution between Brodie's drunken unreason and her sister's weakness, and in a flash she comprehended how much she had built on the friendship of this man before her, understood how great was her regard for him.

"It's splendid for you to have got on so well," she whispered. "But it's only what you deserve. I know you'll do as well in Edinburgh as you've done here. I don't need to wish you success."

"I don't know," he replied, "but I shall like it. Edinburgh is the city to live in—grey yet beautiful. Take Princes Street in the autumn with the leaves crackling in the gardens, and the Castle russet against the sky, and the blue smoke drifting across Arthur's Seat, and the breeze tingling, as clean and crisp as fine wine. No one could help but love it." He glowed at the thought of it and continued: "It's my native place of course—you must forgive my pride.—Still, everything is bigger there —finer and cleaner, like the air."

She followed his words breathlessly, seeing vividly the picture that he drew for her, but filling it always with his own figure, so that it was not only Princes Street which she saw but Renwick, striding along its grey surface, against the mellow background of the Castle Gardens.

"It sounds beautiful. I have never been there but I can picture it all," she murmured, meaning actually that she could picture him there.

"Let me find something for you to do before I go away " he persisted; "something to take you out of that house."

She could feel that he was anxious for her to accept his offer, but she thrust the enticing prospect away from her, saying:

"I came back of my own choice to look after Nessie! I couldn't leave her now. It's been a terrible life for her for the last few months and if I went away again anything might happen to her."

He perceived then that she was fixed upon remaining and immediately a profound concern for her future disturbed him, as if he saw her already immolated on the altar of her own unselfishness, a sacrifice, despite his intervention, to the outrageous pride of her father. What purpose had it served for him to save her, to have helped her to escape from death, were she to drift back once again into the same environment, the same danger in a more deadly form? He was affected even to the point of marvelling at his own emotion, but quickly masking his feelings he exclaimed, cheerfully:

"I'll do my best for Nessie! I'll see Gibson to-day or to-morrow. Everything that I can do shall be done. Don't worry too much about her. Take more heed of yourself."

She felt when he said these words that the purport of her visit had been achieved and, diffident of occupying his time longer, she at once arose from her chair and prepared to go. He, too, got up but made no movement to the door, remaining silent, watching her face which, as she stood erect, was touched lightly by an errant beam of the pale March sunshine, so pale in the interior of the room, that it gleamed upon her skin like moonlight. Moved as another man had been moved by her in moonlight he caught his breath at the sight of her beauty, luminous in this light, showing against the foil of her indifferent and inelegant garments, and in his imagination he clothed her in satin of a faint lavender, visioned her under the silver radiance of a soft Southern moon in a garden in Florence or upon a terrace in Naples. As she poised her small foot in its rough shoe courageously towards her departure, he wished strangely to detain her, but found no words to utter.

"Good-bye," he heard her say, softly. "Thank you for what you have done for me, now, and before."

"Good-bye," he said mechanically, following her into the hall, realising that she was going. He opened the door for her, saw her move down the steps and with the sudden sense of his deprivation he responded to an appeal within him and called out hurriedly, awkwardly, like a schoolboy: "You'll come and see me again soon, won't you?" Then ashamed of his own clumsiness he came down the steps to her and proffered an explanation of his remark, exclaiming: "When I've seen Gibson I'll want you to know what the outcome is to be."

Again she looked at him gratefully and, exclaiming: "I'll come next week," entered the road and walked rapidly away.

As he turned and slowly re-entered his own house he became gradually amazed at his own recent action, at his sudden outspoken request that she should revisit him shortly; but although, at first, he somewhat ashamedly attributed this to the poignant appeal of her beauty in the light that had encircled her in his room, later he more honestly admitted to himself that this was not the sole reason of his conduct. Mary Brodie had always been for him a strangely beautiful figure, a noble, courageous spirit, who had woven her life through his existence in the town with a short and tragic thread. From the moment when he had first seen her unconscious, in the sad predicament of her condition, and against the gross contamination of her surroundings, like a lily uprooted and thrown on the dung hill, he had been drawn to her in her helplessness and immaturity; later he had been fired by her patience and uncomplaining fortitude during her long period of illness and in the suffering visited upon her by the death of her child; he had seen too, and clearly, that, though she had been possessed by another, she was pure, chaste as that light which had recently encompassed her. His admiration and interest had been aroused and he had promised himself that he would assist her to rebuild her life, but she had run from the town the moment her strength had permitted, fluttering away from the net of opprobrium which she must have felt around her. During the years of her absence he had, from time to time, thought of her; often the memory of her figure, thin, white, fragile, had risen before him with a strange insistent appeal, as if to tell him that the thread of her life would return to weave itself once more into the texture of his existence. He sat down at his desk, considering her deeply, praying that there would be no further tragedy in this return of Mary Brodie to the house of tribulation from which she had been so grievously outcast. After a few moments his thoughts moved into another channel, and from a pigeon-hole in his desk he drew out an old letter, the writing of which, now slightly faded after four years' preservation, sloped in rounded characters across the single page. He read it once more, this, her only letter to him, in which she had sent him some money, the pathetic accumulation, no doubt, of her meagre wages, in an attempt to recompense him in some degree for his service to her. With the letter clasped in the fine tapering fingers of his hand he remained staring in front of him, seeing her working as she had now told him she worked, upon her knees, scrubbing, washing, scouring, performing the menial duties of her occupation—working like a servant.

At length he sighed, shook himself, restored the letter to the desk, and observing that he had a full hour before his afternoon consultations were due to begin, determined to visit the Rector of the Academy at once, to enquire discreetly into the condition of Nessie Brodie. Accordingly, having instructed his housekeeper that he would return before four o'clock he left the house and walked slowly towards the school, wrapped in a strange and sober meditation.

It was but a short way to the Academy, that old foundation of the Borough which lay within the town, backing a little from Church Street to exhibit the better the severe, yet proportioned architecture of its weathered front, and now, in the paved space that lay before it, displaying proudly the two high-wheeled Russian guns captured at Balaclava by Maurice Latta's company of the Winton Yeomanry. But Renwick, when he shortly reached the building, passed inside without seeing its frontage or its guns; mounting the shallow, well-worn stone stairs he advanced along the passage, tapped with a preoccupied manner at the head master's door and, as he was bidden, entered.

Gibson, a youngish-looking man for his position, whose face was not yet completely set into the scholastic mould, was seated at his littered desk in the middle of the small book-lined study, and he did not at once look up, but, an engrossed yet unpedantic figure in his smooth suit of dark brown—a colour he habitually affected—continued to observe a document that lay in front of him. Renwick, a faint smile finally twisting his grave face at the other's preoccupation, remarked whimsically, after a moment:

"Still the same earnest student, Gibson," and as the other looked up with a start, continued, "it takes me back again to the old days to see you grinding at it like that."

Gibson, whose eye had brightened at the sight of Renwick, lay back in his chair and, motioning the other to sit down, remarked easily:

"I had no idea it was you, Renwick. I imagined rather one of my inky brigade trembling in the presence, awaiting a just chastisement. It does the little beggars good to keep them in awe of the imperial dignity."

A smile passed between them that was almost as spontaneous as a grin of their schooldays, and Renwick murmured:

"You're the very pattern of old Bulldog Morrison. I must tell him when I get back to Edinburgh. He'd appreciate the compliment."

"The humour of it, you mean," cried Gibson, surveying the past with a distant eye. "Gad! how I wish I were going back to the old place like you! You're a lucky dog." Then fixing his glance on the other suddenly, he remarked: "You haven't come to say good-bye, already?"

"No! No! man," returned Renwick lightly. "I'm not off for six months. I'm not leaving you in the wilderness yet awhile." Then his face changed and he contemplated the floor for a moment before raising his gaze to Gibson and resuming seriously: "My errand is a peculiar one, I want you to treat it in confidence! You're an old friend, yet it is hard for me to explain what I'm about." He again paused, and continued with some difficulty: "You have a child at school here that I am interested in—even anxious about. It is Nessie Brodie. I'm indirectly concerned about her health and her future. Mind you, Gibson, I haven't the least right to come here like this. I'm well aware of that, but you're not like a board of governors. I want your opinion and, if necessary, your help."

Gibson looked at the other intently, then away again, but he made no enquiry as to Renwick's motive and instead replied, slowly:

"Nessie Brodie! she's a clever child. Yes! very intelligent, but with a curious turn of her mind. Her memory is marvellous, Renwick; you could read her a whole page of Milton, and she would repeat it almost word for word; her perception, too, is acute, but her reasoning, the deeper powers of thought, are not proportionate." He shook his head. "She's what I call a smart pupil, quick as a needle, but with, I'm afraid, some pervading shallowness in her intellect."

"She's going up for the Latta," persisted Renwick. "Is she fit for it—will she win it?"

"She may win it," replied Gibson with a shrug of his shoulders, "but to what purpose! And indeed I can't say if she will do so. The matter is not in our hands. The standards of the University are not school standards. Her vocation is teaching—after a Normal education."

"Can't you keep her back, then?" remarked Renwick, with some slight eagerness. "I have information that her health is suffering from the strain of this preparation."

"It's impossible," returned the other. "As I've just said, the matter is out of our hands. It is a scholarship open to the Borough, set by the University authorities, and everyone may enter who is eligible. To be frank, I did drop a hint to her—her esteemed parent," he frowned here momentarily, "but it was useless. He's set on it grimly. And indeed she has such an excellent chance of winning that it sounds like pure folly to wish her to stand down. And yet——"

"What?" demanded Renwick.

In reply the other took the sheet of paper from his desk and, examining it for a moment, handed it to his friend, saying slowly:

"It is a strange coincidence, but I was studying this when you came in. What do you make of it?"

Renwick took the paper and, perceiving that it was a translation of Latin prose—Cicero, probably, he imagined—written in a smooth yet unformed hand, he began to read the free and ingenuously worded rendering, when suddenly his eye was arrested. Interpolated between two sentences of the interesting and artless interpretation lay the words, written in the doric, and in a cramped and almost distorted hand: "Stick in, Nessie! What's worth doing is worth doing well. Ye maun win the Latta or I'll know the reason why"; then, the easy flow of the translation continued undisturbed. Renwick looked up at the other in astonishment.

"Sent along by her form master this morning," explained Gibson, "from Nessie Brodie's exercise book."

"Was this done at home or in school?" enquired the doctor sharply.

"In school! She must have written these words, unconsciously, of course, but none the less written them with her own hand. What does it mean?—some reversion to these famous Scottish ancestors we used to hear so much about from the old man. Or is it dual personality? —you know more about that sort of thing than I do."

"Dual personality be hanged!" retorted Renwick in some consternation. "This is a pure lapse of mind, a manifestation of nervous overstrain, induced, I'm positive from the nature of these words, by some strong force that has been driven into her. Don't you see, man. She became fatigued in the middle of this exercise, her attention wavered and instantly that something beneath the surface of her mind leaped up—tormenting her—forcing her on, so that, indeed, before she resumed coherently, she had unconsciously written this passage." He shook his head. "It reveals only too clearly, I'm afraid, what she fears!"

"We don't work her too hard here," expostulated Gibson; "she's spared in many ways!"

"I know! I know," replied Renwick. "The mischief is being done outside. It's that madman of a father she has got. What are we to do about it? You say you've spoken to him and I'm like a red rag to a bull where he's concerned. It's difficult," then, as he laid the paper again on Gibson's desk he added: "This really alarms me. It's a symptom that I've seen before to presage a thundering bad breakdown. I don't like it a bit."

"You surprise me," said the head master after a pause, during which he regarded his friend shrewdly. "Are you sure you're not taking an extreme view from—from prejudice perhaps?" then, as the other silently shook his head, he continued tentatively: "Would you like to see the child?—only for a moment of course—otherwise we'll alarm her."

The doctor considered for a moment, then replied, decisively:

"Indeed I would! I would like to see for myself. It's good of you to suggest it."

"I'll fetch her along, then," said Gibson, getting to his feet and adding, as he went to the door, "I know you'll not scare her! I want nothing of this slip in her exercise mentioned on any account."

Renwick agreed silently with a motion of his head, and when the other had gone out of the room remained motionless, his brow slightly bent, his eye clouded and fixed upon the writing across the square of paper, as though the strange, incoherent, intruding words had shaped themselves before his gaze into a vision which startled and distressed him. He was aroused by the return of the head master, now accompanied by Nessie, whom Renwick had never seen before, and now, as he observed her thin, drooping body, her mild placating eye, her white, fragile neck, the irresolution of her mouth and chin, he was not surprised that she desired to lean clingingly on Mary, nor that Mary on her part should desire to protect her.

"This is one of our prize pupils," said Gibson diplomatically, turning towards Renwick as he resumed his chair. "We show her off to all the visitors. She has the best memory in the upper school. Is that not so, Nessie?" he added, touching her lightly with his gaze.

Nessie flushed proudly, filled in her small spirit by a profound gratification and a deep awe, amongst which mingled, also, some confusion as to the obscure purpose which had compelled her suddenly before the combined majesty of Dr. Renwick and the Rector. She was, however, silent, and remained with lowered eyes, her thin legs shaking a little in her long well-worn boots and coarse woollen stockings—not from fear, but from the mere agitation of their imposing presence—knowing that the question had been rhetorical. Not for her to speak unless directly addressed!

"You're fond of your work?" enquired Renwick, kindly.

"Yes, sir," replied Nessie timidly, raising her eyes to his like a young and startled doe.

"Does it never tire you?" he continued mildly, afraid to shape his question in a more definite form.

She looked at the Rector for permission to speak, and reassured by his look, replied:

"No, sir! not much! I get a headache, sometimes." She announced this fact diffidently as though it might be a presumption on her part to have a headache, but she continued with more assurance: "My father took me to Dr. Lawrie about six months ago and he said it was nothing." She even added, naïvely: "He said I had a good head on me."

Renwick was silent, conscious of Gibson's slightly satiric eye upon him, yet although he felt the weak, evasive answers of this timid child to be as unreliable as the opinion of his pompous colleague, just quoted, his impression of Nessie's strained and over-driven nerves was further strengthened by her bearing.

"I hear you're going up for the Latta," he at length remarked. "Would you not like to wait another year?"

"Oh! no, sir! I couldn't do that," she replied quickly. "I must take it this year. My father has said——" a shadow fell and deepened upon her brow; she added more reticently, "He would like me to win it—and it's a great thing for a girl to win the Latta. It's never been done, but I think I can do it!" She again blushed slightly, not at this sudden exhibition of her own small self-complacency, but at her hardihood in making such a long speech before them.

"Don't work too hard, then," replied Renwick finally, turning towards Gibson to indicate that he had concluded his observations.

"That's right then, Nessie," said the head master, dismissing her with a cheerful glance. "Run away back to your form now! And remember what Dr. Renwick here has said. The willing horse never needs the spur. Don't overdo the homework."

"Thank you, sir," replied Nessie humbly, as she slipped out of the room, wondering vaguely in her mind what it had all been about, feeling, despite her uncertainty, that it had been a mark of honour for her to be singled out for attention like this, and—remembering warmly the encouraging look in his omnipotent eye—that she must stand high in the Rector's favour. It would, she considered, as she re-entered her classroom with a conscious air, give that impertinent and inquisitive young Grierson something to think about when he knew she had been hobnobbing with the Rector himself.

"I hope I didn't keep her too long," said Renwick, looking at his friend. "It was enough for me to see her."

"You were the epitome of discretion," replied Gibson lightly; "the governors will not throw me out for allowing my discipline to be tampered with." He paused, then added in the same tone: "She gave you a shrewd one about Lawrie."

"Pshaw!" replied Renwick. "To put it bluntly, 'It doesn't do to cry stinking fish,' but as one old friend to another I don't give a snap of the fingers for Lawrie's opinion. He's a pompous ass! That child is not right by a long way."

"Tuts! Renwick," remarked Gibson soothingly, "don't get a bee in your bonnet. I could see nothing wrong with the girl to-day. She's at a bad age and she's got a beastly old sot of a father, but she'll do, she'll do. You're exaggerating. You were always the incorrigible champion of the oppressed, even if it were an ailing, white mouse."

"That's what she is," replied Renwick stubbornly. "A little white mouse, and it might go hard with her if she's not watched. I don't like that cowed look in her eye."

"I was more struck by the neglected look of her," replied Gibson. "She's getting to be conspicuous in the school by it. Did you mark the poorness of her dress?—there's been a difference there in the last year or so, I can assure you. Brodie can't have a penny now but his wages, and most of that he spends on liquor. Strictly between ourselves too, I hear it rumoured that he's behind with the interest on his mortgaged house—that amazing chateau of nonsense of his. What's going to happen there, I don't know, but the man is rushing towards his ruin."

"Poor Nessie," sighed Renwick; but in his mind it was Mary that he visioned amidst the poverty and degradation of her home. It was impossible to judge from Gibson's expression if some vague glimmering of understanding, regarding his friend's motive in the matter, had dawned upon him; and indeed it might, for in the past he had heard him speak feelingly of the strange case of Mary Brodie; but now he patted him upon the shoulder, and remarked encouragingly:

"Cheer up, you miserable sawbones! It's not going to kill anybody. I'll see to that. I'll keep my eye on Nessie."

"Well," said Renwick at length, "it'll do no good to sit glooming here." He looked at his watch and arose from his chair. "I'm keeping you back and I've got my own work to attend to. It's almost four."

"Rich old ladies queueing up for you, you sly dog!" said Gibson quizzically. "What they see in that ugly face of yours I can't imagine!"

Renwick laughed as he replied:

"It's not beauty they want, or I'd refer them to you." He held out his hand. "You're a good sort, Gibson! I'll miss you more than anyone when I leave here."

"I wonder!" said the other as he pressed his friend's hand affectionately.

Renwick left the room quickly, but as he went down the shallow, stone steps, worn through the years by an endless succession of careless footsteps, and passed between the two grey Russian guns, setting his course along the road for his home, his pace insensibly diminished and his thoughts again grew heavy. "Poor Nessie!" He now saw the shrinking figure before him, enveloped by the soft, protecting arms of her sister who, shielding the child's drooping form by her own soft body, looked at him with brave, enduring eyes. As he passed along the street the vision grew in intensity, oppressing him, rendering somehow unattractive the stimulating prospect which had lately filled his mind, dulling the glamour of his new work in Edinburgh, blotting out the freshness of Castle Gardens and the romantic fortress piled against the sky, blunting the ever keen savour of the wind as he felt it sweep to him from off the Calton Hill. It was with a sombre face that he entered his own house and set himself to work.

THE mild April day had advanced for one hour beyond its noontide and, filled by the fresh odours and soft, stirring sounds of the budding spring, lay upon the town of Levenford like a benison. But to Brodie, as at his dinner hour he walked along the road towards his home, there was no blessing in the sweet burgeoning around him. Filled with bitterness, he did not feel the caress of the gentle air or recognise in each new shoot the running sap within the trees; the yellow clumps of nodding daffodils, the white, elusive snowdrops, the glowing, mingled globes of crocuses, which ornamented the front gardens of the road, were by him unseen; the faint cawing of rooks as they circled around their new-built nest amongst the tall trees at the bend of the road was to him a jangle on his irritated ears. Indeed, as he reached these trees and the sound came to him more loudly he sent a venomous glance at the birds, muttering: "Damn their noise—they ring the lugs off a man. I could take a gun to them," when suddenly, as if in answer to his threat, a low-flying crow swept over him and with a derisive "caw-caw" dropped its excrement upon his shoulder. His brow gathered like thunder as he considered that the very birds had turned against him and defiled him; for a moment he looked as though he could have felled each tree, torn apart the nests, and destroyed every bird in the rookery; but with a wry twist of his lips he cleansed his coat with his handkerchief and, his mood set more bitterly, continued upon his homeward way.

The better conditions of his living since the return of Mary had made little difference in his appearance, for although she sponged and pressed his clothing, washed and starched his linen, and brushed his boots to a fine polish, he had now abandoned himself utterly at nights to the bottle with the result that his face had grown more veined, more sallow and sunken, and his neater dress hung upon his gaunt frame with the incongruity of a new suit upon a scarecrow. He looked, although he knew it not, a broken man, and since he had lost Nancy his disintegration had progressed at a more rapid pace. At first he had told himself fiercely that there were other fish in the sea as good as, and indeed, better than she, that he would quickly fill her place in his affections by another and a finer woman; but gradually, and with a cutting injury to his pride, he had been made to see that he was now too old and unattractive to compel the attention of women and, the lordly days of his overflowing purse being ended, that he had become too poor to buy their favour. He realised, too, after a short and resentful period of self-delusion, that it was his Nancy that he desired, that none other could replace her; she had wrapped herself around his flesh so seductively that in her absence he craved for her only, and knew that no one else would do. He drank to forget her, but could not. The whisky soaked his brain, deadened his vivid appreciation of his loss, but still, and even when he was drunk, tormenting pictures floated before his numbed mind, haunting him with visions of Nancy and Matt as they would be together in their new life. As he saw them, they were always together, and, although he cursed himself for the thought, happy, forgetful of him and of his past bearing on their lives; Nancy's laugh, and it was the laugh of an Aphrodite, echoed in his ears, evoked, not by his but by Matt's caresses, and as, with an agonising lucidity, he saw his son supplanting him in her affections his eyes would close, his look become helpless and livid.

At present, however, he was engrossed by another matter, not, let it be said, the offence of the crow, which had merely thrown another coal upon the fire of his resentment, but a greater and more personal affront; and his air was less apathetic than was usual in the public street, his manner more intent as he moved with an unusual rapidity towards his house.

He had a grievance to air and, as Nessie was the only person whom he now addressed with any freedom, and as the affair in some manner concerned her, it was she whom he now hastened to see. As he opened the front door and entered his home, his morose reticence was for the moment abandoned and he immediately called out:

"Nessie! Nessie!" He was in the kitchen before she could reply, and sternly regarded the startled eye that looked back at him from her half-turned head as she sat at table, a spoonful of her broth arrested in mid air, her whole attitude indicative of sudden apprehension. "Has that young whelp o' Grierson's said anything to you about the Latta?" he shot at her fiercely. She let the spoonful of soup splash back into her plate, as, thinking that mercifully his question was not so bad as she had expected, she shook her head nervously, and replied:

"No, father. At least nothing much."

"Think," he cried. "Think hard. What does nothing much mean?"

"Well, father," she quavered, "he's always saying something or another that's not nice about—about us. He sometimes sneers about me and the Latta."

"Did he ever tell you that you shouldna go in for it?" he demanded. "Answer me!"

"Oh! he would like me not to try for it, father," she replied, compressing her small lips. "I know that as well as anything. I suppose he thinks it would give him some small chance of it—not that he's got any."

His discoloured teeth came together, and he displayed them as his lips parted in a grin of wrath.

"So that's it!" he exclaimed. "I was sure o't. Ay, I was right!" He seated himself at table and, ignoring the steaming bowl which Mary silently placed before him, thrust his face close to Nessie's. "Say that again," he muttered.

410

"What, father?"

"About that pup o' Grierson's."

"That's he got no chance of the Latta?" she queried timidly; then seeing that she was pleasing him, she harmonised her mood to his and sniffed indignantly: "No! I should think not. He hasn't a ghost of a chance. Even if I didn't go in for it, there's others have as good a chance as he has. But he'll never git it while I'm about."

"You're the stumblin' block to him."

"Yes, indeed, father!"

"That's fine! That's fine!" he muttered, looking at her with dilated eyes. "God! it does me good to hear that." He paused. "Do ye know what happened to me as I was coming home to-day, like any other respectable townsman?" His nostrils quivered at the memory and his voice rose as he cried: "Yes, comin' home quietly and decently, when that blasted swine came up to me—Provost Grierson—our braw new provost—God! what they made a thing like him provost for beats me, he must have sneaked himself into the position—it's—it's a disgrace to the town. I suppose because he's the provost now he thinks he can do anything, for he had the damned insolence to accost me in the open daylight and tell me not to put you in for the Latta." He looked at her as though he expected her to swell visibly with indignation, and, feeling that some response was expected of her she replied, feebly:

"It was just jealousy, father, that was all!"

"Did I not tax him with that?" he cried. "I should think I did. I told him you had always beaten his measly pup and that you would do it again—and again—and again." He repeated the words in an exultant shout. "The damned cheek of the man to try and cadge the thing for his own son by askin' me to keep you back for another year. And when I flung that in his face he had the impudence to turn round and mealy-mouth me with talk of the dignity of his position, and about him bein' the spokesman of the Borough, saying that he had been told ye werena fit to go up—that you were not strong enough—that he was speakin' in your interests and not in his. But I had him." He clenched his fist in something of his old manner, as he exclaimed: "I had him on all points. I threw Lawrie's own words at his sleekit head. I had the whip hand o' him at every turn!" He laughed exultantly, but after a moment his face darkened and he muttered: "By God! I'll make him pay for it —ay, and for the other things he said to me as well. Why I didna level him to the street I canna think! But never mind—you and me will make him pay for't in other ways. Will we not, Nessie?" He gazed at her wheedlingly. "You'll knock that brat o' his into a cocked hat—will ye not, Nessie? and then we'll look at the grand, chawed look on his face. You'll do it—won't ye, woman?"

"Yes, father," she replied obediently, "I'll do it for ye."

"That's fine. That's real fine," he murmured rubbing his veined hands together in suppressed elation. Then suddenly, at some secret thought his expression grew black, and again thrusting his face into hers he exclaimed: "You better do it. By God! you better beat him. If you don't I'll—I'll grip that thin neck o' yours and fair strangle ye. You've got to win that Latta or it'll be the waur o' ye."

"I'll do it father! I'll do it!" she whimpered.

"Yes, you'll do it, or I'll know why," he cried wildly. "I tell you there's a conspiracy in this town against me. Every man's hand is turned against me. They hate me for what I am. They're jealous. They know that I'm away and above them—that if I had my rights I would wipe my dirty boots on the smug faces o' the lot of them. But never mind," he nodded his head to himself in a wild burst of unreason, "I'll show them yet. I'll put the fear o' me into them! The Latta will be the start o' it. That'll put a spoke in the Lord High Provost's wheel —then we'll begin in real earnest."

At this point Mary, who had been standing in the background, observing her father's paroxysm and his manner towards Nessie with an expression of acute anxiety, came forward and said coaxingly:

"Will you not take your broth before it gets cold, father? I took such pains with it. Let Nessie get hers too—she must eat up if she's going to study as hard as she does."

His exaltation was suddenly arrested at her words. His expression changed, as though something withdrew from it, retired quickly from open view into the hidden recesses of his mind, and he exclaimed angrily:

"What do you want to interfere for? Can you not leave us alone? When we want your advice we'll ask for it." He picked up his spoon and sullenly began his soup; then, after a while, as though he had been brooding on her effrontery in speaking, he exclaimed: "Keep your remarks about Nessie to yourself. I'll manage her my own way."

The meal proceeded for some time in silence, but, when they were partaking of the next simple course Brodie again turned to his younger daughter, and staring at her sideways began, in the ingratiating tone which he invariably adopted for this rote of questions and which, from constant repetition and the manner of his address, now excited her almost to the point of hysteria.

"And how did you get on to-day, Nessie?"

"Quite well, father!"

"Did anybody praise my own lass to-day? Come on now; somebody said something about you. It was your French to-day, was it not?"

She answered him mechanically, at random, anyhow—only to be rid of the nerve-racking necessity of formulating new and gratifying replies to his fatuous, yet pressing queries, of appeasing his insatiable demand for tangible evidence of her prowess, of the attention which his daughter was attracting at school. At length, when he had satisfied himself, although she on her part hardly knew what she had said, he lay back in his chair and, regarding her with a bland, proprietary eye, remarked:

"Good enough! Good enough for the Brodies! That was high praise for them to give us. You're doin' not so badly, woman! But ye maun do better. Better and better. Ye've got to make as sure o' that Latta as if it was lying on that plate in front o' ye. Guidsakes! just think on it. Thirty guineas every year for three years—that makes ninety guineas—or near enough to a hundred, golden sovereigns. There's a hundred, golden sovereigns lying there on that plate o' yours waiting to be picked up. Ye havena got to scramble for them, or stoop for them, you've just got to gather them up! God! if ye don't put these wee hands o' yours out to lift them I'll twist the heid off ye!" He looked at the empty plate before her, seeing it piled high with sovereigns, gleaming with the rich lustre of heaped gold, filled with a sum which in his reduced circumstances, seemed to him enormous. "It's a rich, rich prize," he murmured, "and it's yours! I could see it makes the greedy eyes o' that snipe Grierson drop out o' their sockets to think on it comin' into this house. I'll learn him to affront me in the main street of the town!" He was moved by a short, silent laugh that was like a sneer, then, looking again at Nessie, he lifted his eyebrows and, with a resumption of his absurdly arch manner, said in a tone of high confidence: "I'll be home early to-night, Nessie! We'll make a bend the minute we've finished our tea. Not a minute will we waste! We'll be on with our lessons before we've swallowed the last bite." He looked at her slyly, as he remarked: "You can be at it in the parlour, and I'll bide in here to see that not a soul disturbs ye. Quiet! Quiet! That's what ye want, and I'll see that ye have it. Ye'll have the quiet o' the grave!" He seemed pleased with the force of this comparison and repeated the last words impressively and sonorously. Then in a harder tone he added: "Ye maun stick to it! Stick in hard. Put your back into it. What ye do, do well. Remember you're a Brodie and set your teeth to win through with it." His task of exhortation for the moment completed, filled too, by a consciousness of worthy effort accomplished, he removed his eye from Nessie and allowed it to rest oppressively upon the face of his other daughter, daring her to interfere.

"What are you glowerin' at?" he demanded, after a moment. "Have I not told ye to keep out of the way when me and Nessie are speakin' together? When we want you we'll ask for you. I told you when ye entered this house again that you were to keep your paws off her, so see that you do it. I'm not wantin' her spoiled like her namby-pamby mother spoiled the rest o' ye."

She was about to leave the room, knowing this to be the most effectual manner of curtailing his resentment against her, when suddenly the

front door bell rang loudly, and she paused at the unexpectedness ɔ
the occurrence. Such traffic as came to the house, chiefly from the tradesmen of the Borough, was to the back door, and for the front bell to
ring thus was a rare event, so unusual now that Brodie looked sharply
up, and exclaimed to her, after a moment:

"See what it is!"

She went to the door and opened it, revealing to her own gaze a
messenger, who stood upon the steps of the porch bearing in his hand
a medium-sized parcel, and who now touched his cap, saying interrogatively:

"Miss Mary Brodie?"

She nodded, her eyes fixed in some dismay upon the package which
he was now apparently delivering into her hands and which, from the
smooth brown paper and neat pink cord which enclosed it, she knew
to be no ordinary parcel, no clumsily wrapped groceries from a local
store, neither provisions nor anything which she had herself ordered,
but a paragon of a parcel that she associated immediately in her mind
with others bearing the same exclusive air, which had, at intervals,
descended mysteriously upon her during the last month. But these other
packages had invariably come in the middle of the forenoon, at a fixed
hour when she was always alone in the house and now, with a sudden
anxiety besetting her, she demanded of the messenger the strange
question:

"Are you not late?"

He moved his feet uncomfortably, confirming the suspicion in her
mind as he defended himself.

"I've had a lot of deliveries," he said. "This came from Glasgow. I
had to wait on it." He was glad apparently to see her accept the package
without rebuking him, and clattered off without further speech, leaving
her supporting the light weight of the neatly corded box as though it
pressed her down into an acute discomfiture. These consignments of
delicacies which had regularly arrived for her—enigmatically, yet so
safely and opportunely—and which she had lavished upon Nessie with
an unquestioning delight—was this another? With a beating heart she
slowly closed the door and, her brain moving actively, she slipped into
the parlour, secreted the parcel under the sofa, and again re-entered
the kitchen, hoping uneasily that her father would make no enquiry
into the nature of the visitor. But she saw at once that this faint chance
was impossible, that he was impatiently awaiting her return, even
now lying back in his chair and fixing her with a large and curious
eye.

"Who was that at the door?" Then at her silence he demanded
"Come along! What are ye standing so glaikit for? Who was it?"

"It was only a message boy, father," she replied quietly, essaying to
render her voice composed.

"A message boy!" he repeated incredulously. "Coming to the front door of the house! Gad! what have we got to put up with next." Then, his anger rising at a sudden thought, he exclaimed: "I'm not going to sit down under that sort of insult. Who sent him? Tell me and I'll go in about it myself. Who was he from?"

"I don't know!" she faltered.

"Ye don't know!"

"No!" she answered and still using every effort to conciliate him, hastily added, "Never mind, father—it'll not occur again. Don't upset yourself."

He looked at her for a moment with a lowering eye, noting her suppressed air of embarrassment, faint, yet clearly to be perceived against the pervading candour of her expression.

"Show me the messages he brought," he ground out at her at length. "I didna see you bring them in!"

"They're in the parlour," she replied in a low tone, making as though to move into the scullery. "It's only a parcel—nothing you would want to see."

"Get me what he brought," he insisted. "Look sharp about it too. I've a notion to look at this strange, disappearing parcel."

"Oh! father!" she cried, "can you not believe me?"

"Get it!" he roared, "or I'll know that you're a liar as well as the other thing."

She saw that she must obey and, with a halting step, went out of the room and returned with the package in her hands.

He glared at it, surprised to find that there had, indeed, been a parcel but more astonished now at its unwonted appearance.

"Pink ribbon," he muttered. "Gad, that's rich!" Then changing his voice abruptly, he sneered: "Would ye have me believe they send out our oatmeal with these falderals on it. Open that box at once. I'll see with my own eyes what's inside."

She knew that it was useless to protest further, and, with the fatal calmness of inevitable discovery, she took a knife from the table, cut the string and, after a few seconds, drew from their enwrapping packing of wool a large and luscious bunch of black grapes. He stared at them incredulously as they hung suspended from her hand before his startled eyes. It was an exquisite cluster, hanging in the dull room like an exotic blossom, each fruit large, firm, and perfect, and powdered with a bluish bloom as delicate and seductive as the haze upon a distant landfall. They dangled temptingly upon their thick, smooth stalk, fragrant with a rich sun-drenched odour, filled to bursting with their soft, juicy flesh, ready to melt upon the tongue in a subtle mingling of sweet, succulent flavours. Black grapes at this time! An unheard of, expensive, out of season luxury!

"Where did these come from?" he cried in a loud hectoring voice.

"Who sent these?"

"I don't know, father," she answered truthfully, for, indeed, no note had ever accompanied these mysterious delicacies and she had only guessed vaguely, yet happily, that the sender had been Renwick.

"You do know, you slut," he roared at her; "or why should you hide them." As he looked at her in an angry, baffled fashion, the memory rose before him of the deputation of godly self-righteous women from the church who had called upon his wife during her illness to leave her fruit and jellies, and he cried: "Is it some o' these blasted, snivelling women from the kirk that have sent them? Are we getting charity from the town? Is that what we're come to? I suppose they're sorry for you with such a poor mouth as you're aye puttin' on. Good God! they'll be sending us tracts and soup next." He seized the bunch of grapes roughly from her hand, contemplating them contemptuously, but, as he did so, he realised something of the cost of the exquisite fruit before him, knew suddenly that no collection of church workers, however godly, could have sent them. A slow sneer spread over his face as he exclaimed: "No! I think I see what's at the back o' it. We don't know who sent them. It's what they call an anonymous donor. God Almighty! are ye come back to that again, you trollop—back to your presents from your fancy men! Faugh! you sicken me." He looked at her with a snarl on his face, but she returned his gaze with a calm and steady eye, and it was poor Nessie, fortunately unobserved, who manifested some signs of confusion and distress.

"You're not going to eat them, though," he cried roughly. "No! not a single one. Ye may look at them as greedily as ye like, but you'll not lip them. This is what's going to happen." And, as he uttered the words, he dashed the grapes upon the floor with a pulping sound and in a fury stamped his heavy boots upon them, squelching the rich juice in all directions, crushing them into a dark mass that stained the grey linoleum like blood. "There!" he shouted, "that's the bitter winepress that I'm treading. This is my bitter path—but tread it I will. I only wish the swine that sent them was underneath my feet. I would serve him in like fashion whoever he may be. There—that'll be something for ye to clean up—something to keep your mind off the men—you jade. A bit of scrubbin' will take the itch out of ye," and as he spoke he scattered the residue upon the floor with short kicks into every corner of the room. Seizing her by the shoulders he shoved his face into hers and sneered coarsely: "I understand what you're up to, my bonnie tottie, but don't go too far—ye know what happened to ye the last time." As he concluded he flung her from him, sending her reeling against the wall, from where, with a blush of humiliation upon her face, she still looked at him in silence.

After a moment he turned to Nessie and, in a completely opposite voice, soft, fond, wheedling, rendered deliberately contrasting to his tone to Mary in order to wound her the more, remarked:

"Come on, hinny—pay no attention to what you've seen—or to her, either. Ye don't even need to speak to her in future if you don't want to. This sort of thing does not concern you, and besides it's time you and me had our dauner down the road together—we'll have you late for the school if we don't hurry up, and that would never do." He took Nessie's hand and with a great demonstration of affection, led her timid form from the room, but not before she had flashed one frightened, guilty glance at Mary as she turned to go out into the hall.

When the front door closed behind them Mary sighed. She pulled herself up from where Brodie had thrown her against the wall, and although she gazed sorrowfully at the dirty, scattered remnants of the fruit which Nessie would now never eat, she felt with some relief, despite her own humiliation, that her sister had not been prejudiced by the recent, unfortunate incident. The words which her father had hurled at her shamed her almost beyond endurance, whilst the injustice of his attitude made her bury her teeth into her lip to keep back the hot rush of indignant tears. Although she had no evidence but that of her own intuition, she knew that Dr. Renwick in his kindness had sent her these grapes and indeed the other gifts, and now all the fine feelings of gratitude that she had entertained towards him, all her sacrifice for Nessie's sake, had been degraded, thrust down into the mud by her father's gross interpretation of them. She had been made to feel again her position in the eyes of the world, reminded miserably of the smirch that lay upon her name which would cling to her in this town as long as her life endured.

With a faint shiver she bestirred herself and began to clear the table of its dishes, and when she had carried them into the scullery, she set herself slowly to wash and dry them. As she worked she directed her mind deliberately from her own position, considering with some return of comfort that Nessie seemed to be improving slightly in health, that although her long and forced periods of study continued, she was eating better, that her thin cheeks showed some signs of filling out. Nothing was too much for her to endure if she could protect her sister— make her well and strong. It was a supreme satisfaction to have been able to procure some better clothing for Nessie from her savings—the small stock of money that she had brought home to Levenford—and she cheered herself with the thought of the improved appearance of the child from the neglected state in which she had found her upon her return.

When she had dried and put away the last dish she took a bucket of warm water and a cloth into the kitchen, went down upon her knees, and began to wash the floor. While she was thus engaged she was suddenly confronted by a whimsical vision of Renwick's face could he have observed her in her present occupation and perceived thus the grotesque result of his generosity. She did not, however, smile at her thought, but sighed again, considering that she would be obliged to ask him to discontinue these good-hearted offerings towards Nessie and herself. She had seen him on two occasions since her first visit to his house, and on each she had felt more forcibly how compassionate he had been to interest himself so deeply on Nessie's behalf; but somehow, she had begun to shrink from meeting him, to dread the onset of that strange feeling which swept over her whenever she felt his dark, sympathetic eyes upon hers. The remembrance of her father's recent words now came to her suddenly, and even in her solitude within the room she winced, wondering unhappily what indeed was the nature of her regard for this man who had shown her nothing but kindness and friendship. It was a happy circumstance perhaps that he was soon to leave the town, that the uncertain and troubled state of her mind would soon be ended.

Strange, then, that as she considered this happy circumstance her face should cloud so sadly, that as she finished her washing of the floor, and sat down to busy herself on some mending for Nessie, her thoughts should refuse to leave him. He had told her to make her life a gallery of pictures, but her gallery contained now but one picture, and that was the portrait of his face. The kitchen, once so dirty and untidy, now lay about her clean and spotless; the rest of the house was equally immaculate; her main work was finished for the day; and yet, when she should have taken up a book or engaged herself in some diversion, as he had directed, she could only sit and think of him. It was incredible!

True, her opportunities for relaxation were not unlimited for, although her return had caused no apparent ripple upon the surface of the life of the town, she shunned the public gaze, and lately had formed the habit of going out only when the dusk had fallen. Only once had she departed from this custom, when she had made a pilgrimage to Darroch to see the grave that enclosed Denis and her child. The same train had borne her, the same streets echoed to her sad, returning footsteps, but another name now stretched upon the signboard of the Lomond Vaults, and the doctor whom she had consulted on that last, unhappy visit had answered the call of his destiny and vanished, likewise, into some unknown obscurity. No bitter passion of grief had moved her as she stood by the grave that lay on the slope of Darroch Hill, but only a tender melancholy, directed chiefly towards the form of her infant child that lay so near her kneeling body, and was yet so inseparably divided from it. How strange, she had thought, that the throbbing body of the child that had lived so vigorously within her womb, should now lie buried in earth, detached from her for ever. Strange, too, that she, the mother, had never seen, and now could never see, that child. She had been still unconscious in the Cottage Hospital when, from exposure and its too early advent, it had died without her knowing—without her seeing it.

A sense of the injustice of the infant's death had oppressed her as she rose to her feet and made her way out of the graveyard, feeling that she deserved her punishment, and accepting it, but thinking that her child had surely merited some short happiness of life. As she got into the train at the station upon her homeward journey she had felt that this visit was final—she was never return to that grave—and as the train steamed out of the station she had, through the cloud of her depression, faintly visioned upon the platform an illusive figure—the figure of Denis—waving her a brave, encouraging, and a last good-bye.

Now, as she sat at her sewing with a downward, pensive gaze, it was not the memory of this good-bye which filled her mind but the anticipation of another, a less visionary parting, and in the privacy of her own intimate thoughts she admitted to herself at last, abandoning her attempts at self-delusion, that it was hard for her to contemplate the departure of Dr. Renwick from the town. She knew well the gulf that separated them, bridged only by his charity, but, conscious that her desire did not extend even to the presumption of friendship but merely to a longing for his presence near her, she felt it permissible for her to mourn his going. Levenford would be empty for her, then!

She could sew no longer; her eyes refused to see the stitches, the needle to enter the cotton of the garment; she was weeping at the thought of her loss, prompted, alas, by that emotion which presumed not even to friendship. In her agitation she arose, despising herself, wringing her hands at her own miserable weakness, and, as though she felt the need of a freer air than that within the room, made her way blindly out into the back garden where she paced up and down, striving to calm herself. As she walked, filled at last by a returning tranquillity, she suddenly observed that upon the lilac tree, which in her memory had never flowered, there now grew one large and perfect budding blossom. With a quickening interest she advanced and, gently pulling down the bough which bore it, took the green spray within her fingers, touched and caressed it, and perceived to her surprise, from the faint colour that tinged the tips of the unopened buds, that it was white lilac. Delicious white lilac! She had never known that it was a white lilac bush, but now, like some propitious omen for the future, this melancholy tree had burgeoned, and soon would wave a white and scented spray to cheer her during the coming spring. Nessie would love it, she thought, as, gently releasing the branch, she turned and in a happier spirit made her way back to the house.

The afternoon wore on, dusk fell, tea-time came and passed, Nessie was again inevitably established in the parlour with her books, Brodie seated in the kitchen with his bottle and, the dishes once more washed and her house in order, she decided that she would fulfil her purpose to visit Dr. Renwick and explain, with all the delicacy she possessed, her difficulty in accepting these gifts which he had sent for Nessie. It was permissible for her to go out; her movements, indeed, were not restrained in the evening so long as she did not visibly interfere with the progress of the studies within the parlour, and assuming her hat and coat, she slipped out of the back door—by which inferior avenue her father had now ordained that she should always enter and leave the house.

The night was fresh, the air soothing to her cheek, the unseen flowers more fragrant from the dew, and, hidden by the darkness, she moved down the road at a free and rapid pace. Although she did not immediately question the causes of this lightness of her mood, the throb of the coming springtime was stirring her, moving her as she had been moved by the budding lilac tree, and the nature of her present journey was filling her unconsciously with happiness. But, as she drew near to Wellhall Road she seemed to apprehend dimly the reason of her present cheerfulness, and gradually her steps slowed, and she became confronted by a sudden thought. What right had she to inflict herself upon a busy man who had patients waiting at his house? who was doubtless tired from a hard day's work; further, if it were indeed he who had sent the grapes, what impertinence on her part to refuse them! She was stabbed by the thought that her mission was a ruse, a subterfuge invented by her evasive mind to enable her to see him and, while her father's abusive words again rose before her like a judgment, she began to feel how unnecessary it was, now that Nessie appeared to be improving, for her to visit Dr. Renwick as she proposed. By some strange association of season, or was it of her sensations, her mind flew back to another springtime, and she realised that when she had known Denis in the past he had followed her, pursued her ardently; but now, and she blushed painfully in the darkness, it was she who actually wished to thrust her unworthy presence upon a man who had no desire to see her.

By this time she had reached his house and, on the opposite side of the road, she stopped, rather dejectedly, and surveyed it, considering in her mind the tasteful decorations, the exquisite picture which had compelled her rapt attention. No! she would not go in, but merely watch the house for a moment under cover of the darkness and fill it with his presence, just as in the future she would come to this same spot, and vision him again in that rich room when he had left the town for good.

As she stood there she heard the quick crisp chatter of a horse's trot, saw two high yellow lights gleam in the obscurity and, before she could move away, the doctor's gig came whirling to his house. Drawing back into the shadow of the wall she observed the pleasant bustle at the door, heard the pawing of the horse, the jingle of its harness, then Renwick's firm voice, which shook her by its nearness, saying to his man:

"I shan't be out again to-night, Dick; at least I hope not! Good night to you!

"Good night to you, sir. Hope you won't be disturbed," she heard the groom reply, and clambering back into his seat he drove off to the adjoining stable. With eyes that strained through the blackness she followed Renwick's dim figure to the porch, then, as the door was suddenly flung open and he was silhouetted against the brilliant light within, she saw him vividly. For a moment he turned and surveyed the darkness, looking directly towards her. Although she knew herself to be invisible to him, she trembled as though he had discovered her and would retrace his steps and demand to know the reason of her prying presence at this hour. But he did not return. After a last look at the night he went into his house, closing the door behind him, leaving the darkness unrelieved.

For a moment she remained still, overcome by her thoughts, then she stirred and began to move back towards her home, drooping a little, stealing quietly through the streets, as though some pervading realisation weighed her with a sense of infamy. She knew that she, Mary Brodie, outcast, the despoiled virgin, the mother of a dead and nameless child, loved again, but was herself unloved.

VIII

SUNDAY afternoon still held for Brodie the indulgence of an afternoon repose, for although he rose late and did not dine until two, custom died hard with him, and the blank hours of three until five found him invariably in his shirt-sleeves and upon his back upon the sofa. It was not, however, the parlour sofa, but the couch within the kitchen upon which he rested; the other room was still hallowed to Nessie's studies, which were pursued on this day of rest with an intensity equal to that of week days, and he considered that it was a sacrifice on his part savouring of the heroic to have suggested, and carried into effect, this transference of his repose to a less dignified settee.

On this Sunday the hot July sun had made him feel drowsy and, having seen his younger daughter begin upon her work, exhorting her the more strongly in the face of the nearness of the great day of examination next week, he now laid himself down with the air of one who must not be disturbed and allowed the drone of a fly upon the window to lull him into sleep.

It was, as he had just impressed upon Nessie, the last lap of the race, and whilst he snored, in the happy consciousness of having done his part towards success by relinquishing the parlour, she addressed herself, with a slightly feverish mind, towards her final perusal of the third book of Euclid. Her face was flushed from the heat inside the parlour, and a buzzing of insects, like that which had sent Brodie so comfortably to sleep, annoyed her and distracted her mind from its intent purpose. She had never been quite sure of her geometry, and now, with the examination coming off in a few days' time, her deficiencies in this subject had intimidated her, and impelled her to rush once more through the entire third book. She knotted her brow and moved her lips as she again began to cram the eighth proposition into her brain but, despite her concentration, the words upon the page wavered, the diagrams became blurred, and the lines ran into strange fantastic shapes, not unlike the eccentric figures which had lately filled her troubled dreams and tormented her at nights in her sleep. The axis of the angle to the vertical was the co-efficient of—no, no, what was she talking about— that was perfect nonsense! She must stick into it better than that, or the Latta would slip out of this pocket of hers where it so safely reposed, and run away like a white mouse that would quickly nibble up all these golden sovereigns like so much cheese. How hot it was! And how her head ached! Her English was excellent, Latin perfect, French quite good, algebra splendid—yes, she was a clever girl, everybody said so, and indeed the examiners for the Bursary would realise it the moment they set eyes upon her. When she had made her way proudly and con- fidently to school on the day of an examination she had, in the conscious- ness of her eminence, always felt that people whispered to one another, saying: "That's Nessie Brodie! She's the cleverest scholar in the Acad- emy; she'll come out first in this test as sure as her name's Brodie." Perhaps the professors at the University would put their heads together and talk like that, at least they would do so after they had read her papers. They must do so!—or her father would want to know the reason of it; indeed, if they failed to recognise who she was and to give her the first place he would knock their heads together for them like so many coco-nuts. Coco-nuts! Matt had promised to bring her some when he had left for India and she had wanted a monkey and a parrot, too, but he had somehow forgotten about them, and now that he had gone off with that terrible woman he would never remember about a wee thing like Nessie Brodie. Had he married Nancy? She did not know; but Nancy was wicked, even if Matt had put a ring on her finger, and not like Mary, who was good and kind to her. Yet Mary was not married, although she had somehow had a baby which was dead and never mentioned by anyone. Mary never spoke of it, but had a sadness about her face as though there was something on her mind that she could never forget. Mary was always running after her, giving her soup and eggs and milk, cuddling her and telling her not to work so hard. Mary wanted her to win the Latta, but in a reasonable way, and simply to prevent her from being hurt by their father. Her dear sister would cry if she did not win it—and yet she need not cry. If she failed it would be a wonderful idea never to tell Mary, to let the years run on and never say a single word about it. What was she thinking of? There must be no failing! If she was not sitting high up in that first place—"at the top of the class"—as her father had always called it, she herself would have to take the consequences. "I'll wring that thin neck of yours if you let anybody beat ye—and after the way I've coached ye on for't" —that was what he was always dinning into her ears between his spells of petting and wheedling. He had big hands!

The axis of the angle to the vertical—really it was the height of absurdity that she should be doing this on such a hot day, and on the Sabbath day too, when she might have been at the Bible Class with the white frock and the pink sash that Mamma had made for her. But that was worn out or grown out of now; she was getting a big girl. Yet Mamma had always liked her to go to Sunday School with kid gloves and her face washed after dinner. "Lad and lass, kiss and cas', Nessie's in the Bible Class." She was not in it now though, but working hard, ever so hard at her lessons—"Yes, father, I'm stickin' in hard. What I'm doin', I'm doin' weel." Mamma had liked her to please father, but Mamma was dead. She had no mother and Mary had no baby! Mamma and Mary's baby were together sitting on a cloud, waving to her, and singing: "Nessie Brodie's going to win the Latta." She wanted to join in the chorus with all her might, but something tightened her throat and restrained her. Lately she had not been so sure of herself. No! it was a big thing for a girl, and a Brodie at that, to win the Latta. A big thing and a difficult thing! She had been sure of it at first, so much so that at one time the heap of golden guineas had lain piled upon her plate for everyone to see and admire. But now a dreadful, secret doubt was creeping into her mind as to whether she could do it. No one knew about it—that was a comfort—and no one would ever know. "Yes, father, I'm getting on splendid—couldn't be better. That Grierson hasn't got a chance. I'm the stumbling block. The Latta's mine already." He was pleased at that, rubbing his hands together and smiling at her approvingly—and it was fine for her to feel that she was pleasing him! She would hide everything so cleverly and carefully that he would never see that she was not sure of herself. She had her own ways of doing things, the clever girl that she was! She was inside her own mind, now, creeping about the passages of her brain, admiring, congratulating herself, seeing her very thoughts flow with a marvellous rippling fluency, watching them delightedly as they flashed past her like brilliant, rushing waves of scintillating light.

At last she started suddenly, her eyes lost their vacancy, her face its smooth, unruffled placidity and, as she rubbed her brows with her hand and looked at the clock, she murmured, confusedly: "Good sakes! what have I been thinking about? Have I been asleep or what? There's an hour gone and I can't mind a thing about it!" She shook her head with annoyance at her own weakness, at the loss of this precious hour, and was once more about to apply herself to the Book of Euclid when the door opened quietly and her sister came into the room.

"Here's a glass of milk for you, dear," whispered Mary, tiptoeing up to the table. "Father's asleep now, so I thought I might bring you this. It's cold as can be. I've had the jug in running water for an hour."

Nessie took the glass from her sister and began to sip it in an absent fashion.

"It's cool as cool," she replied, after a moment. "It's as good as ice-cream on a day like this. Did you ever feel it so close?"

Mary pressed her palm lightly against her sister's cheek.

"You're hot!" she murmured. "Will you not take a half an hour off and come out in the air with me?"

"And what would happen to me if he woke up and found I had gone out?" queried Nessie, with a sharp look. "You know you would get it worse than me, too! No! I'll stay where I am. This milk is cooling me fine. Besides, I've got all this book to get through before Friday."

"How is the headache now?" said Mary after a pause, during which she contemplated the other with some anxiety.

"Just the same! It doesn't feel like a headache now. It's more a numbness."

"Would you like me to put on some more cold water and vinegar cloths for you?"

"Never mind, Mary! I don't think they do much good. I'll be better after next Saturday when I've got the exam. over. That's the only thing that'll cure it."

"Is there nothing you can think of that you'd like?"

"No! There's nothing I fancy at all. It's real kind of you though, Mary. You've been wonderful to me, and you've had to put up with so much yourself. But I could never have done without you."

"I've done nothing," replied Mary sadly. "I would like to have done much more. I wish I could have stopped you from going up for the Bursary, but it was impossible! I didn't want you to take it."

"Don't say that!" cried Nessie quickly. "You know I must go up for it. I've thought of nothing else for the last six months, and if I had to draw back now it would fair break my heart. I must take it."

"Do you really want to go on with it?" asked Mary doubtfully.

"Just think how I've worked," replied Nessie with some emotion; "just think how I've been made to work. Am I going to let all that go for nothing? I should hope not. I'm so set on it myself now that I couldn't hold back if I was to try. I feel it now like something that's gripping me and drawing me on."

Mary gazed at the nervous eagerness in her sister's eyes, and, in an attempt to soothe the other, murmured consolingly:

"It'll not be long till it's over now, anyway, Nessie! Don't fret yourself too much about it. Let the work go easy for a day or two."

"How can you talk like that," exclaimed Nessie petulantly. "You know I've got all this ground to get over—and it's most important too. This third book is not right into my head yet. I must get it in. I've— I've got to drive it in like a nail so that it will stay in and never come out. I might get a question on this very thing that you're telling me to leave alone."

"Hush, Nessie, dear! Don't excite yourself," pleaded Mary.

"It's enough to make anybody excited," cried the other wildly. "Here am I working the brains out of myself and you would think that all I had to do was to walk up to that university and ask for the Latta and come home with it in my hand like a stick of toffee. It's not like that at all. I tell you."

"Wheesht, Nessie! Be calm, pettie," soothed Mary. "Don't upset yourself, I didn't mean anything like that."

"You did so!" returned Nessie agitatedly. "Everybody thinks the same thing. They think it's that easy for me because I'm so clever. They don't know the work and the toil that I've been forced to put in. It's been enough to drive me out of my mind."

"I know though, dear," replied Mary softly, stroking the other's brow. "I know all about it and how you've been kept at it! Don't worry yourself though. You're getting tired and anxious. You used to be ever so confident about it. Never mind if you don't win the miserable Bursary. What does it matter!"

Nessie, however, was so strung up that no attitude her sister could have adopted would have pleased her, and now she burst into tears.

"What does it matter," she sobbed hysterically. "That's a good one, that is, for me that's set my very heart on winning it. And to call the good hundred sovereigns that I'll get 'miserable' is enough to discourage anybody. Don't you know what father'll do to me if I don't win it. He'll kill me."

"He'll not do that, Nessie," replied Mary steadily. "I'm here now and I'll protect you from any fear of that. I'll be there when you get the result and if he tries to lay a finger on you it'll be the worse for him."

"What could you do?" cried Nessie. "You talk as if it was better for you to stand up to father than for me to win the Latta."

Mary did not reply to this ungracious speech but stood silent, soothing Nessie by gentle movements of her hands, until at last the other's sobs ceased and, drying her eyes, she remarked with a sudden composure:

"I don't know what we're goin' on about, running round in a circle like that. We've been talkin' nonsense. Of course I'll win the Latta and that's the end of it!"

"That's right, dear," returned Mary, happy to see the other more tranquil. "I know you will. Have you got on well to-day?"

"Splendid!" replied Nessie, in a constrained manner, strangely at variance with her words. "Like a house on fire. I don't know what came over me then. You'll not think any more about what I said will you, Mary!" she continued in a persuasive voice. "Don't say a word about it to anyone! I wouldn't like father to hear I had been so silly. Why, I'm as sure of the Bursary as I am of finishing this milk," and she emptied the remains of the milk at a gulp.

"You know I'll say nothing," answered Mary, looking at her sister perplexedly, considering with some degree of wonder this sudden change in her manner and disposition. Did Nessie really think that she would succeed, or was this attitude assumed to conceal a deeper and more secret fear that she might fail? Thinking anxiously of the immediate future that lay before her sister, Mary said slowly:

"You'll be sure to let me know the result before father, won't you, Nessie? Let me know whenever it comes out."

"Of course I will," replied the other with a continuance of the same manner, but directing her eyes from her sister and looking sideways out of the window. "We'll not know till a fortnight after the examination."

"You're sure now," insisted Mary. "Say that we'll open the letter together."

"Yes! Yes!" cried Nessie fretfully. "Have I not told you that I would long ago. You can open it yourself for all I care. I've promised you and I'll not break my word. You should be letting me get on instead of harping on about that."

Again Mary surveyed her sister with some uneasiness, realising how unlike her usual clinging, artless, mildness was this petulant assumption of assurance, but although she felt troubled in her mind, she decided that this must be the result simply of a natural anxiety at the nearness of the examination and she said, gently:

"I'll go and let you get on then, dear! But please don't tire yourself out too much. I'm anxious for you." Then as she picked up the empty tumbler and retreated to the door she said, tentatively: "You're sure you wouldn't like to come out for a few minutes? I'm going out for my walk now."

"No," cried Nessie with a vehement shake of her head, "I'll not bother about it. I'll get on well and I'll be as right as the mail." She smiled at Mary with a curious complacency—she who a moment ago had been shaken by bitter sobs and whose invariable attitude towards her sister was one of utter dependency. "Away and have your walk, woman!" she added. "I want to have a quiet think to myself."

"About the Euclid?" said Mary doubtfully, from the door.

"Ay! about the Euclid," cried Nessie, with a short laugh. "Away and don't bother me."

Mary shut the parlour door and, as the kitchen was closed to her by its consecration to Brodie's sleep, went slowly up to her room, still bearing in her hand the tumbler which had contained Nessie's milk. She gazed at this empty glass, trying to comfort herself by the recollection of all the care which she had lately bestowed upon her sister, of the additional nourishment which she had obtained for her and induced her to take; but in spite of the reassuring nature of her thoughts she sighed, unable to dismiss from her mind the sudden outburst which had recently occurred, and in which she thought she detected still some evidence of that lack of balance which, since her return, had troubled her in Nessie. While she put on her hat and gloves to take her customary walk, she determined to maintain a closer and more careful observation upon her sister during the climax of Nessie's endeavours, which would be manifested during the coming week.

Outside, the air was warm and still, and the street deserted to that quietude which induced her on Sundays to take her stroll invariably in the afternoon, rather than in the evening, when the same road was crowded by promenading couples. At this time, too, she felt safe in the knowledge that, with Brodie asleep, Nessie would be immune from his hectoring attention for an hour or two, and this assurance gave her a sense of freedom which now she rarely experienced. She proceeded to the head of the road and chose, to-day, the left-hand turn, which led directly towards the distant Winton Hills that stood away from her, rendered more remote by the shimmering haze of heat which almost veiled them. This haze lay also upon the roadway, rising in faint vibrations of the air like a mirage, and giving the illusion of pools of water lying wetly at a distance upon the path in front of her. But there was no wetness, everything was dry with dust which soon covered her shoes with a white, impalpable powder and stirred in little puffs about her skirt with every step she took. The day was delicious, the country lying in a basking warmth, but it was not the hour for walking, and soon the small, front curl which defied always the severity of her brush, lay wisping damply against the whiteness of her brow; her paces dwindled, and she felt tired. With her tiredness came a returning consciousness of Nessie's strange manner to her earlier in the afternoon, the heat all at once became overpowering, and she had made up her mind to turn back towards home when, suddenly, she observed a dogcart coming rapidly in her direction along the road. Immediately, she perceived the nature of the vehicle and the identity of the driver and, in a quick flutter of confusion, she made to turn and retreat, halted, stood indecisively for a moment, looking this way and that as though seeking some place of concealment, then, realising perhaps the futility of flight, she lowered her head and walked rapidly to meet it. As she progressed, she made every effort to compose her features, hoping that she would pass without being observed, but, to her growing agitation, though she observed nothing, she heard the crunching of the advancing wheels gradually subside and come to a halt beside her, heard Renwick's voice saying:

"Good day to you—Miss Brodie!"

She felt it impossible for her to look up to disclose, in her face, the revealing turmoil of her feelings as, thinking unhappily that she was now Miss Brodie to him and not Miss Mary, or even Mary, she stammered out an acknowledgment of his greeting.

"It's a wonderful day," he exclaimed cheerily. "Quite perfect; but it's too hot to be on foot. It must be like crossing the Sahara to walk to-day."

Had he, she asked herself, observed her hot face and the dust upon her boots which must give her the appearance of some dishevelled and disreputable tramp!

"I ought to say, in politeness, that it's a coincidence our meeting here," he continued, "but that's hardly so. I was aware that you took this walk on Sundays when I drove out here to-day. I wanted to know about Nessie."

How wonderful his words would have been without that last explanatory sentence, but, as she stood foolishly with downcast head, she became aware that she must say something in reply or he would consider that she was stupid or uncouth, or both; with a great effort she slowly lifted her eyes to his, thought instantly, despite her embarrassment, how clean cut was his dark, eager face against the background of the sky —and murmured feebly, irrelevantly:

"I haven't been able to tell you about Nessie. I haven't seen you for a long time."

"Far too long," he cried; "and it's been of your own seeking. I haven't seen you about for weeks. I thought you had flown again from Levenford without bidding me good-bye."

"I'm here for good, now," she replied slowly. "It's you that will be saying good-bye to Levenford soon."

His face clouded slightly.

"Yes! it's only another fortnight now. How time flies—like an arrow in its flight." He sighed. "It's curious, but as the day draws near I'm losing interest in the prospect. I was glad to think of going at first, but this old town has its grip on me after all."

"You've so many friends, now, I suppose."

"That's it! I've got friends."

He played idly with his whip, his eyes fixed unseeingly upon the twitching ears of the horse, then he looked at her seriously and said: "Are you free to come for a drive with me, Miss Brodie? I may not see you again and I rather wished to talk to you about one or two matters. Do come if you would care to!"

Of course she would care to come and, thinking of her father resting

428

until five, she realised that no more propitious hour could have been chosen; still, she hesitated, and replied:

"I'm—I'm not dressed for driving, and I should have to be back at five, and——"

"And in that case you're coming," he answered, with a smile, stretching out his hand. "We've got a good hour and a half. As for your dress, it's too good for this old trap of mine."

She was up beside him almost before she knew how, seated close to him on the red velvet cushion, and he had tucked the light, dust cover around her, touched up the horse and she was off with him, gliding forward in an easy yet exhilarating movement. The breeze of their progress through the still air fanned her cheek, the sky lost its glare and became halcyon, the dust was nothing—merely a soft powder to ease the horse's stepping gait—and, after the tedium and fatigue of walking, she was content to sit silent, happy, watching the vivid countryside flit gently past her. But, though she was too conscious of his nearness to look upon him, out of the corner of her gaze she observed the smooth, soft leather of his hand-sewn driving gloves, the silver-plated harness, the monogrammed dust cover, the smart appointments of what he had designated his "old trap," and again, as in his house, she was seized by a feeling of the difference between his life and hers. Now, whatever his early struggles might have been, the manner of his life did not comprise the weighing of every farthing before it was spent, the wearing of clothes until they disintegrated, the stifling of every pleasurable impulse outwith the sphere of a most rigid economy. But she suppressed this rising sense of her inferiority, stifled her thoughts of future sadness and. telling herself that she would not mar her solitary hour of this unusual luxury, abandoned herself to the unfamiliar delight of enjoying herself.

Renwick, on his part, observed her clear profile, the faint colour stirring in her soft cheek, her unwonted animation, with a strange satisfaction, a sense of pleasure more acute than that with which she viewed the countryside. A sudden pressing whim took him to make her turn to him so that he might see into her eyes and he broke the silence, saying:

"You are not sorry you came."

But still she did not look at him, although her lips curved in a faint smile, as she answered:

"I'm glad I came. It's all so wonderful to me. I'm not used to this and I'll be able to look back on it."

"We'll have time to drive up to the Loch shore," he replied pleasantly, "and, if Tim steps out, time for tea there as well."

She was enchanted by the prospect which he proposed and, considering Tim's smoothly groomed back, hoped that he would hasten sufficiently for tea without going so fast as to hurry her home before time.

"Tim," she remarked idly; "what a good name for a horse."

"And a good horse he is too," he replied, calling out in a louder tone, "aren't you, Timmy?"

Tim pricked up his ears at the words and, as though he appreciated them, put a little more mettle into his measured jog-trot.

"You see?' Renwick continued, watching with approval her smile. "He knows that I'm talking about him and is trying not to blush—the wretched hypocrite. He'll be lazier than ever in Edinburgh. Too many oats and not enough exercise!"

"You're taking him with you, then?" she queried.

"Yes. I couldn't sell Timmy. I'm like that somehow." He paused, then continued meditatively: "It's a ridiculous trait in me, but when I've become fond of a thing I can't let it go—pictures, books, a horse— it's the same in every case. When I like a thing I like it. I'm obstinate. I accept no standard of judgment but my own. A critic may tell me a dozen times that such a picture is good, but if I don't like it I won't have it. I take a picture that I do like then, when it's grown upon me, I couldn't bear to part with it."

She looked straight in front of her and remarked:

"That was an exquisite picture in your dining-room."

"Yes," he replied authoritatively, "that is a fine thing—I'm glad you liked it. It's company to me that picture. I bought it at the Institute." Then he added, slyly, "It's not exclusively my taste, though—the critics liked it, too."

The memory of the picture brought before her mind the purpose of her first visit to him and, anticipating his interrogation regarding Nessie, she said:

"I'm grateful for all that you've done about Nessie. You have been more than kind to us both." She had never told him about the tragedy of the grapes, and his favours, these fortunately undiscovered, had continued.

"I wanted to help you," he replied. "How is she getting along, under all the work?"

"She seems better in her health," she answered, with a trace of anxiety in her voice, "but she varies so much. At times she is quite peculiar to me. She's worrying about the nearness of her examination. It's on Saturday. I've done everything I can for her."

"I know you have—everything," he said reassuringly. "Now that she's gone so far without breaking down she ought to be all right! I hope she gets the thing for her own sake." Then, after a considerable silence, he remarked in a serious tone: "I should keep near to her when the results come to hand; and if you want me call on me at once."

She was aware that he would be gone when the result was announced, but, feeling that already he had done enough for her, she made no comment, and remained silent, engrossed by her thoughts. As he had said, Nessie would be all right! She would see to that. She would be with her—watch her, protect her, safeguard her, should she be unsuccessful, from any sudden action of her father.

She was aroused from her meditation, from this strengthening of her resolution, by his voice.

"They've widened the road here. We can get through quite easily, and it's cooler than the other way." Looking up, she was overcome to see that, unconscious of its significance for her, he had branched off the main road and taken that very passage through the fir wood where she had lost herself upon the night of the storm. With a set, startled face she gazed at the wood as it again enclosed her, not now rocking and surging to the passion of the gale, nor crashing with the thunder of uprooting trees, but quiet, appeased, passive with a serene tranquillity. The bright sunbeams stole amongst the sombre foliage of the dark trees, softening them, encrusting their rough branches with gold, and tracing upon their straight, dry trunks a gaily fretted pattern of shimmering light and shadow. As she passed, in her present comfort and security, through the wood, she was stricken by the incredible memory of her own tortured figure, filled then with her living child, rushing blindly through the darkness, staggering, falling, transfixing her hand upon the sharp spear of the branch, beset by mad voices, unseen, unheard.

A tear trembled upon the brink of her humid eye but, clenching her fingers tightly over the long cicatrix upon her palm as though to fortify herself with the remembrance of her endurance then, she refused to let it fall and instead, turned her gaze, as they emerged from the wood, down into the distant valley. Yes! there was the croft where she had lain in her extremity! it stood against the smooth green of the lush meadowland adjoined by the small shed which had contained her anguished body, its white walls rising squarely to its yellow thatched roof, the smoke rising straight from its single chimney like a long, blue ribbon lifting itself tenuously to the sky.

With a wrench she withdrew her eyes and, holding her body tense in the effort to control her emotion, looked straight ahead, whilst Tim's ears blurred and wavered before her swimming gaze. Renwick, perceiving, perhaps instinctively, that some sudden sadness had induced her silence, did not speak for a long time, but as they swept over the crest of Markinch Hill and the placid, smoothly shining sheet of the Loch was revealed stretching below them, he remarked, quietly:

"There's beauty and serenity for you."

It was an exquisite sight. The water, bearing the deep, brilliant blue of the unclouded sky, lay cool and unruffled as a sheet of virgin ice from whose edges the steep and richly wooded slopes of the hills reached back and upwards to the sharp, ridged mountains beyond. Breaking the surface of this still expanse were a series of small islands lying upon the bosom of the Loch like a chain of precious emeralds, green and wooded like the banks, and each mirrored with such perfection that it was impossible for the eyes to distinguish between the islet and its meticulous reflection. Upon the shore nearest to them stood a small hamlet, its aggregation of cottages showing whitely against the vivid background of blue and green, and now Renwick pointed to it significantly.

"There's Markinch—which means tea for you, Mary! Don't let the grandeur of nature spoil your appetite."

Her face, that was serene and beautiful as the surface of the lake, responded to his words, and she smiled with a faint, returning glow of happiness. He had called her Mary!

They descended the winding hill to Markinch where, disdaining the small, somewhat ineffectual inn which stood at the head of the village, Renwick drove on to the last cottage of the row that fringed the shore of the Loch, and with a wise look towards Mary, jumped out and knocked upon the door. The cottage was in perfect harmony with the surrounding beauty, its white walls splashed by the rich yellows of nasturtiums, its green porch embowered by red rambler roses, its garden fragrant with the poignant scent of mignonette—such a cottage, indeed, as she had once visioned for herself in Garshake; and to the door of this small house came a small, bent body of a woman who now lifted her hands and cried, delightedly:

"Doctor! Doctor! It's not yourself? Guidsakes alive! Is it you yourself?"

"Indeed it is, Janet," cried Renwick, in her own tone. "It is I, myself, and a young lady, herself. And the two of us, ourselves, are fair famished from our drive. If we don't get one of your lovely teas, with your own scones, and jam and butter and heaven knows a' what, then we'll just sadly fade awa' and never come back."

"Ye'd no' do that, though," cried Janet vigorously. "Na, na! ye'll have the finest tea in Markinch inside five minutes."

"Can we have it in the garden, Janet?"

"Of course ye can, doctor! Ye can have it on the roof o' my cottage gin ye say the word."

"The garden will do, Janet," replied Renwick with a smile. "And —Janet! let the wee lad look after Tim. And give us a call when you're ready. We'll go along the shore a bit."

"Right! Right, doctor! Ye've only to say the word," answered Janet eagerly, and as she departed to do his bidding, he turned and came back to Mary.

"Shall we go a little way along?" he asked; and at her assent he assisted her from her seat to the ground, saying:

"Janet won't keep us waiting five minutes, but you may well as stretch your legs. You must be cramped from sitting."

432

How delighted the old woman had been to see him, thought Mary, and like all who were in contact with him, how eager to rush to serve him! Thinking of this, as they proceeded along the fine firm shingle of the shore she remarked:

"Janet's an old friend of yours! Her eye actually leaped when she saw you."

"I did something for a son of hers in Levenford once," he replied lightly. "She's a sweet old soul with a tongue like an energetic magpie," —here he looked at her across his nose, adding—"but better than that, she makes delicious scones. You must eat exactly seven of them."

"Why seven?" she queried.

"It's a lucky number," he answered, "and just the right amount of scone food for a healthy, hungry young lady." He looked at her critically. "I wish I had the dieting of you, Miss Mary. There's a sad loveliness in that faint hollow of your cheek, but it means that you've been neglecting your butter and milk. I'll wager you gave all those things I sent you to that wee Nessie of yours."

She blushed.

"No! I didn't really! It was good of you to send them to us."

He shook his head compassionately.

"Will you ever think of yourself, Mary Brodie? It hurts me to think what will come of you when I'm away. You want someone to keep a severe and stern eye upon you, to make you look after yourself. Will you write to me and tell me how you're behaving?"

"Yes," she said slowly, as though a faint coldness had risen to her from the still water beside them, "I'll write when you've gone!"

"That's right," he cried cheerfully. "I'll regard that as a definite promise on your part."

Now they stood looking out upon the sublime tranquillity of the view before them, that seemed to her so remote from the troubled existence within her home, so exalted above the ordinary level of her life. She was overcome by its appeal and, released by the perception of this beauty, all her suppressed feeling for this man by her side swept over her. She was drawn to him with a deeper and more moving emotion than that which had once stirred her; she wished blindly to show her devotion, visibly to demonstrate her homage to him; but she could not, and was compelled to remain quiet by his side, torn by the beating of her straining heart. The faint murmur of the Loch, as it scarcely lapped its shore, swept across the quietude of the scene, whispering to her who and what she was, that she was Mary Brodie, the mother of an illegitimate child, and echoing in her ears in endless repetition that word with which her father had condemned her when he hurled her from the house upon the night of the storm.

"I hear Janet's cracked cow-bell," he said at length. "Are you ready for the scones?"

She nodded her head, her throat too full for speech, and, as he lightly took her arm to assist her across the shingled beach, she was conscious of his touch upon her as more unbearable than any pain which she had ever felt.

"All ready! all ready!" cried Janet, rushing about like a fury. "Table and chairs and everything in the garden for ye, like ye ordered. And the scones are fresh—this mornin's bakin'."

"That's fine!" remarked Renwick, as he seated Mary in her chair and then took his own.

Although his tone had dismissed the old woman, she lingered, and after a full, admiring glance at Mary, moistened her lips, and was about to speak when, suddenly observing the look upon Renwick's face, she arrested, with a prodigious effort, the garrulous speech which trembled upon her tongue, and turned towards the house.

As she departed, shaking her head and muttering to herself a slight constraint settled upon Mary and Renwick; although the tea was excellent and the cool of the garden, spiced by the fragrance of the mignonette, delicious, neither appeared quite at ease.

"Janet's an old footer," he said, with an attempt at lightness. "That's a good Scotch word which just suits her. If I'd given her an opening she'd have deafened us." But after this remark, he fell into an awkward silence which impelled Mary's mind back to that only other occasion in her life when she had sat at table alone with a man, when she had eaten an ice-cream in the gaudy atmosphere of Bertorelli's Saloon, when Denis had pressed her foot with his and charmed her with his gay and sparkling tongue.

How different were her surroundings here, in this cool freshness of the cottage garden filled with the exhaled perfume of a hundred blossoms; how different, too, was her companion, who neither chattered of alluring trips abroad, nor yet, alas, caressed her foot with his. Now, however, he was shaking his head at her.

"You've only eaten two after all," he murmured, looking at her tragically, adding slowly, "and I said seven."

"They're so large," she protested.

"And you're so small—but you would be bigger if you did as you were told."

"I always did as you told me in the hospital!"

"Yes," he replied after a pause, "you did, indeed." A heaviness again seemed to settle upon him while his thoughts flew back to the vision of her as he had first seen her, with her eyes closed, inanimate, blanched, his broken, uprooted lily. At last he looked at his watch, then looked at her with a sombre face. "Time's getting along, I'm afraid. Shall we get back?"

"Yes," she whispered, "if you think it is time."

They arose and went out of the sweet seclusion of the garden—which

434

might have been made for the enclosure of two ardent lovers—without further speech, and when he had helped her into the trap, he returned and paid old Janet.

"I'm not wantin' your siller, doctor," she skirled. "It's a pleasure to do it for you and the bonnie leddie."

"Here, Janet," he cried, "take it now or I'll be cross with you."

She sensed the faint difference in his mood and, as she took the money, whispered in a humble tone:

"Have I put my foot in't? I'm gey and sorry if I've done that. Or was it the scones that werna to your taste?"

"Everything was all right, Janet—splendid," he rejoined, as he mounted into his place. "Good-bye to you."

She waved them a faintly uncomprehending good-bye and, as they disappeared around the bend of the hill, she again shook her head, muttered to herself, and re-entered her cottage.

They spoke little on the way home, and when he had asked her if she were comfortable, or if she wished the covering of a rug—whether she had enjoyed the trip—if he should set Tim to a faster pace—he relapsed into a silence which grew more oppressive the nearer they approached to Levenford.

The tentacles of her home were opening again to receive her, and when they had enclosed her, Brodie, swollen-eyed and with a parched tongue, would awake morosely from his sleep to demand her immediate attention to his tea; Nessie would require her sympathy and consolation; she would be confronted at once by the innumerable tasks which it was her duty to perform. This brief and unexpected departure from the sadness of her life was nearly over and, though she had enjoyed it exquisitely, an exquisitely painful sorrow now filled her heart as she realised, dully, that this was probably—almost certainly—the last time that she would see him.

They were nearly at her gate now, and drawing up a short distance away, he said, in an odd voice:

"Well! here we are back again! It's been very short, hasn't it?"

"Very short," she echoed as she arose from the seat and descended to the ground.

"We should have had longer at Markinch," he said stiffly, then, after a pause: "I may not see you again. I suppose I better say good-bye." They looked at each other a long time and, from beneath him, her eyes shone with a faintly suppliant light; then he drew off his glove and extended his hand to her, saying in a strained tone: "Good-bye."

Mechanically she took his hand and as she felt within her grasp the firm cool strength of his fingers, that she had so often admired, that had once soothed her tortured body but would never again do so, these fingers she loved devotedly, her feelings suddenly overcame her and, with a sob, she pressed her warm lips fervently against his hand

and kissed it, then fled from him down the road and entered her house.

For a moment he looked at his hand incredulously, then raised his head, and, regarding her vanishing figure, made as though to leap out of the trap and follow her; but he did not, and after a long stillness, during which he again gazed at his hand, a strange look entered his eyes, he shook his head sadly, and drawing on his glove he drove slowly down the road.

IX

"BRING in some more porridge for your sister!" cried out Brodie to Mary in a loud voice. "You could put this in your eye what you've given her. How do you expect her to work on an empty stomach, and to-day of all days?"

"But, father," protested Nessie weakly, "I asked Mary not to give me so much. I'm to have a switched egg. The thought of more porridge sickens me this morning."

"Tuts, woman! You don't know what's good for ye," replied Brodie. "It's a good job you've got your father to look after ye and see that ye take what's wholesome. Stick into that porridge, now! That's the stuff to lie against your ribs and fit ye for what's before ye." And he leant back largely in his chair, surveying with a self-satisfied eye the figure of his younger daughter as, with a faintly trembling spoon, she endeavoured to thrust a few further spoonfuls of porridge between her nervous unwilling lips. He did not consider that it nauseated her to eat this morning, or that in her anxiety she might have been happier to be left quietly alone, but, in high fettle at the thought that this was the great day, the day of competition for the Latta, he had not departed for the office at his usual hour but remained to sustain and encourage her with his presence. He would, he thought, be a fine one if he could not see his daughter off to take the Latta. Gad! that was not the style of him, though! He had stuck to his task through all these weary months, ay, and seen that she had stuck to hers, with such perfect thoroughness that now he was not the man to spoil the broth for a halfpennyworth of alt. No! he would not go into the office this morning, would not, indeed, go in all day. He would take a whole holiday for the occasion. It was a festival; he had worked for it, and by God! he would enjoy it. A faint grin marked his features at this consideration and, still surveying her with satisfaction, he cried:

"That's right, woman! Take it steady. There's no need for hurry. Your father's behind ye."

"Has she not taken enough now, father?" ventured Mary, her eyes pleading towards him from out her fine-drawn face. "She's maybe too anxious to eat, this morning. I've a beaten egg for her here."

"Take it up, Ness—take it up," drawled Brodie, ignoring completely the interruption. "We know what puts pith into a body. Ye might be downright starved if it wasna for me. I'm not the one to let ye sit through a three hours examination with nothing inside of ye to stand up to it." He was in his element, reaping the fruits of his labour with her, his vicissitudes forgotten, the stabbing memory of Nancy for the present eased, and, opening his mouth in a broader and more derisive smile, he exclaimed: "Gad! it's just occurred to me that maybe that snipe o' a Grierson is sittin' at the table, watchin' that whelp o' his stap down his breakfast, and wonderin' what'n all the world he's goin' to make o' himself the day. Ay, it's a rich thought for me." His smile dried up, became bitter. "The Provost o' the Borough, forsooth—the fine, easy spokesman o' the town. God! he's lookin' gey small and mean and anxious this mornin', I'll wager." He paused for a moment then, observing that Nessie, who had succeeded in finishing the porridge, was sipping her egg and milk, he cried roughly, as though the bitterness of the thought of Grierson had not quite left him: "Here! take a scone and butter to that slush if ye will drink it." He glowered, too at Mary, adding: "Some folks would make a jaw box o' that stomach of yours!" then, returning his glance to Nessie, he continued, in an admonishing tone: "Don't flicker your een like that, woman; you would think that it was a frichtsome business that you were goin' up for to-day, instead o' an easy osey piece of writin' that you've got to do. It's all in your head waitin' to come out. All that's to do is to take up your pen and write it down. Is that anything to upset ye so that you take a scunner at the good, wholesome porridge?" He reviewed the profound wisdom of his logic blandly, then, as though the absurdity of her nervousness suddenly irritated him, he shot at her questioningly: "What the de'il is it you're feared of? Are ye not my daughter? What is there in this and about it all to make ye grue like that?"

She thought of the lofty examination hall, filled by the scratching of a score of fiercely competitive pens, she saw the silent, black-gowned figure of the examiner upon his rostrum sitting severe and omnipotent like a judge, she saw her own small bowed insignificant figure writing feverishly, but, veiling her gaze, she replied, hurriedly:

"There's nothing I'm afraid of, father! It's maybe the thought of the journey that's upsetting me a bit. I'm not thinkin' of the Latta at all. They might have posted the result already for all the good it'll do the others to go up."

He smiled at her again, broadly, exclaiming:

"That's more like the spirit! That's more like my daughter! We havena put ye through your paces for nothing. Now that I'm showin' you, ye maun step high when you're in the ring." He paused, pleased by his comparison, which, combined with his present elation and the excitement of her departure, reminded him vaguely of those days when he had set out for the Cattle Show, and he cried: "You're on show the day, Nessie, and I'm proud of ye. I know before ye go up who'll come back with the red ticket round her neck. My daughter, Nessie Brodie —that's the name that'll be on everybody's lips. We're goin' to startle the town between us. By God! they'll look the other way along their noses when they meet me now. We'll show them!" He considered her fondly, almost admiringly, remarking, after a moment: "Gad! it fair beats me, when I look at that wee head o' yours and think on all that's in it. Latin and French and mathematics, and heaven knows a' what. And yet it's no bigger than my fist. Ay! it's a true word that good gear gangs in small bulk. It's the quality that counts. It's downright gratifyin' for a man to see his own brains comin' out in his daughter, ay, and to be able to give her the opportunity. When I was your age I never had a chance like you." He sighed, commiseratingly. "No! I would have gone far had I been given the chance, but I had to get out into the world and make my own way. There were no Lattas in those days or I would have lifted the whole jing bang o' them." He lifted his eyes to her and exclaimed in an altered, excited tone: "But it'll be different with you, Nessie. You'll have your chance. I'll see to that. You'll see what I'll do for ye when you've won the Latta. I'll—I'll—I'll push ye on to the highest ye can go." He banged his fist upon the table and considered her triumphantly, adding: "Are ye not pleased with what I'm doin' for ye?"

"Yes, father," she murmured, "I'm—I'm real pleased at it all."

"And I should think so!" he cried. "There's not a man in Levenlord would have done what I've done for ye. See that ye don't forget it! When ye come back with that Latta don't let it fly to your head. Remember who has done it for you!"

She glanced at him timidly, as she remarked in a low voice:

"You're not expecting me to bring it home to-night, father? It'll be a good while before the result comes out—a fortnight anyway!"

As though she had suddenly baulked him of the keen zest of his enjoyment, his look took on a sudden displeasure.

"Are ye off again on that tack? What's all this goin' on about results? Do you think I expect ye to bring the money back in a bag? I know it'll come in good time. I know it's for your studies. I'm not just gaspin' for't. But I seem to feel that you're gettin' anxious as to whether you'll get your fingers on it or not."

"Oh! no, father," she said hastily, "I'm not thinking about that at all. I was just afraid ye might think I would know for sure to-night."

"For sure," he repeated slowly; "are ye not 'for sure' already?"

"Yes! Yes!" she cried, "I'm sure. I'm dead positive about it. I hardly know what I'm saying I'm so excited at going up to the University."

"Don't let all this grand excitement run awa' with you," he replied, warningly. "Remember you're sixteen years old now, and if that's not old enough for you to have some control then you'll never have it. Don't lose your heid, that's all I say! Have ye got a' things that you need —your pen and your nibs and your rubber and what not?"

"I get everything I want up there," she answered meekly. "Everything like that is supplied to us."

"I see! Well in that case ye canna very well say ye had forgotten your pen." He paused and looked at the clock. "It's gettin' near time for your train. Have ye eaten your fill of everything?"

She felt her stomach turn uneasily as she whispered:

"Yes, father."

He arose and went over to his pipe rack, remarking complacently:

"Well, I've done my bit of the business anyway."

As he turned his back Mary moved nearer to his sister, saying in a low tone, close to Nessie's ear:

"I'll go down to the station with you, Nessie, just to keep you company and see that you get away all right. I'll not worry you by speaking."

"What's that?" cried Brodie, turning like a flash. He had, unfortunately, heard something of her words. "You'll go down to the station will ye?" he sneered. "Indeed now! That is verra considerate of ye. You'll do this and you'll do that with your interferin', the same sleekit way that your mother used to have. Is Nessie not capable of walkin' a few yards by herself that you must tie a bit of string round her neck and lead her along?" His sneer became a snarl. "Have I not told ye to leave my Nessie alone? You'll go to no station. You'll do nothing for her. She'll go down by herself." He turned to Nessie. "You don't want her botherin' you, do you, hinny?"

Her eyes fell as she faltered, in a faint voice: "No, father, not if you say it."

Brodie returned his glance to Mary with a dark insolence.

"You see!" he cried, "she doesna want ye! Keep out of what doesna concern ye. I'll do all that's wanted. I'll get her things for her myself this morning. Here! Nessie! Where's your hat and coat? I'm goin' to see you to the door." He swelled at the thought of the honour he was conferring upon her as she dumbly indicated the sofa where, brushed, sponged, and pressed, lay the worn, blue serge jacket of her everyday wear—the only one she now possessed—and her straw hat which now bravely flaunted a new satin band bought by her sister and stitched in place by her devoted fingers. He lifted the coat and hat, handed them to her, assisted her even in the fullness of his service, to assume the coat so that she now stood, a small, indescribably pathetic figure, clothed and ready for her journey. He patted her upon the shoulder with an extravagant flourish, exclaiming, as though he had dressed her fully with his own hands: "There now! you're all set up for the road. Do ye not think it's a great honour for you that I've taken the day off to see you out like this? Come on and I'll take you to the door."

She was, however, strangely disinclined to move, but remained with her head averted from him, her gaze drawn to Mary's dark and tender eyes, her lower lip drooping slightly, her thin fingers interlocked and twisting nervously. The clear skin of her face, denuded of its one-time colour almost to a pale transparency, seemed stretched tightly over the puny framework of her features, its pallor accentuated by the fine-spun sheen of the flaxen hair which, now unplaited, invested loosely the small, drawn countenance. She stood inert, realising that the climax of her endeavours was at hand and that she was loath to face it; then, suddenly appearing to forget the presence of her father, she advanced close to Mary and murmured in a low, almost inaudible tone: "I'm not wanting to go, Mary. I've got that band round my brow again. I would rather stay at home." Yet almost in the same breath, as though she were unaware that she had uttered these whispered words, she cried:

"I'm ready then, father. I've got everything I want. I'm as right as the mail and ready to stick into it."

He stared at her, then relaxed slowly.

"Come on, then, and look sharp about it. What are you moonin' about her for? No more of your silly dawdlin' or you'll miss your train."

"I'll not miss it, father," she cried eagerly, breaking away from Mary without looking at her—as though she had not heard her sister's last murmur of encouragement, or the promise to meet her at the station on her return. "No! No!" she exclaimed, "that wouldn't be like me to do a thing like that. I haven't worked all these six months for nothing. What an idea!" She drew back her narrow shoulders and, demonstrating her willingness by passing him and hastening into the hall, she went to the front door and opened it wide. "I'm away then, father," she cried loudly and in a fashion something after his own manner, "I'll be back when you see me!"

"Hold on a minute," he exclaimed, with a frown, lumbering after her. "I said I was goin' to see ye to the door, did I not? What's come over ye that you're rushing like this." He surveyed her for a moment from beneath his heavy eyebrows, then, reassured by the brightness now manifested in her eyes, he cried: "You'll do, though—you've got the look on ye as if ye couldna get to that examination quick enough. Away wi' ye, then. I'll warrant ye'll put your back into it. I've got ye just in the right fettle. Ye canna help but win it now." He clapped his

440

hands together as though shooing her off, exclaiming: "Off with ye now and put salt on that Grierson's tail."

"Trust me," she returned lightly. "I'll put so much salt on him that I'll pickle him!"

"Good enough," he cried delightedly, following her fondly with his eyes as she went out of the gate and down the road. She did not once look back. As he stood at his door watching her slight figure dwindling into the distance he was filled momentarily by a powerful return of his old, proud, disdainful complacency. Gad! but she was a smarter, was his Nessie! As clever as you make them, with the sharpness of a needle, a sharpness that would prick that big, swollen bladder of a Grierson until the wind rushed out of him like a burst bagpipe. He had primed her well for the event too, made her as keen as a young greyhound to get out of the leash, and when she had left him just now there had been a gleam in her eye that had fairly warmed him. He had done that by his firm handling of the lass, forcing some of his own fire into her blood, filling her with a determination to succeed. "Stick into it, Nessie!" —that had been his slogan, and one which was more than justified! She would walk away with the Latta, putting a hundred miles, or marks, or whatever it might be, between Grierson and herself. Grierson might even be last! With a grim smile at the relish of his thoughts he slowly turned, sniffed the clear air with an added appreciation from his freedom, mounted the steps and went into the house.

Inside he halted, aimlessly, in the hall, losing something of the first flush of his elation in the realisation that, although it was not yet eleven o'clock and he was to-day a free man, he did not quite know what to do with himself; but after a moment he went into the kitchen and gravitated to his chair, where he sat watching Mary, out of the corner of his eye, as she went about her morning tasks. She made no comment upon his absence from the office and was, as always, quiet and composed, though to-day an added darkness lay in and around the pools of her eyes. In her manner she gave him no indication of the nature of her inward thoughts. He opened his lips to speak to her, to make some scathing comment upon the disparity between Nessie and herself barbed with a bitter innuendo concerning her past history, but he did not utter the words, knowing that whatever he said would be met by the same impenetrable silence. He would not speak yet! She could, he thought, be as dour as she liked and as quiet as she liked, but he knew what was at the back of her mind in spite of all her assumption of indifference. She was after his Nessie, interfering whenever she could, obstructing his intentions, laying herself out slyly at every turn to defeat his purpose. Let her wait though! He, too, was waiting and if ever she directly opposed him with Nessie, it would be a sad day for her!

As, without appearing to observe her, he followed the smooth, graceful movements of his daughter, an association of ideas confronted him suddenly with the memory of another woman whom he had loved as much as he hated this one—Nancy, the ultimate object of his waking, yes, even of his dreaming, mind. Now, however, he clenched his teeth firmly and shook the obsessing vision of her from his head, determined that nothing should mar the triumph of his day. It was Nessie that he wanted to think of—Nessie, his solace—who would now be sitting in the train, revolving in her clever brain some of these lessons which he had kept her at so assiduously, or considering, perhaps, the last exhortation he had given her. He had always felt that this would be a great day for him, and now he was aware that he must not let himself become depressed, that he must sustain his spirits at that high level to which they had risen earlier in the morning. He would have a drink—just to liven him a little.

His eye brightened as he arose from his chair and went to the dresser, where he opened the small cupboard on the left, drew out the familiar black bottle and—now kept always in readiness beside it—his own small tumbler. With the tumbler in one hand and the bottle in the other he sat down again in his chair, poured himself out some whisky and at once savoured it gratefully, appreciatively, holding the liquor for a moment between his palate and his tongue. The first drink of the day always passed over his lips with a richer and more satisfying flavour than any other, and now it trickled so warmly down his gullet that he was impelled to follow it quickly by a second. The first had been to himself —this would be in honour of Nessie! She might now be out of the train if she followed, as she undoubtedly would, his directions to get out at Partick Station, and might at this very moment be ascending the steep slope of Gilmorehill towards the grey pile of the University on its summit. He was conscious that this noble building, breathing of erudition, was well suited for the holding of the Latta examination, well worthy for the making of his daughter's mark within it. The professors might already have heard of her cleverness in some stray manner, for reports of brilliant scholars were circulated in devious but far-reaching ways in the academic world, and, even if this were not so, she had a name which they would recognise at once, which was a passport to her, there and anywhere she might choose to go. He drank to the University, to Nessie, and again to the name of Brodie.

This was better! To-day his mind reacted to the whisky in a different manner from that mere dulling of his morose despondency which had lately been the result of his potations; now, the old-time exhilaration of the early days of his toping was returning to him, and as he became aware of this delicious fact, his spirits rose, and he began to cast about in his mind for some channel into which he might direct his new-found animation. It was unconscionably dull for a cheerful man to sit under the sombre eye of his melancholy daughter, and, perceiving that he would have to seek his amusement out of the house, he considered for

a moment the idea of visiting the office, not, of course, to work, bu
merely, in an informal way, to divert those two young sprigs in his room,
and to tweak the offensive nose of the upstart Blair. Being Saturday,
however, it was a half-day at the office—which meant that they would
soon be stopping work and going home—and he felt, too, that the
occasion demanded a more appropriate celebration than merely a
return to the scene of his daily labour. He abandoned this idea with
only a faint regret, which vanished completely as he drowned it in
another glass of Mountain Dew.

Dew! Dew upon the grass—green grass—the bowling green! Ah! he
had it at last! Who said that there was not inspiration in that famous
blend of Teacher which he always favoured? His face lit up with a
lively delight at his aptness in remembering that the summer tournament
of the Levenford Bowling Club was to be held at the Wellhall Green
this afternoon, and he smiled broadly as he considered that all the
worthies would be present—present for a certainty—from wee Johnnie
Paxton up to the Lord High Provost Grierson himself.

"Gad!" he muttered, slapping his thigh, in quite his old manner,
"that's the ticket, right enough! I'll have them all boxed up in that
one place and I'll throw the Latta in their teeth there and then. I'll
show them I'm not feared o' them. It's high time I was makin' myself
heard again. It strikes me I've been over long about it."

He crowned his satisfaction with a bumper, then, raising his voice,
cried:

"Hurry up with my dinner in there. I'm wantin' it quick. I'm goin'
out this afternoon and I want something inside of me first. Let it be
some decent food too, and none o' that swill ye were foistin' off on
Nessie this morning."

"Your dinner's ready, father," Mary replied quietly. "You can have
it now, if you wish."

"I do wish, then," he retorted. "Get on with it and don't stand
glumphin' at me like that."

She quickly laid the table and served him with his meal, but, though
this was to his taste, and, indeed, infinitely better than any which Nancy
had ever prepared for him, he gave neither praise nor thanks. He did
justice to it however, and with an appetite stimulated by the whisky, for
once ate heartily, dividing his thoughts, as he masticated vigorously,
between his plans for the afternoon and the further consideration of
Nessie. She would have begun, actually, the examination by this time,
and would be sitting driving her pen over page after page of paper
whilst the others, and particularly young Grierson, chewed the wooden
ends of theirs and stared at her enviously. Now he saw her, having
entirely finished one exercise book, rise from her place and, her small,
self-conscious face glowing, advance to demand another from the
examiner. She had used up one book already, the first in the room to

do so—Nessie Brodie, his daughter—whilst that young snipe Grierson had not even filled half of his yet! He chuckled slightly at her remarkable prowess and bolted his food with an added gusto from the vision of the other's discomfiture. His thoughts ran chiefly in this strain during the rest of the meal and, when he had finished, he arose and drank again, emptying the bottle to the hope that she would require, not two, but three books to convey to the professors the wide extent of her knowledge.

It was still too early for his descent upon the Wellhall Bowling Green, for he wished to allow a full congregation of the notables to collect, and realising that he was not yet ripe with the careless rapture best suited to such an adventure, confronted, too, by the mere hollow shell which had held the Mountain Dew, he decided to adventure out and rest himself for an hour in the Wellhall Vaults which conveniently adjoined the Green.

Accordingly, he left the house and proceeded down the road not, however, with the set, morose face and unseeing stare which marked him lately in the streets but, fortified by his mood and the knowledge of his daughter's success, with a freer, easier carriage which again invited inspection. Few people were about as yet, but when he had crossed Railway Road he observed on the other side of the street the stately figure of Dr. Lawrie, not driving, but walking, and immediately he crossed over and accosted him.

"Good day to you, Dr. Lawrie," he cried affably. It had been "Lawrie" in the old days and without the affability. "I'm pleased to meet ye."

"Good day," returned the other, thinking of his unpaid bill and speaking with the small store of curtness he possessed.

"It's well met for us just now," retorted Brodie. "Well met! Do ye know what's happening at this very moment?"

Lawrie eyed him warily, as he uttered a cautious: "No."

"My Nessie is up at the University winning the Latta for me while you and me are talkin' here," cried Brodie. "It's a justification of your own words. Don't ye mind what ye told me—that she had a head on her in a thousand?"

"Indeed! Indeed!" returned Lawrie pompously, and with a slight degree of cordiality. "I'm gratified to hear that. Winning the Latta. It all helps. It'll be a little more grist to the mill I suppose." He looked sideways at the other, hoping that he would take the hint, then suddenly he looked directly at Brodie and exclaimed: "Winning?—did ye say she had won the Latta?"

"It's as good as won," replied Brodie comfortably. "She's at it the now—this very minute. I took the day off to see that she got away in the best o' fettle. She went off with a glint in her eye that spoke for victory. She'll fill three books ere she's done!"

444

"Indeed!" said Lawrie again, and, eyeing the other strangely, he drew insensibly away, remarking: "I'll have to be getting along now—an important consultation—my horse just cast a shoe along the road there —I'm late!"

"Don't go yet, man," remonstrated Brodie, buttonholing the embarrassed Lawrie firmly. "I havena told ye half about my daughter yet. I'm real fond o' that lass, you know. In my own way. Just in my own way. I've wrought hard with her for the last six months."

"Pray let me go, Mr. Brodie," cried Lawrie, struggling to free himself.

"We've burned the midnight oil between us, have Nessie and I," retorted Brodie gravely. "It's been a heap o' work—but by gad, it's been worth it!"

"Really sir," exclaimed Lawrie in a shrill, indignant tone, wrenching himself free and looking round to see if his contact with this ruffianly looking individual had been observed, "you've taken a great liberty!. I don't like it! Take care how you address me in future." Then, with a last, outraged look he reinflated his cheeks and bounced off quickly down the road.

Brodie gazed after him in some amazement. He failed to detect anything in his recent conduct which could have aroused indignation, and finally, with a shake of his head, he turned and resumed his way, reaching, without further encounters, the haven of the Wellhall Vaults. Here, he was not known and he remained silent, but drinking steadily, filling himself with liquor and further visions of his daughter's prowess, until three o'clock. Then he got up, set his hat well back upon his head, drew in his lips, and swaggered into the open once more.

The mere step to the Wellhall Green he accomplished with hardly a falter, and soon he was inside the trim enclosure where the smooth square of green lay vivid in the sunshine, marred only by the dark, blurred figures of the players wavering across it before his eye. What a game for grown men, he thought contemptuously; to roll a few balls about like a gang of silly bairns. Could they not take out a gun or a horse, like he had once done, if they wanted their exercise or amusement.

His gaze, however, did not remain long upon the green but, lifting quickly, sought the small group that sat upon the veranda of the pavilion at the further end of the ground, and he smiled with a sardonic gratification as he observed that, even as he had foretold, they were all there—from simple John Paxton to the Lord High Provost of the Borough. He gathered himself together again and advanced deliberately towards him.

For a moment he proceeded unobserved by this small gathering—for they were all concentrating upon the game before them—but suddenly Paxton looked up, observed him and gasped in amazement:

"Guidsakes—just look what's coming!" His tone drew their attention at once, and following his startled gaze, they, too, regarded the strange uncouth, strutting figure as it bore down upon them, and they exclaimed variously:

"Good God! it's Brodie. I havena seen him for months!"

"He's as fou as a lord by the looks o' him."

"Losh! it's the drunken earl himsel'."

"Look at the face o' him and the clothes o' him."

"Ay, but look at the swagger o' the thing!"

They were silent as he drew near, directing their eyes away from him towards the green, disowning him, but still failing to perturb him as, oscillating slightly, he stood encompassing them with his sneer.

"Dear, dear," he snickered, "we're very engrossed in watching the wee, troolin' balls. It's a grand, excitin' pastime. We'll be lookin' on at a game o' peever next if we're not careful, like a band o' silly lassies." He paused and queried pertinently: "Who has won, Provost? Will ye tell me—you that's such a grand spokesman for the town?"

"This game's not finished yet," replied Grierson after a moment's hesitation, and still with his eyes averted. The spite which he had once entertained against Brodie now found nothing in the other's wretched condition with which to justify itself and seemed suddenly to have evaporated. Besides, was he not the Provost? "Nobody has won yet," he added more affably.

"This game's not won yet," echoed Brodie sardonically. "Well, well! I'm sorry to hear it. But I can tell ye a game that *is* won!"

He glared round them all and, his anger rising at their indifference, shouted:

"It's the Latta I m talkin' about. Maybe ye think it's like this rotten game of bowls tha t you're watchin'—not finished yet. But I tell you it is finished—finishe d and done wi'—and it's my Nessie that's won it!"

"Hush! man, hush!" exclaimed Gordon, who sat immediately confronted by Brodie. "I can't see the play for ye. Sit down or stand aside and don't blatter the ears off us."

"I'll stand where I like. Shift me if ye can," retorted Brodie dangerously. Then he sneered: "Who are you to talk, anyway? You're only the ex-provost—you're not the king o' the castle any more—it's our dear friend Grierson that's got your shoes on now, and it's him I'm wantin' to speak to." He directed his sneering gaze at Grierson and addressed him: "Did you hear what I said about the Latta, Provost? No! dinna start like that—I havena forgotten about that braw son o' yours. I know well that he's gone up for it. Provost Grierson's son is up for the Latta. God! it must be as good as in his pocket."

"I never said that yet," replied Grierson, provoked in spite of himself. "My boy can take his chance! It's not as if he was needin' the money for his education, onyway."

Brodie ground his teeth at the sharp implication in the other's careless words and tried fiercely to force his brain to contrive some devastating reply, but as always, when opposing Grierson, he could find no suitable expression of his wrath. The thought that he, who had advanced a moment ago in lordly indifference, had been rendered impotent by a word, goaded him, and, sensing also that he was not creating the impression upon them which he had wished, his temper overcame him and he shouted:

"Why did ye ask me to withdraw my daughter if ye didna want your whelp to win it?—Answer me that, you sneakin' swine! You stopped me at the Cross and asked me to keep back my Nessie."

"Tuts! don't shout like that at my ear, man," retorted Grierson coolly. "I don't like the reek o' your breath. I told ye before I was thinkin' of your Nessie. Somebody that's qualified to speak asked me to mention it to ye. I wasna wantin' to do it, and now I'm sorry I did mention it."

"You're a liar!" bawled Brodie. "You're a damned mealy-mouthed liar!"

"If ye've come here to force a quarrel on me, I'll not let ye do it," returned Grierson. "There's no lying about the matter and no secret either. Now that your daughter has gone up, I don't mind tellin' you it was Dr. Renwick asked me to speak to ye."

"Renwick!" exclaimed Brodie incredulously. He paused, then, as a light dawned upon him, he shot out: "I see! I see it plain. You put him up to it. He's hand in glove with you against me. He hates me just as much as do—as much as ye all do." He swept his arm blindly around them. "I know you're all against me, you jealous swine, but I don't care. I'll win through. I'll trample over ye all yet. Have any of ye got a daughter that can win the Latta? Answer me that!"

"If your daughter does win the Latta," cried someone, "what the de'il does it matter to us? Let her get it and good luck to her. I don't give a tinker's curse who wins it."

Brodie gazed at the speaker.

"Ye don't care?" he replied slowly. "Ye do care—you're leein' to me. It'll spite the faces off ye if a Brodie wins the Latta."

"Away home man, for God's sake," said Gordon quietly. "You're not yourself. You're drivellin'. You can't know what you're sayin'."

"I'll go when I like," mumbled Brodie. The stimulation of the drink suddenly left him, his fierceness waned, he no longer desired to rush upon Grierson and tear him apart, and, as he gazed at their varying expressions of unconcern and disgust, he began to feel profoundly sorry for himself, to ask himself if this could be the same company which he had dominated and overawed in the past. They had never liked him but he had controlled them by his power, and now that they had escaped from out his grasp, his sympathy towards himself grew so excessive that it reached the point of an exceeding sorrow which sought almost to express itself in tears. "I see how it is," he muttered gloomily, addressing

447

them at large. "Ye think I'm all over and done wi'. I'm not good enough for ye, now. God! if it didna make me laugh it would make me greet. To think that ye should sit there and look down your noses at me —at me that comes of stock that's so high above ye they wouldna even use ye as doormats." He surveyed them each in turn, looking vainly for some sign of encouragement, some indication that he was impressing them. Then, although no sign came, he still continued, more slowly, and in a dejected, unconvincing tone: "Don't think that I'm finished! I'm comin' up again. Ye can't keep a good man down—and ye'll not keep me down, however much ye may try. Wait and see what my Nessie will do. That'll show ye that stuff that's in us. That's why I came here. I don't want to know ye. I only wanted to tell ye that Nessie Brodie would win the Latta, and now that I've done it I'm satisfied!" His moody eye swept them, then, finding that he had nothing more to say, that they, too, were silent, he moved off; yet after a few paces he arrested himself, turned, opened his mouth to speak; but no speech came, and at length he lowered his head, swung round, and again shambled off. They let him go without a word.

As he left the confines of the Green and proceeded along the road nursing bitterly his wounded pride, he suddenly perceived in the distance the figures of his two daughters approaching him from the station. He stared at them almost stupidly, at Nessie and Mary Brodie, both of them his children, as though the strange sight of them together in the public street confused him, then all at once he realised that Nessie was returning from her examination, that Mary had disobeyed him by meeting the train. No matter! He could deal later with Mary, but now he desired urgently to know how Nessie had fared, to appease his wounded vanity in the knowledge of her success, and, walking forward quickly, he met them, confronted them in the middle of the pavement. There, absorbing eagerly every detail of the younger girl's tired face he cried:

"How did ye get on, Nessie? Quick! tell me—was everything all right?"

"Yes," she murmured. "Everything was all right."

"How many books did ye fill?—was it two or three?"

"Books?" she echoed faintly. "I only wrote in one book, father."

"Only one book!" he exclaimed. "Ye only filled one book for all the time ye've been away." He considered her in astonishment, then, his face slowly hardening, he demanded harshly: "Can ye not speak, woman? Don't ye see I want to know about the Latta. I'm asking you for the last time. Will you tell me once and for all how ye got on?"

With a great effort she controlled herself, looked at him out of her placating eyes and, forcing her pale lips into a smile, cried:

"Splendid, father! I got on splendid. I couldn't have done better."

He stared down at her for a long time, filled by the recollection of the arrogance with which he had proclaimed her success, then he said slowly, in an odd, strained voice:

"I hope ye have done splendid. I hope so! For if ye haven't then, by God! it'll be the pity of ye!"

X

It was the Saturday following that of the examination for the Latta, the time half-past ten in the morning. Nessie Brodie stood looking out of the parlour window with an expression of expectation upon her face mingled, too, by a hidden excitement which made her eyes shine bright and large out of her small face, as though they awaited the appearance of some sudden, thrilling manifestation in the empty roadway that lay before them. The face, despite its ingenuous weakness, wore something of an unguarded look, for the consciousness that she was alone in the room and unobserved allowed a freer and more unrestrained display of these emotions that she had carefully concealed during the course of the past, uneasy week.

During that week her father's attitude to her had been insupportable, alternating between a fond complacency and a manner so disturbing and threatening that it terrified her; yet she had borne it, comforting herself in the knowledge that she possessed a strategy more subtle, more effective than all his bluster and his bullying. She thought she had won the Latta, had experienced, indeed, with the passage of each of the seven days since the examination, a growing certainty that she had won it. It was impossible that all her work, the compulsory toil, all these long, cold hours of endurance in this same parlour could go unrewarded, and, although a feeling of dissatisfaction with her own paper had possessed her when she left the University last week, now her confidence was completely restored; she felt that she must have taken the Bursary —to use her father's phrase—in her stride. Still, there was always the chance, the faint unreasonable chance that she might not have been successful! It was unthinkable, impossible, yet it was against this chance that by some strange, astute working of her mind she had so cleverly formulated her precaution. They thought, both Mary and her father, that the result of the Latta would not be announced for another week —she had told them so and they had believed her—but she knew better than that, knew that the result would reach her this morning. She was expecting it immediately, for the forenoon delivery of letters at eleven o'clock contained the Glasgow mail, and from enquiries which she had made at the University she knew that the results of the examination had been posted to each competitor on the evening of the day before. She smiled slyly, even now, at the consideration of her own cleverness in deluding them all. It had been a brilliant idea, and daring too—not unlike the sudden sending of that letter to Mary—yet she had accomplished it. Her father had so crushed and oppressed her with the preparation for the examination that she had wanted room to breathe, space to think; and now she had contrived it for herself. It was a triumph. She had a whole week to herself before he would demand threateningly to see the evidence of her success, an entire week during which she could think and cleverly contrive some means of escape from him should she have failed. But she had not failed—she had succeeded—and, instead of using every moment of that precious week to prepare herself against her father's anger, she would treat it like a hidden happiness, treasuring her secret until she could no longer contain it, then delivering it unexpectedly, triumphantly, upon their astounded ears. They would not know until she enlightened them; nobody must know, not even Mary, who had been so good, so kind and loving to her. Surely she should have told Mary? No! That would have spoiled the entire plan. When she did speak she would tell her first, but now everything must be kept secret and sealed within her own mind; she wanted no one peering over her shoulders when she opened that letter, she must be alone, secluded from prying glances that might watch the trembling of her fingers or the eagerness of her eyes.

As she stood there, suddenly she started, and a faint tremor passed over her as she observed an indistinct blue figure at the foot of the road —the postman, who would, in the slow regularity of his routine, reach her within the space of half an hour. In half an hour she would be receiving the letter, must, moreover, be alone to receive it undisturbed! With an effort she withdrew her eyes from the distant figure of the postman and involuntarily, almost automatically, turned and advanced to the door, altering her expression, so that her features lost their revealing look, became secretive, blank, then drew slowly into a frown. This troubled frown intensified as she entered the kitchen and went up to Mary when, pressing her hand against her brow, she exclaimed wearily:

"That headache is on me again, Mary! Worse than ever this time."

Mary looked at her sister sympathetically.

"My poor, wee Nessie!" she exclaimed. "I'm sorry about that! I thought you had got rid of them for good."

"No! No!" cried Nessie, "it's come back. It's hurting me—give me one of my powders, quick!"

From under the cover of her hand she watched Mary as she went to the white cardboard box that stood always on the mantelpiece, observed her open the box and discover that it was empty, then heard her exclaim, condolingly:

"They're all finished, I'm afraid! I'm sorry, dear! I was sure you had one or two left."

"Finished?" exclaimed Nessie. "That's terrible. I can't do without them. My head's bursting. I must have one at once."

Mary looked at her sister's lowered face with solicitude, as she remarked:

"What can I do for you, dear? Would you like a cold cloth and vinegar on it?"

"I told you these were no good," cried Nessie urgently. "You'll need to get me a powder. Go out this very minute for me."

Mary's expression grew doubtful and, after a pause, she said:

"I can hardly go out just now, dearie. There's the dinner to make and everything. Lie down a little and I'll rub your head."

"Away and get the powder," the other burst out. "Can ye not do that one, little thing for me—you that's aye sayin' you want to help me? I'll not be right till I get one—ye know that it's the only thing that eases me."

After a moment's hesitation during which she gazed compassionately at Nessie, Mary moved her hands slowly to the strings of her apron, and untied them even more slowly.

"All right, dear! I can't see you suffer like that. I'll go and get them made up for you right away"; then, as she went out of the room, she added sympathetically: "I'll not be a minute. Lie down and rest till I come back."

Nessie lay down obediently, realising with an inward satisfaction that the minute would be a full hour, that she would have ample time to receive her letter and compose herself again before Mary could make the journey to the town, wait tediously at the chemist's for the compounding of the prescription, and return to her. She smiled faintly as she heard the front door close behind her sister; and this smile again unlocked her restraint, for that strangely artful expression returned to her face and she jumped up and ran eagerly into the parlour.

Yes! there was Mary going down the road, hurrying—the poor thing—to secure the powders, as though there were not two still in the house hidden in the dresser drawer, and passing actually, without a sign, the postman as he made his way towards her. He had something in his bag that would bring more relief than all the powders that Lawrie could ever give her. How slow he was, though! It was, she perceived, Dan, the elder of the two postmen who came upon this round, and the very one who used to hand in Matt's letters with such an air of consequential dignity, exclaiming importantly:

"Something worth while in that one by the look o' it." No letter of Matt's had ever been so important as this one! Why did he not hurry?

As she remained there, she felt vaguely that under the same circumstances of excitement and anticipation she had once before stood at this window in the parlour, and she became aware suddenly, without consciously seeking in her mind, that it had been on that day when Mamma had received the wire that had so upset her. She recollected the delicious thrill it had given her to hold the orange slip within her hand and remembered, too, how cleverly she had manœuvred to ascertain the ignorance of Grandma Brodie upon the matter. Now she did not fear that her letter would be discovered by the old woman who, half blind and almost wholly deaf, kept to her room except when the call of meal-times withdrew her from it.

Dan was getting nearer, leisurely crossing and recrossing the street, hobbling along as though he had corns upon every toe, wearing his heavy bag on his bent back like a packman. Still, how slow he was! Yet now, strangely, she did not wish quite so ardently that he should hurry, but rather that he should take his time, and leave her letter till the last. Everybody in the road seemed to be getting letters to-day, and all, as she desired, before she received hers. Would John Grierson have had his yet? Much good it would do him if he had. She would have liked dearly to see the chawed look upon his face when he opened it. As for herself, she did not now want a letter at all; it was upsetting, and she knew so well she had won the Latta that it was not worth the trouble of opening an envelope to confirm it. Some envelopes were difficult to open!

Yet here was Dan actually advancing to her house, causing her to tremble all over, making her gasp as he passed the gate carelessly—as if aware that there could now be no letters for the Brodies—then, as he stopped suddenly and returned, sending her heart leaping violently into her throat.

An age passed before the door bell rang; but it did ring and she was compelled, whether she now wished it or not, to pull herself away from the window and advance to the door—not with the skipping eagerness that she had displayed when fetching the telegram—but slowly—with a strange detached sense of unreality—as though she still stood by the window and watched her own form move deliberately from the room.

The letter, long, stiff, and important, with a blue shield upon the back, was in Dan's hand and her gaze became fixed upon it as she stood, unconscious of the smile which crinkled his veined, russet cheek and showed his tobacco-stained teeth, almost unconscious of the old postman himself—yet dimly hearing him say, even as she expected: "Something worth while in that one, by the look o' it."

Now it was her hand which was cognisant of the letter, her fingers sensitively perceiving the rich, coarse texture of the paper, her eyes observing the thin, copper-plate inscription of her own name which ran accurately across the centre of its white surface. How long she regarded her name she did not know, but when she looked up Dan had gone, without her having thanked him or even spoken to him, and, as she glanced along the vacant roadway, she felt a vague regret at her lack of courtesy, considered that she must make amends to him in some fashion, perhaps apologise or give him some tobacco for his Christmas box. But first she must open this that he had given her.

She turned, closing the door behind her, and, realising that she need not return to that dismal parlour which she hated so much, traversed the hall without a sound and entered the empty kitchen. There she immediately rid her hand of the letter by placing it upon the table. Then she returned to the door by which she had just entered, satisfied herself that it was firmly shut, advanced to the scullery door, which she inspected in like fashion, and finally, as though at last convinced of her perfect seclusion, came back and seated herself at the table. Everything was as she desired it, everything had befallen as she had so cleverly foreseen, and now, alone, unobserved, concealed, with nothing more to do, nothing for which to wait, she was free to open the letter.

Her eye fell upon it again, not fixedly, as when she had received it, but with a growing, flickering agitation. Her lips suddenly felt stiff, her mouth dried up, and she shook violently from head to foot. She perceived—not the long, white oblong of the letter—but her own form, bent eternally over a book, at school, at home, in the examination hall of the University, and always overcast by the massive figure of her father, which lay above and upon her like a perpetual shadow. The letter seemed to mirror her own face which looked up, movingly, telling her that all she had worked for, all she had been constrained to work for, that the whole object of her life, lay there, upon the table, crystallised in a few written words upon one hidden sheet of paper.

Her name was upon the envelope, and the same name must be upon that hidden sheet within, or else everything that she had done, her very life itself, would be futile. She knew that her name was inside, the single name that was always sent without mention of the failures, the name of the winner of the Latta, and yet she was afraid to view it.

That, clearly, was ridiculous! She need not be afraid of her name which, as her father rightly insisted, was a splendid name, a noble name, and one of which she might justly be proud. She was Nessie Brodie— she was the winner of the Latta! It had all been arranged months beforehand, everything had been settled between her father and herself. My! but she was the clever, wee thing—the smartest lass in Levenford— the first girl to win the Bursary—a credit to the name of Brodie! As in a dream her hand stole towards the letter.

How curious that her fingers should tremble in this strange fashion as, under her own eyes, they opened the stiff envelope. How thin her fingers were! She had not willed them to open the letter and yet they had done so; even now they held the inner sheet in their faintly trembling clasp.

Well! she must see her name—the name of Nessie Brodie. That, surely, was no hardship—to view for one moment her own name. That moment had come!

With a heart that beat suddenly with a frantic, unendurable agitation she unfolded the sheet and looked at it.

The name which met her shrinking gaze was not hers—it was the name of Grierson. John Grierson had won the Latta!

For a second she regarded the paper without comprehension, then her eyes filled with a growing horror, which widened her pupils until the words before her blurred together then faded from her view. She sat motionless, rigid, scarcely breathing, the paper still within her grasp, and into her ears flowed a torrent of words, uttered in her father's snarling voice. She was alone in the room, he at the office a mile away —yet in her tortured imagination she heard him, saw him vividly before her.

"Grierson's won it! You've let that upstart brat beat you. It wouldna have mattered so much if it had been anybody else—but Grierson— the son o' that measly swine. And after all I've talked about ye winnin' it. It's damnable! damnable, I tell ye! You senseless idiot—after the way I've slaved with ye, keepin' ye at it for all I was worth! God! I canna thole it. I'll wring that thin neck o' yours for ye."

She sank deeper into her chair, shrinking from his invisible presence, her eyes still horrified, but cowering too, as though he advanced upon her with his huge open hands. Still she remained motionless, even her lips did not move, but she heard herself cry, feebly:

"I did my best, father. I could do no more. Don't touch me, father."

"Your best," he hissed. "Your best wasna good enough to beat Grierson. You that swore ye had the Latta in your pocket! I've got to sit down under another insult because of ye. I'll pay ye. I told ye it would be the pity of ye if ye failed."

"No! No! father," she whispered. "I didn't mean to fail. I'll not do it again—I promise you! You know I've always been the top of the class. I've always been your own Nessie. You wouldna hurt a wee thing like me. I'll do better next time."

"There'll be no next time for you," he shouted at her. "I'll—I'll throttle ye for what you've done to me."

As he rushed upon her she saw that he was going to kill her and, while she shrieked, closing her eyes in a frantic, unbelievable terror, the encircling band that had bound her brain for the last weary months of her study snapped suddenly and gave to her a calm and perfect peace. The tightness around her head dissolved, she was unloosed from the bonds that had confined her, her fear vanished, and she was free. She opened her eyes, saw that her father was no longer there, and smiled— an easy, amused smile which played over her mobile features like ripples of light and passed insensibly into a high, snickering laugh. Though her laughter was not loud, it moved her like a paroxysm, making the tears roll down her cheeks and shaking her thin body with its utter abandon. She laughed for a long time then, as suddenly as her mirth had begun it ceased, her tears dried instantly, and her face assumed a wise, crafty expression like a gigantic magnification of that slight artfulness which it had worn when she stood thinking in the parlour. Now, however, clearly guided by a force within her, she did not think; she was above the necessity for thought. Pressing her lips into a prim line, she laid the letter, which had all this time remained within her grasp, carefully upon the table like a precious thing, and rising from her chair stood, casting her gaze up and down, moving her head like a nodding doll. When the nodding ceased, a smile, transient this time, flickered across her face and whispering softly, encouragingly to herself: "What ye do, ye maun do well, Nessie dear," she turned and went tiptoeing out of the room. She ascended the stairs with the same silent and extravagant caution, paused in a listening attitude upon the landing, then, reassured, went mincing into her room. There, without hesitation, she advanced to the basin and ewer, poured out some cold water and began carefully to wash her face and hands. When she had washed meticulously, she dried herself, shining her pale features to a high polish by her assiduous application of the towel, then, taking off her old, grey beige dress she took from her drawer the clean cashmere frock which was her best. This, apparently, did not now wholly please her, for she shook her head and murmured:

"That's not pretty enough for ye, Nessie dear. Not near pretty enough for ye, now!" Still, she put it on with the same unhurried precision, and her face lightened again as she lifted her hands to her hair. As she unplaited it and brushed it quickly with long, rapid strokes she whispered, from time to time, softly, approvingly: "My bonnie hair! My bonnie, bonnie hair!" Satisfied at last with the fine, golden sheen which her brushing had produced, she stood before the mirror and regarded herself with a far away, enigmatical smile; then, taking her only adornment, a small string of coral beads, once given her by Mamma to compensate for Matthew's forgetfulness, she made as though to place them round her neck when, suddenly, she withdrew the hand that held them. "They're gey and sharp, these beads," she murmured, and laid them back gently upon her table.

Without further loss of time she marched softly out of her room, descended the stairs, and in the hall put on her serge jacket and her straw hat with the brave, new, satin ribbon that Mary had bought and sewn for her. She was now dressed completely for the street—in her best—dressed, indeed, as she had been on the day of the examination. But she did not go out of the house; instead, she slid stealthily back into the kitchen.

Here her actions quickened. Taking hold of one of the heavy wooden chairs, she moved it accurately into the centre of the room, then turned to her heaped books upon the dresser and transferred these to the chair, making a neat, firm pile which she surveyed with a pleased expression, adjusting some slight deviations from the regular symmetry of the heap with light, fastidious touches of her fingers. "That's a real neat job, my dear," she murmured contentedly. "You're a woman that would have worked well in the house." Even as she spoke she moved backwards from the chair, still admiring her handiwork, but when she reached the door she turned and slipped lightly into the scullery. Here she bent and rummaged in the clothes basket at the window, then, straightening up with an exclamation of triumph, she returned to the kitchen bearing something in her hand. It was a short length of clothes line. Now her movements grew even more rapid. Her nimble fingers worked feverishly with one end of the thin rope, she leaped on the chair and, standing upon the piled books, corded the other end over the iron hook of the pulley on the ceiling. Then, without descending from the chair, she picked up the letter from the table and pinned it upon her bosom, muttering as she did so: "First prize, Nessie! What a pity it's not a red card." Finally, she inserted her neck delicately into the noose which she had fashioned, taking heed that she did not disarrange her hat and, passing the rope carefully under the mane of her hair, tightened it and was ready. She stood gaily poised upon the elevation of the books like a child perched upon a sand castle, her gaze directed eagerly out of the window across the foliage of the lilac tree. As her eyes sought the distant sky beyond, her foot, resting upon the back of the chair, pushed the support from beneath her, and she fell. The hook in the ceiling wrenched violently upon the beam above which still securely held it. The rope strained, but did not break. She hung suspended, twitching like a marionette upon a string, while her body, elongating, seemed to stretch out desperately one dangling foot, straining to reach the floor, yet failing by a single inch to reach it. The hat tilted grotesquely across her brow, her face darkened slowly as the cord bit into her thin, white neck; her eyes that were placating, pleading even, and blue like speedwells, clouded with pain, with a faint wonder, then slowly glazed; her lips purpled, thickened, and fell apart, her small jaw dropped, a thin stream of froth ran silently across her chin. To and fro she oscillated gently, swinging in the room in a silence broken only by the faint flutter of the lilac leaves against the window panes, until, at last, her body quivered faintly and was still.

The house was silent, as with the silence of consummation, but after a long hush the sound was heard of some person stirring above, and slowly, haltingly, descending the stairs. At length the kitchen door opened and Grandma Brodie came into the room. Drawn from her room by the approach of another meal-time and the desire to make herself some

456

especially soft toast, she now tottered forward, her head lowered, totally unobservant, until she blundered against the body.

"Tch! Tch! where am I going?" she mumbled, as she recoiled, mazedly looking upwards out of dim eyes at the hanging figure which the thrust of her arm had once more set in motion, and which now swung lightly against her. Her aged face puckered incredulously as she peered, fell suddenly agape and, as the body of the dead girl again touched her, she staggered back and screamed: "Oh! God in heaven! What—what is't?—She's—she's——" Another scream rent her! Mouthing incoherently, she turned, shambled from the room, and flinging open the front door, stumbled headlong from the house.

Her agitated gait had taken her through the courtyard and into the roadway when, turning to continue her flight, she collided with and almost fell into the arms of Mary, who gazed at her in some distress, and cried:

"What's the matter, Grandma? Are you ill?"

The old woman looked at her, her face working, her sunken lips twitching, her tongue speechless.

"What's wrong with you, Grandma?" repeated Mary in amazement. "Are you not well?"

"There! In there!" stuttered the other, pointing her stark hand wildly to the house. "Nessie! Nessie's in there! She's—she's hangit herself—in the kitchen."

Mary's glance leaped to the house, observed the open door; with a stricken cry she rushed past the old woman, and, still holding the white box of headache powders in her hand, flung herself up the steps, along the lobby, and into the kitchen.

"O God!" she cried, "my Nessie!" She dropped the box she carried, tore out the drawer of the dresser, and, snatching a knife, turned and hacked furiously at the tense rope. In a second this parted, and the warm body of Nessie sagged soundlessly against her and trailed upon the floor. "O God!" she cried again. "Spare her to me. We've only got each other left. Don't let her die!" Flinging her arms around her dead sister, she lowered her to the ground; throwing herself upon her knees, with trembling fingers she plucked at the cord sunk in the swollen neck and finally unloosed it. She beat the hands of the body. stroked the brow, cried inarticulately, in a voice choked by sobs: "Speak to me, Nessie! I love you, dearest sister! Don't leave me." But no reply came from those parted, inanimate lips and in an agony of despair Mary leaped to her feet and rushed again out of the house into the roadway. Looking wildly about, she espied a boy upon a bicycle bearing down on her.

"Stop!" she cried, waving her arms frantically; and as he drew up wonderingly beside her she pressed her hand to her side and gasped, her words tumbling one upon another: "Get a doctor! Get Dr. Renwick!

Quick! My sister is ill! Go quickly! Quickly!" She sped him from her with a last cry and, returning to the house, she rushed for water, knelt again, raised Nessie in her arms, moistened the turgid lips, tried to make her drink. Then, laying the flaccid head upon a cushion, she sponged the dark face, murmuring brokenly:

"Speak to me, dearest Nessie! I want you to live! I want you to live! I should never have left you, but oh! why did you send me away?"

When she had sponged the face she knew of nothing more to do and remained upon her knees beside the prostrate form, tears streaming down her cheeks, her hands pressed distractedly together.

She was kneeling thus when hurried footsteps came through the still open door and Renwick entered the room. He failed at first to observe Nessie's body which was masked by her kneeling form, and seeing only her, stood still, crying in a loud voice:

"Mary! what is wrong?"

But, coming forward, he dropped his gaze, saw the figure upon the floor and in a flash knelt down beside her. His hands moved rapidly over the body while she watched him dumbly, agonisingly, then after a moment he raised his eyes to her across the form of her sister and said, slowly:

"Don't kneel any longer, Mary! Let me—let me put her on the sofa."

She knew then from his tone that Nessie was dead, and while he lifted the body on to the sofa she stood up, her lips quivering, her breast torn by the throbbing anguish of her heart.

"I'm to blame," she whispered brokenly. "I went out to get her headache powders."

He turned from the couch and looked at her gently.

"It's not you that is to blame, Mary! You did everything for her."

"Why did she do it?" she sobbed. "I loved her so much. I wanted to protect her."

"I know that well! She must have lost her reason, poor child," he replied sadly. "Poor, frightened child."

"I would have done anything in life for her," she whispered. "I would have died for her."

He looked at her, her pale face ravaged by her grief, thinking of her past, her present sadness, of the grey uncertainty of her future, and as he gazed into her swimming eyes, an overwhelming emotion possessed him also. Like a spring which had lain deeply buried for long years and now welled suddenly to light, his feelings gushed over him in a rushing flow. His heart swelled at her grief and, swept by the certain knowledge that he could never leave her, he advanced to her, saying in a low voice:

"Mary! don't cry, dear. I love you."

She looked at him blindly through her tears as he drew near to her and in an instant she was in his arms.

458

"You'll not stay here, dear," he whispered. "You'll come with me, now. I want you to be my wife." He comforted her as she lay sobbing in his arms, telling her how he must have loved her from that moment when first he saw her, yet never known it till now.

While they remained thus, suddenly a loud voice addressed them, breaking upon them with an incredulous yet ferocious intensity.

"Damnation! what is the meaning of this in my house?" It was Brodie. Framed in the doorway, his view of the sofa blocked by the open door, he stood still, glaring at them, his eyes starting from his head in rage and wonder. "So this is your fancy man," he cried savagely, advancing into the room. "This is who these bonnie black grapes came from. I wondered who it might be, but by God! I didna think it was this —this fine gentleman."

At these words, Mary winced and would have withdrawn from Renwick but he restrained her and, keeping his arm around her, gazed fixedly at Brodie.

"Don't come that high and mighty look over me," sneered Brodie, with a short, hateful laugh. "You can't pull the wool over my eyes. It's me that's got the whip hand o' you this time. You're a bonnie pillar of the town right enough, to come to a man's house and make a brothel o't."

In answer Renwick drew himself up more rigidly, slowly raised his arm, and pointed to the sofa.

"You are in the presence of death," he said.

Despite himself, Brodie's eyes fell under the coldness of the other's gaze.

"Are ye mad? You're all mad here," he muttered. But he turned to follow the direction of the other's finger and as he saw the body of Nessie he started, stumbled forward. "What—what's this?" he cried dazedly. "Nessie! Nessie!"

Renwick led Mary to the door and, as she clung to him, he paused and cried sternly:

"Nessie hanged herself in this kitchen because she lost the Latta and, in the sight of God, you are responsible for her death." Then, taking Mary with him he drew her out of the room and they passed together out of the house.

Brodie did not hear them go, but, stunned by Renwick's last words and by the strange stillness of the figure before him, he muttered:

"They're tryin' to frighten me! Wake up, Nessie! It's your father that's speakin' to ye. Come on, pettie, wake up!" Putting forward his hand haltingly, to shake her, he perceived the paper on her breast and, seizing it, he plucked it from her dress and raised it tremulously to his eyes.

"Grierson!" he whispered, in a stricken voice. "Grierson's got it. She did lose it then!"

The paper dropped from his hand and involuntarily his glance fell upon her neck, marked by a livid red weal. Even as he saw it, he touched again her inert, flaccid form and his face grew livid like the weal upon her white skin.

"God!" he muttered. "She has—she has hanged herself." He covered his eyes as though unable to bear the sight longer. "My God," he mumbled again, "she has—she has——" And then, as though he panted for breath, "I was fond of my Nessie." A heavy groan burst from his breast. Staggering like a drunken man he backed blindly from the body, and sank unconsciously into his chair. A rush of dry sobs racked him, rending his breast in anguish. With his head sunk into his hands he remained thus, his tortured mind filled by one obsessing thought, yet traversed by other fleeting thoughts, by an endless stream of images which slipped past the central figure of his dead daughter like a procession of shadows floating round a recumbent body on a catafalque.

He saw his son and Nancy, together in the sunshine, saw the drooping form and pathetically inclined head of his wife, the sneering face of Grierson mocking at his distress, Renwick holding Mary in his arms, the bold figure of young Foyle bearding him in his office; he saw the obsequious Perry, Blair, Paxton, Gordon, even Dron—they all marched silently before his shuttered eyes, all with heads averted from him, all condemning him, their eyes turned sadly to the body of his Nessie as she reposed upon the bier.

As though unable to bear longer the torment of these inward visions he raised his head from his hands, uncovered his eyes, and looked furtively towards the sofa. At once his eyes fell upon the thin arm of the dead child as it hung over the edge of the couch—limp, pendent, immobile, the pale waxen fingers of the hand drooping from the small palm. With a shudder he raised his eyes and looked blindly out of the window. As he sat thus the door opened slowly and his mother came into the room. Her recent terror had faded from her senile mind—the whole sad event lost in the maunderings of her doting brain—and now, tottering to her chair, she seated herself opposite her son. Her eyes sought him as she sounded his mood with her dim gaze, then, sensing his silence to be propitious, she muttered:

"I think I'll make myself a bit soft toast." At this she rose—oblivious to all but her own needs—hobbled to the scullery and, returning again, sat down and began to toast the slice of bread she had obtained. "I can soak it in my broth," she muttered to herself, sucking in her cheeks. "It suits my stomach brawly that way." Then, as she again looked at her son across the fireplace, she noticed at last the strangeness of his eyes, her head shook agitatedly, and she exclaimed:

"You're not angry wi' me, are ye, James? I'm just makin' myself some nice, soft toast. I was aye fond o't ye ken. I'll make you a bit yoursel', gin ye want it," and she tittered uneasily, propitiatingly, across at him with a senile, senseless sound that broke the heavy silence of the room. But he did not reply, and still gazed stonily out of the window, where the warm summer wind moved gently amongst the thin leaves of the straggling bushes that fringed his garden. The breeze freshened, disporting itself amongst the shoots of the currant bushes then, circling, it touched the leaves of the three, tall, serene, silver trees, flickering them dark and light with a soft caress, when suddenly, striking the house, it chilled, and passed quickly onwards to the beauty of the Winton Hills beyond.

THE END

THE CITADEL

TO MY WIFE

NOTE

Every character, place and institution in this book
is entirely fictitious and no reference whatever is
intended to any living person.

PART I

I

LATE ONE October afternoon in the year 1924 a shabby young man gazed with fixed intensity through the window of a third class compartment in the almost empty train labouring up the Penowell Valley from Swansea. All that day Manson had travelled from the North, changing at Carlisle and Shrewsbury, yet the final stage of his tedious journey to South Wales found him strung to a still greater excitement by the prospects of his post, the first of his medical career, in this strange, disfigured country.

Outside, a heavy rainstorm came blinding down between the mountains which rose on either side of the single railway track. The mountain tops were hidden in a grey waste of sky but their sides, scarred by ore workings, fell black and desolate, blemished by great heaps of slag on which a few dirty sheep wandered in vain hope of pasture. No bush, no blade of vegetation was visible. The trees, seen in the fading light, were gaunt and stunted spectres. At a bend of the line the red glare of a foundry flashed into sight, illuminating a score of workmen stripped to the waist, their torsos straining, arms upraised to strike. Though the scene was swiftly lost behind the huddled top gear of a mine, a sense of power persisted, tense and vivid. Manson drew a long breath. He felt an answering surge of effort, a sudden overwhelming exhilaration springing from the hope and promise of the future.

Darkness had fallen, emphasising the strangeness and remoteness of the scene when, half an hour later, the engine panted into Drineffy. He had arrived at last. Gripping his bag, Manson leaped from the train and walked quickly down the platform, searching eagerly for some sign of welcome. At the station exit, beneath a wind-blown lamp, a yellow-faced old man in a square hat and a long nightshirt of a mackintosh stood waiting. He inspected Manson with a jaundiced eye and his voice, when it came, was reluctant.

"You Doctor Page's new assistant?"

"That's right. Manson. Andrew Manson is the name!"

"Huh! Mine's Thomas, Old Thomas they mostly call me, dang 'em. I got the gig here. Set in—unless you'd rayther swim."

Manson slung his bag up and climbed into the battered gig behind a tall angular black horse. Thomas followed, took the reins and addressed the horse.

"Hue-up, Taffy!" he said.

They drove off through the town which, though Andrew tried keenly to discern its outline, presented in the lashing rain no more than a blurred huddle of low grey houses ranged beneath the high and ever present mountains. For several minutes the old groom did not speak but continued to dart pessimistic glances at Andrew from beneath the dripping brim of his hat. He bore no resemblance to the smart coachman of a successful doctor but was, on the contrary, wizened and slovenly, and all the time he gave off a peculiar yet powerful odour of the stable. At last he said:

"Only jest got your parchment, eh?"

Andrew nodded.

"I knowed it." Old Thomas spat. His triumph made him more gravely communicative. "Last assistant went ten days ago. Mostly they don't stop."

"Why?" Despite his nervousness, Andrew smiled.

"Work's too hard for one thing, I reckon."

"And for another?"

"You'll find out!" A moment later, as a guide might indicate a fine cathedral, Thomas lifted his whip and pointed to the end of a row of houses, where, from a small lighted doorway a cloud of steam was emerging. "See that. That there's the missus and my little homestead. She takes in washin' like." A secret amusement twitched his long upper lip. "Reckon you might want to know, shortly."

Here the main street ended and, turning up a short uneven side-road, they boggled across a piece of pit ground, and entered the narrow drive of a house which stood amongst the adjacent rows behind a stunted ash tree. On the gate was the name Bryngower.

"This is us," said Thomas, pulling up the horse.

Andrew descended. The next minute, while he gathered himself for the ordeal of his entrance, the front door was flung open and he was in the lighted hall being welcomed cordially by a tall, spare, smiling woman of about fifty with a calm face and clear blue eyes.

"Well! well! This must be Doctor Manson. Come in, please, come in. I'm doctor's sister, Miss Page. I do hope you didn't have a tryin' journey. I *am* pleased to see you. I been out my mind, nearly, since that last awful fellow we had left us. You ought to have seen him. He was a bright one if ever I met one, I can tell you. Oh! but never mind. It's all right now you're here. Come along, I'll show you to your room myself."

Upstairs, Andrew's room was a small camsiled apartment with a brass bed, a yellow varnished chest of drawers and a bamboo table bearing a basin and ewer. Glancing round it, while her clear blue eyes searched his face, he said with anxious politeness:

"This looks very comfortable, Miss Page."

468

"Yes, indeed." She smiled and patted his shoulder maternally. "You'll do famous here, I'm sure. You treat me right and I'll treat you right. I can't say fairer nor that, can I? Now come along before you're a minute older and meet doctor." She paused, her gaze still questioning his, her tone striving to be off-hand. "I don't know if I said so in my letter but, as a matter of fact—doctor hasn't been too well, lately."

Andrew looked at her in sudden surprise.

"Oh, it's nothing much," she went on quickly, before he could speak. "He's been laid up a few weeks. But he'll soon be all right. Make no mistake about that."

Perplexed, Andrew followed her to the end of the passage where she threw open a door, exclaiming blithely:

"Here's Doctor Manson, Edward—our new assistant. He's come to say 'ow do."

As Andrew went into the room, a long fustily furnished bedroom with chenille curtains closely drawn and a small fire burning in the grate, Edward Page turned slowly upon the bed, seeming to do so by a great effort. He was a big, bony man of perhaps sixty with harshly lined features and tired, luminous eyes. His whole expression was stamped with suffering and a kind of weary patience. And there was something more. The light of the oil lamp, falling across the pillow, revealed one half of his face expressionless and waxen. The left side of his body was equally paralysed and his left hand, which lay upon the patchwork counterpane, was contracted to a shiny cone. Observing these signs of a severe and far from recent stroke, Andrew was conscious of a sudden shock of dismay There was an odd silence.

"I hope you'll like it here," Doctor Page remarked at length, speaking slowly and with difficulty, slurring his words a little, "I hope you'll find the practice won't be too much for you. You're very young."

"I'm twenty-four, sir," Andrew answered awkwardly. "I know this is the first job I've had, and all that—but I'm not afraid of work."

"There, now!" Miss Page smiled. "Didn't I tell you, Edward, we'd be lucky with our next one."

An even deeper immobility settled on Page's face. He gazed at Andrew. Then his interest seemed to fade. He said in a tired voice:

"I hope you'll stay."

"My goodness gracious!" cried Miss Page. "What a thing to say!" She turned to Andrew, smilingly and apologetic. "It's only because he's a morsel down to-day. But he'll soon be up and doing again. Won't you, my dear?" Bending, she kissed her brother fondly. "There now! I'll send your supper up by Annie whenever we've had ours."

Page did not answer. The stony look on his one-sided face made his mouth seem twisted. His good hand strayed to the book that lay on the table beside his bed. Andrew saw that it was entitled *The Wild Birds of*

Europe. Even before the paralysed man began to read he felt himself dismissed.

As Andrew went down to supper his thoughts were painfully confused. He had applied for this assistantship in answer to an advertisement in the *Lancet.* Yet in the correspondence, conducted at this end by Miss Page, which had led to his securing the post, there had been no mention whatsoever of Doctor Page's illness. But Page was ill, there could be no question of the gravity of the cerebral hæmorrhage which had incapacitated him. It would be months before he was fit for work, if, indeed, he were ever fit for work again.

With an effort Andrew put the puzzle from his mind. He was young, strong, and had no objection to the extra work in which Page's illness might involve him. Indeed, in his enthusiasm, he yearned for an avalanche of calls.

"You're lucky, doctor," remarked Miss Page brightly as she came into the dining-room. "You can have your bit of snap straight off to-night. No surgery. Dai Jenkins done it."

"Dai Jenkins?"

"He's our dispenser," Miss Page threw out casually. "A handy little feller. And willin' too. 'Doc' Jenkins some folks even call him, though of course he's not to be compared in the same breath with Doctor Page. He's done the surgery and visits also, these last ten days."

Andrew stared at her in fresh concern. All that he had been told, all the warnings he had received regarding the questionable ways of practice in these remote Welsh valleys flashed into his recollection. Again it cost him an effort to be silent.

Miss Page sat at the head of the table with her back to the fire. When she had wedged herself comfortably into her chair with a cushion she sighed in pleasant anticipation and tinkled the little cow-bell in front of her. A middle-aged servant with a pale, well-scrubbed face brought in the supper, stealing a glance at Andrew as she entered.

"Come along, Annie," cried Miss Page, buttering a wedge of soft bread and placing it in her mouth. "This is Doctor Manson."

Annie did not answer. She served Andrew in a contained, silent fashion with a slice of cold boiled brisket. Miss Page had a cut from the same joint with, in addition, a pint of fresh milk. As she poured out the innocuous beverage and lifted it to her lips, her eyes upon him, she explained:

"I didn't have much lunch, doctor. Besides, I have to watch my diet. It's the blood. I have to take a drop of milk for my blood."

Andrew chewed the uninteresting brisket and drank cold water determinedly. Following a momentary dissatisfaction, his main difficulty lay with his own sense of humour. After all, he could not expect to find luxury upon the tables of these spartan valleys.

During the meal Miss Page ate in silence. At length, buttering her last crust of bread, she finished her meat, wiped her lips after the last of the milk and sat back in her chair, her thin figure relaxed, her eyes reserved, appraising. Now she seemed disposed to linger at table, inclined to confidences, perhaps trying in her own way, to sum Manson up.

Studying him, she saw a spare and gawky youngster, dark, rather tensely drawn, with high cheekbones, a fine jaw and blue eyes. These eyes, when he raised them, were, despite the nervous tensity of his brow, extraordinarily steady and inquiring. Although Blodwen Page knew nothing of it, she was looking at a Celtic type. Though she admitted the vigour and alert intelligence in Andrew's face, what pleased her most of all was his acceptance, without demur, of that cut from the three days' old heel of brisket. She reflected that, though he looked hungry, he might not be hard to feed.

"I'm sure we'll get on famous, you and me," she again declared with quite a genial air. "We do need a bit of luck for a change." Mellowed, she told him of her troubles and sketched a vague outline of the practice and its position. "It's been awful, my dear. You don't know. What with Doctor Page's illness, wicked bad assistants, nothin' comin' in and everythin' goin' out—well! you wouldn't believe it! And the job I've had to keep the manager and mine officials sweet—it's them the practice money comes through—what there is of it," she added with a shrug. "You see, the way they work things in Drineffy is like this—the Company has three doctors on its list, though, mind you, Doctor Page is far and away the cleverest doctor of the lot. And besides—the time he's been here! nearly thirty years and more, that's something I should think! Well, then, these doctors can have as many assistants as they like —Doctor Page has you, and Doctor Nicholls has a would-be fellow called Denny—but the assistants don't ever get on the Company's list. Anyway, as I was saying, the Company deducts so much from every man's wages they employ at the mines and the quarries and pays that out to the listed doctors according to how many of the men signs on with them."

She broke off, gazing at him quizzically.

"I think I see how the system works, Miss Page."

"Well, then!" She gave out her short laugh. "You don't have to bother about it any more. All you've got to remember is that you're working for Doctor Page. That's the main thing, doctor. Just remember you're workin' for Doctor Page and you and I will get on a treat."

It seemed to Manson, silent and observant, that she felt she had unbent too far. With a glance at the clock, she straightened herself, restored her napkin to its horn ring. Then she rose. Her voice was different, businesslike.

"By the way, there's a call for Number Seven Glydar Place. It came in the back of five o'clock. You better do it straight away."

II

Andrew went out to the call immediately, with a queer sensation, almost of relief. He was glad of the opportunity to disentangle himself from the curious and conflicting emotions stirred up by his arrival at Bryngower. Already he had a glimmer of a suspicion as to how matters stood and of how he would be called upon by Blodwen Page to run the practice for his disabled principal. It was a strange situation, and very different from any romantic picture which his fancy might have painted. Yet, after all, his work was the important thing, beside it all else was trivial. He longed to begin it. Insensibly he hastened his pace, taut with anticipation, exulting in the realisation—this, this was his first case.

It was still raining when he crossed the smeary blackness of the waste land and struck along Chapel Street in the direction vaguely indicated by Miss Page. Darkly, as he traversed it, the town took shape before him. Shops and chapels—Zion, Capel, Hebron, Bethel, Bethesda, he passed a round dozen of them—then a big Co-operative stores, and a branch of the Western Counties Bank, all lining the main thoroughfare, lying deep in the bed of the valley. The sense of being buried, far down in this cleft of the mountains, was singularly oppressive. There were few people about. At right angles, reaching up a short distance on either side of Chapel Street, were rows and rows of blue roofed workers' houses. And, beyond, at the head of the gorge, beneath a glow that spread like a great fan into the opaque sky, the Drineffy hematite mine and ore works.

He reached 7 Glydar Place, knocked breathlessly upon the door, and was at once admitted to the kitchen where, in the recessed bed, the patient lay. She was a young woman, wife of a steel puddler named Williams, and as he approached the bedside with a fast beating heart he felt, overwhelmingly, the significance of this, the real starting-point of his life. How often had he envisaged it as, in a crowd of students, he had watched a demonstration in Professor Lamplough's wards. Now there was no sustaining crowd, no easy exposition. He was alone, confronted by a case which he must diagnose and treat unaided. All at once, with a quick pang, he was conscious of his nervousness, his inexperience, his complete unpreparedness, for such a task.

While the husband stood by in the cramped, ill-lit stone floored room he examined the patient with scrupulous care. There was no doubt about it, she was ill. She complained that her head ached intolerably. Temperature, pulse, tongue, they all spoke of trouble, serious trouble. What was it? Andrew asked himself that question with a strained intensity as he went over her again. His first case. Oh, he knew that he was over-anxious! But suppose he made an error, a frightful blunder? And worse—suppose he found himself unable to make a diagnosis? He had missed nothing. Nothing. Yet he still found himself struggling towards some solution of the problem, striving to group the symptoms under the heading of some recognised disease. At last, aware that he could protract his investigation no longer, he straightened himself slowly, folding up his stethoscope, fumbling for words.

"Did she have a chill?" he asked, his eyes upon the floor.

"Yes, indeed," Williams answered eagerly. He had looked scared during the prolonged examination. "Three, four days ago. I made sure it was a chill, doctor."

Andrew nodded, attempting painfully to generate a confidence he did not feel. He muttered, "We'll soon have her right. Come to the surgery in half an hour. I'll give you a bottle of medicine."

He took his leave of them and with his head down, thinking desperately, he trudged back to the surgery, a ramshackle wooden erection standing at the entrance to Page's drive. Inside, he lit the gas and began to pace backwards and forwards beside the blue and green bottles on the dusty shelves, racking his brains, groping in the darkness. There was nothing symptomatic. It must, yes, it must be a chill. But, in his heart he knew that it was not a chill. He groaned in exasperation, dismayed and angry at his own inadequacy. He was forced, unwillingly, to temporise. Professor Lamplough, when confronted by obscurity in his wards, had a neat little ticket, which he tactfully applied: P.U.O.—pyrexia of unknown origin—it was noncommittal and exact, and it had such an admirable scientific sound!

Unhappily, Andrew took a six ounce bottle from the recess beneath the dispensary counter and began with a frown of concentration to compound an anti-pyretic mixture. Spirits of nitre, salicylate of sodium —where the dickens was the soda sal.? Oh, there it was! He tried to cheer himself by reflecting that they were all splendid, all excellent drugs, bound to get the temperature down, certain to do good. Professor Lamplough had often declared there was no drug so generally valuable as salicylate of sodium.

He had just finished his compounding and with a mild sense of achievement was writing the label when the surgery bell went "ping," the outer door swung open, and a short, powerfully thick-set red-faced man of thirty strolled in, followed by a dog. There was a silence while the black and tan mongrel squatted on its muddy haunches and the man, who wore an old velveteen suit, pit stockings and hobnail boots with a sodden oilskin cape over his shoulders, looked Andrew up and down. His voice, when it came, was politely ironic and annoyingly well-bred.

"I saw a light in your window as I was passing. Thought I'd look in to welcome you. I'm Denny, assistant to the esteemed Doctor Nicholls, L.S.A. That, in case you haven't met it, is the Licentiate of the Society of Apothecaries, the highest qualification known to God and man."

Andrew stared back doubtfully. Philip Denny lit a cigarette from a crumpled paper packet, threw the match on the floor, and strolled forward insolently. He picked up the bottle of medicine, read the address, the directions, uncorked it, sniffed it, recorked it and put it down, his morose red face turning blandly complimentary.

"Splendid! You've begun the good work already! One tablespoonful every three hours. God Almighty! It's reassuring to meet the dear old mumbo-jummery. But, doctor, why not three times a day? Don't you realise, doctor, that in strict orthodoxy the tablespoonfuls should pass down the œsophagus three times a day." He paused, becoming, with his assumed air of confidence, more blandly offensive than ever. "Now tell me, doctor, what's in it? Spirit of nitre by the smell. Wonderful stuff sweet spirit of nitre. Wonderful, wonderful, my dear doctor! Carminative, stimulant, diuretic, and you can swill it by the tubful. Don't you remember what it says in the little red book? When in doubt give spirit of nitre, or is it pot. lod. Tut! Tut! I seem to have forgotten some of my essentials."

Again there was a silence in the wooden shed broken only by the drumming of the rain upon the tin roof. Suddenly Denny laughed, a mocking appreciation of the blank expression on Andrew's face. He said derisively:

"Science apart, doctor, you might satisfy my curiosity. Why have you come here?"

By this time Andrew's temper was rising rapidly. He answered grimly.

"My idea was to turn Drineffy into a health resort—a sort of spa, you know."

Again Denny laughed. His laugh was an insult, which made Andrew long to hit him. "Witty, witty, my dear doctor. The true Scots steamroller humour. Unfortunately I can't recommend the water here as being ideally suited for a spa. As to the medical gentlemen—my dear doctor, in this valley they're the rag-tag and bobtail of a glorious, a truly noble profession."

"Including yourself?"

"Precisely!" Denny nodded. He was silent a moment, contemplating Andrew from beneath his sandy eyebrows. Then he dropped his mocking irony, his ugly features turned morose again. His tone, though bitter, was serious. "Look here, Manson! I realise you're just passing through on your way to Harley Street, but in the meantime there are one or two things about this place you ought to know. You won't find it conform to the best traditions of romantic practice. There's no hospital, no ambulance, no X-rays, no anything. If you want to operate you use the kitchen table. You wash up afterwards at the scullery bosh. The sanitation won't bear looking at. In a dry summer the kids die like flies with infantile cholera. Page, your boss, was a damn good old doctor, but he's finished now, finished by overwork, and'll never do a hand's turn again.

Nicholls, my owner, is a tight little money-chasing midwife. Bramwell, the Lung Buster, knows nothing but a few sentimental recitations and the Songs of Solomon. As for myself, I better anticipate the gay tidings—I drink like a fish. Oh! and Jenkins, your tame druggist, does a thriving trade, on the side, in little lead pills for female ills. I think that's about all. Come, Hawkins, we'll go." He called the mongrel and moved heavily towards the door. There he paused, his eyes ranging again from the bottle on the counter to Manson. His tone was flat, quite uninterested. "By the way, I should look out for enteric in Glydar Place if I were you. Some of these cases aren't exactly typical."

"Ping" went the door again. Before Andrew could answer Doctor Philip Denny and Hawkins disappeared into the wet darkness.

III

I T W A S not his lumpy flock mattress which caused Andrew to sleep badly that night, but the growing anxiety of the case in Glydar Place. Was it enteric? Denny's parting remark had started a fresh train of doubt and misgiving in his already uncertain mind. Dreading that he had over-looked some vital symptom he restrained himself with difficulty from rising and revisiting the case at an unearthly hour of the morning. In-deed, as he tossed and turned through the long restless night he came to ask himself if he knew anything of medicine at all.

Manson's nature was extraordinarily intense. Probably he derived this from his mother, a Highland woman who, in her childhood, had watched the Northern lights leap through the frosted sky from her home in Ullapool His father, John Manson, a small Fifeshire farmer, had been solid, painstaking and steady. He had never made a success of the land and when he was killed in the Yeomanry in the last year of the War, he had left the affairs of the little steading in a sad muddle. For twelve months Jessie Manson had struggled to run the farm as a dairy, even driving the float upon the milk-round herself when she felt Andrew was too busy with his books to do so. Then the cough which she had un-suspectedly endured for a period of years turned worse and suddenly she surrendered to the lung complaint which ravages that soft skinned, dark haired type.

At eighteen Andrew found himself alone, a first year student at St. Andrews University, carrying a scholarship worth £40 a year, but other-wise penniless. His salvation had been the Glen Endowment, that typically Scottish foundation which in the naïve terminology of the late Sir Andrew Glen "invites deserving and necessitous students of the baptismal name of Andrew to apply for loans not exceeding £50 a year for five years provided they are conscientiously prepared to reimburse such loans whenever they have qualified."

The Glen Endowment, coupled with some gay starvation, had sent Andrew through the remainder of his course at St. Andrews, then on to the Medical Schools in the city of Dundee. And gratitude to the Endowment, allied to an inconvenient honesty, had sent him hurrying down to South Wales—where newly qualified assistants could command the highest remuneration—to a salary of £250 a year, when in his heart he would have preferred a clinical appointment at the Edinburgh Royal and an honorarium of one tenth that sum.

And now he was in Drineffy, rising, shaving, dressing, all in a haze of worry over his first patient. He ate his breakfast quickly, then ran up to his room again. There he opened his bag and took out a small blue leather case. He opened the case and gazed earnestly at the medal inside, the Hunter Gold Medal, awarded annually at St. Andrews to the best student in clinical medicine. He, Andrew Manson, had won it. He prized it beyond everything, had come to regard it as his talisman, his inspiration for the future. But this morning he viewed it less with pride than with a queer, secret entreaty, as though trying to restore his confidence in himself. Then he hurried out for the morning surgery.

Dai Jenkins was already in the wooden shanty when Andrew reached it, running water from the tap into a large earthenware pipkin. He was a quick little whippet of a man with purple veined, hollow cheeks, eyes that went everywhere at once and the tightest pair of trousers on his thin legs that Andrew had ever seen. He greeted Manson ingratiatingly:

"You don't have to be so early, doctor. I can do the repeat mixtures and the certificates before you come in. Miss Page had a rubber stamp made with doctor's signature when he was taken bad."

"Thanks," Andrew answered. "I'd rather see the cases myself." He paused, shaken momentarily from his anxiety by the dispenser's procedure. "What's the idea?"

Jenkins winked. "Tastes better out of here. We know what good old aqua means, eh, doctor, *bach*. But the patients don't. I'd look a proper fool too, wouldn't I, them standin' there watchin' me fillin' up their bottles out the tap."

Plainly the little dispenser wished to be communicative, but here a voice rang out from the back door of the house forty yards away.

"Jenkins! *Jenkins*! I want you—right away."

Jenkins jumped, his nerves were apparently in a very poor state. He muttered: "Excuse me, doctor. There's Miss Page callin' me. I'll . . . I'll have to run."

Fortunately there were few people at the morning surgery, which was over at half past ten and Andrew, presented with a list of visits by Jenkins, set out at once with Thomas in the gig. With an almost painful expectancy he told the old groom to drive direct to 7 Glydar Place.

Twenty minutes later he came out of No. 7, pale, with his lips tightly compressed and an odd expression on his face. He went two doors down, into No. 11, which was also on his list. From No. 11 he crossed the street to No. 18. From No. 18 he went round the corner to Radnor Place where two further visits were marked by Jenkins as having been seen the day before. Altogether, within the space of an hour, he made seven such calls in the immediate vicinity. Five of them, including No. 7 Glydar Place, which was now showing a typical rash, were clear cases of enteric. For the last ten days Jenkins had been treating them with chalk and opium. Now, whatever his own bungling efforts of the previous night had been, Andrew realised with a shiver of apprehension that he had an outbreak of typhoid fever on his hands.

The remainder of his round he accomplished as quickly as possible in a state dithering towards panic. At lunch, during which Miss Page dealt out a dish of boiled fish, which she explained frowningly, "I ordered it for Doctor Page but he don't seem to fancy it somehow," he brooded upon the problem in frozen silence. He saw that he could get little information and no help from Miss Page. He decided he must speak to Doctor Page himself.

But when he went up to the doctor's room the curtains were drawn and Edward lay prostrate with a pressure headache, his forehead deeply flushed and furrowed by pain. Though he motioned his visitor to sit with him a little, Andrew felt it would be cruelty to thrust this trouble upon him at present. As he rose to go, after remaining seated by the bedside for a few minutes, he had to confine himself to asking:

"Doctor Page, if we get an infectious case, what's the best thing to do?"

There was a pause. Page replied with closed eyes, not moving, as though the mere act of speech were enough to aggravate his migraine. "It's always been difficult. We've no hospital, let alone an isolation ward. If you should run into anything very nasty ring up Griffiths at Toniglan. That's fifteen miles down the valley. He's the district medical officer." Another pause, longer than before. "But I'm afraid he's not very helpful."

Reinforced by this information, Andrew hastened down to the hall and rang up Toniglan. While he stood with the receiver to his ear he saw Annie, the servant, looking at him through the kitchen door.

"Hello! Hello! Is that Doctor Griffiths of Toniglan." He got through at last.

A man's voice answered very guardedly. "Who wants him?"

"This is Manson of Drineffy. Doctor Page's assistant." Andrew's tone was overpitched. "I've got five cases of typhoid up here. I want Doctor Griffiths to come up immediately."

There was the barest pause, then with a rush the reply came back in a sing-song intonation, very Welsh and apologetic. "I'm powerful sorry, doctor, indeed I am, but Doctor Griffiths has gone to Swansea. Important official business."

"When will he be back?" shouted Manson. This line was bad.

"Indeed, doctor, I couldn't say for certain."

"But listen . . ."

There was a click at the far end. Very quietly the other had rung off. Manson swore out loud with nervous violence. "Damn it, I believe that was Griffiths himself."

He rang the number again, failed to get a connection. Yet, persisting doggedly, he was about to ring again when turning, he found that Annie had advanced into the hall, her hands folded upon her apron, her eyes contemplating him soberly. She was a woman of perhaps forty-five, very clean and tidy, with a grave, enduring placidity of expression.

"I couldn't help but hear, doctor," she said. "You'll never find Doctor Griffiths in Toniglan this hour of day. He do go to the golf at Swansea afternoons mostly."

He answered angrily, swallowing a lump that hung in his throat.

"But I think that was him I spoke to."

"Maybe." She smiled faintly. "When he don't go to Swansea I've 'eard tell he do say 'e 'ave gone." She considered him with tranquil friendliness before turning away. "I wouldn't waste my time on him if I was you."

Andrew replaced the receiver with a deepening sense of indignation and distress. Cursing, he went out and visited his cases once more. When he got back it was time for evening surgery. For an hour and a half he sat in the little back-shop cubicle which was the consulting-room, wrestling with a packed surgery until the walls sweated and the place was choked with the steam of damp bodies. Miners with beat knee, cut fingers, nystagmus, chronic arthritis. Their wives, too, and their children with coughs, colds, sprains—all the minor ailments of humanity. Normally he would have enjoyed it, welcomed the quiet appraising scrutiny of these dark, sallow-skinned people with whom he felt he was on probation. But now, obsessed by the major issue, his head reeled with the impact of these trifling complaints. Yet all the time he was reaching his decision, thinking, as he wrote prescriptions, sounded chests and offered words of advice, "It was he who put me on to the thing. I hate him. Yes, I loathe him—superior devil—like hell. But I can't help that, I'll have to go to him."

At half past nine when the last patient had left the surgery he came out of his den with resolution in his eyes.

"Jenkins, where does Doctor Denny live?"

The little dispenser, hastily bolting the outer door for fear another straggler might come in, turned with a look of horror on his face that was almost comic.

"You aren't goin' to have anything to do with that fellow, doctor? Miss Page—she don't like him."

Andrew asked grimly:

"Why doesn't Miss Page like him?"

"For the same reason everybody don't. 'E's been so damn rude to her." Jenkins paused, then, reading Manson's look, he added, reluctantly, "Oh, well, if you 'ave to know, it's with Mrs. Seager he stops, Number Forty-nine Chapel Street."

Out again. He had been going the whole day long yet any tiredness he might have felt was lost in a sense of responsibility, the burden of those cases, pressing, pressing, urgently upon his shoulders. His main feeling was one of relief when, on reaching Chapel Street, he found that Denny was at his lodgings. The landlady showed him in.

If Denny was surprised to see him he concealed it. He merely asked, after a prolonged and aggravating stare, "Well! Killed anybody yet?"

Still standing in the doorway of the warm untidy sitting-room Andrew reddened. But, making a great effort, he conquered his temper and his pride. He said abruptly:

"You were right. It was enteric. I ought to be shot for not recognising it. I've got five cases. I'm not exactly overjoyed at having to come here. But I don't know the ropes. I rang the M.O. and couldn't get a word out of him. I've come to ask your advice."

Denny, half slewed round in his chair by the fire, listening, pipe in mouth, at last made a grudging gesture. "You'd better come in." With sudden irritation, "Oh! and for God's sake take a chair. Don't stand there like a Presbyterian parson about to forbid the banns. Have a drink? No! I thought you wouldn't."

Though Andrew stiffly complied with the request, seating himself and even, defensively, lighting a cigarette, Denny seemed in no hurry. He sat prodding the dog Hawkins with the toe of his burst slipper. But at length, when Manson had finished his cigarette, he said with a jerk of his head:

"Take a look at that, if you like!"

On the table indicated a microscope stood, a fine Zeiss, and some slides. Andrew focused a slide then slid round the oil immersion and immediately picked up the rod-shaped clusters of the bacteria.

"It's very clumsily done, of course," Denny said quickly and cynically, as though forestalling criticism. "Practically botched, in fact. I'm no lab. merchant, thank God! If anything I'm a surgeon. But you've got to be jack-of-all-trades under our bloody system. There's no mistake, though, even to the naked eye. I cooked them on agar in my oven."

"You've got cases too?" Andrew asked with tense interest.

"Four! All in the same area as yours." He paused. "And these bugs come from the well in Glydar Place."

Andrew gazed at him, alert, burning to ask a dozen questions, realising

479

something of the genuineness of the other man's work, and beyond everything, overjoyed that he had been shown the focus of the epidemic.

"You see," Denny resumed with that same cold and bitter irony. "Paratyphoid is more or less endemic here. But one day soon, very soon, we're going to have a pretty little blaze up. It's the main sewer that's to blame. It leaks like the devil and seeps into half the low wells at the bottom of the town. I've hammered at Griffiths about it till I'm tired. He's a lazy, evasive, incompetent, pious swine. Last time I rang him I said I'd knock his block off next time I met him. Probably that's why he welshed on you to-day."

"It's a damned shame," Andrew burst out, forgetting himself in a sudden rush of indignation.

Denny shrugged his shoulders. "He's afraid to ask the Council for anything in case they dock his wretched salary to pay for it."

There was a silence. Andrew had a warm desire that the conversation might continue. Despite his hostility towards Denny, he found a strange stimulus in the other's pessimism, in his scepticism, his cold and measured cynicism. Yet now he had no pretext on which to prolong his stay. He got up from his seat at the table and moved towards the door, concealing his feelings, striving to express a formal gratitude, to give some indication of his relief.

"I'm much obliged for the information. You've let me see how I stand. I was worried about the origin, thought I might be dealing with a carrier, but since you've localised it to the well it's a lot simpler. From now on every drop of water in Glydar Place is going to be boiled."

Denny rose also. He growled. "It's Griffiths who ought to be boiled." Then with a return of his satiric humour, "Now, no touching thanks, doctor, if you please. We shall probably have to endure a little more of each other before this thing is finished. Come and see me any time you can bear it. We don't have much social life in this neighbourhood." He glanced at the dog and concluded rudely, "Even a Scots doctor would be welcome. Isn't that so, Sir John?"

Sir John Hawkins flogged the rug with his tail, his pink tongue lolling derisively at Manson.

Yet, going home via Glydar Place, where he left strict instructions regarding the water supply, Andrew realised that he did not detest Denny so much as he had thought.

IV

ANDREW THREW himself into the enteric campaign with all the fire of his impetuous and ardent nature. He loved his work and he counted himself fortunate to have been afforded such an opportunity so early in

480

his career. During these first weeks he slaved joyfully. He had all the ordinary routine of the practice on his hands, yet somehow he got through with it, then turned exultantly to his typhoid cases.

Perhaps he was lucky in this, his first assault. As the end of the month drew near, all his enteric patients were doing well and he seemed to have confined the outbreak. When he thought of his precautions, so rigidly enforced—the boiling of the water, the disinfection and isolation, the carbolic soaked sheet on every door, the pounds of chloride of lime he had ordered to Doctor Page's account and himself shot down the Glydar drains, he exclaimed in elation: "It's working. I don't deserve it. But by God! I'm *doing* it!" He took a secret, detestable delight in the fact that his cases were mending quicker than Denny's.

Denny still puzzled, exasperated him. They naturally saw each other often because of the proximity of their cases. It pleased Denny to exert the full force of his irony upon the work which they were doing. He referred to Manson and himself as "grimly battling with the epidemic" and savoured the cliché with vindictive relish. But for all his satire, his sneers of "don't forget, doctor, we're upholding the honour of a truly glorious profession," he went close to his patients, sat on their beds, laid his hands upon them, spent hours in their sickrooms.

At times Andrew came near to liking him for a flash of shy, self-conscious simplicity, then the whole thing would be shattered by a morose and sneering word. Hurt and baffled, Andrew turned one day in the hope of enlightenment to the Medical Directory. It was a five-year-old copy on Doctor Page's shelf, but it held some startling information. It showed Philip Denny as an honours scholar of Cambridge and Guy's, a M.S. of England, holding—at that date—a practice with an honorary surgical appointment in the ducal town of Leeborough.

Then, on the tenth day of November, Denny unexpectedly rang him up.

"Manson! I'd like to see you. Can you come to my place at three o'clock? It's important."

"Very well. I'll be there."

Andrew went into lunch thoughtfully. As he ate the cottage pie that was his portion he felt Blodwen Page's eye fastened on him with a certain inquiry.

"Who was that on the phone? So it was Denny, eh? You don't have to go around with that fellow. He's no use at all."

He faced her bluntly. "On the contrary, I've found him a great deal of use."

"Go on with you, doctor!" Miss Page seemed put out by his reply. "He's reg'lar queer. Mostly he don't give medicine at all. Why, when Megan Rhys Morgan, who had to have medicine all her life, went to him he told her to walk two mile up the mountain every day and stop bogging herself with hogwash. These was his very words. She came to us after, I can tell you, and has had bottles and bottles of splendid medicine from Jenkins ever since. Oh! he's an insulting devil. He has got a wife somewhere by all accounts. Not livin' with him. See! Mostly he's drunk also. You leave him alone, doctor, and remember you're workin' for Doctor Page."

As she flung the familiar injunction at his head Andrew felt a quick rush of anger sweep over him. He was doing his utmost to please her, yet there seemed no limit to her demands. Her attitude, whether alternating between dryness or jollity, seemed always designed to get the last ounce out of him. He felt a sudden unreasonable anger. His first month's pay was already three days overdue, perhaps an oversight upon her part, yet one which had worried and annoyed him considerably. At the sight of her there, assured and self-contained, sitting in judgment upon Denny, his feelings got the better of him. He said with sudden heat: "I'd be more likely to remember that I'm working for Doctor Page if I had my month's salary, Miss Page."

She reddened so indignantly that he was sure the matter had altogether escaped her mind. She held her head very erect. "You shall have it. The idea!"

For the rest of the meal she sat in a huff, not looking at him, as though he had insulted her. And, indeed, he was conscious of an equal annoyance against himself. He had spoken without thinking, without wishing to offend her. He felt that his quick temper had placed him in a false position.

As he went on with his lunch he could not help reflecting on the relations which existed between Miss Page and himself. The truth was that, from the first moment when he had entered Bryngower, he had sensed that they were unsympathetic to one another. Perhaps the fault lay on his side—the realisation made him moodier than ever—he knew that his manner was stiff and difficult.

And there was no doubt that Blodwen Page was a most estimable woman, a good and economical housewife, who never wasted a moment of her time. She had many friends in Drineffy, everyone spoke well of her. And, indeed, her unsparing devotion to her brother, her unstinted loyalty to his interests made her almost a paragon.

Nevertheless, to Andrew she was always a little sterile, a spare dry spinster whose smile could never quite convince him of real warmth. If only she had been married, been surrounded by a family of romping children, she would have pleased him better.

After lunch she rose and, a moment later, called him into the sitting-room. Her mood was dignified, even austere.

"Here is your money then, doctor. I have found that my assistants prefer to be paid in cash. Sit down and I will count it for you."

She herself was seated in the green plush armchair and in her lap were a number of pound notes and her black leather purse.

Taking up the notes, she began to count them meticulously into Manson's hand—"One, two, three, four." When she had given him twenty she opened her purse and, with the same exactitude, counted out sixteen shillings and eightpence. She then remarked:

"I think that is correct, doctor, for one month. We agreed on a salary of two hundred and fifty a year."

"It's quite correct," he said awkwardly.

She gave him a pale glance.

"So now you know I don't intend to cheat you, doctor."

Andrew left the house in a smouldering irritation. Her rebuke stung him the more because he felt it to be justified.

Only when he reached the post office, bought a registered envelope and posted the twenty pounds to the Glen Endowment—he kept the silver as pocket money for himself—he saw Doctor Bramwell approaching and his expression lightened further. Bramwell came slowly, his large feet pressing down the pavement majestically, his seedy black figure erect, uncut white hair sweeping over the back of his soiled collar, eyes fixed on the book he held at arm's length. When he reached Andrew, whom he had seen from half-way down the street, he gave a theatrical start of recognition.

"Ah! Manson, my boy! I was so immersed, I almost missed you!"

Andrew smiled. He was already on friendly terms with Doctor Bramwell, who, unlike Nicholls, the other "listed" doctor, had given him a cordial welcome on his arrival. Bramwell's practice was not extensive, and did not permit him the luxury of an assistant, but he had a grand manner, and some attitudes worthy of a great healer.

He closed his book, studiously marking the place with one dirty fore-finger, then thrust his free hand picturesquely into the breast of his faded coat. He was so theatrical he seemed hardly real. But there he was, in the main street of Drineffy. No wonder Denny had named him the Lung Buster.

"And how, my dear boy, are you liking our little community? As I told you when you called upon my dear wife and myself at The Retreat, it isn't so bad as it might appear at first sight. We have our talent, our culture. My dear wife and I do our best to foster it. We carry the torch, Manson, even in the wilderness. You must come to us one evening. Do you sing?"

Andrew had an awful feeling that he must laugh. Bramwell was continuing with unction:

"Of course, we have all heard of your work with the enteric cases. Drineffy is proud of you, my dear boy. I only wish the chance had come my way. Is there any emergency in which I can be of service to you, call upon me!"

A sense of compunction—who was he that he should be amused by the older man?—prompted Andrew to reply.

483

"As a matter of fact, Doctor Bramwell, I've got a really interesting secondary mediastinitis in one of my cases, very unusual. You may care to see it with me if you're free."

"Yes?" queried Bramwell with a slight fall in his enthusiasm. "I don't wish to trouble you."

"It's just round the corner," Andrew said hospitably. "And I've got half an hour to spare before I meet Doctor Denny. We'll be there in a second."

Bramwell hesitated, looked for a minute as though he might refuse, then made a damped gesture of assent. They walked down to Glydar Place and went in to see the patient.

The case was, as Manson had inferred, one of unusual interest, involving a rare instance of persistence of the thymus gland. He was genuinely proud to have diagnosed it and he experienced a warm sense of communicative ardour as he invited Bramwell to share the thrill of the discovery.

But Doctor Bramwell, despite his protestations, seemed unattracted by the opportunity. He followed Andrew into the room haltingly, breathing through his nose, and in lady-like fashion approached the bed. Here he drew up and, at a safe range, made a cursory investigation. Nor was he disposed to linger. Only when they left the house, and he had inhaled a long breath of the pure fresh air, did his normal eloquence return. He glowed towards Andrew.

"I'm glad to have seen your case with you, my boy, firstly because I feel it part of a doctor's calling never to shrink from the danger of infection and secondly because I rejoice in the chance of scientific advancement. *Believe it or not, this is the best case of inflammation of the pancreas I have ever seen!*"

He shook hands and hurried off, leaving Andrew utterly nonplussed. The pancreas, thought Andrew dazedly. It was no mere slip of the tongue which has caused Bramwell to make that crass error. His entire conduct at the case betrayed his ignorance. He simply did not know. Andrew rubbed his brow. To think that a qualified practitioner, in whose hands lay the lives of hundreds of human beings, did not know the difference between the pancreas and the thymus, when one lay in the belly and the other in the chest—why, it was nothing short of staggering!

He walked slowly up the street towards Denny's lodging, realising once again how his whole orderly conception of the practice of medicine was toppling about him. He knew himself to be raw, inadequately trained, quite capable of making mistakes through his inexperience. But Bramwell was not inexperienced and because of that his ignorance was inexcusable. Unconsciously Andrew's thoughts returned to Denny who never failed in his derision towards his profession to which they belonged. Denny at first had aggravated him intensely by his weary contention that all over Britain there were thousands of incompetent doctors

484

distinguished for nothing but their sheer stupidity and an acquired capacity for bluffing their patients. Now he began to question if there were not some truth in what Denny said. He determined to reopen the argument this afternoon.

But when he entered Denny's room, he saw immediately that the occasion was not one for academic discussion. Philip received him in morose silence with a gloomy eye and a darkened forehead. Then, after a moment, he said:

"Young Jones died this morning at seven o'clock. Perforation." He spoke quietly, with a still, cold fury. "And I have two new enterics in Ystrad Row."

Andrew dropped his eyes, sympathising, yet hardly knowing what to say.

"Don't look so smug about it," Denny went on bitterly. "It's sweet for you to see my cases go wrong and yours recover. But it won't be so pretty when that cursed sewer leaks your way."

"No, no! Honestly, I'm sorry," Andrew said impulsively. "We'll have to do something about it. We must write to the Ministry of Health."

"We could write a dozen letters," Philip answered, with grim restraint. "And all we'd get would be a doddering commissioner down here in six months' time. No! I've thought it all out. There's only one way to make them build a new sewer."

"How?"

"Blow up the old one!"

For a second Andrew wondered if Denny had taken leave of his senses. Then he perceived something of the other's hard intention. He stared at him in consternation. Try as he might to reconstruct his changing ideas, Denny seemed fated to demolish them. He muttered:

"There'll be a heap of trouble—if it's found out."

Denny glanced up arrogantly.

"You needn't come in with me, if you don't want to."

"Oh, I'm coming in with you," Andrew answered slowly. "But God knows why!"

All that afternoon Manson went about his work fretfully regretting the promise he had given. He was a madman, this Denny, who would, sooner or later, involve him in serious trouble. It was a dreadful thing that he now proposed, a breach of the law which, if discovered, would bring them into the police-court and might even cause them to be scored off the medical register. A tremor of sheer horror passed over Andrew at the thought of his beautiful career, stretching so shiningly before him, suddenly cut short, ruined. He cursed Philip violently, swore inwardly a dozen times that he would not go.

Yet, for some strange and complex reason, he would not, could not draw back.

At eleven o'clock that night Denny and he started out in company

485

with the mongrel Hawkins for the end of Chapel Street. It was very dark with a gusty wind and a fine spatter of rain which blew into their faces at the street corners. Denny had made his plan and timed it carefully. The late shift at the mine had gone in an hour ago. A few lads hung about old Thomas's house at the top end but otherwise the street was deserted.

The two men and the dog moved quietly. In the pocket of his heavy overcoat, Denny had six sticks of dynamite especially stolen for him that afternoon from the powder shed at the quarry by Tom Seager, his landlady's son. Andrew carried six cocoa tins each with a hole bored in the lid, an electric torch, and a length of fuse. Slouching along, coat-collar turned up, one eye directed apprehensively across his shoulder, his mind a whirl of conflicting emotions, he gave only the curtest answers to Denny's brief remarks. He wondered grimly what Lamplough—bland professor of the orthodox—would think of him, involved in this outrageous nocturnal adventure.

Immediately above Glydar Place they reached the main manhole of the sewer, a rusty iron cover set in rotten concrete, and there they set to work. The gangrenous cover had not been disturbed for years but, after a struggle, they prised it up. Then Andrew shone the torch discreetly into the odorous depths, where on the crumbled stonework a dirty stream flowed slimily.

"Pretty, isn't it," Denny rasped. "Take a look at the cracks in that pointing. Take a *last* look, Manson."

No more was said. Inexplicably, Andrew's mood had changed and he was conscious now of a wild upswing of elation, a determination equal to Denny's own. People were dying of this festering abomination and petty officialdom had done nothing. It was not the moment for the bedside manner and a niggling bottle of physic!

They began to deal swiftly with the cocoa tins, slipping a stick of dynamite in each. Fuses of graduated lengths were cut and attached. A match flared in the darkness, startling in its harsh illumination of Denny's pale hard face, his own shaking hands. Then the first fuse spluttered. One by one the live cocoa tins were floated down the sluggish currents, those with the longest fuses going first. Andrew could not see clearly. His heart was thudding with excitement. It might not be orthodox medicine but it was the best moment he had ever known. As the last tin went in with its short fuse fizzing, Hawkins took it into his head to hunt a rat. There was a breathless interlude, filled with the yapping of the dog and the fearful possibilities of an explosion beneath their feet, while they chased and captured him. Then the manhole cover was flung back and they raced frantically thirty yards up the street.

They had barely reached the corner of Radnor Place and stopped to look round when bang! the first can went off.

"By God!" Andrew gasped, exultantly. "We've done it, Denny!"

486

He had a sense of comradeship with the other man, he wanted to grip him by the hand, to shout aloud.

Then swiftly, beautifully, the muffled explosions followed, two, three four, five and the last a glorious detonation that must have been at least a quarter of a mile down the valley.

"There!" said Denny in a suppressed voice, as though all the secret bitterness of his life escaped into that single word. "That's the end of one bit of rottenness!"

He had barely spoken before the commotion broke. Doors and windows were flung open, shedding light upon the darkened roadway. People ran out of their houses. In a minute the street was thronged. At first the cry went up that it was an explosion at the mine. But this was quickly contradicted—the sounds had come from down the valley. Arguments arose and shouted speculations. A party of men set out with lanterns to explore. The hubbub and confusion made the night ring. Under cover of the darkness and the noise, Denny and Manson started to dodge home by the back ways. There was a singing triumph in Andrew's blood.

Before eight o'clock next morning Doctor Griffiths arrived upon the scene by car, fat, veal faced and verging upon panic, summoned from his warm bed with much blasphemy by Councillor Glyn Morgan. Griffiths might refuse to answer the calls of the local doctors but there was no denying the angry command of Glyn Morgan. And, indeed, Glyn Morgan had cause for anger. The Councillor's new villa half a mile down the valley had, overnight, become surrounded by a moat of more than mediæval squalor. For half an hour the Councillor, supported by his adherents, Hamar Davies and Deawn Roberts, told their medical officer, in voices audible to many. exactly what they thought of him.

At the end of it, wiping his forehead, Griffiths tottered over to Denny who, with Manson, stood amongst the interested and edified crowd. Andrew had a sudden qualm at the approach of the health officer. A troubled night had left him less elated. In the cold light of morning, abashed by the havoc of the torn-up road, he was again uncomfortable, nervously perturbed. But Griffiths was in no condition to be suspicious.

"Man, man," he quavered to Philip. "We'll have to get that new sewer for you straight off now."

Denny's face remained expressionless.

"I warned you about that months ago," he said frigidly. "Don't you remember?"

"Yes, yes, indeed! But how was I to guess the wretched thing would blow up this way. It's a mystery to me how it all happened."

Denny looked at him coolly.

"Where's your knowledge of public health, doctor? Don't you know these sewer gases are highly inflammable."

The construction of the new sewer was begun on the following Monday.

V

I T W A S three months later and a fine March afternoon. The promise of spring scented the soft breeze blowing across the mountains where vague streaks of green defied the dominating heaped and quarried ugliness. Under the crisp blue sky even Drineffy was beautiful.

As he went out to pay a call, which had just come in, at 3 Riskin Street, Andrew felt his heart quicken to the day. Gradually he was becoming acclimatised to this strange town, primitive and isolated, entombed by the mountains, and no places of amusement, not even a cinema, nothing but its grim mine, its quarries and ore-works, its string of chapels and bleak rows of houses, a queer and silently contained community.

And the people, they also were strange, yet Andrew, though he saw them so alien to himself, could not but feel stirrings of affection towards them. With the exception of the tradesfolk, the preachers and a few professional people, they were all directly in employment to the Company. At the end and beginning of each shift the quiet streets would suddenly awake, re-echoing to steel-shod footfalls, unexpectedly alive with an army of marching figures. The clothing, boots, hands, even the faces of those from the hematite mine bore bright red powdering of ore dust. The quarry-men wore moleskins with pads and gartered knees. The puddlers were conspicuous in their trousers of blue twill.

They spoke little and much of what they said was in the Welsh tongue. They had the air in their self-contained aloofness of being a race apart. Yet they were a kindly people. Their enjoyments were simple, and were found usually in their own homes, in the chapel halls, on the foreshortened rugby football ground at the top of the town. Their prevailing passion was, perhaps, a love of music—not the cheap melodies of the moment, but stern, classical music. It was not uncommon for Andrew, walking at night along the rows, to hear the sound of a piano coming from one of these poor homes, a Beethoven sonata or a Chopin prelude, beautifully played, floating through the still air, rising to these inscrutable mountains and beyond.

The position in regard to Doctor Page's practice was now clear to Andrew. Edward Page would never see another patient. But the men did not like to "go off" Page who had served them faithfully for over thirty years. And the devoted Blodwen, bringing her forces to bear upon Watkins, the mine manager, through whom the workmen's medical contributions were paid, had succeeded in keeping her brother on the Company's list, and was in consequence receiving a good income, perhaps one sixth of which she paid out to Manson, who did all the work.

Andrew was profoundly sorry for Edward Page. Edward, a gentle,

488

simple soul, who had never had much enjoyment in his lonely bachelor life. He had literally worked himself out in the unswerving pursuit of duty in this harsh valley. Now, broken and bedridden, he was a man without interest. True, he was fond of Blodwen, and she, in a secret intense fashion, was fond of Edward. He, Doctor Page, was her dear brother. Coming into the room while Andrew sat with the sick man she would advance, smiling apparently, yet with a queer jealous sense of exclusion, exclaiming:

"Hey! What are you two talkin' about!"

It was impossible not to love Edward Page, he had so manifestly the spiritual qualities of sacrifice and unselfishness. He would lie there, helpless in bed, a worn out man, submissive to all the attentions of his sister, thanking her merely by a movement of his eyes, a wry contraction of his brows.

There was no need for him to remain in Drineffy and he had occasionally vague desires to get away to a warmer, kindlier place. Once, when Andrew asked: "Is there anything you'd like, sir,' he had sighed: "I'd like to get out of here, my boy. I've been reading about that island —Capri—they're going to make a bird sanctuary there." Then he had turned his face sideways on the pillow. The longing in his voice was very sad.

He never spoke of the practice except to say occasionally in a spent voice: "I daresay I didn't know a great deal. Yet I did my best." But he would spend hours lying absolutely still, watching his window-sill, where Annie every morning devotedly placed crumbs, bacon rind and grated coco-nut. On Sunday forenoons an old miner, Enoch Davies, came in, very stiff in his rusty black suit and celluloid dicky, to sit with Page. The two men watched the birds in silence. On one occasion Andrew met Enoch stamping excitedly downstairs. "Man alive," burst out the old miner, "we've had a rare fine mornin'. Two bluetits playin' pretty as you please on the sill for the best part of an hour." Enoch was Page's only friend. He had great influence with the miners. He swore staunchly that not a man would come off the doctor's list so long as he drew breath. He little knew how great a disservice his loyalty was to poor Edward Page.

Another frequent visitor to the house was the manager of the Western Counties Bank, Aneurin Rees, a long dry bald-headed man whom Andrew at first sight distrusted. Rees was a highly respected townsman who never by any chance met anyone's eye. He came to spend a perfunctory five minutes with Doctor Page and was then closeted for an hour at a time with Miss Page. These interviews were perfectly moral. The question under discussion was money. Andrew judged that Blodwen had a good deal of it invested in sound stocks and that under the admirable direction of Aneurin Rees she was from time to time shrewdly increasing their holdings. Money, at this period, held no significance for Andrew.

It was enough that he was regularly paying off his obligation to the Endowment. He had a few shillings in his pocket for cigarettes. Beyond that he had his work.

Now, more than ever, he appreciated how much his clinical work meant to him. It existed, the knowledge, as a warm ever-present inner consciousness which was like a fire at which he warmed himself when he was tired, depressed, perplexed. Lately, indeed, even stranger perplexities had formed and were moving more strongly than before with him. Medically, he had begun to think for himself. Perhaps Denny, with his radical destructive outlook, was mainly responsible for this. Denny's codex was literally the opposite of everything which Manson had been taught. Condensed and framed, it might well have hung, text-like, above his bed: "I do not believe."

Turned out to pattern by his medical school, Manson had faced the future with a well-bound text-book confidence. He had acquired a smattering of physics, chemistry and biology—at least he had slit up and studied the earthworm. Thereafter he had been dogmatically fed upon the accepted doctrines. He knew all the diseases, with their tabulated symptoms, and the remedies thereof. Take gout, for instance. You could cure it with colchicum. He could still see Professor Lamplough blandly purring to his class, " Vinum Colchici, gentlemen, twenty to thirty minim doses, an absolute specific in gout." But was it?—that was the question he now asked himself. A month ago he had tried colchicum, pushing it to the limit in a genuine case of "poor man's" gout—a severe and painful case. The result had been dismal failure.

And what about half, three-quarters of the other "remedies" in the pharmacopœia? This time he heard the voice of Doctor Eliot, lecturer on Materia Medica. "And now, gentlemen, we pass to elemi—a concrete resinous exudation, the botanical source of which is undetermined, but is probably Canarium commune, chiefly imported from Manilla, employed in ointment form, one in five, an admirable stimulant and disinfectant to sores and issues."

Rubbish! Yes, absolute rubbish. He knew that now. Had Eliot ever tried unguentum elemi? He was convinced that Eliot had not. All of that erudite information came out of a book and that, in its turn, came out of another book and so on, right back, probably to the Middle Ages. The word "issues," now dead as mutton, confirmed this view.

Denny had sneered at him, that first night, for naïvely compounding a bottle of medicine: Denny always sneered at the medicine compounders, the medicine swillers, Denny held that only half a dozen drugs were any use, the rest he cynically classed as "muck." It was something, that view of Denny's, to wrestle with in the night, a shattering thought, the ramifications of which Andrew could as yet only vaguely comprehend.

At this point in his reflections he arrived at Riskin Street and entered

490

No. 3. Here he found the patient to be a small boy of nine years of age, named Joey Howells, who was exhibiting a mild, seasonal attack of measles. The case was of little consequence, yet because of the circumstances of the household, which was a poor one, it promised inconvenience to Joey's mother. Howells himself, a day labourer at the quarries, had been laid up three months with pleurisy, for which no compensation was payable, and now Mrs. Howells, a delicate woman, already run off her feet attending to one invalid, in addition to her work of cleaning Bethesda Chapel, was called upon to make provision for another.

At the end of his visit as Andrew stood talking to her at the door of her house, he remarked with regret:

"You have your hands full. It's a pity you must keep Idris home from school." Idris was Joey's younger brother.

Mrs. Howells raised her head quickly, a resigned little woman with shiny red hands and work swollen finger knuckles.

"But Miss Barlow said I needn't have him back."

In spite of his sympathy Andrew felt a throb of annoyance.

'Oh?" he inquired. "And who is Miss Barlow?"

"She's the teacher at Bank Street School," said the unsuspecting Mrs. Howells. "She come round to see me this morning. And seein' how hard put I was, she's let little Idris stop on in her class. Goodness only knows what I'd have done if I'd had him fallin' over me as well!"

Andrew had a sharp impulse to tell her that she must obey his instructions and not those of a meddling schoolmistress. However, he saw well enough that Mrs. Howells was not to blame. For the moment he made no comment, but as he took his leave and came down Riskin Street his face wore a resentful frown. He hated interference, especially with his work, and beyond everything he hated interfering women. The more he thought of it the angrier he became. It was a distinct contravention of the regulations to keep Idris at school when Joey, his brother, was suffering from measles. He decided suddenly to call upon this officious Miss Barlow and have the matter out with her.

Five minutes later he ascended the incline of Bank Street, walked into the school and, having inquired his way of the janitor, he found himself outside the classroom of Standard I. He knocked at the door, entered.

It was a large detached room, well ventilated, with a fire burning at one end. All the children were under seven and, as it was the afternoon break when he entered, each was having a glass of milk—part of an assistance scheme introduced by the local branch of the M.W.U. His eyes fell upon the mistress at once. She was busy writing out sums upon the blackboard, her back towards him, and she did not immediately observe him. But suddenly she turned round.

She was so different from the intrusive female of his indignant fancy that he hesitated. Or perhaps it was the surprise in her brown eyes which made him immediately ill at ease. He flushed and said:

"Are you Miss Barlow?"

"Yes." She was a slight figure in a brown tweed skirt, woollen stockings and small stout shoes. His own age, he guessed, no, younger—about twenty-two. She inspected him, a little doubtful, faintly smiling, as though, weary of infantile arithmetic, she welcomed distraction on this fine spring day. "Aren't you Doctor Page's new assistant?"

"That's hardly the point," he answered stiffly, "though, as a matter of fact, I am Doctor Manson. I believe you have a contact here. Idris Howells. You know his brother has measles."

There was a pause. Her eyes, though questioning now, were persistently friendly. Brushing back untidy hair she answered:

"Yes, I know."

Her failure to take his visit seriously was sending his temper up again.

"Don't you realise it's quite against the rules to have him here."

At his tone her colour rose and she lost her air of comradeship. He could not help thinking how clear and fresh her skin was, with a tiny brown mole, exactly the colour of her eyes, high on her right cheek. She was very fragile in her white blouse, and ridiculously young. Now she was breathing rather quickly, yet she spoke slowly:

"Mrs. Howells was at her wit's end. Most of the children here have had measles. Those that haven't are sure to get it sooner or later. If Idris had stopped off he'd have missed his milk which is doing him such a lot of good."

"It isn't a question of his milk," he snapped. "He ought to be isolated."

She answered stubbornly. "I have got him isolated—in a kind of way. If you don't believe me look for yourself."

He followed her glance. Idris, aged five, at a little desk all by himself near the fire, was looking extraordinarily pleased with life. His pale blue eyes goggled contentedly over the rim of his milk mug.

The sight infuriated Andrew. He laughed contemptuously, offensively.

"That may be your idea of isolation. I'm afraid it isn't mine. You must send that child home at once."

Tiny points of light glinted in her eyes.

"Doesn't it occur to you that I'm the mistress of this class. You may be able to order people about in more exalted spheres. But here it's my word that counts."

He glared at her, with raging dignity.

"You're breaking the law! You can't keep him here. If you do I'll have to report you."

A short silence followed. He could see her hand tighten on the chalk she held. That sign of her emotion added to his anger against her, yes, against himself. She said disdainfully:

"Then you had better report me. Or have me arrested. I've no doubt it will give you immense satisfaction."

Furious, he did not answer, feeling himself in an utterly false position. He tried to rally himself, raising his eyes, attempting to beat down hers, which now sparkled frostily towards him. For an instant they faced each other, so close he could see the soft beating in her neck, the gleam of her teeth between her parted lips. Then she said:

"There's nothing more, is there?" She swung round tensely to the class. "Stand up, children, and say: 'Good morning, Doctor Manson. Thank you for coming.' "

A clatter of chairs as the infants rose and chanted her ironic bidding. His ears were burning as she escorted him to the door. He had an exasperating sense of discomfiture and added to it the wretched suspicion that he had behaved badly in losing his temper while she had so admirably controlled hers. He sought for a crushing phrase, some final intimidating repartee. But before that came the door closed quietly in his face.

VI

MANSON, AFTER a furious evening during which he composed and tore up three vitriolic letters to the medical officer of health, tried to forget about the episode. His sense of humour, momentarily lost in the vicinity of Bank Street, made him impatient with himself because of his display of petty feeling. Following a sharp struggle with his stiff Scots pride, he decided he had been wrong, he could not dream of reporting the case, least of all to the ineffable Griffiths. Yet, though he made the attempt, he could not so easily dismiss Christine Barlow from his mind.

It was absurd that a juvenile school-mistress should so insistently occupy his thoughts or that he should be concerned by what she might think of him. He told himself it was a stupid case of injured pride. He knew that he was shy and awkward with women. Yet no amount of logic could alter the fact that he was now restless and a little irritable. At unguarded moments, as for example when he was falling off to sleep, the scene in the classroom would flash back to him with renewed vividness and he would find himself frowning in the darkness. He still saw her, crushing the chalk, her brown eyes warm with indignation. There were three small pearly buttons on the front of her blouse. Her figure was thin and agile, with a firm economy of line which spoke to him of much hard running and dauntless skipping in her childhood. He did not ask himself if she were pretty. It was enough that she stood, spare and living, before the screen of his sight. And his heart would turn unwillingly, with a kind of sweet oppression which he had never known before.

A fortnight later he was walking down Chapel Street in a fit of abstraction when he almost bumped into Mrs. Bramwell at the corner of Station Road. He would have gone on without recognising her.

She, however, stopped at once, and hailed him, dazzling him with her smile.

"Why, Doctor Manson! The very man I'm looking for. I'm giving one of my little social evenings to-night. You'll come, won't you?"

Gladys Bramwell was a corn-haired lady of thirty-five, showily dressed, with a full figure, baby blue eyes and girlish ways. Gladys described herself romantically as a man's woman. The gossips of Drineffy used another word. Doctor Bramwell doted upon her and it was rumoured that only his blind fondness prevented him from observing her more than skittish preoccupation with Doctor Gabell, the "coloured" doctor from Toniglan.

As Andrew scanned her he sought hurriedly for an evasion.

"I'm afraid, Mrs. Bramwell, I can't possibly get away to-night."

"But you must, silly. I've got such nice people coming. Mr. and Mrs. Watkins from the mine and," a conscious smile escaped her, "Doctor Gabell from Toniglan—oh, and I almost forgot, the little school-teacher Christine Barlow."

A shiver passed over Manson.

He smiled foolishly.

"Why, of course I'll come, Mrs. Bramwell. Thank you very much for asking me." He managed to sustain her conversation for a few moments until she departed. But for the remainder of the day he could think of nothing but the fact that he was going to see Christine Barlow again.

Mrs. Bramwell's "evening" began at nine o'clock, the late hour being chosen out of consideration for the medical gentlemen who might be detained at their surgeries. It was, in fact, a quarter past nine when Andrew finished his last consultation. Hurriedly, he splashed himself in the surgery sink, tugged back his hair with the broken comb, and hastened to The Retreat. He reached the house which, belying its idyllic name, was a small brick dwelling in the middle of the town, to find that he was the last arrival. Mrs. Bramwell, chiding him brightly, led the way, followed by her five guests and her husband, into supper.

It was a cold meal, spread out on paper doyleys on the fumed oak table. Mrs. Bramwell prided herself upon being a hostess, something of a leader in style in Drineffy, which permitted her to shock public opinion by "doing herself up," and her idea of "making things go" was to talk and laugh a great deal. She always inferred that her background previous to her marriage to Doctor Bramwell, had been one of excessive luxury. To-night, as they sat down she glittered:

"Now! Has everybody got what they want."

Andrew, breathless from his haste, was at first deeply embarrassed. For a full ten minutes he dared not look at Christine. He kept his eyes lowered, overpoweringly conscious of her sitting at the far end of the table between Doctor Gabell, a dark complexioned dandy in spats, striped trousers and pearl pin, and Mr. Watkins, the elderly scrubby-headed mine manager, who in his blunt fashion was making much of her. At last, driven by a laughing allusion from Watkins: "Are ye still my Yorkshire lass, Miss Christine?" he lifted his head jealously, looked at her, found her so intimately there, in a soft grey dress with white at the neck and cuffs, that he was stricken and withdrew his eyes lest she should read them.

Defensively, scarcely knowing what he said, he began to devote himself to his neighbour, Mrs. Watkins, a little wisp of a woman who had brought her knitting.

For the remainder of the meal he endured the anguish of talking to one person when he longed to talk to another. He could have sighed with relief when Doctor Bramwell, presiding at the top of the table, viewed the cleared plates benevolently and made a napoleonic gesture.

"I think, my dear, we have all finished. Shall we adjourn to the drawing-room."

In the drawing-room, when the guests were variously disposed—chiefly upon the three-piece suite—it was plain that music was expected in the order of the evening. Bramwell beamed fondly on his wife and led her to the piano.

"What shall we oblige with first to-night, my love." Humming, he fingered amongst the music on the stand.

"'Temple Bells,'" Gabell suggested. "I never get tired of that one, Mrs. Bramwell."

Seating herself on the revolving music stool Mrs. Bramwell played and sang while her husband, one hand behind his back, the other advanced as in the motion of snuff-taking, stood beside her and deftly turned the sheets. Gladys had a full contralto voice, bringing all her deep notes up from her bosom with a lifting motion of her chin. After the "Love Lyrics" she gave them "Wandering By," and "Just a Girl."

There was generous applause. Bramwell murmured absently, in a pleased undertone: "She's in fine voice to-night."

Doctor Gabell was then persuaded to his feet. Fiddling with his ring, smoothing his well-oiled but still traitorous hair, the olive skinned buck bowed affectedly towards his hostess, and, clasping his hands well in front of him, bellowed fruitily, "Love in Sweet Seville." Then, as an encore, he gave, "Toreador."

"You sing those songs about Spain with real go, Doctor Gabell," commented the kindly Mrs. Watkins.

"It's my Spanish blood, I suppose," laughed Gabell modestly, as he resumed his seat.

Andrew saw an impish glint in Watkins's eye. The old mine manager, a true Welshman, knew music, had last winter helped his men to produce one of Verdi's more obscure operas and now, dormant behind his pipe, was enjoying himself enigmatically. Andrew could not help thinking that it must afford Watkins deep amusement to observe these strangers to his native town affecting to dispense culture in the shape of worthless, sentimental ditties. When Christine smilingly refused to perform he turned to her with a twitch to his lips.

"You're like me, I reckon, my dear. Too fond of the piano to play it."

Then the high light of the evening shone. Doctor Bramwell took the centre of the stage. Clearing his throat, he struck out one foot, threw back his head, placed his hand histrionically inside his coat. He announced: "Ladies and gentlemen. 'The Fallen Star.' A Musical Monologue." At the piano, Gladys started to vamp a sympathetic accompaniment and Bramwell began.

The recitation, which dealt with the pathetic vicissitudes of a once famous actress now come to dire poverty, was glutinous with sentiment and Bramwell gave it with soulful anguish. When the drama rose Gladys pressed bass chords. When the pathos oozed she tinkled on the treble. As the climax came, Bramwell drew himself up, his voice breaking on the final line, "There she was . . ." a pause, "starving in the gutter . . ." a long pause, "only a fallen star!"

Little Mrs. Watkins, her knitting fallen to the floor, turned damp eyes towards him.

"Poor thing, poor thing! Oh, Doctor Bramwell, you always do that most beautiful."

The arrival of the claret-cup created a diversion. By this time it was after eleven o'clock and, on the tacit understanding that anything following Bramwell's effort would be sheer anticlimax, the party prepared to break up. There were laughter, polite expressions of thanks and a movement towards the hall. As Andrew pulled on his coat, he reflected miserably that he had not exchanged a word with Christine all night.

Outside, he stood at the gate. He felt that he must speak to her. The thought of the long wasted evening, in which he had meant so easily, so pleasantly, to put things right between them, weighed on him like lead. Though she had not seemed to look at him, she had been there, near him in the same room and he had kept his eyes doltishly upon his boots. Oh, Lord! he thought wretchedly, I'm worse than the fallen star. I'd better get home and go to bed.

But he did not. He remained there, his pulse racing suddenly as she came down the steps and walked towards him, alone. He gathered all his strength and stammered:

"Miss Barlow. May I see you home."

"I'm afraid," she paused, "I've promised to wait for Mr. and Mrs. Watkins."

His heart sank. He felt like turning away, a beaten dog. Yet something still held him. His face was pale but his chin had a firm line. The words came tumbling one upon another with a rush.

"I only want to say that I'm sorry about the Howell's affair. I came round to give a cheap exhibition of authority. I ought to be kicked— hard. What you did about the kid was splendid. I admire you for it.

496

After all it's better to observe the spirit than the letter of the law. Sorry to bother you with all this but I had to say it. Good night!"

He could not see her face. Nor did he wait for her answer. He swung round and walked down the road. For the first time in many days he felt happy.

VII

THE HALF-YEARLY return of the practice had come in from the Company's offices, giving Miss Page matter for serious reflection and another topic to discuss with Aneurin Rees, the bank manager. For the first time in eighteen months the figures showed an upward jump. There were over seventy more men on "Doctor Page's list" than there had been before Manson's arrival.

Pleased with the increase in the cheque Blodwen nevertheless nursed a most disturbing thought. At mealtimes Andrew caught her unguardedly fixing him with a queer inquiring stare. On the Wednesday following Mrs. Bramwell's social evening Blodwen came into lunch with unusual vivacity.

"I declare!" she remarked. "I've just been thinking. It's nearly four months since you been here, doctor. And you haven't done too badly, either. I'm not complaining. Mind you, it isn't like Doctor Page himself. Oh, dear, no! Mr. Watkins was only saying the other day how they were all looking forward to Doctor Page coming back. Doctor Page is so clever. Mr. Watkins told me they would never dream of having anybody in his place."

She laid herself out to describe, in picturesque detail, the extraordinary skill and ability of her brother. "You wouldn't believe it," she exclaimed nodding her head. "There's nothing he can't do or hasn't done. Operations! You ought to have seen them. Let me tell you this, doctor, he's the cleverest man that's ever been in this valley."

Andrew made no reply. Her purpose was plain to him and he thought it, in its tenacious loyalty, both tragic and kind.

Meanwhile she sat back in her chair and gazed at him, trying to read the effect of her words. Then she smiled confidently.

"There'll be great rejoicings in Drineffy when Doctor Page gets back to work. And it'll be soon too. In the summer, I said to Mr. Watkins, in the summer Doctor Page will be back."

Returning from his afternoon round towards the end of the same week Andrew was shocked to find Edward seated in a chair by the front porch, fully dressed, a rug over his knees and a cap stuck upon his head. A sharp wind was blowing and the gleam of April sunshine which bathed the tragic figure was pale and cold.

"There now," cried Miss Page, coming triumphantly towards Manson from the porch. "You see, don't you. Doctor's *up*! I've just telephoned Mr. Watkins to tell him doctor's better. He'll soon be back at work, won't you, dear?"

Andrew felt the blood rush to his brow.

"Who got him down here?"

"I did," said Blodwen quickly. "And why not? He's my brother. And he's better."

"He's not fit to be up. Far from it." Andrew threw the words at her in a low tone. "Do as I tell you. Help me get him back to bed at once."

"Yes, yes," Edward said feebly. "Get me back to bed. I'm cold. I'm not right. I—I don't feel well." And to Manson's distress the sick man began to whimper.

Instantly Blodwen was in remorseful tears beside him. Down on her knees she dropped, her arms around him, contrite, exclaiming:

"There now, dearest. You shall go back to bed, poor lamb. Blodwen made a mistake. Blodwen'll take care of you. Blodwen loves you, Edward dear."

She kissed his stiff cheek.

Half an hour later, with Edward upstairs and comfortable again, Andrew came to the kitchen, upset.

Annie was now a genuine friend, many a confidence they had exchanged in this same kitchen and many an apple and currant griddle cake the middle-aged woman had slipped out of the larder for him when he came in hungry. Sometimes, indeed, as a last resort she would run down to the town for a double fish supper and they would banquet sumptuously by candle-light at the scullery table. Annie had been at Page's for nearly twenty years. She had many relations in Drineffy, all tidy folk, and her only reason for remaining so long in service was her devotion to Doctor Page.

"Give me my tea in here, Annie," Andrew now declared. "Blodwen and I are out of tune at the moment."

He was in the kitchen before he realised that Annie had visitors—her sister Olwen and Olwen's husband, Emlyn Hughes. He had met them several times before. Emlyn was a shotfirer in the Drineffy High Levels, a solid good-natured man with pale, thickened features.

As Manson, seeing them, hesitated, Olwen, a spry dark-eyed young woman, took an impulsive breath.

"Don't mind us, doctor, if you want your tea. As a matter of fact we were just talkin' about you when you came in."

"Yes?"

"Yes, indeed!" Olwen darted a glance at her sister. "It's no use your lookin' at me that way, Annie, I'll speak what's in my mind. All the men are talkin', Doctor Manson, about how they haven't had such a good young doctor as you for years, about how you take trouble to examine them, and all. You can ask Emlyn if you don't believe me. And they're bothered about how Miss Page is runnin' things. They say you ought to 'ave the practice by rights. Mind you, she fair worships the old boy. She actually believes he'll get better too. Somebody ought to tell her he won't!"

When he had finished his tea Andrew withdrew. Olwen's downright speech made him feel ill at ease. Yet it was flattering to be told that the people of Drineffy liked him. And he took it as an especial tribute when, a few days later, John Morgan, a foreman driller at the hematite mine, came to see him with his wife.

The Morgans were a middle-aged couple, not well off, but highly thought of in the district, who had been married for nearly twenty years. Andrew had heard that they were leaving shortly for South Africa where Morgan had the promise of work in the Johannesburg mines. It was not unusual for good drillers to be tempted out to the gold mines on the Rand where the drill work was similar and the pay much better. Yet no one was more surprised than Andrew when Morgan, seated in the little surgery with his wife, self-consciously explained the purpose of their visit.

"Well, sir, we have done it, at last, it seems. The missus here is goin' to have a baby. After nineteen year, mark you. We are plain delighted, man. And we've decided to put off our leavin' till after the event. For we've been thinkin' about doctors like, and we come to the conclusion that you're the one we must have to handle the case. It means a lot to us, doctor. It'll be a hard job too, I fancy. Missus here is forty-three. Yes, indeed. But here, now, we know you'll give us every satisfaction."

Andrew entered up the case with a warm sense of having been honoured. It was a strange emotion, clear and without material origin, which in his present state was doubly comforting. Lately he had felt lost, completely desolate. Extraordinary currents were moving within him, disturbing and painful. There were times when his heart held a strange dull ache which, as a mature Bachelor of Medicine, he had hitherto believed impossible.

He had never before thought seriously of love. At the university he had been too poor, too badly dressed and far too intent on getting through his examinations to come much in contact with the other sex. At St. Andrews, one had to be a blood, like his friend and classmate Freddie Hamson, to move in that circle which danced and held parties and exhibited the social graces. All this had been denied him. He had really belonged—his friendship with Hamson apart—to that crowd of outsiders who turned up their coat collars, swotted, smoked and took occasional recreation not at the Union but in a down-town billiard saloon.

It is true that the inevitable romantic images had presented themselves to him. Because of his poverty these were usually projected against a lavishly wealthy background. But now, in Drineffy, he stared through

499

the window of the ramshackle surgery, his clouded eyes fastened upon the dirty slag heap of the ore works, longing with all his heart for the skimpy junior mistress of a Council school. The bathos of it made him want to laugh.

He had always prided himself on being practical, upon his strong infusion of native caution, and he attempted, violently and with determined self-interest, to argue himself out of his emotion. He tried, coldly and logically, to examine her defects. She was not beautiful, her figure was too small and thin. She had that mole upon her cheek and a slight crinkling, visible when she smiled, in her upper lip. In addition she probably detested him.

He told himself angrily that he was utterly ill advised to give way to his feelings in this weak fashion. He had dedicated himself to his work. He was still only an assistant. What kind of doctor was he, to form, at the very outset of his career, an attachment which must hamper her future and was even now seriously interfering with his work?

In the effort to take himself in hand, he created loopholes of distraction. Deluding himself that he was missing the old associations of St. Andrews, he wrote a long letter to Freddie Hamson, who had lately gone down to a hospital appointment in London. He fell back a great deal upon Denny. But Philip, though sometimes friendly, was more often cold, suspicious, with the bitterness of a man whom life has hurt.

Try as he would Andrew could not get Christine out of his mind, nor that tormenting yearning for her from his heart. He had not seen her since his outburst at the front gate of The Retreat. What did she think of him? Did she ever think of him? It was so long since he had seen her, despite an eager scanning of Bank Street when he passed it, that he despaired of seeing her at all.

Then, on the afternoon of Saturday, the 25th of May, when he had almost given up hope, he received a note which ran as follows:

Dear Doctor Manson.

Mr. and Mrs. Watkins are coming to supper with me to-morrow, Sunday evening. If you have nothing better to do would you care to come too. Half past seven.

Sincerely,

Christine Barlow.

He gave a cry which brought Annie hurrying from the scullery.

"Eh, doctor, *bach*," reprovingly. "Sometimes you do act silly."

"I have, Annie," he answered, still overcome. "But I—I seem to have got off with it. Listen, Annie, dear. Will you press my trousers for me before to-morrow? I'll sling them outside my door to-night when I go to bed."

On the following evening which, being Sunday, left him free of the evening surgery, he presented himself in tremulous expectation at the house of Mrs. Herbert, with whom Christine lodged, near the Institute. He was early and he knew it, but he could not wait a moment longer.

It was Christine herself who opened the door for him, her face welcoming, smiling towards him.

Yes, she was smiling, actually smiling. And he had felt that she disliked him! He was so overwhelmed he could barely speak.

"It's been a lovely day, hasn't it?" he mumbled as he followed her into her sitting-room.

"Lovely," she agreed. "And I had such a grand walk this afternoon. Right out beyond Pandy. I actually found some celandines."

They sat down. It was on his tongue to inquire nervously if she enjoyed walking but he nipped the gauche futility in time.

"Mrs. Watkins has just sent word," she remarked. "She and her husband will be a little late. He's had to go down to the office. You don't mind waiting a few minutes on them?"

Mind! A few minutes! He could have laughed out of sheer happiness. If only she knew how he had waited all those days, how wonderful it was to be here with her. Surreptitiously he looked about him. Her sitting-room, furnished with her own things, was different from any room he had entered in Drineffy. It held neither plush nor horsehair nor axminster, nor any of those shiny satin cushions which conspicuously adorned Mrs. Bramwell's drawing-room. The floor-boards were stained and polished, with a plain brown rug before the open fireplace. The furniture was so unobtrusive he scarcely noticed it. In the centre of the table, set for supper, was a plain white dish in which floated, like masses of tiny water-lilies, the celandines she had gathered. The effect was simple and beautiful. On the window-sill stood a wooden confectionery box, now filled with earth, from which thin green seedlings were sprouting. Above the mantelpiece was a most peculiar picture, which showed nothing more than a child's small wooden chair, painted red and, he thought, extremely badly drawn.

She must have noticed the surprise with which he viewed it. She smiled with infectious amusement.

"I hope you don't think it's the original."

Embarrassed, he did not know what to say. The expression of her personality through the room, the conviction that she knew things which were beyond him, confounded him. Yet his interest was so awakened he forgot his awkwardness, escaped from the stupid banalities of remarks about the weather. He began to ask her about herself.

She answered him simply. She was from Yorkshire. Her mother had died when she was fifteen. Her father had then been under-manager at one of the big Bramwell Main Collieries. Her only brother John had been trained in the same colliery as a mining engineer. Five years later when she was nineteen and her Normal course completed, her father had been appointed manager of the Porth Pit, twenty miles down the valley. She and her brother had come to South Wales with him, she to keep the house, John to assist his father. Six months after their arrival there had been an explosion in the Porth Pit. John had been underground, killed instantly. Her father, hearing of the disaster, had immediately gone down, only to be met by a rush of black damp. A week later his body and John's were brought out together.

When she concluded there was a silence.

"I'm sorry," Andrew said in a sympathetic voice.

"People were kind to me," she said soberly. "Mr. and Mrs. Watkins especially. I got this job at school here." She paused, her face lighting up again. "I'm like you, though. I'm still strange here. It takes a long time to get used to the valleys."

He looked at her, searching for something which would even faintly express his feeling for her, a remark which might tactfully dispose of the past and hopefully open out the future.

"It's easy to feel cut off down here, lonely. I know. I do often. I often feel I want someone to talk to."

She smiled. "What do you want to talk about?"

He reddened, with a sense that she had cornered him. "Oh, my work, I suppose." He halted, then felt obliged to explain himself. "I seem just to be blundering about, running into one problem after another."

"Do you mean you have difficult cases."

"It isn't that." He hesitated, went on. "I came down here full of formulæ, the things that everybody believes, or pretends to believe. That swollen joints mean rheumatism. That rheumatism means salicylate. You know, the orthodox things! Well I'm finding out that some of them are all wrong. Take medicine, too. It seems to me that some of it does more harm than good. It's the system. A patient comes into the surgery. He expects his 'bottle of medicine.' And he gets it, even if it's only burnt sugar, soda carb. and good old aqua. That's why the prescription is written in Latin—so he won't understand it. It isn't right. It isn't scientific. And another thing. It seems to me that too many doctors treat disease empirically, that's to say, they treat the symptoms individually. They don't bother to combine the symptoms in their own mind and puzzle out the diagnosis. They say, very quick, because they're usually in a rush, 'Ah! headache—try this powder,' or 'you're anæmic, you must have some iron.' Instead of asking themselves what is *causing* the headache or the anæmia——" He broke off sharply. "Oh! I'm sorry! I'm boring you!"

"No, no," she said quickly. "It's awfully interesting."

"I'm just beginning, just feeling my way," he went on tempestuously, thrilled by her interest. "But I do honestly think even from what I've seen that the text-books I was brought up on have too many old-fashioned conservative ideas in them. Remedies that are no use, symptoms that were shoved in by somebody in the Middle Ages. You might say it doesn't matter to the average G.P. But why should the general practitioner be no more than a poultice mixer or a medicine slinger. It's time science was brought into the front line. A lot of people think that science lies in the bottom of a test-tube. I don't. I believe that the out-lying G.P.'s have all the opportunities to *see* things, and a better chance to observe the first symptoms of new disease than they have at any of the hospitals. By the time a case gets to hospital it's usually past the early stages."

She was about to answer quickly when the door bell rang. She rose, suppressing her remark, saying instead, with her faint smile:

"I hope you won't forget your promise to talk of this another time."

Watkins and his wife came in, apologising for being late. And almost at once they sat down to supper.

It was a very different meal from that cold collation which had last brought them together. They had veal cooked in a casserole and potatoes mashed with butter, followed by new rhubarb tart with cream, then cheese and coffee. Though plain, every dish was good and there was plenty of it. After the skimpy meals served to him by Blodwen it was a great treat to Andrew to find hot appetising food before him. He sighed:

"You're lucky in your landlady, Miss Barlow. She's a marvellous cook!"

Watkins, who had been observing Andrew's trencher work with a quizzical eye, suddenly laughed out loud.

"That's a good one." He turned to his wife. "Did you hear him, mother? He says old Mrs. Herbert's a marvellous cook."

Christine coloured slightly.

"Don't pay any attention to him," she said to Andrew. "It's the nicest compliment I've ever had—because you didn't mean it. As it happens, I cooked the supper. I have the run of Mrs. Herbert's kitchen. I like doing for myself. And I'm used to it."

Her remark served to make the mine manager more jovially boister-ous. He was quite changed from the taciturn individual who had stoically endured the entertainment at Mrs. Bramwell's. Blunt and likeably common, he enjoyed his supper, smacked his lips over the tart, put his elbows on the table, told stories which made them laugh.

The evening passing quickly. When Andrew looked at his watch he saw to his amazement that it was nearly eleven o'clock. And he had promised to pay a late visit to see a case in Blaina Place before half past ten.

As he rose, regretfully, to take his leave, Christine accompanied him to the door. In the narrow passage his arm touched her side. A pang of sweetness went over him. She was so different from anyone he had ever known, with her quietness, her fragility, her dark intelligent eyes. Heaven forgive him for daring to have thought her skimpy!

503

Breathing quickly, he mumbled:

"I can't thank you enough for asking me to-night. Please can I see you again? I don't always talk shop. Would you—Christine, would you come to the Toniglan cinema with me, sometime?"

Her eyes smiled up at him, for the first time faintly provocative.

"You try asking me."

A long silent minute on the doorstep under the high stars. The dew-scented air was cool on his hot cheek. Her breath came sweetly towards him. He longed to kiss her. Fumblingly he pressed her hand, turned, clattered down the path and was on his way home with dancing thoughts, walking on air along that dizzy path which millions have tritely followed and still believed themselves unique, rapturously predestined, eternally blessed. Oh! She was a wonderful girl! How well she had understood his meaning when he spoke of his difficulties in practice! She was clever, far cleverer than he. What a marvellous cook too! And he had called her Christine!

VIII

THOUGH CHRISTINE now occupied his mind more than ever the whole complexion of his thoughts was altered. He no longer felt despondent but happy, elated, hopeful. And this change of outlook was immediately reflected in his work. He was young enough to create in fancy a constant situation wherein she observed him at his cases, watched his careful methods, his scrupulous examinations, commended him for the searching accuracy of his diagnosis. Any temptation to scamp a visit, to reach a conclusion without first sounding the patient's chest, was met by the instant thought: "Lord, *no*! What would she think of me if I did that!"

More than once he found Denny's eye upon him, satirical, comprehensive. But he did not care. In his intense, idealistic way he linked Christine with his ambitions, made her unconsciously an extra incentive, in the great assault upon the unknown.

He admitted to himself that he still knew practically nothing. Yet he was teaching himself to think for himself, to look behind the obvious in an effort to find the proximate cause. Never before had he felt himself so powerfully attracted to the scientific ideal. He prayed that he might never become slovenly or mercenary, never jump to conclusions, never come to write "the mixture as before." He wanted to find out, to be scientific, to be worthy of Christine.

In the face of this ingenuous eagerness it seemed a pity that his work in the practice should suddenly and uniformly turn dull. He wanted to scale mountains. Yet for the next few weeks he was presented by a series

of insignificant mole-hills. His cases were trivial, supremely uninteresting, a banal run of sprains, cut fingers, colds in the head. The climax
came when he was called two miles down the valley by an old woman
who asked him, peering yellow faced from beneath her flannel mutch,
to cut her corns.

He felt foolish, chafed at his lack of opportunity, longed for whirlwind
and tempest.

He began to question his own faith, to wonder if it were really possible
or a doctor in this out-of-the-way place to be anything more than a
petty, common hack. And then, at the lowest ebb of all, came an incident
which sent the mercury of his belief soaring once again towards the skies.

Towards the end of the last week in June, as he came over the station
bridge he encountered Doctor Bramwell. The Lung Buster was slipping
out of the side door of the Railway Inn, stealthily wiping his upper lip
with the back of his hand. He had the habit, when Gladys departed, gay
and dressed in her best, upon her enigmatic "shopping" expeditions to
Toniglan, of soothing himself unobtrusively with a pint or two of beer.

A trifle discomfited at being seen by Andrew he nevertheless carried
off the situation with a flourish.

"Ah, Manson! Glad to see you. I just had a call to Pritchard."

Pritchard was the proprietor of the Railway Inn and Andrew had
seen him five minutes ago, taking his bull terrier for a walk. But he
allowed the opportunity to pass. He had an affection for the Lung Buster
whose highflown language and mock heroics were offset in a very human
way by his timidity and the holes in his socks which the gay Gladys
forgot to darn.

As they walked up the street together they began to talk shop. Bramwell was always ready to discuss his cases and now, with an air of gravity,
he told Andrew that Emlyn Hughes, Annie's brother-in-law, was on his
hands. Emyln, he said, had been acting strangely lately, getting into
trouble at the mine, losing his memory. He had turned quarrelsome
and violent.

"I don't like it, Manson." Bramwell nodded sagely. "I've seen mental
trouble before. And this looks uncommonly like it."

Andrew expressed his concern. He had always thought Hughes a
stolid and agreeable fellow. He recollected that Annie had looked
worried lately and when questioned had inferred vaguely, for despite
her proclivity for gossip she was reticent upon family affairs, that she
was anxious about her brother-in-law. When he parted from Bramwell
he ventured the hope that the case might quickly take a turn for the
better.

But on the following Friday at six o'clock in the morning he was
awakened by a knocking on his bedroom door. It was Annie, fully
dressed and very red about the eyes, offering him a note. Andrew tore
open the envelope. It was a message from Doctor Bramwell.

Come round at once. I want you to help certify a dangerous lunatic.

Annie struggled with her tears.

"It's Emlyn, doctor, *bach*. A dreadful thing has happened. I do hope you'll come down quick, like."

Andrew threw on his things in three minutes. Accompanying him down the road, Annie told him as best she could about Emlyn. He had been ill and unlike himself for three weeks, but during the night he had turned violent, and gone clean out of his mind. He had set upon his wife with a bread knife. Olwen had just managed to escape by running into the street in her nightgown. The sensational story was sufficiently distressing as Annie brokenly related it, hurrying beside him in the grey light of morning, and there seemed little he could add, by way of consolation, to alter it. They reached the Hughes's house. In the front room Andrew found Doctor Bramwell, unshaven, without his collar and tie, wearing a serious air, seated at the table, pen in hand. Before him was a bluish paper form, half filled in.

"Ah, Manson! Good of you to come so quickly. A bad business this. But it won't keep you long."

"What's up?"

"Hughes has gone mad. I think I mentioned to you a week ago I was afraid of it. Well! I was right. Acute mania." Bramwell rolled the words over his tongue with tragic grandeur. "Acute homicidal mania. We'll have to get him into Pontynewdd straight away. That means two signatures on the certificate, mine and yours—the relatives wanted me to call you in. You know the procedure, don't you?"

"Yes." Andrew nodded. "What's your evidence?"

Bramwell began, clearing his throat, to read what he had written upon the form. It was a full, flowing account of certain of Hughes's actions during the previous week, all of them conclusive of mental derangement. At the end of it Bramwell raised his head. "Clear evidence, I think!"

"It sounds pretty bad," Andrew answered slowly. "Well! I'll take a look at him."

"Thanks, Manson. You'll find me here when you've finished." And he began to add further particulars to the form.

Emlyn Hughes was in bed and seated beside him—in case restraint should be necessary—were two of his mates from the mine. Standing by the foot of the bed was Olwen, her pale face, ordinarily so pert and lively, now ravaged by weeping. Her attitude was so overwrought, the atmosphere of the room so dim and tense, that Andrew had a momentary thrill of coldness, almost of fear.

He went over to Emlyn and at first he hardly recognised him. The change was not gross, it was Emlyn true enough, but a blurred and altered Emlyn, his features coarsened in some subtle way. His face seemed swollen, the nostrils thickened, the skin waxy, except for a faint

506

reddish patch that spread across the nose. His whole appearance was heavy, apathetic. Andrew spoke to him. He muttered an unintelligible reply. Then, clenching his hands, he came out with a tirade of aggressive nonsense, which, added to Bramwell's account, made the case for his removal only too conclusive.

A silence followed. Andrew felt that he ought to be convinced. Yet inexplicably, he was not satisfied. Why, why, he kept asking himself, *why* should Hughes talk like this? Supposing the man had gone out of his mind, what was the cause of it all. He had always been a happy contented man—no worries, easy going, amicable. Why, without apparent reason, had he changed to *this*!

There must be a reason, Manson thought doggedly, symptoms don't just happen of themselves. Staring at the swollen features before him, puzzling, puzzling for some solution of the conundrum, he instinctively reached out and touched the swollen face, noting subconsciously, as he did so, that the pressure of his finger left no dent in the œdematous cheek.

All at once, electrically, a terminal vibrated in his brain. *Why* didn't the swelling pit on pressure? Because—now it was his heart which jumped!—because it was not true œdema but myxœdema. He had it, by God, he *had* it! No, no, he must not rush. Firmly, he caught hold of himself. He must not be a plunger, wildly leaping to conclusions. He must go cautiously, slowly, be sure!

Curbing himself, he lifted Emlyn's hand. Yes, the skin was dry and rough, the fingers slightly thickened at the ends. Temperature—it was subnormal. Methodically he finished the examination, fighting back each successive wave of elation. Every sign of every symptom, they fitted as superbly as a complex jig-saw puzzle. The clumsy speech, dry skin, spatulate fingers, the swollen inelastic face, the defective memory, slow mentation, the attacks of irritability culminating in an outburst of homicidal violence. Oh! the triumph of the completed picture was sublime.

Rising, he went down to the parlour where Doctor Bramwell, standing on the hearth-rug with his back to the fire, greeted him.

"Well? Satisfied? The pen's on the table."

"Look here, Bramwell," Andrew kept his eyes averted, battling to keep impetuous triumph from his voice. "I don't think we ought to certify Hughes."

"Eh, what?" Gradually the blankness left Bramwell's face. He exclaimed in hurt astonishment, "But the man's out of his mind!"

"That's not my view," Andrew answered in a level tone, still stopping down his excitement, his elation. It was not enough that he had diagnosed the case. He must handle Bramwell gently, try not to antagonise him. "In my opinion Hughes is only sick in mind because he's sick in body. I feel that he's suffering from thyroid deficiency—an absolutely straight case of myxœdema."

Bramwell stared at Andrew glassily. Now, indeed, he was dumbfounded. He made several efforts to speak, a queer sound, like snow falling off a roof.

"After all," Andrew went on persuasively, his eyes on the hearthrug, "Pontynewdd is such a sink of a place. Once Hughes gets in there he'll never get out. And if he does he'll carry the stigma of it all his life. Suppose we try pushing thyroid into him first."

"Why, doctor," Bramwell quavered, "I don't see——"

"Think of the credit for you," Andrew cut in quickly. "If you should get him well again. Don't you think it's worth it. Come on now, I'll call in Mrs. Hughes. She's crying her eyes out because she thinks Emlyn is going away. You can explain we're going to try a new treatment."

Before Bramwell could protest Andrew went out of the room. A few minutes later when he came back with Mrs. Hughes the Lung Buster had recovered himself. Planted on the hearth-rug he informed Olwen in his best manner "that there might still be a ray of hope" while, behind his back, Andrew made a neat tight ball of the certificate and threw it in the fire. Then he went out to telephone to Cardiff for thyroid.

There was a period of quivering anxiety, several days of agonised suspense, before Hughes began to respond to the treatment. But once it had started, that response was magical. Emlyn was out of bed in a fortnight and back at his work at the end of two months. He came round one evening to the surgery at Bryngower, lean and active, accompanied by the smiling Olwen, to tell Andrew he had never felt better in his life. Olwen said:

"We owe everything to you, doctor. We want to change over to you from Bramwell. Emlyn was on his list before I married him. He's just a silly old woman. He'd have had my Emlyn in the—well, you know what—if it hadn't been for you and all you've done for us."

"You *can't* change, Olwen," Andrew answered. "It would spoil everything." He dropped his professional gravity and broke into genuine youthful glee. "If you even try to—I'll come after you with that bread knife."

Bramwell, meeting Andrew in the street, remarked airily:

"Hello, Manson! You've seen Hughes about, I suppose. Ha! They're both very grateful. I flatter myself I've never had a better case."

Annie said:

"That ol' Bramwell, struttin' about the town like he was somebod-ee. He don't know nothing. And his wife, bah! She can't keep her servants no time."

Miss Page said:

"Doctor, don't forget you're workin' for Doctor Page."

Denny's comment was:

"Manson! At present you're too conceited to live with. You're going to make a most hell of a bloomer. Soon. Very soon."

But Andrew, hurrying to Christine full of the triumph of the scientific method, kept everything he had to say for her.

IX

In July of that year the Annual Conference of the British Medical Union was held in Cardiff. The Union, to which, as Professor Lamplough always informed his students in his final address, every reputable medical man ought to belong, was famous for its Annual Conferences. Splendidly organised, these Conferences offered sporting, social and scientific enjoyments to members and their families, reduced terms at all but the best hotels, free charabanc trips to any ruined abbey in the neighbourhood, a memento art brochure, souvenir diaries from the leading surgical appliance makers and drug houses, and pumproom facilities at the nearest spa. The previous year at the end of the week's festivity generous free sample boxes of Non-Adipo biscuits had been sent to each doctor and his wife.

Andrew was not a member of the Union, since the five guinea subscription was, as yet, beyond his means, but he viewed it a little enviously from a distance. Its effect was to make him feel isolated and out of touch in Drineffy. Photographs in the local newspapers of an array of doctors receiving addresses of welcome on a beflagged platform, driving off at the first tee of the Penarth Golf Course, flocking upon a steamer for a sea trip to Weston-super-Mare served to intensify his sense of exclusion.

But midway through the week a letter arrived bearing the address of a Cardiff hotel which caused Andrew a more pleasurable sensation. It was from his friend Freddie Hamson. Freddie, as might be expected, was attending the Conference and he asked Manson to run down and see him. He suggested Saturday, for dinner.

Andrew showed the letter to Christine. It was instinctive now for him to take her into his confidence. Since that evening, nearly two months before, when he had gone round to supper, he was more than ever in love. Now that he could see her frequently, and be reassured by her evident pleasure in these meetings, he was happier than ever he had been in his life. Perhaps it was Christine who had this stabilising effect upon him. She was a very practical little person, perfectly direct and entirely without coquetry. Often he would join her in a state of worry or irritation and come away soothed and tranquillised. She had a way of listening to what he had to say, quietly, then of making some comment which was usually apropos or amusing. She had a lively sense of humour. And she never flattered him.

Occasionally, despite her calmness, they had great arguments, for she had a mind of her own. She told him, with a smile, that her argumentativeness came from a Scottish grandmother. Perhaps her independent spirit came from that source too. He often felt that she had great courage, which touched him, made him long to protect her. She was really quite alone in the world except for an invalid aunt in Bridlington.

When it was fine on Saturday or Sunday afternoons they took long walks along the Pandy Road. Once they had gone to see a film, Chaplin in the *Gold Rush*, and again to Toniglan, at her suggestion, to an orchestral concert. But most of all he enjoyed the evenings when Mrs. Watkins was visiting her and he was able to enjoy the intimacy of her companionship in her own sitting-room. It was then that most of their discussions took place, with Mrs. Watkins, knitting placidly yet primly resolved to make her wool last out the session, no more than a respectable buffer state between them.

Now, with this visit to Cardiff in prospect, he wished her to accompany him. Bank Street School broke up for the summer holidays at the end of the week and she was going to Bridlington to spend her vacation with her aunt. He felt that some special celebration was needed before she took her leave.

When she had read the letter he said, impulsively:

"Will you come with me? It's only an hour and a half in the train. I'll get Blodwen to unchain me on Saturday evening. We might manage to see something of the Conference. And in any case I'd like you to meet Hamson."

She nodded.

"I'd love to come."

Excited by her acceptance he had no intention of being baulked by Miss Page. Before he approached her upon the matter he placed a conspicuous notice in the surgery window:

Closed Saturday Evening.

He went into the house gaily.

"Miss Page! According to my reading of the Sweated Medical Assistants Act, I'm entitled to one half day off a year. I'd like mine on Saturday. I'm going to Cardiff."

"Now look you here, doctor." She bristled at his demand, thinking that he was very full of himself, uppish; but after staring at him suspiciously she grudgingly declared, "Oh, well—you can go, I suppose." A sudden idea struck her. Her eye cleared. She smacked her lips. "Anyhow I'll have you bring me some pastries from Parry's. There's nothing I fancy better than Parry's pastries."

On Saturday, at half past four, Christine and Andrew took train for Cardiff. Andrew was in high spirits, boisterous, hailing porter and booking clerk by their first names. With a smile he looked across at Christine, seated on the opposite seat. She wore a navy blue coat and skirt which intensified her usual air of trimness. Her black shoes were very neat. Her eyes, like her whole appearance, conveyed a sense of appreciation of the expedition. They were shining.

At the sight of her there, a wave of tenderness came over him and a fresh sense of desire. It was all very well, he thought, this comradeship of theirs. But he wanted more than that. He wanted to take her in his arms, to feel her, warm and breathing, close to him.

Involuntarily he said:

"I'll be lost without you—when you're away this summer."

Her cheeks coloured slightly. She looked out of the window. He asked impulsively:

"Shouldn't I have said that?"

"I'm glad you said it, anyway," she answered without looking round.

It was on his tongue to tell her that he loved her, to ask her, in spite of the ridiculous insecurity of his position, if she would marry him. He saw, with sudden lucid insight, that this was the only, the inevitable solution for them. But something, an intuition that the moment was not apt, restrained him. He decided he would speak to her in the train coming home.

Meanwhile he went on, rather breathlessly:

"We ought to have a grand time this evening. Hamson's a good chap. He was rather a blade at the Royal. He's a smart lad. I remember once," his eyes became reminiscent, "there was a charity matinée in Dundee for the hospitals. All the stars were appearing, you know, regular artistes, at the Lyceum. Hanged if Hamson didn't go on and give a turn, sang and danced, and by George! he brought the house down!"

"He sounds more like a matinée idol than a doctor," she said, smiling.

"Now don't be highbrow, Chris! You'll like Freddie."

The train ran into Cardiff at quarter past six, and they made directly for the Palace Hotel. Hamson had promised to meet them there at half past but he had not arrived when they entered the lounge.

They stood together watching the scene. The place was crowded with doctors and their wives, talking, laughing, generating immense cordiality. Friendly invitations flew back and forwards.

"Doctor! You and Mrs. Smith must sit next to us to-night."

"Hey! Doctor! How about these theatre tickets!"

There was a great deal of excited coming and going, and gentlemen with red tabs in their buttonholes sped importantly across the tessellated floor with papers in their hands. In the alcove opposite an official kept up a booming monotone: "Section of O-tology and Larin-Gology *this* way please." Above a passage leading to the annexe was the notice; Medical Exhibition. There were also palms and a string orchestra.

"Pretty social, eh?" Andrew remarked, feeling that they were rather outlawed by the general hilarity. "And Freddie's late as usual, hang him. Let's take a look round the Exhibition."

They walked interestedly round the Exhibition. Andrew soon found his hands full of elegant literature. He showed one of the leaflets to Christine with a smile. *Doctor! Is your surgery empty. We can show you how to fill it!* Also there were nineteen folders, all different, offering the newest sedatives and analgesics.

"It looks like the latest trend in medicine is dope," he remarked, frowning.

At the last stand, on their way out, a young man tactfully engaged them, producing a shiny watch-like contraption.

"Doctor! I think you'd be interested in our new indexometer. It has a multiplicity of uses, is absolutely up to the minute, creates an admirable impression by the bedside, and the price is only two guineas. Allow me, doctor! You see, on the front, an index of incubation periods. One turn of the dial and you find the period of infectivity. Inside," he clicked open the back of the case, "you have an excellent hæmoglobin colour index, while on the back in tabulated form——"

"My grandfather had one of these," Andrew interrupted him firmly, "But he gave it away."

Christine was smiling as they came back through the alcove again.

"Poor man," she said, "nobody ever dared laugh at his lovely meter before!"

At the moment, as they re-entered the lounge Freddie Hamson arrived, leaping from his taxi and entering the hotel with a page-boy carrying his golf-clubs behind him. He saw them at once and advanced with a wide and winning smile.

"Hello! Hello! Here you are! Sorry I'm late. I had my tie to play off in the Lister Cup. I never saw such luck as that fellow had! Well, well! It's good to see you again, Andrew. Still the same old Manson. Ha! Ha! Why don't you buy yourself a new hat, my boy!" He clapped Andrew on the back, affectionate, hail-fellow-well-met, his glance smilingly including Christine. "Introduce me, stick-in-the-mud! What are you dreaming about?"

They sat down at one of the round tables. Hamson decided they must all have a drink. With a crack of his fingers he had a waiter running for them. Then, over the sherry, he told them all about his golf match, how he was absolutely set to win when his opponent had started sinking his mashie shots at every hole.

Fresh complexioned, with blond brilliantine-plastered hair, a nicely cut suit and black opal links in his projecting cuffs, Freddie was a well turned out figure, not good-looking—his features were very ordinary—but good-natured, smart. He looked a trifle conceited perhaps, yet, when he exerted himself, he had an attractive way. He made friends with

512

ease, in spite of which, at the university, Doctor Muir, pathologist and cynic, had once glumly addressed him in the presence of the class. "You know nothing, Mr. Hamson. Your balloon-like mind is entirely filled with egotistical gas. But you're never at a loss. If you are successful in cribbing your way through the nursery games known here as examinations, I prophesy for you a great and shining future."

They went into the grill room for dinner, since none of them were dressed, though Freddie informed them he would have to get into tails later in the evening. There was a dance, a confounded nuisance, but he must show up at it.

Having nonchalantly ordered from a menu gone wildly medical—potage Pasteur, sole Madame Curie, tournedos à la Conference Medicale—he began recalling the old days with dramatic ardour.

"I'd never have thought, then," he ended with a shake of his head, "that old Manson would have buried himself in the South Wales valleys."

"Do you think he's quite buried?" Christine asked, and her smile was rather forced. There was a pause. Freddie surveyed the crowded grill room, grinned at Andrew.

"What do you think of the Conference?"

"I suppose," Andrew answered doubtfully, "it's a useful way of keeping up to date."

"Up to date, my uncle! I haven't been to one of their ruddy sectional meetings all week. No, no, old man, it's the contacts you make that matter, the fellows you meet, mix up with. You've no idea the really influential people I've got in with this week. That's why I'm here. When I get back to town, I'll ring them up, go out and play golf with them. Later on—you mark my words—that means business."

"I don't quite follow you, Freddie," Manson said.

"Why it's as simple as falling off a log. I'm holding down an appointment in the meantime but I've got my eye on a nice little room up West where a smart little brass plate with Freddie Hamson, M.B., on it would look dashed well. When the plate does go up these fellows, my pals, will send me cases. You know how it happens. Reciprocity. You scratch my back and I'll scratch yours." Freddie took a slow appreciative sip of hock. He went on: "And apart from that it pays to push in with the small suburban fellows. Sometimes they can send you stuff. Why, in a year or two, you old dog, you'll be sending patients up to me in town from your stick-in-the-mud Drin—whatever you call it."

Christine glanced quickly at Hamson, made as if to speak, then checked herself. She kept her eyes fastened upon her plate.

"And now tell me about yourself, Manson, old son," Freddie continued, smiling. "What's been happening to you."

"Oh, nothing out of the ordinary. I consult in a wooden surgery, average thirty visits a day—mostly miners and their families."

"Doesn't sound too good to me." Freddie shook his head again, condolingly.

"I enjoy it," Andrew said mildly.

Christine interposed. "And you get in some real work."

"Yes, I did have one rather interesting case lately," Andrew reflected. "As a matter of fact I sent a note of it to the *Journal*."

He gave Hamson a short account of the case of Emlyn Hughes. Though Freddie made a great show of interested listening, his eyes kept rolling round the room.

"That was pretty good," he remarked when Manson concluded. "I thought you only got goitre in Switzerland or somewhere. Anyhow, I hope you socked in a whacking good bill. And that reminds me. A fellow was telling me to-day the best way to handle this fee question——" He was off again, full of a scheme, which someone had suggested to him, for the cash payment of all fees. They had reached the end of the dinner before his voluble dissertation was over. He rose up, flinging down his napkin.

"Let's have coffee outside. We'll finish our pow-wow in the lounge."

At quarter to ten, his cigar burned down, his stock of stories temporarily exhausted, Freddie yawned slightly and looked at his platinum wrist-watch.

But Christine was before him. She glanced at Andrew brightly, sat up straight and remarked:

"Isn't it almost our train time now?"

Manson was about to protest that they had another half-hour when Freddie said:

"And I suppose I must think about this confounded dance. I can't let the party I'm going with down."

He accompanied them to the swing doors, taking prolonged and affectionate farewell of them both.

"Well, old man," he murmured with a final shake of the hand and a confidential pat on the shoulder. "When I put the little plate up in the West End I'll remember to send you a card."

Out in the warm evening air Andrew and Christine walked along Park Street in silence. Vaguely, he was conscious that the evening had not been the success he had anticipated, that it had, at least, fallen short of Christine's expectations. He waited for her to speak but she did not. At last, diffidently, he said:

"It was pretty dull for you, I'm afraid, listening to all these old hospital yarns?"

"No," she answered. "I didn't find that dull in the least."

There was a pause. He asked:

"Didn't you like Hamson?"

"Not a great deal." She turned, losing her restraint, her eyes sparking with honest indignation. "The idea of him, sitting there, all evening, with his waxed hair and his cheap smile, patronising you."

"Patronising me?" he echoed in amazement.

She nodded hotly.

"It was unbearable. 'A fellow was telling me the best way to handle the fee question.' Just after you'd told him about your wonderful case! Calling it a goitre, too. Even I know it was exactly the opposite. And that remark about your sending him patients"—her lip curled—"it was simply superb." She finished quite fiercely. "Oh! I could hardly stand it, the way he put himself above you."

"I don't think he put himself above me," reasoned Andrew, puzzled. He paused. "I admit he seemed rather full of himself to-night. May have been a mood. He's the best natured fellow you could hope to meet. We were great friends at College. We had digs together."

"Probably he found you useful to him," Christine said with unusual bitterness. "Got you to help him with his work."

He protested unhappily.

"Now, don't be mean, Chris."

"It's you," she flared, bright tears of vexation in her eyes. "You must be blind not to see the kind of person he is. And he's ruined our little expedition. It was lovely till he arrived and started talking about himself. And there was a wonderful concert at the Victoria Hall we could have gone to. But we've missed it, we're too late for anything—though he's just in time for his idiotic dance!"

They trudged towards the station some distance apart. It was the first time he had seen Christine angry. And he was angry too—angry at himself, at Hamson, yes, at Christine. Yet she was right when she said that the evening had not been a success. Now, in fact, secretly observing her pale constrained face he felt it had been a dismal failure.

They entered the station. Suddenly, as they made their way towards the up platform, Andrew caught sight of two people on the other side. He recognised them at once: Mrs. Bramwell and Doctor Gabell. At that moment the down train came in, a local which ran out to the seaside at Porthcawl. Gabell and Mrs. Bramwell entered the Porthcawl train together, smiling at one another. The whistle blew. The train steamed off.

Andrew experienced a sudden sensation of distress. He glanced quickly at Christine, hoping she had not observed the incident. Only that morning he had encountered Bramwell who, commenting on the fineness of the day, had rubbed his bony hands with satisfaction, remarking that his wife was going to spend the week-end with her mother at Shrewsbury.

Andrew stood with his head bent, silent. He was so much in love, the scene he had just witnessed, with all its implications, hurt him like a physical pain. He felt slightly sick. It had only wanted this conclusion to make the day thoroughly depressing. His mood seemed to undergo a complete revulsion. A shadow had fallen on his joyfulness. He longed with all his soul to have a long quiet talk with Christine, to open his heart to her, to straighten out their stupid little disagreement. He longed, above everything, to be quite alone with her. But the up-valley train, when it came in, was overcrowded. They had to be content with a compartment packed with miners, loudly discussing the City football match.

It was late when they reached Drineffy and Christine looked very tired. He was convinced that she had seen Mrs. Bramwell and Gabell. He could not possibly speak to her now. There was nothing for it but to see her to Mrs. Herbert's and unhappily bid her good night.

X

THOUGH IT was nearly midnight when Andrew reached Bryngower he found Joe Morgan waiting on him, walking up and down with short steps between the closed surgery and the entrance to the house. At the sight of him the burly driller's face expressed relief.

"Eh, doctor, I'm glad to see you. I been back and forward here this last hour. The missus wants ye—before time too."

Andrew, abruptly recalled from the contemplation of his own affairs, told Morgan to wait. He went into the house for his bag, then together they set out for No. 12 Blaina Terrace. The night air was cool and deep with quiet mystery. Usually so perceptive, Andrew now felt dull and listless. He had no premonition that this night-call would prove unusual, still less that it would influence his whole future in Drineffy. The two men walked in silence until they reached the door of No. 12, then Joe drew up short.

"I'll not come in," he said and his voice showed signs of strain. "But, man, I know ye'll do well for us."

Inside, a narrow stair led up to a small bedroom, clean but poorly furnished, and lit only by an oil lamp. Here Mrs. Morgan's mother, a tall grey-haired woman of nearly seventy, and the stout elderly midwife waited beside the patient, watching Andrew's expression as he moved about the room.

"Let me make you a cup of tea, doctor, *bach*," said the former quickly, after a few moments.

Andrew smiled faintly. He saw that the old woman, wise in experience, realised there must be a period of waiting, that she was afraid he would leave the case, saying he would return later.

"Don't fret, mother. I'll not run away."

Down in the kitchen he drank the tea which she gave him. Overwrought as he was, he knew he could not snatch even an hour's sleep if he went home. He knew, too, that the case here would demand all his attention. A queer lethargy of spirit came upon him. He decided to remain until everything was over.

An hour later he went upstairs again, noted the progress made, came down once more, sat by the kitchen fire. It was still, except for the rustle of a cinder in the grate and the slow tick-tock of the wall clock. No, there was another sound—the beat of Morgan's footsteps as he paced in the street outside. The old woman opposite him sat in her black dress, quite motionless, her eyes strangely alive and wise, probing, never leaving his face.

His thoughts were heavy, muddled. The episode he had witnessed at Cardiff station still obsessed him morbidly. He thought of Bramwell, foolishly devoted to a woman who deceived him sordidly, of Denny, living unhappily, apart from his wife. His reason told him that all these marriages were dismal failures. It was a conclusion which, in his present state, made him wince. He wished to consider marriage as an idyllic state, yes, he could not otherwise consider it with the image of Christine before him. Her eyes, shining towards him, admitted no other conclusion. It was the conflict between his level, doubting mind and his overflowing heart which left him resentful and confused. He let his chin sink upon his chest, stretched out his legs, stared broodingly into the fire.

He remained like this so long, and his thoughts were so filled with Christine, that he started when the old woman opposite suddenly addressed him. Her meditation had pursued a different course.

"Susan said not to give her the chloroform if it would harm the baby. She's a full set upon this child, doctor, *bach*." Her old eyes warmed at a sudden thought. She added in a low tone, "Ay, we all are, I fancy."

He collected himself with an effort.

"It won't do any harm, the anæsthetic," he said kindly. "They'll be all right."

Here the nurse's voice was heard calling from the top landing. Andrew glanced at the clock which now showed half past three. He rose and went up to the bedroom. He perceived that he might now begin his work.

An hour elapsed. It was a long harsh struggle. Then, as the first streaks of dawn strayed past the broken edges of the blind, the child was born, lifeless.

As he gazed at the still form a shiver of horror passed over Andrew. After all that he had promised! His face, heated with his own exertions, chilled suddenly. He hesitated, torn between his desire to attempt to resuscitate the child, and his obligation towards the mother who was herself in a desperate state. The dilemma was so urgent he did not solve it consciously. Blindly, instinctively, he gave the child to the nurse and turned his attention to Susan Morgan who now lay collapsed, almost pulseless, and not yet out of the ether, upon her side. His haste was desperate, a frantic race against her ebbing strength. It took him only an instant to smash a glass ampule and inject pituitrin. Then he flung down the hypodermic syringe and worked unsparingly to restore the flaccid woman. After a few minutes of feverish effort, her heart strengthened, he saw that he might safely leave her. He swung round, in his shirt sleeves, his hair sticking to his damp brow.

"Where's the child?"

The midwife made a frightened gesture. She had placed it beneath the bed.

In a flash Andrew knelt down. Fishing amongst the sodden newspapers below the bed he pulled out the child. A boy, perfectly formed. The limp warm body was white and soft as tallow. The cord, hastily slashed, lay like a broken stem. The skin was of a lovely texture, smooth and tender. The head lolled on the thin neck. The limbs seemed boneless.

Still kneeling, Andrew stared at the child with a haggard frown. The whiteness meant only one thing: asphyxia pallida, and his mind, unnaturally tense, raced back to a case he once had seen in the Samaritan, to the treatment that had been used. Instantly he was on his feet.

"Get me hot water and cold water," he threw out to the nurse. "And basins too. Quick! Quick!"

"But, doctor——" she faltered, her eyes on the pallid body of the child.

"*Quick!*" he shouted.

Snatching a blanket he laid the child upon it and began the special method of respiration. The basins arrived, the ewer, the big iron kettle. Frantically he splashed cold water into one basin; into the other he mixed water as hot as his hand could bear. Then, like some crazy juggler, he hurried the child between the two, now plunging it into the icy, now into the steaming bath.

Fifteen minutes passed. Sweat was now running into Andrew's eyes, blinding him. One of his sleeves hung down, dripping. His breath came pantingly. But no breath came from the lax body of the child.

A desperate sense of defeat pressed on him, a raging hopelessness. He felt the midwife watching him in stark consternation while there, pressed back against the wall, where she had all the time remained, her hand pressed to her throat, uttering no sound, her eyes burning upon him, was the old woman. He remembered her longing for a grandchild, as great as had been her daughter's longing for this child. All dashed away, futile, beyond remedy.

The floor was now a draggled mess. Stumbling over a sopping towel, Andrew almost dropped the child which was now wet and slippery in his hands, like a strange white fish.

"For mercy's sake, doctor," whimpered the midwife. "It's stillborn."

Andrew did not heed her. Beaten, despairing, having laboured in vain for half an hour, he still persisted in one last effort, rubbing the child with

518

a rough towel, crushing and releasing the little chest with both his hands, trying to get breath into that limp body.

And then, as by a miracle the pigmy chest, which his hands enclosed, gave a short convulsive heave. Another. And another. Andrew turned giddy. The sense of life, springing beneath his fingers after all that unavailing striving was so exquisite, it almost made him faint. He redoubled his efforts feverishly. The child was gasping now, deeper and deeper. A bubble of mucus came from one tiny nostril, a joyful iridescent bubble. The limbs were no longer boneless. The head no longer lay back spinelessly. The blanched skin was slowly turning pink. Then, exquisitely, came the child's cry.

"Dear Father in Heaven," the nurse sobbed hysterically. "It's come . . . it's come alive."

Andrew handed her the child. He felt weak and dazed. About him the room lay in a shuddering litter: blankets, towels, basins, soiled instruments, the hypodermic syringe impaled by its point in the linoleum, the ewer knocked over, the kettle on its side in a puddle of water. Upon the huddled bed the mother still dreamed her way quietly through the anæsthetic. The old woman still stood against the wall. But her hands were together, her lips moved without sound. She was praying.

Mechanically Andrew wrung out his sleeve, pulled on his jacket.

"I'll fetch my bag later, nurse."

He went downstairs, through the kitchen into the scullery. His lips were dry. At the scullery he took a long drink of water. He reached for his hat and coat.

Outside he found Joe standing on the pavement with a tense, expectant face.

"All right, Joe," he said thickly. "Both all right."

It was quite light. Nearly five o'clock. A few miners were already in the streets; the first of thé night shift moving out. As Andrew walked with the others under the morning sky he kept thinking blindly, oblivious to all other work he had accomplished in Drineffy: "I've done something, oh, God, I've done something real at last."

XI

AFTER A SHAVE and a bath—thanks to Annie there was always plenty of boiling water in the tap—he felt less tired. But Miss Page, finding his bed unslept in, was dryly ironic at the breakfast table, the more so as he received her shafts in silence.

"Hah! You seem a bit of a wreck this mornin', doctor. Bit dark under the eyes like! Didn't get back from Cardiff till this mornin', eh? And forgot my pastries from Parry's too, like. Been out on the tiles, my boy?

Yes! You can't deceive *me*! I thought you were too good to be true. You're all the same, you assistants. I never found one yet that didn't drink or go wrong somehow!"

After morning surgery and his forenoon round Andrew dropped in to see his case. It had just gone half past twelve as he turned up Blaina Terrace. There were little knots of women talking at their open doorways and as he passed they stopped talking to smile and give him a friendly, "Good morning." Approaching No. 12 he fancied he saw a face at the window. And it was so. They had been waiting on him. The instant he placed his foot on the newly pipe-clayed doorstep the door was swung open and the old woman, beaming unbelievably all over her wrinkled face, made him welcome to the house.

Indeed, she was so eager to make much of him she could barely frame the words. She asked him to come first for some refreshment to the parlour. When he refused she fluttered:

"All right, all right, doctor, *bach*. It's as *you* say. Maybe you'll have time, though, on your way down for a drop of elderberry wine and a morsel of cake." She patted him upstairs with tremulous old hands.

He entered the bedroom. The little room, lately a shambles, had been scoured and polished until it shone. All his instruments, beautifully arranged, gleamed upon the varnished deal dresser. His bag had been carefully rubbed with goose-grease, the snib catches cleaned with metal polish, so that they were as silver. The bed had been changed, spread with fresh linen and there, upon it, was the mother, her plain middle-aged face gazing in dumb happiness towards him, the babe sucking quiet and warm at her full breast.

"Ay!" The stout midwife rose from her seat by the bedside, unmasking a battery of smiles. "They do look all right now don't they, doctor, *bach*? They don't know the trouble they gave us. They don't *care* either, do they!"

Moistening her lips, her soft eyes warmly inarticulate, Susan Morgan tried to stammer out her gratitude.

"Ay, you may well say," nodded the midwife, extracting the last ounce of credit from the situation. "An' don't you forget, my gal, you wouldn't never have another at your age. It was this time or *never* so far as you was concerned!"

"We know that, Mrs. Jones," interrupted the old woman meaningly, from the door. "We know we do owe everything here to *doctor*."

"Has my Joe been to see you yet, doctor?" asked the mother timidly "No? Well he's comin', you may be sure. He's fair overjoyed. He was only sayin' though, doctor, that's the thing we will miss when we're in South Africa, not havin' you to 'tend to us."

Leaving the house, duly fortified with seed cake and home-made elderberry wine—it would have broken the old woman's heart had he refused to drink her grandson's heath—Andrew continued on his round

520

with a queer warmth round his heart. They couldn't have made more of me, he thought self-consciously, if I'd been the King of England. This case became somehow the antidote to that scene he had witnessed upon Cardiff platform. There was something to be said for marriage and the family life when it brought such happiness as filled the Morgan home.

A fortnight later when Andrew had paid his last visit at No. 12 Joe Morgan came round to see him. Joe's manner was solemnly portentous. And, having laboured long with words, he said explosively:

"Dang it all, doctor, *bach*, I'm no hand at talkin'. Money can't repay what you done for us. But all the same the missus and I want to make you this little present."

Impulsively, he handed over a slip to Andrew. It was an order on the Building Society made out for five guineas.

Andrew stared at the cheque. The Morgans were, in the local idiom, tidy folk, but they were far from being well-off. This amount, on the eve of their departure, with expenses of transit to be faced, must represent a great sacrifice, a noble generosity. Touched, Andrew said:

"I can't take this, Joe, lad."

"You *must* take it," Joe said with grave insistence, his hand closing over Andrew's, "or missus and me'll be mortal offended. It's a present for yourself. It's not for Doctor Page. He's had my money now for years and years and we've never troubled him but this once. He's *well* paid. This is a present—for *yourself*—doctor, *bach*. You understand."

"Yes, I understand, Joe," Andrew nodded, smiling.

He folded the order, placed it in his waistcoat pocket and for a few days forgot about it. Then, the following Tuesday, passing the Western Counties Bank he paused, reflected a moment and went in. As Miss Page always paid him in notes, which he forwarded by registered letter to the Endowment offices, he had never had occasion to deal through the bank. But now, with a comfortable recollection of his own substance, he decided to open a deposit account with Joe's gift.

At the grating he endorsed the order, filled in some forms and handed them to the young cashier, remarking with a smile:

"It's not much, but it's a start anyhow."

Meanwhile he had been conscious of Aneurin Rees hovering in the background, watching him. And, as he turned to go, the long-headed manager came forward to the counter. In his hands he held the order. Smoothing it gently, he glanced sideways across his spectacles.

"Afternoon, Doctor Manson. How are you?" Pause. Sucking his breath in over his yellow teeth. "Eh—you want this paid into your new account?"

"Yes." Manson spoke in some surprise. "Is it too small an amount to open with?"

"Oh, no, no, doctor. 'Tisn't the amount, like. We're very glad to have the business." Rees hesitated, scutinising the order then raising his small suspicious eyes to Andrew's face. "Eh—you want it in your *own* name?"

"Why—certainly."

"All right, all right, doctor." His expression broke suddenly into a watery smile. "I only wondered, like. Wanted to make sure. What lovely weather we've havin' for the time of year. Good day to you, Doctor Manson. Go-od day!"

Manson came out of the bank puzzled, asking himself what that bald, buttoned-up devil meant. It was some days before he found an answer to the question.

XII

CHRISTINE HAD left on her vacation more than a week before. He had been so occupied by the Morgan case that he had not succeeded in seeing her for more than a few moments, on the day of her departure. He had not spoken to her. But now that she was gone he longed for her with all his heart.

The summer was exceptionally trying in the town. The green vestiges of spring had long been withered to a dirty yellow. The mountains wore a febrile air and when the daily shotfiring from the mines or quarries re-echoed on the still spent air they seemed to enclose the valley in a dome of burnished sound. The men came out from the mine with the ore dust smeared upon their faces like rust. Children played listlessly. Old Thomas, the groom, had been taken with jaundice and Andrew was compelled to make his rounds on foot. As he slogged through the baking streets he thought of Christine. What was she doing? Was she thinking of him, perhaps, a little? And what of the future, her prospects, their chance of happiness together?

And then, quite unexpectedly, he received a message from Watkins asking him to call at the Company Offices.

The mine manager received him in agreeable fashion, invited him to sit down, pushed over the packet of cigarettes on his desk.

"Look here, doctor," he said in a friendly tone, "I've been wantin' to talk to you for some time—and we better get it over afore I make up my annual return." He paused to pick a yellow shred of tobacco off his tongue. "There's been a number of the lads at me, Emlyn Hughes and Ed Williams are the leadin' spirits, askin' me to put you up for the Company's list."

Andrew straightened in his chair, pervaded by a swift glow of satisfaction, of excitement.

"You mean—arrange for me to take over Dr. Page's practice?"

"Why no, not exactly, doctor," Watkins said slowly. "You see the position is difficult. I've got to watch how I handle my labour question 'ere. I can't put Doctor Page off the list, there's a number of the men wouldn't have *that*. What I was meanin', in the best interests of yourself, was to squeeze you, quiet like, on to the Company's list; then them that wanted to slip away from Doctor Page to yourself could easily manage it."

The eagerness faded from Andrew's expression. He frowned, his figure still braced.

"But surely you see I couldn't do that. I came here as Page's assistant. If I set up in opposition—no decent doctor could do a thing like that!"

"There isn't any other way."

"Why don't you let me take over the practice," Andrew said urgently. "I'd willingly pay something for it, out of receipts—that's another way."

Watkins shook his head bluntly.

"Blodwen won't 'ave it. I've put it up to her afore. She knows she's in a strong position. Nearly all the older men here, like Enoch Davies for instance, are on Page's side. They believe he'll come back. I'd have a strike on my hands if I even tried to shift him." He paused. "Take till to-morrow to think it over, doctor. I send the new list to Swansea head office then. Once it's gone in we can't do anything for another twelve months."

Andrew stared at the floor a moment, then slowly made a gesture of negation. His hopes, so high a minute ago, were now dashed completely to the ground.

"What's the use. I couldn't do it. If I thought it over for weeks."

It cost him a bitter pang to reach this decision and to maintain it in the fact of Watkin's partiality towards him. Yet there was no escaping the fact that he had gained his introduction to Drineffy as Doctor Page's assistant. To set up against his principal, even in the exceptional circumstances of the case, was quite unthinkable. Suppose Page did, by some chance, resume active practice—how well he would look fighting the old man for patients! No, no. He could not, and would not accept.

Nevertheless, for the rest of the day he was sadly cast down, resentful of Blodwen's calm persistence, aware that he was caught in an impossible position, wishing the offer had not been made to him at all. In the evening, about eight o'clock, he went dejectedly to call on Denny. He had not seen him for some time and he felt that a talk with Philip, perhaps some reassurance that he had acted correctly, would do him good. He reached Philip's lodging about half past eight and, as was now his custom, walked into the house without knocking. He entered the sitting-room.

Philip lay on the sofa. At first, in the fading light, Manson thought that he was resting after a hard day's work. But Philip had done no work that day. He sprawled there on his back, breathing heavily, his arm flung across his face. He was dead drunk.

Andrew turned to find the landlady at his elbow, watching him sideways, her eyes concerned, apprehensive.

"I heard you come in, doctor. He's been like this all day. He's eaten nothing. I can't do a thing with him."

Andrew simply did not know what to say. He stood staring at Philip's senseless face, recollecting that first cynical remark, uttered in the surgery on the night of his arrival.

"It's ten months now since he had his last bout," the landlady went on. "And he don't touch it in between. But when he do begin he goes at it wicked. I can tell you it's more nor awkward, with Doctor Nicholls bein' away on holiday. It looks like I must wire him."

"Send Tom up," Andrew said at last. "And we'll get him into bed."

With the help of the landlady's son, a young miner who seemed to regard the matter as something of a joke, they got Philip undressed and into his pyjamas. Then they carried him, dull and heavy as a sack, through to the bedroom.

"The main thing is to see that he doesn't get any more of it, you understand. Turn the key in the door if necessary." Andrew addressed the landlady as they came back into the sitting-room. "And now—you'd better let me have to-day's list of calls."

From the child's slate hanging in the hall he copied out the visits which Philip should have made that day. He went out. By hurrying round he could get most of them done before eleven.

Next morning immediately after surgery he went round to the lodgings. The landlady met him, wringing her hands.

"I don't know where he's got it. I 'aven't done it, I've only done my best for him."

Philip was drunker than before, heavy, insensible. After prolonged shakings and an effort to restore him with strong coffee, which in the end was upset and spilled all over the bed, Andrew took the list of calls again. Cursing the heat, the flies, Thomas's jaundice, and Denny, he again did double work that day.

In the late afternoon he came back, tired out, angrily resolved to get Denny sober. This time he found him astride one of the chairs in his pyjamas, still drunk, delivering a long address to Tom and Mrs. Seager. As Andrew entered Denny stopped short and gave him a lowering, derisive stare. He spoke thickly.

"He! The Good Samaritan. I understand you've done my round for me. Extremely noble. But why should you? Why should that blasted Nicholls clear out and leave us to do the work."

"I can't say." Andrew's patience was wearing thin. "All I know is is would be easier if you did your bit of it."

524

"I'm a surgeon. I'm not a blasted general practitioner. G.P. Huh! What does that mean? D'you ever ask yourself? You didn't? Well, I'll tell you. It's the last and most stereotyped anachronism, the worst, stupidest system ever created by God-made man. Dear old G.P.! And dear old B.P.!—that's the British Public—Ha! Ha!" He laughed derisively. "They made him. They love him. They weep over him." He swayed in his seat, his inflamed eye again bitter and morose, lecturing them drunkenly. "What can the poor devil do about it? Your G.P.— your dear old quack of all trades! Maybe it's twenty years since he qualified. How can he know medicine and obstetrics and bacteriology and all the modern scientific advances and surgery as well. Oh, yes! Oh, yes! Don't forget the surgery! Occasionally he tried a little operation at the cottage hospital Ha! Ha!" Again the sardonic amusement. "Say a mastoid. Two hours and a half by the clock. When he finds pus he's a saviour of humanity. When he doesn't, they bury the patient." His voice rose. He was angry, wildly, drunkenly angry. "Damn it to hell, Manson. It's been going on for hundreds of years. Don't they ever want to *change* the system. What's the use? What's the *use*, I ask you? Give me another whisky. We're all cracked. And it seems I'm drunk as well."

There was a silence for a few moments, then, suppressing his irritation' Andrew said:

"Oughtn't you to get back to bed now. Come on, we'll help you."

"Let me alone," said Denny sullenly. "Don't use your blasted bed-side manner on me. I've used it plenty in my time. I know it too well." He rose abruptly, staggering, and, taking Mrs. Seager by the shoulder, he thrust her into the chair. Then, swaying on his feet, his manner a savage assumption of bland suavity, he addressed the frightened woman. "And how are you to-day, my dear lady? A leetle better, I fancy. A leetle more strength in the pulse. Sleep well? Ha! Hum! Then we mus, prescribe a leetle sedative."

There was, in the ludicrous scene, a strange, alarming note—the stocky, unshaven, pyjama-clad figure of Philip aping the society physician, swaying in servile deference before the shrinking miner's wife. Tom gave a nervous gulp of laughter. In a flash Denny turned on him and violently cuffed his ears.

"That's right! Laugh! Laugh your blasted head off. But I spent five years of my life doing that. God! When I think of it I could die." He glared at them, seized a vase that stood on the mantelpiece, and dashed it hard upon the floor. The next instant the companion piece was in his hands and he sent it shattering against the wall. He started forward, red destruction in his eye.

"For mercy's sake," whimpered Mrs. Seager. "Stop him, stop him——"

Andrew and Tom Seager flung themselves on Philip who struggled with the wild intractability of intoxication. Then, perversely, he suddenly relaxed and was sentimental, fuddled.

"Manson," he drooled, hanging on Andrew's shoulder, "you're a good chap. I love you better than a brother. You and I—if we stuck together we could save the whole bloody medical profession."

He stood, his gaze wandering, lost. Then his head drooped. His body sagged. He allowed Andrew to help him to the next room and into bed. As his head rolled over on the pillow he made a last maudlin request:

"Promise me one thing, Manson! For Christ's sake, don't marry a lady!"

Next morning he was drunker than ever. Andrew gave it up. He half suspected young Seager of smuggling in the liquor, though the lad, when confronted, swore, pale-faced, that he had nothing to do with it.

All that week Andrew struggled through Denny's calls in addition to his own. On Sunday, after lunch, he visited the Chapel Street lodgings. Philip was up, shaved, dressed, and immaculate in his appearance but, though drawn and shaky, cold sober.

"I understand you've been doing my work for me, Manson." Gone was the intimacy of these last few days. His manner was constrained, icily stiff.

"It was nothing," Andrew answered clumsily.

"On the contrary, it must have put you to a great deal of trouble."

Denny's attitude was so objectionable that Andrew flushed. Not a word of gratitude, he thought, nothing but that stiff, hide-bound arrogance.

"If you do want to know the truth," he blurted out, "it put me to a hell of a lot of trouble!"

"You may take it from me something will be done about it!"

"What do you think I am!" Andrew answered hotly. "Some damned cabby that expects a tip from you. If it hadn't been for me Mrs. Seager would have wired Doctor Nicholls and you'd have been thrown out on your neck. You're a supercilious, half-baked snob. And what you need is a damned good punch on the jaw."

Denny lit a cigarette, his fingers shaking so violently he could barely hold the match. He sneered:

"Nice of you to choose this moment to offer physical combat. True Scottish tact. Some other time I may oblige you."

"Oh! Shut your bloody mouth!" said Andrew. "Here's your list of calls. Those with a cross should be seen on Monday."

He flung out of the house in a fury. Damn it, he raged, wincing, what kind of man is he to behave like God Almighty! It's as if he had done me the favour, *allowing* me to do his work!

But, on the way home, his resentment slowly cooled. He was genuinely fond of Philip and he had by now a better insight into his complex nature: shy, inordinately sensitive, vulnerable. It was this alone which made him secrete a shell of hardness round himself. The memory of his recent bout, of how he had exposed himself during it must even now be causing him excruciating torture.

Again Andrew was struck by the paradox of this clever man, using Drineffy as a bolt-hole from convention. As a surgeon Philip was exceptionally gifted. Andrew, administering the anæsthetic, had seen him perform a resection of the gall-bladder on the kitchen table of a miner's house, the sweat dripping from his red face and hairy forearms, a model of swiftness and accuracy. It was possible to make allowances for a man who did such work.

Nevertheless, when Andrew reached home he still smarted from his impact with Philip's coldness. And so, as he came through the front door and hung his hat on the stand, he was scarcely in the mood to hear Miss Page's voice exclaiming:

"Is that you, doctor? Doctor Manson! I want you!"

Andrew ignored her call. Turning, he prepared to go upstairs to his own room. But as he placed his hand on the banister Blodwen's voice came again, sharper, louder.

"Doctor! Doctor Manson! I *want* you."

Andrew swung round to see Miss Page sail out of the sitting-room, her face unusually pale, her blue eyes sparkling with some violent emotion. She came up to him.

"Are you deaf? Didn't you hear me say I *wanted* you!"

"What is it, Miss Page?" he said irritably.

"What is it, indeed." She could scarcely breathe. "I like that. You askin' me! It's me that wants to ask you somethin', my fine Doctor Manson!"

"What, then?" Andrew snapped.

The shortness of his manner seemed to excite her beyond endurance.

"It's *this*. Yes! my smart young gentleman! Maybe you'll be kind enough to explain this." From behind her back she produced a slip of paper and without relinquishing it, fluttered it menacingly before his eyes. He saw it was Joe Morgan's cheque. Then, raising his head, he saw Rees behind Blodwen, standing in the doorway of the sitting-room.

"Ay, you may well look!" Blodwen went on. "I see you recognise it. But you better tell us quick how you come to bank that money for yourself when it's Doctor Page's money and you know it."

Andrew felt the blood rise behind his ears in quick surging waves.

"It's mine. Joe Morgan made me a present of it."

"A *present*! Indeed! I like that. He's not here now to deny it."

He answered between his shut teeth.

"You can write to him if you doubt my word."

"I've more to do than write letters all over the place." In a still louder tone she exclaimed, "I do doubt your word. You think you're a wise one. Huh! Comin' down here and thinkin' you can get the practice

527

into your own hands when you should be workin' for Doctor Page. But this shows what you are, all right. You have no one's interest at heart but your own."

She flung the words at him, half-turning for support to Rees who, in the doorway, was making sounds of expostulation in his throat, his face sallower than usual. Andrew, indeed, saw Rees as the instigator of the whole affair, dallying a few days in indecision, then scurrying to Blodwen with the story. His hands clenched fiercely. He came down the two bottom steps and advanced towards them, his eyes fixed on Rees' thin bloodless mouth with threatening intensity. He was livid with rage and thirsting for battle.

"Miss Page," he said, in a laboured tone. "You've made a charge against me. Unless you take it back and apologise within two minutes I'll sue you for damages for defamation of character. The source of your information will come out in court. I've no doubt Mr. Rees's board of governors will be interested to hear how he discloses his official business."

"I—I only did my duty," stuttered the bank manager, his complexion turning muddier than before.

"I'm waiting, Miss Page." The words came with a rush, choking him. "And if you don't hurry up I'll give your bank manager the worst hiding he's ever had in his life."

She saw she had gone too far, said more, far more than she had intended. His threat, his ominous attitude, sobered her. It was almost possible to follow her swift reflection: Damages! Heavy damages! Oh, Lord, they might take a lot of money off her! She choked, swallowed, stammered:

"I—I take it back. I apologise."

It was almost comic, the gaunt angry woman, so suddenly and unexpectedly subdued. But Andrew found it singularly humourless. He realised, all at once with a great flood of bitterness, that he had reached the limit of his endurance. He could not put up with this impossible situation any longer. He took a quick deep breath.

"Miss Page, there is just one thing I want to tell you. It may interest you to know that last week a deputation of the men approached the manager, who invited me to put my name on the Company's list. It may further interest you to know that on ethical grounds—which you couldn't possibly know anything about—I definitely refused. And now, Miss Page, I'm so absolutely sick of you, I couldn't stay on. You're a good woman, I have no doubt. But to my mind you're a misguided one. And if we spent a thousand years together we should never agree. I give you a month's notice here and now."

She gaped at him, her eyes nearly bursting from her head. Then suddenly she said:

"No, you don't. No, you don't. It's all lies. You couldn't get near the Company's list. And you're *sacked*, that's what you are. No assistant has ever given me notice in his life. The idea, the impudence, the insolence, talking to me like that. I said it first. You're sacked, you are, that's what you are, sacked, sacked, sacked——"

The outburst was loud and penetrating, and at the height of it there was an interruption. Upstairs, the door of Edward's room swung slowly open and, a moment later, Edward himself appeared, a strange, bleak figure, his wasted shanks showing beneath his nightshirt. So strange and unexpected was this apparition Miss Page stopped dead in the middle of a word. From the hall she gazed upwards, as also did Rees and Andrew, while the sick man, dragging his paralysed leg behind him, came slowly, painfully, to the topmost stair.

"Can't I have a little peace." His voice, though agitated, was stern. "What's the matter?"

Blodwen took another gulp, launched into a tearful diatribe against Manson. She concluded, "And so—and so I gave him his notice."

Manson did not contradict her version of the case.

"You mean he's going?" Edward asked, trembling all over with agitation and the exertion of keeping himself upright.

"Yes, Edward." She sniffed. "I did it for your sake. And, anyhow, you'll soon be back."

There was a silence. Edward abandoned all that he wished to say. His eyes dwelt blankly upon Andrew, moved to Rees, passed quickly on to Blodwen, then came to rest sorrowfully on nothing at all. A look of hopelessness yet of dignity formed upon his stiff face.

"No," he said at last. "I'll never be back. You know that—all of you."

He said nothing more. Turning slowly, holding on to the wall, he dragged his way back into his room. The door closed without sound.

XIII

REMEMBERING THE joy, the pure elation which the Morgan case had given him and which, in a few words, his quarrel with Miss Page had turned to something sordid, Andrew brooded angrily, wondering if he should not take the matter further, write to Joe Morgan, demand something more than a mere apology. But he dismissed the idea as both unworthy and mercenary. In the end he picked out the most useless charity in the district and, in a mood of determined bitterness, posted five guineas to the secretary and asked him to send the receipt to Aneurin Rees. After that he felt better. But he wished he might have seen Rees reading that receipt.

And now, realising that his work must terminate here at the end of the month, he began immediately to look for another position, combing the back pages of the *Lancet,* applying for everything which seemed suitable. There were numerous advertisements inserted in the " assistants wanted" column. He sent in good applications, copies of his testimonials and even, as was frequently requested, photographs of himself. But at the end of the first week and again, at the conclusion of the second, he had received not a single answer to his applications. He was disappointed and astounded. Then Denny offered him the explanation in one terse phrase: "You've been in Drineffy."

It dawned upon Andrew, with a pang of dismay, that the fact of his having been in practice in this remote Welsh mining town condemned him. No one wanted assistants from "the valleys," they had a reputation. When a fortnight of his notice had expired Andrew really began to worry. What on earth was he to do? He still owed over £50 to the Glen Endowment. They would allow him to suspend payments, of course. But apart from that if he could not find another job how was he to live? He had two or three pounds in ready cash, no more. He had no equipment, no reserves. He had not even bought himself a new suit since coming to Drineffy and his present garments had been shabby enough when he arrived. He had moments of sheer terror when he saw himself sinking to destitution.

Surrounded by difficulties and uncertainty he longed for Christine. Letters were no use; he had no talent for expressing himself on paper; anything he could write would undoubtedly convey a wrong impression. Yet she was not returning to Drineffy until the first week in September. He turned a fretful, hungry eye upon the calendar, counting the days that intervened. There were still twelve of them to run. He felt, with growing despondency, that they might as well be past, for all the prospect which they held for him.

On the evening of the 30th of August, three weeks after he had given Miss Page his notice and he had begun, from stark necessity, to entertain the idea of trying for a dispenser's post, he was walking dispiritedly along Chapel Street when he met Denny. They had remained on terms of highly strained civility during the past few weeks and Andrew was surprised when the other man stopped him.

Knocking out his pipe on the heel of his boot Philip inspected it as though it demanded all his attention.

"I'm rather sorry you're going, Manson. It's made quite a difference your being here." He hesitated. "I heard this afternoon that the Aberalaw Medical Aid Society are looking for a new assistant. Aberalaw —that's just thirty miles across the valleys. It's quite a decent Society, as these things go. I believe the head doctor—Llewellyn—is a useful man. And as it's a valley town they can't very well object to a valley man. Why don't you try?"

Andrew gazed at him doubtfully. His expectations had recently been raised so high and dashed so hopelessly that he had lost all faith in his ability to succeed.

"Well, yes," he agreed slowly. "If that's the case, I may as well try."

A few minutes later he walked home, through the now heavy rain, to apply for the post.

On the 6th of September there took place a full meeting of the Committee of the Aberalaw Medical Aid Society for the purpose of selecting a successor to Doctor Leslie who had recently resigned in order to take up an appointment on a Malay rubber plantation. Seven candidates had been asked to attend.

It was a perfect summer afternoon and the time, by the big Co-operative Stores clock, was close on four o'clock. Prowling up and down on the pavement outside the Medical Aid offices in Aberalaw Square, darting nervous glances at the six other candidates, Andrew nervously awaited the first stroke of the hour. Now that his foreboding had proved incorrect and he was here, actually being considered for the post, he longed with all his heart to be successful.

From what he had seen of it he liked Aberalaw. Standing at the extreme end of the Gethly valley the town was less in the valley than on top of it. High, bracing, considerably larger than Drineffy—nearly 20,000 inhabitants was his guess—with good streets and shops, two cinemas, and a sense of spaciousness conveyed by green fields on its outskirts, Aberalaw appeared to Andrew, after the sweltering confines of the Penelly ravine, a perfect paradise.

"But I'll never get it," he fretted as he paced up and down—"never, never, *never*." No, he couldn't be so lucky! All the other candidates looked far more likely to be successful than himself, better turned out, more confident. Doctor Edwards, especially, radiated confidence. Andrew found himself hating Edwards, a stoutish, prosperous, middle-aged man who had freely intimated, in the general conversation a moment ago in the office doorway, that he had just sold his own practice down the valley in order to "apply" for this position. Damn him, grated Andrew inwardly, he wouldn't have sold out of a safe berth if he hadn't been sure of this one!

Up and down, up and down, head bent, hands thrust in his pockets. What would Christine think of him if he failed? She was returning to Drineffy either to-day or to-morrow—in her letter she had not been quite sure. Bank Street School reopened on the following Monday. Though he had written her no word of his application here, failure would mean his meeting her gloomily, or worse, with a fictitious brightness, at that very moment when he wished, above everything in the world, to stand well with her, to win her quiet, intimate, exciting smile.

Four o'clock at last. As he turned towards the entrance a fine saloon motor-car swept silently into the Square and drew up at the offices. From the back seat a short, dapper man emerged, smiling briskly, affably, yet with a sort of careless assurance, at the candidates. Before mounting the stairs he recognised Edwards, nodding casually.

"How do, Edwards." Then aside: "It'll be all right, I fancy."

"Thank you, thank you ever so, Doctor Llewellyn," breathed Edwards with tremendous deference.

"Finish!" said Andrew to himself bitterly.

Upstairs, the waiting-room was small, bare, and sour smelling, situated at the end of a short passage leading to the committee-room. Andrew was the third to go in for interview. He entered the big committee-room with nervous doggedness. If the post was already promised he was not going to cringe for it. He took the seat offered him with a blank expression.

About thirty miners filled the room, seated, and all of them smoking, gazing at him with blunt, but not unfriendly curiosity. At the small side-table was a pale quiet man with a sensitive, intelligent face who looked, from his blue pitted features, as if he had once been a miner. He was Owen, the secretary. Lounging on the edge of the table, smiling good naturedly at Andrew, was Doctor Llewellyn.

The interview began. Owen, in a quiet voice, explained the conditions of the post.

"It's like this you see, doctor. Under our scheme, the workers in Aberalaw—there are two anthracite mines here, a steel works and one coal mine in the district—pay over a certain amount to the Society out of their wages every week. Out of this the Society administers the necessary medical services, provides a nice little hospital, surgeries, medicines, splints, etcetera. In addition the Society engages doctors, Doctor Llewellyn, the head physician and surgeon, and four assistants, together with a surgeon dentist, and pays them a capitation fee—so much per head according to the number on their list. I believe Doctor Leslie was making something like five hundred pounds a year when he left us." He paused. "Altogether we find it a good scheme." There was a mutter of approval from the thirty committee men. Owen raised his head and faced them. "And now, gentlemen, have you any questions to ask?"

They began to fire questions at Andrew. He tried to answer calmly, without exaggeration, truly. Once he made a point.

"Do you speak Welsh, doctor?" This from a persistent, youngish miner by the name of Chenkin.

"No," said Andrew, "I was brought up on the Gaelic."

"A lot o' good that would be 'ere!"

"I've always found it useful for swearing at my patients," said Andrew coolly, and a laugh went up against Chenkin.

It was over at last. "Thank you very much, Doctor Manson," Owen said. And Andrew was out again in the sour little waiting-room, feeling as if he had been buffeted by heavy seas, watching the rest of the candidates go in.

Edwards, the last man called, was absent a long, a very long time. He came out smiling broadly, his look plainly saying, "Sorry for you fellows. This is in my pocket."

Then followed an interminable wait. But at last the door of the committee-room opened and out of the smoke swirling depths came Owen, the secretary, a paper in his hand. His eyes searching, rested finally with real friendliness upon Andrew.

"Would you come in a minute, Doctor Manson! The committee would like to see you again."

Pale-lipped, his heart pounding in his side, Andrew followed the secretary back into the committee-room. It couldn't be, no, no, it couldn't be that they were interested in him.

Back in the prisoner's chair again he found smiles and encouraging nods thrown in his direction. Doctor Llewellyn, however, was not looking at him. Owen, spokesman of the meeting, commenced:

"Doctor Manson, we may as well be frank with you. The committee is in some doubt. The committee, in fact, on Doctor Llewellyn's advice, had a strong bias in favour of another candidate, who has considerable knowledge of practice in the Gethly valley."

" 'E's too bloody fat, that Edwards," came an interruption from a grizzled member at the back. "I'd like to see 'im climb to the houses on Mardy Hill."

Andrew was too tense to smile. Breathlessly, he waited on Owen's words.

"But to-day," the secretary went on, "I must say that the committee have been very taken with you. The committee—as Tom Kettles poetically expressed it a minute ago—want young active men!"

Laughter, with cries of " 'Ear! 'Ear!" and "Good old Tom!"

"Moreover, Doctor Manson," continued Owen. "I must tell you that the committee have been exceedin'ly struck by two testimonials, I might even say testimonials *unsolicited* by yourself, which makes them of more value in the eyes of the committee and which reached us by post only this mornin'. These are from two practitioners in your own town, I mean Drineffy. One is a Doctor Denny, who has the M.S., a very high degree as Doctor Llewellyn, who should know, admits. The other, enclosed with Doctor Denny's, is signed by Doctor Page, whose assistant I believe you now are. Well, Doctor Manson, the committee has experience of testimonials and these two refer to your good self in such genuine terms that the committee has been much impressed."

Andrew bit his lip, his eyes lowered, aware for the first time of this generous thing that Denny had done for him.

"There is just one difficulty, Doctor Manson," Owen paused, diffidently moving the ruler on his table. "While the committee is now unanimously disposed in your favour, this position with its—its responsibilities—is more or less one for a married man. You see, apart from the

533

fact that the men prefer a married doctor when it comes to attendin' their families, there's a house, Vale View, and a good house too, that goes with the position. It wouldn't—no, it wouldn't be very suitable for a single man."

A tumultuous silence. Andrew drew a tense breath, his thoughts focused, a bright white light, upon the image of Christine. They were all, even Doctor Llewellyn, looking at him awaiting his answer. Without thinking, entirely independent of his own volition he spoke. He heard himself declaring calmly:

"As a matter of fact, gentlemen, I'm engaged to someone in Drineffy. I've—I've just been waiting on a suitable appointment—such as this—to get married."

Owen slapped down the ruler in satisfaction. There was approval, signified by a tapping of heavy boots. And the irrepressible Kettles exclaimed:

"Good enough, lad. Aberalaw's a rare fine place for an 'oneymoon!'"

"I take it you're agreed then, gentlemen," Owen's voice rose above the noise. "Doctor Manson is unanimously appointed."

There was a vigorous murmur of assent. Andrew experienced a wild thrill of triumph.

"When can you take up your duties, Doctor Manson? The earlier the better, so far as the committee is concerned."

"I could start the beginning of next week," Manson answered. Then he turned cold as he thought: "Suppose Christine won't have me. Suppose I lose her, and this wonderful job as well."

"That's settled then. Thank you, Doctor Manson. I'm sure the committee wishes you—and Mrs. Manson that's to be—every success in your new appointment."

Applause. They were all congratulating him now, the members, Llewellyn, and, with a very cordial clasp, Owen. Then he was out in the waiting-room, trying not to show his elation, trying to appear unconscious of Edwards's incredulous, crestfallen face.

But it was no use, no use at all. As he walked from the Square to the station his heart swelled with excited victory. His step was quick and springy. On his right as he strode down the hill was a small green public park with a fountain and a bandstand. Think of it!—a bandstand!—when the only elevation, the only feature of the landscape in Drineffy was a slag heap. Look at that cinema over there, too; those fine big shops; the hard good road—not a rocky mountain track—under his feet! And hadn't Owen said something about a hospital too, a nice little hospital? Ah! Thinking of what the hospital would mean to his work, Andrew drew a deep, excited breath. He hurled himself into an empty compartment in the train for Cardiff. And as it bore him thither he exulted wildly.

XIV

Though the distance was not great across the mountains, the railway journey from Aberalaw to Drineffy was circuitous. The down train stopped at every station, the Penelly valley train into which he changed at Cardiff would not, simply would not go fast enough. Manson's mood had altered now. Sunk in the corner seat, chafing, burning to be back, his thoughts tormented him.

For the first time he saw how selfish he had been, these last few months, in considering only his side of the case. All his doubts about marriage, his hesitation in speaking to Christine, had centred on his own feelings and had preconceived the fact that she would take him. But suppose he had made a frightful mistake? Suppose she did not love him? He saw himself, rejected, dismally writing a letter to the Committee telling them that "owing to circumstances over which he had no control" he could not accept the position. He saw her now, vividly before him. How well he knew her, that faint inquiring smile, the way in which she rested her hand against her chin, the steady candour in her dark brown eyes. A pang of longing shot through him. Dear Christine! If he had to forgo her he did not care what happened to him.

At nine o'clock the train crawled into Drineffy. In a flash he was out on the platform and moving up Railway Road. Though he did not expect Christine until the morning there was just the chance that she might already have arrived. Into Chapel Street. Round the corner of the Institute. A light in the front room of her lodgings sent a pang of expectation through him. Telling himself that he must contain himself, that it was probably only her landlady preparing the room, he swept into the house, burst into the sitting-room.

Yes! it was Christine. She was kneeling over some books in the corner arranging them on the lower shelf. Finished, she had begun to tidy up the string and paper which lay beside her on the floor. Her suitcase with her jacket and hat upon it lay in a chair. He saw she had not long returned.

"Christine!"

She swung round, still kneeling, a strand of hair fallen over her brow, then with a little cry of surprise and pleasure she rose.

"Andrew! How nice of you to come round."

Advancing towards him, her face alight, she held out her hand. But he took both her hands in his and held them tightly. He gazed down at her. He loved her especially in that skirt and blouse which she was wearing. It somehow increased her slightness, the tender sweetness of her youthfulness. Again his heart was throbbing.

"Chris! I've got to tell you something."

Concern swept into her eyes. She studied his pale and travel grimed face with real anxiety. She said quickly:

"What has happened? Is it more trouble with Miss Page? Are you going away?"

He shook his head, enslaving her small hands more tightly in his. And then, all at once, he broke out:

"Christine! I've got a job, the most wonderful job. At Aberalaw. I was up seeing the committee to-day. Five hundred a year and a house. A house, Christine! Oh, darling—Christine—could you—would you marry me?"

She went very pale. Her eyes were lustrous in her pale face. Her breath seemed to catch in her throat. She said faintly:

"And I thought—I thought it was bad news you were going to tell me."

"No, no," impulsively. "It's the most marvellous news, darling. Oh! if you'd just seen the place. All open and clean with green fields and decent shops and roads and a Park and—oh! Christine, actually a hospital. If only you'll marry me, darling, we can start there straight away."

Her lips were soft, trembling. But her eyes smiled, smiled with that strange and shining lustre towards him.

"Is this because of Aberalaw or because of me?"

"It's you, Chris. Oh, you know I love you, but then—perhaps you don't love me."

She gave a little sound in her throat, came towards him so that her head was buried in his breast. As his arms went round her she said brokenly:

"Oh, darling, darling. I've loved you ever since"—smiling through her happy tears—"oh, ever since I saw you walk into that stupid classroom."

PART II

I

GWILLIAM JOHN LOSSIN's decrepit motor van banged and boiled its way up the mountain road. Behind, an old tarpaulin drooped over the ruined tailboard, the rusted number-plate, the oil lamp that was never lit, dragging a smooth pattern in the dust. At the sides the loose wings flapped and clattered to the rhythm of the ancient engine. And in front, jammed gaily in the driving seat with Gwilliam John were Doctor Manson and his wife.

They had been married that morning. This was their bridal carriage. Underneath the tarpaulin were Christine's few pieces of furniture, a kitchen table bought second-hand in Drineffy for twenty shillings, several new pots and pans, and their suitcases. Since they were without pride they had decided that the best, the cheapest way to bring this grand summation of their worldly goods and themselves to Aberalaw was in Gwilliam John's pantechnicon.

The day was bright, with a fresh breeze blowing, burnishing the blue sky. They had laughed and cracked jokes with Gwilliam John, who obliged occasionally with his special rendering of Handel's *Largo* upon the motor horn. They had stopped at the solitary inn high on the mountain at Ruthin Pass, to make Gwilliam John toast them in Rhymney beer. Gwilliam John, a scatter-brained little man with a squint, toasted them several times and then had a drop o' gin on his own account. Thereafter their career down Ruthin—with its two hairpin bends edging a sheer precipice of five hundred feet—had been demonic.

At last they crested the final rise and coasted down into Aberalaw. It was a moment tinged with ecstasy. The town lay before them with its long and undulating lines of roofs reaching up and down the valley, its shops, churches and offices clustered at the upper end and, at the lower, its mines and oreworks, the chimneys smoking steadily, the squat condenser belching clouds of steam—and all, all spangled by the midday sun.

"Look! Chris, look!" Andrew whispered, pressing her arm tightly. He had all the eagerness of the cicerone. "It's a fine place, isn't it? There's the Square! We've come in the back way. And look! No more oil lamps, darling. There's the gasworks. I wonder where our house is."

They stopped a passing miner and were soon directed to Vale View which lay, he told them, in this very road, right on the fringe of the town. Another minute and they were there.

"Well!" said Christine. "It's—it's nice, isn't it?"

"Yes, darling. It looks—it looks a lovely house."

"By Cor!" Gwilliam John said, shoving his cap to the back of his head. "That's a rum lookin' shop."

Vale View was, indeed, an extraordinary edifice, at first sight something between a Swiss chalet and a Highland shooting box, with a great profusion of little gables, the whole roughcast and standing in half an acre of desolate garden choked with weeds and nettles through which a stream tumbled over a variety of tin cans to be surmounted midway in its course by a mouldering rustic bridge. Though they were not then aware of it, Vale View was their first introduction to the diverse power, the variegated omniscience of the committee, who in the boom year of 1919, when contributions were rolling in, had said largely that they would build a house, a fine house that would do the committee credit, something stylish, a reg'lar smarter. Every member of that committee had had his own positive idea as to what a reg'lar smarter should be. There were thirty members. Vale View was the result.

Whatever their impression of the outside, however, they were speedily comforted within. The house was sound, well-floored and cleanly papered. But the number of rooms was alarming. They both perceived instantly, though neither of them mentioned it, that Christine's few pieces would barely furnish two of these apartments.

"Let's see, darling," Chris said counting practically on her fingers as they stood in the hall after their first breathless tour. "I make it a dining-room, drawing-room, and library, oh, or morning-room—whatever we like to call it, downstairs, and five bedrooms upstairs."

"That's right," Andrew smiled. "No wonder they wanted a married man." His smile faded to compunction. "Honestly, Chris, I feel rotten about this—me, without a bean using your nice furniture, it's as if I was sponging on you, taking everything for granted, dragging you over here at a minute's notice—hardly giving them time to get your deputy into the school. I'm a selfish ass. I ought to have come over first and got the place decently ready for you."

"Andrew Manson! If you'd dared to leave me behind."

"Anyhow I'm going to do something about it," he frowned at her doggedly. "Now listen, Chris——"

She interrupted with a smile.

"I think, darling, I'm going to make you an omelette according to Madame Poulard. At least, the cookery book's idea of it."

Cut off at the outset of his declamation, his mouth opened, he stared at her. Then gradually his frown vanished. Smiling again he followed her into the kitchen. He could not bear her out of his sight. Their footsteps made the empty house sound like a cathedral.

The omelette—Gwilliam John had been sent for the eggs before he took his departure—came out of the pan, hot, savoury and a delicate yellow. They ate it sitting together on the edge of the kitchen table. He exclaimed vigorously:

"By God!—Sorry, darling, forgot I was a reformed character—by Jove! You can cook! That calendar they've left doesn't look bad on the wall. Fills it up nicely. And I like the picture on it—these roses. Is there a little more omelette? Who was Poulard? Sounds like a hen. Thanks, darling. Gosh! You don't know how keen I am to get started. There ought to be opportunities here. *Big* opportunities!" He broke off suddenly, his eyes resting on a varnished wooden case which stood beside their baggage in the corner. "I say, Chris! What's that?"

"Oh, that!" She made her voice sound casual. "That's a wedding present—from Denny!"

"Denny!" His face changed. Philip had been stiff and off-hand when he had charged down upon him to thank him for his help in getting the new job and to tell him he was marrying Christine. This morning he had not even come to see them off. It had hurt Andrew, made him feel that Denny was too complex, too incomprehensible to remain his friend. He advanced slowly, rather suspiciously to the case, thinking, probably an old boot inside—that was Denny's idea of humour. He opened the case. Then he gave a gasp of sheer delight. Inside was Denny's microscope, the exquisite Zeiss, and a note: "I don't really need this, I told you I was a sawbones. Good luck."

There was nothing to be said. Thoughtful, almost subdued, Andrew finished his omelette, his eyes fixed all the time upon the miscroscope. Then, reverently, he took it up and, accompanied by Christine, went into the room behind the dining-room. He placed the microscope solemnly in the middle of the bare floor.

"This isn't the library, Chris—or the morning-room or the study or anything like that. Thanks to our good friend Philip Denny, I hereby christen it the Lab."

He had just kissed her, to make the ceremony really effective, when the phone rang—a persistent shrilling which coming from the empty hall was singularly startling. They gazed at each other questioningly, excitedly.

"Perhaps it's a call, Chris! Think of it! My first Aberalaw case." He dashed into the hall.

It was not a case, however, but Doctor Llewellyn, telephoning his welcome from his home at the other end of the town. His voice came over the wire, distinct and urbane, so that Chris, on her toes at Andrew's shoulder, could hear the conversation perfectly.

"Hel-*lo*, Manson. How are you? Don't fret, now, it isn't work this time. I only wanted to be the first to welcome you and your missus to Aberalaw."

"Thanks, thanks, Doctor Llewellyn. It's awfully good of you. I don't mind if it is work though?"

"Tut! Tut! Wouldn't dream of it till you get straight." Llewellyn gushed. "And look here, if you're not doing anything to-night come over and have dinner with us, you and your missus, no formality, half past seven, we'll be delighted to see you both. Then you and I can have a chat. That's settled then. Good-bye, in the meantime."

Andrew put down the receiver, his expression deeply gratified.

"Wasn't that decent of him, Chris? Asking us over bang off like that! The head doctor, mind you! He's a well-qualified man, too, I can tell you. I looked him up. London hospital—M.D., F.R.C.S., and the D.P.H. Think of it—all these star degrees! And he sounded so friendly. Believe me, Mrs. Manson, we're going to make a big hit here." Slipping his arm round her waist he began jubilantly to waltz her round the hall.

II

THAT NIGHT, at seven o'clock, they set out through the brisk and busy streets for Doctor Llewellyn's house, Glynmawr. It was a stimulating walk. Andrew viewed his new fellow townsmen with enthusiasm.

"See that man coming, Christine! Quick! That fellow coughing over there."

"Yes, dear—but why——?"

"Oh, nothing!" Nonchalantly. "Only, he's probably going to be my patient."

They had no difficulty in finding Glynmawr, a solid villa with well-tended grounds, for Doctor Llewellyn's beautiful car stood outside and Doctor Llewellyn's beautifully polished plate, his qualifications displayed in small chaste letters, was bolted to the wrought-iron gate. Suddenly nervous, in the face of such distinction, they rang the bell and were shown in.

Doctor Llewellyn came out of the drawing-room to meet them, more dapper than ever in frock-coat and stiff gold-linked cuffs, his expression beamingly cordial.

"Well! well! This is splendid. Delighted to meet you, Mrs. Manson. Hope you'll like Aberalaw. It's not a bad little place, I can tell you. Come along in here. Mrs. Llewellyn'll be down in a minute."

Mrs. Llewellyn arrived immediately, as beaming as her husband. She was a reddish-haired woman of about forty-five, with a palish freckled face and, having greeted Manson, she turned towards Christine with an affectionate gasp.

"Oh, my de-ar, you lovely little thing! I declare I've lost my heart to you already. I must kiss you. I must. You don't mind, my dear, do you?"

Without pausing, she embraced Christine, then held her at arm's length, still viewing her glowingly. At the end of the passage a gong sounded. They went in to dinner.

It was an excellent meal—tomato soup, two roast fowls with stuffing and sausages, sultana pudding. Doctor and Mrs. Llewellyn talked smilingly to their guests.

"You'll soon get the hang of things, Manson," Llewellyn was saying. "Yes, indeed. I'll help you all I can. By the way, I'm glad that feller Edwards didn't get himself appointed. I couldn't have stuck him at any price, though I did half promise I'd put a word in for him. What was I sayin'. Oh, yes! Well, you'll be at the West Surgery—that's your end —with old Doctor Urquhart—he's a card, I can tell you—and Gadge the dispenser. Up here at the East Surgery we've got Doctor Medley and Doctor Oxborrow. Oh! They're all good chaps. You'll like them. Do you play golf? We might run out sometimes to the Fernley Course— that's only nine miles down the valley. Of course, I have a lot to do here. Yes, yes, indeed. Myself I don't bother about the surgeries. I have the hospital on my hands, I do the compensation cases for the Company, I'm medical officer for the town, I have the gasworks appointment, I'm surgeon to the workhouse and public vaccinator as well. I do all the approved society examinations with a good deal of county court work. Oh! and I'm coroner, too. And besides"—a gleam escaped his guileless eye—"I do a goodish bit of private practice odd times."

"It's a full list," Manson said.

Llewellyn beamed. "We got to make ends meet, Doctor Manson. That little car you saw outside cost a little matter of twelve hundred pounds. As for—oh, well, never mind. There's no reason why you shouldn't make a good livin' here. Say a round three to four hundred for yourself if you work hard and watch your p's and q's." He paused— confidential, humidly sincere. "There's just one thing I think I ought to put you up to. It's been all settled and agreed amongst the assistant doctors that they each pay me a fifth of their incomes." He went on quickly, guilelessly. "That's because I see their cases for them. When they get worried they have me in. It's worked very well for them, I may tell you."

Andrew glanced up in some surprise. "Doesn't that come under the Medical Aid Scheme."

"Well, not exactly," Llewellyn said, corrugating his brow. "It was all gone into and arranged by the doctors themselves a long time ago."

"But——?"

"Doctor Manson!" Mrs. Llewellyn was calling him sweetly from her end of the table. "I'm just telling your dear little wife we must see a lot of each other. She must come to tea sometime. You'll spare her to me, won't you, doctor. And sometimes she must run down to Cardiff with me in the car. That'll be nice, won't it, my de-ar?"

"Of course," Llewellyn proceeded glossily, "where you'll score—Leslie, that's the feller that was here before you—was a slack devil. Oh, he was a rotten doctor, nearly as bad as old Edwards. He couldn't give a decent anæsthetic anyhow! You're a good anæsthetist, I hope, doctor? When I have a big case, you know, I positively must have a good anæsthetist. But, bless my soul! We'll not talk about that at present. Why, you've hardly started, it isn't fair to bother you."

"Idris!" cried Mrs. Llewellyn to her husband with a kind of delighted sensationalism. "They were only *married* this morning! Mrs. Manson just told me. She's a little bride! Why, would you believe it, the dear innocents."

"Well, well, well, now!" beamed Llewellyn.

Mrs. Llewellyn patted Christine's hand. "My poor lamb! To think of the work you'll have getting straight in that stupid Vale View. I must come sometime and give you a hand."

Manson reddened slightly, collecting his scattered wits. He felt as though Christine and he had somehow become moulded into a soft little ball, played back and forwards, with deft ease between Doctor and Mrs. Llewellyn. However, he judged the last remark propitious.

"Doctor Llewellyn," he said with nervous resolution, "it's quite true what Mrs. Llewellyn says. I was wondering—I hate asking it—but could I have a couple of days off to take my wife to London to see about furnishings for our house and—and one or two other things."

He saw Christine's eyes widen in surprise. But Llewellyn was graciously nodding his head.

"Why not? Why not? Once you start it won't be so easy to get off. You take to-morrow and the next day, Doctor Manson. You see! That's where I'm useful to you. I can help the assistants a lot. I'll speak to the Committee for you."

Andrew would not have minded speaking to the Committee, to Owen, himself. But he let the matter pass.

They drank their coffee in the drawing-room from, as Mrs. Llewellyn pointed out, "hand-painted" cups. Llewellyn offered cigarettes from his gold cigarette case—"Take a look at that, Doctor Manson. There's a present for you! Grateful patient! Heavy, isn't it? Worth twenty pounds if it's worth a penny."

Towards ten o'clock Doctor Llewellyn looked at his fine half-hunter watch—actually he beamed at the watch, for he could contemplate even inanimate objects, particularly when they belonged to him, with that bland cordiality which was especially his own. For a moment Manson thought he was going into intimate details about the watch. But instead he remarked:

"I've got to go to the hospital. Gastro-duodenal I did this morning. How about runnin' round with me in the car and taking a look at it?"

Andrew sat up eagerly. "Why, I'd love to, Doctor Llewellyn."

Since Christine was included in the invitation also, they said good night to Mrs. Llewellyn, who waved them tender farewells from the front door, and stepped into the waiting car which moved with silent elegance along the main street then up the incline to the left.

"Powerful headlights, aren't they?" Llewellyn remarked, switching on for their benefit. "Luxite! They're an extra. I had them fitted specially."

"Luxite!" said Christine suddenly, in a meek voice. "Surely they're very expensive, doctor?"

"You bet they were," Llewellyn nodded emphatically, appreciative of the question. "Cost me every penny of thirty pounds."

Andrew, hugging himself, dared not meet his wife's eye.

"Here we are, then," said Llewellyn two minutes later. "This is my spiritual home."

The hospital was a red-brick building, well constructed and approached by a gravel drive flanked with laurel bushes. Immediately they entered Andrew's eye lit up. Though small the place was modern, beautifully equipped. As Llewellyn showed them round the theatre, the X-ray room, the splint room, the two fine airy wards, Andrew kept thinking exultantly, this is perfect, perfect—what a difference from Drineffy!—God! I'll get my cases well in here!

They picked up the matron on their travels, a tall, raw-boned woman who ignored Christine, greeted Andrew without enthusiasm, then melted into adoration before Llewellyn.

"We get pretty well all we want here, don't we, matron?" Llewellyn said. "We just speak to the Committee. Yes, yes, they're not a bad lot, take them all in all. How's my gastro-enterostomy, matron?"

"Very comfortable, Doctor Llewellyn," murmured the matron.

"Good! I'll see it in a minute!" He escorted Christine and Andrew back again to the vestibule.

"Yes, I do admit, Manson, I'm rather proud of this place. I regard it as my own. Can't blame me either. You'll find your own way home, won't you? And look here, when you get back on Wednesday ring me up. I might want you for an anæsthetic."

Walking down the road together they kept silence for a while then Christine took Andrew's arm.

"Well?" she inquired.

He could feel her smiling in the darkness.

"I like him," he said quickly. "I like him a lot. Did you spot the matron too—as if she was going to kiss the hem of his garment. But by Jove! That's a marvellous little hospital. It was a good dinner they gave us too. They're not mean. Only—oh! I don't know—why should we pay him a fifth of our salary? It doesn't sound fair, or even ethical! And somehow—I feel as if I'd been smoothed and petted and told to be a good boy."

"You were a very good boy to ask or these two days. But really, darling—how can we do it? We've no money to buy furniture with—yet?"

"You wait and see," he answered cryptically.

The lights of the town lay behind, and an odd silence fell between them as they approached Vale View. The touch of her hand upon his arm was precious to him. A great wave of love swept over him. He thought of her, married off hand in a mining village, dragged in a derelict lorry across the mountains, dumped into a half empty house where their wedding couch must be her own single bed—and sustaining these hardships and makeshifts with courage and a smiling tenderness. She loved him, trusted him, believed in him. A great determination swelled in him. He would repay it, he would show her, by his work, that her faith in him was justified.

They crossed the wooden bridge. The murmur of the stream, its littered banks hidden by the soft darkness of night, was sweet in their ears. He took the key from his pocket, the key of their house, and fitted it in the lock.

In the hall it was almost dark. When he had closed the door he turned to where she waited for him. Her face was faintly luminous, her slight figure expectant yet defenceless. He put his arm round her gently. He whispered, strangely:

"What's your name, darling?"

"Christine," she answered wondering.

"Christine what?"

"Christine Manson." Her breath came quickly, quickly, and was warm upon his lips.

III

THE FOLLOWING afternoon their train drew into Paddington Station. Adventurously, yet conscious of their inexperience in the face of this great city which neither of them had seen before, Andrew and Christine descended to the platform.

"Do you see him?" Andrew asked anxiously.

"Perhaps he'll be at the barrier," Christine suggested.

They were looking for the Man with the Catalogue.

On the journey down Andrew had explained, in detail, the beauty, simplicity, and extraordinary foresight of his scheme, of how, realising their needs even before they left Drineffy, he had placed himself in touch with the Regency Plenishing Company and Depositories, of London, E. It wasn't a colossal establishment, the Regency—none of your department store nonsense—but a decent, privately owned emporium which specialised in hire purchase. He had the recent letter from the proprietor in his pocket. Why, in point of fact——

"Ah!" he now exclaimed with satisfaction. "There he is!"

A seedy little man in a shiny blue suit and a bowler hat, holding a large green catalogue like a Sunday school prize, seemed, by some obscure feat of telepathy, to single them out from the crowd of travellers. He sidled towards them.

"Doctor Manson, sir? And Mrs. Manson?" Deferentially raising his hat. "I represent the Regency. We had your telegram this morning, sir. I have the car waiting. May I offer you a cigar?"

As they drove through the strange, traffic-laden streets, Andrew betrayed perhaps the faintest glimmer of disquiet, the corner of one eye on the presentation cigar, still unlighted, in his hand. He grunted:

"We're doing a lot of driving about in cars these days. But this must be all right. They guarantee everything, including free transport to and from the station, *also* our railway fares."

Yet, despite this assurance, their transit along bewilderingly complex and often mean thoroughfares was perceptibly anxious. At length, however, they were there. It was a showier establishment than either of them had expected, and there was a good deal of plate glass and shiny brass about the frontage. The door of the car was opened for them, they were bowed into the Regency Emporium.

Again they were expected, made royally welcome by an elderly sales-man in a frock-coat and high collar, who with his striking air of probity bore some resemblance to the late Prince Albert.

"This way, sir. This way, madam. Very happy to serve a medical gentleman, Doctor Manson. You'd be surprised the number of 'Arley Street specialists I've had the honour of attending to. The testimonials I've 'ad from them! And now, doctor, what would you be requiring?"

He began to show them furniture, padding up and down the aisles of the emporium with a stately tread. He named prices that were inconveniently large. He used the words Tudor, Jacobean and Looez Sez. And what he showed them was fumed and varnished rubbish.

Christine bit her lip and her worried look increased. She willed with all her strength that Andrew would not be deceived, that he would not burden their home with this awful stuff.

"Darling," she whispered swiftly, when Prince Albert's back was turned, "no good—no good at all."

A barely perceptible tightening of his lips was her answer. They inspected a few more pieces. Then quietly, but with surprising rudeness, Andrew addressed the salesman.

"Look here, you! We've come a long way to buy furniture. I said *furniture*. Not this kind of junk." Violently with his thumb he pressed the front of an adjoining wardrobe which, being of plywood, caved in with an ominous cracking.

The salesman almost collapsed. This, his expression said, simply cannot be true.

"But, doctor," he gulped, "I've been showing you and your lady the best in the 'ouse."

"Then show us the worst," Andrew raged. "Show us old second-hand stuff—so long as it's *real*."

A pause. Then, muttering under his breath: "The guv'ner'll give me what for, if I don't sell you!" the salesman padded disconsolately away. He did not return. Four minutes later a short red-faced common man came bustling towards them. He shot out:

"What d'you want?"

"Good second-hand furniture—cheap!"

The short man fired a hard glance at Andrew. Without further speech he spun round and led them to a trade lift at the back which, when manipulated, dropped them to a large chilly basement, crammed to the ceiling with second-hand goods.

For an hour Christine probed amongst the dust and cobwebs, finding a stout chest here, a good plain table there, a small upholstered easy-chair beneath a pile of sacking, while Andrew, following behind, wrangled long and stubbornly with the short man over prices.

Their list was complete at last and Christine, her face smudged but happy, pressed Andrew's hand with a thrilling sense of triumph as they ascended in the lift.

"Just what we wanted," she whispered.

The red-faced man took them to the office, where, laying down his order book on the proprietor's desk with the air of a man who has laboured to do his best, he said: "That's the lot then, Mr. Isaacs."

Mr. Isaacs caressed his nose. His eyes, liquid against his sallow skin, were sorrowful as he studied the order book.

"I'm afraid we can't give you E.P. terms on this, Doctor Manson. You see, it's all second-hand goods." A deprecating shrug. "We don't do our business like that."

Christine turned pale. But Andrew, grimly insistent, sat down upon a chair like a man who meant to stay.

"Oh, yes, you do, Mr. Isaacs. At least it says so in your letter. Printed in black and white on the top of your notepaper. New and second-hand furniture supplied on easy terms."

There was a pause. The red-faced man, bending over Mr. Isaacs, made rapid mutterings accompanied by gesticulations in his ear. Christine plainly caught impolite words which testified to the toughness of her husband's fibre, the power of his racial persistence.

"Well, Doctor Manson," smiled Mr. Isaacs, with an effort. "You shall have your way. Don't say the Regency wasn't good to you. And don't forget to tell your patients. All about how well you were treated here. Smith! Make out that bill on the H.P. sheet and see that

546

Doctor Manson has a copy posted to him first thing to-morrow morning!"

"Thank you, Mr. Isaacs."

Another pause. Mr. Isaacs said, by way of closing the interview, "That's right, then, that's right. The goods will reach you on Friday."

Christine made to leave the office. But Andrew still remained fast to his chair. He said slowly: "And now, Mr. Isaacs! What about our railway fares?"

It was as if a bomb had exploded into the office. Smith, the red-faced man, looked as though his veins would burst.

"My God, Doctor Manson!" exclaimed Isaacs. "What d'you mean. We can't do business like that. Fair's fair, but I ain't a camel! *Railway fares!*"

Inexorably Andrew produced his pocket-book. His voice, though it wavered slightly, was measured.

"I have a letter here, Mr. Isaacs, in which you say in plain black and white that you will pay customers' railway fares from England and Wales on orders over fifty pounds."

"But I tell you," Isaacs expostulated wildly, "you only bought fifty-five pounds worth of goods—and all second-hand stuff——"

"In your letter, Mr. Isaacs——"

"Never mind my letter," Isaacs threw up his hands. "Never mind anything. The deal's off. I never had a customer like you in all my life. We're used to nice young married people which we can talk to. First you insult my Mr. Clapp, then my Mr. Smith can't do nothing with you, then you come here breakin' my heart with talk of *railway fares*. We can't do business, Doctor Manson. You can go try if you can do better somewhere else!"

Christine, in a panic, glanced at Andrew, her eyes holding a desperate appeal. She felt that all was lost. This terrible husband of hers had thrown away all the benefits he had so hardly won. But Andrew, appearing not to see her even, was dourly folding up his pocket-book and placing it in his pocket.

"Very well, then, Mr. Isaacs. We'll say good afternoon to you. But I'm telling you—this won't make very good hearing to all my patients and their friends. I have a large practice. And this is bound to get round. How you brought us up to London, promising to pay our fares, and when we——"

"Stop! Stop!" Isaacs wailed in something like a frenzy. "How much was your fares? Pay them, Mr. Smith! Pay them, pay them, *pay* them. Only don't say the Regency didn't ever do what it promised. *There* now! Are you satisfied?"

"Thank you, Mr. Isaacs. We're very satisfied. We'll expect delivery on Friday. Good afternoon, Mr. Isaacs."

Gravely, Manson shook him by the hand and taking Christine's arm, hastened her to the door. Outside, the antique limousine which had brought them was waiting and, as though he had given the largest order in the history of the Regency, Andrew exclaimed:

"Take us to the Museum Hotel, driver!"

They were off immediately, without interference, swinging out of the East End in the direction of Bloomsbury. And Christine, tensely clutching Andrew's arm, allowed herself gradually to relax.

"Oh, darling," she whispered. "You managed that wonderfully. Just when I thought——"

He shook his head, his jaw still stubbornly set.

"They didn't want trouble, that crowd. I had their promise, their *written* promise——" He swung round to her, his eyes burning. "It wasn't these idiotic fares, darling. You know that. It was the principle of the thing. People ought to keep their word. It put my back up too, the way they were waiting for us, you could see it a mile away—here's a couple of greenhorns—easy money. Oh, and that cigar they dumped on me too, the whole thing reeked of swindle."

"We managed to get what we wanted, anyhow," she murmured tactfully.

He nodded. He was too strung up, too seething with indignation to see the humour of it then. But in their room at the Museum the comic side became apparent. As he lit a cigarette and stretched himself on the bed, watching her as she tidied her hair, he suddenly began to laugh. He laughed so much that he set her laughing, too.

"That look on old Isaacs's face——" he wheezed, his ribs aching. "It was—it was screamingly funny."

"When you," she gasped weakly, "when you asked him for the fares."

"Business, he said, we can't do business." He went off into another paroxysm. " 'Am I a camel,' he said. Oh, lord!—a *camel*——"

"Yes, darling." Comb in hand, tears running down her cheeks, she turned to him, scarcely able to articulate. "But the funniest thing—to me—was the way you kept saying 'I've got it here in black and white' when I—when I—oh dear!—*when I knew all the time you'd left the letter on the mantelpiece at home.*"

He sat up, staring at her, then flung himself down with a yell of laughter. He rolled about, stuffing the pillow into his mouth, helpless, out of all control, while she clung to the dressing-table, shaking, sore with laughter, begging him, deliriously, to stop or she would expire.

Later, when they had managed to compose themselves, they went to the theatre. Since he gave her free choice she selected *Saint Joan*. All her life, she told him, she had wanted to see a play by Shaw.

Seated beside her in the crowded pit he was less engaged by the play— too historical, he told her afterwards, who does this fellow Shaw think he is, anyway?—than by the faint flush upon her eager entranced face.

548

Their first visit to the theatre together. Well, it wouldn't be the last by a long way. His eyes wandered round the full house. They would be back here again some day, not in the pit, in òne of those boxes there. He would see to it; he would show them all a thing or two! Christine would wear a low-necked evening dress, people would look at him, nudge each other, that's Manson, you know, that doctor who did that marvellous work on lungs. He pulled himself up sharply, rather sheepishly, and bought Christine an ice cream at the interval.

Afterwards he was reckless in the princely manner. Outside the theatre they found themselves completely lost, baffled by the lights, the buses, the teeming crowds. Peremptorily Andrew held up his hand. Safely ensconced, being driven to their hotel, they thought themselves, blissfully, pioneers in discovering the privacy afforded by a London taxi.

IV

AFTER LONDON the breeze of Aberalaw was crisp and cool. Walking down from Vale View on Thursday morning to commence his duties, Andrew felt it strike invigoratingly on his cheek. A tingling exhilaration filled him. He saw his work stretching out before him here, work well and cleanly done, work always guided by his principle, the scientific method.

The West Surgery, which lay not more than four hundred yards from his house, was a high vaulted building, white-tiled and with a vague air of sanitation. Its main and central portion was the waiting-room. At the bottom end, cut off from the waiting-room by a sliding hatch, was the dispensary. At the top were two consulting-rooms, one bearing the name of Doctor Urquhart and the other, freshly painted, the mysteriously arresting name, Doctor Manson.

It gave Andrew a thrill of pleasure to see himself identified, already, with his room, which though not large had a good desk and a sound leather couch for examinations. He was flattered too, by the number of people waiting on him—such a crowd, in fact, that he thought it better to begin work immediately without first making himself known, as he had intended, to Doctor Urquhart and the dispenser, Gadge.

Seating himself, he signed for his first case to come in. This was a man who asked simply for a certificate adding, as a kind of afterthought, beat knee. Andrew examined him, found him suffering from beat knee, gave him the certificate of incapacity for work.

The second case came in. He also demanded his certificate, nystagmus. The third case: certificate, bronchitis. The fourth case: certificate, beat elbow.

Andrew got up, anxious to know where he stood. These certificate examinations took a great deal of time. He went to his door and asked: "How many more men for certificates? Will they stand up, please."

There were perhaps forty men waiting outside. They all stood up. Andrew reflected quickly. It would take him the best part of the day to examine them all properly—an impossible situation. Reluctantly, he made up his mind to defer the more exacting examinations until another time.

Even so, it was half past ten when he got through his last case. Then as he glanced up, there stamped into his room a medium sized, oldish man with a brick-red face and a small pugnacious grey imperial. He stooped slightly so that his head had a forward belligerent thrust. He wore cord breeches, gaiters, and a tweed jacket, the side pockets stuffed to bursting point with pipe, handkerchief, an apple, a gum elastic catheter. About him hung the odour of drugs, carbolic and strong tobacco. Andrew knew before he spoke that it was Doctor Urquhart.

"Dammit to hell, man," said Urquhart without a handshake or a word of introduction, "where were ye these last two days? I've had to lump your work for ye. Never mind, never mind! We'll say no more about it. Thank God ye look sound in mind an' limb now ye have arrived. Do ye smoke a pipe?"

"I do."

"Thank God for that also! Can ye play the fiddle?"

"No."

"Neither can I—but I can make them bonny. I collect china too. They've had my name in a book. I'll show ye some day when ye come ben my house. It's just at the side of the surgery ye'll have observed. And now, come away and meet Gadge. He's a miserable devil. But he knows his incompatibles."

Andrew followed Urquhart through the waiting-room into the dispensary where Gadge greeted him with a gloomy nod. He was a long, lean cadaverous man with a bald head streaked with jet-black hair and drooping whiskers of the same colour. He wore a short alpaca jacket, green with age and the stains of drugs, which showed his bony wrists and death's door shoulder blades. His air was sad, caustic, tired; his attitude that of the most disillusioned man in the whole universe. As Andrew entered he was serving his last client, flinging a box of pills through the hatch as though it was rat poison. "Take it or leave it," he seemed to say. "You've got to die in any case!"

"Well," said Urquhart spryly, when he had effected the introduction. "Ye've met Gadge and ye know the worst. I warn ye he believes in nothing except maybe castor oil and Charles Bradlaugh. Now—is there anything I can tell ye?"

"I'm worried about the number of certificates I had to sign. Some of these chaps this morning looked to me quite capable of work."

"Ay, ay. Leslie let them pile up on him anyhow. His idea of examining a patient was to take his pulse for exactly five seconds by the clock. He didn't mind a docken."

Andrew answered quickly. "What can anyone think of a doctor who hands out certificates like cigarette coupons?"

Urquhart darted a glance at him. He said bluntly:

"Be careful how you go. They're liable not to like it if you sign them off."

For the first and last time that morning Gadge made gloomy interjection.

"That's because there's nothing wrong wi' half o' them, ruddy scrimshankers!"

All that day as he went on his visits Andrew worried about these certificates. His round was not easy for he did not know the neighbourhood, the streets were unfamiliar and more than once he had to go back and cover the same ground twice. His district, moreover, or the greater part of it, lay on the side of that Mardy Hill to which Tom Kettles had referred and this meant stiff climbing between one row of houses and the next.

Before afternoon his cogitation had forced him to an unpleasant decision. He could not, on any account, give a slack certificate. He went down to his evening surgery with an anxious yet determined line fixed between his brows.

The crowd, if anything, was larger than at the morning surgery. And the first patient to enter was a great lump of a man, rolling in fat, who smelled strongly of beer and looked as if he had never done a full day's work in his life. He was about fifty and had small pig eyes which blinked down at Andrew.

"Certificate," he said, without minding his manners.

"What for?" Andrew asked.

"'Stagmus." He held out his hand. "The name's Chenkin. Ben Chenkin."

The tone alone caused Andrew to look at Chenkin with quick resentment. Even from a cursory inspection he felt convinced that Chenkin had no nystagmus. He was well aware, apart from Gadge's hint, that some of these old pitmen "swung the lead on 'stagmus," drawing compensation money to which they were not entitled for years on end. However, he had brought his ophthalmoscope with him this evening. He would soon make sure. He rose from his seat.

"Take your things off."

This time it was Chenkin who asked: "What for?"

"I'm going to examine you."

Ben Chenkin's jaw dropped. He had not been examined, so far as he could remember, in the whole of Doctor Leslie's seven years of office. Unwillingly, sulkily, he pulled off his jacket, his muffler, his red and blue striped shirt, revealing a hairy torso swathed in adiposity.

Andrew made a long and thorough examination, particularly of the eyes, searching both retinæ carefully with his tiny electric bulb. Then, sharply, he said:

"Dress up, Chenkin." He sat down and, taking his pen, he began to write out a certificate.

"Ha!" sneered old Ben. "I thought you'd let us 'ave it."

"Next please," Andrew called out.

Chenkin almost snatched the pink slip from Andrew's hand. Then he strode triumphantly from the surgery.

Five minutes later he was back, his face livid, bellowing like a bull, thrusting his way between the men seated waiting on the benches.

"Look what he's done on us! Let us in, will ye! Hey! What's the meanin' of this?" He flourished the certificate in Andrew's face.

Andrew affected to read the slip. It said, in his own handwriting: *This is to certify that Ben Chenkin is suffering from the effects of over indulgence in malt liquors but is perfectly fit to work. Signed A. Manson, M.B.*

"Well?" he asked.

"'Stagmus," shouted Chenkin. "Certificate for 'stagmus. You can't play the bloody fool on us. Fifteen year us got 'stagmus!"

"You haven't got it now," Andrew said. A crowd had gathered round the open door. He was conscious of Urquhart's head popping out curiously from the other room, of Gadge inspecting the tumult with relish through his hatch.

"For the last time—are ye going to give us 'stagmus certificate?" Chenkin bawled.

Andrew lost his temper.

"No, I'm not," he shouted back. "And get out of here before I put you out."

Ben's stomach heaved. He looked as if he might wipe the floor with Andrew. Then his eyes dropped, he turned and, muttering profane threats, he walked out of the surgery.

The minute he was gone Gadge came out of the dispensary and shuffled across to Andrew. He rubbed his hands with melancholy delight.

"You know who that was you just knocked off? Ben Chenkin. His son's a big man on the Committee."

V

THE SENSATION of the Chenkin case was enormous, it hummed round Manson's district in a flash. Some people said it was "a good job"—a few went so far as "a damned good job"—that Ben had been pulled up in his swindling and signed fit for work. But the majority were on Ben's side. All the "compo cases"—those drawing compensation money for disabilities—were especially bitter against the new doctor. As he went on his rounds Andrew was conscious of black looks directed towards him. And at night, in the surgery, he had to face an even worse manifestation of unpopularity.

Although nominally every assistant was allotted a district, the workmen in that district had still the right of free choice of doctor. Each man had a card and by demanding that card and handing it to another doctor he could effect a change. It was this ignominy which now began for Andrew. Every night that week men whom he had never seen dropped into his surgery—some who were disinclined for the personal encounter even sent their wives—to say, without looking at him: "If you don't mind, doctor, I'll 'ave my card."

The wretchedness, the humiliation of rising to extract these cards from the box on his desk, was intolerable. And every card he gave away meant ten shillings subtracted from his salary.

On Saturday night Urquhart invited him into his house. The old man, who had gone about all week with an air of self-justification on his choleric features, began by exhibiting the treasures of his forty years of practice. He had perhaps a score of yellow violins, all made by himself, hung up on his walls, but these were as nothing compared with the choice perfection of his collection of old English china.

It was a superb collection—Spode, Wedgwood, Crown Derby, and, best of all, old Swansea—they were all there. His plates and mugs, his bowls, cups and jugs, they filled every room in the house and overflowed into the bathroom where it was possible for Urquhart, when making his toilet, to survey with pride an original willow pattern tea service.

China was, in fact, the passion of Urquhart's life, and he was an old and cunning master in the gentle art of acquiring it. Whenever he saw a "nice bit"—his own phrase—in a patient's house he would call and call with unwearying attention, meanwhile fixing his eye, with a kind of wistful persistence upon the coveted piece, until at last in desperation the good woman of the house would exclaim:

"Doctor, you seem awful struck on that bit. I can't see but what I'm goin' to let you 'ave it!"

Thereupon Urquhart would make a virtuous protest, then bearing his trophy, wrapped up in newspaper, he would dance home in triumph and place it tenderly on to his shelves.

The old man passed, in the town, as a character. He gave his age as sixty but was probably over seventy and possibly near to eighty. Tough as whalebone, his sole vehicle shoe leather, he covered incredible distances, swore murderously at his patients, and could yet be tender as a woman, lived by himself—since the death of his wife eleven years before—and existed almost entirely upon tinned soup.

This evening, having proudly displayed his collection, he suddenly remarked to Andrew with an injured air:

"Dammit, man! I don't want any of your patients. I've got enough of my own. But what can I do if they come pestering me. They can't all go to the East Surgery, it's too far away."

Andrew reddened. There was nothing that he could say.

"You want to be more careful, man." Urquhart went on in an altered tone. "Oh, I know, I know. You want to tear down the walls of Babylon —I was young myself once. But all the same, go slow, go easy, look before you leap! Good night. My compliments to your wife!"

With Urquhart's words sounding in his ear, Andrew made every effort to steer a cautious course. But, even so, a greater disaster immediately overtook him.

On the Monday following he went to the house of Thomas Evans in Cefan Row. Evans, a hewer at the Aberalaw colliery, had upset a kettle of boiling water over his left arm. It was a serious scald, covering a large area and particularly bad in the region of the elbow. When Andrew arrived he found that the district nurse, who had been in the row at the time of the accident, had dressed the scald with carron oil and had then continued on her round.

Andrew examined the arm, carefully suppressing his horror of the filthy dressing. Out of the corner of his eye he observed the carron oil bottle, corked with a plug of newspaper, holding a dirty whitish liquid, in which he could almost see bacteria seething in shoals.

"Nurse Lloyd done it pretty good, eh, doctor?" said Evans nervously. He was a dark-eyed, highly strung youngster, and his wife, who stood near, closely observing Andrew, was nervous too and not unlike him in appearance.

"A beautiful dressing," Andrew said with a great show of enthusiasm. "I've rarely seen a neater one. Only a first dressing of course. Now I think we'll try some picric."

He knew that if he did not quickly use the antiseptic the arm would almost certainly become infected. And then, he thought, heaven help that elbow joint!

They watched him dubiously while, with scrupulous gentleness, he cleansed the arm and slipped on a moist picric dressing.

"There now," he exclaimed. "Doesn't that feel easier?"

"I don't know as how it does," Evans said. "Are you sure it's goin' to be all right, doctor?"

"Positive!" Andrew smiled reassuringly. "You must leave this to nurse and me."

Before he left the house he wrote a short note to the district nurse, taking extra pains to be tactful, considerate of her feelings, wise. He, thanked her for her splendid emergency treatment and asked her, as a measure against possible sepsis if she would mind continuing with the picric dressings. He sealed the envelope carefully.

Next morning when he arrived at the house, his picric dressings had been thrown in the fire and the arm was redressed with carron oil. Waiting upon him, prepared for battle, was the district nurse.

"What's all this about, I'd like to know. Isn't my word good enough for you, Doctor Manson?" She was a broad, middle-aged woman with untidy iron-grey hair and a harassed, over-wrought face. She could barely speak for the heaving of her bosom.

Andrew's heart sank. But he took a rigid grip upon himself. He forced a smile. "Come now, Nurse Lloyd, don't misunderstand me. Suppose we talk this over together in the front room."

The nurse bridled, swept her eyes to where Evans and his wife, who clutched a little girl of three to her skirts, were listening wide-eyed and alarmed.

"No, indeed, we'll talk it over here. I got nothing to hide. My conscience is clear. Born and brought up in Aberalaw I was, went to school here, married here, 'ad children here, lost my 'usband here, and worked here twenty year as district nurse. And nobody ever told me not to use carron oil on a burn or scald."

"Now listen, nurse," Andrew pleaded. "Carron oil is all right in its way perhaps. But there's a great danger of contracture here." He stiffened up her elbow by way of illustration. "That's why I want you to try my dressing."

"Never 'eard of the stuff. Old Doctor Urquhart don't use it. And that's what I told Mr. Evans. I don't hold with new-fangled ideas of somebody that's been here no more nor a week!"

Andrew's lips were dry. He felt shaky and ill at the thought of further trouble, of all the repercussions of this scene, for the nurse, going from house to house, and talking her mind in all of them, was a person with whom it was dangerous to quarrel. But he could not, he dared not, risk his patient with that antiquated treatment. He said in a low voice:

"If you won't do the dressing, nurse, I'll come in morning and evening and do it myself."

"You can then, for all I care," Nurse Lloyd declared, moisture flashing to her eyes. "And I 'ope Tom Evans lives through it."

The next minute she had flounced out of the house.

In dead silence Andrew removed the dressing once again. He spent nearly half an hour patiently bathing and attending to the damaged arm. When he left the house he promised to return at nine o'clock that night.

That same evening as he entered his consulting-room the first person to enter was Mrs. Evans, her face white, her dark frightened eyes avoiding his.

"I'm sure, doctor," she stammered, "I do hate to trouble you, but can I have Tom's card?"

A wave of hopelessness passed over Andrew. He rose without a word, searched for Tom Evans's card, handed it to her.

"You understand, doctor, you—you won't be callin' any more."

He said unsteadily: "I understand, Mrs. Evans." Then as she made for the door he asked—he had to ask—the question: "Is the carron oil on again?"

She gulped, nodded and was gone.

After surgery, Andrew, who usually tore home at top speed, made the passage to Vale View wearily. A triumph, he thought bitterly, for the scientific method! And again, am I honest or am I simply clumsy?—clumsy and stupid, stupid and clumsy!

He was very silent during supper. But afterwards, in the sitting-room, now comfortably furnished, while they sat together on the couch before the cheerful fire, he laid his head close to her soft young breasts.

"Oh darling," he groaned, "I've made an awful muddle of our start!"

As she soothed him, gently stroking his brow, he felt tears smarting behind his eyes.

VI

Winter set in early and unexpectedly with a heavy fall of snow. Though it was only mid-October, Aberalaw lay so high that hard and bitter frosts gripped the town almost before the leaves had fallen from the trees. The snow came silently through the night, soft drifting flakes, and Christine and Andrew woke to a great glittering whiteness. A herd of mountain ponies had come through a gap in the broken wooden palings at the side of the house and were gathered round the back door. Upon the wide uplands, stretches of rough grass land, all round Aberalaw, these dark wild little creatures roamed in large numbers, starting away at the approach of man. But in snowy weather, hunger drove them down to the outskirts of the town.

All winter Christine fed the ponies. At first they backed from her, shy and stumbling, but in the end they came to eat from her hand. One especially became her friend, the smallest of them all, a black tangle-maned, roguish eyed creature, no larger than a Shetland, whom they named Darkie.

The ponies would eat any kind of food, scraps of loaf, potato and apple rinds, even orange peel. Once, in fun, Andrew offered Darkie an empty match-box. Darkie munched it down, then licked his lips, like a gourmet eating paté.

Though they were so poor, though they had to bear many things, Christine and Andrew knew happiness. Andrew had only pence to jingle in his pockets, but the Endowment debt was almost settled and the furniture instalments were being paid. Christine, for all her fragility and look of inexperience, had the attribute of the Yorkshire woman, she was a house-wife. With the help only of a young girl named Jenny, a miner's daughter from the row behind, who came daily for a few shillings each week, she kept the house shining. Although four of its rooms remained unfurnished, and discreetly locked, she made Vale View a home. When Andrew came in tired, almost defeated by a long day, she would have a hot meal on the table which quickly restored him.

The work of the practice was desperately hard—not alas! because he had many patients, but because of the snow, the difficult "climbs" to the high parts of his district, the long distances between his calls. When it thawed and the roads turned to slush, before freezing hard again at night, the going was heavy and difficult. He came in so often with sodden trouser ends that Christine bought him a pair of leggings. At night when he sank into a chair exhausted she would kneel and take off these leggings, then his heavy boots, before handing him his slippers. It was not an act of service but of love.

The people remained suspicious, difficult. All Chenkin's relations— and they were numerous, since inter-marriage was common in the valleys—had become welded into a hostile unit. Nurse Lloyd was openly and bitterly his enemy and would run him down as she sat drinking tea in the houses which she visited, listened to by a knot of women from the Row.

In addition he had to contend with an ever-increasing irritation. Doctor Llewellyn was using him for anæsthetics far oftener than he judged fair. Andrew hated giving anæsthetics—it was mechanical work which demanded a specialised type of mind, a slow and measured temperament which he certainly did not possess. He did not in the least object to serving his own patients. But when he found himself requisitioned three days a week for cases he had never seen before, he began to feel that he was shouldering a burden which belonged to someone else. Yet he simply dared not risk a protest for fear of losing his job.

One day in November, however, Christine noticed that something unusual had upset him. He came in that evening without hailing her gaily and, though he made pretence of unconcern, she loved him too well not to detect from the deepened line between his eyes and a score of other minute signs, that he had received an unexpected blow.

She made no comment during supper and afterwards she began to busy herself with some sewing beside the fire. He sat beside her, biting on his pipe, then all at once he declared:

"I hate grousing, Chris! And I hate bothering you. God knows I try to keep things to myself!" This, considering that he poured his heart out to her every night, was highly diverting. But Christine did not smile as he continued:

"You know the hospital, darling. You remember going over it our first night. Remember how I loved it and raved about opportunities and chances of doing fine work there, and everything. I thought a lot about that didn't I, darling? I had great ideas about our little Aberalaw Hospital?"

"Yes, I know you did."

He said stonily:

"I needn't have deluded myself. It isn't the Aberalaw Hospital. It's Llewellyn's Hospital."

She was silent, her eyes concerned, waiting for him to explain.

"I had a case this morning, Chris!" He spoke quickly now, at white heat. "You'll note that I say *had*!—a really early apical pneumonia in one of the anthracite drillers, too. I've told you often how terribly interested I am in their lung conditions. I'm positive there's a big field for research work there. I thought to myself—here's my first case for hospital—genuine chance for charting and scientific recording. I rang up Llewellyn, asked him to see the case with me, so that I could get it into the ward!" He stopped to take a swift breath, then rushed on:

"Well! Down came Llewellyn, limousine and all. Nice as you please, and damned thorough in his examination. He knows his work inside out, mind you, he's an absolute topnotch man. He confirmed the diagnosis, after pointing out one or two things I'd missed, and absolutely agreed to take the case into hospital there and then. I began to thank him, saying how much I would appreciate coming into the ward and having such good facilities for this particular case." He paused again, his jaw set. "Llewellyn gave me a look at that, Chris, very friendly and nice. 'You needn't bother about coming up, Manson,' he said, "*I'll* look after him now. We couldn't have you assistants clattering around the wards'—he took a look at my leggings—'in your hob-nail boots——' "

Andrew broke off with a choking exclamation. "Oh! What's the use going over what he said! It all boils down to this—I can go tramping into miners' kitchens, in my sopping raincoat and dirty boots, examining my cases in a bad light, treating them in bad conditions, but when it comes to the hospital—ah! I'm only wanted there to give the ether!"

He was interrupted by the ringing of the telephone. Gazing at him with sympathy she rose, after a moment, to answer it. He could hear her speaking in the hall. Then, very hesitatingly she returned.

"It's Doctor Llewellyn on the phone, I'm—I'm terribly sorry, darling. He wants you to-morrow at eleven for—for an anæsthetic."

He did not answer, but remained with his head bowed despondently between his clenched fists.

"What shall I tell him, darling?" Christine murmured anxiously.

"Tell him to go to hell!" he shouted; then passing his hand across

558

his brow. "No, no. Tell him I'll be there at eleven," he smiled bitterly, "at eleven *sharp*."

When she came back she brought him a cup of hot coffee—one of her effectual devices for combating his moods of depression.

As he drank it he smiled at her wryly.

"I'm so dashed happy here with you, Chris. If only the work would go right. Oh! I admit there's nothing personal or unusual in Llewellyn's keeping me out of the wards. It's the same in London, in all the big hospitals everywhere. It's the system. But why should it be, Chris? Why should a doctor be dragged off his case when it goes into hospital? He loses the case as completely as if he'd lost the patient. It's part of our damn specialist-G.P. system and it's wrong, all wrong! Lord! why am I lecturing you though? As if we hadn't enough worries of our own. When I think how I started here! What I was going to do! And instead —one thing after another—all gone wrong!"

But at the end of the week he had an unexpected visitor. Quite late, when he and Christine were upon the point of going upstairs, the door bell rang. It was Owen, the secretary to the Society.

Andrew paled. He saw the secretary's visit as the most ominous event of all, the climax of these struggling unsuccessful months. Did the Committee want him to resign? Was he to be sacked, thrown out with Christine into the street, a wretched failure? His heart contracted as he gazed at the secretary's thin diffident face, then suddenly expanded with relief and joy as Owen produced a yellow card.

"I'm sorry to call so late, Doctor Manson, but I've been detained late at the office, I didn't have time to look in at the surgery. I was wondering if you would care to have my medical card. It's strange in a way, me being secretary to the society, that I haven't ever bothered to fix up. The last time I visited a doctor I was down in Cardiff. But now, if you'll have me, I'd greatly appreciate to be on your list."

Andrew could scarcely speak. He had handed over so many of these cards, wincing as he did so, that now to receive one, and from the secretary himself, was overwhelming.

"Thank you, Mr. Owen—I'll—I'll be delighted to have you."

Christine, standing in the hall, was quick to interpose.

"Won't you come in, Mr. Owen. Please?"

Protesting that he was disturbing them, the secretary seemed nevertheless willing to be persuaded into the sitting-room. Seated in an armchair, his eyes fixed reflectively upon the fire, he had an air of extraordinary tranquillity. Though in his dress and speech he seemed no different from an ordinary working man he had the contemplative stillness, the almost transparent complexion of the ascetic. He appeared for some moments to be arranging his thoughts. Then he said:

"I'm glad to have the opportunity of talking to you, doctor. Don't be down-hearted if you're havin' a bit of a setback to begin with, like!

They're a little stiff, the folks here, but they're all right at heart. They'll come after a bit, they'll come!" Before Andrew could intervene he continued:

"You haven't heard of Tom Evans, like? No? His arm has turned out very bad. Ay, that stuff you warned them against did exactly what you was afraid of. His elbow's gone all stiff and crooked, he can't use it, he's lost his job at the pit over it. Ay, and since it was at home he scalded himself, he don't get a penny piece of compo."

Andrew muttered an expression of regret. He had no rancour against Evans, merely a sense of sadness at the futility of this case which had so needlessly gone wrong.

Owen was again silent, then in his quiet voice he began to tell them about his own early struggles, of how he had worked underground as a boy of fourteen, attended night school and gradually "improved himself," learned typing and shorthand, and finally secured the secretaryship of the Society.

Andrew could see that Owen's whole life was dedicated to improving the lot of the men. He loved his work in the Society because it was an expression of his ideal. But he wanted more than mere medical services. He wanted better housing, better sanitation, better and safer conditions, not only for the miners, but for their dependants. He quoted the maternity mortality rate amongst miners' wives, the infantile mortality rate. He had all the figures, all the facts at his finger ends.

But, besides talking, he listened. He smiled when Andrew related his experience with the sewer in the typhoid epidemic at Drineffy. He showed a deeper interest in the view that the anthracite workers were more liable to lung trouble than other underground workers.

Stimulated by Owen's presence, Andrew launched into this subject with great ardour. It had struck him, as the result of many painstaking examinations, how large a percentage of the anthracite miners suffered from insidious forms of lung disease. In Drineffy many of the drillers who came to him complaining of a cough or "a bit of phlegm in the tubes" were in reality incipient or even open cases of pulmonary tuberculosis. And he was finding the same thing here. He had begun to ask himelf if there was not some direct connection between the occupation and the disease.

"You see what I mean?" he exclaimed eagerly. "These men are working in dust all day, bad stone dust in the hard headings—their lungs get choked with it. Now I have my suspicion that it's injurious. The drillers, for instance, who get most of it—they seem to develop trouble more frequently than, say, the hauliers. Oh! I may be on the wrong track. But I don't think so! And what excites me so much is— oh, well! it's a line of investigation nobody has covered much. There's no mention in the Home Office list of any such industrial disease. When these men are laid up they don't get a penny piece of compensation!"

Roused, Owen bent forward, a vivid animation kindling his pale face.
"My goodness, doctor. You're really talkin'! I never heard anything
so important for a long time."

They fell into a lively discussion of the question. It was late when the
secretary rose to go. Apologising for having stayed so long, he pressed
Andrew whole-heartedly to proceed with his investigation, promising
him all the help in his power.

As the front door closed behind Owen he left behind him a warm
impression of sincerity. And Andrew thought, as at the Committee-
meeting when he had been given the appointment, that man is my
friend.

VII

THE NEWS that the secretary had lodged his card with Andrew spread
quickly through the district, and did something to arrest the run of the
new doctor's unpopularity.

Apart from this material gain both Christine and he felt better for
Owen's visit. So far the social life of the town had completely passed
them by. Though Christine never spoke of it there were moments during
Andrew's long absences upon his rounds when she felt her loneliness.
The wives of the higher officials of the company were too conscious of
their own importance to call upon the wives of medical aid assistants.
Mrs. Llewellyn, who had promised undying affection, and delightful
little motor trips to Cardiff, left cards when Christine was out and was
not heard of again. While the wives of Doctors Medley and Oxborrow
of the East Surgery—the former a faded white rabbit of a woman, the
latter a stringy zealot who talked West African missions for one hour by
the second-hand Regency clock—had proved singularly uninspiring.
There seemed indeed to be no sense of unity or social intercourse amongst
the medical assistants or their wives. They were indifferent, unresistant
and even down-trodden, in the attitude they presented to the town.

One December afternoon, when Andrew was returning to Vale View
by the back road which led along the brow of the hill he saw approaching
a lanky yet erect young man of his own age whom he recognised at once
as Richard Vaughan. His first impulse was to cross to the other side to
avoid the oncoming figure. And then, doggedly, came the thought:
Why should I? I don't care a damn who he is!

With his eyes averted he prepared to trudge past Vaughan when, to
his surprise, he heard himself addressed in a friendly, half-humorous
tone.

"Hello! You're the chap who put Ben Chenkin back to work, aren't
you?"

Andrew stopped, his gaze lifting warily, his expression saying: "What of it? I didn't do it for you." Though he answered civilly enough he told himself he was not prepared to be patronised even by the son of Edwin Vaughan. The Vaughans were the virtual owners of the Aberalaw Company, they drew all the royalties from the adjacent pits, were rich, exclusive, unapproachable. Now that old Edwin had retired to an estate near Brecon, Richard, the only son, had taken over the managing directorship of the Company. Recently married, he had built himself a large modern house overlooking the town.

Now, considering Andrew and tugging at his spare moustache, he said:

"I'd have enjoyed seeing old Ben's face."

"I didn't find it particularly amusing."

Vaughan's lip twitched behind his hand at the stiff Scots pride. He said easily:

"You're by way of being our nearest neighbours. My missus—she's been away in Switzerland these last weeks—will be calling on yours, now that you're settled in."

"Thanks!" Andrew said curtly, walking on.

At tea that night he related the incident sardonically to Christine:

"What was his idea? Tell me that! I've seen him pass Llewellyn in the street and barely throw him a nod. Perhaps he thought he'd mug me into sending a few more men back to work at his dashed mines!"

' "Now, don't, Andrew," Christine protested. "That's one thing about you! You're suspicious, frightfully suspicious of people."

"Think I would be suspicious of him. Stuck up blighter, rolling in money, old school tie under his ugly phiz—My missus—been yodelling on the Alps while you pigged it on Marcy Hill—will be calling on yours! Huh! I can *see* her looking near us, darling! And if she does," he was suddenly fierce, "take jolly good care you don't let her patronise you."

Chris answered—more shortly than he had ever heard her in all the tenderness of those first months:

"I think I know how to behave."

Despite Andrew's premonitions Mrs. Vaughan did call upon Christine and remained, apparently, much longer than the bare period demanded by convention. When Andrew came in that evening he found Christine gay, slightly flushed, with every appearance of having enjoyed herself. She was reticent to his ironic probings but admitted that the occasion had been a success.

He mocked her. "I suppose you had out the family silver, the best china, the gold-plated samovar. Oh! and a cake from Parry's."

"No. We had bread and butter," she answered equably. "And the brown tea-pot."

He raised his brows derisively.

"And she liked it?"

"I hope so!"

Something rankled queerly in Andrew after this conversation, an emotion which, had he tried, he could not quite have analysed. Ten days later when Mrs. Vaughan rang him up and asked Christine and him to dinner he was shaken. Christine was in the kitchen at the time baking a cake, and he answered the phone himself.

"I'm sorry," he said. "I'm afraid it's impossible. I have surgery till nearly nine every evening."

"But not on Sunday, surely." Her voice was light, charming. "Come to supper next Sunday. That's settled then. We'll expect you!"

He stormed into Christine.

"These dashed high-blown friends of yours have raked us in to supper. We can't go! I've got a positive conviction I'm having a midder case next Sunday evening!"

"Now you listen to me, Andrew Manson!" Her eyes had sparkled at the invitation but nevertheless she lectured him severely. "You've got to stop being silly. We're poor and everybody knows it. You wear old clothes and I do the cooking. But that doesn't matter. You're a doctor and a good doctor, too, and I'm your wife." Her expression relaxed momentarily. "Are you listening to me? Yes, it may surprise you, that I have my marriage lines tucked away in my bottom drawer. The Vaughans have got a lot of money but that's just a detail beside the fact that they're kind and charming and intelligent people. We're marvellously happy together here, darling, but we must have friends. Why shouldn't we be friendly with them if they'll let us? Now don't you be ashamed of being poor. Forget about money and position and everything and learn to take people for what they really are!"

"Oh, well——" he said grudgingly.

He went, on Sunday, expressionless and with apparent docility, merely using the corner of his mouth to remark, as they walked up the well laid out drive beside a new hard tennis court:

"Probably won't let us in, seeing I haven't got on a fish and soup."

Contrary to his expectation they were well received. Vaughan's bony, ugly face smiled hospitably over a silver canister which, for a reason unexplained, he shook heartily. Mrs. Vaughan greeted them with effortless simplicity. There were two other guests, Professor and Mrs. Challis, who were staying over the week-end with the Vaughans.

Over the first cocktail he had ever dealt with in his life Andrew took stock of the long fawn carpeted room with its flowers, books, strangely beautiful old furniture. Christine was talking lightheartedly with Vaughan and his wife and Mrs. Challis, an elderly woman with humorous wrinkles around her eyes. Feeling isolated and conspicuous, Andrew

563

gingerly approached Challis who, despite a large white beard, was successfully and cheerfully despatching his third short drink.

"Will some bright young physician kindly undertake an investigation," he smiled at Andrew, "as to the exact function of the olive in the martini. Mind you, I warn you beforehand—I have my suspicions. But what do you think doctor?"

"Why——" Andrew stammered. "I—I hardly know——"

"My theory!" Challis took pity on him. "A conspiracy of bartenders and inhospitable fellows like our friend Vaughan. An exploitation of the law of Archimedes." He blinked rapidly under his black bushy brows. "By the simple action of displacement they hope to save the gin!"

Andrew could not smile for thinking of his own awkwardness. He had no social graces and he had never been in so grand a house in all his life. He did not know what to do with his empty glass, his cigarette ash, his own—actually his own hands! He was glad when they went in to supper. But here again he felt himself at a disadvantage.

It was a simple but beautifully set out meal—a cup of hot bouillon stood waiting on each plate and this was followed by a chicken salad, all white breast and heart of lettuce and strange delicate flavours. Andrew was next to Mrs. Vaughan.

"Your wife is charming, Doctor Manson," she quietly remarked as they sat down. She was a tall thin elegant woman, very delicate in her appearance, not in the least pretty but with wide intelligent eyes and a manner of distinguished ease. Her mouth had a kind of upturned crookedness, a mobility which somehow conveyed a sense of wit and breeding.

She began to talk to him about his work, saying that her husband had heard of his thoroughness on more than one occasion. She tried kindly to draw him out, asking in an interested fashion, how he felt the conditions of practice could be improved in the district.

"Well—I don't know——" clumsily spilling some soup. "I suppose— I'd like to see more scientific methods used."

Stiff and tongue-tied upon his favourite subject—with which he had entranced Christine for hours—he kept his eyes upon his plate until, to his relief, Mrs. Vaughan slipped into conversation with Challis, on her other side.

Challis—presently revealed as Professor of Metallurgy at Cardiff, lecturer on the same subject at London University, and a member of the exalted Mines Fatigue Board—was a gay and gusty talker. He talked with his body, his hands, his beard, arguing, laughing, exploding, gurgling, meanwhile throwing great quantities of food and drink into himself like a stoker deliriously raising steam. But his talk was good; and the rest of the table seemed to like it.

Andrew, however, refused to admit the value of the conversation, listening grudgingly as it turned to music, to the qualities of Bach, and then, by one of Challis's prodigious leaps, to Russian literature. He heard mentioned the names of Tolstoy, Tchekov, Turgenev, Pushkin with his teeth on edge. Tripe, he raged to himself, all unimportant tripe. Who does this old beaver think he is? I'd like to see him tackle a tracheotomy, say, in a back kitchen in Cefan Row. He wouldn't get far with his Pushkin there!

Christine, however, was enjoying herself thoroughly. Glaring sideways, Andrew saw her smiling at Challis, heard her take her part in the discussion. She made no prĕtence, she was perfectly natural. Once or twice she referred to her Council-schoolroom in Bank Street. It amazed him how well she stood up to the Professor, how quickly, unselfconsciously she made her points. He began to see his wife, as for the first time, and in a strange new light. Seems to know all about these Russian bugs, he grated inwardly, funny she never talks to me about them! And later, as Challis approvingly patted Christine on the hand—can't old bird's nest keep his paws to himself! Hasn't he got a wife of his own!

Once or twice he caught Christine's eyes offering him a bright interchange of intimacy and several times she diverted the conversation in his direction.

"My husband is very interested in the anthracite workers, Professor Challis. He's started a line of investigation. On dust inhalation."

"Yes, yes," puffed Challis, turning an interested glance on Manson.

"Isn't that so, darling?" Christine encouraged. "You were telling me all about it the other night."

"Oh, I don't know," Andrew growled. "There's probably nothing in it. I haven't enough data yet. Perhaps this T.B. doesn't come from the dust at all."

He was furious with himself, of course. Perhaps this man Challis might have helped him, not that he would have asked for assistance, yet the fact that he was connected with the Mines Fatigue Board certainly seemed to offer a wonderful opportunity. For some incomprehensible reason his anger became directed towards Christine. As they walked home towards Vale View at the end of the evening he was jealously silent. And in the same silence he preceded her to the bedroom.

While they undressed, usually a communicative and informal proceeding when, with his braces hanging and a toothbrush in his hand, he would dilate upon the doings of the day, he kept his gaze studiously averted.

When Christine pleaded:

"We did have a nice time, didn't we, darling?" he answered with great politeness. "Oh! An excellent time!" In bed he kept well to the edge, away from her, resisting the slight movement which he felt her make towards him, with a long and heavy snore.

Next morning the same sense of constraint persisted between them.

He went about his work sulking, stupidly unlike himself. About five o'clock in the afternoon while they were having tea a ring came to the front door. It was the Vaughan chauffeur with a pile of books and a great bunch of pheasant's eye narcissi laid on top of them.

"From Mrs. Vaughan, madam," he said smiling, touching his peaked cap as he retreated.

Christine returned to the sitting-room with heaped arms and a glowing face.

"Look, darling," she cried excitedly. "Isn't that too kind. The whole of Trollope loaned me by Mrs. Vaughan. I've always wanted to read him right through! And such lovely—lovely flowers."

He stood up stiffly, sneering:

"Very pretty! Books and flowers from the lady of the manor! You've got to have them, I suppose, to help you to endure living with me! I'm too *dull* for you. I'm not one of those flash talkers that you seemed to like so much last night. I don't know the Russian for boloney! I'm just one of these bloody ordinary medical aid assistants!"

"Andrew!" All the colour had gone out of her face. "How can you!"

"It' rue, isn't it? I could see while I was gawking my way through that : sted supper. I've got eyes in my head. You're sick of me already. I'm only fit for slogging round in the slush, turning over dirty blankets, collecting fleas. I'm too much of a lout for your taste now!"

Her eyes were dark and pitiful in her pale face. But she said steadily:

"How can you talk like that! It's because you *are* yourself that I love you. And I'll never love anybody else."

"Sounds like it," he snarled and banged out of the room.

For five minutes he skulked in the kitchen, tramping up and down, biting his lip. Then all at once he turned, dashed back to the sitting-room, where she stood, her head bent forlornly, staring into the fire. He took her fiercely in his arms.

"Chris, darling!" he cried, in hot repentance. "Darling, darling! I'm sorry! For heaven's sake forgive me. I didn't mean a word of it. I'm just a crazy jealous fool. I adore you!"

They clung to each other wildly, closely. The scent of the narcissi was in the air.

"Don't you know," she sobbed, "that I'd just die without you!"

Afterwards, as she sat with her cheek pressed against his he said sheepishly, reaching forward for a book:

"Who is this chap Trollope, anyway? Will you teach me, darling. I'm just an ignorant hog!"

VIII

THE WINTER passed. He had now the added incentive of his work on dust inhalation which he had begun by planning and conducting a systematic examination of every anthracite worker upon his list. Their evenings together were even happier than before. Christine helped him to transcribe his notes, working before the fine coal fire—it was one advantage of the district that they never lacked an abundance of cheap coal—when he came home from his late surgery. Often they had long talks in which the extent of her knowledge, though she never obtruded it, and her acquaintance with books, astounded him. He began, moreover, to discern in her a fineness of instinct, an intuition which made her judgment of literature, music, and especially of people, uncannily correct.

"Hang it all," he would tease her. "I'm just getting to know my wife. In case you're getting swelled head we'll take half an hour off and I'll beat you at piquet." They had learned the game from the Vaughans.

As the days lengthened, without speaking of it to him, she began on the wilderness that was the garden, Jenny, the maid, had a great-uncle —she was proud of the unique relationship—an elderly, disabled miner who for tenpence an hour became Christine's assistant. Manson, crossing the dilapidated bridge, found them down by the stream bed one March afternoon, starting an assault on the rusty salmon tins that lay there!

"Hey, you below," he shouted from the bridge. "What are you doing? Spoiling my fishing!"

She answered his gibes with a brisk nod:

"You wait and see."

In a few weeks she had grubbed out the weeds and cleared the neglected paths. The bed of the stream was clean, its edges were cut and trimmed. A new rockery, made from loose stones lying about, stood at the foot of the glen. Vaughan's gardener, John Roberts, kept coming over, bringing bulbs and cuttings, offering advice. With real triumph she led Andrew by the arm to view the first daffodil.

Then, on the last Sunday in March, without warning, Denny came over to visit them. They fell upon him with open arms, belaboured him with their delighted welcome. To see the squat figure, that red sandybrowed face again gave Manson a rare pleasure. When they had shown him round, fed him on their best, and thrust him into their softest chair they eagerly demanded news.

"Page is gone," Philip announced. "Yes, the poor chap died a month ago. Another hæmorrhage. And a good thing too!" He drew on his pipe, the familiar cynicism puckering his eyes. "Blodwen and your friend Rees seem all set for matrimony."

"So that's the way of it," Andrew said without bitterness. "Poor Edward!"

"Page was a fine fellow. A good old G.P.," Denny reflected. "You know I hate the very sound of those fatal letters and all that they stand for. But Page let them down lightly."

There was a pause while they thought of Edward Page, who had longed for Capri with its birds and sunshine through all those drudging years amidst the slag heaps of Drineffy.

"And how about you, Philip?" Andrew asked at last.

"Oh, I don't know! I'm getting restless." Denny smiled drily. "Drineffy hasn't seemed quite the same since you people cleared out. I think I'll take a trip abroad somewhere. Ship's surgeon, maybe—if some cheap cargo boat will have me."

Andrew was silent, distressed once again by the thought of this clever man, this really talented surgeon, wasting his life, deliberately, with a kind of self-inflicted sadism. Yet was Denny really wasting his life? Christine and he had often spoken of Philip, trying to solve the enigma of his career. Vaguely they knew that he had married a woman, socially his superior, who had tried to mould him to the demands of a county practice where there was no credit in operating well four days of the week if one did not hunt the other three. After five years of effort on Denny's part she had rewarded him by leaving him, quite casually, for another man. It was no wonder that Denny had fled to the backwoods, despising convention and hating orthodoxy. Perhaps one day he would return to civilisation.

They talked all afternoon and Philip waited till the last train. He was interested in Andrew's account of the conditions of practice in Aberalaw. As Andrew came, indignantly, to the question of Llewellyn's percentage deducted from the assistants' salaries, he said, with an odd smile:

"I can't see you sitting down under that for long!"

When Philip had gone Andrew became gradually aware as the days passed of a gap, an odd vacancy existing in his work. In Drineffy with Philip near him he had always been aware of a common bond, a definite purpose shared between them. But in Aberalaw he had no such bond, felt no such purpose amongst his fellow doctors.

Doctor Urquhart, his colleague in the West Surgery, was, for all his fiery humour, a kindly man. Yet he was old, rather automatic, and absolutely without inspiration. Though long experience enabled him, as he put it, to smell pneumonia the moment he "put his nose in" the sick-room, though he was deft in his application of splints and plasters and an adept in the cruciform treatment of boils, though occasionally he delighted to prove that he could perform some small operation he was nevertheless, in many directions, shatteringly antiquated. He stood out plainly, in Andrew's view, as Denny's "good old type" of family doctor —shrewd, painstaking, experienced, a doctor sentimentalised by his patients and by the public at large, who had not opened a medical book for twenty years and was almost dangerously out of date. Though Andrew was always eager to start discussions with Urquhart, the old man had little time for "shop." When his day's work was over he would drink his tinned soup—tomato was his favourite—sandpaper his new violin, inspect his old china, then clump off to the Masonic Club to play draughts and smoke.

The two assistants at the East Surgery were equally unencouraging. Doctor Medley, the elder of the two, a man of nearly fifty, with a clever sensitive face, was unhappily almost stone deaf. But for this affliction, which for some reason the vulgar always found amusing, Charles Medley would have been a very long way from an assistantship in the mining valleys. He was, like Andrew, essentially a physician. As a diagnostician he was remarkable. But when his patients spoke to him he could not hear a word. Of course, he was a practised lip-reader. Yet he was timid, for he often made laughable mistakes. It was quite painful to see his harassed eyes fastened, in a kind of desperate inquiry, upon the moving lips of the person speaking to him. Because he was so fearful of making a grave error he never prescribed anything but the smallest dose of any drug. He was not well off, for he had met with trouble and expense over his grown-up family, and like his faded wife he had become an ineffectual, strangely pathetic being who went in dread of Doctor Llewellyn and the Committee lest he should be suddenly dismissed.

The other assistant, Doctor Oxborrow, was a very different character from poor Medley and Andrew did not like him nearly so well. Oxborrow was a large pasty man with pudgy fingers and a jerky heartiness. Andrew often felt that with more blood in him Oxborrow would have made an admirable bookmaker. As it was Oxborrow, accompanied by his wife, who played the portable harmonium, betook himself on Saturday afternoons to the near-by tow of Fernely—etiquette precluding his appearing in Aberalaw—and there, in the Market, he would set up his little carpet-covered stand and hold an open-air religious meeting Oxborrow was an evangelist. As an idealist, a believer in a supreme quickening force in life, Andrew could have admired this fervour. But Oxborrow, alas! was embarrassingly emotional. He wept unexpectedly and prayed even more disconcertingly. Once when confronted by a difficult confinement which defeated his own straining skill, he plumped suddenly upon his knees beside the bed and, blubbering, implored God to work a miracle upon the poor woman. Urquhart, who detested Oxborrow, told Andrew of this incident, for it was Urquhart who, arriving, had got upon the bed in his boots, and successfully delivered the patient with high forceps.

The more Andrew considered his fellow assistants and the system under which they worked the more he desired to bring them together. As it was, they had no unity, no sense of co-operation, and little friendliness, amongst themselves. They were simply set up, one against the other, in the ordinary competitive way existing in general practice all over the country, each trying to secure as many patients for himself as he could. Downright suspicion and bad feeling were often the result. Andrew had known Urquhart, for instance, when a patient of Oxborrow's transferred his card to him, take the half finished bottle of medicine from the man's hand in the surgery, uncork it, smell it with contempt, and explode:

"So *this* is what Oxborrow's been givin' ye! Damn it to hell! He's been slowly poisonin' ye!"

Meanwhile, in the face of this diversity, Doctor Llewellyn was quietly taking his cut from each assistant's pay cheque. Andrew burned under it, longed to create a different arrangement, to institute a new and better understanding which would enable the assistants to stand together—without subsidising Llewellyn. But his own difficulties, the sense of his own newness to the place, and above all the mistakes he had made at the start in his own district, caused him to be cautious. It was not until he met Con Boland that he decided to make the great attempt.

IX

ONE DAY early in April Andrew discovered a cavity in a back tooth and went, in consequence, upon an afternoon of the following week, in search of the Society's dentist. He had not yet met Boland and did not know his hours of consultation. When he reached the Square, where Boland's little surgery stood, he found the door closed and pinned upon it, this red-inked notice: *Gone to Extraction. If Urgent apply at House.*

On a moment's reflection Andrew decided that since he was here, he might at least call to make an appointment so, having inquired the way from one of the group of youths lounging outside the Valley Ice Cream Saloon, he set out for the dentist's house.

This was a small semi-detached villa on the upper outskirts of the East side of the town. As Andrew walked up the untidy path to the front door he heard a loud hammering and glancing through the wide-open doors of a dilapidated wooden shed situated at the side of the house he saw a red-haired rangy man in his shirt-sleeves, violently attacking the dismembered body of a car with a hammer. At the same time the man caught sight of him.

"Hello!" he said.

"Hello!" Andrew answered a trifle warily.

"What are ye after?"

"I want to make an appointment with the dentist. I'm Doctor Manson."

"Come in," said the man, hospitably waving the hammer. He was Boland.

Andrew entered the wooden shed which was littered with portions of an incredibly old motor-car. In the middle stood the chassis, supported on wooden egg-boxes, and actually presenting the evidence of having been sawn in half. Andrew glanced from this extraordinary spectacle of engineering to Boland.

"Is this the extraction?"

"It is," Con agreed. "When I'm inclined to be slack in the surgery I just up to my garage and put a little bit in on my car."

Apart from his brogue, which was thick enough to be cut with a knife, he used the words garage, meaning the falling down shed, and car, as applied to the fallen down vehicle, with an accent of unmistakable pride.

"You wouldn't believe what I'm doing now," he went on, "that's to say unless you're mechanical-minded like myself. I've had her five year this little car of mine and, mind ye, she was three year old when I got her. Ye mightn't believe it seeing her *sthripped* but she goes like a hare. But she's small, Manson, she's small by the size of my family now. So I'm in the process of extendin' her. I've cut her, ye see, right across her middle, and that's where I'll slip in a good two feet of insertion. Wait till ye see her finished, Manson!" He reached for his jacket. "She'll be long enough to take a regiment. Come away now, to the surgery, and I'll fix your tooth."

At the surgery which was almost as untidy as the garage and, it must be confessed, equally dirty, Con filled the tooth, talking all the time. Con talked so much and so violently that his bushy red moustache was always dewed with beads of moisture. His shock of chestnut hair, which badly needed cutting, kept getting into Andrew's eyes, as he bent over, using the amalgam filling which he had tucked under his oily finger-nail. He had not bothered to wash his hands—that was a trifle with Con! He was a careless, impetuous, good-natured, generous fellow. The more Andrew knew Con the more he was utterly captivated by his humour, simplicity, wildness and improvidence. Con, who had been six years in Aberalaw, had not a penny to his name. Yet he extracted a vast amount of fun from life. He was mad on "mechanics," was always making gadgets and he idolised his motor-car. The fact that Con should possess a motor-car was in itself a joke. But Con loved jokes, even when they were against himself. He told Andrew of the occasion when, called to extract the decayed molar of an important Committee-man he had gone to the patient's house with, as he imagined, his forceps in his pocket only to find himself reaching for the tooth with a six-inch spanner.

The filling complete, Con threw his instruments into a jelly jar containing lysol, which was his light-hearted notion of asepsis, and demanded that Andrew should return to the house with him to tea.

"Come on, now," he insisted hospitably. "You've got to meet the family. And we're just in time. It's five o'clock."

Con's family were, in fact, in the process of having tea when they arrived but were obviously too accustomed to Con's eccentricities to be disturbed by his bringing in a stranger. In the warm, disordered room Mrs. Boland sat at the head of the table with the baby at her breast. Next came Mary, fifteen, quiet, shy—"the only dark-haired one and her dad's favourite," was Con's introduction—who was already earning a decent wage as a clerk to Joe Larkins, the bookmaker, in the Square. Beside Mary was Terence, twelve, then three other younger children sprawling about, crying out to be taken notice of by their father.

There existed about this family, except perhaps for the shyly conscious Mary, a careless gaiety which entranced Andrew. The room itself spoke with a gorgeous brogue. Above the fireplace beneath the coloured picture of Pope Pius X, which bore a strip of Easter palm, the baby's napkins were drying. The canary's cage, uncleaned but bursting with song, stood on the dresser beside Mrs. Boland's rolled-up stays—she had previously removed them in the cause of comfort—and a split bag of puppy biscuits. Six bottles of stout, newly in from the grocer, were upon the chest of drawers, also Terence's flute. And in the corner were broken toys, odd boots, one rusty skate, a Japanese parasol, two slightly battered prayer books and a copy of *Photo-bits*.

But, as he drank his tea, Andrew was most fascinated by Mrs. Boland —he simply could not keep his eyes from her. Pale, dreamy, unperturbed she sat silently imbibing endless cups of black boiled tea while the children squabbled about her and the baby openly drew his nourishment from her generous fount. She smiled and nodded, cut bread for the children, poured out the tea, drank and gave suck, all with a kind of abstracted placidity, as though years of din, dirt, drabness—and Con's ebullience—had in the end exalted her to a plane of heavenly lunacy where she was isolated and immune.

He almost upset his cup when she addressed him, gazing over the top of his head, her voice meek, apologetic.

"I meant to call on Mrs. Manson, doctor. But I was so busy——"

"In the name of God!" Con rolled with laughter. "Busy, indeed! She hadn't a new dress—that's what she means. I had the money laid by—but damn it all, Terence or one of them had to have new boots. Never mind, mother, wait till I get the car lengthened and we'll whirl ye up in style." He turned to Andrew with perfect naturalness. "We're hard up, Manson. It's the devil! We've plenty of grub, thank God, but sometimes we're not so fancy with the duds. They're a stingy lot on the Committee. And, of course, the big chief gets his whack!"

"Who?" Andrew asked, astonished.

"Llewellyn! He takes his fifth from me as well as you!"

"But what on earth for?"

"Oh! he sees a case or two for me occasionally. He's taken a couple of dentigerous cysts out for me in the last six years. And he's the X-ray expert when that's needed. But it's a bugger." The family had bundled out to play in the kitchen so Con could speak freely. "Him and his big saloon. The damn thing's all paint. Let me inform ye, Manson, once I was comin' up Mardy Hill behind him in my own little bus when I make up my mind to step on the gas, Bejasus! Ye should have seen his face when I give him my dust."

"Look here, Boland," Andrew said quickly. "This business of Llewellyn's cut is a shocking imposition. Why don't we fight it?"

"Eh?"

"Why don't we fight it," Andrew repeated in a louder voice. Even as he spoke he felt his blood rise. "It's a damned injustice. Here we are hard up, trying to make our way—— Listen, Boland, you're the very man I've been wanting to meet. Will you stand in with me on this? We'll get hold of the other assistants. Make a big united effort——"

A slow gleam irradiated Con's eyes.

"Ye mean, ye want to go after Llewellyn?"

"I do."

Con impressively extended his hand.

"Manson, my boy," he declared momentously. "We're together from the start."

Andrew raced home to Christine full of eagerness, thirsting for the fight.

"Chris! Chris! I've found a gem of a chap. A red-headed dentist—quite mad—yes, like me. I knew you'd say that. But listen, darling, we're going to start a revolution." He laughed excitedly. "Oh, Lord! If old man Llewellyn only knew what was in store for him!"

He did not require her caution to go carefully. He was determined to proceed with discernment in everything he did. He began therefore, the following day, by calling upon Owen.

The secretary was interested and emphatic. He told Andrew that the agreement in question was a voluntary one between the head doctor and his assistants. The whole thing lay outside the jurisdiction of the Committee.

"You see, Doctor Manson," Owen concluded. "Doctor Llewellyn is a very clever, well-qualified man. We count ourselves fortunate to have him. But he has a handsome remuneration from the Society for acting as our Medical Superintendent. It is you assistant doctors who think he ought to have more——"

"Do we hell," thought Andrew. He went away satisfied, rang up Oxborrow and Medley, made them agree to come to his house that evening. Urquhart and Boland had already promised to be there. He knew, from past conversations, that every one of the four loathed losing a fifth of his salary. Once he had them together the thing was done.

His next step was to speak to Llewellyn. He had decided on reflection that it would be underhand not to make some disclosure of his intention beforehand. That afternoon he was at the hospital giving an anæsthetic. As he watched Llewellyn go through with the operation, a long and complicated abdominal case, he could not repress a feeling of admiration. Owen's remark was absolutely true: Llewellyn was amazingly clever, not only clever but versatile. He was the exception, the unique instance, which—Denny would have contended—proved the rule. Nothing came amiss to him, nothing floored him. From public health administration, every bye law of which he knew by heart, to the latest radiological technique, the whole range of his multifarious duties found Llewellyn blandly expert and prepared.

After the operation, while Llewellyn was washing up Andrew went to him, jerkily tugging off his gown.

"Excuse me for mentioning it, Doctor Llewellyn—but I couldn't help noticing the way you handled that tumour, it was awfully fine."

Llewellyn's dull skin tinged with gratification. He beamed affably.

"Glad you think so, Manson. Come to speak of it, you're improvin' nicely with your anæsthetics."

"No, no," Andrew muttered. "I'll never be much good at that."

There was a pause. Llewellyn went on soaping his hands equally. Andrew, at his elbow, cleared his throat nervously. Now that the moment had come he found it almost impossible to speak. But he managed to blurt out:

"Look here, Doctor Llewellyn. It's only right to tell you—all we assistants think our salary percentage payments to you unfair. It's an awkward thing to have to say, but I—I'm going to propose they are done away with. We've got a meeting at my house to-night. I'd rather you knew that now, than afterwards. I—I want you to feel I'm at least honest about it."

Before Llewellyn could reply, and without looking at his face, Andrew swung round and left the theatre. How badly he had said it. Yet anyway, he *had* said it. When they sent him their ultimatum, Llewellyn could not accuse him of stabbing him in the back.

The meeting at Vale View was fixed for nine o'clock that evening. Andrew put out some bottled beer and asked Christine to prepare sandwiches. When she had done this, she slipped on her coat and went round to Vaughans' for an hour. Strung with anticipation, Andrew stumped up and down the hall, striving to collect his ideas. And presently the others arrived—Boland first, Urquhart next, Oxborrow and Medley together.

In the sitting-room, pouring beer and proffering sandwiches, Andrew tried to initiate a cordial note. Since he almost disliked him he addressed Doctor Oxborrow first.

"Help yourself, Oxborrow! Plenty more in the cellar."

"Thanks, Manson." The evangelist's voice was chill. "I don't touch alcohol in any shape or form. It's against my principles."

"In the name of God!" Con said, out of the froth on his moustache.

As a beginning it was not auspicious. Medley, munching sandwiches, kept his eyes all the time on the alert, his face wearing the stony anxiety of the deaf. Already the beer was increasing Urquhart's natural belligerence; after glaring steadily at Oxborrow for some minutes he suddenly shot out:

"Now I find myself in your company, *Doctor* Oxborrow, maybe you'll find it convenient to explain how Tudor Evans, Seventeen Glyn Terrace, came off *my* list on to *yours*."

"I don't remember the case," said Oxborrow pressing his finger-tips together aloofly.

"But I do!" Urquhart exploded. "It was one of the cases you stole from me, your medical reverence! And what's more——"

"Gentlemen!" cried Andrew in a panic. "Please, *please*! How can we ever do anything if we quarrel amongst ourselves. Remember what we're here for."

"What *are* we here for?" Oxborrow said womanishly. "I ought to be at a case."

Andrew, standing on the hearth-rug, his expression taut and earnest, took a grab at the slippery situation.

"This is the way of it, then, gentlemen!" He drew a deep breath. "I'm the youngest man here and I'm not long in this practice but I—I hope you'll excuse all that! Perhaps it's because I am new that I get a fresh look at things—things you've been putting up with too long. It seems to me in the first place that our system here is all wrong. We just go hacking and muddling through in the antediluvian way like we were ordinary town and country G.P.'s, fighting each other, not members of the same Medical Society with wonderful opportunities for working together! Every doctor I've met swears that practice is a dog's life. He'll tell you he drudges on, run off his feet, never a minute to himself, no time for meals, always on call! *Why* is that? It's because there's *no attempt at organisation in our profession*. Take just one example of what I mean—though I could give you dozens. Night-calls! You know how we all go to bed at night, dreading we'll be wakened up and called out. We have rotten nights because we *may* be called out. Suppose we knew we *couldn't* be called out. Suppose we arranged, for a start, a co-operative system of night work. One doctor taking all night-calls for one week and then going *free* of all night-calls for the rest of that month, while the others take their turn. Wouldn't that be splendid! Think how fresh you'd be for your day's work——"

He broke off, observing their blank faces.

"Wouldn't work," Urquhart snapped. "Dammit to hell! I'd sooner stay up every night of the month than trust old Foxborrow with one of my cases. Hee, hee! When *he* borrows he doesn't pay back."

Andrew interposed feverishly.

"We'll leave that then—anyway, till another meeting—seeing that we're not agreed on it. But there's one thing we are agreed on. And that's why we're here. This percentage we pay to Doctor Llewellyn." He paused. They were all looking at him now, touched in their pockets, interested. "We've all agreed it's unjust. I've spoken to Owen about it. He says it has nothing to do with the Committee but is a matter for adjustment between the doctors."

"That's right," threw out Urquhart. "I remember when it was fixed. A matter of nine year ago. We had two rank Jonahs of assistants then. One at the East Surgery and one at my end. They gave Llewellyn a lot of trouble over their cases. So one fine day he called us all together and said it wasn't goin' to be worth his while unless we could make some arrangement with him. That's the way it started. And that's the way it's gone on."

"But his salary from the Committee already covers *all* his work in the Society. And he simply rakes in the shekels from his other appointments. He's rolling in it!"

"I know, I know," said Urquhart testily. "But, mind you, Manson, he's damn useful to us, is the same Llewellyn. And he knows it. If he chose to cut up rough we'd be in a pretty poor way."

"Why should *we* pay him?" Andrew kept on inexorably.

"Hear! Hear!" interjected Con, refilling his glass.

Oxborrow cast one glance at the dentist.

"If I may be allowed to get a word in. I agree with Doctor Manson in that it is unjust for us to have our salaries deducted. But the fact is, Doctor Llewellyn is a man of high standing, excellently qualified, who gives great distinction to the Society. And besides he goes out of his way to take our bad cases off our hands."

Andrew stared at the other.

"Do you *want* your bad cases off your hands?"

"Of course," said Oxborrow pettishly. "Who doesn't?"

"I don't," Andrew shouted. "I want to keep them, see them through!"

"Oxborrow's right," Medley muttered unexpectedly. "It's the first rule of medical practice, Manson. You'll realise it when you're older· Get rid of the bad stuff, get rid of it, rid of it."

"But damn it all!" Andrew protested hotly.

The discussion continued, in circles, for three quarters of an hour. At the end of that time, Andrew, very heated, chanced to exclaim:

576

"We've got to put this through. D'you hear me, we've simply got to. Llewellyn knows we're after him. I told him this afternoon."

"What!" The exclamation came from Oxborrow, Urquhart, even from Medley.

"Do you mean to say, doctor, you *told* Doctor Llewellyn——" Half rising, Oxborrow bent his startled gaze on Andrew.

"Of course I did! He's got to know some time. Don't you see, we've only got to stand together, show a united front and *we're bound to win!*"

"Dammit to hell!" Urquhart was livid. "You've got a nerve! You don't know what influence Llewellyn has. He's got a finger in everything! We'll be lucky if we're not all sacked. Think of *me* trying to find another pitch at my time of life." He bullocked his way towards the door. "You're a good fellow, Manson. But you're too *young*. Good *night*."

Medley had already risen hurriedly to his feet. The look in his eye said he was going straight to his telephone to tell Doctor Llewellyn apologetically that he, Llewellyn, was a superb doctor and he, Medley, could hear him perfectly. Oxborrow was on his heels. In two minutes the room was clear of all but Con, Andrew, and the remainder of the beer.

They finished the beverage in silence. Then Andrew remembered that there were six more bottles in the larder. They finished these six bottles. Then they began to talk. They said things touching the origin, parentage and moral character of Oxborrow, Medley and Urquhart. They dwelt especially upon Oxborrow and Oxborrow's harmonium. They did not observe Christine come in and go upstairs. They talked together soulfully, as brothers shamefully betrayed.

Next morning Andrew marched on his rounds with a splitting headache and a scowl. In the Square he passed Llewellyn in his car. As Andrew lifted his head in shamed defiance Llewellyn beamed at him.

X

FOR A WEEK Andrew went about chafing under his defeat, bitterly cast down. On Sunday morning, usually devoted to long and peaceful repose, he suddenly broke loose.

"It isn't the money, Chris! It's the principle of the thing! When I think of it—it drives me crazy! Why can't I let it slip? Why don't I like Llewellyn? At least why do I like him one minute and hate him the next? Tell me honestly, Chris. Why don't I sit at his feet? Am I jealous! What is it?"

Her answer staggered him. "Yes, I think you are jealous!"

"What!"

"Don't break my eardrums, dear. You asked me to tell you honestly.

577

You're jealous, frightfully jealous. And why shouldn't you be? I don't want to be married to a saint. There's enough cleaning in this house already without you setting up a halo."

"Go on," he growled. "Give me all my faults when you're about it. Suspicious! Jealous! You've been at me before! Oh, and I'm too *young*, I suppose. Octogenarian Urquhart rammed that in my teeth the other day!" A pause during which he waited for her to continue the argument. Then, irritably, "Why should I be jealous of Llewellyn?"

"Because he's frightfully good at his work, knows so much, and well— chiefly because he has all these first-class qualifications."

"While I have a scrubby little M.B. from a Scots University! God Almighty! Now I know what you really think of me." Furious, he flung out of bed and began to walk about the room in his pyjamas. "What do qualifications matter anyway? Pure damn swank! It's method, clinical ability that counts. I don't believe all the tripe they serve up in textbooks. I believe in what I hear through the ends of my stethoscope! and in case you don't know it I hear plenty. I'm beginning to find out real things in my anthracite investigation. Perhaps I'll surprise you one fine day, my lady! Damn it all! It's a fine state of affairs when a man wakes up on Sunday morning and his wife tells him he knows *nothing*!"

Sitting up in bed, she took her manicure set and began to do her nails, waiting till he had finished.

"I didn't say all that, Andrew." Her reasonableness aggravated him the more. "It's just—darling, you're not going to be an assistant *all* your life. You want people to listen to you, pay attention to your work, your ideas—oh, you understand what I mean. If you had a really fine degree—an M.D. or—or the M.R.C.P., it would stand you in good stead."

"The M.R.C.P.!" He echoed blankly. Then: "So she's been thinking it out all by her little self. The M.R.C.P.—huh!—take *that* from a mining practice!" His satire should have overwhelmed her. "Don't you understand they only give that to the crowned heads of Europe!"

He banged the door and went into the bathroom to shave. Five minutes later he was back again, one half of his chin shaved, the other lathered. He was penitent, excited.

"Do you *think* I could do it, Chris! You're absolutely right. We need a few pips on the good old name plate so we can hold our end up! But the M.R.C.P.—it's the most difficult medical exam. in the whole shoot. It's—it's *murder*! Still—I believe—wait and I'll get the particulars——"

Breaking off, he dashed downstairs for the Medical Directory. When he returned with it his face had fallen to acute dejection.

"Sunk!" he muttered dismally. "Right bang off! I *told* you it was an impossible exam. There's a preliminary paper in languages. Four languages. Latin, French, Greek, German—and two of them are com-

578

pulsory, before you can even *sit* the cursed thing. I don't know languages. All the Latin I know is dog lingo—mist. alba—mitte decem. As for French——"

She did not answer. There was a silence while he stood at the window gloomily considering the empty view. At last he turned, frowning, worrying, unable to leave the bone alone.

"Why shouldn't I—*damn* it all, Chris—why shouldn't I learn these languages *for* the exam.?"

Her manicure things spread themselves upon the floor as she jumped out of bed and hugged him.

"Oh, I did want you to say that, my dear. That's the real *you*. I could —I could help you perhaps. Don't forget your old woman's a retired schoolmarm!"

They made plans excitedly all day. They bundled Trollope, Tchekov and Dostoevsky into the spare bedroom. They cleared the sitting-room for action. All that evening he went to school with her. The next evening, and the next——

Sometimes Andrew felt the sublime bathos of it, heard from afar off the mocking laughter of the gods. Sitting over the hard table with his wife, in this remote Welsh mining town, muttering after her *caput— capitis*, or *Madame, est-il possible que?*, wading through declensions, irregular verbs, reading aloud from *Tacitus*, and a patriotic reader they had picked up, *Pro Patria*—he would jerk back suddenly in his chair, morbidly conscious—

"If Llewellyn could see us here—wouldn't he grin! And to think this is only the beginning, that I've got all the medical stuff after!"

Towards the end of the following month parcels of books began to arrive periodically at Vale View from the London branch of the International Medical Library. Andrew began to read where, at college, he had left off. He discovered, quickly, how early he had left off. He discovered and was swamped by the therapeutic advance of biochemistry. He discovered renal thresholds, blood ureas, basal metabolism, and the fallibility of the albumen test. As this keystone of his student's days fell from him he groaned aloud.

"Chris! I know nothing. And this stuff is killing me!"

He had to contend with the work of his practice, he had only the long nights in which to study. Sustained by black coffee and a wet towel round his head he battled on, reading into the early hours of the morning. When he fell into bed, exhausted, often he could not sleep. And sometimes when he slept he would awake, sweating from a nightmare, his head ablaze with terms, formulæ, and some drivelling imbecility of his halting French.

He smoked to excess, lost weight, became thinner in the face. But Chris was there, constantly, silently, there, permitting him to talk, to draw diagrams, to explain, in tongue-twisting nomenclature, the extraordinary, the astounding, the fascinating selective action of the kidney tubules. She also permitted him to shout, gesticulate, and, as his nerves grew more ragged, to hurl abuse at her. At eleven o'clock as she brought him fresh coffee he became liable to snarl:

"Why can't you leave me alone? What's this slush for anyway? Caffein—it's only a rotten drug. You know I'm killing myself, don't you. And it's all for you. You're hard! You're damnably hard. You're like a female turnkey, marching in and out with skilly! I'll never get this blasted thing. There are hundreds of fellows trying to get it from the West End of London, from the big hospitals, and me!—from Aberalaw —ha, ha!" His laughter was hysterical. "From the dear old Medical Aid Society! Oh God! I'm so tired and I know they'll have me out to-night for that confinement in Cefan Row and——"

She was a better soldier than he. She had a quality of balance which steadied them through every crisis. She also had a temper but she controlled it. She made sacrifices, refused all invitations from the Vaughans, stopped going to the orchestral concerts in the Temperance Hall. No matter how badly she had slept she was always up early, neatly dressed, ready with his breakfast when he came dragging down, unshaven, the first cigarette of the day already between his lips.

Suddenly, when he had been working six months, her aunt in Bridlington took ill with phlebitis and wrote asking her to come North. Handing him the letter she declared immediately that it was impossible for her to leave him. But he, bunched sulkily over his bacon and egg, growled out:

"I wish you'd go, Chris! Studying this way, I'd get on better without you. We've been getting on each other's nerves lately. Sorry—but—it seems the best thing to do."

She went, unwillingly, at the end of the week. Before she had been gone twenty-four hours he found out his mistake. It was agony without her. Jenny, though working to carefully prepared instructions, was a perpetual aggravation. But it was not Jenny's cooking, or the lukewarm coffee, or the badly made bed. It was Christine's absence: knowing she was not in the house, being unable to call out to her, missing her. He found himself gazing dully at his books, losing hours, while he thought of her.

At the end of a fortnight she wired that she was returning. He dropped everything and prepared to receive her. Nothing was too good, too spectacular for the celebration of their reunion. Her wire had not given him much time but he thought rapidly, then sped to the town on a mission of extravagance. He bought first a bunch of roses. In Kendrick's the fishmonger's he was lucky to find a lobster, fresh in that morning. He seized it quickly, lest Mrs. Vaughan—for whom Kendrick primarily intended all such delicacies—should ring up and forestall him. Then he bought ice in quantity, called at the greengrocer's for salad and finally, with trepidation, ordered one bottle of moselle which Lampert, the grocer in the Square, assured him was "sound."

After tea he told Jenny she might go, for already he could feel her youthful eye fastened inquisitively upon him. He then set to work and lovingly composed a lobster salad. The zinc bucket from the scullery, filled with ice, made an excellent wine pail. The flowers presented an unexpected difficulty, for Jenny had locked up the cupboard under the stairs where all the vases were kept and, to all intents, hidden the key. But he surmounted even this obstruction, placing half the roses in the water jug and the remainder in the tooth-brush holder from the toilet set upstairs. It struck quite a note of variety.

At last his preparations were complete—the flowers, the food, the wine upon the ice, his eye surveyed the scene with shining intensity. After surgery, at half past nine, he raced to meet her train at the Upper Station.

It was like falling in love all over again, fresh, wonderful. Tenderly, he escorted her to the love feast. The evening was hot and still. The moon shone in upon him. He forgot about the intricacies of basal metabolism. He told her they might be in Provence, or some place like that, in a great castle by a lake. He told her she was a sweet, exquisite child. He told her he had been a brute to her but that for the rest of his life he would be a carpet—not red, since she interjected her objection to that colour—on which she might tread. He told her much more than that. By the end of the week he was telling her to fetch his slippers.

August arrived, dusty and scorching. With the finish of his reading in sight he was confronted with the necessity of brushing up his practical work, particularly histology—an apparently insuperable difficulty in his present situation. It was Christine who thought of Professor Challis and his position at Cardiff University. When Andrew wrote to him, Challis immediately replied stating, with verbosity, that he would rejoice to use his influence with the Department of Pathology. Manson, he said, would find Doctor Glyn-Jones a first rate fellow. He concluded with a carolling inquiry for Christine.

"I've got to hand it to you, Chris! It does mean something to have friends. And I very nearly stuck away from meeting Challis that night at Vaughans'. Decent old bouncer! But all the same, I hate asking favours. And what's this about sending tender regards to you!"

In the middle of that month a second-hand Red Indian motor cycle— a low, wickedly unprofessional machine, advertised as "too fast" for its previous owner—made its appearance at Vale View. There were, in the slackness of summer, three afternoon hours which Andrew might reasonably regard as his own. Every day, immediately after lunch, a red streak went roaring down the valley in the direction of Cardiff, thirty miles away And every day towards five o'clock a slightly dustier red streak, moving in the opposite direction, made a target of Vale View.

These sixty miles in the broiling heat with an hour's work at Glyn-Jones' specimens and slides, sandwiched midway, often using the microscope with hands which still shook from the handlebars' vibration, made heavy going of the next few weeks. For Christine it was the most anxious part of the whole lunatic adventure, to see him depart with a swift crackling exhaust, to wait anxiously for the first faint beat of his return, fearing all the time that something must happen to him bent to the metal of that satanic machine.

Though he was so rushed he found a moment occasionally to bring her strawberries from Cardiff. They saved these till after his surgery. At tea he was always parched from the dust and red-eyed, wondering gloomily if his duodenum had not dropped off at that last pothole in Trecoed, asking himself if he could possibly manage before the surgery these two calls which had come in during his absence.

But the final journey was made at last. Glyn-Jones had nothing more to show him. He knew every slide and every single specimen by heart. All that remained was to enter his name and send up the heavy entrance fees for the examination.

On the 15th of October Andrew set out alone for London. Christine saw him to the station. Now that the actual event was so close at hand a queer calmness had settled upon him. All his striving, his frenzied efforts, his almost hysterical outbursts seemed far away and done with. His brain was inactive, almost dull. He felt that he knew nothing.

Yet, on the following day, when he began the written part of the examination which was held at the College of Physicians, he found himself answering the papers with a blind automatism. He wrote and wrote, never looking at the clock, filling sheet after sheet, until his head reeled.

He had taken a room at the Museum Hotel where Christine and he had stayed on their first visit to London. Here it was extremely cheap. But the food was vile, adding the final touch to his upset digestion required to produce a bad attack of dyspepsia. He was compelled to restrict his diet to hot malted milk. A tumberful in an A.B.C. tea-room in the Strand was his lunch. Between his papers he lived in a kind of daze. He did not dream of going to a place of amusement. He scarcely saw the people in the streets. Occasionally, to clear his head, took a ride on the top of an omnibus.

After the written papers the practical and viva voce part of the examinations began and Andrew found himself dreading this more than anything which had gone before. There were perhaps twenty other candidates, all of them men older than himself, and all with an unmistakable air of assurance and position. The candidate placed next to him, for instance, a man named Harrison whom he had once or twice spoken to, had an Oxford B.Ch. an out-patient appointment at St. John's and a consulting-room in Brook Street. When Andrew compared Harrison's charming manners and obvious standing with his own provincial awkwardness he felt his chances of favourably impressing the examiners to be small indeed.

His practical, at the South London Hospital, went, he thought, well enough. His case was one of bronchiectasis in a young boy of fourteen, which, since he knew lungs so intimately, was a piece of good fortune. He felt he had written a good report. But when it came to the viva voce his luck seemed to change completely. The viva procedure at the College of Physicians had its peculiarities. On two successive days each candidate was questioned, in turn, by two separate examiners. If at the end of the first session the candidate was found inadequate he was handed a polite note telling him he need not return on the following day. Faced with the imminence of this fatal missive Andrew found to his horror that he had drawn as his first examiner a man he had heard Harrison speak of with apprehension, Doctor Maurice Gadsby.

Gadsby was a spare undersized man with a ragged black moustache and small, mean eye. Recently elected to his Fellowship, he had none of the tolerance of the older examiners, but seemed to set out deliberately to fail the candidates who came before him. He considered Andrew with a supercilious lift to his brows and placed before him six slides. Five of these slides Andrew named correctly but the sixth he could not name. It was on this slide that Gadsby concentrated. For five minutes he harassed Andrew on this section—which it appeared, was the ovum of an obscure West African parasite—then idly, without interest, he passed him on to the next examiner, Sir Robert Abbey.

Andrew rose and crossed the room with a pale face and a heavily beating heart. All the lassitude, the inertia he had experienced at the beginning of the week was gone now. He had an almost desperate desire to succeed. But he was convinced that Gadsby would fail him. He raised his eyes to find Robert Abbey contemplating him with a friendly, half humorous smile.

"What's the matter?" said Abbey unexpectedly.

"Nothing, sir," Andrew stammered. "I think I've done rather badly with Doctor Gadsby—that's all."

"Never mind about that. Have a look at these specimens. Then just say anything you think about them." Abbey smiled encouragingly. He was a clean shaven, ruddy complexioned man of about sixty-five with a high forehead, a long, humorous upper lip. Though Abbey was now perhaps the third most distinguished physician in Europe he had known hardship and bitter struggles in his earlier days when, coming from his native Leeds, with only a provincial reputation to sustain him, he had encountered prejudice and opposition in London. As he gazed, without seeming to do so, at Andrew, observing his ill-cut suit, the soft collar and shirt, the cheap, ill-knotted tie, and above all, the look of strained intensity upon his serious face, the days of his own provincial youth came

583

back to him. Instinctively his heart went out to this unusual candidate and his eye, ranging down the list before him, noted with satisfaction that his markings, particularly in the recent practical, were above pass level.

Meanwhile Andrew, with his eyes fixed upon the glass jars before him, had been stumbling unhappily through his commentary upon the specimens.

"Good," Abbey said suddenly. He took up a specimen—it was an aneurism of the ascending aorta—and began in a friendly manner to question Andrew. His questions, from being simple, gradually became wider, and more searching in their scope until finally they came to bear upon a recent specific treatment by the induction of malaria. But Andrew, opening out under Abbey's sympathetic manner, answered well.

Finally, as he put down the specimen, Abbey remarked:

"Do you know anything of the history of aneurism?"

"Ambrose Paré"—Andrew answered, and Abbey had already begun his approving nod—"is presumed to have first discovered the condition!"

Abbey's face expressed surprise.

"Why presumed, Doctor Manson? Paré did discover aneurism."

Andrew reddened then turned pale as he plunged on:

"Well, sir, that's what the text-books say. You'll find it in every book —I myself took the trouble to verify that it was in six." A quick breath. "But I happened to be reading Celsus, brushing up my Latin—which needed brushing up, sir—when I definitely came across the word *aneurismus*. Celsus knew aneurism. He described it in full. And that was a matter of thirteen centuries before Paré!"

There was a silence. Andrew raised his eyes, prepared for kindly satire. Abbey was looking at him with a queer expression on his ruddy face.

"Doctor Manson," he said at length, "you are the first candidate in this examination hall who has ever told me something original, something true, and something which I did not know. I congratulate you."

Andrew turned scarlet again.

"Just tell me one thing more—as a matter of personal curiosity," Abbey concluded. "What do you regard as the main principle—the, shall I say, the basic idea which you keep before you when you are exercising the practice of your profession?"

There was a pause while Andrew reflected desperately. At length, feeling he was spoiling all the good effect he had created, he blurted out:

"I suppose—I suppose I keep telling myself never to take anything for granted."

"Thank you, Doctor Manson."

As Andrew left the room, Abbey reached for his pen. He felt young again and suspiciously sentimental. He thought: "If he'd told me he went about trying to heal people, trying to help suffering humanity, I'd have flunked him out of sheer damned disappointment." As it was, Abbey traced the unheard-of maximum, 100, opposite the name of Andrew Manson. Indeed, could Abbey have "got away with it"—his own eloquent reflection—that figure would have been doubled.

A few minutes later Andrew went downstairs with the other candidates. At the foot of the stairs beside his leather hooded cave a liveried porter stood with a little pile of envelopes before him. As the candidates went past he handed an envelope to each of them. Harrison, walking out next to Andrew tore his open quickly. His expression altered: he said quietly, "It would appear I'm not wanted to-morrow." Then, forcing a smile, "How about you?" Andrew's fingers were shaking. He could barely read. Dazedly he heard Harrison congratulate him. His chances were still alive. He walked down to the A.B.C. and treated himself to a malted milk. He thought tensely, if I don't get through now, after all this, I'll—I'll walk in front of a bus.

The next day passed grindingly. Barely half the original candidates remained and it was rumoured that out of these another half would go. Andrew had no idea whether he was doing well or badly: he knew only that his head ached abominably, that his feet were icy, his inside void.

At last it was over. At four o'clock in the afternoon Andrew came out of the cloakroom, spent and melancholy, pulling on his coat. Then he became aware of Abbey standing before the big open fire in the hall. He made to pass. But Abbey, for some reason, was holding out his hand, smiling, speaking to him, telling him—telling him that he was through.

Dear God, he had done it! He had *done* it! He was alive again, gloriously alive, his headache gone, all his weariness forgotten. As he dashed down to the nearest post office his heart sang wildly, madly. He was through, he had done it, not from the West End of London, but from an outlandish mining town. His whole being was a surging exaltation. It hadn't been for nothing after all: these long nights, these mad dashes down to Cardiff, these racking hours of study. On he sped, bumping and cannoning through the crowds, missing the wheels of taxis and omnibuses, his eyes shining, racing, racing to wire news of the miracle to Christine.

XI

WHEN THE train got in, half an hour late, it was nearly midnight. All the way up the valley the engine had been battling against a high head wind and at Aberalaw, as Andrew stepped out on the platform, the force of the hurricane almost bowled him off his feet. The station was deserted. The young poplars planted in line at its entrance bent like bows, whistling and shivering at every blast. Overhead the stars were polished to a high glitter.

Andrew started along Station Road, his body braced, his mind exhilarated by the batter of the wind. Full of his success, his contact with the great, the sophisticated medical world, his ears ringing with Sir Robert Abbey's words, he could not reach Christine fast enough to tell her joyously everything, everything which had taken place. His telegram would have given her the good news; but now he wished to pour out in detail the full exciting story.

As he swung, head down, into Talgarth Street he was conscious, suddenly, of a man running. The man came behind him, labouring heavily, the noisy clatter of his boots upon the pavement so lost in the gale he seemed a phantom figure. Instinctively Andrew stopped. As the man drew near he recognised him, Frank Davis, an ambulance man of Anthracite Sinking No. 3, who had been one of his first-aid class the previous spring. At the same moment Davis saw him.

"I was comin' for you, doctor.· Comin' for you to your house. This wind's knocked the wire all to smash." A gust tore the rest of his words away.

"What's wrong?" shouted Andrew.

"There's been a fall down at Number Three." Davis cupped his hands close to Manson's ear. "A lad got buried there, almost. They don't seem to be able to shift him. Sam Bevan, he's on your list. Better look sharp, doctor, and get to him."

Andrew took a few steps down the road with Davis, then a sudden reflection brought him up short.

"I've got to have my bag," he bawled to Davis. "You go up to my house and fetch it for me. I'll go on to Number Three." He added, "And, Frank!—tell my missus where I've gone."

He was at No. 3 Sinking in four minutes, blown there, across the railway siding and along Roath Lane, by the following wind. In the rescue room he found the under-manager and three men waiting on him. At the sight of him the under-manager's worried expression lifted slightly.

"Glad to see you, doctor. We're all to bits with the storm. And we've had a nasty fall on top of it. Nobody killed, thank God, but one of the lads pinned by his arm. We can't shift him an inch. And the roof's rotten."

They went to the winding shaft, two of the men carrying a stretcher with splints strapped to it and the third a wooden box of first-aid material. As they entered the cage another figure came bundling across the yard. It was Davis, panting, with the bag.

"You've been quick, Frank," Manson said as Davis squatted beside him in the cage.

Davis simply nodded; he could not speak. There was a clang, an instant's suspense, and the cage dropped and rocketed to the bottom. They all got out, moving in single file, the under-manager first, then Andrew, Davis—still clutching the bag—then the three men.

Andrew had been underground before, he was used to the high vaulted caverns of the Drineffy mines, great dark resounding caves, deep down in the earth where the mineral had been gouged and blasted from its bed. But this sinking, No. 3, was an old one with a long and tortuous haulage way leading to the workings. The haulage was less a passage than a low-roofed burrow, dripping and clammy, through which they crawled, often on their hands and knees, for nearly half a mile. Suddenly the light borne by the under-manager stopped just ahead of Andrew who then knew that they were there.

Slowly, he crept forward. Three men, cramped together on their bellies in a dead end, were doing their best to revive another man who lay in a huddled attitude, his body slewed sideways, one shoulder pointing backwards, lost seemingly in the mass of fallen rock around him. Tools lay scattered behind the men, two overturned bait cans, stripped off jackets.

"Well then, lads?" asked the under-manager in a low voice.

"We can't shift him, nohow." The man who spoke turned a sweat grimed face. "We tried everything."

"Don't try," said the under-manager with a quick look at the roof. "Here's the doctor. Get back a bit, lads, and give us room. Get back a tidy bit if I were you."

The three men pulled themselves back from the dead end and Andrew, when they had squeezed their way past him, went forward. As he did so, in one brief moment, there flashed through his head a memory of his recent examination, its advanced bio-chemistry, high sounding terminology, scientific phrases. It had not covered such a contingency as this.

Sam Bevan was quite conscious. But his features were haggard beneath their powdering of dust. Weakly, he tried to smile at Manson.

"Looks like you're goin' to 'ave some amb'lance practice on me proper!" Bevan had been a member of that same first-aid class and had often been requisitioned for bandage practice.

Andrew reached forward. By the light of the under-manager's lamp, thrust across his shoulder, he ran his hands over the injured man. The whole of Bevan's body was free except his left forearm, which lay beneath the fall, so pressed and mangled under the enormous weight of rock, it held him immovably a prisoner.

Andrew saw instantly that the only way to free Bevan was to amputate the forearm. And Bevan, straining his pain tormented eyes, read that decision the moment it was made.

"Go on, then, doctor," he muttered. "Only get me out of here quick."

587

"Don't worry, Sam," Andrew said. "I'm going to send you to sleep now. When you wake up you'll be in bed."

Stretched flat in a puddle of muck under the two foot roof he slipped off his coat, folded it, and slipped it under Bevan's head. He rolled up his sleeves and asked for his bag. The under-manager handed forward the bag and as he did so he whispered in Andrew's ear:

"For God's sake hurry, doctor. We'll have this roof down on us before we know where we are."

Andrew opened the bag. Immediately he smelt the reek of chloroform. Almost before he thrust his hand into the dark interior and felt the jagged edge of broken glass he knew what had occurred. Frank Davis, in his haste to reach the mine, had dropped the bag. The chloroform bottle was broken, its contents irretrievably spilled. A shiver passed over Andrew. He had no time to send up to the surface. And he had no anæsthetic.

For perhaps thirty seconds he remained paralysed. Then automatically he felt for his hypodermic, charged it, gave Bevan a maximum of morphine. He could not linger for the full effect. Tipping his bag sideways so that the instruments were ready to his hand he again bent over Bevan. He said, as he tightened the tourniquet:

"Shut your eyes, Sam!"

The light was dim and the shadows moved with flickering confusion. At the first incision Bevan groaned between his shut teeth. He groaned again. Then, mercifully, when the knife grated upon the bone, he fainted.

A cold perspiration broke on Andrew's brow as he clipped the artery forceps on spurting, mangled flesh. He could not see what he was doing. He felt suffocated here, in this rat-hole, deep down beneath the surface of the ground, lying in the mud. No anæsthesia, no theatre, no row of nurses to run to do his bidding. He wasn't a surgeon. He was guddling hopelessly. He would never get through. The roof would crash upon them all. Behind him the hurried breathing of the under-manager. A slow drip of water falling cold upon his neck. His fingers, working feverishly, stained and warm. The grating of the saw. The voice of Sir Robert Abbey, a long way off: "The opportunity for scientific practice . . ." Oh, God! would he never get through!

At last. He almost sobbed with relief. He slipped a pad of gauze on the bloodied stump. Stumbling to his knees he said:

"Take him out."

Fifty yards back, in a clearing in the haulage way, with space to stand up and four lamps round him he finished the job. Here it was easier. He tidied up, ligatured, drenched the wound with antiseptic. A tube now. Then a couple of holding sutures. Bevan remained unconscious. But his pulse though thin was steady. Andrew drew his hand across his forehead. Finished.

"Go steady with the stretcher. Wrap these blankets round him. We'll want hot bottles whenever we get out."

The slow procession, bent double in the low places, began to sway up the shadows of the haulage. They had not gone sixty paces when a low rumbling subsidence echoed in the darkness down behind them. It was like the last low rumble of a train entering a tunnel. The under-manager did not turn round. He merely said to Andrew with a quiet grimness:

"That's it. The rest of the roof."

The journey out-bye took close upon an hour. They had to edge the stretcher sideways at the bad places. Andrew could not tell how long they had been under. But at length they came to the shaft bottom.

Up, up they shot, out of the depths. The keen bite of the wind met them, as they stepped out of the cage. With a kind of ecstasy Andrew drew a long breath.

He stood at the foot of the steps holding on to the guard rail. It was still dark, but in the mine yard they had hung a big naphtha flare which hissed and leaped with many tongues. Around the flare he saw a small crowd of waiting figures. There were women amongst them, with shawls about their heads.

Suddenly, as the stretcher moved slowly past him, Andrew heard his name called wildly and the next instant Christine's arms were about his neck. Sobbing hysterically she clung to him. Bareheaded, with only a coat above her nightdress, her bare feet thrust into leather shoes, she was a waif-like figure in the gusty darkness.

"What's wrong," he asked, startled, trying to disengage her arms so that he might see her face.

But she would not let him go. Clinging to him frantically like a drowning woman she said brokenly:

"They told us the roof was down—that you wouldn't—wouldn't come out."

Her skin was blue, her teeth chattering with cold. He carried her into the fire of the rescue room, ashamed, yet deeply touched. There was hot cocoa in the rescue room. They drank from the same scalding cup. It was a long time before either of them remembered about his grand new degree.

XII

THE RESCUE of Sam Bevan was commonplace to a town which had known, in the past, the agony and horror of major mine disasters. Yet in his own district it did Andrew a vast amount of good. Had he returned with the bare success of London behind him he would have earned merely an extra sneer for "more newfangled nonsense." As it was, he received nods and even smiles from people who had never seemed to look at him before. The real extent of a doctor's popularity in Aberalaw could be gauged by his passage down the rows. And, where Andrew had hitherto been met by a line of tight shut doors, now he found them open, the off-shift men smoking in their shirt-sleeves ready for a word with him, the women ready to "call him in," as he went by, the children getting him smilingly by name.

Old Gus Parry, head driller in No. 2 and doyen of the West district, summed up the new current of opinion for his mates as he gazed after Andrew's retreating figure.

"Eh, lads! 'E's a bookish chap no doubt. But he can do the real stuff, like, when it's wanted."

Cards began to come back to Andrew, gradually at first and, when it was seen that he did not abuse his returned renegades, with a sudden rush. Owen was pleased at the increase in Andrew's list. Meeting Andrew in the Square one day he smiled:

"Didn't I tell you, now?"

Llewellyn had affected great delight at the result of the examination. He congratulated Andrew effusively upon the phone then blandly raked him in for double duty at the theatre.

"By the way," he remarked, beaming, at the end of the long and ether-ridden session, "did you tell the examiners you were an assistant in a medical aid scheme?"

"I mentioned your name to them, Doctor Llewellyn," Andrew answered sweetly. "And that made it quite all right."

Oxborrow and Medley of the East Surgery took no notice of Andrew's success. But Urquhart was genuinely glad, though his comment took the form of vituperative explosion.

"Dammit to hell, Manson! What d'you think you're doin'? Trying to put my eye out!"

By way of complimenting his distinguished colleague he asked him in consultation to a case of pneumonia he was then attending and demanded to know the prognosis.

"She'll recover," Andrew said and he gave scientific reasons.

Urquhart shook his old head dubiously. He said:

"I never heard tell of your polyvalent sera or your antibodies or your international units. But she was a Powell before her marriage and when the Powells get a swollen belly with their pneumonias they die the eighth day. I know that family backwards. She's got a swollen belly; hasn't she?"

The old man went about with an air of sombre triumph over the scientific method when his patient died on the seventh day.

Denny, now abroad, knew nothing of the new degree. But a final and somewhat unexpected congratulation came in a long letter from

Freddie Hamson. Freddie had seen the results in the *Lancet*, chided Andrew on his success, invited him to London, and then detailed his own exciting triumphs in Queen Anne Street where, as he had predicted that night at Cardiff, his neat brass plate now shone.

"It's a shame the way we've lost touch with Freddie," Manson declared. "I must write to him oftener. I've a feeling we shall run into him again. Nice letter, isn't it?"

"Yes, very nice," Christine answered drily. "But most of it seems to be about himself."

With the approach of Christmas the weather turned colder—crisp frosty days and still, starry nights. The iron hard roads rang under Andrew's feet. The clear air was like an exhilarating wine. Already shaping in his mind was the next step which he would take in his great assault on the problem of dust inhalation. His findings amongst his own patients had raised his hopes high, and now he had obtained permission from Vaughan to extend the field of his investigation by making a systematic examination of all the workers in the three anthracite sinkings —a marvellous opportunity. He planned to use the pit workers and surfacemen as controls. He would begin at the start of the New Year.

On Christmas Eve he returned from the surgery to Vale View with an extraordinary sense of spiritual anticipation and physical well-being. As he walked up the road it was impossible to escape the signs of the impending festival. The miners made much of Christmas here. For the past week the front room in each house had been locked against the children, festooned with paper streamers, toys hidden in the drawers of the chest and a steady accumulation of good things to eat, cake, oranges, sweet sugar biscuits, all bought with the club money paid out at this time of year, laid upon the table.

Christine had made her own decorations of holly and mistletoe in gay expectation. But to-night as he came into the house he saw at once an extra excitement upon her face.

"Don't say a word," she said quickly holding out her hand. "Not a single word! Just shut your eyes and come with me!"

He allowed her to lead him into the kitchen. There, on the table lay a number of parcels, clumsily made up, some merely wrapped in newspaper, but each with a little note attached. In a flash he realised that they were presents from his patients. Some of the gifts were not wrapped up at all.

"Look, Andrew!" Christine cried. "A goose! And two ducks! And a lovely iced cake! And a bottle of elderberry wine! Isn't it kind of them! Isn't it wonderful they should want to give them to you."

He simply could not speak. It overwhelmed him, this kindly evidence that the people of his district had at last begun to appreciate, to like him. With Christine at his shoulder he read the notes, the handwriting

591

laboured and illiterate, some scrawled in pencil upon old envelopes turned inside out. "Your grateful patient at 3 Cefan Row." "With thanks from Mrs. Williams." One lopsided gem from Sam Bevan, "Thanks for gettin' me out for Christmas, doctor, *bach*"—so they went on.

"We must keep these, darling," Christine said in a low voice. "I'll put them away upstairs."

When he had recovered his normal loquacity—a glass of home-made elderberry assisted him—he paced up and down the kitchen while Christine stuffed the goose. He raved beautifully:

"That's how fees should be paid, Chris. No money, no damned bills, no capitation fee, no guinea-grabbing. Payment in kind. You understand me, don't you, darling? You get your patient right, he sends you something that he has made, produced. Coal if you like, a sack of potatoes from his garden, eggs maybe if he keeps hens—see my point. Then you'd have an ethical ideal! By the way, that Mrs. Williams who sent us the ducks—Leslie had her guzzling pills and physic for five stricken years before I cured her gastric ulcer with five weeks' diet. Where was I? Oh, yes! Don't you see. If every doctor was to eliminate the question of *gain* the whole system would be purer——"

"Yes, dear. Would you mind handing me the currants. Top shelf in the cupboard!"

"Damn it all, woman, why don't you listen. Gosh! That stuffing's going to taste good."

Next morning, Christmas Day, came fine and clear. Tallyn Beacons in the blue distance were pearly, with a white icing of snow. After a few morning consultations, with the pleasant prospect of no surgery in the evening, Andrew went on his round. He had a short list. Dinners were cooking in all the little houses and his own was cooking at home. He did not tire of the Christmas greetings he gave and received all along the Rows. He could not help contrasting this present cheerfulness with his bleak passage up those same streets only a year ago.

Perhaps it was this thought which made him draw up, with an odd hesitation in his eyes, outside No. 18 Cefan Row. Of all his patients, apart from Chenkin, whom he did not want, the only one who had not come back to him was Tom Evans. To-day when he was so unusually stirred, perhaps unduly exalted by a sense of the brotherhood of man, he had a sudden impulse to approach Evans and wish him a merry Christmas.

Knocking once, he opened the front door and walked through to the back kitchen. Here he paused, quite taken aback. The kitchen was very bare, almost empty, and in the grate there burned only a spark of fire. Seated before this on a broken-backed wooden chair, with his crooked arm bent out like a wing, was Tom Evans. The droop of his shoulders was dispirited, hopeless. On his knee sat his little girl, four years of age.

They were gazing, both of them, in silent contemplation, at a branch of fir planted in an old bucket. Upon this diminutive Christmas tree which Evans had walked two miles over the mountains to procure, were three tiny tallow candles, as yet unlighted. And beneath it lay the family's Christmas treat—three small oranges.

Suddenly Evans turned and caught sight of Andrew. He started and a slow flush of shame and resentment spread over his face. Andrew sensed that it was agony for him to be found out of work, half his furniture pawned, crippled, by the doctor whose advice he had rejected. He had known, of course, that Evans was down on his luck but he had not suspected anything so pitiful as this. He felt upset and uncomfortable, he wanted to turn and go away. At that moment Mrs. Evans came into the kitchen through the back door with a paper bag under her arm. She was so startled at the sight of Andrew that she dropped her paper bag which fell to the stone floor and burst open revealing two beef faggots, the cheapest meat that Aberalaw provided. The child, glancing at her mother's face, began suddenly to cry.

"What's like the matter, sir," Mrs. Evans ventured at last, her hand pressed against her side. "He hasn't done anything?"

Andrew gritted his teeth together. He was so moved and surprised by this scene he had stumbled upon, only one course would satisfy him.

"Mrs. Evans!" He kept his eyes stiffly upon the floor. "I know there was a bit of a misunderstanding between your Tom and me. But it's Christmas—and—oh! well I want," he broke down lamely, "I mean, I'd be awfully pleased if the three of you would come round and help us eat our Christmas dinner."

"But, doctor——" she wavered.

"You be quiet, lass," Evans interrupted her fiercely. "We're not goin' out to no dinner. If faggots is all we *can* have it's all we *will* have. We don't want any bloody charity from nobody."

"What are you talking about!" Andrew exclaimed in dismay. "I'm asking you as a friend."

"Ah! You're all the same!" Evans answered wretchedly. "Once you get a man down all you can do is fling some grub in his face. Keep your bloody dinner. We don't want it."

"Now, Tom——" Mrs. Evans protested weakly.

Andrew turned towards her, distressed, yet still determined to carry out his intention.

"You persuade him, Mrs. Evans. I'll be really upset now, if you don't come. Half past one. We'll expect you."

Before any of them could say another word he swung round and left the house.

Christine made no comment when he blurted out what he had done. The Vaughans would probably have come to them to-day, but for the fact that they had gone to Switzerland for the ski-ing. And now he had asked an unemployed miner and his family! These were his thoughts as he stood with his back to the fire watching her lay the extra places.

"You're cross, Chris?" he said at last.

"I thought I married Doctor Manson," she answered a trifle brusquely. "Not Doctor Barnardo. Really, darling, you're an incorrigible sentimentalist!"

The Evans arrived exactly upon time, washed and brushed, desperately ill at ease, proud and frightened. Andrew, striving nervously to generate hospitality, had a dreadful premonition that Christine was right, that the entertainment would be a dismal failure. Evans, with a queer look at Andrew, proved to be clumsy at the table because of his bad arm. His wife was obliged to break and to butter his roll for him. And then by good fortune, as Andrew was using the cruet, the top fell off the pepper caster and the entire half ounce of white pepper shot into his soup. There was a hollow silence, then Agnes, the little girl, gave a sudden delighted giggle. Panic stricken, the mother bent to rebuke her, when the sight of Andrew's face restrained her. The next minute they were all laughing.

Free of his dread of being patronised, Evans revealed himself a human being, a staunch rugby football supporter and a great music lover. He had gone to Cardigan three years before to sing at the Eisteddfod there. Proud to show his knowledge he discussed with Christine the oratorios of Elgar, while Agnes pulled crackers with Andrew.

Later, Christine drew Mrs. Evans and the little girl into the other room. Left alone, a strange silence fell between Andrew and Evans. A common thought was uppermost in the mind of each yet neither knew how to broach it. Finally with a kind of desperation Andrew said:

"I'm sorry about that arm of yours, Tom. I know you've lost your work underground over the head of it. Don't think I'm trying to crow over you or anything like that. I'm just damned sorry."

"You're not any sorrier than I am," Evans said.

There was a pause, then Andrew resumed:

"I wonder if you'd let me speak to Mr. Vaughan about you. Shut me up if you think I'm interfering—but I've got a little bit of influence with him and I feel sure I could get you a job on the surface—timekeeper—or something——"

He broke off, not daring to look at Evans. This time the silence was prolonged. At length Andrew raised his eyes only to lower them again immediately. Tears were running down Evans's cheek, his entire body was shaking with his effort not to give way. But it was no use. He laid his good arm on the table, buried his head in it.

Andrew got up and crossed to the window where he remained for a few minutes. At the end of that time Evans had collected himself. He said nothing, absolutely nothing, and his eyes avoided Andrew's with a dumb reticence more significant than speech.

At half past three the Evans family departed in a mood contrasting cheerfully with the constraint of their arrival. Christine and Andrew went into the sitting-room.

"You know, Chris," Andrew philosophised, "all that poor fellow's trouble—his stiff elbow I mean—isn't *his* fault. He distrusted me because I was new. He couldn't be expected to know about that damn carron oil. But friend Oxborrow—who accepted his card—*he* should have known. Ignorance, ignorance, pure damned ignorance. There ought to be a law to make doctors keep up to date. It's all the fault of our rotten system. There ought to be compulsory post-graduate classes—to be taken every five years——"

"Darling!" protested Christine smiling at him from the sofa. "I've put up with your philanthropy all day. I've watched your wings sprouting like an archangel's. Don't give me the Harveian Oration on top of it! Come and sit by me here, I had a really important reason for wanting us to be alone to-day."

"Yes?" Doubtfully; then, indignantly, "You're not complaining, I hope. I thought I had behaved pretty decently. After all—Christmas Day——"

She laughed silently.

"Oh, my dear, you're just too lovely. Another minute there'll be a snowstorm and you'll take out the St. Bernards—muffled to the throat —to bring in somebody off the mountain—late, late at night."

"I know somebody who came down to Number Three Sinking—late, late at night," he grunted in retaliation, "and she wasn't muffled either."

"Sit here." She stretched out her arm. "I want to tell you something."

He went over to seat himself beside her when suddenly there came the loud braying of a Klaxon from outside.

"Krr-krr-krr-ki-ki-ki-krr."

"Damn!" said Christine concisely. Only one motor horn in Aberalaw could sound like that. It belonged to Con Boland.

"Don't you want them?" Andrew asked in some surprise. "Con half said they'd be round for tea."

"Oh, well!" Christine said, rising and accompanying him to the door.

They advanced to meet the Bolands who sat, opposite the front gate, in the reconstructed motor-car, Con upright at the wheel in a bowler hat and enormous new gauntlets with Mary and Terence beside him, the three other children tucked around Mrs. Boland, who bore the infant in her arms, in the rear, all packed, despite the elongation of the vehicle, like herrings in a tin.

595

Suddenly the horn began again: "Krr-krr-krr-krr——" Con had inadvertently pushed the button in switching off and now it was jammed. The Klaxon would not stop. "Krr-krr-krr——" it went, while Con fumbled and swore, and windows went up in the Row opposite and Mrs. Boland sat with a remote expression on her face, unperturbed, holding the baby dreamily.

"In the name of God," Con cried, his moustache bristling along the dashboard. "I'm wastin' juice. What's happened? Am I short circuited or what?"

"It's the button, father," Mary told him calmly. She took her little finger-nail and edged it out. The racket ceased.

"Ah! that's better," Con sighed. "How are you, Manson, my boy? How d'you like the old car now? I've lengthened her a good two feet. Isn't she grand? Mind you there's still a little bother with the gear-box. We didn't quite take the hill in our stride, as ye might say!"

"We only stuck a few minutes, father," interposed Mary.

"Ah! never mind," said Con. "I'll soon have that right when I strip her again. How are ye, Mrs. Manson! Here we all are to wish ye a merry Christmas and take our tea off ye!"

"Come in, Con," Christine smiled. "I like your gloves!"

"Christmas present from the wife," Con answered admiring the flapping gauntlets. "Army Surplus. Would ye believe they were still dishin' them out! Ah! what's gone wrong with this door?"

Unable to open the door he threw his long legs over it, climbed out, helped the children and his wife from the back, surveyed the car—fondly removing a lump of mud from the windscreen—then tore himself away to follow the others to Vale View.

They had a cheerful tea party. Con was in high spirits, full of his creation. "You'll not know her when she has a lick of paint." Mrs. Boland abstractedly drank six cups of strong black tea. The children began upon the chocolate biscuits and ended with a fight for the last piece of bread. They cleared every plate upon the table.

After tea while Mary had gone to wash the dishes—she insisted that Christine looked tired—Andrew detached the baby from Mrs. Boland and played with it on the hearthrug before the fire. It was the fattest baby he had ever seen, a Rubens infant, with enormous solemn eyes and pads of plumpness upon its limbs. It tried repeatedly to poke a finger into his eye. Every time it failed a look of solemn wonder came upon its face. Christine sat with her hands in her lap, doing nothing. Watching him playing with the baby.

But Con and his family could not stay long. Outside the light was fading and Con, worried about his "juice," had doubts which he did not choose to express concerning the functioning of his lamps. When they rose to go he delivered the invitation:

"Come out and see us start."

Again Andrew and Christine stood at the gate while Con packed the car with his offspring. After a couple of swings the engine obeyed and Con, with a triumphant nod towards them, pulled on his gauntlets and adjusted his derby to a more rakish tilt. Then he heaved himself proudly into the driving-seat.

At that moment Con's union broke and the car, with a groan, collapsed. Bearing the entire Boland family the over extended vehicle sank slowly to the ground like some beast of burden perishing from sheer exhaustion. Before the bedazzled eyes of Andrew and Christine, the wheels splayed outwards. There was the sound of pieces dropping off, a vomit of tools from the locker, then the body of the car came to rest, dismembered, on street level. One minute there was a car and the next a fun-fair gondola. In the forepart was Con clutching the wheel, in the aft part his wife, clutching the baby. Mrs. Boland's mouth had dropped wide open, her dreamy eyes well fixed upon eternity. The stupefaction on Con's face, at his sudden loss of elevation, was irresistible.

Andrew and Christine gave out a shriek of laughter. Once they began they could not stop. They laughed till they were weak.

"In the name of God," Con said, rubbing his head and picking himself up. Observing that none of the children were hurt, that Mrs. Boland remained, pale but undisturbed in her seat, he considered the wreckage, pondering dazedly. "Sabotage," he declared at last, glaring at the windows opposite as a solution struck him. "Some of them devils in the Rows has tampered with her." Then his face brightened. He took the helpless Andrew by the arm and pointed with melancholy pride to the crumpled bonnet, beneath which the engine still feebly emitted a few convulsive beats. "See that, Manson! She's still runnin'."

Somehow they dragged the remains into the backyard of Vale View. In due course the Boland family went home on foot.

"What a day!" Andrew exclaimed when they had secured peace for themselves at last. "I'll never forget that look on Con's face as long as I live."

They were silent for a moment, then, turning to her, he asked:
"You did enjoy your Christmas?"
She replied oddly:
"I enjoyed seeing you play with baby Boland."
He glanced at her.
"Why?"
She did not look at him. "I've been trying to tell you all day. Oh, can't you guess, darling?—I don't think you're such a smart physician after all."

XIII

Spring once more. And early summer. The garden at Vale View was a patch of tender colours which the miners often stopped to admire on their way back from their shift. Chiefly these colours came from flowering shrubs which Christine had planted the previous autumn, for now Andrew would allow her to do no manual work at all.

"You've *made* the place!" he told her, with authority. "Now *sit* in it."

Her favourite seat was at the end of the little glen where, beside a tiny water-splash, she could hear the soothing converse of the stream. An overhanging willow offered protection from the rows of houses above. It was the difficulty with the garden of Vale View that they were completely overlooked. They had only to sit outside the porch for all the front windows of the Rows to be tenanted and the murmur to go round: "Eh! There's nice! Come an' 'ave a look, Fan-ee! Doctor and his missis are havin' bit of sun, like!" Once indeed, in their early days, when Andrew slipped his arm round Christine's waist as they stretched by the bank of the stream, he had seen the gleam of focused glass from old Glyn Joseph's parlour. "Damn it!" Andrew had realised hotly. "The old dog—he's got his telescope on us!"

But beneath the willow they were completely screened and here Andrew defined his policy.

"You see, Chris"—fidgeting with his thermometer; it had just occurred to him in a passion of precaution to take her temperature—"we've got to keep calm. It's not as if we were—oh! well—*ordinary* people. After all you're a doctor's wife and I'm—I'm a doctor. I've seen this happen hundreds, at least scores of times before. It's a very *ordinary affair*. A phenomenon of nature, survival of the race, all that sort of thing, see! Now don't misunderstand me, darling, it's *wonderful* for us, of course. The fact is I'd begun to ask myself if you weren't too slight, too much of a kid ever to—oh well, I'm *delighted*. But we're not going to get sentimental. Slushy I mean. No, no! Let's leave that sort of thing to Mr. and Mrs. Smith. It would be rather idiotic, wouldn't it, for me, a doctor, to start—oh, say to start mooning over those little things you're knitting or crocheting, or whatever it is. No! I just look at them and grunt: 'Hope they'll be warm enough!' And all this junk about what colour of eyes she—er—it, will have and what sort of rosy future we'll give her—that's right off the map!" He paused, frowning, then gradually a reflective smile broke over his face. "I say, though, Chris! I wonder if it *will* be a girl!"

She laughed till the tears ran down her cheeks. She laughed so hard that he sat up, concerned.

"Now stop it, Chris! You'll—you might bring on something."

"Oh, my dear." She wiped her eyes. "As a sentimental idealist I adore you. As a hard-boiled cynic—well!—I wouldn't have you in the house!"

He did not quite know what she meant. But he knew he was being scientific and restrained. In the afternoons when he felt she ought to have some exercise he took her for walks in the Public Park, climbing up the uplands being severely forbidden. In the Park they strolled about, listened to the band, watched the miners' children who came to picnic there with bottles of liquorice water and sherbet suckers.

Early one May morning as they lay in bed he became aware, through his light sleep, of a faint movement. He awoke, again conscious of that gentle thrusting, the first movement of the child within Christine. He held himself rigid, scarcely daring to believe, suffocated by a rush of feeling, of ecstasy. Oh, hell! he thought a moment later, perhaps I'm just a Smith after all. I suppose that's why they make the rule a medico can't attend his own wife.

The following week he felt it time to speak to Doctor Llewellyn whom from the outset they had both decided must undertake the case. Llewellyn, when Andrew rang him, was pleased and flattered. He came down at once, made a preliminary examination. Then chatted to Andrew in the sitting-room.

"I'm glad to help you, Manson," accepting a cigarette. "I always felt you didn't like me enough to ask me to do this for you. Believe me, I'll do my best. By the way, it's pretty stifling in Aberalaw at present. Don't you think your little missus ought to have a change of air while she can?"

"What's happening to me?" Andrew asked himself when Llewellyn had gone. "I like that man! He was decent, damned decent. He's got sympathy and tact. He's wizard at his work. And twelve months ago I was trying to cut his throat. I'm just a stiff, jealous, clumsy Highland stot!"

Christine did not wish to go away but he was gently insistent.

"I know you don't want to leave me, Chris! But it's for the best. We've got to think of—oh! everything. Would you rather have the seaside or maybe you'd like to go up North to your aunt. Dash it all, I can afford to send you, Chris. We're pretty well off now!"

They had paid off the Glen Endowment and the last of the furniture instalments and now they had nearly one hundred pounds saved in the bank. But she was not thinking of this when, pressing his hand, she answered steadily:

"Yes! We're pretty well off, Andrew."

Since she must go, she decided to visit her aunt in Bridlington, and a week later he saw her off at the Upper Station with a long hug and a basket of fruit to sustain her on the journey.

He missed her more than he could have believed, their comradeship had become such a part of his life. Their talks, discussions, squabbles, their silences together, the way in which he would call to her whenever he entered the house and wait, his ear cocked, for her cheery answer—he came to see how much these meant to him. Without her, their bedroom became a strange room in an hotel. His meals, conscientiously served by Jenny according to the programme written out by Christine, were arid snatches behind a propped-up book.

Wandering round the garden she had made, he was struck, suddenly, by the dilapidated condition of the bridge. It offended him, seemed an insult to his absent Christine. He had several times spoken to the Committee about this, telling them the bridge was falling to pieces, but they were always hard to move when it came to repairing the assistants' houses. Now, however, in an access of sentiment he rang up the office and pressed the point strenuously. Owen had gone away upon a few days' leave but the clerk assured Andrew that the matter had already been passed by the Committee and referred to Richards the builder. It was only because Richards was busy with another contract that the work had not been put in hand.

In the evenings he betook himself to Boland, twice to the Vaughans who made him remain for bridge and once, greatly to his surprise, he found himself playing golf with Llewellyn. He wrote letters to Hamson and to Denny who had at last left Drineffy and was journeying to Tampico, as the surgeon of a tanker. His correspondence with Christine was a model of illuminating restraint. But he sought distraction, chiefly, in his work.

His clinical examinations at the anthracite sinkings were, by this time, well under way. He could not hasten them since, apart from the demands of his own patients, his opportunity for examining the men came as they went to the minehead baths at the end of the shift and it was impossible to keep them hanging about for any length of time when they wanted to get home for their dinners. He got through on an average two examinations a day, yet already the results were adding further to his excitement. He saw, without jumping to any immediate conclusion, that the incidence of pulmonary trouble amongst the anthracite workers was positively in excess of that existing in the other underground workers in the coal mines.

Though he distrusted text-books, in self-defence, since he had no wish to find afterwards that he had merely put his feet in footprints made by others, he went through the literature on the subject. Its paucity astounded him. Few investigators seemed to have concerned themselves greatly with the pulmonary occupational diseases. Zenker had introduced a high-sounding term, pneumonokoniosis, embracing three forms of fibrosis of the lung due to dust inhalation. Anthracosis, of course, the black infiltration of the lungs met with in coal miners had long been known and was held by Goldman in Germany and Trotter in England to be harmless. There were a few treatises on the prevalence of lung trouble in makers of mill-stones, particularly the French mill-stones, and in knife and axe grinders—"grinder's rot"—and stone cutters. There was evidence, mostly conflicting, from South Africa upon that red rag of Rand labour troubles, gold miners' phthisis, which was undoubtedly due to dust inhalation. It was recorded also that workers in flax and in cotton and grain shovellers were subject to chronic changes in the lungs. But beyond that nothing!

Andrew drew back from his reading with excitement in his eyes. He felt himself upon the track of something definitely unexplored. He thought of the vast numbers of underground workers in the great anthracite mines, the looseness of the legislation upon the disabilities from which they suffered, the enormous social importance of this line of investigation. What a chance, what a wonderful chance! A cold sweat broke over him at the sudden thought that someone might forestall him. But he thrust this from him. Striding up and down the sitting-room before the dead fire long after midnight, he suddenly seized Christine's photograph from the mantelshelf.

"Chris! I really believe I'm going to *do* something!"

In the card-index he bought for the purpose, he carefully began to classify the results of his examinations. Though he never considered this, his clinical skill was now quite brilliant. There, in the changing room the men stood before him, stripped to the waist, and with his fingers, his stethoscope, he plumbed uncannily the hidden pathology of those living lungs: a fibroid spot here, the next an emphysema, then a chronic bronchitis—deprecatingly admitted as "a bit of a cough." Carefully he localised the lesions upon the diagrams printed on the back of every card.

At the same time he took sputum samples from each man and, working till two and three in the morning at Denny's microscope, tabulated his finding on the cards. He found that most of these samples of mucopus—locally described by the men as "white-spit"—contained bright angular particles of silica. He was amazed at the number of alveolar cells present, at the frequency with which he came upon the tubercle bacillus. But it was the presence, almost constant, of crystalline silicon, in the alveolar cells, the phagocytes, everywhere, which riveted his attention. He could not escape the thrilling idea that the changes in the lungs, perhaps even the coincident infections, were fundamentally dependent on this factor.

This was the extent of his advance when Christine returned at the end of June and flung her arms round his neck.

"It's so good to be back. Yes, I enjoyed myself, but oh! I don't

601

know—and you look pale, darling! I don't believe Jenny's been feeding you!"

Her holiday had done her good, she was well and her cheeks had a fine bloom upon them. But she was concerned about him, his lack of appetite, his perpetual fumbling for a cigarette.

She asked him seriously.

"How long is this special work going to take?"

"I don't know." It was the day after her return, a wet day, and he was unexpectedly moody. "It might take a year, it might take five."

"Well, listen to me. I'm not reforming you, one in the family is enough, but don't you think if since it's going on so long as that you'll have to work systematically, keep regular hours, not stay up late and kill yourself!"

"There's nothing the matter with me."

But in some things she had a peculiar insistence. She got Jenny to scrub out the floor of the Lab., brought in an armchair and a rug. It was a room cool on these hot nights and the pine boards had a sweet resinous smell which mingled with the pungent ethereal scent of the reagents he used. Here she would sit, sewing and knitting while he worked at the table. Bent over the microscope he quite forgot about her, but she was there, and at eleven o'clock every night she got up.

"Time for bed!"

"Oh, I say——" Blinking at her near-sightedly over the eye-piece. "You go up, Chris! I'll follow you in a minute."

"Andrew Manson, if you think I'm going up to bed alone, *in my condition——*"

This last phrase had become a comic by-word in the household. They both used it, indiscriminately, facetiously, as a clincher to all their arguments. He could not resist it. With a laugh he would rise, stretch himself, swing round his lenses, put the slides away.

Towards the end of July a sharp outbreak of chicken pox made him busy in the practice, and on the 3rd of August he had an especially heavy list which kept him out from morning surgery until well after three o'clock. As he came up the road, tired, ready for that combination of lunch and tea which would be his meal, he saw Doctor Llewellyn's car at the gate of Vale View.

The implication of that static object caused him to start suddenly, and to hasten, his heart beating rapidly with anticipation, towards his house. He ran up the porch steps, threw open the front door and there, in the hall, he found Llewellyn. Gazing at the other man with nervous eagerness he stammered:

"Hello, Llewellyn. I—I didn't expect to see you here so soon."

"No," Llewellyn answered.

Andrew smiled. "Well?" In his excitement he could find no better words but the question in his bright face was plain enough.

Llewellyn did not smile. After the faintest pause he said:

"Come in here a minute, my dear chap." And he drew Andrew into the sitting-room. "We've been trying to find you, on your round, all morning."

Llewellyn's manner, his hesitation, the strange sympathy in his voice, shot a wave of coldness over Andrew. He faltered:

"Is anything wrong?"

Llewellyn looked through the window, his glance travelling towards the bridge, as if searching for the best, the kindest explanation. Andrew could bear it no longer. He could scarcely breathe, his breast was filled with a stifling agony of suspense.

"Manson," Llewellyn said gently, "this morning—as your wife was going over the bridge—one of the rotten planks gave way. *She's* all right now, quite all right; but I'm afraid——"

He understood even before Llewellyn finished. A great pulse of anguish beat within him.

"You might like to know," Llewellyn went on, in a tone of quiet compassion, "that we did everything. I came at once, brought matron from the hospital, we've been here all day——"

There was a bar of silence. A sob broke in Andrew's throat, another, then another. He covered his eyes with his hand.

"Please, my dear fellow," Llewellyn entreated, "who could help an accident like that? I beg of you—go up and console your wife."

His head lowered, holding to the banister, Andrew went upstairs. Outside the door of the bedroom he paused, scarcely breathing, then, stumblingly, he went in.

XIV

By THE year 1927 Doctor Manson of Aberalaw had a somewhat unusual reputation. His practice was not prodigious—numerically his list had not greatly increased since those first nervous days of his arrival in the town. But everyone upon that list had a convincing belief in him. He used few drugs—indeed, he had the incredible habit of advising his patients against medicine—but when he did use them he prescribed in shattering style. It was no uncommon sight to see Gadge drooping across the waiting-room with a prescription in his hand.

"What's all this, Doctor Manson? *Sixty*-grain doses of KBr. for Evan Jones! And the *Pharmacopœia* says *five.*"

"So does Aunt Kate's dream-book! Go ahead with sixty, Gadge. You know you'd really enjoy knocking off Evan Jones."

But Evan Jones, epileptic, was not knocked off. Instead he was seen, a week later, his fits lessened, taking walks in the Public Park.

The Committee ought to have cherished Doctor Manson tenderly because his drug bill—despite explosive incidents—was less than half that of any other assistant. But alas! Manson cost the Committee three times as much in other directions, and often there was war because of it. He used vaccines and sera for instance, ruinous things which, as Ed Chenkin heatedly declared, none of them had ever heard of. When Owen, defending, instanced that winter month when Manson, using Bordet and Gengou vaccine, had arrested a raging epidemic of whooping cough in his district when all over the rest of the town children were going down with it, Ed Chenkin countered: "How do we know this new-fangled thing did it! Why! When I tackled 'im myself, he said nobody could be *sure!*"

While Manson had many loyal friends, he also had enemies. There were those on the Committee who had never completely forgiven him for his outburst, those agonised words hurled at them, over that matter of the bridge, as they sat in full session three years before. They sympathised, of course, with Mrs. Manson and himself in their bereavement, but they could not hold themselves responsible. The Committee never did things in a hurry. Owen was then on holiday, and Len Richards, who had been given the job, was busy at the time with the new houses in Powis Street. It was preposterous to blame them.

As time went on Andrew had many heartburnings with the Committee for he had a stubborn desire for his own way which the Committee did not like. In addition there was a certain clerical bias against him. Though his wife often went to church he was never seen there—Doctor Oxborrow had been the first to point this out—and he was reported to have laughed at the doctrine of total immersion. He had, moreover, a deadly enemy amongst "the chapel" folk—no less a person than the Reverend Edwal Parry, pastor of Sinai.

In the spring of 1926 the good Edwal, newly married, had sidled, late, into Manson's surgery with an air, thoroughly Christian, yet ingratiatingly man of the world.

"How are you, Doctor Manson! I just happened to be passing. As a rule I attend with Doctor Oxborrow, he's one of my flock, you know, and he's handy at the East Surgery also. But you're a very up-to-date doctor by all accounts and purposes. You're in the way of knowin' everything that's new. And I'd be glad—mind you I'll pay you a nice little fee too—if you could advise me——" Edwal masked a faint priestly blush by show of worldly candour. "You see the wife and I don't want any children for a while yet anyhow, my stipend bein' what it is, like——"

Manson considered the minister of Sinai in a cold distaste. He said carefully:

"Don't you realise there are people with a quarter of your stipend who would give their right hand to have children. What did you get married for?" His anger rose to a sudden white heat. "Get out—quick —you—you dirty little man of God!"

With a queer twist of his face Parry had slunk out. Perhaps Andrew had spoken too violently. But then, Christine, since that fatal stumble, would never have children, and they both desired them with all their hearts.

Walking home from a call on this, the 15th of May, 1927, Andrew was inclined to ask himself why he and Christine had remained in Aberalaw since the death of their child. The answer was plain enough: his work on dust inhalation. It had absorbed him, fascinated him, bound him to the mines.

As he reviewed what he had done, considering the difficulties he had been obliged to face, he wondered that he had not taken longer to complete his findings. Those first examinations he had made—how far removed they seemed in time, yes, and in technique.

After he had made a complete clinical survey of the pulmonary conditions of all the workmen in the district and tabulating his findings, he had plain evidence of the marked preponderance of lung diseases amongst the anthracite workers. For example, he found that ninety per cent of his cases of fibrosed lung came from the anthracite mines. He found also that the death-rate from lung troubles amongst the older anthracite miners was nearly three times that of miners employed in all coal mines. He drew up a series of tables indicating the ratio-incidence of pulmonary disease, amongst the various grades of anthracite workmen.

Next, he set out to show that the silica dust he had found in his examinations of sputum was actually present in the anthracite headings. Not only did he demonstrate this conclusively, but, by exposing glass slides smeared with canada balsam for varying periods in different parts of the mine, he obtained figures of the varying dust concentrations, figures which rose sharply during blasting and drilling.

He now had a series of exciting equations co-relating excessive atmosphere concentrations of silica dust with excessive incidence of pulmonary disease. But this was not enough. He had actually to *prove* that the dust was harmful, that it was destructive to lung tissue and not merely an innocuous accessory after the fact. It was necessary for him to conduct a series of pathological experiments upon guinea-pigs, to study the action of the silica dust upon their lungs.

Here, though his excitement rose, his real troubles began. He already had the spare room, the Lab. It was easy to procure a few guinea-pigs. And the equipment required for his experiments was simple. But though his ingenuity was considerable he was not, and never would be, a pathologist. Awareness of this fact made him angry, more resolved than ever. He swore at a system which compelled him to work alone and pressed Christine to his service, teaching her to cut and prepare sections, the mechanics of the trade which, in no time at all, she did better than he.

Next he constructed, very simply, a dust chamber, in which for certain hours of the day the animals were exposed to concentrations of the dust, other being unexposed—the controls. It was exasperating work, demanding more patience than he possessed. Twice his small electric fan broke down. At a critical stage of the experiment he bungled his system of controls and was forced to begin all over again. But in spite of mistakes and delays he got his specimens, proving in progressive stages the deterioration of the lung and induction of fibrosis from the dust.

He drew a long breath of satisfaction, stopped scolding Christine and, for a few days, was fit to live with. Then another idea struck him and he was off again.

All his investigations had been conducted on the supposition that the damage to the lung was produced in response to mechanical destruction by the hard sharp silicate crystals inhaled. But now, suddenly, he asked himself if there was not some chemical action beyond the mere physical irritation of the particles. He was not a chemist but he was, by this time, too deeply immersed to allow himself to be defeated. He devised a fresh series of experiments.

He procured colloidal silica and injected it under the skin of one of his animals. The result was an abscess. Similar abscesses could, he found, be inducted by the injection of aqueous solutions of amorphous silica which was, physically, a non-irritant. While, in triumphant conclusion, he found that the injection of a mechanically irritating substance, such as particles of carbon, produced no abscess at all. The silica dust *was* chemically active.

He was now almost out of his mind with excitement and delight. He had done even more than he had set out to do. Feverishly he collected his data, drew up in compact form the results of his three years' work. He had decided, months ago, not only to publish his investigation but to send it in as his thesis for the degree of M.D. When the typescript came back from Cardiff, neatly bound in a pale blue folder, he read it exultantly, went out with Christine to post it, then slumped into a backwash of despair.

He felt worn out and inert. He became aware, more vividly than ever, that he was no laboratory worker, that the best, the most valuable part of his work was that first phase of clinical research. He recollected with a pang of compunction how often he had raged at poor Christine. For days he was dispirited and listless. And yet, through it all, there were shining moments when he knew he had accomplished something after all.

XV

THAT MAY afternoon, when Andrew reached home, his mood of preoccupation, this oddly negative phase which had persisted since the
dispatch of his thesis, caused him to miss the look of distress upon
Christine's face. He greeted her absent-mindedly, went upstairs to wash,
then came down to tea.

When he had finished, however, and lit a cigarette he suddenly
observed her expression. He asked, as he reached out for the evening
paper:

"Why? What's the matter?"

She appeared to examine her teaspoon for a moment.

"We had some visitors to-day—or rather I had—when you were out
this afternoon."

"Oh? Who were they?"

"A deputation from the Committee, five of them, including Ed
Chenkin, and escorted by Parry—you know, the Sinai minister—and a
man Davies."

An odd silence fell. He took a long pull at his cigarette, lowered the
paper to gaze at her.

"What did they want?"

She met his scrutiny for the first time, fully revealing the vexation and
anxiety in her eyes. She spoke hurriedly. "They came about four o'clock
—asked for you. I told them you were out. Then Parry said it didn't
matter, they wanted to come in. Of course I was quite taken aback. I
didn't know whether they wanted to wait for you or what. Then Ed
Chenkin said it was the Committee's house, that they represented the
Committee and that in the name of the Committee they could and would
come in." She paused, drew a quick breath. "I didn't budge an inch. I
was angry—upset. But I managed to ask them *why* they wished to come
in. Parry took it up then. He said it had come to his ears, and the ears of
the Committee, in fact it was all over the town, that you were performing experiments on animals, vivisection, he had the cheek to call it. And
because of that they had come to look at your workroom and brought
Mr. Davies, the Prevention of Cruelty to Animals man, along with
them."

Andrew had not moved, nor had his eyes left her face.

"Go on, my dear," he said, quietly.

"Well, I tried to stop them, but it was no use. They just pushed
past, the seven of them, through the hall and into the Lab. Whenever
they saw the guinea-pigs Parry let out a howl—'Oh, the poor dumb
creatures!' And Chenkin pointed to the stain on the boards where I

dropped the fuscine bottle, you remember, dear, and shouted out, ' 'Ave a look at that. *Blood!*' They prowled round everything, went through our beautiful sections, the microtome, everything. Then Parry said, 'I'm not leavin' those poor suffering creatures to be tortured any more. I'd rather have them put out of their pain than that.' He took the bag Davies had with him and shoved them all into it. I tried to tell him there was no question of suffering, or vivisection or any such rubbish. And in any case that those five guinea-pigs were not going to be used for experiments, that we were going to give them to the Boland children, and to little Agnes Evans, for pets. But they simply wouldn't listen to me. And then they—they went away."

There was a silence. Andrew's face was now deeply flushed. He sat up.

"I never heard such rank impertinence in all my life. It—it's damnable you had to put up with it, Chris! But I'll make them pay for it!"

He reflected a minute then started towards the hall to use the telephone. But just as he reached it the instrument rang. He snatched it from the hook.

"Hullo!" he said angrily, then his voice altered slightly. Owen was on the other end of the line. "Yes, it's Manson speaking. Look here, Owen——"

"I know, I know, doctor," Owen interrupted Andrew quickly. "I've been trying to get in touch with you all afternoon. Now listen. No, no, don't interrupt me. We got to keep our heads over this. We're up against a nasty bit o' business, doctor. Don't say any more on the telephone I'm comin' down to see you now."

Andrew went back to Christine.

"What does he mean," he fumed, when he had told her of the conversation. "Anyone would think we were to blame."

They waited for Owen's arrival, Andrew striding up and down in a passion of impatience and indignation, Chris sitting at her sewing with disquieted eyes.

Owen came. But there was nothing reassuring in his face. Before Andrew could speak he said:

"Doctors did you have a licence?"

"A what?" Andrew stared at him. "What kind of licence?"

Owen's face now seemed more troubled. "You've got to have a licence from the Home Office for experimental work on animals. You knew that, didn't you?"

"But damn it all!" Manson protested hotly, "I'm not a pathologist, I never will be. And I'm not running a laboratory. I only wanted to do a few simple experiments to tie up with my clinical work. We didn't have more than a dozen animals altogether—did we, Chris?"

Owen's eyes were averted. "You ought to have had that licence, doctor. There's a section of the Committee are tryin' to play you up pretty bad over this!" He went on quickly. "You see, doctor, a chap like you, that's doin' pioneer work, who's honest enough to speak his mind, he's bound to—well, anyhow, it's only right you should know there's a section here that's dyin' to put a knife in you. But there now! —it'll be all right. There'll be a regular old shindy with the Committee, you'll have to come before them, like. But you've had your troubles with them before. You'll come out on top again."

Andrew stormed. "I'll bring a counter-action. I'll sue them for—for illegal entry. No, damn it, I'll sue them for stealing my guinea-pigs. I want them back, anyway."

A pale amusement twitched Owen's face. "You can't have them back, doctor. Reverend Parry and Ed Chenkin they allowed they'd have to put them out their misery. In the cause of 'umanity they drowned them with their own hands."

Sorrowfully, Owen went away. And the following evening Andrew received a summons to appear before the Committee in one week's time.

Meanwhile the case had flared into prominence like a petrol blaze. Nothing so exciting, so scandalous, so savouring of the black arts had startled Aberalaw since Trevor Day, the solicitor, was suspected of killing his wife with arsenic. Sides were taken, violent factions formed. From his rostrum at Sinai, Edwal Parry thundered the punishments meted out, in this life and the hereafter, to those who tortured animals and little children. At the other end of the town, Reverend David Walpole, chubby minister of the Established Church, to whom Parry was as pig to good Mohammedan, bleated of progress and the feud between the Liberal Church of God and Science.

Even the women were aroused to action. Miss Myfanwy Bensusan, local president of the Welsh Ladies' Endeavour League, spoke to a crowded meeting in the Temperance Hall. It is true that Andrew had once offended Myfanwy by failing to take the chair at the W.L.E. Annual Rally. But her motives, otherwise, were unquestionably pure. After the meeting and on subsequent evenings young lady members of the League normally active in the streets only upon flag days, could be seen distributing gruesome anti-vivisection folders each bearing an illustration of a partially disembowelled dog.

On Wednesday night Con Boland rang up with a joyous tale. "How are ye, Manson, boy? Keepin' the old chin up? Good enough! I was thinking ye might be interested—our Mary was comin' home this evening from Larkin's when one of them simperin' flag sellers stopped her with a pamphlet—these cruelty falderals they've been shovin' around against ye. Do ye know—ha! ha! Do ye know what the bold Mary did! She up with the pamphlet and tore it into bits. Then she up with her hand, boxed the flag-sellin' female's ears, tugged the hat off her head and said—ha! ha!—what do you think our Mary said: 'If it's cruelty

609

you're after,' says she—ha! ha!—'If it's cruelty you're after—*I'll give ye it!'*"

Physical combat was offered by others as loyal as Mary.

Though Andrew's district was solidly behind him, round the East Surgery there was a block of contrary opinion. Fights broke out in the pubs between Andrew's supporters and his enemies. Frank Davies came to the surgery on Thursday night, himself slightly battered, to inform Andrew that he had "knocked the block off two of Oxborrow's patients for saying as 'ow our man was a bloody butcher!"

Thereafter Doctor Oxborrow passed Andrew with a bouncing tread and eyes fixed a long way off. He was known to be working openly with the Reverend Parry against his undesirable colleague. Urquhart came back from the Masonic Club with the meaty Christian's comments, of which perhaps the choicest was: "Why should any doctor have to murder God's living creatures?"

Urquhart had few remarks to make himself. But once, squinting across at Andrew's constrained, tense face, he declared:

"Dammit to hell! When I was your age I'd have enjoyed a scrap like this, too. But now—oh, dammit! I suppose I'm getting old."

Andrew could not help thinking that Urquhart misjudged him. He was far from enjoying the "scrap." He felt tired, irritable, worried. He asked himself fretfully if he was to spend all his life running his head into stone walls. Yet, although his vitality was low, he had a desperate desire to justify himself, to be openly vindicated before the squabbling town.

The week passed at last, and on Sunday afternoon the Committee assembled for what was specified in the agenda as the disciplinary examination of Doctor Manson. There was not a vacant place in the Committee-room and outside in the Square groups of people were hanging about as Andrew entered the offices and walked up the narrow stairs. He felt his heart bumping rapidly. He had told himself he must be calm and steeled. Instead, as he took his seat on that same chair which as a candidate he had occupied five years before, he was stiff, dry lipped, nervous.

The proceedings began—not with prayer, as might have been expected from the sanctimony with which the opposition had conducted their campaign—but with a fiery speech from Ed Chenkin.

"I'm going to put the full facts of this case," said Chenkin, jumping up, "before my fellow members of this Committee." He proceeded, in a loud illiterate speech to enumerate the complaints. Doctor Manson had no right to do this work. It was work done in the Committee's time, work done when he was being paid for doing the *Committee's* work, and work done on the Committee's property. Also it was vivisection, or near neighbour to it. And it was all done without the necessary permit, a very serious offence in the eye of the law!

Here Owen intervened swiftly.

"As regards that last point, I must advise the Committee that if they report Doctor Manson's failure to secure this permit any subsequent action taken would involve the Medical Aid Society as a whole."

"What the 'ell d'you mean?" Chenkin asked.

"As he is our assistant," Owen held. "We are legally responsible for Doctor Manson!"

There was a murmur of assent at this and cries of, "Owen's right! We don't want any trouble on the Society. Keep it amongst ourselves."

"Never mind the bloody permit, then," bawled Chenkin, still upon his feet. "There's enough in the other charges to hang anybody."

"Hear! Hear!" called out someone at the back. "What about all them times he sneaked off to Cardiff on his motor bike—that summer three years back?"

"He don't give medicine," came the voice of Len Richards. "You can wait an hour outside his surgery and not get your bottle filled."

"Order! Order!" Chenkin shouted. When he had stilled them he proceeded to his final peroration. "All these complaints are bad enough! They show that Doctor Manson 'as never been a satisfactory servant to the Medical Aid. Besides which I might add that he don't give proper certificates to the men. But we got to keep our minds on the main item. Here we have an assistant that the whole town's up against for what ought by rights to be a police case, a man who has turned our property into a slaughter-'ouse—I swear by the Almighty, fellow members, I saw the blood on the floor with my own eyes—a man who's nothing but an experimenter and a crank. I ask you, fellow members, if you're goin' to stand it. No! say I. No! say you. Fellow members, I know you are with me one and all, when I say that here and now we demand Doctor Manson's resignation." Chenkin glanced round at his friends and sat down amidst loud applause.

"Perhaps you'll allow Doctor Manson to state his case," Owen said palely, and turned to Andrew.

There was a silence. Andrew sat still for a moment. The situation was worse, even, than he had imagined. Put not your trust in committees, he thought bitterly. Were these the same men who had smiled at him approvingly when they gave him the appointment? His heart burned. He would not, simply would not resign. He got to his feet. He was no speaker and he knew that he was no speaker. But he was angry now, his nervousness lost in a swelling indignation at the ignorance, the intolerant stupidity of Chenkin's accusation, and the acclamation with which the others had received it. He began:

"No one seems to have said anything about the animals Ed Chenkin drowned. That was cruelty if you like—useless cruelty. What I've been doing wasn't that! Why do you men take white mice and canaries down

611

the mine? To test for black damp—you all know that. And when these mice get finished by a whiff of gas—do you call that cruelty? No, you don't. You realise that these animals have been used to save men's lives, perhaps your *own* lives.

"That's what I've been trying to do for you! I've been working on these lung diseases that you get from the dust of the mine headings. You all know that you get chest trouble and that when you *do* get it you don't get compensation. For these last three years I've spent nearly every minute of my spare time on this inhalation problem. I've found out something which might improve your working conditions, give you a fairer deal, keep you in health better than that stinking bottle of medicine Len Richards was talking about would have done! What if I did use a dozen guinea-pigs? Don't you think it was worth it?

"You don't believe me, perhaps. You're prejudiced enough to think I would lie to you. Maybe you still think I've been wasting my time, *your* time as you call it, in a lot of cranky experiments." He was so worked up he forgot his stern resolution not to be dramatic. Diving into his breast pocket he produced the letter he had received earlier in the week. "But this'll show you what other people think of it, people who are qualified to judge."

He walked across to Owen and handed him the letter. It was an intimation from the Clerk of the Senate at St. Andrews that, for his thesis on Dust Inhalation, he had been awarded his M.D.

Owen read the crested, blue-typed letter with a sudden brightening of his face. Thereafter it was passed slowly from hand to hand.

It annoyed Andrew to observe the effect created by the Senate's communication. Although he was so desperately anxious to prove his case he almost regretted his impulse in producing it. If they could not take his word without some sort of official bolstering they must be heavily prejudiced against him. Letter or no letter, he felt moodily that they were bent on making an example of him.

He was relieved when, after a few further remarks, Owen said:

"Perhaps you'll leave us now, doctor, please."

Waiting outside, while they voted on his case, he kicked his heels, simmering with exasperation. It was a wonderful ideal, this group of working men controlling the medical services of the community for the benefit of their fellow workers. But it was only an ideal. They were too biased, too unintelligent ever to administer such a scheme progressively. It was perpetual labour for Owen to drag them along the road with him. And he had the conviction, that on this occasion, even Owen's goodwill would not save him.

But the secretary, when Andrew went in again, was smiling, briskly rubbing his hands. Others on the Committee were regarding him more favourably, at least without hostility. And Owen immediately stood up and said:

"I'm glad to tell you, Doctor Manson—I may even say that personally I'm delighted to tell you—that the Committee have decided by a majority to ask you to remain."

He had won, he had carried them after all. But the knowledge, after one swift throb of satisfaction, gave him no elation. There was a pause. They obviously expected him to express his relief, his gratitude. But he could not. He felt tired of the whole distorted business, of the Committee, Aberalaw, medicine, silica dust, guinea-pigs and himself.

At last he said:

"Thank you, Mr. Owen. I'm glad, after all I've tried to do here, that the Committee don't wish me to go. But, I'm sorry, I can't wait on in Aberalaw any longer. I give the Committee a month's notice from to-day." He spoke without feeling, then he spun round and walked out of the room.

There was a dead silence. Ed Chenkin was the quickest to recover himself. "Good riddance," he called half-heartedly after Manson.

Then Owen startled them all with the first burst of anger he had ever shown in that Committee room.

"Shut your senseless mouth, Ed Chenkin." He flung down his ruler with intimidating violence. "We have lost the best man we ever had."

XVI

ANDREW WOKE up in the middle of that night groaning:

"Am I a fool, Chris? Chucking away our living—a sound job? after all, I *was* getting a few private patients lately. And Llewellyn has been pretty decent. Did I tell you?—he half promised to let me consult at the hospital. And the Committee—they aren't a bad lot when you cut out the Chenkin crowd. I believe in time when Llewellyn retired they might have made me head doctor in his place."

She comforted him, quiet, reasonable, lying beside him in the darkness.

"You don't really want us to stay in a Welsh mining practice all our lives, my dear. We've been happy here, but it's time for us to move on."

"But listen, Chris," he worried, "we haven't enough to buy a practice yet. We ought to have collected some more money before we hoofed it."

She answered sleepily. "What has money got to do with it? Besides, we're going to spend all we've got—almost—on a real holiday. Do you realise you've hardly been away from these old mines for nearly four years."

Her spirit infected him. Next morning the world seemed a gay and careless place. At breakfast, which he ate with new relish, he declared:

"You're not a bad old girl, Chris. Instead of getting up on the platform and telling me you expect Big Things of me now, that it's time for me to go out and make my mark in the world, you just——"

She was not listening to him. Irrelevantly she protested.

"Really, dear, I wish you wouldn't bunch the paper so! I thought it was only women did that. How do you expect me to read my gardening column?"

"Don't read it." On his way to the door he kissed her, smiling. "Think about me."

He felt adventurous, prepared to take his chance with life. Besides, the cautious side of him could not avoid glancing at the assets side of his balance sheet. He had his M.R.C.P., an honours M.D. and over £300 in the bank. With all this behind them surely they would not starve.

It was well that their intention stood firm. A revulsion of sentiment had swept upon the town. Now that he was going of his own free will everybody wished him to remain.

The climax came a week after the meeting when Owen unsuccessfully headed a deputation to Vale View to ask Andrew to reconsider his decision. Thereafter the feeling against Ed Chenkin swelled to the verge of violence. He was booed in the Rows. Twice he was played home from the mine by the penny-whistle band, an ignominy usually reserved by the workmen for a blackleg.

In the face of all these local reverberations it was strange how lightly his thesis appeared to have shaken the outer world. It had gained him his M.D. It had been printed in the *Journal of Industrial Health* in England and published as a brochure in the United States by the Association of American Hygiene. But beyond that it earned him exactly three letters.

The first was from a firm in Brick Lane, E.C., informing him that samples were being forwarded to him of their Pulmo-Syrup, the infallible lung specific for which they had hundreds of testimonials including several from prominent physicians. They hoped he would recommend Pulmo-Syrup amongst the miners in his practice. Pulmo-Syrup, they added, also cured rheumatism.

The second was from Professor Challis, an enthusiastic letter of congratulation and appreciation which ended by asking if Andrew could not call at the Institute in Cardiff some time that week. In a PS., Challis added: *Try and come Thursday.* But Andrew, in the hurry of these last few days, was unable to keep that appointment. Indeed he mislaid the letter and for the time being forgot to answer it.

The third letter he did immediately answer, he was so genuinely thrilled to receive it. It was an unusual, stimulating communication which had crossed the Atlantic from Oregon. Andrew read and re-read the typewritten sheets then took them in excitement to Christine.

"This is rather decent, Chris!—this American letter—it's from a fellow called Stillman, Robert Stillman of Oregon—you've probably never heard of him, but I have—it's full of the most exact appreciation of my Inhalation stuff. More, much more than Challis—damn it, I should have answered his letter! This chap has absolutely understood what I was after, in fact he quietly puts me right on one or two points. Apparently the active destructive ingredient in my silica is serecite. I hadn't enough chemistry to get to that. But it's a marvellous letter, congratulatory—and from Stillman!"

"Yes?" She peeped inquiring. "Is he some doctor out there?"

"No, that's the amazing thing. He's a physicist really. But he runs a clinic for disorders of the lungs, near Portland, Oregon—look, it's on the notepaper. Some of them don't recognise him yet, but he's as a big a man as Spahlinger in his own way. I'll tell you about him when we've time."

It showed how much he thought of Stillman's letter for him to sit down and answer it on the spot.

They were now overwhelmed by preparations for their holiday, arrangements for storing their furniture in Cardiff—the most convenient centre—and by the doleful processes of leave-taking. Their departure from Drineffy had been abrupt, a heroic cleavage. But here they suffered much lingering sentiment. They were entertained by the Vaughans, the Bolands, even by the Llewellyns. Andrew developed "farewell-dyspepsia," symptomatic of these parting banquets. When the actual day arrived Jenny, in tears, told them—to their consternation—that they were to be given a "platform send-off."

At the last moment, on top of this unsettling information, Vaughan came hastening round.

"Sorry to harass you people again. But look here, Manson, what have you been doing to Challis? I've just had a letter from the old boy. Your paper has sent him quite ga-ga—and incidentally—at least so I understand—the Metalliferous Board as well. Anyway he's asked me to get in touch with you. He wants you to see him in London without fail, says it's extremely important."

Andrew answered a trifle peevishly.

"We're going on holiday, man. The first real holiday we've had for years. How *can* I see him?"

"Let's have your address then. He'll obviously want to write to you."

Andrew glanced uncertainly at Christine. They had meant to keep their destination a secret, so that they should be free from all worries, correspondence, interference. But he gave Vaughan the information.

Then they were hurrying to the station, engulfed by the crowd from the district who waited there, shaken by the hand, shouted at, patted on the back, embraced, and finally hustled into their compartment of the moving train. As they steamed off, their friends massed on the platform began lustily to sing "Men of Harlech."

"My God!" Andrew said, trying out his numb fingers. "That was the last straw." But his eyes were glistening, and a minute later he added, "I wouldn't have had us miss it for anything, Chris. Aren't people *decent*. And to think that a month ago half the town was after my blood! You can't get away from the fact—life's damn funny." He gazed at her humorously as she sat beside him. "And this, Mrs. Manson, though you are now an old woman, is your second honeymoon!"

They reached Southampton that evening, took their berths in the cross-channel steamer. Next morning they saw the sun rise behind St. Malo and an hour later Brittany received them.

The wheat was ripening, the cherry-trees were heavy with fruit, goats strayed on the flowering pastures. It had been Christine's idea to come here, to get close to the real France—not its picture galleries or palaces, not historic ruins or monuments, nothing which the tourists's guide-book insisted that they should see.

They reached Val André. Their little hotel was within sound of the sea, within scent of the meadows. Their bedroom had plain scrubbed boards, and their morning coffee came to them steaming in thick blue bowls. They lazed the whole day long.

"Oh, Lord!" Andrew kept repeating. "Isn't this wonderful, darling. I never, never, never want to look a lobar pneumonia in the face again." They drank cider, ate langoustines, shrimps, pastries and whiteheart cherries. In the evenings Andrew played billiards with the proprietor on the antique octagonal table. Sometimes he only lost by fifty in the hundred.

It was lovely, wonderful, exquisite—the adjectives were Andrew's— all but the cigarettes, he would add. A whole blissful month slipped past. And then, more frequently, and with unceasing restlessness, Andrew began to finger the unopened letter, now stained by cherry juice and chocolate, which had remained in his jacket for the past fortnight.

"Go on," Christine urged, at last, one morning. "We've kept our word! Open it."

He slit up the envelope studiously, read the letter lying upon his back in the sunlight, sat up slowly, then read it again. In silence he passed it over to Christine.

The letter was from Professor Challis. It stated that as the direct result of his researches into dust inhalation the C.M.F.B.—Coal and Metalliferous Mines Fatigue Board—had decided to open up the whole question with a view to reporting to the Parliamentary Committee. A whole-time medical officer was, for this purpose, to be appointed by the Board. And the Board, on the strength of his recent investigations, unanimously and without hesitation offered the appointment to him.

When she had read it she looked at him happily:

"Didn't I tell you something would turn up." She smiled. "Isn't it splendid!"

He was throwing stones quickly, nervously at a lobster pot on the beach.

"It's clinical work," he reflected aloud. "Couldn't be anything else. They *know* I'm a clinician."

She observed him with a deepening smile.

"Of course, darling, you remember our bargain. Six weeks here as a minimum, doing nothing, lying still—— You won't let this interrupt our holiday."

"No, no." Looking at his watch. "We'll finish our holiday but—anyhow"—he jumped up and gaily pulled her to her feet—"it won't do us any harm to run down to the telegraph office. And I wonder—I wonder if they've got a time-table there."

PART III

I

THE COAL and Metalliferous Mines Fatigue Board—usually abbreviated to M.F.B.—was housed in a large, impressive grey stone building on the Embankment, not far from Westminster Gardens, conveniently situated to the Board of Trade and the Mines Department, both of which alternately forgot about, and fought fiercely for, a proprietary interest in the Board.

On the 14th of August, a fresh, bright morning, in bustling health and immense spirits, Andrew ran up the steps of the building the look in his eye that of a man about to conquer London.

"I'm the new Medical Officer," he told the commissionaire in the Office of Works uniform.

"Yes, sir, yes, sir," said the commissionaire with a fatherly air. It was gratifying to Andrew that he seemed to be expected. "You'll want to see our Mr. Gill. Jones! Take our new doctor up to Mr. Gill's room."

The lift rose slowly, revealing green tiled corridors and many floors, on which the Office of Works uniform was again sedately visible. Then Andrew was ushered into a large, sunny room where he found himself shaking hands with Mr. Gill, who rose from his desk and put down his copy of *The Times* to welcome him.

"I'm a little late in getting in," Andrew declared with vigour. "Sorry! —we just got back from France yesterday—but I'm absolutely ready to start."

"That's nice!" Gill was a jolly little man, in gold-rimmed glasses, a near-clerical collar, dark blue suit, dark blue tie held in place with a flat gold ring. He looked on Andrew with prim approval.

"Please sit down! Will you have a cup of tea, or a glass of hot milk? I usually have one about eleven. And yes—yes, it's nearly that now——"

"Oh, well——" said Andrew, hesitating, then brightening. "Perhaps you can tell me about the work while we——"

Five minutes later the Office of Works uniform brought in a nice cup of tea and a glass of hot milk.

"I think you'll find that right, Mr. Gill. It 'as boiled, Mr. Gill."

"Thank you, Stevens." When Stevens had gone Gill turned to Andrew with a smile. "You'll find him a useful chap. He makes delicious hot buttered toast. It's rather awkward here—to get really first-class messengers. We're bits and pieces of all departments—Home Office,

618

Mines Department, Board of Trade; I myself"—Gill coughed with mild pride—"am from the Admiralty."

While Andrew sipped his boiled milk and chafed for information about his job, Gill pleasantly discussed the weather, Brittany, the Civil Service pension scheme, and the efficacy of Pasteurisation. Then, rising, he led Andrew to his room.

This also was a warmly carpeted, restful, sunny room with a superb view of the river. A large bluebottle was making drowsy nostalgic noises against the window-pane.

"I chose this for you," said Gill pleasantly. "Took a little bit of arrangement. There's an open coal fireplace, you'll see—nice for the winter. I—I hope you like it?"

"Why—it's a marvellous room, but——"

"Now I'll introduce you to your secretary—Miss Mason." Gill tapped, threw open a communicating door revealing Miss Mason, a nice, elderly girl, neat and composed, seated at a small desk. Rising, Miss Mason put down her *Times*.

"Good morning, Miss Mason."

"Good morning, Mr. Gill."

"Miss Mason, this is Doctor Manson."

"Good morning, Doctor Manson."

Andrew's head reeled slightly under the impact of these salutations, but he collected himself, joined in the conversation.

Five minutes later, as Gill stole pleasantly away, he remarked to Andrew, encouragingly:

"I'll send you along some files."

The files arrived, borne tenderly by Stevens. In addition to his talents as toastmaker and dairyman, Stevens was the best file-bearer in the building. Every hour he entered Andrew's office, with cradled documents which he placed lovingly upon the desk in the japanned tin marked *IN*, while his eye, searching eagerly, besought something to take away from the tin marked *OUT*. It quite broke Stevens's heart when the *OUT* tin was empty. In this lamentable contingency he slunk away, defeated.

Lost, bewildered, irritated, Andrew raced through the files—minutes of past meetings of the M.F.B., dull, stodgy, unimportant. Then he turned urgently to Miss Mason. But Miss Mason, who came, she explained, from the Home Office Frozen Meat Investigation Department, proved a restricted source of enlightenment. She told him that the hours were from ten o'clock till four. She told him of the office hockey team— "the Ladies XI, of course, Doctor Manson"—of which she was vice-captain. She asked him if he would care to have her copy of *The Times*. Her gaze entreated him to be calm.

But Andrew was not calm. Fresh from his holiday, longing to work, he began to weave a pattern on the Office of Works carpet. He gazed chafingly at the brisk river scene where tugs fussed about and long lines of coal barges went spattering against the tide. Then he strode down to Gill.

"When do I start?"

Gill jumped at the abruptness of the question.

"My dear fellow. You quite startled me. I thought I'd given you enough files to last you for a month." He looked at his watch. "Come along. It's time we had lunch."

Over his steamed sole, Gill tactfully explained, while Andrew battled with a chump chop, that the next meeting of the Board did not, and could not take place until September the eighteenth, that Professor Challis was in Norway, Doctor Maurice Gadsby in Scotland, Sir William Dewar, chairman of the Board, in Germany, and his own immediate chief, Mr. Blades, at Frinton with his family.

Andrew went back to Christine that evening with his thoughts in a maze. Their furniture was still in storage and, so that they might have time to look round and find a proper home, they had taken for a month a small furnished flat in Earl's Court.

"Could you believe it, Chris! They're not even *ready* for me. I've got a whole month to drink milk in, and read *The Times*, and initial files— oh! and have long intimate hockey talks with old girl Mason."

"If you don't mind—you'll confine your talks to your own old girl. Oh really, darling, it's lovely here—after Aberalaw. I had a little expedition this afternoon, down to Chelsea. I found out where Carlyle's house is, and the Tate Gallery. Oh! I planned such lovely things for us to do. You can take a penny steamboat up to Kew. Think of the Gardens, darling. And next month Kreisler's at the Albert Hall. Oh, and we must see the Memorial to find out why everyone laughs at it. And there's a play on from the New York Theatre Guild and wouldn't it be lovely if I could meet you some day for lunch." She reached out a small vibrant hand. He had rarely seen her so excited. "Darling! Let's go out and have a meal. There's a Russian restaurant along this street. It looks *good*. Then if you're not too tired we might——"

"Here!" he protested as she led him to the door. "I thought you were supposed to be the matter-of-fact member of this family. But believe me, Chris, after my first day's *toil*, I could do with a lively evening."

Next morning he read every file in his desk, initialled them, and was ranging about his room by eleven o'clock. But soon the cage became too small to hold him and he set out, with violence, to explore the building. It proved uninteresting as a morgue without bodies until, reaching the top storey, he suddenly found himself in a long room, half fitted as a laboratory where, seated on a box which had once held sulphur, was a young man in a long dirty white coat, disconsolately trimming his finger-nails, while his cigarette made yellower the nicotine stain upon his upper lip.

"Hello!" Andrew said.

A moment's pause, then the other answered uninterestedly:

"If you've lost your way, the lift is the third on the right."

Andrew propped himself against the test bench and picked a cigarette from his pocket. He asked:

"Don't you serve tea here?"

For the first time the young man raised his head, jet black and glossily brushed, singularly at variance with the upturned collar of his soiled coat.

"Only to the white mice," he answered with interest. "The tea leaves are particularly nourishing for them."

Andrew laughed, perhaps because the jester was five years younger than himself. He explained:

"My name's Manson."

"I feared as much. So you've come to join the forgotten men." A pause. "I'm Doctor Hope!—at least I used to think I was Hope. Now I am definitely Hope deferred."

"What are you doing here?"

"God only knows—and Billy Buttons—that's Dewar! Some of the time I sit here and think. But most of the time I sit. Occasionally they send me chunks of decomposed miner and ask me the cause of the explosion."

"And do you tell them?" Andrew inquired politely.

"No," Hope said rudely. "I fart!"

They both felt better after that extreme vulgarity and went out to lunch together. Going up to lunch, Doctor Hope explained, was the sole function of the day which enabled him to cling to reason. Hope explained other things to Manson. He was a Backhouse Research Scholar from Cambridge, via Birmingham, which probably—he grinned—accounted for his frequent lapses of good taste. He had been loaned to the Metalliferous Board through the pestering application of Professor Dewar. He had nothing to do but sheer mechanics, a routine which any lab. attendant could have tackled. He inferred that he was surely going mad through indolence and the inertia of the Board, which he now referred to tersely as Maniac's Delight. It was typical of most of the research work in the country: controlled by a quorum of eminent mugs who were too busy squabbling amongst themselves to shove the waggon in any one definite direction. Hope was pulled this way and that, told what to do instead of being allowed to do what he wished, and so interrupted he was never six months on the same job.

He gave Andrew thumb-nail sketches of the council of Maniac's Delight. Sir William Dewar, the doddering but indomitable nonagenarian Chairman, he alluded to as Billy Buttons because of Sir William's propensity for leaving certain essential fastenings unlatched. Old Billy Buttons was chairman of almost every scientific committee in

England, Hope told Andrew. In addition he gave those riotously popular wireless talks: Science for the Children.

Then there was Professor Whinney, aptly known to his students as the Nag, Challis, who wasn't bad when he forgot to dramatise himself, as Rabelais Pasteur Challis, and Doctor Maurice Gadsby.

"Do you know Gadsby?" Hope asked.

"I've met the gentleman." Andrew related his examination experience.

"That's our Maurice," said Hope bitterly. "And he's such a damned little thruster. He's into everything. He'll stick himself into a Royal Apothecaryship one of these days. He's a clever little beast all right. But he's not interested in research. He's only interested in himself." Hope laughed suddenly. "Robert Abbey has a good one about Gadsby. Gadsby wanted to get into the Rumpsteak Club, that's one of those dining-out affairs that occur in London, and a pretty decent one, as it happens! Well, Abbey, who's an obliging pot, promised to do his best for Gadsby, though God knows why. Anyhow a week later Gadsby met Abbey. 'Am I in?' he asked. 'No,' Abbey said. 'You're not.' 'Good God,' blusters Gadsby. 'You don't mean I was blackballed.' 'Blackballed,' Abbey said. 'Listen, Gadsby! *Have you ever seen a plate of caviar?*'" Hope lay back and howled with laughter. A moment later he added: "Abbey happens to be on our Board as well. He's a white man. But he's got too much savvy to come often."

This was the first of many lunches which Andrew and Hope took together. Hope, despite his undergraduate humour and a natural tendency to flippancy, was well endowed with brains. His irreverence had a wholesome ring. Andrew felt that he might one day do something. Indeed, in his serious moments, Hope often exposed his eagerness to get back to the real work he had planned for himself, on the isolation of gastric enzymes.

Occasionally Gill came to lunch with them. Hope's phrase for Gill was characteristic: a good little egg. Though veneered by his thirty years in the Civil Service—he had worked his way from boy clerk to principal—Gill was human underneath. In the office he functioned like a well oiled, easy-moving little machine. He arrived from Sunbury by the same train every morning, returned, unless he was "detained," by the same train every night. He had in Sunbury a wife and three daughters and a small garden where he grew roses. He was superficially so true to type he might have stood as a perfect pattern of smug suburbia. Yet there existed, beneath, a real Gill who loved Yarmouth in winter and always spent his holiday there in December, who had a queer Bible, which he knew almost by heart, in a book named *Hadji Baba*, who—for fifteen years a fellow of the Society—was quite fatuously devoted to the penguins in the Zoo.

Upon the occasion Christine made a fourth at this table. Gill surpassed himself in upholding the civility of the Service. Even Hope behaved with admirable gentility. He confided to Andrew that he was a less likely candidate for the strait jacket since meeting Mrs. Manson.

The days slipped past. While Andrew waited for the meeting of the Board, Christine and he discovered London. They took the steamboat trip to Richmond. They chanced upon a theatre named the Old Vic. They came to know the windy flutter of Hampstead Heath, the fascination of a coffee-stall at midnight. They walked in the Row and rowed on the Serpentine. They solved the delusion of Soho. When they no longer had occasion to study the Underground maps before entrusting themselves to the Tube they began to feel that they were Londoners.

II

THE AFTERNOON of the 18th of September brought the M.F.B. council together, and to Andrew, at last. Sitting beside Gill and Hope, conscious of the latter's flippant glances upon him, Andrew watched the members roll into the long gilt-corniced Boardroom: Whinney, Doctor Lancelot Dodd-Canterbury, Challis, Sir Robert Abbey, Gadsby and finally Billy Buttons Dewar himself.

Before Dewar's entry Abbey and Challis had spoken to Andrew— Abbey a quiet word, the professor an airy gush of graciousness—congratulating him upon his appointment. And whenever Dewar came in he veered upon Gill, exclaiming in his peculiar high-pitched voice:

"Where is our new Medical Officer, Mr. Gill? Where is Doctor Manson?"

Andrew stood up, confounded at Dewar's appearance, which transcended even Hope's description. Billy was short, bowed and hairy. He wore old clothes, his waistcoat much dropped upon, his greenish overcoat bulging with papers, pamphlets and the memoranda of a dozen different societies. There was no excuse for Billy for he had much money and daughters, one of them married to a millionaire peer, but he looked now, and he always looked, like a neglected old baboon.

"There was a Manson at Queens with me in eighteen-eighty," he squeaked benevolently by way of greeting.

"This is he, sir," murmured Hope, to whom the temptation was irresistible.

Billy heard him. "How would *you* know, Doctor Hope?" He squinted urbanely over the steel-rimmed pince-nez on the end of his nose. "You weren't even in swaddling clothes then. Hee! Hee! Hee! Hee!"

He flapped away, chuckling, to his place at the head of the table. None of his colleagues, who were already seated, took any notice of him. Part of the technique of this Board was a proud unawareness of one's neighbours. But this did not dismay Billy. Pulling a wad of papers from his pocket he took a drink of water from the carafe, picked up the little hammer in front of him and hit the table a resounding thwack.

"Gentlemen, gentlemen! Mr. Gill will now read the minutes."

Gill, who acted as secretary to the Board, rapidly intoned the minutes of the last meeting, while Billy, giving to this chanting no attention whatsoever, alternately pawed amongst his papers and let his eye twinkle benevolently down the board towards Andrew whom he still vaguely associated with the Manson of Queens, 1880.

At last Gill finished. Billy immediately wielded the hammer.

"Gentlemen! We are particularly happy to have our new Medical Officer with us to-day. I remember, as recently as nineteen hundred and four, I emphasised the need of a permanent clinician who should be attached to the Board as a solid adjuvant to the pathologists whom we occasionally *filch*, gentlemen—hee! hee!—whom we occasionally filch from the Backhouse Research. And I say this with all respect of our young friend Hope on whose charity—hee! hee!—on whose charity we have been so largely dependent. Now I well remember as recently as eighteen-eighty-nine . . ."

Sir Robert Abbey interposed:

"I'm sure, sir, the other members of the Board wish to join you wholeheartedly in congratulating Doctor Manson on his silicosis paper. If I may say so, I felt this to be a particularly patient and original piece of clinical research and one which, as the Board well knows, may have the most far-reaching effects upon our industrial legislation."

"Hear, hear," boomed Challis, supporting his protégé.

"That is what I was about to say, Robert," said Billy peevishly. To him Abbey was still a young man, a student almost, whose interruptions demanded mild reproof. "When we decided at our last meeting that the investigation must be pursued Doctor Manson's name immediately suggested itself to me. He has opened up this question and must be given every opportunity to pursue it. We wish him, gentlemen," this being for Andrew's benefit he twinkled at him bushily along the table, "to visit all the anthracite mines in the country, and possibly later we may extend this to all the coal mines. Also we wish him to have every opportunity for clinical examination of the miners in the industry. We will afford him every facility—including the skilled bacteriological services of our young friend Doctor Hope. In short, gentlemen, there is nothing we will *not* do to ensure that our new Medical Officer presses this all-important matter of dust inhalation to its ultimate scientific and administrative conclusion."

Andrew drew one quick and furtive breath. It was splendid, splendid —better than he had ever hoped. They were going to give him a free hand, back him up with their immense authority, turn him oose on clinical research. They were angels, all of them, and Billy was Gabriel himself.

624

"But, gentlemen," Billy suddenly piped, shuffling himself a new deal from his coat pockets. "*Before* Doctor Manson goes on with this problem, before we can feel ourselves at liberty to allow him to concentrate his efforts upon it, there is another and more pressing matter which I feel he ought to take up."

A pause. Andrew felt his heart contract and began slowly to sink as Billy continued:

"Doctor Bigsby of the Board of Trade has been pointing out to me the alarming discrepancy in the specifications of industrial first-aid equipments. There is, of course, a definition under the existing Act, but it is elastic and unsatisfactory. There are no precise standards, for example, as to the size and weave of bandages, the length, material and type of splints. Now, gentlemen, this is an important matter and one which directly concerns this Board. I feel very strongly that our medical officer should conduct a thorough investigation and submit a report upon it before he begins upon the problem of inhalation."

Silence. Andrew glanced desperately round the table. Dodd-Canterbury, with his legs outstretched, had his eyes on the ceiling. Gadsby was drawing diagrams upon his blotter, Whinney frowning, Challis inflating his chest for speech. But it was Abbey who said:

"Surely, Sir William, this is matter either for the Board of Trade or the Mines Department."

"We are at the disposal of each of these bodies," squeaked Billy. "We are—hee! hee!—the orphan child of both."

"Yes, I know. But after all, this—this bandage question is comparatively trivial and Doctor Manson . . ."

"I assure you, Robert, it is far from trivial. There will be a question in the House presently. I had that from Lord Ungar only yesterday."

"Ah!" Gadsby said, lifting his ears. "If Ungar is keen we have no choice." Gadsby could toady with deceptive brusqueness, and Ungar was a man he wished particularly to please.

Andrew felt driven to intervene.

"Excuse me, Sir William," he stumbled. "I—I understood I was going to do clinical work here. For a month I have been kicking about in my office and now if I'm to . . ."

He broke off, looking round at them. It was Abbey who helped him.

"Doctor Manson's point is very just. For four years he's been working patiently at his own subject and now, having offered him every facility to expand it, we propose sending him out to count bandages."

"If Doctor Manson has been patient for four years, Robert," Billy squeaked, "he can be patient a little longer. Hee! Hee!"

"True, true," boomed Challis. "He'll be free for silicosis eventually."

Whinney cleared his throat. "Now," Hope muttered to Andrew, "the Nag is about to neigh."

"Gentlemen," Whinney said. "For a long time I have been asking this Board to investigate the question of muscular fatigue in relation to steam heat—a subject which, as you know, interests me deeply, and which, I venture to say, you have hitherto not given the consideration it so richly merits. Now it appears to me, that if Doctor Manson is going to be diverted from the question of inhalation it would be an admirable opportunity to pursue this all-important question of muscular fatigue . . ."

Gadsby looked at his watch. "I have an appointment in Harley Street in exactly thirty-five minutes."

Whinney turned angrily to Gadsby. Co-professor Challis supported him with a gusty:

"Intolerable impertinence."

Tumult seemed about to break.

But Billy's urbane yellow face peered from behind its whiskers at the meeting. He was not disturbed. He had handled such meetings for forty years. He knew they detested him and wanted him to go. But he was not going—he was never going. His vast cranium was filled with problems, data, agenda, obscure formulæ, equations, with physiology and chemistry, with facts and figments of research, a vaulted incalculable sepulchre, haunted by phantoms of decerebrated cats, illumined by polarised light and all rosy hued by the great remembrance that, when he was a boy, Lister had patted him upon the head. He declared guilelessly:

"I must tell you, gentlemen, I have already as good as promised Lord Ungar and Doctor Bigsby that we shall assist them in their difficulty. Six months ought to suffice, Doctor Manson. Perhaps a little longer. It will not be uninteresting. It will bring you into contact with people and things, young man. You remember Lavoisier's remark concerning the drop of water! Hee! Hee! And now, touching Doctor Hope's pathological examination of the specimen from Wendover Colliery in July last . . ."

At four o'clock, when it was all over, Andrew threshed the matter out with Gill and Hope in Gill's room. The effect of this Board, and perhaps of his increasing years, was to implant in him the beginnings of restraint. He neither raved nor furiously split his infinitives but contented himself merely with stabbing a neat pattern with a government pen upon a government desk.

"It won't be so bad," Gill consoled. "It means travelling all over the country, I know—but that can be rather pleasant. You might even take Mrs. Manson with you. There's Buxton now—that's a centre for all the Derbyshire coalfields. And at the end of six months you can begin your anthracite work."

"He'll never get the chance," Hope grinned. "He's a bandage-counter—for life!"

Andrew picked up his hat. "The trouble with you, Hope, is—you're too *young*."

He went home to Christine. And the following Monday, since she resolutely refused to miss a gay adventure, they bought a second-hand Morris for sixty pounds and started out together upon the Great First Aid Investigation. It is to be admitted they were happy as the car sped up the highway to the North, and Andrew, having given a simian impersonation of Billy Buttons steering the car with his feet, remarked:

"Anyway! Never mind what Lavoisier said to the drop of water in eighteen-thirty-two. We're together, Chris!"

The work was imbecile. It consisted in the inspection of the first-aid materials kept at different collieries throughout the country: splints, bandages, cotton wool, antiseptics, tourniquets and the rest. At the good collieries the equipment was good; and at poor collieries the equipment was poor. Underground inspection was no novelty to Andrew. He made hundreds of underground inspections, crawling miles along haulage ways to the coal face to view a box of bandages carefully planted there half an hour beforehand. At small pits in hardy Yorkshire he overheard under-managers whisper aside:

"Run down, Geordie, and tell Alex to go to the chemist's . . ." then, "Have a chair, doctor, we'll be ready for ye in a minute!" In Nottingham he comforted temperance ambulance men by telling them cold tea was a superior stimulant to brandy. Elsewhere, he swore by whisky. But mostly he did the work with alarming conscientiousness. He and Christine found rooms in a convenient centre. Thereafter he combed the district in the car. While he inspected, Christine sat and knitted at a distance. They had adventures, usually with landladies. They made friends, chiefly among the mining inspectors. Andrew was not surprised that his mission provoked these hard-headed, hard-fisted citizens to senseless laughter. It is to be regretted that he laughed with them.

And then in March they returned to London, resold the car for only ten pounds less than they had paid for it, and Andrew set about writing his report. He had made up his mind to give the Board value for its money, to offer them statistics by the tubful, pages of tables, charts and divisional graphs showing how the bandage curve rose as the splint curve fell. He was determined, he told Christine, to show them how well he had done the work and how excellently they had all wasted their time.

At the end of the month when he had rushed a rough draft through to Gill, he was surprised to receive a summons from Doctor Bigsby of the Board of Trade.

"He's delighted with your report," Gill fluttered, as he escorted Andrew along Whitehall. "I shouldn't have let the cat out. But there it is! It's a lucky start for you, my dear fellow. You've no idea how important Bigsby is. He's got the whole factory administration in his pocket!"

It took them some time to reach Doctor Bigsby. They had to sit with their hats in two ante-rooms before gaining admission to the final chamber. But there was Doctor Bigsby, at last, thick-set and cordial, with a dark grey suit and darker grey spats, double-breasted waistcoat and a bustling efficiency.

"Sit down, gentlemen. This report of yours, Manson. I've seen the draft and though it's early to speak I must say I like the look of it. Highly scientific. Excellent graphing. That's what we want in this department. Now as we're out to standardise equipment in factories and mines you ought to know my views. First of all I see you recommend a three inch bandage as the major bandage of the specification. Now, I prefer the two and a half inch. You'll agree there, won't you?"

Andrew was irritated: it may have been the spats.

"Personally, so far as the mines are concerned, I think the bigger the bandage the better. But I don't think it makes a hell of a lot of difference!"

"Eh?—what?" Reddening behind the ears. "No *difference*?"

"Not a bit."

"But don't you see—don't you realise, the whole principle of standardisation is involved. If we suggest two and a half inch and you recommend three inch there may be enormous difficulty."

"Then I'll recommend three inch," Andrew said coolly.

Doctor Bigsby's hackles rose, it was possible to see them rising.

"Your attitude is difficult to understand. We've been working for years towards the two and a half inch bandage. Why—— Don't you know how much this *matters* . . ."

"Yes, I know!" Andrew equally lost his temper. "Have you ever been underground? I have. I've done a bloody operation, lying on my guts in a puddle of water, with one safety lamp and no head room. And I tell you straight any finicky half-inch difference in your bandage doesn't matter a tinker's curse."

He passed out of the building more swiftly than he had entered, followed by Gill who wrung his hands, and lamented all the way to the Embankment.

When he got back Andrew stood in his room, sternly regarding the traffic on the river, and bustling streets, the buses running, trams clanging over bridges, the movement of human people, all the pulsing, vivid flow of life. "I don't belong to this outfit in here," he thought with a surge of impatience. "I should be out there—out there!"

Abbey had given up attending the Board meetings. And Challis had disheartened him, even to the point of panic, by taking him to lunch the week before and warning him that Whinney was lobbying hard, would try to put him on to his muscular fatigue investigation before the silicosis question was touched. Andrew reflected, with a despairing pretence at humour: "If *that* happens, on top of the bandages, I might as well take a reader's ticket for the British Museum."

Walking home from the Embankment he found himself peering

enviously at the brass plates bolted on area railings outside the houses of doctors. He would stop, watch a patient mount to the door, ring the bell, be admitted—then, walking moodily on, he would visualise the ensuing scene, the interrogations, the swift production of stethoscope, the whole thrilling science of diagnosis. He was a doctor, too, wasn't he? At least, once upon a time . . .

Towards the end of May, in this frame of mind, he was walking up Oakley Street about five in the evening when he suddenly saw a crowd of people gathered round a man lying on the pavement. In the gutter alongside was a shattered bicycle and, almost on top of it, a drunkenly arrested motor lorry.

Five seconds later Andrew was in the middle of the crowd, observing the injured man who, attended by a kneeling policeman, was bleeding from a deep wound in the groin.

"Here! Let me through. I'm a doctor."

The policeman, striving unsuccessfully to fix a tourniquet, turned a flustered face.

"I can't stop the bleeding, doctor. It's too high up."

Andrew saw that it was impossible to tourniquet. The wound was too high up in the iliac vessel and the man was bleeding to death.

"Get up," he said to the policeman. "Put him flat on his back." Then making his right arm rigid, he leant over and thrust his fist hard into the man's belly over the descending aorta. The whole weight of his body, thus transmitted to the great vessel, immediately arrested the hæmorrhage. The policeman removed his helmet and wiped his forehead. Five minutes later the ambulance arrived. Andrew went with it.

Next morning Andrew rang up the hospital. The house surgeon answered brusquely after the fashion of his kind:

"Yes, yes, he's comfortable. Doing well. Who wants to know?"

"Oh," mumbled Andrew from the public phone box. "Nobody."

And that, he thought bitterly, was exactly what he was: nobody, doing nothing, getting nowhere. He endured it till the end of the week then quietly, without fuss, he handed in his resignation to Gill for transmission to the Board.

Gill was upset, yet admitted that a premonition of this sad event had troubled him. He made a neat little speech which concluded:

"After all, my dear fellow, I have realised that your place is—well, if I may borrow a wartime comparison—not at the base but—er in the front line with the—er—troops."

Hope said:

"Don't listen to the rose-cultivating penguin fancier! You're lucky. And I'll be after you if I keep my reason—as soon as my three years are up!"

Andrew heard nothing about the Board's activities on the question of dust inhalation until months later when Lord Ungar raised the question dramatically in the House, quoting freely from medical evidence afforded him by Doctor Maurice Gadsby.

Gadsby was acclaimed by the Press as a Humanitarian and a Great Physician. And Silicosis was, in that year, scheduled as an industrial disease.

PART IV

I

THEY BEGAN their search for a practice. It was a jagged business
—wild peaks of expectation followed by wilder plunges of despair.
Stung by a consciousness of three successive failures—at least so he
construed his departures from Drineffy, Aberalaw and the M.F.B.—
Andrew longed to vindicate himself at last. But their total capital,
increased by stringent saving during the last months of salaried security,
was no more than six hundred pounds. Though they haunted the medical
agencies and reached for every opportunity offered in the columns of
the *Lancet* it appeared that this sum was scarcely adequate as purchase
money for a London practice.

They never forgot their first interview. Doctor Brent, of Cadogan
Gardens, was retiring, and he offered a nice nucleus suitable for a well-
qualified gentleman. It seemed, on the face of it, an admirable chance.
An extravagant taxi, for fear that someone speedier might snatch the
plum, rushed them to Doctor Brent whom they found to be a white
haired, pleasant, almost demure little man.

"Yes," Doctor Brent said modestly. "It's a pretty good pitch. Nice
house too. I want only seven thousand pounds for the lease. There's
forty years to run and the ground rent's only three hundred a year. As
to the practice—I thought the usual—two years' premium for cash, eh,
Doctor Manson?"

"Quite!" Andrew nodded gravely. "You'd give a long introduction,
too? Thank you, Doctor Brent. We'll consider it."

They considered it over threepenny cups of tea in the Brompton Road
Lyons.

"Seven thousand—for the lease!" Andrew gave a short laugh. He
thrust his hat back from his corrugated brow, stuck his elbows on the
marble table. "It's pretty damnable, Chris! The way these old fellows
hang on with their back teeth. And you can't prise them loose unless
you've got money. Isn't that an indictment of our system! But rotten
as it is, I'll accept it. You wait! I'm going to attend to this money
question from now on."

"I hope not," she smiled. "We've been moderately happy without
it."

He grunted. "You won't say that when we start to sing in the street.
Check, miss, please."

Because of his M.D., M.R.C.P., he wanted a non-panel, non-dispensing practice. He wanted to be free of the tyranny of the card system. But as the weeks went on he wanted anything, anything that offered him a chance. He inspected practices in Tulse Hill, Islington and Brixton and one—the surgery had a hole in the roof—in Camden Town. He got the length of debating with Hope—who assured him that on his capital it was suicide—the plan of taking a house and setting out his plate on chance.

And then, after two months, when they had reached the point of desperation, all at once Heaven relented and allowed old Doctor Foy to die, painlessly, in Paddington. Doctor Foy's obituary notice, four lines in the *Medical Journal*, caught Andrew's eye. They went, their enthusiasm all spent, to No. 9 Chesborough Terrace. They saw the house, a tall, leaden hued sepulchre with a surgery at the side and a brick garage behind. They saw the books which indicated that Doctor Foy had made perhaps £500 a year, mainly from consultations, with medicine, at the rate of 3s. 6d. They saw the widow, who assured them timidly that Doctor Foy's practice was sound and had once been excellent with many "good patients" coming to the "front door." They thanked her and left without enthusiasm.

"And yet I don't know," Andrew worried. "It's full of disadvantages. I hate the dispensing. It's a baddish locality. D'you notice all these moth-eaten boarding-houses next door. But it's on the *fringe* of a decent neighbourhood. And a corner situation. And a main street. And near enough our price. One and a half years' purchase—and it was decent of her to say she'd flung in the old man's consulting-room and surgery furniture as well—and all ready to step into—that's the advantage of a death vacancy. What do you say, Chris? It's now or never. Shall we chance it?"

Christine's eyes rested upon him doubtfully. For her the novelty of London had worn off. She loved the country and now, in these drab surroundings, she longed for it with all her heart. Yet he was so set upon a London practice she could not bring herself to try, even, to persuade him from it. She nodded slowly.

"If you want to, Andrew."

The next day he offered Mrs. Foy's solicitors £600 in place of the £750 demanded. The offer was accepted, the cheque written. On Saturday the 10th of October they moved their furniture from storage and entered into possession of their new home.

It was Sunday before they collected themselves from the frantic eruption of straw and sacking and wondered shakily how they stood. Andrew took advantage of the moment to launch one of those lectures, rare yet odious, which made him sound like a deacon of a nonconformist chapel.

"We are properly up against it here, Chris. We've paid out every stiver we've got. We've got to live on what we earn. Heaven only knows what that'll be. But we've got to do it. You've got to spruce things up, Chris, economise——"

To his dismay she burst into tears, standing palely there in the large, gloomy, dirty-ceilinged, and as yet uncarpeted, front room.

"For mercy's sake!" she sobbed. "Leave me alone. Economise. Don't I always economise for you? Do I cost you *anything*?"

"Chris!" he exclaimed aghast.

She flung herself frantically against him. "It's this house! I didn't realise. That basement, the stairs, the *dirt*——"

"But hang it all, it's the practice that really matters!"

"We might have had a little country practice, somewhere."

"Yes! With roses round the cottage door. Damn it all——"

In the end he apologised for his sermon. Then they went, his arm still round her waist, to fry eggs in the condemned basement. There he tried to cheer her by pretending that it was not a basement but a section of the Paddington Tunnel through which trains would at any minute pass. She smiled wanly at his attempted humour, but she was in reality looking at the broken scullery sink.

Next morning, at nine o'clock sharp—he decided he must not be early or they would think him too eager!—he opened his surgery. His heart was beating with excitement and a greater, far greater expectation than on that almost forgotten morning when he took the first surgery of all at Drineffy.

Half past nine came. He waited anxiously. Since the little surgery, which had its own door to the side street, was attached by a short passage to the house, he could equally control his consulting-room—the main room on the ground floor, not badly equipped with Doctor Foy's desk, a couch, and a cabinet—to which the "good" patients, by Mrs. Foy's account, were admitted through the front door of the house. He had, in fact, a double net cast out. Tense as any fisherman he waited for what that double cast might bring.

Yet it brought nothing, nothing! It was nearly eleven o'clock now and still no patient had arrived. The group of taxi drivers standing by their cabs at the rank opposite talked equably together. His plate shone on the door, beneath Doctor Foy's old battered one.

Suddenly, when he had almost abandoned hope, the bell on the surgery door tinkled sharply and an old woman in a shawl came in. Chronic bronchitis—he saw it, before she spoke, in every rheumy wheeze. Tenderly, tenderly he seated and sounded her. She was an old patient of Doctor Foy's. He talked to her. In the tiny cubby-hole of a dispensary, a mere lair halfway down the passage between surgery and consulting-room, he made up her physic. He returned with it. And then, without question, as he prepared, tremblingly, to ask her for it, she handed him the fee, three and six.

633

The thrill of that moment, the joy, the sheer relief of these silver coins, there, in the palm of his hand was unbelievable. It felt like the first money he had ever earned in his life. He closed the surgery, ran to Christine, thrust the coins upon her.

"First patient, Chris. It mightn't be a bad old practice after all. Anyhow, this buys us our lunch!"

He had no visits to make, for the old doctor had been dead nearly three weeks now, and no locum had kept the practice going in the interval. He must wait till the calls came in. Meanwhile, aware from her mood that Christine wished to wrestle with her domestic worries in solitude, he occupied the forenoon by walking round the district, prospecting, viewing the peeling houses, the long succession of drab, private hotels, the sooted, grimly arborescent squares, the narrow mews converted into garages, then, at a sudden turn of North Street, a squalid patch of slum—pawnshops, hawkers' barrows, pubs, shop windows showing patent medicines, devices in gaudy rubber.

He admitted to himself that the district had come down in the world since those days when carriages had spun to the yellow painted porticoes. It was dingy and soiled, yet there were signs of new life springing up amidst the fungus—a new block of flats in course of erection, some good shops and offices and, at the end of Gladstone Place, the famous Laurier's. Even he, who knew nothing of women's fashions, had heard of Laurier's and it did not require the long line of elegant motor-cars standing outside the windowless, immaculately white-stoned building to convince him that the little he knew of its exclusiveness was true. He felt it strange that Laurier's should stand incongruously amongst these faded terraces. Yet there it was, indubitable as that policeman opposite.

In the afternoon he completed his inaugural tour by calling upon the doctors in the immediate vicinity. Altogether he made eight such calls. Only three of them made any deep impression on him—Doctor Ince of Gladstone Place, a young man, Reeder at the end of Alexandra Street, and at the corner of Royal Crescent an elderly Scotsman named McLean. But the way in which they all said:

"Oh! It's poor old Foy's practice you've taken on," somehow depressed him. Why that "on," he thought a trifle angrily. He told himself that in six months' time they would change their manner. Though Manson was thirty now, and knew the value of restraint, he still hated condescension as a cat hates water.

That night in the surgery there were three patients, two of whom paid him the three-and-sixpenny fee. The third promised to return and settle up on Saturday. He had, in his first day's practice, earned the sum of ten and six.

But the following day he took nothing at all. And the day after, only seven shillings. Thursday was a good day, Friday just saved from being blank, and on Saturday, after an empty morning, he took seventeen and six at the evening surgery though the patient to whom he had given credit on Monday failed to keep his promise to return and pay.

On Sunday, though he made no comment to Christine, Andrew morbidly reviewed the week. Had he made a horrible mistake in taking this derelict practice, in sinking all their savings in this tomb-like house? What was *wrong* with him? He was thirty, yes, over thirty. He had an M.D., honours, and the M.R.C.P. He had clinical ability, and a fine piece of clinical research work to his credit. Yet here he was, taking barely enough three and sixpences to keep them in bread. It's the system, he thought savagely, it's *senile*. There ought to be some better scheme, a chance for everybody—say, oh, say State control! Then he groaned, remembering Doctor Bigsby and the M.F.B. No, damn it, that's hopeless —bureaucracy, chokes individual effort—it would suffocate me. I must succeed, damn it all, I *will* succeed!

Never before had the financial side of practice so obtruded itself upon him. And no subtler method of converting him to materialism could have been devised than those genuine pangs of appetite—the euphemism was his own—which he carried with him many days of the week.

About a hundred yards down the main bus route stood a small delicatessen shop kept by a fat little woman, a naturalised German, who called herself Smith but who, from her broken speech and insistent s's, was obviously Schmidt. It was typically continental, this little place of Frau Schmidt's, its narrow marble counter loaded with soused herrings, olives in jars, sauerkraut, several kinds of wurstels, pastries, salami, and a delicious kind of cheese named Liptauer. Also it had the virtue of being very cheap. Since money was so scarce at 9 Chesborough Terrace and the cooking stove a choked and antique ruin, Andrew and Christine dealt a great deal with Frau Schmidt. On good days they had hot Frankfurters and apfelstrudel; on bad they would lunch on a soused herring and baked potatoes. Often at night they would drop into Frau Schmidt's, after scanning her display through the steamed window with a selective eye, and come away with something savoury in a string bag.

Frau Schmidt soon got to know them. She developed an especial liking for Christine. Her larded, pastry-cook's face would wrinkle up, almost closing her eyes, beneath her high dome of blonde hair, as she smiled and nodded to Andrew:

"You will be all right. You will succeed. You have a good wife. She iss small, like me. But she iss good. Chust wait—I will send you patients!"

Almost at once, the winter was upon them and fogs hung about the streets, always intensified, it seemed, by the smoke from the great railway station near by. They made light of it, they pretended their struggles were amusing, but never in all their years at Aberalaw had they known such hardship.

Christine did her utmost with their chill barracks. She whitewashed the ceilings, made new curtains for the waiting-room. She re-papered their bedroom. By painting the panels black and gold, she transformed the senile folding doors which disfigured the first floor drawing-room.

Most of his calls, infrequent though these were, took him to the boarding-houses of the neighbourhood. It was difficult to collect the fees from such patients—many of them were seedy, even doubtful characters, and adept in the art of bilking. He tried to make himself agreeable to the gaunt females who kept these establishments. He made conversation in gloomy hallways. He would say, "I'd no idea it was so cold! I should have brought my coat," or "It's awkward getting about. My car's laid up for the moment."

He struck up a friendship with the policeman who usually took point duty at the busy traffic crossing outside Frau Schmidt's delicatessen. Donald Struthers was the policeman's name, and there was kinship between them from the start, for Struthers, like Andrew, came from Fife. He promised in his own style, to do what he could do to help his compatriot, remarking with a grim facetiousness:

"If ever anybody gets run down and killed here, doctor, I'll be sure and fetch them along to ye."

One afternoon, about a month after their arrival, when Andrew got home—he had been calling on the chemists of the district, inquiring brightly for a special 10 c.c. Voss syringe which he knew none of them would keep in stock then casually introducing himself as the new and vigorous practitioner of Chesborough Terrace—Christine's expression apprised him of some excitement.

"There's a patient in the consulting-room," she breathed. "She came by the front door."

His face brightened. This was the first "good" patient who had come to him. Perhaps it was the beginning of better things. Preparing himself, he walked briskly into the consulting-room.

"Good afternoon! What can I do for you?"

"Good afternoon, doctor. Mrs. Smith recommended me."

She rose from her chair to shake hands with him. She was plump, good-natured, thickly made up, with a short fur jacket and a large handbag. He saw at once that she was one of the street-women who frequented the district.

"Yes?" he inquired, his expectation sinking a little.

"Oh, doctor," she smiled diffidently. "My friend just give me a nice pair of gold ear-rings. And Mrs. Smith—I am a customer there—she said you would pierce my ears for me. My friend, he's very anxious I don't get done with a dirty needle or something, doctor."

He took a long steadying breath. Had it actually come to this? He said:

"Yes, I'll pierce your ears for you."

He did this carefully, sterilising the needle, spraying her lobes with ethyl chloride, even fitting the gold rings in for her.

"Oh, doctor, that's lovely." Peering in the mirror of her handbag. "And I never felt a thing. My friend'll be pleased. How much, doctor?"

The statutory fee for Foy's "good" patients, mythical though they might be, was seven and six. He mentioned this sum.

She produced a ten shilling note from her bag. She thought him a kind, distinguished, and very handsome gentleman—she always liked them dark somehow—and she also thought, as she accepted her change, that he looked hungry.

When she had gone he did not wear holes in the carpet, as he would once have done, raving that he, too, had prostituted himself by this petty, servile act. He was conscious of a strange humility. Holding the crumpled note, he went to the window, watching her disappear down the street, swaying her hips, swinging her handbag, proudly wearing her new ear-rings.

II

THROUGH THE rigours of the battle he hungered for medical friendship. He had gone to a meeting of the local medical association without enjoying himself greatly. Denny was still abroad. Finding Tampico to his liking Philip had remained there, taking a post as surgeon to the New Century Oil Company. For the present at least, he was lost to Andrew. While Hope, on a mission to Cumberland, was—as he phrased it in his rudely coloured postcard—counting corpuscles for Maniac's Delight.

Many times Andrew was taken by the impulse to get in touch with Freddie Hamson, but always, though he often got as far as the phone book, the reflection that he was still unsuccessful—not properly settled, he told himself—restrained him. Freddie was still in Queen Anne Street, though he had moved to a different number. Andrew found himself wondering more and more how Freddie had got on, recollecting the old adventures of their student days, until suddenly he found the compulsion too strong for him. He did ring Hamson.

"You've probably forgotten all about me," he grunted, half prepared for a snub. "This is Manson—Andrew Manson. I'm in practice here in Paddington."

"Manson! Forgotten you! You old warhorse!" Freddie was lyrical on the other end of the line. "Good Lord, man! *Why* haven't you rung me?"

"Oh, we've barely got settled," Andrew smiled into the receiver, warmed by Freddie's gush. "And before—on that Board job—we were rushing all over England. I'm married now, you know."

"So am I! Look here, old man, we've got to get together again. Soon! I can't get over it. You, here, in London. Marvellous! Where's my book—— Look here, how about next Thursday? Can you come to dinner then? Yes, yes. That's great. So long then, old man, in the meantime I'll have my wife drop yours a line."

Christine seemed lacking in enthusiasm when he told her of the invitation.

"You go, Andrew," she suggested after a pause.

"Oh! that's nonsense! Freddie wants you to meet his wife. I know you don't care about him much but there'll be other people there, other doctors probably. We may get a new slant on things there, dear. Besides we've had no fun lately. Black tie, he said. Lucky I bought myself that dinner jacket for the Newcastle mines do. But what about you, Chris? You ought to have something to wear."

"I ought to have a new gas cooker," she answered a trifle grimly. These last weeks had taken toll of her. She had lost a little of that freshness which had always been her greatest charm. And sometimes, as just now, her tone was short and jaded.

But on Thursday night when they started out for Queen Anne Street he could not help thinking how sweet she looked in the dress, yes, it was the white dress she had bought for that Newcastle dinner, altered in some way which made it seem newer, smarter. Her hair was done in a new style too, closer to her head, so that it lay darkly about her pale brow. He noticed this as she tied his bow for him, meant to tell her how nice it was, then forgot, in the sudden fear that they would be late.

They were not late, however, but early, so early that an awkward three minutes elapsed before Freddie came gaily in, both hands outstretched, apologising and greeting them in the same breath, telling them he had just come in from hospital, that his wife would be down in a second, offering drinks, pounding Andrew on the back, bidding them be seated. Freddie had put on weight since that evening at Cardiff, there was heavy prosperity in the pink roll of flesh on the back of his neck but his small eyes still glistened and not a single yellow plastered hair was out of its place. He was so well groomed that he shone.

"Believe me!" He elevated his glass. "It's wonderful to see you people again. This time we've got to keep it up. How do you like my place here, old man? Didn't I tell you at that dinner—and *what* a dinner!—I bet we'll do better to-night—that I'd do it. I've the whole house here, of course—not just rooms, bought the freehold last year. And did it cost money?" He patted his tie approvingly. "No need to advertise the fact, of course, even if I am successful. But I don't mind you knowing, old man."

638

It looked an expensive background, there was no doubt: smooth modern furniture, deep-set fireplace, a baby grand player-piano with artificial magnolia blossom shaped from mother of pearl in a big white vase. Andrew was preparing to voice admiration when Mrs. Hamson entered, tall, cool, with a dark middle parting and clothes extraordinarily different from Christine's.

"Come along, my dear." Freddie greeted her with affection, even with deference, and darted to pour and offer her a glass of sherry. She had time negligently to wave away the glass before the other guests— Mr. and Mrs. Charles Ivory, Doctor and Mrs. Paul Deedman—were announced. Introductions followed, with much talk and laughter amongst the Ivorys, the Deedmans and the Hamsons. Then they went in—not too soon—to dinner.

The table appointments were rich and superfine. They closely resembled a costly display, complete with candelabra, which Andrew had seen in the window of Labin & Benn, the famous Regent Street jewellers. The food was unrecognisable as meat or fish yet it tasted extremely well. And there was champagne. After two glasses Andrew felt more confident. He began to talk to Mrs. Ivory who sat on his left, a slender woman in black with an extraordinary amount of jewellery around her neck and large protruding blue eyes which she turned upon him from time to time with an almost babyish stare.

Her husband was Charles Ivory the surgeon—she laughed in answer to his question, she thought everyone knew Charles. They lived in New Cavendish Street round the corner, the whole house was theirs. It was nice being near Freddie and his wife. Charles and Freddie and Paul Deedman were all such good friends, all members of the Sackville Club. She was surprised when he admitted he was not a member. She thought everyone was a member of the Sackville.

Deserted, he turned to Mrs. Deedman on his other side, finding her softer, friendlier, with a pretty, almost oriental bloom. He encouraged her to talk of her husband also. He said to himself: "I want to *know* these fellows, they're so dashed prosperous and smart."

Paul, said Mrs. Deedman, was a physician, and though they had a flat in Portland Place, Paul's rooms were in Harley Street. He had a wonderful practice—she spoke too fondly to be bragging—chiefly at the Plaza Hotel—he must know the big new Plaza, overlooking the Park. Why at lunch-time the Grill Room was crammed with celebrities. Paul was practically the official doctor for the Plaza Hotel. So many wealthy Americans and film stars and—she broke off, smiling—oh, everybody came to the Plaza, which made it rather wonderful for Paul.

Andrew liked Mrs. Deedman. He let her run on until Mrs. Hamson rose, when he jumped up gallantly to draw back her chair.

"Cigar, Manson?" Freddie asked him with a knowledgeable air when the ladies had gone. "You'll find these pretty sound. And I advise you not to miss this brandy. Eighteen-ninety-four. Absolutely no nonsense about it."

With his cigar going and a drain of brandy in the wide bellied glass before him, Andrew drew his chair nearer to the others. It was this he had really been looking forward to, a close lively medical palaver—straight-cut shop, and nothing else. He hoped Hamson and his friends would talk. They did.

"By the way," Freddie said, "I ordered myself one of these new Iradium lamps to-day at Glickert's. Pretty stiff. Something around eighty guineas. But it's worth it."

"M'yes," said Deedman thoughtfully. He was slight, dark-eyed, with a clever Jewish face. "It ought to pay for its keep."

Andrew took an argumentative grip of his cigar.

"I don't think much of these lamps, you know. Did you see Abbey's paper in the *Journal* on bogus Heliotherapy. These Iradiums have got absolutely no infra-red content."

Freddie stared, then laughed.

"They've got a hell of a lot of three-guinea content. Besides, they bronze nicely."

"Mind you, Freddie," Deedman cut in, "I'm not in favour of expensive apparatus. It's got to be paid for before you show a profit. Besides, it dates, loses its vogue. Honestly, old chap, you'll find nothing to beat the good old hypo."

"You certainly use it," said Hamson.

Ivory joined in. He was bulky, older than the others, with a pale shaven jowl, and the easy style of a man about town.

"Talking of that, I booked a course of injections to-day. Twelve. You know, manganese. And I tell you what I did. And I think it pays these days. I said to the fellow, I said, look here, you're a business man. This course is going to cost you fifty guineas but if you care to pay me now and be done with it I'll make it forty-five. He wrote the cheque there and then."

"Ruddy old poacher," Freddie expostulated. "I thought you were a surgeon."

"I am," Ivory nodded. "Doing a curettage at Sherrington's to-morrow."

"Love's labour lost," Deedman muttered absently to his cigar, then returning to his original thought, "There's no getting away from it, thought. Basically, it's interesting. In good-class practice oral administration is definitely demoded. If I prescribed—oh, say a veripon powder, at the Plaza, it wouldn't cut one guinea's worth of ice. But if you give the same thing hypodermically, swabbing up the skin, sterilising and all the rest of the game, your patient thinks, scientifically, that you are the cat's pyjamas!"

Hamson declared vigorously:

"It's a damn good job for the medical profession that oral administration is off the map in the West End. Take Charlie's case here as an example. Suppose he'd prescribed manganese—or manganese and iron, the good old bottle of physic—probably just as much use to the patient—all he knocks out of it is three guineas. Instead of that he splits the medicine into twelve ampules and gets fifty—sorry, Charlie, I mean forty-five."

"Less twelve shillings," murmured Deedman gently. "The price of the ampules."

Andrew's head rocked. Here was an argument in favour of the abolition of the medicine bottle which staggered him with its novelty. He took another swig of brandy to steady himself.

"That's another point," reflected Deedman. "They don't know how little these things cost. Whenever a patient sees a row of ampules on your desk she thinks instinctively, 'Heavens! this is going to mean money!'"

"You'll observe"—Hamson winked at Andrew—"how Deedman's parsing of the good word patient is usually feminine. By the way, Paul, I heard about that shoot yesterday. Dummett's willing to make up a syndicate if you, Charles and I will go in with him."

For the next ten minutes they talked shooting, golf, which they played on various expensive courses round London, and cars—Ivory was having a special body built to his instructions on a new three and a half litre Rex—while Andrew listened and smoked his cigar and drank his brandy. They all drank a deal of brandy. Andrew felt, a trifle muzzily, that they were extraordinarily good fellows. They did not exclude him from their conversation, but always managed to make him feel by a word or look that he was with them. Somehow they made him forget that he had eaten a soused herring for his luncheon. And as they stood up Ivory clapped him on the shoulder.

"I must send you a card, Manson. It'd be a real pleasure to see a case with you—any time."

Back in the drawing-room the atmosphere seemed by contrast, formal, but Freddie, in tremendous spirits, more shining than ever, hands in his pockets, linen spotlessly agleam, decided the evening was still young, that they must finish it altogether at the Embassy.

"I'm afraid"—Christine threw a pale glance at Andrew—"we ought to be going."

"Nonsense, darling!" Andrew smiled roseately. "We couldn't dream of breaking up the party."

At the Embassy, Freddie was obviously popular. He and his party were bowed and smiled to a table against the wall. There was more champagne. There was dancing. These fellows do themselves well, thought Andrew mistily, expansively. "Oh! tha's a—tha's a spleni'd tune they're playing—I won-woner if Chris would like t'dance."

In the taxi, returning at last to Chesborough Terrace, he proclaimed happily:

"First rate chaps these, Chris! 'Sbeen a wonderful evening, hasn't it?"

She answered in a thin steady voice:

"It's been a hateful evening!"

"Eh—what?"

"I like Denny and Hope as—oh, as your medical friends, Andrew—not these, these flashy——"

He broke in "But look here, Chris—— Wha's wrong with——"

"Oh! couldn't you see," she answered in an icy fury. "It was everything. The food, the furniture, the way they talked—money, money all the time. Perhaps you didn't see the way she looked at my dress. Mrs. Hamson I mean. You could see her *realising* that she spends more on one beauty treatment than I do on clothes in a whole year. It was almost funny in the drawing-room when she found out what a nobody I was. She, of course, is the daughter of Whitton—the whisky Whitton! You can't guess what it was like—the conversation—before you came in. Smart-set gossip, who's week-ending with who, what the hairdresser told her, the latest society abortion, not one word of anything *decent*. Why! She actually hinted that she was 'sweet on'—as she put it—the dance-band leader of the Plaza."

The sarcasm in her tone was diabolic. Mistaking it for jealousy he babbled:

"I'll make money for you, Chris. I'll buy you plenty of expensive clothes."

"I don't want money," she said tautly. "And I hate expensive clothes."

"But—darling." Tipsily he reached for her.

"Don't!" Her voice struck him. "I love you, Andrew. But not when you're drunk."

He subsided in his corner, fuddled, furious. It was the first time she had ever repulsed him.

"All right, my girl," he muttered. "If that's the way of it."

He paid the taxi, let himself into the house before her. Then without a word he marched up to the spare bedroom. Everything seemed squalid and dismal after the luxury he had just quitted. The electric switch would not work properly—the whole house was imperfectly wired.

"Damn it," he thought as he flung himself into bed. "I'm going to get out of this hole. I'll show her. I *will* make money. What *can* you do without it?"

Until now in all their married life, they had never slept apart.

III

A T BREAKFAST next morning Christine behaved as though the whole
episode were forgotten. He could see that she was trying to be especially
nice to him. This gratified him and made him sulkier than ever. A
woman, he reflected—pretending absorption in the morning paper—has
got to be shown her place occasionally. But after he had grunted a few
surly replies Christine suddenly stopped being nice to him and retired
within herself, sitting at the table with compressed lips, not looking at
him, waiting till he should finish the meal. Stubborn little devil, he
thought, rising, and walking out of the room. I'll show her!

His first action in his consulting-room was to take down the Medical
Directory. He was both curious and eager to have more precise information of his friends of the previous evening. Quickly he turned the pages,
taking Freddie first. Yes, there it was—Frederick Hamson, Queen Anne
Street, M.B., Ch.B., assistant to out-patients. Walthamwood.

Andrew's brows drew into a frown of perplexity. Freddie had talked
a great deal last night about the hospital appointment—nothing like a
hospital appointment for helping a fellow in the West End, he had said,
gives the patients confidence to know he's a visiting physician. Yet surely
this wasn't it, a poor-law institution—and at Walthamwood, one of the
newer outer suburbs? There couldn't be a mistake, though, this was the
current directory, he had bought it only a month ago.

More slowly, Andrew looked up Ivory and Deedman, then he rested
the big red book on his knees, his expression puzzled, oddly reflective.
Paul Deedman was, like Freddie, an M.B. But without Freddie's distinction. Deedman had no visiting appointment. And Ivory? Mr.
Charles Ivory of New Cavendish Street had no surgical qualification
but the lowest, the M.R.C.S., and no hospital appointment whatsoever.
His record indicated a certain amount of experience in wartime and
pensions hospitals. Beyond that—nothing.

Extremely thoughtful now, Andrew rose and put the book on its
shelf, then his face drew into a sudden resolution. There was no comparison between his own qualifications and those of the prosperous
fellows he had dined with last night. What they could do he could do
also. Better. Despite Christine's outburst, he was more determined than
ever to make a success of himself. But first he must get himself attached,
not to Walthamwood or any such poor-law make-believe, but to one of
the London hospitals. Yes! a real hospital—that must be his immediate
objective. But how?

For three days he brooded, then he went shakily to Sir Robert Abbey.

It was the most difficult task in the world for him to ask a favour, particularly as Abbey received him with such twinkling kindness.

"Well! How is our express bandage enumerator? Aren't you ashamed to look me in the eye? I'm told Doctor Bigsby has developed hypertension. Know anything about that? What is it you want, an argument with me, or a seat on the Board?"

"Well, no, Sir Robert. I was wondering—that's to say—could you help me, Sir Robert, to find an out-patients hospital appointment?"

"Hmm! That's much more difficult than the Board. Do you know how many young fellows there are walking the Embankment? All waiting on honorary appointments. You ought really to be going on with your lung work too—and that narrows the field."

"Well—I—I suppose——"

"The Victoria Chest Hospital. That's your target. One of our oldest London hospitals. Suppose I make some inquiries. Oh! I don't promise anything, but I'll keep an eye scientifically open."

Abbey made him stay to tea. At four o'clock, unvaryingly, he had a ritual of drinking two cups of china tea in his consulting-room, no milk or sugar, and nothing to eat. It was a special tea which tasted of orange blossom. Abbey kept the conversation flowing easily on diverse topics, from Khanghsi saucerless cups to the Von Pirquet skin reaction, then as he showed Andrew to the door he said:

"Still quarrelling with the text-books? Don't give that up. And don't—even if I do get you into the Victoria—for the love of Galen!— don't develop a bedside manner." His eyes twinkled. "That's what has ruined me."

Andrew went home treading the clouds. He was so pleased he neglected to maintain his dignity with Christine. He blurted out:

"I've been to Abbey. He's going to try and fix me up at the Victoria Chest! That practically gives me a consultant's standing." The gladness in her eyes made him suddenly feel shamefaced, small. "I've been pretty difficult lately, Chris! We haven't been getting on too well, I suppose. Let's—oh! let's make it up, darling."

She ran to him, protesting it had all been her fault. Then, for some strange reason, it appeared entirely to be his. Only a small segment of his mind retained the fixed intention of confounding her, at some early date, by the greatness of his material success.

He flung himself into his work with renewed vigour, feeling that something fortunate would surely turn up soon. Meanwhile there was no doubt that his practice was increasing. It was not—he told himself— the class of practice he wanted, these three and sixpenny consultations and five shilling visits. Yet it was genuine practice. The people who came to him or called him out were far too poor to dream of troubling the doctor unless they were really ill. Thus he met diphtheria in queer stuffy rooms above converted stables, rheumatic fever in damp servants' basements, pneumonia in the attics of lodging houses. He fought disease in that most tragic room of all: the single apartment where some elderly man or woman lived alone, forgotten by, friends and relatives, cooking poor meals on a gas ring, neglected, unkempt, forsaken. There were many such cases. He came across the father of a well-known actress—whose name shone in bright lights in Shaftesbury Avenue—an old man of seventy, paralysed, living in filthy squalor. He visited an elderly gentlewoman, gaunt, ludicrous and starving, who could show him her photograph in her Court presentation dress, tell him of the days when she had driven down these same streets in her own carriage. In the middle of the night he pulled back to life—and afterwards hated himself for it— a wretched creature, penniless and desperate, who had preferred the gas oven to the workhouse.

Many of his cases were urgent—surgical emergencies which cried aloud for immediate admission to hospital. And here Andrew encountered his greatest difficulty. It was the hardest thing in the world to secure admission, even for the worst, the most dangerous case. These had a way of happening late at night. Returning, coat and jacket over his pyjamas, a scarf round his neck, hat still on the back of his head he would hang over the telephone, ringing one hospital after another, entreating, imploring, threatening, but always met with the same refusal, the curt, often insolent: "Doctor who? Who? No, no! Sorry! We're full up!"

He went to Christine, livid, blaspheming.

"They're not full up. They've plenty of beds at St. John's for their own men. If they don't know you they freeze you stiff. I'd like to wring that last young pup's neck! Isn't it *hell*—Chris! Here am I with this strangulated hernia and I can't get a bed. Oh! I suppose some of them are full up! And this is London! This is the heart of the bloody British Empire. This is our voluntary hospital system. And some banqueting bastard of a philanthropist got up the other day and said it was the most marvellous in the world. It means the workhouse again for the poor devil. Filling in forms—what do you earn? What's your religion? and was your mother born in wedlock?—and him with peritonitis! Oh, well! Be a good sort, Chris, and get the relieving officer on the phone for me."

Whatever his difficulties, no matter if he railed against the dirt and poverty which he often had to combat, she always had the same reply.

"It's *real* work anyway. And that seems to me to make all the difference."

"Not enough to keep the bugs off me," he growled, going up to the bath to shake himself free.

She laughed; for she was back again to her old happiness. Though the fight had been formidable she had at last subdued the house. Sometimes it would attempt to rear its head and strike at her but in the main it lay

645

clean, furbished, obedient to her eye. She had her new gas cooker, new shades for the lamps, had the loose chair covers freshly cleaned. And her stair rods shone like a guardsman's buttons. After weeks of worry with servants who, in this district, preferred to work in the boarding-houses because of the tips they earned there, Christine had chanced on Mrs. Bennett, a widow of forty, clean and hardworking, who because of her daughter, a child of seven, had found it almost impossible to secure a "living-in" position. Together Mrs. Bennett and Christine had attacked the basement. Now the former railway tunnel was a comfortable bed-sitting-room, with a highly floral wallpaper, furniture brought from "the barrows" and painted cream by Christine, where Mrs. Bennett and little Florrie—now departing regularly with her satchel to Paddington School—felt themselves secure. In return for this security and comfort—after months of straitened uncertainty—Mrs. Bennett could not do enough to prove her worth.

The early spring flowers which made the waiting-room so bright reflected the happiness of Christine's house. She bought them at the street market for a few pence, as she went on her round of morning shopping. Many of the hawkers in Mussleburgh Road knew her. It was possible to buy fruit and fish and vegetables cheaply there. She ought to have been more conscious of her standing as the wife of a professional man, but alas! she was not, and she often brought her purchases back in her neat string bag, stopping at Frau Schmidt's on the way back for a few minutes' conversation and a wedge of the Liptauer cheese which Andrew liked so well.

Frequently, in the afternoons, she walked round the Serpentine. The chestnut trees were breaking into green and the waterfowl went scurrying across the wind-ruffled water. It was a good substitute for the open countryside which she had always loved so much.

Sometimes in the evening Andrew would glance at her in that oddly jealous manner which meant that he was cross because the day had gone past without him noticing her.

"What have you been up to all day?—while I've been busy? If ever I do get a car you'll have to drive the damn thing. That'll keep you close to me."

He was still waiting for those "good" patients who did not come, longing to hear from Abbey about the appointment, fretful because their evening at Queen Anne Street had produced no subsequent opportunity. Secretly he was cut that he had seen nothing of Hamson or his friends since then.

In this condition he sat in his surgery one evening towards the end of April. It was nearly nine o'clock and he was about to close up when a young woman entered. She gazed at him uncertainly:

"I didn't know whether to come this way—or by the front door."

"It's exactly the same," he smiled sourly. "Except that it's half price this end. Come along. What is it?"

"I don't mind paying the full fee." She came forward with a peculiar earnestness and sat down on the Rexine covered chair. She was about twenty-eight, he judged, stockily built, dressed in dark olive green, with bunchy legs and a large plain serious face. To look at her was to have the instinctive thought: No nonsense here!

He relented, saying: "Don't let's talk about the fee! Tell me your trouble."

"Well, doctor!"—she still seemed to wish, gravely, to establish herself. "It was Mrs. Smith—in the little provision shop—who recommended me to come to you. I've known her a long time. I work at Laurier's, quite near. My name is Cramb. But I must tell you I've been to a good many doctors round here." She pulled off her gloves. "It's my hands."

He looked at her hands, the palms of which were covered by a reddish dermatitis, rather like psoriasis. But it was not psoriasis, the edges were not serpiginous. With sudden interest he took up a magnifying-glass and peered more closely. Meanwhile she went on talking in her earnest, convincing voice.

"I can't tell you what a disadvantage this is to me in my work. I'd give anything to get rid of it. I've tried every kind of ointment under the sun. But none of them seem to be the slightest use."

"No! They wouldn't." He put down the glass, feeling all the thrill of an obscure yet positive diagnosis. "This is rather an uncommon skin condition, Miss Cramb. It's no good treating it locally. It's due to a blood condition and the only way to get rid of it is by dieting."

"No medicine?" Her earnestness gave way to doubt. "No one ever told me that before."

"I'm telling you now." He laughed and, taking his pad, drew out a diet for her, adding also a list of foods which she must absolutely avoid.

She accepted it hesitatingly. "Well! Of course I'll try it, doctor. I'd try *anything*." Meticulously she paid him his fee, lingered as though still dubious, then went away. He immediately forgot her.

Ten days later she returned, coming this time by the front door, and entering the consulting-room with such an expression of suppressed fervour that he could barely keep from smiling.

"Would you like to see my hands, doctor?"

"Yes." Now he did smile. "I hope you don't regret the diet."

"Regret it!" She surrendered her hands to him in a passion of gratitude. "Look! Completely cured. Not a single spot on them. You don't know how much it means to me—I can't tell you—such cleverness——"

"That's all right," he said lightly. "It's my job to know these things.

647

You run away and don't worry. Keep off those foods I told you about and you'll never have it again."

She rose.

"And now let me pay you, doctor?"

"You've already paid me." He was conscious of a mild æsthetic thrill. Right gladly would he have taken another three and six, or even seven and six from her, but the temptation to dramatise the triumph of his skill proved irresistible.

"But, doctor——" Unwillingly she allowed herself to be escorted to the door where she paused for the final earnestness. "Perhaps I'll be able to show my gratitude some other way."

Gazing at her upturned moon face a ribald thought crossed his mind. But he merely nodded and closed the door upon her. Again he forgot about her. He was tired, already half regretful at refusing the fee, and, in any case, he had little thought of what any shopgirl might do for him. But here at least he did not know Miss Cramb. Moreover, he quite overlooked a possibility, emphasised by Æsop, which as a bad philosopher, he ought to have remembered.

IV

MARTHA CRAMB was known as the Half-Back to the "juniors" at Laurier's. Sturdy, unattractive, sexless, she seemed a strange person to be one of the senior assistants in this unique shop which dealt luxuriously in smart gowns, exquisite undergarments and furs so rich their prices mounted to hundreds of pounds. Yet the Half-Back was an admirable saleswoman, highly valued by her clients. The fact was that Laurier's, in its pride, employed a special system, each "senior" collecting her own especial clients, a little group of the Laurier customers whom she served exclusively, studied, "dressed" and for whom she "laid aside" things when the new models came in. The relationship was intimate, often existed over many years, and one to which the Half-Back in her earnest sincerity was particularly suited.

She was the daughter of a Kettering solicitor. Many of the Laurier girls were daughters of small professional men in the provinces and outer suburbs. It was esteemed an honour to be allowed to enter Laurier's, to wear the dark green dress which was the uniform of the establishment. Sweated employment and the bad "living-in" conditions which ordinary shop assistants were sometimes made to endure simply did not exist at Laurier's, where the girls were admirably fed and housed and chaperoned. Mr. Winch, the only male buyer in the shop, especially saw to it that they were chaperoned. He particularly esteemed the Half-Back and often held sedate conference with her. He was a pink, motherly old gentleman who had been in millinery for forty years. His thumb was worn flat from appraising material, his back permanently cricked in deferential greetings. Maternal though he might be, Mr. Winch, to the stranger entering Laurier's, exhibited the only trousers in a vast and frothy sea of femininity. He had an unsympathetic eye for those husbands who came with their wives to inspect the mannequins. He knew Royalty. He was almost as great an institution as Laurier's.

The incident of Miss Cramb's cure caused a mild sensation amongst the staff at Laurier's. And the immediate result was that from sheer curiosity a number of the juniors dropped in to Andrew's surgery with mild complaints. Giggling, they told each other that they wanted to see "what the Half-Back's doctor was like!"

Gradually, however, more and more of the Laurier girls began to come to the surgery at Chesborough Terrace. All the girls were insurance patients. They were compelled by law to be "on the panel," but with true Laurier arrogance they repudiated the scheme. By the end of May it was not uncommon for half a dozen of them to be waiting in the surgery—very smart, modelled upon their customers, lip-sticked, young. The result was a marked improvement in the surgery receipts. Also a laughing remark by Christine:

"What *are* you doing with that beauty chorus, darling? Sure they haven't mistaken this for the stage door."

But Miss Cramb's throbbing gratitude—oh, the ecstasy of those healed hands!—was only beginning to express itself. Hitherto, Doctor McLean, safe and elderly, of Royal Crescent, had been regarded as the semi-official doctor of Laurier's, called upon when emergency demanded—as, for instance, when Miss Twigg of the tailoring burned herself badly with a hot iron. But Doctor McLean was on the verge of retiring and his partner and immediate successor, Doctor Benton, was neither safe nor elderly. Indeed, more than once, Doctor Benton's ankle-roving eye and too tender solicitude for the prettier juniors had caused Mr. Winch pinkly to frown. Miss Cramb and Mr. Winch discussed these matters at their little conferences together, Mr. Winch nodding gravely with hands clasped behind his back, as Miss Cramb dwelt upon Benton's inadequacy and the presence of another professional man at Chesborough Terrace, strict and ungaudy, who achieved brilliance without sacrifice to Thaïs. Nothing was settled, Mr. Winch always took his time, but there was a portentous gleam in his eye as he swam away to greet a duchess.

In the first week of June, when Andrew had already come to feel shame for his earlier contempt of her, still another manifestation of Miss Cramb's good offices fell in burning fire upon his head.

He received a letter, very neat and precise—no such informality as a phone call, he afterwards learned, would have befitted the writer—

649

asking him to call on Tuesday, the following forenoon, as near eleven o'clock as possible, at 9 Park Gardens, to see Miss Winifred Everett.

Closing his surgery early, he left with a rising sense of anticipation, to make this visit. It was the first time he had been called out of the drab, neighbourhood which had, up till now, contained his practice. Park Gardens was a handsome block of flats, not altogether modern, but large and substantial, with a fine view of Hyde Park. He rang the bell of 9, expectant and tense, with the odd conviction that this was his chance at last.

An elderly servant showed him in. The room was spacious, with old furniture, books and flowers reminding him of Mrs. Vaughan's drawing-room. The moment he entered it he felt that his premonition was correct. He swung round as Miss Everett appeared, finding her glance, level and composed, fixed appraisingly upon him.

She was a well-made woman of about fifty, dark haired and sallow skinned, severely dressed, with an air of complete assurance. She began immediately, in a measured tone:

"I have lost my doctor—unfortunately—for I had great faith in him. My Miss Cramb recommended you. She's a very faithful creature and I trust her. I've looked you up. You're well qualified." She paused, quite openly inspecting him, weighing him up. She had the look of a woman, well fed, well taken care of, who would not allow a finger near her without due inspection of the cuticle. Then guardedly, "I think perhaps you might suit. I usually have a course of injections at this time of year. I'm subject to hay fever. You know all about hay fever, I presume?"

"Yes," he answered. "Which injections do you have?"

She mentioned the name of a well-known preparation. "My old doctor put me to that. I have great faith in it."

"Oh, that!" Nettled at her manner, he was on the point of telling her that the faithful remedy of her faithful doctor was worthless, that it had achieved its popularity through skilful advertising on the part of the firm who produced it and the absence of pollen in most English summers. But with an effort he restrained himself. There was a struggle between all that he believed and all he wished to have. He thought defiantly, if I let this chance slip, after all these months, I'm a fool. He said, "I think I can give you the injection as well as anyone."

"Very well. And now about your fees. I never paid Doctor Sinclair more than one guinea a visit. May I take it that you will continue this arrangement."

A guinea a visit—it was three times the largest fee he had ever earned! And more important still, it represented his first step into the superior class of practice he had coveted all these months. Again he stifled the quick protests of his convictions. What did it matter if the injections were useless?—that was her lookout, not his. He was sick of failure, tired of being a three-and-sixpenny hack. He wanted to get on, succeed. And he would succeed at all costs.

He came again the following day at eleven o'clock sharp. She had warned him, in her severe way, against being late. She did not wish her forenoon walk interfered with. He gave her the first injection. And thereafter he called twice a week, continuing the treatment.

He was punctual, precise as she, and he never presumed. It was almost amusing the way in which she gradually thawed to him. She was a queer person, Winifred Everett, and a most decided personality. Though she was rich—her father had been a large manufacturer of cutlery in Sheffield and all the money that she had inherited from him was safely invested in the Funds—she set herself out to get the utmost value from every penny. It was not meanness but rather an odd kind of egoism. She made herself the centre of her universe, took the utmost care of her body, which was still white and fine, went in for all sorts of treatments which she felt would benefit her. She must have everything of the best. She ate sparingly, but only the finest food. When on his sixth visit she unbent to offer him a glass of sherry he observed that it was Amontillado of the year 1819. Her clothes came from Laurier's. Her bed linen was the finest he had ever seen. And yet, with all this, she never, according to her lights, wasted a farthing. Not for the life of him could he imagine Miss Everett flinging a half-crown to a taximan without first carefully looking at the meter.

He ought to have loathed her yet strangely he did not. She had developed her selfishness to the point of a philosophy. And she was so eminently sensible. She exactly reminded him of a woman in an old Dutch picture, a Terborch, which Christine and he had once seen. She had the same large body, the same smooth-textured skin, the same forbidding yet pleasure-loving mouth.

When she saw that he was, in her own phrase, really going to suit her, she became much less reserved. It was an unwritten law with her that the doctor's visit should last twenty minutes, otherwise she felt she had not had the value of it. But by the end of a month he was extending this to half an hour. They talked together. He told her of his desire for success. She approved it. Her range of conversation was limited. But the range of her relations was unlimited and it was of them, mostly, that she talked. She spoke to him frequently of her niece, named Catharine Sutton, who lived in Derbyshire and who often came to town since her husband, Captain Sutton, was M.P. for Barnwell.

"Doctor Sinclair used to look after them," she remarked in a non-committal voice. "I don't see why you shouldn't now."

On this last visit she gave him another glass of her Amontillado and, very pleasantly, she said:

"I hate bills coming in. Please let me settle up now." She handed him a folded cheque for twelve guineas. "Of course, I shall have you in again soon. I usually have an anticoryza vaccine in the winter."

She actually accompanied him to the door of the flat and there she stood for a moment, her face drily illumined, the nearest approach to a smile he had ever seen there. But it passed quickly and, gazing at him forbiddingly, she said:

"Will you take the advice of a woman old enough to be your mother. Go to a good tailor. Go to Captain Sutton's tailor—Rogers, in Conduit Street. You've told me how much you wish to succeed. You never will in that suit."

He strode down the road cursing her, the hot indignity still burning on his brow, cursing her in his old impassioned style. Interfering old bitch! What business was it of hers! What right had she to tell him how he should dress? Did she take him for a *lapdog*? That was the worst of compromise, of truckling to convention. His Paddington patients paid him only three and six yet they did not ask him to be a tailor's dummy. In future he would confine himself to them and call his soul his own!

But somehow that mood passed. It was perfectly true that he had never taken the slightest interest in his clothes, a suit off the peg had always served him excellently, covered him, kept him warm without elegance. Christine, too, though she was always so neat, never bothered about clothes. She was happiest in a tweed skirt and a wollen jumper she had knitted herself.

Surreptitiously he took stock of himself, his nondescript worsted, uncreased trousers, mud-spattered at the selvedge. Hang it all, he thought testily, she's perfectly right. How can I attract first-class patients if I look like this? Why didn't Christine tell me? It was *her* job; not old lady Winnie's. What was that name she gave me—Rogers of Conduit Street. Hell! I'm likely to go there!

He had recovered his spirits when he reached home. He flourished the cheque under Christine's nose.

"See that, my good woman! Remember when I came running in with that first wretched three and a bender from the surgery. Bah! That's what I say to it now—bah! This is real money, gen-u-ine fees, like a first rate M.D., M.R.C.P., ought to be earning. Twelve guineas for talking nicely to Winnie the Pooh, and innocuously inoculating her with Glickert's Eptone."

"What's that?" she asked smiling; then suddenly she was doubtful. "Isn't that the stuff I've heard you run down so much?"

His face altered, he frowned at her, completely at a loss. She had made the one remark he did not wish to hear. All at once he felt angry, not with himself, but with her.

"Blast it, Chris! You're *never* satisfied!" He turned and banged out of the room. For the rest of that day he was in a sulky humour. But next day he cheered up. He went then to Rogers, in Conduit Street.

V

HE WAS self-conscious as a schoolboy when, a fortnight later, he came down in one of his two new suits. It was a dark, double-breasted grey, worn, on Rogers' suggestion, with a wing collar and a dark bow-tie which picked up the shade of the grey. There was not the shadow of a doubt, the Conduit Street tailor knew his job, and the mention of Captain Sutton's name had made him do it thoroughly.

This morning, as it fell out, Christine was not looking her best. She had a slight sore throat and had wound her old scarf protectively around her throat and head. She was pouring his coffee when the radiance or his presence burst upon her. For a moment she was too staggered to speak.

"Why, Andrew!" she gasped. "You look wonderful. Are you going anywhere?"

"Going anywhere? I'm going on my rounds, my work of course!" Being self-conscious made him almost snappy. "Well! Do you like it?"

"Yes," she said, not quickly enough to please him. "It's—it's frightfully smart—but"—she smiled—"somehow it doesn't quite seem *you*!"

"You'd rather keep me looking like a tramp, I suppose."

She was silent, her hand, raising her cup, suddenly contracted so that the knuckles showed white. Ah! he thought, I got her there. He finished breakfast and entered the consulting-room.

Five minutes later she followed him there, scarf still round her throat, her eyes hesitant, pleading.

"Darling," she said, "please don't misunderstand me! I'm delighted to see you in a new suit. I want you to have everything, everything that's best for you. I'm sorry I said that a moment ago but you see—I'm accustomed to you—oh! it's awfully hard to explain—but I've always identified you as—now *please* don't misunderstand me—as someone who doesn't give a hang about how he looks or how people think he looks. You remember that Epstein head we saw. That it wouldn't have looked quite the same if—oh, if it had been trimmed and polished up."

He answered abruptly.

"I'm not an Epstein head."

She made no reply. Lately, he had been difficult to reason with and, hurt at this misunderstanding, she did not know what to say. Still hesitating, she turned away.

Three weeks later when Miss Everett's niece came to spend a few weeks in London he was rewarded for his wise observance of the elder lady's hint. On a pretext Miss Everett summoned him to Park Gardens, where she scanned him with severe approval. He could almost see her passing him as a fit candidate for her recommendation. On the following day he received a call from Mrs. Sutton, who, since the condition ran, apparently, in the family, wished the same hay-fever treatment as her aunt. This time he had no compunction about injecting the useless Eptone of the useful Messrs. Glickert. He made an excellent impression upon Mrs. Sutton. And before the end of that same month he was called to a friend of Miss Everett's who also occupied a flat in Park Gardens.

Andrew was highly diverted with himself. He was winning, winning, winning. In his straining eagerness for success he forgot how contrary was his progress to all that he had hitherto believed. His vanity was touched. He felt alert and confident. He did not pause to reflect that this rolling snowball of his high-class practice had been started, in the first place, by a fat little German woman behind the counter of a ham and beef shop near that vulgar Mussleburgh Market. Indeed, almost before he had time to reflect at all the snowball took a further downhill roll—another and more exciting opportunity was offered to his grasp.

One afternoon in June, the zero hour between two o'clock and four, when nothing of consequence normally occurred, he was sitting in the consulting-room, totalling his receipts for the past month, when suddenly the phone rang. Three seconds and he was at the instrument.

"Yes, yes! This is Doctor Manson speaking."

A voice, anguished and palpitant, came back to him.

"Oh, Doctor Manson! I'm relieved to find you in. This is Mr. Winch! —Mr. Winch of Laurier's. We've had a slight mishap to one of our customers. Could you come? Could you come at once?"

"I'll be there in four minutes." Andrew clicked back the receiver and sprang for his hat. A 15 bus, hurtling outside, solidly sustained his impetuous leap. In four minutes and a half he was inside the revolving doors of Laurier's, met by an anxious Miss Cramb, and escorted over swimming surfaces of green-piled carpet, past long gilt mirrors and satinwood panelling against which, as if by chance, there could be seen one small hat on its stand, a lacy scarf, an ermine evening wrap. As they hastened, with rapid earnestness, Miss Cramb explained:

"It's Miss le Roy, Doctor Manson. One of our customers. Not mine, thank goodness, she's always giving trouble. But, Doctor Manson, you see I spoke to Mr. Winch about you——"

"Thanks!" brusquely—he could still, on occasion, be brusque! "What's happened?"

"She seems—oh, Doctor Manson—she seems to have had a fit in the fit-fitting room!"

At the head of the broad staircase she surrendered him to Mr. Winch, pinkly agitated, who fluttered:

"This way, doctor—this way—I hope you can do something. It's most dreadfully unfortunate——"

Into the fitting-room, warm, exquisitely carpeted in a lighter shade of green, with gilt and green panelled walls, a crowd of twittering girls, a gilt chair upturned, a towel thrown down, a spilled glass of water, pandemonium. And there, the centre of it all, Miss le Roy, the woman in the fit. She lay on the floor, rigid, with spasmodic clutching of her hands and sudden stiffenings of her feet. From time to time a straining, intimidating crowing broke from her tense throat.

As Andrew entered with Mr. Winch one of the older assistants in the group burst into tears.

"It wasn't my fault," she sobbed. "I only pointed out to Miss le Roy it was the design she chose herself——"

"Oh, dear. Oh, dear," muttered Mr. Winch. "This is dreadful, dreadful. Shall I—shall I ring for the ambulance."

"No, not yet," Andrew said in a peculiar tone. He bent down beside Miss le Roy. She was very young, about twenty-four, with blue eyes and washed-out silky hair all tumbled under her askew hat. Her rigidity, her convulsive spasms were increasing. On the other side of her knelt another woman, with dark concerned eyes, apparently her friend. "Oh, Toppy, Toppy," she kept murmuring.

"Please clear the room," said Andrew suddenly. "I'd like everyone out but"—his eye fell upon the dark young woman—"but this lady here."

The girls went, a trifle unwillingly—it had been pleasurable diversion assisting at Miss le Roy's fit. Miss Cramb, even Mr. Winch, removed themselves from the room. The moment they had gone the convulsions became terrifying.

"This is an extremely serious case," Andrew said, speaking very distinctly. Miss le Roy's eyeballs rolled towards him. "Get me a chair, please."

The fallen chair was righted, in the centre of the room, by the other woman. Then slowly and with great sympathy, supporting her by the armpits, Andrew helped the convulsed Miss le Roy upright into the chair. He held her head erect.

"There," he said with greater sympathy. Then, taking the flat of his hand, he hit her a resounding smack upon the cheek. It was his most courageous action for many months and remained so—alas!—for many months to come.

Miss le Roy stopped crowing, the spasm ceased, her rolling eyeballs righted themselves. She gazed at him in pained, in infantile bewilderment. Before she could relapse he took his hand again and struck her on the other cheek. Smack! The anguish in Miss le Roy's face was ludicrous. She dithered, seemed about to crow again and then began, gently, to cry. Turning to her friend she wept:

"Darling, I want to go home."

Andrew gazed apologetically at the dark young woman who now regarded him with restrained yet singular interest.

"Sorry," he muttered. "It was the only way. Bad hysteria—carpopedal spasms. She might have harmed herself—I hadn't an anæsthetic or anything. And anyway—it worked."

"Yes—it worked."

"Let her cry this out," Andrew said. "Good safety valve. She'll be all right in a few minutes."

"Wait, though"—quickly—"you must see her home."

"Very well," Andrew said, in his busiest professional tone.

In five minutes' time Toppy le Roy was able to make good her face, a lengthy operation punctuated by a few desultory sobs.

"I don't look too foul, do I, darling," she inquired of her friend. Of Andrew she took no notice whatsoever.

They left the fitting-room thereafter, and their progress through the long showroom was sheer sensation. Wonder and relief left Mr. Winch almost speechless. He did not know, he would never know, how this had come about, how the writhing paralytic had been made to walk. He followed, babbling deferential words. As Andrew passed through the main entrance behind the two women he wrung him fervently with a spongy hand.

The taxi took them along Bayswater Road in the direction of Marble Arch. There was not even pretence of speech. Miss le Roy was sulking now, like a spoiled child who had been punished and she was still jumpy—from time to time, her hands and the muscles of her face gave slight involuntary twitches. She was, now that she could be seen more normally, very thin and almost pretty in a scrawny little way. Her clothes were beautiful yet, despite them, she seemed to Andrew exactly like a young pulled chicken, through which traces of electric current periodically passed. He was himself nervous, conscious of the awkward situation, yet he was determined in his own interests to take advantage of it to the full.

The taxi rounded the Marble Arch, ran alongside Hyde Park, and, wheeling to the left they drew up before a house in Green Street. Then, almost immediately, they were inside. The house took Andrew's breath away, he had never imagined anything so luxurious—the wide soft-pinewood hall, the cabinet gorgeous with jade, the strange single painting set in a costly panel, the reddish-gold lacquer chairs, the wide settees, the skin-thin faded rugs.

Toppy le Roy flung herself down on a satin-cushioned sofa, still ignoring Andrew, and tugged off her little hat which she flung on the floor.

"Press the bell, darling, I must have a drink. Thank God, father isn't home."

Quickly, a manservant brought cocktails. When he had gone Toppy's friend considered Andrew thoughtfully, almost, but not quite, smiling.

"I think we ought to explain ourselves to you, doctor. It's all been rather hurried. I'm Mrs. Lawrence. Toppy here—Miss le Roy—had rather a row over a dress she's having specially designed for the Arts Charity Ball and—well!—she's been doing too much lately, she's a very nervy little person—and the long and the short of it is that although Toppy's very cross with you we're frightfully indebted to you for getting us back here. And I'm going to have another cocktail."

"Me too," said Toppy peevishly. "That bloody Laurier woman. I'll tell father to ring up and get her sacked! Oh, no I won't!" As she tilted her second cocktail a smile of gratification slowly overspread her face. "I did give them something to think about, though, didn't I, Frances? I simply went *wild*! That look on old Mamma Winch's face was too, too funny." Her scraggy little frame shook with laughter. She met Andrew's eyes without ill-will. "Go on, doctor. Laugh! It was priceless."

"No, I don't think it was so amusing." He spoke quickly, anxious to explain himself, establish his position, convince her she was ill. "You really had a bad attack. I'm sorry I had to treat you as I did. If I'd had an anæsthetic I'd have given you that. Much less—less annoying for you. And please don't imagine that I think you tried to bring on that attack. Hysteria—well, that's what it was—is a definite syndrome. People oughtn't to be unsympathetic about it. It's a condition of the nervous system. You see, you're extremely run down, Miss le Roy, all your reflexes are on edge, you're in a very nervous state."

"That's perfectly true," Frances Lawrence nodded. "You've been doing far too much lately, Toppy."

"Would you really have given me chloroform?" Toppy asked Andrew in childish wonder. "That would have been fun."

"But seriously, Toppy," Mrs. Lawrence said, "I wish you'd take yourself up."

"You sound like father," Toppy said, losing her good humour.

There was a pause. Andrew had finished his cocktail. He put the glass down on the carved pine mantelpiece behind him. There seemed nothing more for him to do.

"Well!" he said effectively, "I must get on with my work. Please take my advice, Miss le Roy. Have a light meal, go to bed, and—since I cannot be of any further service to you—call in your own doctor to-morrow. Good-bye."

Mrs. Lawrence accompanied him into the hall, her manner so un-hurried that he was obliged to restrain the busy briskness of his exit. She was tall and slim, with rather high shoulders and a small elegant head. In her dark beautifully waved hair a few iron-grey strands gave her a curious distinction. Yet she was quite young, not more than twenty-seven, he was sure. Despite her height she had fine bones, her wrists especially were small and fine, indeed her whole figure seemed flexible, exquisitely tempered, like a fencer's. She gave him her hand, her greenish hazel eyes fixed upon him in that faint, friendly, unhurried smile.

"I only wished to tell you how I admired your new line of treatment." Her lips twitched. "Don't give it up on any account. I foresee you making it a crashing success."

Walking down Green Street to pick up a bus he saw to his amazement that it was nearly five o'clock. He had spent three hours in the company of these two women. He ought to be able to charge a really big fee for that! And yet, despite this elevating thought—so symptomatic of his brave new outlook—he felt confused, strangely dissatisfied. Had he really made the most of his chance? Mrs. Lawrence had seemed to like him. But you never could tell with people like that. What a marvellous house, too! Suddenly he gritted his teeth in angry exasperation. Not only had he omitted to leave his card, he had forgotten even to tell them who he was. As he took his seat in the crowded bus beside an old workman in soiled overalls he blamed himself bitterly for missing a golden opportunity.

VI

THE FOLLOWING morning at a quarter past eleven, as he was on the point of taking his departure on a round of cheap visits centred about the Mussleburgh Market, the telephone rang. A manservant's voice, gravely solicitous, purred at him.

"Doctor Manson, sir! Ah! Miss le Roy wishes to know, sir, what time you will be calling on her to-day. Ah! Excuse me, sir, hold on—Mrs. Lawrence will speak to you herself."

Andrew hung on, with a quick throbbing excitement while Mrs. Lawrence talked to him in friendly fashion, explaining that they were expecting him to call, without fail.

As he came away from the phone he told himself exultantly that he hadn't missed the opportunity yesterday, he hadn't, no, he hadn't missed it after all.

He dropped all his other calls, urgent or otherwise, and went straight to the house in Green Street. And here, for the first time, he met Joseph le Roy. He found le Roy impatiently awaiting him in the jade-bedizened hall, a bald thick-set figure, downright and bejowled, who abused his cigar like a man who has no time to lose. In one second his eyes bored into Andrew, a swift surgical operation which ended to his satisfaction. He then spoke forcibly in a colonial tongue.

"See here, doc, I'm in a hurry. Mrs. Lawrence had a hell of a bother tracking you down this morning. I understand you're a clever young fellow and you don't stand any nonsense. You're married too, aren't you? That's good. Now you take my girl in hand. Get her right, get her strong, get all this damn hysteria out of her system. Don't spare anything. I can pay. Good-bye."

Joseph le Roy was a New Zealander. And despite his money, his Green Street house, and his exotic little Toppy it was not difficult to believe the truth—that his great-grandfather was one Michael Cleary, an illiterate farm hand on the lands around Greymouth Harbour, who was known colloquially to his fellow "scrubbies" as Leary. Joseph le Roy had certainly faced up to life as Joe Leary, a boy whose first job was that of "milker" on the great Greymouth farms. But Joe was born, as he said himself, to milk more than cows. And thirty years later, in the top-floor office of the first Auckland skyscraper, it was Joseph le Roy who put his signature to the deal unifying the Island dairy farms into a great dried milk combine.

It was a magic scheme—the Cremogen Combine. At this time dried milk goods were unknown, commercially unorganised. It was le Roy who saw their possibility, who led their attack on the world market, advertising them as God-given nourishment for infants and invalids. The cream of the achievement lay, not in Joe's products, but in his own rich audacity. The surplus skim milk, which had been poured down the drain or given to the pigs in hundreds of New Zealand farms, was now sold in the cities of the world in Joe's neat brightly papered tins as Cremogen, Cremax, and Cremafat at three times the price of pure fresh milk.

Co-director in the le Roy Combine, and manager of the English interests, was Jack Lawrence, who had been, illogically enough, a Guards officer before he went into business in the city. Yet it was more than the bare association of commerce which drew Mrs. Lawrence and Toppy together. Frances, rich in her own right and far more at home in the smart society of London than Toppy—who occasionally betrayed her brushwood antecedents—had an amused affection for the *enfant gâté*. When Andrew went upstairs after his interview with le Roy she was waiting for him outside Toppy's room.

Indeed, on subsequent days Frances Lawrence was usually present at the time of his visit, helping with his exacting, wilful patient, ready to see an improvement in Toppy, insistent that she continue with the treatment, asking when they might expect his next call.

Grateful to Mrs. Lawrence, he was still diffident enough to feel it strange that this patrician, self-admittedly selective person whom, before he came to see her photographs in the illustrated weeklies, he knew to be exclusive, should have even this mild interest in him. Her wide and rather sulky mouth usually expressed hostility towards people who were not her intimates, yet for some reason she was never hostile to him. He had an extraordinary desire, greater than curiosity, to fathom her character, her personality. He seemed to know nothing of the real Mrs. Lawrence. It was a delight to watch the controlled actions of her limbs, as she moved about the room. She was always at ease, watchful in everything she did with a mind behind her friendly guarded eyes, despite the graceful casualness of her speech.

He hardly realised that the suggestion was hers yet—though he said nothing to Christine, who still contentedly balanced her housekeeping budget in shillings and pence—he began to ask himself impatiently how any doctor could develop a high-class practice without a smart car? It was ridiculous to think of him stepping along Green Street, carrying his own bag, with dust on his shoes, facing the slightly superior manservant without a car. He had the brick garage at the back of his house, which would considerably reduce the cost of upkeep and there were firms who specialised in supplying cars to doctors, admirable firms who did not mind graciously deferring the terms of payment.

Three weeks later a brown folding-roof coupé, brand new and darkly glittering, drew up at 9 Chesborough Terrace. Easing himself from the driving-seat Andrew ran up the stairs of his house.

"Christine!" he called out, trying to suppress the gloating excitement in his voice. "Christine! Come and see something!"

He had meant to stagger her. And he succeeded.

"Goodness!" She clutched his arm. "Is it *ours*? Oh! what a beauty!"

"Isn't she! Look *out*, dear, don't handle the paintwork! It's—it's liable to mark the varnish!" He smiled at her in quite his old way. "Pretty good surprise, eh, Chris? Me getting it and licensing it and everything and never saying a word to you. Different from the old Morris. Step in, lady, and I'll demonstrate. She goes like a bird."

She could not admire the little car enough as he took her, bareheaded, on an easy spin round the Square. Four minutes later they were back, standing on the pavement, while he still feasted his eyes upon the treasure. Their moments of intimacy, of understanding and happiness together, were so rare now that she was loath to relinquish this one. She murmured:

"It'll be so easy for you to get about now, dear." Then, again, diffidently, "And if we could get out a little bit into the country, say on Sundays, into the woods—oh, it would be *wonderful*."

"Of course," he answered absently. "But it's really for the practice. We can't go gadding about, getting mud all over it!" He was thinking of the effect this dashing little coupé would have upon his patients.

The main effect, however, was beyond his expectation. On Thursday of the following week as he came out of the heavy glass and iron-grilled door of 17a Green Street he ran straight into Freddie Hamson.

"Hello, Hamson," he said casually. He could not repress a thrill of satisfaction at the sight of Hamson's face. At first Hamson had barely recognised him, and as he did so, his expression, falling through various degrees of surprise, was still frankly nonplussed.

"Why, hello!" said Freddie. "What are you doing here?"

"Patient," Andrew answered, jerking his head backwards in the direction of 17a. "I've got Joe le Roy's daughter on my hands."

"Joe le Roy!"

That exclamation alone was worth much to Manson. He put a proprietary hand on the door of his beautiful new coupé.

"Which way are you going? Can I drop you anywhere?"

Freddie recovered himself quickly. He was seldom at a loss, and never for any length of time. Indeed, in thirty seconds, his opinion of Manson, his whole idea of Manson's usefulness to him, had undergone a swift and unexpected revolution.

"Yes," he smiled companionably. "I was going along to Bentinck Street—to Ida Sherrington's Home. Walking to keep the old figure down. But I'll step in with you."

There was a pause for a few minutes while they ran across Bond Street. Hamson was thinking hard. He had welcomed Andrew effusively to London because he hoped Manson's practice might occasionally provide him with a three guinea consultation at Queen Anne Street. But now the change in his old classmate, the car, and above all the mention of Joe le Roy—the name had for him infinitely more worldly significance than it had for Andrew—showed him his mistake. There were Manson's ideal qualifications too, useful, extremely useful. Looking astutely ahead, Freddie saw a better, an altogether more profitable basis for co-operation between Andrew and himself. He would go carefully, of course, for Manson was a touchy, uncertain devil. He said:

"Why don't you come in with me and meet Ida? She's a useful person to know, though she keeps the worst nursing-home in London. Oh! I don't know! She's probably as good as the rest of them. And she certainly charges more."

"Yes?"

"Come in with me and see my patient. She's harmless—old Mrs. Raeburn, Ivory and I are doing a few tests on her. You're strong on lungs, aren't you? Come along and examine her chest. It'll please her enormously. And it'll be five guineas for you."

"What!—you mean——? But what's the matter with her chest?"

"Nothing much," Freddie smiled. "Don't look so stricken! She's probably got a touch of senile bronchitis! And she'd love to see you! That's how we do it here. Ivory and Deedman and I. You really ought to be in on it, Manson. We won't talk about it now—yes, round that first corner there!—but it would amaze you how it works out."

Andrew drew up the car at the house indicated by Hamson, an ordinary town dwelling-house, tall and narrow, which had obviously never been intended for its present purpose. Indeed, gazing at the busy street, along which the traffic racketed and hooted, it was difficult to imagine how any sick person could find peace here. It looked precisely the place to provoke rather than to cure a nervous breakdown. Andrew mentioned this to Hamson as they mounted the steps to the front door.

"I know, my dear fellow," Freddie agreed with ready cordiality. "But they're all the same. This little bit of the West End is jammed with them. You see, we must have them convenient to ourselves." He grinned. "Ideal if they were out somewhere quiet, but—for instance— what surgeon would drive ten miles every day to see his case for five minutes! Oh! You'll get to know about our little West End sick bays in due course." He drew up in the narrow hall into which they passed. "They've all got three smells, you observe—anæsthetics, cooking and excreta—logical sequence—forgive me, old man! And now meet Ida."

With the air of a man who knows his way about, he led the way into a constricted office on the ground floor, where a little woman in a mauve uniform and a stiff white head-dress sat at a small desk.

"Morning, Ida," Freddie exclaimed between flattery and familiarity. "Doing your sums?"

She raised her eyes, saw him, and smiled good-naturedly. She was short, stout and extremely full blooded. But her bright red face was so thickly covered with powder the result was a mauve complexion almost the colour of her uniform. She had a look of coarse bustling vitality, of knowing humour, of pluck. Her teeth were false and ill-fitting. Her hair was grizzled. Somehow, it was easy to suspect her of a strong vocabulary, to imagine her performing admirably as the keeper of a second-rate night club.

Yet Ida Sherrington's nursing-home was the most fashionable in London. Half the peerage had been to Ida, society women, racing men, famous barristers and diplomats. You had only to pick up the morning paper to read that yet another bright young person famous on stage or screen had left her appendix safely in Ida's motherly hands. She dressed all her nurses in a delicate shade of mauve, paid her wine butler two hundred pounds and her chef twice that sum a year. The prices which she charged her patients were fantastic. Forty guineas for a room each week was not an uncommon figure. And on top of that came extras, the chemist's bill—often a matter of pounds—the special night nurse, the theatre fee. But when argued with, Ida had one answer which she often adorned with a free and easy adjective. She had her own worries, with cuts and percentages to be paid out, and often she felt it was she who was being bled.

Ida had a soft side for the younger members of the profession and she greeted Manson agreeably as Freddie babbled:

"Take a good look at him. He'll soon be sending you so many patients you'll overflow into the Plaza Hotel."

"The Plaza overflows into me," Ida nodded her headdress meaningly.

"Ha! Ha!" Freddie laughed. "That's pretty good—I must tell old Deedman that one. Paul'll appreciate it. Come on, Manson. We'll go up top."

The cramped lift, just wide enough to hold a wheeled stretcher diagonally, took them to the fourth floor. The passage was narrow, trays stood outside the doors, and vases of flowers wilting in the hot atmosphere. They went into Mrs. Raeburn's room.

She was a woman of over sixty, propped up on her pillows, expectant of the doctor's visit, holding in her hand a slip of paper on which she had written certain symptoms experienced during the night, together with questions which she wished to ask. Andrew placed her unerringly as the elderly hypochondriac, Charcot's *malade au petit morceau de papier*.

Seated on the bed, Freddie talked to her, felt her pulse—no more— listened to her and gaily reassured her. He told her Mr. Ivory would be calling with the results of some highly scientific tests in the afternoon. He asked her to allow his colleague, Doctor Manson, whose speciality was lungs, to examine her chest. Mrs. Raeburn was flattered. She enjoyed it all very much. It emerged that she had been in Hamson's hands for two years. She was wealthy, without relatives, and spent her time equally between exclusive private hotels and West End nursing-homes.

"Lord!" Freddie exclaimed as they left the room. "You've no idea what a gold mine that old woman has been to us. We've taken nuggets out of her."

Andrew did not answer. The atmosphere of this place slightly sickened him. There was nothing wrong with the old lady's lungs and only her touching look of gratitude towards Freddie saved the matter from being downright dishonest. He tried to convince himself. Why should he be such a stickler? He would never make a success of himself if he continued intolerant, opinionative. And Freddie had meant it kindly, giving him the chance to examine this patient.

He shook hands amicably enough with Hamson before stepping into his coupé. And at the end of the month, when he received a neatly written cheque from Mrs. Raeburn—with her best thanks—for five guineas, he was able to laugh at his silly scruples. He enjoyed receiving cheques now, and to his extreme satisfaction more and more of them were coming his way.

VII

THE PRACTICE, which had shown a promising ncrease, now began a rapid, almost electrifying expansion in all directions, the effect of which was to sweep Andrew more swiftly with the stream. In a sense he was the victim of his own intensity. He had always been poor. In the past, his obstinate individualism had brought him nothing but defeat. Now he could justify himself with the amazing proofs of his material success.

Shortly after his emergency call to Laurier's he had a highly gratifying interview with Mr. Winch and thereafter more of the Laurier juniors, and even some of the seniors, came to consult him. They came chiefly for trivial complaints, yet once the girls had visited him it was strange how frequently they reappeared—his manner was so kind, so cheering, so brisk. His surgery receipts soared. Soon he managed to have the front of the house repainted, and with the help of one of those firms of surgical outfitters—all of them burning to assist young practitioners to enlarge their incomes—he was able to refurnish his surgery and consulting-room with a new couch, a padded swing chair, a dinky rubber-tyred trolley, and sundry elegantly scientific cabinets in white enamel and glass.

The manifest prosperity of the freshly cream-painted house, of his car, of this glitteringly modern equipment, soon traversed the neighbour-hood, bringing back many of the "good" patients who had consulted Doctor Foy in the past but had gradually dropped off when the old doctor and his consulting-room became progressively dingy.

The days of waiting, of hanging about, were finished for Andrew. At the evening surgeries it was as much as he could do to keep going, the front bell purring, the surgery door "pinging," patients waiting for him back and front, causing him to dash between the surgery and the consulting-room. The next step came inevitably. He was forced to evolve a scheme to save his time.

"Listen, Chris," he said one morning. "I've just struck on something that's going to help me a lot in these rush hours. You know—when I've seen a patient in the surgery I come back into the house to make up the medicine. Takes me five minutes usually. And it's a shocking waste of time—when I might be using it to polish off one of the 'good' patients waiting to see me in the consulting-room. Well, d'you get my scheme? From now on, you're my dispenser!"

She looked at him with a startled contraction of her brows.

"But I don't know anything about making up medicine."

He smiled reassuringly.

"That's all right, dear. I've prepared a couple of nice stock mixtures. All you have to do is to fill the bottles, label and wrap them."

"But——" Christine's perplexity showed in her eyes. "Oh, I want to help you, Andrew—only—do you really believe——"

"Don't you see I've *got* to!" His gaze avoided hers. He drank the rest of his coffee irritably. "I know I used to talk a lot of hot air about medicine at Aberalaw. All theories! I'm—I'm a practical physician now. Besides, all these Laurier girls are anæmic. A good iron mixture won't do them any harm." Before she could answer the sound of the surgery bell had pulled him away.

In the old days she would have argued, taken a firm stand. But now,

664

sadly, she reflected on the reversal of their earlier relationships. She no longer influenced, guided him. It was he who drove ahead.

She began to stand in the cubby-hole of the dispensary during those hectic surgery periods, waiting for his tense exclamation, in his rapid transit between "good" and surgery patients: "Iron!" or "Alba" or "Carminative" or something, when she would protest that the Iron mixture had run out, a strung-up, significant bark: "Anything! Damn it! *Anything at all!*"

Often the surgery was not over until half past nine. Then they made up the book, Doctor Foy's heavy ledger, which had only been half used when they took over the practice.

"My God! What a day, Chris!" he gloated. "D'you remember that first measly three and six I took, like a shaky schoolboy. Well, to-day—to-day, we took over eight pounds *cash*."

He tucked the money, heavy piles of silver and a few notes, into the little Afrikander tobacco sack which Doctor Foy had used as his money bag and locked it in the middle drawer of the desk. As with the ledger, he kept on using this old bag in order to continue his luck.

Now, indeed, he forgot all about his early doubts and praised his acumen in taking over the practice.

"We've got it absolutely gilt-edged every way, Chris," he exulted. "A paying surgery and a sound middle-class connection. And on top of that I'm building up a first rate consultant practice on my own. You just watch where we're going."

On the 1st of October he was able to tell her to refurnish the house. After his morning surgery he said, with impressive casualness, his new manner:

"I'd like you to go up West to-day, Chris. Go to Hudson's—or to Ostley's if you like it better. Go to the best place. And get all the new furniture you want. Get a couple of new bedroom suites, drawing-room suite, get *everything*."

She glanced at him in silence as he lit a cigarette, smiling.

"That's one of the joys of making money, being able to give you everything you want. Don't think I'm mean. Lord, no! You've been a little brick, Chris, the whole way through our bad times. Now we're just beginning to enjoy our good times."

"By ordering expensive shiny furniture—and hair-stuffed three-piece suites from Ostley's."

He missed the bitterness in her tone. He laughed.

"That's right, dear. It's high time we got rid of our old Regency junk."

Tears sprang to her eyes. She flashed:

"You didn't think it was junk at Aberalaw. And it isn't either. Oh! those were real days, those were happy days!" With a choking sob she spun round and left the room.

He stared after her in blank surprise. Her moods had been queer recently—uncertain and depressed, with sudden bursts of incomprehensible bitterness. He sensed that they were drifting away from each other, losing that mysterious unity, that hidden bond of comradeship which had always existed between them. Well! It was not his fault. He was doing his best, his utmost. He thought angrily, my getting on means nothing to her, nothing. But he could not dwell upon the unreasonableness, the injustice of her behaviour. He had a full list of calls before him and, since it was Tuesday, his usual visit to the bank.

Twice a week, regularly, he dropped in at the bank to make payments into his account, for he knew it was unwise to let cash accumulate in his desk. He could not but contrast these pleasant visits with his experience in Drineffy when, as a down-at-heel assistant, he had been humiliated, by Aneurin Rees. Here Mr. Wade, the manager, always gave him a warmly deferential smile and often an invitation to smoke a cigarette in his private room.

"If I may say so, doctor, without being personal, you're doing remarkably nicely. Round here we can do with a go-ahead doctor, who's just got the right amount of conservatism. Like yourself, doctor, if I may say so. Now these Southern Railway Guaranteed we were discussing the other day——"

Wade's deference was merely one instance of the general upswing of opinion. He now found the other doctors of the district giving him a friendly salute as their coupés went past his own. At the autumn divisional meeting of the Medical Association, in that same room where, on his first appearance, he had been made to feel himself a pariah, he was welcomed, made much of, given a cigar by Doctor Ferrie, vice-president of the division.

"Glad to see you with us, doctor," fussed little red-face Ferrie. "Did you approve of my speech? We've got to hold out for our fees. On night calls especially, I am taking a firm stand. The other night I was knocked up by a boy—a mere child of twelve, if you please. 'Come round quick, doctor,' he blubbers. 'Father's at work and my mother's taken awful bad.' You *know* that two a.m. conversation. And I'd never seen the kid in my life before. 'My dear boy,' says I, 'your mother's no patient of mine! Away and fetch me my half guinea and *then* I'll come.' Of course he never came back. I tell you, doctor, this district is *terrible*——"

On the week after the divisional meeting Mrs. Lawrence rang him up. He always enjoyed the graceful inconsequence of her telephone conversations, but to-day, after mentioning that her husband was fishing in Ireland, that she might possibly be going later to join him there, she asked him, dropping out her invitation as though it were of no importance, to luncheon on the following Friday.

"Toppy'll be there. And one or two people—less dull, I think, than one usually meets. It might do you some good—perhaps—to know them."

He hung up the receiver between satisfaction and an odd irritation. In his heart he was piqued that Christine had not been invited too. Then, gradually, he came to see that it was not a social but really a business occasion. He must get about and make contacts, particularly amongst the class of people who would be present at this luncheon. And, in any case, Christine need know nothing at all of the affair. When Friday came he told her that he had a luncheon engagement with Hamson and jumped into his car, relieved. He forgot that he was an extremely bad liar.

Frances Lawrence's house was in Knightsbridge, in a quiet street, between Hans Place and Wilton Crescent. Though it had not the splendour of the le Roy mansion its restrained taste conveyed an equal sense of opulence. Andrew was late in arriving and most of the guests were already there: Toppy, Rosa Keane the novelist, Sir Dudley Rumbold-Blane, M.D., F.R.C.P., famous physician and member of the board of Cremo Products, Nicol Watson, traveller and anthropologist, and several others of less alarming distinction.

He found himself at table beside a Mrs. Thornton who lived, she informed him, in Leicestershire, and who came up periodically to Brown's Hotel for a short season in town. Though he was now able calmly to sustain the ordeal of introductions, he was glad to regain his assurance under cover of her chatter, a maternal account of a foot injury, received at hockey by her daughter Sybil, a schoolgirl at Roedean.

Giving one ear to Mrs. Thornton, who took his mute listening for interest, he still managed to hear something of the suave and witty conversation around him—Rosa Keane's acid pleasantries, Watson's fascinatingly graceful account of an expedition he had recently made through the Paraguayan interior. He admired also the ease with which Frances kept the talk moving, at the same time sustaining the measured pedantry of Sir Rumbold, who sat beside her. Once or twice he felt her eyes upon him, half smiling, interrogative.

"Of course," Watson concluded his narrative with a deprecatory smile. "Easily one's most devastating experience was to come home and run straight into an attack of influenza."

"Ha!" said Sir Rumbold. "So you've been a victim too." By the device of clearing his throat and placing his pince-nez upon his richly endowed nose, he gained the attention of the table. Sir Rumbold was at home in this position—for many years now the attention of the great British public had been focused upon him. It was Sir Rumbold who, a quarter of a century before, staggered humanity by the declaration that a certain portion of man's intestine was not only useless but definitely harmful. Hundreds of people had rushed straight away to have the dangerous section removed and, though Sir Rumbold was not himself

667

amongst this number, the fame of the operation, which the surgeons named the Rumbold–Blane excision, established his reputation as a dietitian. Since then he had kept well to the front, successfully introducing to the nation bran food, Yourghout, and the lactic acid bacillus. Later he invented Rumbold–Blane Mastication and now, in addition to his activities on many company boards he wrote the menus for the famous Railey chain of restaurants: *Come, Ladies and Gentlemen, Let Sir Rumbold-Blane, M.D., F.R.C.P., Help You Choose Your Calories!* Many were the muttered grumbles amongst more legitimate healers that Sir Rumbold should have been scored off the Register years ago: to which the answer manifestly was—what would the Register be without Sir Rumbold?

He now said, glancing paternally at Frances:

"One of the most interesting features of this recent epidemic has been the spectacular therapeutic effect of Cremogen. I had occasion to say the same thing at our Company meeting last week. We have—aha!—no cure for influenza. And in the absence of cure the only way to resist its murderous invasion is to develop a high state of resistance, a vital defence of the body against the inroads of the disease. I happened to say, I flatter myself rather aptly, that we have proved incontestably, not on guinea-pigs—aha! aha!—like our laboratory friends—but on *human beings* the phenomenal power of Cremogen in organising and energising the vital antagonism of the body."

Watson turned to Andrew with his odd smile. "What do you think of Cremo productions, doctor?"

Caught unawares, Andrew found himself saying:

"It's as good a way of taking skim milk as any other."

Rosa Keane, with a swift approving side-glance, was unkind enough to laugh. Frances was smiling too. Hurriedly, Sir Rumbold passed to a description of his recent visit, as a guest of the Northern Medical Union, to the Trossachs.

Otherwise the luncheon was harmonious. Andrew eventually found himself joining freely in the conversation. Before he took his leave from her drawing-room, Frances had a word with him.

"You really do shine," she murmured, "out of the consulting-room. Mrs. Thornton hasn't been able to drink her coffee for telling me about you. I have a strange presentiment that you've bagged her—is that the phrase?—as a patient."

With that remark ringing in his ear, he went home feeling that he was much the better, and Christine none the worse for the adventure.

On the following morning, however, at half past ten he had an unpleasant shock. Freddie Hamson rang him to inquire briskly:

"Enjoy your lunch yesterday? How did I know? Why, you old dog, haven't you seen this morning's *Tribune*?"

Dismayed, Andrew went directly into the waiting-room, where the papers were laid out when Christine and he had finished with them. For the second time he went through the *Tribune*, one of the better known pictorial dailies. Suddenly he started. How had he missed it before? There, on a page devoted to society gossip, was a photograph of Frances Lawrence with a paragraph describing her luncheon party of the day before, his name amongst the guests.

With a chagrined face he slipped the sheet from the others, crushed it into a ball, flung it in the fire. Then he realised that Christine had already read the paper. He frowned in an access of vexation. Though he felt sure that she had not seen this confounded paragraph he went scowling into his consulting-room.

But Christine had seen the paragraph. And, after a momentary bewilderment, the hurt of it struck her to the heart. Why had he not told her? Why? Why? She would not have minded his going to this stupid lunch. She tried to reassure herself—it was all too trivial to cause her such anxiety and pain. But she saw, with a dull ache, that its implications were not trivial.

When he went out on his round she attempted to go on with her work in the house. But she could not. She wandered into his consulting-room, from there into his surgery, with that same heavy oppression in her breast. She began in a desultory fashion to dust the surgery. Beside the desk lay his old medical bag, the first he had ever possessed, which he had used at Drineffy, carrying it along the Rows, using it in his emergency calls down the mine. She touched it with a strange tenderness. He had a new bag now, a finer one. It was part of this new, this finer practice which he was striving after so feverishly, and which, deep in her heart, she so distrusted. She knew it was useless to attempt to speak to him about her misgivings on his behalf. He was so touchy now—the sign of his own conflict—a word from her would set him off, instantly provoke a quarrel. She must do her best in other ways.

It was Saturday forenoon and she had promised to take Florrie with her when she set out to do her shopping. Florrie was a bright little girl and Christine had become attached to her. She could hear her waiting now, at the head of the basement stairs, sent up by her mother, very clean and wearing a fresh frock, in a state of great preparedness. They often went out together like this on a Saturday.

She felt better in the open air with the child holding her hand, walking down the Market, talking to her friends amongst the hawkers, buying fruit, flowers, trying to think of something especially nice to please Andrew. Yet the wound was still open. Why, why had he not told her? And why had she not been there? She recollected that first occasion at Aberalaw when they had gone to the Vaughans and it had taken all her efforts to drag him with her. How different was the position now! Was she to blame? Had she changed, withdrawn into herself, become in some way anti-social? She did not think so. She still liked meeting and

669

knowing people, irrespective of who or what they were. Her friendship with Mrs. Vaughan still persisted in their regular exchange of letters.

But actually, though she felt hurt and slighted, her main concern was less for herself than for him. She knew that rich people could be ill as well as poor, that it was possible for him to be as fine a doctor in Green Street, Mayfair, as in Cefan Row, Aberalaw. She did not demand the persistence of such heroic effects as leggings and his old Red Indian motor-cycle. Yet she did feel with all her soul that in those days his idealism had been pure and wonderful, illuminating both their lives with a clear white flame. Now the flame had turned yellower and the globe of the lamp was smudged.

As she went into Frau Schmidt's she tried to erase the lines of worry from her brow. Nevertheless she found the old woman looking at her sharply. And presently Frau Schmidt grumbled:

"You don't eat enough, my dear! You don't look as you should! And you haf a fine car now and money and everything. Look! I will make you taste this. It iss good!"

The long thin knife in her hand, she cut a slice of her famous boiled ham and made Christine ea a soft bread sandwich. At the same time Florrie was provided with an iced pastry. Fraud Schmidt kept talking all the time.

"And now you want some Liptauer. Herr doctor—he has eaten pounds of my cheese and he never grows tired of it. Some day I will ask him to write me a testimonial to put in my window. This is the cheese what has made me famous——" Chuckling, Frau Schmidt ran on until they left her.

Outside, Christine and Florrie stood on the kerb waiting till the policeman on duty—it was their old friend Struthers—should signal them across. Christine kept a restraining hand on the impulsive Florrie's arm.

"You must always watch out for the traffic here," she cautioned. "What would your mother say if you were to get run over?"

Florrie, her mouth stuffed with the end of her pastry, considered this an excellent joke.

They were home at last and Christine began to undo the wrappings from her purchases. As she moved about the front room, putting the bronze chrysanthemums she had bought into a vase, she felt sad again.

Suddenly the telephone rang.

She went to answer it, her face still, her lips slightly drooping. For perhaps five minutes she was absent. When she returned her expression was transfigured. Her eyes were bright, excited. From time to time she glanced out of the window, eager for Andrew's return, her despondency forgotten in the good news she had received, news which was so important to him, yes, important to both of them. She had a happy conviction that nothing could have been more propitious. No better antidote to the poison of a facile success could ever have been decreed. And it was such an advance, such a real step up for him as well. Eagerly she went to the window again.

When he arrived she could not contain herself to wait but ran to meet him in the hall.

"Andrew! I've got a message for you from Sir Robert Abbey. He's just been on the telephone."

"Yes?" His face which had drawn into sudden compunction at the sight of her, cleared.

"Yes! He rang up himself, wanted to speak to you. I told him who I was—oh! he was terribly nice—oh—oh! I'm telling you so badly. Darling! You're to be appointed to out-patients at the Victoria Hospital —immediately!"

His eyes filled slowly with excited realisation.

"Why—that's good news, Chris."

"Isn't it, isn't it," she cried, delighted. "Your own work again— chances for research—everything you wanted on the Fatigue Board and didn't get——" She put her arms round his neck and hugged him.

He looked down at her, indescribably touched by her love, her generous unselfishness. He had a momentary pang.

"What a good soul you are, Chris! And—and what a lout I am!"

VIII

Upon the fourteenth of the following month, Andrew began his duties in the out-patients department of the Victoria Chest Hospital. His days were Tuesdays and Thursdays, the hours from three until five o'clock in the afternoon. It was exactly like his old surgery days in Aberalaw except that now all the cases which came to him were specialised lung and bronchial conditions. And he was, of course, to his great and secret pride, no longer a medical aid assistant but an honorary physician in one of the oldest and most famous hospitals in London.

The Victoria Hospital was unquestionably old. Situated in Battersea in a network of mean streets close to the Thames, it seldom caught, even in summer, more than a stray gleam of sunshine, while in winter its balconies, on to which the patients' beds were intended to be wheeled, were more often than not blanketed in river fog. Upon the gloomy, dilapidated façade was a great placard in red and white, which seemed obvious and redundant. VICTORIA HOSPITAL IS FALLING DOWN.

The out-patients department where Andrew found himself was, in part, a relic of the eighteenth century. Indeed, a pestle and mortar used by Doctor Lintel Hodges, honorary physician to the same section of the hospital from 1761 to 1793, was proudly exhibited in a glass case in the entrance hall. The untiled walls were painted a peculiar shade of dark chocolate, the uneven passages, though scrupulously clean, were so ill-ventilated that they sweated, and throughout all the rooms there hung the musty odour of sheer old age.

On his first day, he went round with Doctor Eustace Thoroughgood, the senior honorary, an elderly, pleasantly precise man of fifty, well under the middle height, with a small grey imperial and kindly manner, rather like an agreeable churchwarden. Doctor Thoroughgood had his own wards in the hospital and under the existing system, a survival of old tradition—in which he was interestingly erudite—he was "responsible" for Andrew and for Doctor Milligan, the other junior honorary.

After their tour of the hospital he took Andrew to the long basement common-room where, although it was barely four o'clock, the lights were already on. A fine fire blazed in the steel grate and on the linenfold walls there hung portraits of distinguished physicians to the hospital—Doctor Lintel Hodges, very pursy in his wig, in the place of honour above the mantelpiece. It was a perfect survival of a venerable and spacious past and from the delicate dilation of his nostrils Doctor Thoroughgood—bachelor and churchwarden though he was—loved it as his own child.

They had a pleasant tea and much hot buttered toast with the other members of the staff. Andrew thought the house physicians very likeable youngsters. Yet as he noted their deference to Doctor Thoroughgood and himself he could not refrain from smiling at the recollection of his clashes with other "insolent pups," not so many months ago, in the frequent struggles to get his patients into hospital.

Seated next to him was a young man, Doctor Vallance, who had spent twelve months studying under the Mayo Brothers in the United States. Andrew and he began to talk about the famous Clinic and its system, then Andrew, with sudden interest, asked him if he had heard of Stillman while he was in America.

"Yes, of course," said Vallance. "They think a lot of him out there. He had no diploma of course, but unofficially they more or less recognise him now. He gets the most amazing results."

"Have you seen his clinic?"

"No," Vallance shook his head. "I didn't get as far as Oregon."

Andrew paused for a moment, wondering if he should speak. "I believe it's a most remarkable place," he said at length. "I happen to have been in touch with Stillman over a period of years—he first wrote me about a paper which I published in the *American Journal of Hygiene*. I've seen photographs and details of his clinic. One couldn't wish for a more ideal place to treat one's cases. High up, in the centre of a pine wood, isolated, glassed balconies, a special air-conditioning system to ensure perfect purity and constant temperature in winter." Andrew broke off, deprecating his own enthusiasm, or a break in the general conversation made everything he said audible to the entire table. "When one thinks of our conditions in London, it seems an unattainable idea."

Doctor Thoroughgood smiled with dry asperity.

"Our London physicians have always managed to get along very well in these same London conditions, Doctor Manson. We may not have the exotic devices of which you speak. But I venture to suggest that our solid, well-tried methods—though less spectacular—bring equally satisfactory and probably more lasting results."

Andrew, keeping his eyes lowered, did not answer. He felt that as a new member of the staff he had been indiscreet in voicing his opinion so openly. And Doctor Thoroughgood, to show that he had intended no snub, went on very pleasantly to turn the conversation. He talked about the art of cupping. The history of medicine had long been his special hobby and he had a mass of information on the subject of the surgeon-barbers of ancient London.

As they rose he declared agreeably to Andrew:

"I actually have an authentic set of cups. I must show you them one day. It really is a shame cupping has gone out. It was—still is—an admirable way of inducing counter-irritation."

Beyond that first slight breeze, Doctor Thoroughgood set himself out to be a sympathetic and helpful colleague. He was a sound physician, an almost unerring diagnostician, and he was always glad to have Andrew round his wards. But in treatment, his tidy mind resented the intrusion of the new. He would have nothing to do with tuberculin, holding that its therapeutic value was still completely unproved. He was chary of using pneumothorax and his percentage of inductions was the lowest in the hospital. He was, however, extremely liberal in the matter of cod-liver oil and malt. He prescribed it for all his patients.

Andrew forgot about Thoroughgood in beginning his own work. It was wonderful, he told himself, after months of waiting, to find himself starting again. He gave, at the outset, quite a good imitation of his old ardour and enthusiasm.

Inevitably his past work on the tubercular lesions induced by dust inhalation had brought him forward to the consideration of pulmonary tuberculosis as a whole. He planned vaguely, in conjunction with the Von Pirquet test, to investigate the earliest physical signs of the primary lesion. He had a wealth of material available in the undernourished children brought by their mothers in the hope of benefiting in Doctor Thoroughgood's well-known liberality with extract of malt.

And yet, though he tried very hard to convince himself, his heart was not in the work. He could not recapture the spontaneous enthusiasm of his inhalation investigations. He had far too much upon his mind, too many important cases in his practice, to be able to concentrate upon obscure signs which might not even exist. No one knew better than he how long it took to examine a case properly. And he was always in a hurry. This argument was unanswerable. Soon he fell into an attitude of admirable logic—humanly speaking, he simply could not do it.

The poor people who came to the dispensary did not demand much of him. His predecessor had, it appeared, been something of a bully and so long as he prescribed generously and made an occasional joke his popularity was never in doubt. He got on, well, too, with Doctor Milligan, his opposite number, and it was not long before he found himself adopting Milligan's method of dealing with the regular patients. He would have them up, in a bunch, to his desk at the beginning of dispensary and rapidly initial their cards. As he scribbled Rep. Mist.— the mixture as before—he had no time to recollect how he had once derided this classic phrase. He was well on the way to being an admirable honorary physician.

IX

Six weeks after he had taken over at the Victoria, as he sat at breakfast with Christine, he opened a letter which bore the Marseilles postmark. Gazing at it unbelievingly for a moment, he gave a sudden exclamation:

"It's from Denny! He's sick of Mexico at last! Coming back to settle down, he says—I'll believe that when I see it! But, Lord! It'll be good to see him again. How long has he been away? It seems ages. He's coming home via China. Have you got the paper there, Chris? Look up when the *Oreta* gets in."

She was as pleased as he at the unexpected news, but for a rather different reason. There was a strong maternal strain in Christine, a queer calvinistic protectiveness towards her husband. She had always recognised that Denny, and indeed, in a lesser degree, Hope, exerted a beneficial effect upon him. Now, especially, when he seemed changing, she was more anxiously alert. No sooner had this letter arrived than her mind was at work planning a meeting which would bring these three together.

The day before the *Oreta* was due at Tilbury she broached the matter.

"I wonder if you'd mind, Andrew—I thought I might give a little dinner next week—just for you and Denny and Hope."

He gazed at her in some surprise. In view of the vague undercurrent of constraint between them it was strange to hear her talk of entertaining. He answered:

"Hope's probably at Cambridge. And Denny and I might as well go out somewhere." Then, seeing her face, he relented quickly. "Oh! All right. Make it Sunday though; that's the best night for all of us."

On the following Sunday Denny arrived, stockier and more brick-red of face and neck than ever. He looked older, seemed less morose, more contented in his manner. Yet he was the same Denny, his greeting to them being:

"This is a very grand house. Sure I haven't made a mistake." Half turning gravely to Christine. "This well-dressed gentleman *is* Doctor Manson, isn't he? If I'd known I'd have brought him a canary."

Seated, a moment later, he refused a drink.

"No! I'm a regular limejuicer now. Strange as it may seem I'm going to set to and get a real pull on the collar. I've had about enough of the wide and starry sky. Best way to get to like this blamed country is to go abroad."

Andrew considered him with affectionate reproof.

"You really ought to settle down, you know, Philip," he said. "After all you're on the right side of forty. And with your talents——"

Denny shot him an odd glance from beneath his brows.

"Don't be so smug, Professor. I may still show you a few tricks one of these days."

He told them he had been lucky enough to be appointed Surgical Registrar of the South Hertfordshire Infirmary, three hundred a year and all found. He did not consider it a permanency, of course, but there was a considerable amount of operative work to be done there and he would be able to refresh his surgical technique. After that he would see what could be done.

"Don't know how they gave me the job," he argued. "It must be another case of mistaken identity."

"No," said Andrew rather stolidly, "it's your M.S., Philip. A first class degree like that will get you anywhere."

"What have you been doing to him?" Denny groaned. "He don't sound like the bloke what blew up that sewer with me."

At this point Hope arrived. He had not met Denny before. But five minutes was enough for them to understand one another. At the end of that time, as they went in to dinner, they were agreeably united in being rude to Manson.

"Of course, Hope," Philip sadly remarked as he unfolded his napkin. "You needn't expect much food here. Oh, no! I've known these people a long time. Knew the Professor before he turned into a woolly Westender. They were thrown out their last home for starving their guineapigs."

"I usually carry a rasher in my pocket," said Hope. "It's a habit I acquired from Billy Buttons on the last Kitchengunga expedition. But unfortunately I'm out of eggs. Mother's hens are not laying at the moment."

There was more of this as the meal went on—Hope's facetiousness seemed especially provoked by Denny's presence—but gradually they settled down to talk. Denny related some of his experiences in the Southern States—he had one or two negro stories which made Christine laugh—and Hope detailed for them the latest activities of the Board. Whinney had at last succeeded in steering his long contemplated muscular fatigue experiments into action.

"That's what I'm doing now," Hope gloomed. "But thank heaven my scholarship has only another nine months to run. Then I'm going to *do* something. I'm tired of working out other people's ideas, having old men stand over me"—his tone dropped into ribald mimicry—" 'how much sarcolactic acid did you find for me this time, Mr. Hope?' I want to do something for myself. I wish to God I had a little lab. of my own!"

Then, as Christine had hoped, the talk became violently medical. After dinner—despite Denny's melancholy prognostication, they had stripped a brace of ducks—when coffee was brought in, she pleaded to remain. And though Hope assured her that the language would not be ladylike she sat, her elbows on the table, chin upon her hands, listening silently, forgotten, her eyes fixed earnestly on Andrew's face.

At first he had appeared stiff and reserved. Though it was a joy to see Philip again he had the feeling that his old friend was a little casual towards his success, unappreciative, even mildly derisive. After all, he had done pretty well for himself, hadn't he? And what had Denny— yes, what had Denny done? When Hope chipped in with his attempts of humour he had almost told them, pretty sharply, to stop being funny at his expense.

Yet now that they were talking shop he was drawn into it unconsciously. Momentarily, whether he wished it or not, he caught the infection from the other two and with not a bad copy of his old rapture, he made himself heard.

They were discussing hospitals which caused him suddenly to express himself upon the whole hospital system.

"The way I look at it is this." He took a long breath of smoke—it was not now a cheap virginian cigarette but a cigar, from the box which he had, braving the devil in Denny's eye, self-consciously produced— "the whole layout is obsolete. Mind you, I wouldn't for anything have you think I'm knocking my own hospital. I love it down there at the Victoria and I can tell you we do great work. But it's the system. Nobody but the good old apathetic B.P. would put up with it—like our roads, for instance, a hopeless out-of-date chaos. The Victoria is falling down. So is St. John's—half the hospitals in London are shrieking that they're falling down! And what are we doing about it? Collecting pennies. Getting a few quid out of the advertisement hoardings we stick up on our frontage. *Brown's Beer is Best.* Isn't that sweet! At the Victoria, if we're lucky, in ten years' time, we'll start to build a new wing, or a nurses' home—incidentally you should see where the nurses *sleep*! But what's the use of patching up the old carcase. What *is* the use of a lung

676

hospital in the centre of a noisy foggy city like London?—damn it all, it's like taking a pneumonia down a coal-mine. And it's the same with most of the other hospitals, *and* the nursing-homes, too. They're bang in the middle of roaring traffic, foundations shaken by the Underground, even the patients' beds rattle when the buses go past. If I went in there, *healthy*, I'd want ten grains of barbitone every night to get to sleep. Think of patients lying in that racket after a serious abdominal, or running a temperature of a hundred and four with meningitis."

"Well, what's the remedy?" Philip lifted an eyebrow in that new irritating fashion. "A joint hospitals' board with you as director in chief?"

"Don't be an ass, Denny," Andrew answered irritably. "Decentralisation is the remedy. No, that isn't just a word out of a book, it's the result of all that I've gone through since I came to London. Why shouldn't our big hospitals stand in a green belt outside London, say fifteen miles outside. Take a place like Benham, for instance, only ten miles out, where there's still green country, fresh air, quiet. Don't think there would be any transportation difficulties. The tube—and why not a specially run hospital service—one straight, silent line, could take you out to Benham in exactly eighteen minutes. Considering that it takes our fastest ambulance forty minutes on the average to bring in an emergency, that sounds to me an improvement. You might say if we moved the hospitals we'd denude each area of its medical service. That's rot! The dispensary stops in the area, the hospital moves on. And while we're talking about it this question of area service is just one large hopeless muddle. When I came here at first, I found here in *West* London that the only place I could get my patient in was the *East* London hospital. Down at the Victoria too, we get patients from all over the shop—Kensington, Ealing, Muswell Hill. There's no attempt to delimit special areas—everything comes pouring in to the centre of the city. I'm telling you fellows straight, the confusion is often unbelievable. And what's being done? Zero, absolute zero. We just drag on in the old, old way, rattling tin boxes, holding flag days, making appeals, letting students clown for pennies in fancy dress. One thing about these new European countries—they get things *done*. Lord, if I had my way I'd raze the Victoria flat and have a new Chest Hospital setting out at Benham with a straight line of communication. And by God! I'd show a rise in our recovery rate!"

This was merely by way of introduction. The crescendo of discussion rose.

Philip got on to his old contention—the folly of asking the general practitioner to pull everything out of the one black bag, the stupidity of making him carry every case on his shoulders until that delightful moment when, for five guineas, some specialist he had never seen before drove up to tell him it was too late to carry anything at all.

Hope, without mildness or restraint, expressed the case of the young bacteriologist, sandwiched between commercialism and conservatism—on the one hand, the bland firm of chemists who would pay him a wage to make proprietary articles, on the other a Board of blithering dotards.

"Can you imagine," Hope hissed, "the Marx brothers sitting in a rickety motor-car with four independent steering wheels and an unlimited supply of motor-horns. That's us at the M.F.B."

They did not stop until after twelve o'clock and then, unexpectedly, they found sandwiches and coffee before them on the table.

"Oh, I say, Mrs. Manson," Hope protested with a politeness which showed that, in Denny's gibe, he was a Nice Young Man at Heart. "We must have bored you stiff. Funny how hungry talking makes one. I'll suggest that to Whinney as a new line of investigation—effect upon the gastric secretions of hot-air fatigue. Ha! Ha! That's a perfect Nag-ism!"

When Hope had gone, with fervent protestations that he had enjoyed the evening, Denny remained a few minutes longer, exacting the privilege of his older friendship. Then, Andrew having left the room to ring for a taxi, he apologetically brought out a small, very beautiful Spanish shawl.

"The Professor will probably slay me," he said. "But this is for you. Don't tell him till I'm safely out of the way." He arrested her gratitude, always for him the most embarrassing emotion. "Extraordinary how all these shawls come from China. They're not really Spanish. I got that one via Shanghai."

A silence fell. They could hear Andrew coming back from the telephone in the hall.

Denny got up, his kind, wrinkled eyes avoiding hers.

"I wouldn't worry too much about him, you know." He smiled. "But we must try, mustn't we, to get him back to Drineffy standards."

X

At the beginning of the Easter school holidays Andrew received a note from Mrs. Thornton asking him to call at Brown's Hotel to see her daughter. She told him briefly, in the letter, that Sybil's foot had not improved and, since she had been much struck by his interest at Mrs. Lawrence's she was anxious to have his advice. Flattered by this tribute to his personality, he made the visit promptly.

The condition which he found upon examination was perfectly simple. Yet it was one which demanded an early operation. He straightened himself, with a smile to the solid, bare-legged Sybil now seated upon the edge of the bed, pulling on her long black stocking, and explained this to Mrs. Thornton.

"The bone has thickened. Might develop into a hammer toe if it's left untreated. I suggest you have it seen to at once."

"That's what the school doctor said." Mrs. Thornton was not surprised. "We are really prepared. Sybil can go into a home here. But—well!—I've got confidence in you, doctor. And I want you to undertake all the arrangements. Whom do you suggest should do it?"

The direct question placed Andrew in a dilemma. His work being almost entirely medical he had met many of the leading physicians, yet he knew none of the London surgeons. Suddenly he thought of Ivory. He said pleasantly:

"Mr. Ivory might do this for us—if he's available."

Mrs. Thornton had heard of Mr. Ivory. Of course! Wasn't he the surgeon who had been in all the newspapers the month before through having flown to Cairo to attend a case of sunstroke. An extremely well-known man! She thought it an admirable suggestion that he should undertake her daughter's case. Her only stipulation was that Sybil should go to Miss Sherrington's Home. So many of her friends had been there she could not think of letting her go anywhere else.

Andrew went home and rang up Ivory, with all the hesitation of a man making a preliminary approach. But Ivory's manner—friendly, confident, charming—reassured him. They arranged to see the case together on the following day and Ivory asserted that though he knew Ida to be bunged up to the attics, he could persuade her to make room for Miss Thornton should this be necessary.

Next morning, when Ivory had agreed emphatically in Mrs. Thornton's presence with all that Andrew had said—adding that immediate operation was imperative—Sybil was transferred to Miss Sherrington's Home and two days later, giving her time to settle down, the operation was performed.

Andrew was there. Ivory insisted that he be present, in the most genuine and friendly fashion imaginable.

The operation was not difficult—indeed in his Drineffy days Andrew would have tackled it himself—and Ivory, though he seemed disinclined to speed, accomplished it with imposing competence. He made a strong cool figure in his big white gown above which his face showed firm, massive, dominant jawed. No one more completely resembled the popular conception of the great surgeon than Charles Ivory. He had the fine supple hands with which popular fiction always endows the hero of the operating theatre. In his handsomeness and assurance he was dramatically impressive. Andrew, who had himself slipped on a gown, watched him from the other side of the table with grudging respect.

A fortnight later, when Sybil Thornton had left the home, Ivory asked him to lunch at the Sackville Club. It was a pleasant meal. Ivory was a perfect conversationalist, easy and entertaining, with a fund of up-to-the-minute gossip, which somehow placed his companion on the same intimate, man-of-the-world footing as himself. The high dining-room of the Sackville, with its Adam ceilings and rock crystal chandeliers, was full of famous—Ivory named them amusing—people. Andrew found the experience flattering, as no doubt Ivory intended it should be.

"You must let me put your name up at the next meeting," the surgeon remarked. "You'd find a lot of friends here, Freddie, Paul, myself— by the way, Jackie Lawrence is a member. Interesting marriage that, they're perfect good friends and they each go their own way! Honestly, I'd love to put you up. I've rather felt, you know, that you've just been a shade suspicious of me, old fellow. Your Scottish caution, eh? As you know I don't visit any of the hospitals. That's because I prefer to freelance. Besides, my dear boy, I'm too *busy*. Some of these hospital fogies don't have one private case a month. I average ten a week! By the by, we'll be hearing from the Thorntons presently. You leave all that to me. They're first class people. And incidentally, while I speak of it, don't you think Sybil ought to have her tonsils seen to. Did you look at them?"

"No—no, I didn't."

"Oh, you ought to have done, my boy. Absolutely pocketed, no end of septic absorption. I took the liberty—hope you don't mind—of saying we might do them for her when the warm weather comes in!"

On his way home Andrew could not help reflecting what a charming fellow Ivory had turned out to be—actually, he ought to be grateful to Hamson for the introduction. This case had passed off superbly. The Thorntons were particularly pleased. Surely there could be no better criterion.

Three weeks later, as he sat at tea with Christine, the afternoon post brought him a letter from Ivory.

My dear Manson,

Mrs. Thornton has just come nicely to scratch. As I am sending the anæsthetist his bit I may as well send you yours—for assisting me so splendidly at the operation. Sybil will be coming to see you at the end of this term. You remember those tonsils I mentioned. Mrs. Thornton is delighted.

Ever cordially yours,

C. I.

Enclosed was a cheque for twenty guineas.

Andrew stared at the cheque in astonishment—he had done nothing to assist Ivory at the operation—then gradually the warm feeling which money always gave him now stole round his heart. With a complacent smile he handed over the letter and the cheque for Christine's inspection.

"Damned decent of Ivory, isn't it, Chris? I bet we'll have a record in our receipts this month."

"But I don't understand." Her expression was perplexed. "Is this your bill to Mrs. Thornton?"

"No—silly," he chuckled. "It's a little extra—merely for the time I gave up to the operation."

"You mean Mr. Ivory is giving you part of his fee."

He flushed, suddenly up in arms.

"Good Lord, no! That's absolutely forbidden. We wouldn't dream of that. Don't you see I earned this fee for assisting, for being *there*, just as the anæsthetist earned his fee for giving the anæsthetic. Ivory sends it all in with his bill. And I'll bet it was a bumper."

She laid the cheque upon the table, subdued, unhappy.

"It seems a great deal of money."

"Well, why not?" He closed the argument in a blaze of indignation. "The Thorntons are tremendously rich. This is probably no more to them than three and six to one of our surgery patients."

When he had gone, her eyes remained fastened upon the cheque with strained apprehension. She had not realised that he had associated himself professionally with Ivory. Suddenly all her former uneasiness swept back over her. That evening with Denny and Hope might never have taken place for all its effect upon him. How fond he now was, how terribly fond, of money. His work at the Victoria seemed not to matter beside this devouring desire for material success. Even in the surgery she had observed that he was using more and more stock mixtures, prescribing for people who had nothing wrong with them, urging them to call and call again. The worried look deepened upon her face, making it pinched and small, as she sat there, confronted by Charles Ivory's cheque. Tears welled slowly to her eyes. She must speak to him, oh, she must, she must.

That evening, after surgery, she approached him diffidently. "Andrew, would you do something to please me? Would you take me out to the country on Sunday in the car? You promised me when you got it. And of course—all winter we haven't been able to go."

He glanced at her queerly.

"Well—oh! all right."

Sunday came fine, as she had hoped, a soft spring day. By eleven o'clock he had done what visits were essential and with a rug and a picnic basket in the back of the car they set off. Christine's spirits lifted as they ran across Hammersmith Bridge and took the Kingston By-Pass for Surrey. Soon they were through Dorking, turning to the right on the road to Shere. It was so long since they had been together in the country that the sweetness of it, the vivid green of the fields, the purple of the budding elms, the golden dust of drooping catkins, the paler yellow of primroses clumped beneath a bank, suffused her being, intoxicating her.

"Don't drive so fast, dear," she murmured in a tone softer than she had used for weeks. "It's so lovely here." He seemed intent upon passing every car upon the road.

Towards one o'clock they reached Shere. The village, with its few red roofed cottages and its stream quietly wandering amongst the watercress beds, was as yet untroubled by the rush of summer tourists. They reached the wooded hill beyond, and parked the car near one of the close turfed bridle paths. There, in the little clearing where they spread the rug, was a singing solitude which belonged only to them and the birds.

They ate sandwiches in the sunshine, drank the coffee from the thermos. Around them, in the alder clumps, the promroses grew in great profusion. Christine longed to gather them, to bury her face in their cool softness. Andrew lay with half closed eyes, his head resting near her. A sweet tranquillity settled upon the dark uneasiness of her soul. If their life together could always be like this!

His drowsy gaze had for some moments been resting on the car and suddenly he said:

"Not a bad old bus, is she, Chris?—I mean, for what she cost us. But we shall want a new one at the Show."

She stirred—her disquiet renewed by this fresh instance of his restless striving. "But we haven't had her any time. She seems to me all that we could wish for."

"Hum! She's sluggish. Didn't you notice how that Buick kept ahead of us. I want one of these new Vitesse saloons."

"But why?"

"Why not? We can afford it. We're getting on, you know, Chris. Yes!" He lit a cigarette and turned to her with every sign of satisfaction. "In case you may not be aware of the fact, my dear little schoolmarm from Drineffy, we are rapidly getting rich."

She did not answer his smile. She felt her body, peaceful and warm in the sunshine, chill suddenly. She began to pick at a tuft of grass, to twine it foolishly with a tassel of the rug. She said slowly:

"Dear, do we really want to be rich? I know I don't! Why all this talk about money? When we had scarcely any we were—oh! we were deliriously happy. We never talked of it then. But now we never talk of anything else."

He smiled again, in a superior manner.

"After years of tramping about in slush, eating sausage and soused herrings, taking dog's abuse from pigheaded committees, and attending miners' wifes in dirty back bedrooms, I propose, for a change, to ameliorate our lot. Any objections?"

"Don't make a joke of it, darling. You usen't to talk that way. Oh! Don't you see, don't you see, you're falling a victim to the very system you used to run down, the thing you used to hate." Her face was pitiful in its agitation. "Don't you remember how you used to speak of life, that it was an attack on the unknown, an assault uphill—as though you had to take some castle that you knew was there, but couldn't see, on the top——"

He muttered uncomfortably.

"Oh! I was young then—foolish. That was just romantic talk. You look round, you'll see that everybody's doing the same thing—getting together as much as they can! It's the only thing to do."

She took a shaky breath. She knew that she must speak now or not at all.

"Darling! It isn't the only thing. Please listen to me. Please! I've been so unhappy at this—the change in you. Denny saw it too. It's dragging us away from one another. You're not the Andrew Manson I married. Oh! If only you'd be as you used to be."

"What have I done?" he protested irritably. "Do I beat you, do I get drunk, do I commit murder? Give me one example of my *crimes*."

Desperately, she replied:

"It isn't the obvious things, it's your whole attitude, darling. Take that cheque Ivory sent you, for instance. It's a small matter on the surface perhaps, but underneath—oh, if you take it underneath it's cheap and grasping and dishonest."

She felt him stiffen, then he sat up, offended, glaring at her!

"For God's sake! Why bring that up again. What's wrong with my taking it?"

"Can't you see?" All the accumulated emotion of the past months overwhelmed her, stifling her arguments, causing her suddenly to burst into tears. She cried hysterically, "For God's sake, darling. Don't, don't sell yourself!"

He ground his teeth, furious with her. He spoke slowly, with cutting deliberation.

"For the last time! I warn you to stop making a neurotic fool of yourself. Can't you try to be a help to me, instead of a hindrance, nagging me every minute of the day!"

"I haven't nagged you." She sobbed. "I've wanted to speak before, but I haven't."

"Then don't." He lost his temper and suddenly shouted. "Do you hear me. *Don't*. It's some complex you've got. You talk as if I was some kind of dirty crook. I only want to get on. And if I want money it's only a means to an end. People judge you by what you are, what you have. If you're one of the have nots you get ordered about. Well, I've had enough of that in my time. In future I'm going to do the ordering. Now do you understand. Don't even mention this damned nonsense to me again."

"All right, all right," she wept. "I won't. But I tell you—some day you'll be sorry."

The excursion was ruined for them, and most of all for her. Though

683

she dried her eyes and gathered a large bunch of primroses, though they spent another hour on the sunny slope and stopped on the way down at the Lavender Lady for tea, though they spoke, in apparent amity, of ordinary things, all the rapture of the day was dead. Her face, as they drove through the early darkness, was pale and stiff.

His anger turned gradually to indignation. Why should Chris of all people set upon him! Other women, and charming women too, were enthusiastic at his rapid rise.

A few days later Frances Lawrence rang him up. She had been away, spending the winter in Jamaica—he had several times in the past two months had letters from the Myrtle Bank Hotel—but now she was back, eager to see her friends, radiating the sunshine she had absorbed. She told him gaily she wanted him to see her before she lost her sunburn.

He went round to tea. As she had inferred, she was beautifully tanned, her hands and slender wrists, her spare interrogative face stained as a faun's. The pleasure of seeing her again was intensified extraordinarily by the welcome in her eyes, those eyes which were indifferent to so many persons and which were, with their high points of light, so friendly to him.

Yes, they talked as old friends. She told him of her trip, of the coral gardens, the fishes seen through the glass-bottomed boats, of the heavenly climate. He gave her, in return, an account of his progress. Perhaps some indication of his thoughts crept into his words for she answered lightly:

"You're frightfully solemn and disgracefully prosy. That's what happens to you when I'm away. No! Frankly I think it's because you're doing too much. *Must* you keep on with all this surgery work? For my part I should have thought it time for you to take a room up West—Wimpole Street or Welbeck Street for instance—and do your consulting there."

At this point her husband entered, tall, lounging, mannered. He nodded to Andrew, whom he now knew fairly well—they had once or twice played bridge at the Sackville Club—and gracefully accepted a cup of tea.

Though he protested cheerfully that he would not for anything disturb them, Lawrence's entrance interrupted the serious turn of the conversation. They began to discuss, with considerable amusement, the latest junketing of Rumbold-Blane.

But half an hour later, as Andrew drove back to Chesborough Terrace, Mrs. Lawrence's suggestion firmly occupied his mind. Why shouldn't he take a consulting-room in Welbeck Street? The time was clearly ripe for it. He wouldn't give up anything of his Paddington practice—the surgery was far too profitable a concern to abandon lightly. But he could easily combine it with a room up West, use the better address for his correspondence, have the heading on his notepaper, his bills.

The thought sparkled within him, nerved him to greater conquest.

What a good sort Frances was, just as helpful as Miss Everett and infinitely more charming, more exciting! Yet he was on excellent terms with her husband. He could meet his eye steadily. He needn't come skulking out of the house like some low boudoir hound. Oh! friendship was a great thing!

Without saying anything to Christine he began to look for a convenient consulting-room up West. And when he found one, about a month later, it gave him great satisfaction to declare in assumed indifference, over the morning paper:

"By the way—you might care to know—I've taken a place in Welbeck Street now. I shall use it for my better-class consultations."

XI

THE ROOM at 57a Welbeck Street gave Andrew a new surge of triumph —I'm there, he secretly exulted, I'm there at last! Though not large, the room was well lit by a bay window and situated on the ground floor, a distinct advantage, since most patients hated to climb stairs. Moreover, although he shared the waiting-room with several other consultants whose neat plates shone beside his own on the front door, this consulting-room was exclusively his own.

On the 19th of April when the lease was signed, Hamson accompanied him as he went round to take possession. Freddie had proved extraordinarily helpful in all the preliminaries and had found him a useful nurse, a friend of the woman whom he employed at Queen Anne Street. Nurse Sharp was not beautiful. She was middle-aged, with a sour, vaguely ill-used, yet capable expression. Freddie explained Nurse Sharp concisely:

"The last thing a fellow wants is a pretty nurse. You know what I mean, old man. Fun is fun. But business is business. And you can't combine the two. We none of us are in this for our health. As a damned hard-headed fellow you'll appreciate that. As a matter of fact I've got a notion you and I are going to come pretty close together now you've moved alongside me."

While Freddie and he stood discussing the arrangement of the room, Mrs. Lawrence unexpectedly appeared. She had been passing and came in, gaily, to investigate his choice. She had an attractive way of turning up casually, of never appearing to obtrude herself. To-day she was especially charming in a black coat and skirt with a necklet of rich brown fur about her throat. She did not stay long but she had ideas, suggestions for decoration, for the window hangings and the curtains behind his desk, far more tasteful than the crude plannings of Freddie and himself.

Bereft of her vivacious presence the room was suddenly empty. Freddie gushed:

"You're a lucky devil, if ever I met one. She's a nice thing." He grinned enviously. "What did Gladstone say in eighteen-ninety about the surest way to advance a man's career."

"I don't know what you're driving at."

Nevertheless when his room was finished he had to agree with Freddie and with Frances, who arrived to view her completed scheme, that it struck exactly the right note—advanced yet professionally correct. Consultations in these surroundings made three guineas seem a right and reasonable fee.

He had not many patients at the start. But by dint of writing politely to every doctor who sent him cases to the Chest Hospital—letters relating, naturally, to these hospital cases and their symptoms—he soon had a network of filaments reaching out all over London which began to bring private patients to his door. He was a busy man these days, dashing in his new Vitesse saloon between Chesborough Terrace and the Victoria, between the Victoria and Welbeck Street, with a full round of visits in addition and always his packed surgery, often running as late as ten o'clock at night.

The tonic of success braced him for everything, tingled through his veins like a gorgeous elixir. He found time to run round to Rogers to order another three suits, then to a shirtmaker in Jermyn Street, Hamson had recommended. His popularity at the hospital was increasing. True, he had less time to devote to his work in the outpatient department, but he told himself that what he sacrificed in time he made up in expertness. Even to his friends he developed a speedy brusqueness, rather taking, with his ready smile: "I must go, old fellow, simply rushed off my legs."

One Friday afternoon five weeks after his installation at Welbeck Street an elderly woman came to consult him about her throat. Her condition was no more than a simple laryngitis but she was a querulous little person and she seemed anxious for a second opinion. Mildly injured in his pride, Andrew reflected to whom he should send her. It was ridiculous to think of her wasting the time of a man like Sir Robert Abbey. Suddenly his face cleared as he thought of Hamson round the corner. Freddie had been extremely kind to him lately. He might as well "pick up" the three guineas as some ungrateful stranger. Andrew sent her along with a note to Freddie.

Three quarters of an hour later she came back, in quite a different humour, soothed and apologetic, satisfied with herself, with Freddie and—most of all—with him.

"Excuse me for coming back, doctor. I only wanted to thank you for the trouble you've taken with me. I saw Doctor Hamson and he confirmed everything you said. And he—he told me the prescription you gave me simply couldn't be improved on."

In June Sybil Thornton's tonsils came out. They were, to a certain extent, enlarged, and lately, in the *Journal*, suspicion had been thrown upon tonsillar absorption in its bearing upon the etiology of rheumatism. Ivory did the enucleation with tedious care.

"I prefer to go slow with these lymphoid tissues," he said to Andrew as they washed up. "I daresay you've seen people whip them out. *I* don't work that way."

When Andrew received his cheque from Ivory—again it came by post—Freddie was with him. They were frequently in and out of each other's consulting-rooms. Hamson had promptly returned the ball by sending Andrew a nice gastritis in return for the laryngitis case. By this time, in fact, several patients had found their way, with notes, between Welbeck and Queen Anne Streets.

"You know, Manson," Freddie now remarked. "I'm glad you've chucked your old dog-in-the-manger, holy-willy attitude. Even now, you know," he squinted across Andrew's shoulder at the cheque, "you're not getting all the juice out of the orange. You hang in with me, my lad, and you'll find your fruit more succulent."

Andrew had to laugh.

That evening, as he drove home, he was in an unusually lighthearted mood. Finding himself without cigarettes he drew up and dashed into a tobacconist's in Oxford Street. Here, as he came through the door he suddenly observed a woman loitering at an adjacent window. It was Blodwen Page.

Though he recognised her at once, she was sadly altered from the bustling mistress of Bryngower. No longer erect, her figure had a listless droop, and the eye which she turned upon him when he addressed her was apathetic, indifferent.

"It is Miss Page," he went up to her. "I ought to say Mrs. Rees now, I suppose. Don't you remember me? Doctor Manson."

She took him in, his well-dressed and prosperous air. She sighed:

"I remember you, doctor. I hope you're very well." Then, as though afraid to linger, she turned to where a few yards along the pavement a long bald-headed man impatiently awaited her. She concluded apprehensively, "I'll have to go now, doctor. My husband's waiting."

Andrew observed her hurry off, saw Rees's thin lips shape themselves to the rebuke: "What d'you mean—keeping me waiting!" while she submissively bent her head. For an instant he was conscious of the bank manager's cold eye directed blankly upon himself. Then the pair moved off and were lost in the crowd.

Andrew could not get the picture out of his head. When he reached Chesborough Terrace and entered the front room he found Christine

687

knitting there, with his tea—which she had rung for at the sound of his car—set out upon a tray. He glanced at her quickly, sounding her. He wanted to tell her of the incident, longed suddenly to end their period of strife. But when he had accepted a cup of tea, and before he could speak, she said quietly:

"Mrs. Lawrence rang you again this afternoon. No message."

"Oh!" He flushed. "How do you mean—again?"

"This is the fourth time she's rung you in a week."

"Well, what of it?"

"Nothing. I didn't say anything."

"It's how you look. Can *I* help it if she rings me."

She was silent, her eyes downcast, upon her knitting. If he had known the tumult in that still breast he would not have lost his temper as he did.

"You would think I was a bigamist the way you go on. She's a perfectly nice woman. Why, her husband is one of my best friends. They're charming people. They don't hang about looking like a sick pup. Oh, hell——"

He gulped down the rest of his tea and got up. Yet the moment he was out of the room he was sorry. He flung into the surgery, lit a cigarette, reflecting wretchedly that things were going from bad to worse between Christine and himself. And he did not want them to get worse. Their growing estrangement depressed and irritated him, it was the one dark cloud in the bright sky of his success.

Christine and he had been ideally happy in their married life. The unexpected meeting with Miss Page had brought back a rush of tender memories of his courtship in Drineffy. He did not idolise her as he once had done, but he was—oh, damn it all!—he was *fond* of her. Perhaps he had hurt her once or twice lately. As he stood there he had a sudden desire to make up with her, to please, propitiate her. He thought hard. Suddenly his eye brightened. He glanced at his watch, found that he had just half an hour before Laurier's closed. The next minute he was in his car on his way to interview Miss Cramb.

Miss Cramb, when he mentioned what he desired, was immediately and fervently at his service. They fell into serious conversation together, then walked into the fur department where various "skins" were modelled for Doctor Manson. Miss Cramb stroked them with expert fingers, pointing out the lustre, the silvering, all that one should look for in this special pelt. Once or twice she disagreed gently with his views, earnestly indicating what was *quality* and what was not! In the end he made a selection which she cordially approved. Then she departed in search of Mr. Winch and presently returned to state glowingly:

"Mr. Winch says you're to have them *at cost*." No such word as "wholesale" had ever sullied the lips of a Laurier employee. "That brings them out at fifty-five pounds and you can take it from me, doctor,

688

it's genuine value. They're beautiful skins, beautiful. Your wife will be proud to wear them."

On the following Saturday at eleven o'clock Andrew took the dark olive-green box, with the inimitable marque artistically scrawled upon its lid, and went into the drawing-room.

"Christine!" he called. "Here a moment!"

She was upstairs with Mrs. Bennett helping to make the beds but she came at once, slightly out of breath, her eyes wondering a little at his summons.

"Look, dear!" Now that the climax approached he felt an almost suffocating awkwardness. "I bought you this. I know—I know we haven't been getting on so well lately. But this ought to show you——" He broke off and, like a schoolboy, handed her the box.

She was very pale as she opened it. Her hands trembled upon the string. Then she gave a little overwhelmed cry:

"What lovely, lovely furs."

There, in the tissue paper, lay a double stole of silver fox, two exquisite skins shaped fashionably into one. Quickly he picked them up, smoothing them as Miss Cramb had done, his voice excited now.

"Do you like them, Chris? Try them on. The good old Half-Back helped me choose them. They're absolutely first-class quality. Couldn't have better. And value too. You see that sheen on them and the silver marking on the back—that's what you want specially to look for!"

Tears were running down her cheeks. She turned to him quite wildly.

"You do love me, don't you, darling? That's all that matters to me in the world."

Reassured at last, she tried on the furs. They were magnificent.

He could not admire them enough. He wanted to make the reconciliation complete. He smiled.

"Look here, Chris. We might as well have a little celebration while we're about it. We'll go out to lunch to-day. Meet me one o'clock at the Plaza Grill."

"Yes, darling," she half questioned. "Only—I've got some shepherd's pie for lunch to-day—that you used to like so much."

"No, no!" His laugh was gayer than it had been for months. "Don't be an old stay-at-home. One o'clock. Meet the dark handsome gentleman at the Plaza. You needn't wear a red carnation. He'll know you by the furs."

All morning he was in a mood of high satisfaction. Fool that he'd been!—neglecting Christine. All women liked to have attention paid to them, to be taken out, given a good time. The Plaza Grill was just the place—all London, or most of it that mattered, could be seen there between the hours of one and three.

Christine was late, an unusual occurrence which caused him to fret slightly, as he sat in the small lounge facing the glass partition watching all the best tables become quickly occupied. He ordered himself a second martini. It was twenty minutes past one when she came hurrying in, flustered by the noise, the people, the ornate flunkeys and the fact that, for the last half-hour, she had been standing in the wrong lounge.

"I'm so sorry, darling," she gasped. "I really did ask. I waited and waited. And then I found it was the restaurant lounge."

They were given a bad table wedged against a pillar beside the service. The place was grotesquely crowded, the tables so close together people seemed to be sitting on each other's laps. The waiters moved like contortionists. The heat was tropical. The din rose and fell like a transpontine college yell.

"Now, Chris, what would you like?" Andrew said determinedly.

"You order, darling," she answered faintly.

He ordered a rich, expensive lunch: caviare, soupe prince de Galles, poulet riche, asparagus, fraises de bois in syrup. Also a bottle of Liebfraumilch, 1929.

"We didn't know much about this in our Drineffy days." He laughed, determined to make merry. "Nothing like doing ourselves well, old girl."

Nobly she tried to respond to his mood. She praised the caviare, made an heroic effort with the rich soup. She pretended interest when he pointed out Glen Roscoe, the cinema star, Mavis Yorke, an American woman celebrated for her six husbands, and other cosmopolitans equally distinguished. The smart vulgarity of the place was hateful to her. The men were over-groomed, smooth and oiled. Every woman visible to her was a blonde, dressed in black, smart, made up, carelessly hard.

All at once Christine felt herself turn a little giddy. She began to lose her poise. Usually her manner was one of natural simplicity. But lately the strain upon her nerves had been great. She became conscious of the discrepancy between her new furs and her inexpensive dress. She felt other women staring at her. She knew she was as out of place here as a daisy in an orchid house.

"What's the matter?" he asked suddenly. "Aren't you enjoying yourself?"

"Yes, of course," she protested, wanly trying to smile. But her lips were stiff now. She could barely swallow, let alone taste, the heavily creamed chicken on her plate.

"You're not listening to a thing I say," he muttered resentfully. "You haven't even touched your wine. Damn it all, when a man takes his wife out——"

"Could I have a little water?" she asked feebly. She could have screamed. She didn't belong to a place like this. Her hair wasn't bleached, her face not made up, no wonder even the waiters watched her now. Nervously she lifted an asparagus stalk. As she did so the head broke and fell, dripping with sauce, on the new fur.

The metallic blonde at the next table turned to her companion with a smile of amusement. Andrew saw that smile. He gave up the attempt at entertainment. The meal ended in a dreary silence.

They went home more drearily. Then he departed, summarily, to do his calls. They were wider apart than before. The pain in Christine's heart was intolerable. She began to lose faith in herself, to ask herself if she was really the right wife for him. That night she put her arms round his neck and kissed him, thanking him again for the furs and for taking her out.

"Glad you enjoyed it," he said flatly. And went to his own room.

XII

At this point an event occurred which, for the time being, diverted Andrew's attention from his difficulties at home. He came upon a paragraph in the *Tribune*, which announced that Mr. Richard Stillman, the well-known health expert of Portland, U.S.A., had arrived on the *Imperial* and was staying at Brooks Hotel.

In the old days he would have rushed excitedly to Christine with the paper in his hand.

"Look here, Chris! Richard Stillman has come over. You remember —I corresponded with him all those months. I wonder if he'd see me—honestly—I'd love to meet him."

But now he had lost the habit of running to Christine. Instead he pondered maturely over the *Tribune*, glad that he could approach Stillman, not as a medical aid assistant, but with the standing of a Welbeck Street consultant. Methodically he typed a letter recalling himself to the American and asking him to lunch at the Plaza Grill on Wednesday.

The following morning Stillman rang him up. His voice was quiet, friendly, alertly efficient.

"Glad to be talking to you, Doctor Manson. I'd be pleased for us to lunch. But don't let's make it the Plaza. I hate that place already. Why don't you come here and lunch with me?"

Andrew found Stillman in the sitting-room of his suite at Brooks, a quietly select hotel which put the racket of the Plaza to shame. It was a hot day, the morning had been a rush, and at the first sight of his host Andrew almost wished he had not come. The American was about fifty, small and slight, with a disproportionately large head and an undershot jaw. His complexion was a boyish pink and white, his light coloured hair thin and parted in the middle. It was only when Andrew saw his eyes, pale, steady and glacially blue, that he realised—almost felt the impact of—the driving force behind this insignificant frame.

"Hope you didn't mind coming here," said Richard Stillman in the quiet manner of one to whom many had been glad to come. "I know we Americans are supposed to like the Plaza." He smiled, revealing himself human. "But it's a lousy crowd that goes there." He paused. "And now I've seen you, let me really congratulate you on that splendid inhalation paper. You didn't mind my telling you about serecite? What have you been doing lately?"

They descended to the restaurant, where the head of many waiters gave Stillman his attention.

"How about you? I'm going to have orange juice," Stillman said then, promptly, without looking at the long French menus, "and two mutton cutlets with peas. Then coffee."

Andrew gave his order and turned with increasing respect to his companion. It was impossible to remain in Stillman's presence long without acknowledging the compelling interest of his personality. His history, which Andrew knew in outline, was in itself unique.

Richard Stillman came of an old Massachusetts family which had, for generations, been connected with the law, in Boston. But young Stillman, despite this continuity, at the age of eighteen at last persuaded his father to allow him to begin his studies at Harvard. For two years he had followed the medical curriculum at this University, when his father died suddenly, leaving Richard, his mother, and his only sister in unexpectedly poor circumstances.

At this point, when some means of support had to be found for the family, old John Stillman, Richard's grandfather, insisted that his grandson should abandon his medical studies in favour of the family tradition of the law. Arguments proved useless—the old man was implacable—and Richard was forced to take, not the medical diploma he had hoped for, but after three tedious years, a legal degree. Then in 1906 he entered the family offices in Boston and for four years devoted himself to the law.

It was, however, a half-hearted devotion. Bacteriology, in particular, microbiology, had fascinated him from his earliest student days and in the attic of his Beacon Hill home he set up a small laboratory, took his clerk as assistant, and devoted every spare moment to the pursuit of his passion. This attic was in fact the beginning of the Stillman Institute. Richard was no amateur. On the contrary he displayed not only the highest technical skill but an originality amounting almost to genius. And when, in the winter of 1908 his sister Mary, to whom he was much attached, died of rapid consumption, he began the concentration of his forces against the tubercle bacillus. He picked up the early work of Pierre Louis and Louis's American disciple, James Jackson, jr. His examination of Laennec's life work on auscultation brought him to the physiological study of the lungs. He invented a new type of stethoscope. He commenced, with the limited apparatus at his disposal, his first attempts to produce a blood serum.

692

In the year 1910, when old John Stillman died, Richard had at last succeeded in curing tuberculosis in guinea-pigs. The results of this double event were immediate. Stillman's mother had all along sympathised with his scientific work. He needed little urging to dispose of the Boston law connection, and, with his inheritance from the old man's estate, to purchase a farm near Portland, Oregon, where he at once flung himself into the real business of his life.

So many valuable years had already been wasted he made no attempt to take a medical degree. He wanted progress, results. Soon he produced a serum from bay horses, succeeded with a bovine vaccine in the mass immunisation of a herd of Jersey cows. At the same time he was applying the fundamental observations of Helmholtz and Willard Gibbs of Yale, and of later physicists like Bisaillon and Zinks, to the treatment of the damaged lung through immobilisation. From this he launched straight into therapeutics.

His curative work at the new Institute soon brought him into prominence with triumphs greater than his laboratory victories. Many of his patients were ambulant consumptives, wandering from one sanatorium to another, reputably adjudged incurable. His success with these cases immediately earned for him disparagement, accusation and the determined antagonism of the medical profession.

There now began for Stillman a different and more protracted struggle, the battle for recognition of his work. He had sunk every dollar he possessed in establishing his Institute and the cost of maintaining it was heavy. He hated publicity and resisted all inducements to commercialise his work. Often it seemed as though mtaerial difficulties, allied to the bitterness of the opposition, must submerge him. Yet Stillman with magnificent courage survived every crisis—even a national newspaper campaign conducted against him.

The era of misrepresentation passed, the storm of controversy subsided. Gradually Stillman won a grudging recognition from his opponents. In 1925 a Washington Commission visited and reported glowingly upon the work at the Institute. Stillman, now recognised, began to receive large donations from private individuals, from trust executives and even from public bodies. These funds he devoted to the extension and perfection of his Institute, which became, with its superb equipment and situation, its herds of Jersey cattle and pure-bred Irish serum horses, a show place in the state of Oregon.

Though Stillman was not entirely free from enemies—in 1929 for instance the grievances of a dismissed laboratory attendant set alight another flare of scandal—he had at least secured immunity to pursue his life work. Unchanged by success, he remained the same quiet and restrained personality who nearly twenty-five years before had grown his first cultures in the attic on Beacon Hill.

And now, seated in the restaurant of Brooks Hotel, he gazed across at Andrew with quiet friendliness.

"It's very pleasant," he said, "to be in England. I like your countryside. Our summers aren't so cool as this."

"I suppose you've come over on a lecture tour?" Andrew said.

Stillman smiled.

"No! I don't lecture now. Is it vanity to say that I let my results lecture for me? As a matter of fact I'm over here very quietly. It so happens your Mr. Cranston—I mean Herbert Cranston who makes those marvellous little automobiles—came to me in America about a year back. He'd been a martyr to asthma all his life and I—well, at the Institute we managed to set him right. Ever since then he's been bothering me to come over and start a small clinic here on the lines of our place at Portland. Six months ago I agreed. We passed the plans and now the place—we're calling it Bellevue—is pretty near completion—out on the Chilterns near High Wycombe. I'm going to get it started, then I'll turn over to Marland—one of my assistants. Frankly, I look upon it as an experiment, a very promising experiment with my methods, particularly from the climatic and racial angles. The financial aspect is unimportant!"

Andrew leaned forward.

"That sounds interesting. What are you specially concentrating on? I'd like to see over your place."

"You must come when we are ready. We shall have our radical asthma régime. Cranston wants that. And then I have particularly specified for a few early tuberculosis cases. I say a few because"—he smiled—"mind you, I don't forget I am just a bio-physicist who knows a little about the respiratory apparatus—but in America our difficulty is to keep ourselves from being swamped. What was I saying? Ah, yes. These early T.B.'s. This will interest you, I have a new method of inducing pneumothorax. It is really an advance."

"You mean the Emile-Weil?"

"No, no. Much better. Without the disadvantages of negative fluctuation." Stillman's face lighted up. "You appreciate the difficulty of the fixed bottle apparatus—that point when the intra-pleural pressure balances the fluid pressure and the flow of gas ceases altogether. Now, at the Institute, we've devised an accessory pressure chamber—I'll show you when you come out—through which we can introduce gas at a decided negative pressure, right at the start."

"But what about gas embolism?" Andrew said quickly.

"We eliminate the risk entirely. Look! It's quite a dodge. By introducing a small bromoform manometer close to the needle we avoid rarefaction. A fluctuation of -14 cm. provides only 1 c.c. of gas at the needle point. Incidentally our needle has a four-way adjustment that goes a little better than Sangman's."

Andrew, in spite of himself—and his honorary appointment at the Victoria—was impressed.

"Why," he said. "If that is so—you're going .to diminish pleural shock right down to nothing. You know, Mr. Stillman—well, it seems strange, quite startling to me, that all this should have come from you. Oh! forgive me, I've said that badly, but you know what I mean—so many doctors, going on with the old apparatus——"

"My dear physician," Stillman answered with amusement in his eyes. "Don't forget that Carson, the first man to urge pneumothorax, was only a physiological essayist!"

After that they plunged into technicalities. They discussed apicolysis and phrenicotomy. They argued over Brauer's four points, passed on to oleothorax and Bernon's work in France—massive intra-pleural injections in tuberculous empyema. They ceased only when Stillman looked at his watch and realised, with an exclamation, that he was half an hour late for an appointment with Churston.

Andrew left Brooks Hotel with a stimulated and exalted mind. But, on the heels of that, came a queer reaction of confusion, dissatisfaction with his own work. I let myself get carried away by that fellow, he told himself, annoyed.

He was not in a particularly amiable frame of mind when he arrived at Chesborough Terrace yet, as he drew up opposite his house, he composed his features into a noncommittal mould. His relations with Christine had come to demand this blankness, for she now presented to him a face so acquiescent and expressionless he felt, however much he raged internally, that he must answer it in kind.

It seemed to him that she had retired within herself, fallen back upon an inner life where he could not penetrate. She read a great deal, wrote letters. Once or twice when he came in he found her playing with Florrie —childish games, played with coloured counters, which they bought at the Stores. She began also, with unobtrusive regularity, to go to church. And this exasperated him most of all.

At Drineffy she had accompanied Mrs. Watkins every Sunday to the parish church and he had found no reason for complaint. But now, unsympathetic and estranged from her, he saw it only as a further slight upon himself, a gesture of pietism directed at his suffering head.

This evening as he entered the front room she was seated alone in the room with her elbows on the table, wearing the glasses she had recently taken to, a book before her, a small occupied figure like a scholar at her lesson. An angry swell of exclusion swept over him. Reaching over her shoulders he picked up the book which, too late, she attempted to conceal. And there, at the head of the page, he read: *The Gospel According to St. Luke*.

"Good God!" He was staggered, somehow furious. "Is this what you've come to? Taken to Bible thumping now."

"Why not? I used to read it before I met you."

"Oh, you did, eh?"

"Yes." A queer look of pain was in her eyes. "Possibly your Plaza friends wouldn't appreciate the fact. But it is at least good literature."

"Is that so! Well let me tell you this in case you don't know it—you're developing into a blasted neurotic woman!"

"Quite probably. That again is entirely my fault. But let me tell you this. I'd rather be a blasted neurotic woman and be spiritually alive than a blasted successful man—and spiritually dead!" She broke off suddenly, biting her lip, forcing back her tears. With a great effort she took control of herself. Looking at him steadily, with pain in her eyes, she said, in a low contained voice:

"Andrew! Don't you think it would be a good thing for us both if I went away for a little while? Mrs. Vaughan has written me, asking me to spend a fortnight or three weeks with her. They've taken a house at Newquay for the summer. Don't you think I ought to go?"

"Yes! Go! Damn it all! Go!" He swung round and left her.

XIII

CHRISTINE'S DEPARTURE for Newquay was a relief, an exquisite emancipation. For three whole days. Then he began to brood, to wonder what she was doing and whether she was missing him, to fret jealously as to when she would return. Though he told himself he was now a free man he had the same sense of incompleteness which had kept him from his work at Aberalaw when she had gone to Bridlington, leaving him to study for his examination.

Her image rose before him, not the fresh young features of that earlier Christine, but a paler, maturer face with cheeks faintly drawn and eyes shortsighted behind their round glasses. It was not a beautiful face but it had some enduring quality which haunted him.

He went out a great deal, played bridge with Ivory, Freddie and Deedman at the club. Despite his reaction to their first meeting he frequently saw Stillman, who was moving between Brooks Hotel and the nearly completed clinic at Wycombe. He wrote asking Denny to meet him in London but it was impossible at this early stage of his appointment for Philip to get to town. Hope was inaccessible in Cambridge.

Fitfully he tried to concentrate on his clinical research at the hospital. Impossible. He was too restless. With this same restless intensity he went over his investments with Wade, the bank manager. All satisfactory; all going well. He began to thresh out a scheme for buying a freehold house in Welbeck Street—a heavy investment but one which should prove highly profitable—of selling the Chesborough Terrace house, merely retaining the surgery at the side. One of the building societies would help him. He woke during the still hot nights, his mind seething with schemes, with his work in the practice, his nerves overwrought, missing Christine, his hand reaching automatically to his bedside table for a cigarette.

In the middle of it all he rang up Frances Lawrence.

"I'm all alone here at present. You wouldn't care to run out somewhere in the evening? It's so hot in London."

Her voice was collected, oddly soothing to him. "That would be frightfully nice. I was hoping somehow you might ring. Do you know Crossways? Flood-lit Elizabethan, I'm afraid. But the river is too perfect there."

The following evening he cleared his surgery in three quarters of an hour. Well before eight, he had picked her up at Knightsbridge and set the car in the direction of Chertsey.

They ran due west through the flat market gardens outside Staines into a great flood of sunset. She sat beside him, as he drove, saying little yet filling the car with her alien, charming presence. She wore a coat and skirt of some thin fawn material, a dark hat close to her small head. He was overwhelmingly conscious of her gracefulness, her perfect finish. Her ungloved hand, near to him, was curiously expressive of this quality —white, slender. Each long finger tipped by an exquisite scarlet oval. Fastidious.

Crossways, as she had inferred, was an exquisite Elizabethan house set in perfect gardens on the Thames, with age-long topiary work and lovely formal lily ponds all outraged, in the conversion from mansion to roadhouse, by modern conveniences and an infamous jazz band. But although a fake lackey sprang to the car as they ran into the courtyard, already filled by expensive cars, the old bricks glowed behind the wistaria vine and the tall angled chimneys clustered serenely against the sky.

They went into the restaurant. It was smart, full, with tables placed round a square of polished floor and a head waiter who might have been brother to the grand vizier of the Plaza. Andrew hated and feared head waiters. But that, he now discovered, was because he had never faced them with a woman like Frances. One swift glance and they were ministered with reverence to the finest table in the room, surrounded by a corps of servitors, one of whom unflicked Andrew's napkin and placed it holily upon his knees.

Frances wanted very little: a salad, toast melba, no wine, only ice water. Undisturbed, the head waiter seemed to see in this frugality a confirmation of her caste. Andrew realised with a sudden qualm of dismay that had he walked into this sanctuary with Christine and ordered such a trivial repast he would have been hounded forth upon the highway with scorn.

He recollected himself to find Frances smiling at him.

"Do you realise we've known each other for quite a period of time now. And this is the first occasion you have asked me to come out with you."

"Are you sorry?"

"Not noticeably so, I hope." Again the charming intimacy of her faintly smiling face elevated him, caused him to feel wittier, more at ease, of a superior status. It was no mere pretentiousness, no silly snobbishness. The stamp of her breeding was somehow extended until it caught up and included him. He was aware of people at the adjoining tables viewing them with interest, of masculine admiration to which she was calmly oblivious. He could not help visualising the stimulus of a more constant association with her.

She said:

"Would it flatter you too much if I told you I had put off a previous theatre engagement to come here. Nicol Watson—do you remember him? He was taking me to the ballet—one of my favourites—what will you think of my infantile taste? Massine in *La Boutique Fantasque*."

"I remember Watson. And his ride through Paraguay. Clever fellow."

"He's frightfully nice."

"But you felt it would be too hot at the ballet?"

She smiled without answering, took a cigarette from a flat enamel box on which was depicted in faded colours an exquisite Boucher miniature.

"Yes, I heard Watson was running after you," he persisted with sudden vehemence. "What does your husband think of that?"

Again she did not speak, merely lifting an eyebrow as if mildly deprecating some lack of subtlety. After a moment she said:

"Surely you understand? Jackie and I are the best of friends. But we each have our *own* friends. He's at Juan at present. But I don't ask him why." Then lightly, "Shall we dance—just once?"

They danced. She moved with that same extraordinarily fascinating grace, light in his arms, impersonal.

"I'm not altogether good," he said when they returned. He was even falling into her idiom—gone, gone were the days when he would have grunted, "Damn it, Chris, I'm no hoofer."

Frances did not reply. That again he felt to be eminently characteristic of her. Another woman would have flattered, contradicted him, made him feel clumsy. Driven by a sudden impulsive curiosity he exclaimed:

"Please tell me something. Why have you been so kind to me? Helping me the way you've done—all those months?"

She looked at him, faintly amused yet without evasion.

"You are extraordinarily attractive to women. And your greatest charm is that you do not realise it."

"No, but, really——" he protested flushing; then he muttered, "I hope I'm some kind of a doctor as well."

She laughed, slowly fanning away the cigarette smoke with her hand.

698

"You will not be convinced. Or I should not have told you. And, of course, you're an excellent doctor. We were talking of you only the other night at Green Street. Le Roy is getting a little tired of our company dietitian. Poor Rumbold!—he wouldn't have enjoyed hearing le Roy bark, 'We must put the skids under grandpa.' But Jackie agrees. They want someone younger, with more drive, on the board—shall I use the cliché?—a coming man. Apparently they plan a big campaign in the medical journals, they want really to interest the profession—from the scientific angle—as le Roy put it. And of course Rumbold is just a joke among his colleagues. But why am I talking like this? Such a waste of a night like this. Now don't frown as though you were about to assassinate me, or the waiter, or the band-leader—I wish you would actually—isn't he odious? You look exactly as you did that first day—when you came into the fitting-room—very haughty and proud and nervous—even a little ridiculous. And then—poor Toppy! By the ordinary convention it is *she* should be here."

"I'm very glad she's not," he said with his eyes upon the table.

"Please don't think me banal. I couldn't bear that. We are fairly intelligent I hope—and we—well, I for one—just do not believe in the grand passion—isn't the phrase enough? But I do think life is so much gayer if one has—a friend—to go a bit of the way with one." Her eyes showed high points of amusement again. "Now I sound completely Rossetti-ish—which is too frightful." She picked up her cigarette-case. "And anyhow it's stuffy here, and I want you to see the moon on the river."

He paid the bill and followed her through the long glass windows which an act of vandalism had inset in the fine old wall. On the balustered terrace the music of the dance band came faintly. Before them a wide avenue of turf led down to the river between dark borders of clipped yew. As she had said, there was a moon which splashed great shadows from the yews and glinted palely upon a group of archery targets standing on the bottom lawns. Beyond lay the silver sheen of water.

They strolled down to the river, seated themselves upon a bench that stood beside the verge. She took off her hat and gazed silently at the slowly moving current, its eternal murmur strangely blended with the muted hum of a high-powered car travelling at speed into the distance.

"What queer night sounds," she said. "The old and the new. And searchlights across the moon there. It's our age."

He kissed her. She gave no sign either way. Her lips were warm and dry. In a minute she said:

"That was very sweet. And very badly done."

"I can do better," he mumbled staring in front of him, not moving. He was awkward, without conviction, ashamed and nervous. Angrily he told himself that it was wonderful to be here on such a night with such a graceful, charming woman. He ought by all the canons of moonshine and the magazines to have swept her madly into his arms. As it was he became aware of his cramped position, of a desire to smoke, of the vinegar in the salad touching up his old indigestion.

And Christine's face in some unaccountable way was mirrored in the water before him, a jaded and rather harassed face, on her cheek a plaintive smudge of paint from the brush with which she had painted the heavy folding doors, when first they came to Chesborough Terrace. It worried and exasperated him. He was here, bound by the obligation of circumstances. And he was a man, wasn't he—not a candidate for Voronoff? Defiantly, he kissed Frances again.

"I thought possibly you were taking another twelve months to make up your mind." Her eyes held that high affectionate amusement. "And now, don't you think we should go, doctor. These night airs—aren't they rather treacherous to the puritanical mind."

He helped her to her feet and she retained his hand, holding it lightly as they walked to the car. He flung a shilling to the baroque retainer, started the engine for London. As he drove her silence was eloquently happy.

But he was not happy. He felt himself a hound and a fool. Hating himself, disappointed in his own reactions, he still dreaded the return to his sultry room, his restless solitary bed. His heart was cold, his brain a mass of tormenting thoughts. The recollection swept before him of the agonising sweetness of his first love for Christine, the beating ecstasy of those early days at Drineffy. He pushed it away from him furiously.

They were at her house and his mind still struggled with the problem. He got out of the car and opened the door for her. They stood together on the pavement while she opened her bag and took out her latchkey.

"You'll come up, won't you? I'm afraid the servants are in bed."

He hesitated, stammered.

"It's very late, isn't it?"

She did not seem to hear him but went up the few flagstone steps with her key in her hand. As he followed, sneaking after her, he had a fading vision of Christine's figure walking down the market, carrying her old string bag.

XIV

THREE DAYS later Andrew sat in his Welbeck Street consulting-room. It was a hot afternoon and, through the screen of his open window, there came the pestering drone of traffic, borne upon the exhausted air. He was tired, over-worked, fearful of Christine's return at the end of the week, expectant yet nervous of every telephone ring, sweating under the task of coping with six three-guinea patients in the space of one hour, and the knowledge that he must rush his surgery to take Frances out to supper. He glanced up impatiently as Nurse Sharp entered, more than usual acrimony on her patchy features.

"There's a man called to see you, a dreadful person. He's not a patient and he says he's not a traveller. He's got no card. His name's Boland."

"Boland?" Andrew echoed blankly; then his face cleared suddenly. "Not Con Boland? Let him in, nurse! Straight away."

"But you have a patient waiting. And in ten minutes Mrs. Roberts——"

"Oh! never mind Mrs. Roberts!" he threw out irritably. "Do as I say."

Nurse Sharp flushed at his tone. It was on her tongue to tell him she was not used to being spoken to like that. She sniffed and went out with her head in the air. The next minute she showed Boland in.

"Why, Con!" said Andrew jumping up.

"Hello, hello, hello," shouted Con, as he bounded forward with a broad and genial grin. It was the red-headed dentist himself, no different, as real and untidy in his oversize shiny blue suit and large brown boots as if he had that moment walked out of his wooden garage, a shade older perhaps, but with no less violence in the beaded brush of his red moustache, still undaunted, wild-haired, exclamatory. He pounded Andrew vehemently on the back. "In the name of God, Manson! It's great to see ye again. Ye're lookin' marvellous, marvellous. I'd have known ye in a million. Well! Well! To think of this now. It's a high-class place you have here and all." He turned his beaming gaze upon the acidulous Sharp who stood watching scornfully. "This lady nurse of yours wasn't for lettin' me in till I told her I was a professional man, myself. It's the God's truth, nurse. This swanky-lookin' fella ye work for was in the same wan horse medical scheme as myself not so long ago. Up in Aberalaw. If ever ye're passin' that way drop in on the missus and me and we'll give ye a cup of tea. Any friend of my old friend Manson is welcome as the day!"

Nurse Sharp gave him one look and walked out of the room. But it was wasted on Con who gushed and bubbled with a pure and natural joy. Swinging round to Andrew irrepressibly:

"No beauty, eh, Manson, my boy? But a decent woman, I'll be bound. Well, well, well! How are ye, now? How *are* ye?"

He refused to relinquish Andrew's hand, but pumped it up and down, grinning away in sheer delight.

It was a rare tonic to see Con again on this devitalising day. When Andrew at last freed himself, he flung himself into his swing chair, feeling himself human again, shoving over the cigarettes to Con. Then Con, with one grubby thumb in an armhole, the other pressing the wet end of a freshly lit cigarette, sketched the reason of his coming.

"I had a bit of a holiday due to me, Manson, my boy, and a couple of matters to attend to, so the wife just told me to pack off and hit it. Ye see, I've been workin' on a sort of a spring invention for tighten' up slack brakes. Off and on I've been devotin' the full candlepower of the old grey mather to th' idee. But devil take them, there's nobody'll look at the gadget! But never mind, never mind, we'll let it go. It's not important besides the other thing." Con cast his cigarette ash upon the carpet and his face took a more serious turn. "Listen, Manson, my boy! It's Mary —you'll remember Mary surely, for I can tell you she remembers you! She's been poorly lately—not up to the mark at all. We've had her to Llewellyn and devil the bit of good he's doin' her." Con grew heated suddenly, his voice was thick. "Damn it all, Manson, he's got the sauce to say she's got a touch of T.B.—as if that wasn't all finished and done with in the Boland family when her Uncle Dan went to the sanatorium fifteen years ago. Now look here, Manson, will ye do something for old friendship's sake? We know ye're a big man now, sure ye're the talk of Aberalaw. Will ye take a look at Mary for us? Ye can't tell what confidence that girl has in you, we've got it ourselves—Mrs. B. and me—for that matter. That's why she says to me she says, 'You go to Doctor Manson when you're in the way of meetin' him. And if he'll see the daughter sure we'll send her up any time that's likely to be convenient.' Now what do you say, Manson? If you're too busy ye've only got to say so and I can easy sling my hook."

Andrew's expression had turned concerned.

"Don't talk that way, Con. Can't you see how delighted I am to see you. And Mary, poor kid—you know I'll do everything I can for her, everything."

Unmindful of Nurse Sharp's significant inthrustings he squandered his precious time in conversation with Con until at last she could bear it no longer.

"You have five patients waiting now, Doctor Manson. And you're more than an hour behind your appointment times. I can't make any more excuses to them, I'm not used to treating patients this way."

Even then, he still clutched at Con, and accompanied him to the front door, pressing hospitality upon him.

"I'm not going to let you rush back home, Con. How long are you up for? Three or four days—that's fine! Where are you staying? The Westland—out Bayswater way! That's no good! Why don't you come and stop with me instead, you're near us already. And we've bag loads of room. Christine'll be back on Friday. She'll be delighted to see you, Con, delighted. We can talk over old times together."

On the following day Con brought his bag round to Chesborough Terrace. After the evening surgery they went together to the second house of the Palladium music-hall. It was amazing how good every turn seemed in Con's company. The dentist's ready laugh rang out, dismaying at first, then infecting the immediate vicinity. People twisted round to smile at Con in sympathy.

"In the name of God!" Con rolled in his seat. "D'ye see that fella with the bicycle! D'y mind the time, Manson——"

In the interval they stood in the bar, Con with his hat on the back of his head, froth on his moustache, brown boots happily planted.

"I can't tell ye, Manson, my boy, what a treat this is for me. Sure you're kindness itself!"

In the face of Con's genial gratitude Andrew somehow felt himself a tarnished hypocrite.

Afterwards they had a steak and beer at the Cadero; then they returned, stirred up the fire in the front room and sat down to talk. They talked and smoked and drank further bottles of beer. Momentarily Andrew forgot the complexities of super-civilised existence. The straining tension of his practice, the prospect of his adoption by le Roy, the chance of promotion at the Victoria, the state of his investments, the soft textured nicety of Frances Lawrence, the dread of an accusation in Christine's distant eyes—these all faded as Con bellowed:

"D'you mind the time we fought Llewellyn. And Urquhart and the rest drew back on us—Urquhart's still goin' strong by the same token, sends his best regards—and then we set to, the both of us, and finished the beer."

But the next day came. And it brought, inexorably, the moment of reunion with Christine. Andrew dragged the unsuspecting Con to the end of the platform, irritably aware of the inadequacy of his self-possession, realising that Boland was his salvation. His heart was beating in painful expectation as the train steamed in. He knew one shattering moment of anguish and remorse at the sight of Christine's small familiar face advancing amongst the crowd of strangers, straining in expectation towards his own. Then he lost everything in the effort to achieve cordial unconcern.

"Hello, Chris! Thought you were never coming! Yes, you may well look at him. It's Con all right! Himself and no other! And not a day older. He's staying with us, Chris—we'll tell you all about it in the car. I've got it outside. Did you have a good time? Oh, look here!—*why* are you carrying your case?"

Swept away by the unexpectedness of this platform reception—when she had feared she might not be met at all—Christine lost her wan expression, and colour flowed back nervously into her cheeks. She also had been apprehensive, nervously keyed, longing for a new beginning. She felt almost hopeful now. Ensconced in the back of the car with Con she talked eagerly, stealing glances at Andrew's profile in the driving seat.

"Oh, it is good to be home." She took a long breath inside the front

703

door of the house; then, quickly, wistfully, "You have missed me, Andrew?"

"I should think I have. We *all* have. Eh, Mrs. Bennett? Eh, Florrie? Con! What the devil are you doing with that luggage?"

He was out in a second, giving Con a hand, performing unnecessarily with suitcases. Then, before anything more could be done or said, he had to leave on his rounds. He insisted that they could expect him for tea. As he slumped into the seat of his car he groaned:.

"Thank God that's over! She doesn't look a lot the better of the holiday. Oh, hell!—I'm sure she didn't notice. And that's the main thing at present."

Though he was late in returning, his briskness, his cheerfulness were excessive. Con was enraptured with such spirits.

"In the name of God! Ye've more go in ye than ever ye had in the old days, Manson, my boy."

Once or twice he felt Christine's eye upon him, half pleading for a sign, a look of understanding. He perceived that Mary's illness was distracting her—a conflicting anxiety. She explained, in an interval of conversation, that she had asked Con to wire Mary to come through at once, to-morrow if possible. She was worried about Mary. She hoped that something, or rather everything, would be done without delay.

It fell out better than Andrew had expected. Mary wired back that she would arrive on the following day before lunch, and Christine was fully occupied in preparing for her. The stir and excitement in the house marked even his hollow heartiness.

But when Mary appeared he suddenly became himself again. It was evident at first sight that she was not well. Grown in these intervening years to a lanky girl of twenty, with a slight droop to her shoulders, she had that almost unnatural beauty of complexion which spoke an immediate warning to Andrew.

She was tired out by her journey and though she wished, in her pleasure at seeing them again, to sit up and continue talking, she was persuaded to bed about six o'clock. It was then that Andrew went up to auscultate her chest.

He remained upstairs for only fifteen minutes but when he came down to Con and Christine in the drawing-room his expression was, for once, genuinely disturbed.

"I'm afraid there's no doubt about it. The left apex. Llewellyn was perfectly right, Con. But don't worry. It's in the primary stage. We can do something with it!"

"You mean," said Con, gloomily apprehensive. "You mean it can be cured?"

"Yes. I'd go as far as to say that. It means keeping an eye on her, constant observation, every care." He reflected, frowning deeply. "It seems to me, Con, that Aberalaw's about the worst place for her—always bad for early T.B. at home—why don't you let me get her into the Victoria? I've got a pull with Doctor Thoroughgood. I'd get her into his ward for a certainty. I'd keep my eye on her."

"Manson!" Con exclaimed impressively. "That's one true act of friendship. If ye only knew the trust that girl of mine has in ye! If any man'll get her right it's yourself."

Andrew went immediately to telephone Thoroughgood. He returned in five minutes with the information that Mary could be admitted to the Victoria at the end of the week. Con brightened visibly and, his bounding optimism responding to the idea of the Chest Hospital, of Andrew's attention and Thoroughgood's supervision, Mary was, for him, as good as cured.

The next two days were fully occupied. By Saturday afternoon when Mary was admitted and Con had boarded his train at Paddington, Andrew's self possession was at last equal to the occasion. He was able to press Christine's arm, and exclaim lightly on his way to the surgery:

"Nice to be together again, Chris! Lord! What a week it has been."

It sounded perfectly in key. But it was as well he did not see the look upon her face. She sat down in the room, alone, her head bent slightly, her hands in her lap, very still. She had been so hopeful when first she came back. But now, within her, was the dreadful foreboding: Dear God! When and how is this going to end?

XV

On and on rushed the spate of his success, a bursting dam sweeping him irresistibly forward in an ever-sounding, ever-swelling flood.

His association with Hamson and Ivory was now closer and more profitable than ever. Moreover, Deedman had asked him to deputise for him at the Plaza, while he flew to Le Touquet for seven days' golf, and by way of acknowledgment, to split the fees. Usually it was Hamson who acted as Deedman's locum, but lately Andrew suspected a rift between these two.

How flattering for Andrew to discover that he could walk straight into the bedroom of a paroxysmal film star, sit on her satin sheets, palpate her sexless anatomy with sure hands, perhaps smoke a cigarette with her if he had time!

But even more flattering was the patronage of Joseph le Roy. Twice in the last month he had lunched with le Roy. He knew there were important ideas working in the other man's mind. At their last meeting le Roy had tentatively remarked:

"You know, doc, I've been feeling my way with you. It's a pretty large thing I'm going on to and I'll need a lot of clever medical advice. I don't want any more double-handed big hats—Old Rumbold isn't worth his own calories, we're going to pin the crape on him right away! —and I don't want a lot of so-called experts goin' into a huddle and pulling me round in circles. I want one level-headed medical adviser and I'm beginning to think you're about it. You see, we've reached a wide section of the public with our products on a popular basis. But I honestly believe the time has come to expand our interests and go in for more scientific derivatives. Split up the milk components, electrify them, irradiate them, tabloid them. Cremo with vitamin B, Cremofax and lethecin for malnutrition, rickets, deficiency insomnia—you get me, doc. And further, I believe if we tackle this on more orthodox professional lines we can enlist the help and sympathy of the whole medical profession, make every doctor, so to speak, a potential salesman. Now this means scientific advertising, doc, scientific approach and that's where I believe a young scientific doctor on the inside could help us all along the road. Now I want you to get me straight, this is all perfectly open and *scientific*. We are actually raising our own status. And when you consider the worthless extracts that doctors do recommend—like Marrobin C and Vegatog and Bonebran—why, I consider in elevating the general standard of health we are doing a great public service to the nation."

Andrew did not pause to consider that there was probably more vitamin in one fresh green pea than in several tins of Cremofax. He was excited, not by the fee he would receive for acting on the board, but at the thought of le Roy's interest.

It was Frances who told him how he might profit by le Roy's spectacular market operations. Ah! it was pleasant to drop in to tea with her, to feel that this charming sophisticated woman had a special glance for him, a swift provoking smile of intimacy! Association with her gave him sophistication too, added assurance, a harder polish. Unconsciously he absorbed her philosophy. Under her guidance he was learning to cultivate the superficial niceties and let the deeper things go hang.

It was no longer an embarrassment to face Christine, he could come into his house quite naturally, following an hour spent with Frances. He did not stop to wonder at this astounding change. If he thought of it at all it was to argue that he did not love Mrs. Lawrence, that Christine knew nothing of it, that every man came to this particular impasse some time in his life. Why should he set himself up to be different?

By way of recompense he went out of his way to be nice to Christine, spoke to her with consideration, even discussed his plans with her. She was aware that he proposed to buy the Welbeck Street house next spring, that they would be leaving Chesborough Terrace whenever the arrangements were complete. She never argued with him now, never threw recriminations at his head, and if she had moods he never saw them. She seemed altogether passive. Life moved too swiftly for him to pause long for reflection. The pace exhilarated him. He had a false sensation of strength. He felt vital, increasing in consequence, master of himself and of his destiny.

And then, out of high heaven, the bolt fell.

On the evening of the 5th of November, the wife of a neighbouring petty tradesman came to his consulting-room at Chesborough Terrace.

She was Mrs. Vidler, a small sparrow of a woman, middle-aged, but bright-eyed and spry, a regular Londoner who had all her life never been further from Bow Bells than Margate. Andrew knew the Vidlers well, he had attended the little boy for some childish complaint when he first came to the district. In those early days, too, he had sent his shoes there to be mended, for the Vidlers, respectable, hard-working trades-people, kept a double shop at the head of Paddington Street named, rather magnificently, *Renovations Ltd.*—one half devoted to boot repairs and the other to the cleaning and pressing of wearing apparel. Harry Vidler himself might often be seen, a sturdy, pale-faced man, collarless and in his shirt-sleeves, with a last between his knees or, though he kept a couple of helpers, using a damping-board, if work in the other depart-ment was urgent.

It was of Harry that Mrs. Vidler now spoke.

"Doctor," she said in her brisk way, "my husband isn't well. For weeks now he's been poorly. I've been at him and at him to come, but he wouldn't. Will you call to-morrow, doctor? I'll keep him in bed."

Andrew promised that he would call.

Next morning he found Vidler in bed, giving a history of internal pain and growing stoutness. His girth had increased extraordinarily in these last few months and inevitably, like most patients who have enjoyed good health all their lives, he had several ways of accounting for it. He sug-gested that he had been taking a drop too much ale, or that perhaps his sedentary life was to blame.

But Andrew, after his investigation, was obliged to contradict these elucidations. He was convinced that the condition was cystic and although not dangerous, it was one which demanded operative treat-ment. He did his best to reassure Vidler and his wife by explaining how a simple cyst such as this might develop internally and cause no end of inconvenience which would all disappear when it was removed. He had no doubt at all in his mind as to the upshot of the operation and he pro-posed that Vidler should go into hospital at once.

Here, however, Mrs. Vidler held up her hands.

"No, sir, I won't have my Harry in a hospital!" She struggled to compose her agitation. "I've had a kind of feeling this was coming—the way he's been overworking in the business. But now it 'as come, thank God we're in a position as can deal with it. We're not well-off people, doctor, as you know, but we 'ave got a little bit put by. And now's the time to use it. I won't have Harry go beggin' for subscribers' letters, and standin' in queues, and goin' into a public ward like he was a pauper."

"But, Mrs. Vidler, I can arrange——"

"No! You can get him in a private home, sir. There's plenty round about here. And you can get a private doctor to operate on him. I can promise you, sir, so long as I'm here no public hospital shall 'ave Harry Vidler."

He saw that her mind was firmly made up. And indeed Vidler himself, since this unpleasant necessity had arisen, was of the same opinion as his wife. He wanted the best treatment that could be had.

That evening Andrew rang up Ivory. It was automatic now for him to turn to Ivory the more so as, in this instance, he had to ask a favour.

"I'd like you to do something for me, Ivory. I've an abdominal here, that wants doing—decent hard-working people but not rich, you understand. There's nothing much in it for you, I'm afraid. But it would oblige me if you did it for—shall we say a third of the usual fee."

Ivory was very gracious. Nothing would please him more than to do his friend Manson any service within his power. They discussed the case for several minutes and at the end of that discussion Andrew telephoned Mrs. Vidler.

"I've just been on to Mr. Charles Ivory, a West End surgeon who happens to be a particular friend of mine. He's coming to see your husband with me to-morrow, Mrs. Vidler, at eleven o'clock. That all right? And he says—are you there?—he says, Mrs. Vidler, that if the operation has to be undertaken he'll do it for thirty guineas. Considering that his usual fee would be a hundred guineas—perhaps more—I think we're not doing too badly."

"Yes, doctor, yes." Her tone was worried yet she made the effort to sound relieved. "It's very kind of you, I'm sure. I think we can manage that some'ow."

Next morning Ivory saw the case with Andrew and on the following day Harry Vidler moved into the Brunsland Nursing Home in Brunsland Square.

It was a clean, old-fashioned home not far from Chesborough Terrace, one of many in the district where the fees were moderate and the equipment scanty. Most of its patients were medical cases, hemiplegics, chronic cardiacs, bedridden old women with whom the main difficulty was the prevention of bedsores. Like every other home which Andrew had entered in London it had never been intended for its present purpose. There was no lift and the operating theatre had once been a conservatory. But Miss Buxton, the proprietress, was a qualified sister and a hardworking woman. Whatever its defects, the Brunsland was spotlessly aseptic—even to the furthest corner of its shining linoleumed floors.

The operation was fixed for Friday and, since Ivory could not come early, it was set for the unusually late hour of two o'clock.

Though Andrew was at Brunsland Square first, Ivory arrived punctually. He drove up with the anæsthetist and stood watching while his chauffeur carried in his large bag of instruments—so that nothing might interfere with his subsequent delicacy of touch. And, though he plainly thought little of the home, his manner remained as suave as ever. Within the space of ten minutes he had reassured Mrs. Vidler, who waited in the front room, made the conquest of Miss Buxton and her nurses, then, gowned and gloved in the little travesty of a theatre, he was imperturbably ready.

The patient walked in with determined cheerfulness, slipped off his dressing-gown, which one of the nurses then whipped away, and climbed upon the narrow table. Realising that he must go through with the ordeal, Vidler had come to face it with courage. Before the anæsthetist placed the mask over his face he smiled at Andrew.

"I'll be better after this is over." The next moment he had closed his eyes and was almost eagerly drinking in deep draughts of ether. Miss Buxton removed the bandages. The iodined area was exposed, unnaturally tumescent, a glistening mound. Ivory commenced the operation.

He began with some spectacular deep injections into the lumbar muscles.

"Combat shock," he threw out gravely to Andrew. "I always use it."

Then the real work began.

His medial incision was large and immediately, almost ludicrously, the trouble was revealed. The cyst bobbed through the opening like a fully inflated wet rubber football. The justification of his diagnosis added, if anything, to Andrew's self-esteem. He reflected that Vidler would do nicely when detached from this uncomfortable accessory and with an eye on his next case he surreptitiously looked at his watch.

Meanwhile Ivory, in his masterly manner, was playing with the football, imperturbably trying to get his hands round it to its point of attachment and imperturbably failing. Every time he attempted to control it the ball slithered away from him. If he tried once he tried twenty times.

Andrew glanced irritably at Ivory, thinking—what is the man doing? There was not much space in the abdomen in which to work but there was space enough. He had seen Llewellyn, Denny, a dozen others at his old hospital, manipulate expertly, with far less latitude. It was a surgeon's job to fiddle through cramped positions. Suddenly he realised that this was the first abdominal operation Ivory had ever done for him. Insensibly, he dropped his watch back into his pocket, drew nearer, rather rigidly, to the table.

Ivory was still straining to get behind the cyst, still calm, incisive, unruffled. Miss Buxton and a young nurse stood trustfully by, not knowing very much about anything. The anæsthetist, an elderly grizzled man, was stroking the end of the stoppered bottle contemplatively with his thumb. The atmosphere of the bare little glass-roofed theatre was flat,

709

supremely uneventful. There was no high sense of tension or steam-heated drama, merely Ivory raising one shoulder, manœuvring with his gloved hands, trying to get behind the smooth rubber ball. But for some reason a sense of coldness fell on Andrew.

He found himself frowning, watching tensely. What was he dreading? There was nothing to be afraid of, nothing. It was a straightforward operation. In a few minutes it would be finished.

Ivory, with a faint smile, as of satisfaction, gave up the attempt to find the cyst's point of attachment. The young nurse gazed at him humbly as he asked for a knife. Ivory took the knife in slow motion. Probably, never in his career had he looked more exactly like the great surgeon of fiction. Holding the knife, before Andrew knew what he was about, he made a generous puncture in the glistening wall of the cyst. After that everything happened at once.

The cyst burst, exploding a great clot of venous blood into the air, vomiting its contents into the abdominal cavity. One second there was a round tight sphere, the next a flaccid purse of tissue lay in a mess of gurgling blood. Frantically Miss Buxton felt in the drum for swabs. The anæsthetist sat up abruptly. The young nurse looked like fainting. Ivory said gravely:

"Clamp, please."

A wave of horror swept over Andrew. He saw that Ivory, failing to reach the pedicule to ligature it, had blindly, wantonly, incised the cyst. And it was a hæmorrhagic cyst.

"Swab, please," Ivory said in his impassive voice. He was fiddling about in the mess, trying to clamp the pedicle, swabbing out the blood-filled cavity, packing, failing to control the hæmorrhage. Realisation broke on Andrew in a blinding flash. He thought: God Almighty! He can't operate, he can't operate at all.

The anæsthetist, with his finger on the carotid, murmured in a gentle, apologetic voice:

"I'm afraid—he seems to be going, Ivory."

Ivory, relinquishing the clamp, stuffed the belly cavity full of blooded gauze. He began to suture up his great incision. There was no swelling now. Vidler's stomach had a caved-in, pallid, an empty look, the reason being that Vidler was dead.

"Yes, he's gone now," said the anæsthetist finally.

Ivory put in his last stitch, clipped it methodically and turned to the instrument tray to lay down his scissors. Paralysed, Andrew could not move. Miss Buxton, with a clay coloured face, was automatically packing the hot bottles outside the blanket. By great force of will she seemed to collect herself. She went outside. The porter, unaware of what had happened, brought in the stretcher. Another minute and Harry Vidler's body was being carried upstairs to his bedroom.

Ivory spoke at last.

"Very unfortunate," he said in his collected voice as he stripped off his gown. "I imagine it was shock—don't you think so, Gray?"

Gray, the anæsthetist, mumbled an answer. He was busy packing up his apparatus.

Still Andrew could not speak. Amidst the dazed welter of his emotion he suddenly remembered Mrs. Vidler, waiting downstairs. It seemed as if Ivory read that thought. He said:

"Don't worry, Manson. I'll attend to the little woman. Come. I'll get it over for you now."

Instinctively, like a man unable to resist, Andrew found himself following Ivory down the stairs to the waiting-room. He was still stunned, weak with nausea, wholly incapable of telling Mrs. Vidler. It was Ivory who rose to the occasion, rose almost to the heights.

"My dear lady," he said, compassionate and upstanding, placing his hand gently on her shoulder, "I'm afraid—I'm afraid we have bad news for you."

She clasped her hands, in worn brown kid gloves, together. Terror and entreaty were mingled in her eyes.

"What!"

"Your poor husband, Mrs. Vidler, in spite of everything which we could do for him——"

She collapsed into the chair, her face ashen, her gloved hands still working together.

"Harry!" she whispered in a heartrending voice. Then again, "Harry!"

"I can only assure you," Ivory went on, sadly, "on behalf of Doctor Manson, Doctor Gray, Miss Buxton and myself that no power on earth could have saved him. And even if he had survived the operation——" He shrugged his shoulders significantly.

She looked up at him, sensing his meaning, aware even at this frightful moment of his condescension, his goodness to her.

"That's the kindest thing you could have told me, doctor." She spoke through her tears.

"I'll send sister down to you. Do your best to bear up. And thank you, thank you for your courage."

He went out of the room and once again Andrew went with him. At the end of the hall was the empty office, the door of which stood open. Feeling for his cigarette-case, Ivory walked into the office. There he lit a cigarette and took a long pull at it. His face was perhaps a trifle paler than usual but his jaw was firm, his hand steady, his nerve absolutely unshaken.

"Well, that's over," he reflected coolly. "I'm sorry, Manson. I didn't dream that cyst was hæmorrhagic. But these things happen in the best regulated circles, you know."

It was a small room with the only chair pushed underneath the desk.

Andrew sank down on the leather covered club fender that surrounded the fireplace. He stared feverishly at the aspidistra in the yellowish-green pot placed in the empty grate. He was sick, shattered, on the verge of a complete collapse. He could not escape the vision of Harry Vidler, walking unaided to the table—"I'll be better after this is over"—and then ten minutes later, sagging on the stretcher, a mutilated, butchered corpse. He gritted his teeth together, covered his eyes with his hand.

"Of course," Ivory inspected the end of his cigarette. "He didn't die on the table. I finished before that—which makes it all right. No necessity for an inquest."

Andrew raised his head. He was trembling, infuriated by the consciousness of his own weakness in this awful situation which Ivory had sustained with such cold-blooded nerve. He said, in a kind of frenzy:

"For Christ's sake stop talking. You know you killed him. You're not a surgeon. You never were—you never will be a surgeon. You're the worst botcher I've ever seen in all my life."

There was a silence. Ivory gave Andrew a pale hard glance. "I don't recommend that line of talk, Manson."

"You don't." A painful hysterical sob shook Andrew. "I know you don't! But it's the truth. All the cases I've given you up till now have been child's play. But this—the first real case we've had—— Oh, God! I should have known—I'm just as bad as you——"

"Pull yourself together, you hysterical fool. You'll be heard."

"What if I am?" Another weak burst of anger seized Andrew. He choked: "You know it's the truth as well as I do. You bungled so much —it was almost murder!"

For an instant it seemed as if Ivory would knock him senseless off the fender, a physical effort which, with his weight and strength, the older man could easily have accomplished. But with a great struggle he controlled himself. He said nothing, simply turned and walked out of the room. But there was an ugly look on his cold hard face which spoke, icily, of unforgiving fury.

How long Andrew remained in the office, his forehead pressed against the cold marble of the mantelpiece, he did not know. But at last he rose, realising dully that he had work which he must do. The dreadful shock of the calamity had caught him with the destructive violence of an explosive shell. It was as though he, also, were eviscerate and empty. Yet he still moved automatically, advancing as might a horribly wounded soldier, compelled by machine-like habit to perform the duties expected of him.

In this fashion he managed, somehow, to drag round his remaining visits. Then, with a leaden heart and an aching head he came back home. It was late, nearly seven o'clock. He was just in time for his surgery and evening consultations.

His front waiting-room was full, his surgery packed to the door.

Heavily, like a dying man, he took stock of them, his patients, gathered, despite the fine summer evening, to pay tribute to his manner, his personality. Mostly women, a great many of them Laurier's girls, people who had been coming to him for weeks, encouraged by his smile, his tact, his suggestion that they persevere with their medicine—the old gang, he thought numbly, the old game!

He dropped into his surgery swing chair, began with a mask-like face, the usual evening rite.

"How are you? Yes, I think you're looking a shade better! Yes. Pulse has much more tone. The physic is doing you good. Hope it's not too nasty for you, my dear girl."

Out to the waiting Christine, handing her the empty bottle, forward along the passage to the consulting-room, stringing out the same interrogative platitudes there, the same bogus sympathy, then back along the passage, picking up the full bottle, back into the surgery again. So it went on, this infernal circus of his own damnation.

It was a sultry night. He suffered abominably but still he went on, half to torture himself and half in empty deadness because he could not stop. As he passed backwards and forwards in a daze of pain he kept asking himself: Where am I going? Where, in the name of God, am I going?

At last, later than usual, at quarter to ten, it was finished. He locked the outer door of the surgery, came through to the consulting-room where, according to routine, Christine waited, ready to call out the lists, to help him make up the book.

For the first time in many weeks he really looked at her, gazed deeply into her face as, with lowered eyes, she studied the list in her hand. Piercing even his numbness, the change in her shocked him. Her expression was still and fixed, her mouth drooped. Though she did not look at him there was a mortal sadness in her eyes.

Seated at the desk before the heavy ledger he felt a frightful straining in his side. But his body, that outer covering of deadness, allowed nothing of that inner throbbing to escape. Before he could speak she had begun to call out the list.

On and on he went, marking the book, a cross for a visit, a circle for a consultation, marking the total of his iniquity. When it was finished she asked, in a voice whose wincing satire he only then observed:

"Well! How much to-day?"

He did not, could not, answer. She left the room. He heard her go upstairs to her room, heard the quiet sound of her closing the door. He was alone: dry, stricken, bemused. Where am I going? Where in the name of God am I going? Suddenly his eyes fell upon the tobacco sack, full of money, bulging with his cash takings for the day. Another wave of hysteria swept over him. He took up the bag and flung it into the corner of the room. It fell with a dull and senseless sound.

He jumped up. He was stifling, he could not breathe. Leaving the consulting-room he rushed into the little back yard of the house, a small well of darkness beneath the stars. Here he leaned weakly against the brick dividing wall. He began, violently, to retch.

XVI

He tossed restlessly in bed all through the night until, at six in the morning, he at last fell asleep. Awakening late he came down after nine o'clock, pale and heavy eyed, to find that Christine had already breakfasted and gone. Normally this would not have upset him. Now, with a pang of anguish, it made him feel how far they were apart.

When Mrs. Bennett brought him his nicely cooked bacon and egg he could not eat it, the muscles of his throat refused to work. He drank a cup of coffee, then, on an impulse, he mixed himself a stiff whisky and soda, drank that too. He then prepared to face the day.

Though the machine still held him, his movements were less automatic than before. A faint gleam, a haggard shaft of light had begun to penetrate his dazed uncertainty. He knew that he was on the verge of a great, colossal breakdown. He knew also that if he once fell into that abyss he would never crawl out of it. Cautiously holding himself in, he opened the garage and took out his car. The effort made the sweat spring out on his palms.

His main purpose this morning was to reach the Victoria. He had made an appointment with Doctor Thoroughgood to see Mary Boland. That, at least, was an engagement he did not wish to miss. He drove slowly to the hospital. Actually he felt better in the car than when he walked—he was so used to driving it had become automatic, reflex.

He reached the hospital, parked his car, went up to the ward. With a nod to sister he passed along to Mary's bed, picking up her chart on the way. Then he sat down on the red blanketed edge of the bed, aware of her welcoming smile, of the big bunch of roses beside her, but all the while studying her chart. The chart was not satisfactory.

"Good morning," she said. "Aren't my flowers beautiful? Christine brought them yesterday."

He looked at her. No flush, but a little thinner than when she came in.

"Yes, they're nice flowers. How do you feel, Mary?"

"Oh!—all right." Her eyes avoided his momentarily, then swept back full of warm confidence. "Anyway I know it won't be for long. You'll soon have me better."

The trust in her words and, above all, in her gaze, sent a great throb of pain through him. He thought, if anything goes wrong here it will be the final smash.

At that moment Doctor Thoroughgood arrived to make his round of the ward. As he came in, he saw Andrew, and at once advanced towards him.

"Morning, Manson," he said pleasantly. "Why? What's the matter? Are you ill?"

Andrew stood up.

"I'm quite well, thank you."

Doctor Thoroughgood gave him an odd glance, then he turned to Mary's bed.

"I'm glad you asked to see this case with me. Let's have the screens, sister."

They spent ten minutes together examining Mary, then Thoroughgood went over to the alcove by the end window, where, though in full view of the ward, they could not be overheard.

"Well?" he said.

Out of the haze Andrew heard himself speak.

"I don't know how you feel, Doctor Thoroughgood, but it seems to me that the progress of this case isn't quite satisfactory."

"There are one or two features," Thoroughgood pulled at his narrow little beard.

"It seems to me that there's some slight extension."

"Oh, I don't think so, Manson."

"The temperature is more erratic."

"'M, perhaps."

"Excuse me for suggesting it—I appreciate our relative positions perfectly, but this case means a great deal to me. Under the circumstances would you not consider pneumothorax. You remember I was very anxious we should use it on Mary, when the case came in."

Thoroughgood glanced sideways at Manson. His face altered, set into stubborn lines.

"No, Manson. I'm afraid I don't see this as a case for induction. I didn't then—and I don't now."

There was a silence. Andrew could not utter another word. He knew Thoroughgood, his crotchety obstinacy. He felt spent, physically and morally, unable to pursue an argument which must be fruitless. He listened with an immobile face while Thoroughgood ran on, airing his own views about the case. When the other concluded and started to go round the remaining beds he went over to Mary, told her he would call again to see her the following day and left the ward. Before he drove away from the hospital he asked the lodge porter to ring up his house to say he would not be in for lunch.

It was now not far off one o'clock. He was still distressed, wrapped in painful self-contemplation, and faint for want of food. Near Battersea Bridge he stopped outside a small cheap tea-room. Here he ordered coffee and some hot buttered toast. But he could only drink the coffee, his stomach revolted at the toast. He felt the waitress gazing at him curiously.

"Ain't it right?" she said. "I'll change it."

He shook his head, asked her for his check. As she wrote it he caught himself stupidly counting the shiny black buttons on her dress. Once, a long time ago, he had gazed at three pearly buttons in a Drineffy schoolroom. Outside, a yellow glare hung oppressively above the river. As from a distance he remembered that he had two appointments this afternoon at Welbeck Street. He drove there slowly.

Nurse Sharp was in a bad temper, her usual humour when he asked her to come in on Saturdays. Yet she also inquired if he felt ill. Then, in a softer voice, for Doctor Hamson was a particular object of her regard, she told him that Freddie had rung him twice since lunch time.

When she went out of the consulting-room he sat at his desk staring straight in front of him. The first of his patients arrived at half past two— a heart case, a young clerk from the Mines Department, who had come to him through Gill, who was genuinely suffering from a valvular complaint. He found that he was spending a long time over this case, taking especial pains, detaining the young man earnestly while he carefully went over the details of the treatment. At the end as the other fumbled for his thin pocket-book he said quickly:

"Please don't pay me now. Wait until I send your bill."

The thought that he would never send the bill, that he had lost his thirst for money and could once again despise it, comforted him strangely.

Then the second case came in, a woman of forty-five, Miss Basden, one of the most faithful of his followers. His heart sank at the sight of her. Rich, selfish, hypochrondriacal, she was a younger, a more egotistic replica of that Mrs. Raeburn he had once seen with Hamson in Sherrington's Home.

He listened wearily, his hand on his brow, while, smiling, she launched nto an account of all that had happened to her constitution since her visit to him a few days before. Suddenly he raised his head.

"Why do you come to me, Miss Basden?"

She broke off in the middle of a sentence, the pleased expression still fixed upon the upper part of her face, but her mouth dropping slowly open.

"Oh, I know I'm to blame," he said. "I told you to come. But there's nothing really wrong with you."

"Doctor Manson!" she gasped, unable to believe her ears.

It was quite true. He realised, with cruel insight, that all her symptoms were due to money. She had never done a day's work in her life, her body was soft, pampered, over-fed. She did not sleep because she did not exercise her muscles. She did not even exercise her brain. She had nothing to do but cut coupons and think about her dividends and scold her maid and wonder what she, and her pet Pomeranian, would eat. If only she would walk out of his room and do something real. Stop all the little pills and sedatives and hypnotics and cholagogues and every other kind of rubbish. Give some of her money to the poor. Help other people and stop thinking about herself! But she would never, never do that, it was useless even to demand it of her. She was spiritually dead and, God help him, so was he!

He said heavily:

"I'm sorry I can't be of any further service to you, Miss Basden. I—I may be going away. But I've no doubt you'll find other doctors, round about here, who will be only too happy to pander to you."

She opened her mouth several times like a fish gasping for air. Then an expression of positive apprehension came upon her face. She was sure, quite sure, that he had gone out of his mind. She did not wait to reason with him. She rose, hastily gathering her belongings together, and hurried from the room.

He prepared to go home, shutting the drawers of his desk with an air of finality. But before he got up Nurse Sharp bounced into the room, smiling.

"Doctor Hamson to see you! He's come round himself instead of telephoning."

The next minute Freddie was there, airily lighting a cigarette, flinging himself into a chair with an air of purpose in his eye. His tone had never been friendlier.

"Sorry to bother you on a Saturday, old man. But I knew you were here, so I brought round the old mountain to Mahomet. Now look here, Manson. I've heard all about the operation yesterday and I don't mind telling you I'm darn well glad. It's about high time you had an inside slant on dear friend Ivory." Hamson's voice took on a sudden vicious twist. "I think you ought to know, old chap, that I've been rather falling out with Ivory and Deedman lately. They haven't been playing the game with me. We've been running a little pool together, and very profitable it was, but now I'm pretty well sure these two are twisting me out of some of my share. Besides which, I'm about sick of Ivory's bloody side. He's no surgeon. You're damned well right. He's nothing but a damned abortionist. You didn't know that, eh? Well, take it from me as gospel. There's a couple of nursing-homes not one hundred miles from this house where they do nothing else—all very pretty and above-board of course—and Ivory's the head scraper! Deedman isn't much better. He's nothing but a sleek dope peddler and he isn't so smart as Ivory. One of these days he's going to get it in the neck from the D.D.A. Now you listen to me, old man, I'm speaking to you for your own good. I'd like you to know the whole inside story about these fellows because I want you to throw them over and come in with me. You've been too damn green. You haven't been getting your proper whack. Don't you know that when Ivory gets a hundred guineas for an operation he hands back fifty—that's how he gets them, you see! And what has he been handling you!—a measly fifteen or maybe twenty. It isn't good enough, Manson! And after this bit of botching yesterday I damn well wouldn't stand for it. Now I've said nothing to *them* yet, I'm too smart for that, but here's my scheme, old man. Let's ditch them altogether, you and me, and start a tight little partnership of our own. After all we were old pals at college, weren't we? I like you. I've always liked you. And I can show you a hell of a lot." Freddie broke off to light another cigarette, then he smiled agreeably, expansively, exhibiting his possibilities as a potential partner. "You wouldn't believe the stunts I've pulled. D'you know my latest. Three guineas a time injections—*of sterile water*! Patient came in one day for her vaccine. I'd forgotten to order the damn thing, so rather than disappoint, pumped in the H_2O. She came back the next day to say she'd had a better reaction than from any of the others. *So I went on*. And why not? It all boils down to faith and the bottle of coloured water. Mind you I can plug the whole pharmacopœia into them when it's necessary. I'm not unprofessional. Lord, no! It's just that I'm wise, and if you and I really got together, Manson—you with your degrees and me with my savvy—we'd simply skim the pool. There's got to be two of us, you see. You want second opinions all the time. And I've got my eye on a smart young surgeon—hell of a lot better than Ivory!—we might snaffle him later. Eventually we might even have our own nursing-home. And *then* we'd be in Klondyke."

Andrew remained motionless and stiff. He had no anger against Hamson, only a bitter loathing of himself. Nothing could have shown him more blastingly how he stood, what he had done, where he had been going, than this suggestion of Hamson's. At last, seeing that some answer was demanded of him, he mumbled:

"I can't go in with you, Freddie. I've—I've suddenly got sick of it. I think I'll chuck it here for a bit. There are too many jackals in this square mile of country. There's a lot of good men, trying to do good work, practising honestly, fairly, but the rest of them are just jackals. It's the jackals who give all these unnecessary injections, whip out tonsils and appendices that aren't doing any harm, play ball amongst one another with their patients, split fees, perform abortions, back up pseudo-scientific remedies, chase the guineas all the time."

Hamson's face had slowly reddened.

"What the hell!" he spluttered. "What about yourself?"

"I know, Freddie," Andrew said heavily. "I'm just as bad. I don't want any ill-feeling between us. You used to be my best friend."

Hamson jumped up.

"Have you gone off your rocker or what?"

"Perhaps. But I'm going to try and stop thinking of money and material success. That isn't the test of a good doctor. When a doctor earns five thousand a year he's not healthy. And why—why should a man try to make money out of suffering humanity?"

"You bloody fool," said Hamson distinctly. He swung round and went out of the room.

Again Andrew sat woodenly at his desk, alone, desolate. He got up at last and drove home. As he approached his house he was conscious of the rapid beating of his heart. It was now after six o'clock. The whole trend of his weary day seemed working upwards to its climax. His hand trembled violently as he turned his latch-key in the door.

Christine was in the front room. The sight of her pale still face sent a great shiver through him. He longed for her to ask, to show some concern as to how he had spent these hours away from her. But she merely said, in that even non-committal voice:

"You've had a long day. Will you have some tea before the surgery?"

He answered:

"There won't be any surgery to-night."

She glanced at him:

"But Saturday—it's your busiest night."

His answer was to write out a notice stating that the surgery was closed to-night. He walked along the passage, pinned it upon the surgery door. His heart was now thumping so violently he felt that it must burst. When he returned along the passage she was in the consulting-room, her face paler still, her eyes distraught.

"What is the matter?" she asked in a strange voice.

He looked at her. The anguish in his heart tore at him, broke through in a great rush that swept him beyond all control.

"Christine!" Everything within him went into that single word. Then he was at her feet, kneeling, weeping.

XVII

THEIR RECONCILIATION was the most wonderful thing that had happened to them since they first fell in love. Next morning, which was Sunday, he lay beside her, as in those days at Aberalaw, talking, talking and, as though years had slipped from him, pouring out his heart to her. Outside the quiet of Sunday was in the air, the sound of bells, soothing and peaceful. But he was not peaceful.

"How did I come to do it?" he groaned restlessly. "Was I mad, Chris, or what? I can't believe it when I look back on it. Me—getting in with that crowd—after Denny, and Hope—God! I should be executed."

She soothed him. "It all happened with such a rush dear. It would have swept anyone off their feet."

719

"No, but honestly, *Chris*. I feel like going off my head when I think about it. And what a hell of a time it must have been for you! Lord! it ought to be a *painful* execution!"

She smiled, actually smiled. It was the most marvellous experience to see her face stripped of that frozen blankness, tender, happy, solicitous of him. Oh, God! he thought: we're both *living* again.

"There's only one thing to be done," he brought his brows together determinedly. Despite his nervous brooding he felt strong now, freed from a haze of illusion, ready to act. "We've got to clear out of here. I'm in too deep, Chris, far too deep. I'd only be reminded at every turn of the fake stuff I'd been doing, yes and maybe get pulled back. We can easily sell the practice. And oh! Chris, I've got a wonderful idea."

"Yes, darling?"

He relaxed his nervous frown to smile at her diffidently, tenderly.

"How long is it since you called me that? I like it. Yes, I know, I deserved it—oh, don't let me start thinking again, Chris!—this idea, this scheme—it hit me whenever I woke up this morning. I was worrying all over again about Hamson having asked me to join up with his rotten team idea—then suddenly it struck me, why not a genuine team? It's the sort of thing they have amongst doctors in America—Stillman always cracks it up to me, even though he isn't a doctor himself—but we just don't seem to have gone in for it here much. You see, Chris, even in quite a small provincial town you could have a clinic, a little team of doctors, each doing his own stuff. Now listen, darling, instead of sticking in with Hamson and Ivory and Deedman why don't I get Denny and Hope together and form a genuine threesome? Denny does all the surgical work—and you know how good he is!—I handle the medical side, and Hope is our bacteriologist! You see the benefit of that, we're each specialising in our own province and pooling our knowledge. Perhaps you remember all Denny's arguments—and mine too—about our hidebound G.P. system—how the general practitioner is made to stagger along, carrying everything on his shoulders, an impossibility! Group medicine is the answer to that, the perfect answer. It comes between State medicine and isolated, individual effort. The only reason we haven't had it here is because the big men like keeping everything in their own hands. But oh! Wouldn't it be wonderful, dear, if we could form a little front-line unit, scientifically and—yes, let me say it—spiritually intact, a kind of pioneer force to try and break down preudice, knock out the old fetishes, maybe start a complete revolution in our whole medical system."

Her cheek pressed against the pillow, she gazed at him with shining eyes.

"It's like old times to hear you talk that way. I can't tell you how I love it. Oh! it's like beginning all over again. I am happy, darling, *happy*."

"I've got a lot to make up for," he reasoned sombrely. "I've been a fool. And worse." He pressed his brow with his hands. "I can't get poor Harry Vidler out of my head. And I won't, either, till I do something really to make up for it." He groaned suddenly! "I was to blame there, Chris, as much as Ivory. I can't help feeling I've got off too easily. It doesn't seem right that I should get away with it. But I'll work like hell, Chris. And I believe Denny and Hope will come in with me. You know their ideas. Denny's really dying to get back into the rough and tumble of a practice again. And Hope—if we give him a little lab. where he can do original stuff between making our sera—he'll follow us anywhere."

He jumped out of bed and began to pace up and down the room in his old impetuous style, torn between elation for the future and remorse of the past, turning things over in his head, worrying, hoping, planning.

"I've so much to settle up, Chris," he cried, "and one thing I must see about. Look, dear! When I've written some letters—and we've had lunch—how about taking a little run into the country with me."

She looked at him questioningly.

"But if you're busy?"

"I'm not too busy for this. Honestly, Chris, I have a fearful weight on my mind over Mary Boland. She's not getting on well at the Victoria and I haven't taken nearly enough notice. Thoroughgood is most unsympathetic and he doesn't properly understand her case, at least not to my way of thinking. God! If anything happened to Mary after me making myself responsible to Con for her I would just about go crazy. It's an awful thing to say of one's own hospital but she'll *never* recover at the Victoria. She ought to be out in the country, in the fresh air, in a good sanatorium."

"Yes?"

"That's why I want us to run out to Stillman's. Bellevue's the finest, the most marvellous little place you could ever hope to see. If only I could persuade him to take Mary in—— Oh! I'd not only be satisfied, I'd feel I'd really done something worth while."

She said with decision:

"We'll leave the minute you're ready."

When he had dressed he went downstairs, wrote a long letter to Denny and another to Hope. He had only three serious cases on his hands and on his way to visit them he posted the letters. Then, after a light meal, he and Christine set out for Wycombe.

The journey, despite the emotional tension persisting in his mind, was a happy one. More than ever it was borne upon him that happiness was an inner state, wholly spiritual, independent—whatever the cynics might say—of worldly possessions. All these months, when he had been striving and tearing after wealth and position and succeeding in every material sense, he had imagined himself happy. But he had not been happy. He had been existing in a kind of delirium, craving more after everything he got. Money, he thought bitterly, it was all for dirty money! First he had told himself he wanted to make £1,000 a year. When he reached that income he had immediately doubled it, and set that figure as his maximum. But that maximum, when achieved, found him dissatisfied. And so it had gone on. He wanted more and more. It would in the end have destroyed him.

He glanced sideways at Christine. How she must have suffered because of him! But now, if he had wished for any confirmation of the sanity of his decision, the sight of her altered, glowing face was evidence enough. It was not now a pretty face for there were marks of the wear and tear of life drawn upon it, a little dark of lines about the eyes, a faint hollowing of the cheeks which had once been firm and blooming. But it was a face which had always worn an aspect of serenity and truth. And this reanimation which kindled it was so bright and moving he felt a fresh pang of compunction strike deeply into him. He swore he would never again in all his life do anything to make her sad.

They reached Wycombe towards three o'clock, then took a side road uphill which led along the crest of the ridge past Lacey Green. The situation of Bellevue was superb, upon a little plateau which though sheltered on the north afforded an outlook over both valleys.

Stillman was cordial in his reception. He was a self-contained, undemonstrative little man, seldom given to enthusiasm, yet he showed his pleasure in Andrew's visit by demonstrating the full beauty and efficiency of his creation.

Bellevue was intentionally small, but of its perfection there could be no question. Two wings, angled to a south-western exposure were united by a central administrative section. Above the entrance hall and offices was a lavishly equipped treatment room, its south wall entirely of vitaglass. All the windows were of this material, the heating and ventilating system the last word in modern efficiency. As Andrew walked round he could not help contrasting this ultra-modern perfection with the antique buildings, built a hundred years before, which served as many of the London hospitals, and with those old dwelling-houses, badly converted and ill-equipped, which masqueraded as nursing-homes.

Afterwards, when he had shown them round, Stillman gave them tea. And here Andrew brought out his request with a rush.

"I hate asking you a favour, Mr. Stillman." Christine had to smile at the almost forgotten formula. "But I wonder if you'd take in a case for me here? Early T.B. Probably requires pneumothorax. You see she's the daughter of a great friend of mine, a professional man—dentist —and she's not getting on where she is——"

Something like amusement gathered behind Stillman's pale blue eyes.

"You don't mean you're proposing to send me a case. Doctors don't send me cases here—though they do in America. You forget that here I'm a fake healer running a quack sanatorium, the kind that makes his patients walk barefooted in the dew—before leading them in to a grated carrot breakfast!"

Andrew did not smile.

"I didn't ask you to pull my leg, Mr. Stillman. I'm dead serious about this girl. I'm—I'm worried about her."

"But I'm afraid I am full up, my friend. In spite of the antipathy of your medical fraternity I have a waiting list as long as my arm. Strange!" Stillman did at last impassively smile. "People want me to cure them in spite of the doctors."

"Well!" Andrew muttered—Stillman's refusal was a great disappointment to him. "I was more or less banking on it. If we could have got Mary in here—oh! I'd have felt *relieved*. Why, you've got the finest treatment centre in England. I'm not trying to flatter you. I know! When I think of that old ward in the Victoria where she's lying now, listening to the cockroaches scramble behind the skirting——"

Stillman leaned forward and picked up a thin cucumber sandwich from the low table before him. He had a characteristic, almost finicky way of handling things as though he had just, with the utmost care, washed his hands and went in fear of soiling them.

"So! It's a little ironic comedy you are arranging. No, no, I mustn't talk that way, I see you are worried. And I will help you. Although you *are* a doctor I'll take your case." Stillman's lip twitched at the blank expression on Andrew's face. "You see, I'm broad-minded. I don't mind dealing with the profession when I'm obliged to. Why don't you smile?—that's a joke. Never mind. Even if you've no sense of humour you're a darn sight more enlightened than most of the brethren. Let me see. I have no room vacant till next week. Wednesday, I think. Bring your case to me a week on Wednesday and I promise you I'll do the best for her I can!"

Andrew's face reddened with gratitude.

"I—I can't thank you enough—I——"

"Then don't. And don't be so polite. I prefer you when you look like throwing things about. Mrs. Manson, does he ever throw the china at you? I have a great friend in America, he owns sixteen newspapers, and every time he gets in a temper he breaks a five cent plate. Well, one day, it so happened——"

He went on to tell them a long—and to Manson—quite pointless story. But, driving home in the cool of the evening Andrew meditated to Christine:

"That's one thing settled anyway, Chris—a big load off my mind. I'm positive it's the right place for Mary. He's a great chap is Stillman. I like him a lot. He's nothing to look at, but underneath he's just pressed steel. I wonder if ever we could have a clinic on these lines—miniature replica—Hope and Denny and me. That's a wild dream, eh? But you never know. And I've been thinking, if Denny and Hope do come in with me and we pitch out in the provinces—we might be near enough one of the coalfields for me to pick up my inhalation work again. What d'you think, Chris?"

By way of answer she leaned sideways and, greatly to the common danger on the public highway, she soundly kissed him.

XVIII

NEXT MORNING he rose early, after a good night's rest. He felt tense, keyed for anything. Going straight to the telephone, he put the practice in the hands of Fulger & Turner, medical transfer agents, of Adam Street. Mr. Gerald Turner, present head of that old established firm, answered personally and in response to Andrew's request he came out promptly to Chesborough Terrace. After a scrutiny of the books lasting all that forenoon he assured him that he would have not the slightest difficulty in effecting a quick sale.

"Of course, we shall have to state a reason, doctor, in our advertisements," said Mr. Turner gently tapping his teeth with his cased pencil. "Any purchaser is bound to ask himself—why should any doctor give up a gold-mine like this?—and excuse me for saying so, doctor, it *is* a gold-mine. I've never seen such spot cash receipts for many a day. Shall we say on account of ill-health?"

"No," said Andrew brusquely. "Tell them the truth. Say——" he checked himself, "oh, say for personal reasons."

"Very well, doctor," and Mr. Gerald Turner wrote, against his draft advertisement: "Relinquished from motives purely personal and unconnected with the practice."

Andrew concluded:

"And remember, I don't want a fortune for this thing—only a good price. There's a lot of tame cats who mightn't follow the new man around."

At lunch time Christine produced two telegrams which had come for him. He had asked both Denny and Hope to wire him in reply to the letters he had written the day before.

The first, from Denny, said simply: *Impressed. Expect me to-morrow evening.*

The second declared with typical flippancy:

Must I spend all my life with lunatics. Feature of English provincial towns pubs stocks cathedrals and pig markets. Did you say laboratory. Signed IN-DIGNANT RATEPAYER.

After lunch Andrew ran down to the Victoria. It was not Doctor Thoroughgood's visiting hour but that suited his purpose admirably. He wanted no fuss or unpleasantness, least of all did he wish to upset his

724

senior who, for all his obstinacy and prim concern with the barber-surgeons of the past, had always treated him well.

Seated beside Mary's bed he explained privately to her what he wished to do.

"It was my fault to begin with," he patted her hand reassuringly. "I ought to have foreseen this wasn't quite the place for you. You'll find a difference when you get to Bellevue—a big difference, Mary. But they've been very kind to you here, there's no need to hurt anybody's feelings. You must just say you want to go out next Wednesday, discharge yourself—if you don't like to do it yourself I'll get Con to write and say he wants you out. They've so many people waiting for beds it'll be easy. Then on Wednesday I'll take you out myself by car to Bellevue. I'll have a nurse with me and everything. Nothing could be simpler—or better for you."

He returned home with a sense of something further accomplished, feeling that he was beginning to clear up the mess into which his life had fallen. That evening in his surgery he set himself sternly to weed out the chronics, ruthlessly to sacrifice his charm school. A dozen times in the course of an hour he declared firmly:

"This must be your last visit. You've been coming a long time. You're quite better now. And it doesn't do to go on drinking medicine!"

It was amazing, at the end of it, how much lighter he felt. To be able to speak his mind honestly and emphatically was a luxury he had long denied himself. He went in to Christine with a step almost boyish.

"Now I feel less like a salesman for bath salts!" He groaned: "God! How can I talk that way. I'm forgetting what's happened—Vidler—everything I've done!"

It was then that the telephone rang. She went to answer it, and it seemed to him that she was a longish time absent and that when she returned her expression was again oddly strained.

"Someone wants you on the phone."

"Who . . .?" All at once he realised that Frances Lawrence had called him up. There was a bar of silence in the room. Then, hurriedly, he said, "Tell her I'm not in. Tell her I've gone away. No, wait!" His expression strengthened, he took an abrupt movement forward. "I'll speak to her myself."

He came back in five minutes to find that she had seated herself with some work in her familiar corner where the light was good. He glanced at her covertly then glanced away, walked to the window and stood there moodily looking out with his hands in his pockets. The quiet click of her knitting needles made him feel inordinately foolish, a sad and stupid dog, cringing home limp tailed and bedraggled from some illicit foray. At last he could contain himself no longer. Still with his back to her he said:

"That's finished too. It may interest you to know it was only my stupid vanity—that and self interest. I loved you all the time." Suddenly he ground out, "Damn it, Chris. It was all my fault. These people don't know any different, but I do. I'm getting out of this too easy—too easy. But let me tell you—while I was at the phone I rang up le Roy, thought I might as well make one job of it. Cremo products won't be interested in me any more. I've wiped myself off their slate, too, Chris. And, God! I'll see that I stay off!"

She did not answer but the click of her needles made, in the silent room, a brisk and cheerful sound. He must have remained there a long time, his shamed eyes upon the movement of the street outside, upon the lights springing up through the summer darkness. When at length he turned the invading dusk had crept into the room but she still sat there, almost invisible in the shadowed chair, a small slight figure occupied with her knitting.

That night he woke up sweating and distressed, turning to her blindly, still anguished by the terrors of his dream.

"Where are you, Chris? I'm sorry. I'm truly sorry. I'll do my best to be decent to you in future." Then quieted, already half asleep. "We'll take a holiday when we sell out here. God! my nerves are rotten —to think I once called you neurotic! And when we settle down, wherever it is, you'll have a garden, Chris. I know how you love it. Remember—remember at Vale View, Chris?"

Next morning he brought her home a great bunch of chrysanthemums. He strove with all his old intensity, to show his affection for her, not by that showy generosity which she had hated—the thought of that Plaza luncheon still made him shiver!—but in small, considerate, almost forgotten, ways.

At tea time when he came home with a special kind of sponge cake that she liked and on top of that silently brought in her house slippers from the cupboard at the end of the passage she sat up in her chair, frowning, mildly protesting:

"Don't, darling, *don't*—or I'm sure to suffer for it. Next week you'll be tearing your hair and kicking me round the house—like you used to in those old days."

"Chris!" he exclaimed, his face shocked, pained. "Can't you see that's all changed. From now on I'm going to make things up to you."

"All right, all right, my dear." Smiling she wiped her eyes. Then with a sudden tensity of which he had never suspected her, "I don't mind how it is so long as we're *together*. I don't want you to run after me. All I ask is that you don't run after anybody else."

That evening Denny arrived, as he had promised, for supper. He brought a message from Hope, who had rung him on the toll line from Cambridge, to say that he would be unable to get to London that evening.

"He said he was detained on business," Denny declared, knocking out his pipe. "But I strongly suspect friend Hope will shortly be taking unto himself a bride. Romantic business—the mating of a bacteriologist!"

"Did he say anything about my idea?" Andrew asked quickly.

"Yes, he's keen—not that it matters, we could just pocket him and take him along with us! And I'm keen too." Denny unfurled his napkin and helped himself to salad. "I can't imagine how a first class scheme like this came out of your fool head. Especially when I fancied you'd tucked yourself up as a West End soap merchant. Tell me about it."

Andrew told him, fully, and with increasing emphasis. They began to discuss the scheme in its more practical details. They suddenly realised how far they had progressed when Denny said:

"My view is that we don't want to pick too large a town. Under twenty thousand inhabitants—that's ideal. We can make things hum there. Look at a map of the West Midlands. You'll find scores of industrial towns served by four or five doctors who are politely at each other's throats, where the good old M.D. drags out half a tonsil one morning and sludges mist. alba the next. It's just there that we can demonstrate our idea of specialised co-operation. We won't buy ourselves in. We just, so to speak, arrive. Lord! I'd like to see their faces, Doctor Brown and Jones and Robinson, I mean. We'll have to stand waggon loads of abuse—incidentally, we may be lynched. Seriously, though, we want a central clinic—as you say—with Hope's lab. attached. We might even have a couple of beds upstairs. We won't be very grand at first—it means conversion rather than building, I suppose—but I've a feeling we'll take root." Suddenly aware of Christine's glistening eyes as she sat following their talk he smiled. "What do you think about it, ma'am? Crazy, isn't it?"

"Yes," she answered a trifle huskily. "But it's—it's the crazy things that matter."

"That's the word, Chris! By God! This does matter."

Andrew bounced the cutlery as he brought down his fist. "The scheme's good. But it's the ideal behind the scheme! A new interpretation of the Hippocratic oath; an absolute allegiance to the scientific ideal, no empiricism, no shoddy methods, no stock prescribing, no fee-snatching, no proprietary muck, no soft-soaping of hypochrondriacs, no—— Oh! for the Lord's sake, give me a drink! My vocal cords won't stand up to this, I ought to have a drum."

They talked on until one o'clock in the morning. Andrew's tense excitement was a stimulus felt even by the stoic Denny. His last train had long since departed. That night he occupied the spare room and as he hurried off after breakfast on the following day he promised to come to town again on the following Friday. Meanwhile he would see Hope and—final proof of his enthusiasm—buy a large scale map of the West Midlands.

"It's on, Chris, it's on!" Andrew came back triumphant from the door. "Philip's as keen as mustard. He doesn't say much. But *I know*."

That same day they had the first inquiry for the practice. A prospective buyer arrived and he was followed by others. Gerald Turner came in person with the more likely purchasers. He had a beautiful flow of elegant language which he even directed upon the architecture of the garage. On Monday, Doctor Noel Lowry called twice, alone in the morning and escorted by the agent in the afternoon. Thereafter Turner rang up Andrew, suavely confidential:

"Doctor Lowry is interested, doctor, *very* interested I may say. He's particularly anxious we don't sell till his wife has a chance to see the house. She's at the seaside with the children. She's coming up Wednesday."

This was the day on which Andrew had arranged to take Mary to Bellevue but he felt the matter could be left in Turner's hands. Everything had gone as he anticipated at the hospital. Mary was due to leave at two o'clock. He had fixed up with Nurse Sharp to accompany them in the car.

It was raining heavily as, at half past one, he started off by driving to Welbeck Street to pick up Nurse Sharp. She was in a sulky humour waiting but unwilling, when he reached No. 57A. Since he had told her he must dispense with her service at the end of the month her moods had been even more uncertain. She snapped an answer to his greeting and stepped into the car.

Fortunately he had no difficulty with Mary. He drew up as she came through the porter's lodge and the next moment she was in the back of the saloon with Nurse Sharp, warmly wrapped in a rug with a hot bottle at her feet. They had not gone far, however, before he began to wish he had not brought the sulky and suspicious nurse. It was evident that she considered the expedition far beyond the scope of her duties. He wondered how he had managed to put up with her so long. At half past three they reached Bellevue. The rain had now ceased and a burst of sun came through the clouds as they ran up the drive. Mary leaned forward, her eyes fastened nervously, a little apprehensively, upon the place from which she had been led to expect so much.

Andrew found Stillman in the office. He was anxious to see the case with him at once for the question of pneumothorax induction weighed heavily on his mind. He spoke of this as he smoked a cigarette and drank a cup of tea.

"Very well," Stillman nodded as he concluded. "We'll go up right now."

He led the way to Mary's room. She was now in bed, pale from her journey and still inclined to apprehensiveness, gazing at Nurse Sharp who stood at one end of the room folding up her dress. She gave a little start as Stillman came forward.

728

He examined her meticulously. His examination was an illumination to Andrew, quiet, silent, absolutely precise. He had no bedside manner. He was not impressive. He did not, indeed, resemble a physician at work. He was like a business man engaged with the complications of an adding machine which had gone wrong. Although he used the stethoscope, most of his investigation was tactile, a palpation of the inter-rib and supra-clavicular spaces as if, through his smooth fingers, he could actually sense the condition of the living, breathing lung cells beneath.

When it was over he said nothing to Mary but took Andrew beyond the door.

"Pneumothorax," he said. "There's no question. That lung should have been collapsed weeks ago. I'm going to do it right away. Go back and tell her."

While he went off to see to the apparatus Andrew returned to the room and informed Mary of their decision. He spoke as lightly as he could yet it was evident that the immediate prospect of the induction upset her further.

"You'll do it?" she asked in an uneasy tone. "Oh! I'd much rather you did it."

"It's nothing, Mary. You won't feel the slightest pain. I'll be here. I'll be helping him! I'll see that you're all right."

He had meant actually to leave the whole technique to Stillman. But as she was so nervous, so palpably depending upon him and as, indeed, he felt himself responsible for her presence here, he went to the treatment-room and offered his assistance to Stillman.

Ten minutes later they were ready. When Mary was brought in he gave her local anæsthesia. He then stood by the manometer, while Stillman skilfully inserted the needle, controlling the flow of sterile nitrogen gas into the pleura. The apparatus was exquisitely delicate and Stillman undoubtedly a master of the technique. He had an expert touch with the cannula, driving it deftly forward, his eye fixed upon the manometer for the final "snap" which announced perforation of the parietal pleura. He had his own method of deep manipulation to prevent the occurrence of surgical emphysema.

After an early phrase of acute nervousness Mary's anxiety gradually faded. She submitted to the operation with increasing confidence and at the end she could smile at Andrew, completely relaxed. Back again in her room she said:

"You were right. It was nothing. I don't feel as if you'd done anything at all."

"No?" He lifted an eyebrow; then laughed. "That's how it should be—no fuss, no sense of anything terrible happening to you—I wish every operation could go that way! But we've immobilised that lung of yours all the same. It'll have a rest now. And when it starts breathing again—believe me!—it will be healed."

Her glance rested upon him then wandered round the pleasant room, through the window to the view of the valley beyond.

"I'm going to like it here, after all. He doesn't try to be nice—Mr. Stillman, I mean—but somehow you feel he is nice. Do you think I could have my tea?"

XIX

It was nearly seven o'clock when he left Bellevue. He had remained longer than he had anticipated, talking to Stillman on the lower verandah, enjoying the cool air and the quiet conversation of the other man. As he drove off he was pervaded by an extraordinary sense of placidity, of tranquillity. He derived that benefit from Stillman whose personality, with its repose, its indifference to the trivialities of life, reacted favourably upon his own impetuous disposition. Moreover, he was now easy in his mind about Mary. He contrasted his previous hurried action, her summary dispatch into an out-of-date hospital, with all that he had done for her this afternoon. It had caused him inconvenience, a great deal of troublesome arrangement. It was quite unorthodox. Though he had not discussed the question of payment with Stillman, he realised that Con was in no position to meet the Bellevue fees and that, in consequence, the settlement of the bill would fall upon himself. But all this became as nothing beside the glowing sense of real achievement which pervaded him. For the first time in many months he felt that he had done something which, to his own belief, was worthy. It pervaded him warmly, a cherished thought, the beginning of his vindication.

He drove slowly, enjoying the quiet of the evening. Nurse Sharp once again sat in the back seat of the car but she had nothing to say and he, with his own thoughts, was almost unconscious of her. When they drew into London, however, he asked where he should drop her and, on her reply, drew up at Notting Hill Tube Station. He was glad to be rid of her. She was a good nurse but her nature was repressed and unhappy. She had never liked him. He decided to post her month's salary to her the next day. Then he would not see her again.

Strangely, his mood had altered as he came along Paddington Street. It always affected him to pass the Vidler's shop. Out of the corner of his eye he saw it—*Renovations Ltd*. One of the assistants was pulling down the shutters. The simple action was so symbolic it sent a shiver through him. Subdued, he reached Chesborough Terrace and ran the car into his garage. He went into his house with a curious sadness pressing upon him.

Christine met him joyfully in the hall. Whatever his mood might be, hers was vivid with success. Her eyes were shining with her news.

"Sold!" she declared gaily. "Knocked down, lock, stock, and basement. They waited and waited for you, darling—they've only just gone.
Doctor and Mrs. Lowry, I mean. He got so agitated," she laughed,
"because you weren't here for the surgery that he set to and did it
himself. Then I gave them supper. Then we made more conversation.
I could almost see Mrs. Lowry deciding that you'd had a motor smash.
Then *I* began to worry! But now you are here, dear! And it's all *right*.
You've to meet him at Mr. Turner's office to-morrow at eleven to sign
the contract. And—oh! yes—he's given Mr. Turner a deposit."

He followed her into the front room, where the supper had been
cleared from the table. He was pleased, naturally, that the practice
should be sold, yet he could not, at present, summon any great show of
elation.

"It is good, isn't it," Christine went on, "that it should all be settled
up so quickly. I don't think he expects a very long introduction. Oh!
I've been thinking so much before you come in. If only we could have
a little holiday at Val André again, before we start work—it was lovely
there, wasn't it, darling—and we had such a wonderful time——" She
broke off, gazing at him. "Why, what's the matter, dear?"

"Oh, nothing," he smiled, sitting down. "I'm a little tired, I think.
Probably because I missed my dinner——"

"What!" she exclaimed, aghast. "I made certain you'd had it at
Bellevue, before you left." Her glance swept round. "And I've cleared
everything away, and let Mrs. Bennett out to the pictures."

"It doesn't matter."

"But it *does*. No wonder you didn't jump when I told you about the
practice. Now you just sit there one minute and I'll bring up a tray. Is
there anything you'd especially like? I could heat up some soup—or
make you some scrambled egg—or *what*?"

He considered.

"The egg, I think, Chris. Oh! but don't bother. Well, if you like,
then—and perhaps a bit of cheese afterwards."

She was back in no time with a tray on which stood a plate of
scrambled eggs, a glass of celery heart, bread, biscuits, butter and the
cheese-dish. She placed the tray upon the table. As he pulled in his
chair she brought out a bottle of ale from the sideboard cupboard.

While he ate she watched him solicitously. She smiled.

"You know, dear, I've often thought—if we'd lived in Cefan Row,
say a kitchen and one bedroom, we'd have fitted in perfectly. High life
doesn't agree with us. Now I'm going to be a working-man's wife again
I'm awfully happy."

He went on with his scrambled egg. The food was certainly making
him feel better.

"You know, darling," she continued, placing her hands beneath her
chin in her characteristic way, "I've thought such a lot these last few

731

days. Before that my mind was stiff, somehow, all closed up. But since we're together—oh, since we're ourselves again everything has seemed so clear. It's only when you've got to fight for things that they really become worth while. When they just drop into your lap there's no satisfaction in them. Don't you remember those days at Aberalaw— they've been living, simply living in my mind all day—when we had to go through all those rough times together. Well! now I feel that the same thing is starting for us all over again. It's our kind of life, darling. It's *us*! And oh! I'm so happy about it."

He glanced towards her.

"You're really happy, Chris?"

She kissed him lightly.

"Never happier in my life than I am at this moment."

There was a pause. He buttered a biscuit and lifted the lid of the dish to help himself to cheese. But there was anticlimax in the action which revealed, not his favourite Liptauer but no more than a barren end of cheddar, which Mrs. Bennett used for cooking. The instant she saw it Christine gave a self-reproachful cry.

"And I meant to call at Frau Schmidt's to-day!"

"Oh! it's all right, Chris."

"But it isn't all right." She whipped the dish away before he could help himself. "Here am I mooning like a sentimental schoolgirl, giving you no dinner at all—when you come in tired—starving you. Fine sort of working-man's wife I'd be!" She jumped up, her eye upon the clock. "I've just time to rush across for it now before she closes."

"Don't bother, Chris——"

"*Please*, darling." She silenced him gaily. "I *want* to do it. I want to—because you love Frau Schmidt's cheese and I—I love you."

She was out of the room before he could protest again. He heard her quick step in the hall, the light closing of the outer door. His eyes still were faintly smiling—it was so like her to do this. He buttered another biscuit waiting for the arrival of the famous Liptauer, waiting for her return.

The house was very still: Florrie sleeping downstairs, he reflected, and Mrs. Bennett at the cinema. He was glad Mrs. Bennett was coming with them on their new venture. Stillman had been great this afternoon. Mary would be all right now, right as rain. Marvellous how the rain had cleared off this afternoon—beautiful it had been coming home through the country, so fresh and quiet. Thank God! Christine would soon have her garden again. He and Denny and Hope might get themselves lynched by the five doctors in Muddletown. But Chris would always have her garden!

He began absently to eat one of the buttered biscuits. He'd lose his appetite if she didn't hurry up. She must be talking to Frau Schmidt. Good old Frau; sending him his first cases. If he'd only gone on decently instead of—oh, well, that was finished with now, thank God! They were together again, Christine and he, happier than ever they had been. Wonderful to hear her say that a minute ago. He lit a cigarette.

Suddenly the door-bell rang violently. He glanced up, laid down his cigarette, went into the hall. But not before the bell had been wrenched again. He opened the front door.

Immediately he was conscious of the commotion outside, a crowd of people on the pavement, faces and heads interwoven with the darkness. But before he could resolve the mingling pattern, the policeman who had rung the bell loomed up before him. It was Struthers, his old Fife friend, the pointsman. What seemed strange about Struthers was the staring whiteness of his eyes.

"Doctor," he breathed with difficulty like a man who has been running. "Your wife's got hurted. She ran, oh! God Almighty! She ran right out of the shop in front of the bus."

A great hand of ice enclosed him. Before he could speak the commotion was upon him. Suddenly, dreadfully, the hall was filled with people. Frau Schmidt weeping, a bus conductor, another policeman, strangers, all pressing in, forcing him back, into the consulting-room. And then, through the crowd, carried by two men, the figure of his Christine. Her head drooped backwards upon the thin white arch of her neck. Still entwined by its string in the fingers of her left hand was the little parcel from Frau Schmidt. They laid her upon the high couch of his consulting-room. She was quite dead.

XX

HE BROKE down completely and for days was out of his mind. Moments of lucidity there were when he became aware of Mrs. Bennett, of Denny, and, once or twice, of Hope. But for the most part he went through life, performed the actions demanded of him in sheer automatism, his whole being concentrated deep within himself in one long nightmare of despair. His frayed out nervous system intensified the agony of his loss, by creating morbid fancies and terrors of remorse from which he awoke, sweating, crying out in anguish.

Dimly he was conscious of the inquest, the drab informality of the coroner's court, of the evidence given so minutely, so unnecessarily by the witnesses. He stared fixedly at the squat figure of Frau Schmidt upon whose plump cheeks the tears kept rolling, rolling down.

"She was laughing, laughing all the time she came into my shop. Hurry, please—she kept on telling me—I don't want to keep my husband waiting——"

When he heard the coroner expressing sympathy with Doctor Manson in his sad bereavement he knew that it was over. He stood up mechanically, found himself walking upon grey pavements with Denny.

How the arrangements for the funeral were made he did not know, they all came mysteriously to pass without his knowledge. As he drove to Kensal Green his thoughts kept darting hither and thither, backwards through the years. In the dingy confines of the cemetery he remembered the wide and wind-swept uplands behind Vale View where the mountain ponies raced and reared their tangled manes. She had loved to walk there, to feel the breeze upon her cheeks. And now she was being laid in this grimy city graveyard.

That night in the stark torture of his neurosis he tried to drink himself insensible. But the whisky only seemed to goad him to fresh anger against himself. He paced up and down the room, late into the night, muttering aloud, drunkenly apostrophising himself.

"You thought you could get away with it. You thought you *were* getting away with it. But my God! you weren't. Crime and punishment, crime and punishment! You're to blame for what happened to her. You've *got* to suffer." He walked the length of the street, hatless, swaying, to stare wild-eyed at the blank shuttered windows of the Vidler shop. He came back muttering, through bitter maudlin tears, "God is not mocked! Chris said that once—God is not mocked, my friend."

He staggered upstairs, hesitated, went into her room, silent, cold, deserted. There on the dressing-table lay her bag. He picked it up, pressed it against his cheek, then fumblingly opened it. Some coppers and loose silver lay inside, a small handkerchief, a bill for groceries. And then, in the middle pocket he came upon some papers—a faded snapshot of himself taken at Drineffy and—yes, he recognised them with a throbbing pang—those little notes he had received at Christmas from his patients at Aberalaw: *With grateful thanks*—she had treasured them all those years. A heavy sob broke from his heart. He fell on his knees by the bed in a passion of weeping.

Denny made no effort to stop him drinking. It seemed to him that Denny was about the house almost every day. It was not because of the practice, for Doctor Lowry was doing that now. Lowry was living out somewhere but coming in to consult and pick up the calls. He knew nothing, nothing whatever of what was going on, he did not wish to know. He kept out of Lowry's way. His nerves had gone to pieces. The sound of the door-bell made his heart palpitate madly. A sudden step made the sweat break out on the palms of his hands. He sat upstairs in his room with a rolled-up handkerchief between his fingers, wiping his sweating palms from time to time, staring at the fire, knowing that when night came he must face the spectre of insomnia.

This was his condition when Denny walked in one morning and said: "I'm free at last, thank God. Now we can go away."

There was no question of refusal, his power of resistance was completely gone. He did not even ask where they were going. In silent apathy he watched Denny pack a suitcase for him. Within an hour they were on their way to Paddington Station.

They travelled all afternoon through the south-west counties, changed at Newport and struck up through Monmouthshire. At Abergavenny they left the train and here, outside the station, Denny hired a car. As they drove out of the town across the River Usk and through the rich autumnal tinted countryside he said:

"This is a small place I once used to come to—fishing. Llantony Abbey. I think it ought to suit."

They reached their destination, through a network of hazel fringed lanes, at six o'clock. Round a square of close green turf lay the ruins of the Abbey, smooth grey stones, a few arches of the cloisters still upstanding. And adjoining was the guest-house, built entirely from the fallen stones. Near at hand a small stream flowed with a constant soothing ripple. Wood smoke rose, straight and blue, into the quiet evening air.

Next morning Denny dragged Andrew out to walk. It was a crisp dry day but Andrew, sick from a sleepless night, his flabby muscles failing on the first hill, made to turn back when they had gone only a short way. Denny, however, was firm. He walked Andrew eight miles that first day and on the next he made it ten. By the end of the week they were walking twenty miles a day and Andrew, crawling up to his room at night, fell immediately into insensibility upon his bed.

There was no one to worry them at the Abbey. Only a few fishermen remained, for it was now close to the end of the trout season. They ate in the stone-flagged refectory at a long oak table before an open log fire. The food was plain and good.

During their walks they did not speak. Often they walked the whole day long with no more than a few words passing between them. At the beginning Andrew was quite unconscious of the countryside through which they tramped, but as the days passed the beauty of its woods and rivers, of its sweeping bracken-covered hills penetrated gradually, imperceptibly, through his numbed senses.

The progress of his recovery was not sensationally swift, yet by the end of the first month he was able to stand the fatigue of their long marches, eat and sleep normally, bathe in cold water every morning and face the future without cowering. He saw that no better place could have been chosen for his recovery than this isolated spot, no better routine than this spartan, this monastic existence. When the first frost bit hard into the ground he felt the joy of it instinctively in his blood.

He began unexpectedly to talk. The topics of their discussion were inconsequential at the outset. His mind, like an athlete performing simple exercises before approaching greater feats, was guarded in its approach to life. But imperceptibly he learned from Denny the progress of events.

His practice was sold to Doctor Lowry, not for the full amount which Tucker had stipulated—since under the circumstances no introduction had been given—but for a figure near enough that sum. Hope had at last completed the full term of his scholarship, and was now at his home in Birmingham. Denny also was free. He had given up his registrarship before coming to Llantony. The inference was so clear that Andrew suddenly lifted up his head.

"I ought to be fit for work at the beginning of the year."

Now they began to talk in earnest and within a week his hard-faced listlessness was gone. He felt it strange and sad that the human mind should be capable of recovering from such a mortal blow as that which had struck him. Yet he could not help it, the recovery was there. Previously he had trudged with stoic indifference, a perfectly functioning machine. Now he breathed the sharp air with real vigour, switched at the bracken with his stick, took his correspondence out of Denny's hands, and cursed when the post did not bring the *Medical Journal*.

At night Denny and he pored over a large scale map. With the help of an almanac they made a list of towns, weeded out that list, then narrowed their selection down to eight. Two of the towns were in Staffordshire, three in Northampton and three in Warwickshire.

On the following Monday Denny took his departure and was away a week. During these seven days Andrew felt the rushing return of his old desire to work, his own work, the real work he could do with Hope and Denny. His impatience became colossal. On Saturday afternoon he walked all the way to Abergavenny to meet the last train of the week. Returning, disappointed, to endure two further nights and one whole day of this intensifying delay, he found a small dark Ford drawn up at the guest-house. He hurried through the door. There in the lamp-lit refectory, Denny and Hope sat at a ham and egg tea with whipped cream and tinned peaches on the sideboard.

That week-end they had the place entirely to themselves. Philip's report delivered at that richly composite meal was a fiery prelude to the excitement of their discussions. Outside rain and hail battered on the windows. The weather had finally broken. It made no difference to them.

Two of the towns visited by Denny—Franton and Stanborough— were, in Hope's phrase, ripe for medical development. Both were solid semi-agricultural towns upon which recently a new industry had been grafted. Stanborough had a freshly erected plant for the manufacture of motor engine bearings, Franton a large sugar beet factory. Houses were springing up on the outskirts, the population increasing. But in each case the medical services had lagged behind. Franton had only a cottage hospital and Stanborough none at all. Emergency cases were sent to Coventry, fifteen miles away.

These bare details were enough to set them off like hounds upon a scent. But Denny had information even more stimulating. He produced a plan of Stanborough torn from an A.A. midland route itinerary. He remarked:

"I regret to say I stole it from the hotel at Stanborough. Sounds like a good beginning for us there."

"Quick," impatiently declared the once facetious Hope, "what's this mark here?"

"That," Denny said, as they bent their heads over the plan, "is the market square—at least, that's what it amounts to, only for some reason they call it the Circle. It's bang in the centre of the town, high up, too, with a fine situation. You know the kind of thing, a ring of houses and shops and offices, half residential, half old established business, rather a Georgian effect, with low windows and porticoes. The chief medico of the place, a whale of a fellow, I saw him, important red face and mutton chops, incidentally he employs two assistants, has his house in the Circle." Denny's tone was gently ironic. "Directly opposite, on the other side of the charming granite fountain in the middle of the Circle, are two empty houses, large rooms, sound floors, good frontage *and* for sale. It seems to me——"

"And to me," said Hope with a catch in his breath, "off hand I should say there's nothing I should like better than a little lab. opposite that fountain."

They went on talking. Denny unfolded further details, interesting details.

"Of course," he concluded, "we are probably all quite mad. This idea has been brought to perfection in the big American cities by thorough organisation and tremendous outlay. But here—in Stanborough! And we none of us have a lot of cash! We shall also probably fight like hell amongst ourselves. But somehow——"

"God help old mutton chops!" said Hope, rising and stretching himself.

With the prospect of a full day before him Hope left early next morning, dashing off in his Ford in a spatter of mud before the others had finished breakfast. The sky was still heavily overcast but the wind was high, a gusty, exhilarating day. After breakfast Andrew went out by himself for an hour. It was good to feel fit again, with his work reaching out to him once more in the high adventure of the new clinic. He had not realised how much his scheme meant to him until now, quite suddenly it was near fruition.

When he returned at eleven o'clock the post had come in, a pile of letters forwarded from London. He sat down at the table with a sense of anticipation to open them. Denny was beside the fire behind the morning paper.

His first letter was from Mary Boland. As he scanned the closely written sheets his face warmed to a smile. She began by sympathising with him, hoping he had now recovered fully. Then briefly she told him about herself. She was better, infinitely better, almost well again. Her temperature had been normal for the last five weeks. She was up, taking graduated exercise. She had put on so much weight he would scarcely recognise her. She asked him if he could not come to see her. Mr. Stillman had returned to America for several months leaving his assistant, Mr. Marland, in charge. She could not thank him sufficiently for having sent her to Bellevue.

Andrew laid down the letter, his expression still bright with the thought of Mary's recovery. Then, throwing aside a number of circulars and advertising literature, all in flimsy envelopes with halfpenny stamps, he picked up his next letter. This was a long official-looking envelope. He opened it, drew out the stiff sheet of notepaper within.

Then the smile left his face, He stared at the letter with disbelieving eyes. His pupils widened. He turned deadly pale. For a full minute he remained motionless, staring, staring at the letter.

"Denny," he said, in a low voice. "Look at this."

XXI

Eight weeks before, when Andrew set down Nurse Sharp at Notting Hill Station she went on by tube to Oxford Circus and from there walked rapidly in the direction of Queen Anne Street. She had arranged with her friend Nurse Trent, who was Doctor Hamson's receptionist, to spend the evening at the Queen's Theatre where Louis Savory, whom they both adored, was appearing in *The Duchess Declares*. But since it was now quarter past eight and the performance began at eight forty-five the margin of time left for Nurse Sharp to call for her friend and be in the upper circle of the Queen's was narrow. Moreover, instead of having leisure for a nice hot meal at the Corner House as she had planned, they would be obliged to snatch a sandwich on the way down or perhaps do without altogether. Nurse Sharp's mood, as she thrust her way along Queen Anne Street, was that of a woman bitterly ill-used. As the events of the afternoon kept turning in her mind she seethed with indignation and resentment. Mounting the steps of No. 17c she hurriedly pressed the bell.

It was Nurse Trent who opened the door, her expression patiently reproachful. But before she could speak Nurse Sharp pressed her arm.

"My dear," she said, speaking rapidly, "I'm ever so sorry. But *what* a day I've had! I'll tell you later. Just let me pop in to leave my things. If I come as I am I think we can just do it."

At that moment as the two nurses stood together n the passage

Hamson came down the stairs, groomed, shining and in his evening clothes. Seeing them he paused. Freddie could never resist an opportunity to demonstrate the charm of his personality. It was part of his technique, making people like him, getting the most out of them.

"Hello, Nurse Sharp!"—rather gaily, as he picked a cigarette from his gold case. "You look weary. And why are you both so late? Didn't I hear something from Nurse Trent about a theatre to-night?"

"Yes, doctor," said Nurse Sharp. "But I—I was detained over one of Doctor Manson's cases."

"Oh?" Freddie's tone held just a hint of interrogation.

It was enough for Nurse Sharp. Rankling from her injustices, disliking Andrew and admiring Hamson, she suddenly let herself go.

"I've never had such a time in all my life, Doctor Hamson. Never. Taking a patient from the Victoria and sneaking her out to that Bellevue place and Doctor Manson keeping me there all hours while he does a pneumothorax with an unqualified man——" She poured out the whole story of the afternoon, repressing her smarting tears of vexation with difficulty.

There was a silence when she concluded. Freddie's eyes held an odd expression.

"That was too bad, nurse," he said at length. "But I hope you won't miss your theatre. Look, Nurse Trent—you must take a taxi and charge it to me. Put it on your expense sheet. Now if you'll excuse me, I must go."

"*There's* a gentleman," Nurse Sharp murmured, following him admiringly with her eyes. "Come, dear, get the taxi."

Freddie drove thoughtfully to the club. Since his quarrel with Andrew he had, almost of necessity, pocketed his pride and fallen back to a closer association with Deedman and Ivory. To-night the three were dining together. And as they dined, Freddie, less in malice than from a desire to interest the other two, to pull himself up with them again, airily remarked:

"Manson seems to be playing pretty parlour tricks since he left us. I hear he's started feeding patients to that Stillman fellow."

"What!" Ivory laid down his fork.

"And co-operating, I understand." Hamson sketched a graceful version of the story.

When he finished Ivory demanded with sudden harshness:

"Is this true?"

"My dear fellow," Freddie answered in an aggrieved tone, "I had it from his own nurse not half an hour ago."

A pause followed. Ivory lowered his eyes and went on with his dinner. Yet beneath his calm he was conscious of a savage elation. He had never forgiven Manson for that final remark after the Vidler operation. Though he was not thin-skinned, Ivory had the sultry pride of a man who

739

knows his own weakness and guards it jealously. He knew deep in his heart that he was an incompetent surgeon. But no one had ever told him with such cutting violence the full extent of his incompetence. He hated Manson for that bitter truth.

The others had been talking a few moments when he raised his head. His voice was impersonal.

"This nurse of Manson's—can you get her address?"

Freddie broke off, gazing at him across the table.

"Absolutely."

"It seems to me," Ivory reflected coolly, "that something ought to be done about this. Between you and me, Freddie, I never had much time for this Manson of yours, but that's neither here nor there. I'm thinking purely of the ethical aspect. Gadsby happened to be speaking to me about this Stillman only the other evening—we were guests at the Mayfly Dinner. He's getting into the papers—Stillman, I mean. Some ignorant jackass in Fleet Street has got together a list of alleged cures by Stillman, cases where doctors had failed, you know the usual twaddle. Gadsby is pretty hot about it all. I believe Churston was a patient of his at one time—before he ditched him for this quack. Now! Just what is going to happen if members of the profession are going to *support* this rank outsider. Gad! the more I think about it the less I like it. I'm going to get in touch with Gadsby straight off the handle. Waiter! Find out if Doctor Maurice Gadsby is in the Club. If not, have the porter ring up and find out if he's at his house."

Hamson, for once, looked uncomfortable about his collar. He had no rancour in his disposition and no ill-will towards Manson, whom, in his easy, egotistic fashion he had always liked. He muttered:

"Don't bring me into it."

"Don't be a fool, Freddie. Are we going to let that fellow sling mud at us and then get away with *this*?"

The waiter returned to say that Doctor Gadsby was at home. Ivory thanked him.

"I'm afraid this means the end of my bridge, you fellows. Unless Gadsby happens to be engaged."

But Gadsby was not engaged and later that evening Ivory called upon him. Though the two were not exactly friends they were good enough acquaintances for the physician to produce his second best port and a reputable cigar. Whether or not Doctor Gadsby knew something of Ivory's reputation he was at least aware of the surgeon's social standing, which ranked high enough for Maurice Gadsby, aspirant to fashionable honours, to treat him with adequate good-fellowship.

When Ivory mentioned the object of his visit Gadsby had no need to assume interest. He leaned forward in his chair, his small eyes fastened upon Ivory, listening intently to the story.

"Well! I'm damned!" he exclaimed with unusual vehemence at

the end of it. "I know this Manson. We had him for a short time on the M.F.B. and I assure you we were extremely relieved to see the end of him. A complete outsider, hasn't the manners of an errand boy. And do you actually mean to tell me that he took a case from the Victoria, it must have been one of Thoroughgood's cases—we'll hear what Thoroughgood has to say about *that*—and turned it over to Stillman."

"More than that, he actually assisted Stillman at the operation."

"If that is true," Gadsby said, carefully, "the case is one for the G.M.C."

"Well," Ivory hesitated becomingly. "That was precisely my own view. But I rather held back. You see I knew this fellow at one time rather better than you. I didn't really feel like lodging the complaint myself."

"I will lodge it," said Gadsby authoritatively. "If what you tell me is indeed a fact I will lodge it personally. I should consider myself failing in my duty if I did not take immediate action. The point at issue is a vital one, Ivory. This man Stillman is a menace, not so much to the public, as to the profession. I think I told you my experience of him the other night at dinner. He threatens our status, our training, our tradition. He threatens everything that we stand for. Our only remedy is to ostracise him. Then, sooner or later, he runs into disaster over the question of certification. Observe that, Ivory! Thank God! we have kept that in the hands of the profession. We alone can sign a death certificate. But if—mark you—if this fellow and others like him can secure professional collaboration then we're lost. Fortunately the G.M.C. have always come down like a ton of bricks upon that sort of thing in the past. You remember the case of Jarvis, the manipulator, several years ago, when he got some cad of a doctor to anæsthetise for him. *He* was struck off, instanter. The more I think of that bounder Stillman the more I'm determined to make an example of this. If you'll excuse me one minute now I'll ring Thoroughgood. And then to-morrow I shall want to nterrogate that nurse."

He rose and telephoned Doctor Thoroughgood. On the following day, in Doctor Thoroughgood's presence he took a signed statement from Nurse Sharp. So conclusive was her testimony he immediately put himself in touch with his solicitors, Messrs. Boon & Everton of Bloomsbury Square. He detested Stillman, of course. But he had already a soothing premonition of the benefit likely to accrue to a public upholder of the medical morality.

While Andrew, oblivious, went to Llantony, the process raised against him moved steadily upon its way. It is true that Freddie, coming, in dismay, on a paragraph reporting the inquest upon Christine's death, had telephoned Ivory to try to stop the case. But by then it was too late. The complaint had been lodged.

Later the Penal Cases Committee considered that complaint and upon its authority a letter was dispatched summoning Andrew to attend at the November meeting of the Council to answer the charge laid against him. This was the letter which he now held in his hand, white with anxiety, confronted by the menace of its legal phrasing:

"That you, Andrew Manson, knowingly and wilfully, on August 15th, assisted one Richard Stillman, an unregistered person `practising in a department of medicine, and that you associated yourself in a professional capacity with him in carrying out such practice. And that in relation thereto you have been guilty of infamous conduct in a professional respect."

XXII

THE CASE was due to be heard on the 10th November and Andrew was in London a full week before that date. He was alone, for he had asked Hope and Denny to leave him entirely to himself. And he stayed, with a bitter, melancholy sentiment, at the Museum Hotel.

Though outwardly controlled, his state of mind was desperate. He swung between dark fits of bitterness and an emotional suspense which came not only from his doubts about the future but from the vivid remembrance of every past moment of his medical career. Six weeks ago this crisis would have found him still benumbed by the agony of Christine's death, heedless, uncaring. But now, recovered, eager and ready to begin work again, he felt the shock of it with cruel intensity. He realised, with a heavy heart, that if all his reborn hopes were killed then he too might just as well be dead.

These and other painful thoughts perpetually thronged his brain, producing at times a state of bewildering confusion. He could not believe that he, Andrew Manson, was in this horrible situation, really facing the dreaded nightmare of every doctor. Why was he called before the Council? Why did they wish to strike him off the register? He had done nothing disgraceful. He was guilty of no felony, no misdemeanour. All that he had done was to cure Mary Boland of consumption.

His defence was in the hands of Hopper & Co., of Lincoln's Inn Fields, a firm of solicitors Denny had strongly recommended to him. At first sight Thomas Hopper was not impressive, a small red-faced man with gold-rimmed glasses and a fussy manner. Through some defect in his circulation he was subject to attacks of suffusion of his skin which gave him a self-conscious air, a peculiarity that certainly did not serve to inspire confidence. Nevertheless Hopper had decided views upon the conduct of the case. When Andrew, in his first burst of agonised indignation, had wished to rush to Sir Robert Abbey, his one influential friend in London, Hopper had wryly pointed out that Abbey was a member of the Council. With equal disapproval the fussy little solicitor had vetoed Andrew's frantic plea that they cable Stillman to return immediately from America. They had all the evidence that Stillman could give them and the actual presence of the unqualified practitioner could serve only to exasperate the Council members. For the same reason Marland, now acting at Bellevue, must stay away.

Gradually Andrew began to see that the legal aspect of the case was utterly different from his own. His frenzied logic as, in Hopper's office, he protested his innocence, caused the solicitor disapprovingly to wrinkle up his brow. At last Hopper was forced to declare:

"If there is one thing I must beg of you, Doctor Manson, it is that you will *not* express yourself in such terms during the hearing on Wednesday. I assure you nothing would be more fatal to our case."

Andrew stopped short, his hands clenched, his eyes burning on Hopper.

"But I want them to know the *truth*. I want to show them that getting this girl cured was the best thing I'd done for years. After mucking about for months doing ordinary material practice I'd actually done something fine and that—*that's* what they're having me up for."

Hopper's eyes behind his glasses were deeply concerned. In his vexation the blood rushed into his skin.

"Please, *please*, Doctor Manson. You don't *understand* the gravity o our position! I must take this opportunity to tell you frankly that at the *best* I consider our chances of—of success to be slender. Precedent is dead against us—Kent in nineteen-nine, Louden in nineteen-twelve, Foulger in nineteen-nineteen, they were all deleted for unprofessional associations. And, of course, in the famous Hexam case, in nineteen-twenty-one, Hexam was struck off for administering a general anæsthetic for Jarvis the bonesetter. Now, what I wish to entreat of you is this—answer questions in the affirmative or negative or, failing that, as briefly as possible. For I solemnly warn you that if you launch into one of these digressions which you have recently been offering me we will unquestionably lose our case and you will be struck off the register as sure as my name is Thomas Hopper."

Andrew saw dimly that he must try to hold himself in check. Here he must, like a patient laid upon the table, submit to the formal operations of the Council. But it was difficult for him to reach that passive state. The mere idea that he must forgo all attempt at self-exoneration and dully answer "yes" or "no" was more than he could bear.

On the evening of Tuesday the 9th November, when his febrile expectation of what the next day would bring had reached its zenith, he found himself unaccountably in Paddington, walking in the direction of the Vidlers' shop, driven by a strange subconscious impulse. Deeply buried in his mind lay the morbid, still unconquered, fancy that all the calamity of these last months came in punishment for Harry Vidler's death. The inference was involuntary, unadmitted. Yet it was there, springing from the deep roots of his earliest belief. He was drawn irresistibly to Vidler's widow as though the mere sight of her might help him, give him, in some strange manner, appeasement from his suffering.

It was a wet, dark night and there were few people in the streets. He had a sense of queer unreality, walking unrecognised in this district where he had been known so well. His own dark figure became a shadow amongst other phantoms all hurrying, hurrying through the teeming rain. He reached the shop just before closing time, hesitated, then as a customer came out, hurriedly he went in.

Mrs. Vidler was alone, behind the counter of the cleaning and pressing department, folding a woman's coat which had just been left with her. She wore a black skirt and an old blouse, dyed black, gaping a little at the neck. Her mourning made her somehow smaller. Suddenly she lifted her eyes and saw him.

"It's Doctor Manson," she exclaimed, her face lighting up. "How are you, doctor?"

His answer came stiffly. He saw that she knew nothing of his present trouble. He remained standing in the doorway, rigid, gazing at her, the rain dripping slowly from his hat brim.

"Come in, doctor. Why, you're drenched. It's a wicked night——"

He interrupted her, his voice strained, unreal.

"Mrs. Vidler, I've wanted to come and see you for a long time. I've often wondered how you were getting on——"

"I'm managing, doctor. Not so bad. I've a new young man in the cobbling. He's a good worker. But come in and let me give you a cup of tea."

He shook his head.

"I'm—I'm just passing." Then he went on, almost desperately. "You must miss Harry very much."

"Well, yes, I do. At least, at first I did. But it's wonderful"—she even smiled at him—"how you come to get used to things."

He said rapidly, confusedly:

"I reproach myself—in a way. Oh! it all happened so suddenly for you, I've often felt you must blame me——"

"Blame you!" She shook her head. "How can you say such a thing, when you done everything, even to the home, and getting the finest surgeon——"

"But you see," he persisted huskily, a rigid coldness in all his body, "if you had done differently, perhaps if Harry had gone to hospital——"

"I wouldn't have had it any different, doctor. My Harry had the best that money could give him. Why, even his funeral, I wish you could have seen it, the wreaths. As for *blaming* yourself—why, many's the time I've said in this shop Harry couldn't have had a better nor a kinder nor a cleverer doctor than yourself——"

As she went on talking he saw with a conclusive pang that, though he made open confession, she would never believe him. She had her illusion of Harry's peaceful, inevitable, costly passing. It would be cruelty to shake her from this pillar to which she clung so happily. He said, after a pause:

"I'm very glad to have seen you again, Mrs. Vidler. As I've said—I wanted to look you up."

He broke off, shook hands with her, bade her good night, and went out.

The encounter, far from reassuring or consoling him, served only to intensify his wretchedness. His mood underwent a complete revulsion. What had he expected? Forgiveness, in the best fictional tradition? Condemnation? He reflected bitterly that now she probably thought more highly of him than ever. As he tramped back through the sopping streets he had the sudden conviction that he must lose his case to-morrow. The conviction deepened to a terrifying certainty.

Not far from his hotel, in a quiet side street, he passed the open doorway of a church. Once again impulse caught him, caused him to stop, retrace his steps and enter. It was dark inside, empty and warm, as though a service had not long ended. He did not know what church it was, nor did he care. He simply sat down in the back seat of all and fixed his haggard gaze upon the dark enshrouded apse. He reflected how Christine in their estrangement had fallen back upon the thought of God. He had never been a church-goer, but now, here he was, in this unknown church. Tribulation brought people here, brought people to their senses, brought people to the thought of God.

There he sat, bowed, like a man resting at the end of a journey. His thoughts flowed outwards, not in any considered prayer, but winged with the longing of his soul. God! don't let me be struck off. Oh, God! don't let me be struck off. For perhaps half an hour he remained in this strange meditation, then he rose and went straight to his hotel.

Next morning, though he had slept heavily, he woke to an even greater sense of sick anxiety. As he dressed his hands trembled slightly. He blamed himself for having come to this hotel with its associations of his membership examination. The feeling he now experienced was exactly that pre-examination dread, intensified a hundredfold.

Downstairs he could eat no breakfast. The time of his case was eleven o'clock and Hopper had asked him to be early. He estimated it would take him not more than twenty minutes to get to Hallam Street and he fretted, in nervous pretence, with the newspapers in the hotel lounge until half past ten. But when he started his taxi was caught in a long traffic jam due to an obstruction in Oxford Street. It was striking eleven when he reached the G.M.C. offices.

He hurried into the Council Chamber with only a disturbed impression of its size, of the high table where the Council sat with the President,

745

Sir Jenner Halliday, in the chair. Seated at the far end were the partici-
pants in his own case, oddly like actors waiting for their cue. Hopper
was there, Mary Boland, accompanied by her father, Nurse Sharp,
Doctor Thoroughgood, Mr. Boon, Ward Sister Myles—his glance
travelled along the line of chairs. Then hastily he seated himself beside
Hopper.

"I thought I told you to be early," the solicitor said in an aggrieved
tone. "This other case is almost over. With the Council it's fatal to be
late."

Andrew made no answer. As Hopper had said, the President was even
now pronouncing judgment on the case before his own, an adverse
judgment, erasure from the register. Andrew could not keep his eye from
the doctor convicted of some drab misdemeanour, a seedy down-at-heel
individual who looked as though he had struggled hard to make a living.
His utterly hopeless expression as he stood condemned by this august
body of his fellows, sent a shiver over Andrew.

But he had no time for thought, for more than a passing wave of pity.
The next minute his own case was called. His heart contracted as the
proceedings began.

The charge was formally read through. Then Mr. George Boon, the
prosecuting solicitor, rose to open. He was a thin, precise, frock-coated
figure, clean shaven, with a wide black ribbon to his eyeglasses. His voice
came deliberately.

"Mr. President, gentlemen, this case which you are about to consider
has, I submit, nothing to do with any theory of medicine as defined under
Section Twenty-eight of the Medical Act. On the contrary, it exhibits
a clear-cut instance of professional association with an unregistered
person, a tendency which, I may perhaps observe, the Council has
recently had cause to deplore.

"The facts of the case are these. The patient, Mary Boland, suffering
from apical phthisis, was admitted to the wards of Doctor Thoroughgood
at the Victoria Chest Hospital on the 18th of July. There she remained
under the care of Dr. Thoroughgood until the 14th of September when
she discharged herself on the pretext that she wished to return to her
home. I say pretext because, on the day of her discharge, instead of
returning home, the patient was met at the lodge of the hospital by
Doctor Manson, who immediately took her to an institution by the name
of Bellevue which purports, I believe, to undertake the cure of pulmonary
disorders.

"On arrival at this place, Bellevue, the patient was put to bed and
examined by Doctor Manson in conjunction with the proprietor of the
establishment, Mr. Richard Stillman, an unqualified person and—er—
I understand, an alien. Upon examination, it was decided in consultation—I particularly call the Council to mark that phrase—in consultation, by Doctor Manson and Mr. Stillman, to operate upon the patient

746

and to induce the condition of pneumothorax. Thereupon Doctor Manson administered the local anæsthetic and the induction was performed by Doctor Manson and Mr. Stillman.

"Now, gentlemen, having briefly outlined the case I propose with your permission to call further evidence. Doctor Eustace Thoroughgood, please."

Doctor Thoroughgood rose and came forward. Removing his eyeglasses, and holding them in readiness to emphasise his points, Boon began his interrogation.

"Doctor Thoroughgood, I have no wish to embarrass you. We are well aware of your reputation, I might say your eminence, as a consulting physician upon diseases of the lungs and I have no doubt you may be actuated by a sense of leniency towards your junior colleague, but, Doctor Thoroughgood, is it not the fact that on Saturday, the morning of the 10th of September, Doctor Manson pressed you to a consultation upon this patient Mary Boland?"

"Yes."

"And is it not also the fact that in the course of this consultation he pressed you to adopt a line of treatment which you thought to be unwise?"

"He wished me to perform A.P.T."

"Exactly! And in the best interests of the patient you refused."

"I did."

"Was Doctor Manson's manner in any way peculiar when you refused?"

"Well——" Thoroughgood hesitated.

"Please, Doctor Thoroughgood! We respect your natural reluctance."

"He didn't seem altogether himself that morning. He seemed to disagree with my decision."

"Thank you, Doctor Thoroughgood. You had no reason to imagine that the patient was dissatisfied with her treatment at the hospital"—at the mere idea a watery smile touched Boon's arid face—"that she had any grounds for complaint against you or the staff."

"None whatever. She always seemed well pleased, happy and contented."

"Thank you, Doctor Thoroughgood." Boon picked up his next paper. "And now, Ward Sister Myles, please."

Doctor Thoroughgood sat down. Ward Sister Myles came forward. Boon resumed:

"Sister Myles, on the forenoon of Monday, the 12th of September, the next day but one after this consultation between Doctor Thoroughgood and Doctor Manson, did Doctor Manson call to see the patient?"

"He did."

"Was it a usual hour for him to call?"

"No."

"Did he examine the patient?"

"No. We had no screens that morning. He just sat and talked with her."

"Exactly, Sister—a long and earnest conversation, if I may use the wording of your statutory declaration. But tell us, Sister, in your own words now, what took place immediately subsequent to Doctor Manson's departure."

"About half an hour after, Number Seventeen, that's to say, Mary Boland, said to me, 'Sister, I've been thinking things over and I've made up my mind to go. You've been very kind to me. But I want to leave next Wednesday.' "

Boon interrupted quickly.

"Next Wednesday. Thank you, Sister. It was that point I wished to establish. That will be all at present."

Ward Sister Myles stepped back.

The solicitor made a politely satisfied gesture with his beribboned eyeglasses.

"And now—Nurse Sharp, please." A pause. "Nurse Sharp. You are in a position to bear out the statement relating to Doctor Manson's movements on the afternoon of Wednesday the 14th of September."

"Yes, I was there!"

"I gather from your tone, Nurse Sharp, that you were there un-willingly."

"When I found out where we were going and who this man Stillman was, not a doctor or anything, I was——"

"Shocked," Boon suggested.

"Yes, I was," shot out Nurse Sharp. "I've never had to do with anybody but proper doctors, real specialists, all my life."

"Exactly," Boon purred. "Now, Nurse Sharp, there is just one point which I wish you to make quite clear once again for the benefit of the Council. Did Doctor Manson actually co-operate with Mr. Stillman in—in performing this operation?"

"He did," Nurse Sharp answered vindictively.

At this point Abbey leaned forward and put a question suavely, through the President.

"Is it not the case, Nurse Sharp, that when the events in question took place you were under notice to Doctor Manson?"

Nurse Sharp reddened, violently, lost her composure and stammered: "Yes, I suppose so."

As she sat down a minute later Andrew was conscious of a faint spark of warmth—Abbey, at least, remained his friend.

Boon turned to the Council table, mildly aggrieved at the interruption.

"Mr. President, gentlemen, I might continue to call witnesses but I am too sensible of the value of the Council's time. Moreover, I submit that I have proved my case conclusively. There seems not the slightest

748

doubt that the patient Mary Boland was removed, entirely through the connivance of Doctor Manson, from the care of an eminent specialist in one of the best hospitals in London to this questionable institute—which in itself constitutes a grave breach of professional conduct—and that there Doctor Manson deliberately associated himself with the unqualified proprietor of this institute in the performance of a dangerous operation already stated to be contra-indicated by Doctor Thoroughgood, the specialist ethically responsible for the case. Mr. President, gentlemen, here, I submit, we are not dealing, as might appear at first sight, with an isolated instance, an accidental misconduct, but with a planned, preconceived, and almost systematic infringement of the medical code."

Mr. Boon sat down, well pleased, and began to polish his glasses. There was a moment's silence. Andrew kept his eyes firmly upon the floor. It had been torture for him to endure the biased presentation of the case. Bitterly he told himself they were treating him like some hole-and-corner criminal. Then his solicitor came forward and prepared to address the Council.

As usual, Hopper seemed flustered, his face was red and he had difficulty in arranging his papers. Yet, strangely, this seemed to gain him the indulgence of the Council. The President said:

"Yes, Mr. Hopper?"

Hopper cleared his throat.

"May it please you, Mr. President, gentlemen—I am not in dispute with the evidence brought by Mr. Boon. I have no wish to go behind the facts. But the manner of their interpretation gravely concerns us. There are, besides, certain additional points which throw a complexion upon the case much more favourable to my client.

"It has not yet been stated that Miss Boland was primarily Doctor Manson's patient, since she consulted him, previous to seeing Doctor Thoroughgood, on the 11th of July. Further, Doctor Manson was personally interested in the case. Miss Boland is the daughter of a close friend. Thus, all along, he regarded her as his own responsibility. We must frankly admit that Doctor Manson's action was completely misguided. But I suggest respectfully it was neither dishonourable nor malicious.

"We have heard of this slight difference of opinion over the question of treatment between Doctor Thoroughgood and Doctor Manson. Bearing in mind Doctor Manson's great interest in the case it was not unnatural for him to wish to take it back into his own hands. Naturally, he wished to cause his senior colleague no distress. That, and nothing more, was the reason of the subterfuge upon which Mr. Boon has laid such stress." Here Hopper paused, pulled out a handkerchief and coughed. He had the air of a man approaching a more difficult hurdle. "And now we come to the matter of association, of Mr. Stillman and

749

Bellevue. I assume members of the Council are not ignorant of Mr. Stillman's name. Although unqualified, he enjoys a certain reputation and is even reported to have brought about certain obscure cures."

The President interrupted gravely:

"Mr. Hopper, what can you, a layman, know of these matters?"

"I agree, sir," Hopper said hurriedly. "My real point is that Mr. Stillman would appear to be a man of character. It so happens that he introduced himself to Doctor Manson many years ago through a letter complimenting Doctor Manson upon some research work he had done upon the lungs. The two met later on a purely unprofessional footing when Mr. Stillman came here to establish his clinic. Thus, though it was ill-considered, it was not unnatural that Doctor Manson, seeking a place where he could himself give treatment to Miss Boland, should avail himself of the convenience offered him at Bellevue. My friend Mr. Boon has referred to Bellevue as a 'questionable' establishment. On that point I feel the Council might be interested to hear evidence. Miss Boland, please."

As Mary rose the scrutiny of the Council members fell upon her with marked curiosity. Though she was nervous and kept her gaze on Hopper, not once glancing at Andrew, she seemed well, in normal health.

"Miss Boland," said Hopper, "I want you to tell us frankly—did you find anything to complain of while you were a patient at Bellevue?"

"No! Quite the reverse." Andrew saw at once that she had been carefully instructed beforehand. Her answer came with guarded moderation.

"You suffered no ill effects?"

"On the contrary. I am better."

"In fact the treatment carried out there was really the treatment Doctor Manson suggested for you at your first interview with him on— let me see—on July the 11th."

"Yes."

"Is this relevant?" the President asked.

"I have finished with this witness, sir," Hopper said quickly. As Mary sat down he threw out his hands towards the Council table in his deprecatory style. "What I am venturing to suggest, gentlemen, is that the treatment effected at Bellevue was in actuality Doctor Manson's treatment carried out—unethically perhaps—by other persons. There was, I contend, within the meaning of the act, no professional co-operation between Stillman and Doctor Manson. I should like to call Doctor Manson."

Andrew stood up, acutely conscious of his position, of every eye directed towards him. He was pale and drawn. A sense of cold emptiness lay in the pit of his stomach. He heard Hopper address him.

"Doctor Manson, you received no financial gain in respect of this alleged co-operation with Mr. Stillman?"

750

"Not a penny."

"You had no ulterior motive, no base objective, in doing as you did?"

"No."

"You meant no reflection on your senior colleague, Doctor Thorough-good?"

"No. We got on well together. It was just—our opinions did not coincide on this case."

"Exactly," Hopper intervened rather hastily. "You can assure the Council then, honestly and sincerely that you had no intention of offending against the medical code nor the remotest idea that your conduct was in any degree infamous."

"That is the absolute truth."

Hopper suppressed a sigh of relief as, with a nod, he dismissed Andrew. Though he had felt himself obliged to produce this evidence he had feared his client's impetuosity. But now it was safely over, and he felt that, if his summing up were brief, they might now possibly have a slender chance of success. He said with a contrite air:

"I have no wish to keep the Council further. I have tried to show that Doctor Manson made merely an unhappy mistake. I appeal, not only to the justice, but to the mercy of the Council. And I should like finally to draw the Council's attention to my client's attainments. His past history is one of which any man might be proud. We are all aware of cases in which brilliant men have been guilty of a single error, and failing to secure mercy, their careers were eclipsed. I hope, and indeed I pray, that this case which you are about to judge may not be such as these."

The apology and humility in Hopper's tone were quite admirable in their effect upon the Council. But almost at once Boon was on his feet again, craving the indulgence of the President.

"With your permission, sir, there are one or two questions I should like to put to Doctor Manson." He swung round, inviting Andrew to his feet by an upward movement of his eyeglasses. "Doctor Manson, your last answer was scarcely clear to me. You say you had no know-ledge that your conduct was in any degree infamous. Yet you *did* know that Mr. Stillman was not a qualified gentleman."

Andrew considered Boon from beneath his brows. The attitude of the finicky solicitor had, during the entire hearing, made him feel guilty of some disgraceful act. A slow spark kindled in the chilly void within him. He said distinctly:

"Yes, I knew he was not a doctor."

The little wintry smirk of satisfaction showed on Boon's face. He said goadingly:

"I see. I see. Yet even that did not deter you."

"Even that didn't," echoed Andrew with sudden bitterness. He felt his control going. He took a long breath. "Mr. Boon, I've listened to you asking a great many questions. Will you allow me to ask you one? Have you heard of Louis Pasteur?"

"Yes," Boon was startled into the reply. "Who hasn't!"

"Exactly! Who hasn't? You are probably unaware of the fact, Mr. Boon, but perhaps you will allow me to tell you that Louis Pasteur, the greatest figure of all in scientific medicine, was *not* a doctor. Nor was Ehrlich—the man who gave medicine the best and most specific remedy in its entire history. Nor was Haffkine—who fought the plague in India better than any *qualified gentleman* has ever done. Nor was Metchnikoff, inferior only to Pasteur in his greatness. Forgive me for reminding you of these elementary facts, Mr. Boon. They may show you that every man fighting disease who hasn't got his name on the register isn't necessarily a knave or a fool!"

Electric silence. Hitherto the proceedings had dragged along in an atmosphere of pompous dreariness, a musty staleness, like a second-hand law court. But now every member at the Council table sat erect. Abbey, in particular, had his eyes upon Andrew with a strange intentness. A moment passed.

Hopper, with his hand before his face, groaned in dismay. Now, indeed, he knew the case was lost. Boon, though horribly discomfited, made an effort to recover himself.

"Yes, yes, these are illustrious names, we know. Surely you don't compare Stillman with them?"

"Why not," Andrew rushed on in burning indignation "They're only illustrious because they're dead. Virchow laughed at Koch in his lifetime—abused him! We don't abuse him now. We abuse men like Spahlinger and Stillman. There's another example for you—Spahlinger—a great and original scientific thinker. He's not a doctor. He has no medical degree. But he's done more for medicine than thousands of men *with* degrees, man who ride about in motor-cars and charge their fees, free as air, while Spahlinger is opposed and disparaged and accused, allowed to spend his fortune in research and treatment, and then left to struggle on in poverty."

"Are we to take it," Boon managed a sneer, "that you have an equal admiration for Richard Stillman?"

"Yes! He's a great man, a man who has devoted his whole life to benefiting mankind. He's had to fight jealousy and prejudice and misrepresentation too. In his own country he has overcome it. But apparently not here. Yet I'm convinced that he's done more against tuberculosis than any man living in this country. He's outside the profession. Yes! But there are plenty inside it who have been running up against T.B. all their lives and have never done an atom of good in fighting it."

There was sensation in the long high room. Mary Boland's eyes now fixed on Andrew were shining between admiration and anxiety. Hopper, slowly and sadly, was gathering his papers, slipping them into his leather case.

The President intervened.

"Do you realise what you are saying?"

"I do." Andrew gripped the back of his chair tensely, aware that he had been carried into grave indiscretion but determined to stand by his opinions. Breathing quickly, strung to breaking pitch, a queer kind of recklessness took hold of him. If they were going to strike him off, let him give them cause to do so. He rushed on, "I've listened to the pleading that's been going on to-day on my behalf and all the time I've been asking myself what harm I've done. I don't want to work with quacks. I don't believe in bogus remedies. That's why I don't open half the highly scientific advertisements that come pouring into my letter box by every post. I know I am speaking more strongly than I should, but I can't help it. We're not nearly liberal enough. If we go on trying to make out that everything's wrong outside the profession and everything is right within, it means the death of scientific progress. We'll just turn into a tight little trade protection society. It's high time we starting putting our own house in order, and I don't mean the superficial things either. Go to the beginning, think of the hopelessly inadequate training doctors get. When I qualified I was more of a menace to society than anything else. All I knew was the names of a few diseases and the drugs I was supposed to give for them. I couldn't even lock a pair of midwifery forceps. Anything I know I've learned since then. But how many doctors do learn anything beyond the ordinary rudiments they pick up in practice. They haven't got time, poor devils, they're rushed off their feet. That's where our whole organisation is rotten. We ought to be arranged in scientific units. There ought to be compulsory post-graduate classes. There ought to be a great attempt to bring science into the front line, to do away with the old bottle-of-medicine idea, give every practitioner a chance to study, to co-operate in research. And what about commercialism?—the useless guinea-chasing treatments, the unnecessary operations, the crowds of worthless pseudo-scientific proprietary preparations we use—isn't it time some of these were eliminated? The whole profession is far too intolerant and smug. Structurally, we're static. We never think of advancing, altering our system. We say we'll do things and we don't. For years we've been bleating about the sweated conditions under which our nurses work, the wretched pittances we pay them. Well? They're still being sweated, still paid their pittances. That's just an example. What I really mean is deeper than that. We don't give our pioneers a chance. Doctor Hexam, the man who was brave enough to give anæsthetics for Jarvis, the manipulator, when he was beginning his work, got struck off the register. Ten years later when Jarvis had cured hundreds of cases which had baffled the best surgeons in London, when he had been given a knighthood, when all the 'best

753

people' proclaimed him a genius, then we crawled back and gave him an honorary M.D. By that time Hexam was dead of a broken heart. I know I have made plenty of mistakes, and bad mistakes, in practice. And I regret them. But I made no mistake with Richard Stillman. And I don't regret what I did with him. All I ask you to do is to look at Mary Boland. She had apical phthisis when she went to Stillman. Now she's cured. If you want any justification of my infamous conduct here it is, in this room, before you."

Quite abruptly he ended and sat down. At the high Council table there was a queer light upon Abbey's face. Boon, still upon his feet, gazed at Manson with mixed feelings. Then, reflecting vengefully that he had at least given this upstart doctor enough rope to hang himself with, he bowed to the President and took his chair.

For a minute a peculiar silence filled the chamber, then the President made the customary declaration.

"I ask all strangers to withdraw."

Andrew went out with the rest. Now his recklessness was gone and his head, his whole body was throbbing like an overtaxed machine. The atmosphere of the coucil chamber stifled him. He could not endure the presence of Hopper, Boland, Mary and the other witnesses. He dreaded especially that melancholy reproach on the face of his solicitor. He knew he had behaved like a fool, a wretched declamatory fool. Now he saw his honesty as sheer madness. Yes, it was madness to attempt to harangue the Council as he had done. He ought to have been not a doctor but a stump orator in Hyde Park. Well! Soon he would cease to be a doctor. They would simply wipe him off the list.

He went into the cloak-room, desiring only to be alone, and sat on the edge of one of the washbasins, mechanically feeling for a cigarette. But the smoke was tasteless on his parched tongue and he crushed the cigarette beneath his heel. It was strange, despite the hard things, the true things he had said of the profession a few moments ago, how miserable he should feel at being cast out from it. He realised that he might find work with Stillman. But this was not the work he wanted. No! He wished to be with Denny and Hope, to develop his own bent, drive the spearhead of his scheme into the hide of apathy and conservatism. But all this must be done from within the profession, it could never, in England, never, never be accomplished from outside. Now Denny and Hope must man the Trojan horse alone. A great wave of bitterness swept over him. The future stretched out before him desolately. He had already that most painful sense of all—the feeling of exclusion—and allied to it, the knowledge that he was finished, done for —this was the end.

The sound of people moving in the corridor brought him wearily to his feet. As he joined them and re-entered the council chamber he told himself sternly that only one thing remained to him. He must not grovel. He prayed that he would give no sign of subservience, of weakness. With his eyes fixed firmly on the floor immediately before him, he saw no one, gave no glance towards the high table, remained passive, motionless. All the trivial sounds of the room re-echoed maddeningly about him—the scraping of chairs, the coughing, whispering, even the incredible sound of someone tapping idly with a pencil.

But suddenly there was silence. A spasm of rigidity took hold of Andrew. Now, he thought, now it is coming! The President spoke. He spoke slowly, impressively.

"Andrew Manson, I have to inform you that the Council has given very careful consideration to the charge brought against you and to the evidence brought in support of it. The Council is of opinion that, despite the peculiar circumstances of the case and your own particularly unorthodox presentation of it, you were acting in good faith and were sincerely desirous of complying with the spirit of the law demanding a high standard of professional conduct. I have to inform you, accordingly, that the Council has not seen fit to direct the Registrar to erase your name."

For one dazed second he did not comprehend. Then a sudden shivering thrill passed over him. They had not struck him off. He was free, clear, vindicated.

He raised his head shakily towards the Council table. Of all the faces, strangely blurred, turned towards his own, the one he saw most distinctly was that of Robert Abbey. The understanding in Abbey's eyes distressed him even more. He knew, in one illuminating flash, that it was Abbey who had got him off. Gone now was his pretence of indifference. He muttered feebly—and though he addressed the President it was to Abbey that he spoke:

"Thank you, sir."

The President said:

"That terminates the case."

Andrew stood up, instantly surrounded by his friends, by Con, Mary, the astounded Mr. Hopper, by people he had never seen before, who now shook him warmly by the hand. Somehow he was in the street outside, still being beaten about the shoulders by Con, oddly reassured in his nervous confusion by the passing buses, the normal stream of traffic, recapturing every now and then, with a start of joy, the unbelievable ecstasy of his release. He looked down unexpectedly to see Mary gazing up at him, her eyes still filled with tears.

"If they'd done anything to you—after all you've done for me, I'd—oh! I'd have killed that old President."

"In the name of God!" Con irrepressibly declared, "I don't know what ye were worrying about! The minute old Manson started to get goin', sure, I knew he would knock the stuffing outa them."

Andrew smiled weakly, doubtfully, joyously.

755

The three reached the Museum Hotel after one o'clock. And there, waiting in the lounge, was Denny. He sauntered towards them, gravely smiling. Hopper had telephoned the news. But he had no comment to make. He merely said:

"I'm hungry. But we can't feed here. Come along, all of you, and lunch with me."

They lunched at the Connaught Restaurant. Though no flicker of emotion crossed Philip's face, though he talked mainly of motor-cars to Con, he made it a happy celebration. Afterwards he said to Andrew:

"Our train leaves at four o'clock. Hope's in Stanborough—at the hotel, waiting on us. We can get that property dirt cheap. I've got some shopping to do. But I'll meet you at Euston at ten to four!"

Andrew gazed at Denny, conscious of his friendship, of all that he owed him since the first moment of their meeting, in the little Drineffy surgery. He said suddenly:

"Supposing I'd been struck off?"

"You're not." Philip shook his head. "And I'll see to it that you never will be."

When Denny left to make his purchases Andrew accompanied Con and Mary to their train at Paddington. As they waited on the platform, rather silent now, he repeated the invitation he had already given them.

"You must come and see us at Stanborough."

"We will that," Con assured him. "In the spring—whenever I get the little bus tuned up."

When their train steamed out he still had an hour to spare. But there was no doubt in his mind as to what he wished to do. Instinctively, he boarded a bus and soon he was in Kensal Green. He entered the cemetery, stood a long time at Christine's grave, thinking of many things. It was a bright, fresh afternoon, with that crispness in the breeze which she had always loved. Above him, on the branch of a grimy tree, a sparrow chirped merrily. When at last he turned away, hastening for fear he should be late, there, in the sky before him, a bank of cloud lay brightly, bearing the shape of battlements.

THE END

THE KEYS OF THE KINGDOM

"And I will give to thee the keys
of the kingdom of heaven."
— CHRIST TO PETER

To

MY FRIEND F.M.

For twenty years a missionary in China

CONTENTS

NOTE

Every character in this book is entirely fictitious
and no reference whatever is intended to any
living person.

BEGINNING OF THE END

1

LATE ONE AFTERNOON in September 1938 old Father Francis Chisholm limped up the steep path from the church of St. Columba to his house upon the hill. He preferred this way, despite his infirmities, to the less arduous ascent of Mercat Wynd; and, having reached the narrow door of his walled-in garden, he paused with a kind of naïve triumph—recovering his breath, contemplating the view he had always loved.

Beneath him was the River Tweed, a great wide sweep of placid silver, tinted by the low saffron smudge of autumn sunset. Down the slope of the northern Scottish bank tumbled the town of Tweedside, its tiled roofs a crazy quilt of pink and yellow, masking the maze of cobbled streets. High stone ramparts still ringed this Border burgh, with captured Crimean cannon making perches for the gulls as they pecked at partan crabs. At the river's mouth a wraith lay upon the sand bar, misting the lines of drying nets, the masts of smacks inside the harbour pointing upwards, brittle and motionless. Inland, dusk was already creeping upon the still bronze woods of Derham, towards which, as he gazed, a lonely heron made laboured flight. The air was thin and clear, stringent with wood smoke and the tang of fallen apples, sharp with the hint of early frost.

With a contented sigh, Father Chisholm turned into his garden: a patch beside his pleasance upon the Hill of Brilliant Green Jade, but a pretty one, and, like all Scots gardens, productive, with a few fine fruit trees splayed on the mellow wall. The jargonelle espalier in the south corner was at its best. Since there was no sign of the tyrant Dougal, with a cautious glance towards the kitchen window he stole the finest pear from his own tree, slid it under his soutane. His yellow, wrinkled cheek was ripe with triumph as he hobbled—dot and carry—down the gravelled drive, leaning on his one indulgence, the new umbrella of Chisholm tartan which replaced his battered favourite of Pai-tan. And there, standing at the front porch, was the car.

His face puckered slowly. Though his memory was bad and his fits of absent-mindedness a perpetual embarrassment, he now recollected the vexation of the Bishop's letter, proposing, or rather announcing, this visit of his secretary Monsignor Sleeth. He hastened forward to welcome his guest.

Monsignor Sleeth was in the parlour, standing, dark, thin, distinguished, and not quite at ease, with his back to the empty fireplace—his youthful impatience heightened, his clerical dignity repelled, by the mean surroundings in which he found himself. He had looked for a note of individuality: some piece of porcelain perhaps, or lacquer, a souvenir from the East. But the apartment was bare and nondescript, with poor linoleum, horsehair chairs and a chipped mantelpiece on which, out of the corner of a disapproving eye, he had already noted a spinning top beside an uncounted litter of collection pennies. Yet he was resolved to be pleasant. Smoothing his frown, he stifled Father Chisholm's apology with a gracious gesture.

"Your housekeeper has already shown me my room. I trust it will not disturb you to have me here for a few days. What a superb afternoon it has been. The colourings!—as I drove up from Tynecastle I almost fancied myself in dear San Morales." He gazed away, through the darkening window, with a studied air.

The old man nearly smiled at the imprint of Father Tarrant and the Seminary—Sleeth's elegance, that bladelike look, even the hint of hardness in the nostril, made him a perfect replica.

"I hope you'll be comfortable," he murmured. "We'll have our bite presently. I'm sorry I can't offer you dinner. Somehow we've just fallen to the habit of a Scots high tea!"

Sleeth, head half-averted, nodded noncommittally. Indeed, at that moment, Miss Moffat entered and, having drawn the drab chenille curtains, stealthily began to set the table. He could not but reflect, ironically, how the neutral creature, darting him one frightened glance, matched the room. Though it caused him a passing asperity to observe her lay places for three, her presence enabled him to lead the conversation safely into generalities.

As the two priests sat down at table he was eulogizing the special marble which the Bishop had brought from Carrara for the transept of the new Tynecastle pro-cathedral. Helping himself with good appetite from the ashet of ham, eggs and kidneys before him, he accepted a cup of tea poured from the Britannia metal teapot. Then, busy buttering brown toast, he heard his host remark mildly:

"You won't mind if Andrew sups his porridge with us. Andrew—this is Monsignor Sleeth!"

Sleeth raised his head abruptly. A boy about nine years of age had come silently into the room and now, after an instant's indecision, when he stood tugging at his blue jersey, his long pale face intense with nervousness, slipped into his place, reaching mechanically for the milk jug. As he bent over his plate a lock of dank brown hair—tribute to Miss

Moffat's sponge—fell over his ugly bony forehead. His eyes, of a remarkable blue, held a childish prescience of crisis—they were so uneasy he dared not lift them up.

The Bishop's secretary relaxed his attitude, slowly resumed his meal. After all, the moment was not opportune. Yet from time to time his stare travelled covertly towards the boy.

"So you are Andrew!" Decency demanded speech, even a hint of benignness. "And you go to school here?"

"Yes . . ."

"Come then! Let us see how much you know." Amiably enough, he propounded a few simple questions. The boy, flushed and inarticulate, too confused to think, betrayed humiliating ignorance.

Monsignor Sleeth's eyebrows lifted. "Dreadful," he thought. "Quite a gutter brat!"

He helped himself to another kidney—then suddenly became aware that while he trifled with the rich meats of the table the other two kept soberly to porridge. He flushed: this show of asceticism on the old man's part was insufferable affectation.

Perhaps Father Chisholm had a wry perception of that thought. He shook his head: "I went without good Scots oatmeal so many years I never miss it now I have the chance."

Sleeth received the remark in silence. Presently, with a hurried glance, out of his downcast muteness, Andrew begged permission to depart. Rising to say his grace, he knocked a spoon spinning with his elbow. His stiff boots made an uncouth scuffling towards the door.

Another pause. Then, having concluded his meal, Monsignor Sleeth rose easily and repossessed, without apparent purpose, the fleshless hearth-rug. With feet apart and hands clasped behind his back he considered, without seeming to do so, his aged colleague, who, still seated, had the curious air of waiting. Dear God, thought Sleeth, what a pitiable presentation of the priesthood—this shabby old man, with the stained soutane, soiled collar and sallow, desiccated skin! On one cheek was an ugly weal, a kind of cicatrix, which everted the lower eyelid, seemed to tug the head down and sideways. The impression was that of a permanent wry neck, counterpoising the lame and shortened leg. His eyes, usually lowered, took thus—on the rare occasions that he raised them—a penetrating obliqueness which was strangely disconcerting.

Sleeth cleared his throat. He judged it time for him to speak and, forcing a note of cordiality, he inquired: "How long have you been here, Father Chisholm?"

"Twelve months."

"Ah, yes. It was a kindly gesture of His Grace to send you—on your return—to your native parish."

"And his!"

Sleeth inclined his head suavely. "I was aware that His Grace shared with you the distinction of having been born here. Let me see . . . what age are you, Father? Nearly seventy is it not?"

Father Chisholm nodded, adding with gentle senile pride: "I am no older than Anselm Mealey."

Sleeth's frown at the familiarity melted into a half-pitying smile. "No doubt—but life has treated you rather differently. To be brief,"—he gathered himself up, firm, but not unkind,—"the Bishop and I both have the feeling that your long and faithful years should now be recompensed; that you should, in short, retire!"

There was a moment of strange quiet.

"But I have no wish to retire."

"It is a painful duty for me to come here"—Sleeth kept his gaze discreetly on the ceiling—"to investigate . . . and report to His Grace. But there are certain things which cannot be overlooked."

"What things?"

Sleeth moved irritably. "Six—ten—a dozen things! It isn't my place to enumerate your—your Oriental eccentricities!"

"I'm sorry." A slow spark kindled in the old man's eyes. "You must remember that I spent thirty-five years in China."

"Your parish affairs are in a hopeless muddle."

"Am I in debt?"

"How are we to know? No returns on your quarterly collections for six months." Sleeth's voice rose, he spoke a little faster. "Everything so . . . so unbusinesslike. . . . For instance when Bland's traveller presented his bill last month—three pounds for candles, and so forth— you paid him entirely in coppers!"

"That's how it comes to me." Father Chisholm viewed his visitor thoughtfully, as though he looked straight through him. "I've always been stupid about money. I've never had any, you see. . . . But after all . . . Do you think money so dreadfully important?"

To his annoyance Monsignor Sleeth found himself reddening. "It makes talk, Father." He rushed on. "And there is other talk. Some of your sermons . . . the advice you give . . . certain points of doctrine." He consulted a Morocco-covered notebook already in his palm. "They seem dangerously peculiar."

"Impossible!"

"On Whitsunday you told your congregation, 'Don't think heaven is in the sky . . . it's in the hollow of your hand . . . it's everywhere and anywhere.'" Sleeth frowned censoriously as he turned the pages. "And again . . . here is an incredible remark you made during Holy Week. 'Atheists may not all go to hell. I knew one who didn't. Hell is only for those who spit in the face of God!' And, good gracious, this atrocity: 'Christ was a perfect man, but Confucius had a better sense of humour!'" Another page was turned indignantly. "And this incredible incident . . . when one of your best parishioners, Mrs. Glendenning, who cannot of course help her extreme stoutness, came to you for spiritual guidance you looked at her and replied, 'Eat less. The gates of Paradise are narrow.' But why should I continue?" Decisively, Monsignor Sleeth closed the gilt-edged book. "To say the least, you seem to have lost your command of souls.'"

"But . . ." Calmly: "I don't want to command anyone's soul."

Sleeth's colour heightened disagreeably. He did not see himself in theological discussion with this shambling dotard.

"There remains the matter of this boy whom you have so misguidedly adopted."

"Who is to look after him—if I don't?"

"Our own Sisters at Ralstone. It is the finest orphanage in the diocese."

Again Father Chisholm raised his disconcerting eyes. "Would you have wished to spend your own childhood at that orphanage?"

"Need we be personal, Father? I've told you . . . even conceding the circumstances . . . the situation is highly irregular and must be ended. Besides . . ." He threw out his hands. "If you are going away— we must find some place for him."

"You seem determined to be rid of us. Am I to be entrusted to the Sisters too?"

"Of course not. You can go to the Aged Priests' Home at Clinton. It is a perfect haven of rest."

The old man actually laughed—a dry short laugh. "I'll have enough perfect rest when I'm dead. While I'm alive I don't want to be mixed up with a lot of aged priests. You may think it strange—but I never have been able to stand the clergy in bulk."

Sleeth's smile was pained and flustered. "I think nothing strange from you, Father. Forgive me, but to say the least of it . . . your reputation, even before you went to China . . . your whole life has been peculiar!"

There was a pause. Father Chisholm said in a quiet voice: "I shall render an account of my life to God."

The younger man dropped his eyelids with an unhappy sense of indiscretion. He had gone too far. Though his nature was cold he strove always to be just, even considerate. He had the grace to look uncomfortable. "Naturally I don't presume to be your judge—or your inquisitor. Nothing is decided yet. That is why I am here. We must see what the next few days bring forth." He stepped towards the door. "I am going to the church now. Please don't trouble. I know my way." His mouth creased into an unwilling smile. He went out.

Father Chisholm remained seated, motionless, at the table, his hand shading his eyes, as though thinking deeply. He felt crushed by this threat which had gathered, so suddenly, above the quiet of his hard-won retreat. His sense of resignation, long overtaxed, refused acceptance of it. All at once he felt empty and used-up, unwanted by God or man. A burning desolation filled his breast. Such a little thing; and yet so much. He wanted to cry out: My God, my God, why hast thou forsaken me? He rose heavily, and went upstairs.

In his attic above the spare room the boy Andrew was already in bed and asleep. He lay upon his side, one skinny arm crooked before him on the pillow, defensively. Watching him, Father Chisholm took the pear from his pocket and placed it on the clothes folded upon the cane-bottomed chair beside the bed. There seemed nothing more for him to do.

A faint breeze swayed the muslin curtains. He moved to the window and parted them. Stars were quivering in the frosty sky. Under these stars the span of his years reached out in all its ineptitude, built of his puny strivings, without form or nobility. It seemed such a short time since he had been a boy himself, running and laughing in this same town of Tweedside. His thoughts flew back. If there were any pattern in his life at all the first fateful stroke was surely drawn on that April Saturday sixty years ago when, out of untroubled happiness, so deep it passed unrecognized . . .

II

STRANGE VOCATION

I

THAT SPRING MORNING, at early breakfast in the snug dark kitchen, with the fire warm to his stockinged feet and the smell of kindling wood and hot oat-cakes making him hungry, he was happy, despite the rain, because it was Saturday and the tide was right for salmon.

His mother finished her brisk stirring with the wooden spurtle, and placed the blue-ringed bowl of pease brose on the scrubbed table between his father and himself. He reached for his horn spoon, dipped in the bowl, then in the cup of buttermilk before him. He rolled his tongue over the smooth golden brose, made perfectly, without lumps or gritty unmixed meal.

His father, in worn blue jersey and darned fishing stockings, sat opposite, his big frame bowed, supping in silence, with quiet slow movements of his red hands. His mother shook the last batch of oat-cakes from the griddle, set them on their ends against the bowl, and sat down to her cup of tea. The yellow butter melted on the broken oat-cake which she took. There was silence and comradeship in the little kitchen, with the flames leaping across the bright fender and the pipe-clayed hearth. He was nine years of age and he was going to the bothy with his father.

There, he was known—he was Alex Chisholm's laddie, accepted by the men in their woollen jerseys and leather hip-boots with a quiet nod or, better still, a friendly silence. He had a dark secret glow of pride as he went out with them, the big flat cobble sweeping wide round the butt, the rowlocks creaking, the seine skilfully payed out by his father in the stern. Back on the butt, their tackets rasping the wet stones, the men huddled themselves low against the wind, some squatting with a yellowed sailcloth across their shoulders, others sucking warmth from a blackened inch-long clay. He stood with his father, apart. Alex Chisholm was the head man, the watcher of Tweed Fisheries Station No. 3. Together, not speaking, cut by the wind, they stood watching the far circle of corks dancing in the choppy back-lash where the river met the sea. Often the glare of sun upon the ripples made his head swim. But he would not, he could not blink. Missing even a single second might mean the missing of a dozen fish—so hard to come by, these days, that in distant Billingsgate they brought the Fisheries Company a good half-crown a pound. His father's tall figure, the head sunk a little on the shoulders, the profile keen beneath the øld peaked cap, a fine blood whipped into the high cheekbones, had the same still unswerving tensity. At times, mingled exquisitely in his consciousness with the smell of wrack, the distant strike of the Burgess Clock, the cawing of the Derham rooks, the sense of this unspeaking comradeship drew moisture to the boy's already smarting eyes.

Suddenly his father shouted. Try as he might Francis could never win first sight of the dipping cork: not that tidal bobbing which sometimes caused him foolishly to start, but the slow downward tug which to long experience denoted the thrusting of a fish. At the quick high shout there was an instant clatter as the crew jumped to the windlass which hauled the net. Usage never staled that moment: though the men drew a poundage bonus on their catch, the thought of money did not stir them; this deep excitement sprang from far primeval roots. In came the net, slowly, dripping, flaked with kelp, the guide ropes squeaking on the wooden drum. A final heave, then, in the purse of the billowing seine, a molten flash, powerful, exquisite—salmon.

One memorable Saturday they had taken forty at a cast. The great shining things arched and fought, bursting through the net, slithering back to the river from the slippery butt. Francis flung himself forward with the others, desperately clutching at the precious escaping fish. They had picked him up, sequined with scales and soaked to the bone, a perfect monster locked in his embrace. Going home that evening, his hand inside his father's, their footfalls echoing in the smoky twilight, they had stopped, without comment, at Burley's in the High Street, to buy a pennyworth of cockles, the peppermint ones that were his special choice.

Their fellowship went further still. On Sundays, after mass, they took their rods and slipped secretly—lest they shock finer sensibilities—through the back ways of the Sabbath-stricken town, out into the verdant valley of the Whitadder. In his tin, packed with sawdust, were luscious maggots, picked the night before from Mealey's boneyard. Thereafter the day was heady with the sound of the stream, the scent of meadowsweet,—his father showing him the likely eddies,—the crimson-speckled trout wriggling on bleached shingle,—his father bent over a twig fire,—the crisp sweet goodness of the frizzled fish . . .

At other seasons they would go to gather blueberries, wood strawberries, or the wild yellow rasps which made good jam. It was a gala day when his mother accompanied them. His father knew all the best places and would take them deep into devious woods, to untouched cane-brakes of the juicy fruit.

When snow came and the ground was clamped by winter, they stalked between the frozen trees of Derham "policies," his breath a rime before him, his skin pricking for the keeper's whistle. He could hear his own heart beating as they cleared their snares, under the windows, almost, of the great house itself—then home, home with the heavy game-bag, his eyes smiling, his marrow melting to the thought of rabbit pie. His mother was a grand cook, a woman who earned—with her thrift, her knack of management and homely skill—the grudging panegyric of a Scots community: "Elizabeth Chisholm is a well-doing woman!"

Now, as he finished his brose, he became conscious that she was speaking, with a look across the breakfast table towards his father.

"You'll mind to be home early tonight, Alex, for the Burgess."

There was a pause. He could see that his father, preoccupied,—perhaps by the flooded river and the indifferent salmon season,—was caught unawares, recalled to the annual formality of the Burgess Concert which they must sustain that evening

"You're set on going, woman?" With a faint smile.

She flushed slightly; Francis wondered why she should seem so queer. "It's one of the few things I look forward to in the year. After all, you are a Burgess of the town. It's . . . it's right for you to take your seat on the platform with your family and your friends."

His smile deepened, setting lines of kindness about his eyes—it was a smile Francis would have died to win. "Then it looks like we maun gang, Lisbeth." He had always disliked "the Burgess," as he disliked teacups, stiff collars, and his squeaky Sunday boots. But he did not dislike this woman who wanted him to go.

"I'm relying on you, Alex. You see," her voice, striving to be casual, sounded an odd note of relief, "I have asked Polly and Nora up from Tynecastle—unfortunately it seems Ned cannot get away." She paused. "You'll have to send someone else to Ettal with the tallies."

He straightened with a quick look which seemed to see through her, right to the bottom of her tender subterfuge. At first, in his delight, Francis noticed nothing. His father's sister, now dead, had married Ned Bannon, proprietor of the Union Tavern in Tynecastle, a bustling city some sixty miles due South. Polly, Ned's sister, and Nora, his ten-year-old orphan niece, were not exactly close relations. Yet their visits could always be counted occasions of joy.

Suddenly he heard his father say in a quiet voice: "I'll have to go to Ettal all the same."

A sharp and throbbing silence. Francis saw that his mother had turned white.

"It isn't as if you had to. . . . Sam Mirlees, any of the men, would be glad to row up for you."

He did not answer, still gazing at her quietly, touched on his pride, his proud exclusiveness of race. Her agitation increased. She dropped all pretence of concealment, bent forward, placed nervous fingers upon his sleeve.

"To please me, Alex. You know what happened last time. Things are bad again there—awful bad, I hear."

He put his big hand over hers, warmly, reassuringly.

"You wouldn't have me run away, would you, woman?" He smiled and rose abruptly. "I'll go early and be back early . . . in plenty time for you, our daft friends, and your precious concert to the bargain."

Defeated, that strained look fixed upon her face, she watched him pull on his hip-boots. Francis, chilled and downcast, had a dreadful premonition of what must come. And indeed, when his father straightened it was towards him he turned, mildly, and with rare compunction.

"Come to think of it, boy, you'd better bide home today. Your mother could do with you about the house. There'll be plenty to see to before our visitors arrive."

Blind with disappointment, Francis made no protest. He felt his mother's arm tensely, detainingly about his shoulders.

His father stood a moment at the door, with that deep contained affection in his eyes, then he silently went out.

Though the rain ceased at noon the hours dragged dismally for Francis. While pretending not to see his mother's worried frown, he was racked by the full awareness of their situation. Here in this quiet burgh they were known for what they were—unmolested, even warily esteemed. But in Ettal, the market town four miles away where, at the Fisheries Head Office, his father, every month, was obliged to check the record of the catches, a different attitude prevailed. A hundred years before the Ettal moors had blossomed with the blood of Covenanters; and now the pendulum of oppression had relentlessly swung back. Under the leadership of the new Provost a furious religious persecution had recently arisen. Conventicles were formed, mass gatherings held in the Square, popular feelings whipped to frenzy. When the violence of the mob broke loose, the few Catholics in the town were hounded from their homes, while all others in the district received solemn warning not to show themselves upon the Ettal streets. His father's calm disregard of this threat had singled him for special execration. Last month there had been a fight in which the sturdy salmon-watcher had given good account of himself. Now, despite renewed menaces, and the careful plan to stay him, he was going again. . . . Francis flinched at his own thoughts and his small fists clenched violently. Why could not people let each other be? His father and his mother had not the same belief; yet they lived together, respecting each other, in perfect peace. His father was a good man, the best in the world . . . why should they want to do him harm? Like a blade thrust into the warmth of his life came a dread, a shrinking from that word "religion," a chill bewilderment that men could hate each other for worshipping the same God with different words.

Returning from the station at four o'clock, sombrely leaping the puddles to which Nora, his half-cousin, gaily dared him,—his mother walking with Aunt Polly, who came, dressed up and sedate, behind,— he felt the day oppressive with disaster. Nora's friskiness, the neatness of her new brown braided dress, her manifest delight in seeing him, proved but a wan diversion.

Stoically, he approached his home, the low neat greystone cottage, fronting the Cannelgate, behind a trim little green where in summer his father grew asters and begonias. There was evidence of his mother's passionate cleanliness in the shining brass knocker and the spotless door-step. Behind the immaculately curtained windows three potted geraniums made a scarlet splash.

By this time, Nora was flushed, out of breath, her blue eyes sparkling with fun, in 'one of her moods of daring, impish gaiety. As they went round the side of the house to the back garden where, through his mother's arrangements, they were to play with Anselm Mealey until teatime, she bent close to Francis' ear so that her hair fell across her thin laughing face, and whispered in his ear. The puddles they had barely missed, the sappy moisture of the earth, prompted her ingenuity.

At first Francis would not listen—strangely, for Nora's presence stirred him usually to a shy swift eagerness. Standing small and reticent, he viewed her doubtfully.

"I know he will," she urged. "He always wants to play at being holy. Come on, Francis. Let's do it. Let's!"

A slow smile barely touched his sombre lips. Half-unwilling, he fetched a spade, a watering can, an old news sheet from the little tool-shed at the garden end. Led by Nora, he dug a two-foot hole between the laurel bushes, watered it, then spread the paper over it. Nora artistically sprinkled the sheet with a coating of dry soil. They had barely replaced the spade when Anselm Mealey arrived, wearing a beautiful white sailor suit. Nora threw Francis a look of terrible joy.

"Hello, Anselm!" she welcomed brilliantly. "What a lovely new suit. We were waiting on you. What shall we play at?"

Anselm Mealey considered the question with agreeable condescension. He was a large boy for eleven, well-padded, with pink and white cheeks. His hair was fair and curly, his eyes were soulful. The only child of rich and devoted parents,—his father owned the profitable bone-meal works across the river,—he was already destined, by his own election and that of his pious mother, to enter Holywell, the famous Catholic college in Northern Scotland, to study for the priesthood. With Francis he served the altar at St. Columba's. Frequently he was to be found kneeling in church, his big eyes fervent with tears. Visiting nuns patted him on the head. He was acknowledged, with good reason, as a truly saintly boy.

"We'll have a procession," he said. "In honour of St. Julia. This is her feast day."

Nora clapped her hands. "Let's pretend her shrine is by the laurel bushes. Shall we dress up?"

"No." Anselm shook his head. "We're praying more than playing. But imagine I'm wearing a cope and bearing a jewelled monstrance. You're a white Carthusian Sister. And Francis, you're my acolyte. Now, are we all ready?"

A sudden qualm swept over Francis. He was not of the age to analyse his relationships; he only knew that, though Anselm claimed him fervently as his best friend, the other's gushing piety evoked in him a curious painful shame. Towards God he had a desperate reserve. It was a feeling he protected without knowing why, or what it was, like a tender nerve, deep within his body. When Anselm burningly declared in the Christian Doctrine class "I love and adore our Saviour from the bottom of my heart," Francis, fingering the marbles in his pockets, flushed a deep dark red, went home sullenly from school and broke a window.

Next morning when Anselm, already a seasoned sick-visitor, arrived at school with a cooked chicken, loftily proclaiming the object of his charity as Mother Paxton,—the old fishwife, sere with hypocrisy and cirrhosis of the liver, whose Saturday-night brawls made the Cannelgate a bedlam,—Francis, possessed, visited the cloakroom during class and opened the package, substituting for the delicious bird—which he consumed with his companions—the decayed head of a cod. Anselm's tears, and the curses of Meg Paxton, had later stirred in him a deep dark satisfaction,

Now, however, he hesitated, as if to offer the other boy an opportunity of escape. He said slowly: "Who'll go first?"

"Me, of course," Anselm gushed. He took up his position as leader. "Sing, Nora: Tantum Ergo."

In single file, at Nora's shrill pipe, the procession moved off. As they neared the laurel bushes Anselm raised his clasped hands to heaven. The next instant he stepped through the paper and squelched full-length in the mud.

For ten seconds no one moved. It was Anselm's howl as he struggled to get up that set Nora off. While Mealey blubbered clammily, "It's a sin, it's a sin!" she hopped about laughing, taunting wildly, "Fight. Anselm, fight. Why don't you hit Francis?"

"I won't, I won't," Anselm bawled. "I'll turn the other cheek."

He started to run home. Nora clung deliriously to Francis—helpless, choking, tears of laughter running down her cheeks. But Francis did not laugh. He stared in moody silence at the ground. Why had he stooped to such inanity while his father walked those hostile Ettal causeways? He was still silent as they went in to tea.

In the cosy front room, where the table was already set for the supreme rite of Scots hospitality, with the best china and all the electroplate the little household could muster, Francis' mother sat with Aunt Polly, her open rather earnest face a trifle flushed from the fire, her stocky figure showing an occasional stiffening towards the clock.

Now, after an uneasy day, shot equally with doubt and reassurance,—when she told herself how stupid were her fears,—her ears were tuned acutely for her husband's step: she was conscious of an overwhelming longing for him. The daughter of Daniel Glennie, a small and unsuccessful baker by profession, and by election an open-air preacher, leader of his own singular Christian brotherhood in Darrow, that shipbuilding town of incomparable drabness which lies some twenty miles from the city of Tynecastle, she had, at eighteen, during a week's holiday from the parental cake counter, fallen wildly in love with the young Tweedside fisher, Alexander Chisholm, and promptly married him.

In theory, the utter incompatibility of such a union foredoomed it. Reality had proved it a rare success. Chisholm was no fanatic: a quiet, easy-going type, he had no desire to influence his wife's belief. And she, on her side, sated with early piety, grounded by her peculiar father in a strange doctrine of universal tolerance, was not contentious.

Even when the first transports had subsided she knew a glowing happiness. He was, in her phrase, such a comfort about the place; neat, willing, never at a loss when it came to mending her wringer, drawing a fowl, clearing the bee-skeps of their honey. His asters were the best in Tweedside, his bantams never failed to take prizes at the show, the dovecot he had finished recently for Francis was a wonder of patient craftsmanship. There were moments, in the winter evenings when she sat knitting by the hearth, with Francis snug in bed, the wind whistling cosily around the little house, the kettle hissing on the hob, while her long raw-boned Alex padded the kitchen in his stocking feet, silently intent upon some handiwork, when she would turn to him with an odd, tender smile: "Man, I'm fond of you."

Nervously she glanced at the clock: yes, it was late, well past his usual time of homecoming. Outside a gathering of clouds was precipitating the darkness and again heavy raindrops splashed against the window-panes. Almost immediately Nora and Francis came in. She found herself avoiding her son's troubled eye.

"Well, children!" Aunt Polly summoned them to her chair and wisely apostrophized the air above their heads. "Did you have a good play? That's right. Have you washed your hands, Nora? You'll be looking forward to the concert tonight, Francis. I love a tune myself. God save us, girl, stand still. And don't forget your company manners, either, my lady—we're going to get our tea."

There was no disregarding this suggestion. With a hollow sensation of distress, intensified because she concealed it, Elizabeth rose.

"We won't wait on Alex any longer. We'll just begin." She forced a justifying smile. "He'll be in any moment now."

The tea was delicious, the scones and bannocks home-made, the preserves jelled by Elizabeth's own hands. But an air of strain lay heavily about the table. Aunt Polly made none of those dry remarks which usually gave Francis such secret joy, but sat erect, elbows drawn in, one finger crooked for her cup. A spinster, under forty, with a long, worn, agreeable face, somewhat odd in her attire, stately, composed, abstracted in her manner, she looked a model of conscious gentility, her lace handkerchief upon her lap, her nose humanly red from the hot tea, the bird in her hat brooding warmly over all.

"Come to think, Elizabeth——" She tactfully filled a pause. "They might have brought in the Mealey boy—Ned knows his father. A wonderful vocation, Anselm has." Without moving her head she touched Francis with her kindly omniscient eye. "We'll need to send you to Holywell too, young man. Elizabeth, you'd like to see your boy wag his head in a pulpit?"

"Not my only one."

"The Almighty likes the only ones." Aunt Polly spoke profoundly.

Elizabeth did not smile. Her son would be a great man, she was resolved, a famous lawyer, perhaps a surgeon; she could not bear to think of him as suffering the obscurity, the sorry hardships of the clerical life. Torn by her growing agitation she exclaimed: "I do wish Alex would come. It's . . . it's most inconsiderate. He'll keep us all late if he doesn't look sharp."

"Maybe he's not through with the tallies," Aunt Polly reflected considerately.

Elizabeth flushed painfully, out of all control. "He must be back at the bothy by now . . . he always goes there after Ettal." Desperately she tried to stem her fears. "I wouldn't wonder if he'd forgotten all about us. He's the most heedless man." She paused. "We'll give him five minutes. Another cup, Aunt Polly?"

But tea was over and could not be prolonged. There was an unhappy silence. What had happened to him? . . . Would he never, never come? Sick with anxiety, Elizabeth could restrain herself no longer. With a last glance, charged with open foreboding, towards the marble timepiece, she rose. "You'll excuse me, Aunt Polly, I'll have to run down, and see what's keeping him. I'll not be long."

Francis had suffered through these moments of suspense—haunted by the terror of a narrow wynd, heavy with darkness and surging faces and confusion, his father penned . . . fighting . . . falling under the crowd . . . the sickening crunch of his head upon the cobblestones. Unaccountably he found himself trembling. "Let me go, Mother," he said.

"Nonsense, boy." She smiled palely. "You stay and entertain our visitors."

Surprisingly, Aunt Polly shook her head. Hitherto she had betrayed no perception of the growing stress. Nor did she now. But with a penetrating staidness she remarked: "Take the boy with you, Elizabeth. Nora and I can manage fine."

There was a pause during which Francis pleaded with his eyes.

"All right . . . you can come."

His mother wrapped him in his thick coat; then, bundling into her plaid cape, she took his hand and stepped out of the warm bright room.

It was a streaming, pitch-dark night. The rain lathered the cobble-stones, foamed down the gutters of the deserted streets. As they struggled up the Mercat Wynd past the distant Square and the blurred illumination of the Burgess Hall, new fear reached at Francis from the gusty blackness. He tried to combat it, setting his lips, matching his mother's increased pace with quivering determination.

Ten minutes later they crossed the river by the Border Bridge and picked their way along the waterlogged quay to Bothy No. 3. Here his mother halted, dismayed. The bothy was locked, deserted. She turned indecisively, then suddenly observed a faint beacon, vaporous in the rainy darkness, a mile up-river: Bothy No. 5, where Sam Mirlees, the underwatcher, made his lodging. Though Mirlees was an aimless, tippling fellow, he could surely give them news. She started off again, firmly, plodding across the sodden meadows, stumbling over unseen tussocks, fences, ditches. Francis, close at her side, could sense her apprehension, mounting with every step.

At last they reached the other bothy, a wooden shanty of tarred boards, stoutly planted on the riverbank, behind the high stone butt and a swathe of hanging nets. Francis could bear it no longer. Darting forward with throbbing breast, he threw open the door. Then, at the consummation of his day-long fear, he cried aloud in choking anguish, his pupils wide with shock. His father was there with Sam Mirlees, stretched on a bench, his face pale and bloodied, one arm bound up roughly in a sling, a great purple weal across his brow. Both men were in their jerseys and hip-boots, glasses and a mutchkin jar on the near-by table, a dirty crimsoned sponge beside the turbid water dipper, the hurricane swing lamp throwing a haggard yellow beam upon them, while beyond the indigo shadows crept, wavered in the mysterious corners and under the drumming roof.

His mother rushed forward, flung herself on her knees beside the bench. "Alex . . . Alex . . . are ye hurt?"

Though his eyes were muddled he smiled, or tried to, with his blenched and battered lips.

"No worse nor some that tried to hurt me, woman."

Tears sprang to her eyes, born of his wilfulness and her love for him, tears of rage against those who had brought him to this pass.

"When he came in he was near done," Mirlees interposed with a hazy gesture. "But I've stiffened him up with a dram or two."

She threw a blazing look at the other man: fuddled, as usual on Saturday night. She felt weak with anger that this sottish fool should have filled Alex up with drink on top of the dreadful hurt he had sustained. She saw that he had lost a great quantity of blood . . . she had nothing here to treat him with . . . she must get him away at once . . . at once. She murmured, tensely:

"Could you manage home with me, Alex?"

"I think so, woman . . . if we take it slow."

She thought feverishly, battling her panic, her confusion. All her instinct was to move him to warmth, light and safety. She saw that his worst wound, a gash to the temple bone, had ceased to bleed. She swung round towards her son.

"Run back quick, Francis. Tell Polly to get ready for us. Then fetch the doctor to the house at once."

Francis, shivering as with ague, made a blind, convulsive gesture of understanding. With a last glance at his father he bent his head and set off frantically along the quay.

"Try, then, Alex . . . let me give you a hand." Bitterly dismissing Mirlees' offer of assistance which she knew to be worse than none, she helped her husband up. He swayed slowly, obediently to his feet. He was dreadfully shaky, hardly knew what he was doing. "I'll away then, Sam," he muttered, dizzily. "Good night to ye."

She bit her lip in a torment of uncertainty, yet persisted, led him out, met by the stinging sheets of rain. As the door shut behind them and he stood, unsteady, heedless of the weather, she was daunted by the prospect of that devious return, back through the mire of the fields with a helpless man in tow. But suddenly, as she hesitated, a thought illuminated her. Why had it not occurred to her before? If she took the short cut by the Tileworks Bridge she could save a mile at least, have him home and safe in bed within half an hour. She took his arm with fresh resolution. Pressing into the downpour, supporting him, she pointed their course up-river towards the bridge.

At first he did not apparently suspect her purpose, but suddenly, as the sound of rushing water struck his ear, he halted.

"Whatna way's this to come, Lisbeth? We cannot cross by the Tileworks with Tweed in such a spate."

"Hush, Alex . . . don't waste your strength by talking." She soothed him, helped him forward.

They came to the bridge, a narrow hanging span, fashioned of planks with a wire rope handrail, crossing the river at its narrowest, quite sound, though rarely used, since the Tileworks which it served had long ago shut down. As Elizabeth placed her foot upon the bridge, the blackness, the deafening nearness of the water, caused a vague doubt, perhaps a premonition, to cross her mind. She paused, since there was not room for them to go abreast, peering back at his subdued and sodden figure, swept by a rush of strange maternal tenderness.

"Have ye got the handrail?"

"Ay, I have the handrail."

She saw plainly that the thick wire rope was in his big fist. Distracted, breathless and obsessed, she could not reason further. "Keep close to me, then." She turned and led on.

They began to cross the bridge. Halfway across his foot slid off a rain-slimed board. It would have mattered little another night. Tonight it mattered more, for the Tweed, in flood, had risen to the planking of the bridge. At once the racing current filled his thighboot. He struggled against the pull, the overpowering weight. But they had beaten the strength from him at Ettal. His other leg slipped, both boots were waterlogged, loaded as with lead.

At his cry she spun round with a scream and caught at him. As the river tore the handrail from his grip her arms enfolded him; she fought closely, desperately, for a deathless instant to sustain him. Then the sound and the darkness of the waters sucked them down.

All that night Francis waited for them. But they did not come. Next morning they were found, clasped together, at low tide, in the quiet water near the sand bar.

II

One Thursday evening in September four years later, when Francis Chisholm ended his nightly tramp from Darrow Shipyard by veering wearily towards the blistered double headboard of Glennie's Bakery, he had reached a great decision. As he trudged down the floury passage dividing the bakehouse from the shop—his smallish figure oddly suppressed by an outsize suit of dungarees, his face grimy, beneath a man's cloth cap worn back to front—and went through the back door, placing his empty lunch pail on the scullery sink, his dark young eyes were smouldering with this purpose.

In the kitchen Malcom Glennie occupied the table—its soiled cover now, as always, littered with crockery—lolling on his elbow over *Locke's Conveyancing*, a lumpish pallid youth of seventeen, one hand massaging his oily black hair, sending showers of dandruff to his collar, the other attacking the sweetbread cooked for him by his mother on his return from the Armstrong College. As Francis took his supper from the oven—a twopenny pie and potatoes cremated there since noon—and cleared a place for himself, aware, through the torn opaque paper on the half glazed partition door, of Mrs. Glennie serving a customer in the front shop, the son of the house threw him a glance of peevish disapproval. "Can't you make less noise when I'm studying? And God! What hands! Don't you ever wash before you eat?"

In stolid silence—his best defence—Francis picked up a knife and fork in his calloused, rivet-burned fingers.

The partition door clicked open and Mrs. Glennie solicitously scuffled in. "Are you done yet, Malcom dear? I have the nicest baked custard—just fresh eggs and milk—it won't do your indigestion a mite of harm."

He grumbled: "I've been gastric all day." Swallowing a deep bellyful of wind, he brought it back with an air of virtuous injury. "Listen to that!"

"It's the study, son, that does it." She hurried to the range. "But this'll keep your strength up . . . just try it . . . to please me."

He suffered her to remove his empty plate and to place a large dish of custard before him. As he slobbered it down she watched him tenderly, enjoying every mouthful he took, her raddled figure, in broken corsets and dowdy, gaping skirt, inclined towards him, her shrewish face with its long thin nose and pinched-in lips doting with maternal fondness.

She murmured, presently: "I'm glad you're back early tonight, son. Your father has a meeting."

"Oh, no!" Malcom reared himself, in startled annoyance. "At the Mission Hall?"

She shook her narrow head. "Open air. On the Green."

"We're not going?"

She answered with a strange, embittered vanity: "It's the only position your father ever gave us, Malcom. Until he fails at the preaching too, we'd better take it."

He protested heatedly. "You may like it, Mother. But it's damned awful for me, standing there, with Father Bible-banging, and the kids yelling 'Holy Dan.' It wasn't so bad when I was young, but now when I'm coming out for a solicitor!" He stopped short, sulkily, as the outer door opened and his father, Daniel Glennie, came gently into the room.

Holy Dan advanced to the table, absently cut himself a slice of cheese, poured a glass of milk and, still standing, began his simple meal. Changed from his working singlet, slacks and burst carpet slippers, he was still an insignificant and drooping figure in shiny black trousers, an old cutaway coat too tight and short for him, a celluloid dickey and a stringy black tie. His cuffs were of celluloid too, to save the washing; they were cracked; and his boots might have done with mending. He stooped slightly. His gaze, usually harassed, often ecstatically remote, was now

778

thoughtful, kind, behind his steel-rimmed spectacles. As he chewed, he let it dwell in quiet consideration on Francis.

"You look tired, grandson. Have you had your dinner?"

Francis nodded. The room was brighter since the baker's entry. The eyes upon him now were like his mother's.

"There's a batch of cherry cakes I've just drawn. You can have one, if you've a mind to—on the oven rack."

At the senseless prodigality Mrs. Glennie sniffed: casting his goods about like this had made him twice a bankrupt, a failure. Her head inclined in greater resignation.

"When do you want to start? If we're going now I'll shut the shop."

He consulted his big silver watch with the yellow bone guard. "Ay, close up now, Mother, the Lord's work comes first. And besides"—sadly—"we'll have no more customers tonight."

While she pulled down the blinds on the fly-blown pastries he stood, detached, considering his address for tonight. Then he stirred. "Come, Malcom!" And to Francis: "Take care of yourself, grandson. Don't be late out your bed!"

Malcom, muttering beneath his breath, shut his book and picked up his hat. He sulkily followed his father out. Mrs. Glennie, pulling on tight black kid gloves, assumed her martyred "meeting" face. "Don't forget the dishes, now." She threw a meaning sickly smile at Francis. "It's a pity you're not coming with us!"

When they had gone he fought the inclination to lay his head upon the table. His new heroic resolution inflamed him, the thought of Willie Tulloch galvanized his tired limbs. Piling the greasy dishes into the scullery he began to wash them, rapidly probing his position, his brows tense, resentful.

The blight of enforced benefactions had lain upon him since that moment, before the funeral, when Daniel had raptly told Polly Bannon: "I'll take Elizabeth's boy. We are his only blood relations. He must come to us!"

Such rash benevolence alone would not have uprooted him. It took that later hateful scene when Mrs. Glennie, grasping at the small estate, money from his father's insurance and the sale of the furniture, had beaten down Polly's offer of guardianship, with intimidating invocations of the law.

This final acrimony had severed all contact with the Bannons—abruptly, painfully, as though he, indirectly, had been to blame: Polly, hurt and offended, yet with the air of having done her best, had undoubtedly erased him from her memory.

On his arrival at the baker's household, with all the attraction of a novelty, he was sent, a new satchel on his back, to the Darrow Academy: escorted by Malcom; straightened and brushed by Mrs.

779

Glennie, who watched the departing scholars from the shop door with a vague proprietary air.

Alas! The philanthropic flush soon faded. Daniel Glennie was a saint, a gentle noble derided soul who passed out tracts of his own composition with his pies and every Saturday night paraded his van horse through the town with a big printed text on the beast's rump: "*Love thy neighbour as thyself*." But he lived in a heavenly dream, from which he periodically emerged, careworn, damp with sweat, to meet his creditors. Working unsparingly, with his head on Abraham's bosom and his feet in a tub of dough, he could not but forget his grandson's presence. When he remembered he would take the small boy by the hand to the back yard, with a bag of crumbs, to feed the sparrows.

Mean, shiftless yet avaricious, viewing with a self-commiserating eye her husband's progressive failure,—the sacking of the van man, of the shopgirl, the closing of one oven after another, the gradual decline to a meagre output of twopenny pies and farthing pastries,—Mrs. Glennie soon discovered in Francis an insufferable incubus. The attraction of the sum of seventy pounds she had acquired with him quickly faded, seemed dearly bought. Already wrung by a desperate economy, to her the cost of his clothing, his food, his schooling became a perpetual Calvary. She counted his mouthfuls resignedly. When his trousers wore out she "made down" an old green suit of Daniel's, a relic of her husband's youth, of such outlandish pattern and colour it provided derisive outcry in the streets, shrouded the boy's life in misery. Though Malcom's fees at the Academy were paid upon the nail she usually succeeded in forgetting Francis' until, trembling, pale with humiliation, having publicly been called as a defaulter before the class, he was forced to approach her. Then she would gasp, feign a heart attack by fumbling at her withered bosom, count out the shillings as though he drew away her very blood.

Though he bore it with stoic endurance the sense of being alone . . . alone . . . was terrible for the little boy. Demented with sorrow, he took long solitary walks, combing the sick country vainly for a stream in which to guddle trout. He would scan the outgoing ships, consumed with longing, stuffing his cap between his teeth to stifle his despair. Caught between conflicting creeds, he knew not where he stood; his bright and eager mind was dulled, his face turned sullen. His only happiness came on the nights that Malcom and Mrs. Glennie were from home, when he sat opposite Daniel by the kitchen fire watching the little baker turning the pages of his Bible, in perfect silence, with a look of ineffable joy.

Daniel's quiet but inflexible resolve not to interfere with the boy's religion—how could he, when he preached universal tolerance!—was an added, ever-present goad to Mrs. Glennie. To a "Christian" like herself, who was saved, this reminder of her daughter's folly was anathema. It made the neighbours talk.

The climax came at the end of eighteen months when Francis, with ungrateful cleverness, had the bad taste to beat Malcom in an essay competition open to the school. It was not to be endured. Weeks of nagging wore the baker down. He was on the verge of another failure. It was agreed that Francis' education was complete. Smiling archly for the first time in months, Mrs. Glennie assured him that now he was a little man, fit to contribute to the household, to take his coat off and prove the nobility of toil. He went to work in Darrow Shipyard as a rivet-boy, twelve years old, at three and six a week.

By quarter-past seven he had finished the dishes. With greater alacrity, he spruced himself before the inch of mirror and went out. It was still light, but the night air made him cough and turn up his jacket as he hurried into High Street, past the livery stable and the Darrow Spirit Vaults, reaching at length the doctor's shop on the corner, with its two bulbous red and green vials and its square brass plate: DR. SUTHERLAND TULLOCH: PHYSICIAN AND SURGEON. Francis' lips were parted, faintly, as he entered.

The shop was dim and aromatic with the smell of aloes, assafœtida and liquorice root. Shelves of dark green bottles filled one side and at the end three wooden steps gave access to the small back surgery where Dr. Tulloch held his consultations. Behind the long counter, wrapping physic on a marble slab spattered with red sealing wax, stood the doctor's eldest son, a sturdy freckled boy of sixteen with big hands, sandy colouring and a slow taciturn smile.

He smiled now, staunchly, as he greeted Francis. Then the two boys looked away, avoiding one another, each reluctant to view the affection in the other's eyes.

"I'm late, Willie!" Francis kept his gaze intently on the skirting of the counter.

"I was late myself . . . and I've to deliver these medicines for Father, bless him." Now that Willie had begun his medical curriculum at the Armstrong College, Dr. Tulloch had, with solemn facetiousness, accredited him his assistant.

There was a pause. Then the older boy threw a secret glance towards his friend.

"Have you decided?"

Francis' gaze was still downcast. He nodded broodingly, his lips set. "Yes."

"You're right, Francis." Approval flooded Willie's plain and stolid features. "I wouldn't have stood it so long."

"I wouldn't . . . either . . ." Francis mumbled, "except for . . . well . . . my grandfather and you." His thin young face, concealed and sombre, reddened deeply as the last words came out with a rush.

Flushing in sympathy, Willie muttered: "I found out the train for you. There's a through leaves Alstead every Saturday at six-thirty-five . . . Quiet. Here's Dad." He broke off, with a warning glance, when the surgery door opened and Dr. Tulloch appeared, showing his last patient out. As the doctor returned toward the boys, a brusque, bristling dark-skinned figure in pepper-and-salt tweeds, his bushy hair and glossy whiskers seemed to spark with sheer vitality. For one who bore the awful reputation of the town's professed free-thinker, open adherent of Robert Ingersoll and Professor Darwin, he had a most disarming charm, and the look of one who would be useful in a sick-room. Because the hollows in Francis' cheeks made him grave, he cracked a frightful joke. "Well, my lad—that's another one killed off! Oh, he's not dead yet! Soon will be! Such a nice man too, leaves a large family." The boy's smile was too drawn to please him. He cocked his clear, challenging eye, mindful of his own troubled boyhood: "Cheer up, young housemaid's knee— it'll all be the same in a hundred years." Before Francis could reply the doctor laughed briefly, thrust his hard square hat on the back of his head and began pulling on his driving gloves. On his way out to his gig he called back: "Don't fail to bring him for supper, Will. Hot prussic acid served at nine!"

An hour later, with the physic delivered, the two boys made their way in unspeaking comradeship towards Willie's house, a large dilapidated villa facing the Green. As they talked in low voices of the daring promise of the day beyond tomorrow, Francis' spirits lifted. Life never seemed so hostile in Willie Tulloch's company. And yet, perversely, their friendship had begun in strife. After school, one day, larking down Castle Street with a dozen classmates, Willie's gaze had strayed to the Catholic church, ugly but inoffensive, beside the gasworks. "Come on," he shouted, in animal spirits. "I've got sixpence. Let's go in and get our sins forgiven!" Then, glancing round, he saw Francis in the group. He reddened with healthy shame. He had not meant the stupid jibe, which would have passed unheeded if Malcom Glennie had not pounced on it and fanned it skilfully into the occasion for a fight.

Incited by the rest, Francis and Willie fought a bloody indecisive battle on the Green. It was a good fight, rich in uncomplaining courage, and when the darkness stopped it, though neither was the victor, each had clearly had enough. But the spectators, with the cruelty of youth, refused to let the quarrel rest. On the next night, after school, the con-testants were brought together, whetted with the taunt of cowardice and set to batter each other's already battered head. Again, bloody, spent, yet dogged, neither would concede the victory. Thus for a dreadful week they were matched, like gamecocks, to make sport for their baser fellows. The inhuman conflict, motiveless and endless, became, for each, a nightmare. Then, on the Saturday, the two met unexpectedly, face to face, alone. An agonizing moment followed, then the earth opened, the sky melted and each had an arm round the other's neck, Willie blubbering: "I don't want to fight you, I like ye, man!"—while Francis, knuckling his purple eyes, wept back: "Willie, I like you best in the whole of Darrow!"

They were halfway across the Green, a public open space carpeted by dingy grass, with a forlorn bandstand in the centre, a rusty iron urinal at the far end and a few benches, mostly without backs, where pale-faced children played and loafers smoked and argued noisily, when suddenly Francis saw, with a tightening of his skin, that they must pass his grandfather's meeting. At the end farthest from the urinal a small red banner had been planted bearing the words in tarnished gilt: "*Peace on Earth to Men of Goodwill.*" Opposite the banner stood a portable harmonium furnished with a campstool on which Mrs. Glennie sat, wearing her victim's air, with Malcom, glumly clasping a hymn-book, beside her. Between the banner and the harmonium on a low wooden stand, surrounded by some thirty persons, was Holy Dan.

As the boys drew up on the fringe of the gathering Daniel had finished his opening prayer and, with his uncovered head thrown back, was beginning his address. It was a gentle and beautiful plea. It expressed Daniel's burning conviction, bared his simple soul. His doctrine was based on brotherhood, the love of one another and of God. Man should help his fellow man, bring peace and goodwill to earth. If only he could lead humanity to that ideal! He had no quarrel with the churches but chastised them mildly: it was not the form which mattered but the fundamentals, humility and charity. Yes, and tolerance! It was worthless to voice these sentiments if one did not practise them.

Francis had heard his grandfather speak before, and felt a throb of dogged sympathy for these views which made Holy Dan the laughing-stock of half the town. Now, edged by his wild intention, his heart swelled in understanding and affection, in longing for a world free of cruelty and hate. Suddenly, as he stood listening, he saw Joe Moir, the skip of his riveting squad at the Shipyard, sidle up the outskirts of the meeting. Accompanying Joe was the gang that hung about the Darrow Vaults, with an armament of bricks, decayed fruit, and oily waste thrown out from the boiler works. Moir was a ribald likeable giant, who, when drunk, gleefully pursued salvation rallies and other outdoor conclaves. He fingered a fistful of dripping waste and shouted: "Hey! Dan! Give us a song and dance!"

Francis' eyes dilated in his pale face. They were going to break up the meeting! He had a vision of Mrs. Glennie, clawing a ripe tomato from her splattered hair, of Malcom, with a greasy rag plastering his hateful face. His being exulted with a wild ecstatic joy.

Then he saw Daniel's face: still unconscious of the danger, lit by a strange intensity, every word throbbing, born of unquenchable sincerity, from the depths of his soul.

He started forward. Without knowing how, or why, he found himself at Moir's side, restraining his elbow, pleading breathlessly: "Don't Joe! Please don't! We're friends, aren't we?"

"Hell!" Moir glanced down, his boozy scowl melting to friendly recognition. "For Christ's sake, Francis!" Then, slowly, "I forgot he was your grandpa." A desperate pause. Then, commandingly, to his followers: "Come on lads, we'll go up to the Square and take it out on the Hallelujas!"

As they moved off the harmonium wheezed with life. No one but Willie Tulloch knew why the thunderbolt had not fallen.

A minute later, entering his house, he asked, baffled yet impressed: "Why did you, Francis?"

Francis answered shakily: "I don't know . . . There's something in what he says . . . I've had enough hating these last four years. My father and mother wouldn't have got drowned if people hadn't hated him . . ." He broke off, inarticulate, ashamed.

Silently, Willie led the way to the living room, which, after the outer dusk, glowed with light and sound and a prodigal untidy comfort. It was a long high maroon-papered chamber, asprawl with broken red plush furniture, the chairs castorless, the vases cracked and glued together, the bell pull tugged out, a litter of vials, labels, pillboxes on the mantelpiece and of toys, books and children upon the worn ink-stained Axminster. Though it was shockingly near nine o'clock none of the Tulloch family was abed. Willie's seven young brothers and sisters, Jean, Tom, Richard,—a list so complex even their father admitted to forgetting it,—were diversely occupied in reading, writing, drawing, scuffling and swallowing their supper of hot bread and milk while their mother Agnes Tulloch, a dreamy voluptuous woman with her hair half down and her bosom open, had picked the baby from his crib upon the hearth and, having removed its steaming napkin, now placidly refreshed the nuzzling bare-bottomed infant at her creamy, fire-lit breast.

She smiled her welcome, unperturbed, to Francis. "Here you are then, boys. Jean, set out more plates and spoons. Richard, leave Sophia alone. And Jean, dear, a fresh diaper for Sutherland from the line! Also see that the kettle's boiling for your father's toddy. What lovely weather we are having. Dr. Tulloch says there is much inflammation about though. Be seated, Francis. Thomas, didn't your father tell you to keep away from the others!" The doctor was always bringing home some disorder: measles one month, chicken-pox the next. Now Thomas, aged six, was the victim. His poll shorn and smelling of carbolic, he was happily disseminating ringworm through the tribe.

Squeezed on the crowded twanging sofa beside Jean, at fourteen the image of her mother, with the same creamy skin, the same placid smile, Francis supped his bread and milk flavoured with cinnamon. He was still upset from his recent outburst; there was an enormous lump inside his chest, his mind was a maze of confusion. Here was another problem for his aching brain. Why were these people so kind, happy, and contented? Reared by an impious rationalist to deny, or rather to ignore, the existence of their God, they were damned, hell fire already licked their feet.

At quarter-past nine the crunch of the dogcart's wheels was heard on the gravel. Dr. Tulloch strode in, a shout went up, he was at once the centre of an attacking mob. When the tumult stilled the doctor had bussed his wife heartily, was in his chair, a glass of toddy in his hand, slippers on his feet, the infant Sutherland goggling on his knee.

Catching Francis' eye, he raised his steaming tumbler in friendly satire. "Didn't I tell you there was poison going! Strong drink is raging—eh, Francis?"

Seeing his father in high humour, Willie was tempted to relate the story of the prayer meeting. The doctor slapped his thigh, smiling at Francis. "Good for you, my wee Roman Voltaire. I will disagree to the death with what you say and defend with my life your right to say it! Jean, stop making sheep's eyes at the poor laddie. I thought ye wanted to be a nurse! Ye'll have me a grandfather before I'm forty. Eh, well——" He sighed suddenly, toasting his wife. "We'll never get to heaven, woman—but at least we get our meat and drink."

Later, at the front door, Willie gripped Francis by the hand. "Good luck . . . Write to me when you're there."

At five next morning, while all was still dark, the Shipyard hooter sounded, long and dolorous, over the cowering dreariness of Darrow. Half senseless with sleep, Francis tumbled out of bed and into his dungarees, stumbled downstairs. The frigid morning, pale yet murky, met him like a blow as he joined the march of silent shivering figures, hurrying with bent head and huddled shoulders towards the Shipyard gates.

Over the weighbridge, past the checker's window, inside the gates . . . Gaunt spectres of ships rose dimly in their stocks around him. Beside the half-formed skeleton of a new ironclad Joe Moir's squad was mustering: Joe and the assistant plater, the holders-on, the two other rivet-boys and himself.

He lit the charcoal fire, blew the bellows beneath the forge. Silently, unwillingly, as in a dream, the squad set itself to work. Moir lifted his sledge, the hammers rang, swelled and strengthened, throughout the Shipyard.

Holding the rivets, white-hot from the brazier, Francis shinned up the ladder and thrust them quickly through the bolt-holes in the frame, where they were hammered flat and tight, annealing the great sheets of metal which formed the ship's hull. The work was fierce: blistering by the brazier, freezing on the ladders. The men were paid by piece work. They wanted rivets fast, faster than the boys could give them. And the rivets must be heated to the proper incandescence. If they were not malleable the men threw them back at the boys. Up and down the ladder, to and from the fires, scorched, smoky, with inflamed eyes, panting, perspiring, Francis fed the platers all day long.

In afternoon the work went faster: the men seemed careless, straining every nerve, unsparing of their bodies. The closing hour passed in a swimming daze with ear drums tense for the final hooter.

At last, at last it sounded. What blessed relief! Francis stood still, moistening his cracked lips, deafened by the cessation of all sound. On the way home, grimed and sweaty, through his tiredness, he thought: Tomorrow . . . tomorrow. That strange glitter returned to his eye, he squared his shoulders.

That night he took the wooden box down from its hiding place in the disused oven and changed his hoard of silver and coppers, saved with agonizing slowness, into half a sovereign. The golden coin, clutched deep in his trouser pocket, fevered him. With a queer, exalted flush he asked Mrs. Glennie for a needle and thread. She snubbed him, then threw him suddenly a veiled appraising glance.

"Wait! There's a reel in the top drawer—by that card of needles. You can take it." She watched him go out.

In the privacy of his bare and wretched room above the bakehouse he folded the coin in a square of paper, sewed it firm and tight inside the lining of his coat. He had a sense of glad security as he came down to give her back the thread.

The following day, Saturday, the Shipyard closed at twelve. The thought that he would never enter these gates again so elated him that at dinner he could scarcely eat; he felt his flushed restlessness more than enough to raise some sharp inquiry from Mrs. Glennie. To his relief she made no comment. As soon as he left the table, he edged out of the house, slipped down East Street, then fairly took to his heels.

Outside the town, he slipped into a brisk walk. His heart was singing within him. It was pathetic commonplace: the time-worn flight of all unhappy childhood. Yet for him it was the road to freedom. Once he was in Manchester he could find work at the cotton-mills, he was sure, doubly sure. He covered the fifteen miles to the railway Junction in four hours. It was striking six o'clock as he entered Alstead Station.

Seated under an oil lamp on the draughty deserted platform, he opened his penknife, cut the sewing on his jacket, removed the folded paper, took the shining coin from within. A porter appeared on the platform, some other passengers, then the booking office opened.

He took his place at the grille, demanded his ticket.

"Nine and six," the clerk said, punching the green cardboard slip into the machine.

Francis gasped with relief: he had not, after all, miscalculated the fare. He pushed his money through the grille.

There was a pause. "What's the game? I said nine and six."

"I gave you half a sovereign."

"Oh, you did! Try that again young feller and I'll have you run in!" The clerk indignantly flung the coin back at him.

It was not a half-sovereign but a bright new farthing.

In anguished stupor, Francis saw the train tear in, take up its freight, and go whistling into the night. Then his mind, groping dully, struck the heart of the enigma. The sewing, when he ripped it open, was not his own clumsy stitching but a close firm seam. In a withering flash he knew who had taken his money: Mrs. Glennie.

At half-past nine, outside the colliery village of Sanderston, in the dank wet mist which blurred his gig-lamps, a man in a dogcart almost ran down the solitary figure keeping the middle of the road. Only one person was likely to be driving in such a place on such a night. Dr. Tulloch, holding in his startled beast, peered downwards through the fog, his masterly invective suddenly cut short.

"Great Lord Hippocrates! It's you. Get in. Quick, will you—before the mare pulls my arms from their sockets." Tulloch wrapped the rug about his passenger; proceeded without questions; he knew the virtue of a healing silence.

By half-past ten Francis was drinking hot broth before the fire in the doctor's living room, now bereft of its occupants and so unnaturally still the cat slept peacefully on the hearth-rug. A moment later Mrs. Tulloch came in, her hair in plaits, her quilted dressing gown open above her night gown. She stood with her husband studying the dead-beat boy, who seemed unconscious of their presence, their murmured converse, wrapped in a curious apathy. Though he tried to smile, he could not when the doctor came forward, producing his stethoscope with a jocular air: "I'll bet my boots that cough of yours is a put-up job." But he submitted, opening his shirt, letting the doctor tap, and listen to, his chest.

Tulloch's saturnine face wore a queer expression as he straightened himself. His fund of humour had surprisingly dried up. He darted a look at his wife, bit his full lip, and suddenly kicked the cat.

"Damn it to hell!" he cried. "We use our children to build our battleships. We sweat them in our coal mines and our cotton-mills. We're a Christian country. Well! I'm proud to be a pagan." He turned brusquely, quite fiercely, to Francis. "Look here, boy, who are these folks you knew in Tynecastle? What's that—Bannon, eh? The Union Tavern. Get away home now and into bed unless you want treble pneumonia."

Francis went home, resistance crushed in him. All the next week Mrs. Glennie wore a martyred frown and Malcom a new checked waistcoat: price half a sovereign at the stores.

It was a dire week for Francis. His left side hurt him, especially when he coughed; he had to drag himself to work. He was aware, dimly, that his grandfather fought a battle for him. But Daniel was beaten down, defeated. All the little baker could do was to offer, humbly, some cherry cakes that Francis could not eat.

When Saturday afternoon came round he had not the strength to go out. He lay upstairs in his bedroom gazing in hopeless lethargy through the window.

Suddenly he started, his heart gave a great and unbelieving bound. In the street below, slowly approaching, like a barque navigating strange and dangerous waters, was a hat, a thing of memory, unique, unmistakable. Yes, yes: and the gold-handled umbrella, tightly rolled, the short sealskin jacket with the braided buttons. He cried out weakly, with pale lips: "Aunt Polly."

The shop door pinged below. Dithering to his feet, he crept downstairs, poised himself, trembling, behind the half-glazed door.

Polly was standing, very erect, in the centre of the floor, her lips pursed, her gaze sweeping the shop, as though amusedly inspecting it. Mrs. Glennie had half-risen, to confront her. Lounging against the counter, his mouth half-open, gaping from one to the other, was Malcom.

Aunt Polly's vision came to rest above the baker's wife. "Mrs. Glennie, if I remember right!"

Mrs. Glennie was at her worst: still unchanged, wearing her dirty forenoon wrapper, her blouse open at the neck, a loose tape hanging from her waist.

"What do you want?"

Aunt Polly raised her eyebrows. "I have come to see Francis Chisholm."

"He's out."

"Indeed! Then I'll wait till he comes in." Polly arranged herself on the chair by the counter as though prepared to remain all day.

There was a pause. Mrs. Glennie's face had turned a dirty red. She remarked, aside: "Malcom! Run round to the bakehouse and fetch your father."

Malcom answered shortly: "He went to the Hall five minutes ago. He won't be back till tea."

Polly removed her gaze from the ceiling, brought it critically to bear on Malcom. She smiled slightly when he flushed, then, entertained, she glanced away.

For the first time Mrs. Glennie showed signs of uneasiness. She burst

788

out angrily: "We're busy people here, we can't sit about all day. I've told you the boy is out. Like enough he won't be back till all hours— with the company he keeps. He's a regular worry with his late hours and bad habits. Isn't that so, Malcom?"

Malcom nodded sulkily.

"You see!" Mrs. Glennie rushed on. "If I was to tell you everything you'd be amazed. But it makes no difference, we're Christian people here, we look after him. You have my word for it—he's perfectly well and happy."

"I'm glad to hear it," Polly spoke primly, politely stifling a slight yawn with her glove, "for I've come to take him away."

"What!" Taken aback, Mrs. Glennie fumbled at the neck of her blouse, the colour flooding, then fading from, her face.

"I have a doctor's certificate," Aunt Polly enunciated, almost masticated, the formidable phrase with a deadly relish, "that the boy is underfed, overworked and threatened with pleurisy."

"It's not true."

Polly pulled a letter from her muff and tapped it significantly with the head of her umbrella. "Can you read the Queen's English?"

"It's a lie, a wicked lie. He's as fat and well fed as my own son!"

There was an interruption. Francis, flat against the door, following the scene in an agony of suspense, leaned too heavily against the rickety catch. The door flew open, he shot into the middle of the shop. There was a silence.

Aunt Polly's preternatural calm had deepened. "Come over, boy. And stop shaking. Do you want to stay here?"

"No, I don't."

Polly threw a look of justification towards the ceiling. "Then go and pack your things."

"I haven't anything to pack."

Polly stood up slowly, pulling on her gloves. "There's nothing to keep us."

Mrs. Glennie took a step forward, white with fury. "You can't walk over me. I'll have the law on you."

"Go ahead, my woman." Polly meaningly restored the letter to her muff. "Then maybe we'll find out how much of the money that came from the sale of poor Elizabeth's furniture has been spent on her son and how much on yours."

Again there was a shattered silence. The baker's wife stood, pale, malignant and defeated, one hand clutching at her bosom.

"Oh, let him go, Mother," Malcom whined. "It'll be good riddance."

Aunt Polly, cradling her umbrella, examined him from top to toe.

"Young man, you're a fool!" She swung round towards Mrs. Glennie. "As for you, woman," looking straight over her head, "you're another!"

Taking Francis triumphantly by the shoulder, she propelled him, bare-headed, from the shop.

They proceeded in this fashion towards the station, her glove grasping the fabric of his jacket firmly, as though he were some rare and captive creature who might at any moment escape. Outside the station she bought him, without comment, a bag of Abernethy biscuits, some cough drops, and a brand-new bowler hat. Seated opposite him in the train, serene, singular, erect, observing him moisten the dry biscuits with tears of thankfulness, extinguished almost by his new hat which enveloped him to the ears, she remarked with half-closed, judicial eyes:—

"I always knew that creature was no lady, I could see it in her face. You made an awful mistake letting her get hold of you, Francis dear. The next thing we'll do is get your hair cut!"

III

It was wonderful these frosty mornings to lie warm in bed until Aunt Polly brought his breakfast, a great plate of bacon and eggs still sizzling, boiling black tea and a pile of hot toast, all on an oval metal tray stamped *Allgood's Old Ale*. Sometimes he woke early, in an agony of apprehension; then came the blessed knowledge that he need no longer fear the hooter. With a sob of relief he burrowed more deeply into his thick yellow blankets, in his cosy bedroom with its paper of climbing sweet peas, its stained boards and woolwork rug, a lithograph of Allgood's Prize Brewery Dray Horse on one wall, of Pope Gregory on another, and a little china holy-water font with a sprig of Easter palm stuck sideways in it by the door. The pain in his side was gone, he seldom coughed, his cheeks were filling out. The novelty of leisure was like a strange caress and, though the uncertainty of his future still troubled him, he received it gratefully.

On this fine morning of the last day of October, Aunt Polly sat on the edge of his bed exhorting him to eat. "Lay in, boy! That'll stick to your ribs!" There were three eggs on the plate, the bacon was crisp and streaky, he had forgotten that food could taste so good.

As he balanced the tray on his knees, he sensed an unusual festivity in her manner. And soon she gave him one of her profound nods.

"I've news for you today, young man—if you can stand it."

"News, Aunt Polly?"

"A little excitement to cheer you up—after your dull month with Ned and me." She smiled dryly at the quick protest in his warm brown eyes. "Can't you guess what it is?"

He studied her with the deep affection which her unceasing kindness had awakened in him. The homely angular face—poor-complexioned, the long upper lip downed with hair, a tufted blemish at the angle of the cheek—was now familiar and beautiful.

"I can't think, Aunt Polly."

She was moved to her short rare laugh, a little snort of satisfaction at her success in provoking his curiosity.

"What's happened to your wits, boy? I believe too much sleep has addled them."

He smiled happily in sympathy. It was true that the routine of his convalescence had hitherto been tranquil. Encouraged by Polly, who had feared for his lungs,—she had a dread of "consumption₀" which "ran" in her family,—he had usually lain abed until ten. Dressed, he accompanied her on her shopping, a stately progress through the main streets of Tynecastle which, since Ned ate largely and nothing but the best, demanded great prodding of poultry and sniffing of steak. These excursions were revealing. He could see that it pleased Aunt Polly to be "known," deferred to, in the best stores. She would wait, aloof and prim, until her favourite shopman was free to serve her. Above all, she was ladylike. That word was her touchstone, the criterion of her actions, even of her dresses, made by the local milliner in such dreadful taste they sometimes evoked a covert snigger from the vulgar. In the street she had a graduated series of bows. To be recognized, greeted by some local personage—the surveyor, the sanitary inspector or the chief constable— afforded her a joy which, though sternly concealed, was very great. Erect, the bird in her hat atwitter, she would murmur to Francis: "That was Mr. Austin, the tramway manager . . . a friend of your uncle's . . . a fine man." The height of her gratification was reached when Father Gerald Fitzgerald, the handsome portly priest of St. Dominic's, gave her in passing his gracious and slightly condescending smile. Every forenoon they would stop in at the church and, kneeling, Francis would be conscious of Polly's intent profile, the lips moving silently, above her rough chapped reverent hands. Afterwards she bought him something for himself, a stout pair of shoes, a book, a bag of aniseed drops. When he protested, often with tears in his eyes, as she opened her worn purse, she would simply press his arm and shake her head. "Your uncle won't take 'no.'" She was touchingly proud of her relationship with Ned, her association with the Union Tavern.

The Union stood near the docks at the corner of Canal and Dyke Streets, with an excellent view of the adjacent tenements, of coal barges, and the terminus of the new horse tramway. The brown painted stucco building was of two stories, and the Bannons lived above the tavern. Every morning at half-past seven Maggie Magoon, the scrubwoman, opened the saloon and began, talking to herself, to clean it. At eight precisely Ned Bannon came down, in his braces, but closely shaved, with his forelock oiled, and strewed the floor with fresh sawdust from the box behind the bar. It was unnecessary: a kind of ritual. Next, he inspected the morning, took in the milk and crossed the back yard to feed his whippets. He kept thirteen—to prove that he was not superstitious.

Soon the first of the regulars began to drop in, Scanty Magoon always in the van, hobbling on his leather padded stumps to his favourite corner, followed by a few dockers, a tram driver or two, returning from the night shift. These workmen did not stop: only long enough to down their half of spirits and chase it with a glass, a schooner, or a pint of beer. But Scanty was a permanent, a kind of faithful watchdog, gazing pro-pitiatingly at Ned as he stood bland, unconscious, behind the bar with its sombre woodwork and the framed notice: GENTLEMEN BEHAVE OTHERS MUST.

Ned, at fifty, was a big thick figure of a man. His face was full and yellowish, with prominent eyes, very solemn in repose, matching his dark clothes. He was neither genial nor flashy, the qualities popularly attributed to a publican. He had a kind of solemn, bilious dignity. He was proud of his reputation, his establishment. His parents had been driven out of Ireland by the potato famine, he had known poverty and starvation as a boy, but he had succeeded against inconceivable odds. He had a "free" house, stood well with the licensing authorities and the brewers, had many influential friends. He said, in effect, The drink trade is respectable and I prove it. He set his face against young men drinking and refused rudely to serve any woman under forty: there was no *Family Department* in the Union Tavern. He hated disorder, at the first sound of it he would rap crossly with an old shoe—maintained handy for that purpose—on the bar, and keep rapping till the discord ceased. Though a heavy drinker himself he was never seen the worse for it. Perhaps his grin was loose, his eye inclined to wander on those rare evenings which he deemed "an occasion," such as St. Patrick's night, Halloween, Hogmanay, or after a day's dog racing when one of his whippets had added another medal to the galaxy on the heavy watchchain that spanned his stomach. At any rate, on the following day he would wear a sheepish air and send Scanty up for Father Clancy, the curate at St. Dominic's. When he had made his confession he rose heavily, dusting his knees, from the boards of the back room and pressed a sovereign for the poor-box into the young priest's hand. He had a healthy respect for the clergy. For Father Fitzgerald, the parish priest, he had, indeed, considerable awe.

Ned was reputed "comfortable," he ate well, gave freely and, dis-trusting stocks and shares, had money invested in "bricks and mortar." Since Polly had a competence of her own, inherited from Michael, the dead brother, he had no anxiety on her account.

Though slow to form an affection, Ned was, in his own cautious word, "taken" with Francis. He liked the boy's unobtrusiveness, the sparseness of his speech, the quiet way he held himself, his silent gratitude. The sombreness of the young face, caught unguarded, in repose, made him frown dumbly, and scratch his head.

In the afternoon Francis would sit with him in the half-empty bar, drowsy with food, the sunlight slanting churchwise through the musty air, listening with Scanty to Ned's genial talk. Scanty Magoon, husband and encumbrance of the worthy witless Maggie, was so named because there was not enough of him, only in fact a torso. He had lost his legs from gangrene caused by some obscure disorder of the circulation. Capitalizing on his complaint, he had promptly "sold himself to the doctors," signing a document which would deliver his body to the dissecting slab on his demise. Once the purchase price was drunk, a sinister aura settled on the bleary, loquacious, wily, unfortunate old scamp. An object now of popular awe, in his cups he indignantly declared himself defrauded. "I never got enough for myself. Them bloody scalpers! But they'll never get ahold of me poor old Adam! God damn the fear! I'll enlist for a sailor and drown myself."

Occasionally Ned would let Francis draw a beer for Scanty, partly for charity, partly to give the boy the thrill of the "engine." As the ivory-handled pull came back, filling the mug—Scanty prompting anxiously, "Get a head on her, boy!"—the foamy brew smelled so nutty and good Francis wanted to taste it. Ned nodded permission, then smiled in slow delight at the wryness of his nephew's face. "It's a acquired taste," he gravely asserted. He had a number of such clichés, from "Women and beer don't mix," to "A man's best friend is his own pound note," which, through frequency and profundity of utterance, had been hallowed into epigrams.

Ned's gravest, most tender affection was reserved for Nora, daughter of Michael Bannon. He was devoted to his niece who when three had lost her brother from tuberculosis, and her father through that same murderous malady, so fatal to the Celtic race, two years later. Ned had brought her up, sent her off at the age of thirteen to St. Elizabeth's, the best convent boarding school in Northumberland. It was a genuine pleasure for him to pay the heavy fees. He watched her progress with a fond indulgent eye. When she came home for the holidays he was a new man: spryer, never seen in braces, ponderously devising excursions and amusements and, lest anything should offend her, much stricter in the bar.

"Well——" Aunt Polly was gazing half-reproachfully across the breakfast tray at Francis. "I see I'll have to tell you what it's all about. In the first place your uncle's decided to give a party to-night to celebrate Halloween . . . and"—momentarily she dropped her eyes—"for another reason. We'll have a goose, a four-pound black bun, raisins for the snapdragon, and of course the apples—your uncle gets special ones at Lang's market garden in Gosforth. Maybe you'll go over for them this afternoon. It's a nice walk."

"Certainly, Aunt Polly. Only, I'm not quite sure of where it is."

"Someone'll show you the way." Polly composedly produced her main surprise. "Someone who's coming home from her school to spend a long week-end with us."

"Nora!" he exclaimed abruptly.

"The same." She nodded, took up his tray and rose. "Your uncle's pleased as punch she's got leave. Hurry up and dress now, like a good boy. We're all going to the station to meet the little monkey at eleven."

When she had gone Francis lay staring in front of him with a queer perplexity. This unexpected announcement of Nora's arrival had taken him aback, and strangely thrilled him. He had always liked her, of course. But now he faced the prospect of meeting her again with an odd new feeling, between diffidence and eagerness. To his surprise and confusion he suddenly found himself reddening to the roots of his hair. He jumped up hurriedly and began to pull on his clothes.

Francis and Nora started off, at two o'clock, on their excursion, taking the tram across the city to the suburb of Clermont, then walking across country toward Gosforth, each with a hand on the big wicker basket, swinging it between them.

It was four years since Francis had seen Nora and, stupidly tongue-tied all through lunch, when Ned had surpassed himself in massive playfulness, he was still painfully shy of her. He remembered her as a child. Now she was nearly fifteen and, in her modestly long navy-blue skirt and bodice, she seemed quite grown-up, more elusive and unreadable than ever before. She had small hands and feet and a small, alert provoking face, which could be brave or suddenly timid. Though she was tall and awkward from her growth her bones were fine and slender. Her eyes were teasing, darkly blue against her pale skin. The cold made them sparkle, made her little nostrils pink.

Occasionally, across the basket handle, his fingers touched Nora's. The sensation was remarkable: sweet and warmly confusing. Her hands were the nicest things to touch that he had ever known. He could not speak, did not dare look at her, though from time to time he felt her looking at him and smiling. Though the golden blaze of the autumn was past, the woods still glowed with bright red embers. To Francis the colours of the trees, of the fields and sky, had never appeared more vivid. They were like a singing in his ears.

Suddenly she laughed outright and, tossing back her hair, began to run. Attached to her by the basket he raced like the wind alongside

794

until she drew up, gasping, her eyes sparkling like frost on a sunny morning.

"Don't mind me, Francis. I get wild sometimes. I can't help it. It's being out of school, perhaps."

"Don't you like it there?"

"I do and I don't. It's funny and strict. Could you believe it?" She laughed, with a little rush of disconcerting innocence. "They make us wear our nightgowns when we take a bath! Tell me, did you ever think of me all the time you were away?"

"Yes." He stumbled out the answer.

"I'm glad . . . I thought of you." She threw him a swift glance, made as though to speak, and was silent.

Presently they reached the Gosforth market garden. Geordie Lang, Ned's good friend and the owner of the garden, was in the orchard, among the half-denuded trees, burning leaves. He gave them a friendly nod, an invitation to join him. They raked the crackling brown and yellow leaves towards the great smouldering cone he had already built, until the smell of the leaf smoke impregnated their clothing. It was not work but glorious sport. They forgot their earlier embarrassment, competed as to who should rake the most. When he had raked a great pile for himself Nora mischievously despoiled it. Their laughter rang in the high clear air. Geordie Lang grinned in broad sympathy. "That's women, lad. Take your pile and laugh at ye."

At last Lang waved them towards the apple shed, a wooden erection at the end of the orchard.

"You've earned your keep. Go and help yourself!" he called after them. "And give my best respects to Mr. Bannon. Tell him I'll look in for my drop of spirits sometime this week."

The apple shed was soft with crepuscular twilight. They climbed the ladder to the loft where, spaced out on straw, not touching, were rows and rows of the Ribston Pippins for which the garden was renowned. While Francis filled the basket, crouching under the low roof, Nora sat crosslegged on the straw, picked an apple, shone it on her bony hip and began to eat.

"Oh, my, it's good," she said. "Have one, Francis?"

He sat down opposite, took the apple she held out to him. The taste was delicious. They watched each other eating. When her small teeth bit through the amber skin into the crisp white flesh, little spurts of juice ran down her chin. He did not feel so shy in the dark little loft, but dreamy and warm, suffused with the joy of living. He had never liked anything so much as being here, in the garden, eating the apple she had given him. Their eyes, meeting frequently, smiled; but she had a half-smile, strange and inward, that seemed entirely for herself.

"I dare you to eat the seeds," she teased suddenly; then added quickly:

"No, don't, Francis! Sister Margaret Mary says they give you colic. Besides a new apple tree will grow from each of those seeds. Isn't it funny! Listen, Francis . . . you're fond of Polly and Ned?"

"Very." He stared. "Aren't you?"

"Of course . . . except when Polly coddles me every time I get a cough . . . and when Ned pets me on his knee—I hate that."

She hesitated, lowered her gaze for the first time. "Oh, it's nothing, I shouldn't, Sister Margaret Mary thinks I'm impudent, do you?"

He glanced away awkwardly, his passionate repudiation of the charge condensed in a clumsy: "No!"

She smiled almost timidly. "We're friends, Francis, so I will say it, and spite old Margaret Mary. When you're a man what are you going to be?"

Startled, he stared at her. "I don't know. Why?"

She picked with sudden nervousness at the serge of her dress. "Oh, nothing . . . only, well . . . I like you. I've always liked you. All those years I've thought of you a lot and it wouldn't be nice if you . . . sort of disappeared again."

"Why should I disappear?" He laughed.

"You'd be surprised!" Her eyes, still childish, were wide and wise. "I know Aunt Polly . . . I heard her again today. She'd give anything to see you made a priest. Then you'd have to give up everything, even me." Before he could reply she jumped up, shaking herself, with a great show of animation. "Come on, don't be silly, sitting here all day. It's ridiculous with the sun shining outside, and the party tonight." He made to rise. "No, wait a minute. Shut your eyes and you might get a present."

Even before he thought of complying she darted over and gave him a hurried little kiss on the cheek. The quick warm contact, the touch of her breath, the closeness of her thin face with the tiny brown mole on the cheekbone, stunned him. Blushing deeply, unexpectedly she slipped down the ladder and ran out of the shed. He followed slowly, darkly red, rubbing the small moist spot upon his cheek as though it were a wound. His heart was pounding.

That night the Halloween party began at seven o'clock. Ned, with a sultan's privilege, closed the bar at five minutes to the hour. All but a few favoured patrons were politely asked to leave. The guests assembled upstairs, in the parlour, with its glass cases of wax fruit, the picture of Parnell above the blue-glass lustres, the velvet-framed photograph of Ned and Polly at the Giant's Causeway, the bog oak jaunting car,—a present from Killarney,—the aspidistra, the varnished shillelagh hung on the wall with green ribbon, the heavy padded furniture which emitted a puff of dust when heavily sat upon. The mahogany table was fully extended, with legs like a dropsical woman, and set for twenty. The coal fire, banked halfway up the chimney, would have prostrated an African explorer. The smell, off, was of rich basting birds. Maggie Magoon, in cap and apron, ran about like a maniac. In the crowded room were the young curate, Father Clancy, Thaddeus Gilfoyle, several of the neighbouring tradesmen, Mr. Austin the manager of the tramways, his wife and three children, and, of course, Ned, Polly, Nora and Francis.

Amidst the din, with beaming benevolence and a sixpenny cigar, Ned stood laying down the law to his friend Gilfoyle. A pale, prosaic and slightly catarrhal young man of thirty was Thaddeus Gilfoyle, clerk at the gasworks,—who in his spare time collected the rents of Ned's property in Varrell Street, was a sidesman at St. Dominic's, a steady-going chap who could always be relied on to do an odd job, to fill the breach, to "come forward," as Ned phrased it,—who never had two words to rub against one another or a single idea that might be called his own, yet who somehow managed to be there, hanging around, on the spot when he was wanted, dull and dependable, nodding in agreement, blowing his nose, fingering his confraternity badge, fish-eyed, flat-footed, solemn, safe.

"You'll be for making a speech tonight?" he now inquired of Ned, in a tone which implied that if Ned did not make a speech the world would be desolate.

"Ah, I don't know now." Modestly yet profoundly, Ned considered the end of his cigar.

"Ah, you will now, Ned!"

"They'll not expect it."

"Pardon me, Ned, if I beg to differ."

"Ye think I should?"

With solemnity, "Ned, ye both should and would!"

"Ye mean . . . I ought to?"

"You must, Ned, and you will."

Delighted, Ned rolled the cigar across his mouth. "As a matter of fact, I had," he cocked his eye, significantly, "I have a announcement . . . a important announcement I want to make. I'll say a few words later, since you press me."

Led by Polly as a kind of overture to the main event, the children began to play Halloween games—first snapdragon, scrambling for the flat blue raisins, ablaze with spirit, on a big china dish, then duck-apple, dropping a fork from between the teeth over the back of a chair into a tub of swimming apples.

At seven o'clock the "gowks" came in: working lads from the neighbourhood, with soot-blackened faces and grotesque attire, mumming their way around the district, singing for sixpences, in the strange tradition of All Hallows Eve. They knew how to please Ned. They sang "Dear Little Shamrock," "Kathleen Mavourneen," and "Maggie

Murphy's Home." Largesse was distributed. They clattered out. "Thank you, Mr. Bannon! Up the Union! Good night, Ned!"

"Good lads. Good lads all of them!" Ned rubbed his hands, his eye still moist with Celtic sentiment. "Now, Polly, our friends' stomachs will be thinking their throats is cut."

The company sat down at table, Father Clancy said grace, and Maggie Magoon staggered in with the largest goose in Tynecastle. Francis had never tasted such a goose—it dissolved, in rich flavours, upon the tongue. His body glowed from the long excursion in the keen air and from a strange interior joy. Now and then his eyes met Nora's across the table, shyly, with exquisite understanding. Though he was so quiet her gaiety thrilled him. The wonder of this happy day, of the secret bond which lay between them, was like a pain.

When the repast was over Ned got up slowly, amidst applause. He struck an oratorical attitude, one thumb in his armpit. He was absurdly nervous.

"Your Reverence, Ladies and Gentlemen, I thank you one and all. I'm a man of a few words,"—a cry of "No, No" from Thaddeus Gilfoyle,—"I say what I mean, and I mean what I say!" A short pause while Ned struggled for more confidence. "I like to see my friends happy and contented round about me—good company and good beer never hurt any man." Interruption at the doorway from Scanty Magoon, who had sneaked in with the gowks and contrived to remain. "God save you, Mr. Bannon!"—brandishing a drumstick of the goose. "You're a fine man!" Ned remained unperturbable—every great man has his sycophants. "As I was remarkin' when Mrs. Magoon's husband flung a brick at me . . ." Laughter. ". . . I favour the social occasion. I'm sure we're proud and pleased, every mother's son of us,—and daughter,—to welcome into our midst my poor wife's brother's boy!" Loud applause and Polly's voice: "Take a bow, Francis." "I'm not going into recent history. Let the past bury its dead, I say. But I say and say it I will, Look at him now, I say, and when he came!" Applause and Scanty's voice in the corridor: "Maggie, for the love of God, will ye bring some more of the goose!" "Now, I'm not one to blow my own trumpet! I try to do fair between God and man and beast. Look at my whippets if ye don't believe me." Gilfoyle's voice: "The best dogs in Tynecastle!" A longer pause, during which Ned lost the thread of his speech. "Where am I?" "Francis!" Polly prompted quickly. "Ah, yes." Ned raised his voice. "When Francis came, I said to myself, says I, Here's a boy that might be useful. Shove him behind the bar and let him earn his keep? No, by God—Saving your presence, Father Clancy— that's not us. We talk it over, Polly and me. The boy's young, the boy's been ill-treated, the boy has a future before him, the boy's my poor dead wife's brother's boy. Let's send him to college, we say; we can manage it between us." Ned paused. "Your Reverence, Ladies and Gentlemen, I'm pleased and proud to announce that next month Francis starts off for Holywell!" Making the name the triumphant keystone of his peroration, Ned sat down, perspiring, amidst loud applause.

IV

Though the elm shadows were long upon the cropped lawns of Holywell, the northern June evening was still light as noon. The darkness would come late, so close to dawn the aurora borealis would but briefly glitter across the high pale heavens. As Francis sat at the open window of the high little study which he shared, since his election to the "Philosophers," with Laurence Hudson and Anselm Mealey, he felt his attention wander from the notebook, drawn, almost sadly, with a pense of the transience of beauty, to the lovely scene before him.

From the steep angle of his vision he could see the school, a noble grey granite baronial mansion, built for Sir Archibald Frazer in 1609, and endowed, this century, as a Catholic College. The chapel, styled in the same severity, lay at right angles, linked by a cloister, to the library, enclosing a quadrangle of historic turf. Beyond were the fives and handball courts, the playing fields, the end of a game still in progress, wide reaches of pasture threaded by the Stinchar River with stumpy black Polled Angus cattle grazing stolidly, woods of beech and oak and rowan clustering the lodge, and in the ultimate distance the backdrop, blue, faintly serrated, of the Aberdeenshire Grampians.

Without knowing, Francis sighed. It seemed only yesterday that he had landed at Doune, the draughty northern junction, a new boy, scared out of his wits, facing the unknown and that first frightful interview with the Headmaster, Father Hamish MacNabb. He remembered how "Rusty Mac," great little Highland gentleman, blood cousin to MacNabb of the Isles, had crouched at his desk beneath his tartan cape, peering from bushy red eyebrows, dreadfully formidable.

"Well, boy, what can you do?"

"Please, sir . . . nothing."

"Nothing! Can't you dance the Highland Fling?"

"No, sir."

"What! With a grand name like Chisholm?"

"I'm sorry, sir."

"Humph! There's not much profit in you, is there boy?"

"No, sir, except sir . . ." Trembling: ". . . Maybe I can fish."

"Maybe, eh?" A slow dry smile. "Then maybe we'll be friends." The smile deepened. "The clans of Chisholm and MacNabb fished together, ay, and fought together, before you or I were thought of. Run now, before I cane ye."

And now, in one more term, he would be leaving Holywell. Again his gaze slanted down to the little groups promenading to and fro on the gravelled terraces beside the fountain. A seminary custom! Well, what of it? Most of them would go from here to the Seminary of San Morales in Spain. He discerned his room-mates walking together: Anselm, as usual, extrovert in his affections, one arm tenderly linking his companion's, the other gesticulating, but nicely, as befitted the outright winner of the Frazer Good Fellowship Prize! Behind the two, surrounded by his coterie, paced Father Tarrant—tall, dark, thin . . . intense yet sardonic . . . classically remote.

At the sight of the youngish priest Francis' expression tightened oddly. He viewed the open notebook before him on the window ledge with distaste, picked up his pen and began, after a moment, his imposition. His frown of resolution did not mar the clean brown moulding of his cheek or the sombre clearness of his hazel eyes. Now, at eighteen, his body had a wiry grace. The chaste light heightened absurdly his physical attractiveness, that air, unspoiled and touching, which—inescapable—so often humiliated him.

"*June 14th, 1887.* Today there occurred an incident of such phenomenal and thrilling impropriety I must revenge myself on this beastly diary, and Father Tarrant, by recording it. I oughtn't really to waste this hour before vespers—afterwards I shall be dutifully cornered by Anselm to play handball—I should jot down *Ascension Thursday : Fine day; memorable adventure with Rusty Mac,* and leave it. But even our incisive Administrator of Studies admitted the virtue of my breed—conscientiousness—when he said to me, after his lecture: 'Chisholm! I suggest you keep a diary. Not of course for publication,'—his confounded satire flashed out,—'as a form of examen. You suffer, Chisholm, inordinately, from a kind of spiritual obstinacy. By writing your inmost heart out . . . if you could . . . you might possibly reduce it.'

"I blushed, of course, like a fool, as my wretched temper flared. 'Do you mean I don't do what I'm told, Father Tarrant?'

"He barely looked at me, hands tucked away in the sleeves of his habit, thin, dark, pinched in at the nostrils and oh, so unanswerably clever. As he tried to conceal his dislike of me, I had a sharp awareness of his hard shirt, of the iron discipline I know he uses unsparingly upon himself. He said vaguely: 'There is a mental disobedience . . .' and walked away.

"Is it conceit to imagine he has his knife in me because I do not model myself upon him? Most of us do. Since he came here two years ago he has led quite a cult of which Anselm is deacon. Perhaps he cannot

800

forget the occasion when, at his instruction to us upon the 'one, true, and apostolic religion' I suddenly remarked: 'Surely, sir, creed is such an accident of birth God can't set an exclusive value on it.' In the shocked hush which followed he stood nonplussed, but icy cold. 'What an admirable heretic you would have made, my good Chisholm.'

"At least we have one point in common: agreement that I shall never have a vocation.

"I'm writing ridiculously pompously for a callow youth of eighteen. Perhaps it is what is named the affectation of my age. But I'm worried . . . about several things. Firstly, I'm terribly, probably absurdly, worried about Tynecastle. I suppose it's inevitable that one should lose touch, when one's 'home-leave' is limited to four short summer weeks. This brief annual vacation, Holywell's only rigour, may serve its purpose of keeping vocations firm, but it also strains the imagination. Ned never writes. His correspondence during my three years at Holywell has been effected through the medium of sudden and fantastic gifts of food: that colossal sack of walnuts for instance, from the docks, in my first winter, and last spring, the crate of bananas, three quarters of which were over-ripe and created an undignified epidemic amongst the 'clergy and laity' here.

"But even in Ned's silence there's something queer. And Aunt Polly's letters make me more apprehensive. Her dear inimitable gossip about parochial events has been replaced by a meagre catalogue of, mainly, meteorological facts. And this change in tone arrived so suddenly. Naturally Nora hasn't helped me. She is the original postcard girl, who scribbles off her obligations in five minutes, once a year, at the seaside. It seems, however, centuries since her last brilliant *Sunset from Scarborough Pier* and two letters of mine have failed even to produce a *Moon over Whitley Bay*. Dear Nora! I shall never forget your Eve-like gesture in the apple loft. It's because of you that I anticipate these coming holidays so eagerly. Shall we walk again, I wonder, to Gosforth? I have watched you grow, holding my breath—seen your character—by which I mean your contradictions—develop. I know you as someone quick, shy, bold, sensitive and gay, a little spoiled by flattery, full of innocence and fun. Even now, I see your impudent sharp little face, lit up from within as you indulge your amazing gift of mimicry—'taking off' Aunt Polly . . . or me—your skinny arms akimbo, blue eyes provoking, reckless, ending by flinging yourself into a dance of gleeful malice. Everything about you is so—human and alive, and—even those flashes of petulance and fits of temper which shake your delicate physique and end in such tremendous weepings. And I know, despite your faults, how warm and impulsive is your nature, making you run, with a quick and shamefaced blush, towards someone you have hurt . . .

unconsciously. I lie awake thinking of you, of the look in your eyes, the tender pathos of your collar bones above your small round breasts . . ."

Francis broke off here, and with a sudden flush scored out the last line he had written. Then, conscientiously, he resumed.

"Secondly, I am selfishly concerned about my future. I'm now educated above—here again Fr. Tarrant would agree—my station. I've only another term at Holywell. Am I to return gracefully to the beer-pulls of the Union? I can't continue to be a charge on Ned—or more justly Polly, since I recently ascertained quite by accident that my fees have been discharged, out of her modest income, by that wonderful woman! My ambitions are so muddled. My fondness for Aunt Polly, my overbrimming gratitude, make me long to repay her. And it is her dearest wish to see me ordained. Again, in a place like this, where three quarters of the students and most of one's friends are predestined for the priesthood, it is hard to escape the inevitable pull of sympathy. One wants to line up in the ranks. Tarrant apart, Father MacNabb thinks I should make a good priest—I can feel it in his shrewd, friendly provocativeness, his almost Godlike sense of waiting. And as Principal of this College he should know something about vocations.

"Naturally I'm impetuous and hot-tempered; and my mixed upbringing has left me with a schismatic quirk. I can't pretend to be one of these consecrated youths—our college library teems with them— who lisp prayers throughout their infancy, make boyish shrines in the woods and sweetly rebuke the little girls who jostle them at the village fair. 'Keep away, Thérèse and Annabelle, I am not for thee.'

"Yet who can describe those moments that come to one suddenly: alone upon the back road to Doune, waking in the darkness in one's silent room, remaining behind, quite solitary, when the scraping, coughing, whispering mob has gone in the empty yet breathing church. Moments of strange apprehension, of intuition. Not that sentimental ecstasy which is as loathsome to me as ever—Query: why do I want to vomit when I see rapture on the Master of Novices' face?—but a sense of consolation, of hope.

"I'm distressed to find myself writing like this—though it is for no other eye than mine. One's private ardours make chilling stuff on paper. Yet I must record this inescapable sense of belonging to God which strikes at me through the darkness, the deep conviction, under the measured, arranged, implacable movement of the universe, that man does not emerge from, or vanish into, nothing. And here—is it not strange?—I feel the influence of Daniel Glennie, dear, cracked Holy Dan, feel his warm unearthly gaze upon me. . . .

"Confound it! And Tarrant! I *am* literally pouring out my heart.

If I am such a Holy Willie why don't I set out and do something for God, attack the great mass of indifference, of sneering materialism in the world today . . . in short, become a priest? Well . . . I must be honest. I think it is because of Nora. The beauty and tenderness of my feeling for her overfills my heart. The vision of her face, with its light and sweetness, is before me even when I am praying to Our Lady in church. Dear, dear Nora. You are the real reason why I don't take my ticket on the celestial express for San Morales!"

He stopped writing and let his gaze travel into the distance, a faint frown on his brow, but his lips smiling. With an effort, he again collected himself.

"I must, I must get back to this morning and Rusty Mac. This being a holiday of obligation, I had the forenoon on my hands. On my way down to post a letter at the lodge I ran into the Headmaster coming up from the Stinchar with his rod and without fish. He stopped, supporting his short burly form on the gaff, his ruddy face screwed up, rather put out, beneath his blaze of red hair. I do love Rusty Mac. I think he has some fondness for me and perhaps the simplest explanation is that we are so dourly Scottish and both of us fishers . . . the only two in the school. When Lady Frazer endowed the College from her Stinchar properties, Rusty claimed the river as his own. The jingo in the *Holywell Monitor* beginning,

> I'll not have my pools
> Whipped to ribbons by fools . . .

neatly takes off his attitude—for he's a mad fisher. There's a story of him, in the middle of mass at Frazer Castle, which Holywell serves, when his staunch friend, the Presbyterian Gillie, stuck his head through the window of the oratory, bursting with suppressed excitement. 'Your reverence! They're rising like fury in Lochaber Pool!' Never was a mass more quickly completed. The stupefied congregation, including Her Ladyship, was pattered over, blessed at breakneck speed; then a dark streak, not unlike the local concept of the Devil, was seen flying from the sacristy. 'Jock! Jock! What flee are they taking?'

"Now, he looked at me disgustedly. 'Not a fish in sight. Just when I wanted one for the notables!' The Bishop of the diocese and the retiring principal of our English Seminary at San Morales were coming to lunch at Holywell that day.

"I said, 'There's a fish in the Glebe Pool, sir.'

" 'There's no fish in the river at all, not even a grilse . . . I've been out since six.'

" 'It's a big one.'

" 'Imaginary!'

" 'I saw it there yesterday, under the weir, but of course I didn't dare try for it.'

"From beneath his sandy brows he gave me his dour smile. 'You're a perverse demon, Chisholm. If you want to waste your time—you've my dispensation.' He handed me his rod and walked off.

"I went down to the Glebe Pool, my heart leaping as it always does at the sound of running water. The fly on the leader was a Silver Doctor, perfect for the size and colour of the river. I began to fish the pool. I fished it for an hour. Salmon are painfully scarce this season. Once I thought I saw the movement of a dark fin in the shadows of the opposite bank. But I touched nothing. Suddenly I heard a discreet cough. I swung round. Rusty Mac, dressed in his best blacks, wearing gloves and his ceremonial top hat, had stopped, on his way to meet his guest at Doune Station, to condole with me.

" 'It's these large ones, Chisholm——' he said with a sepulchral grin—'they're always the hardest!'

"As he spoke, I made a final cast thirty yards across the pool. The fly fell exactly on the spume eddying beneath the far edge of the weir. The next instant I felt the fish, struck, and was fast in it.

" 'Ye have one!' Rusty cried. Then the salmon jumped—four feet in the air. Though for my own part I nearly dropped, the effect on Rusty was stupendous. I could feel him stiffen beside me. 'In the name of God!' he muttered in stricken awe. The salmon was the biggest I had ever seen, here, in the Stinchar, or in my father's Tweedside bothy. 'Keep his head up!' Rusty suddenly shouted. 'Man, man—give him the butt!'

"I was doing my best. But now the fish was in control. It set off, downstream, in a mad tearing rush. I followed. And Rusty followed me.

"The Stinchar, at Holywell, is not like the Tweed. It runs in a brown torrent through pines and gorges, making not inconsiderable somersaults over slippery boulders and high shaley ledges. At the end of ten minutes, Rusty Mac and I were half a mile downstream, somewhat the worse for wear. But we still stayed with the fish.

" 'Hold him, hold him!' Mac was hoarse from shouting. 'You fool, you fool, don't let him get in that slack!' The brute, of course, was already in the slack, sulking in a deep hole, with the leader ensnared in a mess of sunken roots.

" 'Ease him, ease him!' Mac hopped in anguish. 'Just ease him while I give him a stone.'

"Gingerly, breathlessly, he began flipping stones, trying to start out the fish without snapping the cast. The game continued for an agony of time. Then *whirr!*—off went the fish, to the scream of the reel. And off again went Rusty and I.

"An hour later, or thereabouts, in the slow wide flats opposite Doune village, the salmon at last showed signs of defeat. Exhausted, panting, torn by a hundred agonizing and entrancing hazards, Rusty gave a final command.

" 'Now, now! On this sand!' He croaked: 'We've no gaff. If he takes you down farther, he's gone for good.'

"My mouth was gulpy and dry. Nervously, I stood the fish close. It came, quiet, then suddenly made a last frantic scuttle. Rusty let out a hollow groan. 'Lightly . . . lightly! If you lose him now I'll never forgive you!'

"In the shallows the fish seemed incredible. I could see the frayed gut of the leader. If I lost him!—an icy lump came under my shirt. I slid him gently to the little flat of sand. In an absolute tense silence Mac bent over, whipped his hand in the gills and heaved the fish, monstrous, on to the grass.

"It made a noble sight on the green meadow, a fish of over forty pounds, run so freshly the sea lice still were on its arching back.

" 'A record, a record!' Mac chanted, swept, as was I, by a wave of heavenly joy. We had joined hands and were dancing the fandango. 'Forty-two pounds if it's an ounce . . . we'll put it in the book.' He actually embraced me. 'Man, man—You're a bonny, bonny fisher.'

"At that moment, from the single railway line across the river, came the faint whistle of an engine. Rusty paused, gazed in bewildered fashion at the plume of smoke, at the toylike red-and-white signal which had suddenly dipped over Doune village station. Recollection flooded him. He dug in consternation for his watch. 'Good Heavens, Chisholm!' His tone was that of the Holywell Headmaster. 'That's the Bishop's train.'

"His dilemma was apparent: he had five minutes to meet his distinguished visitors and five miles of roundabout road to reach the station —visible, only two fields away, across the Stinchar.

"I could see him slowly make up his mind. 'Take the fish back, Chisholm, and have them boil it whole for luncheon. Go quickly now. And remember Lot's wife and the pillar of salt. Whatever you do, *don't look back!*'

"I couldn't help it. Once I reached the first bend of the stream, from behind a bush, I risked a salty ending. Father Mac had already stripped to the buff and tied his clothing in a bundle. Wearing his top hat firmly on his head, with the bundle uplifted like a crozier, he stepped stark naked into the river. Wading and swimming, he reached the other side, scrambled into his suit and sprinted manfully towards the approaching train.

"I lay on the grass, rolling, in a kind of ecstasy. It was not the vision— which would live with me forever—of the top hat planted dauntlessly upon the nubile brow, but the moral pluck which lay behind the escapade. I thought: He too must hate our pious prudery, which shudders at the sight of human flesh, and cloaks the female form as though it were an infamy.''

A sound outside made Francis pause and he ceased writing as the door opened. Hudson and Anselm Mealey came into the room. Hudson, a dark quiet youth, sat down and began to change his shoes. Anselm had the evening mail in his hand.

"Letter for you, Francis," he said effusively.

Mealey had grown into a fine pink-and-white young man. His cheek had the smoothness of perfect health. His eye was soft and limpid, his smile ready. Always eager, busy, smiling: without question he was the most popular student in the school. Though his work was never brilliant, the masters liked him—his name was usually on the prize list. He was good at fives and racquets and all the less rough games. And he had a genius for procedure. He ran half a dozen clubs—from the Philatelists to the Philosophers. He knew, and glibly employed, such words as "quorum," "minutes" and "Mr. Chair." Whenever a new society was proposed, Anselm's advice was sure to be invoked—automatically he became its president. In praise of the clerical life he was lyrical. His only cross was this singular paradox: the Headmaster and a few odd lonely souls cordially disliked him. To the rest he was a hero, and he bore his successes with open smiling modesty.

Now, as he handed Francis the letter, he gave him that warm disarming smile. "Hope it's full of good news, dear fellow."

Francis opened the letter. Undated, it was written in pencil upon an invoice headed:

Dr. to Edward Bannon
Union Tavern,
Corner Dyke and Canal Streets,
Tynecastle.

Dear Francis,

I hope this finds you well as it leaves me. Also please excuse pencil. We are all upset. It grieves me to tell you Francis you won't be able to come home this holiday. No one is more sick and sorry than me about it not having seen you since last summer and all. But believe me it is impossible and we must bow to the will of God. I know you are not one to take no for an answer but this time you must the B.V.M. be my witness. I won't disguise we have trouble as you must guess but it is nothing you can help or hinder. It is not money nor sickness so do not worry. And it will all pass by the help of God and be forgotten. You can easy arrange to stay the holidays at the college. Ned will pay all extras. You'll have your books and your nice surroundings and all. Maybe we'll fix for you to come down at Christmas, so don't fret. Ned has sold his whippets but not for the money. Mr. Gilfoyle is a comfort to all. You are not missing much in the weather, it has been terrible wet. Now don't forget Francis we have people in the house, there isn't no room, you are not [underlined twice] to come.

Bless you my dear boy and excuse haste.

Yours affectionately,

POLLY BANNON

At the window, Francis read the letter several times: though its purpose was plain, its meaning remained troubling and inscrutable. With a strained look he folded the sheet and placed it in his pocket.

"Nothing wrong I hope?" Mealey had been studying his face solicitously.

Francis, uncomfortably silent, hardly knew what to say.

"My dear fellow, I am sorry." Anselm took a step forward, placed his arm lightly, comfortingly, around the other's shoulders. "If there's anything I can do for mercy's sake let me know. Perhaps,"—he paused earnestly,—"perhaps you don't feel like handball tonight?"

"No," Francis mumbled. "I believe I'd rather not."

"Quite all right, my dear Francis!" The vespers bell rang. "I can see there is something bothering you. I'll remember you tonight in my prayers."

All through vespers Francis worried about Polly's incomprehensible letter. When the service was over he had a sudden impulse to take his trouble to Rusty Mac. He went slowly up the wide staircase.

As he entered the study he became aware that the Headmaster was not alone, Father Tarrant sat with him, behind a pile of papers; and from the odd sudden silence his appearance provoked, Francis had the extraordinary feeling that the two had been discussing him.

"I'm sorry, sir." He cast an embarrassed glance towards Rusty Mac. "I didn't know you were engaged."

"That's all right, Chisholm. Sit down."

The quick warmth of the tone compelled Francis, already half-turned towards the door, into the wicker chair beside the desk. With slow movements of his stubby fingers Rusty went on stuffing shag into his corroded briar pipe. "Well! What can we do for you, my good man?"

Francis coloured. "I . . . I rather thought you'd be alone."

For some queer reason the Headmaster avoided his appealing gaze. "You don't mind Father Tarrant? What is it?"

There was no escape. Without guile to invent further excuse Francis stumbled out: "It's a letter I've had . . . from home." He had meant to show Polly's note to Rusty Mac but, in Tarrant's presence, his pride restrained him. "For some obscure reason they don't seem to want me back for the vacation."

"Oh!" Was he mistaken: was there again swift interchange between the two? "That must be something of a disappointment."

"It is, sir. And I feel worried. I was wondering . . . in fact I came to ask you what I should do."

Silence. Father MacNabb himself sank more deeply into his old cape, still fumbling at his pipe. He had known many boys, known them inside-out; yet there was about this youth who sat beside him a fineness, beauty, and dogged honesty which lit a fire in his heart. "We all have our disappointments, Francis." His meditative voice was sad, more than unusually mild. "Father Tarrant and I have suffered one today. Retirements are the order of the day at our Seminary in Spain." He paused. "We are appointed there, I as Rector, Father Tarrant as my Administrator of Studies."

Francis stammered a reply. San Morales was, indeed, a coveted advancement, next step to a bishopric; but whatever Tarrant's reaction— Francis shot a quick glance at the expressionless profile—MacNabb would not so regard it. The dry Aragon plains would be alien for a man who loved the green woods and rushing waters of Holywell with all his soul. Rusty Mac smiled gently. "I had my heart set on staying here. You had set yours on going away. What d'you say? Shall we both agree to take a beating from Almighty God?"

Francis strove to pluck the proper phrase from his confusion. "It's just . . . being anxious . . . I wondered if I shouldn't find out what's wrong and try to help?"

"I question if I should." Father MacNabb answered quickly. "What would you say, Father Tarrant?"

In the shadow, the younger master stirred. "Troubles resolve themselves best, in my experience, without outside interference."

There appeared nothing more to be said. The Headmaster turned up his desk lamp which, while it brightened the dark study, seemed to terminate the interview. Francis got up. Though he faced them both, haltingly, from his heart, he spoke to Rusty Mac.

"I can't say how sorry I am that you are leaving for Spain. The school . . . I . . . I shall miss you."

"Perhaps we shall see you there?" There was hope, quiet affection in the voice.

Francis did not answer. As he stood there, indecisively, hardly knowing what to say, torn by conflicting difficulties, his downcast gaze struck suddenly upon a letter, lying open on the desk. It was not so much the letter—illegible at that distance—as the letter's bright blue-stamped heading which caught his eye. Quickly he glanced away. But not before he had read *St. Dominic's Presbytery, Tynecastle.*

A shiver went through him. Something was wrong at home. Now he was sure. His face revealed nothing, remained impassive. Neither of the two masters was aware of his discovery. But as he moved towards the door he knew, despite all persuasion to the contrary, that one course at least was clear before him.

V

The train arrived at two o'clock that sultry June afternoon. Carrying his handbag, Francis walked rapidly from the station, his heart beating faster as he approached the familiar quarter of the city.

A queer air of quiet hung outside the tavern. Thinking to take Aunt Polly by surprise, he ran lightly up the side stairs and entered the house. Here, too, it was quiet and oddly dim after the glare of the dusty pavements; no one in the lobby or the kitchen, no sound but the thunderous ticking of a clock. He went into the parlour.

Ned was seated at the table, both elbows on the red drugget cover, gazing endlessly at the opposite blank wall. Not the attitude alone, but the alteration in the man himself, drew from Francis a stifled exclamation. Ned had lost three stones in weight, his clothes hung upon him, the rotund beaming face had turned dreary and cadaverous.

"Ned!" Francis held out his hand.

There was a pause, then Ned sluggishly slewed round, perception slowly dawning through his settled wretchedness.

"It's you, Francis." His smile was bewitching, evasive. "I'd no idea you were expected."

"I'm not really, Ned." Through his anxiety Francis essayed a laugh. "But the minute we broke up I simply couldn't wait. Where's Aunt Polly?"

"She's away. . . . Yes . . . Polly's away for a couple of days to Whitley Bay."

"When'll she be back?"

"Like enough . . . tomorrow."

"And where's Nora?"

"Nora!" Ned's tone was flat. "She's away with Aunt Polly."

"I see." Francis was conscious of a throb of relief. "That's why she didn't answer my wire. But Ned . . . you . . . you're well yourself, I hope?"

"I'm all right, Francie. A trifle under the weather maybe . . . but the like of me'll come to no harm." His chest took a sudden grotesque heave. Francis was horrified to see tears run down the egg-shaped face. "Away now and get yourself a bite. There'll be plenty in the cupboard. Thad'll get you anything you want. He's below in the bar. A great help he's been to us, has Thad." Ned's gaze wavered, then wandered back to the opposite wall.

In a daze, Francis turned, put his bag in his own small room. As he came along the passage the door of Nora's room was open: the neat white privacy caused him to withdraw his eyes in sudden confusion. He hastened downstairs.

The saloon was empty, even Scanty vanished, his vacant corner arresting, unbelievable, like a gap blown through the solid structure of the wall. But behind the bar, in his shirt sleeves, smugly drying glasses, was Thaddeus Gilfoyle.

Thad stopped his silent whistle as Francis entered. Slightly taken aback, an instant elapsed before he offered a welcome with his limp and dampish hand.

"Well, well!" he exclaimed. "Here's a sight for sore eyes."

Gilfoyle's air of proprietorship was hateful. But Francis, now thoroughly alarmed, succeeded in affecting indifference. He said lightly: "I'm surprised to see you here, Thad? What's happened to the gasworks?"

"I've give up the office," Thad answered composedly.

"What for?"

"To be here. Permanent." He picked up a glass and eyed it professionally, breathed on it softly, and began to polish. "When they asked me to come forward . . . I couldn't do more!"

Francis felt his nerves tighten beyond endurance. "In the name of heaven, what's all this about, Gilfoyle?"

"*Mister* Gilfoyle, if you don't mind, Francis!" Thad rolled his tongue smugly around the reproach. "It heartbreaks Ned not to see me get my place. He's not the same man, Francis. I doubt he'll ever be himself again."

"What's happened to him? You talk as if he were out of his mind!"

"He was, Francis, he was . . ." Gilfoyle groaned, "but he's come to senses now, poor man." His eye watchful, he stopped Francis' angry interruption with a whine. "Now don't take on that way with me. I'm the one that's doin' right. Ask Father Fitzgerald if you disbelieve me. I know you've never liked me much. I've seen ye on vacations making sport of me as you growed up. I've the best intentions towards you, Francis. We ought to pull together . . . now, especially."

"Why now especially?" Francis gritted his teeth.

"Oh, yes, yes . . . you wouldn't know . . . to be sure." Thad darted a fearful smirk. "The banns was only put up for the first time last Sunday. You see, Francis, me and Nora's going to be wed!"

Aunt Polly and Nora returned late the following evening. Francis, sick with apprehension, with his failure to penetrate Gilfoyle's fish-

810

like secrecy, had awaited their arrival in an agony of impatience. He tried immediately to corner Polly.

But Polly, after her first start, her wail of recognition,—"Francis, I told you not to come,"—had fled upstairs with Nora, her ears closed to his importunities, reiterating the formula, "Nora's not well . . . she's sick I tell you . . . get out of my road . . . I've got to tend to her."

Rebuffed, he climbed sombrely to his room, chilled by the mounting premonitions of this unknown dread. Nora, having scarcely given him a look, had gone immediately to bed. And for an hour he heard Polly, scurrying with trays and hot-water bottles, entreating Nora in a low voice, persecuting her with agitated attentions. Nora, thin as a wand, and pale, somehow had the air of sick-rooms. Polly, worn and harassed, even more negligent in her dress, had acquired a new gesture—a quick pressing of her hand against her brow. Late into the night, from her adjoining room, he heard the mutter of her prayers. Torn by the enigma, Francis bit his lip, turning restlessly between his sheets.

Next morning dawned clear. He rose and, according to his habit, went out to early mass. When he returned he found Nora seated outside on the back-yard steps warming herself in a patch of sunshine while at her feet some chickens cheeped and scuttled. She made no move to let him pass, but when he had stood a moment, she raised her head contemplatively.

"It's the holy man . . . been out already, saving his soul!"

He reddened at her tone, so unexpected, so quietly bitter.

"Did the Very Reverend Fitzgerald officiate?"

"No. It was the curate."

"The dumb ox in the stall! Ah, well, at least he's harmless."

Her head drooped, she stared at the chickens, propping her thin chin upon a thinner wrist. Though she had always been slight he was startled to discover this almost childish fragility which matched so ill the sullen maturity in her eyes, and the new grey dress, womanly and costly, which stiffly adorned her. His heart melted, his breast was filled with a white fire, an unsupportable pain. Her hurt plucked at the chords of his soul. He hesitated, his gaze averted. His voice was low.

"Have you had breakfast?"

She nodded. "Polly shoved it down my throat. God! If she'd only leave me be!"

"What are you doing today?"

"Nothing."

He paused again, then blurted out, all his feelings for her flooding through the anxiety in his eyes, "Why don't we go for a walk, Nora? Like we used to. It's so glorious a day!"

She did not move. Yet a faint tinge of animation seemed to penetrate her hollow, shadowed cheek.

"I can't be bothered," she said heavily. "I'm tired!"

"Oh, come on, Nora . . . please."

A dull pause. "All right."

His heart gave another great painful thud. He hurried into the kitchen and cut, with nervous haste, some sandwiches and cake, wrapped them clumsily into a packet. There was no sign of Polly and now, indeed, he was eager to avoid her. In ten minutes Nora and he sat in the red tram, clanging across the city. Within the hour, they tramped side by side, unspeaking, towards the Gosforth Hills.

He wondered at the impulse which had sent him to this familiar stretch. Today the burgeoning countryside was lovely; but its very loveliness was tremulous, unbearable. As they came upon Lang's orchard, now foamy with blossom, he paused, tried to break the steely silence which lay between them.

"Look, Nora! Let's take a stroll round. And have a word with Lang."

She threw one glance at the orchard, the trees standing spaced and stiff, like chessmen, around the apple shed. She said rudely, bitterly: "I don't want to. I hate that place!"

He did not answer. Dimly he knew her bitterness was not towards him.

By one o'clock they reached the summit of Gosforth Beacon. He could see that she was tired and, without consulting her, stopped under a tall beech, for lunch. The day was unusually warm and clear. In the flat distance beneath them, sparkling with golden light, lay the city, domed and spired, and from afar, ineffably beautiful.

She scarcely touched the sandwiches he produced and, remembering Polly's demonstrative tyranny, he did not press her. The shade was soothing. Overhead the new green flickering leaves sent quiet patterns chasing across the moss, carpeted with dry beechnuts, on which they sat. There was a smell of flowing sap; the throaty call of a thrush came from a high twig overhead.

After a few moments she leaned back against the bole of the tree, tilted her head, and closed her eyes.

Her relaxation seemed somehow the greatest tribute she could pay him. He considered her with a deeper surge of tenderness, stirred to undreamed-of compassion by the arch of her neck, so thin and unprotected. The welling tenderness within him made him strangely protective. When her head slipped a little from the tree he scarcely dared touch her. Yet, fancying her asleep, he moved his arm instinctively to support her. The next instant she wrenched herself free, struck him repeatedly on the face and chest with her clenched knuckles, hysterically breathless.

"Leave me alone! You brute! You beast!"

"Nora, Nora! What's the matter?"

Panting, she drew back, her face quivering, distorted. "Don't try to get round me that way. You're all the same. Every one of you!"

"Nora!" He pleaded with her desperately. "For pity's sake . . . let's get this straight."

"Get what straight?"

"Everything . . . why you're going on like this . . . why you're marrying Gilfoyle."

"Why shouldn't I marry him?" She threw the question at him, with a bitter defensiveness.

His lips were dry, he could scarcely speak. "But Nora, he's such a poor creature . . . He's not your sort."

"He's as good as anybody. Haven't I said you're all the same? At least I'll keep him in his place."

Confounded, he stared at her with a pale and stricken face. And there was that in his unbelieving eyes which cut her so cruelly, she more cruelly cut back.

"Perhaps you think I should be marrying you . . . the bright-eyed altar boy . . . the half-baked carpet priest!" Her lip twitched with the bitterness of her sneer. "Let me tell you this. I think you're a joke . . . a sanctimonious scream. Go on, turn up your blessed eyes. You don't know how funny you are . . . you holy pater noster. Why if you were the last man in the world I wouldn't . . . ." She choked and shuddered violently, tried, painfully, uselessly, to check her tears with the back of her hand and then, sobbing, flung her head upon his breast. "Oh, Francis, Francis, dear, I'm sorry! You know I've always loved you. Kill me if you want to . . . I don't care."

While he quieted her, clumsily, stroking her brow, he felt himself trembling as much as she. The racking violence of her sobs diminished gradually. She was like a wounded bird in his arms. She lay, spent and passive, her face hidden against his coat. Then slowly she straightened herself. With averted eyes, she took her handkerchief, rubbed her ravaged, tear-stained face, straightened her hat, then said, in an exhausted neutral tone: "We'd better get home."

"Look at me, Nora?"

But she would not, only remarking in that same odd monotone: "Say what you want to say."

"I will then, Nora." His youthful vehemence overcame him. "I'm not going to stand this! I can see there's something behind it. But I'll get to the bottom of it. You're not going to marry that fool Gilfoyle. I love you, Nora. I'll stand by you."

There was a pitiful stillness.

"Dear Francis," she said, with an oddly hollow smile. "You make me feel as though I'd lived a million years." And rising, she bent and

kissed him, as she had kissed him once before, upon the cheek. As they
went down the hill the thrush had ceased its singing in the high tree.

That evening, with fixed intention, Francis set out for the dockside
tenement inhabited by the Magoons. He found the banished Scanty
alone, since Maggie was still out charring, squatting by a spark of fire
in the single "back to back" apartment, glumly working a wool-rug
shuttle by the light of a tallow dip. As he recognized his visitor there was
no mistaking the pleasure in the exile's bleary eye, a gleam that
heightened when Francis uncovered the gill bottle of spirits he had
privily removed from the bar. Quickly, Scanty produced a chipped
delft cup, solemnly toasted his benefactor.

"Ah, that's the stuff!" he muttered, across the back of his ragged
sleeve. "Devil the sup have I had since that skinflint Gilfoyle took over
the bar."

Francis drew up the backless wooden chair. He spoke with dark
intensity, the shadows heavy beneath his eyes.

"Scanty! What's happened at the Union—to Nora, Polly, Ned? I've
been back three days and I'm still no wiser. You've got to tell me!"

A look of alarm invaded Scanty's expression. He glanced from Francis
to the bottle—from the bottle to Francis.

"Ah! How would I know?"

"You do know! I can see it in your face."

"Didn't Ned say nothing?"

"Ned! He's like a deaf-mute these days!"

"Poor ould Ned!" Scanty groaned, blessed himself, and poured
out more whisky. "God save us! Who would ever have dreamed it.
Sure there's bad in the best of us." With a sudden hoarse emphasis: "I
couldn't tell ye, Francis, it's a shame to remember, it don't do no good."

"It will do good, Scanty," Francis urged. "If I know, I can do something."

"Ye mean, Gilfoyle . . ." With head cocked, Scanty considered,
then he nodded slowly. He took another tot to stiffen himself, his battered face oddly sober, his tone subdued. "I'll tell you then, Francis,
if you swear to keep it dark. The truth of it is . . . God pity us . . .
that Nora's had a baby."

Silence: long enough for Scanty to take another drink. Francis said:
"When?"

"Six weeks ago. She went down to Whitley Bay. The woman there
has the child . . . a daughter. . . . Nora can't bear the sight of it."

Cold, rigid, Francis struggled with the tumult in his breast. He made
himself ask: "Then Gilfoyle is the father?"

"That gutless fish!" Hatred overcame Scanty's caution. "No, no,
he's the one that came forward, as he's pleased to call it, to give the

814

little one a name, and get his foot in the Union to the bargain, the bla'g'ard! Father Fitzgerald's behind him, Francis. It's all settin' pretty as a pictur', the way they've pulled it. Marriage lines in the drawer, not a soul the wiser, and the daughter brought here later on, as it were, at the end of a long vaycation. God strike me down dead, if it don't turn the stomach of a pig!"

A band, an insupportable constriction, girded Francis' heart. He fought to keep his voice from breaking.

"I never knew Nora was in love with anyone? Scanty . . . Do you know who it was . . . I mean . . . the father of her child?"

"Before God I don't!" The blood rushed to Scanty's forehead as he thumped the floor boards in vociferous denial. "I don't know nothing about that at all. How should a poor creature like me! And Ned don't either, that's gospel truth! Ned always treated me right, a fine generous upstanding man, except for occasions, like when Polly was away, and the drink took hold of him. No, no, Francis, take it from me, there's not a hope of findin' the man!"

Again a silence, frozen, prolonged. A film clouded Francis' eyes. He felt deathly sick. At last, with a great effort he got up.

"Thank you, Scanty, for telling me."

He quitted the room, went giddily down the bare flights of tenement stairs. His brow, the palms of his hands, were bedewed with icy sweat. A vision haunted, tormented him: the trim neatness of Nora's bedroom, white and undisturbed. He had no hatred, only a searing pity, a dreadful convulsion of his soul. Outside in the squalid courtyard he leaned, suddenly overcome, against the single lamp-post and retched his heart out, into the gutter.

Now he felt cold, but firmer in his intention. He set out resolutely in the direction of St. Dominic's.

The housekeeper at St. Dominic's admitted him with that noiseless discretion which typified the Presbytery. In a minute, she glided back to the half-lit hall, where she had left him, and for the first time faintly smiled at him. "You're fortunate, Francis. His Reverence is free to see you."

Snuff-box in hand, Father Gerald Fitzgerald rose as Francis entered, his manner a mixture of cordiality and inquiry, his fine handsome presence matching the French furniture, the antique prie-dieu, the choice copies of Italian primitives upon the walls, the vase of lilies on the escritoire, scenting the tasteful room.

"Well young man, I thought you were up North? Sit down! How are all my good friends in Holywell?" As he paused to take snuff, his eye touched upon the College tie, which Francis wore, with affectionate approval. "I was there myself, you know, before I went to the Holy City . . . a grand gentlemanly place. Dear old MacNabb. And Father

Tarrant. A classmate of mine at the English College in Rome. There's a fine, a coming man! Well now, Francis." He paused, his needled glance sheathed by a courtier's suavity. "What can we do for you?"

Painfully distressed, breathing quickly, Francis kept his eyes down. "I came to see you about Nora."

The stammered remark rent the room's serenity, its note of mannered ease.

"And what about Nora, pray?"

"Her marriage with Gilfoyle . . . She doesn't want to go through with it . . . she's miserable . . . it seems so stupid and unjust . . . such a needless and horrible affair."

"What do you know about the horrible affair?"

"Well . . . everything . . . that she wasn't to blame."

There was a pause. Fitzgerald's fine brow expressed annoyance, yet he gazed at the distraught youth before him with a kind of stately pity.

"My dear young man, if you enter the priesthood, as I trust you will, and gain even half the experience which unhappily is mine, you will comprehend that certain social disorders demand equally specific remedies. You are staggered by this——" He returned the phrase with an inclination of his head—"horrible affair. I am not. I even anticipated it. I know and abominate the whisky trade for its effect upon the brute mentality of the clods who constitute this parish. You and I may sit down and quietly enjoy our Lachryma Christi, like gentlemen. Not so Mr. Edward Bannon. Enough! I make no allegations. I merely say, we have a problem, unhappily not unique to those of us who spend drab hours in the confessional." Fitzgerald paused to take snuff, with a distinguished wrist. "What are we to do with it? I will tell you. First, legitimize and baptize the offspring. Secondly, marry the mother if we can, to as decent a man as will have her. We must regularize, regularize. Make a good Catholic home out of the mess. Weave the loose ends into our sound social fabric. Believe me, Nora Bannon is highly fortunate to get Gilfoyle. He's not so bright, but he's steady. In a couple of years you'll see her at mass with her husband and family . . . perfectly happy."

"No, no." The interruption was wrenched from Francis' shut lips. "She'll never be happy—only broken and miserable."

Fitzgerald's head was a trifle higher. "And is happiness the ultimate objective of our earthly life?"

"She'll do something desperate. You can't compel Nora. I know her better than you."

"You seem to know her intimately." Fitzgerald smiled with withering suavity. "I hope you have no physical interest in the lady yourself."

A dark red spot burned on Francis' pale cheek. He muttered: "I am very fond of Nora. But if I love her—it's nothing that would make your confessional more drab. I beg you——" His voice held a low, desperate entreaty. "Don't force her into this marriage. She's not common clay . . . she's a bright sweet spirit. You can't thrust a child upon her bosom and a husband into her arms—because—in her innocence, she's been . . ."

Stung to the quick, Fitzgerald banged his snuff-box on the table. "Don't preach at me, sir!"

"I'm sorry. You can see I don't know what I'm saying. I'm trying to beg you to use your power." Francis mustered his flagging forces in a final effort. "At least give her a little time."

"That is enough, Francis!"

The parish priest, too much master of himself, and of others, to lose his temper or his countenance for long, rose abruptly from his chair and looked at his flat gold watch. "I have a confraternity meeting at eight. You must excuse me." As Francis got up, he patted him reproachfully on the back. "My dear boy, you are very immature. Might I even say a little foolish? But thank God you have a wise old mother in Holy Church. Don't run your head against the walls, Francis. They've stood for generations—against stronger batterings than yours. But there now— I know you're a good lad. Come up and have a chat about Holywell when the wedding's over. And meanwhile—as a little act of reparation for your rudeness will you say the Salve Regina for my intention?"

A pause. It was useless, quite useless. "Yes, Father."

"Good night then, my son . . . and God bless you!"

The night air was raw and chill. Defeated, crushed by the impotence of his youth, Francis dragged himself away from the Presbytery. His footsteps echoed dully on the closed pathway. As he passed the chapel steps, the sacristan was closing the side doors. When the last chink of light was gone, Francis stood, hatless, in the darkness, his eyes fixed on the wraith-like windows of the clerestory. He blurted out, in a kind of final desperation: "Oh, God! Do what's best for all of us."

As the wedding day approached, consuming Francis with a deadly, sleepless fever, the atmosphere of the tavern seemed insensibly to settle, like a stagnant pool. Nora was quiet, Polly vaguely hopeful; and though Ned still cringed in solitude, the muddled terror in his eyes was less. The ceremony would, of course, be private. But no restraint need operate upon the trousseau, the dowry, the elaborate honeymoon to Killarney. The house was littered with robes and rich materials. Polly, beseeching another "try-on," with a mouthful of pins, waded through bales of cloth and linen, enveloped in merciful fog.

Gilfoyle, smugly observant, smoking the Union's best cigars, would occasionally hold conference, upon matters of finance, with Ned. There was a deed of partnership, duly signed, and great talk of building, to accommodate the new ménage. Already Thad's numerous poor relatives hung about the house, sycophantic yet assertive. His married sister, Mrs. Neily, and her daughter Charlotte, were perhaps the worst.

Nora had little enough to say. Once, meeting Francis in the passage she stopped.

"You know . . . don't you?"

His heart was breaking, he dared not meet her eye. "Yes, I know."

There was a suffocating pause. He could not sustain the torture in his breast. Incoherently he burst out, boyish tears starting in his eyes: "Nora . . . We can't let this happen. If you knew how I've felt for you . . . I could look after you—work for you. Nora . . . let me take you away."

She considered him with that strange and pitying tenderness. "Where would we go?"

"Anywhere." He spoke wildly, his cheek wet and shining.

She did not answer. She pressed his hand without speaking, then went on, quickly, to be fitted for a dress.

On the day before the wedding, she unbent a little, losing something of her marble acquiescence. Suddenly, over one of those cups of tea which Polly inflicted upon her, she declared: "I believe I'd like to go to Whitley Bay today."

Astounded, Polly echoed: "Whitley Bay?"—then added in a flutter, "I'll come with you."

"There's no need." Nora paused, gently stirring her cup. "But of course if you want to . . ."

"I do indeed, my dear!"

Reassured by that lightness in Nora's manner,—as though a bar of that old mischievous gaiety re-echoed, like distant music, in her being, —Polly came to view the excursion without disfavour. She had a gratified, bewildered idea that Nora was "coming round." As she finished her tea she discoursed upon the beautiful Lake of Killarney, which she had once visited as a girl. The boatman there had been most amusing.

The two women, dressed for the expedition, left for the station after the dinner hour. As she turned the corner Nora looked up towards the window where Francis stood. She seemed to linger for a second, smiled gravely, and waved her hand. Then she was gone.

News of the accident reached the district even before Aunt Polly was brought home, in a state of collapse, in a cab. The sensation throughout the city was impressive. Popular interest could never have been so stirred by the mere stupidity of a young woman stumbling between a platform and a moving train. It was the prenuptial timing which made the thing so exquisite. Around the docks women ran out of their doorways, gathering in groups, beshawled, arms akimbo. Blame for the tragedy was finally pinned upon the victim's new shoes. There was enormous sympathy for Thaddeus Gilfoyle, for the family, for all young women about to be married and under the necessity of travelling by train. There was talk of a public funeral—with the confraternity band—for the mangled remains.

Late that night, how he knew not, Francis found himself in St. Dominic's church. It was quite deserted. The flickering wick of the sanctuary lamp drew his haggard eyes, a feeble beacon. Kneeling, stiff and pale, he felt, like an embrace, the remorseless foreclosure of his destiny. Never had he known such a moment of desolation, of abandonment. He could not weep. His lips, cold and stricken, could not move in prayer. But from his tortured mind there soared an offering of anguished thought. First his parents; and now Nora. He could no longer ignore these testaments from above. He would go away . . . he must go . . . to Father MacNabb . . . to San Morales. He would give himself entirely to God. He must become a priest.

VI

During Easter, in the year 1892, an event occurred in the English Seminary of San Morales which set the place humming with a note of consternation. One of the students, in the subdiaconate, disappeared completely for the space of four entire days.

Naturally the Seminary had witnessed other seditions since its foundation in these Aragon uplands fifty years before. Students had mutinied for an hour or so, skulking to the *posada* outside the walls, hurriedly deranging conscience and digestion with long *cigarros* and the local *aguardiente*. Once or twice it had been necessary to drag some tottering recusant by the ears from the dingy parlours of the Via Amorosa in the town. But this—for a student to march out through the open gates in broad daylight and, half a week later, by the same gates, in even brighter light of day, to limp in again, dusty, unshaven, dishevelled, offering every evidence of horrible dissipation, and then, with no other excuse than "I've been for a walk!" to fling himself upon his bed and sleep the clock round—it was apostasy.

At the recreation the students discussed it in awed tones—little groups of dark figures on the sunny slopes, between the bright green copperas-sprayed vineyards, with the Seminary, white and gleaming against the pale pink earth, beneath them.

It was agreed that Chisholm would undoubtedly be expelled.

The Committee of Examination had immediately been constituted. According to precedent, as in all grave breaches of discipline it was composed of the Rector, the Administrator, the Director of Novices and the Head Seminarian. After some preliminary discussion, the tribunal opened its proceedings, in the theological atrium, on the day following the runagate's return.

Outside the *solano* was blowing. The ripe black olives fell from the blade-leafed trees and burst beneath the sun. A scent of orange flowers swept across from the grove above the infirmary. The baked earth crackled with the heat. As Francis entered the white and lofty-pillared room, its polished empty benches cool and dark, he had a quiet air. The black alpaca soutane stressed the thinness of his figure. His hair, cropped and tonsured, gave tautness to his face-bones, intensified the darkness of his eyes, his dark contained reserve. There was an odd tranquillity about his hands.

Before him, on the platform reserved for protagonists in debate, were four desks, already occupied by Father Tarrant, Monsignor MacNabb, Father Gomez and Deacon Mealey. Conscious of a mingling of displeasure and concern in the united gaze now upon him, Francis hung his head, while in a rapid voice Gomez, Director of Novices, read out the accusation.

There was a silence. Then Father Tarrant spoke.

"What is your explanation?"

Despite the quietness which enclosed him Francis suddenly began to flush. He kept his head down.

"I went for a walk!" The words resounded lamely.

"That is sufficiently apparent. We use our legs whether our intentions are good or bad. Apart from the obvious sin of leaving the Seminary without permission, were your intentions bad?"

"No."

"During your absence did you indulge in alcoholic liquor?"

"No."

"Did you visit the bullfight, the fair, the casino?"

"No."

"Did you consort with women of ill fame?"

"No."

"Then what did you do?"

Silence again, then the muttered inarticulate reply. "I've told you. You wouldn't understand. I . . . I went for a walk!"

Father Tarrant smiled thinly. "Do you wish us to believe that you spent these entire four days ceaselessly perambulating the countryside?"

"Well . . . practically."

"What destination did you reach eventually?"

"I—I got to Cossa!"

"Cossa! But that is fifty miles away!"

"Yes, I suppose so."

"You were there for some specific purpose?"

"No."

Father Tarrant bit his thin lip. He could not brook obstruction. He had a sudden wild longing for the rack, the boot, the wheel. Small wonder the mediævalists had recourse to such instruments! There were circumstances which fully justified them.

"I believe you are lying, Chisholm."

"Why should I lie—to you?"

A muffled exclamation came from Deacon Mealey. His presence was purely formal. As the chief prefect he sat there as a symbol, perhaps a cipher, expressive of the student body. Yet he could not restrain his earnest pleading.

"Please, Francis! For the sake of all of the students . . . all of us who love you . . . I . . . I implore you to own up."

As Francis remained silent, Father Gomez, the young Spanish novice master, inclined his head and murmured to Tarrant: "I've had no evidence . . . none whatever, from the town. But we might write to the priest at Cossa."

Tarrant shot a swift glance at the Spaniard's subtle face.

"Yes. That is decidedly an idea."

Meanwhile the Rector had taken advantage of the lull. Older, slower than at Holywell, he leaned forward. He spoke slowly and kindly.

"Of course, you must realize, Francis, that in the circumstances, so general an explanation is barely adequate. After all, it is a serious matter to play truant—not merely the breaking of the Seminary rule— the disobedience—but rather the underlying motive which prompted you. Tell me! Are you not happy here?"

"Yes, I am happy."

"Good! And you've no reason to doubt your vocation?"

"No! I want more than ever to try to do some good in the world."

"That pleases me greatly. You don't wish to be sent away?"

"No!"

"Then tell us in your own words how you came to—to take your remarkable adventure."

At the quiet encouragement, Francis raised his head. He made a great effort, his eyes remote, his face troubled.

"I . . . I had just been to the chapel. But I couldn't pray, I couldn't seem to settle. I was restless. The *solano* was blowing—the hot wind seemed to make me more restless, the routine of the Seminary suddenly seemed petty and vexatious. Suddenly, I saw the road outside the gates, white and soft with dust. I couldn't help myself. I was on the road, walking. I walked all night, miles and miles. I walked——"

"All the next day." Father Tarrant bit out the satiric interruption. "And the next!"

"That's what I did."

"I never heard such a pack of rubbish in my life! It is an insult to the intelligence of the Committee."

The Rector, with frowning resolution, suddenly straightened himself in his chair.

"I propose that we temporarily adjourn." While the two priests stared at him in surprise, he said decisively to Francis: "You may go for the present. If we think it necessary we will recall you."

Francis left the room in a dead silence. Only then did the Rector turn to the others. He declared coldly: "I assure you that bullying will do no good. We must go carefully. There is more in this than meets the eye."

Smarting under the interference, Father Tarrant moved fretfully.

"It is the culmination of an unruly career."

"Not at all." The Rector demurred. "He's been eager and persevering ever since he came here. There is nothing damaging in his record, Father Gomez?"

Gomez turned the pages, on the desk, before him.

"No." He spoke slowly, reading from the record. "A few practical jokes. Last winter he set fire to the English newspaper when Father Despard was perusing it in the common room. Asked why . . . he laughed and answered, 'The Devil finds work for idle hands!'"

"Never mind that." The Rector spoke sharply. "We all know Father Despard corners every paper that comes into this Seminary."

"Then," Gomez resumed, "when deputed to read aloud in the refectory he smuggled in and substituted for *The Life of St. Peter of Alcantara* a C. R. S. tract entitled *When Eva Stole the Sugar* which—until he was stopped—induced much unseemly hilarity."

"Harmless mischief."

"Again . . ." Gomez turned another page. "In the comical procession the students got up, representing the Sacraments—you may remember, one dressed up as a baby representing Baptism, two others were got up as Matrimony, and so on—it was all done with permission of course. But," Gomez shot a dubious glance at Tarrant, "on the back of the corpse carried in for Extreme Unction, Chisholm pinned a card:

> " Here lies Father Tarrant
> I've gladly signed his warrant.
> If ever——"

"That's enough." Tarrant broke in sharply. "We've more to concern us than these absurd lampoons."

The Rector nodded. "Absurd, yes. But not malicious. I like a young man who can knock some fun out of life. We cannot ignore the fact that Chisholm is an unusual character—most unusual. He has great depth and fire. He's sensitive, inclined to fits of melancholy. He conceals it behind these high spirits. You see, he's a fighter, he'll never give in. He's a queer mixture of childlike simplicity and logical directness. And, above all, he's a complete individualist!"

"Individualism is rather a dangerous quality in a theologian," Tarrant interposed acidly. "It gave us the Reformation."

"And the Reformation gave us a better-behaved Catholic Church." The Rector smiled mildly at the ceiling. "But we're getting from the point. I don't deny there's been a gross breach of discipline. It must be punished. But the punishment cannot be rushed. I can't expel a student of Chisholm's quality without first knowing positively that he deserves expulsion. Therefore, let us wait a few days." He rose, innocently. "I'm sure you all agree."

As the three priests left the platform, Gomez and Tarrant went off together.

During the next two days an air of suspended doom overhung the unhappy Francis. He was not restrained. No apparent ban was placed upon his studies. But wherever he went—to the library, refectory or common room—an unnatural silence struck his fellows, followed swiftly by an exaggerated casualness which deceived no one. The knowledge that he was the universal topic gave him a guilty look. His Holywell companion, Hudson, also in the subdiaconate, pursued him with affectionate attentions and a worried frown. Anselm Mealey led another faction which clearly felt itself outraged. At recreation they consulted, approached the solitary figure. Mealey was the spokesman.

"We don't want to hit you when you're down, Francis. But this touches all of us. It's a slur upon the student body as a whole. We feel that it would be so much finer and manlier if you would make a clean breast and own up to it."

"Own up to what?"

Mealey shrugged his shoulders. There was a silence. What more could he do? As he turned away with the others he said:

"We've decided to make a novena for you. I feel it worse than the others. I hoped you were my best friend."

Francis found it harder to maintain his pretence of normality. He would start off to walk in the Seminary grounds, then stop, sharply, recollecting that walking had been his ruin. He drifted about, aware that for Tarrant and the other professors he had ceased to exist. At the lectures he found he was not listening. The summons to the Rector he half hoped for did not come.

His sense of personal stress increased. He failed to understand himself. He was a purposeless enigma. He brooded over the justification of those who had predicted that he had no vocation. He had wild conceptions of setting out as a lay brother to some dangerous and distant mission. He began to haunt the church—but secretly. Above all there existed the necessity of putting on a face to meet his little world.

It was on the morning of the third day, Wednesday, that Father Gomez received the letter. Shocked but deeply gratified, his resourcefulness confirmed, he ran with it to the Administrator's office. He stood, while Father Tarrant read the note, like an intelligent dog awaiting its reward, a kind word or a bone.

Mi Amigo,

In reply to your honoured communication of Whit-Sunday, I deeply regret to inform you that inquiries have elicited the fact that a Seminarian, of such bearing, height and colour as you define, was observed in Cossa on April 14th. He was seen to enter the house of one Rosa Oyarzabal late that evening and to leave early the following morning. The woman in question lives alone, is of a known character, and has not frequented the altar rail for seven years.

I have the honour to remain, dear Padre,
Your devoted brother in Jesus Christus,

SALVADOR BOLAS
P. P. Cossa

Gomez murmured: "Don't you agree it was good strategy?"

"Yes, yes!" With a brow of thunder Tarrant brushed the Spaniard aside. Bearing the letter like something obscene, he strode into the Rector's room at the end of the corridor. But the Rector was saying his mass. He would be occupied for half an hour.

Father Tarrant could not wait. He crossed the courtyard like a whirlwind and, without knocking, burst into Francis' room. It was empty.

Checked, realizing that Francis must also be at mass, he struggled with his fury as an ungovernable horse might fight its bit. He sat down, abruptly, forcing himself to wait, his dark thin figure charged with lightning.

The cell was barer even than others of its kind, its inventory a bed, a chest, a table, the chair he occupied. Upon the chest stood one faded photograph, an angular woman in a frightful hat holding the hand of a white-clad little girl: *Love from Aunt Polly and Nora.*

Tarrant repressed his sneer. But his lip curled at the single picture on the whitewashed walls, a tiny replica of the Sistine Madonna, Our Lady of Chastity.

Suddenly, upon the table, he saw an open notebook: a diary. Again he started, like a nervous horse, his nostrils dilated, a dark red fire in his eye. For a moment he sat, battling his scruples, then rose and went slowly towards the book. He was a gentleman. It was repugnant to pry like a vulgar chambermaid, into another's privacy. But it was his duty.

324

Who could guess what further iniquities this scroll contained? With relentless austerity upon his face, he picked up the written page.

". . . was it Saint Anthony who spoke of his 'ill-judged, obstinate and perverse behaviour'? I must console myself in the greatest despondency I have ever known, with that single thought! If they send me away from here my life will be broken. I'm a miserable crooked character, I don't think straight like the others, I cannot train myself to run with the pack. But with my whole soul I desire passionately to work for God. In our Father's house there are many mansions! There was room for such diversities as Joan of Arc and . . . well, Blessed Benedict Labre who let even the lice run over him. Surely there is room for me!

"They ask me to explain to them. How can one explain nothing—or what is so obvious as to be shameful? Francis de Sales said: 'I will be ground to powder rather than break a rule.' But when I walked out of the Seminary I did not think of rules, or of breaking them. Certain impulses are unconscious.

"It helps me to write this down: it gives my transgression the semblance of reason.

"For weeks I had been sleeping badly, tossing through these hot nights in a fever of unrest. Perhaps it is harder for me here than for the others —judged at least by the voluminous literature on the subject, wherein the steps to the priesthood are represented as sweet untroubled joys, piled one upon another. If our beloved laity knew how one has to fight!

"Here my greatest difficulty has been the sense of confinement, of physical inaction—what a bad mystic I should make!—always aggravated by echoes, stray sounds, penetrating inwards from the outer world. Then I realize that I am twenty-three, that I have done nothing yet to help a single living soul, and I am fevered with unrest.

"Willie Tulloch's letters provide—in Father Gomez' phrase—the most pernicious stimuli. Now that Willie is a qualified doctor and his sister Jean a certified nurse, both working for the Tynecastle Poor Law Board and enjoying many thrilling, if verminous adventures, in the slums, I feel that I should be out and fighting too.

"Of course I shall, one day. . . . I must be patient. But my present ferment seems heightened by the news of Ned and Polly. I was happy when they decided to remove from above the tavern and have Judy, the child, to live with them in the little flat which Polly had taken at Clermont, on the outskirts of the city. But Ned has been ill, Judy troublesome, and Gilfoyle—left to manage Union Tavern—a most unsatisfactory business partner. Ned, in fact, has gone to pieces, refuses to go out, sees no one. That one impulse of blind unthinkable stupidity has finished him. A baser man would have survived it.

"The pattern of life sometimes demands great faith. Dear Nora! That

825

tender platitude conceals a thousand avenues of thought and feeling. When Father Tarrant gave us that practical talk—*agendo contra*—he said most truly: 'Some temptations cannot be fought—one must close one's mind and fly from them!' My excursion to Cossa must have been that kind of flight.

"At first, though walking fast, I did not mean to go far when I passed through the Seminary gates. But the relief, the sense of escape from myself which the violent exercise afforded, drove me on. I sweated gloriously, like a peasant in the fields—that salty running sweat which seems to purge one of human dross. My mind lifted, my heart began to sing. I wanted to go on and on until I dropped!

"I walked all day without food or drink. I covered a great distance, for, when evening drew near, I could smell the sea. And as the stars broke out in the pale sky, I came over the hill and found Cossa at my feet. The village, harboured on a sheltered creek where the sea barely lapped, with blossoming acacia trees lining its single street, had an almost heavenly beauty. I was dead with tiredness. There was an enormous blister on my heel. But as I came down the hill the place welcomed me with its quiet pulse of life.

"In the little square the villagers were enjoying the cool air, scented with acacia flowers, the dusk made dimmer by the lamps of the little inn, where at an open doorway stood two pine benches. Before the benches in the soft dust some old men were playing bowls with wooden balls. From the creek came the booming of frogs. Children laughed and ran. It was simple and beautiful. Though I now realized that I had not a peseta in my pocket, I seated myself on one of the benches outside the door. How good it was to rest. I was stupid with fatigue. Suddenly, in the quiet darkness beneath the trees, the sound of Catalan pipes rang out. Not loud—low, attuned to the night. If one has not heard these reeds, or the shrill, sweet native tunes, one cannot fully estimate the gladness of that moment. I was enchanted. I suppose, as a Scot, I've the lilt of the pipes in my blood. I sat as though drugged by the music, the darkness, the beauty of the night, my utter weakness.

"I had resolved to sleep out on the beach. But presently, as I thought to move there, a mist rolled in from the sea. It fell like a mystery upon the village. In five minutes the square was choked with twisting vapour, the trees dripping, and everybody going home. I had reached the conclusion, unwillingly, that I must go to the local priest ' give myself up,' and get a bed, when a woman seated on the other bench suddenly spoke to me. For some time I had felt her gazing at me with that mixture of pity and contempt which the mere sight of a religious seems to provoke in Christian countries. Now, as if she read my thoughts, she said: 'They are tight people there. They will not take you in.'

"She was about thirty years of age, dressed quietly in black, with a pale face, dark eyes and a thickened figure. She continued indifferently:

" 'There is a bed in my house if you wish to sleep in it.'

" 'I have no money to pay for a lodging.'

"She laughed scornfully. 'You can pay me with your prayers.'

"It had now begun to rain. They had closed the *fonda*. We both sat on the wet benches under the dripping acacia trees in the deserted square. The absurdity of this seemed to strike her. She rose.

" 'I am going home. If you are not a fool you will accept my hospitality.'

"My thin soutane was soaked. I had begun to shiver. I reflected that I could send her money for my room on my return to the Seminary. I got up and walked with her down the narrow street.

"Her house was halfway down the row. We descended two steps into the kitchen. When she had lit the lamp, she threw off the black shawl, put a pot of chocolate on the fire and took a new loaf from the oven. She spread a red-checked tablecloth. Bubbling chocolate and hot bread made a good smell in the small clean room.

"As she poured the chocolate into thick cups she looked at me across the table. 'You had better say grace. That improves the flavour!' Though now there was no mistaking the irony in her voice, I said grace. We began to eat and drink. The flavour needed no improvement.

"She kept watching me. She had once been a very pretty woman, but the remnants of her beauty made her dark-eyed olive face seem hard. Her small ears were close to her head and pierced with heavy gold rings. Her hands were plump like the hands of a Rubens Madonna.

" 'Well, little padre, you are lucky to be here. I have no liking for the priests. In Barcelona, when I pass them I break into open laughter!'

"I couldn't help smiling. 'You don't surprise me. It's the first thing we learn—to be laughed at. The best man I ever knew used to preach in the open air. The whole town turned out to laugh at him. They named him, in mockery, Holy Daniel. You see, there's so little doubt nowadays that anyone who believes in God is a hypocrite or a fool!'

"She took a slow drink of chocolate, watching me over her cup. 'You are no fool. Tell me, do I please you?'

" 'I think you are charming and kind.'

" 'It is my nature to be kind. I've had a sad life. My father was a Castilian noble who was dispossessed by the Madrid Government. My husband commanded a great ship in the Navy. He was lost at sea. I myself am an actress—living quietly here at present until my father's estate is recovered. Of course you understand that I am lying.'

" 'Perfectly!'

"She didn't take this as a joke as I had hoped. She reddened slightly. 'You are too clever. But I know why you are here, my runaway priestling; you are all the same.' She got over her fit of pique, and mocked: 'You forsake Mother Church for Mother Eve.'

"I was puzzled, then her meaning dawned on me. It was so absurd I

827

wanted to laugh. But it was annoying too—I supposed I'd have to clear out. I had finished my bread and chocolate. I rose and took my hat. 'Thank you exceedingly for my supper. It was excellent.'

"Her expression changed, all the malice driven out of it by surprise. 'So you are a hypocrite then.' She bit her lip sulkily. As I went to the door she said suddenly: 'Don't go!'

"A silence. She said defiantly:

" 'Don't look at me like that. I'm entitled to do as I choose. I enjoy myself. You should see me Saturday evenings, sitting in the Cava at Barcelona—more fun than ever you'll have in your miserable little life. Go upstairs and sleep.'

"There was a pause. Her attitude now seemed reasonable; and I could hear the rain outside. I hesitated, then moved towards the narrow stairs. My feet were swollen and smarting. I must have limped badly, for she exclaimed suddenly, coldly: 'What is the matter with your precious foot?'

" 'It's nothing . . . only blistered.'

"She studied me with those strange unfathomable eyes.

" 'I will bathe it for you.'

"In spite of all my protests she made me sit down. When she had filled a basin with warm water she knelt and took off my boot. My sock was sticking to the raw flesh. She softened it with water and drew it off. Her unexpected kindness embarrassed me. She bathed both my feet and put some ointment on them. Then she stood up.

" 'That should feel better. Your socks will be ready for you in the morning.'

" 'How can I thank you?'

"She said unexpectedly in an odd dull tone: 'What does one do with a life like mine!' Before I could answer she raised the pitcher in her right hand. 'Do not preach at me or I will break your head. Your bed is on the second landing. Good night.'

"She turned away towards the fire. I went upstairs, found a small room beneath the skylight. I slept as though stunned.

"Next morning when I came down, she was moving about the kitchen, making coffee. She gave me breakfast. As I took my leave I tried to express my gratitude. But she cut me short. She gave me her sad peculiar smile. 'You are too innocent to be a priest. You will be a great failure.'

"I started back for San Morales. I was lame and rather scared of my reception. I was afraid. I took my time."

Father Tarrant remained motionless at the window for a long moment, then quietly replaced the diary upon the table, reminded by a glint of recollection that it was he who had first asked Francis to keep it. Methodically he tore the Spanish priest's letter into fragments. The expression on his face was quite remarkable. For once it lacked its bleakness, that iron austerity seared into every feature by pitiless self-mortification. It became a young face, flooded with generosity and thoughtfulness. With his clenched hand still holding the pieces of the letter, slowly, almost unconsciously, he struck his breast three times. Then he spun round and left the room.

As he descended the broad staircase Anselm Mealey's solid head came up and around the spiral balustrade. Observing Father Tarrant, the model seminarian dared to pause. He admired the Administrator to excess. To be noticed by him was a heavenly joy. He ventured modestly:

"Excuse me, sir. We are all very anxious. I am wondering if there is any more news . . . concerning Chisholm?"

"What news?"

"Well . . . of his leaving."

Tarrant contemplated his creature with remote distaste. "Chisholm is not leaving." He added, with sudden violence, "You fool!"

That evening as Francis sat in his study, dizzy and unbelieving under the miracle of his redemption, one of the college servants silently handed in a packet. It contained a superb figure of the Virgin of Montserrat carved in ebony, a tiny masterpiece of fifteenth-century Spanish craftsmanship. No message accompanied the exquisite thing. Not a word of explanation. Suddenly, with a wild consuming thought, Francis remembered he had seen it above the prie-dieu in Father Tarrant's room.

It was the Rector, meeting Francis at the end of the week, who put his finger on the manifest inconsistency. "It strikes me, young sir, that you have escaped gey lightly, through a sinister screen of sanctity. In my young days playing truant—'plunking' we called it—was a punishable crime." He fixed on Francis his shrewd and twinkling gaze. "As a penance you might write me an essay—two thousand words—on 'The Virtue of Walking.'"

In the small universe of a seminary the very walls have ears, the keyholes diabolic vision. The story of Francis' escapade came gradually to light, was fitted, piece by piece, together. It grew, gained indeed, as it passed from lip to ear. Assuming the facets of the finished gem, it seemed likely to descend—a classic in the Seminary's history. When Father Gomez had the final details, he wrote fully to his friend the parish priest of Cossa. Father Bolas was much impressed. He wrote back, a glowing five-page letter, of which, perhaps, the final paragraph merits quotation:

Naturally, the pinnacle of achievement would have been the conversion of the woman, Rosa Oyarzabal. How wonderful it would have been had she come to me and wept, on her knees, in true contrition, as the result of our young apostle's visitation! But alas! She has gone into partnership with another madam and opened a brothel in Barcelona, which I grieve to report is flourishing.

III

AN UNSUCCESSFUL CURATE

I

IT WAS RAINING steadily, early that Saturday evening in January when Francis arrived at Shalesley, on the branch line, some forty miles from Tynecastle. But nothing could damp the eagerness, the burning of his spirit. While the train disappeared into the mist, he stood expectantly on the wet open platform, his alert eyes sweeping its dreary vacancy. No one had come to meet him. Undismayed, he picked up his bag and swung into the main street of the colliery village. The Church of the Redeemer should not be hard to find.

It was his first appointment, his first curacy. He could scarcely believe it. His heart sang . . . at last, at last, newly ordained, he had his chance to get into the battle and fight for human souls.

Though he had been forewarned, Francis had never seen greater ugliness than that which now surrounded him. Shalesley consisted of long grey rows of houses and poor cheap shops, interspaced with plots of waste land, slag heaps,—smoking even in the rain,—a refuse dump, several taverns and chapels, all dominated by the high black headstocks of the Renshaw Colliery. But he told himself gaily that his interest lay in the people, not the place.

The Catholic church stood on the east side of the village, adjacent to the colliery, harmonizing with the scene. It was a big erection of raw red brick with Gothic blue-stained windows, a dark red corrugated iron roof, and a sawed-off rusty spire. The school lay on one side; the Presbytery, fronted by a weedy plot and girded by a broken-toothed fence, upon the other.

With a deep, excited breath, Francis approached the small, ramshackle house and pulled the bell. After some delay, when he was about to ring again, the door was opened by a stout woman in a blue striped apron. Inspecting him, she nodded.

"It'll be yourself, Father! His Reverence is expecting you. In there!" She pointed with privileged good nature to the parlour door. "What weather to be sure. I'll away and put on the kippers."

Francis sturdily entered the room. Already seated at a table covered with a white cloth and laid for a repast, a thickset priest of about fifty stopped his impatient knife-tapping to greet his new curate.

"You're here at last. Come in."

Francis extended his hand. "Father Kezer, I imagine?"

"That's right. Who did you expect? King William of Orange? Well, you're just in time for supper. Trust you!" Tilting back, he called to the adjoining kitchen. "Miss Cafferty! Are you going to be all night?" Then, to Francis: "Sit down and stop looking like the lost chord. I hope you play cribbage. I like a game of an evening."

Francis took a chair at the table and soon Miss Cafferty hurried in with a large covered dish of kippers and poached eggs. As Father Kezer helped himself to two eggs and a brace of kippers she laid another place for Francis. Then Father Kezer passed over the dish, his mouth full.

"Go ahead and help yourself. Don't stint. You'll have to work hard here so you'd better eat."

He himself ate rapidly, his strong crunching jaws and capable hands, felted with black hairs, never at rest. He was burly, with a round cropped head, and a tight mouth. His nose was flat, with wide nostrils out of which sprouted two dark snuff-stained tufts. He conveyed the impression of strength, of authority. Every movement was a masterpiece of unconscious self-assertion. As he cut an egg in two and slipped one half into his mouth his little eyes watched, formed an opinion of Francis, as a butcher might weigh the merits of a steer.

"You don't look too hardy. Under eleven stone, eh? I don't know what you curates are coming to. My last was a weak-kneed effort! Should have called himself flea—not Lee—he hadn't the guts of one. It's this Continental la-de-da that ruins you. In my time—well, the fellows that came out of Maynooth with me were men."

"I think you'll find me sound in wind and limb." Francis smiled.

"We'll soon see." Father Kezer grunted. "Go in and hear confessions when you've finished. I'll be in later. There won't be many tonight though . . . seeing it's wet. Give them an excuse! They're bone lazy—my beautiful lot!"

Upstairs, in his thin-walled room, massively furnished with a heavy bed and an enormous Victorian wardrobe, Francis washed his hands and face at the stained washstand. Then he hastened down towards the church. The impression Father Kezer had given him was not favourable, but he told himself he must be fair: immediate judgements were so often unjust. He sat for a long time in the cold confessional box,—still marked with the name of his predecessor, FR. LEE,—hearing the drumming of the rain on the tin roof. At last he came out and wandered round the empty church. It was a depressing spectacle—bare as a barn and not very clean. An unhappy attempt had been made to marble the nave with dark green paint. The statue of Saint Joseph had lost a hand and been clumsily repaired. The stations of the cross were sad little daubs. On the altar some gaudy paper flowers, in vases of tarnished brass, hit the eye like an affront. But these little shortcomings only made his opportunity the greater. The tabernacle was there. And Francis knelt before it, with throbbing fervour, dedicating his life anew.

Habituated to the cultured atmosphere of San Morales, a halfway house for scholars and preachers, men of breeding and distinction moving between London, Madrid and Rome, Francis found the next few days increasingly difficult. Father Kezer was not an easy man. Naturally irascible and inclined to surliness, age, experience, and failure to win affection from his flock had made him hard as nails.

At one time he had held an excellent parish in the seaside resort of Eastcliffe. He had proved himself so disagreeable that important people in the town had petitioned the Bishop to remove him. The incident, at first bitterly resented, had been hallowed by time into an act of personal sacrifice. He would remark, soulfully: "Of my own free will I stepped from the throne to the footstool . . . but, ah! . . . those were the days."

Miss Cafferty, his cook and housekeeper combined, alone stood by him. She had been with him for years. She understood him, she was of his own kidney, she could take his slangings and heartily slang him back. The two respected each other. When he departed on his annual six weeks' holiday to Harrogate he allowed her to go home for her own vacation.

In his personal habits he had scant refinement. He stamped around his bedroom, opened and slammed the single bathroom door. The matchboard house reverberated with his wind.

Unwittingly, he had reduced his religion to a formula—with no conception of interior meanings, of the unsubstantial, no elasticity of outlook. "Do this or be damned" was imprinted on his heart. There were certain things to be accomplished with words, water, oil and salt. Without them, hell was ready, hot and gaping. He was deeply prejudiced, loudly voicing his detestation of every other denomination in the village —an attitude which did little to gain him friends.

Even in his relations with his own congregation he was not at peace. The parish was a poor one with a heavy debt upon the church and despite a stringent economy he was often desperately pressed to make ends meet. He had a legitimate case to place before his people. But his natural ire was a poor substitute for tact. In his sermons, planted solidly on his feet, head thrust aggressively forward, he lashed the sparse congregation for its neglect.

"How do you expect me to pay the rent, and the taxes, and the insurance? And keep the church roof over your heads? You're not giving it to me, you're giving it to Almighty God. Now listen to me, every man and woman of ye. It's silver I want to see in the plate, not your miserable brass farthings. You're most of you in work you men, thanks to the generosity of Sir George Renshaw. You've no excuse! As for the wimmen of the parish—if they'd put more in the offertory and less on their backs it would fit them better." He thundered on, then took up the collection himself, glaring accusingly at each of his parishioners as he shoved the plate beneath their noses.

His demands had provoked a feud, a bitter vendetta between himself and his parishioners. The more he berated them the less they gave. Enraged, he devised schemes, took to distributing little buff envelopes. When they left the empty envelopes behind he went round the church after the service, gathering up the litter and muttering furiously: "That's how they treat Almighty God!"

In this gloomy financial sky there was one bright sun.

Sir George Renshaw, who owned the Shalesley colliery, with, indeed, fifteen other coal mines in the county, was not only a man of immense resources and a Catholic but an inveterate philanthropist. Though his country seat, Renshaw Hall, was seventy miles away, on the other side of the shire, the Church of the Redeemer had somehow gained a place upon his list. Every Christmas, with the utmost regularity, a cheque for one hundred guineas reached the parish priest. "Guineas, mind ye!" Father Kezer anointed the word. "Not just measly pounds. Ah! There's a gentleman for ye!" He had seen Sir George only twice, at public gatherings in Tynecastle many years before, but he spoke of him with reverence and awe. He had a lurking fear that, through no fault of his, the magnate might discontinue the charity.

By the end of his first month at Shalesley, close association with Father Kezer began to take effect on Francis. He was continually on edge. No wonder young Father Lee had had such a bad nervous break-down. His spiritual life became overcast, his sense of values confused. He found himself regarding Father Kezer with growing hostility. Then he would recollect himself with an inward groan, and strive wildly for obedience, for humility.

His parochial work was desperately hard, particularly in this wintry weather. Three times a week he had to bicycle to Broughton and Glenburn, two distant wretched hamlets, to say mass, hear confessions, and take the catechism class in the local town hall. The lack of response amongst his people increased his difficulties. The very children were lethargic, shuffling. There was much poverty, heartrending destitution; the whole parish seemed steeped in apathy, savourless and stale. Passionately he told himself he would not surrender to routine. Conscious of his clumsiness and inefficiency, he had a burning desire to reach these poor hearts, to succour and revive them. He would kindle a spark, blaze the dead ashes into life, if it were the last thing he did.

What made it worse was the fact that the parish priest, astute and watchful, seemed to sense, with a kind of grim humour, the difficulties his curate was experiencing, and to anticipate slyly a readjustment of the other's idealism to his own practical common sense. Once when

833

Francis came in, tired and wet, having bicycled ten miles through wind and rain to an outlying sick call at Broughton, Father Kezer compressed his attitude into a single gibe. "Handing out haloes isn't what you thought it was—eh?" He added, naturally: "A good-for-nothing lot."

Francis flushed hotly. "Christ died for a good-for-nothing lot."

Deeply upset, Francis began to mortify himself. At meals he ate sparingly, often only a cup of tea and some toast. Frequently, when he woke up in the middle of the night, tortured by misgivings, he would steal down to the church. Shadowed and silent, washed in pale moonlight, the bare edifice lost its distracting crudity. He flung himself down on his knees, begging for courage to embrace the tribulations of this beginning, praying with impetuous violence. At last, as he gazed at the wounded figure on the cross, patient, gentle, suffering, peace would fill his soul.

One night, shortly after midnight, when he had made a visit of this nature and was tiptoeing upstairs, he found Father Kezer waiting on him. Wearing his nightshirt and an overcoat, a candle in his hand, the parish priest planted his thick hairy legs on the top landing, angrily barred the way.

"What d'you think you're doing?"

"Going to my room."

"Where have you been?"

"To the church."

"What! At this time of night!"

"Why not?" Francis forced a smile. "Do you think I might wake our Lord up?"

"No, but you might wake me up." Father Kezer lost his temper. "I won't have it. I never heard such nonsense in my life. I'm running a parish, not a religious order. You can pray all you want in the day, but while you're under my orders you'll sleep at night."

Francis suppressed the hot answer on his tongue. He walked to his bedroom in silence. He must curb himself, make a great effort to get on with his superior, if he were to do any good in the parish at all. He tried to concentrate on Father Kezer's good points: his frankness and courage, his odd jocularity, his adamantine chastity.

A few days later, choosing a moment which he thought propitious, he diplomatically approached the older priest.

"I've been wondering, Father . . . we've such a scattered district, so out of the way, with no proper places of amusement . . . wondering if we couldn't have a club for the youngsters of the parish."

"Aha!" Father Kezer was in his jocular mood. "So you're out for popularity, my lad!"

"Good gracious, no." Francis took up an equal heartiness, so intent was he on winning his point. "I don't want to presume. But a club might take the young people off the streets—and the older ones out of the pubs. Develop them physically and socially." He smiled. "Even make them want to come to church."

"Ho, ho!" Father Kezer guffawed. "It's well you're young. I believe you're worse than Lee. Well, go ahead if you want to. But you'll get all your thanks in one basket from the good-for-nothing crowd that hangs out here."

"Thank you, thank you. I only wanted your permission."

With thrilling eagerness Francis immediately began to carry out his plan. Donald Kyle, the manager at Renshaw Colliery, was a Scot and a steady Catholic who had showed signs of good will. Two other officials at the pit, Morrison the check-weigher, whose wife occasionally came in to help at the Presbytery, and Creeden, the head shot-firer, were also members of the church. Through the manager, Francis received permission to use the Colliery first-aid hall three nights a week. With the help of the other two he set out to stir up interest in the proposed club. His own money, added up, made less than two pounds, and he would have died sooner than ask assistance from the parish. But he wrote to Willie Tulloch—whose work brought him into touch with the Tynecastle Corporation Recreation Centres—begging him to send along some old and cast-off athletic gear.

Puzzling how he might best launch the venture, he decided that nothing could draw the young people better than a dance. There was a piano in the room and Creeden was a first-rate performer on the fiddle. He posted up a notice on the Red Cross door, and when Thursday arrived, he expended his capital on a buffet of cakes, fruit and lemonade.

The success of the evening, after a stiff start, surpassed his wildest expectations: so many turned out they managed eight sets of lancers. Most of the lads had no shoes, they danced in their pit boots. Between the dances they sat on the benches round the room, red-faced and happy, while the girls went to the buffet to find them refreshment. When they waltzed they all sang the words of the refrain. A little group of pitmen going off shift gathered at the entrance, the gaslight showing their teeth white against their grimed faces. Towards the end they joined in the singing, and one or two of the brighter sparks amongst them nipped in and stole a dance. It was a merry evening.

As he stood at the door, with their good-nights ringing in his ears, Francis thought with a surge of trembling joy: "They've begun to come alive. Dear God, I've made a start."

Next morning Father Kezer came in to breakfast in a towering rage. "What's this I hear? A fine to-do! A right royal example. You ought to be ashamed of yourself."

Francis looked up in amazement. "What on earth do you mean?"

"You know what I mean! That infernal stew you put on last night."

"You gave me permission—only a week ago."

Father Kezer snarled: "I didn't give you permission to start a promiscuous rigadoon on the very doorstep of my church. I've had trouble enough to keep my young girls pure without your introducin' your immodest pawing and prancing!"

"The entire evening was perfectly innocent."

"Innocent!—As God is above us!" Father Kezer was dark red with anger. "Don't you know what that sort of gallantry leads to—you poor dolt—clutching and clasping and bodies and legs together? It starts bad thoughts working in these young folks' minds. It leads to concupiscence, carnality and lusts of the flesh."

Francis was very pale, his eyes were blazing with indignation.

"Aren't you confusing lust with sex?"

"Holy St. Joseph! What's the difference?"

"As much as there is between disease and health."

Father Kezer's hands made a convulsive gesture. "What in the foul fiend's name are you talking about?"

The pent-up bitterness of the past two months broke over Francis in a tempestuous wave. "You can't suppress nature. If you do it'll turn on you and rend you. It's perfectly natural and good for young men and women to mix together, to dance together. It's a natural prelude to courtship and marriage. You can't keep sex under a dirty sheet like a stinking corpse. That's what starts the sly laugh, the prurient sneer. We must learn to educate and transmute sex, not choke it as though it were an adder. If you try that you'll fail, besides making something filthy out of what is clean and fine!"

A horrible silence. The veins in Father Kezer's neck were swollen, purple. "You blasphemous pup! I'll not have my young folks couplin' in your dance halls!"

"Then you'll drive them to couple—as you call it—in the dark lanes and fields."

"You lie," Father Kezer stuttered. "I'll keep the maidenhood of this parish undeflowered. I know what I'm about."

"No doubt," Francis answered bitterly. "But the fact remains that statistics show the Shalesley illegitimacy rate to be the highest in the diocese."

For a moment it seemed as though the parish priest must have a fit. His hands clenched and unclenched, as though seeking something to strangle. Rocking slightly on his feet, he raised his finger and levelled it at Francis.

"Statistics'll show another thing. And that is there's no club within five miles of this spot I'm standing on. Your fine plan is finished, smashed, done for. I say that! And in this case *my* word is final!" He flung himself down at the table and furiously began his breakfast.

Francis finished quickly and went upstairs to his room, pale and shaken. Through the dusty panes he could see the first-aid room, with the packing case of boxing gloves and Indian clubs outside, which had arrived yesterday from Tulloch, all useless now, forbidden. A terrible emotion rose up in him. He thought rigidly: I cannot continue to submit, God cannot demand such subservience, I must fight, fight, on Father Kezer's level, fight, not for myself, but for this pitiful, broken-winded parish. He was rent by an overflowing love, an undreamed-of longing to help these poor people, his first charge from God.

During the next few days, as he went through the routine of the parish, he sought feverishly for some means of lifting the ban upon his club. Somehow the club had become the symbol of the parish's emancipation. But the more he dwelt upon it the more unassailable Father Kezer's position appeared.

Drawing his own conclusions from Francis' quietness the older priest showed an ill-concealed jubilation. He was the one to tame them, to bring these young pups to heel. The Bishop must know how good he was to send him so many, one after the other. His sour grin broadened.

Quite suddenly, Francis had an idea. It struck him with overwhelming force, a slender chance, perhaps, yet one which might succeed. His pale face coloured slightly, he almost cried out loud. With a great effort, he calmed himself. He thought: I'll try, I must try . . . whenever Aunt Polly's visit is over.

He had arranged for Aunt Polly and Judy to come to Shalesley for a holiday during the last week in June. Shalesley, it is true, was not a health resort. But it stood high, the air was good. The fresh green of spring had touched its bleakness with a transient beauty. And Francis was particularly anxious that Polly should have the rest she so richly deserved.

The winter had been hard for her, physically and financially. Thaddeus Gilfoyle was, in her own phrase, "ruining" the Union, drinking more than he sold, failing to show receipts, trying to get the remnants of the business into his own hands. Ned's chronic illness had taken a peculiar turn, for twelve months now he had lost the power of his legs and was quite beyond business. Confined to a wheeled chair, he had lately become irresponsible and irrational. He had absurd delusions, spoke to the smirking, toadying Thaddeus of his steam yacht, his private brewery in Dublin. One day he had escaped her care and attended by Scanty—a grotesque spectacle of motion—had propelled himself to the Clermont shops and ordered himself two dozen hats. Dr. Tulloch, called in at Francis' request, had pronounced Ned's condition no stroke, but a tumour of the brain. It was he who had procured the male nurse who was now relieving Polly.

Francis would have greatly preferred Judy and Aunt Polly to occupy the guest room at the Presbytery—indeed, one of his dreams was a parish of his own where Polly would be his housekeeper and Judy his particular charge. But Father Kezer's attitude made a request for hospitality out of the question. Francis found a comfortable lodging for them at Mrs. Morrison's. And on June 21st, Aunt Polly and Judy arrived.

Welcoming them at the station, he felt a sudden pain in his heart. Polly, a stiff valiant figure, advanced from the train, leading by the hand, as she had led Nora, the small, dark, glossy-haired child.

"Polly. Dear Polly." He spoke as to himself. She was little changed, a trifle shabbier perhaps, her gaunt cheeks more drawn. She had the same short coat, gloves, and hat. She never spent a penny on herself, always on others. She had cared for Nora and himself, for Ned and now for Judy. She was so utterly selfless, his breast filled. He stepped forward and hugged her.

"Polly, I'm so glad to see you . . . you're . . . you're eternal."

"Oh, dear." She fumbled in her bag for her handkerchief. "It's windy here. And there's something in my eye."

He took her arm and Judy's, and escorted them to their rooms.

He did his utmost to give them a happy time. In the evenings he had long talks with Polly. Her pride in him, in what he had become, was touching. She made light of her troubles.

But she admitted one anxiety—Judy was a problem.

The child, now ten years of age and attending the day school at Clermont, was a queer mixture. Superficially she had an engaging frankness, but beneath she was suspicious and secretive. She hoarded all sorts of odds and ends in her bedroom, and would shake with temper if they were disturbed. She had wild enthusiasms which quickly faded. In other moods she was timid and uncertain. She could not bear to admit a fault and would wander glibly from the t ruth to hide it. The hint that she was lying brought floods of indignant tears.

With this before him Francis made every effort to win her confidence. He had her frequently to the Presbytery where, with the complete unconsciousness of the young, she made herself at home, often wandering off into Father Kezer's room, climbing on his sofa, fingering his pipes and paperweights. It was embarrassing, but since the parish priest made no protest, Francis did not restrain the child.

On the last day of their short holiday, when Aunt Polly had gone for a final walk and Judy had at length come to rest with a picture book in the corner of Francis' room, a knock sounded on the door. It was Miss Cafferty. She addressed Francis.

"His Reverence wants to see you immediately."

Francis' brows lifted at the unexpected request. There was something ominous in the housekeeper's words. He rose, slowly.

Father Kezer stood waiting in his own room. For the first time in weeks he looked straight at Francis.

"That child is a thief."

Francis said nothing. But he felt a sudden hollow in his stomach.

"I trusted her. I let her play about the place. I thought she was a nice little thing even though——" Kezer broke off angrily.

"What has she taken?" Francis said. His lips were stiff.

"What do thieves usually take?" Father Kezer swung round to the mantelpiece where a row of little pillars stood, each made up of twelve pennies, wrapped in white paper by his own careful hands. He picked one up. "She's stolen from the collection money. It's worse than thievery. It's simony. Look at this."

Francis examined the packet. It had been opened and clumsily retwisted at the top. Three of the pennies were missing.

"What makes you think Judy did this?"

"I'm not a fool," Father Kezer snapped. "I've been missing pennies all week. Every copper in these packets is marked."

Without a word Francis turned towards his own room. The parish priest followed him.

"Judy. Show me your purse."

Judy looked as though she had been struck. But she recovered quickly. She smiled innocently.

"I left it at Mrs. Morrison's."

"No, here it is." Francis bent forward and took the purse from the outside patch pocket of her dress. It was a new little strap purse which Aunt Polly had given her before the holiday. Francis opened it with a sinking heart. There were three pennies inside. Each had a cross scratched on the back.

Father Kezer's scowl was both outraged and triumphant. "What did I tell you? Ah! You wicked little brat, stealing from God!" He glared at Francis. "She ought to be prosecuted for this. If she were my responsibility I'd march her straight down to the police."

"No, no." Judy burst into tears. "I meant to put it back, truly, I did."

Francis was very pale. The situation was horrible for him. He took his courage in both hands.

"Very well," he said quietly. "We'll go down to the police station and charge her before Sergeant Hamilton straightaway."

Judy's grief became hysterical. Father Kezer, taken aback, sneered: "I'd like to see you."

Francis picked up his hat and took Judy's hand.

"Come along, Judy. You must be brave. We're going down to Sergeant Hamilton to tell him Father Kezer charges you with stealing three pennies."

As Francis led the child towards the door, confusion, then positive apprehension, flared up in Father Kezer's eyes. He had let his tongue run away with him. Sergeant Hamilton, an Orangeman, was no friend of his: they had often clashed bitterly in the past. And now . . . this trivial charge . . . he saw himself jeered at all over the village. He mumbled suddenly:

"Ye needn't go!"

Francis did not seem to hear.

"Stop!" Father Kezer shouted. He fought down his temper, choked out: "We'll . . . we'll forget about it. Talk to her yourself."

He walked out of the room seething with rage.

When Aunt Polly and Judy returned to Tynecastle, Francis had a quick revulsion: he wanted to explain, to express his regret for Judy's petty pilfering. But Father Kezer froze him. A sense of being balked had further embittered the older man. Besides, he was shortly leaving on his vacation. He wanted to put the curate thoroughly in his place before he left.

He ignored Francis with tight-mouthed surliness. By arrangement with Miss Cafferty he took his meals alone, before the junior priest was served. On the Sunday before his departure, he preached a violent sermon, every word aimed at Francis, on the seventh commandment: "Thou shalt not steal."

The sermon decided Francis. Immediately the service was over he went direct to Donald Kyle's house, took the manager aside, and talked to him with restrained intensity. Gradually a light broke over Kyle's face, still dubious perhaps, but hopeful, aroused. He muttered, finally: "I doubt if we can do it! But I'm with ye all the way." The two men shook hands.

On Monday morning Father Kezer left for Harrogate where, for the next six weeks, he would drink the waters. That evening Miss Cafferty went off to her native Rosslare. And on Tuesday, early, Francis met Donald Kyle by appointment at the station. Kyle carried a portfolio of papers and a glossy new brochure recently issued by a large rival coal combine in Nottingham. He wore his best clothes and an air only slightly less resolved than Francis'. They took the eleven o'clock train from Shalesley.

The long day passed slowly, they did not return until late evening. They came up the road together in silence; each looked straight ahead. Francis seemed tired, his expression revealed nothing. It was perhaps significant that the colliery manager smiled with grim solemnity as they said "Good night."

The next four days passed normally. Then, without warning, there began a period of strange activity.

The activity seemed centred upon the colliery, not unnaturally, since the colliery was the centre of the district. Francis was there a good deal between the works of the parish, consulting with Donald

Kyle, studying the architect's blue prints, watching the squads of men at work. It was remarkable how quickly the new building grew. In a fortnight it had risen above the adjoining aid-room, in a month the structure was complete. Then the carpenters and plasterers came in. The sound of hammering fell exquisitely on Francis' ears. He sniffed the aroma of fresh wood shavings. Occasionally he set to and did a job with the men. They liked him. He had inherited from his father a fondness for working with his hands.

Alone in the Presbytery, except for the unobtrusive daily visits of Mrs. Morrison, his temporary housekeeper, free of the nagging of his superior, his fervour knew no limits, a pure white glow pervaded him. He felt himself getting close to the people, breaking down suspicion, gradually entering their dulled lives, bringing to hidden stolid eyes a sudden startled gleam. It was a glorious sensation, a mingling of purpose and achievement, as though, embracing the poverty and wretchedness about him, he drew near in pity and soaring tenderness to the threshold of the unseen God.

Five days before Father Kezer's return, Francis sat down and wrote a letter. It ran as follows:

Shalesley,
September 15th, 1897.

Dear Sir George,

The new recreation centre which you have so generously donated to Shalesley Village is now practically complete. It should prove a tremendous boon, not only to your own colliery workers and their families, but to everyone else in this scattered industrial district, irrespective of class or creed. A non-partisan committee has already been formed and a syllabus drawn up on the lines we discussed. From the copy I enclose you will see how comprehensive is our winter programme: boxing and singlestick classes, physical culture, first-aid instruction and a weekly dance every Thursday.

When I consider the unhesitating liberality with which you met the diffident and perhaps unwarranted approach of Mr. Kyle and myself I am quite overwhelmed. Any words of gratitude which I might use would be hopelessly inadequate. Your real thanks will come from the happiness which you bring to the working people of Shalesley and from the good which must undoubtedly result from their increased social unity.

We propose holding a gala opening night on September 21st. If you would consent to honour us with your presence our gratification would be complete.

Believe me,
Yours most sincerely,
FRANCIS CHISHOLM,
Curate of the Church of the Redeemer.

He posted the letter with a strange taut smile. His words were heart-felt, burningly sincere. But his legs were trembling.

At midday on the nineteenth, one day after his housekeeper's return, Father Kezer reappeared. Fortified by the saline waters, he was bursting with energy—in his own phrase: fair itching to get his fingers on the reins. Reinfusing the Presbytery with his loud, black, hairy essence, with his shouted greeting to Miss Cafferty, his demand for substantial food, he ran through his correspondence. Then he bustled in to lunch, rubbing his hands. On his plate lay an envelope. He ripped it open, drew out the printed card.

"What's this?"

Francis moistened his dry lips, mustered all his courage. "It appears to be an invitation to the opening night of the new Shalesley Athletic and Recreation Club. I've had one too."

"Recreation Club. What's that to us!" Holding it at arm's length, he glared redly at the card. "What is it?"

"A fine new centre. You can see it from the window." Francis added, with a tremor: "The gift of Sir George Renshaw."

"Sir George . . ." Kezer broke off, stupefied, then stamped to the window. He gazed through the window, a long time, at the impressive proportions of the new erection. Then he returned, sat down and slowly began his lunch. His appetite was scarcely that of a man with a purified liver. He kept darting glances at Francis out of his small, lowering eyes. His silence blasted the room.

At length Francis spoke—awkwardly, with tense simplicity. "You must decide, Father. You've put a ban on dancing and all mixed recreation. On the other hand if our people don't co-operate, ostracize the club, and stop away from the dances, Sir George will feel himself mortally insulted." Francis kept his eyes on his plate. "He's coming down, in person, on Thursday, for the opening."

Father Kezer could eat no more. The thick and juicy beefsteak on his plate might have been dishcloth. He rose abruptly, crushing the card in his hairy fist with sudden, dreadful violence. "We'll not go to the foul fiends' opening! We'll not. Do you hear me? Once and for all, I've said it!" He rampaged out of the room.

On the Thursday evening, freshly shaved, in clean linen and his best black, his face a dreadful compromise of gaiety and gloom, Father Kezer stalked over to the ceremony. Francis followed behind him.

The new hall was warm with lights and excitement, filled to capacity with the working people of the community. On the raised platform a number of the local notables were seated, Donald Kyle and his wife, the colliery doctor, the council schoolmaster, and two other ministers of religion. As Francis and Father Kezer took their seats there was prolonged cheering, then a few catcalls and loud laughter. Father Kezer's jaws snapped sourly together.

The sound of a car arriving outside heightened the expectation and a minute later, amidst a great ovation, Sir George appeared on the platform. He was a medium-sized man of about sixty with a shining bald head fringed with white hair. His moustache was silvery also, and his cheeks were brightly coloured. He had that remarkably fresh pink-and-whiteness achieved by some fair-haired persons in their declining years. It seemed preposterous that one so quiet in his dress and manner should command such enormous power.

He listened agreeably while the ceremony proceeded, sustained the address of welcome from Mr. Kyle, then delivered a few remarks himself. He concluded amiably:

"I should like in fairness to state that the first suggestion of this very worthy project came directly from the vision and broadmindedness of Father Francis Chisholm."

The applause was deafening and Francis flushed, his eyes, pleading and remorseful, bent on his superior.

Father Kezer raised his hands automatically, brought them soundlessly together twice, with a grin of sickly martyrdom. Later, when the impromptu dance started, he stood watching Sir George swing round the hall with young Nancy Kyle. Then he faded into the night. The music of the fiddlers followed him.

When Francis returned, late, he found the parish priest sitting up in the parlour, with no fire, his hands on his knees.

Father Kezer seemed oddly inert. All the fight had gone out of him. In the last ten years he had knocked out more curates than Henry VIII had wives. And now a curate had knocked him out. He said tonelessly:

"I'll have to report you to the Bishop!"

Francis felt his heart turn over in his breast. But he did not flinch. No matter what happened to him, Father Kezer's authority was shaken. The older priest continued glumly: "Perhaps you'd be the better of a change. The Bishop can decide. Dean Fitzgerald needs another curate in Tynecastle . . . your friend Mealey's there, isn't he?"

Francis was silent. He did not wish to leave this now faintly stirring parish. Yet even if he were forced to do so things would be easier for his successor. The club would continue. It was a beginning. Other changes would come. He had no personal exultation, but a quiet, almost visionary, hope. He said in a low voice: "I'm sorry if I have upset you, Father. Believe me, I was only trying to help . . . our good-for-nothing lot."

The eyes of the two priests met. Father Kezer's fell first.

One Friday towards the end of Lent, in the dining room of St. Dominic's Presbytery, Francis and Father Slukas were already seated at the meagre midday repast of boiled stock-fish and butterless brown toast served on Victorian silver and fine blue Worcester china, when Father Mealey returned from an early sick call. From the suppression of his manner, his indifferent mode of helping himself, Francis was immediately aware that Anselm had something on his mind. Dean Fitzgerald dined upstairs at this season of the Church and the three junior priests were alone. But Father Mealey, munching without taste, a faint colour beneath his skin, kept silence till the end of the meal. Only when the Lithuanian had brushed the crumbs from his beard, risen, bowed, and departed, did his tension relax. He drew a long pressing breath.

"Francis! I want you to come with me this afternoon. You've no engagements?"

"No . . . I'm free till four o'clock."

"Then you must come. I'd like you as my friend, as my fellow priest, to be the first . . ." He broke off, would say no more to lift the heavy mystery of his words.

For two years Francis had been the second curate at St. Dominic's, where Gerald Fitzgerald, now Dean Fitzgerald, still remained, with Anselm his senior assistant and Slukas, the Lithuanian Father, a necessary encumbrance on account of the many Polish immigrants who kept crowding into Tynecastle.

The change from the backwoods of Shalesley to this familiar city parish where the services went like clockwork and the church was elegantly perfect had left a curious mark on Francis. He was happy to be near Aunt Polly, to maintain an eye on Ned and Judy, to see the Tullochs, Willie and his sister, once or twice a week. He had a queer consolation, a sense of indefinable support, in the recent elevation of Monsignor MacNabb from San Morales to be Bishop of the diocese. Yet his new air of maturity, the lines about his steady eyes, the spareness of his frame, gave silent indications that the transition had not been easy.

Dean Fitzgerald, refined and fastidious, priding himself on being a gentleman, stood at the opposite pole from Father Kezer. Yet, though he strove to be impartial, the Dean was not without a certain lofty prejudice. While he warmly approved Anselm—now his prime favourite —and blankly ignored Father Slukas,—whose broken English and table habits, a napkin tucked beneath the beard at every meal, coupled with a strange predilection for wearing a derby hat with his soutane placed him far beyond the pale,—towards his other curate he had a strange wariness. Francis soon realized that his humble birth, his association with the Union Tavern, with, indeed, the whole stark Bannon tragedy, must prove a handicap he could not lightly overcome.

And he had made such a bad beginning! Tired of the shopworn platitudes, the same old parrot sermons that came, almost by rote, on the appointed Sundays of the year, Francis had ventured, soon after his arrival, to preach a simple homily, fresh and original, his own thoughts, on the subject of personal integrity. Alas, Dean Fitzgerald had cuttingly condemned the dangerous innovation. Next Sunday, at his behest, Anselm had mounted the pulpit and given forth the antidote: a magnificent peroration on The Star of the Sea, in which harts panted for the water and barques came safe across the bar; ending dramatically with arms outstretched, a handsome suppliant for Love, on the admonition "Come!" All the women of the congregation were in tears, and afterwards, as Anselm ate a hearty breakfast of mutton chops, the Dean pointedly congratulated him. "That!—Father Mealey—was eloquent. I heard our late Bishop deliver practically the same sermon twenty years ago."

Perhaps these opposite orations set their courses: as the months passed Francis could not but dejectedly compare his own indifferent showing with Anselm's remarkable success. Father Mealey was a figure in the parish, always cheerful, even gay, with a ready laugh and a comforting pat on the back for anyone in trouble. He worked hard and with great earnestness, carrying a little book full of his engagements in his waistcoat pocket, never refusing an invitation to address a meeting or make an after-dinner speech. He edited the *St. Dominic's Gazette*: a newsy and often humorous little sheet. He went out a good deal and, though no one could call him a snob, took tea at all the best houses. Whenever an eminent cleric came to preach in the city, Anselm was sure to meet him and to sit admiringly at his feet. Later he would send a letter, beautifully composed, expressing ardently the spiritual benefit he had derived from the encounter. He had made many influential friends through this sincerity.

Naturally there were limits to his capacity for work. While he vigorously assumed the post of secretary to the new Diocesan Foreign Missionary Centre in Tynecastle—a cherished project of the Bishop—and worked unremittingly to please His Grace he had been obliged reluctantly to decline, and depute to Francis, the management of the Working Boy's Club in Shand Street.

The property round Shand Street was the worst in the city, tall tenements and lodging houses, a network of slums, and this, properly enough, had come to be regarded as Francis' district. Here, though his results seemed trivial and meaningless, he found plenty to do. He had

845

to train himself to look destitution in the eye, to view without shrinking the sorrow and the shame of life, the eternal irony of poverty. It was not a communion of saints that grew about him but a communion of sinners, rousing such pity in him it brought him sometimes to the brink of tears.

"Don't say you're taking forty winks," said Anselm reproachfully.

Almost with a start Francis came out of his reverie to find Father Mealey, waiting on him, hat and stick in hand, beside the lunch table. He smiled and rose in acquiescence.

Outside, the afternoon was fresh and fine, with a rousing, bustling breeze, and Anselm strode along with a brisk swing, clean, honest and healthy, greeting his parishioners bluffly. His popularity at St. Dominic's had not spoiled him. To his many admirers his most engaging characteristic was the way in which he deprecated his achievements.

Soon Francis saw that they were making for the new suburb recently added to the parish. Beyond the city boundary, a housing development was in progress, on the parklands of an old country property. Workmen were moving with hods and barrows. Francis subconsciously noted a big white board: *Hollis Estate, Apply Malcom Glennie, Solicitor.* But Anselm was pushing on, over the hill, past some green fields, then down a wooded pathway to the left. It was a pleasant rural stretch to be so near the chimney-pots.

Suddenly Father Mealey halted, with the still excitement of a pointing hound.

"You know where we are, Francis? You've heard of this place?"

"Of course."

Francis had often passed it: a little hollow of lichened rocks, screened with yellow broom and enclosed by an oval copse of copper beeches. It was the prettiest spot for miles around. He had often wondered why it was known as "The Well" and sometimes, indeed, as "Marywell." The basin had been dry for fifty years.

"Look!" Clutching his arm, Father Mealey led him forward. From the dry rocks gushed a crystal spring. There was an odd silence, then, stooping with cupped hands, Mealey took an almost sacramental drink.

"Taste it, Francis. We ought to be grateful for the privilege of being among the first."

Francis bent and drank. The water was sweet and cold. He smiled. "It tastes good."

Mealey regarded him with wise indulgence, not without its tinge of patronage. "My dear fellow, I could call it a heavenly taste."

"Has it been flowing long?"

"It began yesterday afternoon at sundown."

Francis laughed. "Really, Anselm, you're a Delphic oracle today—full of signs and portents. Come on, give me the whole story. Who told you about this?"

Father Mealey shook his head. "I can't . . . yet."

"But you've made me so confoundedly curious."

Pleased, Anselm smiled. Then his expression regained its solemnity. "I can't break the seal yet, Francis. I must go to Dean Fitzgerald. He's the one who must deal with this. Meantime, of course, I trust you . . . I know you will respect my confidence."

Francis knew his companion too well to press him further.

On their return to Tynecastle, Francis parted from his fellow curate and went on to Glanville Street to make a sick call. One of his club members, a boy named Owen Warren, had been kicked on the leg in a football game some weeks before. The youngster was poor and under-nourished and heedless of the injury. When the Poor Law doctor was eventually called in, the condition had developed into an ugly ulcer of the shin.

The affair had upset Francis—the more so since Dr. Tulloch seemed dubious of the prognosis. And this evening, in his endeavour to bring some comfort to Owen and his worried mother, the peculiar and inconclusive excursion of the afternoon was driven completely from his mind.

Next morning, however, loud and minatory sounds emerging from Dean Gerald Fitzgerald's room brought it back before him.

Lent was a deadly penance for the Dean. He was a just man, and he fasted. But fasting did not suit his full elegant body, well habituated to the stimuli of rich and nourishing juices. Sorely tried in health and temper, he kept to himself, walked the Presbytery with no recognition in his hooded eye, and each night marked another cross upon the calendar.

Although Father Mealey stood so high in Fitzgerald's favour it demanded considerable resourcefulness to approach him at such a time, and Francis heard Anselm's voice full, persuasive and pleading, across the Dean's irascible abruptness. In the end the softer voice triumphed—like drops of water, Francis reflected, wearing out granite through sheer persistence.

An hour later, with a very bad grace, the Dean came out of his room. Father Mealey was waiting on him in the vestibule. They departed together in a cab in the direction of the centre of the town. They were absent three hours. It was lunchtime when they returned and for once the Dean broke his rule. He sat down at the curate's table. Though he would eat nothing he ordered a large pot of French coffee, his one luxury in a desert of self-denial. Sitting sideways, his legs crossed, a handsome elegant figure, sipping the black and aromatic brew, he diffused an air of warmth, almost of comradeship, as though a little taken out of himself by an inner, thrilling exaltation. He said, meditatively, to Francis and the Polish priest—it was notable that he included Slukas in his friendly glance:

"Well, we may thank Father Mealey for his persistence . . . in the face of my somewhat violent disbelief. Naturally it is my duty to maintain

847

the utmost scepticism towards certain . . . phenomena. But I have never seen, I had never hoped to see, such a manifestation, in my own parish——" He broke off and, taking up his coffee cup, made a generous gesture of renunciation towards the senior curate. "Let it be your privilege to tell them, Father."

That faint excited colour persisted in Father Mealey's cheek. He cleared his throat and began, readily and earnestly, as though the incident he related demanded his most formal eloquence:

"One of our parishioners, a young woman, who has been delicate for a considerable time, was out walking on Monday of this week. The date, since we wish above everything to be precise, was March fifteenth, and the time, half-past three in the afternoon. The reason for her excursion was no idle one—this girl is a devout and fervent soul not given to giddiness or loitering. She was walking in accordance with her doctor's instructions—to get some fresh air—the medical man being Dr. William Brine of 42 Boyle Crescent, whom we all know as a physician of unimpeachable, I might say, of the highest, integrity. Well!" Father Mealey took a tense gulp of water and went on. "As she was returning from her walk, murmuring a prayer, she chanced to pass the place which we know as Mary's Well. It was twilight, the last rays of the sun lingering in pure radiance upon the lovely scene. This young girl stopped to gaze and admire when suddenly to her wonder and surprise she saw standing before her a lady in a white robe and a blue cape with a diadem of stars upon her forehead. Guided by holy instinct our Catholic girl immediately fell upon her knees. The lady smiled to her with ineffable tenderness and said: 'My child, sickly though you are, you are the one to be chosen!' Then, half-turning, still addressing the awestruck yet comprehending girl: 'Is it not sad that this Well which bears my name is dry? Remember! It is for you and those like you that this shall happen.' With a last beautiful smile she disappeared. At that instant a fount of exquisite water sprang from the barren rock."

There was a silence when Father Mealey concluded.

Then the Dean resumed: "As I have said, our approach to this delicate matter was made in the frankest incredulity. We don't expect miracles to grow on every gooseberry bush. Young girls are notoriously romantic. And the starting of the spring might have been a sheer coincidence. However——" His tone took on a deeper gratification. "I've just completed a long interrogation of the girl in question with Father Mealey and Dr. Brine. As you may imagine, the solemn experience of her vision was a great shock to her. She went to bed immediately after it and has remained there ever since." The voice became slower, fraught with immense significance. "Though she is happy, normal and physically well-nourished, in these five days she has touched neither food nor drink." He gave the amazing fact its due weight in

848

silence. "Moreover . . . moreover, I say, she shows plainly, unmistakably and irrefutably, the blessed stigmata!" He went on triumphantly: "While it is too early to speak yet, while final evidence must be collected, I have the strongest premonition, amounting almost to conviction, that we in this parish have been privileged by Almighty God to participate in a miracle comparable to, and perhaps far-reaching as, those which gave our holy religion the new-found Grotto at Digby and the older and more historic Shrine at Lourdes."

It was impossible not to be affected by the nobility of his peroration.

"Who is the girl?" Francis asked.

"She is Charlotte Neily!"

Francis stared at the Dean. He opened his lips and closed them again. The silence remained impressive.

The next few days brought a growing excitement to the Presbytery. No one could have been better equipped to deal with the crisis than Dean Gerald Fitzgerald. A man of sincere devotion, he was wise also in worldly ways. Long and hard-won experience on the local school board and urban councils gave him an astute approach to temporal affairs. No news of the event was permitted to escape, not a whisper, even, in the parochial halls. The Dean had everything under his own hand. He would raise his hand only when he was ready.

The incident, so miraculously unexpected, was a breath of new life to him. Not for many years had he known such inner satisfaction: both spiritual and material. He was a strange mixture of piety and ambition. His exceptional attributes of mind and body had seemed to destine him, automatically, for advancement in the Church. And he longed passionately for that advancement as much, perhaps, as he longed for the advancement of Holy Church herself. A keen student of contemporary history, he likened himself often in his own mind to Newman. He merited equal eminence. Yet he remained, becalmed, at St. Dominic's. The only preferment they had given him, the reward of twenty distinguished years, was this petty elevation to the rank of Dean, an infrequent title in the Catholic Church and one which often embarrassed him on his journeying beyond the city, causing him to be mistaken for an Anglican clergyman, an inference he most cordially resented.

Perhaps he realized that while he was admired he was not liked. With the passage of each day he was growing more and more a disappointed man. He strove for resignation. Yet when he bent his head and said "O Lord, Thy will be done!" deep down beneath his humility was the burning thought: "By this time they should have given me my mozzetta."

Now everything was changed. Let them keep him at St. Dominic's. He would make St. Dominic's a shrine of light. Lourdes was his exemplar and, nearer in time and space, the recent striking instance of Digby in the Midlands, where the foundation of a miraculous grotto, with many authenticated cures, had transformed the dreary hamlet into a thriving town, and elevated, at the same time, an unknown but resourceful parish priest to the status of a national figure.

The Dean sank into a splendid vision of a new city, a great basilica, a solemn triduum, himself enthroned in stiff vestments . . . then sharply took himself in hand and scrutinized the draft contracts. His first action had been to place immediately a Dominican nun, Sister Teresa, trustworthy and discreet, in Charlotte Neily's home. Reassured by her impeccable reports he had taken to the law.

It was fortunate that Marywell and all the land adjacent formed the estate of the old and wealthy Hollis family. Though not a Catholic, Captain Hollis had married one, Sir George Renshaw's sister. He was friendly and well-disposed. He and his solicitor, Malcom Glennie, were closeted with the Dean upon successive days, holding long conferences over sherry and biscuits. A fair and amicable arrangement was at length worked out. The Dean had no personal interest in money. He regarded it contemptuously as so much dross. But the things that money could purchase were important and he must ensure the future of his shining project. No one but a fool could fail to realize that the value of the land would rocket to the sky.

On the last day of the negotiations Francis ran into Glennie in the upper corridor. Frankly, he was surprised to find Malcom dealing with the Hollis affairs. But the solicitor, when articled, had shrewdly bought himself into an old established firm with his wife's money and quietly succeeded to some first-rate practice.

"Well, Malcom!" Francis held out his hand. "Glad to see you again."

Glennie shook hands with damp effusiveness.

"But I'm amazed," Francis smiled, "to find you in the house of the Scarlet Woman!"

The solicitor's answering smile was thin. He mumbled: "I'm a liberal man, Francis . . . besides being obliged to chase the pennies."

There was a silence. Francis had often thought to restore his relationship with the Glennies. But news of the death of Daniel had dissuaded him—and a chance encounter with Mrs. Glennie in Tynecastle when, as he crossed the street to greet her, she had sighted him from the corner of her eye, and shied away, as though she spied the Devil.

He said: "It made me very sad to hear of your father's death."

"Ay, ay! We miss him of course. But the old man was such a failure."

"It's no great failure to get into heaven," Francis joked.

"Well, yes, I suppose he's there." Glennie vaguely twisted the emblem on his watchchain. He was already tending towards an early middle age, his figure slack, shoulders and stomach pendulous, his thin hair plastered in streaks over his bare scalp. But his eye, though palely evasive, was

850

gimlet sharp. As he moved towards the stairs he threw off a tepid invitation.

"Look us up when you have time. I'm married, as you know—two of a family—but Mother still lives with us."

Malcom Glennie had his own peculiar interest in the beatific vision of Charlotte Neily. Since his early youth he had been patiently seeking an opportunity to acquire wealth. He inherited from his mother a burning avarice and something of her long-nosed cunning. He smelled money in this ridiculous Romish scheme. Its very uniqueness convinced him of its possibilities. His opportunity was here, dangling like a ripe fruit. It would never occur again, never in a lifetime.

Working disingenuously for his client, Malcom remembered what everyone else had forgotten. Secretly, and at considerable expense, he had a geological survey carried out. Then he was sure of what he had already suspected. The flow of water to the property came exclusively through an upper tract of heath land, above and remote from the estate.

Malcom was not rich. Not yet. But by taking all his savings, by mortgaging his house and business, he had just enough to execute a three months' option on this land. He knew what an artesian bore would do. That bore would never be driven. But a bargain would be driven, later, on the threat of that bore, which would make Malcom Glennie a landed gentleman.

Meanwhile the water still gushed clear and sweet. Charlotte Neily still maintained her rapture and her stigmata, still existed without sustenance. And Francis still prayed, broodingly, for the gift of faith.

If only he could believe like Anselm who, without a struggle, blandly, smilingly, accepted everything from Adam's rib to the less probable details of Jonah's sojourn in the whale! He did believe, he did, he did . . . but not in the shallows, only in the depths . . . only by an effort of love, by keeping his nose to the grindstone in the slums, when shaking the fleas from his clothing into the empty bath . . . never, never easily . . . except when he sat with the sick, the crippled, those of stricken, ashen countenance. The cruelty of this present test, its unfairness, was wrecking his nerves, withering in him the joy of prayer.

It was the girl herself who disturbed him. Doubtless he was prejudiced: he could not overlook the fact that Charlotte's mother was Thaddeus Gilfoyle's sister. And her father was a vague and windy character, pious yet lazy, who stole away from his small chandler's premises every day, to light candles before the side altar for success in his neglected business. Charlotte had all her father's fondness for the Church. But Francis had a worried suspicion that the incidentals drew her, the smell of incense and of candle grease, that the darkness of the confessional struck overtures upon her nerves. He did not deny her unblemished goodness, the regularity with which she carried out her duties. As against that, she washed sketchily, and her breath was rancid.

On the following Saturday as Francis walked down Glanville Street, feeling absurdly depressed, he observed Dr. Tulloch come out of Number 143, the house of Owen Warren. He called, the doctor turned, stopped, then fell into step beside his friend.

Willie had broadened with the years, but had otherwise changed little. Slow, tenacious and canny, loyal to his friends, hostile to his enemies, he had, in manhood, all his father's honesty, but little of his charm and nothing of his looks. His blunt-nosed face was red and stolid, topped by a shock of unmanageable hair. He had an air of plodding decency. His medical career had not been brilliant, but he was sound and enjoyed his work. He was quite contemptuous of all orthodox ambitions. Though he spoke occasionally of "seeing the world," of pursuing adventure in far-off romantic lands, he remained in his Poor Law appointment—which demanded no hateful bedside falsities and enabled him at most times to speak his mind—anchored by the humdrum, by his matter-of-fact capacity of living from day to day. Besides, he never could save money. His salary was not large; and much of it was spent on whisky.

Always careless of his appearance, this morning he had not shaved. And his deepset eyes were sombre, his expression unusually put out: as though today he had a grudge against the world. He indicated briefly that the Warren boy was worse. He had been in to take a shred of tissue for pathological examination.

They continued along the street, linked by one of their peculiar silences. Suddenly on an unaccountable impulse, Francis divulged the story of Charlotte Neily.

Tulloch's face did not change, he trudged along, fists in his deep coat pockets, collar up, head down.

"Yes," he said at last. "A little bird told me."

"What do you think of it?"

"Why ask me?"

"At least you're honest."

Tulloch looked oddly at Francis. For one so modest, so conscious of his mental limitations, the doctor's rejection of the myth of God was strangely positive. "Religion isn't my province, I inherited a most satisfying atheism . . . which the anatomy room confirmed. But if you want it straight—in my old dad's words, I have my doubts. See here, though! Why don't we take a look at her? We're not far from the house. We'll go in together."

"Won't that get you into trouble with Dr. Brine?"

"No. I can square it with Salty tomorrow. In dealing with my colleagues I find it pays to act first and apologize afterwards." He threw Francis a singular smile. "Unless you're afraid of the hierarchy?"

Francis flushed but controlled his answer. He said a minute later: "Yes, I'm afraid, but we'll go in."

It proved surprisingly easy to effect an entrance. Mrs. Neily, worn-out by a night of watching, was asleep. Neily, for once, was at his business. Sister Teresa, short, quiet and amiable, opened the door. Since she came from a distant section of Tynecastle she had no knowledge of Tulloch, but she knew and recognized Francis, at once. She admitted them to the polished, immaculately tidy room where Charlotte lay on spotless pillows, washed and clothed in a high white nightgown, the brasses of the bedstead shining. Sister Teresa bent over the girl, not a little proud of her stainless handiwork.

"Charlotte, dear. Father Chisholm has come to see you. And brought a doctor who is a great friend of Dr. Brine."

Charlotte Neily smiled. The smile was conscious, vaguely languid, yet charged with curious rapture. It lit up the pale, already luminous face motionless upon the pillow. It was deeply impressive. Francis felt a stir of genuine compunction. There was no doubt that something existed, here, in this still white room, outside the bonds of natural experience.

"You don't mind if I examine you, Charlotte?" Tulloch spoke kindly.

At his tone, her smile lingered. She did not move. She had the cushioned repose of one who is watched, who knows that she is watched, yet is undisturbed, rather exalted, by such watching: a consciousness of inner power, a mollification, a dreamy and elevated awareness of the deference and reverence evoked amongst the watchers. Her pale eyelids fluttered. Her voice was untroubled, remote.

"Why should I mind, doctor? I'm only too glad. I'm not worthy to be chosen as God's vessel . . . but since I am chosen I can only joyfully submit."

She allowed the respectful Tulloch to examine her.

"You don't eat anything, Charlotte?"

"No, doctor."

"You've no appetite?"

"I never think of food. I just seem sustained by an inner grace."

Sister Teresa said quietly: "I can assure you she hasn't put a bite in her mouth since I came into this house."

A silence fell in the hushed white room. Dr. Tulloch straightened himself, pushing back his unruly hair. He said simply:

"Thank you, Charlotte. Thank you, Sister Teresa. I'm much indebted to you for your kindness." He went towards the bedroom door.

As Francis made to follow the doctor a shadow fluttered over Charlotte's face.

"Don't you want to see too, Father? Look . . . my hands! My feet are just the same."

She extended both her arms, gently, sacrificially. Upon both her pale palms, unmistakably, were the blood-stained marks of nails.

Outside, Dr. Tulloch maintained his attitude of reserve. He kept his lips shut until they reached the end of the street. Then at the point where their ways diverged, he spoke rapidly. "You want my opinion I suppose. Here it is. A borderline case—or just over: manic depressive in the exalted stage. Certainly a hysteric bleeder. If she steers clear of the asylum, she'll probably be canonized!" His composure, his perfect manner left him. His red plain face became congested. His words choked him. "Damn it to hell! When I think of her trigged up there in her simpering holiness, like an anæmic angel in a flour bag—and little Owney Warren, stuck in a dirty garret, with worse pain than your hellfire in his gangrenous leg, and the threat of malignant sarcoma over him, I could just about explode. Bite on that when you say your prayers. You're probably going back to say them now. Well, I'm going home to have a drink." He walked rapidly away before Francis could reply.

That same evening when Francis returned from tenebræ an urgent summons awaited him, written on the slate which hung in the Presbytery vestibule. With a premonition of misfortune, he went upstairs to the study. The Dean was wearing out his temper and his carpet with short exasperated paces.

"Father Chisholm! I am both amazed and indignant. Really, I expected better of you than this. To think that you should bring in—from the streets—an atheistic doctor—I resent it violently!"

"I'm sorry." Francis answered heavily. "It's just—oh, well, he happens to be my friend."

"That in itself is highly reprehensible. I find it wildly improper that one of my curates should associate with a character like Dr. Tulloch."

"We . . . we were boys together."

"That is no excuse. I'm hurt and disappointed. I'm thoroughly and justifiably incensed. From the very beginning your attitude towards this great event has been cold and unsympathetic. I daresay you are jealous that the honour of the discovery should have fallen to the senior curate. Or is there some deeper motive behind your manifest antagonism?"

A sense of wretchedness flowed over Francis. He felt that the Dean was right. He mumbled:

"I'm terribly sorry. I'm not disloyal. That's the last in the world I'd want to be. But I admit I've been lukewarm. It's because I've been troubled. That's why I took Tulloch in today. I have such doubts——"

"Doubts! Do you deny the miracles of Lourdes?"

"No, no. They're unimpeachable. Authenticated by doctors of all creeds."

854

"Then why deny us the opportunity to create another monument of faith—here—in our very midst?" The Dean's brow darkened. "If you disregard the spiritual implications, at least respect the physical." He sneered. "Do you fondly imagine that a young girl can go nine days without food or drink—and remain well and perfectly nourished—unless she is receiving other sustenance?"

"What sustenance?"

"Spiritual sustenance." The Dean fumed. "Didn't Saint Catherine of Siena receive a spiritual mystic drink which supplanted all earthly food? Such insufferable doubting! Can you wonder that I lose my temper?"

Francis hung his head. "Saint Thomas doubted. In the presence of all the disciples. Even to putting his fingers in our Lord's side. But no one lost their temper."

There was a sudden shocked pause. The Dean paled, then recovered himself. He bent over his desk, fumbling at some papers, not looking at Francis. He said in a restrained tone:

"This is not the first time you have proved obstructive. You are getting yourself into very bad odour in the diocese. You may go."

Francis left the room with a dreadful sense of his own deficiencies. He had a sudden overwhelming impulse to take his troubles to Bishop MacNabb. But he suppressed it. Rusty Mac seemed no longer approachable. He would be too fully occupied by his new high office to concern himself with the worries of a wretched curate.

Next day, Sunday, at the eleven o'clock high mass, Dean Fitzgerald broke the news in the finest sermon he had ever preached.

The sensation was immediate and tremendous. The entire congregation stood outside the church talking in hushed voices, unwilling to go home. A spontaneous procession formed up and departed, under the leadership of Father Mealey, for Marywell. In the afternoon crowds collected outside the Neily home. A band of young women of the confraternity, to which Charlotte belonged, knelt in the street reciting the rosary.

In the evening the Dean consented to be interviewed by a highly curious press. He conducted himself with dignity and restraint. Already esteemed in the city, rated as a public-spirited clergyman, he produced a most favourable impression. Next morning the newspapers gave him generously of their space. He was on the front page of the *Tribune*, had a eulogistic double spread inside the *Globe*. "Another Digby," proclaimed the *Northumberland Herald*. Said the *Yorkshire Echo*, "Miraculous Grotto Brings Hope to Thousands." The *Weekly High Anglican* hedged, rather cattily, "We await further evidence." But the London *Times* was superb with a scholarly article from its theological correspondent tracing the history of the Well back to Aidan and Saint Ethelwulf. The Dean flushed with gratification. Father Mealey could eat no breakfast, and Malcom Glennie was beside himself with joy.

Eight days later Francis paid an evening visit to Polly's little flat in Clermont, at the north end of the city. He was tired, after a long day's visiting in the dingy tenements of his district, and most desperately depressed. That afternoon a note had come round from Dr. Tulloch which curtly signed young Warren's death warrant. The condition had been revealed as malignant sarcoma of the leg. There was no hope whatsoever for the boy: he was dying and might not last the month.

At Clermont, Polly was her indomitable self, Ned, perhaps, a trifle more trying than usual. Hunched in his wheeled chair, a blanket wrapped about his knees, he talked much and rather foolishly. Some sort of final settlement had at last been squeezed out of Gilfoyle on account of the remnants of Ned's interest in the Union Tavern. A pitiful sum. But Ned had boasted as though it were a fortune. As the result of his complaint his tongue seemed too large for his mouth, he was distressingly inarticulate.

Judy was already asleep when Francis arrived, and although Polly said nothing there was a hint in her manner that the child had misbehaved and been sent off early. The thought saddened him further.

Eleven o'clock was striking when he left the flat. The last tram to Tynecastle had gone. Tramping home, his shoulders drooping slightly under this final discomfiture, he entered Glanville Street. As he drew opposite the Neily home he observed that the double window on the ground floor, which marked Charlotte's room, was still illuminated. He made out the movements of figures, vague shadows on the yellow blind.

A rush of contrition overcame him. Oppressed by the realization of his obduracy, he had a sudden desire to see the Neilys and make amends. The instinct of reparation was strong within him as he crossed the street and went up the three front steps. He raised his hand towards the knocker, altered his mind and turned the old-fashioned handle of the door. He had acquired that facility, common to priests and physicians, of making his sick visits unannounced.

The bedroom, opening off the small lobby, projected a wide slant of gaslight. He tapped gently on the lintel and entered the room. Then he stood, suddenly transformed to stone.

Charlotte, propped up in bed, with an oval tray before her laden with breast of chicken and a custard, was stuffing herself with food. Mrs. Neily, wrapped in a faded blue dressing gown, bent with solicitude, was noiselessly decanting stout.

It was the mother who saw Francis first. Arrested, she gave a neighing cry of terror. Her hand flew to her throat, dropping the glass, spilling the stout upon the bed.

856

Charlotte raised her gaze from the tray. Her pale eyes dilated. She gazed at her mother, her mouth opened, she began to whimper. She slid down on the bed, shielding her face. The tray crashed on to the floor. No one had spoken. Mrs. Neily's throat worked convulsively. She made a stupid, feeble effort to secrete the bottle in her dressing gown. At last she gasped: "I've got to keep her strength up somehow . . . all she's been through . . . it's invalid's stout!"

Her look of frightened guilt revealed everything. It sickened him. He felt debased and humiliated. He had difficulty in finding words.

"I suppose you've given her food every night . . . when Sister left her, thinking she was asleep?"

"No, Father! As God is my witness!" She made a last desperate attempt at denial, then broke down, lost her head completely. "What if I did? I couldn't see my poor child starve, not for nobody. But dear Saint Joseph . . . I'd never have let her do it if I'd known it would mean so much . . . with the crowds . . . and the papers . . . I'm glad to be through with it. . . . Don't . . . don't be hard on us, Father."

He said in a low voice: "I'm not going to judge you, Mrs. Neily." She wept.

He waited patiently until her sobs subsided, seated on a chair at the door, gazing at his hat, between his hands. The folly of what she had done, the folly, at that moment, of all human life, appalled him. When the two were quieter he said: "Tell me about it."

The story came, gulped out, mostly by Charlotte.

She had read such a nice book, from the church library, about Blessed Bernardette. One day when she was passing Marywell, it was her favourite walk, she noticed the water running. That's funny, she thought. Then the coincidence struck her, between the water, Bernardette and herself. It was a shock. She had almost, in a sort of way, fancied she saw the Blessed Virgin. When she got home, the more she thought of it the surer she became. It gave her quite a turn. She was all white and trembling, she had to take to her bed and send for Father Mealey. And before she knew where she was, she was telling him the whole story.

All that night she'd lain in a kind of ecstasy, her body seemed to go rigid, stiff as a board. Next morning, when she woke up, the marks were there. She'd always bruised terrible but these were different.

Well, that convinced her. All that day, when food came, she refused it, just waved it away. She was too happy, too excited to eat. Besides, lots of Saints had lived without food. That idea fixed itself on her, too. When Father Mealey and the Dean heard she was living on Grace—and perhaps she was too—it was a glorious feeling. The attention she had, it was like she was a bride. But of course, after a bit, she got dreadfully hungry. She couldn't disappoint Father Mealey and the Dean: the way she was looked up to by Father Mealey especially. She just told her

857

mother. And things had gone so far her mother had to help her. She had a big meal, sometimes two, every night.

But then, oh, dear, things had gone even further. "At first, as I told you, Father, it was wonderful. The best of all was the confraternity girls praying to me outside the window!" But when the newspapers started and all that, she got really frightened. She wished to God she had never done it. Sister Teresa was harder to pull the wool over. The marks on her hands were getting faint, instead of being all lifted up and excited she was turning low, depressed . . .

A fresh burst of sobbing terminated the pitiful revelation—tawdry as an illiterate scrawl upon a wall. Yet tragic, somehow, with the idiocy of all humanity.

The mother interposed.

"You won't tell Dean Fitzgerald on us, will you, Father?"

Francis was no longer angry, only sad and strangely merciful. If only the wretched business had not gone so far. He sighed.

"I won't tell him, Mrs. Neily, I won't say a word. But——" He paused. "I'm afraid you must."

Terror leaped again in her eyes. "No, no . . . for pity's sake no, Father."

He began, quietly, to explain why they must confess, how the scheme which the Dean contemplated could not be built upon a lie, especially one which must soon be palpable. He comforted them with the thought that the nine days' wonder would soon subside and be forgotten.

He left them an hour later, somewhat appeased, and with their faithful promise that they would follow out his advice. But as he directed his echoing footsteps homewards through the empty streets his heart ached for Dean Gerald Fitzgerald.

The next day passed. He was out visiting most of the time, and did not see the Dean. But a curious hollowness, a kind of suspended animation, seemed to float within the Presbytery. He was sensitive to atmosphere. He felt this strongly.

At eleven o'clock on the following forenoon, Malcom Glennie broke into his room.

"Francis! You've got to help me. He's not going on with it. For God's sake, come in and talk to him."

Glennie was painfully distressed. He was pale, his lips worked, there was a wildness in his eye. He stuttered:

"I don't know what's taken him. He must be out of his mind. It's such a beautiful scheme. It'll do so much good——"

"I have no influence with him."

"But you have—he thinks the world of you. And you're a priest. You owe it to your flock. It'll be good for the Catholics——"

"That hardly interests you, Malcom."

"But it does," Glennie babbled. "I'm a liberal man. I admire the Catholics. It's a beautiful religion. I often wish—Oh, for God's sake, Francis, come in, quick, before it's too late."

"I'm sorry, Malcom. It's disappointing for all of us." He turned away towards the window.

At that Glennie lost all control of himself. He caught hold of Francis' arm. He snivelled abjectly.

"Don't turn me down, Francis. You owe everything to us. I've bought a little bit of land, put all my savings in it, it's worthless if the scheme falls through. Don't see my poor family ruined. My poor old mother! Think of how she brought you up, Francis. Please, please persuade him. I'd do anything in the world. I'll even turn a Catholic for you!"

Francis kept staring out of the window, his hand gripping the curtain, his eyes fixed on the church gable, pointed with a grey stone cross. A dull thought crossed his mind. What would mankind do for money? Everything. Even to selling its immortal soul.

Glennie exhausted himself at last. Convinced, finally, that nothing could be gained from Francis, he struggled for the remnants of his dignity. His manner altered.

"So you won't help me. Well, I'll remember you for this." He moved towards the door. "I'll get even with you all. If it's the last thing I do."

He paused on his way out, his pallid face contorted with malice. "I should have known you'd bite the hand that fed you. What else could you expect from a lot of dirty papists!"

He slammed the door behind him.

The hollowness continued within the Presbytery: that kind of vacuum in which people lose their clear outlines, become unsubstantial, transitory. The servants moved on tiptoe, as though it were a house of death. The Lithuanian Father wore a look of sheer bewilderment. Father Mealey went about with his eyes cast down. He had received a grave hurt. But he kept silence, which in one so naturally effusive was a singular grace. When he spoke it was of other matters. He distracted himself, passionately, with his work at the Foreign Missions office.

For more than a week after Glennie's outburst Francis had no encounter with Fitzgerald. Then, one morning, as he entered the sacristy, he found the Dean unvesting. The altar boys had gone; the two were alone.

Whatever his personal humiliation, the Dean's control of the disaster had been consummate. Indeed, in his hands it ceased to be disaster. Captain Hollis had willingly torn up the contracts. An occupation had been found for Neily in a distant town: the first step towards discreet withdrawal of the family. The clangour in the journals was tactfully stilled. Then, on Sunday, the Dean climbed again into the pulpit. Facing the hushed congregation, he gave the text: "O Ye of Little Faith!"

Quietly, with still intensity, he developed his thesis: What need had the Church of additional miracles? Had she not fully justified herself, miraculously, already? Her foundations were planted deep, foursquare, upon the miracles of Christ. It was pleasant, no doubt exciting, to meet a manifestation like that of Marywell. They had all, himself included, been carried away with it. But on sober reflection, why all this outcry about a single blossom, when the very flower of heaven bloomed here in the church, before their eyes? Were they so weak, so pusillanimous in their faith they needed further material evidence? Had they forgotten the solemn words: "Blessed are they that have not seen, and have believed"? It was a superb feat of oratory. It surpassed his triumph of the previous Sunday. Gerald Fitzgerald, still a Dean, alone knew what it cost him.

At first, in the sacristy, the Dean seemed about to maintain his inflexible reserve. But, when ready to leave, with his black coat cast about his shoulders, he suddenly swung round. In the clear light of the sacristy Francis was shocked to see the deep lines on the handsome face, the weariness in the full grey eyes.

"Not one lie, Father, but a tissue of lies. Well! God's will be done!" He paused. "You're a good fellow, Chisholm. It's a pity you and I are incompatible." He went out of the sacristy, erect.

By the end of Easter the event had almost been forgotten. The neat white railing which had been erected round the Well in the Dean's first ardour still stood; but the little entrance gate remained unlocked, swinging, rather pathetically, in the light spring air. A few good souls went occasionally to pray and bless themselves with the sparkling, ever-gushing water.

Francis, caught by a spurt of parish work, rejoiced in his own forgetfulness. The smear of the experience was gradually wearing off. What remained was only a faint ugliness at the back of his mind, which he quickly suppressed and would soon bury completely. His idea of a new playing field for the boys and young men of the parish had taken tangible form. He had been offered the use of a strip of the Public Park by the local council. Dean Fitzgerald had given his consent. He was now immersed in a pile of catalogues.

On the eve of Ascension Day he received an urgent call to visit Owen Warren. His face clouded. He rose immediately, the cricket folder falling from his knee. Though he had expected this summons for many weeks, he dreaded it. He went quickly to the church and, with the viaticum upon his person, hurried through the crowded town to Glanville Street.

His expression was fixed and sad as he saw Dr. Tulloch pacing restlessly outside the Warren home. Tulloch was attached to Owen too. He looked deeply upset as Francis approached.

"Has it come at last?" Francis said.

"Yes, it's come!" As an afterthought: "Yesterday the main artery thrombosed. It wasn't any use—even to amputate."

"Am I too late?"

"No." Tulloch's manner held a subdued violence. He shouldered roughly past Francis. "But I've been in three times at the boy while you've been strolling along. Come in, damn it . . . if you're coming in at all."

Francis followed the other up the steps. Mrs. Warren opened the door. She was a spare woman of fifty, worn out by the weeks of anxiety, plainly dressed in grey. He saw that her face was wet with tears. He pressed her hand in sympathy.

"I'm so sorry, Mrs. Warren."

She laughed—weakly, chokingly.

"Go into the room, Father!"

He was shocked. He thought that grief had momentarily turned her mind. He went into the room.

Owen was lying on the counterpane of his bed. His lower limbs were unbandaged, bare. They were rather thin, showing the wasting of disease. Both were sound, unblemished.

Dazed, Francis watched Dr. Tulloch lift up the right leg and run his hand firmly down the sound straight shin which yesterday had been a festering malignant mass. Finding no answer in the doctor's challenging eyes, he turned giddily to Mrs. Warren, saw that her tears were tears of joy. She nodded blindly, through these tears.

"I bundled him up warm in the old gocar' this morning before anybody was about. We wouldn't give up, Owney and me. He had always believed . . . if he could only get up there to the Well . . . We prayed and dipped his leg in the water. . . . When we got back . . . Owney . . . took the bandage off himself!"

The stillness in the room was absolute. It was Owen who finally broke it.

"Don't forget to put me down for your new cricket team, Father."

In the street, outside, Willie Tulloch stared doggedly at his friend.

"There's bound to be a scientific explanation beyond the scope of our present knowledge. An intense desire for recovery—psychological regeneration of the cells." He stopped short, his big hand trembling on Francis' arm. "Oh, God!—if there is a God!—let's all keep our bloody mouths shut about it!"

That night Francis could not rest. He stared with sleepless eyes into the blackness above his head. The miracle of faith. Yes, faith itself was the miracle. The waters of Jordan, Lourdes, or Marywell—they mattered not a jot. Any muddy pool would answer, if it were the mirror of God's face.

Momentarily, the seismograph of his mind faintly registered the shock: a glimmering of the knowledge of the incomprehensibility of God. He prayed fervently. O dear God, we don't even know the beginning. We are like tiny ants in a bottomless abyss, covered with a million layers of cotton wool, striving . . . striving to see the sky. O God . . . dear God, give me humility . . . and give me faith!

III

It was three months later when the Bishop's summons arrived. Francis had expected it for some time now, yet its actual arrival somewhat dismayed him. Heavy rain began as he walked up the hill towards the palace; only by racing the intervening distance did he avoid a thorough drenching. Out of breath, wet and splashed with mud, he felt his arrival somewhat lacking in dignity. Insensibly his anxiety increased as he sat, slightly shivering, in the formal parlour, gazing at his mired boots, so incongruous upon the red pile carpet.

At last the Bishop's secretary appeared, ushered him up a shallow flight of marble stairs, and silently indicated a dark mahogany door. Francis knocked and went in.

His Lordship was at his desk, not bent at work but resting, his cheek against his hand, elbow on the arm of his leather chair. The fading light, striking sideways through the velvet pelmets of the tall window, enriched the violet of his biretta but found his face in shadow.

Francis paused uncertainly, disconcerted by the impassive figure, asking himself if this were really his old friend of Holywell and San Morales. There was no sound but the faint ticking of the Buhl clock on the mantelpiece. Then a severe voice said:

"Well, Father, any miracles to report tonight? And by the by, before I forget, how is the dance-hall business doing now?"

Francis felt a thickness in his throat, he could have cried for sheer relief. His Lordship continued his scrutiny of the figure marooned on the wide rug. "I must confess it affords some relief to my old eyes to see a priest so manifestly unprosperous as you. Usually they come in here looking like successful undertakers. That's an abominable suit you're wearing—and dreadful boots!" He rose slowly, and advanced towards Francis. "My dear boy, I am delighted to see you. But you're horribly thin." He placed his hand on the other's shoulder. "And good gracious, horribly wet, too!"

"I got caught in the rain, your Grace."

"What! No umbrella! Come over to the fire. We must get you something warm." Leaving Francis, he went to a small escritoire and produced a decanter and two liqueur glasses. "I am not yet properly acclimatized to my new dignity. I ought to ring and command some of these fine vintages used by all the Bishops one reads about. This is only Glenlivet, but it's fit tipple for two Scots." He handed Francis a tiny glassful of the neat spirit, watched him drink it, then drank his own. He sat down on the other side of the fireplace. "Speaking of dignity, do not look so scared of me. I'm bedizened now—I admit. But underneath is the same clumsy anatomy you saw wading through the Stinchar!"

Francis reddened. "Yes, your Grace."

There was a pause, then His Lordship said, directly and quietly: "You've had a pretty thin time, I imagine, since you left San Morales."

Francis answered in a low voice. "I've been a pretty good failure."

"Indeed?"

"Yes, I felt this coming . . . this disciplinary interview. I knew I wasn't pleasing Dean Fitzgerald lately."

"Just pleasing Almighty God, eh?"

"No, no. I'm really ashamed, dissatisfied with myself. It's my incorrigibly rebellious nature." A pause.

"Your culminating iniquity seems to be that you failed to attend a banquet in honour of Alderman Shand . . . who has just made a magnificent donation of five hundred pounds to the new high altar fund. Can it be that you disapprove of the good Alderman—who, I am told, is slightly less pious in his dealings with the tenants of his slum property in Shand Street?"

"Well . . ." Francis halted in confusion. "I don't know. I was wrong not to go. Dean Fitzgerald specially advised us we must attend . . . he attached great importance to it. But something else cropped up . . ."

"Oh?" The Bishop waited.

"I was called to see someone that afternoon." Francis spoke with great reluctance. "You may remember . . . Edward Bannon . . . though he's unrecognizable now, in his illness, paralyzed, drooling, a caricature of God-made man. When it was time for me to go he clutched my hand, implored me not to leave him. I couldn't help myself . . . or restrain a terrible sick pity for this . . . grotesque, dying outcast. He fell asleep mumbling, 'John the Father, John the Son, John the Holy Ghost,' saliva running down his grey unshaven chin, holding my hand. . . . I remained with him till morning."

A longer pause. "No wonder the Dean was annoyed that you preferred the sinner to the saint."

Francis hung his head. "I am annoyed with myself. I keep trying to do better. It's strange—when I was a boy I had the conviction that priests were all quite infallibly good . . ."

"And now you are discovering how terribly human we are. Yes, it's unholy that your 'rebellious nature' should fill me with joy, but I find it a wonderful antidote to the monotonous piety I am subjected to.

You are the stray cat, Francis, who comes stalking up the aisle when everyone is yawning their head off at a dull sermon. That's not a bad metaphor—for you *are* in the church even if you don't match up with those who find it all by the well-known rule. I am not flattering myself, when I say that I am probably the only cleric in this diocese who really understands you. It's fortunate I am now your Bishop."

"I know that, your Grace."

"To me," His Lordship meditated, "you are not a failure, but a howling success. You can do with a little cheering up—so I'll risk giving you a swelled head. You've got inquisitiveness and tenderness. You're sensible of the distinction between thinking and doubting. You're not one of our ecclesiastical milliners who must have everything stitched up in neat little packets—convenient for handing out. And quite the nicest thing about you, my dear boy, is this—you haven't got that bumptious security which springs from dogma rather than from faith."

There was a silence. Francis felt his heart melt towards the old man. He kept his eyes cast down. The quiet voice went on.

"Of course, unless we do something about it you're going to get hurt. If we go on with cudgels there'll be too many bloody heads—including your own! Oh, yes, I know—you're not afraid. But I am. You're too valuable to be fed to the lions. That's why I have something to put before you."

Francis raised his head quickly, met His Lordship's wise and affectionate gaze. The Bishop smiled.

"You don't imagine I'd be treating you as a boon companion if I didn't want you to do something for me!"

"Anything . . ." Francis stumbled on the words.

There was a long pause. The Bishop's face was gravely chiselled. "It's a big thing to ask . . . a great change to suggest . . . if it is too much . . . you must tell me. But I think it is the very life for you." Again a pause. "Our Foreign Missions Society has at last been promised a vicariate in China. When all the formalities are completed, and you've had some preparation, will you go there as our first unprincipled adventurer?"

Francis remained completely still, numb with surprise. The walls seemed to crumble about him. The request was so unexpected, so tremendous, it took his breath away. To leave home, his friends, and move into a great unknown void . . . He could not think. But slowly, mysteriously, a strange animation filled his being. He answered haltingly: "Yes . . . I will go."

Rusty Mac leaned over and took Francis' hand in his. His eyes were moist and had a poignant fixity. "I thought you would, dear boy. And I know you'll do me credit. But you'll get no salmon fishing there, I warn you."

864

I V

THE CHINA INCIDENT

1

EARLY IN THE year 1902 a lopsided junk making dilatory passage up the endless yellow reaches of the Ta-Hwang River in the province of Chek-kow, not less than one thousand miles inland from Tientsin, bore a somewhat unusual figurehead in the shape of a medium-sized Catholic priest wearing list slippers and an already wilted topee. With his legs astride the stubby bowsprit and his breviary balanced on one knee, Francis ceased momentarily his vocal combat with the Chinese tongue, in which every syllable seemed to his exhausted larynx to have as many inflections as a chromatic scale, and let his gaze rest on the drifting brown-and-ochre landscape. Fatigued after his tenth night in the three-foot den between-decks which was his cabin, he had, in the hope of a breath of air, forced himself forward into the bows through the packed welter of his fellow passengers: farm labourers, basket and leather workers from Sen-siang, bandits and fishermen, soldiers and merchants on their way to Pai-tan, squatting elbow to elbow, smoking, talking and tending their cooking pots amongst the crates of ducks, the pig-pens and the heaving net which held the solitary but fractious goat.

Although Francis had vowed not to be fastidious the sounds, sights and smells of this final yet interminable stage of his journey had tried him severely. He thanked God and Saint Andrew that tonight, short of further delay, he would at last reach Pai-tan.

Even yet he could not believe himself a part of this new fantastic world, so remote and alien, so incredibly divorced from all that he had known, or hoped to know. He felt as if his life had suddenly been bent, grotesquely, away from its natural form. He checked his sigh. Others lived to a smooth and normal pattern. He was the oddity, the misfit, the little crooked man.

It had been hard to say good-bye to those at home. Ned, mercifully, had passed away three months ago, a blessed ending to that grotesque and pitiful epilogue of life. But Polly . . . he hoped, he prayed he might see Polly in the future. There was consolation in the fact that Judy had been accepted as a shorthand-typist in the Tynecastle Council offices—a post which offered security and good chances of promotion.

As if to steel himself anew he pulled from his inside pocket the final letter relating to his appointment. It was from Father Mealey, now relieved of his parish duties at St. Dominic's to devote himself exclusively to the F.M.S. Administration.

Addressed to him at Liverpool University, where for the past twelve months he had hammered out his language course, the letter ran:

My Dear Francis,

I am overjoyed to be the bearer of glad tidings! We have just received news that Pai-tan, in the Vicariate of Chek-kow, which, as you well know, was presented to us by the A.F.M.S. in December, has now been ratified by the Congregation of Propaganda. It was decided at our meeting held at the F. M. S. in Tynecastle tonight that nothing need delay your departure. At last, at last, I am able to speed you on your glorious mission to the Orient.

So far as I can ascertain Pai-tan is a delightful spot, some miles inland, but on a pleasant river, a thriving city specializing in the manufacture of baskets, with an abundance of cereal, meat, poultry, and tropical fruits. But the supremely important, the blessed fact is that the mission itself, while somewhat remote and for the past twelve months unfortunately without a priest, is in a highly flourishing condition. I'm sorry we have no photographs but I can assure you the layout is most satisfactory: comprising chapel, priest's house and compound. (What an exciting sound that word "compound" has! Don't you remember as boys when we played Indians? Forgive my enthusiasm.)

But *la crème de la crème* lies in our proved statistics. Enclosed you will find the annual report of the late incumbent, Father Lawler, who, a year ago, returned to San Francisco. I don't propose to analyze this for you since you will indubitably con it over, nay, digest it in the wee small hours. Nevertheless I may stress these figures: that although established only three years ago the Pai-tan mission can boast of four hundred communicants and over one thousand baptisms, only a third of which were *in articulo mortis*. Is it not gratifying, Francis? An example of how the dear old grace of God leavens even heathen hearts amidst pagan temple bells.

My dear fellow, I rejoice that this prize is to be yours. And I have no doubt that by your labours in the field you will materially increase the vineyard's crop. I look forward to your first report. I feel that you have at last found your métier and that the little eccentricities of tongue and temper which have been your trouble in the past will no longer be part and parcel of your daily life. Humility, Francis, is the life blood of God's Saints. I pray for you every night.

I will be writing you later. Meanwhile don't neglect your outfit. Get good strong durable soutanes. Short drawers are the best and I advise

866

a body belt. Go to Hanson & Son; they are sound people; and cousins of the organist at the Cathedral.

It is just possible I may be seeing you sooner than you imagine. My new post may make me quite a globe trotter. Wouldn't it be grand if we met in the shady compound of Pai-tan?

Again my congratulations and with every good wish,

I remain, your devoted brother in J. C.

ANSELM MEALEY

Secretary to the Foreign Missions Society,

Diocese of Tynecastle.

Towards sundown a heightening of the commotion in the junk indicated the imminence of their arrival. As the vessel yawed round a bend into a great bight of dirty water, mobbed by a pack of sampans, Francis eagerly scanned the low tiered reaches of the town. It seemed like a great low hive, humming with sound and yellow light, fronted by the reedy mud flats with their flotsam of rafts and boats, backed distantly by mountains, pink and of a pearly translucency.

He had hoped the mission might send a boat for him but the only private wherry was for Mr. Chia, merchant and wealthy resident of Pai-tan, who now emerged for the first time, silent and satin-clad, from the recesses of the junk.

This personage was about thirty-five, but of such composure he looked older, with a supple golden skin and hair so black it seemed moist. He stood with leisurely indifference while the kapong fussed around him. Though his lashes did not once flicker in the direction of the priest, Francis had the odd conviction he was being taken in minutely.

Owing to the preoccupation of the purser, some time elapsed before the new missioner secured passage for himself and his japanned tin trunk. As he stepped down to the sampan he clutched his large silk umbrella, a glorious thing covered in Chisholm tartan which Bishop MacNabb had pressed upon him as a parting gift.

His excitement rose when, nearing the bank, he saw a great press of people on the landing steps. Was it a welcome from his congregation? What a splendid thought for the end of his long, long journey! His heart began to beat almost painfully, with happy expectation. But alas, when he landed he saw he was mistaken. No one greeted him. He had to push his way through the staring yet incurious throng.

At the end of the steps, however, he stopped short. Before him, smiling happily, dressed in neat blue and bearing, as a symbol of their credentials, a brightly coloured picture of the Holy Family, were a Chinese man and woman. As he stood, the two small figures approached him, their smile deepening, overjoyed to see him, bowing and zealously blessing themselves.

Introductions began—less difficult than he had supposed. He asked warmly:

"Who are you?"

"We are Hosannah and Philomena Wang—your beloved catechists, Father."

"From the mission?"

"Yes, yes, Father Lawler made a most excellent mission, Father."

"You will conduct me to the mission?"

"By all means, let us go. But perhaps Father will honour us and come first to our humble abode."

"Thank you. But I am eager to reach the mission."

"Of course. We will go to the mission. We have bearers and a chair for Father."

"You are very kind, but I would prefer to walk."

Still smiling, though less perceptibly, Hosannah turned and in a rapid unintelligible exchange, which had some semblance of an argument, dismissed the sedan chair and the string of porters which he had in tow. Two coolies remained: one shouldered the trunk, the other the umbrella, and the party set off on foot.

Even in the tortuous and dirty streets it was agreeable for Francis to stretch his legs, cramped from confinement in the junk. A quick fervour stirred his blood. Amidst the strangeness he could feel the pulse of humanity. Here were hearts to be won, souls to be saved!

He became aware of one of the Wangs, pausing, to address him.

"There is an agreeable dwelling in the Street of the Netmakers . . . only five taels by the month . . . where Father might wish to spend the night."

Francis looked down in amused surprise. "No, no, Hosannah. Onwards to the mission!"

There was a pause. Philomena coughed. Francis realized that they were standing still. Hosannah politely smiled.

"Here, Father, is the mission."

At first he did not fully understand.

Before them on the riverbank was an acre of deserted earth, sun-scorched, gullied by the rains, encircled by a tramped-down piece of kaolin. At one end stood the remnants of a mud-brick chapel, the roof blown off, one wall collapsed, the others crumbling. Alongside lay a mass of caved-in rubble which might once have been a house. Tall feathery weeds were sprouting there. A single meagre shell remained, amidst the ruins, leaning yet still straw-roofed—the stable.

For three minutes Francis stood in a kind of stupor, then he slowly turned to the Wangs, who were close together, watching him, neat, unfathomable, similar as Siamese twins.

"Why has this taken place?"

"It was a beautiful mission, Father. It cost much—and we made many financial arrangements for its building. But alas, the good Father Lawler placed it near the river. And the Devil sent much wicked rain."

"Then where are the people of the congregation?"

"They are wicked people without belief in the Lord of Heaven." The two spoke more rapidly now, helping each other, gesticulating. "Father must understand how much depends upon his catechists. Alas! Since the good Father Lawler has gone away we have not been paid our lawful stipend of fifteen taels each month. It has been impossible to keep these wicked people properly instructed."

Crushed and devastated, Father Chisholm removed his gaze. This was his mission, these two his sole parishioners. The recollection of the letter within his pocket sent a sudden upsurge of passion over him. He clenched his hands, stood thinking, rigidly.

The Wangs were still talking fluently, trying to persuade him to return to the town. With an effort he rid himself of their importunities, their unctuous presence. It was, at least, a relief to be alone.

Determinedly, he carried his box into the stable. At one time a stable had been good enough for Christ. Gazing round he saw that some straw still littered the earthen floor. Though he had neither food nor water, at least he had a bed. He unpacked his blankets, began to make the place as habitable as he could. Suddenly a gong sounded. He ran out of the stable. Across the decapitated fence, outside the nearest of the temples which stippled the adjacent hill, stood an aged bonze wearing thick stockings and a quilted yellow robe, beating his metal plaque into the short unheeding twilight with measured boredom. The two priests—of Buddha and of Christ—inspected each other in silence; then the old man turned, expressionless, mounted the steps and vanished.

Night fell with the swiftness of a blow. Francis knelt down in the darkness of the devastated compound and lifted his eyes to the dawning constellations. He prayed with fierce, with terrible intensity. Dear God, you wish me to begin from nothing. This is the answer to my vanity, my stubborn human arrogance. It's better so! I'll work, I'll fight for you. I'll never give up . . . never . . . never!

Back in the stable, trying to rest, while the shrill ping of mosquitoes and the crack of flying beetles split the sweltering air, he forced himself to smile. He did not feel heroic, but a dreadful fool. Saint Teresa had likened life to a night in a hotel. This one they had sent him to was not the Ritz!

Morning came at last. He rose. Taking his chalice from its cedar box, he made an altar of his trunk and offered up his mass, kneeling on the stable floor. He felt refreshed, happy and strong. The arrival of Hosannah Wang failed to discompose him.

"Father should have let me serve his mass. That is always included in our pay. And now—shall we find a room in the Street of the Netmakers?"

Francis reflected. Though he had stubbornly made up his mind to live here till the situation cleared, it was true that he must find a more fitting centre for his ministrations. He said: "Let us go there now."

The streets were already thronged. Dogs raced between their legs, pigs were rooting for garbage in the gutter. Children followed them, jeering and shouting. Beggars wailed with importunate palms. An old man setting out his wares, in the Street of the Lanternmakers, spat sullenly across the foreign devil's feet. Outside the yamen of justice, a peripatetic barber stood twanging his long tongs. There were many poor, many crippled and some, blinded by smallpox, who tapped their way forward with a long bamboo and a queer high whistle.

It was an upper room Wang brought him to, clumsily partitioned with paper and bamboo, but sufficient for any service he would conduct. From his small store of money he paid a month's rent to the shopkeeper, named Hung, and began to set out his crucifix and solitary altar cloth. His lack of vestments, of altar furnishings, fretted him. Led to expect a full equipment at the "flourishing" mission, he had brought little. But his standard, at least, was planted.

Wang had preceded him to the shop below and as he turned to descend he observed Hung take two of the silver taels which he had given him and pass them, with a bow, to Wang. Though he had early guessed the worth of Father Lawler's legacy Francis was conscious of a sudden mounting of his blood. Outside, in the street, he turned quietly to Wang.

"I regret, Hosannah, I cannot pay your stipend of fifteen taels a month."

"Father Lawler could pay. Why cannot the Father pay?"

"I am poor, Hosannah. Just as poor as was my Master."

"How much will the Father pay?"

"Nothing, Hosannah! Even as I am paid nothing. It is the good Lord of Heaven who will reward us!"

Wang's smile did not falter. "Perhaps Hosannah and Philomena must go where they are appreciated. At Sen-siang the Methodys pay sixteen taels for highly respected catechists. But doubtless the good Father will change his mind. There is much animosity in Pai-tan. The people consider the *feng shua* of the city—the Laws of Wind and Order—destroyed by the intrusion of the missionary."

He waited for the priest's reply. But Francis did not speak. There was a strained pause. Then Wang bowed politely and departed.

A coldness settled upon Francis as he watched the other disappear. Had he done right in alienating the friendly Wangs? The answer was that the Wangs were not his friends, but lick-spittle opportunists who believed in the Christian God because of Christian money. And yet . . .

his one contact with the community was severed. He had a sudden, frightening sense of being alone.

As the days passed this horrible loneliness increased, coupled with a paralyzing impotence. Lawler, his predecessor, had built upon sand. Incompetent, credulous, and supplied with ample funds, he had rushed about, giving money and taking names, baptizing promiscuously, acquiring a string of "rice-Christians," filling long reports, unconsciously the victim of a hundred subtle squeezes, sanguine, bombastic, gloriously triumphant. He had not even scratched the surface. Of his work nothing remained except perhaps—in the city's official circles—a lingering contempt for such lamentable foreign folly.

Beyond a small sum set for his living expenses, and a five-pound note pressed into his hand by Polly on his departure, Francis had no money whatsoever. He had been warned, too, on the futility of requesting grants from the new society at home. Sickened by Lawler's example, he rejoiced in his poverty. He swore, with a feverish intensity, that he would not hire his congregation. What must be done would be done with God's help and his own two hands.

Yet so far he had done nothing. He hung a sign outside his makeshift chapel; it made no difference: none appeared to hear his mass. The Wangs had spread a wide report that he was destitute, with nothing to distribute but bitter words.

He attempted an open-air meeting outside the courts of justice. He was laughed at, then ignored. His failure humiliated him. A Chinese laundryman preaching Confucianism in pigeon-English in the streets of Liverpool would have met with more success. Wildly he fought that insidious demon, the inner whisper of his own incompetence.

He prayed, he prayed most desperately. He ardently believed in the efficacy of prayer. "Oh God, you've helped me in the past. Help me now, for God's sake, please."

He had hours of raging fury. Why had they sent him, with plausible assurances, to this outlandish hole? The task was beyond any man, beyond God Himself! Cut from all communications, buried in the hinterland, with the nearest missioner, Father Thibodeau, at Sen-siang, four hundred miles away, the place was quite untenable.

Fostered by the Wangs, the popular hostility towards him increased. He was used to the jeers of the children. Now, on his passage through the town, a crowd of young coolies followed, throwing out insults. When he stopped a member of the gang would advance and perform his natural functions in the vicinity. One night, as he returned to the stable, a stone sailed out of the darkness and struck him on the brow.

All Francis' combativeness rose hotly in response. As he bandaged his broken head, his own wound gave him a wild idea, making him pause, rigid and intent. Yes . . . he must . . . he must get closer to the people

. . . and this . . . no matter how primitive . . . this new endeavour might help him to that end.

Next morning, for two extra taels a month, he rented the lower back room of the shop from Hung and opened a public dispensary. He was no expert—God knew. But he had his St. John's certificate, and his long acquaintance with Dr. Tulloch had grounded him soundly in hygiene.

At first no one ventured near him; and he sweated with despair. But gradually, drawn by curiosity, one or two came in. There was always sickness in the city and the methods of the native doctors were barbaric. He had some success. He exacted nothing in money or devotion. Slowly his clientèle grew. He wrote urgently to Dr. Tulloch, enclosing Polly's five pounds, clamouring for an additional supply of dressings, bandages, and simple drugs. While the chapel remained empty the dispensary was often full.

At night, he brooded frantically amongst the ruins of the mission. He could never rebuild on that eroded site. And he gazed across the way in fierce desire at the pleasant Hill of Brilliant Green Jade where, above the scattered temples, a lovely slope extended, sheltered by a grove of cedars. What a noble situation for a monument to God!

The owner of this property, a civil judge named Pao, member of that inner intermarried community of merchants and magistrates who controlled the city's affairs, was rarely to be seen. But on most afternoons his cousin, a tall dignified mandarin of forty, who managed the estate for Mr. Pao, came to inspect and to pay the labourers who worked the clay-pits in the cedar grove.

Worn by weeks of solitude, desolate and persecuted, Francis was undoubtedly a little mad. He had nothing; he was nothing. Yet one day, on an impulse, he stopped the tall mandarin as he crossed the road towards his chair. He did not understand the impropriety of this direct approach. In fact he knew little of what he did: he had not been eating properly, and was lightheaded from a touch of fever.

"I have often admired this beautiful property which you so wisely administer."

Taken wholly by surprise, Mr. Pao's cousin formally viewed the short alien figure with its burning eyes, and the soiled bandage on its forehead. In frigid politeness he bore with the priest's continued assaults upon the syntax, briefly deprecated himself, his family, his miserable possessions, remarked on the weather, the crops, and the difficulty the city had experienced last year in buying off the Wai-Chu bandits; then pointedly opened the door of his chair. When Francis, with swimming head, strove to return the conversation to the Green Jade land, he smiled coldly.

"The Green Jade property is a pearl without price, in extent more than sixty mous . . . shade, water, pasture . . . in addition a rich and extraordinary clay-pit for the purpose of tiles, pottery and bricks. Mr. Pao has no desire to sell. Already, for the estate, he has refused . . . fifteen thousand silver dollars."

At the price, ten times greater than his most fearful estimate, Francis' legs shook. The fever left him, he suddenly felt weak and giddy, ashamed at the absurdity into which his dreams had led him. With splitting head, he thanked Mr. Pao's cousin, muttered a confused apology.

Observing the priest's disappointed sadness, the lean, middle-aged, cultured Chinese allowed a flicker of disdain to escape his watchful secrecy.

"Why does the Shang-Foo come here? Are there no wicked men to regenerate in his own land? For we are not wicked people. We have our own religion. Our own gods are older than his. The other Shang-Foo made many Christians by pouring water from a little bottle upon dying men and singing 'Ya . . . ya!' Also, by giving food and clothing, to many more who would sing any tune to have their skins covered and their bellies full. Does the Shang-Foo wish to do this also?"

Francis gazed at the other in silence. His thin face had a worn pallor, there were deep shadows beneath his eyes. He said quietly: "Do you think that is my wish?"

There was a strange pause. All at once, Mr. Pao's cousin dropped his eyes.

"Forgive me," he said, in a low tone. "I did not understand. You are a good man." A vague friendliness tinctured his compunction. "I regret that my cousin's land is not available. Perhaps in some other manner I may assist you?"

Mr. Pao's cousin waited with a new courtesy, as if anxious to make amends. Francis thought for a moment, then asked heavily: "Tell me, since we are being honest. . . . Are there no true Christians here?"

Mr. Pao's cousin answered slowly: "Perhaps. But I should not seek them in Pai-tan." He paused. "I have heard, however, of a village in the Kwang Mountains." He made a vague gesture towards the distant peaks. "A village Christian for many years . . . but it is far away, many many li from here."

A gleam of light shot into the haggard gloom of Francis' mind.

"That interests me deeply. Can you give me further information?"

The other shook his head regretfully. "It is a small place on the uplands—almost unknown. My cousin only learned of it from his trade in sheepskins."

Francis' eagerness sustained him. "Could you procure directions for me . . . perhaps a map?"

Mr. Pao's cousin reflected, then nodded gravely. "It should be possible. I shall ask Mr. Pao. Moreover I shall be careful to inform him that you have spoken with me in a most honourable fashion."

He bowed and went away.

Overwhelmed with this wholly unexpected hope, Francis returned to the ruined compound where, with some blankets, a water-skin and the few utensils purchased in the town, he had made his primitive encampment. As he prepared himself a simple meal of rice, his hands trembled, as from shock. A Christian village! He must find it—at all costs. It was his first sense of guidance, of divine inspiration, in all these weary, fruitless months.

As he sat tensely thinking in the dusk he was disturbed by a hoarse barking of crows, fighting and tearing at some carrion by the water's edge. He went over at length, to drive them off. And there, as the great ugly birds flapped and squawked at him, he saw their prey to be the body of a newly born female child.

Shuddering, he took up the infant's torn body from the river, saw it to be asphyxiated, thrown in and drowned. He wrapped the little thing in linen, buried it in a corner of the compound. And as he prayed he thought: yes, despite my doubts, there is need for me, in this strange land, after all.

II

Two weeks later, when the early summer burgeoned, he was ready. Placing a painted notice of temporary closure on his premises in Netmaker Street, he strapped a pack of blankets and food upon his back, took up his umbrella and set off briskly on foot.

The map given him by Mr. Pao's cousin was beautifully executed, with wind-belching dragons in the corners and a wealth of topographic detail as far as the mountains. Beyond it was sketchy, with little drawings of animals instead of place names. But from their conversations and his own sense of direction Francis had in his head a fair notion of his route. He set his face towards the Kwang Gap.

For two days the journey lay through easy country, the green wet ricefields giving place to woods of spruce, where the fallen needles made a soft resilient carpet for his feet. Immediately below the Kwangs he traversed a sheltered valley aflame with wild rhododendrons, and later that same dreamy afternoon, a glade of flowering apricots whose perfume prickled the nostrils like the fume of sparkling wine. Then he began the steep ascent of the ravine.

It grew colder with every step up the narrow stony track. At night he folded himself under the shelter of a rock, hearing the whistle of the wind, the thunder of snow-water in the gorge. In the daytime, the cold blazing whiteness of the higher peaks burned his eyes. The thin iced air was painful to his lungs.

On the fifth day he crossed the summit of the ridge, a frozen wilderness

874

of glacier and rock, and thankfully descended the other side. The pass led him to a wide plateau, beneath the snowline, green with verdure, melting into softly rounded hills. These were the grasslands of which Mr. Pao's cousin had spoken.

Thus far the sheer mountains had defined his twisted course. Now he must rely on Providence, a compass and his good Scots sense. He struck out directly towards the west. The country was like the uplands of his home. He came on great herds of stoic grazing goats and mountain sheep that streamed off wildly at his approach. He caught the fleeting image of a gazelle. From the bunch-grass of a vast dun marsh thousands of nesting ducks rose screaming, darkening the sky. Since his food was running low, he filled his satchel gratefully with the warm eggs.

It was trackless, treeless plain: he began to despair of stumbling on the village. But early on the ninth day when he felt he must soon turn back, he sighted a shepherd's hut, the first sign of habitation since he'd left the southern slopes. He hastened eagerly towards it. The door was sealed with mud, there was no one inside. But as he swung round, his eyes sharp with disappointment, he saw a boy approaching over the hill behind his flock.

The young shepherd was about seventeen, small and wiry, like his sheep, with a cheerful and intelligent face now caught between wonderment and laughter. He wore short sheepskin trousers and a woollen cape. Round his neck was a small bronze Yuan cross, wafer-thin with age and roughly scratched with the symbol of a dove. Father Chisholm gazed from the boy's open face to the antique cross in silence. At last he found his voice and greeted him, asking if he were from the Liu village.

The lad smiled. "I am from the Christian village. I am Liu-Ta. My father is the village priest." He added, not to be thought boasting, "One of the village priests!"

Again, there was a silence. Father Chisholm thought better of questioning the boy further. He said: "I have come a long distance, and I too am a priest. I should be grateful if you would take me to your home."

The village lay in an undulating valley five li farther to the westward, a cluster of some thirty houses, tucked away in this fold of the uplands, surrounded by little stone-walled fields of grain. Prominent, upon a central hillock, behind a queer conical mound of stones shaded by a ginkgo tree, was a small stone church.

As he entered the village the entire community immediately surrounded him, men, women, children and dogs, all crowding round in curiosity and excited welcome, pulling at his sleeves, touching his boots, examining his umbrella with cries of admiration, while Ta threw off a rapid explanation in a dialect he could not understand. There were perhaps sixty persons in the throng, primitive and healthy, with naïve, friendly eyes and features that bore the imprint of their common family. Presently, with a proprietary smile, Ta brought forward his father Liu-Chi, a short and sturdy man of fifty with a small grey beard, simple and dignified in his manner.

Speaking slowly, to make himself understood, Liu-Chi said: "We welcome you with joy, Father. Come to my house and rest a little before prayer."

He led the way to the largest house, built on a stone foundation next the church, and showed Father Chisholm, with courteous urbanity, into a low cool room. At the end of the room stood a mahogany spinet and a Portuguese wheel clock. Bewildered, lost in wonder, Francis stared at the clock. The brass dial was engraved: *Lisbon* 1632.

He had no time for closer inspection, Liu-Chi was addressing him again. "Is it your wish to offer mass, Father? Or shall I?"

As in a dream Father Chisholm nodded his head towards the other. Something within him answered: "You . . . please!" He was groping in a great confusion. He knew he could not rudely break this mystery with speech. He must penetrate it graciously, in patience, with his eyes.

Half an hour later they were all within the church. Though small it had been built with taste in a style that showed the Moorish influence on the Renaissance. There were three simple arcades, beautifully fluted. The doorway and the windows were supported by flat pilasters. On the walls, partly incomplete, free mosaics had been traced.

He sat in the front row of an attentive congregation. Every one had ceremonially washed his hands before entering. Most of the men and a few of the women wore praying caps upon their heads. Suddenly a tongueless bell was struck and Liu-Chi approached the altar, wearing a faded yellow alb and supported by two young men. Turning, he bowed ceremoniously to Father Chisholm and the congregation. Then the service began.

Father Chisholm watched, kneeling erect, spellbound, like a man beholding the slow enactment of a dream. He saw now that the ceremony was a strange survival, a touching relic of the mass. Liu-Chi must know no Latin, for he prayed in Chinese. First came the confiteor, then the creed. When he ascended the altar and opened the parchment missal on its wooden rest, Francis clearly heard a portion of the gospel solemnly intoned in the native tongue. An original translation. . . . He drew a quick breath of awe.

The whole congregation advanced to take communion. Even children at the breast were carried to the altar steps. Liu-Chi descended, bearing a chalice of rice wine. Moistening his forefinger he placed a drop upon the lips of each.

Before leaving the church, the congregation gathered at the Statue of the Saviour, placing lighted joss-sticks on the heavy candelabrum before the feet. Then each person made three prostrations and reverently withdrew.

Father Chisholm remained behind, his eyes moist, his heart wrung by the simple childish piety—the same piety, the same simplicity he had so often witnessed in peasant Spain. Of course this ceremony was not valid —he smiled faintly, visualizing Father Tarrant's horror at the spectacle —but he had no doubt it was pleasing to God Almighty none the less.

Liu-Chi was waiting outside to conduct him to the house. There a meal awaited them. Famished, Father Chisholm did full justice to the stew of mountain mutton—little savoury balls floating in cabbage soup—and the strange dish of rice and wild honey which followed. He had never tasted such a delicious sweet in all his life.

When they had both finished, he began tactfully to question Liu-Chi. He would have bitten out his tongue rather than give offence. The gentle old man answered trustingly. His beliefs were Christian, quite childlike and curiously mingled with the traditions of *Táo-tê*. Perhaps, thought Father Chisholm, with an inward smile, a touch of Nestorianism thrown in for value. . . .

Chi explained that the faith had been handed down from father to son through many generations. The village was not dramatically isolated from the world. But it was sufficiently remote; and so small, so integrated in its family life, that strangers rarely troubled it. They were one great family. Existence was purely pastoral and self-supporting. They had grain and mutton in plenty even through the hardest times; cheese, which they sealed in the stomach of a sheep, and two kinds of butter, red and black, both made from beans and named *chiang*. For clothing they had home-carded wool, sheepskins for extra warmth. They beat a special parchment from the skins that was much prized in Pekin. There were many wild ponies on the uplands. Rarely, a member of the family went out with a ponyload of vellum.

In the little tribe there were three Fathers, each chosen for this honoured position while still in infancy. For certain religious offices a fee of rice was paid. They had a special devotion to the Three Precious Ones —the Trinity. Within living memory they had never seen an ordained priest.

Father Chisholm had listened with rapt attention and now he put the question uppermost in his mind.

"You have not told me how it first began!"

Liu-Chi looked at his visitor with final appraisal. Then with a faint reassured smile he got up and went into the adjoining room. When he returned he bore under his arm a sheepskin-covered bundle. He handed it over silently, watched Father Chisholm open it, then, as the priest's absorption became apparent, silently withdrew.

It was the journal of Father Ribiero, written in Portuguese, brown, stained and tattered, but mostly legible. From his knowledge of Spanish, Francis was able slowly to decipher it. The fascinating interest of the document made the labour as nothing. It held him riveted. He remained motionless, except for the slow movement of his hand turning, at intervals, a heavy page. Time flew back three hundred years: the old stopped clock took up its measured tick.

Manoel Ribiero was a missioner of Lisbon who came to Pekin in 1625. Francis saw the Portuguese vividly before him: a young man of twenty-nine, spare, olive-skinned, a little fiery, his swart eyes ardent yet humble. In Pekin the young missionary had been fortunate in his friendship with Father Adam Schall, the great German Jesuit, missionary, courtier, astronomer, trusted friend and canon founder extraordinary to the Emperor Tchoun-Tchin. For several years Father Ribiero shared a little of the glory of this astounding man who moved untouched through the seething intrigues of the Courts of Heaven, advancing the Christian Faith, even in the celestial harem, confounding virulent hatreds with his accurate predictions of comets and eclipses, compiling a new calendar, winning friendship and illustrious titles for himself and all his ancestors.

Then the Portuguese had pressed to be sent on a distant mission to the Royal Court of Tartary. Adam Schall had granted his request. A caravan was sumptuously equipped and formidably armed. It started from Pekin on the Feast of the Assumption, 1629.

But the caravan had failed to reach the Tartar Royal Courts. Ambushed by a horde of barbarians on the northern slopes of the Kwang Mountains the formidable defenders dropped their arms and fled. The valuable caravan was plundered. Father Ribiero escaped, desperately wounded by flint arrows, with only his personal belongings and the least of his ecclesiastical equipment. Benighted in the snow, he thought his last hour had come and offered himself, bleeding, to God. But the cold froze his wounds. He dragged himself next morning to a shepherd's hut, where he lay for six months neither dead nor alive. Meanwhile an authentic report reached Pekin that Father Ribiero was massacred. No expedition was sent out to search for him.

When the Portuguese decided he might live, he made plans to return to Adam Schall. But time went on and he still remained. In these wide grasslands, he gained a new sense of values, a new habit of contemplation. Besides, he was three thousand li from Pekin, a forbidding distance, even to his intrepid spirit. Quietly he took his decision. He collected the handful of shepherds into one small settlement. He built a church. He became friend and pastor—not to the King of Tartary but to this humble little flock.

With a strange sigh Francis put down the journal. In the failing light he sat thinking, thinking, and seeing many things. Then he rose and went out to the great mound of stones beside the church. Kneeling, he prayed at Father Ribiero's tomb.

He remained at the Liu village for a week. Persuasively, in a manner to hurt no one, he suggested a ratification of all baptisms and marriages. He said mass. Gently he dropped a hint, now here, now there, suggesting an emendation of certain practices. It would take a long time to regularize the village to hidebound orthodoxy: months—no, years. What did that matter? He was content to go slowly. The little community was as clean and sound as a good apple.

He spoke to them of many things. In the evenings a fire would be lit outside Liu-Chi's house, and when they had all seated themselves about it, he would rest himself on the doorstep and talk to the silent, flame-lit circle. Best of all they liked to hear of the presence of their own religion in the great outside world. He drew no captious differences. It enthralled them when he spoke of the churches of Europe, the great cathedrals, the thousands of worshippers flocking to St. Peter's, great kings and princes, statesmen and nobles, all prostrating themselves before the Lord of Heaven, that same Lord of Heaven whom they worshipped here, their master too, their friend. This sense of unity, hitherto but dimly surmised, gave them a joyful pride.

As the intent faces, flickering with light and shadow, gazed up at him in happy wonderment, he felt Father Ribiero at his elbow smiling a little, darkly, not displeased with him. At such moments he had a terrible impulse to throw up Pai-tan and devote himself entirely to these simple people. How happy he could be here! How lovingly he would tend and polish this jewel he had found so unexpectedly in the wilderness! But no, the village was too small, and too remote. He could never make it a centre for true missionary work. Resolutely, he put the temptation away from him.

The boy Ta had become his constant follower. Now he no longer called him Ta but Joseph, for that was the name the youngster had demanded at his conditional baptism. Fortified by the new name, he had begged permission to serve Father Chisholm's mass; and though he naturally knew not a shred of Latin, the priest had smilingly consented. On the eve of his departure Father Chisholm was seated at the doorway of the house when Joseph appeared, his usually cheerful features set and woebegone, the first arrival for the final lecture. Studying the boy the priest had an intuition of his regret, followed by a sudden happy thought.

"Joseph! Would it please you to come with me—if your father would permit it? There are many things you might do to help me."

The boy jumped up with a cry of joy, fell before the priest and kissed his hand.

"Master, I have waited for you to ask me. My father is willing. I will serve you with all my heart."

"There may be many rough roads, Joseph."

"We shall travel them together, Master."

Father Chisholm raised the young man to his feet. He was moved and pleased. He knew he had done a wise thing.

Next morning the preparations for departure were completed.

Scrubbed and smiling, Joseph stood with the bundles beside the two shaggy mountain ponies he had rounded up at dawn. A small group of younger boys surrounded him, already he was aweing his companions with the wonders of the world. In the church Father Chisholm was finishing his thanksgiving. As he rose, Liu-Chi beckoned him to the crypt-like sanctuary. From a cedar chest he drew an embroidered cope, an exquisite thing, stiff with gold. In parts the satin had rubbed paper-thin but the vestment was intact, usable and priceless. The old man smiled at the expression on Francis' face.

"This poor thing pleases you?"

"It is beautiful."

"Take it. It is yours!"

No protestations could prevent Liu-Chi from making the superb gift. It was folded, wrapped in clean flax-cloth, and placed in Joseph's pack.

At last Francis had to bid them all farewell. He blessed them, gave repeated assurances that he would return within six months. It would be easier next time, mounted, and with Joseph as his guide. Then the two departed, together, their ponies nodding neck-to-neck, climbing to the uplands. The eyes of the little village followed them with affection.

With Joseph beside him, Father Chisholm set a good round pace. He felt his faith restored, gloriously fortified. His breast throbbed with fresh hope.

III

The summer which followed their return to Pai-tan had passed. And now the cold season fell upon the land. With Joseph's help he made the stable snug, patching the cracks with fresh mud and kaolin. Two wooden bunks now buttressed the weakest wall and a flat iron brazier made a hearth upon the beaten earth floor. Joseph, whose appetite was healthy, had already acquired an interesting collection of cooking pots. The boy, now less angelic, improved upon acquaintance: he was a great prattler, loved to be praised and could be wilful at times, with a naive facility for abstracting ripe musk melons from the market garden down the way.

Francis was still determined not to quit their lowly shelter until he saw his course ahead. Gradually a few timid souls were creeping to his chapel room in Netmaker Street, the first an old woman, ragged and ashamed, furtively pulling her beads from the sacking which served her for a coat, looking as though a single word would send her scurrying. Firmly, he restrained himself, pretended not to notice her. Next morning she returned with her daughter.

The pitiful sparsity of his followers did not discourage him. His resolve neither to cajole nor to buy his converts was tempered, like fine steel.

His dispensary was going with a swing. Apparently his absence from the little clinic had been regretted. On his return he found a nondescript assembly awaiting him outside Hung's premises. With practice, his judgement, and indeed his skill, increased. All sorts of conditions came his way: skin diseases, colics and coughs, enteritis, dreadful suppurations of the eyes and ears; and most were the result of dirt and overcrowding. It was amazing what cleanliness and a simple bitter tonic did for them. A grain of potassium permanganate was worth its weight in gold.

When his meagre supplies threatened to run out, an answer came to his supplication to Dr. Tulloch—a big nailed-up box of lint, wool and gauze, iodine and antiseptics, castor oil and chlorodyne, with a scrawled torn-off prescription sheet crumpled at the foot.

"Your Holiness: I thought I was the one to go doctoring in the tropics! And where is your degree? Never mind—cure what you can and kill what you can't. Here is a little bag of tricks to help you."

It was a neatly packed first-aid case of lancet, scissors, and forceps. A postscript added: "For your information, I am reporting you to the B.M.A., the Pope and Chung-lung-soo."

Francis smiled at the irrepressible facetiousness. But his throat was tight with gratitude. With this stimulation of his own endeavour and the comfort of Joseph's companionship, he felt a new and thrilling exaltation. He had never worked harder, nor slept sounder, in his life.

But one night in November his sleep was light and troubled and after midnight he suddenly awoke. It was piercing cold. In the still darkness he could hear Joseph's deep and peaceful breathing. He lay for a moment trying to reason away his vague distress. But he could not. He got up, cautiously, so that he might not wake the sleeping boy, and slipped out of the stable into the compound. The frozen night stabbed him: the air was razor-edged with cold, each breath a cutting pain. There were no stars, but from the frosted snow came a strange and luminous whiteness. The silence seemed to reach a hundred miles. It was terrifying.

Suddenly, through that stillness, he fancied he heard a faint and uncertain cry. He knew he was mistaken, listened, and heard no more. But as he turned to re-enter the stable the sound was repeated, like the feeble squawking of a dying bird. He stood indecisively, then slowly crunched his way across the crusted snow, towards the sound.

Outside the compound, fifty paces down the path, he stumbled on a stiff dark shadow: the prostrate form of a woman, her face sunk into the snow, starkly frozen. She was quite dead, but under her, in the garments about her bosom, he saw the feeble writhings of a child.

He stooped and lifted up the tiny thing, cold as a fish, but soft. His heart was beating like a drum. He ran back, slipping, almost falling, to the stable, calling in a loud voice to Joseph.

When the brazier was blazing with fresh wood, throwing out light and heat, the priest and his servant bent over the child. It was not more than twelve months old. Its eyes were dark and wild, unbelieving towards the warmth of the fire. From time to time it whimpered.

"It is hungry," Joseph said in a wise tone.

They warmed some milk and poured it into an altar vial. Father Chisholm then tore a strip of clean linen and coaxed it, like a wick, into the flask's narrow neck. The child sucked greedily. In five minutes the milk was finished and the child asleep. The priest wrapped it in a blanket from his own bed.

He was deeply moved. The strangeness of his premonition, the simplicity of the coming of the little thing, into the stable, out of the cold nothingness, was like a sign from God. There was nothing upon the mother's body to tell who she might be, but her features, worn by hardship and poverty, had a thin, fine Tartar cast. A band of nomads had passed through the daybefore: perhaps she had been overcome by cold, had fallen behind to die. He sought in his mind for a name for the child. It was the feast day of Saint Anna. Yes, he would name her Anna.

"Tomorrow, Joseph, we shall find a woman to take care of this gift from heaven."

Joseph shrugged. "Master, you cannot give away a female child."

"I shall not give the child away," Father Chisholm said sternly.

His purpose was already clear and fixed. This babe, sent to him by God, would be his first foundling—yes, the foundation of his children's home . . . that dream he had cherished since his arrival in Pai-tan. He would need help of course, the Sisters must one day come—it was all a long way off. But, seated on the earth floor, by the dark red embers, gazing upon the sleeping infant, he felt it was a pledge from heaven that he would, in the end, succeed.

It was Joseph, the prize gossip, who first told Father Chisholm that Mr. Chia's son was sick. The cold season was late in breaking, the Kwang Mountains were still deep in snow; and the cheerful Joseph blew upon his nipped fingers as he chattered away after mass, assisting the priest to put away his vestments. " *Tch!* My hand is as useless as that of the little Chia-Yu."

Chia-Yu had scratched his thumb upon no one knew what; but in consequence, his five elements had been disturbed and the lower humours had gained ascendancy, flowing entirely into one arm, distending it, leaving the boy's body burning and wasted. The three highest physicians of the city were in attendance and the most costly remedies had been applied. Now a messenger had been despatched to Sen-siang for the *elixir vitae:* a priceless extract of frog's eyes, obtained only in the circle of the Dragon's moon.

"He will recover," Joseph concluded, showing his white teeth in a sanguine smile. "This *hao kao* never fails . . . which is important for Mr. Chia, since Yu is his only son."

Four days later, at the same hour, two closed chairs, one of which was empty, drew up outside the chapel shop in the Street of the Netmakers, and a moment later the tall figure of Mr. Pao's cousin, wrapped in a cotton-padded tunic, gravely confronted Father Chisholm. He apologized for his unseemly intrusion. He asked the priest to accompany him to Mr. Chia's house.

Stunned by the implication of the invitation, Francis hesitated. Close relationship, through business and marriage ties, existed between the Paos and the Chias, both were highly influential families. Since his return from the Liu village he had not infrequently encountered the lean, aloof, and pleasantly cynical cousin of Mr. Pao, who was, indeed, also first cousin to Mr. Chia. He had some evidence of the tall mandarin's regard. But this abrupt call, this sponsorship, was different. As he turned silently to get his hat and coat, he felt a sudden hollow fear.

The Chia house was very quiet, the trellised verandahs empty, the fish pond brittle with a film of ice. Their steps rang softly, but with a momentous air, upon the paved, deserted courtyards. Two flanking jasmine trees, swathed in sacking, lolled like sleeping giants, against the tented, red-gold gateway. From the women's quarters across the terraces came the strangled sound of weeping.

It was darkish in the sick-chamber, where Chia-Yu lay upon a heated *kang,* watched by the three bearded physicians in long full robes seated upon fresh rush matting. From time to time one of the physicians bent forward and placed a charcoal lump beneath the boxlike *kang.* In the corner of the room, a Taoist priest in a slate-coloured robe was mumbling, exorcising, to the accompaniment of flutes behind the bamboo partition.

Yu had been a pretty child of six, with soft cream colouring and sloe-black eyes, reared in the strictest traditions of parental respect, idolized, yet unspoiled. Now, consumed by remorseless fever and the terrible novelty of pain, he was stretched upon his back, his bones sticking through his skin, his dry lips twisting, his gaze upon the ceiling, motionless. His right arm, livid, swollen out of recognition, was encased in a horrible plaster of dirt mixed with little printed paper scraps.

When Mr. Pao's cousin entered with Father Chisholm there was a tiny stillness; then the Taoist mumbling was resumed, while the three physicians, more strictly immobilized, maintained their vigil by the *kang.*

Bent over the unconscious child, his hand upon the burning brow, Father Chisholm knew the full import of that limpid and passionless restraint. His present troubles would be as nothing to the persecution which must follow a futile intervention. But the desperate sickness of the boy and this noxious pretence of treatment whipped his blood. He began, quickly yet gently, to remove from the infected arm the *hao kao*, that filthy dressing he had so often met with in his little dispensary.

At last the arm was free, washed in warm water. It floated almost, a bladder of corruption, with a shiny greenish skin. Though now his heart was thudding in his side Francis went on steadfastly, drew from his pocket the little leather case which Tulloch had given him, took from that case the single lancet. He knew his inexperience. He knew also that if he did not incise the arm the child, already moribund, would die. He felt every unwatching eye upon him, sensed the terrible anxiety, the growing doubt gripping Mr. Pao's cousin as he stood motionless behind him. He made an ejaculation to Saint Andrew. He steeled himself to cut, to cut deep, deep and long.

A great gush of putrid matter came heaving through the wound, flowing and bubbling into the earthenware bowl beneath. The stench was dreadful, evil. In all his life Francis had never savoured anything so gratefully. As he pressed, with both his hands, on either side of the wound, encouraging the exudation, seeing the limb collapse to half its size, a great relief surged through him, leaving him weak.

When, at last, he straightened up, having packed the wound with clean wet linen, he heard himself murmur, foolishly, in English: "I think he'll do now, with a little luck!" It was old Dr. Tulloch's famous phrase: it demonstrated the tension of his nerves. Yet on his way out he strove to maintain an attitude of cheerful unconcern, declaring to the completely silent cousin of Mr. Pao, who accompanied him to his chair: "Give him nourishing soup if he wakes up. And no more *hao kao*. I will come tomorrow."

On the next day little Yu was greatly better. His fever was almost gone, he had slept naturally and drunk several cups of chicken broth. Without the miracle of the shining lancet he would almost certainly have been dead.

"Continue to nourish him." Father Chisholm genuinely smiled as he took his departure. "I shall call again tomorrow!"

"Thank you." Mr. Pao's cousin cleared his throat. "It is not necessary." There was an awkward pause. "We are deeply grateful. Mr. Chia has been prostrate with grief. Now that his son is recovering, he also is recovering. Soon he may be able to present himself in public!" The mandarin bowed, hands discreetly in his sleeves, and was gone.

Father Chisholm strode down the street—he had angrily refused the chair—fighting a dark and bitter indignation. This was gratitude. To be thrown out, without a word, when he had saved the child's life, at the risk, perhaps, of his own . . . From first to last he had not even seen the wretched Mr. Chia, who, even on the junk, that day of his arrival, had not deigned to glance at him. He clenched his fists, fighting his familiar demon: "O God, let me be calm! Don't let this cursed sin of anger master me again. Let me be meek and patient of heart. Give me humility, dear Lord. After all it was Thy merciful goodness, Thy divine providence, which saved the little boy. Do with me what Thou wilt, dear Lord. You see, I am resigned. But, O God!"—with sudden heat: "You must admit it was such damned ingratitude after all!"

During the next few days Francis rigorously shunned the merchant's quarter of the city. More than his pride had been hurt. He listened in silence while Joseph gossiped of the remarkable progress of little Yu, of the largesse distributed by Mr. Chia to the wise physicians, the donation to the Temple of Lao-tzŭ, for the exorcising of the demon which had troubled his beloved son. "Is it not truly remarkable, dear Father, how many sources have benefited by the mandarin's noble generosity?"

"Truly remarkable," said Father Chisholm dryly, but wincing.

A week later, when about to close his dispensary after a stale and profitless afternoon, he suddenly observed, across the flask of permanganate he had been mixing, the discreet apparition of Mr. Chia.

He started hotly, but said nothing. The merchant wore his finest clothes: a rich black satin robe with yellow jacket, embroidered velvet boots in one of which was thrust the ceremonial fan, a fine flat satin cap, and an expression both formal and dignified. His too-long fingernails were protected by gold metal cases. He had an air of culture and intelligence, his manners expressed perfect breeding. There was a gentle, enlightened melancholy on his brow.

"I have come," he said.

"Indeed!" Francis' tone was not encouraging. He went on stirring with his glass rod, mixing the mauve solution.

"There have been many matters to attend to, much business to settle. But now,"—a resigned bow,—"I am here."

"Why?" Shortly, from Francis.

Mr. Chia's face indicated mild surprise. "Naturally . . . to become a Christian."

There was a moment of dead silence—a moment which, traditionally, should have marked the climax of these meagre toiling months, the thrilling first fruits of the missionary's achievement: here, the leading savage, bowing the head for baptism. But there was little exultation in Father Chisholm's face. He chewed his lip crossly, then he said slowly: "Do you believe?"

"No!" Sadly.

"Are you prepared to be instructed?"

"I have not time to be instructed." A subdued bow. "I am only eager to become a Christian."

"Eager? You mean you want to?"

Mr. Chia smiled wanly. "Is it not apparent—my wish to profess your faith?"

"No, it is not apparent. And you have not the slightest wish to profess my faith. Why are you doing this?" The priest's colour was high.

"To repay you," Mr. Chia said simply. "You have done the greatest good to me. I must do the greatest good for you."

Father Chisholm moved irritably. Because the temptation was so alluring, because he wished to yield and could not, his temper flared. "It is not good. It is bad. You have neither inclination nor belief. My acceptance of you would be a forgery for God. You owe me nothing. Now please go!"

At first Mr. Chia did not believe his ears.

"You mean you reject me?"

"That is putting it politely," growled Father Chisholm.

The change in the merchant was seraphic. His eyes brightened, glistened, his melancholy dropped from him like a shroud. He had to struggle to contain himself; but although he had the semblance of desiring to leap into the air he did contain himself. Formally, he made the kowtow three times. He succeeded in mastering his voice.

"I regret that I am not acceptable. I am of course most unworthy. Nevertheless, perhaps in some slight manner . . ." He broke off, again he made the kowtow three times and, moving backwards, went out.

That evening, as Father Chisholm sat by the brazier with a sternness of countenance which caused Joseph, who was cooking tasty river mussels in his rice, to gaze at him timidly, there came the sudden sound of firecrackers. Six of Mr. Chia's servants were exploding them, ceremoniously, in the road outside. Then Mr. Pao's cousin advanced, bowed, handed Father Chisholm a parchment wrapped in vermilion paper.

"Mr. Chia begs that you will honour him by accepting this most unworthy gift—the deeds of the Brilliant Green Jade property with all land and water rights and the rights to the crimson clay-pit. The property is yours, without restraint, forever. Mr. Chia further begs that you accept the help of twenty of his workmen till any building you may wish to carry out is fully accomplished."

So completely taken aback was Francis he could not speak a word. He watched the retreating figure of the cousin of Mr. Pao, and of Mr. Chia, with a strange still tensity. Then he wildly scanned the title deeds and cried out joyfully, "Joseph! Joseph!"

Joseph came hurrying, fearing another misfortune had befallen them. His master's expression reassured him. They went together to the Hill of Brilliant Green Jade and there, standing under the moon amidst the tall cedars, they sang aloud the Magnificat.

Francis remained bare-headed, seeing in a vision what he would create on this noble brow of land. He had prayed with faith, and his prayer had been answered.

Joseph, made hungry by the keen wind, waited uncomplainingly, finding his own vision in the priest's rapt face, glad he had shown the presence of mind to take his rice-pot from the fire.

IV

Eighteen months later, in the month of May, when all Chek-kow province lay basking in that span of short perfection between the winter snows and the swelterings of summer, Father Chisholm crossed the paved courtyard of his new Mission of St. Andrew.

Never, perhaps, had such a sense of quiet contentment suffused him. The crystal air, where a cloud of white pigeons wheeled, was sweet and sparkling. As he reached the great banyan tree which, through his design, now shaded the forecourt of the mission, he threw a look across his shoulder, partly of pride, part in wry wonderment, as though still apprehensive of a mirage which might vanish overnight.

But it was there, shining and splendid: the slender church sentinelled between the cedars, his house, vivid with scarlet lattices, adjoining the little schoolroom, the snug dispensary opening through the outer wall, and a further dwelling screened by the foliage of papaw and catalpa, which sheltered his freshly planted garden. He sighed, his lips smiling, blessing the miracle of the fruitful clay-pit which had yielded, through many blendings and experimental bakings, bricks of a lovely soft pale rose, making his mission a symphony in cinnabar. He blessed, indeed, each subsequent wonder: the implacable kindness of Mr. Chia; the skilful patience of his workers; the incorruptibility—almost complete— of his sturdy foreman; even the weather, this recent brilliant spell, which had made his opening ceremony, held last week and politely attended by the Chia and Pao families, a notable success.

For the sole purpose of viewing the empty classroom he took the long way round: peering, like a schoolboy, through the window at the brand new pictures upon the whitewashed wall, at the shining benches which, like the blackboard, he had carpentered himself. The knowledge that his handiwork was in that particular room lay warmly round his heart. But recollection of the task he had in mind drove him to the end of the garden where, near the lower gate, and beside his private workshop, was a small brick kiln.

Happily, he jettisoned his old soutane and, in stained denim trousers, shirt sleeves and suspenders, he took a wooden spade and began to puddle-up some clay.

Tomorrow the three Sisters would arrive. Their house was ready—cool, curtained, already smelling of beeswax. But his final conceit, a secluded loggia in which they might rest and meditate, was not quite finished, demanding at least another batch of bricks from his own especial oven. As he shaped the marl he shaped the future in his mind.

Nothing was more vital than the advent of these nuns. He had seen this from the outset, he had worked and prayed for it, sending letter upon letter to Father Mealey and even to the Bishop, while the mission slowly rose before his eyes. Conversion of the Chinese adult was, he felt, a labour for archangels. Race, illiteracy, the tug of an older faith—these were formidable barriers to break down honestly, and one knew that the Almighty hated being asked to do conjuring tricks with each individual case. True, now that he was sustained in "face" by his fine new church, increasing numbers of repentant souls were adventuring to mass. He had some sixty persons in his congregation. As their pious cadences ascended at the Kyrie it sounded quite a multitude.

Nevertheless, his vision was focused, brightly, on the children. Here, quite literally, children went two for a penny. Famine, grinding poverty, and the Confucianism of masculine perpetuation made female infants, at least, a drug upon the market. In no time at all he would have a school, ful of children, fed and cared for by the Sisters, here in the mission-spinning their hoops, making the place gay with laughter, learning their letters and their catechism. The future belonged to the children: and the children . . . his children . . . would belong to God!

He smiled self-consciously at his thoughts as he shoved the moulds into the oven. He could not call himself, precisely, a ladies' man. Yet he had hungered, these long months, amidst this alien race, for the comfort of intercourse with his own kind. Mother Maria-Veronica, though Bavarian by birth, had spent the past five years with the Bon Secours in London. And the two whom she led, the French Sister Clotilde and Sister Martha, a Belgian, had equal experience in Liverpool. Coming direct from England they would bring him, at least, a friendly breath of home.

A trifle anxiously—for he had taken enormous trouble—he reviewed his preparations for their arrival on the following day: A few fireworks in the best Chinese style, but not enough to alarm the ladies, at the river landing stage, where the three best chairs in Pai-tan would await them. Tea served immediately they reached the mission. A short rest followed by benediction—he hoped they would like the flowers—and then, a special supper.

He almost chuckled as he conned, in his mind's eye, the menu of that supper. Well . . . they'd get down to hard-tack soon enough, poor things! His own appetite was scandalously meagre. During the building of the mission he had subsisted abstractedly, standing on scaffolds, or fingering a plan with Mr. Chia's foreman, upon rice and bean curd. But now he had sent Joseph scouring the city for mangos, chowchow and, rarest delicacy of all, fresh bustard from Shon-see in the North.

Suddenly, across his meditation, came the sound of footsteps. He lifted his head. As he turned, the gate was thrown open. Signed forward by their guide, a ragged riverside coolie, three nuns appeared. They were travel-stained, with a vague uneasiness in their uncertain glances. They hesitated, then advanced wearily up the garden path. The foremost, about forty years of age, had both dignity and beauty. There was high breeding in the fine bones of her face and in her wide heavy blue eyes. Pale with fatigue, impelled by a kind of inward fire, she forced herself on. Barely looking at Francis, she addressed him in fair Chinese.

"Please take us immediately to the mission, Father."

Dreadfully put out at their obvious distress, he answered in the same tongue.

"You were not expected till tomorrow."

"Are we to return to that dreadful ship?" She shivered with continued indignation. "Take us to your master at once."

He said slowly, in English: "I am Father Chisholm."

Her eyes, which had been searching the mission buildings, returned incredulously to his short shirt-sleeved figure. She stared with growing dismay at his working clothes, dirty hands and caked boots, the smear of mud across his cheek. He murmured awkwardly: "I'm sorry . . . most distressed you weren't met."

For a moment her resentment mastered her. "One might have supposed some welcome at the end of six thousand miles."

"But you see . . . the letter said quite definitely——"

She cut him short with a repressed gesture.

"Perhaps you will show us to our quarters. My companions"—with a proud negation of her own exhaustion—"are completely worn-out."

He was about to make a final explanation, but the sight of the two other Sisters, staring and very frightened, restrained him. He led the way in painful silence to their house. Here he stopped.

"I hope you will be comfortable. I will send for your baggage. Perhaps . . . perhaps you will dine with me tonight."

"Thank you. It is impossible." Her tone was cold. Once again her eyes, holding back haughty tears, touched his disreputable garments. "But if we could be spared some milk and fruit . . . tomorrow we shall be fit for work."

Subdued and mortified, he returned slowly to his house, bathed and changed. From amongst his papers he found and carefully examined the letter from Tientsin. The date given was May 19th, which, as he had said, was tomorrow. He tore the letter into little pieces. He thought of that fine, that foolish bustard. He flushed. Downstairs he was confronted by Joseph, bubbling with spirits, his arms full of purchases.

"Joseph! Carry the fruit you have bought to the Sisters' house. Take everything else and distribute it to the poor."

"But, Master. . . ." Stupefied at the tone of the command, the expression on the priest's face, Joseph swallowed rapidly; then, his jubilation gone, he gulped: "Yes, Master."

Francis went towards the church, his lips compressed as though they sealed an unexpected hurt.

Next morning the three Sisters heard his mass. And he hurried, unconsciously, through his thanksgiving, hoping to find Mother Maria-Veronica awaiting him outside. She was not there. Nor did she come, for her instructions, to his house. An hour later he found her writing in the schoolroom. She rose quietly.

"Please sit down, Reverend Mother."

"Thank you." She spoke pleasantly. Yet she continued to stand, pen in hand, notepaper before her on the desk. "I have been waiting on my pupils."

"You shall have twenty by this afternoon. I've been picking them for many weeks." He strove to make his tone light and agreeable. "They seem intelligent little things."

She smiled gravely. "We shall do our utmost for them."

"Then there is the dispensary. I am hoping you will assist me there. I've very little knowledge—but it's amazing what even a little does here."

"If you will tell me the dispensary hours I shall be there."

A brief silence. Through her quiet civility, he felt her reserve deeply. His gaze, downcast, moving awkwardly, lit suddenly upon a small framed photograph which she had already established on the desk.

"What a beautiful scene!" He spoke at random, striving to break the impersonal barrier between them.

"Yes, it is beautiful." Her heavy eyes followed his to the picture of a fine old house, white and castellated against a dark wall of mountain pines, with a sweep of terraces and gardens running down towards the lake. "It is the Schloss Anheim."

"I have heard that name before. It is historic, surely. It is near your home?"

She looked at him for the first time straight in the face. Her expression was completely colourless. "Quite near," she said.

Her tone absolutely closed the subject. She seemed to wait for him to speak, and when he did not she said, rather quickly—

"The sisters and I . . . we are most earnest in our desire to work for the success of the mission. You have only to mention your wishes and they will be carried out. At the same time——" Her voice chilled slightly. "I trust you will afford us a certain freedom of action."

He stared at her oddly. "What do you mean?"

"You know our rule is partly contemplative. We should like to enjoy as much privacy as possible." She gazed straight in front of her. "Take our meals alone . . . maintain our separate establishment."

He flushed. "I never dreamed of anything else. Your little house is your convent."

"Then you permit me to manage all our convent affairs."

Her meaning was quite plain to him. It settled like a weight upon his heart. He smiled, unexpectedly, rather sadly.

"By all means. Only be careful about money. We are very poor."

"My order has made itself responsible for our support."

He could not resist the question. "Does not your order enforce holy poverty?"

"Yes," she gave back swiftly, "but not meanness."

There was a pause. They remained standing side by side. She had broken off sharply, with a catch in her breath, her fingers tight upon the pen. His own face was burning; he had a strange reluctance to look at her.

"I will send Joseph with a note of the dispensary hours . . . and of church services. Good morning, Sister."

When he had gone she sat down, slowly, at the desk, her gaze still fixed ahead, her expression proudly unreadable. Then a single tear broke and rolled mysteriously down her cheek. Her worst forebodings were justified. Passionately, almost, she dipped her pen in the inkwell and resumed her letter.

" . . . It has happened, already, as I feared, my dear, dear brother, and I have sinned again in my dreadful . . . my ineradicable Hohenlohe pride. Yet who could blame me? He has just been here, washed free of earth and approximately shaved—I could see the scrubby razor cuts upon his chin—and armed with such a dumb authority. I saw instantly, yesterday, what a little bourgeois it was. This morning he surpassed himself. Were you aware, dear count, that Anheim was historic? I almost laughed as his eyes fumbled at the photograph: you remember the one I took from the boathouse that day we went sailing with Mother on the lake—it's gone with me everywhere—my sole temporal treasure. He said, in effect, 'Which Cook's tour did you take to view it?' I felt like saying, 'I was born there!' My pride restrained me. Yet had I done so he would probably have kept on gazing at his boots, still creviced with mud, where he had failed to clean them—and muttered: 'Oh, indeed! Our Blessed Lord was born in a stable.'

"You see, there is something about him which strikes at one. Do you recollect Herr Spinner, our first tutor . . . we were such brutes to him . . . and the way he had of looking up suddenly with such hurt, yet humble restraint? His eyes, here, are the same. Probably his father was a woodcutter like Herr Spinner's, and he too has struggled up, precariously, with dogged humility. But, dear Ernst, it is the future that I dread, shut up in this strange and isolated spot which intensifies every aspect of the situation. The danger is a lowering of one's inborn standards, yielding to a kind of mental intimacy with a person one instinctively despises. That odious familiar cheerfulness! I must drop a hint to Martha and Clotilde—who has been such a poor sick calf all the way from Liverpool. I am resolved to be pleasant and to work myself to the bone. But only complete detachment, an absolute reserve, will . . . ."

She broke off, gazing again, remote and troubled, through the window.

Father Chisholm soon perceived that the two under Sisters went out of their way to avoid him.

Clotilde was not yet thirty, flat-bosomed and delicate, with bloodless lips and a nervous smile. She was very devout and when she prayed, with her head inclined to one side, tears would gush from her pale green eyes. Martha was a different person: past forty, stocky and strong, a peasant type, dark-complexioned and with a net of wrinkles round her eyes. Bustling and outspoken, a trifle coarse in manner, she looked as though she would be immediately at home in a kitchen or a farmyard.

When by chance he met them in the garden the Belgian sister would drop a quick curtsey while Clotilde's sallow face flushed nervously as she smiled and fluttered on. He knew himself to be the subject of their whisperings. He had the impulse, often, to stop them violently. "Don't be so scared of me. We've made a stupid beginning. But I'm a much better fellow than I look."

He restrained himself. He had no grounds whatsoever for complaint. Their work was executed scrupulously, with minute perfection of purpose. New altar linen, exquisitely stitched, appeared in the sacristy; and an embroidered stole which must have taken days of patient labour. Bandages and dressings, rolled, cut to all sizes, filled the store-cupboard in the surgery.

The children had come and were comfortably housed in the big ground-floor dormitory of the Sisters' house. And presently the schoolroom hummed with little voices, or with the chanted rhythm of a much-repeated lesson. He would stand outside, open breviary in hand, sheltered by the bushes, listening. It meant so much to him, this tiny school, he had so joyfully anticipated its opening. Now he rarely went in; and never without a sense of his intrusion. He withdrew into himself, accepting the situation with a sombre logic. It was very simple. Mother Maria-Veronica was a good woman, fine, fastidious, devoted to her work. Yet from the first she had conceived a natural aversion to him. Such things cannot be overcome. After all, he was not a prepossessing character, he had been right when he judged himself no squire of dames. It was a sad disappointment, nevertheless.

The dispensary brought them together on three afternoons each week when, for four hours at a stretch, Maria-Veronica worked close beside him. He could see that she was interested, often so deeply as to forget her aversion. Though they spoke little he had on such occasions a strange sense of comradeship with her.

One day, a month after her arrival, as he finished dressing a severe whitlow, she exclaimed, involuntarily: "You would have made a surgeon."

He flushed. "I've always liked working with my hands."

"That is because you are clever with them."

He was ridiculously pleased. Her manner was friendlier than it had ever been. At the end of the clinic, as he put away his simple medicines, she gazed at him questioningly. "I've been meaning to ask you . . . Sister Clotilde has had too much to do lately, preparing the children's meals with Martha in the kitchen. She isn't strong and I'm afraid it is too much for her. If you have no objection I would like to get some help."

"But of course." He agreed at once—even happier that she should have asked his permission. "Shall I find you a servant?"

"No thank you. I already have a good couple in mind!"

Next morning when crossing the compound, he observed on the convent balcony, airing and brushing the matting, the unmistakable figures of Hosannah and Philomena Wang. He stopped short, his face darkening, then he took immediate steps towards the Sisters' house.

He found Maria-Veronica in the linen room checking over the sheets. He spoke hurriedly: "I'm sorry to disturb you. But—these new servants—I'm afraid you won't find them satisfactory."

She turned slowly from the cupboard, sudden displeasure in her face. "Surely I am the best judge of that?"

"I don't want you to think I'm interfering. But I'm bound to warn you that they are far from reliable characters."

Her lip curled. "Is that your Christian charity?"

He paled. She was placing him in a horrible position. But he went on determinedly. "I am obliged to be practical. I am thinking of the mission. And of you."

"Please do not trouble about me." Her smile was icy. "I am quite capable of looking after myself."

"I tell you these Wangs are a really bad lot."

She answered with peculiar emphasis: "I know they've had a really bad time. They told me."

His temper flared. "I advise you to get rid of them."

"I won't get rid of them!" Her voice was cold as steel. She had always suspected him, and now she knew. Because she had relaxed her vigilance yesterday, for a moment, in the dispensary, he had rushed to interfere, to show his authority, on this frivolous pretext. Never, never would she be weak with him again. "You already agreed that I am not responsible to you for the administration of my house. I must ask you to keep your word."

He was silent. There was nothing more that he could say. He had meant to help her. But he had made a bad mistake. As he turned away he knew that their relationship, which he had thought to be improving, was now worse than it had been before.

The situation began to affect him seriously. It was hard to keep his expression unruffled when the Wangs passed him, with an air of muted triumph, many times a day. One morning, towards the end of July, Joseph brought him his breakfast of fruit and tea with swollen knuckles and a sheepish air—part triumphant, part subdued.

"Master, I am sorry. I have had to give that rascal Wang a beating."

Father Chisholm sat up sharply, his eye stern: "Why so, Joseph?"

Joseph hung his head. "He says many unkind words about us. That Reverend Mother is a great lady and we are simply dust."

"We all are dust, Joseph." The priest's smile was faint.

"He says harder words than that."

"We can put up with hard words."

"It is more than words, Master. He has become puffed-up beyond measure. And all the time he is making a bad squeeze on the Sisters' housekeeping."

It was quite true. Because of his opposition, the Reverend Mother was indulgent towards the Wangs. Hosannah was now the majordomo of the Sisters' house while Philomena departed, every day, with a basket on her arm, to do the shopping as if she owned the place. At the end of each month, when Martha paid the bills with the roll of notes which the Reverend Mother gave her, the precious pair would depart for the town, in their best clothes, to collect a staggering commission from the tradesmen. It was barefaced robbery, anathema to Francis' Scottish thrift.

Gazing at Joseph he said grimly: "I hope you did not hurt Wang much."

"Alas! I fear I hurt him greatly, Master."

"I am cross with you, Joseph. As a punishment you shall have a holiday tomorrow. And that new suit you have long been asking of me."

That afternoon, in the dispensary, Maria-Veronica broke her rule of silence. Before the patients were admitted she said to Francis:

"So you have chosen to victimize poor Wang again?"

He answered bluntly: "On the contrary. It is he who is victimizing you."

"I do not understand you."

"He is robbing you. The man is a born thief and you are encouraging him."

She bit her lip fiercely. "I do not believe you. I am accustomed to trust my servants."

"Very well then, we shall see." He dismissed the matter quietly.

In the next few weeks his silent face showed deeper lines of strain. It was dreadful to live in close community with a person who detested, despised, him—and to be responsible for that person's spiritual welfare. Maria-Veronica's confessions, which contained nothing, were torture to him. And he judged they were equal torture for her. When he placed the sacred wafer between her lips while her long delicate fingers upheld the altar cloth in the still and pallid dawn of each new day, her upturned pale face, with eyelids veined and tremulous, seemed still to scorn him. He began to rest badly and to walk in the garden at night. So far, their disagreement had been limited to the sphere of her authority. Constrained, more silent than ever, he waited for the moment when he must enforce his will.

It was autumn when that necessity arose, quite simply, out of her inexperience. Yet he could not pass it by. He sighed as he walked over to the Sisters' house.

"Reverend Mother . . ." To his annoyance he found himself trembling. He stood before her, his eyes upon those memorable boots. "You have been going into the city these last few afternoons with Sister Clotilde?"

She looked surprised. "Yes, that is true."

There was a pause.

On guard, she inquired with irony: "Are you curious to know what we are doing?"

"I already know." He spoke as mildly as he could. "You go to visit the sick poor of the city. As far away as the Manchu Bridge. It is commendable. But I'm afraid it must cease."

"May I ask why?" She tried to match his quietness but did not quite succeed.

"Really, I'd rather not tell you."

Her fine nostrils were tense. "If you are prohibiting my acts of charity . . . I have a right . . . I insist on knowing."

"Joseph tells me there are bandits in the city. Wai-Chu has begun fighting again. His soldiers are dangerous."

She laughed outright proudly, contemptuously.

"I am not afraid. The men in my family have always been soldiers."

"That is most interesting." He gazed at her steadily. "But you are not a man, nor is Sister Clotilde. And Wai-Chu's soldiers are not exactly the kid-gloved cavalry officers infallibly found in the best Bavarian families."

He had never used that tone with her before. She reddened, then paled. Her features, her whole figure seemed to contract. "Your outlook is common and cowardly. You forget that I have given myself to God. I came here prepared for anything—sickness, accident, disaster, if necessary death—but not to listen to a lot of cheap sensational rubbish."

His eyes remained fixed on her, so that they burned her, like points of light. He said unconditionally: "Then we will cease to be sensational. It would, as you infer, be a small matter if you were captured and carried off. But there is a stronger reason why you should restrain your charitable promenades. The position of women in China is very different from that to which you are accustomed. In China women have been rigidly excluded from society for centuries. You give grave offence by walking openly in the streets. From a religious standpoint it is highly damaging to the work of the mission. For that reason I forbid you, absolutely, to enter Pai-tan unescorted, without my permission."

She flushed, as though he had struck her in the face. There was a mortal stillness. She had nothing whatever to say.

He was about to leave her when there came a sudden scud of footsteps in the passage and Sister Martha bundled into the room. Her agitation was so great she did not observe Francis, half-hidden by the shadow of the door. Nor did she guess the tension of the moment. Her gaze, distraught beneath her rumpled wimple, was bent on Maria-Veronica. Wringing her hands, she lamented wildly:

"They've run away . . . taken everything . . . the ninety dollars you gave me yesterday to pay the bills . . . the silver . . . even Sister Clotilde's ivory crucifix . . . they've gone, gone . . ."

"Who has gone?" The words came, with a dreadful effort, from Maria-Veronica's stiff lips.

"The Wangs, of course . . . the low, dirty thieves. I always knew they were a pair of rogues and hypocrites."

Francis did not dare to look at the Mother Superior. She stood there, motionless. He felt a strange pity for her. He made his way clumsily from the room.

V

As Father Chisholm returned to his own house he became aware, through the strained preoccupation of his mind, of Mr. Chia and his son, standing by the fish pond, watching the carp, with a quiet air of waiting. Both figures were warmly padded against the chill,—it was a "six-coat cold day,"—the boy's hand was in his father's, and the slow dusk, stealing from the shadows of the banyan tree, seemed reluctant to envelop them, and to efface a charming picture.

The two were frequent visitors to the mission and perfectly at home there; they smiled, as Father Chisholm hurried over, greeted him with courteous formality. But Mr. Chia, for once, gently turned aside the priest's invitation to enter his house.

"We come instead to bid you to our house. Yes, tonight, we are leaving for our mountain retreat. It would afford me the greatest happiness if you would accompany us."

Francis stood amazed. "But we are entering upon winter!"

"It is true, my friend, that I and my unworthy family have hitherto ventured to our secluded villa in the Kwangs only during the inclement heat of summer." Mr. Chia paused blandly. "Now we make an innovation which may be even more agreeable. We have many cords of wood and much store of food. Do you not think, Father, it would be edifying to meditate, a little, amongst these snowy peaks?"

Searching the maze of circumlocution with a puzzled frown, Father Chisholm shot a swift glance of interrogation at the merchant.

"Is Wai-Chu about to loot the town?"

Mr. Chia's shoulders mildly deprecated the directness of the query but his expression did not falter. "On the contrary, I myself have paid Wai considerable tribute and billeted him comfortably. I trust he will remain in Pai-tan for many days."

A silence. Father Chisholm's brows were drawn in complete perplexity.

"However, my dear friend, there are other matters which occasionally make the wise man seek the solitudes. I beg of you to come."

The priest shook his head slowly. "I am sorry, Mr. Chia—I am too busy in the mission. . . . How could I leave this noble place which you have so generously given me?"

Mr. Chia smiled amiably. "It is most salubrious here at present. If you change your mind do not fail to inform me. Come, Yu . . . the wagons will be loaded now. Give your hand to the holy Father in the English fashion."

Father Chisholm shook hands with the little wrapped-up boy. Then he blessed them both. The air of restrained regret in Mr. Chia's manner disturbed him. His heart was strangely heavy as he watched them go.

The next two days passed in a queer atmosphere of stress. He saw little of the Sisters. The weather turned worse. Great flocks of birds were seen flying to the South. The sky darkened and lay like lead upon all living things. But except for a few flurries no snow came. Even the cheerful Joseph showed unusual signs of grievance, coming to the priest and expressing his desire to go home.

"It is a long time since I have seen my parents. It is fitting for me to visit them."

When questioned, he waved his hand around vaguely, grumbling that there were rumours in Pai-tan of evil things travelling from the North, the East, the West.

"Wait till the evil spirits come, Joseph, before you run away." Father Chisholm tried to rally his servant's spirits. And his own.

Next morning, after early mass, he went down to the town, alone, in determined quest of news. The streets were teeming, life apparently pulsed undisturbed, but a hush hung about the larger dwellings and many of the shops were closed. In the Street of the Netmakers, he found Hung boarding up his windows with unobtrusive urgency.

"There is no denying it, Shang-Foo!" The old shopkeeper paused to give the Father a calamitous glance over his small pebble spectacles. "It is sickness . . . the great coughing sickness which they name the Black Death. Already six provinces are stricken. People are fleeing with the wind. The first came last night to Pai-tan. And one of the women fell dead inside the Manchu Gate. A wise man knows what that portends. Ay, ay, w hen there is famine we march and when there is pestilence we march again. Life is not easy when the gods show their wrath."

Father Chisholm climbed the hill to the mission with a shadow upon his face. He seemed already to smell the sickness in the air.

Suddenly he drew up. Outside the mission wall, and directly in his path, lay three dead rats. Judging by the priest's expression there was, in this stiff trinity, a dire foreboding. He shivered unexpectedly, thinking of his children. He went himself for kerosene, and poured it on the corpses of the rats, ignited the oil, and watched their slow cremation. Hurriedly, he took up the remains with tongs and buried them.

He stood thinking deeply. He was five hundred miles from the nearest telegraph terminal. To send a messenger to Sen-siang by sampan, even by the fastest pony, might take at least six days. And yet he must at all costs establish some contact with the outer world.

Suddenly his expression lifted. He found Joseph and led him quickly by the arm to his room. His face was set with gravity as he addressed the boy.

"Joseph! I am sending you on an errand of the first importance. You will take Mr. Chia's new launch. Tell the kapong you have Mr. Chia's permission and mine. I even command you to steal the launch if it is necessary. Do you understand?"

"Yes, Father." Joseph's eyes flashed. "It will not be a sin."

"When you have the boat, proceed with all speed to Sen-siang. There you will go to Father Thibodeau at the mission. If he is away go to the offices of the American oil company. Find someone in authority.

898

Tell him the plague is upon us, that we need immediately medicine, supplies, and doctors. Then go to the telegraph company, send these two messages I have written for you. See . . . take the papers . . . the first to the Vicariate at Pekin, the second to the Union General Hospital at Nankin. Here is money. Do not fail me, Joseph. Now go . . . go. And the good God go with you!"

He felt better an hour later as the lad went padding down the hill, his blue bundle bobbing on his back, his intelligent features screwed to a staunch tenacity. The better to view the departure of the launch, the priest hastened to the belfry tower. But here, as he perched himself against the pediment, his eye darkened. On the vast plain before him he saw two thinly moving streams of beasts and straggling humans, reduced, alike, by distance to the size of little ants—two moving streams, the one approaching, the other departing from the city.

He could not wait; but, descending, crossed immediately to the school. In the wooden corridor Sister Martha was on her knees scrubbing the boards. He stopped.

"Where is Reverend Mother?"

She raised a damp hand to straighten her wimple. "In the classroom." She added, in a sibilant, confederate's whisper: "And lately much disarranged."

He went into the classroom, which, at his entry, fell immediately to silence. The rows of bright childish faces gave him, suddenly, a gripping pang. Quickly, quickly, he fought back that unbearable fear.

Maria-Veronica had turned towards him with a pale, unreadable brow. He approached and addressed her in an undertone.

"There are signs of an epidemic in the city. I am afraid it may be plague. If so, it is important for us to be prepared." He paused, under her silence, then went on. "At all costs we must try to keep the sickness from the children. That means isolating the school and the Sisters' house. I shall arrange at once for some kind of barrier to be put up. The children and all three Sisters should remain inside, with one Sister always on duty at the entrance." He paused again, forcing himself to be calm. "Don't you think that wise?"

She faced him, cold and undismayed. "Profoundly wise."

"Are there any details we might discuss?"

She answered bitterly: "You have already familiarized us with the principle of segregation."

He took no notice. "You know how the contagion is spread?"

"Yes."

There was a silence. He turned towards the door, sombre from her fixed refusal to make peace. "If God sends this great trouble upon us, we must work hard together. Let us try to forget our personal relations."

"They are best forgotten." She spoke in her most frigid tone, submissive upon the surface, yet charged, beneath, with high disdainful breeding.

He left the classroom. He could not but admire her courage. The news he had conveyed to her would have terrified most women. He reflected tensely that they might need all their spirit before the month was past.

Convinced of the need of haste, he recrossed the compound and despatched the gardener for Mr. Chia's foreman and six of the men who had worked on the church. Immediately, when these arrived, he set them to build a thick fence of kaolin on the boundary he had marked off. The dried stalks of maize made an excellent barricade. While it rose under his anxious eyes, girding the school and convent house, he trenched a narrow ditch around the base. This could be flooded with disinfectant if the need arose.

The work went on all day and was not completed until late at night. Even after the men had gone he could not rest, a mounting tide of dread was in his blood. He took most of his stores into the enclosure, carrying sacks of potatoes and flour on his shoulders, butter, bacon, condensed milk, and all the tinned goods of the mission. His small stock of medicines he likewise transferred. Only then did he feel some degree of relief. He looked at his watch: three o'clock in the morning. It was not worth while to go to bed. He went into the church and spent the hours remaining until dawn in prayer.

When it was light, before the mission was astir he set out for the yamen of the Chief Magistrate. At the Manchu Gate fugitives from the stricken provinces were still crowding unhindered into the city. Scores had taken up their lodging beneath the stars, in the lee of the Great Wall. As he passed the silent figures, huddled under sacking, half-frozen by the bitter wind, he heard the racking sound of coughing. His heart flowed out towards these poor exhausted creatures, many already stricken, enduring humbly, suffering without hope; and a burning impetuous desire to help them suffused his soul. One old man lay dead and naked, stripped of the garments he no longer needed. His wrinkled toothless face was upturned towards the sky.

Spurred by the pity in his breast, Francis reached the yamen of justice. But here a blow awaited him. Mr. Pao's cousin was gone. All the Paos had departed, the closed shutters of their house stared back at him like sightless eyes.

He took a swift and painful breath and turned, chafing, into the courts. The passages were deserted, the main chamber a vault of echoing emptiness. He could see no one, except a few clerks scurrying with a furtive air. From one of these he learned that the Chief Magistrate had been called away to the obsequies of a distant relative in Tchientin, eight hundred li due south. It was plain to the harassed priest that all but the lowest court officials had been "summoned" from Pai-tan. The civil administration of the city had ceased to exist.

The furrow between Francis' eyes was deeply cut, a haggard wound. Only one course lay open to him now. And he knew that it was futile. Nevertheless, he turned and made his way rapidly to the cantonment.

With the bandit Wai-Chu complete overlord of the province, ferociously exacting voluntary gifts, the position of the regular military forces was academic. They dissolved or seceded as a matter of routine on the bandit's periodic visits to the town. Now, as Francis reached the barracks, a bare dozen soldiers hung about, conspicuously without arms, in dirty grey-cotton tunics.

They stopped him at the gate. But nothing could withstand the fire which now consumed him. He forced his way to an inner chamber, where a young lieutenant in a clean and elegant uniform lounged by the paper-latticed window, reflectively polishing his white teeth with a willow twig.

Lieutenant Shon and the priest inspected one another, the young dandy with polite guardedness, his visitor with all the dark and hopeless ardour of his purpose.

"The city is threatened by a great sickness." Francis fought to inject his tone with deliberate restraint. "I am seeking for someone with courage and authority, to combat the grave danger."

Shon continued dispassionately to consider the priest. "General Wai-Chu has the monopoly of authority. And he is leaving for Tou-en-lai tomorrow."

"That will make it easier for those who remain. I beg of you to help me."

Shon shrugged his shoulders virtuously. "Nothing would afford me greater satisfaction than to work with the Shang-Foo entirely without prospect of reward, for the supreme benefit of suffering mankind. But I have no more than fifty soldiers. And no supplies."

"I have sent to Sen-siang for supplies." Francis spoke more rapidly. "They will arrive soon. But meanwhile we must do all in our command to quarantine the refugees and prevent the pestilence from starting in the city."

"It has already started." Shon answered coolly. "In the Street of the Basket-makers there are more than sixty cases. Many dead. The rest dying."

A terrible urgency tautened the priest's nerves, a surge of protest, a burning refusal to accept defeat. He took a quick step forward.

"I am going to aid these people. If you do not come I shall go alone. But I am perfectly assured that you are coming."

For the first time the Lieutenant looked uncomfortable. He was a bold youngster, despite his foppish air, with ideas of his own advancement and a sense of personal integrity which had caused him to reject the price offered him by Wai-Chu, as dishonourably inadequate. Without the slightest interest in the fate of his fellow citizens, he had been, on the priest's arrival, idly debating the advisability of joining his few remaining men in the Street of the Stolen Hours. Now, he was disagreeably embarrassed and reluctantly impressed. Like a man moving against his own will, he rose, threw away his twig and slowly buckled on his revolver.

"This does not shoot well. But as a symbol it encourages the unswerving obedience of my most trusted followers."

They went out together into the cold grey day.

From the Street of the Stolen Hours they routed some thirty soldiers and marched to the teeming warrens of the basket-weavers' quarters by the river. Here the plague had already settled, with the instinct of a dunghill fly. The river dwellings, tiers of cardboard hovels, leaning one on top of another, against the high mud bank, were festering with dirt, vermin, and the disease. Francis saw that unless immediate measures were taken the contagion would spread in this congestion like a raging conflagration.

He said to the Lieutenant, as they emerged, bent double, from the end hovel of the row:

"We must find some place to house the sick."

Shon reflected. He was enjoying himself more than he had expected. This foreign priest had shown much "face" in stooping close to the stricken persons. He admired "face" greatly.

"We shall commandeer the yamen of the *yu shih*—the imperial recorder." For many months Shon had been at violent enmity with this official, who had defrauded him of his share of the salt tax. "I am confident that my absent friend's abode will make a pleasing hospital."

They went immediately to the recorder's yamen. It was large and richly furnished, situated in the best part of the city. Shon effected entry by the simple expedient of breaking down the door. While Francis remained with half a dozen men to make some preparations for receiving the sick, he departed with the remainder. Presently the first cases arrived in litters and were arranged in rows on quilted mats upon the floor.

That night, as Francis went up the hill towards the mission, tired from his long day's work, he heard above the faint incessant death music the shouts of wild carousing and sporadic rifle shots. Behind him, Wai-Chu's irregulars were looting the shuttered shops. But presently the city fell again to silence. In the still moonlight he could see the bandits, streaming from the Eastern Gate, spurring their stolen ponies across the plains. He was glad to see them go.

At the summit of the hill the moon suddenly was dimmed. It began at last to snow. When he drew near the gateway in the kaolin fence the air was alive and fluttering. Soft dry blinding flakes came whirling out of the darkness, settling on eyes and brow, entering his lips like tiny hosts, whirling so dense and thick that in a minute the ground was carpeted in white. He stood outside, in the white coldness, rent by anxiety, and called in a low voice. Immediately Mother Maria-Veronica came to the gate, holding up a lantern which cast a beam of spectral brightness on the snow.

He scarcely dared to put the question. "Are you all well?"

"Yes."

His heart stopped pounding in sheer relief. He waited, suddenly conscious of his fatigue and the fact that he had not eaten all that day. Then he said: "We have established a hospital in the town . . . not much . . . but the best we could do." Again he waited, as if for her to speak, deeply sensible of the difficulty of his position, and the greatness of the favour he must ask. "If one of the Sisters could be spared . . . would volunteer to come . . . to help us with the nursing . . . I should be most grateful."

There was a pause. He could almost see her lips shape themselves to answer coldly: "You ordered us to remain in here. You forbade us to enter the town." Perhaps the sight of his face, worn, drawn and heavy-eyed, through the maze of snowflakes, restrained her. She said: "I will come."

His heart lifted. Despite her fixed antagonism towards him she was incomparably more efficient than Martha or Clotilde. "It means moving your quarters to the yamen. Wrap up warmly. And take all you need."

Ten minutes later he took her bag; they went down to the yamen together in silence. The dark lines of their footprints in the fresh snow were far apart.

Next morning sixteen of those admitted to the yamen were dead. But three times that number were coming in. It was pneumonic plague and its virulence surpassed the fiercest venom. People dropped with it as if bludgeoned and were dead before the next dawn. It seemed to congeal the blood, to rot the lungs, which threw up a thin white speckled sputum, swarming with lethal germs. Often one hour spaced the interval between a man's heedless laugh and the grin that was his death-mask.

The three physicians of Pai-tan had failed to arrest the epidemic by the method of acupuncture. On the second day they ceased prickling the limbs of their patients with needles, and discreetly withdrew to a more salubrious practice.

By the end of that week the city was riddled from end to end. A wave of panic struck through the apathy of the people. The southern exits of the city were choked with carts, chairs, overburdened mules and a struggling, hysterical populace.

The cold intensified. A great blight seemed to lie on the afflicted land, here and beyond. Dazed with overwork and lack of sleep, Francis nevertheless dimly sensed the calamity at Pai-tan to be but a portion of the major tragedy. He had no news. He did not grasp the immensity of the disaster: a hundred thousand miles of territory stricken, and half a million dead beneath the snow. Nor could he know that the eyes of the civilized world were bent in sympathy on China, that expeditions quickly organized in America and Britain had arrived to combat the disease.

His torturing suspense deepened daily. There was still no sign of Joseph's return. Would help never reach them from Sen-siang? A dozen times each day he plodded to the wharfside for the sight of the up-coming boat.

Then, at the beginning of the second week, Joseph suddenly appeared, weary and spent, but with a pale smile of achievement. He had encoun-tered every obstacle. The countryside was in a ferment, Sen-siang a place of torment, the mission there ravaged by the disease. But he had persisted. He had sent his telegrams and bravely waited, hiding in his launch in a creek of the river. Now he had a letter. He produced it with a grimed and shaking hand. More: a doctor who knew the Father, an old and respected friend of the Father, would arrive on the supply boat!

With beating excitement, and a strange wild premonition, Father Chisholm took the letter from Joseph, opened it and read:

> *Lord Leighton Relief Expedition*
> *Chek-kow*

DEAR FRANCIS,

I have been in China five weeks now with the Leighton expedition. This should not surprise you if you remember my youthful longings for the decks of ocean-going freighters and the exotic jungles that lay beyond. Quite truly, I thought I had forgotten all that nonsense myself. But at home, when they began asking for volunteers for the relief party, I suddenly surprised myself by joining up. It certainly was not the desire to become a National Hero which prompted the absurd impulse. Probably a reaction, long deferred, against my hum-drum life in Tynecastle. And perhaps, if I may say it, a very real hope of seeing you.

Anyhow, ever since we arrived, I've been working my way up-country, trying to push myself into your sacred presence. Your tele-gram to Nankin was turned over to our headquarters there and word of it reached me at Hai-chang next day. I immediately asked Leighton, who is a very decent fellow, despite his title, if I might push off to give you a hand. He agreed and even let me have one of our few remaining power boats. I've just reached Sen-siang and am collecting supplies. I will be along full steam ahead, probably arriving twenty-four hours behind your servant. Take care of yourself till then. All my news later.

In haste,

Yours,

WILLIE TULLOCH

The priest smiled, slowly, for the first time in many days, and with a deep and secret warmth. He felt no great amazement; it was so typical of Tulloch to sponsor such a cause. He was braced, fortified by the unexpected fortune of his friend's arrival.

It was difficult to hold his eagerness in check. Next day when the relief boat was sighted he hastened to the wharf. Even before the launch drew alongside, Tulloch had stepped ashore, older, stouter, yet unchangeably the same dour quiet Scot, careless as ever in his dress, shy, strong and prejudiced as a Highland steer, as plain and honest as homespun tweed.

The priest's vision was absurdly blurred.

"Man, Francis, it's you!" Willie could say no more. He kept on shaking hands, confused by his emotion, debarred by his Northern blood from more overt demonstration. At last he muttered, as if conscious of the need of speech: "When we walked down Darrow High Street we never dreamed we'd forgather in a place like this." He tried a half-laugh, but with little success. "Where's your coat and gumboots? You can't stroll through the pest in these shoes. It's high time I kept an eye on you."

"And on our hospital." Francis smiled.

"What!" The doctor's sandy eyebrows lifted. "You have a hospital of sorts? Let's see it."

"As soon as you are ready."

Instructing the crew of the launch to follow him with the supplies, Tulloch set off, at the priest's side, agile despite his increased girth, his eyes intent in his red hard-wearing face, his thinned hair showing a mass of freckles on his ruddy scalp as he punctuated his friend's brief report with comprehending nods.

At the end of it, as they reached the yamen, he remarked with a dry twinkle: "You might have done worse. Is this your centre?" Across his shoulder he told his bearers to bring in the cases.

Inside the hospital he made a quick inspection, his eyes darting right, left, and with an odd curiosity towards Mother Maria-Veronica, who now accompanied them. He took a swift glance at Shon, when the young dandy came in, then firmly shook hands with him. Finally as they stood, all four, at the entrance to the long suite of rooms which formed the main ward, he addressed them quietly.

"I think you have done wonders. And I hope you don't expect melodramatic miracles from me. Forget all your preconceived ideas and face the truth—I'm not the dark handsome doctor with the portable laboratory. I'm here to work with you, like one of yourselves, which means . . . flatly . . . like a navvy. I haven't a drop of vaccine in my bag—in the first place because it isn't one damn bit of good outside the story-books. And in the second because every flask we brought to China was used up in a week. Ye'll note," he inserted mildly, "it didn't check the epidemic. Remember! This is practically a fatal disease once it gets you. In such circumstances, as my old dad used to say," he smiled faintly, "an ounce of prevention is better than a ton of cure. That's why, if you don't mind, we'll turn our attention—not to the living—but to the dead."

There was a silence while they slowly grasped his meaning. Lieutenant Shon smiled.

"Cadavers are accumulating in the side streets at a disconcerting rate. It is discouraging to stumble in the darkness and fall into the arms of an unresponsive corpse."

Francis shot a quick glance at Maria-Veronica's expressionless face. Sometimes the young Lieutenant was a little indiscreet.

The doctor had moved to the nearest crate and, with stolid competence, was prying off the lid.

"The first thing we do is fit you out properly. Oh! I know you two believe in God. And the Lieutenant in Confucius." He bent and produced rubber boots from the case. "But I believe in prophylaxis."

He completed the unpacking of his supplies, fitting white overalls and goggles upon them, berating their negligence of their own safety. His remarks ran on, matter-of-fact, composed. "Don't you realize, you confounded innocents . . . one cough in your eye and you're done for . . . penetration of the cornea. They knew that even in the fourteenth century . . . they wore vizors of isinglass against this thing . . . it was brought down from Siberia by a band of marmoset hunters. Well, now, I'll come back later, Sister, and have a real look at your patients. But first of all, Shon, the Reverend and myself will take a peek round."

In his stress of mind, Francis had overlooked the grim necessity of swift interment before the germ-infested bodies were attacked by rats. Individual burial was impossible in that iron ground and the supply of coffins had run out long ago. All the fuel in China would not have burned the bodies—for as Shon again remarked, nothing is less inflammable than frozen human flesh. One practical solution remained. They dug a great pit outside the walls, lined it with quicklime, and requisitioned carts. The loaded carts, driven by Shon's men, bumped through the streets and shot their cargo into this common grave.

Three days later, when the city was cleared and the stray carcasses, half-devoured and dragged away by dogs, collected from the ice-encrusted fields, stricter measures were enforced. Afraid lest the spirits of their ancestors be defiled by an unholy tomb, people were hiding the bodies of their relatives, storing scores of infected corpses under the floorboards of their houses and in the kaolin roofs.

At the doctor's suggestion Lieutenant Shon promulgated an edict that all such hoarders would be shot. When the death carts rumbled through the city his soldiers shouted: "Bring out your dead. Or you yourselves will die."

Meanwhile, they were ruthlessly destroying certain properties which Tulloch had marked as breeding grounds of the disease. Experience and dire necessity made the doctor vengefully efficient. They entered, cleared the rooms, demolished the bamboo partitions with axes, spread kerosene, and made a pyre for the rats.

The Street of the Basket-makers was the first they razed. Returning, scorched and grimed, a hatchet still in his hand, Tulloch cast a queer glance at the priest, walking wearily beside him through the deserted streets. He said, in sudden compunction:

"This isn't your job, Francis. And you're worn so fine you're just about to drop. Why don't you get up the hill for a few days, back to those kids you're worrying yourself stiff over?"

"That would be a pretty sight. The man of God taking his ease while the city burns."

"Who is there to see you in this out-of-the-way hole?"

Francis smiled strangely. "We are not unseen."

Tulloch dropped the matter abruptly. Outside the yamen he swung round, gazing glumly at the redness still smouldering in the low dim sky. "The fire of London was a logical necessity." Suddenly his nerves rasped. "Damn it, Francis, kill yourself if you want to. But keep your motives to yourself."

The strain was telling on them. For ten days Francis had not been out of his clothes, they were stiff with frozen sweat. Occasionally he dragged his boots off, obeyed Tulloch's command to rub his feet with colza oil—even so his right great toe was inflamed with agonizing frost-bite. He was dead with fatigue, but always there was more . . . more to be done.

They had no water, only melted snow, the wells were solid ice. Cooking was near impossible. Yet every day, Tulloch insisted that they all meet to have their midday meal together, to counteract the growing nightmare of their lives. At this hour, doggedly, he exerted himself to be cheerful, occasionally giving them Edison Bell selections on the phonograph he had brought out with him. He had a fund of North Country anecdotes, stories of the Tynecastle "Georgies," which he drew on freely. Sometimes he had the triumph of bringing a pale smile to Maria-Veronica's lips. Lieutenant Shon could never understand the jokes, though he listened politely while they were explained to him.

Sometimes Shon was a little late in coming to the meal. Though they guessed that he was solacing some pretty lady who still, like themselves, survived, the empty chair took an unsuspected toll upon their nerves.

As the third week began Maria-Veronica showed signs of breaking down. Tulloch was bewailing the lack of floor space in the yamen, when she remarked: "If we took hammocks from the Street of the Netmakers we could house double our number of patients . . . more comfortably, too."

The doctor paused, gazed at her with grim approbation. "Why didn't I think of that before? It's a grand suggestion."

She coloured deeply under his praise, cast down her eyes and tried to go on with her dish of rice. But she could not. Her arm began to shake. It shook so violently the food dropped off her fork. She could not raise a grain of rice towards her lips. Her flush deepened, spread into her neck. Several times she repeated the attempt and failed. She sat with bent head, enduring the absurd humiliation. Then she rose without a word and left the table.

Later, Father Chisholm found her at work in the women's ward. He had never known such calm and pitiless self-sacrifice. She performed the most hateful duties for the sick, work which the lowest Chinese sweeper would have spurned. He dared not look at her, so unbearable had their relationship become. He had not addressed her directly for many days.

"Reverend Mother, Dr. Tulloch thinks . . . we all think you have been doing too much . . . that Sister Martha should come down to relieve you."

She had regained only a vestige of her cold aloofness. His suggestion disturbed her anew. She drew herself up. "You mean that I am not doing enough?"

"Far from it. Your work is magnificent."

"Then why attempt to keep me from it?" Her lips were trembling.

He said clumsily, "We are considering you."

His tone seemed to sting her to the quick. Holding back her tears, she answered passionately: "Do not consider me. The more work you give me . . . and the less sympathy . . . the better I shall like it."

He had to leave it at that. He raised his eyes to look at her but her gaze was fixedly averted. He sadly turned away.

The snow which had held off for a week suddenly began again. It fell and fell unendingly. Francis had never seen such snow, the flakes so large and soft. Each added snowflake made an added silence. Houses were walled up in the silent whiteness. The streets were choked with drifts, hindering their work, increasing the sufferings of the sick. His heart was wrung again . . . again. In the endless days he lost all sense of time and place and fear. As he bent over the dying, succouring them with deep compassion in his eyes, stray thoughts swam through his dizzy brain. . . . Christ promised us suffering . . . this life was given us only as a preparation for the next . . . when God will wipe all sorrow from our eyes, weeping and mourning shall be no more.

Now they were halting all nomads outside the walls, disinfecting and holding them in quarantine until assured of their freedom from the disease. As they came back from the isolation huts they had thrown up, Tulloch inquired of him, overtaxed, frayed to a raw anger:

"Is hell any worse than this?"

He answered, through the fog of his fatigue, blundering forward, unheroic, yet undismayed: "Hell is that state where one has ceased to hope."

None of them knew when the epidemic eased. There was no climax of achievement, no operatic crowning of their efforts. Visible evidence of death no longer lingered in the streets. The worst slums lay as dirty ashes on the snow. The mass flight from the Northern Provinces gradually ceased. It was as if a great dark cloud, immovably above them, were at last rolling slowly to the southwards.

Tulloch expressed his feelings in a single dazed and jaded phrase. "Your God alone knows if we've done anything, Francis . . . I think . . ." He broke off, haggard, limp, and for the first time seemed about to break. He swore. "The admissions are down again today . . . let's take time off or I'll go mad."

That evening the two took a brief respite, for the first time, from the hospital and climbed to the mission to spend the night at the priest's house. It was after ten o'clock and a few stars were faintly visible in the dark bowl of sky.

The doctor paused on the brow of the snow-embowered hill, which they had ascended with great effort, studying the soft outlines of the mission, lit by the whiteness of the earth. He spoke with unusual quietness: "It's a bonny place you've made, Francis. I don't wonder you've fought so hard to keep your little brats safe. Well, if I've helped at all, I'm mortal glad." His lips twitched. "It must be pleasant to spend your days here with a fine-looking woman like Maria-Veronica."

The priest knew his friend too well to take offence. But he answered, with a strained and wounded smile:

"I'm afraid she does not find it agreeable."

"No?"

"You must have seen that she loathes me."

There was a pause. Tulloch gave the priest a queer glance.

"Your most endearing virtue, my holy man, has always been your painful lack of vanity." He moved on. "Let's go in and have some toddy. It's something to have worked through this scourge and to have the end of it in sight. It sort of lifts one up above the level of the brutes. But don't try to use that on me as an argument to prove the existence of the soul."

Seated in Francis' room they knew a moment of exhausted exaltation, talked of home late into the night. Briefly, Tulloch satirized his own career. He had done nothing, acquired nothing but a taste for whisky. But now, in his sentimental middle age, aware of his limitations, having proved the fallacy of the world's wide-open spaces, he was hankering for his home in Darrow and the greater adventure of matrimony. He excused himself with a shamed smile.

"My dad wants me in the practice. Wants to see me raise a brood of young Ingersolls. Dear old boy, he never fails to mention you, Francis . . . his Roman Voltaire."

He spoke with rare affection of his sister Jean, now married and comfortably settled in Tynecastle. He said, oddly, not looking at Francis:

"It took her a long time to reconcile herself to the celibacy of the clergy."

His silence on the subject of Judy was strangely suspect. But he could not speak enough of Polly. He had met her six months ago in Tynecastle, still going strong. "What a woman!" He nodded across his glass. "Mark my words, she may astound you one day. Polly is, was, and always will be a holy trump." They slept in their chairs.

By the end of that week the epidemic showed further indications of abatement. Now the death carts seldom rattled through the streets, vultures ceased to swoop from the horizon and snow no longer fell.

On the following Saturday Father Chisholm stood again on his balcony at the mission, inhaling the ice-cold air, with a deep and blessed thankfulness. From his vantage he could see the children playing in complete unconsciousness behind the tall kaolin fence. He felt like a man towards whom sweet daylight slowly filters after a long and dreadful dream.

Suddenly his gaze was caught by a figure of a soldier, dark against the snowbanks, moving rapidly up the road towards the mission. At first he took the man for one of the Lieutenant's followers. Then, with some surprise, he saw that it was Shon himself.

This was the first time the young officer had visited him. A puzzled light hovered about Francis' eyes as he turned and went down the stairs to meet him.

On the doorstep, the sight of Shon's face stopped the welcome on his lips. It was lemon pale, tight-drawn, and of a mortal gravity. A faint dew of perspiration on the brow bespoke his haste, as did the half-unbuttoned tunic, an unbelievable laxity in one so precise.

The Lieutenant wasted no time. "Please come to the yamen at once. Your friend the doctor is taken ill."

Francis felt a great coldness, a cold shock, like the impact of a frigid blast. He shivered. He gazed back at Shon. After what seemed a long time he heard himself say: "He has been working too much. He has collapsed."

Shon's hard dark eyes winced imperceptibly. "Yes, he has collapsed."

There was another pause. Then Francis knew it was the worst. He turned pale. He set out, as he was, with the Lieutenant.

They walked half the way in complete silence. Then Shon, with a military precision that suppressed all feeling, revealed briefly what had occurred. Dr. Tulloch had come in with a tired air and gone to take a drink. While he poured the drink he had coughed explosively, and steadied himself against the bamboo table, his face a dingy grey, except for the prune-juice froth upon his lips. As Maria-Veronica ran to help him, he gave her before he collapsed a weak, peculiar smile: "Now is the time to send for the priest."

When they reached the yamen a soft grey mist was drooping, like a tired cloud, across the snow-banked roofs. They entered quickly. Tulloch lay in the small end room, on his narrow camp bed, covered with a quilted mat of purple silk. The rich deep colour of the quilt intensified his dreadful pallor, threw a livid shadow upon his face. It was agony for Francis to see how swiftly the fever had struck. Willie might have been a different man. He was shrunken, unbelievably, as though after weeks of wasting. His tongue and lips were swollen, his eyeballs glazed and shot with blood.

Beside the bed Maria-Veronica was kneeling, replenishing the pack of snow upon the sick man's forehead. She held herself erect—tensely, her expression rigid in its fixed control. She rose as Francis and the Lieutenant entered. She did not speak.

Francis went over to the bedside. A great fear was in his heart. Death had walked with them these past few weeks, familiar and casual, a dreadful commonplace. But now that death's shadow lay upon his friend, the pain that struck at him was strange and terrible.

Tulloch was still conscious, the light of recognition remained in his congested gaze. "I came out for adventure." He tried to smile. "I seem to have got it." A moment later, he added, half-closing his eyes, as a kind of afterthought: "Man, I'm weak as a cat."

Francis sat down on the low stool at the head of the bed. Shon and Maria-Veronica were at the end of the room.

The stillness, the painful sense of waiting, was insupportable, growing, alike, with a frightful feeling of intrusion upon the privacy of things unknown.

"Are you quite comfortable?"

"I might be worse. Spare me a drop of that Japanese whisky. It'll help me along. Man, it's an awful conventional thing to die like this . . . me that damned the story-books."

When Francis had given him a sip of spirits he closed his eyes and seemed to rest. But soon he lapsed into a low delirium.

"Another drink, lad. Bless you, that's the stuff! I've drunk plenty in my time, round the slums of Tynecastle. And now I'm away home to dear old Darrow. On the banks of Allan Water, when the sweet springtime had fled. D'you mind that one, Francis . . . it's a bonny song. Sing it Jean. Come on, louder, louder . . . I cannot hear you in the dark." Francis gritted his teeth, fighting the tumult in his breast. "That's right, Your Reverence. I'll keep quiet and save my strength . . . It's a queer business . . . altogether . . . we've all got to toe the line sometime." Muttering, he sank into unconsciousness.

The priest knelt in prayer by the bedside. He prayed for help, for inspiration. But he was strangely dumb, gripped by a kind of stupor. The city outside was ghostly in its silence. Twilight came. Maria-Veronica rose to light the lamp, then returned to the far corner of the room outside the beam of lamplight, her lips unmoving, silent, but her fingers steadily enumerating the beads beneath her gown.

Tulloch was getting worse: his tongue black, his throat so swollen his bouts of vomiting were an agony to watch.

But suddenly he seemed to rally; he dimly opened his eyes.

"What o'clock is it?" His voice crouped huskily. "Near five . . . at home . . . that's when we had our tea. D'you mind, Francis, the crowd of us at the big round table . . . ?" A longer pause . . . "Ye'll write the old man and tell him that his son died game. Funny . . . I still can't believe in God."

"Does that matter now?" What was he saying? Francis did not know. He was crying and, in the stupid humiliation of his weakness, the words came from him, in blind confusion. "He believes in you."

"Don't delude yourself . . . I'm not repentant."

"All human suffering is an act of repentance.'

There was a silence. The priest said no more. Weakly, Tulloch reached out his hand and let it fall on Francis' arm.

"Man, I've never loved ye so much as I do now . . . for not trying to bully me to heaven. Ye see——" His lids dropped wearily. "I've such an awful headache."

His voice failed. He lay on his back, exhausted, his breathing quick and shallow, his gaze upturned as though fixed far beyond the ceiling. His throat was closed, he could not even cough.

The end was near. Maria-Veronica was kneeling now, at the window, her back towards them, her gaze directed fixedly into the darkness. Shon stood at the foot of the bed. His face was set immovably.

Suddenly Willie moved his eyes, in which a lingering spark still flickered. Francis saw that he was trying, vainly, to whisper. He knelt, slipped his arm about the dying man's neck, brought his cheek close to the other's breath. At first he could hear nothing. Then weakly came the words: "Our fight . . . Francis . . . more than sixpence to get my sins forgiven."

The sockets of Tulloch's eyes filled up with shadow. He yielded to an unaccountable weariness. The priest felt rather than heard the last faint sigh. The room was suddenly more quiet. Still holding the body, as a mother might hold her child, he began blindly, in a low and strangled voice, the De Profundis.

"Out of the depths have I cried unto thee, O Lord. Lord, hear my voice . . . because with the Lord there is mercy: and with him plentiful redemption."

He rose at last, closed the eyes, composed the limp hands.

As he went out of the room he saw Sister Maria-Veronica still bowed at the window. As though still within a dream he gazed at the Lieutenant. He saw, in a kind of dim surprise, that Shon's shoulders were shaking convulsively.

VI

The plague had passed, but a great apathy gripped the snowbound land. In the country the rice fields were frozen lakes. The few remaining peasants could not work a soil so mercilessly entombed. There was no sign of life. In the town survivors emerged as from a painful hibernation, began dully to gather up their daily lives. The merchants and magistrates had not yet returned. It was said that many distant roads were quite impassable. None could remember such evil weather. All the passes were reported blocked and avalanches hurtled down the distant Kwangs like puffs of pure white smoke. The river, in its upper reaches, was frozen solid, a great grey wasteland over which the wind drove powder snow, in blinding desolation. Lower down there was a channel. Huge lumps of ice crashed and pounded in the current under the Manchu Bridge. Hardship was in every home and famine lurked not far behind.

One boat had risked the jagged floes and steamed up-river from Sen-siang, bringing food and medical comforts from the Leighton Expedition, and a long-delayed packet of letters. After a brief stay it had cast off, taking the remaining members of Dr. Tulloch's party back to Nankin.

In the mail which arrived one communication surpassed the others in importance. As Father Chisholm came slowly up from the end of the mission garden where a small wooden cross marked Dr. Tulloch's grave, he bore this letter in his hand and his thoughts were busy with the visit it announced. He hoped his work was satisfactory—the mission was surely worthy of his pride in it. If only the weather would break—thaw quickly—in the next two weeks!

When he reached the church Mother Maria-Veronica was coming down the steps. He must tell her—though he had come to dread these rare occasions when official business forced him to break the silence which lay between them.

"Reverend Mother . . . the provincial administrator of our Foreign Missions Society, Canon Mealey, is making a tour of inspection of the Chinese missions. He sailed five weeks ago. He will arrive in about a month's time . . . to visit us." He paused. "I thought you'd like to have notice . . . in case there is anything you wish to put before him."

Muffled against the cold, she raised her gaze, impenetrable, behind the rimed vapour of her breath. Yet she started faintly. Now she so seldom saw him closely, the change which those last weeks had brought was strikingly manifest. He was thin, quite emaciated. The bones of his face had become prominent, the skin drawn tighter, cheeks slightly sunken, so that his eyes seemed larger and oddly luminous. A terrible impulse took possession of her.

"There is only one thing I wish to put before him." She spoke instinctively, the sudden news lifting from the recesses of her soul a deeply buried thought. "I shall ask to be transferred to another mission."

There was a long pause. Though not wholly taken by surprise, he felt chilled, defeated. He sighed. "You are unhappy here?"

"Happiness has nothing to do with it. As I told you, when I entered the religious life I prepared myself to endure everything."

"Even the enforced association of someone whom you despise?"

She coloured with a proud defiance. That deep throbbing in her bosom drove her to continue. "You mistake me completely. It is obvious. It is something deeper . . . spiritual."

"Spiritual? Will you try to tell me?"

"I feel"—she took a quick breath—"that you are upsetting me . . . in my inner life . . . my spiritual beliefs."

"That is a serious matter." He stared at the letter unseeingly, twisting it in his bony hands. "It hurts me . . . as much, I am sure, as it hurts you to say it. But perhaps you have misunderstood me. To what do you refer?"

"Do you think I have prepared a list?" Despite her control she felt her agitation rising. "It is your attitude . . . For instance, some remarks you made when Dr. Tulloch was dying . . . and afterwards, when he was dead."

"Please go on."

"He was an atheist, and yet you virtually promised he would have his eternal reward . . . he who didn't believe . . ."

914

He said quickly: "God judges us not only by what we believe . . . but by what we do."

"He was not a Catholic . . . not even a Christian!"

"How do you define a Christian? One who goes to church one day of the seven and lies, slanders, cheats his fellow men the other six?" He smiled faintly. "Dr. Tulloch didn't live like that. And he died—helping others . . . like Christ himself."

She repeated stubbornly: "He was a free-thinker."

"My child, our Lord's contemporaries thought him a dreadful free-thinker . . . that's why they killed him."

She was pale now, quite distraught. "It is inexcusable to make such a comparison—outrageous!"

"I wonder! . . . Christ was a very tolerant man—and humble."

A rush of colour again flooded her cheek. "He made certain rules. Your Dr. Tulloch did not obey them. You know that. Why, when he was unconscious, at the end, you did not even administer extreme unction."

"No, I didn't! And perhaps I should have." He stood, thinking worriedly, rather depressed. Then he seemed to cheer up. "But the good God may forgive him none the less." He paused, with simple frankness. "Didn't you love him too?"

She hesitated, lowered her eyes. "Yes . . . Who could help that?"

"Then don't let us make his memory the occasion of a quarrel. There is one thing we most of us forget. Christ taught it. The Church teaches it . . . though you wouldn't think so to hear a great many of us today. No one in good faith can ever be lost. No one. Buddhists, Mohammedans, Taoists . . . the blackest cannibals who ever devoured a missionary . . . If they are sincere, according to their own lights, they will be saved. That is the splendid mercy of God. So why shouldn't He enjoy confronting a decent agnostic at the Judgement Seat with a twinkle in his eye: 'I'm here you see, in spite of all they brought you up to believe. Enter the Kingdom which you honestly denied.'" He made to smile, then, seeing her expression, sighed and shook his head. "I'm truly sorry you feel as you do. I know I'm hard to get on with, and perhaps a little odd in my beliefs. But you've worked so wonderfully here . . . the children love you . . . and during the plague . . ." He broke off. "I know we haven't got on very well . . . but the mission would suffer terribly if you should go."

He gazed at her with a queer intentness, a sort of strained humility. He waited for her to speak. Then, as she did not, he slowly took his leave.

She continued on her way to the refectory where she superintended the serving of the children's dinner. Later, in her own bare room, she paced up and down in a strange continuance of her agitation. Suddenly, with a gesture of despair, she sat down and set herself to complete a further passage in another of those lengthy letters in which, from day to day, as the outlet for her emotions, a penance and a consolation, she compiled the record of her doings for her brother.

Pen in hand, she seemed calmer; the act of writing seemed to tranquillize her.

"I have just told him I must ask to be transferred. It came suddenly, a sort of climax to all I have suppressed, and something of a threat as well. I was amazed at myself, startled by the words issuing from my lips. Yet when the opportunity presented itself I could not resist, I wanted instantly to startle, to hurt him. But, my dear dear Ernst, I am no happier. . . . After that second of triumph when I saw dismay cloud his face I am even more restless and distressed. I look out at the vast desolation of these grey wastes—so different from our cosy winter landscape with its golden air, its sleighbells and clustered chalet roofs—and I want to cry . . . as if my heart would break.

"It is his silence which defeats me—that stoic quality of enduring, and of fighting, all without speech. I've told you of his work during the plague, when he went about amongst foul sickness and sudden repulsive death as carelessly as if he were walking down the main street of his dreadful Scottish village. Well, it wasn't merely his courage, but the muteness of that courage, which was so unbelievably heroic. When his friend, the doctor, died, he held him in his arms, unmindful of the contagion, of that final cough which spattered his cheek with clotted blood. And the look upon his face . . . in its compassion and utter selflessness . . . it pierced my heart. Only my pride saved me the humiliation of weeping in his sight! Then I became angry. What irks me most of all is that I once wrote you that he was despicable. Ernst, I was wrong,— what an admission from your stubborn sister!—I can no longer despise him. Instead I despise myself. But I detest him. And I won't, I won't let him beat me down to his level of harrowing simplicity.

"The two others here have both been conquered. They love him —that is another mortification I must sustain. Martha, the stolid peasant, with bunions but no brains, is prepared to adore anything in a cassock. But Clotilde, shy and timid, flushing on the slightest provocation, a gently sweet and sensitive creature, has become a perfect devotee. During her enforced quarantine she worked him a thick quilted bed-mat, soft and warm, really beautiful. She took it to Joseph, his servant, with instructions to place it on the Father's bed—she is much too modest even to whisper the word 'bed' in his hearing. Joseph smiled: 'I am sorry, Sister, there is no bed!' It appears he sleeps upon the bare floor, with no covering but his overcoat, a greenish garment of uncertain age, which he is fond of, and of which, caressing the frayed and threadbare

916

sleeves, he says proudly, 'Actually! I had it when I was a student at Holywell!'

"Martha and Clotilde have been making inquiries in his kitchen, nervous and perturbed, convinced that he does not look after himself. Their expressions, like shocked tabbies, almost made me laugh as they told me what I already knew, that he eats nothing but black bread, potatoes and bean curd.

" 'Joseph has instructions to boil a pot of potatoes and place them in a wicker basket,' Clotilde mewed. '*He* eats one cold when he is hungry, dipping it in bean curd. Often they are quite musty before the basketful is finished.'

" 'Isn't it dreadful?' I answered curtly. 'But then some stomachs have never known a good cuisine—it is not hardship for them to do without it.'

" 'Yes, Reverend Mother,' murmured Clotilde, blushing, and retreating.

"She would do penance for a week to come and see him eat one nice hot meal. Oh, Ernst, you know how I abominate the sedulous and fawning nun who in the presence of a priest exposes the whites of her eyes and dissolves in obsequious rapture. Never, never, will I descend to such a level. I vowed it at Coblenz when I took the veil, and again at Liverpool . . . and will keep that vow . . . even in Pai-tan. But bean curd! *You* will not encounter it. A thin pinkish paste tasting of stagnant water and chewed wood!" She raised her head at an unexpected sound. "Ernst . . . It is unbelievable . . . it is raining . . ." She stopped writing, as if unable to continue, and slowly laid down her pen. With dark and self-distrustful eyes she sat watching the novelty of the rain, which trickled down the pane like heavy tears.

A fortnight later it was still raining. The skies, dull as tallow, were open sluices from which a steady deluge fell. The drops were large, pitting the upper crust of yellowish snow. It seemed everlasting . . . the snow. Great frozen slabs of it still came sliding from the church roof, with unpremeditated acceleration, landing soddenly upon the slushy snow beneath. Rivulets of rain went rushing across the dun-coloured sludge, channeling, undercutting the banks, which toppled with a slow splash into the stream beneath. The mission was a quagmire of slush.

Then the first patch of brown earth appeared, momentous as the tip of Ararat. Further patches sprouted and coalesced, forming a landscape of bleached grass and scabby desert all fissured and cratered with the flood. And still the rain continued. The mission roofs broke down at last and leaked incessantly. Water came in cataracts from the eaves. The children sat, green and miserable, in the classroom, while Sister Martha placed pails for the larger drips. Sister Clotilde had a dreadful cold and took lessons at her desk beneath Reverend Mother's umbrella.

The light soil of the mission garden could not withstand the scouring fusion of rain and thaw. It swept down the hill in a yellow turbulence on which floated uptorn sareta plants and oleander shrubs. Carp from the fish pond darted frightened, through the flood. The trees were slowly undermined. For a painful day the lychees and catalpas stood upright on their naked roots, which groped like pallid tentacles, then slowly toppled. The young white mulberries followed next, then the lovely row of flowering plum, these on the day that the lower wall was washed away. Only the toughened cedars stood, with the giant banyan, amidst the muddied desolation.

On the afternoon before Canon Mealey's arrival Father Chisholm heavily surveyed the dreary havoc, on his way to children's benediction. He turned to Fu, the gardener, who stood beside him.

"I wished for a thaw. The good God has punished me by sending one."

Fu, like most gardeners, was not a cheerful man. "The great Shang-Foo who arrives from across the seas will think much ill of us. Ah! If only he had seen my bloom of lilies last spring!"

"Let us be of good heart, Fu. The damage is not irreparable."

"My plantings are lost." Fu gloomed. "We shall have to begin all over again."

"That is life . . . to begin again when everything is lost!"

Despite his exhortation, Francis was deeply depressed as he went into the church. Kneeling before the lighted altar, while the rain still drummed upon the roof, he seemed to hear, above the childish treble of the Tantum Ergo, a liquid murmuring beneath him. But the sound of flowing water had long been echoing in his ears. His mind was burdened by the wretched appearance which the mission must present to his visitor upon the following day. He put the thing away as an obsession.

When the service was over and Joseph had snuffed the candles and left the sacristy he came slowly down the aisle. A dank vapour hung about the whitewashed nave. Sister Martha had taken the children across the compound for their supper. But still in prayer upon the damp boards were Reverend Mother and Sister Clotilde. He passed them in silence; then suddenly stopped short. Clotilde's running head catarrh made her a spectacle of woe and Maria-Veronica's lips were drawn with cold. He had an extraordinary inner conviction that they should neither of them be allowed to remain.

He stepped back to them and said: "I am sorry, I'm going to close the church now."

There was a pause. This interference was unlike him. They seemed surprised. But they rose obediently, in silence, and preceded him to the

918

porch. He locked the front doors and followed them through the streaming dusk.

A moment later the sound broke upon them. A low rumble, swelling to a roll of subterranean thunder. As Sister Clotilde screamed, Francis swung round to see the slender structure of his church in motion. Glistening, wetly luminous, it swayed gracefully in the fading light; then like a reluctant woman, yielded. His heart stood still in horror. With a rending crash, the undermined foundations broke. One side caved in, the roof's spire snapped, the rest was a blinding vision of torn timbers and shattered glass. Then his church, his lovely church, lay dissolved into nothing, at his feet.

He stood rooted, for an instant, in a daze of pain, then ran towards the wreckage. But the altar lay smashed to rubble, the tabernacle crushed to splinters beneath a beam. He could not even save the sacred species. And his vestments, the precious Ribiero relic, these were in shreds. Standing there, bare-headed in the teeming rain, he was conscious, amidst the frightened babble which now surrounded him, of Sister Martha's lamentations.

"Why . . . why . . . why has this come on us?" She was moaning, wringing her hands. "Dear God! What worse could you have done to us?"

He muttered, not moving, desperately sustaining his own faith rather than hers:

"Ten minutes sooner . . . we should every one of us have been killed."

There was nothing to be done. They left the fallen wreckage to the darkness and the rain.

Next day, at three o'clock punctually, Canon Mealey arrived. Because of the turbulence of the flooded river, his junk had dropped anchor in a backwater five li below Pai-tan. There were no chairs available: only some wheelbarrows, long-shafted like ploughs, with solid wooden wheels which, since the plague, were used by the few remaining runners to transport their passengers. The situation was difficult for a man of dignity. But there was no alternative. The Canon, mud-spattered and with dangling legs, reached the mission in a wheelbarrow.

The modest reception rehearsed by Sister Clotilde—a song of welcome, with waving of little flags, by the children—had been abandoned. Watching from his balcony, Father Chisholm hurried to the gate to meet his visitor.

"My dear Father!" cried Mealey, stiffly straightening himself and warmly grasping both Francis' hands. "This is the happiest day in many months—to see you again. I told you I should one day run the gamut of the Orient. With the interest of the world centred upon suffering China it was inevitable my resolve should crystallize to action!" He broke off, his eyes bulging across the other's shoulder at the scene of desolation. "Why . . . I don't understand. Where is the church?"

"You see all that is left of it."

"But this mess . . . You reported a splendid establishment."

"We have had some reverses." Francis spoke quietly.

"Why, really, it's incomprehensible . . . most disturbing."

Francis intervened with a hospitable smile. "When you have had a hot bath and a change I will tell you."

An hour later, pink from his tub, in a new tussore suit, Anselm sat stirring his hot soup, with an aggrieved expression.

"I must confess this is the greatest disappointment of my life . . . to come here, to the very outposts . . ." He took a mouthful of soup, meeting the spoon with plump, pursed lips. He had filled out in these last years. He was big now, full-shouldered and stately, still smooth-skinned and clear-eyed, with big palps of hands, hearty or pontifical at will. "I had set my heart on celebrating high mass in your church, Francis. These foundations must have been badly laid."

"It is a wonder they were laid at all."

"Nonsense! You've had lots of time to establish yourself. What in heaven's name am I to tell them at home?" He laughed shortly, dolefully. "I even promised a lecture at London Headquarters of the F.M.S.— 'St. Andrew's: or God in Darkest China.' I'd brought my quarter-plate Zeiss to get lantern slides. It places me . . . all of us . . . in a most awkward position."

There was silence.

"Of course I know you've had your difficulties," Mealey continued between annoyance and compunction. "But who hasn't? I assure you we've had ours. Especially lately since we merged the two divisions . . . after Bishop MacNabb's death!"

Father Chisholm stiffened, as in pain.

"He's dead?"

"Yes, yes, the old man went at last. Pneumonia—this March. He was past his best, very muddled and queer, quite a relief to all of us when he went, very peacefully. The coadjutor, Bishop Tarrant, succeeded him. A great success."

Again a silence fell. Father Chisholm raised his hand to shield his eyes. Rusty Mac gone . . . A rush of unbearable recollection swept him: that day by the Stinchar, the glorious salmon, those kind wise peering eyes and the warmth of them when he was worried at Holywell; the quiet voice in the study at Tynecastle before he sailed, "Keep fighting, Francis, for God and good old Scotland."

Anselm was reflecting, with friendly generosity: "Well, well! We must face things. I suppose. Now that I'm here I'll do my best to get things straight for you. I've a great deal of organizing experience. It may interest you, some day, to hear how I have put the Society on its feet. In my personal appeals, delivered in London, Liverpool and Tynecastle, I raised thirty thousand pounds—and that is only the beginning." He showed his sound teeth in a competent smile. "Don't be so depressed, my dear fellow. I'm not unduly censorious . . . the first thing we'll do is have Reverend Mother over to lunch—she seems an able woman— and have a real round-table parochial conference!"

With an effort Francis pulled himself back from the dear forgotten days. "Reverend Mother doesn't care to take her meals outside the Sisters' house."

"You haven't asked her properly." Mealey gazed at the other's spare figure with a hearty, pitying kindliness. "Poor Francis! I'd hardly expect you to understand women. She'll come all right . . . just leave it to me!"

On the following day, Maria-Veronica did, in fact, present herself for lunch. Anselm was in high spirits after an excellent night's rest and an energetic morning of inspection. Still benevolent from his visit to the schoolroom, he greeted the Reverend Mother, though he had parted from her only five minutes before, with effusive dignity.

"This, Reverend Mother, is indeed an honour. A glass of sherry? No? I assure you it is fine—pale Amontillado. A little travelled perhaps," he beamed, "since it came with me from home. Coddlesome, maybe . . . but a palate, acquired in Spain, is hard to deny."

They sat down at table.

"Now Francis, what are you giving us? No Chinese mysteries, I trust, no birds'-nest soup or purée of chopsticks. Ha! Ha!" Mealey laughed heartily as he helped himself to boiled chicken. "Though I must confess I am somewhat enamoured of the Oriental cuisine. Coming over on the boat—a stormy passage, incidentally; for four days no one appeared at the skipper's table but your humble servant—we were served with a quite delicious Chinese dish, chow mein."

Mother Maria-Veronica raised her eyes from the tablecloth. "Is chow mein a Chinese dish? Or an American edition of the Chinese custom of collecting scraps?"

He stared at her, mouth slightly agape. "My dear Reverend Mother! Chow mein! Why . . ." He glanced at Francis for support, found none, and laughed again. "At any rate, I assure you, I chewed mine! Ha! Ha!"

Swinging round, for better access to the dish of salad which Joseph was presenting, he ran on: "Food apart, the lure of the Orient is immensely fascinating! We Occidentals are apt to condemn the Chinese as a greatly inferior race. Now I for one will shake hands with any Chinaman, provided he believes in God and . . ." he bubbled . . . "carbolic soap!"

Father Chisholm shot a quick glance at Joseph's face, which, though expressionless, showed a faint tightening of the nostrils.

"And now," Mealey paused suddenly, his manner dropping to pontifical solemnity. "We have important business on our agenda. As a boy, Reverend Mother, our good mission father was always leading me into scrapes. Now it's my task to get him out of this one!"

Nothing definite emerged from the conference. Except, perhaps, a modest summary of Anselm's achievements at home.

Free of the limitations of a parish, he had set himself whole-heartedly to work for the missions, mindful that the Holy Father was especially devoted to the Propagation of the Faith and eager to encourage the workers who so selflessly espoused his favourite cause.

It had not been long before he won recognition. He began to move about the country, to preach sermons of impassioned eloquence in the great English cities. Through his genius for collecting friends, no contact of any consequence was ever thrown away. On his return from Manchester, or Birmingham, he would sit down and write a score of charming letters, thanking this person for a delightful lunch, the next for a generous donation to the Foreign Mission Fund. Soon his correspondence was voluminous, and employed a whole-time secretary.

Presently, London acknowledged him as a distinguished visitor. His debut, in the pulpit of Westminster, was spectacular. Women had always idolized him. Now he was adopted by the wealthy coterie of Cathedral spinsters who collected cats and clergymen in their rich mansions south of the Park. His manners had always been engaging. That same year he became a country member of the Athenæum. And the sudden engorgement of the F.M. moneybags evoked a most gracious token of appreciation, direct from Rome.

When he became the youngest canon in the Northern Diocese, few grudged him the success. Even the cynics who traced his exuberant rise to an overactive thyroid gland admitted his business acumen. For all his gush he was no fool. He had a level head for figures and could manage money. In five years he had founded two fresh missions in Japan and a native seminary in Nankin. The new F.M.S. offices in Tynecastle were imposing, efficient and completely free of debt.

In brief, Anselm had made a fine thing of his life. With Bishop Tarrant at his elbow there was every chance that his most admirable work would continue to expand.

Two days after his official meeting with Francis and Reverend Mother, the rain ceased and a watery sun sent pale feelers towards the forgotten earth. Mealey's spirits bounded. He joked to Francis.

"I've brought fine weather with me. Some people follow the sun around. But the sun follows me."

He unlimbered his camera and began to take countless photographs. His energy was tremendous. He bounded out of bed in the morning shouting "Boy! Boy!" for Joseph to get his bath. He said mass in the schoolroom. After a hearty breakfast he departed in his solar topee, a stout stick in hand, the camera swinging on his hip.

He made many excurisons, even poking discreetly for souvenirs amongst the ashes of Pai-tan's plague-spots. At each scene of blackened desolation he murmured reverently: "The hand of God!" He would stop suddenly at a city gate, arresting his companion with a dramatic gesture. "Wait! I must get this one. The light is perfect."

On Sunday, he came in to lunch greatly elated. "It's just struck me, I can still give that lecture. Treat it from the angle of Dangers and Difficulties in the Mission Field. Work in the plague and the flood. This morning I got a glorious view of the ruins of the church. What a slide it will make, titled 'God Chastiseth His Own'! Isn't that magnificent?"

But on the eve of his departure Anselm's manner altered and his tone, as he sat with the mission priest on the balcony after supper, was grave.

"I have to thank you for extending hospitality to a wanderer, Francis. But I am not happy about you. I can't see how you are going to rebuild the church. The Society cannot let you have the money."

"I haven't asked for it." The strain of the past two weeks was beginning to tell on Francis, his stern self-discipline was wearing thin.

Mealey threw his companion a sharp glance. "If only you had been more successful with some of the better-class Chinese, the rich merchants. If only your friend Mr. Chia had seen the light."

"He hasn't." Father Chisholm spoke with unusual shortness. "And he has given munificently. I shall not ask him for another tael."

Anselm shrugged his shoulders, annoyed. "Of course that's your affair. But I must tell you, frankly, I'm sadly disappointed in your conduct of this mission. Take your convert rate. It doesn't compare with our other statistics. We run them as a graph at headquarters, and you're the lowest in the whole chart."

Father Chisholm gazed straight ahead, his lips firmly compressed. He answered with unusual irony: "I suppose missionaries differ in their individual capabilities."

"And in their enthusiasm." Anselm, sensitive to satire, was now justly incensed. "Why do you persist in refusing to employ catechists? It's the universal custom. If you had even three active men, at forty taels a month, why, one thousand baptisms would only cost you fifteen hundred Chinese dollars!"

Francis did not answer. He was praying desperately that he might control his temper, suffer this humiliation as something he deserved.

"You're not getting behind your work here," Mealey went on. "You live, personally, in such poor style. You ought to impress the natives, keep a chair, servants make more of a show."

"You are mistaken." Francis spoke steadily. "The Chinese hate ostentation. They call it *ti-mien*. And priests who practice it are regarded as dishonourable."

Anselm flushed angrily. "You're referring to their own low heathen prietss, I presume."

"Does it matter?" Father Chisholm smiled palely. "Many of these priests are good and noble men."

There was a strained silence. Anselm drew his coat about him with a shocked finality.

"After that, of course, there is nothing to be said. I must confess your attitude pains me deeply. Even Reverend Mother is embarrassed by it. Ever since I arrived it has been plain how much she is at variance with you." He got up and went into his own room.

Francis remained a long time in the gathering mist. That last remark had cut him worst of all: the stab of a premonition confirmed. Now he had no doubt that Maria Veronica had submitted her request to be transferred.

Next morning Canon Mealey took his departure. He was returning to Nankin to spend a week at the Vicariate and would go from there to Nagasaki to inspect six mssions in Japan. His bags were packed, a chair waited to bear him to the junk, he had taken his farewells of the Sisters and the Children. Now, dressed for the journey, wearing sun-glasses, his topee draped with green gauze, he stood in final conversation with Father Chisholm in the hall.

"Well, Francis!" Mealey extended his hand in grudging forgiveness. "We must part friends. The gift of tongues is not given to all of us. I suppose you are a well-meaning fellow at heart." He threw out his chest. "Strange! I'm itching to be off. I have travel in my blood. Good-bye. *Au revoir. Auf Wiedersehen.* And last but not least—God bless you!"

Dropping the mosquito veil he stepped into his chair. The runners groaningly bent their shoulders, supported him and shuffled off. At the sagging mission gates he leaned through the window of the chair, fluttered his white handkerchief in farewell.

At sundown, when he took his evening walk, his beloved hour of stealing twilight and far-off echoing stillness, Father Chisholm found himself meditating, amongst the débris of the church. He seated himself upon a lump of rubble, thinking of his old Headmaster—somehow he always saw Rusty Mac with schoolboy's eyes—and of his exhortation to courage. There was little courage in him now. These last two weeks, the perpetual effort to sustain his visitor's patronizing tone, had left him void. Yet perhaps Anselm was justified. Was he not a failure, in God's sight and in man's? He had done so little. And that little, so laboured and inadequate, was almost undone. How was he to proceed? A weary hopelessness of spirit took hold of him.

Resting there, with bent head, he did not hear a footstep behind him. Mother Maria-Veronica was compelled to make her presence known to him.

"Am I disturbing you?"

He glanced up, quite startled. "No . . . no. As you observe,"—he could not suppress a wincing smile,—"I am doing nothing."

There was a pause. In the indistinctness her face had a swimming pallor. He could not see the nerve twitching in her cheek yet he sensed in her figure a strange rigidity.

Her voice was colourless. "I have something to say to you. I——"

"Yes?"

"This is no doubt humiliating for you. But I am obliged to tell you. I —I am sorry." The words, torn from her, gained momentum, then came in a tumbled flood. "I am most bitterly and grievously sorry for my conduct towards you. From our first meeting I have behaved shamefully, sinfully. The devil of pride was in me. It's always been in me, ever since I was a little child and flung things at my nurse's head. I have known now for weeks that I wanted to come to you . . . to tell you . . . but my pride, my stubborn malice restrained me. These past ten days, in my heart, I have wept for you . . . the slights and humiliations you have endured from that gross and worldly priest, who is unworthy to untie your shoe. Father, I hate myself—forgive me, forgive me . . ." Her voice was lost, she crouched, sobbing into her hands, before him.

The sky was strained of all colour, except the greenish afterglow behind the peaks. This faded swiftly and the kind dusk enfolded her. An interval of time, in which a single tear fell upon her cheek. . . .

"So now you will not leave the mission?"

"No, no . . ." Her heart was breaking. "If you will let me stay. I have never known anyone whom I wished so much to serve . . . Yours is the best . . . the finest spirit I have ever known."

"Hush, my child. I am a poor and insignificant creature . . . you were right . . . a common man . . ."

"Father, pity me." Her sobs went choking into the earth.

"And you are a great lady. But in God's sight we are both of us children If we may work together . . . help each other . . ."

"I will help with all my power. One thing at least I can do. It is so easy to write to my brother. He will rebuild the church . . . restore the mission. He has great possessions, he will do it gladly. If only you will help me . . . help me to defeat my pride."

There was a long silence. She sobbed more softly. A great warmth filled his heart. He took her arm to raise her but she would not rise. So he knelt beside her and gazed, without praying, into the pure and peaceful night where, across the ages, amongst the shadows of a garden, another poor and common man also knelt and watched them both.

VII

One sunny forenoon in the year 1912 Father Chisholm was separating beeswax from his season's yield of honey. His workshop, built in Bavarian style, at the end of the kitchen garden—trim, practical, with a pedal lathe and tools neatly racked, as much a source of delight to him as on the day Mother Maria-Veronica had handed him the key—was sweet with the fume of melted sugar. A great bowl of cool yellow honey stood among fresh shavings upon the floor. On the bench, setting, was the flat copper pan of tawny wax from which, tomorrow, he would make his candles. And such candles—smooth-burning and sweet-scented; even in St. Peter's one would not find the like!

With a sigh of contentment, he wiped his brow, his short fingernails blobbed with the rich wax. Then, shouldering the big honey jar, he pulled the door behind him and set off through the mission grounds. He was happy. Waking in the morning with the starlings chattering in the eaves, and the coolness of the dawn still dewed upon the grass, his second thought was that there could be no greater happiness than to work—much with his hands, a little with his head, but mostly with his heart—and to live, simply, like this, close to the earth which, to him, never seemed far from heaven.

The province was prospering and the people, forgetting flood, pestilence and famine, were at peace. In the five years which had elapsed since its reconstruction, through the generosity of Count Ernst von Hohenlohe, the mission had flourished in a quiet fashion. The church was bigger, stouter than the first. He had built it solidly, with grim compunction, using neither plaster nor stucco, after the monastic model which Queen Margaret had introduced to Scotland centuries before. Classic and severe, with a simple bell-tower, and aisles supported by groined arches, its plainness grew on him until he preferred it to the other. And it was safe.

The school had been enlarged, a new children's home added to the building. And the purchase of the two adjoining irrigated fields provided a model home farm with pigpen, byre, and a chicken run down which Martha stalked, thin-shanked, in wooden shoes and kilted habit, casting corn and clucking joyously in Flemish.

Now his congregation comprised two hundred faithful souls, not one of whom knelt under duress before his altar. The orphanage had trebled in size and was beginning to bear the first fruits of his patient foresight. The older girls helped the Sisters with the little ones, some were already novices, others would soon be going into the world. Why, last Christmas he had married the eldest, at nineteen, to a young farmer from the Liu village. He smiled ruefully at the implications of his cunning. At his recent pastoral visit to Liu—a happy and successful expedition from which he had returned only last week—the young wife had hung her head and told him he must return presently to perform another baptism.

As he shifted the heavy honey to his other shoulder, a bent little man of forty-three, growing bald, with rheumatism already nibbling at his joints, a bough of jessamine flailed him on the cheek. The garden had seldom been so lovely: that, also, he owed to Maria-Veronica. Admitting some adroitness with his hands, he could not remotely claim to have green fingers. But Reverend Mother had revealed an unsuspected skill in growing things. Seeds had arrived from her home in Germany, bundles of shoots wrapped tenderly in sacking. Her letters, begging for this cutting and for that, had sped to famous gardens in Canton and Peking—like his own swift white doves, importunate and homing. This beauty which now surrounded him, this sun-shot sanctuary, alive with twittering hum, was her work.

Their comradeship was not unlike this precious garden. Here, indeed, when he took his evening walk, he would find her, intent, coarsely gloved, cutting the full white peonies that grew so freely, training a stray clematis, watering the golden azaleas. There they would briefly discuss the business of the day. Sometimes they did not speak. When the fireflies flitted in the garden they had gone their separate ways.

As he approached the upper gate he saw the children march in twos across the compound. Dinner. He smiled and hastened. They were seated at the long low table in the new annex to the dormitory, two-score little blue-black polls and shining yellow faces, with Maria-Veronica at one end, Clotilde at the other. Martha, aided by the Chinese novices, was ladling steaming rice broth into a battery of blue bowls. Anna, his foundling of the snow, now a handsome girl, handed round the bowls with her usual air of dark and frowning reserve.

The clamour stilled upon his entry. He shot a shamed boyish look at the Reverend Mother, craving indulgence, and placed the honey jar triumphantly on the table.

"Fresh honey today, children! It is a great pity. I am sure no one wishes it!"

Shrill, immediate denial rose like the chatter of little monkeys. Suppressing his smile he shook his head dolefully at the youngest, a solemn mandarin of three who sat swallowing his spoon, swaying dreamily, his soft small buttocks unstable on the bench.

"I cannot believe a good child could enjoy such monstrous depravity! Tell me, Symphorien—" It was dreadful the way in which new converts chose the most resounding saint names for their children—"Tell me, Symphorien . . . would you not rather learn nice catechism than eat honey?"

"Honey!" answered Symphorien dreamily. He stared at the lined brown face above him. Then, surprised by his own temerity, he burst into tears and fell off the bench.

Laughing, Father Chisholm picked up the child. "There, there! You are a good boy, Symphorien. God loves you. And for speaking the truth you shall have double honey."

He felt Maria-Veronica's reproving gaze upon him. She would presently follow him to the door and murmur: "Father . . . we must consider discipline!" But today—it seemed so long since he stood outside the buzzing classroom, troubled and unhappy, afraid to penetrate the chill unfriendly air—nothing could restrain his manner with the children. His fondness towards them had always been absurd, it was what he named his patriarchal privilege.

As he expected, Maria-Veronica accompanied him from the room but, though her brow seemed unusually clouded, she did not even mildly rebuke him. Instead, after some hesitation, she remarked: "Joseph had a strange story this morning."

"Yes. The rascal wants to get married . . . naturally. But he is deafening me with the beauties and convenience of a lodge . . . to be built at the mission gate . . . not, of course, for Joseph or for Joseph's wife . . . but solely for the benefit of the mission."

"No, it isn't the lodge." Unsmiling, she bit her lip. "The building is taking place elsewhere, in the Street of the Lanterns—you know that splendid central site—and on a grander scale, much grander than anything we have accomplished here." Her tone was strangely bitter. "Scores of workmen have arrived, barges of white stone from Sen-siang. Everything. I assure you money is being spent as only American millionaires can spend it. Soon we shall have the finest establishment in Pai-tan, with schools, for both boys and girls, a playground, public rice kitchen, free dispensary, and a hospital with resident doctor!" She broke off, gazing at him with tears in her troubled eyes.

"What establishment?" He spoke automatically, stunned by a presage of her answer.

"Another mission. Protestant. The American Methodists."

There was a long pause. Secure in the remoteness of his situation, he had never contemplated even the possibility of such intrusion. Reverend Mother, recalled to the refectory by Clotilde, left him in painful silence.

He walked slowly towards his house, all the brightness of the morning dimmed. Where was his mediaeval fortress now? In a quick throwback to his childhood, he had the same sensation of injustice as when, out berry-picking, another boy had encroached upon a secret bush of his own discovery and rudely begun to strip it of its fruit. He knew the hatreds which developed between rival missions, the ugly jealousies, above all,

928

the bickerings on points of doctrine, the charge and countercharge, the raucous denunciation which made the Christian faith appear, to the tolerant Chinese mind, an infernal tower of Babel where all shouted at lung-pitch: "Behold, it is here! Here! Here!" But where? Alas! When one looked, there was nothing but rage and sound and execration.

At his house he found Joseph, duster in hand, idling about the hall, in pretence of work, waiting to bemoan the news.

"Has the Father heard of the hateful coming of these Americans who worship the false God?"

"Be silent, Joseph!" The priest answered harshly. "They do not worship the false God, but the same true God as we. If you speak such words again you will never get your gate-house!"

Joseph edged away, grumbling beneath his breath.

In the afternoon Father Chisholm went down to Pai-tan and, in the Street of the Lanterns, received the fateful confirmation of his eyes. Yes, the new mission was begun—was rising rapidly under the hands of many squads of masons, carpenters, and coolies. He watched a string of labourers, swaying along a strip of planking, bearing baskets of the finest Soochin glaze. He saw that the scale of operations was princely.

As he lingered there, with his thoughts for company, he suddenly discovered Mr. Chia at his elbow. He greeted his old friend quietly.

As they talked of the fineness of the weather and the general excellence of trade, Francis sensed more than usual kindness in the merchant's manner.

Suddenly, having appeased the proprieties, Mr. Chia guilelessly remarked: "It is pleasant to observe the excess growth of goodness, though many would consider it a superfluity. For myself I much enjoy walking in other mission gardens. Moreover, when the Father came here many years ago he received much ill-usage." A gentle and suggestive pause. "It seems highly probable, even to such an uninfluential and lowly-placed citizen as I, that the new missioners could receive such execrable treatment on their arrival that they might be most regretfully forced to depart."

A shiver passed over Father Chisholm as an unbelievable temptation assailed him. The ambiguity, the forced understatement, of the merchant's remark was more significant than the direst threat. Mr. Chia, in many subtle and subterranean ways, wielded the greatest power in the district. Francis knew that he need only answer, gazing into space: "It would certainly be a great misfortune if disaster befell the coming missioners . . . But then, who can prevent the will of heaven?" to foredoom the threatened invasion of his pastorate. But he recoiled, abhorring himself for the thought. Conscious of a cold perspiration on his brow, he replied as calmly as he could:

"There are many gates to heaven. We enter by one, these new preachers by another. How can we deny them the right to practise virtue in their own way? If they desire it, then they must come."

He did not observe that spark of singular regard which for once irradiated Mr. Chia's placid eye. Still deeply disturbed, he parted from his friend and walked homeward up the hill. He entered the church and seated himself, for he was tired, before the crucifix on the side altar. Gazing at the face, haloed with thorns, he prayed, in his mind, for endurance, wisdom, and forbearance.

By the end of June the Methodist mission was near completion. For all his fortitude, Father Chisholm had not brought himself to view the successive stages of construction; he had sombrely avoided the Street of the Lanterns. But when Joseph, who had not failed as a baleful informant, brought news that the two foreign devils had arrived, the little priest sighed, put on his one good suit, took his tartan umbrella, and steeled himself to call.

When he rang the door bell the sound echoed emptily into the new smell of paint and plaster. But after waiting indeterminately for a minute under the green-glass portico, he heard hastening steps within, and the door was opened by a small faded middle-aged woman in a grey alpaca skirt and high-necked blouse.

"Good afternoon. I am Father Chisholm. I took the liberty of calling to welcome you to Pai-tan."

She started nervously and a look of quick apprehension flooded her pale blue eyes.

"Oh, yes. Please come in. I am Mrs. Fiske. Wilbur . . . my husband . . . Dr. Fiske . . . he's upstairs. I'm afraid we are all alone, and not quite settled yet!" Hurriedly, she silenced his regretful protest. "No, no . . . you must step in."

He followed her upstairs to a cool, lofty room, where a man of forty, clean-shaven, with a short-cropped moustache, and of her own diminutive size, was perched on a stepladder methodically arranging books upon the shelves. He wore strong glasses over his intelligent, apologetic, short-sighted eyes. His baggy cotton knickers gave his thin little calves an indescribable pathos. Descending the ladder, he stumbled, almost fell.

"Do be careful, Wilbur!" Her hands fluttered protectively. She introduced the two men. "Now let's sit down . . . if we can." She unsuccessfully attempted a smile. "It's too bad not having our furniture . . . but then one gets used to anything in China."

They sat down. Father Chisholm said pleasantly:

"You have a magnificent building here."

"Yes." Dr. Fiske deprecated. "We're very lucky. Mr. Chandler, the oil magnate, is most generous with us."

A strained silence. They so little fulfilled the priest's uneasy expectations, he felt taken unawares. He could not claim gigantic stature, yet the Fiskes, by the very sparseness of their physical economy, silenced the merest whisper of aggression. The little doctor was mild, with a bookish, even timid air, and a smile, deprecating, about his lips, as though afraid to settle. His wife, more clearly distinguishable in this good light, was a gentle, steadfast creature, her blue eyes easily receptive of tears, her hands alternating between her thin gold locket chain and a frizzy pad of rich, net-enclosed, brown hair which, with a slight shock, Francis perceived to be a wig.

Suddenly Dr. Fiske cleared his throat. He said, simply: "How you must hate our coming here!"

"Oh, no . . . not at all." It was the priest's turn to look awkward.

"We had the same experience once. We were up-country in the Lan-hi province, a lovely place. I wish you'd seen our peach trees. We had it all to ourselves for nine years. Then another missionary came. Not," he inserted swiftly, "a Catholic priest. But, well . . . We did resent it, didn't we, Agnes?"

"We did, dear." She nodded tremulously. "Still . . . we got over it. We are old campaigners, Father."

"Have you been long in China?"

"Over twenty years! We came as an insanely young couple the day we were married. We have given our lives to it." The moisture in her eyes receded before a bright and eager smile. "Wilbur! I must show Father Chisholm John's photograph." She rose, proudly took a silver-framed portrait from the bare mantelpiece. "This is our boy, taken when he was at Harvard, before he went as Rhodes Scholar to Oxford. Yes, he's still in England . . . working in our dockland settlement in Tynecastle."

The name shattered his strained politeness. "Tynecastle!" He smiled. "That is very near my home."

She gazed at him, enchanted, smiling back, holding the photograph to her bosom with tender hands.

"Isn't that amazing? The world is such a small place after all." Briskly she replaced the photograph on the mantel. "Now I'm going to bring in coffee, and some of my very own doughnuts . . . a family receipt." Again she silenced his protests. "It's no trouble. I always make Wilbur take a little refreshment at this hour. He has had some bother with his duodenum. If I didn't look after him who would?"

He had meant to stay for five minutes; he remained for more than an hour.

They were New England people, natives of the town of Biddeford, in Maine, born, reared and married in the tenets of their own strict faith. As they spoke of their youth he had a swift and strangely sympathetic vision of a cold crisp countryside, of great salty rivers flowing between wands of silver birches to the misty sea, past white wooden houses amidst the wine of maples, and sumac, velvet-red in winter, a thin white steeple above the village, with bells and dark silent figures in the frosted street, following their quiet destiny.

But the Fiskes had chosen another and harder path. They had suffered. Both had almost died of cholera. During the Boxer rebellion, when many of their fellow missioners were massacred, they had spent six months in a filthy prison under daily threat of execution. Their devotion to each other, and to their son, was touching. She had, for all her tremulousness, an indomitable maternal solicitude towards her two men.

Despite her antecedents, Agnes Fiske was a pure romantic whose life was written in a host of tender souvenirs she so carefully preserved. Soon she was showing Francis a letter of her dear mother's, a quarter of a century old, with the formula for these doughnuts, and a curl from John's head worn within her locket. Upstairs in her drawer were many more such tokens: bundles of yellowing correspondence, her withered bridal bouquet, a front tooth her son had shed, the ribbon she had worn at her first Biddeford Church Social. . . .

Her health was frail and presently, once this new venture was established, she was leaving for a six months' vacation which she would spend in England with her son. Already, with an earnestness that presaged her goodwill, she pressed Father Chisholm to entrust her with any commissions he might wish executed at home.

When, at last, he took his leave, she escorted him beyond the portico, where Dr. Fiske stood, to the outer gate. Her eyes filled up with tears. "I can't tell you how relieved, how glad I am at your kindness, your friendliness in calling . . . especially for Wilbur's sake. At our last station he had such a painful experience . . . hatreds stirred up, frightful bigotry. It got so bad, latterly, when he went out to see a sick man he was struck and knocked senseless by a young brute of a . . . a missionary who accused him of stealing the man's immortal soul." She suppressed her emotion. "Let us help one another. Wilbur is such a clever doctor. Call on him any time you wish." She pressed his hand quickly and turned away.

Father Chisholm went home in a curious state of mind. For the next few days he had no news of the Fiskes. But on Saturday a batch of home-baked cookies arrived at St. Andrew's. As he took them, still warm and wrapped in the white napkin, to the children's refectory, Sister Martha scowled.

"Does she think we cannot bake here—this new woman?"

"She is trying to be kind, Martha. And we also must try."

For several months Sister Clotilde had suffered from a painful irritation of her skin. All sorts of lotions had been used, from calamine to carbolic, but without success. So distressing was the affliction she made a special novena for a cure. The following week Father Chisholm saw her rubbing her red excoriated hands in a torment of itching. He frowned and, fighting his own reluctance, sent a note to Dr. Fiske.

The doctor arrived within half an hour, quietly examined the patient in Reverend Mother's presence, used no resounding words, praised the treatment that had been given and, having mixed a special physic to be taken internally every three hours, unobtrusively departed. In ten days the ugly rash had vanished and Sister Clotilde was a new woman. But after the first radiance she brought a troubling scruple to her confession.

"Father . . . I prayed to God so earnestly . . . and . . ."

"It was the Protestant missionary who cured you?"

"Yes, Father."

"My child . . . don't let your faith be troubled. God did answer your prayer. We are his instruments . . . every one of us." He smiled suddenly. "Don't forget what old Lao-tzu said—'Religions are many, reason is one, we are all brothers.'"

That same evening as he walked in the garden Maria-Veronica said to him, almost unwillingly:

"This American . . . he is a good doctor."

He nodded. "And a good man."

The work of the two missions marched forward without conflict. There was room for both in Pai-tan, and each was careful not to give offence. The wisdom of Father Chisholm's determination to have no rice-Christians in his flock was now apparent. Only one of his congregation betook himself to Lantern Street, and he was returned with a brief note: "Dear Chisholm, The bearer is a bad Catholic but would be a worse Methodist. Ever, Your friend in the Universal God, Wilbur Fiske, M.D. P.S. If any of your people need hospitalization send them along. They'll receive no dark hints on the fallibility of the Borgias!"

The priest's heart glowed. Dear Lord, he thought, kindness and toleration—with these two virtues how wonderful Thy earth would be!

Fiske's accomplishments were not worn on his sleeve: he was revealed gradually as an archaeologist and Chinese scholar of the first order. He contributed abstruse articles to the archives of obscure societies at home. His hobby was Chien-lung porcelain and his collection of eighteenth-century *famille noire*, picked up with unobtrusive guile, was genuinely fine. Like most small men ruled by their wives, he loved an argument, and it was not long before Francis and he were friends enough to debate, warily, with cunning on both sides, and sometimes, alas, with rising heat, certain points which separated their respective creeds. Occasionally, carried away by the fervour of their opposite views, they parted with a certain tightness of the lips—for the pedantic little doctor could be querulous when roused. But it soon passed.

Once, after such a disagreement, Fiske met the mission priest. He stopped abruptly. "My dear Chisholm, I have been reflecting on a sermon which I once heard from the lips of Dr. Elder Cummings, our eminent divine, in which he declared: 'The greatest evil of today is the growth of the Romish Church through the nefarious and diabolical intrigues of its priests.' I should like you to know that since I have had the honour of your acquaintance I believe the Reverend Cummings to have been talking through his hat."

Francis, smiling grimly, consulted his theological books and ten days later formally bowed.

"My dear Fiske, in Cardinal Cuesta's catechism I find, plainly printed, this illuminating phrase: 'Protestantism is an immoral practice which blasphemes God, degrades man, and endangers society.' I should like you to know, my dear Fiske, that even before I had the honour of your acquaintance I considered the Cardinal unpardonable!" Raising his hat he solemnly marched off.

Neighbouring Chinese thought the "doubled-up-with-laughter small-foreign-devil Methody" had completely lost his reason.

One gusty day towards the end of October Father Chisholm met the doctor's good lady on the Manchu Bridge. Mrs. Fiske was returning from marketing, one hand holding a net bag, the other clasping her hat securely to her head.

"Goodness!" she exclaimed cheerfully. "Isn't this a gale? It does blow the dust into my hair. I shall have to shampoo it again tonight!"

Familiar now with this one eccentricity, this single blot upon a blameless soul, Francis did not smile. Upon every possible occasion she guilelessly assumed her dreadful toupee to be a perfect mane of hair. His heart went out to her for the gentle little lie.

"I hope you are all well."

She smiled, head inclined, being very careful of her hat. "I am in rude health. But Wilbur is sulking—because I am off tomorrow. He will be so lonely, poor fellow. But then you are always lonely—what a solitary life you have!" She paused. "Do tell me, now that I am going to England, if there is anything I can do for you. I am bringing Wilbur back some new winter underwear—there's no place like Britain for woollens. Shall I do the same for you?"

He shook his head, smiling; then an odd thought struck him. "If you have nothing better to do one day . . . look up a dear old aunt of mine in Tynecastle. Miss Polly Bannon is the name. Wait, I'll write down her address."

He scribbled the address with a stub of pencil on a scrap of paper torn from a package in her shopping bag. She tucked it into her glove.

"Shall I give her any message?"

"Tell her how well and happy I am . . . and what a grand place this is. Tell her I'm—next to your husband—the most important man in China."

934

Her eyes were bright and warm towards him. "Perhaps I shall tell her more than you think. Women have a way of talking when they get together. Good-bye. See that you look in on Wilbur occasionally. And do take care of yourself."

She shook hands and went off, a poor weak woman with a will of iron.

He promised himself he would call on Dr. Fiske. But as the weeks slipped past he seemed never to have an hour of leisure. There was the matter of Joseph's house to be arranged, and, when the little lodge was nicely built, the marriage ceremony itself, a full nuptial mass with six of the youngest children as train-bearers. Once Joseph and his bride were suitably installed, he returned to the Liu village with Joseph's father and brothers. He had long cherished the dream of an outpost, a small secondary mission at Liu. There was talk of a great trade route being constructed through the Kwangs. At some future date he might well have a younger priest to help him, one who might operate from this new centre in the hills. He had a strange impulse to set his plans in motion by increasing the area of the village grain-fields, arranging with his friends in Liu to clear, plough and sow an additional sixty mu of arable upland.

These affairs offered a genuine excuse, yet he experienced a sharp twinge of self-reproach as, some five months later, he unexpectedly encountered Fiske. The doctor, however, was in good spirits, lit by a guarded, oddly jocose animation, which permitted only one deduction.

"Yes." He chuckled, then corrected himself to a fitting gravity. "You're quite right. Mrs. Fiske rejoins me at the beginning of next month."

"I'm glad. It has been a long journey for her to take alone."

"She was fortunate in finding a most congenial fellow-passenger."

"Your wife is a very friendly person."

"And with a great talent," Dr. Fiske seemed to suppress a preposterous tendency to giggle, "for not minding her own business. You must come and dine with us when she arrives."

Father Chisholm rarely went out, his mode of life did not permit it, but now compunction drove him to accept. "Thank you, I will."

Three weeks later he was reminded of his commitment, not altogether willingly, by a copper-plate note from the Street of the Lanterns: "Tonight, without fail, seven-thirty."

It was inconvenient, when he had arranged for vespers at seven o'clock. But he advanced the service by half an hour, sent Joseph to procure a chair, and that evening set out in formal style.

The Methodist Mission was brightly illuminated, exuding an unusual air of festivity. As he stepped out into the courtyard he hoped it would not be a large or lengthy affair. He was not anti-social, but his life had grown increasingly interior in these last years and that strain of Scots

935

reserve, inherited from his father, had deepened into an odd guardedness towards strangers.

He was relieved, on entering the upper room, now gay with flowers and festoons of coloured paper, to find only his host and hostess, standing together on the hearth-rug, rather flushed from the warm room, like children before a party. While the doctor's thick lenses scintillated rays of welcome, Mrs. Fiske came quickly forward and took his hand.

"I am so glad to see you again, my poor neglected and misguided creature."

There was no mistaking the warmth of her greeting. She seemed quite taken out of herself. "You're happy to be back anyway. But I'm sure you've had a wonderful trip."

"Yes, yes, a wonderful trip. Our dear son is doing splendidly. How I wish he were with us tonight." She rattled on, ingenuous as a girl, her eyes bright with excitement. "Such things I have to tell you. But you'll hear . . . indeed, you'll hear . . . when our other guest comes in."

He could not prevent a questioning elevation of his brows.

"Yes, we are four tonight. A lady . . . in spite of our different viewpoints . . . now a most particular friend of mine. She is here on a visit." She stumbled, aware of his amazement, then faltered nervously. "My dear good Father, you are not to be cross with me." She faced the door and clapped her hands, in prearranged signal.

The door opened and Aunt Polly came into the room.

VIII

In the convent kitchen on that September day of 1914 neither Polly nor Sister Martha gave the slightest heed to the faint familiar sound of rifle-fire in the hills. While Martha cooked the dinner, using her spotless battery of copper pans, Polly stood by the window ironing a pile of linen wimples. In three months the two had become as inseparable as two brown hens in a strange farmyard. They respected each other's qualities. Martha had acclaimed Polly's crochet as the finest she had ever seen while Polly, after fingering Martha's cross-stitch, admitted her own inferior for the first time in her life. And they had, of course, a topic which never failed them.

Now, as Polly damped the linen and raised the iron expertly to her cheek to test its heat, she complained: "He is looking very poorly again." With one hand Martha put some more wood into the stove while she stirred the soup reflectively with the other. "What would one expect? He eats nothing."

"When he was a young man he had a good appetite."

The Belgian Sister shrugged her shoulders in exasperation. "He is the worst feeder of all the priests I have known. Ah! I have known some great feeders. There was our abbé at Metiers—six courses of fish in Lent. Of course I have a theory. When one eats little the stomach contracts. Thereafter it becomes impossible."

Polly shook her head in mild disagreement. "Yesterday when I took him some new baked scones he looked at them and said, 'How can one eat when thousands are hungry, within sight of this room?'"

"Bah! They are always hungry. In this country it is customary to eat grass."

"But now he says it will be worse because of all this fighting that is going on."

Sister Martha tasted the soup, her famous *pot-au-feu*, and her face registered critical approval. But as she turned to Polly she made a grimace. "There is always fighting. Just as there is always starving. We have bandits with our coffee in Pai-tan. They pop a few guns—like you hear now. Then the city buys them off and they go home. Tell me, did he eat my scones?"

"He ate one. Yes, and said it was excellent. Then he told me to give the set to Reverend Mother for our poor."

"That good Father will drive me to distraction." Though Sister Martha was, outside her kitchen, as mild as mother's milk, she scowled as if she were a creature of splendid rages. "Give, give, give! Until one's skin cracks with the strain. Shall I tell you what occurred last winter? One day in the town when it was snowing he took his coat off, his fine new coat that we sisters had made for him of best imported wool cloth, and gave it to some already half-frozen good-for-nothing. I would have let him have a tonguing, I assure you. But Mother Superior chose to correct him. He looked at her with those surprised eyes which hurt you deep inside. 'But why not? What's the use of preaching Christianity if we don't live as Christians? The great Christ would have given that beggar his coat. Why shouldn't I?' When Reverend Mother answered very crossly that the coat was a gift from us he smiled, standing there, shivering with cold. 'Then you are the good Christians—not I.' Was not that incredible? You wouldn't believe it, if like me you were brought up in a country where thrift is inculcated. Enough! Let us sit and drink our soup. If we wait until these greedy children have done we may faint for weakness."

Walking past the uncurtained window on his way back from the town Father Chisholm caught a glimpse of the two seated at their early lunch. The deep shadow of anxiety lifted momentarily from his face, his lips faintly smiled.

Despite his first premonitions, the accident of Polly's visit was an immense success; she fitted miraculously into the frame of the mission,

937

and was enjoying herself with the same placidity that she would have displayed during a short week-end at Blackpool. Undismayed by clime or season, she would stalk silently to her seat in the kitchen garden and knit for hours among the cabbages with shoulders squared, elbows angled, and needles flashing, her mouth slightly pursed, her eyes remotely complacent, the yellow mission cat purring like mad, crouched half beneath her skirts. She was the closest crony of old Fu and became a hub round which the gloomy gardener revolved, exhibiting prodigious vegetables for her approval and prognosticating the weather with signs and baleful portents.

In her contact with the Sisters she never interfered, never assumed a privilege. Her tact was instinctive and beautiful, springing from her gift of silence, from the prosaic simplicity of her life. She had never been happier. She was realizing her cherished longing to see Francis at his missionary work, a priest of God, helped, perhaps, to the worthy end—though she would never have dreamed of voicing such a thought—by her own humble effort. The length of her stay, set primarily at two months, had been extended until January.

Her one regret, naïvely expressed, was that she had been unable to take this trip earlier in her life. Though she had served Ned hand and foot so long, his death had not freed her from responsibility. Judy remained, a constant anxiety, with her whims and giddiness, her capricious inconstancy of purpose. From her first employment with the Tynecastle Council she had passed through half a dozen secretarial positions, each acclaimed as perfect in the beginning, then presently thrown up in disgust. From a business career she had turned to pupil-teaching, but her course at the Normal College soon bored her, and she vaguely entertained the idea of entering a convent. At this stage, when twenty-seven years of age, she had suddenly discovered that her true vocation was to become a nurse and had joined the staff of the Northumberland General Hospital as a probationer. This was the circumstance which had provided Polly with her present opportunity—a freedom which, alas, seemed only momentary. Already, after four short months, the hardships of the probationer's life were discouraging Judy, and letters kept coming, full of petulance and grievance, hinting that Aunt Polly must return soon to look after her poor neglected niece.

As Francis pieced together the pattern of Polly's life at home— gradually, for she was never garrulous—he came to see her as a saint. Yet her fixity was not that of a plaster image. She had her foibles, and her genius for the malapropos still remained. For instance, with remarkable initiative, and a loyal desire to aid Francis in his work, she had practically reconverted two errant souls, who on one of her staid excursions through Pai-tan obsequiously attached themselves to her person and her purse. It had cost Francis some trouble to rid her of Hosannah and Philomena Wang.

If only for the consolation of their daily conversations, he had reason to value this amazing woman. Now, in the trials which had suddenly confronted him, he clung to her common sense.

As he reached his house, there, awaiting him on the porch verandah, stood Sister Clotilde and Anna. He sighed. Was he never to have peace to consider the disquieting news he had received?

Clotilde's sallow face wore a nervous flush. She stood close to the girl, almost like a gaoler, restraining her with a freshly bandaged hand. Anna's eyes were dark with defiance. She also smelled of perfume.

Under his interrogating gaze Clotilde took a quick breath. "I had to ask Reverend Mother to let me bring Anna over. After all, in the basket workroom, she's under my special charge."

"Yes, Sister?" Father Chisholm forced himself to speak patiently. Sister Clotilde was quivering with hysterical indignation.

"I've put up with so much from her. Insolence and disobedience and laziness. Watching her upset the other girls. Yes, and steal! Why, even now she's reeking of Miss Bannon's Eau-de-Cologne. But this last——"

"Yes, Sister?"

Sister Clotilde reddened more deeply. It was a greater ordeal for her than for the graceless Anna.

"She's taken to going out at night. You know the place is infested with soldiers just now. She was out all last night with one of Wai-Chu's men, her bed not even slept in. And when I reasoned with her this morning, she struggled with me and bit me."

Father Chisholm turned his eyes on Anna. It seemed incredible that the little child he had held in his arms that winter night, who had come to him like a gift from heaven, should now confront him as a sulky and unruly young woman. In her teens, she was quite mature, with a full bosom, heavy eyes, and a plummy ripeness on her lips. She had always been different from the other children: uncaring, bold, never submissive. He thought: For once the copy-books are wrong—Anna has turned out no angel.

The heavy burden upon his mind made his voice mild. "Have you anything to say, Anna?"

"No."

"No, Father," Sister Clotilde hissed. Anna gave her a sullen glance of hatred.

"It seems a pity, after all we've tried to do for you, Anna, that you should repay us like this. Aren't you happy here?"

"No, I am not."

"Why?"

"I didn't ask to come to the Convent. You didn't even buy me. I came for nothing. And I am tired of praying."

"But you don't pray all the time. You've got your work."

"I don't want to make baskets."

"Then we'll find something else for you to do."

"What else? Sewing? Am I to go on sewing all my life?"

Father Chisholm forced a smile. "Of course not. When you've learned all those useful things, one of our young men will want to marry you."

She gave him a sullen sneer, which said plainly: "I want something more exciting than your nice young men."

He was silent; then he said, somewhat bitterly, for her lack of gratitude hurt him: "No one wishes to keep you against your will. But until the district is more settled you must remain. Great trouble may be coming to the town. Indeed, great trouble may be coming to the world. While you are here you are safe. But you must keep the rule. Now go with Sister and obey her. If I find that you do not I shall be very angry."

He dismissed them both, then as Clotilde turned he said: "Ask Reverend Mother to come and see me, Sister." He watched them cross the compound, then went slowly to his room. As if he had not enough to weigh him down!

Five minutes later when Maria-Veronica entered he stood at the window viewing the city below. He let her join him there, keeping silent. At last he said: "My dear friend, I have two bad pieces of news for you, and the first is that we are likely to have a war here—before the year is out."

She gazed at him calmly, waiting. He swung round and faced her.

"I have just come from Mr. Chia. It is inevitable. For years the province has been dominated by Wai-Chu. As you know, he has bled the peasants to death with taxation and forced levies. If they didn't pay, their villages were destroyed—whole families slaughtered. But—brute though he is—the merchants of Pai-tan have always managed to buy him off." He paused. "Now another war lord is moving into the district —General Naian, from the lower Yangtze. He's reported to be not so bad as Wai—in fact our old friend Shon has gone over to him. But he wants Wai's province, that is, the privilege of squeezing the people there. He will march into Pai-tan. It is impossible to buy off both leaders. Only the victor can be bought off. So this time they must fight it out."

She smiled slightly. "I knew most of this before. Why are you so ominous today?"

"Perhaps because war is in the air." He gave her a queer strained glance. "Besides, it will be a bitter battle."

Her smile deepened. "Neither you nor I are afraid of a battle."

There was a silence. He glanced away. "Of course, I am thinking of ourselves, exposed here outside the city walls—if Wai attacks Pai-tan we shall be in the middle of it. But I am thinking more of the people—

940

so poor, so helpless and so hungry. I have come to love them here with all my heart. They only beg to be left in peace, to get a simple living from the soil, to live in their homes quietly with their families. For years they've been oppressed by one tyrant. Now, because another appears on the scene, guns are being thrust into their hands, yes, into the hands of the men of our congregation, flags are being waved, the usual cries are already raised—Freedom and Liberty. Hatreds are being worked up. Then, because two dictators wish it, these poor creatures will fall upon one another. And to what purpose? After the slaughter, when the smoke and the shooting have cleared away, there will be more taxation, more oppression, a heavier yoke than before." He sighed, "Can one help feeling sad for poor mankind?"

She moved somewhat restively. "You have not a great opinion of war. Surely some wars can be just and glorious? History proves it. My family has fought in many such."

He did not answer for a long time. When at last he turned to her the lines about his eyes had deepened. He spoke slowly, heavily. "It is strange you should say that at this moment." He paused, averting his eyes. "Our little trouble here is only the echo of a greater disorder." He found it difficult, most difficult, to continue. But he forced himself on. "Mr. Chia has had word by special courier from his business associates in Sen-siang. Germany has invaded Belgium and is at war with France and Britain."

There was a short pause. Her face altered, she did not speak, but stood silent, her head immobile, unnaturally arrested.

At length he said: "The others will soon know. But we must not let it make any difference to us at the mission."

"No, we must not." She answered mechanically, as though her gaze were fixed thousands of miles away.

The first sign came some days later: a small Belgian flag, sewn hurriedly with coloured threads upon a square of silk, and placed prominently in Sister Martha's bedroom window. That same day, indeed, Martha scurried in early to the Sisters' house from the dispensary, with her new eagerness, then gave a cluck of nervous satisfaction. They had come—what she looked forward to with all her soul: the newspapers. It was the *Intelligence*, an American daily published in Shanghai, and it arrived, in batches, erratically, about once a month. Hurriedly, her fingers trembling between expectation and apprehension, she undid the wrappers at the window.

For a minute she turned the pages, hastily. Then she gave an outraged cry.

"What monsters! Oh my God, it is insupportable!" She beckoned urgently, not lifting her head, to Clotilde, who had come quickly into the room, drawn by the same magnetic force. "Look, Sister! They are in Louvain—the Cathedral is in ruins—shelled to pieces. And Metrieux —ten kilometres from my home—destroyed to the ground. Oh, dear God! Such a fine and prosperous town!"

Linked by common calamity, the two Sisters bent over the sheets, punctuating their reading with exclamations of horror.

"The very altar blown to pieces!" Martha wrung her hands. "Metrieux! I drove there with my father in the high cart when I was a little thing of seven. Such a market! We bought twelve grey geese that day . . . so fat and beautiful . . . and now . . . ."

Clotilde, with dilated eyes, was reading of the battle of the Marne. "They are slaughtering our brave people. Such butchery, such vileness!"

Though Reverend Mother had entered and seated herself quietly at the table, Clotilde remained unconscious of her presence. But Martha saw her, from the corner of her eye, and Martha was beside herself.

Suffused with indignation, her voice shaking, she pointed her finger to a paragraph. "Consider this, Sister Clotilde. 'It is reliably reported that the convent of Louvain was violated by the German invaders. Unimpeachable sources confirm the fact that many innocent children have been mercilessly butchered.'"

Clotilde was pale as ivory. "In the Franco-Prussian War it was the same. They are inhuman. No wonder, in this good American journal, they already call them Huns." She hissed the word.

"I cannot allow you to speak in such terms of my people."

Clotilde spun round, supporting herself on the window frame, taken aback. But Martha was prepared.

"Your people, Reverend Mother? I would not be so proud to own them if I were you. Brutal barbarians. Murderers of women and little children."

"The German Army is comprised of gentlemen. I do not believe that vulgar sheet. It is not true."

Martha spread her hands on her hips; her harsh peasant voice grated with resentment. "Is it true when the vulgar sheet reports the ruthless invasion of a little peaceful country by your gentlemanly army?"

Reverend Mother was paler now than Clotilde.

"Germany must have her place in the sun."

"So she kills and plunders, blows up cathedrals, and the market place I went to as a girl, because she wants the sun and the moon, the greedy swine——"

"Sister!" Dignified even in her agitation, Reverend Mother rose up. "There is such a thing as justice in this world. Germany and Austria have never had justice. And do not forget that my brother is fighting even now to forge the new Teutonic destiny. Therefore I forbid you both, as your superior, to speak any such slanders as have just defiled your lips."

There was an intolerable pause, then she turned to leave the room. As she reached the door Martha cried: "Your famous destiny isn't forged yet. The Allies will win the war."

Maria-Veronica gave her a cold and pitying smile. She went out.

The feud intensified, fanned by the stray news that filtered to the far-off mission itself under threat of war. Though the French Sister and the Belgian had never greatly liked each other, now they were linked in bosom friendship. Martha was protective towards the weaker Clotilde, solicitous for her health, dosing her troublesome cough, giving her choice pieces from every dish. Together, openly, they knitted mittens and socks to be sent to the brave *blessés*. They would talk of their beloved countries, over Reverend Mother's head, with many sighs and innuendoes—careful, oh so careful to give no offence. Then Martha with a strange significance would remark: "Let us go over a moment to pray for our intention."

Maria-Veronica endured it all with a proud silence. She, too, prayed for victory. Father Chisholm could see the three faces in a row, beatifically upturned, praying for opposing victories while he, careworn and harassed, watching Wai's forces march and countermarch amongst the hills, hearing of Naian's final mobilization, prayed for peace . . . safety for his people . . . and enough food for the children.

Presently Sister Clotilde began to teach her class the *Marseillaise*. She did it secretly, when Reverend Mother was engaged in the basket room at the other end of the mission. The class, being imitative, picked it up quickly. Then, one forenoon as Maria-Veronica came slowly across the compound, her air fatigued and noticeably constrained, there burst, through the open windows of Clotilde's classroom, to the accompaniment of a thumped piano, the full-throated blast of the French national anthem.

" *Allons, enfants de la patrie . . .* "

For an instant Maria-Veronica's step faltered; then her figure, which showed signs of softening, became steeled. All her fortitude was summoned to sustain her. She walked on with her head high.

One afternoon towards the end of the month, Clotilde was again in her schoolroom. The class, having given its daily rendering of the *Marseillaise,* had now concluded its catechism lesson. And Sister Clotilde, following her recently instituted custom, remarked:

"Kneel down, dear children, and we will say a little prayer for the brave French soldiers."

The children knelt down obediently and repeated the three Hail Marys after her.

Clotilde was about to signal them to rise when, with a slight shock, she became aware of Reverend Mother standing behind her. Maria-Veronica was calm and pleasant. Gazing across Sister Clotilde's shoulder she addressed the class.

"And now, children, it is only right that you should say the same prayer for the brave German soldiers."

Clotilde turned a dirty green. Her breath seemed to choke her.

"This is my classroom, Reverend Mother."

Maria-Veronica ignored her. "Come now, dear children, for the brave Germans, 'Hail Mary full of Grace . . .'"

Clotilde's breast heaved, her pale lips retracted from her narrow teeth. Convulsively, she drew back her hand and slapped her superior on the face.

There was a terrified hush. Then Clotilde burst into tears and ran sobbing from the room.

Maria-Veronica moved not a muscle. With that same agreeable smile she said to the children:

"Sister Clotilde is unwell. You see how she knocked against me. I will finish the class. But first, children, three Hail Marys for the good German soldiers."

When the prayer concluded she seated herself, unruffled, at the high desk and opened the book.

That evening, entering the dispensary unexpectedly, Father Chisholm surprised Sister Clotilde measuring herself a liberal dose of chlorodyne. She whipped round at his step and almost dropped the full minim glass, her cheek flooded by a painful flush. The episode in the classroom had strung her to breaking pitch.

She stammered: "I take a little for my stomach. We have so much to worry us these days." He knew, from the measure and her manner, that she was using the drug as a sedative.

"I wouldn't take it too often, Sister. It contains a good deal of morphine."

When she had gone he locked the bottle in the poison cupboard. As he stood in the empty dispensary, torn by the anxiety of their danger here, weighed down by the sheer futility of that far-off, awful war, he felt a slow surge of anger at the senseless rancour of these women. He had hoped it would settle. But it had not settled. He compressed his lips in sudden resolution.

After school that day he sent for the three Sisters. He made them stand before his desk, his face unusually stern, choosing his words, almost with bitterness.

944

"Your behaviour at a time like this is greatly distressing me. It must cease. You have no justification for it whatsoever."

There was a short pause. Clotilde was shaking with contention. "But we have justification." She fumbled in the pocket of her robe and agitatedly thrust into his hand a much-creased, cut-out section of newsprint. "Read this, I beg of you. From a prince of the Church."

He scanned the cutting, slowly read it aloud. It was the report of a pronouncement by Cardinal Amette, from the pulpit of the Cathedral of Notre Dame in Paris. " 'Beloved Brethren, Comrades in Arms of France and her Glorious Allies, Almighty God is upon our side. God has helped us to our greatness in the past. He will help us once again in our hour of need. God stands beside our brave soldiers in the battlefield, strengthening their arms, girding them against the enemy. God protects his own. God will give us victory . . .'"

He broke off, he would go no further.

A rigid silence followed. Clotilde's head trembled with nervous triumph and Martha's face was dogged with vindication. But Maria-Veronica remained undefeated Stiffly, from the black cloth bag she wore upon her girdle, she unfolded a neat square clipping.

"I know nothing of the prejudiced opinion of any French Cardinal. But here is the joint statement to the German people of the Archbishops of Cologne, Munich and Essen." In a cold and haughty voice she read: " 'Beloved People of the Fatherland, God is with us in this most righteous struggle which has been forced upon us. Therefore we command you in God's name to fight to the last drop of your blood for the honour and glory of our country. God knows in his wisdom and justice that we are in the right and God will give us . . .'"

"That is enough."

Francis stopped her, struggling for self-control, his soul suffused by wave upon wave of anger and despair. Here, before him, was the essence of man's malice and hypocrisy. The senselessness of life seemed suddenly to overwhelm him. Its hopelessness crushed him.

He remained with his head resting upon his hand, then in a low voice he said: "God knows God must get sick of all this crying out to God!"

Mastered by his emotion he rose abruptly and began to pace the room. "I can't refute the contradictions of cardinals and archbishops with still more contradictions. I wouldn't presume to. I'm nobody—an insignificant Scottish priest stuck in the wilds of China on the edge of a bandit's war. But don't you see the folly and the baseness of the whole transaction? We, the Holy Catholic Church—yes, all the great Churches of Christendom—condone this world war. We go further—we sanctify it.

We send millions of our faithful sons to be maimed and slaughtered, to be mangled in their bodies and their souls, to kill and destroy one another, with a hypocritical smile, an apostolic blessing. Die for your country and all will be forgiven you. Patriotism! King and Emperor! From ten thousand smug pulpits: 'Render to Cæsar the things that are Cæsar's . . .'" He broke off, hands clenched, eyes remotely burning. "There is no Cæsar nowadays—only financiers and statesmen who want diamond mines in Africa and rubber in the slave-driven Congo. Christ preached everlasting love. He preached the brotherhood of man. He did not climb the mountain and shout, 'Kill! kill! Go forth in hatred and plunge a bayonet into thy brother's belly!' It isn't His voice that resounds in the churches and high cathedrals of Christendom today— but the voice of time-servers and cowards." His lips quivered. "How in the name of the God we serve can we come to these foreign lands, the lands we call pagan, presuming to convert the people to a doctrine we give the lie to by our every deed? Small wonder they jeer at us. Christianity—the religion of lies! Of class and money and national hatreds! Of wicked wars!" He stopped short, perspiration beading his brow, his eyes dark with anguish. "Why doesn't the Church seize her opportunity? What a chance to justify herself as the Living Bride of Christ! Instead of preaching hatred and incitement, to cry, in every land, with the tongues of her pontiff and all her priests: 'Throw down your weapons. Thou shalt not kill. We command you *not* to fight.' Yes, there would be persecutions and many executions. But these would be martyrdoms—not murders. The dead would decorate, not desecrate, our altars." His voice dropped, his attitude was calmer, strangely prophetic. "The Church will suffer for its cowardice. A viper nourished in one's bosom will one day strike that bosom. To sanction the might of arms is to invite destruction. The day may come when great military forces will break loose and turn upon the Church, corrupting millions of her children, sending her down again—a timid shadow—into the Catacombs."

There was a strained stillness when he concluded. Martha and Clotilde hung their heads, as though touched, against their will. But Maria-Veronica, with something of the arrogance that marked those early days of strife, faced him with a cold clear gaze, hardened by a glint of mockery.

"That was most impressive, Father . . . worthy of these cathedrals you decry. . . . But aren't your words rather empty if you don't live up to them . . . here in Pai-tan?"

The blood rushed to his brow, then quickly ebbed. He answered without anger.

"I have solemnly forbidden every man in my congregation to fight in this wicked conflict which threatens us. I have made them swear to come with their families inside the mission gates, when trouble breaks. Whatever the consequences I shall be responsible."

All three Sisters looked at him. A faint tremor passed over Maria-Veronica's cold still face. Yet, as they filed from the room, he could see they were not reconciled. He suddenly felt a shiver of unnameable fear. He had the strange sensation that time swung suspended, balanced in fateful expectation of what might come to pass.

IX

On a Sunday morning, he was awakened by a sound which he had dreaded for many days—the dull concussion of artillery in action. He jumped up and hurried to the window. On the western hills, a few miles distant, six light field-pieces had begun to shell the city. He dressed rapidly and went downstairs. At the same moment Joseph came running from the porch.

"It has begun, Master. Last night General Naian marched into Pai-tan and the Wai forces are attacking him. Already our people are arriving at the gates."

He glanced swiftly over Joseph's shoulder. "Admit them at once."

While his servant went back to unlock the gates he hastened over to the home. The children were collected at breakfast and amazingly undisturbed. One or two of the smaller girls whimpered at the sudden distant banging. He went round the long tables, forcing himself to smile. "It is only firecrackers, children. For a few days we are going to have big ones."

The three Sisters stood apart at the head of the refectory. Maria-Veronica was calm as marble but he saw at once that Clotilde was upset. She seemed to hold herself in, and her hands were clenched in her long sleeves. Every time the guns went off she paled. Nodding toward the children, he joked expressly for her. "If only we could keep them eating all the time!"

Sister Martha cackled too quickly: "Yes, yes, then it would be easy." As Clotilde's stiff face made the effort to smile the far-off guns rolled again.

After a moment he left the refectory and pressed on to the lodge where Joseph and Fu stood at the wide-open gates. His people were pouring in with their belongings, young and old, poor humble illiterate creatures, frightened, eager for safety, the very substance of suffering mortality. His heart swelled as he thought of the sanctuary he was giving them. The good brick walls would afford them sound protection. He blessed

947

the vanity which had made him build them high. With a queer tenderness, he watched one aged ragged dame, whose withered face bespoke a patient resignation to a long life of privation, stumble in with her bundle, establish herself quietly in a corner of the crowded compound, and painstakingly begin to cook a handful of beans in an old condensedmilk can.

At his side, Fu was imperturbable but Joseph, the valiant, showed a slight variation of his normal colour. Marriage had altered him, he was no longer a careless youth, but a husband and a father, with all the responsibilities of a man of property.

"They should hurry," he muttered restively. "We must lock and barricade the gates."

Father Chisholm put his hand on his servant's shoulder. "Only when they are all inside, Joseph."

"We are going to have trouble," Joseph answered with a shrug. "Some of our men who have come in were conscripted by Wai. He will not be pleased when he finds they prefer to be here rather than to fight."

"Nevertheless they will not fight." The priest answered firmly. "Come, now, don't be despondent. Run up our flag, while I watch at the gate."

Joseph departed, grumbling, and in a few minutes the mission flag, of pale blue silk with a deeper blue St. Andrew's cross, broke and fluttered on the flagstaff. Father Chisholm's heart gave an added bound of pride, his breast was filled with a quick elation. That flag stood for peace and goodwill to all men, a neutral flag, the flag of universal love.

When the last straggler had entered they locked the gates provisionally. At that moment Fu drew the priest's attention to the cedar grove, some three hundred yards to the left, on their own Jade hillside. In this clump of trees a long gun had unexpectedly appeared. Indistinctly, between the branches, he could see the quick movements of soldiers, in Wai green tunics, trenching and fortifying the position. Though he knew little of such matters the gun seemed a far more powerful weapon than the ordinary field-pieces now in action. And even as he gazed there came a swift flash, followed instantly by a terrifying concussion and the wild scream of the shell overhead.

The change was devastating. As the new heavy gun deafeningly pounded the city, it was answered by a Naian battery of ineffectual range. Small shells, falling short of the cedar grove, rained about the mission. One plunged into the kitchen garden, erupting a shower of earth. Immediately a cry of terror rose in the crowded compound and Francis ran to shepherd his congregation from the open into the greater safety of the church.

The noise and confusion increased. In the classroom the children were in a milling stampede. It was Reverend Mother who stemmed the panic. Calm and smiling, but shouting above the bursting shells, she drew the children round her, made them close their ears with their fingers and sing at the pitch of their lungs. When they became calmer they were herded quickly across the courtyard into the cellars of the convent. Joseph's wife and the two children were already there. It was strange to see all these small yellow faces, in the half-light, amongst stores of oil and candles and sweet potatoes, below the long shelves on which stood Sister Martha's preserves. The screaming of the shells was less down below. But from time to time there was a heavy shock, the building shook to its foundations.

While Polly remained below with the children, Martha and Clotilde scurried to fetch them lunch. Clotilde, always highly strung, was now almost out of her wits. As she crossed the compound a spent piece of metal struck her lightly on her cheek.

"Oh, God!" she cried, sinking down. "I'm killed!" Pale as death she began to make an act of contrition.

"Don't be a fool." Martha shook her fiercely by the shoulder. "Come and get these wretched brats some porridge."

Father Chisholm had been called by Joseph to the dispensary. One of the women had been slightly wounded in the hand. When the bleeding was controlled and the wound bandaged, the priest sent both Joseph and the patient over to the church, then hurried to the window, anxiously gauging the effects of the bursts, damaging puffs of débris, as the shells from the Wai gun exploded in Pai-tan. Sworn to neutrality, he could not repress a terrible desire, surging and devastating, that Wai, the unspeakable, might be defeated.

Suddenly, as he stood there, he saw a detachment of Naian soldiers strike out from the Manchu Gate. They flowed out like a stream of grey ants, perhaps two hundred of them, and began in a ragged line to mount the hill.

He watched them with a dreadful fascination. They came quickly, at first, in little sudden rushes. He could see them vividly against the untroubled green of the hillside. Bent double, each man bolted forward, carrying his rifle, for a dozen yards, then flung himself, desperately, upon the earth.

The Wai gun continued firing into the city. The grey figures drew nearer. They were crawling now, flat on their stomachs, completing their toiling ascent in that blazing sun. At a distance of a hundred paces from the cypress grove they paused, hugging the slope, for a full three minutes. Then their leader gave a sign. With a shout they jumped erect and rushed on the emplacement.

They covered half the distance rapidly. A few seconds and they would have reached their objective. Then the harsh vibration of machine guns resounded in the brilliant air.

There were three, manned and waiting, in the cypress grove. At their jarring impact the rushing grey figures seemed to stop, to fall in sheer bewilderment. Some fell forwards, others on their backs, some for a moment upon their knees, as though in prayer. They fell all ways, comically, then lay still, in the sunshine. At that, the rattling of the Maxims ceased. All was stillness, warm and quiet, until the heavy concussion of the big gun boomed again, reawakening everything to life— all but those quiet little figures on the green hillside.

Father Chisholm stood rigid, consumed by the torment of his mind. This was war. This toylike pantomime of destruction, magnified a million times, was what was happening now on the fertile plains of France. He shuddered, and prayed passionately: O Lord, let me live and die for peace.

Suddenly his haggard eye picked up a sign of movement on the hill. One of the Naian soldiers was not dead. Slowly and painfully, he was dragging himself down the slope in the direction of the mission. It was possible to observe the ebbing of his strength in the gradual slowing of his progress. Finally he came to rest, utterly spent, lying on his side, some sixty yards from the upper gate.

Francis thought, He is dead . . . this is no time for mock-heroics, if I go out there I will get a bullet in my head . . . I must not do it. But he found himself leaving the dispensary and moving towards the upper gate. He had a shamed consciousness as he opened the gate: fortunately no one was watching from the mission. He walked out into the bright sunshine upon the hillside.

His short black figure and long black shadow were shockingly obvious. If the mission windows were blank he felt many eyes upon him from the cypress grove. He dared not hurry.

The wounded soldier was breathing in sobbing gasps. Both hands were pressed weakly against his lacerated belly. His human eyes gazed back at Francis with an anguished interrogation.

Francis lifted him on his back and carried him into the mission. He propped him up while he relocked the gate. Then he pulled him gently into shelter. When he had given him a drink of water he found Maria-Veronica and told her she must prepare a cot in the dispensary.

That afternoon another unsuccessful raid was made on the gun position. And when night fell Father Chisholm and Joseph brought in five more wounded men. The dispensary assumed the appearance of a hospital.

Next morning the shelling continued without interruption. The noise was interminable. The city took severe punishment, and it looked as if a breach were being driven in the western wall. Suddenly, at the angle of the Western Gate, about a mile away, Francis saw the main body of the Wai forces bearing in upon the broken parapet. He thought with a sinking heart, They are in the city. But he could not judge.

The remainder of the day passed in a state of sick uncertainty. In the late afternoon he liberated the children from a cellar and his congregation from the church to let them have a breath of air. At least they were unharmed. As he went among them, heartening them, he buoyed himself with this simple fact.

Then, as he finished his round, he found Joseph at his side, wearing for the first time a look of unmistakable fear.

"Master, a messenger has come over from the Wai gun in the cedar grove."

At the main gate three Wai soldiers were peering between the bars while an officer, whom Father Chisholm took to be the captain of the gun crew, stood by. Without hesitation Francis unlocked the gate and went outside.

"What do you wish of me?"

The officer was short, thickset and middle-aged, with a heavy face and thick mulish lips. He breathed through his mouth, which hung open, showing his stained upper teeth. He wore the usual peaked cap and green uniform with a leather belt, bearing a green tassel. His puttees ended in a pair of broken canvas plimsols.

"General Wai favours you with several requests. In the first place you are to cease sheltering the enemy wounded."

Francis flushed sharply, nervously. "The wounded are doing no harm. They are beyond fighting."

The other took no notice of this protest. "Secondly, General Wai affords you the privilege of contributing to his commissariat. Your first donation will be eight hundred pounds of rice and all American canned goods in your storerooms."

"We are already short of food." Despite his resolution, Francis felt his temper rise; he spoke heatedly. "You cannot rob us in this fashion."

As before, the gun captain let the argument pass unheeded. He had a way of standing sideways, with his feet apart, delivering each word across his shoulder, like an insult.

"Thirdly, it is essential that you clear your compound of all whom you are protecting there. General Wai believes you are harbouring deserters from his forces. If this is so they will be shot. All other able-bodied men must enlist immediately in the Wai army."

This time Father Chisholm made no protest. He stood tense and pale, his hands clenched, his eyes blazing with indignation. The air before him vibrated on a red haze. "Suppose I refuse to comply with these most moderate solicitations?"

The obstinate face before him almost smiled. "That, I assure you, would be a mistake. I should then most reluctantly turn our gun upon you and in five minutes reduce your mission, and all within, to an inconsiderable powder."

There was a silence. The three soldiers were grimacing, making signs to some of the younger women in the compound. Francis saw the situation as cold and clear-cut as a picture etched on steel. He must yield, under threat of annihilation, to these inhuman demands. And that yielding would be but the prelude to greater and still greater demands. A dreadful sweep of anger conquered him. His mouth went dry, he kept his burning eyes on the ground.

"General Wai must realize that it will take some hours to make ready these stores for him . . . and to prepare my people . . . for their departure. How much time does he afford me?"

"Until tomorrow." The officer answered promptly. "Provided you deliver to me before midnight at my gun position a personal offering of tinned goods together with sufficient valuables to constitute a suitable present."

Again there was a silence. Francis felt a dark choking swelling of his heart. He lied in a suppressed voice: "I agree. I have no alternative. I will bring you your gift tonight."

"I commend your wisdom. I shall expect you. And I advise you not to fail."

The captain's tone held a heavy irony. He bowed to the priest, shouted a command to his men, and marched off squatly towards the cedar grove.

Francis re-entered the mission in a trembling fury. The clang of the heavy iron gate behind him set a chain of febrile echoes ringing through his brain. What a fool he had been, in his fatuous elation, to imagine he could escape this trial. He . . . the dove-like pacifist. He gritted his teeth as wave after wave of pitiless self-anger assailed him. Abruptly, he rid himself of Joseph and of the silent gathering who timidly searched his face for the answer to their fears.

Usually he took his troubles to the Church, but now he could not bow his head and tamely murmur: Lord, I will suffer and submit. He went to his room and flung himself violently into the wicker chair. His thoughts for once ran riot, without the rein of meekness or forbearance. He groaned as he thought of his pretty gospel of peace. What was to happen to his fine words now? What was to happen to them all?

Another barb struck him—the needlessness, the crass inanity of Polly's presence in the mission at such a time. Under his breath he cursed Mrs. Fiske for the interfering officiousness which had subjected his poor old aunt to this fantastic tribulation. God! He seemed to have the cares of all the world upon his bent incompetent shoulders. He jumped up. He could not, he would not, yield, weakly, to the maddening menace of Wai's threat and the deadlier menace of that gun which grew in his feverish imagination, swelled to such gigantic size it became the symbol of all wars, and of every brutal weapon built by man for the slaughter of mankind.

As he paced his room, tense and sweating, there came a mild knock at his door. Polly entered the room.

"I don't like to disturb you, Francis . . . but if you have a minute to spare. . . ." She smiled remotely, using the privilege of her affection to disturb his privacy.

"What is it, Aunt Polly?" He composed his features with a great effort. Perhaps she had further news, another message from Wai.

"I'd be glad if you'd try on this comforter, Francis. I don't want to get it too large. It should keep you nice and warm in the winter." Under his bloodshot gaze she produced a woollen Balaclava helmet she was knitting him.

He scarcely knew whether to weep or laugh. It was so like Polly. When the crack of doom resounded she would no doubt pause to offer him a cup of tea. There was nothing for it but to comply. He stood and let her fit the half-finished capote upon his head.

"It looks all right," she murmured critically. "Maybe a trifle wide about the neck." With her head on one side and her long wrinkled upper lip pursed, she counted the stitches with her bone knitting-needle. "Sixty-eight. I'll take it in four. Thank you, Francis. I hope I haven't troubled you."

Tears started to his eyes. He had an almost irresistible desire to put his head on her hard shoulder and cry brokenly, outrageously: "Aunt Polly! I'm in such a mess. What in God's name am I to do?"

As it was, he gazed at her a long time. He muttered: "Don't you worry, Polly, about the danger we're all in here?"

She smiled faintly. "Worry killed the cat. Besides . . . aren't you looking after us?"

Her ineradicable belief in him was like a breath of pure cold air. He watched her wrap up her work, skewer it with needles and, giving her competent nod, silently withdraw. Somehow, beneath her casualness, her air of commonplace, there lay a hint of deeper knowledge. He had no doubts now as to what he must do. He took his hat and coat, made his way secretly towards the lower gate.

Outside the mission the deep darkness blindfolded him. But he went down the Brilliant Green Jade road towards the city, rapidly, heedless of any obstacle.

At the Manchu Gate he was sharply halted and a lantern thrust close against his face, while the sentries scrutinized him. He had counted on being recognized—he was, after all, a familiar figure in the city—yet his luck went further still. One of the three soldiers was a follower of Shon who had worked all through the plague epidemic. The man vouched for him immediately and after a short exchange with his companions agreed to take him at once to the Lieutenant.

The streets were deserted, choked in parts with rubble and ominously silent. From the distant eastern section there came occasional bursts of firing. As the priest followed the quick padding footsteps of his guide he had a strange exhilarating sense of guilt.

Shon was in his old quarters at the cantonment, snatching a short rest, fully dressed, on that same camp bed which had been Dr. Tulloch's. He was unshaven, his puttees white with mud, and there were dark shadows of fatigue beneath his eyes. He propped himself upon his elbow as Francis entered.

"Well!" he said slowly. "I have been dreaming about you, my friend, and your excellent establishment on the hill."

He slid from the bed, turned up the lamp and sat down at the table. "You do not want some tea? No more do I. But I am glad to see you. I regret I cannot present you to General Naian. He is leading an attack on the East section . . . or perhaps executing some spies. He is a most enlightened man."

Francis sat down at the table, still in silence. He knew Shon well enough to let him talk himself out. And tonight the other had less to say than usual. He glanced guardedly at the priest. "Why don't you ask it, my friend? You are here for help which I cannot give. We should have been in your mission two days ago except that then we should merely have been blown to pieces together by that infamous Sorana."

"You mean the gun?"

"Yes, the gun," Shon answered with polite irony. "I have known it too well for a period of years . . . It came originally from a French gunboat. General Hsiah had it first. Twice I took it from him with great trouble, but each time he bought it back from my commandant. Then Wai had a concubine from Pekin who cost him twenty thousand silver dollars. She was an Armenian lady, very beautiful, named Sorana. When he ceased to regard her with affection he exchanged her to Hsiah for the gun. You saw us try to capture it yesterday. It is not possible. . . . Fortified . . . Across that open country . . . with only our *piff-paff* battery to protect us. Perhaps it is going to lose us our war . . . just when I am making a great personal advancement with General Naian."

There was a pause. The priest said stiffly: "Suppose it were possible to capture the gun?"

954

"No. Do not entice me." Shon shook his head with concealed bitterness. "But if ever I get near that dishonourable weapon I shall finish it for good."

"We can get very near the gun."

Shon raised his head deliberately, sounding Francis with his eyes. A glint of excitement enlivened him. He waited.

Father Chisholm leaned forward, his lips making a tight line. "This evening under threat of shelling the mission, the Wai officer who commands the gun crew ordered me to bring food and money to him before midnight . . ."

He went on, gazing at Shon, then abruptly broke off, conscious that he need say no more. For a full minute nothing was said. Shon was thinking, behind his careless brow. At last he smiled—at least the muscles of his face went through the act of smiling, but there was nothing of humour in his eyes.

"My friend, I must continue to regard you as a gift from heaven."

A cloud passed over the priest's set face. "I have forgotten about heaven tonight."

Shon nodded, not thinking of that remark. "Now listen and I will tell you what we shall do."

An hour later Francis and Shon left the cantonment and made their way through the Manchu Gate towards the mission. Shon had changed his uniform for a worn blue blouse and a pair of coolie's slacks, rolled to the knee. A flat pleated hat covered his head. On his back he carried a large sack, tightly sewn with twine. Following silently, at a distance of some three hundred paces, were twenty of his men.

Halfway up the Brilliant Green Jade road Francis touched his companion on the arm. "Now it is my turn."

"It is not heavy." Shon shifted the bundle tenderly to his other shoulder. "And I am perhaps more used to it than you."

They reached the shelter of the mission walls. No lights were showing, the outline which compassed everything he loved lay shadowy and unprotected. The silence was absolute. Suddenly, from within the lodge, he heard the melodious strike of the American chiming clock he had given Joseph for a wedding present. He counted automatically. Eleven o'clock.

Shon had given the men a final word of instruction. One of them, squatting against the wall, suppressed a cough which seemed to echo out across the hill. Shon cursed him in a violent whisper. The men were not important. It was what Shon and he must do together that mattered. He felt his friend peering at him through the silent darkness.

"You know exactly what is going to occur?"

"Yes."

"When I fire into the can of gasoline it will ignite instantly and explode the cordite. But before that, even before I raise my revolver, you must begin to move away. You must be well away. The concussion will be extreme." He paused. "Let us go if you are ready. And for the love of your Lord of Heaven keep the torch away from the sack."

Nerving himself, Francis took matches from his pocket and let the split reed flare. Then, holding it up, he stepped from the cover of the mission wall and walked openly towards the cypress grove. Shon came behind him, like a servant, bearing the sack on his back, as if groaning beneath its weight, taking care to make a noise.

The distance was not great. At the edge of the grove he halted, called out into the watchful stillness of the invisible trees:

"I have come as requested. Take me to your leader."

There was an interval of silence; then, close behind them, a sudden movement. Francis swung round and saw two of Wai's men standing in the pool of smoky glare.

"You are expected, Bewitcher. Proceed without undue fear."

They were escorted through a formidable maze of shallow trenches and sharp-ended bamboo stakes to the centre of the grove. Here the priest's heart sharply missed a beat. Behind a breastwork of earth and cedar branches, the crew dispersed in attitudes of care beside it, stood the long-muzzled gun.

"Have you brought all that was demanded of you?"

Francis recognized the voice of his visitor earlier that evening. He lied more readily this time.

"I have brought a great load of tinned goods . . . which will certainly please you."

Shon exhibited the sack, moving nearer, a trifle nearer, to the gun.

"It is not so great a load." The captain of the gun crew stepped into the light. "Have you brought money also?"

"Yes."

"Where is it?" The captain felt the neck of the sack.

"Not there." Francis spoke hurriedly, with a start. "I have the money in my purse."

The captain gazed at him, diverted from his examination of the sack, his expression lit by a sudden cupidity. A group of soldiers had collected, their staring faces all bent upon the priest.

"Listen, all of you." Francis held their attention, with a desperate intensity. He could see Shon edging imperceptibly into the fringe of shadow, closer, still closer to the gun. "I ask you—I beg you—to leave us unmolested in the mission."

Contempt showed in the captain's face. He smiled derisively. "You shall be unmolested . . . until tomorrow." Someone laughed in the background. "Then we shall protect your women."

Francis hardened his heart. Shon, as though exhausted, had un-loaded the sack under the breech of the gun. Pretending to wipe the perspiration from his brow he came back a little towards the priest. The crowd of soldiers had increased and were growing impatient. Francis strove to gain one minute of extra time for Shon.

"I do not doubt your word but I should value some assurance from General Wai."

"General Wai is in the city. You will see him later."

The captain spoke curtly and stepped out to get the money. From the corner of his eye, Francis saw Shon's hand go beneath his blouse. It is coming now, he thought. In the same moment, he heard the loud report of the revolver shot and the impact of the bullet as it struck the oil tin inside the sack. Braced for the convulsion, he could not under-stand. There was no explosion. Shon in swift succession fired three further shots into the tin. Francis saw the gasoline flood all over the sacking. He thought, with a kind of sick disillusionment yet quicker than the thudding shots: Shon was mistaken, the bullets won't ignite the gasoline, or perhaps it is only kerosene they put inside the tin. He saw Shon shooting into the crowd now, struggling to free his gun, shouting hopelessly to his own men to rush in. He saw the captain and a dozen soldiers closing on him. It all happened as swiftly as his thought. He felt a final, devastating wave of anger and despair. Deliberately, as though casting with a salmon rod he drew back his arm and threw his torch.

His accuracy was beautiful. The blazing flare arched like a comet through the night and hit the oil-soaked sacking squarely in the centre. Instantly a great sheet of sound and light struck at him. He no more than sensed the brilliant flash when the earth erupted and amidst a frightful detonation a blast of scorching air blew him backwards into crashing darkness. He had never lost consciousness before. He seemed falling, falling, into space and blackness, clutching for support and finding none, falling to annihilation, to oblivion.

When his senses returned he found himself stretched in the open, limp but unhurt, with Shon pulling his ear-lobes to bring him round. Dimly he saw the red sky above him. The whole cypress grove was ablaze, crackling and roaring like a pyre

"Is the gun finished?"

Shon stopped the ear-tweaking and sat up, relieved.

"Yes, it is finished. And some thirty of Wai's soldiers blown to pieces with it." His teeth showed white in his scorched face. "My friend, I congratulate you. I have never seen such a lovely killing in my life. Another such and you may have me for a Christian."

The next few days brought a terrible confusion of mind and spirit to Father Chisholm. The physical reaction to his adventure almost

957

prostrated him. He was no virile hero of romantic fiction but a stubby, short-winded little man well over forty. He felt shaken and dizzy. His head ached so persistently he had to drag himself to his room several times a day to plunge his splitting brow in the tepid water of his ewer. And through this bodily suffering ran the greater anguish of his soul, a chaotic mixture of triumph and remorse, a heavy and relentless wonder that he, a priest of God, should have raised his hand to slay his fellow men. He could barely find self-vindication in the safety of his people. His strangest torment lay in the stabbing recollection of his own unconsciousness under the shock of the explosion. Was death like that? A total oblivion . . .

No one but Polly suspected that he had left the mission grounds that night. He could feel her tranquil gaze travelling from his own silent and diminished form to the charred cedar stumps which marked the remnants of the gun emplacement. There was infinite understanding in the banal phrase she spoke to him:

"Somebody has done us a good turn by getting that nuisance out of the way."

Fighting continued in the outskirts of the city and in the hills to the eastward. By the fourth day reports reaching the mission indicated that the struggle was turning against Wai.

The end of that week came grey and overcast, with heavy gathering clouds. On Saturday the firing in Pai-tan dwindled to a few spasmodic rattles. Watching from his balcony Father Chisholm saw strings of figures in the Wai green retreating from the Western Gate. Many of these had thrown away their arms in the fear of being captured and shot as rebels. This Francis knew to be an indication of Wai's reverses and of his inability to effect a compromise with General Naian.

Outside the mission, behind the upper wall where some bamboo canes screened them from observation from the city, a number of these scattered soldiers had collected. Their voices, indeterminate and plainly frightened, could be heard inside the mission.

Towards three o'clock in the afternoon Sister Clotilde came with renewed agitation to Father Chisholm as he paced the courtyard, too disturbed to rest.

"Anna is throwing food over the upper wall." She wailed out the complaint. "I am sure her soldier is there . . . they were talking together."

His own nerves were near to breaking point. "There is no harm in giving food to those who need it."

"But he is one of those dreadful cut-throats. Oh, dear, we shall all be murdered in our beds!'

"Don't think so much about your own throat." He flushed with annoyance. "Martyrdom is an easy way to heaven."

As twilight fell, masses of the beaten Wai forces poured from all the city gates. They came by the Manchu Bridge, swarming up the Brilliant Green Jade road past the mission, in great confusion. The dirty faces of the men were stamped with the urgency of flight.

The night that followed was one of darkness and disorder, filled with shouting and shots, with galloping horses and the flare of torches on the far-off plain below. The priest watched with a strange melancholy from the lower mission gate. Suddenly, as he stood there, he heard a cautious step behind him. He turned. As he had half-expected, it was Anna, her mission coat buttoned closely to her chin, a cloth-wrapped bundle in her hand.

"Where are you going, Anna?"

She drew back with a stifled cry, but immediately regained her sullen boldness.

"It is my own affair."

"You will not tell me?"

"No."

His mood had fallen to quieter key, his attitude was changed. What was the use of more compulsion here?

"You have made up your mind to leave us, Anna. That is evident. And nothing that I can say or do will change it."

She said bitterly: "You have caught me now. But the next time you will not do so."

"There need be no next time, Anna." He took the key from his pocket and unlocked the gate. "You are free to go."

He could feel her start in sheer amazement, feel the impact of those full sultry eyes. Then without a word of gratitude or farewell she gripped her bundle and darted through the opening. Her running form was lost in the crowded roadway.

He stood, bare-headed, while the rabble swept past him. Now the exodus had turned to a rout. Suddenly there was a louder shouting, and he saw in the bobbing glare of upheld torches a group of men on horses. They approached rapidly, beating their way through the slow un-mounted stream that hindered them. As they reached the gate one of the riders wrenched his lathered pony to a stop. In the torchlight the priest had a vision of incredible evil, a death's-head face, with narrowed slits of eyes, and a low receding brow. The horseman shouted at him, an insult charged with hatred, then raised his hand with immediate deadly menace. Francis did not move: His perfect immobility, uncaring and resigned, seemed to disconcert the other. While he hesitated for an instant a pressing cry was raised from behind. "On, on, Wai . . . to Tou-en-lai . . . they are coming!"

Wai dropped his hand, holding the weapon, with a queer fatalism. As he spurred his beast forward he bent in the saddle and spat venomously in the priest's face. The night enclosed him.

Next morning, which dawned bright and sunny, the mission bells were ringing gaily. Fu, of his own accord, had clambered to the tower. He swung on the long rope, his thin beard wagging with delight. Most of the refugees were ready to go home, their faces jubilant, waiting only to have the mission Father's word before departing. All the children were in the compound, laughing and skipping, watched by Martha and Maria-Veronica, who had patched up their differences sufficiently to stand no more than six feet apart.

Even Clotilde was playing, the gayest of all, bouncing a ball, running with the little ones, giggling. Polly, upright in her favourite place in the vegetable garden, sat winding a new skein of wool as though life were nothing but a round of calm normality.

When Father Chisholm came slowly down the steps of his house Joseph met him joyfully, carrying his chubby infant on his arm. "It is over, Master. Victory for the Naians. The new general is truly great. No more war in Pai-tan. He promises it. Peace for all of us in our time." He bounced the baby tenderly, triumphantly. "No fighting for you my little Joshua, no more tears and blood. Peace! Peace!"

Inexplicably, a shaft of utter sadness pierced the priest's heart. He took the babe's tiny cheek, soft and golden, between his thumb and finger, caressingly. He stifled his sigh and smiled. They were all running towards him, his children, his people whom he loved—whom, at the cost of his dearest principle, he had saved.

X

The end of January brought the first glorious fruits of victory to Pai-tan. And Francis felt relief that Aunt Polly was spared the sight of them. She had departed for England the week before, and although the parting had been difficult he knew in his heart that it was wiser for her to go.

This morning as he crossed to the dispensary he speculated on the length of the rice line. Yesterday it had stretched the whole length of the mission wall. Wai, in the fury of defeat, had burned every stalk of grain for miles around. The sweet potato crop was poor. The rice fields, tended only by the women, with men and water-oxen commandeered by the army, had produced less than half the usual yield. Everything was scarce and costly. In the city, the value of tinned goods had multiplied five times. Prices were soaring daily.

He hastened into the crowded building. All three Sisters were there, each with a wooden measure and a black japanned bin of rice, engaged in the interminable task of scooping three ounces of the grain, running it into the proffered bowls.

He stood watching. His people were patient, quite silent. But the motion of the dry kernels made a constant hissing in the room. He said in a low voice to Maria-Veronica: "We can't keep this up. Tomorrow we must cut the allowance in half."

"Very well." She made a gesture of acquiescence. The strain of the past weeks had taken toll of her, he thought her unusually pale. She kept her eyes on the bin.

He went to the outer door, once or twice, counting the numbers. At last, to his relief, the line began to thin. He recrossed the compound, and descended to the store cellars, recasting the inventory of their supplies. Fortunately he had placed an order with Mr. Chia two months ago and it had been faithfully delivered. But the stock of rice and sweet potatoes, which they used in great quantity, was dangerously low.

He stood thinking. Though prices were exorbitant, food could still be purchased in Pai-tan. He took a sudden resolution and decided, for the first time in the mission's history, to cable the Society for an emergency grant.

A week later he received the answering cable:

Quite impossible allocate any monies. Kindly remember we are at war. You are not and therefore extremely lucky. Am immersed Red Cross work. Best regards Anselm Mealey.

Francis crumpled the green slip with an expressionless face. That afternoon he mustered all the available financial resources of the mission and went to the town. But now it was too late—he could buy nothing. The grain market was closed. The principal shops showed only a minimum of perishable produce: some melons, radishes, and small-river fish.

Disturbed, he stopped at the Lantern Street mission, where he had a long conversation with Dr. Fiske. Then, on his way back, he visited Mr. Chia's house.

Mr. Chia made Francis welcome. They drank tea together in the latticed little office, smelling of spice and musk and cedar.

"Yes," Mr. Chia agreed gravely, when they had fully discussed the shortage. "It is a matter of some small concern. Mr. Pao has gone to Chek-kow to endeavour to procure certain assurances from the new government."

"With some chance of success?"

"With every chance." The mandarin added, with the nearest approach to cynicism Father Chisholm had heard from him: "But assurances are not supplies."

"It was reported that the granary held many tons of reserve grain."

"General Naian took every bushel for himself. He has gutted the city of food."

"But surely," the mission Father spoke frowningly, "he cannot see the people starve. He promised them great benefit if they fought for him."

"Now he has mildly expressed the belief that some slight depopulation might benefit the community."

There was a silence. Father Chisholm reflected. "At least it is a blessing that Dr. Fiske will have large supplies. He is promised three full junkloads from his headquarters in Pekin."

"Ah!"

Again the silence.

"You are dubious?"

Mr. Chia responded with his gentle smile. "It is two thousand li from Pekin to Pai-tan. And there are many hungry people on the way. In my unworthy opinion, my most esteemed friend, we must prepare for six months of greatest hardship. These things come to China. But what matter? We may go. China remains."

Next morning Father Chisholm was obliged to turn back the rice line. It cut him to the heart to do so, yet he had to close the doors. He instructed Joseph to paint a notice that cases of utter destitution might leave their names at the lodge. He would investigate them personally.

Back in his house he set himself to work out a plan for rationing the mission. And the following week he introduced it. As the scheme began to operate the children wondered, then passed through fretfulness into a kind of puzzled dullness. They were lethargic and they asked for more at every meal. The insufficiency of sugar and starchy stuffs seemed to cause them most discomfort. They were losing weight.

From the Methodist mission came no word of the relief stores. The junks were now nearly three weeks overdue, and Dr. Fiske's anxiety was too significant to be mistaken. His public rice-kitchen had been closed for more than a month. In Pai-tan the people had a sluggish air, a heavy apathy. There was no light upon their faces, no briskness in their movements.

Then it began and gradually gathered strength: the timeless transmigration, old as China itself, the silent departure of men and women with their children from the city towards the South.

When Father Chisholm saw this symptom his heart chilled. A horrible vision attacked him of his little community, emaciated, relaxed in the final debility of starvation. He drew the lesson, swiftly, from the slow procession now beginning before his eyes.

As in the days of plague, he summoned Joseph to him, spoke to him and sped him upon an urgent errand.

On the morning following Joseph's departure he came over to the refectory and ordered an extra portion of rice to be given to the children. One last box of figs remained in the larder. He went down the long table giving each child a sweet sticky mouthful.

This sign of better feeding made the community more cheerful. But Martha, with one eye on the almost empty store-cellar and the other upon Father Chisholm, muttered her perplexity.

"What is in the wind, Father? There's something . . . I'm sure."

"You shall know on Saturday, Martha. Meanwhile, please tell Reverend Mother we shall continue on the extra rice for the remainder of this week."

Martha went off to do his bidding but could not find Reverend Mother anywhere. It was strange.

All that afternoon Maria-Veronica did not appear. She failed to take her weaving class, which was always held on Wednesdays, in the basket room. At three o'clock she could not be found. Perhaps it was an oversight. Shortly after five, she came in for refectory duty as usual, pale and composed, offering no explanation of her absence. But that night in the convent both Clotilde and Martha were awakened by a startling sound which came, unmistakably, from Maria-Veronica's room.

Appalled, they talked of it next morning in whispers, in the corner of the laundry, watching Reverend Mother through the window as she crossed the courtyard, dignified and upright, yet much slower than before.

"She has broken at last." Martha's words seemed constricted in her throat. "Blessed Virgin, did you hear her weep last night?"

Clotilde stood twisting an end of linen in her hands. "Perhaps she has news of a great German defeat we have not heard of yet."

"Yes, yes . . . it is something terrible." Martha's face suddenly puckered up. "Truly, if she were not an accursed Boche I would feel almost sorry for her."

"I have never known her to weep before." Clotilde meditated, her fingers twisting indecisively. "She is a proud woman. That must make it doubly hard."

"Pride goeth before a fall. Would she have had sympathy for us if we had yielded first? Nevertheless I must admit—Bah! Let us continue with our ironing."

Early on Sunday morning a small cavalcade approached the mission, winding downwards from the mountains. Advised by Joseph of its arrival, Father Chisholm hastened to the lodge to welcome Liu-Chi and his three companions from the Liu village. He clasped the old shepherd's hands as though he would never let them go.

"This is true kindness. The good God will bless you for it."

Liu-Chi smiled, naïvely pleased by the warmth of his reception. "We would have come sooner. But we took much time to collect the ponies."

There were perhaps thirty of the short shaggy uplands ponies, bridled but unsaddled, with big double panniers strapped upon their backs. They were contentedly munching the swathes of dried grass strewn for them. The priest's heart lifted. He pressed the four men to the refreshments which Joseph's wife had already prepared in the lodge, told them they must rest when they had eaten.

He found Reverend Mother in the linen room silently passing out fresh white bundles of the week's requirements: tablecloths, sheets and towels, to Martha, Clotilde and one of the senior students. He no longer attempted to conceal his satisfaction.

"I must prepare you for a change. Because of the threat of famine we are moving to the Liu village. You'll find plenty there, I assure you." He smiled. "Sister Martha, you'll find many ways of cooking mountain mutton before you return. I know you will enjoy the experience. And for the children . . . it will be a fine holiday."

There was a moment's sheer surprise. Then Martha and Clotilde both smiled, conscious of a coming break in the monotony of life, already stirring to the excitement of the adventure.

"Doubtless you will expect us to be organized in five minutes," Martha grumbled amiably, casting her eye instructively, for the first time in many weeks, upon Reverend Mother, as if for her approval.

It was the first faint gesture of atonement. But Maria-Veronica, standing by, with a colourless face, gave no answering sign.

"Yes, you must look sharp." Father Chisholm spoke almost gaily. "The little ones will be packed into the panniers. The others must take turns of walking and riding. The nights are warm and fine. Liu-Chi will look after you. If you leave today you should reach the village in a week."

Clotilde giggled. "We shall be like one of the tribes of Egypt."

The priest nodded. "I am giving Joseph a basket of my fantails. Every evening he must release one to bring me a message of your progress."

"What!" Martha and Clotilde exclaimed together. "You are not coming with us?"

"I may follow at a later date." Francis felt happy that they should want him. "You see, someone must remain at the mission. Reverend Mother and you two will be the pioneers."

Maria-Veronica said slowly: "I cannot go."

There was a silence.

At first he thought it a continuation of her pique, a disinclination to accompany the other two, but one glance at her face told him otherwise.

He said persuasively: "It will be a pleasant trip. The change would do you good."

She shook her head slowly. "I shall be obliged to take a longer trip . . . quite soon."

There was a longer pause. Then standing very still, she spoke with a toneless lack of emotion. "I must return to Germany . . . to see about the disposal . . . to our order . . . of my estate." She gazed into the distance. "My brother has been killed in action."

The previous silence had been deep, but now there was a mortal stillness. It was Clotilde who burst into violent tears. Then Martha, as though trapped, like an animal, hung her head unwillingly, in sympathy. Father Chisholm glanced from one to the other in deep distress, then walked silently away.

A fortnight after the party had arrived at Liu the day of Maria-Veronica's departure was, incredibly, upon him. The latest information from the village, received by pigeon post, indicated that the children were primitively yet comfortably billeted, and wild with health in the keen high air. Father Chisholm had good reason to congratulate himself upon his own resourcefulness. Yet as he walked beside Maria-Veronica to the landing steps, preceded by two bearers with long poles, supporting her baggage upon their shoulders, he felt a desperate forlornness.

They stood on the jetty while the men placed the bundles in the sampan. Behind them the city lay, murmuring in still dejection. Before them, in mid-river, lay the outgoing junk. The dun water which lapped its hull reached out to a grey horizon.

He could find no words to express himself. She had meant so much to him, this gracious and distinguished woman, with her help, encouragement, and comradeship. The future had stretched before them, indefinitely, a future filled with their work together. Now she was going, unexpectedly, almost furtively. it seemed, in a haze of darkness and confusion.

He sighed, at last, giving her his troubled smile. "Even if my country remains at war with yours . . . remember . . . I am not your enemy."

The understatement was so like him, and all that she admired in him, it shook her determination to be strong. As she gazed at his spare figure, gaunt face and thinning hair, tears clouded her beautiful eyes.

"My dear . . . dear friend . . . I will never forget you."

She gave him her warm firm clasp and stepped quickly into the little craft which would take her to the junk.

He stood there, leaning on his old tartan umbrella, his eyes screwed against the water's glitter, until the vessel was a speck, floating, vanishing beyond the rim of the sky.

Unknown to her, he had placed amongst her baggage the little antique figure of the Spanish Virgin which Father Tarrant had given him. It was his sole possession of any value. She had often admired it.

He turned and slowly plodded home. In the garden which she had made and loved so much, he paused, grateful for the silence and the peace there. The scent of lilies was in the air. Old Fu, the gardener, his sole companion in the deserted mission, was pruning the azalea bushes with gentle, inquiring hands. He felt worn-out by all that he had lately undergone. A chapter in his life was ended: for the first time, he dimly sensed that he was growing old. He seated himself on the bench beneath the banyan tree, rested his elbows on the pinewood table she had placed there. Old Fu, pruning the azaleas, pretended not to see him as, after a moment, he laid his head upon his arms.

XI

The broad leaves of the banyan tree still shaded him as he sat at the garden table turning the pages of his journal with hands which, as by by some strange illusion, were veined and vaguely tremulous. Of course, old Fu no longer watched him, unless through a chink of heaven. Instead, two young gardeners bent by the azalea bed while Father Chou, his Chinese priest, small, gentle and demure, pacing with his breviary at a respectful distance, kept a warm brown filial eye upon him.

In the August sunshine the mission compound was aquiver with dry light, like the sparkle of a golden wine. From the playground the happy shouts of the children at their playtime told him the forenoon hour: eleven o'clock. His children, or rather, he corrected himself wryly, his children's children . . . How unfairly time had flashed across him, tumbling the years into his lap, one upon another, too fast for him to marshal them.

A jolly red face, plump and smiling, swam into his abstracted vision, above a tumblerful of milk. He forced a frown as Mother Mercy Mary drew near, annoyed to be reminded of his age by another of her coddling tricks. He was only sixty-seven . . . well, sixty-eight next month . . . a mere nothing . . . and fitter than any youngster.

"Haven't I told you not to bring me that stuff?"

She smiled soothingly—vigorous, bustling, and matronly. "You need it today, Father, if you will insist on taking that long unnecessary trip." She paused. "I don't see why Father Chou and Dr. Fiske couldn't go themselves?"

"Don't you?"

"No, indeed."

"Dear Sister, that's too bad. Your mind must be breaking up." She laughed indulgently and tried to coax him.

"Shall I tell Joshua you've decided not to go?"

"Tell him to have the ponies saddled in an hour."

He saw her depart, shaking her head reproachfully. He smiled again, with the dry triumph of a man who has had his way. Then, sipping his milk, without, now that she was gone, the necessity of a grimace, he resumed his leisured perusal of the diary before him. It was a habit into which he had lately fallen, a kind of wilful retrospection, evoked by turning the frayed and dog-eared pages at random.

This morning it opened, strangely, first at the date *October* 1917.

"Despite the improving conditions in Pai-tan, the good rice crop and the safe homecoming of my little ones from Liu, I have been downcast lately; yet today a simple incident gave me preposterous happiness.

"I had been away for four days at the annual conference which the Prefect Apostolic has thought fit to institute at Sen-siang. As the farthest outpost of the Vicariate I had fancied myself immune from such junketings. Indeed, we missioners are so widely scattered and so few—only Father Surette, poor Thibodeau's successor, the three Chew-kow Chinese priests and Father Van Dwyn the Dutchman from Rakai— that the occasion seemed scarcely worth the long river journey. But there we were 'exchanging viewpoints.' And naturally I talked indiscreetly against 'aggressive Christianizing methods,' got hot under the collar and quoted Mr. Pao's cousin: 'You missionaries walk in with your Gospel and walk off with our land.' I fell into disgrace with Father Surette, a bustling Father who rejoices in his muscles, which he has used to destroy all the pleasant little Buddhist wayside shrines within twenty li of Sen-siang, and who in addition claims the amazing record of 50,000 pious ejaculations in one day.

"On my return trip I was overcome with remorse. How often have I had to write in this journal: 'Failed again. Dear Lord, help me restrain my tongue!' And they thought me such a queer fish at Sen-siang!

"To mortify myself I had dispensed with a cabin on the boat. Next to me on deck was a man with a cage of prime rats which he dined on, progressively, under my jaundiced eye. In addition it rained hard, blew down streams and I was, as I deserved to be, extremely sick.

"Then, as I stepped off the vessel at Pai-tan, more dead than alive, I found an old woman waiting for me on the drenched deserted jetty. As she approached I saw her to be my friend, old mother Hsu, she who cooked beans in the milk-can in the compound. She is the poorest, the lowest person in my parish.

"To my amazement her face was illuminated at the sight of me. Quickly she told me she had missed me so much she had stood there in the rain these past three afternoons, waiting my arrival. She produced six little ceremonial cakes of rice flour and sugar, not for eating—the kind they place before the images of Buddha—the same images that Father Surette knocks down. A comic gesture . . . But the joy of knowing that to one person at least one is dear . . . and indispensable . . .

"*May* 1918. This lovely morning my first batch of young settlers departed for Liu, twenty-four in all,—I might discreetly add, twelve of each kind,—amidst great enthusiasm and many knowing nods and practical admonitions from our good Reverend Mother Mercy Mary. Though I resented her coming intensely—weighing her sulkily against the memory of Maria-Veronica—she is a fine, capable, cheerful person, and for a holy nun she has an amazing insight into the exigencies of the marriage bed.

"Old Meg Paxton, the Cannelgate fishwife, used to reassure me that I wasn't such a fool as I looked; and I'm quite proud of my inspiration to colonize Liu—with the finest produce of this mission of St. Andrew's. There simply aren't enough jobs here for my growing-up young people. It would seem the worst kind of stupidity, having pulled them out of the gutter, to throw them back again, benevolently, now they are educated. And Liu itself will profit by an infusion of fresh blood. There is ample land, a stirring climate. Once the numbers are adequate I shall establish a young priest there. Anselm must send me one, until he does so I shall deafen him with my importunities. . . .

"I am tired tonight from the excitement and the ceremonies—these mass marriages are no joke, and Chinese ceremonial oratory leaves the vocal cords in ruins. Perhaps my depression is reactionary, perhaps physical. I do need a holiday quite badly, I am a little stale. The Fiskes have gone off for their routine six months' rest, to visit their son, now established in Virginia. I miss them. Their relief, the Reverend Ezra Salkins, makes me realize how fortunate I am to have such sweet and gentle neighbours. Shang-Foo Ezra is neither—a big man with a fixed beam, a Rotarian handshake, and a smile like melting lard. He boomed at me as he cracked my fingerbones: 'Anything I can do to help you, brother, anything at all.'

"The Fiskes would be my honoured guests at Liu. But to Ezra I am dumb. In just sixty seconds he would have Father Ribiero's tomb plastered with bill-heads: *Brother are you saved?* Oh, blow! I am crabbed and sour, it's that plum pie Mercy Mary. made me eat at the wedding breakfast. . . .

"I have been made truly happy by a long letter dated June 10th, 1922 from Mother Maria-Veronica. After many vicissitudes, the trials of the

968

war and the humiliations of the armistice, she has at last been rewarded by her appointment as Superior of the Sistine Convent in Rome. This is the mother house of her order, a fine old foundation on the high slopes between the Corso and the Quirinal overlooking the Saporelli and the lovely church of Santi Apostoli. It is an office of the first importance but no more than she deserves. She seems contented . . . at peace. Her letter brings me such a fragrance of the Holy City—that might be one of Anselm's phrases!—always the object of my tender longings, I have dared to make a plan. When my sick-leave, already twice postponed, does arrive, what is to prevent my visiting Rome, wearing my boots out on the mosaics of St. Peter's, and seeing Mother Maria-Veronica in the bargain? When I wrote in April congratulating Anselm on his appointment as Rector of the Tynecastle Cathedral Church he assured me, in his reply, that I should have an assistant priest within six months and my 'much-needed vacation' before the year was out.

"An absurd thrill pervades my sun-bleached bones when I think that such happiness may be in store for me. Enough! I must start to save to buy myself a suit of clothes. What would the good Abbess of Santi Apostoli think if the little bricklayer who claimed her acquaintance turned out to have a patch on the backside of his pants. . . .

"*September* 17th, 1923. Breathless excitement! Today, my new priest arrived, at last I have a colleague, and it seems almost too good to be true.

"Although, at first, Anselm's voluminous hieratics gave me hope of a stout young Scot, preferably with freckles and sandy hair, later advices had prepared me for a native Father from the College at Pekin. It was like my perverted humour to tell the Sisters nothing of the coming dénouement. For weeks they had been gathering themselves to coddle the young missioner from home—Clotilde and Martha wanted something Gallic with a beard, but poor Mother Mercy Mary had made a very special novena for an Irish one. The look on her honest Hibernian face as she burst into my room, purple with tragedy! 'The new Father is a Chinese!'

"But Father Chou seems a splendid little fellow, not only quiet and amiable, but conveying a deep sense of that extraordinary interior life which is such an admirable characteristic of the Chinese. I have met several native priests on my infrequent pilgrimages to Sen-siang and I have always been impressed. If I wished to be pompous I should say that the good ones appear to combine the wisdom of Confucius with the virtue of Christ.

"And now I am off to Rome next month . . . my first holiday in nineteen years. I am like a Holywell schoolboy, at the end of term, banging his desk and chanting:

969

'Two more weeks and I shall be,
Outside the gates of mis-er-ee.'

"I wonder if Mother Maria-Veronica has lost her taste for fine stem ginger. I shall take her a jar and risk being told she has turned to macaroni. Heigh-ho! This life is most jolly. Through my window I see the young cedars swaying in the wind with a wild joy. I must write now to Shanghai for my tickets. Hurrah!

"*October* 1923. Yesterday the cable came cancelling my trip to Rome and I have just returned from my evening walk by the river-bank where I stood a long time in a soft mist watching the cormorant fishers. It is a sad way of catching fish, or perhaps I had a sad way of looking at it. The great birds are ringed by the neck to prevent their swallowing the fish. They crouch indolently on the gunwale of the boat as though dreadfully bored with the whole proceeding. Suddenly there is a dip and a splutter and up comes the great bill, pouched with fish, a tail wriggling at the tip. An embarrassing undulation of the neck follows next. When relieved of their catch the birds shake their heads, disconsolate, yet as though experience had taught them nothing. Then they squat again, brooding blackly, recuperating for a fresh defeat.

"My own mood was dark and defeated enough, God knows. As I stood by the slaty water, from which the night wind threw waves upon the weed coiled like hair upon the shore, my thoughts, strangely, were not of Rome but of the streams of Tweedside, with myself, barefoot in the rippling crystal, casting a withy rod for trout.

"More and more of late I find myself living in the memory of my childhood, recollected so vividly it might be yesterday—a sure symptom of approaching age! . . . I even dream, tenderly, wistfully—isn't this unbelievable?—of my boyish love: my own dear Nora.

"You see, I have reached the sentimental stage of disappointment, which is next to getting over it, but when the telegram arrived, in old Meg's words, 'it was hard to thole.'

"Now I am almost resigned to the utter finality of my exile. The principle is probably correct that a return to Europe unsettles the missionary priest. After all, we give ourselves entirely, there is no retreat. I am here for life. And I'll lay myself, at last, in that little piece of Scotland where Willie Tulloch rests.

"Moreover, it is certainly logical and just that Anselm's trip to Rome is more necessary than mine. The funds of the Society cannot sustain two such excursions. And he can better tell the Holy Father of the advances of 'his troops'—as he calls us. Where my tongue would be stiff and clumsy his will captivate—garner funds and support for all the F. S. missions. He has promised to write me fully of his doings. I must enjoy

Rome vicariously, have my audience in imagination, meet Maria-Veronica in spirit. I could not bring myself to accept Anselm's suggestion of a short vacation in Manila. Its gaiety would have troubled me, I should have laughed at the solitary little man, poking round the harbour, fancying himself on the Pontine Hill. . . .

"*A month later.* . . . Father Chou is nicely established in the Liu village and our pigeons pass one another at celestial speed. What a joy that my scheme is working so beautifully. I wonder if Anselm will mention it, perhaps, when he sees the Holy Father, just a word of that tiny jewel, set in the great wilderness, once forgotten . . . by all but God. . . .

"*22nd November,* 1928. How can one compass a sublime experience in mere words—in one bald and arid phrase? Last night Sister Clotilde died. Death is a topic I have not often dwelt upon in this sketchy record of my own imperfect life.

"Thus, twelve months ago when Aunt Polly passed away in her sleep at Tynecastle, uneventfully and of pure goodness and old age, and the news reached me in Judy's tear-smudged letter, I made no comment here beyond the simple entry: '*Polly died, 17th October,* 1927.' There is an inevitability in the death of those whom we know to be good. But there are others . . . sometimes we tough old priests are staggered, as by a revelation.

"Clotilde had been ailing, slightly it seemed, for several days. When they called me just after midnight I was shocked to see the change in her. I sent at once to tell Joshua, Joseph's eldest boy—to run for Dr. Fiske. But Clotilde, with a strange expression, restrained me. She indicated, with a peculiar smile, that Joshua might spare himself the journey. She said very little; but enough.

"When I recollected how, years ago, I tartly reproached her for that inexplicable recourse to chlorodyne, I could have wept for my stupidity. I had never thought enough of Clotilde: the tension of her manner, which she could not help, her morbid dread of flushing, of people, of her own overcharged nerves, made her superficially unattractive, even ridiculous. One should have reflected on the struggles of such a nature to overcome itself, one should have thought of the invisible victories. Instead, one thought only of the visible defeats.

"For eighteen months she had been suffering from a growth of the stomach arising out of a chronic ulcer. When she learned from Dr. Fiske that nothing could be done she pledged him to secrecy and set herself to fight an unsung battle. Before I was called the first bad hemorrhage had prostrated her. At six next morning she had the second and succumbed quite quietly. Between, we talked . . . but I dare not make a record of that conversation. Broken and disjointed, it would seem meaningless, . . . a prey for easy sneers . . . and alas, the world cannot be reformed by a sneer . . .

"We are all much upset, Martha especially. She is like me, strong as a mule, and will go on forever. Poor Clotilde! I think of her as a gentle creature so strung to sacrifice that sometimes she vibrated harshly. To see a face become at peace, a quiet acceptance of death, without fear . . . it ennobles the heart of man.

"*November 30th*, 1929. Today Joseph's fifth child was born. How life flies on! Who would have dreamed that my shy, brave, garrulous, touchy youngster had in him the makings of a patriarch? Perhaps his early fondness for sugar should have warned me! Really, he is quite a personage now—officious, uxorious, a little pompous, very curt to callers he thinks I should not see—I am rather scared of him myself. . . .

"*A week later*. More local news . . . Mr. Chia's dress boots have been hung up at the Manchu Gate. This is a tremendous honour here . . . and I rejoice for my old friend, whose ascetic, contemplative, generous nature has always been devoted to the reasonable and the beautiful, to that which is eternal.

"Yesterday, the mail came in. Even without the presage of his immense success in Rome, I had long realized that Anselm must achieve high honour in the Church. And at last his work for the foreign missions has earned him a fitting reward from the Vatican. He is the new Bishop of Tynecastle. Perhaps the greatest strain is thrown upon our moral vision by the spectacle of another's success. The dazzle hurts us. But now, in my approaching old age, I'm short-sighted. I don't mind Anselm's lustre, I'm rather glad, because I know that he will be supremely glad himself. Jealousy is so hateful a quality. One should remember that the defeated still have everything if they still have God.

"I wish I might take credit for my magnanimity. But this is not magnanimity, merely an awareness of the difference between Anselm and myself . . . of the ridiculous presumption of myself aspiring to the crozier. Though we started from the same mark Anselm has far outstripped me. He has developed his talents to the full, is now, I observe from the *Tynecastle Chronicle*, 'an accomplished linguist, a notable musician, a patron of arts and science in the diocese, with a vast circle of influential friends.' How lucky! I have had no more than six friends in my uneventful life, and all except one were humble folk. I must write to Anselm to congratulate him, making it clear, however, that I do not presume upon our friendship and have no intention of asking for preferment. *Viva Anselmo!* I am sad when I think how much you have made of your life and how little I have made of mine. I have bumped my head so often . . . and so hard, in my strivings after God.

"*December 30*, 1929. I have not written in this journal for almost a month . . . not since the news of Judy arrived. I still find it difficult to set down even the barest outline of what has taken place at home . . . and here, within myself.

"I flattered myself I had achieved a beatific resignation towards the finality of my exile. Two weeks ago today, I was remarkably complacent. Having made a survey of my recent additions to the mission, the four rice-fields by the river which I bought last year, the enlarged stockyard beyond the white mulberry grove, and the new pony farm, I came into the church to help the children make the Christmas crib. This is a job I particularly enjoy, partly from that lamentable obsession which has stuck to me all my life, I suppose the ribald would call it a suppressed paternal instinct: a love of children—from the dear Christ child down to the meanest little yellow waif who ever crawled into this mission of St. Andrew's.

"We had made a splendid manger with a snowy roof of real cotton wool and were arranging the ox and ass in their stall behind. I had all sorts of things up my sleeve too, coloured lights, and a fine crystal star to hang on the spruce-branched sky. As I saw the shining faces about me and listened to the excited chatter—this is one of the occasions when distractions are permissible in church—I had a wonderful sense of lightness, a vision of all the Christmas cribs in all the Christian churches of the world, dignifying this sweet festival of the Nativity, which, even to those who cannot believe, must at least be beautiful as the feast of all motherhood.

"At that moment one of the bigger boys, sent by Mother Mercy Mary, hurried in with the cablegram. Surely ill-tidings come fast enough without flashing them round the earth. As I read my expression must have changed. One of the smallest girls began to cry. The brightness in my breast was quenched.

"Perhaps I might be judged absurd for taking this so much to heart. I lost Judy when in her teens, on my departure for Pai-tan. But I have lived her life with her in thought. The infrequency of her letters made them stand out like beads upon a chain.

"The hand of heredity propelled Judy forward without mercy. She never quite knew what she wanted or where she was going. But so long as Polly stood beside her she could not become the victim of her own caprice. All through the war she prospered, like many other young women, working for high wages in a munitions factory. She bought a fur coat and a piano—how well I recollect the letter in which the joyful information reached me—and was keyed to sustain her effort by the sense of emergency in the air. This was her heyday. When the war ended, she was over thirty, opportunities were scarce, she gradually abandoned all thought of a career and lapsed into a quiet life with Polly, sharing the small flat in Tynecastle and gaining, one hoped, with maturity, an added balance.

"Judy seemed always to have a queer suspicion towards the other sex and had never been attracted by the thought of marriage. She was forty when Polly died and one never dreamed that she would change her single state. Nevertheless, within eight months of the funeral, Judy was married . . . and later deserted.

"One does not disguise the brutal fact that women do strange things before the climacteric. But this was not the explanation of the pitiful comedy. Polly's legacy to Judy was some two thousand pounds, enough to provide a modest annual competence. Not until Judy's letter arrived did I guess how she had been persuaded to realize her capital, to transfer it to her sober, upright and gentlemanly husband whom she had first met, apparently, in a boarding house at Scarborough.

"No doubt whole volumes might be written on this basic mundane theme . . . dramatic . . . analytical . . . in the grand Victorian manner . . . perhaps with that sly smirk which sees a rich deep humour in the gullibility of our human nature. But the epilogue was briefly written in ten words on the telegraph form that I held in my hands before the Christmas crib. A child had been born to Judy of this belated, transitory union. And she had died in bearing it.

"Now I reflect there had always been a dark thread running through the flimsy fabric of Judy's inconsequential life. She was the visible evidence, not of sin—how I detest and distrust that word!—but of man's weakness and stupidity. She was the reason, the explanation of our presence here on earth, the tragic evidence of our common mortality. And now, differently, yet with the same essential sadness, that mortal tragedy is again perpetuated.

"I cannot bring myself to contemplate the fate of this unlucky infant, with no one to look after it but the woman who attended Judy—she who has now sent me the news. It is easy to fit her to the pattern of events: one of those handywives who take in expectant mothers, in straitened, slightly dubious circumstances. I must reply to her at once . . . send some money, what little I have. When we bind ourselves to holy poverty we are strangely selfish, forgetful of the awful obligations which life may place upon us. Poor Nora . . . poor Judy . . . poor unnamed little child . . .

"*June* 19*th*, 1930. A grand day of early summer sunshine and my heart is lighter for the letter received this afternoon. The child is baptized Andrew, after this same infamous mission, and the news makes me chuckle with senile vanity, as though I, myself, were the little wretch's grandfather. Perhaps, whether I wish it or not, this relationship will devolve on me. The father has vanished and we shall make no attempt to trace him. But if I send a certain sum each month, this woman, Mrs. Stevens, who seems a worthy creature, will care for Andrew. Again I can't help smiling . . . my priestly career has been a hotch-potch of peculiarities

. . . to rear an infant at a distance of eight thousand miles will be its crowning oddity!

"Wait a moment! I've flicked myself on the raw with that phrase: 'my priestly career.' The other day, during one of our friendly tiffs, on Purgatory I think it was, Fiske declared—heatedly, for I was getting the better of him: 'You argue like a mixed Convention of Holy Rollers and High Anglicans!'

"That brought me up short. I daresay my upbringing, and that early bit of the uncalculable influence of dear old Daniel Glennie, shaped me towards undue liberality. I love my religion, into which I was born, which I have taught, as best I could, for over thirty years, and which has led me unfailingly to the source of all joy, of everlasting sweetness. Yet in my isolation here my outlook has simplified, clarified with my advancing years. I've tied up, and neatly tucked away, all the complex, pettifogging little quirks of doctrine. Frankly, I can't believe that any of God's creatures will grill for all Eternity because of eating a mutton chop on Friday. If we have the fundamentals—love for God and our neighbour—surely we're all right? And isn't it time for the churches of the world to cease hating one another . . . and unite? The world is one living, breathing body, dependent for its health on the billions of cells which comprise it . . . and each tiny cell is the heart of man . . .

"*December 15th*, 1932. Today the new patron saint of this mission was three years old. I hope he had a pleasant birthday and didn't eat too much of the toffee I wrote Burley's, in Tweedside, to send him.

"*September 1st*, 1935. Oh Lord, don't let me be a silly old man . . . this journal is becoming more and more the fatuous record of a child I have not seen and shall never see. I cannot return and he cannot come here. Even my obstinacy balks at that absurdity . . . though I did in fact inquire of Dr. Fiske, who told me that the climate would be deadly for an English child of such tender years.

"Yet I must confess I'm troubled. Reading between her letters it would seem as though Mrs. Stevens had lately come down a little in her luck. She has moved to Kirkbridge, which, as I remember it, is a cotton town, not prepossessing, near Manchester. Her tone has altered, too, and I am beginning to wonder if she is more interested in the money she receives than in Andrew. Yet her parish priest gave her an excellent character. And hitherto she has been admirable.

"Of course, it's all my own fault. I could have secured Andrew's future, after a fashion, by turning him over to one of our excellent Catholic institutions. But somehow . . . he's my one 'blood relation,' a living memento of my dear lost Nora . . . I can't and I won't be so impersonal . . . it's my inveterate crankiness, I suppose, which makes me fight against officialdom. Well . . . if that is so . . . I . . . and Andrew . . . must take the consequences . . . we are in God's hands and he will . . ."

Here, as Father Chisholm turned another page, his concentration was disturbed by the sound of ponies stamping in the compound. He hesitated, listening, half unwilling to relinquish his mood of precious reverie. But the sound increased, mingled with brisk voices. His lips drew together in acceptance. He turned to the last entry in the journal and, taking his pen, added a paragraph.

"*April* 30*th*, 1936. I am on the point of leaving for the Liu settlement with Father Chou and the Fiskes. Yesterday Father Chou came in, anxious for my advice about a young herdsman he had isolated at the settlement, fearing he might have the smallpox. I decided to go back with him myself—with our good ponies and the new trail, it is only a two days' journey. Then I amplified the idea. Since I have repeatedly promised to show Dr. and Mrs. Fiske our model village, I decided we might all four take the trip. It will be my last opportunity to fulfil my long-outstanding pledge to the doctor and his wife. They are returning home to America at the end of this month. I hear them calling now. They are looking forward to the excursion . . . I'll tackle Fiske en route on his confounded impudence . . . Holy Roller, indeed! . . ."

XII

The sun was already dropping towards the bare rim of the hills which enclosed the narrow valley. Riding ahead of the returning party, occupied by thoughts of Liu, where they had left Father Chou with medicine for the sick herdsman, Father Chisholm had resigned himself to another night encampment before reaching the mission when, at a bend of the road, he met three men in dirty cotton uniforms slouching head-down with rifles on their hips.

It was a familiar sight: the province was swarming with irregulars, disbanded soldiers with smuggled weapons who had formed themselves into roving gangs. He passed them with a muttered, "Peace be with you," and slowed down till the others of the party made up to him. But as he turned he was surprised to see terror on the faces of the two porters from the Methodist mission and a sudden anxiety in his own servant's eyes.

"These look like followers of Wai." Joshua made a gesture towards the road ahead. "And there are others."

The priest swung round stiffly. About twenty of the grey-green figures were approaching down the path kicking up a cloud of slow white dust. On the shadowed hill, straggling in a winding line, were at least another score. He exchanged a glance with Fiske.

"Let's push on."

The two parties met a moment later. Father Chisholm, smiling, with his usual greeting, kept his beast moving steadily down the middle of the path. The soldiers, gaping stupidly, gave way automatically. The only mounted man, a youngster with a broken peaked cap and some air of authority, enhanced by a corporal's stripe misplaced upon his cuff, halted his shaggy pony indecisively.

"Who are you? And whither are you going?"

"We are missionaries, returning to Pai-tan." Father Chisholm gave the answer calmly across his shoulder, still leading the others forward. They were now almost through the dirty, puzzled, staring mob: Mrs. Fiske and the doctor behind him, followed by Joshua and the two bearers.

The corporal was uncertain but partly satisfied. The encounter was robbed of danger, reduced to commonplace, when suddenly the elder of the two porters lost his head. Prodded by a rifle butt in his passage between the men, he dropped his bundle with a screech of panic and bolted for the cover of the brushwood on the hill.

Father Chisholm suppressed a bitter exclamation. In the gathering twilight, there was a second's dubious immobility. Then a shot rang out, another, and another. The echoes went volleying down the hills. As the blue figure of the bearer, bent double, vanished into the bushes, a loud defrauded outcry broke amongst the soldiers. No longer dumbly wondering, they crowded around the missionaries, in furious chattering resentment.

"You must come with us." As Father Chisholm had foreseen, the corporal's reaction was immediate.

"We are only missionaries," Dr. Fiske protested heatedly. "We have no possessions. We are honest people."

"Honest people do not run away. You must come to our leader, Wai."

"I assure you——"

"Wilbur!" Mrs. Fiske interposed quietly. "You'll only make it worse. Save your breath."

Bundled about, surrounded by the soldiers, they were roughly pushed along the path which they had recently traversed. About five li back, the young officer turned west into a dry watercourse which took a tortuous and stony course into the hills. At the head of the gully the company halted.

Here perhaps a hundred ill-conditioned soldiers were scattered about in postures of ease—smoking, chewing betel nut, scraping lice from their armpits and caked mud from between their bare toes. On a flat stone, cross-legged, eating his evening meal before a small dung fire, with his back against the wall of the ravine, was Wai-Chu.

Wai was now about fifty-five, gross but full-bellied, with a greater and more evil immobility. His ghee-oiled hair, worn long and parted in the middle, fell over a forehead so drawn down by a perpetual frown as to narrow the oblique eyes to slits. Three years before, a bullet had sheared away his front teeth and upper lip. The scar was horrible. Despite it, Francis plainly recognised the horseman who had spat into his face at the mission gate that night of the retreat. Hitherto he had sustained their detention with composure. But now, under that hidden, subhuman gaze, charged beneath its blankness with an answering recognition, the priest was conscious of a sharp constriction of his heart.

While the corporal volubly related the circumstances of the capture, Wai continued unfathomably to eat, the twin sticks sending a stream of liquid rice and pork lumps into his gullet from the bowl pressed beneath his chin. Suddenly two soldiers broke up the ravine at the double, dragging the fugitive bearer between them. With a final heave they threw him into the circle of fire-glow. The unhappy man fell on his knees close to Wai, his arms skewered behind him, panting and gibbering, in an ecstasy of fear.

Wai continued to eat. Then, casually, he pulled his revolver from his belt and fired it. Caught in the act of supplication, the porter fell forward, his body still jerking against the ground. A creamy pinkish pulp oozed from his blasted skull. Before the stunning reverberations of the report had died Wai had resumed his meal.

Mrs. Fiske had screamed faintly. But beyond a momentary lifting of their heads, the resting soldiers took no notice of the incident. The two who had brought in the bearer now pulled his corpse away and systematically dispossessed it of boots, clothing, and a string of copper cash. Numb and sick, the priest muttered to Dr. Fiske, who stood, very pale, beside him.

"Keep calm . . . show nothing . . . or it is hopeless for all of us."

They waited. The cold and senseless murder had charged the air with horror. At a sign from Wai the second bearer was driven forward and flung upon his knees. The priest felt his stomach turn with a dreadful premonition. But Wai merely said, addressing them all, impersonally:

"This man, your servant, will leave immediately for Pai-tan and inform your friends that you are temporarily in my care. For such hospitality a voluntary gift is customary. At noon on the day following tomorrow two of my men will await him, half a li outside the Manchu Gate. He will advance, quite alone." Wai paused blankly. "It is to be hoped he will bring the voluntary gift."

"There is little profit in making us your guests." Dr. Fiske spoke with a throb of indignation. "I have already indicated that we are without worldly goods."

"For each person five thousand dollars is requested. No more."

Fiske breathed more easily. The sum, though large, was not impossible to a mission as wealthy as his own.

"Then permit my wife to return with the messenger. She will ensure that the money is paid."

Wai gave no sign of having heard. For one apprehensive moment the priest thought his overwrought companion was about to make a scene. But Fiske stumbled back to his wife's side. The messenger was dispatched, sent bounding down the ravine with a last forceful injunction from the corporal. Wai then rose and, while his men made preparations for departure, walked forward to his tethered pony, so casually that the dead man's bare upturned feet, protruding from an arbutus bush, struck the eye like a hallucination.

The missionaries' ponies were now brought up, the four prisoners forced to mount, then roped together by long hemp cords. The cavalcade moved off into the gathering night.

Conversation was impossible at this bumping gallop. Father Chisholm was left to the mercy of his thoughts, which centred on the man now holding them for ransom.

Lately Wai's waning power had driven him to many excesses. From a traditional war lord, dominating the Chek-kow district of the province with his army of three thousand men, bought off by the various townships, levying taxes and imposts, living in feudal luxury in his walled fortress at Tou-en-lai, he had slowly fallen to ruinous days. At the height of his notoriety he had paid fifty thousand taels for a concubine from Pekin. Now he lived from hand to mouth by petty forays. Beaten decisively in two pitched battles with neighbouring mercenaries, he had thrown in his lot first with the *Min-tuan*, then, in a fit of malice, with the opposing faction, the *Yu-chi-tui*. The truth was that neither desired his doubtful aid. Degenerate, vicious, he fought solely for his own hand. His men were steadily deserting. As the scale of his operations dwindled his ferocity intensified. When he reached the humiliation of a bare two hundred followers, his round of pillage and burnings stood as a dreadful theme of terror. A fallen Lucifer, his hatreds fed on the glories he had lost, he was at enmity with mankind.

The night was interminable. They crossed a low range of hills, forded two rivulets, spattered for an hour through low-lying swamplands. Beyond that, and his conjecture from the pole star that they were travelling due west, Father Chisholm had no knowledge of the terrain they traversed. At his age, used to the quiet amble of his beast, the rapid jolting shook his bones until they rattled. But he reflected, with commiseration, that the Fiskes, too, were enduring the bone-shaking, for the

979

good God's sake. And Joshua, poor lad, though supple enough, was so young he must be sadly frightened. The priest told himself that on the return to the mission he would assuredly give the boy the roan pony he had coveted, silently, these past six months. Closing his eyes, he said a short prayer for the safety of their little party.

Dawn found them in a wilderness of rock and windblown sand, quite uninhabited, with no vegetation but scattered clumps of yellowish tuft grass. But within an hour, the sound of rushing water reached them and there, behind an escarpment, was the ruined citadel of Tou-en-lai, a huddle of ancient mud-brick houses on the cliff slope, surrounded by a crenellated wall, scarred and scorched by many sieges, the old glazed pillars of a Buddhist temple standing roofless, by the riverside.

Within the walls, the party dismounted, and Wai, without a word, entered his house, the only habitable dwelling. The morning air was raw. As the missionaries stood shivering on the hard mud courtyard, still roped together, a number of women and older men came crowding from the little caves which honeycombed the cliff and joined the soldiers in a chattering inspection of the captives.

"We should be grateful for food and rest." Father Chisholm addressed the company at large.

"Food and rest." The words were repeated, passed from mouth to mouth, amongst the onlookers, as an amusing curiosity.

The priest proceeded patiently. "You observe how weary is the missionary woman." Mrs. Fiske was, indeed, half-fainting, on her feet. "Perhaps some well-disposed person would offer her hot tea."

"Tea . . . hot tea," echoed the mob, crowding closer.

They were now within touching distance of the missionaries and suddenly, with a simian acquisitiveness, an old man in the front rank snatched at the doctor's watch-chain. It was the signal for a general spoliation—money, breviary, Bible, wedding ring, the priest's old silver pencil—in three minutes the little group stood divested of everything except their boots and clothing.

As the scramble ended, a woman's eye was caught by the dull sparkle of a jet buckle on the band of Mrs. Fiske's hat. Immediately, she clutched at it. Aware, desperately, of her awful hazard, Mrs. Fiske struggled, with a shrill defensive cry. But in vain. Buckle, hat and wig came off together in her assailant's tenacious grasp. In a flash her bald head gleamed, like a bladder of lard, with grotesque and terrible nakedness, in the remorseless air.

There was a hush. Then a babble of derision broke, a paroxysm of shrieking mockery. Mrs. Fiske covered her face with her hands and burst into scalding tears. The doctor, attempting tremulously to cover his wife's scalp with his handkerchief, saw the coloured silk snatched away.

Poor woman, Father Chisholm thought, compassionately averting his eyes.

The sudden arrival of the corporal ended the hilarity as quickly as it had begun. The crowd scattered as the missionaries were led into one of the caves, which possessed the distinction of a hatch. This heavy-ribbed door was slammed and fastened. They were left alone.

"Well," said Father Chisholm after a pause, "at least we have this to ourselves."

There was a longer silence. The little doctor, seated on the earth floor with his arm about his weeping wife, said dully: "It was scarlet fever. She caught it the first year we were in China. She was so sensitive about it. We took such pains never to let a soul know."

"And no one will know," the priest lied swiftly. "Joshua and I are silent as the grave. When we return to Pai-tan the—the damage can be repaired."

"You hear that, Agnes, dear? Pray stop crying, my dearest love."

A slackening, then cessation of the muffled sobs. Mrs. Fiske slowly raised her tear-stained eyes, red-rimmed in that ostrich orb.

"You are very kind," she choked.

"Meanwhile, they seem to have left me with this. If it can be of any service." Father Chisholm produced a large maroon bandana from his inner pocket.

She took it humbly, gratefully; tied it, like a mob-cap, with a butterfly knot behind her ear.

"There now, my dear." Fiske patted her on the back. "Why, you look quite captivating again."

"Do I, dear?" She smiled wanly, coquettishly. Her spirits lifted. "Now let's see what we can do to put this wretched *yao-fang* in order."

There was little they could do: the cave, no more than nine feet deep, held nothing but some broken crockery and its own dank gloom. The only light and air came from chinks in the barricaded entry. It was cheerless as a tomb. But they were worn-out. They stretched themselves on the floor. They slept.

It was afternoon when they were wakened by the creak of the opening hatch. A shaft of fantastic sunshine penetrated the *yao-fang*, then a middle-aged woman entered with a pitcher of hot water and two loaves of black bread. She stood watching as Father Chisholm handed one loaf to Dr. Fiske, then silently broke the other between Joshua and himself. Something in her attitude, in her dark and rather sullen face, caused the priest to gaze at her attentively.

"Why!" He gave a start of recognition. "You are Anna!" She did not answer. After sustaining his gaze, boldly, she turned and went out.

"Do you know that woman?" Fiske asked quickly.

"I am not sure. But yes, I am sure. She was a girl at the mission who . . . who ran away."

"Not a great tribute to your teaching." For the first time Fiske spoke acidly.

"We shall see."

That night they all slept badly. The discomforts of their confinement grew hourly. They took turns lying next to the hatch, for the privilege of breathing in the damp moist air. The little doctor kept groaning: "That awful bread! Dear heaven, it's tied my duodenum in a knot."

At noon, the next day, Anna came again with more hot water and a bowl of millet. Father Chisholm knew better than to address her by name.

"How long are we to be kept here?"

At first it seemed as though she would make no reply, then she said indifferently:

"The two men have departed for Pai-tan. When they return you will be free."

Dr. Fiske interposed restively: "Cannot you procure better food for us and blankets? We will pay."

She shook her head, scared off. But when she had retreated and let down the hatch she said, through the bars: "Pay me if you wish. It is not long to wait. It is nothing."

"Nothing." Fiske groaned again when she had gone. "I wish she had my insides."

"Don't give way, Wilbur." From the darkness beyond Mrs. Fiske exhorted him. "Remember, we've been through this before."

"We were young, then. Not old crocks on the verge of going home. And this Wai . . . he's got his knife in us missionaries especially . . . for changing his good old order when crime paid."

She persisted: "We must all keep cheerful. Look, we've got to distract ourselves. Not talk—or you two will start quarrelling about religion. A game. The silliest we can think of! We'll play 'animal, vegetable or mineral.' Joshua, are you awake? Good. Now listen and I'll explain how it goes."

They played the guessing game with heroic vigour. Joshua showed surprising aptitude. Then Mrs. Fiske's bright laugh cracked suddenly. They all fell very quiet. A dragging apathy succeeded; snatches of fitful sleep; uneasy, restless movements.

"Dear God, they must surely be back by now." All next day that phrase fell incessantly from Fiske's lips. His face and hands were hot to the touch. Lack of sleep and air had made him feverish. But it was evening before a loud shouting and the barking of dogs gave indication of a late arrival. The silence which followed was oppressive.

At last, footsteps approached and the hatch was flung open. On being commanded, they scrambled out on their hands and knees. The freshness of the night air, the sense of space and freedom, induced a delirium, almost, of relief.

"Thank heaven!" Fiske cried. "We're all right now."

An escort of soldiers took them to Wai-Chu.

He was seated, in his dwelling, on a coir mat, a lamp and a long pipe beside him, the lofty dilapidated room impregnated with the faintly bitter reek of poppy. Beside him was a soldier with a soiled blood-stained rag tied round his forearm. Five others of his troop, including the corporal, stood by the walls with rattans in their hands.

A penetrating silence followed the introduction of the prisoners. Wai studied them with deep and meditative cruelty. It was a hidden cruelty, sensed rather than seen, behind the mask of his face.

"The voluntary gift has not been paid." His voice was flat, unemotional. "When my men advanced to the city to receive it one was killed and the other wounded."

A shiver passed over Father Chisholm. What he had dreaded had come to pass. He said:

"Probably the message was never delivered. The bearer was afraid and ran away to his home in Shansee without going to Pai-tan."

"You are too talkative. Ten strokes on the legs."

The priest had expected this. The punishment was severe, the edge of the long square rod, wielded by one of the soldiers, lacerating his shins and thighs.

"The messenger was our servant," Mrs. Fiske spoke with suppressed indignation, a high spot of colour burning on her pale cheek. "It is not the Shang-Foo's fault if he ran away."

"You are also too talkative. Twenty slaps on the face."

She was beaten hard with the open palm on both cheeks while the doctor trembled and struggled beside her.

"Tell me, since you are so wise. If your servant ran away why should my emissaries be waited upon and ambushed?"

Father Chisholm wished to say that, in these times, the Pai-tan garrison was perpetually on the alert and would shoot any of Wai's men on sight. He knew this to be the explanation. He judged it wiser to hold his tongue.

"Now you are not so talkative. Ten strokes on the shoulders for keeping unnatural silence."

He was beaten again.

"Let us return to our missions." Fiske threw out his hands, gesticulating, like an agitated woman. "I assure you on my solemn oath that you will be paid without the slightest hesitation."

"I am not a fool!"

"Then send another of your soldiers to Lantern Street with a message which I will write. Send him now, immediately."

"And have him slaughtered also? Fifteen blows for assuming that I am a fool."

Under the blows the doctor burst into tears. "You are to be pitied," he blubbered. "I forgive you but I pity, I pity you."

There was a pause. It was almost possible to observe the dull flicker of gratification in Wai's contracted pupils. He turned to Joshua. The lad was healthy and strong. He desperately needed recruits.

"Tell me. Are you prepared to make atonement by enlisting under my banner?"

"I am sensible of the honour." Joshua spoke steadily. "But it is impossible."

"Renounce your foreign devil god and you will be spared."

Father Chisholm endured an instant of cruel suspense, preparing himself for the pain and humiliation of the boy's surrender.

"I will die gladly for the true Lord of Heaven."

"Thirty blows for being a contumacious wretch."

Joshua did not utter a cry. He took the punishment with eyes cast down. Not a moan escaped him. But every blow made Father Chisholm wince.

"Now will you advise your servant to repent?"

"Never." The priest answered firmly, his soul illuminated by the boy's courage.

"Twenty blows on the legs for reprehensible obduracy."

At the twelfth blow, delivered on the front of his shins, there was a sharp brittle crack. An agonizing pain shot through the broken limb. Oh Lord, thought Francis, that's the worst of old bones.

Wai considered them with an air of finality. "I cannot continue to shield you. If the money does not arrive tomorrow I have a foreboding that some evil may befall you."

He dismissed them blankly. Father Chisholm could barely limp across the courtyard. Back in the *yao-fang* Mrs. Fiske made him sit down and, kneeling beside him, stripped off his boot and sock. The doctor, somewhat recovered, then set the broken limb.

"I've no splint . . . nothing but these rags." His voice had a high and tremulous ring. "It's a nasty fracture. If you don't rest it'll turn compound. Feel how my hands are shaking. Help us, dear Lord! We're going home next month. We're not so——"

"Please, Wilbur." She soothed him with a quiet touch. He completed dressing the injury in silence. Then she added: "We must try to keep our spirits up. If we give in now, what's going to happen to us tomorrow?"

Perhaps it was well that she prepared them.

In the morning the four were led out into the courtyard, which was lined with the population of Tou-en-lai, and humming with the promise of a spectacle. Their hands were tied behind their backs and a bamboo-pole passed between their arms. Two soldiers then seized the ends of each spit and, raising the prisoners, marched them in procession round the arena six times, in narrowing circles, bringing up before the bullet-pocked façade of the house where Wai was seated.

Sick with the pain of his broken leg, Father Chisholm felt, through the stupid ignominy, a terrible dejection, amounting to despair, that the creatures of God's hand should make a careless festival out of the blood and tears of others. He had to still the dreadful whisper that God could never fashion men like this . . . that God did not exist.

He saw that several of the soldiers had their rifles, he hoped that a merciful end was near. But after a pause, at a sign from Wai, they were turned about and frog-marched down the steep path, past some beached sampans on a narrow spit of shingle, to the river. Here, before the reassembled crowd, they were dragged through the shallows and each secured with cord to a mooring stake in five feet of running water.

The switch from the threat of sudden execution was so unexpected, the contrast to the filthy squalour of the cave so profound, it was impossible to escape a sensation of relief. The shock of the water restored them. It was cold from mountain springs, and clear as crystal. The priest's leg ceased to pain him. Mrs. Fiske smiled feebly. Her courage was heartrending.

Her lips shaped the words: "At least we shall get clean."

But after half an hour a change set in. Father Chisholm dared not look at his companions. The river, at first so refreshing, gradually grew colder, colder, losing its gentle numbness, compressing their bodies and lower limbs in an algid vice. Each heartbeat, straining to force the blood through frozen arteries, was a throb of pulsing agony. The head, engorged, floated disembodied, in a reddish haze. With his swimming senses the priest still strove to find the reason of this torture, which now he dimly recollected as "the water ordeal," an intermittent sadism, hallowed by tradition, first conceived by the tyrant Tchang. It was a punishment well suited to Wai's purpose, since it probably expressed his lingering hope that the ransom might still be paid. Francis suppressed a groan. If this were true, their sufferings were not yet over.

"It's remarkable." With chattering teeth the doctor tried to talk. "This pain . . . perfect demonstration of angina pectoris . . . intermittent blood supply through constricted vascular system. O blessed Jesus!" He began to whimper. "O Lord God of Hosts—why hast thou forsaken us? My poor wife . . . thank God she has fainted. Where am I? . . . Agnes . . . Agnes . . ." He was unconscious.

The priest painfully turned his eyes towards Joshua. The boy's head, barely visible to his congested gaze, seemed decapitated, the head of a young Saint John the Baptist on a streaming charger. Poor Joshua—and poor Joseph! How he would miss his eldest-born. Francis said gently:

"My son, your courage and your faith—they are very pleasing to me."

"It is nothing, Master."

A pause. The priest, deeply moved, made a great effort to stem the torpor stealing over him.

"I meant to tell you, Joshua. You shall have the roan pony when we return to the mission."

"Does the Master think we shall ever return to the mission?"

"If not, Joshua, the good God will give you a finer pony to ride in heaven."

Another pause, Joshua said faintly:

"I think, Father, I should prefer the little pony at the mission."

A great surging flowed into Francis' ears, ending their conversation with waves of darkness. When the priest came to himself again they were all back in the cave, flung together in a sodden heap. As he lay a moment, gathering his senses, he heard Fiske talking to his wife, in that querulous plaint to which his speech had fallen.

"At least we are out of it . . . that dreadful river."

"Yes, Wilbur dear, we are out of it. But unless I mistake that ruffian, tomorrow we shall be into it again." Her tone was quite practical as though she were discussing the menu for his dinner. "Don't let's delude ourselves, dearest. If he keeps us alive it's only because he means to kill us as horribly as possible."

"Aren't you . . . afraid, Agnes?"

"Not in the least, and you mustn't be either. You must show these poor pagans . . . and the Father . . . how good New England Christians die."

"Agnes dear . . . you're a brave woman."

The priest could feel the pressure of her arm about her husband. He was greatly stirred, reshaken by a passionate concern for his companions, these three people, so different, yet each so dear to him. Was there no way of escape? He thought deeply, with gritted teeth, his brow pressed against the earth.

An hour later when the woman entered with a dish of rice he placed himself between her and the door.

"Anna! Do not deny that you are Anna! Have you no gratitude for all that was done for you at the mission? No——" She tried to push past him. "I shall not let you go until you listen. You are still a child of God. You cannot see us slowly murdered. I command you in His name to help us."

"I can do nothing." In the darkness of the cave it was impossible to see her face. But her voice, though sullen, was subdued.

"You can do much. Leave the hatch unfastened. No one will think to blame you."

"To what purpose? All the ponies are guarded."

"We need no ponies, Anna."

A spark of inquiry flashed in her lowering gaze. "If you leave Tou-en-lai on foot you will be retaken next day."

"We shall leave by sampan . . . and float down-river."

"Impossible." She shook her head with vehemence. "The rapids are too strong."

"Better to drown in the rapids than here."

"It is not my business where you drown." She answered with sudden passion: "Nor to help you in any manner whatsoever."

Unexpectedly, Dr. Fiske reached out in the darkness and gripped her hand. "Look, Anna, take my fingers and give heed. You must make it your business. Do you understand? Leave the door free tonight."

There was a pause.

"No." She hesitated, slowly withdrew her hand. "I cannot tonight."

"You must."

"I will do it tomorrow . . . tomorrow . . . tomorrow." With an odd change of manner, a sudden wildness, she bent her head and darted from the cave. The hatch closed behind her with a heavy slam.

And a heavier silence settled upon the cave. No one believed that the woman would keep her word. Even if she meant it, her promise was a feeble thing to weigh against the prospects of the coming day.

"I'm a sick man," Fiske muttered peevishly, laying his head against his wife's shoulder. In the darkness they could hear him percussing his own chest. "My clothes are still sopping. D'you hear that . . . it's quite dull . . . lobar consolidation. Oh, God, I thought the tortures of the inquisition were matchless."

Somehow the night passed. The morning was cold and grey. As the light filtered through and sounds were heard in the courtyard, Mrs. Fiske straightened herself with a look of sublime resolution on her peaked and pallid face, still girded by the shrunken head-dress. "Father Chisholm, you are the senior clergyman here. I ask you to say a prayer before we go out to what may be our martyrdom."

He knelt down beside her. They all joined hands. He prayed, as best he could, better than he had prayed in all his life. Then the soldiers came for them.

Weakened as they were, the river seemed colder than before. Fiske shouted hysterically as they drove him in. To Father Chisholm it now became a hazy vision.

Immersion, his thoughts ran mazily, purification by water, one drop and you were saved. How many drops were here? Millions and millions

. . . four hundred million Chinese all waiting to be saved, each with a drop of water. . . .

"Father! Dear good Father Chisholm!" Mrs. Fiske was calling him, her eyes glassy with a sudden feverish gaiety. "They are all watching us from the bank. Let us show them. An example. Let us sing. What hymn have we in common? The Christmas Hymn, of course. A sweet refrain. Come, Joshua . . . Wilbur . . . all of us."

She struck up, in a high quavering pipe:

" Oh, come, all ye faithful,
Joyful and triumphant . . ."

He joined with the others:
" Oh, come ye, oh, come ye, to Bethlehem."

Late afternoon. They were back in the cave again. The doctor lay on his side. His breath came raspingly. He spoke with an air of triumph.

"Lobar pneumonia. I knew it yesterday. Apical dullness and crepitations. I'm sorry, Agnes, but . . . I'm rather glad."

No one said anything. She began to stroke his hot forehead with her bleached sodden fingers. She was still stroking when Anna came to the cave. This time, however, the woman brought no food with her.

She did no more than stand in the entrance staring at them with a kind of grudging sullenness. At last she said:

"I have given the men your supper. They think it is a great joke. Go quickly before they discover their mistake."

There was an absolute silence. Father Chisholm felt his heart bound in his racked, exhausted body. It seemed impossible that they might leave the cave of their own free will. He said: "God will bless you, Anna. You have not forgotten Him and He has not forgotten you."

She gave no answer. She stared at him with her darkly inscrutable eyes which he had never read, even on that first night amidst the snow. Yet it gave him a burning satisfaction that she should justify his teaching, openly, before Dr. Fiske. She stood for a moment, then glided silently away.

Outside the cave it was dark. He could hear laughter and low voices from the neighbouring *yao-fang*. Across the courtyard there was a light in Wai's house. The adjacent stables and soldiers' quarters showed a feeble illumination. The sudden barking of a dog sent a shock through his tortured nerves. This slender hope was like a new pain, suffocating in its intensity.

Cautiously, he tried to stand upon his feet. But it was impossible, he fell heavily, beads of perspiration breaking on his brow. His leg, swollen to three times its natural size, was quite unusable.

In a whisper he told Joshua to take the half-unconscious doctor on

988

his back and carry him very quietly to the sampans. He saw them go off, accompanied by Mrs. Fiske, Joshua bent under his sacklike burden, keeping cleverly to the dense shadows of the rocks. The faint clatter of a loose stone came back to him, so loud it seemed to wake the dead. He breathed again; no one had heard it but himself. In five minutes Joshua returned. Leaning on the boy's shoulder, he dragged slowly and painfully down the path.

Fiske was already stretched out on the bottom of the sampan with his wife crouched beside him. The priest seated himself in the stern. Lifting his useless leg with both hands he arranged it out of the way, like a piece of timber, then propped himself against the gunwale with his elbow. As Joshua climbed into the bow and began to untie the mooring rope he seized the single stern oar in readiness to push off.

Suddenly a shout rang out from the top of the cliff, followed by another and the sound of running. A loud commotion broke, dogs set up a violent barking. Then two torches flared in the upper darkness and came rapidly, amidst shrill voices and excited, clattering footsteps, down the river path.

The priest's lips moved, in the anguished immobility of his body. But he remained silent. Joshua, fumbling and tearing at the matted rope, knew the danger, without the added confusion of a command.

At last, with a wild gasp, the boy pulled the rope loose, falling backwards against the thwarts. Instantly, Father Chisholm felt the sampan float free and with all his remaining strength he fended it into the current. Out of the slack water, they spun aimlessly, then began to slide downstream. Across and behind them, the flares now showed a group of running figures on the bank. A rifle-shot cracked, followed by an irregular volley. The lead skipped the water with a twanging hum. They were sliding faster now, much faster; they were almost out of range. Father Chisholm was staring into the dark wall ahead with almost feverish relief when suddenly, amidst the scattered shooting, a great weight struck at him out of the night. His head rocked under the impact of what seemed a heavy flying stone. Beyond the crashing blow he had no pain. He raised his hand to his wet face. The bullet had smashed through his upper jaw, torn out by his right cheek. He kept silent. The firing ceased. No one else was hit.

The river now moved them forward at intimidating speed. He was quite sure in his own mind that it must ultimately join the Hwang— no other outlet was possible. He leaned forward towards Fiske and, seeing him conscious, made an effort to cheer him.

"How do you feel?"

"Pretty comfortable, considering I'm dying." He repressed a short cough. "I'm sorry I've been such an old woman, Agnes."

"Please don't talk, dear."

The priest straightened himself, sadly. Fiske's life was ebbing away. His own resistance was almost gone. He had to fight an almost irresistible impulse to weep.

Presently an increase in the volume of the river's sound heralded their approach to broken water. The noise seemed to blot out what vision was left him. He could see nothing. With his single oar he pulled the sampan straight with the current. As they shot down, he commended their souls to God.

He was beyond caring, beyond realizing how the craft lived in that unseen thunder. The roar dulled him into stupor. He clung to the useless oar as they lurched and plunged, invisibly. At times they seemed to drop through empty space, as if the bottom had fallen from the boat. When a splintering crash arrested their momentum, he thought numbly that they must founder. But they plunged off again, the boiling water surging in on them as they whirled, down, down. Whenever he felt they must be free, a new roaring reared itself ahead, reached out, engulfed them. At a narrow bend they hit the rocky bank with stunning force, ripping low branches from overhanging trees, then bounced, spun, crashed on again. His brain was caught in the swirl, battered and jarred, down, down, down.

The peace of the quiet water, far below, brought him feebly to his senses. A faint streak of dawn lay ahead of them, limning a broad expanse of gentle pastoral waters. He could not guess what distance they had come, though dimly he surmised it must be many li. All he knew was this: they had reached the Hwang and were floating calmly on its bosom towards Pai-tan.

He tried to move, but could not, his weakness held him fettered. His damaged limb felt heavier than lead, the pain of his smashed face was like a raging toothache. But with incredible effort he turned and pulled himself slowly down the boat with his hands. The light increased. Joshua was huddled in the bow, his body limp, but breathing. He was asleep. In the bottom of the sampan Fiske and his wife lay together, her arm supporting his head, her body shielding him from the water they had shipped. She was awake and calmly reasonable. The priest was conscious of a great wonder as he gazed at her. She had shown the highest endurance of them all. Her eyes answered his unspoken inquiry with a wan negation. He could see that her husband was almost gone.

Fiske was breathing in little staccato spasms, with intervals when he did not breathe at all. He muttered constantly but his eyes, though fixed, were open. And, suddenly, there appeared in them a vague, uncertain light of recognition. The shadow of a movement crossed his lips—nothing, yet in that nothingness hovered the suggestion of a smile. His muttering took on coherent form.

"Don't pride yourself . . . dear fellow . . . on Anna." A little gasp of breathing. "Not so much your teaching as——" Another spasm. "I bribed her." Weakly, the flutter of a laugh. "With the fifty-dollar bill I always carried in my shoe." A feeble triumphant pause. "But God bless you, dear fellow, all the same."

He seemed happier now he had scored his final point. He closed his eyes. As the sun rose in a flood of sudden light they saw that he was gone.

Back in the stern Father Chisholm watched Mrs. Fiske compose the dead man's hands. He looked dizzily at his own hands. The backs of both his wrists were covered peculiarly with raised red spots. When he touched them they rolled like buckshot beneath his skin. He thought, Some insect has bitten me while I slept.

Later, through the rising morning vapours, he saw down-river, in the distance, the flat boats of cormorant fishers. He closed his throbbing eyes. The sampan was drifting . . . drifting in the golden haze, towards them.

XIII

One afternoon six months later the two new missionary priests, Father Stephen Munsey, M.B. and Father Jerome Craig, were earnestly discussing the arrangements over coffee and cigarettes.

"Everything has got to be perfect. Thank God the weather looks good."

"And settled." Father Jerome nodded. "It's a blessing we have the band."

They were young, healthy, full of vitality, with an immense belief in themselves and God. Father Munsey, the American priest, with a medical degree from Baltimore, was slightly the taller of the two, a fine six-footer, but Father Craig's shoulders had gained him a place in the Holywell boxing team. Though Craig was British he had a pleasant touch of American keenness, for he had taken a two years' missionary preparatory course at the College of St. Michael's in San Francisco. Here, indeed, he had met Father Munsey. The two had felt, instinctively, a mutual attraction, had soon become, affectionately, "Steve" and "Jerry" to each other—except on those occasions when a burst of self-conscious dignity induced a more formal tone. "Say, Jerry, old boy, are you playing basketball this afternoon?—And oh, er, by the way, Father, what time is your mass tomorrow?" To be sent to Pai-tan together had set the seal upon their friendship.

"I asked Mother Mercy Mary to look in." Father Steve poured himself fresh coffee. He was clean-cut and virile, two years senior to Craig, admittedly the leader of the partnership. "Just to discuss the final touches. She's so cheery and obliging. She's going to be a great help to us."

"Yes, she's a grand person. Honestly, Jerry, we'll make things hum here when we have it to ourselves."

"Hist! Don't talk so loud," Father Steve warned. "The old boy's not so deaf as you'd think."

"He's a case." Father Jerry's blunt features melted to a reminiscent smile. "Of course I know you pulled him through. But at his age to shake off a broken leg, a smashed jaw, and the smallpox on top of it— well!—it says something for his pluck."

"He's terribly feeble though." Munsey spoke seriously. "It's quite finished him. I'm hoping the long voyage home'll do him good."

"He's a funny old devil—sorry, Father, I mean fogy. D'you remember, when he was so sick and Mrs. Fiske sent up the four-poster bed before she left for home? The awful trouble we had to get him into it? Remember how he kept saying 'How can I rest if I'm comfortable?' " Jerry laughed.

"And that other time he threw the beef tea at Mother Mercy Mary's head——" Father Steve stifled his grin. "No, no, Father, we mustn't let our tongues get the better of us. After all he's not so bad if you take him the right way. Anybody would get a bit queer in the topknot after being over thirty years out here alone. Thank God we're a pair. Come in."

Mother Mercy Mary entered, smiling, red-cheeked, her eyes friendly and merry. She was very happy with her new priests, whom she thought of, instinctively, as two nice boys. She would mother them. It was good for the mission to have this infusion of young blood. It would be more human for her to have a proper priest's laundry to oversee, decent thick underwear to darn.

"Afternoon, Reverend Mother. Can we tempt you to the cup that cheers but doesn't inebriate? Good. Two lumps? We'll have to watch that sweet tooth of yours in Lent. Well now, about tomorrow's farewell ceremonies for Father Chisholm."

They talked together, amicably and earnestly, for half an hour. Then Mother Mercy Mary seemed to prick up her ears. Her expression of maternal protectiveness deepened. Listening acutely, she sounded a note of concern with her tongue.

"Do you hear him about? I don't. God bless my soul, I'm sure he's away out without telling us." She rose. "Excuse me, Fathers. I'll have to find out what he's up to. If he goes and gets his feet wet it'll ruin everything."

Leaning on his old rolled umbrella, Father Chisholm had made a last pilgrimage of his mission of St. Andrew's. The slight exertion fatigued him absurdly; he realized, with an inward sigh, how sadly useless his long illness had left him. He was an old man. The thought was quite staggering—he felt so little different, within his heart, so unchanged. And tomorrow he must leave Pai-tan. Incredible! When he had made up his mind to lay his bones at the foot of the mission garden alongside Willie Tulloch. Phrases in the Bishop's letter recurred to him: ". . . not up to it, solicitous your health, deeply appreciative, end your labours in the foreign mission field." Well, God's will be done!

He was standing, now, in the little churchyard, swept by a flood of tender, ghostly memories, noting the wooden crosses—Willie's, Sister Clotilde's, the gardener Fu's, a dozen more, each an end and a beginning, the milestones of their common pilgrimage.

He shook his head like an old horse amidst a hum of insects in a sunny field: really he must not yield to reverie. He fixed his gaze across the low wall in the new pasture field. Joshua was putting the roan pony through its paces while four of his younger brothers watched admiringly. Joseph himself was not far off. Fat, complacent and forty-five, shepherding the remainder of his nine children back from their afternoon stroll, he slowly pushed a wicker perambulator towards the lodge. What richer instance, thought the priest with a faint slow smile, of the subjugation of the noble male?

He had made the grand tour, as unobtrusively as possible, for he guessed what lay in store for him tomorrow. School, dormitory, refectory, the lace and mat-making workrooms, the little annex he had opened last year to teach basket-weaving to the blind children. Well . . . why continue the meagre tally? In the past he had judged it some small achievement. In his present mood of gentle melancholy he measured it as nothing. He swung round stiffly. From the new hall came the ominous stertor of wind on brass. Again he suppressed a crooked smile, or was it perhaps a frown? These young curates with their explosive ideas! Only last night, when he was trying—vainly, of course—to instruct them in the topography of the parish, the doctor one had whispered: *Aeroplane*. What were things coming to! Two hours by air to the Liu village. And his first trip had taken him two weeks on foot!

He ought not to go farther, for the afternoon was turning chill. But, though he knew his disobedience would earn a merited scolding, he pressed harder on his umbrella and went slowly down the Hill of Brilliant Green Jade towards the deserted site of the first forgotten mission. Though the compound was now rank with bamboo, the lower edge eroded to a muddy swamp, the mud-brick stable still remained.

He bowed his head and passed under the sagging roof, assailed, immediately, by another host of recollections, seeing a young priest, dark, eager and intent, crouched before a brazier, his sole companion a Chinese boy. That first mass he had celebrated here, on his japanned tin trunk without bell or server, no one but himself—how sharply it struck the taut chords of his memory. Clumsily, a stiff ungainly figure, he knelt down, and begged God to judge him less by his deeds than by his intention.

Back at the mission he let himself in by the side porch and went softly upstairs. He was fortunate; no one saw him come in. He did not wish "the grand slam," as he had come to call it, a flurry of feet and doors, with hot-water bottles and solicitous profferings of soup. But, as he opened the door of his room, he was surprised to find Mr. Chia inside. His disfigured face, now grey with cold, lit up to a sudden warmth. Heedless of formality, he took his old friend's hand and pressed it.

"I hoped you would come."

"How could I refrain from coming?" Mr. Chia spoke in a sad and strangely troubled voice. "My dear Father, I need not tell you how deeply I regret your departure. Our long friendship has meant much to me."

The priest answered quietly: "I, too, shall miss you much. Your kindness and benefactions have overwhelmed me."

"It is less than nothing," Mr. Chia waved the gratitude away, "beside your inestimable service to me. And have I not always enjoyed the peace and beauty of your mission garden? Without you, the garden will hold a great sadness." His tone lifted to a fitful gleam. "But then . . . perhaps, on your recovery . . . you may return to Pai-tan?"

"Never." The priest paused, with the suspicion of a smile. "We must look forward to our meeting in the celestial hereafter."

An odd silence fell. Mr. Chia broke it with constraint. "Since our time together is limited it might not be unfitting if we talked a moment regarding the hereafter."

"All my time is dedicated to such talk."

Mr. Chia hesitated, beset by unusual awkwardness. "I have never pondered deeply on what state lies beyond this life. But if such a state exists it would be very agreeable for me to enjoy your friendship there."

Despite his long experience, Father Chisholm did not grasp the import of the remark. He smiled but did not answer. And Mr. Chia was forced in great embarrassment to be direct.

"My friend, I have often said: There are many religions and each has its gate to heaven." A faint colour crept beneath his dark skin. "Now it would appear that I have the extraordinary desire to enter by your gate."

Dead silence. Father Chisholm's bent figure was immobilized, rigid.

"I cannot believe that you are serious."

"Once, many years ago, when you cured my son, I was not serious. But then I was unaware of the nature of your life . . . of its patience, quietness and courage. The goodness of a religion is best judged by the

994

goodness of its adherents. My friend . . . you have conquered me by example."

Father Chisholm raised his hand to his forehead, that familiar sign of hidden emotion. His conscience had often reproached him for his initial refusal to accept Mr. Chia, even without a true intention. He spoke slowly. "All day long my mouth has been bitter with the ashes of failure. Your words have rekindled the fires in my heart. Because of this one moment I feel that my work has not been worthless. In spite of that I say to you . . . don't do this for friendship—only if you have belief."

Mr. Chia answered firmly. "My mind is made up. I do it for friendship and belief. We are as brothers, you and I. Your Lord must also be mine. Then, even though you must depart tomorrow, I shall be content, knowing that in our Master's garden our spirits will one day meet."

At first the priest was unable to speak. He fought to conceal the depth of his feeling. He reached out his hand to Mr. Chia. In a low uncertain tone he said:

"Let us go down to the church." . . .

Next morning broke warm and clear. Father Chisholm, awakened by the sound of singing, escaped from the sheets of Mrs. Fiske's bed and stumbled to the open window. Beneath his balcony twenty little girls from the junor school, none more than nine years of age, dressed in white and blue sashes, were serenading him: *Hail, Smiling Morn* . . . He grimaced at them. At the end of the tenth verse he called down:

"That's enough. Go and get your breakfast."

They stopped, smiled up at him, holding their music sheets. "Do you like it, Father?"

"No . . . Yes. But it's time for breakfast."

They started off again from the beginning and sang it all through with extra verses while he was shaving. At the words "on thy fresh cheek" he cut himself. Peering into the minute mirror at his own reflection, pocked and cicatrized, and now gory, he thought mildly, Dear me, what a dreadful-looking ruffian I've become, I really must behave myself today.

The breakfast gong sounded. Father Munsey and Father Craig were both waiting on him, alert, deferential, smiling—the one rushing to pull out his chair, the other to lift the cover from the kedgeree. They were so anxious to please they could scarcely sit still. He scowled.

"Will you young idiots kindly stop treating me like your great-grandmother on her hundredth birthday?"

Must humour the old boy, thought Father Jerry. He smiled tenderly. "Why, Father, we're just treating you like one of ourselves. Of course you can't escape the honour due to a pioneer who blazed the first trails. You don't want to, either. It's your natural reward and don't you have any doubt about it."

"I have a great many doubts."

Father Steve said heartily: "Don't you worry, Father. I know how you feel, but we won't let you down. Why, Jerry—I mean Father Craig and I have schemes in hand for doubling the size and efficiency of St. Andrew's. We're going to have twenty catechists—pay them good wages too—start a rice kitchen in Lantern Street, right opposite your Methodist pals there. We'll poke them in the eye all right." He laughed good-naturedly, reassuringly. "It's going to be downright, honest, four-square Catholicism. Wait till we get our plane! Wait till we start sending you our conversion graphs. Wait till——"

"The cows come home," said Father Chisholm dreamily.

The two young priests exchanged a sympathetic glance. Father Steve said kindly:

"You won't forget to take your medicine in the trip home, Father? One tablespoonful *ex aqua*, three times a day. There's a big bottle in your bag."

"No, there isn't. I threw it out before I came down." Suddenly Father Chisholm began to laugh. He laughed until he shook. "My dear boys, don't mind me. I'm a cantankerous scoundrel. You'll do grandly here if you're not too cocksure . . . if you're kind and tolerant, and especially if you don't try to teach every old Chinaman how to suck eggs."

"Why . . . yes . . . yes, of course, Father."

"Look! I have no aeroplanes to spare but I'd like to leave you a useful little souvenir. It was given me by an old priest. It's been with me on most of my travels." He left the table, handed them from the corner of the room the tartan umbrella Rusty Mac had given him. "It has a certain status amongst the state umbrellas of Pai-tan. It may bring you luck."

Father Jerry took it gingerly as though it were a sort of a relic.

"Thank you, thank you, Father. What pretty colours. Are they Chinese?"

"Much worse, I'm afraid." The old priest smiled and shook his head. He would say no more.

Father Munsey put down his napkin with a surreptitious signal to his colleague. There was an organizing glitter in his eye. He rose.

"Well, Father, if you'll excuse Father Craig and myself. Time is getting on, and we're expecting Father Chou any moment now . . ."

They departed briskly.

He was due to leave at eleven o'clock. He returned to his room. When he had completed his modest packing he had still an hour in which to wander round. He descended, drawn instinctively towards the church. There, outside his house, he drew up, genuinely touched. His entire congregation, nearly five hundred, stood awaiting him, orderly and silent, in the courtyard. The contingent from the Liu village, under Father Chou, stood on one flank, the older girls and handicraft workers upon the other, with his beloved children, shepherded by Mother Mercy Mary, Martha, and the four Chinese Sisters, in front. There was something in the mass attention of their eyes, all bent affectionately upon his insignificant form, which gripped him with a sudden pang.

A deeper hush. From his nervousness it was clear that Joseph had been entrusted with the honour of the address. Two chairs were produced like a conjuring trick. When the old Father was seated in one, Joseph mounted unsteadily upon the other, almost overbalancing, and unrolled the vermilion scroll.

"Most Reverend and Worthy Disciple of the Lord of Heaven, it is with the utmost anguish that we, thy children, witness thy departure across the broad oceans . . ."

The address was no different from a hundred other eulogies suffered in the past except that it was lachrymose. Despite a score of secret rehearsals before his wife, Joseph's delivery was vanquished by the open courtyard. He began to sweat and his paunch quivered like a jelly. Poor dear Joseph, thought the priest, staring at his boots and thinking of a slim young boy running, unfaltering, at his bridle rein thirty years ago.

When it was over the entire congregation sang the *Gloria laus* quite beautifully. Still looking at his boots, as the clear voices ascended, the priest felt a melting of his old bones. "Dear God," he prayed, "don't let me make a fool of myself."

For the presentation, they had chosen the youngest girl in the basket-weaving centre for the blind. She came forward, in her black skirt and white blouse, uncertain yet sure, guided by her instinct and Mother Mercy Mary's whispered instructions. As she knelt before him, holding out the ornate gilt chalice of execrable design, bought by mail order from Nankin, his eyes were sightless as her own. "Bless you, bless you, my child," he muttered. He could say no more.

Mr. Chia's number-tone chair now swam into the orbit of his hazy vision. Disembodied hands helped him into it. The procession formed and set off amidst the popping of firecrackers and a sudden burst of Sousa from the new school band.

As he swayed slowly down the hill, borne pontifically on the shoulders of the men, he tried to rivet his consciousness upon the gimcrack comedy of the band: twenty schoolboys in sky-blue uniforms, blowing their cheeks out, preceded by a Chinese majorette aged eight in fleecy shako and high white boots, strutting, twirling a cane, kicking up her knees. But somehow, his sense of the ridiculous had ceased to function. In the town the doorways were crowded with friendly faces. More firecrackers welcomed him at every street crossing. As he neared the landing stage flowers were cast before him.

Mr. Chia's launch lay waiting at the steps, the engines quietly running. The chair was lowered, he stepped out. It had come at last. They were surrounding him bidding him farewell: the two young priests, Father Chou, Reverend Mother, Martha, Mr. Chia, Joseph, Joshua . . . all of them, some of the women of the congregation weeping, kneeling to kiss his hand. He had meant to say something. He could not mumble one incoherent word. His breast was overflowing.

Blindly, he boarded the launch. As he turned again to face them there fell a bar of silence. At a prearranged signal, the children's choir began his favourite hymn: the *Veni Creator*. They had saved it till the last.

> " Come, Holy Spirit, Creator, come,
>   From thy bright heav'nly throne."

He had always loved these noble words, written by the great Charlemagne in the ninth century, the loveliest hymn of the Church. Everyone on the landing was singing now.

> " Take possession of our souls,
>   And make them all thy own."

Oh, dear the thought, yielding at last, that's kind, that's sweet of them . . . but oh, how wickedly unfair! A convulsive movement passed over his face.

As the launch moved away from the stage and he raised his hand to bless them, tears were streaming down his battered face.

V

THE RETURN

I

His grace bishop mealey was extremely late. Twice a nice young priest of the household had peeped round the parlour door to explain that His Lordship and His Lordship's secretary were detained, unavoidably, at a Convocation. Father Chisholm blinked formidably over his copy of the *Tablet*.

"Punctuality is the politeness of prelates!"

"His Lordship is a very busy man." With an uncertain smile, the young priest withdrew, not quite sure of this old boy from China, half-wondering if he could be trusted with the silver. The appointment had been for eleven. Now the clock showed half-past twelve.

It was the same room in which he had awaited his interview with Rusty Mac. How long ago? Good heavens . . . thirty-six years! He shook his head dolefully. It had amused him to intimidate the pretty stripling, but his mood was far from combative. He felt rather shaky this morning, and desperately nervous. He wanted something from the Bishop. He hated asking favours, yet he must ask this one, and his heart had jumped when the summons to the interview arrived at the modest hotel where he had been staying since the ship unloaded him at Liverpool.

Valiantly, he straightened his wrinkled vest, spruced up his tired collar. He was not really old. There was plenty of go in him yet. Now that it was well past noon, Anselm would undoubtedly ask him to remain to luncheon. He would be spry, curb his outrageous tongue, listen to Anselm's stories, laugh at his jokes, not be above a little, or perhaps a lot of, flattery. He hoped to God the nerve wouldn't start twitching in his damaged cheek. That made him look a perfect lunatic!

It was ten minutes to one. At last there came a commotion of importance in the corridor outside and, decisively, Bishop Mealey entered the room. Perhaps he had been hurrying; his manner was brisk, his eye beaming towards Francis, not unconscious of the clock.

"My dear Francis. It's splendid to see you again. You must pardon this little delay. No, don't get up, I beg of you. We'll talk here. It's . . . it's more intimate than in my room."

Briskly, he pulled out a chair and seated himself with an easy grace beside Father Chisholm at the table. As he rested his fleshy, well-tended hand affectionately upon the other's sleeve, he thought: Good heavens, how old and feeble he has become!

"And how is dear Pai-tan? Not unflourishing, Monsignor Sleeth tells me. I vividly remember when I stood in that stricken city, amidst deadly plague and desolation. Truly the hand of God lay upon it. Ah, those were my pioneering days, Francis. I pine for them sometimes. Now," he smiled, "I'm only a Bishop. Do you see much change in me since we parted on that Orient strand?"

Francis studied his old friend with an odd admiration. There was no doubt of it—the years had improved Anselm Mealey. Maturity had come late to him. His office had given him dignity, toned his early effusiveness to suavity. He had a fine presence and held his head high. The soft full ecclesiastic face was lit by the same velvety eye. He was well preserved, still had his own teeth, and a supple vigorous skin.

Francis said simply, "I've never seen you look better."

The Bishop inclined his head, pleased. "*O tempora! O mores!* We're neither of us so young as we were. But I don't wear too badly. Frankly, I find perfect health essential to efficiency. If you knew what I have to cope with! They've put me on a balanced diet. And I have a masseur, a husky Swede, who literally pummels the fear of God into me. . . . I'm afraid," with a sudden genuine solicitude, "you've been very careless of yourself."

"I feel like an old ragman beside you, Anselm, and that is God's truth. . . . But I keep young in heart . . . or try to. And there's still some service left in me. I . . . I hope you're not altogether dissatisfied with my work in Pai-tan."

"My dear Father, your efforts were heroic. Naturally we're a little disappointed in the figures. Monsignor Sleeth was showing me only yesterday . . ." The voice was quite benevolent. ". . . In all your thirty-six years you made less conversions than Father Lawler made in five. Please don't think I'm reproaching you—that would be too unkind. Someday when you have leisure we'll discuss it thoroughly. Meanwhile——" His eye was hovering round the clock. "Is there anything we can do for you?"

There was a pause; then, in a low tone, Francis answered: "Yes . . . There is, your Grace . . . I want a parish."

The Bishop almost started out of his benign, affectionate composure. He slowly raised his brows as Father Chisholm continued, with that quiet intensity: "Give me Tweedside, Anselm. There's a vacancy at Renton . . . a bigger, better parish. Promote the Tweedside priest to Renton. And let me . . . Let me go home."

The Bishop's smile had become fixed, rather less easy, upon his handsome face. "My dear Francis, you seem to wish to administer my diocese."

"I have a special reason for asking you. I would be so very grateful . . ." To his horror Father Chisholm found his voice out of control. He broke off, then added huskily: "Bishop MacNabb promised I should have a parish if ever I came home." He began to fumble in his inside pocket. "I have his letter . . ."

Anselm raised his hand. "I can't be expected to honour the posthumous letters of my predecessor." A silence; then, with kindly urbanity, His Lordship continued: "Naturally, I will bear your request in mind. But I cannot promise. Tweedside has always been very dear to me. When the weight of the pro-cathedral is off my shoulders I had thought of building myself a retreat there—a little Castle Gondolfo." He paused—his ear, still keen, picking up the sound of an arriving car, followed by voices in the hall outside. Diplomatically his eye sought the clock. His pleasant manner quickened. "Well . . . It is all in God's hands. We shall see, we shall see."

"If you would let me explain——" Francis protested humbly. "I'm . . . rather anxious to make a home . . . for someone."

"You must tell me some other time." Another car outside and more voices. The Bishop gathered up his violet cassock, his tone honeyed with regret. "It is quite a calamity, Francis, that I must slip away, just as I was looking forward to our long and interesting talk. I have an official luncheon at one. The Lord Mayor and City Council are my guests. More politics, alas . . . school board, water board, finance . . . a *quid pro quo* . . . I have to be a stockbroker these days . . . But I like it Francis, I like it!"

"I wouldn't take more than a minute . . ." Francis stopped short, dropped his gaze to the floor.

The Bishop had risen blandly. With his arm lightly on Father Chisholm's shoulder he aided him affectionately to the door. "I can't express what a great joy it has been for me to welcome you home. We will keep in touch with you, never fear. And now, I must leave you. Good-bye, Francis . . . and bless you."

Outside, a stream of large dark limousines flowed up the drive towards the high portico of the palace. The old priest had a vision of a purple face beneath a beaver hat, of more faces, hard and bloated, of miniver, gold chains of office. A wet wind was blowing and it cut his old bones, used to sunshine and covered only by his thin tropic suit. As he moved away a car-wheel churned near the kerb and a spurt of mud flew up and hit him in the eye. He wiped it off with his hand, gazing down the arches of the years, reflecting, with a faint grim smile: Anselm's mud bath is avenged.

His breast was cold, yet through his disappointment, his sinking weakness, a white flame burned, unquenchably. He must find a church at once. Across the street the great domed bulk of the new cathedral loomed, a million pounds in sterling, transmuted to massive stone and marble. He limped urgently towards it.

He reached the broad entrance steps, mounted them, then suddenly drew up. Before him, on the wet stone of the topmost step, a ragged cripple crouched in the wind, with a card pinned upon his chest: *Old Soldier, Please Help.*

Francis contemplated the broken figure. He pulled out the solitary shilling from his pocket, placed it in the tin cup. The two unwanted soldiers gazed at each other in silence, then each gazed away.

He entered the pro-cathedral, an echoing vastness of beauty and silence, pillared in marble, rich in oak and bronze, a temple of towering and intricate design, in which his mission chapel would have stood unnoticed, forgotten, in a corner of the transept. Undaunted, he marched towards the high altar. There he knelt and fiercely, with unshaken valour, prayed.

"Oh, Lord, for once—not Thy will, but mine, be done."

II

Five weeks later Father Chisholm made his expedition, long deferred, to Kirkbridge. As he left the railway station the cotton-thread mills of that large industrial centre were disgorging their workers for the dinner hour. Hundreds of women with shawls wrapped about their heads went hurrying through the drenching rain, yielding only to an occasional tram clanging over the greasy cobbles.

At the end of the main street he inquired his way, then took to the right, past an enormous statue erected to a local thread magnate, and entered a poorer locality: a squalid square imprisoned by high tenements. He crossed the square and plunged into a narrow alley, fetid with smells, so dark that, on the brightest day, no gleam of sun could penetrate. Despite his joy, his high excitement, thè priest's heart sank. He had expected poverty but not this. . . . He thought: What have I done in my stupidity and neglect! Here, it was like being at the bottom of a well.

He inspected the numbers on the tenement entrances, singled out the right one, and began to climb the stairs, which were without light or air, the windows foul, the gas brackets plugged. A cracked soil pipe had drenched one landing.

Three flights up he stumbled and almost fell. A child was seated upon the stairs, a boy. The priest stared through the foggy gloom at the small rachitic figure, supporting his heavy head with one hand, bracing his sharp elbow against his bony knee. His skin was the colour of candle tallow. He was almost transparent. He looked like a tired old man. He might have been seven years of age.

Suddenly the boy lifted his head so that a shaft from the broken skylight fell upon him. For the first time Francis saw the child's face. He gave a stifled exclamation and a heavy wave of terrible emotion broke over him, he felt it as a ship might feel the buffet of a heavy wave. That pallid upturned face was unmistakable in its likeness to Nora's face. The eyes, especially, enormous in the pinched skin, could never be denied.

"What is your name?"

A pause. The boy answered: "Andrew."

Behind the landing door there was a single room where, cross-legged on a dirty mattress stretched on the bare boards, a woman stitched rapidly, her needle flying with deadly, automatic speed. Beside her, on an upturned egg-box, was a bottle. There was no furniture, only a kettle, some sacking, and a cracked jug. Across the egg-box lay a pile of half-finished coarse serge trousers.

Torn by his distress, Francis could barely speak. "You are Mrs. Stevens?" She nodded. "I came . . . about the boy."

She let her work fall nervously into her lap: a poor creature, not old, nor vicious, yet worn-out by adversity, sodden through and through. "Yes, I had your letter." She began to whimper out an explanation of her circumstances, to exonerate herself, to produce irrelevant evidence proving how misfortune had lowered her to this.

He stopped her quietly; the story was written in her face. He said: "I'll take him back with me today."

At this quietness, she dropped her eyes to her swollen hands, the fingers blue-stippled by countless needle-pricks. Though she made an effort to conceal it, his attitude agitated her more than any rebuke. She began to weep.

"Don't think I'm not fond of him. He helps me in a heap of ways. I've treated him well enough. But it's been a sore struggle." She looked up with sudden defiance, silent.

Ten minutes later he left the house. Beside him, clutching a paper bundle to his pigeon chest, was Andrew. The priest's feelings were deep and complex. He sensed the child's dumb alarm at the unprecedented excursion, yet felt he could best reassure him by silence. He thought, with a slow deep joy: God gave me my life, brought me from China . . . for this!

They walked to the railway station without a word between them. In the train, Andrew sat staring out of the window, hardly moving, his legs dangling over the edge of the seat. He was very dirty, grime was ingrained into his thin pallid neck. Once or twice he glanced sideways at Francis, then immediately he glanced away again. It was impossible to guess his thoughts, but in the depths of his eyes there lurked a dark glimmer of fear and suspicion.

"Don't be afraid."

"I'm not afraid." The boy's underlip quivered.

Once the train had quitted the smoke of Kirkbridge it sped across the country and down the riverside. A look of wonder dawned slowly on the boy's face. He had never dreamed that colours could be so bright, so different from the leaden squalor of the slums. The open fields and farmlands gave place to a wilder scene, where woods sprang up about them, rich with green bracken and the hart's-tongue fern, where the glint of rushing water showed in little glens.

"Is this where we are going?"

"Yes, we're nearly there."

They ran into Tweedside towards three in the afternoon. The old town, clustered on the riverbank, so unchanged he might have left it only yesterday, lay basking in brilliant sunshine. As the familiar landmarks swam into his gaze Francis' throat constricted with a painful joy. They left the little station and walked to St. Columba's Presbytery together.

VI

END OF THE BEGINNING

I

FROM THE WINDOW of his room Monsignor Sleeth frowned down towards the garden where Miss Moffat, basket in hand, stood with Andrew and Father Chisholm, watching Dougal fork up the dinner vegetables. The tacit air of companionship surrounding the little group heightened his fretful feeling of exclusion, hardened his resolution. On the table behind him, typed on his portable machine, lay his finished report—a terse and lucid document, crammed with hanging evidence. He was leaving for Tynecastle in an hour. It would be in the Bishop's hands this evening.

Despite the keen, incisive satisfaction of accomplishment it was undeniable that the past week at St. Columba's had been trying. He had found much to annoy, even to confuse him. Except for a group centred round the pious yet obese Mrs. Glendenning, the people of the parish had some regard, he might even say affection, for their eccentric pastor. Yesterday, he had been obliged to deal severely with the delegation that waited on him to protest their loyalty to the parish priest. As if he didn't know that every native son must have his claque! The height of his exasperation was touched that same evening when the local Presbyterian minister dropped in and, after hemming and hawing, ventured to hope that Father Chisholm was not "leaving them"—the "feeling" in the town had lately been so admirable. . . . Admirable—indeed!

While he meditated, the group beneath his eye broke up and Andrew ran to the summerhouse to get his kite. The old man had a mania for making kites, great paper things with waving tails, which flew—Sleeth grudgingly admitted—like monster birds. On Tuesday, coming upon the two breezily attached to the clouds by humming twine, he had ventured to remonstrate.

"Really, Father. Do you think this pastime dignified?"

The old man had smiled—confound it, he was never rebellious, always that quiet, maddeningly gentle smile.

"The Chinese do. And they're a dignified people."

"It's one of their pagan customs, I presume."

"Ah, well! Surely a very innocent one!"

He remained aloof, his nose turning blue in the sharp wind, watching them. It appeared that the old priest was merging pleasure with instruction. From time to time, while he held the string, the boy would sit in the summerhouse taking down dictation on strips of paper. Completed, these laboured scrawls were threaded on the string, sent soaring to the sky, amidst joint jubilation.

An impulse of curiosity had mastered him. He took the latest missive from the boy's excited hands. It was clearly written and not ill-spelled. He read: "I faithfully promise to oppose bravely all that is stupid and bigoted and cruel. Signed, ANDREW. *P.S.* Toleration is the highest virtue. Humility comes next."

He looked at it bleakly, for a long time, before surrendering it. He even waited with a chilled face until the next was prepared. "Our bones may moulder and become the earth of the fields but the Spirit issues forth and lives on high in a condition of glorious brightness. God is the common Father of all mankind."

Mollified, Sleeth looked at Father Chisholm. "Excellent. Didn't Saint Paul say that?"

"No." The old man shook his head apologetically. "It was Confucius."

Sleeth was staggered. He walked away without a word.

That night he misguidedly began an argument, which the old man evaded with disconcerting ease. At the end he burst out, provoked:

"Your notion of God is a strange one."

"Which of us has any notion of God?" Father Chisholm smiled. "Our word 'God' is a human word . . . expressing reverence for our Creator. If we have that reverence, we shall see God . . . never fear."

To his annoyance, Sleeth had found himself flushing. "You seem to have a very slight regard for Holy Church."

"On the contrary . . . all my life I have rejoiced to feel her arms about me. The Church is our great mother, leading us forward . . . a band of pilgrims, through the night. But perhaps there are other mothers. And perhaps even some poor solitary pilgrims who stumble home alone."

The scene, of which this was a fragment, seriously disconcerted Sleeth and gave him, when he returned that night, a shockingly distorted nightmare. He dreamed that while the house slept his guardian angel and Father Chisholm's knocked off for an hour and went down to the living room for a drink. Chisholm's angel was a slight cherubic creature, but his own was an elderly angel with discontented eyes and a ruffled angry plumage. As they sipped their drink, wings at rest on the elbows of their chairs, they discussed their present charges. Chisholm, although indicted as a sentimentalist, escaped lightly. But he . . . he was torn to shreds. He sweated in his sleep as he heard his angel dismiss him with a final malediction. "One of the worst I ever had . . . prejudiced, pedantic, over-ambitious, and worst of all a bore."

Sleeth wakened with a start in the darkness of his room. What a hateful, disgusting dream. He shivered. His head ached. He knew better than to give credence to such nightmares, no more than odious distortions of one's waking thoughts, altogether different from the good, authentic scriptural dreams, that of Pharaoh's wife, for instance. He dismissed his dream violently, like an impure thought. But it nagged him now, as he stood at the window: *Prejudiced, pedantic, over-ambitious, and worst of all, a bore.*

Apparently he had misjudged Andrew, for the child emerged from the summerhouse bearing, not his kite, but a large wicker trug into which, with Dougal's aid, he began to place some fresh-picked plums and pears. When the task was accomplished the boy moved towards the house, carrying the long basket on his arm.

Sleeth had an inexplicable impulse to retreat. He sensed that the gift was for him. He resented it, was vaguely, absurdly disconcerted. The knock on his door made him pull his scattered wits together.

"Come in."

Andrew entered the room and put the fruits upon the chest of drawers. With the shamed consciousness of one who knows himself suspected he delivered his message, memorized all the way upstairs. "Father Chisholm hopes you will take these with you—the plums are very sweet—and the pears are the very last we'll get."

Monsignor Sleeth looked sharply at the boy, wondering if a double meaning were intended in that final simple phrase.

"Where is Father Chisholm?"

"Downstairs. Waiting on you."

"And my car?"

"Dougal has just brought it round for you to the front door."

There was a pause. Andrew began, hesitantly, to move away.

"Wait!" Sleeth drew up. "Don't you think it would be more convenient . . . altogether politer . . . if you carried down the fruit and put it in my car?"

The boy coloured nervously and turned to obey. As he lifted the basket from the chest one of the plums fell off and rolled below the bed. Darkly red, he stooped and clumsily retrieved it, its smooth skin burst, a trickle of juice upon his fingers. Sleeth watched him with a cold smile.

"That one won't be much good . . . will it?"

No answer.

"I said, will it?"

"No, sir."

Sleeth's strange pale smile deepened. "You are a remarkably stubborn child. I've been watching you all the week. Stubborn and ill-bred. Why don't you look at me?"

With a tremendous effort the boy wrenched his eyes from the floor. He was trembling, like a nervous foal, as he met Sleeth's gaze.

"It is the sign of a guilty conscience not to look straight at a person. Besides being bad manners. They'll have to teach you better at Ralstone."

Another silence. The boy's face was white. Monsignor Sleeth still smiled. He moistened his lips.

"Why don't you answer? Is it because you do not wish to go to the Home?"

The boy faltered: "I don't want to go."

"Ah! But you want to do what is right, don't you?"

"Yes, sir."

"Then you will go. In fact, I may tell you that you are going very soon. Now you may put the fruit in the car. If you can do so without dropping all of it."

When the boy had gone, Monsignor Sleeth remained motionless, the contour of his lips fixed into a stiff, straight mould. His arms stretched down at his sides. His hands were clenched.

With that same stiff look upon his face he moved to the table. He could not have believed himself capable of such sadism. But that very cruelty had purged the darkness from his soul. Without hesitation, inevitably, he took up his compiled report, and tore it into shreds. His fingers ripped the sheets with methodical violence. He threw the torn and twisted fragments from him, scattered them irrevocably on the floor. Then he groaned and sank upon his knees.

"Oh, Lord." His voice was simple and pleading. "Let me learn something from this old man. And dear Lord . . . Don't let me be a bore."

That same afternoon, when Monsignor Sleeth had gone, Father Chisholm and Andrew came guardedly through the back door of the house. Though the boy's eyes were still swollen, their brightness was that of expectation, his face, at last, was reassured.

"Be careful of the nasturtiums, laddie." Francis urged the boy forward with a conspirator's whisper. "Heaven knows we've had enough trouble in one day without Dougal starting on us."

While Andrew dug the worms in the flower-bed the old man went to the tool-shed, brought out their trout rods, and stood waiting at the gate. When the child arrived, breathless, with a wriggling tinful, he chuckled.

"Aren't you the lucky boy to be going trouting with the best fisher in all Tweedside? The good God made the little fishes, Andrew . . . and sent us here to catch them."

Their two figures, hand in hand, dwindled and disappeared, down the pathway, to the river.

THE END